The Mary Ann Omnibus

Catherine Cookson

THE
Mary Ann Omnibus

A Grand Man

The Lord and Mary Ann

The Devil and Mary Ann

Love and Mary Ann

Life and Mary Ann

Marriage and Mary Ann

Mary Ann's Angels

Mary Ann and Bill

A Macdonald Book

Copyright © Catherine Cookson 1981

This edition first published in Great Britain by
Macdonald & Co (Publishers) Ltd · London & Sydney
Reprinted in 1986

CONDITIONS OF SALE NOTICE

British Library Cataloguing in Publication Data

Cookson, Catherine
The Mary Ann omnibus.
I. Title
823'.914[F]   PR6053.0525

ISBN 0-356-12770-2

This edition specially produced for
The Leisure Circle Limited
by
Macdonald & Co (Publishers) Ltd
Greater London House
Hampstead Road
London NWI 7QX

A BPCC plc company

Printed in West Germany by
Mohndruck Graphische Betriebe GmbH, Gütersloh

Macdonald & Co (Publishers) Ltd
Greater London House
Hampstead Road
London NW1 7QX

A BPCC plc company

A Grand Man first published in Great Britain by Macdonald & Co. in 1954
The Lord and Mary Ann first published in Great Britain by Macdonald & Co. in 1956
The Devil and Mary Ann first published in Great Britain by Macdonald & Co. in 1958
Love and Mary Ann first published in Great Britain by Macdonald & Co. in 1961
Life and Mary Ann first published in Great Britain by Macdonald & Co. in 1962
Marriage and Mary Ann first published in Great Britain by Macdonald & Co. in 1964
Mary Ann's Angels first published in Great Britain by Macdonald & Co. in 1965
Mary Ann and Bill first published in Great Britain by Macdonald & Co. in 1967

Contents

A Grand Man

*Everything in this story is fictitious,
except that which you yourself know to be true.*

1

A BIT OF IMAGINATION

In the quiet corner of the school yard Mary Ann stood surrounded by a little band of open-mouthed, silent admirers. With waving movements of her thin arms she drew them closer about her, and when they were pressed near she warmed to her theme.

"And besides the great big house," she said, here eyes moving from one to the other, like revolving saucers, "we've got three servants and two cars and two horses . . . galloping ones." She curved her arms into what she considered was the shape of the horses' legs, and she jerked them at a great speed to indicate the velocity of the steeds. "And," she finished in a voice weighed with awe, "some day I'll show you them; and our house, and the car besides, some day when I have a party."

The children stared at her in admiration. Then one after the other they put forth tentative offers that might act as a sprat to catch a mackerel.

"Would you like a stot of me ball, Mary Ann?"

"I'll lend you me thick skipping rope at the week-end, Mary Ann."

"When I spend me penny on Saturda' I'll save you some, Mary Ann."

Whether Mary Ann would have accepted any of these offers cannot be known, for at that moment an indignant figure came rushing round the corner of the school wall and startled them all by crying, "Oh, you big liar, Mary Ann Shaughnessy! I've been listening behind the wall. You don't live in a big house, and you ain't got no servants or cars or horses. Oh, was there ever such a liar as you?"

The little crowd turned its eyes from the black-haired, vicious-faced accuser back to Mary Ann, and expectantly awaited developments.

Mary Ann felt no immediate anger against her enemy . . . Sarah Flannagan was always spoiling people's fun. And anyway, it wasn't lies she was telling, it was more in the nature of a story. Yes, that was it. This soothed her conscience, but she couldn't tell them that it was just a story. No, oh no. She felt a sudden spasm of pity for them; they had listened to her so intently—they were the best lot she had talked to for a long time. Looking back into the eyes of her audience, she realized that she owed them something, a show of defence at any rate. So she cocked her elfin face on one side and blinked her large brown eyes at Sarah Flannagan, and said quite calmly, "You know nothing whatever about our house, or me da's car, Sarah Flannagan; and I'll thank you to mind your own business." She nodded at the children, and the nod said, "There, that's settled her hash."

The dark spoiler of dreams gasped, and for a moment was struck speechless; then sucking in her lips and making a sound that was a good imitation of frying bacon, she turned to the eager group, head wagging as quickly as her tongue as she cried, "Why! of all the whopping liars she's one. She lives right opposite us; and not in a house like ours either, but in Mulhattans' Hall. They've only got two wee rooms and a cupboard of a kitchen. And as for her da having a car . . . Why! my! huh! He can't even keep down a job 'cause he's always on the booze."

Knowing she had played her trump card, Sarah Flannagan's vituperation ceased, but her chin, thrust out towards the slight, quivering figure of Mary Ann, was defying her to get over that shattering piece of integrity.

Now the poised calm of Mary Ann had vanished, and her eyes were blazing with an anger that lent to her little frame the energy of lightning. She almost sprang on the indignant stickler for truth, stopped only, it would seem, by the jutting chin of her enemy. Her voice shaking with an emotion that could be classed as uncontrollable rage, she shouted, "You! you pig face! you wicked thing. I'll slap your face, so I will, if you dare say me da drinks. Oh . . . h!" She cast her eyes heavenwards. "It's a wonder God doesn't strike you down dead. But you'll go to hell for your wickedness . . . Oh, yes you will." She pointed an accusing finger, and had only to add "I'll see to it" to give the stamp of absolute authority to this last statement.

Sarah Flannagan was not in the least intimidated by this threat to her future, but turned her fishy eyes on to the group that had widened and spread itself away from Mary Ann.

Mary Ann too looked at her late admirers, and beseechingly she entreated them, "Don't believe a word she says. Me da's a lovely man. He gets sick at times but he never drinks. And he tells the loveliest stories. Look, some day I'll take you . . . home. . . ."

The words trailed away at Sara Flannagan laughed: "She thinks she's safe with you lot that comes from the Fifteen Streets; she doesn't tell them lies to anybody living round our way."

The faces, whose attention Mary Ann had held so eagerly a few minutes ago, now looked at her in silence and condemnation, for to partake in the make-believe world of childhood is not to lie unless the word lie is actually uttered, but once it is then make-believe is wrong; it immediately becomes a sin—another weight to be carried on the head until the priest removes it in confession; lies were connected with penance and purgatory. Mary Ann Shaughnessy had been found out.

With one accord they backed away. Then turning together like pigeons in flight, they went hitching and skipping around the personification of truth as she walked triumphantly out of the school yard with a backward leer to where Mary Ann stood with trembling lips and the burning sting of tears in the backs of her eyes.

The blazing indignation had died out of her as quickly as it had arisen, and after waiting in order to give her tormentor a good start, she too walked out of the yard and made her way home. And to comfort herself, she decided that if she could cover the whole distance homewards without once stepping a crack in the pavement any wish she might make would be bound to come true.

To this end she began a series of hops, jumps and long and short strides, of stepping into the gutter when confronted by a paving stone so cracked that it was impossible to hop, jump or stride over it. It was when confronted by such a stretch of pavement that she was knocked right into the middle of it by two boys rushing out of Stanley Street. Their wild stampede carried her before them and left her staring down at her feet lying bang across a crack.

Her face worked and her lips trembled, and she could have cried with vexation. She had so wanted a wish, just another wish to make doubly sure of the week-end. She couldn't have too many wishes to . . . keep the week-end right. And the week-end started to-night, because it was Friday night and her da got his pay packet that night. She stood uncertain for a moment, plucking at her lip. Then her face brightened and she hopped clean off the diseased pavement on to a whole but greasy slab. She knew what she would do; she'd go and have a talk with The Holy Family. If anybody could make sure of the week-end, they could.

This decision made, she hurried back along the main road, charitably forgetful of the times when the Holy Family had slipped up in their duty and the week-ends had been a failure.

As she neared the church, its external severity filled her with nothing but hope, and its interior gaudiness lifted her heart and clothed her with peace.

Going up to the small side altar she knelt down below the life-size statues of the Virgin, with the Child in her arms, and St. Joseph standing protectingly near. She gazed up at them for some moments in silence before beginning her routine. First she blessed herself; then she lifted the Sacred Heart Medal that was reposing on her chest at the end of a narrow brass chain, which she would have assured you was solid gold, and she laid this on the front of her coat so that it would not escape the notice of the influential ones. Then bringing to her face what she called her 'good look', she said, in a voice that was a mixture of Tyneside and Irish, "Oh, Holy Family, I've come to ask you something; and I'll do anything you like for you if you'll grant my request."

She waited, as if to let her offer sink in, before going on, "I want you to keep me da from being sick at the week-end, 'cause he's a lovely da, as you know, and he doesn't mean to make me ma cry. He told her so last night himself when he thought I was asleep in bed. He told her it was sorry he was to the heart, and if only we could all get back into the country he'd give up the . . . I mean he wouldn't be sick any more; it's having to work in the shipyard and them factories that makes him want to be sick. And there's nothing but yards round here to work in. But mind," she put in, hastily, "I'm not blaming you for making so many yards; you've had to put them some place." She nodded, expressing her sympathy at what must have been a dilemma to them.

Then she went on, "But you see, me da doesn't like them; he likes the country. And he won't go into it to work without me ma and me and our Michael. And that's where the cottage comes in. You'll mind I asked you about it last week. If only you could see your way clear to getting us a cottage, just a little weeny one would do, I'd do anything for you, Jesus, Mary and Joseph. I'll even stop telling lies about the servants and the horses. I will, honest to God."

She had a vague idea that something should happen at this point, a clapping of hands at least. She gazed up at the group of statuary in strained, expectant silence, and had to be content when the infant child looked up at his mother with a "Well, what about it?" look on his face.

The Virgin must have taken the cue, for quite suddenly Mary Ann experienced a feeling of relief, and tears, which she was sure she had not started, ran down her cheeks, and she was powerless to stop them.

She blessed herself, and having risen, she genuflected deeply; then turned away and walked almost into the arms of Father Owen.

The old priest, with his bald head and long solemn face, hung over her for a moment and affected astonishment at seeing her. He made not the smallest reference to her tear-stained face, but he bent down and whispered, "You've a great devotion to the Holy Family, I notice, Mary Ann."

Blinking, smiling and sniffing, all in one movement, she whispered back confidentially, "Yes, Father, 'cause it's nearly the same size as our family."

"Oh, of course. Yes, yes," he nodded at her. "You're a good girl." He patted her cheek, and the smile left her face and her head drooped, and she took small, quiet steps on her toes up the aisle, the priest walking as noiselessly by her side.

When she whispered something that he could not catch, he bent his long frame towards her, asking, "What is it? And she, still with eyes averted, whispered, "I'm not a good girl, Father, I'm a howling liar."

The priest's eyebrows moved slightly, and he said, "Oh, indeed?"

And Mary Ann nodded to the heating grid over which she stepped carefully, and said, "Yes."

In silence they reached the end of the church and came to a halt where the holy water font was attached to a pillar. Mary Ann dipped in her fingers and once again blessed herself, and the priest, standing looking at her, sighed and exclaimed, "Ah well. It's a good thing when we know what we are, but I think you're too hard on yourself. That's a bit too strong a name for you, Mary Ann."

"It isn't, Father. Oh, it isn't," she whispered emphatically.

She had called herself a howling liar, and the priest must take her word that that was what she was; he mustn't take things lightly like this. She stretched up to him and went on to explain, still in a whisper, "You see, Father, I tell people we've got cars and horses and servants, and we haven't."

"Oh, you do?" The priest's eyebrows moved again.

"Yes."

"Dear, dear. Cars, horses and servants?"

"Yes."

They stared at each other.

"Well, well; this is serious. They couldn't be just nice daydreams you've been having?"

"No, oh no, Father."

"Dear, dear me. Cars, horses and servants. What are we going to do about it?"

"I've talked to the Holy Family, Father."

"You have?"

"Yes, Father. And I promised them I won't lie again. And I meant to promise them I won't get into any more rages either, but. . . ."

"Do you get into rages, Mary Ann?"

"I do, Father;when anybody says me da . . ." She hesitated and her eyes drooped once more, and she toyed with her hair ribbon which was hanging perilously on the end of one plait.

"Yes, Mary Ann," prompted Father Owen. "And what do they say?"

"Well"—she looked straight up into the priest's eyes—"people say me da drinks; and you know yourself, Father, he doesn't. You know he never touches a drop."

The child and the priest regarded each other intently; and as Mary Ann watched the priest's nostrils quiver and his right eyebrow jerk spasmodically, very like the head of Mr. Lavey, who lived on the ground floor of their house and who had the tick, she felt forced to press her point again.

"He might get sick now and then, but he doesn't drink. Does he, Father?"

The appeal in the great eyes, the strain visible in the thin wisp of a body, did not touch the priest as much as did the unseen but evident conflict of loyalties raging in the heart of this child who had the art of conjuring up and of living numbers of separate lives, each with the same focal point, her father . . . and him a drunken agitator, and not of the faith either! Which, in a way, was something to be thankful for. No, no—he chided himself for his thoughts—it could be the saving of him if he'd come in. . . .

"Does he, Father?" The whispered insistence made him pinch his quivering nose between his finger and thumb, and with a sliding glance at the cross hanging above the holy water font, he said, almost defiantly, "Not a drop, Mary Ann. Not a drop. I know that."

Mary Ann sighed, and she smiled, and her young mouth stretched wide in happiness as she said, "I knew you would speak the truth, Father."

Her pleasure, however, turned to immediate concern when she saw her dear, dear Father Owen almost choke. Something must have stuck in his throat, for he was going red in the face with coughing.

Still coughing, the priest led Mary Ann to the door, and patting her head, he nodded to her in farewell, for he was unable to speak.

In grave concern, Mary Ann watched him re-enter the church. Poor Father Owen; he had a bad cold. Eeh . . . the thought swept over her making her hot . . . what if he were to get the 'flu and die? Oh, but he wouldn't. God wouldn't let Father Owen die. She could not see the Creator being such a cold-blooded monster as to take away her confidant, friend, and what was more, her ally in defence of her father.

Suddenly she skipped off the church step. Wouldn't that be one in the eye for Sarah Flannagan when she told her what Father Owen had said? "Sarah Flannagan," she would say to her, "now shut your big gob and listen to this. Father Owen said . . . and mind he was standing near the holy water font and the cross above him when he said it, and not even you'll dare to say Father Owen tells lies . . . Well, standing there, he said, 'I've never known your da to touch a drop of drink, Mary Ann. And anybody that says it will go to Hell and be shrivelled up.' So there!" By, that would be like a slap across her nasty big face.

For the moment she felt very happy. Father Owen was the bestest man in the world, next to her da. Eeh. Well, was her da better than the priest?

She spent most of her time that it took her to reach home in debating in which position of goodness she should place the two men who were a power in her life.

2

MULHATTAN'S HALL

Mulhattan's Hall was a small tenement house jammed between two-storey houses consisting of two rooms upstairs and two down. In any other part of the country these would have been termed flats, but in Jarrow and the surrounding towns two rooms so placed was called a house, and if, as sometimes happened, the back-yard had been designed that each occupant had a slit of private concrete with a high wall cutting him off from his near neighbour, then that occupant had a right to feel that he was socially on the upgrade. It can therefore be guessed how far down the social scale were the five families living in Mulhattan's Hall, for here there was only one communal back-yard, and from it water for all uses had to be carried.

The official name of Mulhattan's Hall was sixteen Burton Street. It had come by its title from a family of that name who had lived there some years before, and from occupying one 'house' the family, through marriage, had spread into the other four parts; and since they were all sons who had married the house had become a hive of Mulhattans, and far from a peaceful hive; and although the last of these Mulhattans had long since gone the name still remained.

Five families still occupied the Hall; the Shaughnessys on the attic floor, Miss Harper and the Quigleys on the first floor, and on the ground floor, on one side the McBrides, on the other the Laveys.

Tonight being Friday was bath night. Mary Ann didn't mind the bath, in fact she liked it, but she hated having to provide the means for it, for no matter how she talked to herself or what games she played she found that, even with their Michael on the other side of the handle, a bucket of water weighed a ton by the time she had reached the twenty-eighth step and the top landing. If possible she would have preferred to carry the bucket herself, for their Michael was the worst one on earth for playing games. What was more, tonight being Friday her grannie was sure to be visiting. That together with the bath was enough to try an angel with nothing on her mind; Mary Ann was no angel and she had a lot on her mind.

Once upon a time, she had hated to go into the house and find her grannie there, for as sure as her life her grannie would want her to go and stay with her for the week-end, and to be in her grannie's company for just one hour seemed like a long nightmare, but now, although she still hated to find her there, all fear that she would make any such disagreeable request of her was past. If she thought her grannie was going to be so foolish as to ask her to go and stay with her, she had just to look at her with a certain look, which she kept now especially for her grannie, and that terrible old lady would dry up.

For years Mrs. McMullen had put so many fears into Mary Ann's mind that it became difficult for the child to know which she was afraid of most . . . of hell, where she'd be made to sit on a red-hot gridiron all day without her knickers on, of being thrown clean out of the Catholic Church and plumb into the Salvation Army, or of being put away in a home so that she would never be able to see her ma or her da again till she would be an old woman of twenty. But now the old lady no longer instilled fear into Mary Ann with her prophecies; if possible, she kept out of her granddaughter's way, for Mary Ann had at last got her, if not exactly where she wanted her, at least under a certain control, and here she hoped to keep her. But Mary Ann knew she could only do this if she remained strong enough not to tell her da what had changed her grannie, for once she divulged the reason, her power, she knew, would vanish as quickly as a soap bubble, for he would roar for a month, and nothing she could think of would keep him from throwing his knowledge at his mother-in-law by way of a small repayment for what he had suffered at her hands during the past years.

Panting, Mary Ann reached the eighteenth stair and the landing before her own, and there, as usual, was Miss Harper, with her door open and sitting just where she could see who passed up and down..

"Hallo, there, Mary Ann," Miss Harper called; "your grannie's up."

"Hallo, Miss Harper," said Mary Ann. "Is she?"

Unsmiling, she mounted her own flight of stairs. Miss Harper knew everybody's business, and she was the biggest borrower from here to John O'Groats.

She pushed open her own door, and there was her grannie, sitting like a lady in her astrakhan coat, and her hat, with the blue feather and veil on, cocked high upon her head.

"Hallo, Mary Ann," said Mrs. McMullen primly.

"Hallo, Grannie," said Mary Ann.

"Have you just come from school?"

"Yes, Grannie." What a silly daft question. Where would she have come from? Whitley Bay?

"Get your hands washed, and you can have your tea now," said her mother.

"Aw . . . w," Mary Ann protested, her face screwed up; "can't I wait until me da comes?"

"Get your hands washed."

When her mother spoke in that tone there was nothing to do but get your hands washed.

The ritual over, Mary Ann held up her hands for her mother's inspection; then sat down at the table. It was adorned with the best cloth, with the fancy work at the corners, and on a tray stood the three best cups, which if you held them up to the light you could see through, and the best tea-pot, which was of the same blue colour as the cups, but didn't match and had an odd lid.

In front of her grannie was a plate of boiled ham and a jar of pickled onions, and in the centre of the table was a plate of square, thin slices of bread which told all who beheld it that it was a 'cut loaf'.

Mary Ann watched her grannie eyeing the plate, and she said to herself, "If she says a thing about it I'll say . . . 'Milk Bottles!' I will, you'll see." And she could almost hear her grannie thinking: Bought bread again, huh! Thought she didn't hold with it . . . nothing but brown, home-made wholemeal for her children. Must have their fancy vitamins. She hasn't a penny left to get the flour, that's it. And she got the loaf and ham on tick from Fennell's, I bet.

And Mary Ann also watched her mother avoid her grannie's eye and go to the fireplace.

But she became so intent on again staring at her grannie that she did not not notice her mother come back to the table; and she jumped when she said, "Will you have jam or syrup?"

She eyed the small amount of jam in the dish, and knowing that Michael liked jam and hated syrup and thinking of last night and the names he had called their da, she said, "Jam."

"Jam what?" asked her mother.

"Please."

"They hadn't to be told in my day," said her grannie. Then almost choking on a mouthful of ham, she added hastily and in oiled tones to make up for her censure, "Have you been picked for the procession, Mary Ann?"

Mary Ann attacked her jam and bread with vigour, but made no reply; and her mother said sharply, "You heard your grannie talking to you?"

So Mary Ann, her eyes fixed on her plate, said, "No, Grannie." Oh, how she hated her grannie. She always asked about things that hurt you. For two pins she'd lean across the table and look her right in her old wrinkled eyes and say, "Milk Bottles!" But once she had said it her hold would be gone, so she contented herself with just staring at her grannie in an irritating way and thinking back to that Sunday morning and the milk bottles.

She could see herself—it was very early and she had wakened with a cramp in her stomach. She was staying in Shields with her grannie, and as she usually did on such visits she was sleeping on the couch behind the kitchen door. It was the plums that were causing the cramp. Her grannie had made her eat them because she said they shouldn't be wasted. Yet they had been all soft and nasty. She'd got up and unbolted the back door and gone out to the lavatory. She had sat there for a long time, for the cramp kept on coming and going, and during the times her stomach was at peace she thought of home and her da and whether it had been a nice week-end. If it had he would be taking some tea to her ma in bed; and if she had been at home she'd have got some too, just as if she were grown up.

It was then she saw her grannie through the crack in the door. She watched her coming stealthily down the yard; then she disappeared from her sight as she went to the back door. Puzzled, she had listened, and she had heard her grannie open the back door and close it, and when she came within sight again she was carrying two pints of milk. She saw her stand within the shelter of the staircase wall, which also kept her out of the view of the upper window; and she watched her skilfully remove the milk-caps by inserting a needle under their edges, then pour the cream off both bottles into the screw-top jar, which she took from beneath her apron. This done, she filled one of the bottles to brim out of the other, and after carefully replacing the cap, left the bottle inside the back door.

It was at this point that Mary Ann showed herself, and she watched her grannie hang on to the door for a moment and fight for breath as she exclaimed, "Eeh! I saw what you did."

She thought her grannie was going to have a fit; but before she could add anything further to her accusation she was grabbed by the collar of the coat she was wearing over her nightie and lifted clean off her feet and run up the yard as if the devil had her by the neck.

But if the terrifying Mrs. McMullen had hoped to frighten Mary Ann she was mistaken. When at last Mary Ann was able to get a word in, with enraging calm and in her own words she reminded her grannie that it was only two weeks ago that Mrs. Baker from upstairs, her that was deaf, had stood in the kitchen and complained of there being no cream on the milk, and she had blamed the milkman for swiping it and feeding his large, robust family with it.

There had followed a verbal barrage for power, which ended with Mary Ann putting on her clothes and saying she thought she'd go to mass in Jarrow this morning, and if her grannie would give her the threepence now for the bus instead of the night she'd be obliged.

Mrs. McMullen had handed over the money, whilst her eyes had consigned her grandchild to the place from where through continued chastisement she had hoped to save her.

Mary Ann's last words as she left the house, which were apropos of nothing that had been said that morning, almost caused the final collapse of Mrs. McMullen, for just a second before closing the door behind her Mary Ann said, "Me da's a grand man."

She had often wished since she had stayed just a little longer to have seen the effect of her words on her grannie, for even through the closed door she had heard the sound of her choking.

She looked now at the old woman guzzling the last of the ham. She hadn't been offered even the smallest piece. But what did it matter? She had more than ham on her grannie, and her grannie knew it. She could keep her ham and she hoped it stuck half-way down. She looked to where her mother was refilling her grannie's cup and wondered, and not for the first time, if her grannie was really her mother's mother. Her da likely wasn't joking when he had said her grannie had stolen her mother when she was a baby and she really never had been Lizzie McMullen at all but one of the first ladies of the land. Her da joked a lot at times, but still he was probably right about this, for what connection had her lovely mother with her grannie? None; none in the wide world. Her mother's hair was fair, like silver, and straight; not even a kink in it; while her grannie's was black and white and frizzed up like a nigger's. She got it that way by sticking it in thousands of papers. And her grannie's eyes were as round as aniseed balls but black, while her mother's were long and grey. And then again her grannie was little and stumpy and fat, and her mother was a grand height, and if she'd had nice clothes like Mrs. Tullis, who kept the outdoor beershop at the corner, she'd have looked like a queen. No, like a princess; for in spite of her mother's great age of twenty-nine, she could be gay at times, like a young princess. No; her mother was no relation to her grannie. Would her mother have golloped all that ham herself? She wouldn't even eat any food if there wasn't much for her and their Michael. Her grannie was just what her da said she was, pig, guts, hog and artful!"

"You can get down now." Lizzie's voice brought Mary Ann's fixed gaze from her grandmother. "Say your grace."

Mary Ann said her grace. She knew why she had been ordered to leave the table, because she'd been staring at her grannie and her ma was afraid she'd say something.

Never slow to take advantage of a situation, she asked, "Can I look at the album, Ma?"

Now the album was a treasure chest which, through an odd assortment of snaps, kept fresh the memories of the happy incidents that had taken place in the early years of Elizabeth Shaughnessy's married life, and as time went on she found it more and more necessary to refer to it to confirm that these memories were the stamp on her mind of incidents that had once actually taken place and were not just vague dreams.

Mary Ann could remember when she first saw the album. She was sitting between her ma and da and they were laughing and laughing as they turned the pages. She could remember the firelight shining on their faces, and they had both appeared so beautiful to her that instead of laughing with them she had cried. She could remember her da picking her up and carrying her upstairs to bed. Yes, she'd gone upstairs to bed, where Michael and her had a real bedroom. She couldn't remember very much about that house, only the real bedroom. There had been other houses; then rooms; and finally Mulhattan's Hall. In each place the furniture got less and less, until now none of it was familiar . . . only the album. The table and chairs might change, and even the beds, but the album . . . never. It was to her a land wherein she could wander and dream; but rare were the times she was allowed to wander alone. Only on such occasions as the present when her mother desired to keep her quiet was there a chance of getting the album to herself.

She saw that her mother was annoyed with her because she had asked for the album in front of her grannie, for it was a subject of controversy between them; Mrs. McMullen considered that it belonged to her by right, having ignored the fact that her late husband had given it to his daughter on her sixteenth birthday.

"Wash your hands again," said Lizzie; "and be careful how you get it out of the trunk. And mind, don't disarrange the things. And stay in the room with it."

Mary Ann did as she was bidden; and as she knelt on the floor to open the lid of the trunk that stood beside the little window which came down to the floor, she paused to wonder why the album should have been put into the trunk, for although it was usually placed out of her reach it was generally on show, for it was indeed a showpiece, being backed with fine leather and bound with brass hinges that spread across the back and front of it; it had once been owned by her mother's granda who came from Norway.

She lifted it tenderly out of the trunk, smoothed again into order the assortment of clothes, then went to the bed and, laying it there, she fell on her stomach across the bed, her heels playing a silent tattoo on her small buttocks. Sucking in her breath in anticipation of coming enjoyment, she lifted back the heavy cover and looked once more on Great-Granda Stenson. But his sidewhiskers had long ceased to be funny. She turned a number of thick pages, ignoring with an upward tilt of her nose the photographs they held; she knew them all; they were merely pictures of her grannie from the time she was a baby until she was married . . . and who'd want to look at them? But following the picture of her grandmother's wedding group the real pictures began.

Now she burrowed her knees into the bed. There was her ma with nothing on; and there was her ma on the sands with her spade and pail; and there she was again with her great long fair plaits and holding her school prize in her hand. There were many more snaps of her ma. Then they too abruptly stopped, and Mary Ann was confronted with two blank pages. They were like a curtain ending an act of a play, and although she was anxious to raise the curtain and continue the story, she did not hurry, but savoured what was to come. She knew there was not a lot more to follow, but it was the best, and, like the pork cracknel she sometimes had on a Sunday, she always conserved the nice things until the end.

Slowly now she turned the page, and there they were, her ma and da. She drew the air up through her nose as if inhaling a scent. Oh, didn't they look lovely? Anybody would know that her ma was a bride although she wasn't dressed in white but just in a costume. It was the . . . lovely look on her face that told you. And there was her da, dressed as a soldier. Oh, better than a soldier . . . an airman. And he wasn't like any airman, for he had two stripes on his arm. He'd been a grand man in the Air Force, had her da. He had told her about the marshal, the one that sent the aeroplanes up. He had thought the world of her da, and he wouldn't think about lifting a finger unless first asking her da about it. . . . Oh my, yes; it was as her da said, the Air Force knew it the day he left.

Her ma, at one time, had laughed until she cried when her da was telling her about what a grand man he was in the Air Force. But not lately, not since they came to live here. In fact, when she came to think about it, her da never looked at the album at all now.

Suddenly her interest in the pictures waned; she found she didn't want to look at herself and their Michael in the various stages of undress. She looked up from the book and around the room. Its only articles of furniture were the bed, the trunk and a white-painted wardrobe. The floor had no covering except a clippie rug, but the boards were stained and polished and would have looked fine, she thought, had there not been so many wide gaps that let both draught and dust up through them.

Slowly she closed the book and wriggled back off the bed; and lifting the album, she returned it to the trunk. And not until she had closed the lid did she realize that it was the very first time she had put it away without being told . . . always her mother had to tell her again and again before she could be induced to close it. A pain not unlike a toothache came into her chest, and she stepped to the window and stood looking down into the street. Some of her friends were playing tiggie in the middle of the road, while others on the pavement opposite were endeavouring to walk on tin cans which they held tight to the soles of their shoes by pulling on string reins. The hurt feeling was pressing on her so heavily that it took away the wish that she might join them.

Her mind became a confused jumble of desires. They swirled around in her head and became tangled, as always, about the mainspring of her life; if only her ma and da laughed together like they used to; if only their Michael didn't make her wild by saying the things he did about her da; if only there were no week-ends in the week and men didn't get paid on a Friday; and if only her grannie could be wafted away to some far place; not hell; no, but some place from where she would find it impossible to come and visit her ma and talk in a quiet voice in the scullery, telling her what she should do about her da—her ma was always short with him after her grannie had been.

She leaned her head against the top of the attic window—it was just the right height for leaning against—and filled now with a pain that was almost of an adult quality, she stared unseeing through it.

Usually she was only too well aware that the Flannagan's window was straight below theirs on the opposite side of the street; but this evening with so much on her mind she gave no thought to it, until the curtains being jerked violently together attracted her attention. Then she straightened herself up, thinking, Eeh, I wasn't looking in. Eeh, I wasn't. She was about to withdraw when a too-well-known face suddenly appeared between the curtains and a tongue of remarkable length was thrust up at her. Before she could retaliate the owner of the tongue had withdrawn it, and the curtains were again closed.

For the moment, the weight of the family worry was lifted from her, and she compressed her lips and shook her head from side to side before muttering, "Oh, Sarah Flannagan, you cheeky thing, you. Oh, you are! Just you wait."

She could see by the bunched curtains that her enemy was still behind them, so keeping to one side of the attic window she waited, and it was no time at all before the curtains were jerked apart, and Mary Ann was ready at the instant. Not only did her tongue shoot out but it wagged itself violently for a second before returning limply to its residence.

Gasping with indignation, Mrs. Flannagan threw up the window; but Mary Ann did not wait to hear what she had to say. With her fingers pressed to her lips she ran across the room, but before pulling open the door she composed herself to enter the kitchen so as not to give herself away. But she need not have troubled, for her mother and her grannie were in the scullery, as her grannie's voice proclaimed.

It came softly, but clearly audible, to her. "You're a fool," it said.

She stood, her ear cocked towards the scullery, and when her grannie's voice came again, her body began to tremble as if she was freezing with cold. "Leave him. Get a court order; he'll have to pay. I'll take the bairns. And if you don't want to go back to office work there's plenty of clean factories to pick from now. If ever there's been a fool, its's been you. If only you'd stuck to Bob Quinton you'd be living like a lady now. Look at the building business he's got up. And him never married. Oh, I wish the other one would fall into the Don on a dark night, I do, so help me God. And there's never a night goes by but I pray for it. God forgive me."

There was a crash that brought the two women running into the kitchen, and for a moment they stood looking down at the blue cup and saucer lying in fragments on the hearth. Then they looked towards Mary Ann standing by the table, her face white and drained and her eyes stretched wide.

Mrs. McMullen was the first to speak. Forgetting for the moment all caution, she reverted to her old manner. "Well now, would you believe it? Anybody can see with half an eye that she threw it. Well, I ask you. And one of the good ones, an' all."

"Shut up! Shut up! Shut up!" The words rose to a scream in Mary Ann's throat. The tears rained from her eyes, blinding her. As her mother's arms went about her she started to moan, and Lizzie, holding her tightly, cried, "It's all right. It's all right. It doesn't matter about the cup or anything. We'll get another. Sh! . . . Sh! now."

"A good smacked backside, that's what she wants."

"Mother. Please." Lizzie's voice checked the old woman. "Go, will you; I'll be down on Sunday."

Even the feather on Mrs. McMullen's hat seemed to bristle. "You're telling me to get out because of that 'un?"

"Yes. Yes. Don't you see? Just this once. Go on."

Completely outraged, Mrs. McMullen buttoned up her coat and marched to the door. But there she turned and said, "Very well. But I'll expect you as usual on Sunday, mind. What's things coming to, anyway? Ordered out!" Her voice was cut off abruptly from them as the door banged.

For a moment Lizzie's eyes rested on the closed door; then lifting Mary Ann up she set her on her knee and rocked her gently, saying nothing but looking away out of the window, over the roof tops, into a narrow stretch of clear sky, unpierced by even one tall chimney or crane or mast.

Was it wrong to wish to die? Was it wrong to wish from the bottom of her heart that she had never set eyes on Mike Shaughnessy? How much longer could she go on? . . . All her life, she supposed, until she was an old woman, inured to it all like Mrs. Lavey down below . . . hope dead, love and respect burnt out. What more could she do? Only pray for something to happen. She shook her head. Pray? She was always praying, until now it had become only a form of talking to herself. Sometimes she thought her appeals never left her head—there was no force left in her to push them out. Her belief in the goodness of God was going, if not already gone. To believe in God's inevitable pattern for good you had to be made like Mary Ann and swear black was white, or be a saint. She was long past the Mary Ann stage, and she wasn't made of the stuff of saints. She wanted to lead a decent life and to have Mike the way he used to be. She wouldn't grow into a Mrs. Lavey; she'd leave him.

She almost sprang to her feet, forgetting that she held the child.

The jerk caused Mary Ann to slip to the floor, and she stood dazed, and asked, "Is he coming? Is it me da?"

"No," said Lizzie, getting up; "you slipped."

"Ma."

"Me grannie . . ."

"Now"—Lizzie smoothed the tumbled hair back from Mary Ann's forehead—"forget what you heard your grannie say."

"But she said . . ."

"It doesn't matter what she said. Everthing's going to be all right."

"Honest?"

Lizzie pressed her teeth into her lip and her head moved slightly. "Honest," she said. Mary Ann sniffed and turned away. "Will I start getting the water up?"

"No. Wait until Michael comes in," said Lizzie.

"But he won't be in until six. Didn't he say that Mr. Wilson wanted him for two hours the night?"

"Yes, I know. But it can wait until he comes in. You go out and play for a little while."

"I don't want to go."

Lizzie looked down on her daughter, and she thought, Oh, let her want to go out to play. Don't let her start to reason and feel yet. But hadn't she always reasoned and felt, especially where he was concerned? If things came to a pitch, it would be her that would be the stumbling-block. If she were deprived of him she would die. She said, "Do you want the album again?"

"No." Mary Ann shook her head. And as Lizzie stared at her the sound of footsteps on the stairs caused them both to turn and face the door, but almost instantly they recognized the steps weren't his.

There came a knock on the door, and when Lizzie opened it there stood Mrs. Flannagan dressed for the street; and besides wearing her best things she was using her best voice, the one that Mike Shaughnessy called her refeened twang.

"Mrs. Shaughnessy, I must have a word with you. I'm sorry to trouble you as you've plenty on your plate, God knows, but I really must make a stand. It's getting that way that a body can't look out of her window."

"What has she done now?" Lizzie Shaughnessy's voice was flat.

"Stuck her tongue out at me. A yard long it was. I was just pulling back me curtains before I went out. I was just off to the confraternity . . . I'll let the sun in, I thought, to warm up the room. It's a pity you don't get it across this way in the evening, it'd make all the difference. But there I was at the window, and she came and with real intent and purpose she leant forward and stuck her tongue out at me. I was so taken aback, Mrs. Shaughnessy, I was really. It was uncalled for."

"Did you?" Lizzie looked over her shoulder to where Mary Ann was standing behind her.

"Not at her, Ma. At Sarah. She had stuck her tongue out at me and dived behind the curtains; and I was waiting for her."

"Now, now, now, Mary Ann." Mrs. Flannagan looked and sounded distinctly shocked. "My Sarah was nowhere in the room when I went to the window. You must not preevaritate."

"I'm not," said Mary Ann from behind her mother. "She was. I saw her through the curtains."

"Well! . . . That child!" To Mrs. Flannagan's feelings was added indignation. "It's one thing to weave tales as I know you do, but it's another thing to tell downright lies. I'll say no more, Mrs. Shaughnessy. But I thought I'd come and tell you . . . one must make a stand. And I'm not the person to cause trouble, especially to those who are heavily burdened already."

Mary Ann saw her mother's shoulders lift and heard her voice take on that note that made her different. "You came to tell me about Mary Ann putting her tongue out. You have told me, Mrs. Flannagan. I shall chastise Mary Ann. Is there anything more you want to say to me?"

There followed a short silence while the two women regarded each other. Then the older woman burst out, "Don't come your hoity-toity with me, Mrs. Shaughnessy; it won't wash. I pity you, I do, but I'll only stand so much."

"Your pity is entirely wasted, Mrs. Flannagan. . . ."

"It is that. It is that." The deep rocketing voice came from the stairs, and Mary Ann sprang forward, only be stopped by her mother's hip. She watched her father come into view, but he didn't look to where she was or at her mother, but straight at Mrs. Flannagan.

"Good evening to you, Mrs. Flannagan." He doffed his black, grease-laden cap, and standing over the now wide-eyed Mrs. Flannagan, he held it to his chest and moved it round between his hands in mock obsequiousness, and his voice took on a matching whine. "Your pity's wasted on me wife, Mrs. Flannagan. But now me, it's the very thing I'm needing. I'm needing pity so badly that you could bathe me in it; you could hold me down in a bath full of it and I would't drown. It has the same effect on me as beer, you know. Now, now, what's your hurry?" He obstructed her means of escape by standing at the head of the stairs. "Don't go away, Mrs. Flannagan, without sprinkling on me shamed head a few drops of your pity. It'd be about as effective as your holy water."

"Mike!"

Mike took not the slightest notice of his wife's sharp demand, but advanced one step further towards the now retreating woman saying, "Come now. Come now. You must make a stand. That's it, isn't it? That's your slogan . . . you must make a stand."

"I'll call me husband, mind."

Mike Shaughnessy's head went back and he bellowed forth a laugh. "You've got a sense of humour, I'll grant you that." Then of a sudden he dropped his posing and his voice lost its bantering tone, and he stood to one side and, pointing to the stairs, said, "Get down there, and don't come up here again unless you're asked, for if I find you at this door again I'll put me toe in your backside. That's if I'm sober. God knows what I'll do to you if I'm drunk." He watched her scurrying down the stairs; then he turned to his own doorway, which was now empty, and entered the room.

Lizzie was at the table and did not look towards him, nor he to her, but he threw his cap to Mary Ann and she caught it deftly. Then she took his greasy mackintosh and dived into the inner pocket where his bait tin was, and opening it, discovered there one sausage. She smiled at him, and taking it out sniffed its smoky, stale flavour; then began to eat it hurriedly before her ma should remember it was Friday and stop her.

Mike divested himself of his coat, and, rolling up his sleeves, went towards the scullery, saying, "What brought her here?"

Mary Ann and Lizzie exchanged glances. Then Mary Ann said, "I put me tongue out at her; I thought she was Sarah behind the curtains."

His head went up again, and he laughed: "Good for you."

Mary Ann lifted the kettle from the hob and followed him into the scullery. She poured the water into a dish and stood waiting at his side with the towel while he washed himself. He did this with a lot of puffing and blowing, interspersed with remarks about Mrs. Flannagan.

"You know the saying: Put a beggar on horseback and he'll ride to Hell? Well, it was started by just such another as her. Did you know that?"

"No, Da."

"Well, it was. She means to rise, that 'un, or die in the attempt. It's a good job the poor are kept down." He blew into the towel. Then peering over the top of it his brown eyes twinkled down at her. "You remember the time she sent the note to your school saying Sarah had an illustrated throat?"

Mary Ann laughed up at him. She remembered it well. The note had been passed among the teachers and they had not been discreet about the cause of their laughter.

"And there was the time she asked in Funnell's for the liquidated milk. Do you mind that?"

Mary Ann nodded and chuckled, saying, "If she couldn't have said evaporated she should have said unsweetened, shouldn't she?"

"She should that." He buttoned up his shirt neck. "Take my tip, Mary Ann. Anyone who tries to use long words in an aim to get above themselves, they're not much good. You can say all you want to say with your own kind of language."

"But if you could get to the Grammar School you'd learn big words then properly, wouldn't you?"

"Yes . . . yes, you would then."

"If Michael goes, he'll learn big words."

Mike stopped in the act of rolling down his shirt sleeves and stared at her; but she did not flinch from the look in his eyes.

She might fight with Michael because he called this man names—Michael sometimes lay on the floor and beat his fists on the mat, grinding out from between his teeth such words as "Big, rotten, drunken beast!" At such times she hated Michael and would think nothing of kicking out at him. Yet she knew why Michael said these things. He loved their mother and he was hurt when she was hurt, and he was ashamed of their da. He was going in for an exam for the Grammar School and he couldn't see himself holding a place there when his father's name was becoming a byword wherever drunks were mentioned—but her eyes were now telling Mike Shaughnessy that no matter how she fought with Michael she wanted him to go to the Grammar School, not so as she could brag about him, but because it would make her ma happy.

Suddenly Mike took her small face between his great hands and pressed it gently, and she pressed her hands over his before turning swiftly and running into the kitchen.

"Where's the kettle?" asked her mother.

"Oh!" She turned about again and collided with her father, and they both laughed.

Mike went to the table and looked significantly down on to the empty plates set there, and Lizzie, still not looking at him said, "I didn't get anything ready."

Mike gazed at his wife in silence for a moment before saying, "You didn't believe me then?"

Lizzie moved towards the fire, and his eyes followed her.

"I swore to you."

"You've sworn before."

"But I thought it was a fresh start?"

Lizzie stood looking down into the fire, and he came and stood behind her, his red head topping her silver one. "Liz"—his arms went about her—"help me; I'm trying hard."

She did not answer but made a choking sound, and he swung her round to him and held her pressed tightly against his chest.

Mary Ann stood at the door of the scullery, her eyes bright, watching them. It caused her no embarrassment to see her parents loving; rather, it filled her with bubbling joy. She listened now to her da's voice deep in his throat, and soft.

"Darlin', darlin'. I swear before God I'll make a go of it this time. Liz, Oh Liz. I should be hung for the things I've done to you." His voice became lower. "Never leave me, Liz. Promise you'll never leave me."

No answer came from her mother, only the sound of her sobs. They were too much for Mary Ann and she turned into the scullery and, leaning against the wall, began to cry. Oh it was going to be a lovely week-end. Oh her da was wonderful.

There was no connection between the man in there saying such words as darlin', beloved and precious, and the man who, just a week to-night, had rolled up the stairs at eleven o'clock singing at the top of his voice and proclaiming to all who would listen to him that at this time tomorrow he'd be a rich man, for hadn't he put three pounds on a sure winner, and the Sporting Pink would be red with his success.

There was no sound now from the kitchen, and after drying her eyes Mary Ann went in. Her mother was standing by the table opening her da's pay packet. She watched her shake out the contents. It was all happening as she had heard him saying last night it would.

Lizzie counted the notes, then moved the silver about with her finger. There was thirteen shillings, and she looked up at her husband and said, "Will that do?"

He stared at it for a moment; then smiled with the corner of his mouth drawn in. "Make it a quid. That'll do for me baccy an' all."

She handed him the pound, and taking another four from the bundle of seven she stuck them in a jug on the mantelpiece saying, "That'll clear the rent."

"Ah, Liz-a-beth. Must you do it all at once?"

His tone was joking, but Mary Ann knew that he didn't like what her ma had done. "Look"—he caught hold of Lizzie's arm—"pay two weeks. You can clear it next week. You'll have more next week. I'm telling you, you will. What do you think? Look at me now"—he drew himself up in a mock attitude—"and listen to what I am saying. Mike Shaughnessy is working the morrer—overtime till five."

Lizzie and Mary Ann stared at him but said nothing, and he dived across the kitchen and, lifting a chair, brought it to Lizzie, saying, "Hold on to that, for you'll need it." He put her hands on the back of it, then stood away from her and proclaimed in an awful voice, "Sunday an' all!"

Now Lizzie did show her surprise, and her expression gave him great delight; and Mary Ann stared up at her father, her eyes like pools of gladness. He was going to do overtime; he was going to work on a Sunday; he must have forgotten clean about the things he called theories, for they usually stopped him doing overtime. He often had these theories when he was having a period of . . . sickness, and then he would talk a lot about them. She had come to understand that if all the men did overtime there soon wouldn't be enough work for them in the middle of the week, and they would be standing at the street corners again. She couldn't imagine the men standing at the street corners in the middle of the week, except Willie James, and he'd neither work nor want. Sometimes her da's theories took a different turn, as they had done last week-end when he talked all the time about the men stopping work on account of Harry Bancroft being sacked. He said Harry Bancroft had asked for it for he'd never done a decent day's work in his life; then he got bitter and said nobody had wanted to strike when he'd got the push, yet he did more work in a day than some of them did in a week, for he wasn't a gaffer watcher; and if every man pulled his weight there'd be no need for overtime. And he knew why he had got the sack. It was because he'd made his mouth go against the Union.

And now he was going to do overtime, and they'd have a lot of money next week and her ma would be happy and not listen to her grannie.

She ran to him, and throwing her arms round his leg clutched it to her. Mike laid his hand upon his daughter's head, and still looking at his wife, said, "See? You see? I have me public." Then hoisting Mary Ann into his arms, he kissed her and asked, "Do you know what your da's going to do the morrer night?" And she, holding his beloved face gently between her hands as if it were something delicate and precious, said, "Take us into Shields."

He sniffed loudly. "Shields! Newcastle it is the morrer night, and we're going to do a show; and in style."

"Don't buoy her up." Lizzie spoke quietly. "I'm paying all the rent and you'll want your pound for baccy and for fares. And there's a bill to pay to Funnell's."

"But I tell you I'll make a fiver over the week-end—you can pay it off next week." He put Mary Ann down and moved towards his wife, saying, "Ah Liz, be reasonable."

But Lizzie moved away from him and went to the mantelpiece, and, taking the four pounds out of the jug, she turned to Mary Ann saying, "Straighten your hair and put your hat and coat on."

"What you going to do?" Mike's voice was stiff now.

"Send it to him." Lizzie sat down at the table, and having written a note, put it with the money in an envelope, and when Mary Ann stood by her side, she said, "Now you know where to go, don't you? Along Grange Road and turn to the right."

"I know," said Mary Ann. Her voice, too, was flat and had a touch of impatience in it. Oh, if only her ma hadn't got to do it. But she had; and there was her da looking at them, his face all hard again.

Her mother pinned the envelope inside the breast pocket of her school frock. "Go on now, and don't speak to anyone; and keep to the main roads."

As she moved towards the door no-one spoke, and when she went out, closing the door after her, and stood on the landing, still no sound came from the room to her. An urgent, turbulent feeling filled her stomach. It had a voice of its own which cried loudly in her ears, "Make them speak. Oh, make them speak. It'll soon be all right if they'll only speak." She waited, her head bent towards the door; she couldn't go all the way down Western Road and Ormond Street across Dee Street to Grange Road to the rent man's house knowing they were not speaking.

"You're not taking any chances on me, are you?"

In spite of her relief, the tone of her father's voice hurt her; and her mother's added to the pain as she said, "I've been taken before; you wouldn't have rested until you'd had that rent."

"My God! After all I said last night. All I was asking was that you paid two weeks and cleared it next. I wanted to give you a treat . . . take you away out of here for a while."

"I'd rather get out of here permanently."

"You shall, Liz—you shall, but I can't do it all at once."

Her father's voice was so convincing; how could anyone not believe him. And it went on, "Do you know it's Hell now—this minute my innards are burning for a drink."

"Mike. Oh, Mike!"

There was a scrambling sound, and she knew her mother had flown to her da and that her arms were about him and that she was soothing and mothering him like she did Michael and herself when they were bad. Filled now with a sad happiness, she was about to turn from the door when a voice hissing between the banisters caused her to jump.

"You sneaking little pig. Just you wait—I'll tell me ma. Listening at the key-hole again."

"Aw! you," she hissed back at her brother, "I wasn't listening."

When Michael reached the landing he towered above her, his indignation making him seem even taller. In looks at least he took after his father; and he already looked more than his eleven years, whereas Mary Ann looked less than her eight; but in repartee and temper they were equally matched.

"I'd like to box your ears."

"I know." She pursed up her lips and wagged her head at him. "But you'll have to grow a bit more, Michael Shaughnessy; and if you raise a hand to me I'll bite a lump out of you—see?" She edged round him and made her way down a number of stairs before turning and looking up into his angry countenance, and calling softly, "Ginger! you're barmy."

She did not stop to find out whether or not he was after her but took the stairs at a dangerous speed, almost taking Miss Harper's dustbin with her. But once she had gained the hall and found that she wasn't being pursued, her bearing suddenly changed and took on a graveness, as befitted anyone with a fortune pinned on her chest.

3

SATURDAY

It was a funny Saturday, Mary Ann reflected, her da being at work in the afternoon; and it was pouring from the heavens and she couldn't go out; and it was cold, too. She was sitting on the fender near the oven where she was both warm and lapped around with the appetizing aroma of baking. The bread was out and arranged on the rack above her head, and inside the oven a bacon and egg pie was cooking. Her da liked bacon and egg pie. And her mother looked happier to-day and nearly young again—twice she had laughed at her when she'd had to push her along the fender to get to the oven.

Michael was sitting at the corner of the table writing on scraps of paper. He was doing sums. He hadn't passed the exam last year, and she wasn't a bit surprised, getting sums like he had to do. His teacher said he should have passed on his head. The teacher had come and talked to her ma and said Michael was worried and highly-strung and nervous. She was glad she wasn't going in for any exam. She didn't hate Michael to-day, she was sorry for him, yet last night she had stamped hard on his bare foot and pretended it was an accident. She had done that because he wouldn't answer their da nicely when he talked to him. Her da wasn't sick, even a little bit, because he had never been out, and he had asked Michael about the exam, and Michael had been surly and said, "Oh, what's the use?" And he had gone out of the room and she had followed him and stamped on his bare toe. But to-day he too seemed happier, and he had been working at his sums all afternoon, except when he talked to their ma. Sometimes he talked quietly so that she wouldn't hear. She wasn't in the least annoyed at this because she liked to talk to her da in that way. Michael was talking quietly now, and she was pretending to read her comic while straining her ears to hear what he was saying. He was talking about clothes.

"I'd need a sweater and sports things; it wouldn't matter about a top coat, I never feel the cold."

"Don't worry about anything." His mother's voice was as low as his. "You'll get all things you need; you must keep all you earn from now on to help buy what's necessary."

"Oh, no."

"Well, I will just this week."

Why, Mary Ann wondered, should he want to keep his money just this week? And then with a start she remembered April the twenty-third was her mother's birthday, and to-day. . . . What was to-day? Yesterday at school had been the fifteenth; then this was the sixteenth. A week to-day! And she had nothing saved up. Well, only threepence. Still, she had to get her pay from her da yet. But that would only be sixpence at the most. She looked towards her mother's back. The skirt and jumper she was wearing both had a washed-out look. Oh, if only she had a lot of money and could go and buy her a dress. If she had a pound she'd buy her a lovely dress. There was a shop down Ormond Street that had lovely dresses. She had touched one once. There was a rack just inside the door and she had seen a woman pushing the dresses back and forward, and she had slipped in and stood behind the rack and fingered the dresses until the shop-woman had found her and chased her. Now, if she could buy her mother one of those dresses. If she could make a lot of money . . . oh, if only she knew the way to make some money. She was no good at knitting and selling things, or making kettle holders. Perhaps if she asked the Holy Family they'd show her the way. Yes, that was it. Bowing her head further over her comic and pretending to read, she began supplicating conversation with the Holy Family.

"Are you in, Lizzie?" A voice broke in on her prayers, and exclaiming, "Oh bust!" she raised her head.

It was Mrs. McBride. Not that she disliked Mrs. McBride, but she talked a lot and everything had been so nice, just the three of them; and now their Michael would go into the other room to do his work and it was cold in there.

"Come in, Mrs. McBride." Her mother never called Mrs. McBride Fanny, like the other women in the house.

"Oh, these stairs, I don't know how you stand them."

"Sit down. Get Mrs. McBride a chair, Michael."

Michael brought a chair forward and placed it near the fat old woman, then without a word he gathered up his papers from the table and went out of the room.

"Thanks, lad," Fanny called after him. "He still working at his books?" She looked up at Lizzie, and without waiting for any comment she went on, "What I came up about was Lady Golightly. I've just heard this minute that she was over here last night and that Mike put a flea in her ear. Oh, I wish I'd been in; I'd have had a reception committee on the ground floor for her, fit for the Mechanics Institute. What was she after, Lizzie?"

"Oh"—Lizzie measured the jam into the tarts—"Mary Ann and Sarah had been having a squabble."

"And what did Mike say to her?" Fanny asked, leaning across the table, eagerness expressed in each wrinkle of her sagging cheeks.

Lizzie laughed tolerantly and shook her head. "I can't remember."

Fanny sat back and with a sidelong glance looked up at Lizzie. She scratched herself under the breasts, then rubbed the end of her nose before asking "Is it true what I'm hearing the day?"

With a touch of asperity Lizzie replied, "Yes, it's true."

"Well, well." Fanny's face was beaming. "He'll be workin' on a Sunday next."

"He is."

"Glory be to God! The things you live to see." This indeed had the power to startle Mrs. McBride and she shook her head. Then pointing a grimy finger at Lizzie, she cried, "But you'll stand by me when I say I've always upheld Mike. Now, haven't I? Haven't I said time and again he's got one fault, and apart from that there's not a better fellow living?"

Mary Ann raised her eyes from the comic. Oh, she liked Mrs. McBride. Oh, she did.

"And he's got eyes for no one but yourself—that's another thing in his favour—drunk or sober."

"Sh!" Lizzie's voice came sharply.

"Oh, she's reading," said Fanny, waving Mary Ann's presence away with her hand; and she went on, "And I'm telling you, in a way you're lucky, for some of the flaming Janes round here would put up with his weakness just to have him around the house, for where will you see a better set-up man when he's sober? Or drunk, for that matter? I've known him for longer than anybody—I should know."

"Sh! sh!"

Fanny sighed in exasperation. "Why bother what they hear? You cannot keep them in glasshouses, they'll go their own road, some up, some down. Oh"—she leant back and began to laugh—"that reminds me. You'll never guess who our Phil's taken up with. Oh my, talk about reforming. What a week we've had! He's started courting a lass from Binns'—Binns' mind." Her watery blue eyes narrowed. "Stick that in your gullet and try to swallow. From no potty little draper's shop, but Binns' in King Street, in Shields!"

"Well, why shouldn't he? Phil's a nice lad."

"Ay, he's nice enough; but we aren't." Again she leaned back and laughed. "Oh, my God!"—she slapped her thick thigh—"you should have heard him last night at our Peggy's young Joe. 'You shouldn't say backside,' he said, 'you should say bottom.' He had cornered him in the scullery. And there was me—I had to sit down on the fender or I'd have collapsed. Joe's backside was no longer a backside but a bottom, and all because of a lass from Binns'."

Lizzie, trying hard not to laugh, said, "I shouldn't tease him—he wants to get on and he likely wants the girl—you should help him."

"Help him!" Fanny's voice rose in a crescendo. "Me help our Phil? Why Lizzie, nobody can help our Phil. It's him that's out to reform the world. You know he's never been one of us, has Phil; you could never tell where you had him or what he was up to; not like our Jack. Now he's as clear as daylight, is Jack." She sat back, quiet for a time, savouring the affinity between herself and her youngest son. Then suddenly leaning forward again, she said, "Did you hear about Lady Jane Collins and the rent man?"

"Mary Ann!" Lizzie turned sharply. "Go in and play with Michael."

"But he's doing his homework, Ma."

"Here," Fanny beckoned Mary Ann to her, "go down to our house, there's nobody in, and in the pantry behind the basin of dripping on the top shelf you'll find a bar of taffy. Take half of it. Go on now."

"Can I?" Mary Ann looked at her mother, and Lizzie nodded. Mary Ann knew why she was being allowed to go in to Mrs. McBride's. Her ma was afraid she'd hear something, like the time Mrs. McBride had talked of how she had first seen her da as a little baby in the workhouse nursery. Mary Ann didn't want to recall this, although it didn't hurt now like it used to, not since her ma had made it into a story.

She did not immediately go down to Mrs. McBride's but sat on the top stair thinking of and loving and pitying her da for not having had a ma and a da and for having been brought up in a Cottage Home.

She had first heard about this when Mrs. McBride had laughed at her da for talking stronger Irish when he was—sick. Mrs. McBride had stood in their kitchen and said, "Ah, Mike, it's real funny to hear you, and you never having set foot in the country. You talk it better than either me or me Colin ever did. God have mercy on him wherever He's put him."

Mrs. McBride had said a lot more, and her da had laughed, but it wasn't his nice laugh and her ma had pushed her outside and she had sat just here and cried. She had cried at intervals for a long time after that and then her ma had told her the story. And it went like this: Once upon a time an angel laid a baby in a basket outside Harton Institution gates. . . . No, no, she wouldn't think about it. She shuffled her bottom along the bare stair board to the wall. She'd begin where her da was a grand looking lad and worked on a farm, and her ma used to cycle past and watch him work the plough. . . . No, for that was a sad part too, for her grannie had found out and evacuated her ma miles and miles away. No; she'd begin where her ma was going along the platform on Hereford Station and she turned and looked towards the barrier, and there waving wildly was a man in R.A.F. uniform, and he was waving to her, and it was the boy with the red hair. She had walked back and through the barrier to his side, and when she stood near him he hadn't the sense to open his mouth.

Mary Ann sighed. That was the nice part of the story. It wasn't her ma, though, who told her how her grannie had tried to stop them getting married, it was her da, one day when he was—sick. Nor did her ma tell her that when her da came out of the Air Force he went to work on a farm near Kibblesworth, but that he wouldn't stay because he couldn't get a place where they could all live together; and he had come into the town and had worked for a time in Lord's yard before getting another job on a farm. But again he couldn't get a cottage, so once more he had come back to where they were then living in a house that had its own back-yard, and even a three foot wide piece of garden in front with an iron rail round it. Yet even in all this space he said he couldn't breathe—there was no air in his lungs. It was in that house she first remembered seeing him sick. Her ma never spoke of these things, but her grannie did.

Slowly now she went downstairs, past Miss Harper's open door, down the next flight and to the hall-way, and as there was no one in she did not trouble to knock on the McBride's door but pushed it open and walked across the room that was cluttered with furniture, all very much the worse for wear. But before reaching the scullery door she stopped and her head went to one side as it was wont to do when she was surprised or interested, and added to this her eyes now opened wide and her lips slowly parted, for her astonished gaze was resting on a couple locked tightly in each other's arms. Although their faces were so close together as to be one, she knew the man to be Jack McBride and the girl, Joyce Scallen.

Now she was not unused to seeing courting couples. When she came from confession on a Thursday night and it was dark she often bumped into them at the corner of the back lane, and their bemused swaying only evoked the term "Sloppy doppies!" from her. But this couple was different. This girl was Joyce Scallen and she was a Protestant. Worse than a Protestant—her da was in the Salvation Army, and everybody knew that Protestants, especially Salvationists, were destined for Hell. This had always made Mary Ann feel sorry, at least for Joyce, for she was so nice, and up to now she had steadfastly refused to believe that every one of the Protestants would go to Hell, for this would include her da. Yet somewhere in her was the knowledge that once the Holy Family had had time to answer her special prayer on that subject and her da . . . turned, then there would be no further anxiety about the destination of the Protestant tribe, singly or collectively. But eeh! for Joyce Scallen to be kissing Jack McBride—and in the McBride's scullery an' all.

The joined figures parted and Joyce's voice came pleadingly, "Oh Jack, let me go. You shouldn't have pulled me in; there'll be murder if I'm caught."

"It's all right, she's upstairs; she wont't be down for a while and you can hear her coming a mile off."

"But I must go; me ma'll be in shortly and someone may come."

"Will you see me the night?"

"I can't get out—there's a meeting."

"Then tomorrow?"

"Oh—I don't know."

"Look, we can't go on like this. Anyway, everybody knows about us but your folks and mine, and they're laughing, waiting for the balloon to go up."

"Yes, and when it goes up think of me da. And just imagine how your ma'll go on."

Yes, Mary Ann thought, Mr. Scallen would create, but what would Mrs. McBride do? Eeh! she couldn't make her mind imagine the scene that would ensue when Mrs. McBride got to know.

At this point her quick ears heard a familiar voice—it was Don McBride talking to his wife as they came up the steps of the house. In a matter of seconds they'd be in the room and Jack and Joyce would be caught. Wildly, she looked about her as if she herself were trapped; then she decided there was only one thing for it. Swiftly, she dived into the scullery and her sudden appearance brought a scream from Joyce. But standing with her back to the door, she did a wild pantomime that could not have been misunderstood by the dimmest. Joyce needed no other warning. Like lightning she darted out of the back door, down the yard and into her own door opposite, while Jack stood looking down at Mary Ann, who was now beginning to enjoy herself and feeling completely in command of any wits that were left to the short thick-set young man.

"Taffy," she whispered. "Bunk me up to the top shelf." The need for caution was gone but she wished to continue her part as long as possible.

As the voice of his brother came from the room Jack hoisted Mary Ann up to the shelf and hissed as he did so, "How long have you been here?"

On the ground once more and calmly breaking the bar of toffee in two Mary Ann said, "Oh a long time—I'll go out this way."

"Did you see—?"

She nodded, looking straight up at him.

She had reached the door when he thrust his hand into his pocket and brought forth a handful of silver. He raked amongst it and taking out half-a-crown pushed it into her hand, saying, "You won't let on to me ma?"

Mary Ann looked down at this gift from Heaven and murmured, "Thank you, oh thank you, Jack."

She was half out of the door when she turned back and whispered, "But I wouldn't have let on anyway, you know."

Suddenly they smiled at each other and she darted away out of the yard, round the corner and up the front steps again, and not until she had reached the comparative privacy of her own landing did she open her closed fist to make sure her eyes had not deceived her. Half-a-crown! And just for doing that. She had only to help another seven courting couples ahd she'd have a pound! She looked up at the stained and peeling sloping ceiling of the staircase.

. . . Oh Jesus, Mary and Joseph, thank you very much for showing me the way. . . . Now who would have believed they would have been as quick as that? She had only asked them a few minutes since. She shook her head at the tangible power of the Holy Family.

.   .   .   .   .

At half-past five the table was set ready and Mary Ann, surveying it, thought that she had never seen a better. There was a knife and fork laid for her da, which meant he was going to have a dinner; then there was the bacon and egg pie, and besides that jam tarts and tea-cakes, and a big sly cake. She moved around the table examining it from all angles. Her mouth was watering and she was hungry, but she resisted the desire to ask for even a piece of bread because she wanted to eat a big tea; her da liked to see her eat well.

She looked at the clock. Only another five minutes and he'd be in. She looked at her mother. Lizzie was sitting by the fire patching, and occasionally she too would look up at the mantelpiece and glance at the clock. She hadn't spoken for a long time now.

Mary Ann went and sat on the fender near Michael. For once he wasn't writing, but just sitting gazing into the fire. The three of them were all tidied up as if it was an occasion. These last five minutes, she decided, were going to be the longest in the afternoon.

She nudged Michael and asked, "Can I have a look at your Eagle?"

"I haven't got it," he mumbled; "I swapped Ned Potter."

"Well, can I have a look at your swap then?" she asked.

"I didn't get a comic."

"What did you get?"

"Oh—nothing."

"You must have got something."

He did not explain or argue further and Mary Ann's attention was drawn away from him, for the clock made a sound like a hiccup as it always did when it passed the six. It was half-past five. She looked towards the door, waiting and listening; her mother went on sewing, not lifting her head; and Michael continued to gaze into the fire.

The seconds ticked by, getting louder and slower in her ears, and just a small tremor of panic seized her when she found herself counting them. She had counted sixty eleven times when she rose from the fender. Their Michael was still staring into the fire and her ma was still sewing. She went and stood by the table, still counting. She counted sixty twice more, then she attempted to speak, but she got a frog in her throat and she croaked instead. It would have been funny at any other time, but not now.

When her throat was clear she asked, "Can I go down to the front door, Ma?"

"No," said Lizzie.

She stood staring at her mother, whose face seemed the same colour as her hair. Then she looked at the clock. It said a quarter to six. Well, he could have lost the bus—there were hundreds and hundreds of workmen waiting near the Mercantile for the buses. The feeling of panic swelled. Not on a Saturday though.

Then her mother spoke the words that sent the panic swirling through her body. Lizzie had risen from her chair and was folding up the mending, and she said, "Come and get your tea."

"No, no, not yet—oh, not yet."

"There's no use waiting." Her mother moved about the room as she spoke.

"Just a few minutes more—oh, Ma!"

"Now stop it!" Lizzie's voice was sharp as she turned on her, but it immediately softened as she said, "It's no use."

What was no use wasn't explained, and they looked at each other until Mary Ann's head sank, and, moving a step to the side, she slid on to her chair. Her mother then said, "Michael." But Michael's answer was to screw himself further round until his face was hidden completely from them.

Lizzie passed a hand over her brow. She looked from the back of her son to the face of her daughter. If there were only Michael she knew what she would do—pack up this minute and go. And when he came rolling in at eleven o'clock, then perhaps he'd believe what she said. But there was her. She'd never get her from the house no matter what ruse she used.

"Start your tea."

"I don't want any."

"Now do what you're told. Michael . . . come along."

The boy did not move, and she went to him and, taking his arm, led him to the table.

With her eyes Mary Ann watched her mother mash the tea but with her ears she was trying to separate the sounds of the house and leave a wide space for the sound for which she was waiting. The clock said six, then five past, then ten past, and she still had her first piece of tea-cake on her plate. Michael across from her was eating slowly and stubbornly, and suddenly she had a deep concern for him as she had for her da. She thought, Oh don't let him cry, for if he cries he'll be wild at himself; and the blame would be her da's and Michael would hate him more.

By half past six the panic feeling had given place to the awfulness, which was how she described to herself the anxiety, the fear and the love which combined to cause the feeling of utter sadness.

"Are you finished?"

"What?" Mary Ann blinked at her mother—she had been brought back from her listening. "I mean—pardon?"

"Are you finished?"

"Yes." They had all been finished a long time.

"Then say your Grace."

"Bless us, O Lord, and these Thy gifts, which we have received through Thy bounty. Through Christ, our Lord, A——" She stopped. There were thundering footsteps on the stairs, not sick footsteps and yet not her da's usual steps. They sounded like someone bounding up the stairs two at a time.

All their eyes were on the door when it burst open, and Mike Shaughnessy came into the room, red of face and laughing . . . and sober.

"Da, oh Da." She was hanging on to his arm, jumping up and down like a Jack-in-the-box, and he said, "Here, here. Hold on. Stop it. Look, you'll have old Miss Harper's ceiling down."

He looked from her to Lizzie. "I'm sorry I'm late," he said.

Lizzie stared at him, her face a mixture of relief and astonishment.

"You'll never guess what happened." He moved towards her, and her head moved slightly.

"I got an accumulator up."

"An accumulator?" Only her lips showed that she was repeating the word.

"I took a chance and backed Bird's Eye. It was a rank outsider in the two-thirty. I put ten shillings on. Yes I know, I know." He quelled the protest in her eyes. "But it came off. It was ten to one and the lot went on to Fancy Fair, and, God alive, that came up and then every penny was on Raindrop. It was the favourite and only two to one. If it had been anything of a price . . . Liz, don't cry. Aw, I knew what you'd be thinking, but I wanted to come home with the money, and I had to wait until the Anchor opened and Reg Brown paid out—I was afraid he might skedaddle with that lot—but I didn't even. . . ." He paused, and suddenly Liz sat down and dropped her face into her hands.

"Ma, don't." Michael was on one side of her and Mary Ann on the other and Mike in front, and Michael repeated again, "Oh Ma, don't."

Mike said nothing, but drew her hands from her face and, taking a wad of notes from his pocket, he closed her fingers about them.

The tears dropping on their joined hands, she looked down on the notes.

"There's over thirty there. I've kept three, and no-one's going to stop me from spending them." He took hold of her chin, lifting her face up to him. "We're all going to Newcastle."

Lizzie could only blink and say, "It's too late."

"You haven't had your tea."

"All I want is a wash."

"But——"

"Ma, Ma, come on." Mary Ann pulled at her mother's arm, and even Michael added to her entreaty and said, "Let's go, Ma."

"Where's that water?" Mike swung round and Mary Ann dashed to the fire and lifted the kettle from the hob and had the water in a dish by the time her da had stripped himself to the waist. She watched him lather his hair, and when he gave a particular grunt she lifted an enamel jug of cold water, and as she poured it over his head, turning his thick hair into spirals of rust-coloured ringlets, her thoughts too flowed with it like benediction, bathing him with her admiration and love.

4

THE BLINDNESS OF FATHER OWEN

Why was it, Mary Ann wondered, that happiness lasted for only short periods whereas unhappiness seemed to go on for ever? Or was it, she pondered, that unhappiness was made of stronger stuff than happiness? It must be something like that, for she could recall vividly the numerous times she had been unhappy, yet when she tried to recall the happy times the memories were weak and elusive, like the vapour that floated over the river; she couldn't pin them down. Even that wonderful week-end when her da had won all that money and had taken them to Newcastle, that seemed now like something she had seen at the pictures, it wasn't real; yet it had happened only four weeks ago.

The week-end following it had promised to be the same, too, but her grannie had stepped in and spoilt it. Oh, how she hated her grannie. Why hadn't she said "Milk bottles!" to stop her. But it would have been no use saying "Milk bottles" or trying any other means of stopping her grannie that time. It had all happened on a Sunday. Her ma had taken her and Michael down to their grannie's in the afternoon because their da was at work, and Mr. Quinton was there, and her grannie had a fancy tea all set out in the front room. And then Michael had made them all laugh, except, of course, her grannie, by saying for his Grace "Oh Lord, make us able to eat all that's on the table." She could remember being amazed at their Michael making anyone laugh; but since their da had been working overtime and hadn't been—sick, Michael had been different, even to their da. And all this had made their ma look really like a girl again, especially with the new dress and coat her da had bought her for her birthday. She herself hadn't been able to buy that frock she had set her heart on for her ma, although she had looked out for courting couples until she was tired. She had even got a clip on the ear off one girl who was having a row with her lad up a back lane off Ferry Street. It had been no use trying to explain she was only listening so as to be able to help.

But it didn't matter now, nothing seemed to matter any more since that Sunday night. She had become deader and deader inside since then. If she could feel mad, or scream or cry, it would be better than this feeling that made her want to die. She had actually been praying to the Holy Family for them to make her die this last week, and all through her grannie.

The scene, like all unhappy things, was held fast in her mind and she couldn't get rid of it. She had only to shut her eyes to see it all as plain as plain. They were having their tea and her ma was laughing at something funny Mr. Quinton had said, when her da walked in. For a moment he had looked terrifying as he glared down on Mr. Quinton, then he had laughed and said something to her grannie about when she was making plans she should always be prepared for set-backs. Mr. Quinton had got up from the table and stared back at her da, but he hadn't spoken to him. Then he said goodbye to her grannie and her ma and he called her ma Elizabeth, and when he had gone her da had said, "And now E-liz-a-beth, with your mother's permission, we will go home. It seems a great pity I was finished early, I spoilt the party. And your mother must have gone to great pains to organize it." Then he had suddenly dropped his quiet voice and, turning on her grannie, had cried, "You old devil, you!"

After that she couldn't really remember what was said, except the feeling of terror her grannie's admission had brought to her, for her grannie had said she would go on planning until she had her daughter away from him. She could recall the terrifying stillness of the room and then her da saying, "But what about a divorce? There's no divorce for a Catholic, is there? If your plan worked out you'd be making her live in sin, wouldn't you? You old hypocrite."

On this her ma had got them all out of the house and they had come back to Jarrow, and no one spoke at all on the way until they got home; and then her da wouldn't believe that her ma didn't know Mr. Quinton was going to be at her grannie's, and they fought in the bedroom, a different kind of fighting, talking low and quiet and bitterly. And at intervals during the following week they had talked like that. But still her da hadn't been sick until last Saturday, and even then he hadn't meant to be, for he had come in at half-past five after doing overtime, and it was then her ma had told him she'd had the offer of a house, one of the newer ones, up Primrose Way. At first he had been pleased, and then he had begun to question her, and in a sudden burst of temper her ma had admitted it was through Mr. Quinton's influence that the offer had been made. Her da had gone out then and got sick, not blind sick but just sick enough to talk and talk and talk; and twice during the week he had gone and got sick like that again; and last night as she held the towel for him he asked her quite suddenly: "Do you like Mr. Quinton?" and she had lied promptly, saying, "No, no, I hate him." And as he dried himself he had said flatly, "You can't lie to me—you like him because he's smart and has a fine big car and he never swears."

"I don't."

"And what's more, he doesn't get—sick—does he?"

She had fallen against him and clung to his leg and he had said something to himself that made her shiver. "Life's hell," he had said. He had loosened her hands from him and walked away. There seemed to be a deadness about him—he didn't bounce or rush or laugh any more—and the deadness was on her too, and she wished that she was really dead—dead as dead and in purgatory, and so taken up with going through it for her sins that she wouldn't have time to feel like this.

"If I have to speak to you again, Mary Ann Shaughnessy, you'll know about it. Are you going to confession?"

"Yes, oh yes, Miss Johnson." Mary Ann dragged herself up out of her misery and from her desk.

"Then stop dreaming. . . . Now you'll all walk three abreast, and if there's any carry-on in the street like there was last Thursday you'll all be for it in the morning. Grace Smith, stop that pushing there. . . . All those going to Father Beaney at the front and those for Father Owen at the back here."

Mary Ann joined the latter group. Not only did she not scramble for the front place but she took the inner side of the last three in the ranks which ensured her the unenviable position of being the last to go into confession, but that was what she wanted, for when she was last she could talk to her heart's content and the priest wouldn't hurry her on. Once she had told Father Owen all that was on her mind she knew that she would get some relief from this feeling. She had seen him a number of times during the past week but of course she couldn't tell him her trouble in any other place but the confessional box, for she didn't want him to know it was she who was troubled, or what she was troubled by, and in the confessional box he wouldn't know it was her, for as everybody knew God struck priests blind once they entered their part of the box so as they wouldn't know who was talking. They might peer through the grid but they couldn't see a styme. That's why you could tell them everything that was in your heart and not be afraid they'd split on you.

As the crocodile swung out of the school-yard it touched on a group of the bigger girls. They, too, were on their way to confession, but, because of their years, free and unhampered, and among them and near to Mary Ann's side of the ranks was Sarah Flannagan.

After mimicking the marching by striding along the gutter swinging her arms, Sarah addressed herself to Mary Ann's averted face and hissed, "Convict!" whereupon Mary Ann, without turning her head but mouthing each syllable widely, said, "Cas-i-bi-anca, flannel face!"

This retort had the effect of infuriating Sarah and with her fist she pushed Mary Ann in the back and knocked her flying into the girl in front, who, in turn, fell on to the girl in front of her. The result was four children lying on the pavement and Miss Johnson standing over them, saying, "Who did this?"

There was a chorus of "Mary Ann Shaughnessy, miss."

"It wasn't!" Mary Ann denied emphatically. "It was Sarah Flannagan."

But since there was neither sight nor sound of Sarah Flannagan Miss Johnson said, "You come to me to-morrow morning," which added bitterness to Mary Ann's collection of negative feelings and a new resentment against so-called justice.

In church she found it impossible to make her preparation for confession—she could only keep thinking that she wished she were dead. With one thing and another, she was fed-up and tired of it all. If only it was possible to die quickly—like that. She snapped her finger and thumb against her bent forehead. If something could happen and she could be struck dead. Laurie Carter had said her mother knew a man who had been struck dead because he swore at a priest. . . . She lifted her eyes over the back rest and looked across the church to where the Holy Family were enthroned in deep shadow. If she was struck dead she'd likely go straight to them. For the moment she had forgotten the required passage through purgatory. Suppose she swore at Father Owen. Eeh, what had put that into her head? Fancy thinking about swearing at Father Owen! But if it would make her die . . . No, not Father Owen. Well, which other priest did she know but Father Beaney? and she wouldn't have the courage to go up to Father Beaney and swear at him. She stared through the dimness towards the altar, and presently she thought, "If I'm going to do it, Father Owen will be the best." Suppose, as she was kneeling in the box, she did just a little swear at him. Perhaps that would do, and when he died he'd know she hadn't meant it. But what would she swear? Should she say damn? No, that wasn't quite big enough. Bloody? Eeh! no, that was too awful. She might be sent to Hell for ever for that.

The last penitent came stumbling out of the box, and, rising from her knees, she sent up a quick prayer to the Holy Family in an appeal to be provided with the swear words necessary to cause her demise. She groped her way into the dark confessional and knelt down below the grid and began in her customary way, "Pray Father give me thy blessing for I have sinned. It is a week since my last confession."

"Yes. Go on." The priest's voice seemed to come from a great distance and did not for the moment seem to be the soothing voice of Father Owen but of a priest who already knew all her sins and the blackness of her heart, so, quickly, she gathered her wits together and presented them to him, "Please, Father, I have given way to the sin of hate."

"Who do you hate?"

"Me grannie."

"Why?"

"Well, she's always saying nasty things about me da and she wants me ma to leave him and she's got another man all ready for her. The other man's nice enough but he's not me da."

There was a movement of the priest's feet, and he said, "Your mother—what does she say about all this?"

"Nothing, Father—at least they fight a bit. She gets sick to the heart because he goes and gets a skinful. I mean he gets drunk."

There, she had said the word. It was only in here in the fast secretness of this box with this blind priest that she could utter that word.

"When was he last drunk?"

"He had a few last night, Father."

"Go on with your confession."

"I've kicked our——" She stopped herself saying the word Michael, he might recognise her through that name; so she said, "Me brother. And I've torn up the scraps of paper he writes on, and made him wild by calling him Ginger. And I've missed my morning prayers because I got up late, and I've looked over Cissy Tollard's shoulder into her exercise book."

"Yes; go on."

She was raking round in her mind for her other great sins when it came back to her that not a few minutes ago she had committed the worst sin of all by deciding to swear at him.

"Go on, my child."

But she couldn't go on. And after waiting a while he said, "Come on, my child, finish your confession."

"I wanted . . ."

"Yes?" he encouraged.

"In the church, a minute back, I made up my mind to swear at you, Father."

"You what?"

Two white bulbs came close to the grid and looked down on Mary Ann, but she looked fearlessly back into them knowing that the eyes were sightless. After a while they were withdrawn and the priest said, "And why did you want to swear at me?"

" 'Cause I wanted to die."

"Because you wanted to die?" There was utter bewilderment in his tone.

"Yes, I heard tell that if you swore at a priest you'd be struck down dead."

Father Owen gave two short coughs, then he blew his nose before saying, "And why, may I ask, do you want to die?"

"I told you, Father, it's about me da. I'm miserable and I never want me dinner and I don't care if I can go out to play or not. I even thought if I could find some poison I'd take it and when I was dead me da might be sorry and not get drunk again."

"Poison?" The priest's voice was crisp now. "Poison's no use, I've tried it."

"You have, Father?" She was brought clean out of her own trouble with surprise and she stretched up to see better into the dimness beyond the grid.

"Yes, it only gives you the gripes in your inside and you're no better off."

"Oh——" The thought of gripes in her inside turned her for ever from the thought of poison, but she went on, warming up to the situation, "Last night I was so miserable, Father, and me ma wouldn't let me go out and look for me da and I thought if I could get out I'd a good mind to throw meself under the bus where it rounds the Ben Lomond in Ellison Street."

"Under a bus? Oh, that's a worse idea altogether."

"Is it Father?"

"I'd say it is. What happens when you throw yourself under a bus? It chops off either your arms or your legs and you live on, and it's not a very pleasant state having no arms or legs, is it?"

"No, Father."

"Well, forget about the bus, and pray to the. . . . Who do you usually pray to?"

"To the Holy Family, Father."

"Oh, the Holy Family . . . well, you couldn't pray to a better Family, and you pray to them to-night and ask them for something nice to happen to you. What would you like to happen?"

"Oh, Father. For me da. . . ."

"Oh"—he cut her short—"leave your da to God. Now isn't there something you want to happen to yourself?"

"Well, I wanted to get into the procession, Father."

"And you're not in it?"

"No, Father, and all of them have been picked."

"Yes. . . . Ah well, you go on praying to the Holy Family and you can be assured they'll make something nice happen to you."

"They will, Father?"

"They will that. They never fail. Now for your penance say the first Joyful Mystery of the Rosary, and make your act of contrition."

"O my God, I am very sorry I have sinned against Thee because Thou art so good, and by the help of Thy Holy Grace I will never sin again."

"Good night and God bless you."

"Good night, Father."

Out of the confessional box, Mary Ann decided it would not be wise to stay in a now empty church to say her penance, for the priest, once out of the box and his sight back, would know it was her he had been talking to. And he'd remember about the drink and connect it with her da.

On her way home she wondered what nice thing the Holy Family would make happen to her; but this only played on the fringe of her thoughts, for deep in the permanency of her mind she knew there was only one thing that really mattered, one thing that would make her happy, and that was the happiness of her ma and da.

.　　.　　.　　.　　.

Friday was usually a nice day. It began by having your breakfast packed up and going off to Communion, then going straight to school and eating your breakfast in the hall, that's if you hadn't already eaten it on the road. Then there was Bible History, and one Friday in every four Father Owen or Father Beaney came and heard your Catechism. It was nice on the days Father Owen came, for he made you laugh. Then the class acted pages from history—to-day it was to be Flora Macdonald and Bonnie Prince Charlie. And in the afternoon there was the poetry lesson. She liked poetry and could remember long bits of it.

When she was in Miss Harrington's class she used to get pennies for being the first to learn, but Miss Johnson didn't give you anything . . . only the stick if you didn't know it. But she never got the stick for not knowing her poetry. She knew long stretches of Hiawatha's childhood. It was easy stuff to learn because the man who wrote it kept repeating everything so as to make it easy to remember—like:

> "He was a marvellous story-teller,
> He was a traveller and a talker,
> He was a friend of old Nokomis,
> Made a bow for Hiawatha;
> From a branch of ash he made it,
> From an oak-bough made the arrows,
> Tipped with flint, and winged with feathers . . ."

Oh, she knew yards and yards of it.

> "I have given you streams to fish in,
> I have given you bear and bison,
> I have given you roe and reindeer,
> I have given you brant and beaver . . ."

Sometimes at night she put herself to sleep saying it.

Yes, she usually liked Fridays, at school anyway, but to-day the misery from last night still lay heavily upon her. She had arrived home from Confession to find her ma out, and she hadn't got back before her da came in, and they didn't speak. And he'd gone out after he'd had his tea and got a little sick; and in the night she had woken up on the camp bed where she slept under the sloping roof by the side of the scullery door and there, lying on the mat in front of the dead fire, was her da, with just a blanket over him. She felt so bad at the sight of him lying there in the cold that she began to cry. She had got up and the noise she caused brought her ma out of the room, and she made her get back into bed. And now here she was in school, with her breakfast still uneaten, and feeling more than ever that she wanted to die.

This morning was Catechism test and all the partitions of the school had been pushed back and Father Owen was up now on the platform talking. She wasn't paying much attention to him, for she was having her work cut out to keep her six inches of bottom space on the edge of the desk seat. All about her was a mass of heads and shoulders, except to the right of her where there was a little altar. It was St. Anthony's altar, and he was standing on a pedestal in his brown habit with no shoes on, and his feet looked cold, she thought, and there were bits of dirt in between his toes. In a detached way she decided that when she was moved up into this class after the summer holidays she'd scrape out all that dirt. She didn't like dirt between her toes—her ma made her and Michael wash their feet every night before they went to bed. They were a rare family for washing, especially her da. The thought of her da brought back the thought of dying, and she looked once again at St. Anthony. She had never laid much stock by him, yet she heard he was quite good at finding things for you if you lost them. She wondered, if she prayed to him now, how long he would take to bring about her wish. Anyway, it would pass the time away for there was nothing to see in front of her and nothing to hear but a mumbling of voices.

There had been quite a bit of stir at the beginning of proceedings because Betty Paul, who was to lead the procession dressed in a blue cloak and a crown like Our Lady, had gone and got the measles. Fancy anybody going and getting the measles when they were going to lead the May Procession and walk bang behind the statue of Our Lady hoisted on a platform and carried by four boys. She wouldn't have done a silly thing like that. But what did it matter, she wanted to die.

She looked up into the face of St. Anthony and with first a little placation just to soothe him and make up for her neglect of him, she began, "Dear St. Anthony, I haven't prayed to you because I've been so busy, but I know full well how clever you are, and you could perform any miracle you like if you wanted to. Dear St. Anthony, I'm very miserable, and you being in Heaven will know why. And please, St. Anthony, I want to die, Oh, I want to die. I can't bear to think about me da. . . ."

"Mary Ann Shaughnessy—where is she?"

The priest's voice was lost to her, but a thump between the shoulders was an effective way of recalling her to it. A number of voices hissed at her "Go on out." "Are you daft?" "Don't you hear Father Owen calling you?" "What's up with her?" The voices brought her to her feet and she looked towards the platform, and there was Father Owen laughing and beckoning to her with his hand.

"Come on, come on, Mary Ann," he called. "Were you asleep?"

As dazed as if she had been, she walked towards the platform wondering all the while what she had done to be called out. Surely it wasn't because of last night—she was going to report to Miss Johnson when her class assembled again. Her teacher was at the bottom of the steps, but said nothing to her, only pushed her up them, and not too gently either, and, still in a daze, Mary Ann found herself in front of Father Owen and with a whole sea of faces around her, for on the platform was the headmistress and a lot of the teachers, and not one of them was looking pleasant.

What had she done to be brought up here? Only if you stole anything or broke somebody's windows were you yanked up on the platform and made an example of.

"Well, there it is. One person's bad luck is another's good." Father Owen put his hand on Mary Ann's head and slowly screwed her around to face the school. "As I've already said, nobody was more upset than myself when I knew that Betty had the measles and I had to find someone to take her place, so as it is my privilege to pick from the school the leader of the procession, I have decided on Mary Ann Shaughnessy here. Granted Mary Ann is small"—he looked down on her—"but I've a notion that the Holy Mother herself was a slight body, and the gown may have to be shortened, but that can easily be done. I have chosen her because there is no black mark against her in school, and since she made her first confession fifteen months ago there has not been one week but she has attended Confession and Communion. Now let us give her a great big clap."

He led the clapping by banging his long bony hands together. Mary Ann gazed up at him, then at the obedient clapping hands in front of her, then to the side where the teachers were clapping in such a way that would not have disturbed a sleeping baby, and she asked herself whether she was in bed having another of her dreams. But no, she wasn't, for her eyes were on a level with the bottom button of Father Owen's slack waistcoat and she could feel his fingers moving in her hair. She was just about to realise the wonderful enormity of the thing that was happening to her when out of the blue came the answer to her eager prayer of a moment ago. She felt it first starting in her legs as a shooting pain which screwed itself up through her chest and into her head. All the faces about her began to run into one. She made a great effort to steady herself and to keep her feet on the ground but it was no use, and when, without any warning, Father Owen's long thin figure began to swell before her eyes she knew, in an illuminating flash, what was happening—her earnest prayer to the Saint was being answered and she was about to die. The inadvisability of dealing with two firms for the one product was brought home to her—competition could evoke disastrous results. The efficacy of St. Anthony's power was terrifying—he was as sharp as the Devil himself. She spun round to where his statue showed dimly in the distance, and there he stood laughing at her—she could hear him. She turned about to where the statue of Our Lady dominated the side wall above the platform and cried, "Put it right with him, will you? I don't want to die now . . . well not just yet."

But neither the Virgin nor the complete Holy Family had anything, it would appear, on St. Anthony for quick service, for he strode from his pedestal shouting, "It's nice to be able to play God," and he picked her up in his arms and carried her off and rushed her straight through the air heavenwards.

The rush of the air made her gasp and his voice boomed in her ears as he shouted from the clouds down to the headmistress, "I consider her need the greatest."

Suddenly he dropped her and she gasped and gasped for breath as she fell. Having landed with a thump, she opened her eyes; then after one startled glance about her she lay back in contentment as she realised she was in the sanctuary of the Teachers' Room, lying on a couch, with the Headmistress on one side of her and Father Owen on the other.

"You're feeling better? That's it. Ah—that's it. You've been to Communion and haven't eaten your breakfast, I bet. Now, am I right?"

She made a slight movement with her head and he laughed and said, "I knew it."

"Father."

"Yes?"

"It's true . . . about . . .?"

"You going to lead the procession?"

She nodded again.

"As true as life, but only if you drink a glass of hot milk and eat up a good breakfast."

"I'm not going to die?"

"Die?" His long body seemed to fold up with laughter. "I should say not. And you're going to wear that lovely blue gown."

She gazed up at him. He didn't know it was her he had told last night to pray for something nice to happen, and she couldn't tell him for it would give the show away. But lifting her hands, she caught hold of his fingers and pressed them to her cheek. "Oh, Father, Father," she said.

5

MR. FLANNAGAN, THE CORONATION, AND MIKE SHAUGHNESSY

Nowhere in Jarrow was the Coronation looked forward to and prepared for more than in Burton Street. For weeks there had been Committee Meetings. That the Committee grew in numbers and became divided in policy was to be expected, but that the divided parties should break up within themselves into smaller factions was to be regretted. Some were for teas in the street with games afterwards for the bairns, some, remembering rain-soaked street parties from the past, were all for the Baptists' Hall; but as Mrs. McBride said, who'd want to get drunk in the Baptists' Hall? This called down censure from most of the factions. Who wanted to get drunk at all? Those who wanted that kind of a party had better take themselves down to the Fifteen Streets and not join in the festivities of a respectable neighbourhood. There was a nodding of heads and the murmuring of the name Shaughnessy. Then there were those who suggested that every adult in the street should subscribe five shillings, the accumulated wealth to be used for sending three of them, these to be determined by a draw, up to London to see the actual procession. Before protests could rain down on this proposal it was haughtily thrust aside by Mrs. Flannagan saying that if the Flannagans wanted to go to London they were quite able to provide their own train fare, thank you, and they had already refused the offer to accompany her sister and husband from Hartlepools who were going to her sister's husband's cousin and he had an excellent view already for them, from the window of the office where he worked, slap on the Coronation route.

At this, a combined murmur like the wash of the tide on a pebble beach came from all quarters, and it could have been translated into "Oh ye-ah!"

Finally, after many meetings, a street party was decided upon, which as some of the Committee said, had been inevitable from the first. One stipulation was made: should it rain the bairns were to have their tea in the Baptists' Hall and Mr. Gallon engaged to do his Punch and Judy Show. Of course there was one snag here, as those people who were not tired of arguing pointed out, they couldn't leave it until June 2nd to say if it was going to rain before engaging Mr. Gallon—he'd have to be engaged wet or dry.

The day dawned and it does not need testifying that it was wet, but it took more than rain to damp the enthusiasm of the tenants of Burton Street and Mulhattan's Hall in particular. The children were wild with excitement, and the adults got rid of much of their suppressed emotion in trying to quell the exuberance of their young.

But put two hundred and twenty six people in a hall that would be crowded with half that number and you will find all emotions subsidiary to the feeling of self-preservation. So at least thought Mike Shaughnessy.

He was sober and dressed in his best and standing in the corner of the hall. It would have been impossible to sit down had there been anything to sit on. The only advantage he had was his view—his head topped every other man's and woman's in the room—and he looked down on the rows of trestle tables lined with children and the rows of their admiring parents watching them eating as if they were accomplishing the feat for the first time in their lives.

Mike was not unaware that he was a subject of interest; that he was sober on such a day as this was a source of wonder to his neighbours. From different quarters he had seen covert glances and heard whispered words. At least he was a man who wasn't unknown. He smiled wryly to himself as his eyes roamed over the crowd, halting here and there to hold a gaze fixed on him in curiosity, and he wondered if anyone in this room would believe that ten years ago he hadn't known the taste of beer or whisky. Yes, there was one . . . she knew.

His eyes went to Lizzie. It was easy for him to find her, for he hadn't allowed her to move far from his sight all afternoon. She was like a queen among peasants, standing out far above them. My God, if ever there was a fool in this world he was one—to exchange her for a skinful of beer! He could only blame himself, not Quinton. He would lose her; then what would become of him? He'd be finished. Why did he do it? Why wasn't he as big and tough inside as he was out? Why did the smell of oil and tar and rope and the singey smell of hot rivets fill his stomach with the craving? Yet it was no use blaming the work and the sweat; he recalled the periods when he had sweated on the land. He had burned then for a drink, but a draught of spring water or a canful of milk had swilled it away. He was weak and he knew it.

It seemed like the twisting that Fate was apt to indulge in that he couldn't settle on a farm away from her and the youngsters, yet if she left him and he was adrift with nothing to hold him to this blasted town he would still be unable to return to the land. She mustn't leave him . . . ever. His heart began to beat rapidly, pumping as if at the end of a run, and he felt his pulse beat, as it had often seemed to do of late, in his eyes. Just the thought of losing her filled him with the terror of loneliness, that loneliness that he had known as a child and then as a boy, the loneliness that made him shun crowds and people, the loneliness that for its easing required only one heart to beat against. If she left him, the loneliness he had known before would be as nothing to what would come in the years ahead. But it needn't happen. It was up to him; he had only to go steady. She didn't mind him having a glass or two if he could stop at that. Yes, if he could. And then there was the other one tugging at the secret place in his heart. If anyone could keep a man straight it should be that child. His son, he knew, wouldn't care if he was gone the morrer, but Mary Ann. . . . He looked towards her and her eyes were waiting for him. She waved her hand and he waved back. The pride of him showed in her face, and he thought that she could be proud at any rate of her achievement in getting him here to-day. God knew she had worked hard enough at it, but he did not know for how much longer he could stand this crush and the warm, damp air of the room. The noise was a bedlam vying with that of the dry-dock, and he was feeling it pressing down on him. If only he could make his way towards that door and stand in the street a moment and get himself a mouthful of air. Judiciously he began to edge his way forward. He even got past the entrance to the hall kitchen where plates and trays were being handed overhead from hand to hand, but just beyond this and within a few steps of the door his progress was halted and he found himself wedged in another corner to make room for the hasty exit of a child who had eaten well but not wisely. She was being pushed through the crowd with the fiercesome admonition from her mother to "Hold it." The dire penalty of her refusing to comply with this order rose above the clamour. The situation amused Mike and he laughed, and so did the man at his side, and Mike turned his head towards him and said, "Poor little beggar, she's between the devil and the deep blue sea." The man looked back at him for a moment without speaking, then he laughed again, but not such a hearty laugh this time and said, "Yes. Yes, you're right."

"And," commented Mike to himself, "you're another poor little devil." Anyone unfortunate enough to have to spend a lifetime with that upstart woman Flannagan had his sympathy. Mike chuckled inwardly. How often had he been threatened that he would suffer for his insolence at the hands of this little chap, and up to the present this was the nearest they had got to each other.

He said quite pleasantly, "I'm trying to make for the door to get some air," and Mr. Flannagan replied with equal pleasantness, "I'm heading that way meself."

They nodded at each other, a strange, comradely nod that said, "We may as well make it together then."

"London's got nothing on this," said Mike, when at last the double doors were reached.

"You're right there, Mr. Shaughnessy."

Oh, thought Mike, we're getting our title the day—Mr. Shaughnessy it is. And to think we've seen each other every day for two years with never a "Whatcher there!"

"Harry!" The astonished, strident voice brought Mr. Flannagan swiftly round and he stood with his back to the door and faced his wife. "Where you off to?"

Mr. Flannagan did not answer for a moment, but his eyes flitted to Mike's back where he stood struggling with the long iron bar of the door. Then he said briefly, "Outside."

"Why?" asked Mrs. Flannagan. "What do you want to go outside for?"

Mr. Flannagan's answer to this was drowned by Mike's laugh. Perhaps he was laughing at himself being unable to get the door open. With a quick jerk the bar went upwards and the double doors shot apart, and as he turned to close them his eyes met the malevolent glare of Mrs. Flannagan, and he laughed in her face and closed the door on her words, "Stay where you are till the air's clearer."

Mike stood in the shelter of the porch for a moment and looked at the rain falling like a solid lead sheet across the opening, and Mrs. Flannagan's voice, muffled now but still audible, came to him. He could not distinguish what she was saying but her tone told him that the poor little devil was getting it hot and heavy. As the door behind him opened again he turned his collar up and stepped out into the rain. He found it was not amusing to hear the little fellow being slated; rather, he was embarassed. When a woman made a man look small it touched all men.

"Do you hear me?" Mrs. Flannagan's voice followed him through the opened door. Then on a pitch of a scream it came down the empty street, crying, "Harry!" and it told Mike that Mr. Flannagan must be somewhere behind him. He did not turn round, but he thought with a glow of satisfaction, "So he stood his ground . . . good for him." And he slowed his pace until the little man came abreast. The odd thing was that Mr. Flannagan made no effort to pass on, but suited his steps to Mike's, having to lengthen his stride to do so. This must have conveyed the worst to Mrs. Flannagan, for her voice crying, "Do you hear me, Harry Flannagan? Come back here this minute!" seemed to hit the two men in the neck. Anyway, it sent them forward at a quicker pace until they rounded the corner of the street. There Mr. Flannagan, his face running with rain, looked up at Mike and asked quite solemnly, "Would you mind me company, Mr. Shaughnessy?" and Mike, successfully keeping his eyebrows stationary, replied in his politest tone, "Not at all, Mr. Flannagan, not at all."

.   .   .   .   .

Mary Ann saw her da leave the hall, and for a moment the brightness of this wonderful day vanished, until she told herself that he had only gone out for a mouthful of air and he would be back in a minute. But he didn't come back in a minute.

The tea over, the children were bidden to sit where they were to see the Punch and Judy Show. Mary Ann tried to catch her mother's eye and ask her permission to attempt to leave the table, but Lizzie's eyes seemed to rest everywhere but on her daughter. Mary Ann did not care for Punch and Judy—the sight of poor Judy being beaten unmercifully with a stick always made her close her eyes—so at this point in the entertainment she followed the ruse of so many other children who were bored with sitting in one spot for so long, she put up her hand. It seemed to her that almost immediately her mother was behind her, and with a warning injunction for quiet, she lifted her off the form and carried her with some difficulty through the press, but not towards the backyard of the hall, but to the main door. Once outside, she put her down, saying, "There are too many waiting, we'd better go home." She did not say, "You had better run home and then come back," and Mary Ann knew that her ma wanted to go and see if her da was home.

It had stopped raining now and they hurried along hand in hand. Mulhattan's Hall was quiet and had the air of a house that had been vacated in a hurry, especially in the hallway outside Mrs. McBride's door, for there reposed a welter of oddments, the possessions undoubtedly of Mrs. McBride's numerous grandchildren. Mary Ann ran ahead up the stairs and pushed open their door.

She did not call down to her mother that her da wasn't in, but her silence was telling enough for Lizzie, and when she entered the room she made no comment one way or the other but an anger rose in her against the man who was so weak and so selfish that he would not keep his promise to this child even for a day. The promise had not been given in words; but in a thousand and one ways Mary Ann had tried to impress on him the importance of Coronation Day and extract from him a laugh or the slow shaking of the head or a quick hoist in the air, and all these she took as signs that he would stay with them on that day and enter into the jollification.

Her own heart had softened towards him as it hadn't done for some time when she had seen him standing patiently with the crowd in the hall, for she knew how human contact in the mass could irritate him. But it had been too much for him. She had expected too much of him. Her anger made her silently vehement. He was weak, he was cowardly, he was rotten to the core. Let him hurt her, she could in a way stand up to it, but the look on the child's face when yet once again he had let her down was heart-rending. She turned to Mary Ann who was standing near the table picking at her fingers and said, "I thought you wanted to leave the room?"

"I did." Mary Ann turned and walked out and down the stairs, and Lizzie went into the scullery, and after staring down into the sink for some time she beat her fist three times in quick succession on the draining-board, and when the sound of Mary Ann's footsteps mounting the stairs again came to her she sighed heavily and went into the kitchen, and with an effort towards brightness she greeted her daughter, "Well, shall we go back?"

"No, I don't want to."

"Why?"

"Well, it will be nearly over."

That was true. "But," said Lizzie, "now that it's fair there'll be the races in the street and you've been practising for long enough."

"I'm tired."

"Now listen," Lizzie spoke sharply. "You're no more tired than I am," which, if this had been strictly true, would have made Mary Ann very weary indeed.

"I am," persisted Mary Ann, sitting down.

"What about the prizes you were after? The big box of chocolates Mr. Funnell's giving, and the doll to the best skipper?"

"I'm tired."

Lizzie moved her head impatiently; then as a noise like a stampede of cattle came from the street she said, "There they are, all back."

"I don't want to go."

"But we were going to see all the bonfires later on—what about that?"

Mary Ann looked straight at her mother and the look said, "If he comes in roarin' will we leave him and go and see the bonfires?"

Lizzie turned and went to the fireplace, and with the raker pulled from the back of the grate a little more coal on to the low embers, then swinging round almost fiercely, she cried, "Well, you'll go to bed mind, I'm not having you sitting there with a face like that."

Even this threat could not bring Mary Ann out of her misery, and when she said, "All right", Lizzie gave her one helpless look before walking into the bedroom.

She sat on the edge of the bed and rocked herself slowly. Oh, dear God, dear God. Was this to be her life? There was no likelihood at all that he would return before he was well soaked, and he would say, "Well now, take you for a spoil-sport. Isn't it every creature that's drinking the Queen's health the night?" His voice would be thick with the Irish brogue, a tongue she had come to detest, for the deeper his cup the thicker it came. Once he had tried to explain to her the reason why he spoke broad Irish when he was drunk. You've got to belong somewhere, he had said; there are two things a man must have, a mate and a country. When you grow up knowing that you belong to nowhere or to no one and that no one belongs to you, that your very name was given to you by a committee, and one name being as good as another, they let you be called after the man who had picked you up from the gate, when a thing like that is the kind of thought you live with from the time you start thinking you begin to make up places and people that do belong to you. It was natural I should pick on Ireland with a name like Mike Shaughnessy, and for people it was as natural as breathing that I should pick on you the moment I saw you, with your golden hair and your promise of another world.

Oh, Mike, Mike. She leant her head on the bed-rail and her pity was resurrected. Why had life to be like this? Why wasn't she big enough to fill the loneliness that ate him up at times? He loved her, she was the only creature he wanted. He was capable of killing any man who would come between them, yet he could not kill or would not kill that which was a greater danger to their happiness than any man. Oh, Mike, Mike.

He had been gone three hours now. It would be another two or three before he would be back. She was weary and tired of thinking, tired of counting time, tired of worrying, tired of anxiety, tired of living. She raised her head and looked towards the window, for the noise and shouting from the street had suddenly increased. Was it only the echo of her worry or had she heard Mike's name called above the yelling and the shouting? She sat bolt upright, her ears strained. There it was again. Mike and Mr. Shaughnessy. Mr. Shaughnessy, the voices said.

Darting to the window she stooped and peered down into the street. The twilight had not yet deepened into darkness but the street lamps were lit and in the half-light she could not at first make out one figure from another; then her eyes were drawn over the crowd to a clearing, in the middle of which a man was dancing with his hands above his head. He was dancing a weird imitation of a Scotch reel, accompanied by the clapping and stamping of the crowd. But it was not Mike—it was Mr. Flannagan. She dropped on to her knees and lowered her head to the bottom of the window to confirm that she was seeing aright. It couldn't really be Mr. Flannagan, the solemn, miserable-looking little man, who rarely opened his mouth to anyone and was known never to have touched drink for years, not since he was converted to sobriety by the visiting mission. Without closer confirmation she knew that only if he had . . . 'had some' would he be dancing in the street. But Mike; they had been calling Mike. Where was he? Her eyes roamed wide over the crowd, peering through the distorted reflections of the lamps, only to come back to the cleared space. And then she saw him, and her amazement grew, for Mr. Flannagan, who had stopped dancing, was pulling him by the arm in an effort to induce him to join the fray.

That Mike should need inducement to join in a bit of jollification was a sure guarantee that he was sober. She was completely mystified by it all; everything was topsy-turvy, Mike sober and Mr. Flannagan drunk. Slowly she raised her eyes from the street to the window below on the far side of the road, and seeing the outline of Mrs. Flannagan's face behind the curtain and being only human, she voicelessly said, "Now how do you like it, Mrs. Flannagan?" Then remembering the torture she herself had endured she added, "But I wouldn't wish it on you, no matter what you're like."

"Lizzie! Are you there, Lizzie?"

Lizzie turned from the window as Mrs. McBride's voice came from the other room; and before she could reach the door it was thrust open, and Fanny, puffing and yelling, cried, "Was there ever such a crowning to a day as that? Have you seen him?"

She carried Lizzie towards the window again with a sweep of her arm. "Look at him!" She pointed into the street. Then looking across to Mrs. Flannagan's window, she voiced the same sentiments as Lizzie had restrained. "Ah, me fine madam. How d'you like it? This'll knock some of the stinking brag out of you. . . . Oh"—she turned to Lizzie, her broad beaming smile making her face resemble nothing so much as a dented and rather discoloured bag of tripe—"oh, if I've lived to see nothing else, this"—she indicated with a jerk of her thumb the again dancing figure of Mr. Flannagan—"this would have been worth all me struggles. And if it doesn't keep the Duchess of Dam' All quiet for the rest of her life I'm a Hallelujah. Oh, isn't Mike the boy that gets his own back! If he had tried for a thousand years he couldn't have thought of anything better."

"Mike?" Lizzie looked at the old woman. "What's Mike got to do with it?"

"He did it. Took him along and got him bottled up. Didn't you see them leaving the hall together? Mary Prout said there was a do in the street with Lady Golightly."

Lizzie's face hardened as she stared down on to the back of Mrs. McBride's head. The things these people said. Mike had his faults, God knew, but petty vindictiveness was not one of them. Yet what about Mr. Flannagan trying to get him to dance? If they hadn't been together would he have done that?

"The street's alive with it," went on Fanny, again cocking her head up to Lizzie. "Everybody knows the things she's said about Mike. Aw, who says the devil doesn't look after his own? Do you want to look down, hinny?" She put her hand out to where Mary Ann was standing now near her mother. "Come and see your da. He's down there as sober as a judge, and it's Coronation Day an' all."

"I wouldn't say that, Fanny."

The three of them turned abruptly to where Mike was filling the doorway. His face was not clearly discernible in the dimness of the room, but his voice, the inflection of which could tell Lizzie whether he had been on beer, whisky, or both, told her now that he'd had a few beers, but that was all.

"Oh, there you are, Mike. How did you get away from him? You've got yourself a drinking pal from now on. But what in the name of God gave you the idea? If you'd spat clean in her eye you wouldn't have hit her harder."

As Fanny threw her laughing remarks to him, Mary Ann darted across the room. She did not shout, "Da! Oh, Da!" but just clung on to his arm, pressing her face against his sleeve in a passionate expression of relief.

Mike fondled her head and asked of Fanny, "Who says it was my idea getting him drunk?"

"Who says! . . . Ah, what d' you take me for, Mike?" She pushed past him. "Who says? Why everybody in the street, and they're all having a dam' good laugh, knowing the way she's held you up as a disgrace to the neighbourhood."

"Has she now?"

"Has she now? Why are you playing so dumb all of a sudden? Has she now? Oh, you'll kill me with your fun one of these days. Well, here I am now going to see what happens when old Flannagan knocks on his door for admittance. I'll be seeing you, Lizzie. . . . Has she now?" She leered at Mike in farewell.

Lizzie made no comment, and not until the outer door had banged did Mike speak. "I didn't get him full," he said.

"Who did then? He's been with you, hasn't he?" Lizzie's voice conveyed neither displeasure nor amusement.

"Yes, he was along of me; I couldn't shake him off. It was at his suggestion we had a pint together. . . . And then—" Suddenly Mike's voice broke, and his head went up and back, and his rocketing laugh filled the room. He took out his handkerchief and dabbed his eyes and said between gasps, "Me. I had to put the brake on because of him. Can you see me putting the brake on because of Harry Flannagan? I kept saying, 'No. I'll just have a gill. . . . No, no,' I said, 'I never touch whisky.' And there he was with a double and a pint at his elbow. I tell you I had to get him out while he was still on his legs. If I'd waited any longer I'd have to've carried him back." His laughter eased to a gentle shaking, and he looked at Lizzie and said, quietly, "It's funny, don't you think, me having to keep him steady to look after him? He wouldn't leave me; I couldn't shake him off."

It was funny; the anxiety, the worry, the pain, and her recrimination of him were once again washed away with his elusive endearingness, the unfair endearingness that had the power to blot out all but the feelings of the moment. With one accord they moved swiftly to each other, and his laughter rolling out again, he caught her up and swung her about.

Mary Ann's laughter joined his, but it was a little too loud and a little too high to be natural, and it was too full of relief to stay as laughter. This was the first time since her da had won that money that she had seen him and her ma laughing together and with their arms about each other. It meant that everything was going to be all right, no matter what her grannie did or how nice Mr. Quinton was.

Her laughter broke on a cry, and she fled from the room and through the kitchen into the scullery, and she leant her head on the sink and sobbed. But almost immediately she felt herself lifted up, and hiding her face, she buried it in her father's neck. And when Lizzie, stroking her head, said, "Come, come now, we're going to see the bonfires," her crying mounted, for it was the only way in which she could express her happiness at this moment.

6

SUNDAY

The world was a beautiful place; there had never been any rain, or dullness, or darkness; for was not the sun shining brightly, and wasn't she walking in the country? In the country, mind, where the big trees grew, hand in hand with her da!

Not only was Mike solid and sober but he had on a new suit, and to crown his well-set-up appearance he was wearing on his head not the usual cap but a trilby. Mary Ann's gaze continually lifted from his face to the hat, and her heart was so swollen with pride that it was ready to burst from her body. Oh, he looked lovely in his new hat. Never, never in all the world was there anybody who looked so wonderful as her da. Only one cloud touched him and the morning—Sarah Flannagan's eyes had not beheld the glory of him. Before they had left the house she had watched Sarah depart for Mass, and she had failed to induce her da to walk round by the church on their journey to the country in the hope that they would encounter Sarah coming out.

The thought of her enemy made Mary Ann once again put her hand tentatively towards the back of her head and feel the lump that even after a week had subsided very little. She touched it almost lovingly, for had she not received it in defence of her da?

On the morning following the events of Coronation Day Sarah had cornered her round the bottom of the back lane between the store shed of Tullis's outdoor beer shop and the Colyers' backyard wall. There in the narrow alley she had pinned her against the wall, and in language not strictly of school standard had accused Mike of making her da drunk and making her ma nearly throw a fit, and keeping them all up half the night, and, what was more, causing her da to lose the first shift in years because his head was so bad he couldn't raise it from the pillow.

Mary Ann had stoutly denied these accusations, saying that her da was solid and sober as everybody in the street knew, and he had never been inside a bar or smelt beer. As for Mr. Flannagan, he was a disgrace. Hadn't she seen him with her very own eyes being dragged into the house by Mrs. Flannagan? That was when her da was taking them all to see the bonfires. And hadn't Mr. Flannagan made a show of himself by fighting Mrs. Flannagan because he wanted to go along with her da?

That Sarah's rage only led her to bang Mary Ann's head repeatedly against the wall said something for her control. Whether she would have continued this restrained retaliation until she had accomplished Mary Ann's entire insensibility cannot be known, for Mary Ann's cries brought Mrs. Colyer from her house, and Sarah reluctantly departed at a run.

The attitude of her parents concerning this attack was not quite clear to Mary Ann; even her da gave her little sympathy, and her ma did not show the slightest sign of going to Mrs. Flannagan and telling her off. There was, she felt, injustice somewhere; but to explain it, even to herself, was beyond her. Only one thing was sure in her mind concerning the affair, she had got this great bump on her head and nearly died in defence of her da.

"That's the farm," said Mike.

"Oh."

Mary Ann looked over the yellow-green fields towards the flat-faced red-brick house and asked, "Will the cottage be that size?"

"No. No, of course not," said Mike. "You know the size of cottages; they're like the little houses at the Quay Corner, two or three rooms at the most. But there's bound to be a good patch of garden."

"And how'll I get to school?"

"You'll have to take the bus. But wait, I haven't got it yet."

The altered tone of her father's voice made her lift her eyes searchingly up to him. His smile had gone and there was a stiff straightness about his face that brought the shadow of anxiety back for a moment to dim the sun, and caused her to resort to praying rapidly that the job might be his.

There was no one in the farmyard except a sow with its stomach almost trailing the ground, and the sight of it brought Mary Ann from an anxious conversation with the Holy Family. She had never seen such a fat pig. She stared at it amazed, fascinated by the wobbling enormity of its flesh.

Mike left her to her wonderment and went towards a brick cowshed standing stark in its newness from amongst the time-worn, rather tumble-down buildings of the yard.

"Mr. Campbell?" He spoke to a man who was unscrewing a nozzle from a pipe, and the man turned his and said peremptorily, "Yes, I'm Campbell. What is it?"

The tone slightly nonplussed Mike. But he went forward, and in a carefully guarded voice, said, "I've come about the job; I was told you wanted a hand."

"Oh, that." Mr. Campbell straightened his back, his eyes still directed towards the nozzle. "You're too late, that's been filled nearly a week."

The expression on Mike's face did not change, but he stood staring down at the bowed head of this under-sized little man and making a great effort to check a swift rush of temper. He hadn't got the job. That was bad, but by now he was, in a way, inured to disappointment; it was the offhandedness of the man that had angered him. He was still intent on the pipe; it was as if he were alone, that nothing existed for him but the nozzle of the artificial milker.

Abruptly Mike turned and walked away, out of the cowshed, across the yard towards the road again, holding out his hand silently to Mary Ann as he went. His return was so quick and unexpected that she had to drag her thoughts back from the fascinating ugliness of the pig to take in exactly what this quick departure meant.

She moved towards him and put her hand in his. And so swift was his stride that she had to run to keep abreast of him. She could see he was flaming mad—she used his own expression to describe his temper—and she was sensible enough not to anger him further by asking senseless questions.

They had gone some way down the road when they were both halted by a shout. "Hi! Hi, there!"

Mike turned slowly, paused a moment, then walked back towards the farmer. They stopped within a few yards of each other, and there was no prelude in the farmer's speech. "Old Lord will be needing men; he's bought Coffin's farm. . . . You know Lord's place?"

Mike nodded.

"It was only sold yesterday. Coffin's taking his men with him. There'll be two empty cottages. . . . I suppose you want a cottage?"

"Yes."

"Well, I would try there." Then as if to explain his previous disinterest he added before turning away, "I'm having trouble with the new machine. Not used to it yet."

He had almost reached his farm-gate when Mike shouted, "Thank you, sir."

The man raised his hand in acknowledgement, and Mike and Mary Ann went on their way again.

"Are we going to Mr. Lord's, Da?"

"No."

"What for not?"

"Because it would be no use."

"Why?"

"Oh." Mike moved his head impatiently.

"If there's a cottage, Da?"

"You know who Mr. Lord is, don't you?"

At the moment Mary Ann didn't know; she had to delve back in her mind. . . . Mr. Lord? . . . Mr. Lord? . . . "Oh yes." She smiled. "He's the man with the big stone walls round his house, with the big trees inside. You can't see the house. It's up beyond the cemetery."

Mike nodded.

"And he's got a wood farther along with barbed wire round and you can't get in."

Mike nodded again.

But Mary Ann could see no reason why this should keep them from visiting Mr. Lord. Her mind groped to understand all her da had left unsaid. Then suddenly she understood. Mr. Lord was . . . the Lord. It was the nickname the men gave him in the yard, and her da had once worked in Lord's yard. And he had left when he was having a lot of talk about his theories. . . . Mr. Lord and the Lord were the same person. Her spirits sank to a still lower ebb, and any hope of the cottage sank with them.

They boarded a bus that took them into Hebburn and then on to Jarrow, and when they alighted at the Ben Lomond, Mike said, "You run off home, I won't be long." And after one long look at him, Mary Ann turned silently away. The sun had gone, the day was dull, almost dark again.

She walked through the empty streets. The shops were shut and there was no one even sitting on a step, because it was Sunday. Everywhere looked bare and deserted and the atmosphere touched her low spirits and sent her off at a run to seek the security of the kitchen and the comfort of her mother. But her running ceased abruptly when she entered her street, for there she saw small groups gathered together on the pavement. There must, she surmised, have been a row. But not on a Sunday, surely. You could have rows up to quite late on a Saturday night, and they'd be quite in order, but it was shocking to have them on a Sunday. Smugly the thought came to her that it couldn't be her family, anyway. No, but it was in Mulhattan's Hall where the row was. She had evidence of this as she neared her home, and her surprise was almost stupefying as she mounted the stairs, for the shouting was coming right from the top of the house, and it was Mrs McBride who was doing it.

She passed Miss Harper's open door, and also the Quigleys', and when she reached her own landing Mrs. McBride was shouting at her mother, "Why didn't you tell me, you could have tipped me the wink?"

She stood in the doorway watching them. Mrs. McBride was all dressed up in her Mass clothes, the tight black coat and the black felt hat she wore only on Sundays. Her mother was wearing the big apron she put round her when she was doing the dinner; she had the oven cloth in one hand and she kept pulling through the other; but she didn't answer Mrs. McBride; and Fanny cried: "The whole place has known except me, and never a thing would I have heard yet but for something Mary Prout said at the church door. She was talking to May Brice. 'Join the army and see the world,' she said, 'and join the Salvation

Army and see the other world. Wait till old Fan gets wind of it, Jack'll wonder which cuddy's kicked him.' It wasn't long afore I had it out of her, and I nearly died when I heard. And let her take what she got, for I wouldn't believe a word of it. Yet there's no smoke without a fire, and I came tearing home and tackled him, and he admitted it."

She became silent for a moment, and her gaze turned inwards. She was seeing the astonishment on her son's face and feeling the tearing hurt of his words. "Yes, it's Joyce Scallen. And I'm going to marry her. And just you try and stop me. And you make that rowdy tongue of yours go about it and I'll do it right away, I won't wait."

But her tongue was her only weapon, the only weapon she knew of, and she had lashed it at him, and not only at him but at the whole family of Scallens.

Lizzie said gently, "It might turn out all right. Just give them a chance."

"A chance! A chance to do what, I ask you? Lead a hell of a life? What chance is there for happiness between a Hallelujah and a Catholic . . . because she won't turn? Do you know what her father said to me? 'It must be the will of God,' he said. And he said that God was showing Jack the way and he'd be saved yet."

"You see," said Lizzie, "Mr. Scallen's taking it quietly. There'd be more chance with Jack if you could take it quietly an' all; you'd beat Mr. Scallen at his own game them."

"So you think like me," cried Fanny, "he means something? Perhaps he's known about it all along, although the old swine said he hadn't." She flung her short arms wide apart and lifted her eyes to the ceiling. "Oh, what am I to do? Before you know it there'll be our Jack leading the band and knocking bloody hell out of the big drum, and I'll never be able to raise me head again on the whole Tyneside."

Try as she might Lizzie could not suppress a smile, but her concern for the old woman was genuine, so much so that she addressed her by her Christian name as she said, "Don't worry, Fanny, he'll not do anything silly; he's a sensible lad, is Jack; only be patient with him."

"Patient!" Fanny spoke quietly now. She looked suddenly deflated. "I've always been patient with him. Now if our Phil had done this I could have understood it. But not Jack. Not him." Shaking her head, she moved towards the door saying, "This is what comes of missing Mass and neglecting his duties. It's two years since he was at them." She paused near Mary Ann, and in a broken voice, said, "There's worse things than drink, hinny. Remember that." She patted her on the head, then went slowly down the stairs.

Mary Ann watched her. There was a lump the size of an egg in her throat—Mrs. McBride was crying.

Her mother was standing by the table waiting for her to speak, but she couldn't for the moment, and Lizzie said, "He didn't get it?"

She shook her head.

"Where is he?"

"At the Ben Lomond. He won't be long."

Lizzie turned away and Mary Ann said, "The farmer was nice. . . . He was sorry and he told me da about another job."

"Where?" Lizzie turned about again.

"At Mr. Lord's."

"Lord's?"

"Yes. Beyond the cemetery."

"The shipyard man?"

"Yes. Me da said it was no use going."

"He was right."

Mary Ann watched her mother go into the scullery. She too looked deflated. There was no comfort or security even here; and the whole world must be sad when Mrs. McBride was crying.

7

THE LAST STRAW

Although during the following week Mike was never paralytic, his inability to reach this stage being, he himself confessed, merely owing to the weakness of the beer, he was at times well set. Yet he had made no oration in the street, and hadn't sung until he reached the stairs. And although on this particular night he had to be alternately pulled and coaxed away from Miss Harper's fast-closed door, where he insisted on serenading her, not untunefully, with "He was her man, but he did her wrong", this had been the only incident of the week.

But this incident, which had amused everyone in the house with the exception of Miss Harper and the Shaughnessys themselves, was the means of snapping the taut thread of Michael's strained nerves. He had sat for the examination, and during the waiting period prior to the results being made known, he was up in the clouds and down in the depths ten times a day . . . yes, he would be telling Lizzie, he felt he had answered most of the questions correctly; or no, he was sure he hadn't and had mugged everything.

It was earlier in the evening of Mike's serenading that Michael's pal had dashed in to say his parents had received a letter saying he had passed for the Grammar School. The last post of the day had been to Mulhattan's Hall and Michael had done his best to be pleased for his pal, but even his best was a poor effort, and Lizzie, keen disappointment filling her together with a heart torn with pity for her son, tried to reassure him that there was still tomorrow and that they wouldn't send all the notices out together. Michael had made no response to this except to shrug her hand off his shoulder and go into the other room and close the door after him.

It was eleven o'clock the same night, when Lizzie had to arouse Mary Ann from her bed to go down and coax Mike from Miss Harper's door, that Michael had begun to cry. His crying at first had been the broken sobs of a child, but when his father staggered into the room his sobs turned to angry gasps and when Mike, still singing, flopped into a chair he sat up and screamed at him: "Shut up, you drunken pig you! I hate you, you rotten drunken pig!"

There followed a short surprised silence, which was suddenly broken by Michael crying again, "Damn! damn! damn!" He thumped the bedcothes with his fist, and when Lizzie rushing to the bed tried to draw him to her he sprang up, thrusting her aside, and ran to where Mike, silent now, was surveying him. "I wish you were dead, do you hear?" He pushed his face towards his father, who was now wearing a fuddled, surprised expression. "They wouldn't let me pass because they knew about you . . . everybody knows about you. I wish you'd fall from the top of a mast and be smashed to bits."

"Michael!" Lizzie dragged at him, but with the strength of his passion he again thrust her off, crying at her now, "Why don't you go away and leave him? Why do you make us stay here? I won't stay; I'll go to me grannie's."

With the aid of the chair Mike rose. He seemed much steadier than when he had sat down and his voice was only slightly fuddled when he said, "Be quiet, do you hear?"

"I won't! I won't! I loathe you. I wish you were. . . ."

"Quiet!" The shout vibrated from the walls, and in the silence that followed they all stood still, seeming to be stunned by the force of the order.

Mike was staring down into his son's face and his expression was frightening, but it seemed powerless wholly to intimidate Michael, who continued to glare up at him, and after a moment Mike turned from the loathing in the boy's eyes and, with only a slight sway in his walk, went towards the room.

Mary Ann watched her mother lead Michael to the bed. She watched her tenderly cover him up, then lie down on top of the bed beside him, and not until she began to shiver did she go to the corner where her bed was, and, climbing in, turn her face to the wall and thrust her fingers into her ears to shut out the sound of Michael's crying.

It was a long time later when her mother came and stood over her. She did not let her know she was awake, but kept her eyes closed. She heard her walk softly away and turn the light out, and when the darkness fell on her lids she opened her eyes and stared into the blackness. She felt her mother move across the room and into the bedroom. The door clicked softly. Then there was no sound. She could not even hear Michael's breathing. Poor Michael. Her thoughts were tender towards him. If only he had passed the exam, then he might not have minded about her da so much.

The words Michael had used to her father had not shocked her, for he had expressed them many times to her, and whereas she had always fought him when he upbraided Mike, to-night for the first time she felt in sympathy with him. But this did not mean she was less sorry for her father or that she condemned him, it only meant that within her small body was the capacity for understanding the agony of the personal disappointments of childhood.

For what seemed to her hours and hours she lay on her back staring into the darkness. Once a car passed down the street, and once Miss Harper had a fit of coughing and it sounded as if she was in the room. She was slowly falling into sleep when she was recalled to her wakefulness by the foghorn wailing up the river, and she felt a little guilty that she should sleep when there was all this trouble in the house. Hastily she determined that she must keep awake. This was her last thought before sleep overtook her, but then it was a troubled sleep, for her dreams were on the surface and once or twice as was usual with her she told herself she was dreaming. Once she imagined she heard Michael get out of bed and go into the scullery, the door of which was near the foot of her bed, but it was all mixed up in her dreams.

She was not sure what woke her; perhaps it was the smell—she had been dreaming that she was being choked by the smell. She tried to sit up but found that her head was heavy and that she felt very sleepy. She also felt a little sick. Now why should she be feeling sick, for she had eaten no supper and she hadn't eaten any sweets for two days? It was a gassy smell, like when her mother turned the tap on and dropped the match and the gas came out of the oven and filled the scullery.

She was never to know exactly what drove her to rise against all her opposing inclinations and stagger to Michael's bed. It was empty, but she knew where he was . . . he was in the scullery. The scullery door was closed, and when she pushed it open the gas met her in a sickening wave. She could not see Michael but she knew he was there.

Staggering in her run, she burst into the bedroom and having groped her way to the bed pulled madly at her mother.

"What is it?" Lizzie was sitting up. "My God!" Almost immediately she got the smell of the gas and was out of bed.

"Michael."

"He's in the scullery." Mary Ann's words were cut short by being knocked on her bottom in Lizzie's dive for the door.

"Wha's up? Wha's the row?" Mike's voice, thick with sleep, came from the bed, and Mary Ann, scrambling to him, shook him by his slack hanging arm, crying, "It's Michael—he's in the scullery and the gas is on."

Again she was almost knocked flat, and by the time she reached the door she heard her father's voice coming from the other side of the kitchen, saying, "God in Heaven, what's he done?"

It was many hours later that Mary Ann recollected they were the only words she heard her da speak that night. It was her ma who did the talking. Fiercely she whispered, "Open the window, and the scullery one, too, and let a draught through . . . and do it quietly."

As Mike swiftly obeyed her command she said to Mary Ann, "Get me the torch from the cupboard—mind the table."

Mary Ann groped her way to the cupboard, groped for the torch, then groped her way back to where her mother was kneeling on the floor. Lizzie snatched the torch from her fingers and, switching it on, plunged its light on to Michael's face.

Mary Ann stared down at her brother. His face looked pink and smooth and swollen. He looked sound asleep, very sound asleep. She watched her mother grab him by the shoulders and shake him. She allowed her eyes to travel to her father's legs and up to where they disappeared beneath his shirt-tail, but she could not lift them to his face . . . until he bent his body over his son and his face came into the beam of the torch, and then she saw it was grey, an awful whitish grey, and that his eyes, although sunk deep into his head, had, at the same time, a popping look. His whole appearance looked wild and not a little fantastic. His strong wiry hair was standing up from his head in points and his shirt seemed too short and tight for his body.

Mary Ann moved swiftly back as he hauled Michael from the floor and carried him to the window. Her mother followed, directing the light towards the floor. Mary Ann looked to where her father, silhouetted against the darkness of the night and the blackness of the houses opposite, was shaking Michael, and when after a moment Michael's head lolled against his shoulder Lizzie turned to Mary Ann gasping, "Get your things on, quick." And she followed her to the bed saying, "Run for the doctor, the nearest—that one off Ormond Road—Pimsel." Her talking was in staccato whispers. "Tell him . . . tell him that Michael . . . wait." She stopped, and Mary Ann saw her turn to the window. "No, don't go yet. Look, run down to Mrs. McBride's. Go quietly without your shoes. Let yourself out the back door. She sleeps with the window open a bit. Try not to raise the house. Ask her to come. Go on now." She pushed Mary Ann to the door, putting a coat about her petticoat and her thin bare arms as she went.

Mary Ann did not need to be told to hurry or to make no noise. She was used to the stairs in the dark, and when her swift light tread made them creak she took no notice for she knew they always creaked at night—it was the souls in purgatory being made to use them as a tread-mill that caused the creaking.

The cold of the yard struck up through her stockinged feet as she closed the back hall door softly after her and she knew a moment of fear at finding herself in the back-yard made unfamiliar with the night. When she reached Mrs. McBride's bedroom window she raised herself to the sill by digging her toes into the wall, and she called softly through the narrow opening, "Mrs. McBride." On her third call she heard a rustling and she knew that she had woken the old woman, but not until she had repeated the call did she hear her speak.

"Holy Mother of God," said Mrs. McBride; and Mary Ann said, "It's me, Mrs. McBride . . . Mary Ann."

There was a pause before Mrs. McBride answered, "Mary Ann Shaughnessy? In the name of God, what's up?"

"Sh!" said Mary Ann. "Listen. Me ma sent me for you . . . our Michael's bad."

"Bad?"

"Yes."

Mrs. McBride didn't seem to be unduly disturbed by this and Mary Ann had to say the dreaded words, "He's put his head in the gas oven."

It seemed to Mary Ann that almost in a single blinking of her eyelids Mrs. McBride was at the back door. Dragging a coat over her dirty nightdress with one hand, she pulled Mary Ann into the scullery with the other and pushed her ahead into the room and across it; then quietly unbolting her door she drew Mary Ann into the hallway and preceded her up the stairs. She did all this, to Mary Ann's amazement, with the quietness and swiftness of a cat.

From the moment Mrs. McBride entered the room she took command of the situation. She bent over Michael where he was now lying on the bed and put her hand inside his pyjama jacket for a moment, then turning to Mike, she said, "Hoist him up and get him walking, he's not gone. . . . That's it." She got on to one side of him. "Come on now, keep him going. Make up a good dose of hot salt water, Lizzie." She turned her head in Lizzie's direction without pausing in her walk. "He'll come to. That's it, keep him at it Mike, it's air he wants."

In the light of the torch Mary Ann stood watching her da and Mrs. McBride dragging Michael back and forward between the window and the bed, his feet trailing like dead things. It was a strange and weird trio, made more fantastic still by the torchlight. Suddenly Michael's body stiffened, his head came up and his chest swelled out and he retched and was sick over the floor.

"That's the ticket, get it up lad. He won't need the salt water now." When they got him back to the bed again and Lizzie held a dish under his head, Mrs. McBride exclaimed in much the same tone as another would use when viewing an objet d'art, "Lovely . . . beautiful."

Mary Ann moved a little closer. Michael was lying gasping now, his head moving heavily from side to side, and she could have thrown herself into Mrs. McBride's arms when she heard her say, "He'll be as right as rain; there's no need to worry."

"Could I light the gas now?" asked Lizzie.

"Aye, of course, it'll all be gone by now. But I'd pull down the blinds," said Fanny, "or Nancy Cooper'll have her two bleary eyes glued to her window . . . she never sleeps."

It was not until the gas was lit that Mary Ann saw her father clearly. He didn't seem like her da at all . . . his face seemed altered completely. It looked to her as if something had sucked all the blood from it, and his eyes looked—she could not allow herself even to think how his eyes looked, for fear was the last thing she would associate with her da.

It wasn't until Mike dragged his eyes from his son's face to gaze from one to the other of them in stupefied perplexity that he became conscious of his state of undress. He turned from the bed and went slowly into the room, and Lizzie, bending over the boy, called softly, "Michael, Michael." For answer he rolled his head and retched again, and Fanny, straightening her back with an effort, said, "Ah, he'll do fine. There's nothing to worry about. You should have seen my Florrie the night she did it, when she found young Bob Lancaster had given her a bellyful. It was nearly touch and go that night and many's the time I've wondered since if it wouldn't have been better to let her go, for there she is now with seven round her, and to a no-good waster like Fred Boyle, and her young Bob gone off God knows where, and him the only one she gives a hoot for. Life's crazy, I've said it afore, but thank God even at the longest it's short. And it can't be short enough for me." She sighed heavily, and Mary Ann knew she was thinking of Jack who was really going to marry Joyce Scallen. But what was that to worry about compared with what had nearly happened.

She shivered, and Mrs. McBride turned to her saying, "What, are you cold, hinny? Why don't you jump into bed?" She bent over her, her breasts pressing out the front of her coat like great inflated balloons. And Mary Ann wanted to lay her head between them and put her arms about the not too clean neck and cry with relief, for had she not saved their Michael and was she not as anxious as her ma to keep the disgrace from the neighbours, for Mary Ann was fully aware of the disgrace that clung to a family should one of them stick their head in the gas oven. You were put in the papers then and everybody knew about you. That was why her mother had stopped her going for the doctor, for if the doctor had come it would have been all over the place and her da would have got all the blame. She glanced towards the bedroom door and Mrs. McBride said, "Don't worry, hinny, he'll be all right an' all, he's only getting into his things. Jump into bed with you now."

Slowly she did as she was told and when Fanny's lips came down to hers she did not offer her cheek but returned the old woman's kiss. She watched her go and bend over Michael again, then walk towards the door pulling her coat about her. She saw her ma follow and she could hear them talking but not what they said. She saw Mrs. McBride patting her mother, then she went out and her mother closed the door softly after her and returned to Michael.

It was some little time before her father came out of the room. He did not go to the bed but stood looking towards it to where Lizzie knelt stroking the boy's head. Michael was recovered sufficiently to cry again, but softly, and after a time, during which Lizzie gave no heed to Mike's presence, he went back into the room. Mary Ann watched her mother make a drink for Michael, she watched him refuse it and then be coaxed to drink it, then she saw Lizzie lie on top of the bed and put her arms about him, and she felt nothing but pity, until once again her father entered the kitchen. And when he stood silently looking at his wife and son the pity for Michael and sorrow for her mother combined into a fear, and the fear was formed around their allegiance and what it would mean to her da.

When once again her father returned to the room she saw her mother gently disengage herself from Michael and follow him. She had not turned out the light, so that meant she was coming back. Mary Ann sat swiftly up in bed and pressed her ears in the direction of the bedroom but the only sound she could hear was of a low murmur, and it was of her mother's voice. Her ears were so attuned to listening that she could distinguish what emotion was present in the murmuring of her parents' speech, but even without this facility she would have recognised disaster from the low, dead murmur of her mother's voice.

Knowing that she might be caught in the act did not prevent her from getting out of bed and moving swiftly towards the door. She had no need to bend down to the keyhole, for the door was ajar. She stood at the side nearest the opening, close to the wall, and listened to her mother. At first she could not disentangle the quick, low speech, but then she began to make out the words. They were dead words, yet alive with dread significance. They came to Mary Ann, bearing all the sorrow in the world. "Don't think this silent, remorseful attitude of yours will touch me. You've tried everything in the past. You found talking yourself silly didn't work; well, you can save yourself this effort for it won't work either. If he had died I would have killed you, do you hear? Oh how I loathe you, you great weak hulk. . . . Well, it's finished, finally finished. I'm going."

In the awful silence that followed, into which Mike threw no plea, Mary Ann stumbled back to bed; whatever more there was to be said could not surpass this. She lay watching the door. Her breathing seemed to have ceased, until suddenly, her lungs demanding air, she drew into her narrow chest deep gulps that almost choked her.

Lizzie came out of the room and stood for a moment, her hand pressed to her throat, before slowly moving towards the light and turning it down to a mere glimmer. After the springs of Michael's bed creaked, there was no more sound.

Mary Ann lay for a long time trying to discern objects through the glimmer, trying to shut out the thoughts that conjured up the future without her da, trying to stave off the dawn. Yet when its first light showed on the paper blind she realised she must have fallen asleep, for the gas was out and she hadn't seen her mother get up and turn it off. Soon she knew her da would come out of the room and get ready for work, and he would leave the house, and perhaps before he returned her mother would have taken them away to their grannie's. This might be the last time she would see him leave for work. The thought brought her from the bed. She must say something to him, tell him she would always love him and when she grew up she would look after him.

Gently she pushed the open door wider, and her eyes peered towards the bed. But he wasn't in it, he was sitting on the box to the side of the window. She could see the great dark huddled shape of him, and she was about to move softly forward when her step was checked by a sound coming from him. It was a familiar enough sound when connected with herself or Michael, or her mother, or anyone else in the world, but not with her da. It filled her body with a great, deep, unbearable pity. She stood listening to the sound until she could stand it no longer. It did not drive her to him to spread her comfort over him but back to her bed to lie huddled and sobbing herself. A god had fallen, not through his sins but through his weakness—for gods did not cry.

By the nine o'clock post the letter had arrived to say that Michael had passed for the Grammar School, but it did not make much difference; it had come too late.

8

SOME CALL IT AUTO-SUGGESTION
(IT'S THEIR IGNORANCE, GOD HELP THEM)

As Father Owen listened to the child his heart grew heavy, not only with the weight of her sorrow but with the sorrow that seemed to be the heritage of all such as Mary Ann. Their very joy was tinged with sorrow, made so by their sensitiveness, a quality which should have been used merely to appreciate the finer things of life but which was deformed by constant worry. As he listened to her voice relating the happenings of the last few days his mind rebelled against the sentence inflicted on childhood, a sentence inflicted by the parents themselves. Life at this stage should be a joyous thing; God made it so; away with all the twaddle that it was He who sent suffering.

Mary Ann was saying, "He doesn't talk, Father . . . he says nothing, and he hasn't been full. He went out last night but he came back solid and sober."

"When is your mother going?"

"Saturday, Father, I think."

"And you're not going to your grandmother's?"

"No. She said only last night she'd got a furnished room round Hope Street and we go in on Saturday, and she's got the promise of a job, and Michael and me are to have our dinner at school."

"And your da says nothing?"

"No, nothing; and he wouldn't let me pour the water over his head when he washed."

"And does he seem upset at your mother going?"

Mary Ann did not answer the priest for the moment—upset could not describe the state her da was in, he seemed gone away somehow, dead. She was no consolation to him, and she knew, without knowing how she had come to the knowledge, that without her mother she had no power of her own to hold him. She herself could have done without even her mother as long as she had him, but in him it was her ma that infused the power to live. So she answered, "When me ma goes I don't know what he'll do. I'm frightened, Father."

"Now there's no need to be frightened. Just trust in God and everything will come out all right. For your penance, say one Our Father and one Hail Mary . . . make a good act of contrition."

Slowly Mary Ann said the set piece—it was as if she were loath to leave the confessional and the comfort of the priest—she spread it out and was only induced to finish when Father Owen said, "Now, good night, my child, and trust in God."

"Good night, Father."

When she left the box the priest, after a murmured prayer, followed her. There would be no other children after Mary Ann. He was so used to her manoeuvres that he almost judged the time by her now. He saw her light a candle, then kneel with uplifted face to the altar of the Holy Family, and he turned to the church door and went through the porch and stood on a step, drawing in the fresh air as he looked up and down the street.

It was quiet now, the traffic of the day having eased. The shops on the other side were closed, their doors locked and barred, all except the door leading to the office of Mayland's, the solicitor. Likely, Father Owen surmised, there was a meeting going on up in the Board Room there. Ah, he shook his head at himself, he wished he had just the smell of the money that had changed hands in that room today. . . . But what was he thinking about? There would be no board meeting at this time of the evening. It was now six o'clock. Didn't his stomach tell him so? And what was more there were no cars about except one, and if he was not mistaken it was old Lord's. Likely it was him up there alone, settling the business of more land. What did he hope to do with it all? One thing was sure, he couldn't take it with him. Oh dear, dear; what men strove for. He shook his head again, this time at Mr. Lord.

Peter Lord was an old man now, and what was in his life? Money and land. Yet God help him, he wasn't to blame entirely. Thirty years ago he had been a man splendid in his prime and if he had only managed his private affairs with the same sagacity as he did his business he would undoubtedly have had an exceptionally happy life, but like many another able man before him he had to go and pick on a feather-brained vain piece of a girl, and what a life she had led him. And she had given him nothing, not even a child; and then to leave him when she thought he was going broke. Oh, she had been a right bad piece that. And there he was alone in that barracks of a house where he lived like a hermit. Life was strange. Just imagine, if he had had someone to pour out love on him as did that child back in the church there on that hot-headed devil of a father of hers, it would have made all the difference in the world.

"Oh, there you are, Mary Ann." He stood to one side and made room for her on the step beside him in the half-open doorway. "Have you been to confession?"

He was well aware, perhaps not that he was blind in the confessional, but that he was to Mary Ann an entirely different being when once out of the box, and of being quite incapable of recognising her as the same child who a few minutes before had poured her heart out to him.

"Yes, Father," said Mary Ann, but there was no smile on her face to-night as she said it.

"That's a good girl . . . you'll be qualifying to lead the procession again next year, I can see that."

"Yes, Father." She managed a very faint smile. As he patted her head the sound of a car starting up made him turn his gaze up the street and as he watched it approach his hand became still on her head; then swiftly, without looking at her again, he gave her a little push backwards, saying, "Stay there now." And as Mary Ann stood within the shelter of the porch he stepped briskly to the kerb and hailed the driver of the car.

"Have you a minute?"

The car had not gathered any speed and Mr Lord brought it to a standstill, saying, "Hallo—what are you after now?"

"Have you a minute?"

"Yes, and nothing else, and even that is valuable."

The priest laughed and was in no way put out at the brusqueness of the tone. "Oh yes,

yes. Don't I know." He bent his face down to the open window and cast his eyes sidelong at the erect forbidding figure sitting behind the wheel. "Well it's only two minutes of your time I want, and I'll pay you when my ship comes in, or perhaps I'll just leave it to God and good neighbours."

"What are you after now?"

"What makes you think I'm after anything?"

"If I know you it's something to do with money."

"You're wrong then, this time at any rate. But if you've got any going . . ."

"Not a penny. Three hundred you had out of me last year."

"Was it that much? Good gracious."

"Was it that much!"

"Well, well, doesn't it mount up?"

Mr. Lord surveyed the priest with a hard, forbidding look which did not intimidate Father Owen, who, putting his head and shoulders farther into the car, changed his tone and said, "You can do me a favour if you would."

There was no Yes or Nay or What is it? from Mr. Lord, but in still silence he waited for the priest to go on.

"I heard you'd bought up Coffin's farm."

Still silence surrounded Mr. Lord.

"And I've heard," said Father Owen, "that Coffin took his hands with him, at least that's what I'm given to understand. They must have been fine workers; when a man gets good farm-hands these days he keeps them. Of course Coffin was good to the men. Didn't he have those two fine cottages built for them?"

Mr. Lord closed his blue-veined eyelids for a second, then stared ahead through the windscreen and said, "Come to the point, I want to get home."

"All right—I want you to give a man I know a job—it may be the making of him. Have you stocked up? Have you got your men?"

"No." Mr. Lord turned his head slowly towards the priest. "And I'm not stocking up with any of your riff-raff. I've had experience of your recommendations before and whoever you're wanting to palm off on me now would likely not be able to recognise one end of a cow from the other."

"Ah, but you're wrong there—he's a right fine man with cows."

Whether intentionally or otherwise Father Owen had adopted Mary Ann's voice and her words, and he had to laugh at himself for so doing. But his hilarity had an irritating effect on Mr. Lord. He moved his hand on the wheel saying, "You're wasting your time."

"Look, just a minute." Father Owen stretched out his hand and laid it gently on Mr. Lord's arm. "If you were to give this man a chance it would likely mean the saving of a family."

"Why should that particular point be any concern of mine?"

The two old men stared at each other. Then Father Owen brought back the dim past when this man and he had been firm friends before the bitterness of life had erected the barrier between Peter Lord and all men, by saying, "Peter, do this one thing for me."

The use of his Christian name seemed to have little or no effect upon Mr. Lord's feelings, for his countenance remained forbidding, but after a moment during which he seemed about to drive off despite the fact that Father Owen was half in and half out of the car, he asked, "Who is it, and why are you so bent on getting him on a farm?"

Father Owen kept all eagerness from his voice as he said, "Because it's his natural work—he's like a fish out of water in the yards."

"But there's plenty of farm work going, they're crying out for farm hands."

"Yes, but they're not issuing cottages to go with them; and you know yourself there are no set hours for a good farm-hand, and the farms are so few and far between here that a man would have to stay on the job and travel home at odd times, and this fellow can't stick that. He's tried it. He wants his family with him. He's the kind of fellow who . . ." He did not finish this and add, "who falls to pieces without his wife", but said: "Well, he'd pay you a good dividend in labour if you could settle him and his family in a cottage."

"What's his name?"

"Shaughnessy."

Mr. Lord turned in his seat until he was square to the priest. "Shaughnessy?" he asked heavily.

"Yes, that's him . . . a big red-headed chap."

"Ha, ha!" It was supposed to be a laugh, but resulted in a dry splitting crack of a sound. "You want me to take Mike Shaughnessy on? Why, if he was the last man on God's earth I wouldn't give him breathing space. Do you know what he did in my yard last year, or tried to do?"

The priest remained sadly silent.

"He would have had the men out—like that." He snapped his fingers; and Father Owen said lamely, "I hear he's a good worker."

"A good worker!—he won't do a bat of overtime except with his tongue, besides which he's never sober. What do you take me for? Good-bye, Father."

The farewell salutation was weighed with sarcasm and Father Owen withdrew himself from the car, which almost immediately shot forward and away.

As he turned towards the church again there was Mary Ann looking at him from the step, and he walked up to her, and they surveyed each other in silence.

How much had she heard? Her eyes were so full of strangled hope. He said, "Mr. Lord has a job and a cottage going for a farm-hand. I thought I might get it for your da."

She did not reply but continued to gaze up at him.

"He's not feeling too well to-night—he's in a bit of a bad mood—or perhaps I just didn't put the case properly." He smiled gently down at her. "Now you, Mary Ann, would likely have put his case much better—I mean your da's." His voice trailed off and he became uneasy under the fixed pain of her eyes. "Well, we must never give up hope. Keep on praying, Mary Ann; it's amazing the miracles the Holy Family perform. Just you ask them for advice. They never fail you. Now I must be off to my tea. Good night, my child."

He moved hastily into the church and her eyes followed him, but she did not speak, not even to answer his farewell, and after a moment she too moved awway, walking slowly in the direction of home.

.   .   .   .   .

The kitchen was empty when she arrived, but she knew that both her parents were in, for her da's black cap was hanging on the back of the door and the table had not been cleared and her mother never went out without first clearing the table. She was removing her coat and hat when their voices came to her from the bedroom. They sounded normal, quiet voices and her hands became still and hope sprang afresh into her being and overwhelmed her for a moment, until, moving farther into the room, her father's voice, like the backwash of a mighty wave, sucked it away again.

"I'll allow you so much. . . . But don't take my word for it, have it done legally; you'll be safe then. . . . When are you going?"

"Saturday."

"To your mother's?"

"No—a place in Hope Street."

"Are you taking the bits?"

"No, it's furnished."

"Well, you may as well sell them because I won't be staying here. Can I . . . see the bairns sometime?"

There was a pause before Lizzie answered, "Yes."

To Mary Ann the voices sounded even and untroubled; they sounded the same as when they were discussing something that had appeared in the *Shields Gazette*. They sounded like that but they weren't like that; they were final voices, voices that had ceased to shout or yell or fight, or even plead; they were voices from which emotion had been drained; and they frightened Mary Ann more than any other voices could have done. She fled into the scullery and, covering her face with her hands and pressing herself into the corner of the wall between the sink and the cupboard, she began to pray.

9

THE LORD

The steps were very wide, the widest she had even seen attached to any house, and the house was the biggest she had ever seen. When she had pulled herself below the barbed wire and into the wood she had been scared at the size of the trees, at the thickness of the undergrowth and of the dim, weird light, but when she had emerged from the wood and seen across the meadow the house looking gaunt and weary with a sort of stripped look in the early morning sunshine she had been more than scared. It had taken her quite a time to cross the meadow and get through the fence. She hadn't seen a gate and she had walked through the pathless tangled garden, and here she was, standing on the top step, her hand hovering towards the great knobbly door-bell, and she was, in truth, scared out of her wits.

She knew she had had the dream in the night and that the Holy Family had told her to come and see the Lord himself, but they, as far as she could see, hadn't come with her, and never in all her life had she known fear such as this. She tried to recall the courage she had felt in the night when she had talked with the Virgin. She had actually gone right up to Heaven and seen the Virgin busy with her task of making babies, and the Holy Mother had stopped her work and took her on her knee and had listened to all that she had to say, and then she had told her what she must do. And St. Joseph himself had set her to the gate. And then she had woken up full of courage. The courage had kept her awake until daylight. It had helped her to dress and get past her mother, who was asleep on a shake-down near the fireplace, and out of the door without awakening anyone.

She reached up a little farther and touched the bell, and of its own volition it seemed to come out of the wall for a surprising length, and the clatter it made would have raised the dead. She was still gasping with the shock of it when the door opened.

To say whose face showed the more surprise would be difficult. Mary Ann had expected to be confronted by . . . the Lord; instead, before her stood a thin old man in a baggy old suit. His head was long and pointed and without hair, and his shoulders stooped as if he were carrying a weight upon them, but it was his face that surprised Mary Ann. If she had not been overcome with fright and worry she would have laughed at it. His mouth hung open and his nose twitched like a rabbit's and sent the wrinkles across his cheeks with each twitch.

But of the two, she was the first to find her voice, and even if at first the words wobbled round her mouth reluctant to come out she made the effort and stammered, "P . . . please I came to see the Lord."

"What?" The old man's voice sounded cracked.

"The Lord—I've come to see . . . the Lord. I want to t-talk to him, if you please."

"How did you get in here?"

"Through the hedge—the gate was fastened."

"Through the hedge?" The baggy suit appeared to swell with indignation. "You got in through the hedge?"

"Yes, under the barbed wire."

"Well, the quicker you get out the better it will be for you. Now away with you."

He pointed a shaking finger over her head, but she did not move, and he said, "Did you hear me?"

Slowly Mary Ann's mouth drew to a button which would have been a warning to anyone who knew her, and she answered with deceptive quietness, "I'm not going till I see the Lord."

"You're not what?" The bones seemed to rattle within the suit. "We'll see about that." His hand made as if to descend on her, and she rasped at him, "You touch me and I'll bite a piece out of you."

His hand remained threateningly over her, but it said much for her attitude that it didn't descend on her, but his voice rose to a shrill yet muffled cry as he exclaimed, "Get out of this!"

"Not until I've seen the Lord." As she spoke she placed herself in front of the stanchion, making it impossible for him to close the door.

"In the name of all . . . !" Her defence staggered him, and his pursed lips threw bubbles from his mouth. "You would . . . defy me? Well, we'll see about that."

"I'll scream, mind, if you touch me." This threat seemed to intimidate him for a moment and he cast a backward glance over his shoulder; then whispered fiercely, "You do if you dare."

He made a grab at her but with a wriggle of her body she slipped past him and into the hall.

For a moment he stood looking at her as if she were something uncanny wafted into the morning from another world, and he asked, not without a trace of fear in his own voice, "What are you after?"

"I want to see the Lord."

"Who told you to come here?"

"The Holy Family."

"The what——?"

"The Holy Family."

Now understanding and a trace of compassion touched his face. The child was mad. But mad or no, he must get her out of this before the master came down, so he said softly, "The Holy Family sent you?"

"Yes." Mary Ann nodded emphatically.

"Ah, well, yes, now I quite believe that. And what did they send you for?"

"To speak to the Lord."

"What about?"

"About me da."

"And what about your da?"

"I'm going to tell the Lord."

"Now come, come." He advanced slowly towards her. "You tell me and I'll tell the mast . . . the Lord. How about that—eh?" As the old man came on Mary Ann backed away from him until she was at the foot of the stairs. Here she stopped and said, "I won't tell nobody, only the Lord."

"Now look here"—the old man's patience was swept away by the defiance that embodied this minute child—"I'm having no more of it, " he declared. "Do you hear? You get out of here this minute."

"I'll scream mind . . . I will." Mary Ann's warning cry had no effect this time and as his hand caught her none too gently by the shoulder she let out a high, shrill scream.

By now almost on the verge of hysteria himself, he was attempting to muffle her cries when a voice thundered over them. What it said neither of them knew but its mighty tone flung them apart and Mary Ann and the old man gazed up the staircase to where stood a figure with a pose of the avenging angel. Step by step the master of the house descended upon them, until he stood on the last step but one.

Had he, by one movement of his hand, now ordered them both to be shrivelled up in consuming flames it would not have been of the smallest surprise to Mary Ann. As he gazed down on her she actually stopped breathing, and when he thundered, "What's this, may I ask?" she released her breath and opened her mouth still wider in an attempt to speak, but the old manservant forestalled her.

"I found her at the door, sir—she darted in."

"What is she doing here?"

"She says she wants to see you."

"Me?" Mr. Lord brought his eyes from Mary Ann and laid them on his servant, as if to extract without further preamble the meaning of the outrage.

"That's all I could get out of her, sir. I don't think she is"—he made an effort to straighten his bent shoulders as he delivered his verdict—"compos mentis, sir. She says she was sent here by the Holy Family."

Mr. Lord looked once more at Mary Ann, and Mary Ann made haste to press home the advantage she imagined the servant had unwittingly opened for her.

"He's right," she said, in a voice that was a mere reflection of her normal and anything but quiet tone, "They did, last night. Go to the Lord, they said, and tell him what a grand man your da is, and everything will come all right."

Mr. Lord's bushy eyebrows gathered and hung over his cheek-bones like miniature palm trees.

At this point, collecting the shreds of her shattered courage, she half turned her back on the servant, and stretching to her fullest height, whispered confidentially in much the same tone as she used when addressing God, "Lord, I want to talk to you."

After staring down at her for a moment longer Mr. Lord made an impatient movement and he shook himself as if throwing off some benumbing spell. "Not this morning, no time." He thrust her aside as he descended the last stair and grimly, in an aside, said to the old servant, "Get rid of her."

Mary Ann heard. The new world that seemed almost within her grasp was dissolving before her eyes. She was in the actual presence of the Lord whose power equalled God's and to whom all things were possible. This man could give her da a job; he could give them a cottage, and in a cottage in the country they would be fast closed round and safeguarded from separation—if only her da could offer her ma a cottage in the country then she wouldn't leave him; she couldn't leave him if he'd give her a cottage in the country.

"Lord. Lord." She dived at him and gripped his hand. "If you only knew what a grand man me da is you'd give him the job."

Mr. Lord's veined hand hung slackly between the two small hands that clawed at it. "What job?" he asked quietly.

"On the farm—he's a grand man with horses and things—he knows all about. . . ."

"Who sent you here?" Mr. Lord released his hand slowly from hers.

"I told you Lord—the Holy Family."

"Now, now"—the voice was grim—"none of that. Father Owen sent you, didn't he?"

"He did not . . . Father Owen? No."

"Don't lie. You were the child that was standing at the church door last night, weren't you, while we were talking?"

"I was standing there, but he didn't send me, and I couldn't hear all you said—I heard some, and I knew you had a job going that would have just suited me da and I went home and prayed to the Holy Family. . . ."

"Father Owen told you to do that?"

"Yes . . . no . . . No, I always pray to them on me own."

"The scheming old rascal!" Mary Ann heard the muttered words and her own troubles were forgotten for the moment as she came to the defence of her beloved priest.

"He's not a rascal; he's a fine man, as fine as me da, and don't you say a word against him. And anyway you'll burn in Hell for daring to call a priest a rascal. Maggie Simmond's Aunt Nellie spilled a big panful of boiling fat over herself and she died, and that was just after she'd had words with the priest, so there . . . look out."

"Here, here, don't be cheeky. And come along. You've told enough lies and trash."

The old servant once again bore down on Mary Ann, and this time she turned on him like a wild cat. "I'm not telling lies, I'm telling the truth. After I had the dream I kept awake and I got up when the blind got a bit light on it and I come all this way to talk to the Lord about me da. And Father Owen's a lovely priest. D'you hear? And he put me in the May Procession, right at the head." She seemed to be watching her voice as she sent it yelling up at the old bent figure. Then for a moment her face showed comical surprise as she heard it change. It began to wobble and crack, and her mouth began to quiver. She knew what was about to happen, and she fought against it with all her might, shouting even louder. "There's a pair of you, so there is. You don't believe anything. You're like Sarah Flannagan, that's what you are. You wouldn't do much for God if the divil was dead." And now, feeling that her case was hopeless and that her plea had failed, she turned on Mr. Lord, crying in deep earnest, "You can keep your job and your old horses, and the cottage; me da'll get a job on a farm. They'll jump at him, for he's a fine, steady man—he can work like a black. And me ma'll go back to him when he gets a job with a cottage. You'll see. So there." She nodded her head up at him in short, sharp nods; then turning blindly to what she thought was the front door, she stumbled into the dining-room.

The manservant, about to haul her out, was checked by Mr. Lord, who thrust his arm across the doorway, and after a moment of watching Mary Ann walking bewilderedly about the room, he said, "Bring my breakfast."

"But sir, she——"

"You heard what I said."

One old man looked at the other. Then the servant who gave off his displeasure like the skunk does its smell, walked reluctantly away kitchenwards; and Mr. Lord went into the room and sat down at the table.

He did not look at Mary Ann who was standing now before the great empty fireplace staring down on to the dusty hearth, her back turned purposely to him, but he moved the crockery which was set on a none too clean cloth on the corner of the long massive dining table first one way then another. Then abruptly he commanded, "Come here!"

Mary Ann did not at once turn towards him; she sniffed a number of times and moved her shoulders. Thus having expressed her independence, she turned slowly about and walked to the table, her eyes cast down.

"Your name is Shaughnessy, isn't it?"

"Yes." It was a very small voice.

"Does your father know you've come here?"

"Oh no. He said it was no use coming."

"So he did know you were coming?"

"No. No; he didn't He said that the Sunday we went to the farm up Pelaw way. The job was gone there, the farmer told him about you."

"And he said it was no use coming?"

"Yes."

"How right he was."

"Well, he doesn't want your job. You can keep. . . ."

"All right. All right." He hastily lifted his hand to check her swiftly rising voice.

"He's a grand man."

"Yes. Yes."

"He is. He is." Twice her chin was jerked up at him.

"Very well. . . . Ah, there you are." It was with evident relief that he hailed the servant entering the room with a tray. And when the man, placing a dish before him, lifted the cover, the audible sniff from Mary Ann caused him to look at her with a swift searching glance.

She had been unable to prevent the sniff and she bowed her head in shame. She was hungry, but she'd rather starve to death than take even a bit of fried bread from the nasty old devil.

"Have you had any breakfast?"

". . .No." Her eyes, half raised, were just on a level with the big plate on which lay two pieces of fried bread, two rashers of bacon, an egg and two halves of a tomato.

"That'll do." Mr. Lord, making to attack his breakfast, gave the curt order. But on this occasion, the old man was apparently deaf.

"Ben."

"Yes, sir."

"You heard me."

Ben walked slowly to the door and passed into the hall, where Mr. Lord's voice, which nearly lifted Mary Ann from the ground, halted him.

"Ben!"

"Yes, sir?" Ben's disapproving body appeared in the doorway again.

"Close that door and don't come back till I ring."

Ben closed the door, and his master, in much the same curt tone, said to Mary Ann, "Sit down!"

Slowly she eased the big chair from under the table and wriggled herself on to its seat, only to find that even when she perched on its edge she was too far away from the table; so she got down again, pushed the chair further in and squeezed herself between it and the table and on to its seat again. But now, not a little to her consternation, she found she was much nearer . . . the Lord. She watched him place half a tomato on a slice of bacon which was already reposing on a piece of fried bread. This he had put on his side plate, and when he pushed it towards her she wanted to say in a very civil voice, "No, thank you, I'm not hungry;" but what she did was to take the knife he handed her and cut the bread and bacon by holding it firmly with one hand, since there was no fork available, and despatching it without further quibble or hesitation.

"What do you drink? Tea or milk?"

"Tea."

"Then get a cup. You'll find one in there." He pointed to a china cabinet, and she struggled off the chair again and went to the cabinet, and opening the doors took out a cup. It was thin and felt so light in her hand that for a moment she stood staring at it before returning to the table with it.

"Where do you live?"

"Mulhattan's Hall."

"Where is that?"

"In Burton Street. Off Walter Street."

"How old are you?"

"Gone eight."

"Are you the only child?"

"No. There's our Michael. . . . He's going to the Grammar School; he passed an exam."

"Indeed."

"He's going to be a great scholar and earn a lot of money." She offered this information in an ordinary conversational tone; but this soon changed when she heard him say, "That's impossible, he can't do both." The words were muttered more to himself, but immediately she took them up.

"He will! His teacher says he will. You don't believe anything."

The cessation of hostilities was forgotten; the fact that she had just partaken of a miracle in the form of half his breakfast was neither appreciated nor understood.

"You're just the spit of Sarah Flannagan!" she finished.

"Who, may I ask, is Sarah Flannagan? Do you want a piece of bread and marmalade?"

"No. No, I don't . . . I mean, no, thank you. She's a girl lives opposite us. She goes to our school, and she's a big liar, and she never believes anything."

"And I'm like her?" He helped himself to marmalade, while Mary Ann paused to reconsider her verdict, blinking at him the while.

"Well, you don't believe anything, do you? You don't believe about me da, and that's like her. It's a wonder she's not struck down dead the things she's said about me da."

"What kind of things?"

"Well." Mary Ann paused as if there was need to recollect. "Well, she said me da drinks. Now would you believe that?" She leant a little towards him; and he leaned back in his chair and surveyed her.

"And you say she's lying?"

"Yes. She's a bigger liar than Tom Pepper."

"You did say your name was Shaughnessy, didn't you?"

"Yes." Mary Ann was quite emphatic about this.

"And your father is called . . . Mike. Is that right?"

"Yes."

"And he's a big man, with red hair?" He waved his hand round his own white head as he spoke.

"Yes, that's him. Do you know me da?"

He ignored her question and said, "And you say he doesn't drink?"

She stared at him, unblinking. Then she said quietly, "Yes."

As his head moved down towards her, her body began to stiffen but she continued to look him defiantly in the eye.

"Do you mean to sit there and tell me that your father doesn't drink at all?"

She moved her bottom quickly back and forward on the seat until the leather began to squeak. Then she brought out, "I do. And," she continued, slipping off the seat, "I don't want any more of your tea or your breakfast, for you're as like as two pins with her. You can ask Father Owen about me da. He'll tell you what a right fine man he is." She bounced her head once at him with finality. Then turning on her heels she marched towards the door.

"Where are you going now?"

"I'm going home." She threw this over her shoulder.

"Come here."

Mary Ann found that she was forced to turn at the command, and when once again she was standing by the side of the chair she had just left, he said again, "You say your father doesn't drink?"

"I've told you."

"You're a Catholic, aren't you?"

"Yes."

"And still you say your father doesn't drink? Be careful now."

Mary Ann stared at him, and her answer did not come immediately. But when it did it was still quite firm. "I do."

"Would you swear on it?" Now he seemed to be towering over her, and there was an odd look on his lined face. It had shed its stiff, hard mask and had taken on an expression that could only be called excitement; it sat strangely upon him, and he looked like a man who was watching a race.

Mary Ann's eyes widened, stretching across her face until they seemed almost to encompass it. It was one thing to fight the whole world for something that you wanted to believe, but to be made to swear on it . . . that was another thing entirely; and to be reminded that she was a Catholic into the bargain made things a thousand times worse. The Holy Family, with hurt expressions, were on one side of her, purgatory, hell and damnation gaped widely on the other; but in front of her, blotting out them all, even the face of this terrifying old man, stood her da, looking as she saw him last night before she went to bed, a drawn, changed, different da. Her lips began to tremble and her nose to twitch, but her eyes met Mr. Lord's without flinching. "I would swear on it," she said.

There was a taut silence in the room; then it was split by a laugh, the strangest laugh that Mary Ann had ever heard. She watched Mr. Lord lean back in his chair, and his thin body seemed to crack each time a staccato sound escaped his lips. The sounds mounted, and when he pressed his hands to his side Mary Ann's concern for him brought her to his knee.

"Have you got a stitch?"

Her attitude and concern only aggravated the stitch, for his laughter mounted. Neither of them noticed Ben come into the room and it was not until he spoke, asking in an awed voice, "Are you all right, sir?" that Mr. Lord, with a noticeable effort, took hold of himself. His laughter weakened and became spasmodic, but Ben's concern grew when his master, looking at him with streaming eyes, said, "The greatest of these is loyalty."

The old man looked at Mary Ann and there was fear in his eyes, and when he turned to his master once again Mr. Lord waved him away. "Go on—go on," he said; but as the old servant went again reluctantly out of the room his master's eyes followed him.

Mr. Lord had never considered before that he had been the recipient of loyalty for over forty years. He had taken Ben for granted. He had growled at and abused him, first because no other servant would live with him, then because of the state of the house, then just because it had become a habit. He had sacked him countless times; he had even stopped his money to make him go, but it had made no difference. For years he had seen Ben as an old nuisance who hung on because he wouldn't be able to get a job anywhere else. Ben was twenty-eight when he first came to work for him, and he knew everything there was to know about him. He had witnessed the madness of his marriage; he had seen its end; and as isolation had become his defence he had clung closer to him. Yet, it was strange, he had never before this morning looked upon Ben's service as loyalty. It had taken this child, who could lie with the innocence of an angel and the purpose of a priest, to show him just how much of the same loyalty had he himself been receiving all these years?

Mr. Lord wiped his eyes. But why should he have laughed? It was many a long year since his body had shaken with such laughter as this child had inspired. He looked at her through his swimming eyes. Her face was like a film flickering the thoughts of her mind across its surface; she imagined that she had only to stick to her guns and he would see her father as she saw him. If he hadn't known Mike Shaughnessy he would have, without doubt, believed every word she said. She did not look a bit like Red Mike, yet there was something of him there. Perhaps it was her tenacity—given an idea she would hang on to it until she died—that was him. If only he had the right ideas. But apparently, to him, they were right for he was willing to lose his job for them—yes, and to cause strikes through them. No, he must be fair to the man—he would have caused no strike in his yard; he was too much of an individualist; he could sway neither side completely for he pointed too blatantly to the rottenness of both. It was because his own conscience had been pricked by the man that he was so mad at him. Yet it was strange that all this big red-headed hulk wanted was to work on the land and have his family near him.

"Are you all right now?"

He nodded to her. "Yes, yes, I'm all right."

"I get like that when I go to the pictures and I see a comic, the stitch gets me in the side and I want to cry when I'm laughing . . . it's awful. Will I pour you out another cup of tea?"

"Yes—can you?"

"Oh yes, I often do the tea at home. There." She pushed a cup towards him, and he lifted it and drank while he continued to look down at her.

"What are you going to do when you go back home this morning?" he asked.

Her eyes dropped from his, and she replied dully, "Nothing."

He handed the cup back to her and with the side of his finger he smoothed down his white moustache; then hesitantly, almost as if he wanted to find favour with her, he said, "Will you have time then to take a little ride with me to . . . to the farm?"

They looked at each other. The significance of the request took on a tangible form; it shone between them, blinding Mary Ann with its promise; it formed a fairy-like castle on a high mountain; and she was choked with its wonder. She could bear no more. She flung herself at his feet, her arms about his legs, and when he, making strange tut-tutting sounds, attempted to quieten her noisy sobs, her crying only increased. With gruff tenderness he coaxed her up, and when she leant against him it seemed the natural sequence that he should then lift her on to his knee.

He had in his time been kissed both passionately and falsely by women, but never had he been kissed by a child, never had he felt that ecstatic grip of thin arms about his neck. In this moment he would willingly have changed places with Mike Shaughnessy.

10

THE TRUTH, AND NOTHING BUT . . .

It had been a grand morning, a lovely morning. Mary Ann wanted it to go on for ever, but there was her ma and her da and the letter. Lovingly she touched the pocket in which the letter reposed and edging herself further towards the front of the car seat, she smiled up at Mr. Lord. "Will you take me round by our school?"

"Where's that?"

"Not far from the church, you know. Round Dee Street."

"Oh."

"Do you think we might be able to have a dog and a cat?"

"I don't see why not."

"Have you a dog?"

"No."

"You should have, in a big house like that, because it would scare burglars."

"Yes . . . yes, you're quite right."

"Haven't you anyone to tidy up for you besides him?"

A spasm passed over Mr. Lord's face, moving the wrinkled skin like small lapping waves on a ridge of sand, but he answered quite seriously, "No, only him."

Mary Ann shook her head. "Me ma's the right one for tidying up."

"Is she?"

"Yes. Our house is like a new pin. Look . . . there's our school. You see that second window along the top? That's our class."

Mr. Lord bent his head and looked up at the window, saying, "Yes. Ah yes, I see." Then he added, "Can I put you down here? Can you find your own way home?"

"Yes. Why yes," she laughed up at him.

He was funny. Find her way home indeed . . . she could find her way all over Jarrow by herself.

It was at this point when Mr. Lord was about to apply his brakes that Mary Ann, peering through the windscreen, saw in the distance a group of children, five in number, and all well known to her. One head in particular was so familiar that she almost choked with excitement and actually nudged him. "Look . . . along there. See those girls? Can I get off there? Will you ride me along there?"

Mary Ann, thinking she detected a slight hesitancy in Mr. Lord's manner, added urgently, "The long one, that's Sarah Flannagan."

"Oh-h."

The car moved on again, and Mary Ann, her eyes starting from her head with the force of her feelings volunteered the information, "She's the one as I told you of. When I've been telling girls about our car and horses she's always spoilt it . . . she never believes it."

"Dear, dear, doesn't she?" said Mr. Lord.

"No. But I was only making on, you know. But still, she should have believed it, shouldn't she?"

"Of course. Of course."

"Well, now she'll see. She'll get the shock of her life. It wouldn't be any use me telling her on Monday that I'd been for a ride with you in a car. She'd say I was loopy and wanted me head looking."

"She would indeed." Mr. Lord brought the car to a slow stop just where the group of girls stood on the pavement, and leaning across Mary Ann he opened the door. With a grateful sidelong smile at him she edged herself off the seat, gave a little jump and landed on the pavement, face to face with Sarah Flannagan.

That Sarah was surprised is an understatement. She goggled, her mouth as it fell open looking out of all proportion to her face. Mary Ann gazed up at her, long and steadily, before allowing her shining eyes to flicker over the rest of the group, two of whom had been listeners to the . . . big house, cars and horses tale, which Sarah Flannagan had shattered that particular night in the school-yard. Now Mary Ann, addressing herself solely and pointedly to Sarah, said, "I've been for a ride and I've had me breakfast in a great big house. Like a palace it is. And we're going to move into a fine grand cottage with a great lump of garden, and me da's going to be somebody and me ma'll have nice clothes."

To give Sarah her due she did try to speak. Her lips formed the usual phrase, but soundlessly, and they only got as far as "Oh you great big . . ." for her eyes lifted to the old man in the car. She knew who he was, everybody in Jarrow knew who he was, and Mary Ann Shaughnessy had just stepped out of his car.

Mr. Lord watched the little play, and groping back and clutching at a faint spark of devilment from his youth, suddenly brought all eyes towards himself, including Mary Ann's, when he said with slow pomp and using her name for the first time, "Where did you say you wanted to go for a ride tomorrow, Mary Ann?"

A message that could only be read by Mary Ann came from his eyes, and she answered it with one that was touched with love. She moved towards the car window, "Oh, Whitley Bay."

"Whitley Bay it is then. And what time will I come?"

"Come for me, in the car?"

The proposal was filled with such phantasy that even she didn't for the moment believe it was true.

"Of course." Mr. Lord's voice had a touch of the old asperity about it, and this itself conveyed to all present the serious and truthful intent of his purpose.

"Oh." On a surge of rising joy came an inspiration to Mary Ann, and after casting a glance about her at the amazed faces she swallowed hard and said, "Would you call for me then after Mass, the ten o'clock, at the church door?"

The meeting place obviously was a surprise to Mr. Lord, and his brows contracted for a moment as he repeated, "The church door?"

"Yes."

It was evident that the church door did not meet with Mr. Lord's approval. The sound that came from him was akin to a groan, and Mary Ann, looking apprehensively, said in a small voice, "Well, can you?"

He moved back in his seat pulling the car door closed as he did so. His expression looked to Mary Ann very like the one he was wearing before he'd had his breakfast.

"Goodbye," she said softly.

"Goodbye," said Mr. Lord.

Suddenly she knew she couldn't let him go like this. Reaching up, she peered over the lowered glass of the window and whispered, "Are you vexed?"

For a moment he looked at her; then his eyes crinkled into a smile and his hand came out to her cheek, "I'll be there."

Until the car had passed from sight around the corner of the street Mary Ann did not move, and when she did it was to walk away with her chin in the air and without even a glance at or word to Sarah Flannagan and the girls. The ground was still shaking under her feet; she fully realized it had been touch and go about the church door; also that its accomplishment was a glory that wouldn't come her way twice. Tomorrow morning when all the school was coming out of church there would be the car to meet her. Sarah Flannagan and all the lot of them, even the teachers would see her. The emotion was partly agony.

She had reached the corner of the street before she realized that not a solitary jeer had followed her, not even the usual gibe of "Mary Ann, frying pan!" She turned round, and there they were where she had left them, standing like dummies. Unable to resist a parting shot she turned her back, lifted up her short skirt, and thrust her bottom out at them.

· · · · ·

The voice of Fanny McBride rang up the staircase with the force of a sergeant-major on the barrack-square. She was holding on to the bottom banister with both hands as she cried once again, "Mike! Mike! You, Lizzie—she's here, walking down the street as large as life."

She had scarcely finished before Mike was descending the last flight of stairs towards her.

"Look for yourself." She followed him to the door and called out over her shoulder, "What did I tell you, Liz? I knew she would turn up. She's not the kind to go and tip herself in the river . . . not Mary Ann."

Mary Ann walked up the steps towards her parents. Her eyes darted from one to the other. She spared no glance for Mrs. McBride or Miss Harper, or the Laveys who were now crowded the hallway, but the suppressed excitement about her made itself felt, and she asked in an airy tone, "What's the matter, Ma?"

"Listen to her. What's the matter, Ma?" Fanny's laugh vibrated round the hall. "Only half the town looking for you, polismen an' all."

Mike and Lizzie both stood staring down on her as if they were finding it hard to believe the evidence of their eyes, and it was Mike who eventually spoke. "Where've you been?" he asked.

Mary Ann did not at first reply, but looked up at her father. His voice was harsh and his face looked even worse than it had done last night, and his manner had the power to crush her gaiety and she replied meekly, "In the country."

"In the country . . . well, I'll be damned!" Fanny slapped her thigh, and Lizzie, saying nothing, reached out and taking Mary Ann's hand led her through the little press and up the stairs.

Once in the room and the door closed, Lizzie suddenly sat down. It was as if her legs had been whipped from under her. She put her hand for a moment to her brow and covered her eyes, then softly she asked, "Where've you been? I want the truth, mind."

"In the country, Ma."

"Why did you go out like that . . . so early?"

Mary Ann looked from her mother to where Mike was standing glaring down at her, and she found she couldn't say. There wasn't very much time left, so she substituted, "I wanted to get back soon but we went for a ride in the car."

The room became so still that Mary Ann scraped her foot on the lino in order to make some familiar sound.

"Whose car? Who have you been with? Now no lies." The tone of her father's voice wiped the remaining joy from the morning. It was as if she had done something wrong . . . and him saying 'no lies'. As if she told lies for herself—she told lies only to make things come right for him. Her lips trembled and her head drooped and she muttered "Mr. Lord's."

"Mr. Whose?"

"Lord's . . . him who has the farm."

Slowly Mike came to her. "You went to Mr. Lord's? What for?"

"To tell him . . . to tell him . . ." Now she was sniffling and Lizzie said, "Sh! There now. Just tell us what happened and you won't get wrong."

"I went to tell him what a . . . a grand man you were with . . . horses and cows and things."

For a brief moment Mike's eyes held Lizzie's; then he turned slowly towards the fire, and Lizzie, gathering the child to her said, "Tell me what happened. How did you get into Mr. Lord's place?"

"I got through the barbed wire, and the old man let me in, and Mr. Lord give me half his breakfast. Then we went to see the cottage." She lifted her head from her mother's breast and still sniffing continued, "Oh it's a lovely cottage, Ma; he's given us the best one."

As Mike swung round exclaiming, "What did you say?" Lizzie pressed Mary Ann away from her, and holding her at arm's length demanded, "What are talking about, child?"

"The cottage that goes with the farm, Ma. He gave me a letter—here——" she pulled the letter from her pocket, and turning, handed it to Mike who took it and opened it without taking his eyes from her. When he did begin to read both Lizzie and Mary Ann watched him. Then he slowly lifted his head and silently contemplated Mary Ann. His head shaking with a slight bewildered movement, he handed the letter to Lizzie and went into the room, walking, Mary Ann thought to herself, as if he'd already had a few.

After a moment Lizzie's hands dropped into her lap and she too stared at Mary Ann in a bewildered fashion; then without any warning she began to cry, not a quiet easy crying, but a crying that was tinged with laughter and touched on hysteria. It brought Mike back to the kitchen and after only a moment's hesitation, during which his face worked convulsively, he went to her and gathered her into his arms and smothered her wild cries against his breast.

Mary Ann stood apart, watching. The emotions that were coursing through her were too tangled and complex for her to experience any one of them consciously; she could not put a name to the feeling of deflation their combined force created; she could not even think that her da holding her ma in his arms again portended nothing but good. One thing was evident to her, everything had turned out quite differently from what she had imagined. Her news hadn't been greeted with open arms; she hadn't been hugged and kissed and told what a clever girl she was; instead, she had been accused of lying. Why, when she came to think of it, the only one who believed her was the Lord himself. He thought she was a clever girl; he had told her so when he put the letter into her hand. And because he realized she was a clever girl she had given him her entire confidence—she had related graphically just how Sarah Flannagan had banged her head against the wall because of what happened on Coronation Day, and he had laughed and laughed. She had even told him about how she went in the black dark for Mrs. McBride the night their Michael put his head in the gas oven. The more she told him the more he laughed and she knew he believed everything she said.

She had decided much earlier in the morning that she liked Mr. Lord. She had even decided to take him under her wing, for all he needed was a good laugh and his house tidying up and he'd be all right.

She watched her da lead her ma into the bedroom, and when the door closed on them she felt indeed alone. She stood irresolute for a moment; then with a flop she sat on a chair and was preparing herself to feel very misused when the outer door burst open and Michael appeared. He gave no welcome cry at the sight of her but in his brotherly fashion advanced towards her demanding, "Where do you think you've been?"

She did not answer but looked up at him with a sidelong glance fully calculated to aggravate his already harassed feelings.

"Where's me Ma and Da? The motor cops are looking for you." He looked around the room. "Where's me Ma?"

Still Mary Ann said no word, and her air of superiority, which at any time had the power to annoy him, infuriated him now. Without further words he stretched both hands out to grab her, but like lightning she slipped beneath them and, still without speaking, she aimed one well-cobbled toecap at his shin.

On his cry of real pain the morning suddenly balanced itself again and her depression lifted. Life was normal, the world was full of magic, she was cleverer than their Michael even if he was going to the Grammar School; they had a cottage in the country, her ma and her da weren't going to leave each other . . . and there was Mr. Lord. And tomorrow morning he'd be at the church waiting for her for all the world to see.

Michael, hopping on one leg, cried, "For two pins I'd . . ." and she answered pertly, "Oh, would you? Well wait a minute and I'll get them for you."

"Mary Ann." On her name being called softly from the bedroom door, she swung round and there stood her da. They looked at each other for a moment before he held out his arms to her and almost in one leap she was in them, hugging and being hugged with such intensity that even Sunday morning became blotted out.

．　　　．　　　．　　　．　　　．

Now came the Elevation of the Host. Mary Ann knelt with bowed head and beat her narrow chest with clenched fist as each tinkle of the bell came from the altar and she murmured with every thump, "Lord be merciful to me, a sinner; Lord be merciful to me, a sinner." She drew a deep breath as she raised her head after the last tinkle. Ah, that was over. There wasn't much more now. Soon John Finlay would carry the big book from one side of the altar to the other and then Father Owen would say 'Our Father' and 'Hail Mary' and a little bit more, and then. . . . The excitement began to tear round inside her again, almost making her feel sick. Eeh, she mustn't be sick. She had been last night, but she hadn't minded for both her ma and her da had held her head, and it wasn't because she had eaten any sweets or anything or had had anything fancy for her tea. She had felt the sickness coming on in the afternoon while she waited for her da to come back. He had gone out all dressed up to see Mr. Lord and he hadn't returned till nearly seven o'clock, but for once her ma hadn't looked worried. She had looked quiet and calm—she had looked like that since she had unpacked their clothes—and her da had looked quiet too. She remembered at dinner time they had all sat round a makeshift meal, and Mrs. McBride had come up and had cried, "Lord, ye're as quiet as a bunch of survivors from a wreck," and her da had said in an odd way, "Just as quiet, Fanny." And when he came back from Mr. Lord's he was still quiet and he wasn't quite himself, but he wasn't sick or anything. Oh no, for she knew he hadn't touched a drop. But he seemed as if he must have her near him; and after she was sick he had even washed her himself and put her to bed. Oh, it had been a grand week-end, a lovely week-end. And it wasn't over. Oh no, not by a long time—there was all to-day.

Oh, if Father Owen would only put a move on . . . Eeh, what was she saying? After all the Holy Family had done for her, and . . . She tut-tutted to herself. Would you believe it, she had never even thanked them properly. She turned her face to the side altar and found to her surprise that as she had nothing at the moment to ask of them she was a little at a loss for words. Hesitatingly she began, "Dear Blessed Holy Family, thank you for all you have done for me, for getting me da a job and for the cottage." It all sounded so inadequate, sort of mean. She felt that something was expected of her, some present of some sort. Well, she'd light a candle the morrer—she just couldn't spare the time this morning. The mean feeling persisted and she thought, "I know what . . . I know what'll please them more than anything." She unlaced her fingers and put her hands finger-tip to finger-tip as she usually did when dealing with matters of import. "Dear Holy Family. I promise you faithfully, so help me, that I'll never tell another lie. May I be struck down dead if I do." There, she felt better, and the Holy Family looked very pleased, but it still felt funny not having anything to ask them to do. She was about to turn her attention back to the main altar where John Finlay was now moving the book when she suddenly thought of her grannie. Now there was something they could do to get on with. Solemnly and fluently now she beseeched them, "Dear Holy Family, could you do something about me grannie to stop her coming out to our cottage? Could you give her a bad leg or something? You needn't kill her off, just stop her. In the name of the Father, Son, Holy Ghost, Amen."

She got that in just in time to give the responses with the rest of the children to the priest saying the first half of the 'Our Father.' On the third 'Hail Mary' her responses were loud and clear and very definite, as if she herself had some proprietary right in their saying . . . 'Holy Mary—Mother of God—pray for us sinners—now and at the hour of our death—Ah-men.'

Ah . . . there, it was over. Father Owen had not disappeared through the vestry door before she was on her feet.

"Sit down and wait until the class is out." A hand on her shoulder and the hissed command from Miss Johnson brought her bottom abruptly into contact with the hard seat.

Oh, Miss Johnson! She had eyes like a gimlet. Oh dear! Bust! Now as like as not she'd keep her back till the very last.

Which was exactly what Miss Johnson did. Row after row of children swarmed methodically into the aisle. With noisy caution they kicked against the wooden kneelers, gasped audibly as they genuflected towards the altar, and invariably scraped their feet on the heating grids.

Mary Ann kept her eyes riveted on Miss Johnson's back, but Miss Johnson seemed to have entirely forgotten Mary Ann's presence. She was standing six rows away and apparently in another world.

Oh the beast . . . oh she was awful. Mary Ann wriggled on her seat as if she were already on that gridiron so often prophesied by her grannie. Everybody would be gone home. Perhaps even Mr. Lord would think she'd gone, and he'd go away. There was no fear strong enough to keep her in her seat; she rose to her feet and, moving quietly into the aisle, genuflected and bowed her head to the altar, only to lift it to Miss Johnson's legs which she surmised had been whipped in front of her by lightning, or the devil.

"I thought I told you to wait until the church emptied?"

You don't argue with a teacher or Mary Ann would have said, "You said wait until the class had gone, which is quite a different thing from waiting until the church was empty."

Perhaps the swish of Father Owen's gown had some influence on Miss Johnson's censure, for she murmured softly, "Go on now; but come to me in the morning."

Without a word Mary Ann turned away, and it was only with the greatest restraint that she stopped herself from running up the aisle—or was it the fact that she was 'twixt the devil and the deep sea, with Miss Johnson behind her and Father Owen in front?

Father Owen paused before going out into the porch and patted the heads of self-conscious philanthropists as she or he made a great show of putting a penny into the poor box or lighting a candle to their favourite saint. Mary Ann did neither, but she was going past him, actually without looking at him and on the verge of a run now, when his hand descended on her head.

"What have you been up to?" he whispered.

"Nothing, Father."

"You were kept in."

"Yes, Father, 'cause I wanted to get out quick."

A twinkle in his eye softened the harshness of his words. "Out quick? away from God as quickly as you can?"

"No, Father. But you see, it's a special morning."

Oh dear, dear. Wouldn't he take his hand off her head? She glanced with evident longing towards the door.

"What's extra special about it?"

"Mr. Lord—he's come to take me for a ride . . . I was going to come and tell you last night but I was sick and vomited all over the place."

"Mr. Lord?" The pressure on her head became heavier and her hat was hurting her ears. The priest bent nearer to her. "What were you saying about Mr. Lord?"

"He's given me da a job and a fine cottage. I prayed to the Holy Family and they told me to go and have a talk with him, just like you said yourself, Father. Oh Father, can I go now?"

He took his hand from her head but said, "Wait a minute. When did you talk to him?"

"Yesterday morning, Father. I got up early and crawled through the barbed wire and knocked on his door."

Father Owen straightened up. He could not step back for he was already against the wall, but he drew his chin in and half closed his eyes as if to focus her better, then he began to chuckle.

Mary Ann could not go without his word, but she moved from one foot to the other just to show him the extent of her need to hurry. But he only continued to chuckle. "Where is he going to meet you?"

"Outside, Father, just outside——" she pointed to the door and moved a step towards it, trying to draw him with her.

"Did you ask him to meet you outside here?"

"Yes, Father."

He continued to stare at her, but he remained where he was. He knew exactly why she had requested the car to be brought to the church just after Mass but he could not for the life of him imagine what form her persuasion had taken to make Peter Lord agree to bringing it. His head wagged. "Well, well." And he had given Mike the job. Again "Well, well." And all through this little mite's tongue. . . . Nothing she would do or say would ever surprise him.

But here Father Owen was wrong.

"Will you come and see, Father, or else he'll be away?"

"No. No, Mary Ann . . . you run along."

This was her hour. He knew his presence out on the street would only deflect some of the children's attention from her and he guessed he'd be the last person Peter Lord would wish to see this morning. No, he'd stay where he was.

"I'll come and tell you all about it the morrer. Goodbye, Father."

She was gone; and after waiting a few seconds Father Owen's good intentions were also gone. Cautiously he went into the porch and towards the main doorway.

The crowd that awaited Mary Ann was somewhat disappointing. There weren't more than twenty-five altogether. . . . It was that beastly Miss Johnson's fault. They had all gone home; and the car wasn't right opposite the church door either, but some way along the street.

However, the number of the crowd did not matter so much, it was the quality of it that counted. And the quality to her was of the best, for it consisted of most of her class and, pleasure upon pleasure, Sarah Flannagan.

The car was facing her and as she ran towards it holding on to her hat with one hand she waved to the grim face behind the wheel with the other, and it was no imagination on her part that the face relaxed into a smile and a hand was raised in response to her salute.

"Get by!" Mary Ann directed this command to Sarah Flannagan who was standing on the pavement well to the side of the car door. In fact, all the children had kept a respectful distance from the car. Sarah was no more in Mary Ann's way than were two or three of the other children, and she did not, as some of the others did, shuffle a few steps to the side, but she stood her ground. "Get by yersel," she said.

Mary Ann got by. She walked round her enemy with her lips and her nose pursed and eye to eye with her, for Sarah slowly pivoted in the same direction.

As Mary Ann reached the car door it opened, but she gave no word of greeting to Mr. Lord, only smiled warmly at him before ducking beneath his outstretched arm to sit herself with dignity on the edge of the seat. The door banged and there was a soft purr, then from the open window she faced the little crowd of children, now gathered closer about the car; but her eyes rested only on one, and to Sarah she addressed herself.

"Now you see who's a liar, Sarah Flannagan. You wouldn't believe about our house and the cars and the horses, would you? Well, we're going into our new house the morrer, and there's four horses, and me da's got a right fine job, better than your da will ever have, 'cause he's a drunken no-good and"—her voice rose to a shrill pipe and all her dignity vanished—"if you dare to call me a liar again you won't half catch it, because this . . " she cried finally, sticking her head out of the window now and jerking her thumb over her shoulder, "is me Granda!"

There was a shocked silence in Heaven, while down in the church porch Father Owen bent his head and covered his face with one hand.

·   ·   ·   ·   ·

"There you go—I tell you it did happen. Ooh! you'll believe nothing—it's like Sarah Flannagan you are."

The Lord
and Mary Ann

1

A RESPECTABLE COW

The cowshed was full. It was full of cows and activity, of pails clanging, of nooses like jets of escaping steam, of deep lowings,of snuffles and swishes, of hooves meeting stone, of steaming flesh, and of contentment. Mike Shaughnessy leaned his head against the warm, brown skin. His brow moved gently over a rib, and the cow, a dappled Jersey, turned a deeply soft eye on him. Her jaws moved twice; she turned away again and let her milk run freely.

"Mike."

"Aye?" He did not turn his head from the beast's side, but screwed it round to look at the man who was addressing him.

"It's rainin' again. What d'you bet he doesn't send you out to the top field?"

Mike lifted his head and looked full at the undersized man who, hose in hand, was directing a jet of water along the gutter flanking the byres.

"Well, if he does, what of it?"

The other man stared for a moment before saying, "Why, man, I can't understand you. You're a damn fool. What d'you put up with it for? When it's wet you're out, when it's fine you're in. He gives you all the muck. You'll never get the tractor through that bog."

"I'll try. And look, Jonesy"—Mike stood up, and his height and breadth dwarfed the man still further—"It's like this: if I don't make a hullabaloo about it I don't see any reason why you should. So don't keep on."

"You needn't take it like that. I'm not keeping on. But what I maintain is, if he does it to one he's just as likely to do it to another. . . . I'd like to see him try it on me. I was engaged for one job. I didn't even mind doin' two or three, but I wouldn't stand for what he dishes out to you. Aw, man," Jones leaned towards Mike, and continued quietly, "why don't you tell him to go to hell? What can he do but give you the sack?"

"Da."

Both men turned, and Jones, his manner jovial now, said, "Hallo there, Mary Ann."

"Hallo, Mr. Jones."

Mary Ann loked at the farmhand. She wasn't sure, even after having known Mr. Jones for three months, whether she liked him or not. Sometimes he made her laugh . . . but not when he was talking to her da.

She turned to Mike, saying, "Me ma says, are you comin'? Your breakfast's been ready for ages."

"I'll be there in a minute." Mike lifted the brimming pail, and Jones said, "Give it here, I'll see to it. You should be comin' back now 'stead of goin'."

Mike handed over the pail and with no further words left the cowshed, Mary Ann walking somewhat soberly by his side.

"Da, can we have a dog?"

"What do you want a dog for? There's two on the farm already, and you've got Tibby."

"I know, but a cat's not a dog. And Mr. Ratcliffe doesn't like us to play with the farm dogs."

"Well, we'll see," said Mike.

"Da—" The inflexion Mary Ann now gave to the word told Mike that whatever was to follow was of grave importance.

"Aye, what is it?" he said.

"Isn't a heifer a bull?"

One side of Mike's mouth pulled up, but restraining his smile, he said, "Hardly that."

"But it is, Da." Mary Ann paused in her walk to add emphasis to this statement.

But when Mike continued to move steadily on she ran and caught him up and pulled at his hand. "But it is, Da. It must be."

"Well, if you say it is, it is."

They continued across the yard in silence, and out on to the road. Away over the fields the rain looked like a swaying sheet let down from the surrounding fells. Even the knowledge that the weather looked set and that in a very short time he would be out working in it did not affect Mike adversely. Each day was good, for his feet were on the ground. No longer did he have to listen to the banging and hammering of the shipyard; no longer climb the gantries and tremble at their height; no longer was he hemmed in by people, people as thickly packed as the bricks in the walls of their houses. He was in the open once again doing the job he was created for. He had no religious beliefs, had Mike, but of this he was sure: each man had been made for a specific purpose, and his was to tend animals and to work under the open sky. Time and again he had tried it, only to be driven back to the towns and the yards. But now he was settled—thanks to this mite.

He put out his hand and grasped his daughter's, and this to Mary Ann was the signal that her da didn't want to be quiet any longer and that he wouldn't mind if she chattered. So once again she pressed her point regarding the sex of a heifer.

"It must be a bull, Da."

Mike's head suddenly went back in its old carefree fashion and his laugh ran along the hedges like wind and sent the birds into a chirruping and chittering. Mary Ann, too, was forced into laughter, and she pulled his hand, saying, "Oh Da, give over and tell me—come on. Aw!"

"Look"—Mike nodded along the road—"There's your mother. I'm in for it."

Elizabeth Shaughnessy was standing by the cottage gate. She was a tall, blonde woman, as tall as her husband, and with a carriage that had something of defiance in its straightness. Mary Ann looked along the road towards her, and, as oft-times happened, she was so struck by the beauty of her mother's face that all else was sent spinning from her mind. She had always considered her ma bonnie, even when they were living in the attics in Mulhattan's Hall and her da had got sick at times and didn't come home with his pay, when her ma's face would become drawn and her voice sharp. Even then she had remained bonnie. But since they'd come to the farm the word bonnie no longer fitted her, for now she was beautiful, and she laughed with her da and they larked on in the kitchen at nights. Even their Michael was happy and all swanky now that he was at the Grammar School.

The wonder of life shot through Mary Ann, and she leapt clean off the road and with a shout dashed to the gate and to Elizabeth.

"Now look, stop it! What's come over you? Don't go mad. Go on, start your breakfast or you'll miss the bus." Lizzie pushed Mary Ann up the path, then turned to greet her husband: "You get later . . . anything wrong?"

"Wrong? What could be wrong?" He paused a moment and looked into her eyes, which were on a level with his own. "Why can't you stop worrying?"

She sighed and smiled quietly. "Come on, have your breakfast."

Midst the warm smell of fried bacon they sat down: Mike and Elizabeth on one side of the table, Michael and Mary Ann on the other.

Michael ate hurriedly, his eyelids blinking as his thoughts darted to and fro in his mind.

"Don't gollop your food," Lizzie cautioned him, and Mary Ann, crunching a crisp piece of bacon rind, added slyly, "He's hurrying to the bus stop to meet Lena Ratcliffe."

"I'm not! I'm not!" His face scarlet, and almost choking on his food, Michael glared at Mary Ann.

"Yes, you are; you both talk swanky." She now proceeded to pull her nose and lengthen her upper lip until it completely covered her lower one, whilst she mimicked, "My form mistress . . . my form master."

"You—" Michael was on his feet.

"Sit down. Sit down." Mike's voice was gentle to his son. But to his beloved daughter his voice took a sternness: "And you get on with your breakfast if you don't want your backside skelped."

Mary Ann took this threat for what it was worth. Her head wagged, and she continued her breakfast in hurt silence. And in the quiet that followed, her thoughts returned to the troublesome problem that must be straightened out before she went to school. She must make quite sure that a heifer was a bull, for as soon as she should set her foot in the school yard this morning Sarah Flannagan would start again trying to be clever and making on she knew everything.

This time she appealed to her mother, saying, "Ma, isn't a heifer a baby bull?"

Lizzie almost looked startled. "A baby . . .?" She did not finish but glanced towards Mike. But Mike was very intent on his breakfast.

"A baby bull?" Michael's voice now was full of scorn. "You're daft!"

"It is! It is!" Mary Ann attacked him.

"Now stop shouting," Lizzie cautioned her, "and go and wash your hands."

"But, Ma, isn't it? I must tell Sarah Flannagan."

Mary Ann's face looked full of misery.

"But why do you want to tell Sarah that?" asked Lizzie.

"Because she talks potty," said Mary Ann. "She says it isn't a bull, she says it's nothing. She says her ma says it becomes a cow when it gets married."

There was a great spluttering and choking. Mike had been in the act of drinking his last mouthful of tea; now most of it sprayed across the table. Rising swiftly, he went into the scullery.

Mary Ann watched the scullery door until he reappeared. He was red in the face. "I'm afraid Sarah's got one on you this time," he said.

"But, Da—"

"Now, now, it's no use arguing that point. Sarah's right."

"Aw, but—"

"Look. Get your hands washed this minute!"

And Lizzie enforced this command by pushing Mary Ann from the table towards the scullery. Then her glance met Mike's, and her silent laughter joined his.

"Trust Nellie Flannagan," said Mike, under his breath, "to bring the sanctity of marriage to a cow."

Lizzie walked with Mary Ann to the gate. Her daughter was looking anything but pleased—the fact that Sarah had scored over her had the power to darken her sky, and, incidentally, to put her in a fighting mood. If Mary Ann's retaliation could be directed solely against Sarah this morning, Lizzie would not have felt the slightest qualm. But before Mary Ann would meet Sarah she would meet Lena, and the farm manager's daughter had in some odd way assumed the embodiment of a threat to the family's new-found security. She wanted at this moment to bend down and grasp hold of Mary Ann's hand and beg of her, "Be nice to Lena, will you? And don't brag about Mr. Lord."

As if Mary Ann had heard the echo of Mr. Lord's name, she looked up at her mother and said, "If the Lord—I mean Mr. Lord—comes afore the bus he'll take us into Jarrow, and if he does can I spend me bus fare, Ma?"

"No," said Lizzie, buttoning up the collar of Mary Ann's mackintosh. "You've done that twice this week already. It's to go into your money-box. Don't forget Christmas isn't so far off. And Mary Ann—" Lizzie paused and adjusted the round school hat.

"Don't be cheeky to Lena, will you?"

The stark injustice of this remark widened Mary Ann's brown eyes and brought her mouth to a button.

"I'm not, Ma. She's cheeky to me, and always swanking. She's—"

"All right! All right! Only I'm telling you. And pay heed. Go on now." Lizzie kissed the pained face, then with a push sent Mary Ann on her way down the lane. She watched her until she reached the bend, and when the child turned and gave a desultory wave she waved back, then went thoughtfully into the cottage.

.   .   .   .   .

The bus stop was at the crossroads and was indicated by a heap of gravel lying by the side of the road at the foot of a signpost, one arm of which pointed to Gateshead and the other to Shields. At the far side of the gravel stood Lena Ratcliffe, a thick-set girl of eleven. Her hair was brown and fluffy, and her face could have been pretty had it not shown so much petulance. Michael was standing somewhat self-consciously in front of the heap and Mary Ann on the near side. Each was constrained. Mary Ann, not because of the presence of the other two but because once again she had been put in the wrong.... Her ma saying, "Don't be cheeky to Lena"! She had never been half as cheeky to Lena as she had wanted to be. If she'd done all the things she'd wanted to do to Lena her ma might have room to talk. She often wanted to butt her in the stomach, or knock her into the big pig trough.

But the thought of Lena vanished as a large black car turned the bend and moved swiftly towards them. Simultaneously the two girls stepped on to the road. Mary Ann said nothing, only her eyes widened and her face took on a look of happy expectancy, not unmixed with self-satisfied propriety.

As the car drew to a halt, Lena, with studied dignity, went to the window and said, "Good morning, Mr. Lord. May I sit in the front?"

Mr. Lord did not return the greeting. His brows were beetling over the top of his eyes, shadowing the deep blue to black, his white moustache was bristling on his pursed upper lip, and his whole attitude expressed barely controlled rage.

"Get in the back."

With a sound like "Huh!" Lena opened the door and climbed into the back seat.

Michael, who was standing behind Mary Ann, said respectfully and a little apprehensively, "Good morning, sir."

"Morning. Get in."

Michael got in and sat beside Lena.

With the air of a duchess taking her rightful place, Mary Ann now opened the front door of the car and wriggled herself on to the seat.

"Hullo!" She grinned at the old man—the Lord, as she always thought of him.

He cast a swift sidelong glance at her. A light gleamed in the shadows of his eyes for a moment; his moustache moved and he muttered something that could have been "Hallo!"

As the car bounded forward, Lena placed her head between Mary Ann and Mr. Lord, and in her politest tone, which was saying a great deal, she said, "It's very kind of you to take us into Jarrow, Mr. Lord. Mammy says we do appreciate it."

Mr. Lord's shoulder jerked, and Mary Ann making an imperceptible movement nearer to him, forced Lena to remove her head. She glanced up at him, wondering if he appreciated the move she had made. But he was intent on his driving; and just as her father's silence often warned her when to keep her tongue quiet, her quick perception bade her to do so now.

Lena, in her condescending prim way, was talking to Michael, and for quite some distance the one-sided conversation centred around school. There she goes again, thought Mary Ann, always swanking . . . and he wants to be quiet. He'll go for her. I hope he does.

Her own silence gave her a definite feeling of superiority, which would have continued for the remainder of the journey had not Lena changed her topic to one which annoyed her more than did the described glories of the high school. Lena was once again mesmerising Michael with the splendour of the big house she had lived in before coming north. It was a lovely house, she was saying, big and white, with japonica all round.

Mary Ann's self-denial was weighed and found wanting. Mr. Lord's unspoken demand for quiet could not stand up to the desire to do a bit of swanking on her own account, so she screwed herself round, bringing her chin to the top of the seat.

"Us used to live in a big house an' all," she said. She ignored the flushed face of her brother and his look which was plainly saying, "Shut up, you fool."

Mulhattan's Hall and the garrets at the top in which they had lived were still painfully clear in Michael's mind, and try as he might he could not wholly remove the dread of returning there.

Staring coldly back at Mary Ann with cutting correctness and ignoring the subject-matter of the conversation, Lena said, "You shouldn't say 'Us used to'; you should say 'We used to'."

Now it was Mary Ann's turn to colour. But if she was aware of her facial betrayal she ignored it, and replied with a well-feigned airiness, even adding emphasis, "It was us—me da and ma, and me and our Michael."

"Be quiet, and don't be so soft!"

Michael's censorious tone brought her battling to her knees. She might have to be civil to Lena Ratcliffe, but their Michael was a different kettle of fish.

"You!—Who d'you think—?"

"Sit down this minute!"

The thunder of Mr. Lord's voice shut off her own as if with a switch. Slowly she slipped into a sitting position again, and into the purring silence came Lena's polite tones, this time addressed directly to Mr. Lord. "It is 'We used to', isn't it, Mr. Lord?" And to Mary Ann's utter astonishment, amazement, indignation and mystification, Mr. Lord answered quietly but also with emphasis, "Yes, it is . . . 'We used to.' "

After staring at Mr. Lord's stiff profile for almost a quarter of a mile Mary Ann looked ahead again. He had said that! He had taken Lena Ratcliffe's part, even though he didn't like her. Without any proof but that of her intuition, she knew this. Mr. Lord was hers. He might be the owner of a shipyard and run the farm as a hobby; he might be a man whom people were afraid of; but he had given her da a job when she had gone to him and asked him even though he had refused this to Father Owen and had once sacked her da from his yard.

It was when her ma had been going to leave her da, after their Michael had tried to gas himself, that she had got up in the dark and gone right out into the country and squeezed under the barbed wire round Mr. Lord's great house and knocked on his door. And the old servant had wanted to throw her out and had told the Lord that she was loopy because she had said that the Holy Family had sent her to tell him what a grand man her da was with cows and things. Mr. Lord had taken a bit of convincing, but he had given her da the job after she had made him laugh.

She liked to make him laugh—he had nobody to make him laugh, stuck away in that big house all on his own. And what was more, he always believed everything she said; not like Sarah Flannagan and Lena Ratcliffe and their Michael, and even her ma and da at times. Even these last two, in varying degrees, doubted her word; but never Mr. Lord. She had even told Sarah Flannagan in front of him that he was her granda, and he had believed her. He was hers.

The car came to a stop and Michael got out, saying in an awkward fashion, "Thank you, sir."

Mr. Lord nodded abruptly and drove on. The car stopped again, but Lena did nothing so common as get out. She alighted, definitely pleased with herself, and said, "Thank you so much, Mr. Lord. And goodbye."

Again Mr. Lord nodded and drove on. And yet again he stopped. This time he leant across Mary Ann and opened the door.

Without glancing at him, she slid off the seat and on to the pavement, then turned a pained, blank countenance towards him.

"Ta."

"Don't say 'Ta', say 'Thank you'."

Mary Ann's eyes popped.

Mr. Lord's brows like miniature sweeping brushes, moved up and down as he glared at the small elfin figure on the pavement. "Don't you know when to use 'us' and 'we'? What do they teach you at school?"

Closing her mouth and trying to still its trembling, she muttered, "Sums and things."

"Don't they teach you grammar?"

"Yes."

"Then don't say 'us' when it should be 'we'."

They stared at each other, the very small girl and the tall, bristling old man. Then, swinging round, Mary Ann darted like a rabbit up the street towards the school gate. And if she heard him call her name she took no heed . . . she was hurt and bewildered, she wanted to go to the lavatory and cry and cry. But this solace was denied her, for waiting for her, together with a number of cronies, was Sarah Flannagan, and the change in sex of a heifer had to be faced and somehow got over.

.   .   .   .   .

It had been an awful day. Sarah Flannagan had crowed about the heifer during the two playtimes, even going as far as to produce a book which said that a heifer was a young cow. And Miss Thompson had been awful, too; she was always awful; she was even worse than Miss Johnson, and had never been impressed by the grandness of her da or his new job, or the cottage, or even Mr. Lord. And if knowing Mr. Lord didn't make people sit up and take notice of you, nothing would.

Mary Ann closed her desk and marched out with the others to the cloak-room. There, her best friend, Cissie Bailey, told her that she would be unable to set her to the bus stop as she had to go straight home and mind the baby 'cos her ma was going in to Shields. And when her next best friend, Agnes Wilkins, said she couldn't come either because she had to go home and have her shoes mended, the world for Mary Ann became dull, almost dead. She'd have to walk the length of three long streets without an admiring audience—all her grandiose thoughts would be wasted!

She turned from them in a huff and marched away, determined never to speak to either of them again . . . and after her sharing her taffee with them an' all!

The need for Cissie's and Agnes's support became more apparent as she passed through the school gateway, for there waiting for her, was Sarah with three of her friends. Against all rules they remained silent as she passed them with her chin cocked in the air. And even when she had gone some distance they didn't shout after her, which was most unusual. Her curiosity forced her to look round. Although they weren't calling they were following her, and Sarah's dark, vicious face had a leer on it that Mary Ann knew portended no good. Nevertheless, she could not resist the opportunity of showing that lot, and Sarah in particular, that she wasn't afraid of them. And she did so by sticking out her tongue and wagging it violently.

This indeed was the signal for retaliation, and it came in the form of a chant, Sarah's voice being louder than the others':

> *"Swanky Shaughnessy—there she goes:*
> *Two boss eyes and turned-in toes;*
> *She cannot even wipe her nose.*
> *Swanky Shaughnessy—there she goes!"*

Mary Ann's gait became dignified. The serpent of pride slithered round inside her—it was nice to be called swanky. But it was usual, of course, to deny it strongly, saying, "I'm not! I'm not!" And this would be accompanied by a bobbing of the head. But on this occasion she did not retort; she was alone against four, and she was wise enough to know how far she could go. It would have been different had Cissie or Agnes been with her; then she could have revelled in the battle of tongues.

Suddenly the swanky feeling disappeared, swept away by Sarah's voice alone chanting:

> *"Pig's belly,*
> *Wobble jelly;*
> *Pig's fat,*
> *Dirty cat;*
> *Pig's skin,*
> *Double chin;*
> *Pig's cheek,*
> *Shiny beak;*
> *Pig's lug,*
> *Ugly mug—*
> *And that's Mary Ann Shaughnessy!"*

Oh . . . h! Her lips were pursed, and her face was wearing its tightest buttoned-up look. Just wait, she'd let her have it. Wait till the bus was just going so she couldn't get at her, and she'd yell, "Pig's snout, you great big lout!"

She turned into the street where the bus stop was, and Sarah and her cronies were for the moment wiped from her mind, for there, standing near the lamp post, was Lena Ratcliffe. She was staring at the back of Mitchell's factory wall. Lena never caught the bus at this stop, she caught it near the cemetary. What was she doing here? Perhaps she had to go a message. Mary Ann was overcome with an uneasiness quite inexplicable to herself. But she did not want Lean Ratcliffe to meet Sarah Flannagan, so, forming her own rearguard action, she turned on the advancing girls.

"Go on. Stop following me."

"Huh! Listen to her," said Sarah. "Who d'you think you are? Is it your street now?"

"I'll tell me da on you, mind."

"Ho! ho! ho!" Sarah bellowed derisively. "I'll tell me da! Did you hear her? I'll tell me da! Her da!"

Boiling inwardly, Mary Ann was forced to move on, until she come up to Lena. Lena was still staring at the wall on which there was some large writing in red and white chalk. But becoming aware of Mary Ann, she turned and looked down on her, and her expression was puzzling, for it was triumphant and very like Sarah Flannagan's when she had scored a victory.

Lena said nothing, no word of greeting, but slowly she looked at the wall again. Mary Ann's eyes were drawn to it, and with sagging jaw she read: "MARY ANN

SHAUGHNESSY IS A BIG LIAR AND HER DA'S A DRUNKEN NO-GOOD AND EVERYBODY KNOWS IT."

The new life seemed to drain from Mary Ann's body as she stood gazing at the large chalked words, and the old life crept back, making her shiver—the old life she knew before they went to the farm to live, the life that was full of sickness and fear.

It was not because Sarah had written that she was a big liar, and it was not the first time that Sarah had called her da a drunken no-good, but it was because Lena had read it. Her mother's voice came to her with that strange quality it had held this morning when she said, "Don't be cheeky to Lena." It was as if her ma was afraid. Of what, Mary Ann could not exactly explain, yet it was to do with Lena, or her mother, or her father—and her own da.

A hot sickly feeling of anxiety filled her. If anything should happen to her da. . . . If he should lose this job, and all through Sarah Flannagan. . . . Suddenly the anxiety and fear fled before a wave of fury which seemed to animate every inch of her. She turned to where Sarah was standing in the gutter grinning, and she leapt at her, tearing at her hair with her hands and using her feet against the taller girl's shins. For a moment, Sarah was taken off her guard. But it was only for a moment. She struck out and slapped Mary Ann such a ringing blow across the ear that Mary Ann's anger was knocked completely out of her, together with her wind. Her feet left the ground, and she found herself lying wher Sarah had been standing.

Sarah was now on the pavement being comforted by her friends. There was a deep scratch down the length of her cheek, and her face was dark with both pain and anger. She glared down at Mary Ann and cried, "I'll get you wrong for this, so I will. Wait till I tell me ma. And your da isn't any good . . . he is a drunk, a great big drunk! And me ma says she gives him six months in that job afore he's thrown out; and you'll all be glad to come crawling back to Mulhattan's Hall!"

On this enlightening tirade, Sarah flung round, and together with her cronies marched off. From a sitting position Mary Ann watched them. No one of them seemed to be walking straight; nothing was straight, the houses, the pavement . . . or Lena . . . And Lena had heard.

The fury was gone, and her mind was once again full of the dark foreboding. It did not lessen as she pulled herself to her feet and looked towards the disdainful girl coldly surveying her. With a definite look of pleading in her eyes, and in an almost humble voice, Mary Ann said, "You don't believe her, do you, Lena—what she said about me da—what's on the wall? Cos me da doesn't drink, he never goes into a bar. You've never seen him go into the village bar, have you?"

She waited for an answer. But Lena's only reply was to lift her chin and to shrug her shoulders.

The bus came round the corner. Mary Ann watched Lena move to the edge of the kerb and stick her arm straight out. She looked down at her own hands, all mud, and at her coat and stockings, thick with dirt. If she went home like this her ma would get out of her what had happened, and she'd be upset.

The bus stopped, and Lena got on, but Mary Ann stood where she was. It wasn't even any satisfaction to her to witness Lena's surprised expression through the window as the bus moved off without her.

For quite some time Mary Ann stood, her fingers trying to still her trembling lips. Then she thought of Mrs. McBride. She would go to her . . . Mrs. McBride would clean her up.

.   .   .   .   .

"Did you wallop her?" asked Mrs. McBride.
"I scratched her face."

"Well, I hope it was a good long scratch."

Fanny McBride held up Mary Ann's coat, saying, "Don't worry, it'll be as good as new. Go and wash your hands and knees, then have a sup of tea, an' you'll feel your old self again."

"Me da won't lose his job cos Lena knows, will he?"

Mrs. McBride let out a disdainful laugh which shook her fat and made the myriad wrinkles on her face quiver. "Lose his job? I should say not! And after Mr. Lord taking such a fancy to you."

"Sarah said we'd have to come back here and live."

"Not on your life. That 'un's like her mother, her venom would poison a rattlesnake. Anyway"—Fanny turned on Mary Ann—"where's that old spunk of yours? Surely if you could manage Sarah Flannagan and Mr. Lord, you're a match enough for this Lena, or whoever she is."

"But her da's me da's boss, and he doesn't like him very much."

"Who? Your da or his boss?"

"Mr. Ratcliffe doesn't like me da."

"Who said so?"

"Well he's always giving him the worst jobs, and Mr. Jones says he wouldn't stand for it."

"What does your da say?"

"Nothing. He just gets on with his work."

"And a good job, too. Does Mr. Lord say anything?"

"No. But he's not nice to me da, or pleasant, or anything."

"If I know old Lord, is he ever pleasant? Is he pleasant to the others?"

"No. He's grumpy all the time . . . except to me. And he was grumpy with me this morning cos I said 'us' instead of 'we'."

"Oh my God!" Fanny put her hand to her head. "The people who go in for fine words! You stick to your guns and don't let them make a lady out of you, or you'll turn into another Mrs. Flannagan and choke yourself."

"I don't want to be like her," said Mary Ann with emphasis. "I won't let then make a lady out of me."

"That's the ticket. Now go and get washed."

Mary Ann did as she was told, then had her sup of tea and an inch-thick slice of bread and dripping whilst Fanny cleaned her coat. And when she was ready to go again she stood at the door and smiled at the old woman. "Me da always talks about you, Mrs. McBride."

"Does he now? Well I hope he says something good."

"Yes, he does. He says to me ma that he misses your patter."

Fanny let out a laugh. "Does he so? Well I miss him an' all, tell him. I miss you all more than you know. But go now, else you'll miss that bus again, and it'll be black dark. And tell your ma I'll be over to see her. Goodbye now.

"Goodbye, Mrs. McBride . . . and ta . . . thanks for me coat and the tea." Mary Ann ran down the steps. She felt better now; she always felt better after talking with Mrs. McBride, because Mrs. McBride liked her da and she liked people who liked her da.

But once in the street she did not hurry, because she wasn't going to catch the quarter-to-five bus. She was late now and she would likely get wrong in any case, so she would catch the quarter past five, for there were two things she must do—she must pay a visit to the Holy Family and chalk out the writing on the wall. The thought of the Holy Family caused her conscience to move restlessly. She had neglected them for weeks, because there had been nothing to ask them to do, because everything had been nice, but now there would be plenty for them to get on with if things were to remain nice.

With somewhat of the air of a culprit she entered the church and made her way to the altar. But for a half-moon of candles burning below the altar and the sanctuary lamp, the church was in darkness. But it was not a darkness that could frighten Mary Ann.

She knelt, looking up at the three figures. They looked warm, drawn together in the candlelight; only the Virgin's face was in shadow under her blue hood. After gazing at them for some time, she felt their expressions changing, and her eyes slid down to her joined hands. They looked a bit vexed cos she hadn't been here for months; they looked like her grannie used to look when she went down to Shields to visit her. "You only come when you're dragged or when you want something," her grannie would say. But in this present case she had a defence, for she prayed to them in her night prayers, and she looked across the church at them when she was at Mass. But still, it wasn't the same as paying a visit.

She raised her eyes and began, "I'm sorry, Jesus, Mary and Joseph; I know I should have come afore, after all you did for us . . . getting me da the job and us the cottage, and putting our Michael to the grammar school, and making me ma happy. But I've been so full up with things. And it gets dark at nights and I've got to catch the half-past-four bus else me ma worries."

This thought stopped her colloquy . . . Eeh! Her ma would be worrying now. Well, it was no use, it was done. She had missed the quarter-to-five. . . . She returned to her prayers.

"I've come to tell you, Jesus, Mary and Joseph, what Sarah Flannagan did. She wrote something on the wall about me da. And Lena Ratcliffe saw it, and if she tells her ma and da they might . . ." She stopped again, unable to find words to formulate the vague uneasiness that filled her should the knowledge that her da had drunk heavily ever reach the ears of the farm manager and his wife. She did not reason to herself that Mr. Lord had engaged her father, and that only he could sack him, for she could feel that there were ways and means of bringing about the desired result other than by direct assault . . . subtle, frightening ways.

She began again, " Well, they might think me da was a bad man, and you know he's not, you know he's the finest da in the world. And he hasn't been . . . sick, even a little bit since we went to the farm. But if Lena tells her ma about him . . . " She paused and glanced down. "I don't like Lena Ratcliffe. Me ma says I've got to be nice to her but she's like me grannie and Sarah Flannagan, and I can't. And she's swanky and thinks she's somebody cos her da's the farm boss. And she's jealous of the Lord liking me. Yes, she is." Her thoughts were loud in her head and the three members of the Holy Family brought their frowns to bear on her.

Eeh! What had she said?

Their censure weighed her down, and her head drooped again and she muttered, "I'm sorry." But somehow that did not seem adequate, for they still looked ratty, so she added the confessional formula, "I am very sorry I have sinned against thee and by the help of Thy Holy Grace I'll never sin again." But even this did not soften them; so, self-consciously blessing herself, she stood up, genuflected, then walked up the church and into the blackness.

At the font she blessed herself with the holy water, and stood for a moment thinking: "And just because I said that . . . Well, she is jealous—I don't care." It was on this bold and wicked note she went to open the swing door that led into the porch, but as she touched it, it swung in on her, and for the second time that evening she found herself sitting on her bottom. It was as if the Holy Family with one accord had knocked her there.

"In the name of goodness, child, have I hurt you?"

Father Owen picked her up and peered at her. "Why, it's Mary Ann. Are you hurt?"

"No, Father."

She didn't sound quite sure.

"What are you doing here so late? You should have been home by now."

"I've been to Mrs. McBride's, and I missed the bus, Father, so I thought I'd pay a visit to the Holy Family." She hesitated to add what they had done to her through the instrument of himself.

"A very good thought an' all. And now are you all right?" He led her out to the church door, and there, in the light from a street lamp, he looked at her. "You're a bit white. Did I hurt you now?"

"No, Father . . . no."

"That's all right then."

He still continued to stare at her, his hand placed firmly on the top of her hat. "Is anything wrong, Mary Ann?"

"No, Father."

He paused a while. "Is your da all right?"

"Oh yes . . . yes, Father."

"He hasn't . . . ?"

"No, no, no." She brought the denial out rapidly. She couldn't bear that the priest should even say the word, even if he should say sick instead of drunk. "Me da's fine, and so's me ma and our Michael."

"Well, I'm glad to hear that. . . . Now, you're sure you're all right?"

"Yes, Father."

"Then off you go. Good night, my child."

"Good night, Father."

Mary Ann turned away, but before re-entering the church the priest gazed after her for a moment, and he scratched the sparse grey hair above his ear. He knew Mary Ann, none better, and there was something wrong with her, or else he was a Dutchman. . . .

Mary Ann glanced into Harry Siddon's, the watchmaker. His big clock said five minutes past five. In the light from his window she groped in her school bag and found a piece of chalk. Then she started to run; she'd just have time to scratch the words out before the bus came.

As she turned into Frank Street she saw with relief that there was no one waiting by the stop, so nobody would make any remark when she began to chalk the wall.

The down bus had stopped on the opposite side of the road, and as it moved on a man came hurrying from behind it. He stepped on to the pavement just as she reached the wall.

"Mary Ann!"

So great was the start she gave that the chalk sprang from her hand.

"Where've you been?"

"To . . . to Mrs. McBride's, Da."

"Why couldn't you tell your mother you were going?"

"I didn't know I was going, Da."

She could see he was flaming mad, the kind he got when he was worried; he seemed twice as tall and twice as broad. She didn't really mind him being mad at her, she'd rather him be mad at her than at her ma or their Michael, but she was worried nevertheless.

"Lena said you were fighting. Who were you fighting with?"

"Sarah Flannagan."

"Sarah Flannagan!" he repeated. "If you don't stop it I'll take the hide off you. D'you hear?"

She made no answer.

"You're like a hooligan."

They were staring at each other, the father and the daughter, and as a mighty ship can be turned by the slightest touch on the wheel, she turned him to face the road. She did it by holding his eye and moving towards the kerb. Whatever happened he mustn't see what was on the wall. He could be as mad as a hatter with her now but the morrow they'd be all right again. . . . But if he saw what was on the wall . . .

He stood now looking across the road and talking at her. He had his hands in his pockets so that he would not be softened by her touch. She stood a little away from him, her head down, pretending that she was sulking. . . . And then she remembered her chalk. It was the only piece she had and she'd dropped it. All the subtlety of her past manoeuvre she lost in turning to retrieve the chalk.

Mike turned and watched her looking on the pavement. He saw her pick up a piece of chalk, and as if it were activated by a malevolent power and wanted to point out to him its purpose, it caused Mary Ann to raise her eyes to the wall. Mike's gaze followed hers, and before she could swing round again to the kerb he had read what was there.

After one glance at his face. Mary Ann stared at the road again.

"Give me that chalk."

Silently she handed him the chalk but she did not look at him as he scrubbed out the words. When the scraping stopped he came to the kerb again and handed her all that was left, a tiny stump. Then he took her hand and held it tightly in his.

When Sarah Flannagan had knocked her into the gutter she hadn't cried; when the priest had knocked her on to her bottom and she'd thought her hip bones were coming through her shoulders she hadn't cried; but now the tears came into her throat and the pain of them choked her and dragged from her a groan. Mike's hands came about her and she was lifted into his arms, and as the bus came she turned her head into his coat so that the people should not see.

2

GOING UP IN THE WORLD

"Come on, man, and have a pint. What's a Saturda' afternoon for?" Mr. Jones adjusted his cap and buttoned up his coat. "What're you going to do with yersel'?"

Mike gave a short laugh. "I can find plenty to do with meself. I've got that back garden to dig."

"Oh, to hell, man. Come on, the back garden'll be there when you're not. Look, there's no use in working night and day. What's life for? I'm like yersel', I mean to get on, but I'm not goin' to work me guts out. I'll go up in the world without doing that, ye'll see. Are you comin'?"

"Da, can I weed?"

Mike turned and looked at Mary Ann standing in the doorway. "Yes, get on with it," he said, somewhat shortly.

But Mary Ann did not go and get on with it; she stared at Mr. Jones. She had come to a definite decision about Mr. Jones: she didn't like him. He was always egging her da on to do something or other, and she was terrified that repetition would wear Mike down and that one Saturday he would go with Mr. Jones to the village bar.

The four men on the farm had alternate Saturday afternoons off, and every other Saturday, when Mike and he were off together, Mr. Jones would repeat his invitation. He liked Mike. He considered him a man's man, but he couldn't understand why he was sticking so hard to the water waggon. He guessed that it was his wife who was at the bottom of it. She was a bit high-hat, at least his missus thought so. But then Clara thought everyone high-hat who was different from herself. She had to remember, as he was continually pointing out to her, that they were lucky to have the Shaughnessys as neighbours, for they didn't grumble about having their rightful half of the yard.

The yard behind the cottages had once been part of a second stable-yard, and no dividing fence separated the cottages. The two back doors and the kitchen and bedroom windows all faced the yard. Except for a rain barrel, a lean-to and a stack of logs the Shaughnessys' side was clear, but on the Joneses' side was a conglomeration of old motor-bikes because Mr. Jones was mechanical-minded.

"Mary Ann!" Lizzie called from the kitchen; and Mary Ann, going hurriedly into the room, said, "I'm going to weed, Ma."

"Stay in here a minute."

"But Ma."

"Sit down, I say, and leave your da alone."

"But Ma, Mr. Jones . . . " Mary Ann sat down without finishing.

"You needn't worry about Mr. Jones," said Lizzie.

Screwing uneasily on her chair, Mary Ann watched her mother hanging the cups of the new half set of china she had bought that morning on the hooks of the dresser. She watched her stand back and survey the result. But all the time her irritation was rising, and when there came the clutter of Mike's boots on the stones of the yard, she jumped up, asking eagerly, "Can I go now, Ma?"

"Yes," said Lizzie; "but don't bother him."

Mary Ann ran out, grabbing a small garden fork from under the lean-to as she went, and she joined Mike as he started to turn over the patch of ground at the side of the cottage.

"Where can I do, Da?"

"Along by the wall there," he said.

Mary Ann started to dig up the weeds with vigour. She did not chatter, for when her ma said "Don't bother him" it meant something. It was only four days ago that he had scratched the writing out and he had been funnily quiet since, not boisterous and laughing and throwing her up to the ceiling and carrying on with her ma in the kitchen.

Mrs. Jones, coming out of her front door dressed for town, said, "Hallo there, Mike. At it again?"

"Aye," said Mike, "at it again."

"You should give yourself a break, man," said Mrs. Jones, laughing.

Mary Ann watched her go down the path. Mrs. Jones was all right, but she wasn't like Mrs. McBride. She wished Mrs. McBride could live next door. . . . The futility of this wish made her attack the soil with renewed vigour until she became hot with her efforts. She looked at Mike. He didn't look hot, he was digging steadily. She wished he would talk. She had been quiet so long, hours and hours.

The sound of a church clock striking came to her. She didn't know whether the chimes came from Felling or Hebburn, but much to her surprise it struck only two. She'd just have to say something. She straightened her aching back, made a number of coughing sounds and was just about to lead Mike into conversation when Michael came tearing across the yard.

"Da . . . can I buy some fireworks? Look, Mr. Lord gave it to me." He held out his palm, with a shilling on it.

"Mr. Lord? Where's he?" Mary Ann dropped her fork and darted to Michael.

"At the farm."

"You'd better ask your ma," said Mike. "I thought you had some for tonight."

"Only a few." Michael turned to Mary Ann. "He gave Lena a shilling an' all."

Mary Ann started at her brother, then with an exaggerated show of indifference she said, "I don't care."

"Do you know what, Da? Mr. Lord's going to build a house here."

Mike straightened up. "Who told you that?"

"I heard him and Mr. Ratcliffe talking. I wasn't meaning to listen or anything." Michael cast a scathing glance at his sister which dissociated him from any connection with her tactics of getting information. "He was talking over in the yard. The architect's coming on Monday."

Mike, pulling a face, raised his eyebrows and pursed his lips, but he made no comment; but Mary Ann's comments came tumbling over each other. "Build a house here! Oh, goody. He'll take us to school every morning and I'll be able to go in the house every day and . . . and he won't be lonely, and he'll likely get rid of old Ben, cos you couldn't have him in the new house, and he'll get a young servant who won't be so bossy."

Michael sniffed disdainfully and went into the house. Within a few minutes Mary Ann watched him come out again and run across the yard and along the narrow lane which led to the village.

"I bet me ma's let him spend it, and she wouldn't me." On this thought, she too sped into the house, crying, "Ma, have you let our Michael buy fireworks?"

"Yes," said Lizzie. "And go and tell your da there's a cup of tea ready."

"Aw . . . w, you wouldn't let me. Can I spend me da's sixpence?"

Lizzie sighed. "You've got fireworks for tonight."

"Only a few, Ma. And now our Michael and Lena'll have piles."

"Oh, go on then," said Lizzie; "there'll be no peace until you do. But mind, don't start moaning at Christmas because there's nothing in your box."

Christmas was as a thousand light-years away from the fifth of November; in fact it might never come at all. She dashed to her school purse which was hanging on a long strap at the back of the cupboard door, extracted a solitary sixpence and dashed out of the house. She had reached the lane before she remembered the tea, and from there she shouted, "There's some tea for you, Da," then ran like the wind in case their Michael and Lena Ratcliffe should buy up the shop.

Wilson's stores, standing between the Boar's Head and a row of grey stone cottages and dead opposite the Methodist chapel, sold everything but beer, coke and coal. Inside the shop, in the small space left for customers, stood Michael and Lena. They had already made their purchases and seemed to have acquired a considerable amount for their money, but, Mary Anne noticed scornfully, they were all little 'uns that wouldn't make very big bangs, so, just to show them, she decided to spend the entire sixpence at one go.

"I want a One o'Clock Gun, please," she said.

Swiftly Michael turned on her. "You're not to buy One o'Clock Guns, me ma said so."

"She didn't so," said Mary Ann. And this was true, for Lizzie had not forbidden her to buy such a firework, never dreaming that she would attempt to do so, knowing that she was afraid of big bangs.

"You'll get into trouble," said Michael.

She hesitated. Yes, that was true, she likely would. She was still hesitating when Lena said, "We've got two One o'Clock Guns for to-night."

That did it. Had Mary Ann suspected that secreted within the firework was a time bomb she would still have bought it.

"Now, do you want it or not?" asked Mrs. Wilson.

"Yes, please."

Michael walked out of the shop and Lena followed, and when Mary Ann joined them, with a fat red stick of gunpowder in her hand, Michael said, "You won't half catch it if me ma finds you with that, you'll see."

"Tell-tale, long tongue!" said Mary Ann.

"Come on," said Lena.

"Where're you going?" asked Mary Ann.

"To our hut."

"Can I come?"

"No," said Lena.

Mary Ann watched Michael. It was his turn to hesitate. He half turned to her, but finally succumbed to Lena's delicate manoeuvre of pulling him forcibly by the arm.

"Spoonies!" cried Mary Ann after them. "Sloppy doppies!"

She had the satisfaction of seeing Michael bounce round and make for her. She did not, however, wait for his coming, but scampered away in the opposite dirction, homewards. Once in the lane, her running turned into a slow walk, for ahead of her was Mr. Jones, and he wasn't walking quiet straight but with his usual Saturday-afternoon gait. She let him enter his cottage before she crossed the yard. She was no longer carrying the One o'Clock Gun in her hand, for she knew quite well that she would lose it if her ma saw it. There were some matches kept just inside the scullery door. She proposed to pinch a few, then light the firework and throw it as far away from her as possible.

The kitched door was closed, and the sound of voices came from behind it, but so intent was Mary Ann on securing the matches that for once her curiosity was not to the fore. The matches safely tucked under the elastic of her bloomers, and trembling at her daring, she made her way into the lane again and stood silently considering where would be the best place to let it off. The bottom field where the cows were would do. This decision spurred her to climb three gates—she preferred the arduous climb to shutting the gates after her—and to make her way round the edges of two ploughed fields. After all this labour she reached the selected field only to decide against it. The placidity of the cows at their munching stayed her hand, for it brought back their teacher's warning to all the class not to set fireworks off when there were any animals about.

Slowly now, and rather dismally, she wandered back to the lane. The only thing for it was to set if off here. It wouldn't be much fun, but she could see no other safe place.

She struck a match, but before it got within an inch of the fuse she dropped it. Refusing to admit her fear, she lit another. This she only allowed to singe the end of the fuse before dropping that, too. She was busy with the fourth attempt when she heard coming from the main road, which was screened from her by the bank and the hedge, the sound of Lena's voice, and a great idea sprang into her head. It lifted her feet off the ground and sent her flying along the lane. She'd set it off and give them the shock of their lives. Reaching the yard, she darted in a zig-zag fashion through Mr. Jones's jumble of bikes and entered his lean-to, which was about three feet from the cottage bedroom window, and there crouched down.

As once again she fumbled with the matches the sound of deep snores came to her, and glancing to her left she saw between the curtains and through the partly opened window the prostrate figure of Mr. Jones fast asleep in bed. His mouth was open and he was anything but a pleasant sight. He looked awful, Mary Ann thought.

The match struck, she applied it with a steadier hand now that she had a definite purpose. When they crossed the yard she'd throw it behind them, not too near, but near enough to make them jump out of their skins, cos her ma had said if you must throw squibs never throw them in anybody's face, it might blind them. Her whole body was shaking with excitement. The fuse was nearly alight, and there was Lena and their Michael just entering the yard. Her heart pumping rapidly, she was holding the sizzling stick out ready to throw, when a terrible thing happended. From out of her own doorway stepped Mr. Lord and her da.

He mind, usually as nimble as mercury, refused to suggest what she should do now. Her main feeling at the moment was that Mr. Lord had been in their house and she hadn't known—she had missed something. Then her mind swung back to the job in hand and she became petrified . . . if she threw the One o'Clock Gun it would explode right between her da and Mr. Lord and Lena and their Michael.

Mr. Lord hated fireworks—he had said so only yesterday. Now her agile brain was working at such a speed that the flame, travelling along the fuse, seemed to become stationary. She must do something with the thing. It had ceased to be a One o'Clock Gun or even a firework, it had become a Thing—an awful Thing. Throw it near Mr. Lord she couldn't. The only alternative was to let it go off here . . . and die. Eeh! but she couldn't do that either, she was scared of big bangs. Eeh . . . Hail Mary, full of Grace . . . Mary Ann felt she had been holding the firework at least a week instead of a few seconds, and the fuse, racing now with her thoughts, was getting shorter at a speed that both fascinated and terrified her and almost robbed her of the power to fling the Thing anywhere at all. Then, seemingly of its own volition, the firework sprang from her hand and flew through the open window and right under Mr. Jones's bed.

The sound of the explosion, hemmed in as it was by the cottage walls, had differing effects on those who heard it. It caused Mr. Lord to jump as if the firework had been tied to his coat tails, and Mike to start and gaze in perplexity towards his neighbour's door. It acted on both Michael and Lena in the same way. It sprang open their eyes and mouths to their widest, for instantly they both knew what had caused the bang and who had caused it, and their astonishment made them look senseless. But the effect on Mary Ann was to lift her off her feet and precipitate her into the middle of the spare parts, where she lay covering her head with her hands to stop the cottage from falling on her.

What effect her sudden appearance had on the four people in the yard was lost in that of a greater surprise, for following on an unearthly wail the cottage door was pulled open and there raced into the yard the apparition of Mr. Jones.

Clad only in his shirt and linings, and making almost animal sounds, Mr. Jones had the appearance of a madman intent on winning a marathon, and it took all Mike's strength, which was considerable, to bring the little man to a halt and to hold him.

"Steady, man, steady!" cried Mike.

Mr. Jones, panting as if at the end of a race, and his face working in much the same way as that of a straining and spent runner, gasped, "In the n . . . name of G . . . God, Mike. . . . "

"Steady, man!" said Mike again.

"B-but, Mike . . . "

Mary Ann rose from her knees with all eyes on her, including Lizzie's. Mr. Jones, still jangling, was holding on to Mike as he stared at the perpetrator of the crime. No one spoke as she moved forward. Mr. Lord's face was very red and her da's unusually white. That was temper, Mary Ann knew. Michael and Lena looked at if they had been struck dead.

Lizzie's voice was low as she said, "Get inside."

Mary Ann got inside. She was so frightened she thought she was going to vomit. She sat on the kitchen chair with her legs tightly crossed and waited. After a while Lena came to the open door and looked at her as if she were some strange specimen in a cage, then she walked away again without saying a word.

Mary Ann sat for a long while. She heard voices and movement in the cottage next door. Then there was quiet for a moment before they all came back into the kitchen: her ma and da, their Michael and Mr. Lord. And when she looked at her da she wanted to leave the room, so affected was she by the anger she saw in his face.

Then before her da could say a word Mr. Lord suddenly sat down, his red face turned to purple as if he, too, were on the verge of exploding. And then he did, but not with the sudden impact of the firework. First the muscles of his face worked, then his body shook and he groaned and put his hand to his side, then he strained back in his chair and said, "Oh dear! oh dear! . . . the funniest sight . . . the funniest sight." As the tears began to rain down his cheeks the tension in the room slackened somewhat. Mary Ann, with one eye on Mike, gave the semblance of a watery smile; Lizzie and Michael seemed to breathe more freely; only Mike remained the same. He was apparently unaffected by Mr. Lord's laughter, and glared at Mary Ann.

"Why did you do it?" he demanded.

"I didn't mean to, Da."

"Then why?"

Mary Ann made no answer, and Mike's voice, rising, demanded again, "Why?"

Trembling now, Mary Ann said, "Cos I was frightened of it going off near me, and if I'd thrown it at Michael and Lena it would have frightened——" Her eyes slid to where Mr. Lord sat dabbing at his eyes.

"Why did you throw it at all? I've warned you about big crackers, haven't I?"

Mary Ann didn't stress the fine point here that it was Michael he had warned, but with her eyes stretched wide she continued to stare at him. Even when Mr. Lord said, "Don't worry, don't worry. He wanted stirring up anyway, that fellow," she still continued to gaze at her da.

"It might have turned the man's mind." Mike spoke down to the top of Mr. Lord's head and there was not the slightest deference in his voice.

And now Mary Ann looked a little fearfully from Mike to Mr. Lord, but Mr. Lord still seemed amused and he said, "What, a bang like that, and the fellow been through the war?"

"That's a different thing," said Mike, "you're expecting bangs then."

"He shouldn't have been in bed on a Saturday afternoon. And he was likely half drunk," said Mr. Lord, tersely.

Was it her imagination or was there a sort of warning in Mr. Lord's voice? But it was no imagination that her da stiffened, and the stiffness came over in his tone: "It was the man's own time."

"Yes, yes, his own time." Mr. Lord stood up abruptly, and Lizzie, looking fearfully from one to the other, asked: "Won't you stay and have a cup of tea, sir?"

"No, no thank you," he said, and much to her amazement he smiled kindly at her. "I've had all the beverage I want for one afternoon," His hand went out and he rumpled Mary Ann's hair, and Mike, seeming to become more hostile and addressing Mary Ann pointedly, said: "You're not getting off with this this time, you're in for a good smacked backside, and don't you forget it."

"Nothing of the kind." The old man swung round on Mike. "You're treating the thing too seriously."

"I know me own business, sir, if you don't mind."

Now they were facing each other, hostility in their eyes.

Lizzie's hand went to her throat. She prayed that Mike might keep his temper. Oh, were things never to run smoothly? She knew that Mike's nerves were on edge—the desire for a drink had been in him for days. He had been coping, and had himself well in hand, until last Tuesday and the incident of the writing on the wall. Things like that affected him. "I might as well just be at it again," he had said. "They're waiting for me to start . . . I can feel it." And she had cried back at him. "Nonsense! The doings of a girl like Sarah Flannagan. And you know her mother, she hasn't a good word for God." And on top of this Mr. Jones had to come in today when he was well under way and jabber and jabber. It was all telling on Mike. If only Mr. Lord would go and she could talk to him.

Mr. Lord turned from Mike and moved to the door, and there he turned again and said, "Don't thrash her." And although he said it quietly, it was an order.

Now anger rose in Lizzie against her daughter. Mike had been made to appear as if thrashing Mary Ann was a pastime of his, when the truth was he had never raised a hand to her in his life . . . he had spoilt her. He may, for a time, have made her own life a hell, but never intentionally Mary Ann's. Even before Mr. Lord was out of earshot, she cried to Mary Ann, "Get up those stairs and into bed."

Without a word, and at the double, Mary Ann went.

"And you too!" cried Lizzie to Michael.

"But, Ma, I've done nothing . . . and I'll not go up with her."

"Then go on out."

Michael went out, his face expressing the injustice of the dismissal.

Lizzie looked to where Mike was standing staring into the fire, his hands thrust into his pockets, and said softly, "Take no heed."

He swung round on her. "Take no heed! He acts as if he owns me, body and soul. And not only me . . . he gave me the job because of her, and he's taken her."

"Don't be silly." Lizzie moved to him, and placing her hands beneath his loose cardigan she gripped his braces and pulled him to her. "Nobody can take her from you."

"No? Why is he gong to build his house here?"

"Oh!" she leant back from him. "Mike, that's madness. He's fond of her, I know, but he's got no need to build a house here to see her. He can come in the car as often as he likes. . . . Oh, that's a silly idea, if ever there was one."

"I don't know so much."

"It is. You know what he said. He's retiring from an active part in his yard, and now feels he must have something to fill his time. It's only reasonable he wants to build a house on his own land and be near his farm."

"Why did he have to come and explain it to us? It's none of our business, is it? I'm only a hand here."

"He's lonely," said Elizabeth. "Can't you see? For all his money he's lonely, and he doesn't get on with people—he's kept away from them too long."

"All I can see is he wants to run her life and mine. Well, I'll give him a good working day, but from then on me life's me own . . . and hers is mine an' all, until she can look after herself."

He jerked himself from her hands and, taking up his cap, went out, whilst Lizzie, after staring at the closed door for a moment, braced herself before going up the stairs.

Mary Ann was sitting on the side of the bed, her eyes fixed wide in her drawn face.

"You see what you've done? You've got your da into trouble with Mr. Lord. Are you satisfied?"

Mary Ann's face became even whiter, and her eyelids drooped as if she were about to faint. Her silence was more telling than any verbal defence.

The tenseness went out of Lizzie's body, and moving her head in bewilderment she went to the bed and, sitting down, slowly drew her daughter into her arms.

Like a small avalanche Mary Ann's pent-up emotion was released. Sobbing and crying, she clung to her monther, while Lizzie rocked her, saying, "There now, there now, it's all over. It's all right, it's all right. Stop that crying, it's all right." But as she was saying it she wondered in her own mind whether it was all right. Mary Ann would forget most of the happenings of today; only the funny parts would remain, and tomorrow the whole family would likely be laughing at the recollection of Mr. Jones tearing from the house. Yes . . . even Mike, for it bore out Mr. Jones's oft-used prophecy that he would rise in the world. But would the deep implications that the event had brought to the surface be forgotten? There had always seemed to be a state of undeclared war existing between Mike and Mr. Lord, but this incident had brought about an open declaration. There could be only one victor in such a war—Mike. And what would the victory entail?

Suddenly Lizzie felt very weary.

3

CHRISTMAS

The kitchen was rich with the smells of cooking. There was the pastry smell, a mince smell, a herb smell, the smell of boiling bacon, and the warm sweet smell of cocoa.

Mary Ann let the steam from her mug waft about her face; then she stuck her tongue down into the froth on the surface of the cocoa and licked at it.

"Don't do that!" said Lizzie, turning from the baking board.

"Well, it's hot, Ma. Ma . . . "

"Yes?"

"Lena says that Mr. Lord's goin' t'give her a great big present."

"That's nice."

"Do you think he will?"

"Lena must think so, else she wouldn't have said so."

"I think she's a liar."

"Don't use that word!"

"Well," Mary Ann took a sip of her cocoa, "Sarah Flannagan calls me that, and"—she glanced covertly at Lizzie—"others do an' all."

Lizzie suppresed her smile while redoubling her efforts with the rolling-pin.

"Look, there's me da." Mary Ann jumped from her chair and made for the window, spilling her cocoa as she did so. And Lizzie cried, "Look what you're doing!"

She, too, looked through the window across the yard to where Mike was striding towards the cottage. It was eleven o'clock in the morning, and not the usual time for him to come in; he had his break at ten. But his brows weren't drawn, and he looked cheery . . . and handsome, she thought, like he did when they were first married. The winter sun was shining on his mop of red hair and lightening still further the new clearness of his skin. He was looking ten years younger than he did when they lived in Jarrow. But what was bringing him here at this time?

"Da, d'you want some cocoa?" asked Mary Ann.

"Yes. And anything else that's going . . . something smells good." He came and stood near Lizzie, and dipping his finger into the flour he rubbed it on to her cheek.

Mary Ann gurgled. It always gave her a feeling of joy to see her ma and da larking on.

"Give over." Lizzie pushed him with her elbow. "What are you here for, anyway?"

Mike, hitching up his trousers, said with slow, exaggerated airiness, "His lordship's asked me to accompany him into Newcastle. Me, Mike Shaughnessy, as ever was."

"Mr. Lord?"

"Mr. Lord . . . his honour . . . his worship."

"Oh, Da, can I come?"

"You cannot . . . Bejapers! Not even a queen would I allow to accompany me the day."

Mike was amused, he was happy; and although he scoffed and put on the Irish twang, Lizzie could see he was pleased.

"What are you going in for?" she asked.

"I haven't a notion, me darlin'."

Mary Ann laughed out loud, and Mike, looking at Lizzie, made a tiny movement with his eyes towards her. And after a pause Lizzie said, "It's time you were going to meet your grannie. Go on, get your coat on."

Mary Ann's face suddenly fell. She knew she was being got rid of. "Aw! . . . it's ten minutes afore the bus comes; and it'd freeze you out."

"Get your coat on," said Lizzie callously, "and freeze. You haven't frozen, I notice, during the last two hours you've been out . . . And mind," she warned her daughter, "of what I told you last night."

Mary Ann got into her coat, hat, scarf and gloves at a snail's pace, and saying to anyone it might concern, "I never get taken nowhere," she went out.

Mike and Lizzie looked at each other and smiled.

"Why is he taking you?" asked Lizzie.

"I'm not exactly sure," said Mike, "but I think it's to buy me Lady Jane something." He nodded in the direction of the window, through which Mary Ann could be seen slowly cross ing the yard. "But I know this much," he added, "I'll have to pay for me jaunt. Ratcliffe's furious; in fact, he tried to stop me going. He told him I was needed to load beet, and the old boy said why not put one of the others outside, it'd do them good. He keeps his eyes open, I'll grant him that. But Ratcliffe'll swear I've been mewing to him."

"Let him swear what he likes," said Lizzie. She was happy to think Mr. Lord held no feeling of animosity towards Mike, for she had been worried sick since the firework episode. "Do you think someone's told him about Ratcliffe giving you all the tough jobs?" she asked.

"Not on your life. Which of them would concern himself about me?" said Mike scornfully. "Jonesy might tell me what to say, but he'd never say it for me. And Stan and Joe are for ever sucking up to Ratcliffe . . . No, the old fellow's not blind. He engaged me as cowman afore Ratcliffe came, and what does he see when he comes around. . . . I'm anywhere but in the byres."

"Then why doesn't he say something to Ratcliffe?"

"Well, I suppose fair's fair. You put a man in as manager, you've got to let him manage."

Lizzie, turning to the board, cut a spray of leaves from out of the pastry and placed them on top of a pie. Then she said quietly, "I don't like him, Mike . . . I don't trust him. Nor her, I'd be careful if I was you."

He came close to her side again, but did not immediately answer her. Instead he stood looking at the gold coils of her hair lying low down on her neck, and his finger traced the curve of the twined braids before he said softly, "Don't you worry, I know what's at stake. It'll take more than Ratcliffe to get me on the wrong foot. The old fellow can do it more easily than him."

"Oh Mike, be careful." Lizzie turned her face to his and her eyes added a plea to her voice. "Don't say anything to him you'll be sorry for. Don't, Mike."

"Now look," he pulled her round, gathering her floured hands into his great fists. "Haven't I behaved meself and kept me tongue quiet . . . and haven't I done what I said about the other business? I've never touched a drop. And it hasn't been easy, mind."

"Oh Mike, I know, I know. Only I get frightened."

"Well, don't."

She leant her face towards him and rested her cheek against his. His lips touched her ear, and she stayed still for a moment. Then, suddenly pulling herself from him she exclaimed in indignant tones, "Eleven o'clock on a Saturday morning and tomorrow Christmas Eve! And I suppose Mr. Lord's waiting patiently for you?" Her face was flushed and her eyes happy and he brought his hand with a resounding whack upon her buttocks, saying, "Big Liz."

"Oh Mike, that hurts!" She held the affected parts.

"You asked for it," said Mike, putting on his cap. "Turning a man's head. I'm off now and I don't know what time I'll be back . . . that's if I come back at all. If I should see a nice little piece in Newcastle, something on the lines of Nellie Flannagan . . . "

He was gone, leaving Lizzie laughing and happy. But still in the midst of it she turned her eyes to the corner of the room where hung a passe-partout framed picture of the Virgin, the work of Mary Ann, and voicelessly she prayed, "Let it last."

. . . . . .

Mary Ann stood at the cross-roads, the wind chafing the only exposed part of her, which was her face. She did not turn her back to it but faced it squarely and told herself she would freeze to death and it would serve them right. There followed in her mind a distinct picture of her death-bed scene. She was lying in bed dressed all in white. Her ma was begging her not to die, her da was crying like anything and so was their Michael, and Father Owen was there, and Mr. Lord and Mrs. McBride . . . and Lena Ratcliffe and Sarah Flannagan. She had, with the beneficence always attached to the dying, sent for these two to bestow on them her forgiveness. She had reached the scene where she was telling Sarah, in a very weak voice of course, that if she would swear that she had never heard her, Mary Ann, tell a lie in her life she'd speak to the Holy Family for her when she got up to Heaven, when the loud honk-honk of a motor horn made her swing round, and there was her da and Mr. Lord waving. Frantically she waved back, but she doubted if they saw her, or if they cared for that matter. Fancy them not stopping. This affront wiped out even her mother's callousness. And yet as the car disappeared into the distance the wonder of what she had just witnessed dawned on her . . . Mr. Lord was taking her da to Newcastle. Mr. Lord must like her da very much. Suddenly her body became alive with activity. She jumped, she skipped, she took giant strides along the grass verge to a field gate and back again. She flung her arms about the sign-post and endeavoured to climb it. After numerous failures she was half-way up it when the bus stopped on the other side of the road and her grannie alighted.

Mary Ann, lost in her present joy and forgetting why she was at the cross-roads at all, did not see Mrs. McMullen trotting across the road. She was not aware of her presence until she spoke.

"You get your clothes cheap."

Mary Ann, gripping the pole, was now on eye level with her grannie, and that small, dark, energetic lady, who carried her sixty-seven years with a lightness that chilled the hope of those who relied upon years alone to carry her off, drew in her mouth before opening it to command, "Get down out of that! Are you stuck there for life?"

Mary Ann's convulsive grasp on the pole slackened, and she sped the short distance to the ground so quickly that she lost her balance and fell down the heap of beach on to the road.

"That's right," cried Mrs. McMullen, "roll in the mud! You get worse. You were bad enough afore. Look at the sight of you."

Mary Ann did not follow her grannie's pointing finger and look at her coat. She continued to stare glumly at her grannie, and some private section of her mind, kept solely to deal with her hated relative and kept closed these past months, opened and addressed itself to whoever was responsible for her grannie's presence on this globe at all. Why had you to go and let her come, it said, after I asked you to keep her away? You could've done something to her, given her rheumatics or something. But, she ended with truth, nothing ever happens to me grannie.

"Well, come on. Are you going to stand here and freeze us? How far is it? Why didn't your mother come?"

"It's not far, just along the road and down the lane. Me ma's baking."

They walked away with at least four feet separating them, Mrs. McMullen looking about her with critical eyes. Bare trees, wet brown fields and not a house to be seen; you couldn't even see the top of the gantries in the shipyards only a couple of miles away. Her eyes fell or seemed to be dragged down to her grand-daughter, and she noticed with disapproval that there was colour in her cheeks. But it wouldn't last long, she comforted herself. The child was small and puny by nature and she wouldn't be surprised if there wasn't T.B. there somewhere, brought over from the Shaughnessy family. Even her embittered mind could not actually pin the consumption on the great brawny Mike.

"It's a God-forsaken place you've come to. Your ma didn't get out much afore, she'll get out less here."

"She does get out. Me da takes her on a Saturda' night, and us an' all, me and our Michael. We go to the pictures. Sometimes we go to Newcastle."

Mrs. McMullen's eyes and head jerked upwards, and her hat, perched high on top of her abundant hair, looked in danger of toppling off. "Another brilliant start," she said, backing up her words with a significant cough.

Mary Ann's eyes, screwed up like gimlets, fixed themselves on her grannie's profile. She was starting again. Why had she to come, anyway? No one had asked her. She had written asking to come, and her ma had said last night, "Well, she's got to come sometime. And it's Christmas; we must bury the hatchet."

Mary Ann wished with swift urgency that somebody would spring out of the hedge and hit her grannie with a hatchet . . . and run away again, for she wouldn't want anyone to get wrong for hitting her grannie.

"What's the people like?"

"Who . . . who d'you mean?"

"The farm men and the manager, of course." Mrs. McMullen looked at her grand-daughter as if she was a halfwit, for Mary Ann was weighing her answer. If she were to say what she thought, it would be, "Mr. Ratcliffe's awful, and Mrs. Ratcliffe's snooty, like Lena, and I don't like Mr. Jones, but Stan and Joe are all right," but being wise to the fact that her grannie would immediately take sides with those she disliked and connect the reason for her dislike with her da, she said, "They're all right."

"That's a change."

This caustic remark demanded no reply, and in silence they continued down the lane. The silence was enforced on the old woman for she had to keep her feet clear of the potholes. But at last she exclaimed, "Never seen anything like it . . . you could break your neck on a dark night."

Maybe this statement gave rise to the hope in her mind that this would happen to her son-in-law, for she followed it immediately with, "How often has your da been drunk since he's been here?"

Mary Ann stopped dead and watched her grannie step over a puddle near the grass verge. She had an almost overwhelming desire to take a running jump at the old woman and push her into the ditch.

The word "drunk" when connected with her da always had the power to make her feel sick. The word was a weapon so powerful that it overshadowed not only her own life but also that of the entire family. What it had almost done in the past it could do again. It had almost parted her ma and da and it had made their Michael gas himself. And there was the other thing it had nearly done, vague in her mind now but still recognised as a bad thing, and made more bad still because her grannie came into it. In fact her grannie seemed to be the master of this particular evil. Her grannie could do again what she had done at Mulhattans' Hall, talk and talk to her ma in the scullery about her da drinking, then end up by mentioning Mr. Quinton and his fine car—she always ended up with Mr. Quinton.

"What you looking like that for? Don't you start any of your tantrums afore I get me foot inside the door. And answer me question."

"Me da doesn't drink, he' a grand——"

"Yes, yes, I know. He's a grand man, and for God's sake don't start that again."

"Well, he is."

"All right, have it your own way. And don't you bawl at me or I'll take the side of your ear off you."

"I'm not bawling . . . me da doesn't drink. He doesn't even go in the village bar, so there. He's fine and respected and everybody likes him. Mr. Lord's taken him in his own car right into Newcastle, and he was sitting aside Mr. Lord and . . . "

"Oh my God! that's enough. " Mrs. McMullen flapped her hand in the air. "He'll be the Archangel Gabriel next and covered with down. How much further have we got to go along this God-forsaken road?"

Mary Ann gave her no answer, but her indignation carried her some distance ahead of the old woman until they reached the gate, then she ran up the path and round to the back and into the kitchen.

"Where's your grannie?" Lizzie turned from the oven.

Mary Ann tore off her hat. "She's comin'."

Lizzie, looking keenly at her daughter, said, "Now mind, I'm having no trouble. Keep that tongue of yours quiet."

"She's——"

"That's enough. Where did you leave her?"

"At the gate."

A hammering on the front door told Lizzie that her mother was no longer at the gate. Forcing a smile to her lips and stiffening her shoulders as if she were going into battle, she went to open the door, saying over her shoulder, "You stay out to play. Go over to the byres, it's warm there."

.   .   .   .   .

The afternoon had passed off not unpleasantly. Mrs. McMullen had shown no approval of anything in the cottage, but still she had not voiced her disapproval, except about the condition of the road and the distance from the bus. This latter grouse had not been displeasing to Lizzie, for she thought that it would hasten her mother's departure before Mike should come in. Although he knew of his mother-in-law's proposed visit, there had been no mention of it between them, and as he had not returned to dinner she hoped now that he would not return before tea-time. He had not forbidden Mrs. McMullen the house, yet Lizzie knew he would hate to see her in it. Perhaps he was already back on the farm and was not going to put in an appearance until she was gone.

When it was half-past three, however, and Mrs. McMullen was showing not signs of taking her leave, Lizzie became uneasy. And not about this alone. She knew from experience that if into her mother's small talk there should creep a note of mystery, it brooked no good. Three times already during the afternoon her mother had alluded to a surprise that was in store for her, and now she was at it again. Sipping at her seventh cup of tea since her arrival, she was saying, musingly, "Funny how things turn out. . . . By! it is. But you'll get a surprise one of these days . . . you will that. I've told you, I know more than you think."

"Look, Mother"—Lizzie endeavoured to keep her impatience from being revealed in her voice—"don't be so mysterious. What can surprise me? I think I've had all the surprises I want in my life. If this is something unpleasant, let me know now."

"Who said it was unpleasant?"

Mrs. McMullen put her cup down carefully into the saucer and surveyed it, first from one angle, then from another, before continuing, "It might be for some. It all depends how you look at it, and who looks at it, and what you look at."

Lizzie went into the scullery. She could not trust her tongue. It might be for some. She knew what that portended—trouble with or for Mike. Why was her mother so vindictive?

Why did she continue to hate him?

"Aren't you going to put a light on, I can hardly see a finger afore me?"

In answer to the querulous demand, Lizzie returned to the kitchen and switched on the light, saying, "Yes, it's darker than ever to-night." Then she added, "You're going to find it difficult getting to the bus."

"I got here, didn't I? Well, I'll get back. Don't worry about me. Where's that 'un? Running the roads, and it near dark."

"She'll likely be somewhere on the farm. There's no worry about her being out in the dark here."

"No? You'll always have worry with that madam, you mark my words. And Michael, I've only seen him for five minutes. Why couldn't you keep him in? It isn't as if I'm on the doorstep every day."

"He'll be in the byres . . . he likes to help. Will you have another cup of tea?"

"No."

A silence settled on the room. The glow from the fire, the pink-shaded light reflecting on the Christmas decorations, and the homely furniture gave it an atmosphere of comfort and of gaiety; but it ceased to charm Lizzie. She knew why her mother was sitting tight. She had no intention of going until she had seen Mike. But why? Even in the past she had always taken her leave before the time Mike was due home.

But any further speculation Lizzie might have made was cut short by Mike's entry—he came in like a strong wind, bursting into the room, seeming to fill it. His presence, like the wind, stirred things with unseen power, although the gay light in his eyes shadowed on the sight of his mother-in-law. Lizzie felt his excitement, his vitality, his joy at being home again even after only a few hours away from her, and the love in herself answered his. But she kept it veiled from her eyes.

Now Mrs. McMullen rose to her feet. "I'll have me hat and coat," she said. She did not look towards Mike, but took her hat from Lizzie and slowly pinned it on her head. Lizzie next helped her into her coat, and as she did so Michael came in, and she said to him, "Your grannie's just going, are you coming with us to the bus?"

"All right," said Michael. He did not appear at all eager, and he added, "But if you want the half-past four you'll have to hurry." Turning from his mother he said to Mike, "Have you just got back, Da?"

"Just this minute," said Mike. He spoke pleasantly to the boy while reaching for one of three pipes from a rack to the side of the fireplace. Scraping the bowl, he sat down by the hearth.

Mrs. McMullen paused in her dressing, and her eyes darted from father to son. The friendliness between them was not lost on her, and it both surprised and annoyed her. The boy had never liked Mike, which had been mostly of her doing, and so to think that now Michael could tolerate his father seemed to her entirely wrong. The wicked should be made to suffer, not only hereafter but now, and they would be. She wasn't done yet, not by a long chalk. She'd have her own back on that big gormless Irishman, if it took the last breath she breathed.

She stood drawing on her gloves, glancing covertly at the back of Mike's head as she did so. Then looking up at her daughter and in a manner which would have led anyone to believe that she was picking up the threads of a conversation just recently dropped, she exclaimed, "So old skinflint Lord's going to spend some of his ill-gotten gains and build himself a house here, is he.?"

Lizzie stared at her mother. Mr. Lord's name had not been mentioned, nor the building of his house. Her face, screwed up in perplexity, was asking her mother silently how she knew this, when Mrs. McMullen continued, "It's a small world. Fancy Bob getting that contract. That's a feather in his cap, that. Ten thousand pounds the house will cost afore it's finished.

That's some money, isn't it? That's a contract. Well, come on. . . . "

Lizzie stood stiffly watching her mother go from the room. It was almost diabolical the way in which she had manoeuvred this piece of news to hit Mike. This, then, was the surprise.

She could find it in her heart to hate this woman, who was relentless in her attempts to achieve a separation between her and Mike, and all under the guise of wanting nothing but her happiness.

Outwardly Mike had not moved except to draw deeply on his pipe, but the news had caused something to leap within him, a mixture of fear and hate and envy. Slowly he lifted his eyes and looked into the mirror above the mantelpiece. In it he could see Lizzie. Her face was turned from him, and she did not turn towards him or speak a word to him as she followed her mother out. He kept himself still, although some vital part of him had flown through the room and grasped his mother-in-law by the neck and swung her round and away; and he watched her, spinning away and over the hills, over the river, away, away into Eternity, nevermore to touch their lives with her bitteness and venom.

Suddenly he leant forward and sharply knocked out his pipe upon the bar, knocking the nodule completely out. So Quinton was coming to build the old fellow's house. Well what of it! What of it? Lizzie would see him—she wouldn't be able to help it. His fine car would come into the lane and she would watch him daily directing operations on the hill practically opposite the kitchen window. He would come in here—he was an old friend of hers, he should have been her husband—he would sit in this chair and look at her; and they would laugh together while he was at his work.

As he stood up abruptly the front door banged and Lizzie came into the room. There had not been time for her to go to the crossroads and back again, and Mike looked towards her as she stood within the door pulling off her coat. Neither of them spoke for a moment. Then she said softly, "Look Mike, I knew nothing about it until a minute ago."

He stared at her. "Who's saying anything?"

"But you don't believe me."

"Who's saying I don't believe you?"

"But I can tell. She sprang it on me—his name had not been mentioned, or the house, or anything."

Mike gave a tight laugh. "Well, now, ask yourself if that doesn't take some believing. The old bitch was full of it. It's hard to imagine her keeping that up her sleeve, and it didn't sound as if she had."

"But Mike, that's just the point, she had. She did it to cause trouble. She's my mother, and at this moment I hate her."

So intent was Lizzie in trying to convince Mike of the truth that she took no heed of the click of the outer door. Nor did Mike as he turned from her and looked into the fire and rasped his hands over the dark stubble on his chin before saying, "She'll never rest till she's done it."

As Lizzie went to his side and gripped his arm Mary Ann's head came round the door. She had been about to give her da a fright, but her mischievous intent was checked and the impish gleam died out of her eyes as she stared at them. They were fighting, the quiet fighting like they had done in the bedroom at Mulhattan's Hall. Yet they couldn't be fighting, they hadn't had time. Their Michael had just told her that their grannie had gone and their da had just come in.

She saw Lizzie put her arms about Mike and pull him almost fiercely round to her. As she listened to her mother's low, urgent words, the old fear, that at one time had made her want to die, came flooding over her again.

"How often have I told you she can't separate us? Nor can Bob. You're the only one that can do that. Haven't I told you, Mike? Let him come and build the house, what does it matter? I don't want a car or a fine house; I only want you and what you can give me. Do you believe me? Mike, tell me. . . . "

Mary Ann watched her da look into her mother's eyes with that lost look she knew so well; then with a suddenness that drove the breath from Lizzie's body he pulled her into his arms.

The fact that they were kind again was no solace to Mary Ann. Quietly she retreated, her gloved fingers pushed deep into her mouth. It was her grannie had done it. She had made Mr. Quinton come and build the house for Mr. Lord and upset her da. . . . Oh, her grannie! If only she would drop down dead.

She stood under the lean-to biting her fingers for some time. She stood until she felt the cold creep up past her knees, and one foot went dead. But what did it matter? All of a sudden everything was spoiled, Christmas and Mr. Lord's house, even the reason for the visit to Newcastle.

With flooding eyes she stared upwards into the sky. Venus was making its way towards its zenith. Tomorrow night that big star, she knew, would come to rest over the stable, and Jesus would be born. And as she stared, she was not surprised to see the star wink at her. It grew brighter and bigger still, until right in the centre she actually saw the Infant Himself.

Her hands under the arm-pits, she swayed now backwards and forwards trying to still the cold, and as she swayed the Child nodded to her. "Go on in," He said. "Go on in now and be nice to your da. And the morrow pay a visit to the Crib and we'll see what can be done."

After she had blown her nose, the star decreased to its normal size, and slowly she went indoors.

Her da was sitting before the fire as if nothing had happened, and her ma turned and smiled at her. She took off her hat and coat and went and stood between her da's knees and pressed herself close to him.

"You're cold," he said. "Are you all right?"

"Yes," she answered.

"Don't you want to ask me anything about Newcastle?"

She shook her head.

Mike lifted his eyes to Lizzie and she came and, bending over Mary Ann, asked, "Do you feel bad?"

"No."

"Have you been fighting?"

"No."

"Put your tongue out then."

Mary Ann stuck her tongue out to its surprising length, and Lizzie said, "Well just in case you'll have a dose of syrup of figs, and off to bed with you."

When there was no objection to this, Lizzie and Mike looked at each other with knowledge in their eyes. They knew the reason for their daughter's quietness. As usual, with or without intention, she had been listening.

Lizzie turned away, and Mike bent his head and rubbed his face reassuringly against his daughter's cheek.

4

THE OLD FIRM

Lizzie lifted the square box on to the bus platform and said to the conductor, "Will you help her off with it at Pratt's Lane, please?" But before that obliging man could agree.Mary Ann exclaimed for the twenty-sixth time that morning, "I tell you I can carry it meself!"

Lizzie stepped back, not so much to avoid being knocked over as to restrain herself from lifting Mary Ann off the bus and boxing her ears.

As the bus began to move, Mary Ann looked from her mother's set face to Michael, who was standing by her side, and, as was her way, she was suddenly overcome with remorse—it was because of her persistence and tantrums that Michel wasn't coming with her to give Mr. Lord the cake. Gripping the rail, she leant forward and shouted, "You can take me own Christmas box to him by yourself this afternoon, you can."

But Michael's reaction to this offer was lost on her, for the conductor, holding her securely by the collar, pushed her into the bus and on to a seat. He placed the box by her side, saying, "You're going to have your work cut out carrying that, it's nearly as big as you. Is anybody meeting you?"

"No—and I can carry it."

"Well, if you say you can, you can."

Left to her own thoughts Mary Ann looked at the box, and her eye penetrated the wrapping and saw lying snugly in layers of soft paper the Christas cake, all iced and beautiful. She gave a deep sigh; she was taking it on her own to him. And she was surprised that she was, for it was only just before going to sleep last night that she had decided she must take the cake to Mr. Lord all by herself, because if their Michael went with her as arranged it would be impossible for her to talk to Mr. Lord, and it was absolutely necessary now, after what she had heard, that she should do so. The new threat to her parents' happiness had even made the news that Mr. Lord had given Lena a pair of ballet shoes for her Christmas box lose its sting.

She sat lost in her plan of campaign. After he had opened the box and been overcome by the beauty of the cake's green-and-white trellis-work icing, she would make her request. Of course, she would do it properly and nicely. And what with the cake and it being Christmas Eve, he would not, of course, refuse her so simple a thing.

Long before they reached Pratt's Lane, Mary Ann was on the platform, the box at her feet. When the bus stopped and the conductor lifted the box off and placed it in her arms, she thought for one horrifying moment that she was going to drop it. The conductor's caustic comments followed her as she moved along the road towards the big iron gates. Once there, she propped the corner of the box on a low spike and, panting heavily, rested against it. Then she pushed the other half of the gate open, and when she had passed through she was careful, even under her present difficulties, to follow the same procedure and close it, for it wouldn't do to annoy the Lord this morning. She was actually staggering to the end of the long drive when she saw him coming down the dilapidated broad stone steps of the house.

Mr. Lord's brows had gathered in surprise at the sight of Mary Ann carrying a box as broad as herself and apparently twice as heavy, and it must be admitted that at the sight of him her staggering became so exaggerated as to suggest she was either on a heavy sea or drunk. As neither of these things was possible, it could only be the tremendous weight of the box that was weighting the child down.

The old man moved swiftly towards her, and as Mary Ann relinquished her burden to him with a sigh that was not altogether acting, he demanded, "Who sent you with this?"

"Me ma," she gasped.

"Your mother?"

"Yes, it's for you, for Christmas."

"You mean to say she sent you with this great box? Where's your brother? What's he doing he couldn't bring it, if it had to come?"

Mary Ann remained silent, and Mr. Lord, glancing at her, knew without further explanation why Michael had not been allowed to carry the box and whatever was in it.

And so they entered the house. In the hall they passed Ben, or it would be more correct to say Ben passed them. He passed them as if he were blind, for on no account could Ben be brought on to the side of Mary Ann. To Ben the child was uncanny. Most of his life had been spent with the man who was his master, and there was nothing that he didn't know about him. He knew him to be a hard man and not always just; he was a bitter man and had cause to be; he had for many long years hated women, and children he abhorred, and no female foot had entered these doors for twenty-seven years, until that child came in early one morning. Like a mist she came in, for only a mist could have penetrated the barbed-wire fencing and the high stone walls that bordered the house. Now the gate was left open, the master drove children to school in his car, and, latest madness of all, he was going to build a new house . . . at his age! And all this since that child had been allowed in here, that uncanny child who had the temper of a banshee and the coaxing ways of the wee folk. Well, the master could build the house, but would never get him inside it, he would die before that. His usefulness was done. He shambled on into the kitchen.

Mary Ann, standing by the table in the dining-room said, "Aren't you going to open it?"

"What is it?"

"It's your Christmas box from me ma, she made it herself. And you know what?" Her voice sank to an awed whisper. "There's a glass of brandy in it."

"Brandy?" he said.

"Yes. Go on, open it and see."

Mr. Lord somewhat slowly undid the string and opened the box, and lifting the many papers, he unveiled the cake.

Mary Ann's eyes had not left his face, and after some time, noticing no ecstatic change taking place, she rose on her toes and peered into the box. Yes, there it was. She cast an eye up at him. "Isn't it lovely?"

"Yes—yes, very."

"Me ma made it all herself . . . she knew he"—nodding her head as though towards Ben in the kitchen—"could never manage one. She sent something for him an' all. I've got it here in me pocket; it's three hankies. They were one and elevenpence ha'penny each."

Mr. Lord turned from contemplating the cake. "Your mother is very kind—very thoughtful. It's a long time since I had a home-made Christmas cake; or Ben . . . any hankies."

"You'll like it. And she didn't put all marge in either, like ours; she put half butter in yours."

Slowly Mr. Lord smiled, and putting his hand on her head he wobbled it gently back and forth, and moving towards a chair he guided her to it.

Standing beside his knee she gazed down on his blue-veined hand lying along the arm of the chair and wondered how she would begin to make her request. She took her finger and gently traced a knotted vein to where it disappeared under his cuff, but this meditation gave her no clue.

"What are you going to get for Christmas?"

Quickly she looked up at him—here was the opening. "I'm gonna get a school bag and a box of paints, but"—she added, her face taking on a melancholy look—"that's not what I want."

"It isn't? What do you want?" He bent above her, his eyes narrowed with enquiry.

"Well, you see, it's a different thing to what you get in your stocking."

His head came down to hers and he whispered mysteriously, "I know what it is."

"You don't," said Mary Ann.

"I do."

"What is it then?"

"Ah, that's telling."

Mary Ann stared at him. He couldn't know, but he was in a fine temper, and that augured only good. "You can't know," she said, "'cos I didn't know meself till last night."

"Oh!" There seemed a trace of disappointment in the old man's face. "Well, come on, tell me what it is."

Mary Ann wriggled a little. She hitched up her knickers, which, no matter how tight the elastic might be, would slip down. She put her head first on one side then on the other, then, keeping her eyes lowered and tracing her finger round his hand again, she said, "You know the house you're going to get built? Well, I know the man who's going to build it."

Puzzled, Mr. Lord's brows drew together.

"It's Mr. Quinton, isn't it?"

"Yes, but what of it? What's that got to do with your Christmas-box?"

"That's it—that's me Christmas-box. I don't want him to build it."

Utter perplexity showed in Mr. Lord's face. His turkey neck fell into deeper folds as he drew his chin in; his lips attempted to meet his nose and his eyes became pin points of pale-blue light; but he said nothing—he just waited. And Mary Ann went on, eagerly now, "That'd be me Christmas-box, if you did that . . . if you got someone else to build your house. I wouldn't want nothing else and I'd do anything for you."

"Why?"

"Why?"

"Why do you want me to change my builder?"

This was the difficult part. Mary Ann moved uneasily. "Well, you see, me ma knows Mr. Quinton, and me da . . ."

"Yes?"

"Well, me da . . ."

"Go on."

"Me da doesn't like Mr. Quinton to be near me ma, and me grannie's always wanting Mr. Quinton to be near her, and—"

Mr. Lord rose, pushing her gently to one side; human triangles always irritated him. The part he himself had played in one had long since ceased to pain him, and people who became so involved were fools. He had been a fool once.

He blew into his moustache and said sharply, "You must not talk about your parents' affairs."

"But I can't help it, it's me grannie. . . . Will you get somebody else?"

"No."

The syllable was final, but Mary Ann refused to recognise it. "But there's lots of men who build houses."

"There might be, but I want Mr. Quinton. Now we'll say no more about it. You must not concern yourself about such things, child." He turned to her again and addressed her gently now. "Thank your mother for the cake, and come tomorrow and tell me what you get in your stocking." The last could have been an appeal, but it did not touch Mary Ann.

"I don't want nothing in me stocking."

Mr. Lord sighed. He had been acquainted with this morsel of humanity for only four months but he recognised only too well the signs of battle.

Mary Ann's mouth was now a button. "I don't want nothing off you." Her chin jerked at him.

"Very well."

"Nothing . . . and I don't care about you buying Lena Ratcliffe ballet shoes."

Mr. Lord's eyebrows jerked and his face showed surprise at this piece of news. He had certainly given Lena a pound, but ballet shoes. . . .

"She'd never be able to dance in them, anyway, she's too big . . . like a Corporation horse."

Mr. Lord turned quickly away, saying, "Well, she can but try."

"She'd look daft in a ballet dress—she's a pig-face."

"Now, now."

"She is. And she's a rotten, swanky, stuck-up . . . "

"Now that's enough, quite enough. And stop shouting."

"I'm not shouting."

"Well, if you're not, I never hope to hear you do so."

"I'm going."

"Very well."

"And I'll go to church and ask the Holy Family. They'll stop him building the house for you, you'll see."

She marched to the door, but no voice bade her come back; not even when she opened the door and halted there did Mr. Lord bid her stay.

In the dim vastness of the hall she stood pulling at the ends of her woollen gloves with her teeth. Her temper was seeping rapidly away.

Ben, coming from a dark corridor carrying a broom, stopped in his tracks at the sight of her. She turned and, seeing him, remembered the packet in her pocket.

Ben's face was a study as he watched her approach, and whatever his reactions were when she handed him the Christmas-paper wrapped packet, saying flatly, "Me ma sent you these and she says a Happy Christmas," he did not allow them to show. But he took the gift from her hand and stood staring at her. She stared back at him. Then, as if he were a confederate, friend, and joint guardian with her of the master of the house, she nodded to him and whispered, "He's in a bad temper, he won't do nothing."

There was no word about her own temper, yet her conscience was working at a great rate and she was already thinking, Eeh! I shouldn't have been so cheeky, and after him being so nice and kind and all. I won't half get it if me ma knows.

Ben watched her walk towards the drawing-room door again, open it quietly and go in, and he looked down on the first wrapped Christmas gift he'd had in years. Slowly he turned and went back into the kitchen again.

In the drawing-room once more, Mary Ann leaned her back against the door and looked towards the forbidding figure standing before the tall window looking out into the wet, unkempt garden.

She coughed; she coughed again. Then putting her hands behind her, she gently rattled the door handle. But Mr. Lord either did not hear or did not want to hear. Reluctantly leaving the door, she walked slowly up the big room, and skirting the massive table and chairs she came to his side. Once more she coughed, quite loud this time, but its effect was lost and it did not even make him look at her. So, tentatively, with one finger she poked at his coat pocket, and concentrated her gaze on her hand as she said "I'm sorry. I didn't mean it."

There was quite a long pause before he turned and looked down on her. A slight tremor passed over his face but his voice showed no amusement when he said, "I should hope so."

He turned and went to the file, and she followed him saying, "Are you vexed?"

"No."

There seemed nothing more to say for a long while. Then, moving nearer to him, she asked, "Will you be going into Jarrow this mornin'?"

"Yes."

"Will you take me in with you?"

"Where do you want to go?"

"To church—to pay a visit to the Holy Family . . . "Her voice trailed off as Mr. Lord groped for a chair and sat down—he always had to sit down when he laughed, for that unusual emotion seemed to shake his entire frame.

Mary Ann, pleased and happy at the un-hoped for turn of events, stood at his knee and joined in his laughter. He was in a good mood and, who knew, he might get another builder . . . he might. She took his hand, and as his laughter rose, her voice vied with his for supremacy. She had only to keep him laughing and everything would be all right.

5

A CHILD IS BORN

When Mary Ann had a project in hand which centred round the happiness of her parents, time itself was ignored. It was only something into which she could cram her efforts. That she was answerable to her parents for what she did with her time was periodically forgotten; it had to be if she wished to achieve anything. Didn't it stand to reason that when every part of her mind, wit and energy was being used on their behalf they should understand? And yet she did not really expect anyone to understand for people were . . . funny, all except her da and Father Owen, and sametimes Mr. Lord.

But with him it was just sometimes, for look at him today and what he had done, or not done. Still laughing, he had left her at the church door, but had damped her spirits with his parting shot: "This is one time the old firm is not going to help you; you can take my word for that, Mary Ann," he had said. She knew by the "old firm" that he meant the Holy Family, and she was downcast by his prophecy. And what was more he seemed to be right, for she had been unable to get near Jesus, Mary or Joseph at all, not even in her mind.

Inside the church, she had been astonished to see that the group of the Holy Family had been moved, and that in its place stood the Crib. There was some solace, however, in remembering the Star last night and what the Infant had said, but she couldn't get a word in to talk to Him, for there were so many people inside the altar rails messing about with things. There was Miss Honeysett, the priest's housekeeper, and two nuns, and John Findlay and Walter Hewitt, who were altar boys. You couldn't kneel and have a talk with them about, so after saying one desultory "Our Father" and three equally desultory "Hail Marys" she went out into the dull, bleak day again, and decided that if she went to see Mrs. McBride she might get a bit dinner. By that time they should have finished messing about with the Crib and she would come back.

Mrs. McBride was delighted to see Mary Ann. Not only did she give her a bit of dinner but kept her for nearly two hours listening to her crack, and when, just on the point of her departure, Mrs. McBride's daughter-in-law and five children swarmed in. Mary Ann was detailed yet again and drawn without any hesitation into going out to play Tommy-noddy.

This particular section of Mrs. McBride's grandchildren consisted of four boys and a girl, all under twelve, and all admirers of Mary Ann. What better company in which to meet Sarah Flannagan. And they were no sooner on the street than Sarah made her appearance. She advanced on Mary Ann with slow and deadly intent, exclaiming, "What you doing here? Get yersel' away, this is our street."

Mary Ann's courage being greatly reinforced by the McBride squadron, she not only attacked the solitary Sarah with her tongue, but also joined in the fray of pelting her. This game, however, was abruptly brought to a stop by the furious figure of Mrs. Flannagan descending on the gang, as if airborne, and scattering them. Unfortunately, Mary Ann's courage far outstrode her wisdom, and standing to make one last sally at Sarah she was caught by the scruff of the neck and shaken like a rat by the indignant and enraged lady who, apparently, had heard nothing as yet of "Peace on Earth to men of goodwill." If she had she was taking this occasion to prove the utter lack of goodwill towards her and hers by this imp of the devil, for that is what she called Mary Ann. She spoke in so loud a voice that Mrs. McBride was brought to her window, and from there seemingly catapulted into the street and to Mary Ann's defence.

Mrs. McBride was ready to do war with Lady Golightly, as she had nicknamed Mrs. Flannagan, at any season of the year. Very often she didn't wait for an excuse, but were there one to hand it helped to intensify the heat of the battle.

Mary Ann now found herself wrenched from Mrs. Flannagan's hands and almost flung into the middle of the road. As she saw Mrs. McBride going for Mrs. Flannagan and Mrs. Flannagan looking down her thin nose with utter scorn at the vibrating, wobbling flesh of Fanny, Mary Ann hastily made her retreat and didn't stop running until she had reached Ormond Street, where she tidied her hair, composed herself, and thought, "Eeh! it's getting dark, I'd better hurry to church, then get the bus home."

She expected to find the church, at this darkening hour, empty and quietly awaiting her presence and prayers, but instead, to use her own words, it was crushed full. This exaggerated impression was caused by a number of mothers with small children kneeling at various distances from the Crib, waiting to get a better view, and at the other side of the church a number of rows of seats holding scattered penitents waiting to go into Confession in preparation for the Midnight Mass Communion. She stood hesitating near the holy-water font, and definite annoyance filled her—there was a laxity of arrangement somewhere. Here she had, she told herself, been waiting all day to see the Infant Jesus and she was further away from this than ever. It was no good waiting her turn to get near the Crib, for she'd never be able to talk to Him properly with all these people about, and she'd likely have wilful distractions at prayers, and that'd be a sin, and she'd have to tell it in Confession, and it wouldn't be her fault.

The thought of Confession turned her eyes towards Father Owen's box. That was an idea. Father Owen was next to the Holy Father as the recipient of her troubles. She could talk to him to her heart's content in the confessional box, that is, if she went in last, and she could tell him about everything, even about her da and Mr. Quinton, and her confidence would be as safe as houses. For Mary Ann firmly believed what her imagination and innate desire to shield her father from all censure bid her believe; namely, that God struck a priest blind the minute he entered the confessional box, so that he, not knowing who was talking, would naturally not be able to split on the penitent should he ever be assailed by the desire to do so.

She now went and knelt at the very end of the row, and slowly she moved upwards as, one after the other, the men and women left the pew. But bewilderment filled her when she realised that, as she had been moving up, others had been moving in, and only the fact, although somewhat belated, that she had to get home deterred her from again going to the end of the seat in the hope of being the last. Finally, when it was her turn to go into the box, she realised she had not made any of the usual preparations. But still, she told herself, it didn't really matter, for she hadn't committed any sins, not big 'uns, anyway.

In the dark confessional, with her chin barely reaching the elbow rests, she looked at the dim outline of Father Owen's face which was reflected behind the grid by the light of one candle, and she began her confession. "Pray, Father, give me thy blessing for I have sinned. It is five days since my last confession."

There was no word from the priest, so she went on: "I haven't said me Grace after meals, and I punched me brother and called after Lena Ratcliffe...and...and...I've wanted to push me grannie into the ditch and wished she was dead...."

"That's very wicked."

Mary Ann stared at the grid. He didn't know her grannie; he couldn't know her grannie or he wouldn't have said that.

"Why do you wish your grannie dead?"

"It's because she doesn't like me da, Father, and she's trying to take me ma away from him, like she did afore."

The priest's head turned sharply, and with his sightless eyes he peered down at Mary Ann. "What makes you think that?" he asked.

Mary Ann told him why she thought so. Without once mentioning a name she gave him exact details about the building of the house by Mr. Quinton. In fact, she also informed herself, as she talked, of what would happen. It became like a picture unfolding in her mind. She could see Mr. Quinton in their kitchen, and her da coming in and looking mad....

She became so lost in her story that the priest checked her with "All right, all right." She stopped and waited, and listened to Father Owen coughing in little short, sharp coughs. Then he said, "Now you must not worry yourself any more about this matter. Take no heed of it. Why, don't you know what day it is? It's Christmas Eve. Have you been to the Crib?"

"I can't get near it, Father, there's a crush there."

"Well, go and have another try. Then get off home and to bed, else Santa Claus will be here before you know where you are. What are you going to get in your stocking?"

Somewhat sadly, Mary Ann said, "A school bag and a box of paints."

"Well, isn't that what you want?"

"Not very much, Father. I wanted a bike, a two-wheeler, but me ma says it would be years afore I get that, and anyway I'm too little."

"Ah, you'll grow, and by the time you're ready to reach a bike you'll get one, you'll see. But, anyway, you go and have a talk with the Infant about it, and you can be assured if it's for your good you'll get it. Always remember that . . . your tiniest prayer is answered if it's for your good. Now for your penance say three 'Hail Marys'. Say your act of contrition."

Mary Ann said the act of contrition and left the box, and, wonder of wonders, the church was nearly empty. Apart from the few people waiting to go into confession, there was no one about, and not a soul at the Crib.

Reverently, on tiptoe, she now approached the stable, and it was a real stable, with a donkey and a goat and piles of straw, and there amid the straw sat Our Lady, and there stood Joseph, and there, with hardly a stitch on him, was the Baby. Mary Ann gazed and gazed at Him. In spite of His nakedness He looked warm and snug. She continued to gaze, held spellbound by the wonder of Him. He was lying so quiet; everything in the stable looked quiet. They were all waiting for twelve o'clock, waiting for Him to be born. She found she couldn't pray, or ask anything of Him. He was so little, not at all like He was when seated in His Mother's arms on the altar of the Holy Family.

A lump came into her throat and she sniffed. If she could only touch Him, just a little touch, just put her finger on Him. A quick glance to either side told her she was alone.

Trembling, even to her kneecaps, she rose, and skirting the short altar rail she crept up the altar steps. Another three steps and she had passed the imitation rocks and was right behind the donkey. Another quick glance about her to ensure that she was alone, and she knelt down. Now she was looking through the donkey's legs, and there was the Baby, startlingly close but still far away. Four wriggles under the donkey's belly and she was at the side of the Crib.

Heaven and Earth trembled; she was in the stable. There was Our Lady and St. Joseph and the goat, and up above her was the donkey, and before her, in His cradle of straw, was the Baby. Her body shook as her hand went towards Him. When it hovered over His open palm she put out one finger and with a touch like thistledown she rested it on the moulded plaster. The contact was not hard, cold, and lifeless; the warmth from His soft flesh flowed through her little body and made her life His. Like that she stayed for a number of Eternities; then, crawling backwards, she went out the way she had come.

She didn't remember leaving the altar, but as she walked up the aisle she knew she had . . . a holy feeling. She could even hear angelic voices singing "Venite adoremus". she felt good, in fact, saintly. It may have been the lights from the many candle sconces that danced around her, or it may have been the halo of light that circled round her own saintly head, but she knew she was walking in light and felt . . . holy.

History has told us that saints have always been sorely tried, and mostly by their relatives; that they have had to call from time to time on God to fortify their patience when dealing with the ignorance and thick-headedness of members of their families, especially brothers.

Mary Ann, floating in a holy mist out of the church door, was dragged with startling force to earth. "Where do you think you've been?" Michael, gripping hold of her arm, took on the appearance of the devil himself; but still in her holy state. Mary Ann was proof even against the tempter, and remembering that a gentle word turneth away wrath, she replied in an unnaturally soft voice, "To the Crib."

"I've been in church twice for you in the last hour."

"I was at Confession." Still the angelic voice.

"Well, don't you think that'll get you off; you're in for it this time."

"Aw—you!" Like a feather wafted away by a gale of wind, the holy feeling vanished, and she pulled herself from Michael's hands as he said, "You had to come straight back home . . . me ma's nearly mad with worry, and on Christmas Eve an' all, and everybody's looking for you."

"They're not!" She turned on him with scorn. "Don't tell lies."

"They are. It's close on six o'clock. Me da's out, and Mr. Lord an' all. Me da's gone to Mrs. McBride's again, and Mr. Lord's taken me ma down to me grannie's."

"Me grannie's!" Mary Ann's scorn reached the heavens. "I wouldn't be at me grannie's, would I?"

Michael didn't argue this point, but griping her firmly by the hand, said, "Come on. We're all to meet at Ellison Street."

"Leave go."

"I won't."

"If you don't I'll kick your shins, mind."

"You do if you dare."

"There then take that!"

"Oooh! you." Wincing in pain, Michael released her hand, and she sped away towards Ellison Street with him in hot pursuit.

The light had gone, and with it the holy feeling. She was once more on earth, being buffeted by the ungratefulness of her family. And this was made only too apparent when her da, who was, if the truth be told, really the source of all her troubles, brought her running to a stop by a mighty hand on her shoulder and a mightier voice in her ear demanding the same stupid question, "Where do you think you've been?"

"To church, Da."

It seemed for a moment that Mike might explode, he looked so angry, and he almost spluttered as he said, "You'll do this once too often, mind."

Standing under the lamp they regarded each other, and Michael regarded them. Then Mary Ann, her head drooping, turned away and looked at the lamp-post, and the three of them stood silent, waiting.

The damp cold was piercing; the only glow of warmth came from the coloured lights in the bar on the opposite side of the street. The bar was decorated gaily, ivy and holly intertwining the bottles on the high shelves, and from it, too, came the sound of laughter and merry talk. Mary Ann's glance slowly raised to Mike. He was staring straight across the street, and in his eyes was that look she knew but could not name. Rapidly now she began to pray for the car to come, and when, in almost immediate answer to her prayer, it drew up close to the kerb in front of them, she forgot she was the culprit and smiled her relief at the occupants. But her smiling was brief, for not only did her mother go for her, but also Mr. Lord as well.

"If it wasn't Christmas Eve," Lizzie said in a low voice, "I'd give you the best hiding you ever had in your life."

"I endorse that, I do firmly." Mr. Lord stared down on her, and she was almost startled at his ferocity. "Get in," he said. "Never again will I give you a ride. Why didn't you tell me you had to return home? Frightening people."

She got into the car and sat crouched in the corner, hurt and solitary, listening to their voices all joined together against her. Her da spoke little, but when he did he agreed with Mr. Lord. That was the only solace of the journey.

. . . . . .

The misery of last night was past, and the weight that had been placed upon her shoulders, of spoiling everybody's fun, had slid away in sleep.

Jesus was born now—that was her first awakening thought. The next was . . . me stocking! She was out of bed and around the curtain that divided her portion of the room from Michael's before she was fully awake, and shaking him by the arm, she hissed, "Come on, are you coming downstairs?"

Michael, awake at once, muttered, "Yes, all right; but be quiet." For him, too, last night was past.

Cautiously, and holding on to each other, they went down the narrow steep stairs to the kitchen. Michael groped for the light, and when it flooded the room they made no dive towards their stockings hanging from the brass rod above the fireplace. Their eyes were glued in hypnotic stares at the table. Even when they moved towards it, they did so slowly. Michael's mouth was agape and Mary Ann's whole expression had taken on the semblance of her . . . holy look.

Two shining cycles were propped against the table, one large and one small, and the labels attached said briefly, "From Mr. Lord".

One hand on the seat and one hand holding the label, Mary Ann was still in a state of stupor when Michael was proclaiming his grateful astonishment with gasps and grunts. The label might say from Mr. Lord, but it could only have been at the instigation of the Holy Family that this miracle had been performed, and because of the star last night and her touching the baby. . . .

Michael, in the midst of his joy, glanced at her. Then staightening himself, he exclaimed in astonishment, "What you crying for now? Oh! You're barmy!"

6

A MATTER OF EDUCATION

Mike pushed his unfinished dinner away from him, and Lizzie, putting down her own knife and fork, asked anxiously, "What is it ? Something's wrong . . . you've been like this for days now."

Without answering, but passing his hand tightly over his mouth, Mike rose from the table and took his pipe from the mantelpiece. And Lizzie said again, "Tell me what it is."

Staring down at the pipe, he said, "I'm worried, that's all."

"Is it Ratcliffe?"

"Aye."

"What has he done?"

"Nothing. . . . Blast them bikes!" He gnawed at his lower lip and thrust his pipe into his pocket.

"But you couldn't help that, Mike."

"I know, but had I known the old boy wasn't getting Lena one an' all, I wouldn't have accepted them two, seeing how things stood between Ratcliffe an' me. How was I to know he wasn't giving her the same, or something of like value? It's his fault, he shouldn't make flesh of one and fish of the other. It's a wonder he bought Michael one . . . I suppose he couldn't get out of that, being in the same house."

"Oh, Mike, don't talk like that, he's been so good. We should be grateful."

"Well I'm not grateful." Mike spoke quietly and without rancour. "He does it to buy her, and you know it. And Ratcliffe's taking it out of me because his wife's taking it out of him."

"But in what way is he doing it; can't you speak about it?"

Mike gave a jerk of his head. He could not tell Lizzie the number of small humiliations he had suffered lately; the dirtiest jobs pushed his way, the placing of a young lad, the latest addition to the farm staff, over him. But the most telling incident had happened yesterday. Coming out of the cattle market after the sale, he had encountered Ratcliffe standing by the best end of the Three Horseshoes. Ratcliffe had looked him straight in the eye and said, "Coming in for one?" There had been no invitation in the words, only a challenge. Ratcliffe wasn't the kind of boss who drank with his men, but he would have taken him in then and let him drink till he was blind. Mike had been aware, in that instant, that Ratcliffe knew all there was to know about him, and he could date the source of his knowledge from the night Lena had come home and said Mary Ann was fighting with a girl at the bus stop—the writing on the wall had not escaped Lena.

The Ratcliffes were not local people, and Jarrow being six miles from the farm, it was unlikely that his reputation for the bottle would have spread this far. One thing Mike was sure of, Ratcliffe was only waiting his chance to give him the push. Any so he would eventually pin something on him, insolence, negligence . . . or drink.

He picked up his cap, saying, "Well, I'll be off." Then he turned and smiled at her, and she came to him.

"Don't worry; only keep your temper. Promise you will."

He patted her cheek and laughed. "I promise I won't hit him."

He went out, and she stood at the window watching him cross the yard. Why were things made so difficult for him? He was trying so hard, God knew he was. Not a drop had passed his lips even at Christmas. It was over six months now since he had tasted liquor of any kind. If only he could be given a fair chance and allowed to work peaceably, that was all he asked. But there were so many conflicts raging in and around him. There was Ratcliffe taking it out of him, and Mr. Lord vying with him for Mary Ann—Lizzie admitted to herself what she wouldn't for worlds have admitted to Mike, that Mr. Lord was angling for the child's affection. And she was afraid of the old man's power, the power of his money . . . and his loneliness. Of the two, it was his loneliness that would be the most telling. It even affected herself. She knew Mr. Lord's history, as did everyone in and around Jarrow. Except for going daily to the ship-yard, he had lived like a hermit for years. Some of the older folk remembered the big splash his wedding had made, when at past forty he married a girl less than half his age, and spent so much on her whims that he nearly went broke. And then she had left him. Now in his old age, Mary Ann had brought him back to life and he saw in her what might have been had he been given a child to rule and mould, and in whose affection he could warm his thinning blood.

But that a child of his would not have resembled Mary Ann in the least, Mr. Lord did not consider, for he thought he saw in Mary Ann's tenacity of purpose and courage a reflection of himself. This, coupled with her being so endearing made her almost irresistible to him.

Sensing all this, Lizzie saw a bitter struggle ahead. But its end she would not even try to see.

Mike had long since passed from her sight, and she was about to turn from the window when two figures on the hill opposite caught her attention. She knew them both. One was the man who had been filling her mind for the past few minutes and the other was a man who had filled her early life, the unformed years of her teens. Even when the image of the red-headed farm boy had occupied her nightly dreams, her waking thoughts guided by her mother, had seen in Bob Quinton not only a husband but a man who was going to rise. Bob had risen, beyond even his own dreams, and he hadn't married . . . She turned from the window.

It was many months now since she had seen him. The last time was the night he had kindly given her a lift home from a bus stop, only to be seen by Mike. The repercussion of the events of that evening had resulted in Michael almost killing himself. She turned her mind from it now and from the man himself, and busied herself with clearing the table and washing-up.

She was sitting by the fire, hurriedly finishing off a pair of socks for Michael before the light of the short afternoon should fade, when there came a knock on the back door, and on opening it she was faced by the two men.

She did not look at the tall, pleasant-faced, fair man or give him any greeting. It was to Mr. Lord she looked and spoke: "Won't you come in?" she said.

"Thank you; we will for a moment. This is my builder . . . I understand you know each other?"

"Hallo, Elizabeth."

"Hullo, Bob. Will you take a seat? It's very cold out." There was restraint in her voice.

"Yes, it's nippy. No, I won't sit down. You're looking very well, Elizabeth, farm life agrees with you. How are the children?"

"Oh, excellent."

The exchange of pleasantries was all very stilted and correct.

As Mr. Lord's glance moved quickly from one to the other, he thought, Fool of a woman . . . women are all fools. They would have made a fine pair, if there is such a thing . . . and she would have had an easy mind.

"May I get you a cup of tea?" asked Lizzie. But both men answered together "No, no."

As she stood in an uneasy calm by the side of the table, Bob looked at her with the penetrating look she knew so well. During times of heartache in the past she had thought of this look, but now it embarrassed her. She pulled a chair forward. "Do sit down," she said.

"Thanks all the same, Elizabeth, but I'm due in Newcastle in fifteen minutes. I just wanted to come in and say hullo." He glanced at his watch. "Yes, I must make a move, but I'll be seeing you again, that's sure."

The "that's sure" disturbed her, although she knew it meant nothing. It was as natural for him to be nice and pleasant as it was for Mike to be hot-headed, but Mike would read a personal meaning into every gesture Bob was likely to make in her presence.

"Goodbye, sir," he said to Mr. Lord. "Goodbye, Elizabeth; remember me to the children."

He had not mentioned Mike. Well, it was to be understood. She went to the door with him, and there he did not repeat his farewells but smiled at her quietly before leaving. The smile was disturbing, and she returned to the kitchen thinking: Pray God Mike and he never come in together.

"I want to discuss something with you, Mrs. Shaughnessy."

"Yes, Mr. Lord." Lizzie seated herself on the opposite side of the hearth and looked at the old man. Even with the kindly note in his voice he appeared forbidding, and she marvelled once again how Mary Ann had ever got round him.

"I am going to come to the point, Mrs. Shaughnessy. I don't believe in a lot of palaver." Lizzie waited.

"It's about the child."

A queer little pain touched her just below her ribs; it tightened the muscles and caused her to take a deep breath.

"Her education."

Still Lizzie waited.

"I want to have here educated—properly educated; sent away to a good school right away from all this." He waved his hand about the room, yet his meaning excluded it but encompassed the whole of the Tyne.

"No." Lizzie stood up.

"Why do you say no without even considering the matter?"

"Her father—he wouldn't hear of that . . . not for her to go away."

"If it's for the child's good . . . ?"

"He would miss her so."

"He won't be the only one. Don't think I haven't given the matter thought." He paused and turned his eyes from her and looked into the fire. "I'm fond of the child."

"Yes, yes, I know." Lizzie was breathing heavily. "Then why want to send her away, there are plenty of fine schools about here?"

"There may be, but not for her. Don't you see woman, if she were near, the pull of you and him, and even me, would interfere with any form of higher education."

For a moment Lizzie's shoulders went back as she faced the autocratic figure. "I don't want Mary Ann changed, not fundamentally."

"Don't you want her to have the chances you have dreamed of?" He turned further round in his chair. "You are an intelligent woman, Mrs. Shaughnessy. With the right sort of education you could have gone far. Think of Mary Ann at your age. What will she be if left where she is now?"

"It's quite a good school."

"For some it might be . . . not for Mary Ann. She hardly knows anything. She hasn't the faintest knowledge of English, her grammar makes me squirm. She uses 'us' instead of 'we'. Everything is 'me this', 'me that', and 'us has got'. It's criminal in a child of her intelligence."

"She'll get out of all that; children do."

"They don't . . . most of them get worse once they leave school. 'Ganging hyem', they say. 'Had on', they say. You know they do. Do you want her to speak like that?"

"I don't think it matters very much how one speaks, it's how one acts that counts."

"Don't be silly, woman." He stood up. "They act mostly as they speak."

Lizzie put her hand to her trembling lips. "I know you mean well, sir, and you have been kindness itself to us all, but I would ask you to forget about this and leave Mary Ann where she is. In any case, it's hopeless—Mike will never agree to it."

"Mike!" Mr. Lord's head swung from his shoulders as if it would leave his body; it was as if Mike's name had set his nerves jangling. "Look, I'll have this settled now—send for him. He's no fool about the child, no matter what else he is. He will put her first."

Lizzie put her hand on the table and steadied herself. "It's no use, sir; besides, there's no one here to go for him."

"Then I'll soon find someone."

She watched him march out of the cottage, and to her amazement she heard him imperiously request Mrs. Jones to bring Mike at once. She sat down as if to give herself respite before the coming battle. The old man, she could see, was on his high horse, when he would brook no interference from anyone. But Mike wasn't anyone, he was Mary Ann's father. He was her life-spring, and she, to a greate extent, was his. They couldn't do without each other. Mike's words came back: "He does it to buy her." He was right.

Mr. Lord returned and sat down, but did not speak. The room, warm and still, took on the atmosphere of a court room where the judge, who was also the prisoner, was awaited.

.　　　.　　　.　　　.

Even as they fought they jumped about, clapped their hands and stamped their feet to ward off the penetrating cold. Sarah and her army of three were ranged on one side while Mary Ann with only Cissy and Agnes were on the other.

"You think you're everybody because you've been picked to say poetry," said Sarah, skipping in an imaginary rope. "Any fool can learn poetry."

"They why don't you?" said Mary Ann pertly.

"'Cause I wouldn't want to be like you, for all the tea in China, because you're the biggest liar from here to Frenchmen's Bay and back—telling people that the Infant Jesus bought you that bike."

"I didn't say that, so there." Mary Ann bounced her head at the grim-visaged Sarah. "I said that I prayed to Him and He told Mr. Lord to get it . . . Father Owen told me to do it. 'Go on and ask the Bay, Mary Anne,' he said, 'and He'll give you anything you want because He knows you're good.' That's what he said. So there!"

Thumping her forehead with her fist, Sarah turned amazed eyes to her followers, and together they followed her example and thumped their own heads. "She's barmy!" cried Sarah. "She'll end up in the looney bin."

"I'll not," said Mary Ann, blowing on her gloved hands, "but I know where you'll go for certain—Hell—down there!" She thumbed the earth. "Hell! Hell! Hell!" Every word was emphasised with a jump, and on the loudest "Hell!" and the highest jump, a voice said: "Mary Ann Shaughnessy! you come to me in the morning."

The injustice meted out by teachers in general and this one in particular kept Mary Ann, in spite of the intense cold, immovable as she watched the departing figure. Then a splutter from Sarah brought her round in fury: "You! you great big goat-face! I'll tell me da on you," she cried.

"I'll tell me da on you," mimicked Sarah. "Me da's a grand man."

"So he is, an' all."

"And a grand drinker."

Still mimicking, Sarah turned on her heel with this shot, and taking her friends with her, ran out of the school yard, with Mary Ann's voice helping her on her way, crying, "Oh you!

you . . . you big liar! You'll burn in . . . " She stopped abruptly and glanced round, but there were only the questioning eyes of her friends upon her. "She's jealous of me bike," she ended lamely. Then, "Come on," she said, "else I'll miss the bus. And"—she added, by way of payment to her reserve army—"I'll give you a ride on me bike when the weather's fine and me ma lets me ride it."

By the time Mary Ann reached the bus stop she was once more in harmony with her own particular world, for she had regaled her admiring friends with the wonders of the farm: their cottage, which had now reached the proportions of a mansion house; Mr. Lord, who was the good genie and bestower of all gifts; but lastly and covering all, her da and his high position on the farm.

She waved to her friends from the bus, and they waved back, even running along the streets to get a last glimpse of her from the window. She was happy. And wait till her da knew she had been picked from the whole school to say poetry at the monthly assembly, when all the classes would be there. Wasn't it lucky she had been asked to recite bits from Hiawatha? She liked Hiawatha because it was sing-songy.

To the rhythmic purr of the bus she began to recite to herself from Hiawatha's Childhood, shaking her head each time she repeated the plea of the animals and birds, "Do not shoot us, Hiawatha," until she reached the end and rendered triumphantly to herself,

> *"All the village came and feasted,*
> *All the guests praised Hiawatha,*
> *Called him Strong-Heart, Soan-ge-taha!*
> *Called him Loon-Heart, Mahn-go-taysee!"*

But long before the bus reached the cross-roads her thoughts had sunk to a less literary level and she was endeavouring to compose a rhyme that would make Sarah Flannagan mad. Line after line was discarded as not bad enough, and by the time the bus stopped she had given up the attempt. But she still felt happy; so, to the rhythm of

> *"Boxy, boxy, push it down your socksy;*
> *Umper, umper, push it up your jumper,"*

she hitched down the lane home.

"Boxy, boxy" was a very good thing to hitch to—it got you along—and so happy was she to be home that she continued to chant in no small voice right across the yard and into the scullery, but stopped dead at the kitchen door.

In the kitchen, and all looking at her, were her ma and da and Mr. Lord, and she did not need her eyes to tell her that there had been a row. The atmosphere was enough. The tension conveyed itself to her and touched her nerves like a vibrating wire.

"Say that again."

"What?" She looked at Mr. Lord.

"That jingle you were saying as you came in."

Mary Ann looked from Lizzie to Mike, then at Mr. Lord again, and she repeated slowly and flatly, "Boxy, boxy, push it down your socksy; umper, umper, push it up your jumper."

It didn't sound right like that, you had to hitch to it.

Mr. Lord turned on Mike. "The school is good enough for her, she is learning fast! That's what she is learning."

Mike's face was unusually pale. He wet his lips a number of times before saying, "Look, sir, let's get this straight once and for all. She's my daughter, she'll have the education I can afford and that's all."

There was almost a sneer on Mr. Lord's face. "And what do you pay for her present education?"

"Nothing," barked Mike, with startling suddenness, "and that's what I can afford!"

Lizzie closed her eyes and her hand went to her throat as she waited, but unexpectedly Mr. Lord did not answer Mike with a similar bark. His voice became even quieter. "Look," he said, "will you let her decide for herself?"

"No—a child of her age doesn't know what she wants."

"True in most cases, but this case I think is different. She knows what she wants, if anybody does. Will you take a chance on it? I promise you I'll stand by it, and you won't hear me mention the matter again if it goes against me."

Lizzie brought Mike's eyes to hers, and he saw the fear in them, not of Mary Ann being allowed to choose, but of his reactions to this affair no matter what the child's choice should be. Fear for him was ever present with Lizzie, and nothing he ever did seemed to allay it. The anger that was boiling in him suddenly lost its intense heat. "All right," he said, "have it your way."

Now they all looked at Mary Ann, but no one offered to tell her what she had to choose, and she gazed from one to the other in troubled perplexity. Heavily, Lizzie moved towards her, and, taking her hand, drew her to a chair. She sat down and brought Mary Ann to face her squarely, and in a low voice began to talk to her as one does to a child when another is asleep.

"You know the stories you read in your *Girl's Own* and *The Schoolgirl* about the big schools where the girls sleep in dormitories and have parties at the end of term before they go home?"

"Yes, Ma."

"Do you like those stories?"

"Yes, Ma."

Lizzie paused and looked away from Mary Ann to Mr. Lord's feet. They were thin feet, she noticed, long and thin. He was all long and thin, not capable surely of such tenacity to a whim, for that's all it was, a whim.

She looked at Mary Ann again. "You know at those schools the girls learn different things from what you do at your school?"

"Yes, Ma. But"—Mary Ann brightened a little—"I've been picked for poetry, I'm going to say Hiawatha before the whole school, and Sarah Flannagan . . . "

"Yes, yes, you can tell me later. I'm glad you've been picked. But listen—would you like to learn French and German, and play hockey?"

"Oh yes, Ma."

Lizzie paused again—she dare not look at Mike—"And talk properly?"

Now Mary Ann's bewilderment vanished. She became herself again. Her chin edged upwards, just the slightest and she enquired in no meek voice, "Like Lena Ratcliffe?"

"Something like Lena—perhaps better."

Mary Ann turned and glanced at Mr. Lord. Then she asked, "Grammar and things?"

"Yes."

"I don't want to be like Lena Ratcliffe, but . . . " She paused. There was another side to this. Imagine being able to talk swanky and boast about your house matches to Sarah Flannagan, like Gwendolyn Tremayne did in *The Prefect of the Fourth*. She would say to her, in her best swanky voice, "So you see, Sarah Flannagan, I'm a prefect, and you've got to do as I say or I'll have you chucked out—no, thrown out, on your great big ugly mug, and . . . "

"You'll have to go a long way from home and only come back in the holidays."

Only come home in the holidays. . . . Mary Ann swung round and looked at Mike. He was staring at her, but she could get nothing from his face. It looked blank, as if he was asleep with his eyes open. If she went to this school she wouldn't see him, not for weeks and weeks. She wouldn't hear him laughing, she wouldn't be here to pour the water over his head when he washed, and she always poured the water over his head, and when he was sad and had his gone-away look she wouldn't be here to make him laugh. And she wouldn't see her ma or their Michael either. Suddenly the thought of not seeing Michael became painful, too, in spite of the fact that last night he had punched her because she had slapped him on the back with the cold, wet flannel when he was taking off his shirt. Everything quite suddenly became painfully dear to her. Above all, far above all, the dearness of her da. Yet, as her answer came into her mind, her head drooped, for there came over her a feeling of pity for Mr. Lord. He was nice, in spite of his growling when he talked, and he was kind, and she would like to please him, 'cos hadn't he bought her that bike. But if she pleased him, she would displease her da.

"I don't want to go to any school if I have to go away."

Neither Mike nor Mr. Lord moved, nor did their expressions change. Lizzie, glancing from one to another, and relief rising in her, made herself say, "Now are you sure? Remember you will have nice clothes and meet nice girls."

"But I don't want to—not to go away."

Mr. Lord picked up his hat from the chair and without a word made for the door, and before Lizzie could rise to open it he was gone.

Mary Ann went towards Mike. She felt all of a sudden quiet and somehow tired. She leant against his leg and his hand moved gently on her hair.

"Get your things off," said Lizzie; and to Mike she said, "Are you going back now before your tea?"

"Yes, I'm going back now." He spoke quietly; then he eased Mary Ann from his leg and went out.

"Get your hands washed," said Lizzie.

Mary Ann washed her hands. Everything was as it had been, except that she felt sorry for Mr. Lord.

7

THE LAPSE

"And you know what I said to him next, Mrs. McBride?"

"No." Fanny pushed her folded arms, which supported her huge breasts, further on to the table. "Go on, hinny, and tell me; me ears are like cuddy's lugs."

"Well"—Mary Ann became lost in recalling the scene of three weeks ago—"well, I said to him: I'm not going to your fancy school 'cos I don't want to be a lady and talk posh and swanky, an' I said I'm gonna stay home with me ma and da."

"And what did the old boy say to that?" Fanny's eyes were lost in deep wrinkles of amusement.

"Oh, he said lots, he kept on and on and on."

"And you wouldn't give in?"

"No."

"Good on you. You stick to your ma and da."

"I'm going to." Mary Ann now also leaned her elbows on the table. It was nice being in Mrs. McBride's kitchen, although it wasn't clean like theirs for it smelt of onions and soapsuds and baking herrings; and it was nice being with Mrs. McBride, for she made you feel fine and important, and she took away all the things that kept niggling inside of you. She had even dulled the one terrifying thing, the fear. Yet the terrifying thing itself seemed more at home now in this house than it did in the cottage, for it had nearly happened here last year, and now it was starting again. She had no name for it, this thing which existed between her ma and da and Mr. Quinton, but just a fortnight ago it had come into their lives again. She had seen it almost take on tangible form and and fill the kitchen, when her da walked in upon her ma and Mr. Quinton having a cup of tea, and her ma had the best cloth on and the good china out, and it was Saturday and the men weren't working on the house. Mr. Quinton had spoken nicely to her da and her da had spoken nice back, but even as they talked about the house the terrifying thing was there. Yet it did not leap to real life until her ma and da went to bed, when they fought quietly, their words hissing unintelligibly, well into the night.

The next day her ma's face was stiff and white. And then there was yesterday and the snow-balling. Her and their Michael were pelting their ma with snowballs in the lane when Mr. Quinton came along—he was walking, because he couldn't get his car up the lane—and he joined in the fight, helping their ma, and they all had a rare game; and nobody came past, only Mr. Ratcliffe. Yet her da knew, because when he came in he said, "Well, did you have some fine sport?" and it wasn't really to her and Michael he said it but to their ma. And this morning her face was all white again. And then straight after dinner her da had gone out. That's why she was here.

In the soothing company of this fat, grubby old woman she had forgotten for the moment why she had been sent into Jarrow. Lizzie, in her agony of uncertainty as to what Mike in the throes of his jealousy might do, had sent Mary Ann to his old haunt in the hope, not that she might find him sober, but that, with the usual power the child had over him, she might induce him to return home quietly, for Mike, under the influence, was a one-man show. Beer did not make him belligerent but gave him the desire to entertain. Contrary to his attitutde towards the mass in his sober state, when in drink he sought out his fellows, and with song and dance regaled them. It was this regaling that filled Lizzie with shame and gave a sourness to Mike's own awakening.

"And what are you in Jarrow for the day on your own?" enquired Mrs. McBride. And when Mary Ann, with a betraying nonchalance, said, "Oh, just to look round," Mrs. McBride squinted at her and drew her chins in, fold upon fold.

"Just to look round!" she said.

"M'm."

The squint became narrower. "Don't tell me Mike's at it again."

The blood rushed to Mary Anne's face.

"Dear God, is he mad? To jeopardise a fine job! What's come over him this time?"

Mary Ann stood up. "He hasn't done it . . . I mean I just come to look for him." Then her small show of defiance slid away. This old woman knew all there was to know—hadn't she saved their Michael's life after he gassed himself, and didn't she like her da and always stood up for him? She said quietly, "He went out all on his own, and he usually takes us on a Saturday, and me ma was worried and sent me to look for him. And I waited till the Ben Lomond came out and he wasn't there; nor at the Long Bar; nor at Rafferty's."

"He's a blasted fool if ever there was one!" cried Fanny indignantly. "And old Lord won't stand for him and the bottle again. He should tread warily there."

This last remark put into words another worry. Everyone had to tread warily with Mr. Lord now; he wasn't like he used to be. He didn't pass the cross-roads in the morning and give them all a lift to school, and he never came into their house at all now; and he had refused to take her hand that day in the farmyard. And Lena Ratcliffe had seen and had crowed over her the next morning.

"You've been put in your place," she had said, "and Mammie says it's not before time."

When she had jumped at Lena and slapped her face she had expected their Michael to go for her, but strangely enough he didn't, he went for Lena instead. That had made her feel . . . funny towards him, and that night she had lent him her paint-box.

"Look, get on your coat and get off to the bus and away home, and it's ten to one you'll find him there, solid and sober . . . Well, it's to be hoped to God you will, anyway," added Fanny.

After buttoning Mary Ann up to the eyes against the biting, snow-filled wind, Fanny pushed a packet of bullets into her pocket and sixpence into her hand, and setting her to the top of the steps, called a cheery farewell to her. Mary Ann's farewell was equally cheery, but as soon as she was out the old woman's sight her cheeriness vanished.

Cold as she was, both inside and out, and filled with longing to get home to see if her da was back, she made her way to the church. Her misery seemed to draw her there. There was no Crib to-day, no glowing lights, in fact the Holy Family looked perished to the bone themselves, for there wasn't even one candle lit to keep them warm. And there was no heat from the hot-water pipes—they weren't on, as hers and hundreds of other sets of chattering teeth had confirmed only yesterday morning, for there had been a burst.

Before kneeling down, she lit one candle, with tuppence left from her pocket money; then slowly withdrawing the newly acquired sixpence, she gazed at it. The silver piece represented a comic, two ounces of shelled monkey nuts and a single stick of spearmint. She could make these entertaining purchases on her way home, and the night after she had bathed all over she could sit on the fender close to the fire and read her comic while she chewed her nuts. And in bed, so that her ma wouldn't see, she could chew the spearmint and make bubbles with it—she was a dandy hand at making bubbles with gum. But would she do all this if her da was . . . sick? The answer came with the tinkle of the sixpence as it fell into the tin box.

She had not consciously decided to devote this enormous sum to the benefit of the Holy Family. But it was done now, so she took up three more candles. She had never lit four candles at one go in her life before, but this was an emergency, and she hoped that the Holy Family would appreciate that fact. They did so immediately, for they all looked warmer. Saint Joseph smiled at her and his smile thanked her.

Kneeling down before them, she began, "Please, Jesus, Mary and Joseph, I can't stay a minute because I've got to catch the bus. I only come into Jarrow to look for me da, but I was so cold I went into Mrs. McBride's to get a warm. I didn't find me da. Please, oh please, Jesus, Mary and Joseph, you can stop doing anything for me, you can make me bad and have the 'flu or let me fall down or let me teacher go for me or even Sarah Flannagan get one on me, but please don't let me da start to get . . . sick again. Oh, please!"

The candles, in a draught of air, flickered wildly, the statues moved and the Virgin hitched the Infant further up into her arms before bending forward and saying, "Go home; everything will be all right."

The candle flames steady once more, Mary Ann blessed herself, then rose and went out. She felt sort of empty and quiet inside. It was a relieved sort of feeling, but it did not cause her to feel boisterous, she did not want to run, skip or jump. She walked decorously to the bus stop, boarded the bus, sat quietly in the corner seat, and so came home.

And it was as the Holy Family had said—there he was, solid and sober, sitting before the fire. He had on his good suit and he looked nice, but not happy.

As she entered the door a signal passed between Mary Ann and Lizzie, and the signal said, "Say nothing; don't tell him where you've been. But as her da looked at her, Mary Ann knew that he knew where she had been—it was in his eyes like a deep hurt.

.   .   .   .   .

It was nearly a fortnight later when Mary Ann learned where her da had been that

Saturday afternoon, he had been after another farm job. This had distressed her, for she told herself, I like it here, and our nice house; and I wouldn't see Mr. Lord again. Though this last should not have troubled her, for he was still nasty, and never spoke to her. She had followed him one Saturday morning when he had gone up the hill to see his house. It was slowly rising from its foundations, and she had stood quite near him and offered her opinion. "It's nice," she had said, "and you're gonna have a lot of windows, aren't you?" But he had only grunted; and after a while she had walked away because she had wanted to cry. But she had stopped herself by saying, "He's a bad-tempered, nasty old beast." And when he had come down the hill to his car she had kept close, but not too close, and, just to let him see she didn't care, she had skipped with her ropes to "Boxy, boxy, stick it down your socksy." But he had suddenly yelled at her, "Stop that!" and had stared at him, and he had got into his car and banged the door and gone off.

Mr. Lord had just this minute gone from the cowshed. She was keeping out of his way, staying up in the loft until he was well passed. He was talking now to Mr. Ratcliffe about Clara. Clara was going to have a baby, and when Mary Ann heard Mr. Lord mention her da's name she nearly fell out of the loft, straining to hear what he had to say. Only the tail end of it came to her: "If there should be any trouble, let Shaughnessy deal with her."

There was no response from Mr. Ratcliffe that Mary Ann could hear, and preening with pride she nodded in the direction of the departing men. That was one in the eye for Mr. Ratcliffe. Mr. Lord wanted her da to see to Clara because he was a right fine man with cows, and Clara had been bad and had had the doctor.

She came down from the loft and went into the cowshed. Her da wasn't there. There was no one there except Clara and Mr. Jones. Clara looked very large, very soft and very warm. Mr. Jones looked very small, very hard, and his expression was anything but warm as he stared at her. Mr. Jones and Mary Ann were not not on speaking terms. Mr. Jones's memory was long and his sense of humour only really active when he himself was the cause of its rising.

She came out of the cowshed and went to the pigsties. Her da wasn't there, either, only Joe and their Michael. Michael looked happy. He was whistling, and she said to him, "Have you see me da?"

"Yes," he said, "he's gone up to mend the fence in the long field. And you know what"—his voice fell and he leaned nearer to her over the sty wall—"he's going to let me keep one of Daisy's puppies."

"Oh goody—if it's a girl I'll call it Pat."

"You'll call it nothing of the kind, it's gonna be mine."

The usual relations were resumed, and Mary Ann cried, "Aw—you! it won't be all your dog—I'll ask me da."

Michael's voice followed her as she sped out of the yard and up the lane.

The long field lay some way beyond the cottages, and it was a chance glance when speeding past them that brought her to a dead stop. The cottage door which led into the scullery was open, and standing outside round the corner under the lean-to was her da. Mary Ann herself was so versed in the art of listening that she recognised immediately that that was what her da was doing. After a long moment during which she presented to herself many reasons for her da's eavesdropping but would not allow herself to think of the true one, she moved towards him, walking softly, and she was within a few feet of him before he became aware of her presence. And when he did he ordered her away, but silently. With a quick movement of the head and hand he bid her be gone, and he looked as if he were about to enforce this when the low, pleasantly deep voice of Bob Quinton came from just beyond the door. It stiffened Mike's half-turned body, and Mary Ann's eyes, riveted on his profile, actually saw the colour drain from it and leave it looking like dirty snow as Mr. Quinton's voice came to them, saying, "You know, Elizabeth, there was only you. All those years there was only you." She wanted to dash to the door and bang it, or yell and shout so that her da wouldn't hear any more, but as if anticipating this move, Mike's hand pressed back on her.

The sound of Bob's voice still came to them, but his words now were not audible. Then there followed a silence that filled Mary Ann's mind with wild pictures and she saw the silence stretch her da's body until she thought his head would shoot up through the corrugated roof. She knew that in another second he would fling himself into the house and hit Mr. Quinton. It was then her ma's voice came, whispering softly, and instead of adding impetus to Mike's taut limbs it seemed as if Lizzie's hushed words drew the very sinews out of them. "It makes me very happy, Bob, to hear you say that," she was saying. "I've waited a long time for you to tell me that . . . I've prayed for it."

That's what her ma had said. The words themselves held no particular meaning—it was the nice way her ma had said them that gave Mary Ann the feeling that her own slight body was shrinking. The earth shuddered under her feet, the trees swayed, and the heavens became tilted. She closed her eyes against a rocking world, and when she opened them her da had moved.

Mary Ann had witnessed all kinds of emotions on Mike's face, from such gentleness that made her cry to tearing rage that terrified her. She had seen him look lost and pitiful, but never had she seen him look as he was doing now, like a blind man. And like a blind man he put his hand out and touched the post of the lean-to and stood for the moment looking away up the hill to the house Mr. Quinton was building. Then he lifted his shoulders, pressing them until his back, turned towards Mary Ann was straight as a die, and like that he walked towards the long field.

Mary Ann went across the yard to the lavatory, and through the air holes she watched Mr. Quinton take his leave and her ma smile at him with her nice smile. When the yard was empty once more she still continued to strain up and look through the holes as though she were fixed there. Then, as if she had been suddenly cut down, she dropped on to the seat and, pressing her hands tightly between her knees, she rocked herself, muttering, "Eeh! no. Eeh! no." One part of her mind refused to believe what the other half was telling her—her ma was bad.

She came out from the lavatory and, without glancing towards the cottage, she went up the road to the long field. Mike was mending the fence and from a distance he looked as he did on any other day. She knew she could not bear to see him hurt at close quarters, but she watched him from the side of the gate until he finished the job, and when he went back to the farmyard she went slowly into the house. She felt drawn there—to look at her ma and see how changed she was.

But Lizzie wasn't changed, except that she looked happier. She was actually humming to herself. After one searching glance, Mary Ann turned towards the fire, and Lizzie, who was ironing on the table, said, "I'm nearly finished. Put the dinner plates on top of the oven and then you can set the table." She didn't look towards her daughter but seemed preoccupied with her own thoughts.

Mary Ann did as she was bidden. She did it quickly, because she wanted to get out again; she didn't want to be in when her da came in.

Fifteen minutes later she was standing behind the stone pillar that had once supported a gate to the farmyard. She wanted to see her da come out without him seeing her. She saw him pass into the road, but he didn't turn up towards the lane which led to the back door of the cottages, or keep on the main road which led to the front door, but he jumped the fence bordering the field opposite the gate.

Her mouth agape, she watched him striding along the outskirts of the field. She wanted to shout after him, but she couldn't, there was no voice left in her. All expression for the moment was weighed down with the awful knowledge that her da was making for the bus and Jarrow . . . and the Ben Lomond, or some other bar, and with him he was taking all his week's wages. The men usually got paid on a Friday night, but Mr. Ratcliffe had been away all day yesterday at a cattle sale and he would have paid the men this morning. She put a hand across her mouth to stop the moaning sound that was escaping, then, running like the wind, she went home. Gone now was the thought that her ma was bad. Bursting into the kitchen, she gasped, "Me da! he's got on the bus."

Lizzie looked at her dumbfounded. "Your da?" she said. "What bus?"

"For Jarrow."

"Jarrow?" Lizzie repeated stupidly. She stared at Mary Ann, and Mary Ann stared back at her. She was now feeling bewildered at the expression of her mother, who looked absolutely stunned. "But why?" she muttered.

Mary Ann turned her head away, then her body, and stared at the table leg; only to be swung furiously about. "What is it?" Lizzie demanded.

Mary Ann looked hard at her mother for a moment before saying, "He heard—when you were with Mr Quinton—in the scullery."

"My God!"

Lizzie stood back from her daughter. Her fingers went to her lips, and for the moment Mary Ann thought she was going to burst into tears. But she didn't. Instead, going to her purse, she grabbed a shilling out of it and, thrusting it into Mary Ann's hand, cried, "Look. Go on after him, tell him to come home. Tell him"—she passed her hand over her face and drew in a long breath—"tell him Mr. Quinton is going to be married."

"Married, Ma? Oh!" Relief gushed into Mary Ann's body and so activated her limbs that she was out of the door and halfway across the yard before she pulled up, swung on her heel and retraced her steps.

"It's nearly another half-hour afore the next bus, Ma."

Lizzie seemed to become smaller. She sat down on a chair and Mary Ann stood gazing pitifully at her, until, rousing herself, she said, "I'd better go myself."

"No, no, Ma"—Mary Ann pressed her back—"he'll come for me . . . and quiet. I'll bring him. Look; I'll run to Morpeth Lane, the Shields bus that goes down Robin Hood way passes there. That'll take me."

"Go on then," said Elizabeth. "And run."

Mary Ann ran, as she neared the corner of Morpeth Lane she screamed and yelled and waved her arms as she saw the bus speeding away from her. Then, as if by a miracle, it stopped some way down the road, and she stumbled on to it almost in a state of collapse.

A woman, lifting her on to the seat, said, "You shouldn't run like that, hinny, there's other buses."

Mary Ann said nothing, only pressed her hand to her side to ease the stitch.

When she left the bus she ran again, along streets, up back lanes, down alley-ways, across main roads, until she came to the Ben Lomond; and there she stopped and waited, for she could not see inside the bar and she dared not open the door. But when a man came out, she asked him, "Is me da there? He's Mr. Shaughnessy . . . Mike Shaughnessy. Will you tell him to come out a minute, please?" And the man, pushing open the door, called, "Anybody by the name of Shaughnessy here? Mike Shaughnessy?"

It was the bar-man's voice which answered, "Mike Shaughnessy? No, he's not here. Haven't seen Mike for weeks. Who wants him?"

"His bairn."

"Oh well, tell her he's not here."

"He's not in there, hinny," said the man.

"Ta," said Mary Ann, and walked away.

He might be in the Long Bar. . . . Running again, she came to Staple Road and the Long Bar, and here she followed the same procedure, and with the same result. She stood on the edge of the pavement blinking down at the muddy gutter. It was nearly one o'clock. She would go to Rafferty's, and if he wasn't there she would go home and like that other Saturday she would find him sitting in the kitchen, but happy now because Mr.Quinton was going to be married.

At Rafferty's her meeting with two men coming out of the bar took all thought of speeding home from her. Yes, they said, Mike Shaughnessy had been in, but he had gone not ten minutes ago.

"Where?" she asked.

That they couldn't say but she could try the Long Bar.

She went back to the Long Bar; she went back to the Ben Lomond. He had been to neither. So she now started a round of the other bars, foreign places, because she had never before stood outside them. She paraded High Street from the Wellington to the Duke of York, and then to the Telegraph. Outside the small bar stood a number of people. They were in groups, and the groups informed Mary Ann that in one way her search was ended, for it was closing time. She did not ask if anyone had seen her da, but stood against a house windowsill and rested for a moment. She was very tired, her legs ached and she felt sick.

There was no thought in her mind now of going home. Her da had been in the bar; and from one he would have gone to another, on and on till closing time, and even then he wouldn't go straight home—her da liked a bit of jollification when he was full. She moved from the wall. It would be easier finding him now anyway. She just had to walk until she heard somebody singing out loud, and she would find him, and likely see him dancing an' all.

The sickness deepened as she made her way towards Burton Street. Why Burton Street she didn't question, but Mulhattan's Hall was in Burton Street and Mrs. McBride was there; he could laugh with Mrs. McBride. And Mrs. Flannagan was there; he would laugh at Mrs. Flannagan and very likely, in spite of his good humour, say rude things to her.If she didn't find him before she got there she would find him in Burton Street.

Five streets away from Mulhattan's Hall she heard him—no one could sing "Acushla" like her da, drunk or sober.

A group of boys came scampering out of a back lane, one crying to the others, "Come on, there's a drunk in Burton Street, he'll make yer split yer sides. Remember? He used to live there—big Mike Shaughnessy."

She stood against the wall to let them pass; there was no movement from her to defend her right to the pavement now. As she entered Burton Street she saw the boys come to a halt outside a ring of children that surrounded the dancing figure. The street was out, but the grown-ups were keeping to the pavement and their doors and windows.

She did not hurry now—the damage was done. Sorrow, deep and leaden, born of love and humiliation, dragged at her feet. It was the ageless sorrow of a child, old, elemental, welling from depths buried in past eternities, not understood, beyond reason, outbidding its cause, but felt, and felt to be unbearable. Oh Jesus, Mary and Joseph, make him stop. All the people looking at him, and Mrs. Flannagan at her window. Oh blessed Lord, do something.

"MY FRIEND, HE IS THE FRIEND OF ALL FRIENDS," Mike was singing now. His head was back and his arms stretched wide and the people listened.

Mary Ann, moving past a group of chuckling women, heard one exclaim, "He can sing, can Mike. Ah, it's good to have him back, say what you like. What's done this, I wonder? His lady wife left him? I wouldn't be a bit surprised at that an' all."

A sharp nudge stilled the woman's tongue, and the eyes were turned on Mary Ann. She took no heed but went to the circle in the middle of the road, and slowly pushed herself through the crowd. She was almost within touching distance of Mike when a voice crying above his, swept over her head and those in the road and turned all eyes towards the Flannagans' upper window. Sarah was leaning out, and what she had called was "Me da's a grand man!" She was looking triumphantly down on Mary Ann, and behind her, standing back in the shadow, was her mother, with unadulterated satisfaction covering her thin face.

Mike had not seen Mary Ann. He was looking up now to the window, and with an exaggerated Irish twang he cried, "Oh, there you are, me darlin' Mrs. Flannagan—the light of me life."

Reeling towards the pavement, with the circle giving way to him, he flung up his arms to her, crying, "Come on down , me darlin', and let me hear the clatter of your refeened twang, for it's that desire alone that has brought me back to me old haunts. And where's me friend Harry? Have you got him tied up under the bed?"

The bedroom window closed with a bang, and Mike shouted, stuttering and stammering, "Ah don't break me heart. Ah Nellie, come on down, come on woman and tell me how to get all the heifers on the farm married and made into respectable cows."

A howl went up from the street, and Mike, appealing to all at large, cried, "Did you know that? It's the God's own truth as I stand here. Mrs. Falnnagan is going to get a bill passed to make every heifer into a decent woman. It'll be a Bull of a Bill, that."

Mary Ann's trembling lips were shaping the word "Da" when she was pushed roughly aside by the enraged figure of Mrs. McBride. Mrs. McBride was in her shopping clothes, a black shiny coat and a large black felt hat,lightened here and there with dust and a greenish hue. Grabbing Mike by the arm, she pulled him round, shouting, "Shut that big mouth of yours and come inside this minute!"

"Here, here! who're you pulling?" Mike's voice became truculent. Then he laughed down on her, "Aw! Fan. Fat old Fan." And he attempted to put his arms about her and waltz her around, but Fanny was more than a match for him. She'd had a great deal of training in handling drunks, and before he knew what was happening it was he who was being waltzed round, and in the direction of Mulhattan's Hall. A jerk of her head brought her eldest son from the pavement where he had been enjoying the fun, and Don McBride said pleasantly, "Come on, away in, Mike, and let's have a crack."

"Take your hands off me!"

Don took his hands off and retreated, laughing sheepishly, out of harm's way.

"Da! Da! come on."

Mike's countenance lightened once more, and he exclaimed. "Why, it's me Mary Ann." His tone was scoffing as he swayed above her. "Put me in hell an' me Mary Ann would be there. . . . But you didn't catch up with me, did you?"

He almost fell on her, and she steadied him and took his hand, and guiding him with the forcible assistance of Mrs. McBride from behind she got him up the steep steps and into the house.

Mike was laughing now. Like one child who had got the better of another, he preened himself at Mary Ann.

"I did you, didn't I? O, aye, you thought I'd go to the Long Bar or the Ben Lomond, didn't you? I know! Your da knows all you think! So I beat you. . . . I did a round. But I didn't start where you thought I would. And you know why?"

"No, Da. Lie back, and I'll get you some tea. Can I, Mrs. McBride?"

"Aye, hinny. And I'll give him more than tea," exclaimed Fanny, busying herself with a number of tins she had taken down from the top shelf of the cupboard.

"Shut up, you old hag, I'm talking to me girl. And you know why, me darlin'?"

"No, Da. Lie back."

"Well, I'll tell you. . . . 'Cos I knew that if I looked into those eyes of yours I'd be done. I couldn't go and get . . . sick,if I looked into those eyes . . . could I now, not real sick? A pint or two, but not real sick. And I'm real sick now, aren't I?"

"Da. Listen." With her hands on his face Mary Ann tried to rivet his attention.

"Aye, I'm listenin'." Mike's head rolled on his shoulders. "I listened to Ratcliffe. I listened to Jonesy. Ratcliffe said to young Len, 'You see to Clara,' he said. And Jonesy said he heard the old boy say Shaughnessy had to see to Clara . . . Shaughnessy may be no good, he won't give his daughter away, but he knows cows. . . . He can handle cows, can't he, me darlin'?''

"Yes, Da. . . . And listen. Listen."

"I'm listenin'. Ratcliffe knows as much about a farm as me Aunt Fanny. . . . That's not you, Fan. Never you, Fan . . . aw! never you." The laughter rumbled thick and deep in his throat and he became launched on a list of Fanny's good points, while Mrs. McBride, pulling Mary Ann to one side, whispered, "What's happened at all. Has he had a row with the boss?"

"No."

"Well, what in the name of God is it? He's back where he was."

The sickness deepened in Mary Ann's breast. As she told her story she glanced at Mike, sprawled now like a giant in the chair. He was rambling again about the farm: Ratcliffe, Len, Jonesy and the cows, but he let slip not the slightest hint about the real reason for his present state. He made no mention of either Lizzie or Bob. That which was eating him up was temporarily buried. His faith in the bottle had not been broken. Once full of liquor, he would be merry . . . the trials of his life would be dulled, even forgotten—if no one raked them up.

Her eyes cast down, Mary Ann finished the dreaded sentence: "And he thought me ma was goin' off."

"The blasted fool!" muttered Fanny. "And Mr. Quinton goin' to be married. Well, you tell him. Git it into his thick skull whilst I mix him a concoction that'll skite the drink out of him quicker'n the corporation sewer cleaner."

Mary Ann stood between Mike's legs, her hands on his lapels, and trying to shake his great relaxed body, she said, "Da . . . listen. Will you listen!"

"Aren't I listenin'?"

"No. Stop a minute . . . It's about me ma."

Mike stopped. The good humour faded from his face, his brows drew down and his lips pushed at each other, and with his forearm he went to thrust Mary Ann away, but she hung on to his coat.

"When you listened, Da, it was all wrong what you heard—I want to tell you— listen."

Mike's eyes became narrow slits of fiery light. In another minute she would not be able to hold him—he would fling her aside and his rage would break. There could be no gentle words leading up to the enlightenment point. Quickly the words came tumbling out, "Mr Quinton's goin' to be married . . . to a girl. He was tellin' me ma."

Mike's rage did not vanish, but it was checked. And Mary Ann, bringing her imagination to her aid to help penetrate his befuddled state, added hastily, "She's nice, lovely, an' they're gonna be married in a big church and have it in the papers. Me ma says she is glad and . . . and," she added finally, "she wants you home. Me ma wants you home, Da."

Mike blinked at her, then looked away to the wall above the cluttered mantelpiece as if he expected to find there, written large, words that would further bear out this news . . . this disturbing news, that was going to make him look a fool, for that's what he would be, his reeling brain told him, if this were true. And he was no fool. No, by God! he was not. With a great show of effort, he was making to rise from the chair when Fanny checked him.

"Here! Get this down you."

"What's it, eh? Poison?"

"Aye . . . get it down you."

"Fan," he took the cup from her, "do you know . . . what . . . the child's tellin' me?"

"I know well enough. Drink up!"

"Now listen . . . listen. I'm no fool, I've been duped afore. Once bitten."

"Drink!" The order would have done credit to a sergeant-major.

Mike drank, throwing the contents of the cup against the back of his throat at one go, and in the next instant the cup was flung across the room and he was out of the chair, coughing and gasping. And between the gasps he spluttered, "In . . . in the name of God! . . ."

"Ah, it won't kill you."

"M . . . m . . . m . . . my God . . . Fan!"

"Ah, be quiet, will you!"

Coughing as though his lungs were burning, he leant over the high back of the armchair, his mouth wide open.

"Come on . . . get your head under the tap and you'll be nearly yourself again, And stop making such a to-do. That was me old man's tonic. It's a corpse reviver, if ever there was one. The quick an' the dead, he called it. You had to be quick if you didn't want to be dead. Come on, now, under the tap."

Half leading, half pushing him, she got him into the scullery, and, pointing to the sink, said, "Get your head down."

Shaken into temporary docility by her command, Mike obeyed Fanny and put his head under the tap.

Standing now close to the sink, her eyes unblinking, Mary Ann watched his every movement with patient concern, and when finally he lifted his dripping head and almost fell on his face, she steadied him, stiffening her tiny weight to check his fall. Then she led him into the kitchen once again and to his chair. Standing on a stool, she helped him to dry his head. When this was completed Fanny surveyed him. "You're a blasted fool!" she said.

"Shut up!"

"I'll not shut up. Have you any money left?"

"Why?"

"If you have, I'd sport a taxi."

"Taxi, be damned!" Mike got to his feet. "I'll be all right."

He stood swaying a little; but he no longer reeled. As yet he was not sober enough to feel shame-faced, but he was sober enough not to want to walk the street again.

Fanny, sensing this, said, "Go on out the back way with you then. . . . And look, put this dry muffler round your neck."

Mary Ann said no word of thanks. She only looked at the old woman who was looking at Mike as he slowly tucked the muffler into his braces. And when Fanny turned and nodded encouragingly to her, Mary Ann, incapable of using her voice in any way because of the lump that was blocking her windpipe, followed the shambling figure of her father into the backyard. Without having to turn, Mary Ann knew that Mrs. McBride was following their progress up the lane, and she knew that her head would be shaking. For some reason this increased the size of the lump still further.

She led Mike through all the side ways she knew towards the bus stop, and they met no one who took any notice of them until they turned the corner of Delius Street, and there, on the opposite side of the road and coming towards them, was Father Owen. His long length bent against the wind he was holding on to his hat, and at the sight of him, Mary Ann's heart gave a painful leap. Father Owen was the last person in the world she wished to meet at this moment. Father Owen thought her da a grand man; he didn't know he drank; hadn't he sworn when he was standing beneath the cross that he knew her da never touched a drop? Even if her da only looked . . . a little sick now, Father Owen mustn't see him.

Being unable to work it out, but feeling that for the priest's own peace of mind he must not find himself to have been mistaken, she suddenly pulled at Mike's arm and, turning him about, guided him round the corner and steered him up Delius Street's back lane. Had she kept straight on it is possible that Father Owen would have passed without noticing them, but the scurry she made and Mike's protesting arm flung wide attracted the priest's attention. Father Owen had no need to question who they were, Mike could never hope to disguise himself, and Mary Ann . . . well back view or front view there was only one Mary Ann.

His face took on a sadness and he slowed his pace to allow her sufficient time to make the desired get-away with her burden—her cross, he thought, her beloved cross. He, too, shook his head.

Breathing now more easily, Mary Ann neared the bus stop. Soon they would be home and her da would be in bed, and nobody would have seen him. The crowds in Burton Street did not matter now, they belonged to a past world that had no connection with the farm.

The bus came, and Mike, pushing her before him, hoisted himself on board, and since the only empty seats were at the far end of the bus they made their way towards these and sat down, right opposite Lena and Mrs. Ratcliffe!

After staring for a moment at the wife of his boss, Mike ran his tongue over his lips, and, ironically, he laughed to himself. His mind was clear enough to make him realize that there was no hope of disguising his condition, so with exaggerated bravado he doffed his cap and exclained loudly, "Good day to you, Mrs. Ratcliffe."

Mary Ann prayed swifly that the Ratcliffes might be struck blind and, incidentally, deaf; that some act of God might waft them out of the bus and drop then in the road somewhere; and at last, in desperation, she prayed that the bus might collide with something and that they would all be killed.

God did not apparently hear any of her prayers, or if He did, He chose to ignore them. And after a journey during which her agony was, she knew, only a foretaste of that which was to come, they reached the cross-roads. After alighting, by some strange manoeuvre the Ratcliffes managed to walk down the line behind them. And to Mary Ann's bewilderment, her da's swaying became worse. Then came the final humiliation, he raised his voice in song.

.   .   .   .   .

"Listen to me." Stooping quietly and swiftly, Lizzie dragged Michael up from the fender where he sat slumped. Her handling of him was rough and her whispering fierce. "It was a mistake, I tell you; it won't happen again."

She stared at him, forcing him to believe her, but his eyes dropped from hers and his head sank, and he muttered, "It will, it's Mulhattan's Hall all over again."

"It isn't . . . He didn't mean to do it . . . It was my fault."

Michael looked quickly up at her. And Lizzie, drawing in her breath, said haltingly, "It was something that . . . that happened."

It was impossible to explain to this son of hers exactly what had happened. Mary Ann could witness the intricacies, the pitfalls, and the tightrope walkings of marriage, and even handle them, but not Michael. His father's weakness found only two reactions in him, depression and anger—and now the anger was to the fore.

Pulling himself from her hands, he cried, "He's spoilt eveything, as he always does. The whole place knows . . . Singing in the lane! And bringing the Joneses out. And Mrs. Ratcliffe there."

"Stop shouting, our Michael, you'll wake him." Mary Ann, who had been standing aside watching her mother fighting to keep Michael's respect for the man who was now snoring upstairs, pushed at her brother with doubled fists and hissed, "Shut up! It's like me me says, he won't do it again."

"Aw, you!" Michael rounded on her fiercely. "You'd always stick up for him, you like to see him drunk."

"Oh . . . h!" The injustice of this remark left her for the moment verbally dry, but the "Oh . . . h!" expressed her hurt, and Michael, more quiet now, said again, "Well, you always stick up for him."

"Be quiet!" said Lizzie tersely. "Here's Len coming across the yard. She stood watching the farmhand approach, and when he neared the window she went and opened the back door.

Looking somewhat sheepish, the young fellow said, "Is Mike in, Mrs. Shaughnessy?"

Lizzie did not immediately answer him—the whole farm community knew Mike was in—but then she said flatly, "Yes, he's in."

"It's . . . it's the boss. He wants him in the byres. He says he wants him to see to Clara."

Lizzie's eyes became cold. "It's his half day."

"I know, Mrs. Shaughnessy." The young man's tone was genuinely apologetic. "It isn't me. I was quite willing to see to her, but them's his orders."

Lizzie's expression did not alter. "Very well," she said, "I'll tell him."

She closed the door and walked into the kitchen, where both Michael's and Mary Ann's eyes asked her the same question. She did not answer them.

Mary Ann stood listening to her mother ascending the stairs, and putting her thumb into the side of her mouth, she started systematically to bite hard round the nail. He had only been upstairs for half an hour, and she'd had a job getting him up, for he would sing and laugh, and he hadn't spoken to her ma, nor her ma to him—their talking would come later, she knew, when he was sober. And now she was going to waken him, and he'd still be . . . a bit sick. Not even in the most secret places of her mind did she imprint the word drunk. She heard him snort loudly, then shout something. Then there was silence. Presently her mother came downstairs, and a few minutes later Mike followed, and to Mary Ann's deepening distress she saw he was in a bad mood, like he used to be after he had sobered up in the mornings. Only now he wasn't sober, not really sober. His face was heavy with sleep and his eyes angry. He passed his hands through his matted hair, then said to Mary Ann, "Fetch me boots."

Quickly Mary Ann brought the boots. He took them from her, but looked at Lizzie where she was standing with her back to him staring into the fire. His voice deep in his throat and still fuddled, he said, "You see the plan of campaign, don't you? Ratcliffe's got a line at last. With me very own hands I've given him a line. I'm to look after a sick cow, a valuable sick cow, and I'm in no condition to see to even a mountain goat. He's hoping, is Ratcliffe."

Lizzie said nothing, but continued to stare into the fire. And as Mike pulled savagely on his laces, he went on speaking as if to himself, "Jonesy heard the old man leave orders for me to see to her this morning; but Ratcliffe wasn't letting the old boy give him any orders, so Len was detailed. But now that his lady wife has informed him I am drunk he sees his chance. Well"—Mike knotted the laces and gritted his teeth—"I'll show him. Drunk or sober, I'll show him I could buy and sell him where a cow's concerned. Where's me coat?"

"Here, Da."

Mary Ann, the coat already on her arm, handed it to him. Thrusting his arms into it, Mike noticed Michael for the first time. He stared at the boy. Then pulling his cap from his pocket he pressed it onto his head, saying fiercely, "And don't you look at me like that or I'll wring your blasted ear for you."

The door banged behind him, and Mary Ann, moving slowly to the window, watched him cross the yard, his step still uncertain.

8

THE LOFT

Mike leaned against the stanchion of the sick bay and wiped the running sweat from his face with his forearm. There was no sound, not even a secretive night sound to bring comfort. There was only the heavy, sweet warm smell pressing down on him and the dead cow and calf lying at his feet. He gazed pityingly down on the animals. Clara had been so human, she had fought to the last. After seeming to hold the calf for an unnecessarily long time, she had struggled valiantly to bring it, but to no purpose. It was just after twelve when she turned her head and looked at him and made a sound, a quiet uncowlike sound. Remembering it now, he thought, she knew she couldn't bring if off.

He looked at his watch. It was a quarter-past three. He felt as tired as though he had done a double shift in the shipyard. He moved out of the bay and sat down on a low box and leant his head against the byre. He'd have to go and tell Ratcliffe, and there'd be hell to pay. Without a doubt, he'd push the blame on him. In the back of his now sober but sleep-hazy mind, he vaguely sensed Ratcliffe's plan. . . . A man couldn't be sacked for being drunk off the job, but he could be sacked for what he did, or didn't do, when drunk on the job. Ratcliffe had been in three times during the evening, the last time just before twelve o'clock. However fuddled he may have appeared earlier on, Ratcliffe could certainly not deny that he was sober then, for they has spoken together quite ordinarily; and Ratcliffe had suggested that Clara would hang on for at least another twelve hours.

Well, Clara was dead, and besides Ratcliffe's reactions, the old man would go sky high. She had been his best cow. He had paid a great deal of money for her, hoping to start a stock.

Mike rasped his chin with his hand, then pressed his eyeballs. He was dead beat, and he would no sooner get into bed than he would have to get up again. His mind swung to Lizzie, and he moved restlessly. He had her to face, too, and explain yet once again why he had been a blasted weak fool. Other fellows could get knocks and stand up to them, but he always had to seek consolation. But when the knock hadn't been a knock at all, only the result of the fermentation in his mind, the explanation was going to be harder than ever before.

Well, that was one scene that could be put off. He would sleep here, and then he'd be in better shape to face her in the morning. He'd go now and get this business over with Ratcliffe before turning in on the straw.

The arrangement settled in his mind, he sat on, and the warm quietness settled upon him like a blanket.

.   .   .   .   .

Mike was brought sharply from the far depths of sleep by a blow in the middle of his back. There is no mistaking a heavy-booted foot, and the fact that he had been kicked brought him out of the straw and to his feet as if he 'had been suddenly stung into life. He looked a ferocious and forbidding sight, his hair with the straw in it standing up on end and his arm drawn back ready to strike.

"What the hell d'you think you're doin'?" he yelled.

Ratcliffe, his face grim and his voice cutting in its meaning, said, "And what the hell do you think doing? Look at that!" He swung round and pointed to the dead animals. "Gone; both of them, while you lie snoring your head off."

Mike's arm had dropped, but his voice was still menacing: "Don't be a blasted fool . . . !"

"What!" Ratcliffe roared. "You remember who you're talking to."

"I know who I'm talking to all right. I did me utmost, but I could save neither of them. The calf was strangled afore it came, you can see that."

"Why didn't you come for me?"

"How could I, I couldn't leave her? If you had done the right thing you would have left the lad with me."

"Don't you tell me what I should do. But if I had let the lad see to her I'd have had a live cow and calf this morning. They wouldn't have died time he was sleeping his drink off."

The two men glared at each other. The dislike, born at their first meeting and fostered on Ratcliffe's part by his wife, now flared into open hatred. His brows drawn down and his lips thrust out, Mike growled, "So that's your game. I knew it. I got drunk yesterday and gave you the chance you've been waiting for. Clara being sick just fitted in, didn't it? When I was sober you wouldn't let me near her, although you had your orders from the old man. Aye, I know all about that, an' all."

"I'm in charge of this farm and I'll put my men where I like."

"Well, here's one you won't put where you like."

"Won't I? We'll see . . . you're fired!"

"Da! Da!" The cry cut through their shouting and caused them both to swing round to where Mary Ann stood hugging a coat about her. Her face was chalk coloured and her brown eyes looked like great black sloes, and, as such incapable of blinking. Her gaze was not fixed on Mike but on Mr. Ratcliffe, as if, instead of his flesh and blood, she saw him embodied in the fiery tissues of the devil himself.

Even when Mike rapped out, "What you doin' here? get yourself back home," she still did not lift her gaze from Ratcliffe, who, finding the intensity of her eyes more unnerving than any expression of Mike's, swung round, saying over his shoulder as he marched away, "Come to the office at nine tomorrow morning."

"Be damned to you!" cried Mike, stepping forward.

"Da, oh Da! don't." Mary Ann was now tugging at Mike's hand. "Be quiet, Da . . . Oh, Da!"

"You be quiet and get yourself home to bed." Mike made to thrust her away, then stopped. The sight of her face, so pinched with fear, and her eyes so weighed with sadness, checked his harshness, for he saw in her expression all the unhappiness that was about to descend on them again, and as usual through him. Yet the blame was not entirely his. Ratcliffe had meant to get rid of him; it had to come sooner or later.

"Oh, Da . . . Da."

"It's all right. Be quiet now," he said roughly.

His anger was seeping from him and he put his hand gently on her head. "Why did you come out at this time of the morning, and it still dark? What if your mother finds you gone?"

"I couldn't sleep, Da, and I went to the landing window to see if the light was still on here. And it was. And I had to come. . . . Will you come to bed now, Da?"

"No. No, I can't. Anyway it's near time to get up, and I've got some work to do."

Although his eyes did not turn towards the byre, Mary Ann's gaze slid fearfully round. Before he could move in front of her to block her view she had seen Clara and the calf.

Even to her child's eyes the animals did not look merely asleep, their relaxation was too complete. She took several shuddering breaths, then, turning swiftly to Mike, she buried her face in his thigh and bit on his trousers to still her crying.

"There now, there now." He lifted her into his arms.

"They're all right, they're just fast asleep. They've gone to. . . . " He found it difficult to use the jargon that was as natural to her as breathing, but finally he brought out . . . "heaven." But it brought no comfort; her crying mounted. So pulling his coat off a peg, he put it round his shoulders and about her, and made his way in the bleak dawn towards the cottage. As he went, strangely enough, it wasn't the coming meeting with Lizzie he thought of, or yet that with Ratcliffe or the old man, but he thought of Mrs. McMullen and how she would gloat over this latest development, which would prove conclusively that he wasn't any good. And in his own mind, for the first time, drunk or sober, he was agreeing with her.

.   .   .   .   .

At twenty-past nine on the same Saturday morning Mary Ann was waiting for the bus to take her into Jarrow and to Mass. She had refused to be persuaded to go to Mass in Felling with Michael, although Felling was much nearer to the farm. Now she was wondering whether, if she attended the grown-up Mass at eleven o'clock, Miss Thompson would consider it the same as her going to Children's Mass. Miss Thompson might not even miss her presence at the ten o'clock Mass; but Sarah Flannagan would, and she would find some way to suggest to the teacher that she hadn't been to Mass at all. With a slight movement of her head, she dismissed the consequences of her premeditated action, for this worry was infinitesimal compared with the grief now loading her mind. Sarah Flannagan and Miss Thompson were irritants that, given time, she could deal with, but there was no time to deal with this other thing.

In the freshly budding flecked green of the hawthorn hedge flanking the opposite side of the road she saw her mother's face as it had looked a few minutes earlier when she left the house. It bore the old look of Mulhattan's Hall again. And yet her ma and da hadn't fought.

Her mother's attitude had beenn disturbing. The quiet way she had taken Mike's report of the scene with Ratcliffe; the sadness and pity in her face as she had looked at him created an odd effect in Mary Ann. It had increased instead of diminished her fear of the future, for although her ma had said, "Well, there are other jobs," there had been a hopelessness about her. Like the return of a dread disease, once imagined gone for ever, it seemed now useless to fight against the sentence it imposed, even though her mother herself had seemed to grasp at hope when she said, "Why don't you go to Mr. Lord and tell him everything?"

"Go to hir..? Not likely," Mike had said. "I'm crawling to no man. And what would be the good anyway; won't Ratcliffe phone him as soon as he's out of bed?"

What time did Mr. Lord get out of bed? It was Sunday morning and likely he'd be having a lie in. Mary Ann prayed fervently that this would be so. This morning of all mornings she prayed that sleep would lie heavily on the old man, that the bed would drag and that if Ben came to call him he would growl at him and turn over.

She sent up these urgent requests while she gazed steadfastly down on her prayer book held tightly between her two hands, as if her prayer, being filtered through this passport to heaven, would reach the celestial quarters so coated with piety that a refusal on the part of the Holy Family to grant her desires would be practically impossible. Already she had a plan of campaign mapped out . . . roughly sketched would be more accurate. She would go to Mr. Lord and get the first one in. If she could get her say in before Mr. Ratcliffe, all would—she imagined—be well. Not about Clara. No, that was something beyond her province. In any case, although sorrow for Clara's fate was still touching her, it bore no comparison with the sorrow for the fate that awaited her da should Mr. Lord hear he had been drunk yesterday. It was this and this alone she must work on; she must in some way convince him that her da had been solid and sober when he went to the cowshed. . . . But how?

The how did not unduly worry her either. It was a long way in the bus to Mr. Lord's . . . two miles. By then she would have thought of something.

As always when Mary Ann left her subconscious to deal with her difficulties it never failed her. She was sitting in the bus looking disconsolately out of the window when her eyes saw a post depicting a number of startling scenes from *The Robe* . . . There she had the solution. She would tell him her da had taken her to see that picture. She had studied this poster before, for there was one on her way to school, and she had been fascinated by the physique of the two men and the beauty of the lady, but mostly she had been touched by the three crosses on the hill and . . . the poor Lord, hanging there.

But not until she had left the bus and was half-way up the drive was her enthusiasm for her plan dampened and her courage halved, for she remembered, literally with a start that brought her to a stop, that the feeling between Mr. Lord and herself was not as it had once been. The Lord she was going to now was as formidable as the man into whose house she had gate-crashed a few months previously. Now her steps were slow and she approached the door with the same trepidation she had experienced on that first visit.

Ben answered her ring, and she looked up into his wizened face and said "Hullo" with unusual humility. To her surprise, he didn't growl at her and say, "What d'you want?" but stood aside to let her in. And she was forced for the moment to take her mind off Mr. Lord and look at his servant, for he was not scowling at her. It was a very strange and surprising thing to see, but in his eyes there was a look of kindness. He almost looked as if he were glad to see her, which placed him immediately in the category of an ally. Her glance moved away across the large dim hall towards the dining-room, then back again. And she strained up to him and whispered, "Is he all right?"

Ben moved his head slowly from side to side, and Mary Ann's mouth formed a soundless "Oh", while she watched with widening eyes Ben's creaking length being bent towards her. And when his parchment-skin face was on a level with her own, she was so taken aback by his cordiality that she could scarcely take in the dread import of what he was saying.

"Mr. Ratcliffe's phoned about the cow, and the master is"—Ben paused before adding—"very annoyed" as if he found the expression inadequate to describe the master's reaction.

Mary Ann dragged her gaze from the interesting spectacle of Ben's face at close quarters and looked down at her thumb, then conveyed it to her mouth and nibbled at the nail. That Mr. Ratcliffe was a nasty rotten beast, he was. She wished he would drop down dead, she did. Yet hope never utterly dead in her, prompted the thought that although Mr. Ratcliffe had phoned about Clara he may not have mentioned her da and yesterday. There was a possibility that she had still time to prove to Mr. Lord that her da couldn't have been sick yesterday.

After a pathetic glance in Ben's direction she went slowly towards the dining-room door, tapped once, and without waiting for an answer, opened it and went in.

It was at once evident to her that Mr. Lord was not surprised to see her. He was sitting by the fire filling his pipe. She saw from the table that he had just finished his breakfast. His head moved a little and his eyes slid towards her, but without resting on her or seeming to take in her presence. Then they returned to his pipe, and he went on filling it, pushing the tobacco into the bowl with gentle pressures that misled Mary Ann and made her think: He's not really mad or else he'd be poking it in.

"Hallo," she said.

There was no return greeting to this, but she moved closer—she was used to him being grumpy. "I'm going to Mass. I was on me way and I thought . . . " She paused. This was too much like real lying. She had been about to add, "I thought I'd look in and see you." She knew that only the present emergency had brought her here, yet there was something she was unable to explain to herself, for she was glad to be here, glad to see him. She was experiencing a similar feeling to that which she had when she played houses and wrapped her doll against the cold and nursed it on her knee by the fire. Bertha roused her pity by the coldness of its china body; this old man by his loneliness, visible to her even through the layers of his severity. She wanted to put her hand on his and say something funny—daft funny, to make him laugh.

"Well what do you want; you want something, don't you?"

This direct attack nonplussed her for the moment, and she said, "Yes . . . no . . . yes. I mean——" She stopped. She could see now that he was in a bad temper . . . he was in a flaming temper. And like her da he was worse when he was quiet, and more unmanageable. If he would bawl at her she would know what to do.

Mr. Lord stopped pushing at his pipe, and he looked at her with a look that sent hope fleeing from her. Then he said, "You have come to tell me that the cow isn't dead, nor her calf. The calf is alive and kicking, isn't it? And you have come to tell me"—his neck moved out of his collar, and his head with small jerks emphasised each word—"that your father was not drunk yesterday."

She stared back at him. Tragedy filled the space between them, the tragedy of her da getting the sack, of her ma packing up their things.

"He was drunk yesterday, wasn't he?" Mr. Lord seemed to derive some satisfaction in repeating this statement, for it was accompanied by a sneer, which reminded her of Sarah Flannagan when she said, "Aw, you! You see, I told you so." Mostly from habit, the denial slipped from her lips: "He wasn't."

"What!"

The force of the word, which owed nothing to loudness but everything to its intensity, sent her back from him. He heaved himself out of the chair. "Why do I listen to you? Get yourself away!"

He spoke to her, not as to a child, but as to an adult, an equal, for that was how he thought of her. Had she appeared to him merely as a child, he would have lost interest in her after their first encounter. But from the first he had recognized in her an adult quality, a similar quality to one which he himself possessed and which centered around his tenacity. No one of his experience had fought for what he wanted against heavy odds as he had done, and as she was continually doing. Yet this knowledge at the same time irked him, for with this very trait she would grow up defending that waster. All her efforts and thoughts would be centred around him, and she would emerge into womanhood like millions of other women, ordinary, except for the doubtful quality of a father fixation. Whereas, had she received the proper schooling to train her nimble mind there was, he imagined, no limit to the height she could eventually reach . . . away from Mike's influence, and himself behind her. He turned to the window. He would not allow himself to follow up this thought, or look at her while she spoke.

"I'm going, and whoever told you that's a liar. . . . Mr. Ratcliffe's a liar, I know he is. He wouldn't let me da look after Clara. He put Len on, and I heard you tell him to let me da do it."

She knew she had caught his attention with this last piece of news, for she saw his head lift. She went on, nodding at his back, "Mr. Ratcliffe's got it in for me da; he always has. He gives him the worst jobs. Mr. Jones says if it was him he would have left. And me ma's wanted me da to mention it to you but he wouldn't. And Mr. Ratcliffe only sent for me da last night out of spite because . . . " Her flow ceased, and Mr. Lord turned from the window and finished the sentence for her, " . . . Because he knew your father was drunk. That's it, isn't it?"

"He wasn't"—now her chin was jerking up at him—"he was solid and sober!"

"Stop that!" Mr. Lord's voice had risen. And hers went to an even higher key as she replied with heat, "I won't! . . . he wasn't . . . he took me out, he did, and we went into Jarrow."

"And he got drunk."

"He didn't, I tell you!"

"I don't want any of your shouting."

"I'm not shouting. You'll believe nothing, nothing at all. He didn't get drunk, so there, 'cos he couldn't, we went to the pictures. You can ask anybody."

"Who's anybody?" It sounded now as if he wanted to believe her.

"Mrs. McBride . . . and . . . and . . . " Her mind rushed madly around, searching for another likely defender . . . and found one . . . "and Father Owen," she added. "He knows we went. 'Enjoy the picture, Mary Ann,' he said, "cos it's about Jesus.' "

Eeh! She stood petrified at the length her imagination had stretched, and also at what it was achieving, for Mr. Lord's brows were drawn together in a decided question.

"You saw Father Owen?"

"Yes." It was a very small yes.

"And he knew you were going to the pictures with your father?"

" . . . Yes."

The bushy brows were drawn over the eyes. "What did you see at the pictures?"

"The Robe."

"The Robe?"

"Yes."

"What was it about?"

"About two men and a beautiful lady."

"Yes?"

"And . . . and Our Lord being crucified."

"Go on."

"And . . . and . . . " She stared fixedly at him, trying to conjure up the poster again. But it would not be brought up, and all she had to defend her cause now was her knowledge of Bible history, and she had never liked Bible history, for she had never been any good at it. "And Peter and the cock crowing three times," she said haltingly. "And Our Lord giving everybody fish and bread and saying, if there's anybody here who hasn't told a lie he can do the pelting. It was a nice picture." Her voice trailed off.

The silence pressed down on the room, and it told her more plainly than any words that she had failed. He had likely seen the picture.

When he turned from her she stood for a while longer. Then taking heed of the rising lump in her throat she swung round and ran out of the room and into the hall, where her swift entry startled Ben in his eavesdropping. Still running, she dashed through the doorway and down the drive. . . .

·   ·   ·   ·   ·

It was nearly one o'clock when she returned home. Mass had brought no comfort. Being the grown-ups' Mass, Father Owen had been inaccessible. He Holy Family too had offered not the slightest solace; they had stared back at her as if they couldn't care less. And now, it seemed unbelievable but it was true, there was her grannie sitting at the table with her hat off, and from the expression on her face, Mary Ann judged that she already knew everything. Her grannie, she had always known, was like the devil—she received first-hand information about the bad things. But it would now seem that she was quicker than the devil.

"Hallo . . . you been to Mass?"

Mrs. McMullen's tone was civil, which in itself was a bad sign.

"Yes." Mary Ann turned to her mother. "Ma, where's me . . . "

Lizzie cut short her enquiry: "Get your things off," she said.

"Which Mass were you at?" asked Mrs. McMullen.

"The eleven o'clock."

"Why didn't you go to the ten, that's your Mass, isn't it?"

"Yes."

"Then why didn't you go?"

"'Cos I didn't want to!" The shouted words startled both Mrs. McMullen and Lizzie, but before Lizzie could remonstrate with her daughter, Mrs. McMullen's hand came across Mary Ann's ear in a resounding slap.

Lizzie caught her as she reeled back and held her tightly, and looking straight at her mother, she said, quietly, "Don't do that again, I'm telling you."

"Then teach her some manners . . . Shouting at me. And after asking her a civil question. . . . It's like him, she is, uncivilised, bringing trouble wherever she goes."

"That's enough," said Lizzie. She pushed Mary Ann from her.

"It isn't enough. I've prophesied this time and again. I've been waiting for it."

"Then you're not disappointed," said Lizzie.

"No, I'm not. And neither was the whole of Burton Street. Mrs. Flannagan said it was the peak of his career, the way he went on yesterday. He made a holy show of himself. The whole of Jarrow was out."

"It wasn't. Shut up you!" Mary Ann's face, except where her grandmother's fingers had left their imprint, was white. "Shut up! You're . . . you're a cheeky bitch. You are! . . . you are!"

Lifting Mary Ann bodily, Lizzie carried her from the room and up the stairs. There was the sound of a door banging overhead, followed by load sobbing; then Lizzie came slowly back into the kitchen.

Mrs. McMullen was standing now, her hat perched on one hand, while with the other she pulled the velvet bow into shape. Lizzie stood just inside the door. Her face wore the protecting tightness bred of past encounters with her mother.

"What," she asked quietly, "do you hope to gain from it?"

"What do you mean? . . . Go on . . . go on and put the blame on me for her being like a gutter-snipe."

"If," went on Lizzie, ignoring her mother's side-tracking, "I was to do what you want and leave him, and suppose I couldn't earn enough myself to keep us like you imagine whe should be kept, who would you have me turn to now that Bob is going to be married?" And having sprung this piece of news, she waited.

Mrs. McMullen's hands remained poised over her hat. The news was evidently a shock to her, for her prim features were sagging with surprise as she brought out, "Bob! . . . I don't believe it. He wouldn't."

"He told me himself yesterday."

"I don't believe it, not a word. There's only ever been you."

"He is marrying a girl from Jesmond. Pringle's daughter . . . the fruit people."

Mrs. McMullen sat down. The muscles of her face were tight again. "The turncoat," she muttered. "He wouldn't dare come and tell me. Why, he said only afore Christmas that the greatest pleasure he'd get from building the old man's house would be that he could see you." She turned her small sharp eyes on to her daughter. "It's a broken heart he's doing it out of . . . that's what it is."

"You can stop deluding yourself on that point too," said Lizzie. "I happen to know she is young and very lovely. And what is more, she'll be quite rich one day."

Mrs. McMullen seemed unable to find an answer to this. She sat for a while longer in silence; then rising, she pulled on her hat without the fuss she usually accorded this operation, grabbed her coat from a hook on the door, and for the very first time in her life left her daughter without a word of admonition.

After her mother's departure, Lizzie sat down, and resting her elbows on the table and her head in her hands, she said with utter weariness, "Dear God. Dear God."

.   .   .   .   .

On Monday morning Mary Ann said she was feeling bad.

"Where?" asked her mother. "Have you a pain?"

"No," said Mary Ann. "I'm just sick."

This was true enough; she was feeling sick, the sickness born of anxiety. But she had experienced this before, and it hadn't prevented her from getting up and going to school. This morning, however, she didn't want to go to school; it was as urgent as a matter of life and death that she should be here when Mr. Ratcliffe sacked her da, as he would do at nine o'clock.

Lizzie wasn't fooled, but her mind, dwelling on the same thing as Mary Ann's, was too harassed to cope with her daughter. She could only say, "Well, you'll go at dinner time, mind."

"Yes, Ma."

The victory had been easy. She lay, not curled up as she usually did when she was enjoying a lie in, but with her short length stretched tautly out. Soon Michael would come up for his schoolbag and things, then she would get up and go to the farm.

She turned her head and stared at the wall. On her eye level were three humpty elephants following a giraffe, a tiger and a penguin. Her da had pasted the animals all round her corner. He had cut them out of a book especially for her. And now she would have to leave them; some other girl would have this corner. She stared at the ceiling. Where would they go to live? They couldn't go back to Mulhattan's Hall because the attics had been taken. Perhaps Mrs. McBride would take them in . . . But she had only two rooms.

Her da had offered no opinion as to what was going to happen to them. He had been quiet; he hadn't opened his mouth all day yesterday, nor had he eaten anything, not a bit of dinner, nor yet supper. But twice he had made himself some tea, thick black tea.

"You're not sick."

Michael's appearance from behind the curtain and his accusation startled her, and she stammered, "I . . . I . . . I am."

"You're not . . . you only want to nose around."

They continued to stare hostilely at each other. Then Michael, turning away to close the door stealthily, came back to her bed and, sitting on it, said, "Listen. If you want to hear anything go up in the loft."

"But who'll I hear there?" Mary Ann was sitting up now.

"Mr. Ratcliffe. . . . Look, listen to what I'm saying. You know the long loft where the feed's kept. Well, the end of it runs over the dairy, doesn't it?"

"Yes." Mary Ann was not certain.

"Well, next to the dairy is the store Mr. Ratcliffe turned into an office, isn't it?"

"Yes." She was still not certain, for the topographical situation as Michael explained it was not clear to her.

"Well, get up in the loft. Go behind the bales until you come to where there's just the beams, and if you lie along the end one, nearest the back of the loft, you can hear them talking down below."

"Who?"

"Well, anybody who's there. And Mr. Lord'll be there. And Mr. Ratcliffe'll be telling his the tale, and you can see if he tells him the truth."

Their faces were close together, and she saw from the troubled hurt look in his eyes that in his own way Michael was as concerned for their da as she was. But she couldn't as yet see what good it was going to do listening to Mr. Ratcliffe talking to Mr. Lord, and she said so.

"It'll be no use if I do hear."

"It will. Me da can go and deny it."

"He won't."

"He will if me ma puts her foot down."

The idea of her da being forced to defend himself under the pressure of a foot being put down, whether her ma's or anybody else's was enough to make her obstinate. "I'm not going to listen," she said.

Michael sprang up from the bed, his face almost as red as his hair. "Oh you. . . . You little . . . !"

"I'm not." Mary Ann denied her sub-title before it was uttered. "if me ma makes me da do something, they'll row, and then things'll be just as bad."

"Nothing can be as bad as him being out of work and likely having to go back to the yards."

They stared at each other for a moment longer. Then Michael turned away, collected his bag from behind the curtain and went downstairs. When she heard the outer door bang, she got up and dressed hurriedly; but her descent of the stairs was slow, as befitted a sick person.

Lizzie, clearing the table, said, "Can you eat anything?"

"No," said Mary Ann.

And this was true, too, for she had no appetite. she fiddled about with her hair ribbon. She sat down. She stood up. She opened a picture book and turned the pages without seeing anything. The she asked quietly, "Can I go out for a walk, Ma?"

"Yes," said Elizabeth.

That was all. She did not question whither the walk would take her; she knew. She did not say, "If you are sick, you had better stay in," for she also knew that that would aggravate the particular kind of sickness.

Immediately she reached the lane, Mary Ann started to run. She did not turn into the main road which would lead her to the farmyard, but cut across the a field that would bring her to the back of the barn. Through a knot-hole in the barn she saw her da. He was cleaning a machine, rubbing it with an oily rag. He was working slowly as if he was tired. She saw Mr. Jones come in and heard him ask, "We gonner start on the binder, Mike?" and her da reply, "Might as well."

From the time she saw Mike and Mr. Jones move into the far dimness of the barn until she climbed the ladder to the loft was only a matter of seconds, for she knew that if she was spotted by her da she would be ordered home.

The loft was warm and had a stingy smell that made her want to sneeze, and it was not a little frightening, for it seemed bigger than usual and the stacked bales higher. Cautiously she followed Michael's instructions, until she came to the beams naked of floor-boards. There were only four of them and they could not have measured more than three feet before they disappeared into the slope of the roof, but to Mary Ann they appeared to be yards long. She stretched cautiously over them and looked down. It was dark, and she could make out nothing. When tentatively she put her hand down in between the beams, it touched the roughness of bricks, and she could not tell what was actually beneath her, but Michael had said if she lay across the last beam she would be able to hear. Trembling, she attempted the feat.

A man, or even a boy, could have rested easily over the beams, but her slight body would have fallen in between them, and as her courage was not of the kind that could perform physical feats, it took a great deal more of it to lie along a beam than it would have taken to swear her own life away.

After easing herself back and forwards a number of times for practice she sat and waited for voices to come to her. The minutes took on the length of hours, and the only sound that she heard was the distant closing of a door. It was strange but there weren't even any farm sounds here. The bales made the corner a silent world in which she could hear only her own breathing, and she didn't like the sound of that. It was like being all alone in the lane on a dark night. . . . And then she heard a voice . . . or the echo of one. It came as if from the bottom of a well. In a second she was lying along the beam. Now the voice was joined by another; but it wasn't her da's, it was Mr. Lord's. But what was he saying, she couldn't make out a thing?

The urgency of the situation overcoming her fear, she thrust her head down between the beams, and, like the voices of the old records Mrs. McBride used to play on her gramaphone, she heard them talking. They came quietly at first, then rose swiftly.

"You didn't carry out my instructions."

"Am I managing this farm or not?"

"You are managing it, but what you seem to forget is that you don't own it. I told you to let Shaughnessy see to her."

"He's not capable."

"There you know you are wrong. Whatever else he lacks it's not a knowledge of animals. Remember Douglas's bull. It was he who warned you against buying it. Isn't that so?"

"The bull was all right. . . . We are not talking about the bull but about the cow."

"Why did you send for him on Saturday night after putting Morley on?"

"Because Morley wanted a break."

"He didn't. You sent for Shaughnessy because you knew he was drunk. You were to ring for the vet if the animal got worse, but what did you do? You wanted a handle, didn't you?"

"Look here, Mr. Lord, you want to be careful."

"You wanted to get rid of him."

"I didn't."

"All right, then, why do you say you mean to sack him?"

"Because he neglected his work."

"What if I say he didn't neglect his work, and he stays on?"

"You won't."

"Won't I?"

"No . . . because if you do I go."

Mary Ann stared into the darkness, waiting breathlessly for the silence to end. And then Mr. Lord's voice broke it, it was so low and quiet that she could scarcely make out his words.

"Very well; you go, Mr. Ratcliffe."

Now came Ratcliffe's voice in a spate of words, forcing their way up through the blocked-in chimney and into Mary Ann's ear, so loud and so rapid that she could distinguish none of them until their speed lessened. And then they came slower than was ordinary and filled with such scorn that she was thrown on to the defensive.

"Your smallholding! You fancy yourself as a gentleman farmer. Why, the piggeries in my last job were bigger than this."

"Doubtless. Then can you leave the smallholding as soon as possible?"

The tone should have shrivelled Mr. Ratcliffe dead.

"I am due for three months' notice."

"Your money will be paid to you. I want you off my farm at the earliest possible moment."

A door banged, and no more sound came up through the chimney. Mary Ann wriggled back along the beam and sat down. Mr. Ratcliffe had got the sack, not her da. The loft became filled with light. It streaked between the bales; it was not due to the sun coming out, but to the turn of events. Mr. Lord was going to keep her da on; Mr. Ratcliffe was going; they'd get a new manager, and he'd be nice . . . he must be nice.

Mr. Ratcliffe had classed the farm as a smallholding. She wasn't exactly sure what this was, but it was something only as big as his last pigsties. She got to her feet. The sickness had left her chest and in its place was a bubbling joy. She'd dash down and tell her da, and then her ma. Oh yes, she must fly and tell her ma. And their Michael . . . Michael wouldn't know till the night. And Lena Ratcliffe would soon be gone and she wouldn't have to put up with her swanking any more.

Almost bursting with excitement, she reached the top of the ladder, only to find her escape cut off for the time being, for there was Mr. Lord talking to Len, and by the sound of Mr. Lord's voice Len was getting it. . . . But she must get down somehow and let her da know.

A suggestion of a means of escape rising in her mind turned her about, and she looked towards a square of floor-board with a ring in the middle. That was where they dropped the things through. Her da would be just under there, for she could hear him now calling to Jones to start her up. That would be the machine they were cleaning. She'd have to shout to him before they got that going or he'd never hear her.

Scampering to the trapdoor she pulled at the ring. But her effort made no impression. And then she laughed to herself as she looked down at her feet. How could she open it, she was standing on it? But much to her consternation she found that when she stood outside the trapdoor she couldn't reach the ring.

In a flurry now, she knelt down at the opposite side to where it was hinged and, into the gap made by the countless hands that had grabbed its edge, thrust her own hands and pulled. And behold, the door came upwards towards her. But only for a short way, for she hadn't the strength to give it the final lift that would throw it back. This she decided didn't really matter, for she knew what she would do. She'd squeeze her head and shoulders in and call to her da . . . "Sst! sst!" Like that.

Lying flat, she forced her head into the aperture, and then her shoulders, and from this unusual angle she looked down into the barn. The new aspect of the familiar place stilled her cry—things looked funny. She was looking on to the side of the binder. It was all sharp knives—shiny, sharp knives—and through them she could see her da at the other side of the machine bending down and rubbing something. The open door of the barn looked as if it was stuck to the ceiling; everything was topsyturvy.

She said "Sst!" And when Mike looked about him, not knowing from where the voice was coming, she gurgled inside and let him return to his job before putting her tongue to her teeth again. But the instant she did this, Mike's voice called, "Let her go," and her "Sst!" was drowned by the terrific noise and whirl of the blades beneath her. She became frozen with terror, and powerless to pull herself into the loft again.

Suddenly she screamed, a long piercing scream that cut into the din below and brought Mike's eyes upwards and paralysed his senses for a moment. From where he stood her threshing arms seemed to be waving directly over the machine. With a gabbled cry that re-echoed around the barn he sprang forward. His cry was to Jones and said "Shut her off!" His right hand emphasising his demand, was thrust towards Jones, and his left, in a blind instinctive movement to save, towards the machine.

Mary Ann's eyes, already blinded by her fear, were now only able to take in part of what was happening, but piercing through her terror was the knowledge that her da was hurt. And when the machinery stopped and she heard his deep tearing groans and saw him staggering back against the barn wall clutching something red and running to his chest, her own screams filled her head and her body. Her world became swamped with nothing but her screaming. Even when she felt her legs gripped and she was being lifted into someone's arms, she still saw the barn and heard the groans. And to her screaming she added her struggles. She fought frantically to free herself, tearing like a wild animal for release.

"Me da! Me da! Me da! Me da!" It was as if her lungs drew fresh strength with each scream. . . . "Me da! Me da! Me da! Me da!"

There were other arms about her, and she was dimly conscious of Mr. Lord's voice commanding her to cease her screaming. But she would not listen to it; she continued to fight and struggle and scream, always aiming to turn towards the barn.

Later, she knew she was in the kitchen and lying between the warmth of her mother's breasts and being rocked and rocked, always rocked. When the screams came the rocking would start. And quite suddenly they both stopped, the rocking and the screams.

9

ABSOLUTION

Mr. Lord stood in the kitchen with his back to the fire and looked from one to the other of the cheap pieces of furniture with which he had become very familiar during the past week. For instance, he knew that there were only eight blue roses bordering the saucers arrayed on the delf-rack, whereas there were nine on each of the tea plates. He knew that although there was a felt pad under the table cloth covering the little dining table, the top was badly marked. He also knew that one of the chairs had a short leg, which irritated him whenever it was his misfortune to sit on it. The furniture displeased him, and was saved from his utter condemnation only because of its scrupulous cleanliness.

He raised his eyes to the ceiling and moved uneasily. They were a long while up there. As he lowered his gaze again it touched on a farm calendar which said Monday March 14th: Gregsons for all Farm Machinery. . . . Machinery. He turned abruptly towards the fire. It was almost a week to the very minute since all this trouble had started. Never would he want another week like it. And what was to be the outcome of it? A man with only one hand and a child half crazy? Of the two it was the child for whom he was more concerned. Something would be done for Shaughnessy. What he did not as yet know, farm work being out of the question. But what could be done for the child who had come, despite the persistent denials to himself, to be of an almost overpowering interest in his life? For nearly five days she had been kept asleep, and now, although she was awake and quite conscious, she was as lifeless as a rag doll.

The kitchen door opened and Lizzie entered, followed by the doctor.

After waiting a moment, Mr. Lord said, "Well?"

The doctor drew on his gloves before replying. "If it's possible, I advise that the father be brought home. I cannot see an improvement in her until he is."

"But it's only a week, will they allow him out so soon?" he asked.

"I can find out. He can attend the out-patients' ward. If he can come out perhaps you'll be good enough to pick him up."

The doctor's manner was brusque, and under other circumstances Mr. Lord's hackles would have risen and his own brusqueness would have overshadowed the doctor's. But on this occasion he said nothing, only followed him outside.

Lizzie stood at the window and watched them crossing the yard. In their ways they were both like gods. Mr. Lord had the power of their material future in his hands, and on the doctor Mary Ann's mental state seemed to depend. He was right, she knew, to bring Mike back, for only through him could Mary Ann become alive again. But the Mike she had seen yesterday was not the man who could inspire life in a child, or in anyone else. Her husband had always been a virile man. He had, she knew, been proud of his physique, of his tall, thick body, and of his strength, which drink had not yet impaired. Many a time he had picked her up bodily and held her aloft, glorying in his power to do so. But now, like a Samson without his hair, the loss of his hand had seemingly cut the virility out of him—he appeared to her like a child.

"What am I to do, Liz? What job can I do with one hand, other than night watchman? That would kill me, Liz. They won't give me compen, it was me own fault." He had not said it was Mary Ann's fault, and she knew he would not say so. And he must not. All blame must be taken from the child. Mary Ann must never be allowed to take to herself the blame for the loss of his hand. It was this guilt, she knew, that was hovering in the drugged layers of the child's mind, and only Mike, the old hearty Mike, could push it so far down that it would never rise again.

The door opened and Michael came in. He appeared to have grown older and taller during the past few days. He stood looking at her and stretching his school cap between his hands.

"What does he say?" he asked.

"That your da must come home," she said.

"Ma."

"Yes,"

"I'm going to leave school when I'm fifteen."

"All right," said Lizzie dully, "there's plenty of time to talk about that."

"But I am." His tone was emphatic, yet held a tremor. And she looked at him and was touched at the trouble she saw in his face.

"And for as long as we're here I'm going to get paid for what I do on the farm, nights and week-ends."

"Who says so?"

"Mr. Lord. . . . Ma."

"Yes?"

She saw that he was unable to speak, and he turned from her and hid his face in his arms against the wall.

Gently she pulled him round to her and pressed his head against her shoulder. She knew he was torturing himself, taking the primary blame because he had sent Mary Ann to listen. He sniffed hard and pulled away from her.

"She'll be all right," she said, "and your da'll get well. . . . And Michael . . . when he comes home, and he may be home today, be . . . be nice to him, will you?"

He did not answer, but sat down on the fender and looked into the fire . . .

.   .   .   .   .

Mike came home at three o'clock, and Mr. Lord, using an unused but natural tact, found something to busy himself with in the car. And so Mike came in alone. Like that of a man who had undergone a severe illness, his skin was shades lighter than was natural, and his eyes, sunk in his head, looked big and dark . . . and dead. Smiling her greeting, Lizzie put her arms about him, taking care of the arm strapped to his chest. And when only the pressure of his one hand touched her, leaving her body somehow cold, all her resolutions to put on a brave face vanished.

"Come on, come on," he muttered gruffly. "Stop your bubbling, I'm not dead yet."

It sounded so much like the old Mike that she raised her eyes to his face, but it was still the face she had come to know during the past week. She drew away from him, and, trying to adopt a lighter tone, she said, "Come and have a cup of tea."

He sat down like a stranger by the side of his own table, and he had drunk half the tea before Mr. Lord put in an appearance.

"Can I offer you a cup of tea, sir?" asked Lizzie.

"Thank you, I'd like one very much."

He, too, sat down by the table, and the room became as quiet as though there was no one in it. . . .

Upstairs Mary Ann lay looking at the elephants on the wall. They were not running after the giraffe and butting him with their trunks as they usually did when she concentrated her gaze upon them; they were standing stock still as paper elephants should do. She turned her head slowly and looked across the room. It seemed very big now that the curtain had been drawn back. The sun was shining through the little window and making a square of colour on the mat. But it was just the sun shining into a poorly furnished bedroom. It was no longer the most wonderful room in the world set in the best cottage in the world. It was drab and colourless, and she was aware of it. And it was this awareness that was partly the cause of the pain that was in her head and in her chest, for her life had been stripped of wonder.

When she had woken from the funny sleep the screaming was still in her head. If she kept her eyes open it wasn't so loud; but it was difficult to keep her eyes open. And then gradually it had died away, and in the strange quiet that followed she knew what she had screamed about. Since she had been awake no one had mentioned her da to her, her ma, or Mr. Lord, or the doctor, or their Michael. She knew why; because they were frightened to. She was waiting for someone to say, "Your da's gone away on a long journey and you'll see him again one day." That's what they said to Mary Fitzgerald when her da died. Mary had told them all in the school yard. But Mary Fitzgerald hadn't caused her da . . . to go away, whereas she had. Beacause she had almost fallen through the roof her da had . . . gone away, and she wouldn't see him again ever, not till she died. But now no suggestion came to her as to how she could bring about her demise; even this faculty was dormant. She looked at the foot of her bed where, on a bamboo table, stood her little altar. Her eyes rested on the figures of Our Lady and the Infant. They brought no solace. If any emotion touched her, it was resentment that they had let her do this thing, that their guidance and protection were fallible.

When her eyes were brought to the doorway by the dark bulk filling it, she looked at Mike for a moment without recognition. Then the scream entered her head again, brought her hands to her mouth. But it did not escape, for Mike's voice saying, "Hallo, there," stilled it.

The "Hallo there" was so ordinary—it was his usual greeting, and he was saying it. He was walking towards her. He sat on her bed and said it again. . . . "Hallo, there."

Her eyes moved from his face to the arm strapped across his chest, then up to his face again.

"Well, aren't you going to give me a kiss?"

She made no move, and Mike said, "Here am I, come rushing out of hospital to see you, and all you do is sit there and stare. Aren't you pleased to see me?"

Slowly she pulled herself up. But still did not speak. Then her hand moved to his arm and touched it, just below the elbow. She looked at him again, and he smiled; then her arms were about his neck, pulling him towards her, and whatever pain he suffered by her contact with the raw stump of his wrist he gave no sign of it.

"Da. Oh, Da!"

"Now, what's all the fuss about?" He stroked her hair and talked to her as she lay quivering but dry-eyed against his breast. "Here you are in bed with a cold when you should have been downstairs helping your ma to get the tea ready for me coming home. . . . And you never came to the hospital to see me, and there was me waiting every day. And all you could hear was, 'She's in bed with a cold.' So I said to meself, 'Well, if she can't come to me I'm going to her . . . a bit cut on the hand's not goin' to keep me in bed.'"

It all sounded very brave and airy. It was make-believe such as Mary Ann herself would have used. Yet he felt better for having said it. It was the first time he had actually referred to his hand. He had forbidden his mind to touch on it, and it had obeyed him except during his sleep, when he would dream that his hand was being sliced off his body . . . but slowly; and he would awake, thinking, My God! what a dream, only to realise that the dream was a reality. And there would follow a period of retrospection, when he would go over his life and ask why everything he touched had the mark of failure on it. Was it the heritage from the parents he had never known? Or was it due to his ingrained sense of inferiority born of his life in a Cottage Home? Whatever the cause, his efforts seemed doomed. He had come to the farm with the firm intention of making a go of it, and nobody but himself knew what it had cost him those first few months to go without his drink. And then Quinton had to crop up again. Quinton, in himself, might be a decent enough fellow, but his very name had the power to show up his own shortcomings; and the knowledge that Quinton had loved Liz, and that had she married him her life would have been smooth and free from the perpetual worry she now knew, had been enough to raise the tearing demon of his jealousy.

But his troubles could have been halved, he knew, had he been able to conquer his weakness for the bottle.

Lying in hospital the future had seemed so dark that he could see not even the smallest ray of light. What lay before him but public assistance, the very thought of which brought his teeth grating over each other. There would be no compensation for the accident, it had been his own fault. He would not say Mary Ann's. . . . He could not think blame on the child who would sell her soul for him, but he knew that if her head had not come through the trap-door he would have his hand now. And they all knew it. Especially the old man. The old fellow might be fond of Mary Ann, but he would not fork out a couple of thousand for which she was the cause. And he wouldn't keep him on the farm. What good would he be on the farm, anyway?

The thoughts had revolved on each other, creating a fear. And there had been only one person to whom he could voice it . . . Liz. And she had pooh-poohed it.

"That's nothing," she had said, "we'll manage somehow. It's the bairn we must think of. She knows she's to blame, and it's doing something to her."

He looked down now on the small white profile. It had done something. There was no spark of the old Mary Ann here. She was not even crying as she was wont to do with joy or sorrow. Talk about your hand, the doctor had said. Make light of it to her. It will help to balance her, and indirectly, yourself, too.

It was all right for them to ladle out advice. Nobody should give advice unless he had been in the same boat. . . . He wetted his lips, cleared his throat, and made an effort:

"You've got a stupid bloke for a da, haven't you?"

Her head pressed closer to him.

"I was never much good at anything, was I? Wouldn't listen to anybody, always the big fellow." He felt sick at himself for talking this stuff, but as her head moved and her face was lost in his waistcoat he went on, "Jonesy warned me. 'You'll get your hand off one of these days,' he said, 'cleaning while the machine's on.' . . . Well"—he stopped and the sigh he gave was not altogether feigned.—"Jonesy was right. I wouldn't listen. Third time's catchy time, Jonesy said, and it was. It served me right, I suppose. The only thing I'm sorry for is"—again he paused—"that you had to be up in the loft and see it."

Her head came up from his chest, and she looked at him, taking in this new aspect of the situation; and her spirit, gazing from her eyes, beseeched him to still her conscience for ever. Of its own accord, it demanded that he do for her what she was continually doing for him. It demanded now that he lie with the sincerity of sacrifice and redeem something of himself in absolving this child from all blame.

Words came to him, flowing with the smoothness of heavenly-endowed truth. He listened to himself uttering them, not knowing from where they sprang. And as he talked he saw the shadow of his Mary Ann return. It came back into her eyes; the sand-dryness became moist, and slowly she began to cry.

The new picture of her da, incompetent with machinery, stubbornly refusing all advice, even spurning the guiding hand of Mr. Ratcliffe, and admitting that any farm flair he had lay entirely with animals, brought her protective instinct surging up, and as it came it pressed down the numbing guilt into the secret chambers of her mind.

"Oh Da!" Her hand moved along his arm to where the neatly crossed bandages began. And again she said, "Oh Da."

"Look," he said, "I want cheering up. What you goin' to do about it? Are you coming downstairs with me?"

She hesitated.

"Come on, stand up."

Obediently, she stood up, rocking on her feet. Slipping his good arm about her he gathered her to him, and carried her down the stairs.

10

THE DEAL

Although Mary Ann's conscience was at rest once more, her mind was still troubled, for the anxiety that was eating into both Mike and Lizzie could not fail to make itself felt by her. Her da's pay packet had been brought to the cottage as if he was working, and Mr. Lord himself had said, "Don't worry." But she could feel that this statement instead of soothing her da's anxiety had only irritated him.

Mike did not want to be pensioned off out of charity. He wanted to work. At what? He didn't as yet know. He attended the out-patients' department; he read the "wanted" columns; he gazed for hours out of the window in the direction of the farm; and he chafed at his lot. Finally and boldly, he approached Mr. Lord, saying, "I'm not ungrateful, sir, but I can't go on like this."

"Like what?" Mr. Lord had asked. "You have been out of hospital for only ten days and I understand you have to attend for some time yet."

"That's all very well," said Mike, "but what's to follow?"

Mr. Lord had given no direct answer to this question; all he said was to go home and rest and wait.

What was to follow Mr. Lord did not himself know. He had been racking his brains as to what course he should take. If he gave him a small lump sum and let him go, the child would go. Yet how to give him a job? He would, of course, eventually get a hook for his hand, but even then would he be able to do a day's work with the other men? It was very doubtful. To use a hook skilfully needed long practice, and his knowledge of men was too wide to think that their present sympathy for Shaughnessy would stand the test of years. Nor would a man like Shaughnessy tolerate being carried. No, he could not see Shaughnessy back on the farm. His labour troubles were bad enough without adding to them.

For the first time Mr. Lord regretted his farm venture; he regretted the expensive house he was building; he regretted very much paying Ratcliffe three months' money in lieu of notice and leaving the farm without a directive; and above all he regretted the incident that had caused a place in his heart to open when Mary Ann had boldly claimed him as her granda. Material things could be rejected or replaced, but when carefully guarded feelings were exposed to the light of a child's charm a man became vulnerable.

In mid-week Mary Ann suddenly expressed a desire to return to school, and Lizzie, without protest, let her go, for she felt that the atmosphere of the house was unhealthy for her. Daily, she witnessed Mike's attempt at cheerfulness when in Mary Ann's presence, and it hurt her. And she knew it hurt the child. For with Mike, Mary Ann was like a watchful mother—no shade of his feelings escaped her. She knew he was worried, so therfore she was worried.

It was Father Owen's unexpected visit that precipitated Mary Ann's return to school. As she sat listening to his cheerful talk in the kitchen she had wanted to pour out her troubles to him; but only in church or Confession could she do this. So she went back to school.

The reception she received from her class would, at any other time, have filled her with unholy pride. She would have grabbed at the opportunity to let her imagination have full rein, for had she not been hanging head first from a hole in the ceiling, with below a whirling machine and ten thousand blades ready to cut her up? And hadn't her da rushed in and saved her? The children themselves made it sound something like this, anyway; and in this instance she did not deny them the use of their imaginations. But she added nothing of her own. Her only comment, when in the playground one sympathiser said, "Your poor da's got only one hand now," was to add, "That's nothing, he's still a grand man for all that."

Let it be noted here that Sarah Flannaghan did not attack this docile Mary Ann. After one scrutinising look at her, she had walked off. The white, sapped-looking being was not a worthy recipient of her powers of invective.

There was no Confession on a Wednesday night, and Mary Ann knew that unless she bumped into Father Owen in the church there was no way of seeing him other than to go boldly to his front door and ask for him. But she didn't feel equal to making that effort now, for Miss Honeysett was a tartar. There was, however, always the Holy Family to fall back on.

So after school she went to them, not hitching or skipping, just walking. And when she knelt before them she found it was difficult to talk to them. Like everything and everyone else They had changed; They all had that "gone away" look that her da had. She tried to commence in her usual way, but it was no good. She said a "Hail Mary" and "Our Father" and a "Glory Be To God", but still her troubles would not flow. It was as if they were tightly locked within her and she had lost the key for their release. So she blessed herself, rose from her knees, and turned away, only to turn as quickly to them again, when her old self flashed through for a second as she implored "Do something, will you?" But their look of hurt surprise seemed to reproach her for her imperious demand and lack of faith, and her head drooped and she muttered, "I am sorry," and to placate them, she added, "Blessed be the Holy and Undivided Trinity now and for ever. Amen."

Almost immediately upon this the vestry door creaked, and Father Owen, with a handkerchief to his nose, walked towards the altar. He stopped and sneezed twice, reached the bottom of the steps, genuflected, went up to the altar, lifted the heavy cross and descended the steps again. And there, through his streaming eyes he saw Mary Ann standing immediately in front of the altar rails, and having no regard for the millions of germs that he was letting loose on the world, and on Mary Ann in particular, he flapped his handkerchief at her and beckoned her towards the vestry. He sneezed as he put the cross down, and turning to her said "Oh, I'm in a right bad fix, aren't I; but it sounds much worse than it is. You're back at school then, Mary Ann?"

"Yes, Father."

"That's good. Far better at school. And how's everything . . . all right?"

"Yes, Father . . . No, Father . . . No, it's not all right."

"Oh dear! oh dear! Come and sit down. Have you had your tea? Of course you haven't, you haven't been home yet. Well, I've a bit of chocolate here." He rummaged in his pockets, then exclaimed with astonishment, "I've eaten it. I remember now, I've eaten it."

"It's all right, Father," she assured him unsmilingly, "I've got some bullets in me bag." She indicated her school bag hanging at her side.

He said, "You're a clever girl to be able to save your bullets; meself, I'm a greedy hog and eat them as they come. How's your da?"

They were still standing looking at each other, but now Mary Ann's eyes dropped. "His . . . his arm's getting better," she said.

"That's good. He'll be as right as rain in no time and back to work."

"What work, Father?" Her eyes were on his again.

Father Owen, peering at her over the top of his glasses, thought: That was a stupid thing to say. She's right, what work? A sneeze gave him a little breathing space and he dabbed at his nose as he asked, "Has he said anything . . . what he wants to do or anything?"

"No, Father; but he keeps looking towards the farm."

"Then he'll go back to the farm."

"He says he won't . . . he can't."

"Mr. Lord'll give him a light job, never fear."

"Me da says there are no light jobs on a farm."

"That's true . . . well, what I mean is, it's heavy work farming."

"Yes, Father."

"Aye. Mm. Well . . . " Father Owen pushed his fingers through his thin hair. He was feeling in no mood to listen to troubles or to dole out advice. All he desired was to get his head down on a pillow; or one of his heads, for there seemed to be a dozen of them at the moment all spinning in different directions. But the child's face would haunt him if he left her in the air like this . . . bad stress to the man! He was always doing something to make her carry a weight much too heavy for her; yet poor fellow, it wasn't his fault this time. He was to be pitied. He took a fit of coughing and when it was over he said, "Oh this head of mine!"

"Does it ache, Father?"

"It does, it does. But as I was saying"—which he hadn't been saying—"your da's a fine man and he'll get a job. Anyway, I think he'll be glad to leave the farm for he didn't take to the manager, did he?"

"No, Father." Mary Ann's pleasure at the unsolicited compliment paid to her da was shining from her eyes. "But Mr. Ratcliffe's gone, Father," she said, "and Lena an' all."

"Gone?"

"Yes; he got the sack. He had a row with Mr. Lord."

Father Owen was genuinely surprised at this news. He had been speaking to Peter Lord only yesterday and never a word had he said about losing his manger. Oh, the conceit of the old boy! He wouldn't let on he was having labour troubles on so small a place. He must be finding the farm as difficult to run as his yard. . . . A thought suddenly entering the priest's head made it wag and sent his eyes flickering over the vestry, and when finally they came to rest on Mary Ann they were screwed up into small points of light. "Has your da got a good hand, Mary Ann?" To this faux pas he added, "I mean, can he write nicely?"

"Oh yes, Father. He does me homework for me . . . me sums and things, and he writes lovely." She paused—she had given herself away with a vengeance. But her uneasiness on this point was negligible—Father Owen wouldn't split to Miss Thompson. She swallowed and added, "He does write lovely."

"Does he now? That's good. Well, do you know what I'm thinking?"

"No, Father."

"I'm thinking he should go after a job where there's writing to do, but on a farm you know, buying and selling . . . a manager. That's what he should go after. Or something like that—perhaps an assistant to start with—for he's got a good eye for cattle, and but for the few years he spent in the yards he's been on farms all of his life. Now that's what I advise. Of course, it would have to be a little farm."

"But Father . . . " All her features were stretching away from one another in amazement at this suggestion.

"Now be quiet. I'm sure it would be the very thing. You see, Mary Ann . . . Come here." He pulled her down on to the polished form that usually seated the scrambling altar boys when changing their shoes, and taking her hand, went on, "Have you ever noticed it, Mary Ann, the way God works? If He wants to give you something He waits until you lose something. You see, everything in some way has got to be paid for. Do you know that, Mary Ann?"

"No, Father."

"Well, it has. It's ten to one your da would never have thought of using his head to earn his living if he hadn't lost his hand. Now do you see?"

Mary Ann's eyes, although wide, were not seeing.

"It's like this," said Father Owen. "Leaving things as they were, your da would have remained a farmhand all his life, and content to do so; but then there was the accident, although mind"—the priest wagged a warning finger at her—"God doesn't make accidents happen, you must remember that, Mary Ann. It's our foolishness and neglect that causes them. But when they do happen, in He steps and points out a way to bring happiness and contentment to the sufferer. Oh, I've seen it again and again. But of course it's no use His pointing out the way if we don't take advantage of it, is it?" He poked his head forward, and Mary Ann, beginning to see a dim light in the distance, said, "No, Father."

"It's up to us, Mary Ann, it's always up to us." Here Father Owen took another bout of sneezing.

Mary Ann counted eight atishoos with concern; he sounded as if he was going to blow his head off. He was bad, poor soul, very bad.

After his streaming eyes had been dried, Father Owen began again, but a little heavily. "As I was saying, farmers these days go to colleges and things, and that to my mind is a fanciful idea if ever there was one. Cows have given milk and lambs been born for many years now without the help of a college. And anyway your da could, if he gave his mind to it, pick up from books any added knowledge he wants, so why don't you ask him to have a shot at it, eh? Tell him not to aim at too big a farm, mind." He turned his head a little to one side and glanced down at her. "But one a bit bigger than Mr. Lord's . . . that's very small." His nose wrinkled at the smallness of Mr. Lord's farm.

Mary Ann could not find it in her heart to be annoyed with this beloved friend who was also . . . bad, but her tone conveyed slight censure as she said, "It's a nice farm, and not really little, not like a . . . smallholding. And it's bigger than a pigery, isn't it?"

Father Owen could not, of course, follow these comparisons, but he said, "No, no, of course not," to the first part, and "Yes, yes," to the second; then went on, a trifle wearily, "There it is, that's what I advise your da to do. You needn't tell him I said so. Just put it in your own way and you'll see it will work out all right. Now, Mary Ann, my head's bursting and I'm going to me bed this very minute. . . . Do you feel any easier about things?"

"Yes, Father. I do, Father."

And it was true. she did feel easier. There was a surging of the old excited feeling in her stomach. What she wanted now was to get to some place quiet, like bed, and think. So she said, "Good-night, Father. And I'll say a 'Hail Mary' to Our Lady to look after your cold for you."

The priest was laughing now as he cried, "I don't want her to look after me cold, you stipulate that I want to get rid of it. Get on with you, now, home to your tea, and don't worry. Leave everything to God. Good-night."

"Good-night, Father."

He watched her for a moment from the vestry door, and as he turned away he put his hand to his head. What had he done this time? To put an idea into the head of that child was like supplying her with a bomb. Ah well, it was done. He only hoped that when she held the explosive under Mr. Lord's nose and put the match to it he would descend to earth again whole, which was asking for a miracle.

.   .   .   .   .

Mary Ann was feeling considerably better, for her mind was working. It was tackling a problem. She lay staring into the darkness. The house was quiet, but it was an uneasy quiet. No sound came from Michael behind the curtain, and across the landing the unrest was even greater, making itself evident by its complete stillness. There was no dim whisper of murmuring voices, not even a creaking bedspring or a cough. . . . The morrer, her da was going to tackle Mr. Lord finally. He had said so. And this was enough to cause her concern, for she knew that, left to themselves, the interview would not be successful—her da wouldn't knuckle under even in pretence to Mr. Lord. Without somebody, as she put it to herself, doing something, they would get on at each other.

She was also fully aware that the relationship between herself and Mr. Lord had shown little improvement; not even when she was bad had they got on to the old footing. He had been nice to her and sent her flowers and things, but he wasn't the same as when she had first come to the farm. No; he had wanted her to do something and she hadn't done it, and that had made him get his . . . back up. Also she was aware that she could not approach him using her old tactics; they would not carry weight with him now. Some new way, she felt, must be found if she was to carry out the scheme thought up by the Holy Family and suggested by Father Owen.

With a matureness beyond her years and accepted without question, she now realised that any success she could hope for with Mr. Lord would best be brought about by a frontal attack. As she so plainly put it to herself in the darkness: Tell him straight what you'll do for him if he'll do something for you. That was to be the strong structure of the scheme— exchange. What the exchange would mean to her she did not dwell on. First things first. If her da was settled, then her world would be all right . . . somehow.

She left for school as usual the following morning, but alighted from the bus at Pratt's Lane. This daring act alone made her knees weak, for she was about to play truant, and although she would tell Miss Thompson she had felt bad again and couldn't come to school, there was still Confession to be faced.

The door of Mr. Lord's house was open, and outside on the gravel drive was a car. It was painted blue and had a big dent in the mudguard, besides which it had no top. She had seen this car before. Only last night when she was going down the lane home it had come up from the farm. Why it should cause her uneasiness she didn't know, but it did. Ben explained the reason. He was mounting the stairs when her "Psst!" halted him. He actually came down again and asked how she was. His face wore his habitual look of disapproval but his voice had a touch of kindness. "And how's your Father?" he enquired.

"He's not bad," she said. "Mr. Ben"—this was the title she had bestowed on him since Christmas—"Mr. Ben, is The Lord with somebody?"

Ben nodded. "He is. He's interviewing a young fellow who's after the farm manager's job. And there's another one due any minute. I wouldn't trouble him this morning . . . he's very busy."

"Oh!" The bottom dropped out of her world. Her bright shining scheme became like a much-used comic . . . dull. Even the abrupt opening of a door to a room she had never entered and the appearance of Mr. Lord himself did little to lighten it. But immediately the owner of the blue car appeared in the doorway the scheme took on a glow again, faint, but nevertheless a glow. The young man wore knee breeches, polished gaiters, a lovely tweed coat, and he carried a short stick. Anything so unlike Lord's farm could not be imagined. Mary Ann's innate sense of fitness told her that he looked . . . too swanky. And soon, also, she sensed the Lord's reactions, for his leave-taking of the man was peremptory, while the owner of the blue car was all but condescending.

Mary Ann's presence at that time of the morning caused Mr. Lord some surprise. He came back from the hall door before the owner of the old and battered but still impressive Jaguar had gone on his way.

"Hullo, what are you after, eh?" His tone was kindly, as if she was still sick.

"I want to talk to you."

There was an exchange of glances between the old servant and his master as they remembered that these were the the very same words she had spoken early one morning in this hall some months ago. Mr. Lord peered down on her. This was not the cheeky imp who had demanded audience with him that morning. This was an older Mary Ann, if a frailer one. He felt a strange longing for the battling, intrepid fighter, the loyal liar; and his tone was kind as he voiced his refusal. "I'm busy this morning, I've got someone coming."

"It won't take a minute . . . well, not long." Sincerely she prayed that it wouldn't take long.

Mr. Lord cleared his throat. "Why aren't you at school?"

"I told you, I wanted to talk to you."

There was only one thing that she would want to talk about, and he was in no mood to hear talk of Shaughnessy this morning. "Later perhaps," he muttered, and was visibly startled at the keenness of her perception when she said, "It isn't only about me da."

"No, then?" he asked. "What is it?"

"Well . . . " She hesitated. Ben was still standing there, and as her eyes involuntarily slid to him, he grunted and departed. Mr. Lord, glancing at his watch, said, "Only a few minutes, mind."

She trotted after him into the room he used as an office, and the lumber of books and papers that met her eye took her interest for a moment from the vital matter in hand. She stood looking round as Mr. Lord seated himself at his desk, and when he said, "Well, what is this you have to tell me?" she turned to him and said, "You want cleaning up."

"What?"

She waved her hand round the room. "It's mucky. Me ma would soon do it for you, she's a . . . "

"Yes, yes. Leave the room alone. What is this you want to say to me?"

She turned to his desk, and, standing at the side, lifted up a sheet of paper from the top of a pile of letters.

"Put that down!" His hands snatched the letter from her. "Now, what is it you want?"

He was in a bad temper. If he got in a stew just because she touched his papers what would he do when she asked him about the farm job?

"Well?"

She looked up into the pale-blue eyes. They were the colour of the glass vase on the cottage mantelpiece, the one you couldn't see through. "Do you still want me to go to that school?"

Mr. Lord made no immediate answer, but the swivel chair moved slowly round and brought him to face her.

"I'll go if you want me."

There was not the slightest change in his expression. "Since when have you wanted to go?"

"Since last night, in bed."

"Why?"

"'Cos I want to go . . . if . . . "

"Yes?"

"Well, if I do something for you, will . . . ?"

"Will I do something for you?" he ended tersely.

"Yes."

Mr. Lord drew in his breath and his head moved slightly. "You don't think I'd be doing something for you by sending you to this school?"

"No—I mean—not what I want."

"Then you don't really want to go to this school?"

"Yes . . . yes, I do."

"Why are you willing to go?"

"Because you want me to."

He leant a little towards her. "You would go to please me?"

"Yes . . . if——"

He sighed again. "If I did something for you?"

She could not find words to placate his tone, so she remained silent.

"What is it you want?" His voice was dull.

She stared at him. It had sounded quite an easy thing when in bed to say "I'll go to this school on condition that you make me da manager," but now the enormity of the request assumed its rightful proportions and she knew that the bargain was quite unequal; in fact, she didn't think she could bring herself to ask it.

"Well—come on."

Her tongue was sticking to the roof of her mouth, and there it would have remained for some time no doubt had not the jangling sound of the front-door bell released it. That ring she knew was the . . . other fellow, so, gulping, she began, "Me da must have a job. He wouldn't be happy anywhere else but on a farm, for he's grand with animals as you know. But now he can't use his hands . . . only the one. Mr. Ratcliffe didn't use his hands either; he never dirtied his hands. Me da said he was a book farmer and a hard day's work would have killed him. Me da's cleverer than Mr. Ratcliffe. He writes a good hand an' all, and he said last night he was going to . . . to . . ." She stopped. Where was it Father Owen said some farmers went? School? No, college.

Mr. Lord hadn't moved, but his expression had changed for the worse and Mary Ann's voice had a distinct tremble as she continued: "To college or some such, where they learn to be managers." Her voice was small now. "There, that's it."

Mr. Lord's colour had deepened and his brows were aiming to reach his pursed lips as he growled, "What are you asking? That I should make your father manager of my farm?"

The "my" carried a weight all its own, and Mary Ann's voice reached a croak as she said, "He'd be a fine manager, and its only a little farm—bigger than a smallholding though—but me da would work hard for you and I'd go to school for you and everything'd be all right."

"Who put this idea into your head—your father?"

"No—he knows nothing about being a manager." She stopped; she was getting into deep waters, her father was supposed to be going to college.

"Father Owen?"

"Father Owen?" she repeated, as if for the first time in her life she had heard the name. "Father Owen? No. I went to church and I prayed . . . "

"All right"— he held up his hand abruptly in protest—"that's enough. Now"— he pushed back his thin shoulders—"go along and forget all this business that you've hatched up. School and farm included. It's out of the question."

"But——"she moved nearer to him.

"That's enough." As they stared at each other a tap came on the door.

"What is it?" He looked towards Ben.

"Mr. Dukes, sir."

"Show him in. . . . Now, off you go." His manner of dismissal was neither of his usual ones. There was no flaring temper nor was his voice barking, it was quiet, but not kindly quiet. It left no vestige of hope that might guide her back to a point from where she could resume her attack; there was a dead finality about it.

As she went out, Mr. Dukes came in, and had she been possessed of hope it would have fled on the sight of the sturdy workaday-looking man. She could see this one on the farm, and coping.

The hallway was empty and she stood amidst its dim dustiness and gnawed at her thumbnail, and as she gnawed the tears came. Slow, painful tears; tears for her ma when she had to leave the cottage; tears for their Michael, unsettled once again and morose; but most of all there were tears for her da and the sadness piled up within him. She heard the creak of footsteps on the landing above and she moved back and stood in the dark corner by the panelling that flanked the broad stairs. Ben came downstairs and went into the kitchen, but she did not move towards the hall door. Whether by accident or design she was standing right opposite the office door and she could hear the voices in the room rising and falling. But from where she stood it was impossible to hear what they were saying, so she cautiously moved nearer, taking the precaution to hold her nose so that she wouldn't sniff. Her head bent to the keyhole, the voices came as clear as if she were in the room, yet what they were saying was like a foreign language to her, and not really connected with the job for a farm manager. And most distressing of all, the voices were friendly. First the man's, talking about pigs at twenty-eight shillings a score. She knew what a score was—it was twenty, so that meant you could get twenty pigs for twenty-eight shillings. and twenty hundredweights of protein, the man said.

They were talking like sums at school, and then Mr. Lord's voice. "Seven shillings a week on wages," he was saying, "and it won't stop there." "Land Race. They were the ones," the man said. Then, "wheat at twenty-two and eightpence, with a good fertiliser. . . . And a sprayer attachment." Mr. Lord's voice, quiet now, saying it wasn't paying its way. Then no more from Mr. Lord, and the man going on and on. Potash, nitro-chalk, winter feed. Then the miracle. He kept on about the miracle. Mary Ann never knew that miracles were needed to get milk from cows, but apparently they were, and they were attached to a bucket milker.

The voices droned on, mostly the man's, but both were still friendly. They even laughed together. The sound of the laughter must have dulled her senses for she was unaware that the voices had ceased, and the next thing she knew was that the support of the door left her and she was on her knees with a pair of feet on either side of her. Her startled glance darted from one set of boots to the other. Then an exclamation from the man drowned by a roar from Mr. Lord shot her to her feet, and without raising an eye to either of them she was off and out of the door and down the drive. As she ran, panting, towards the gate, the bus passed, then stopped, and when she reached the road the bus conductor called, "Come on, divvn't hang aboot."

She got on, assisted by his hand on her collar, and not till she was seated did she realise that she was bound Jarrow-wards. And she didn't want to go to Jarrow, someone might see her and ask her why she wasn't at school. But it was done now. She could, she decided after some thought, go to Mrs. McBride's till dinner time, and perhaps she would get a bite of dinner there as she would miss her school dinner. This settled, she left the bus, not at her usual stop, but near Burton Street, to where she slowly made her way.

It was unfortunate that ouside Mackintosh's shop at the corner she should come across a number of under fives playing the game of mothers and fathers. It was a different version altogether from her own in that they had a live set of twins to give authenticity to the game. These were being forced, at the hands of a distracted four-year-old mother with a running nose, to sit on the cold pavement, but, as the twins were the ripe and obstinate age of two years and one had a large rent in her knickers which made contact with the pavement still less desirable, a howling match was in progress.

Mary Ann, with time on her hands and unable, even at this stage of mental unrest, to pass anyone who so obviously stood in need of advice, stopped to add the wisdom of her years to the slight knowledge of the new mother. And she was doing it quite effectively when her arm was caught in an extremely tight grip and she was swung about to face, of all people at this time of the morning, Sarah Flannagan.

"What you doing here?" Sarah glared at Mary Ann, and any feeling of sympathy that the general attitude had forced her to show towards Mary Ann was swept away by the sight of her enemy, apparently herself again, playing happily in the street in school hours, and, what was more, in their street!

"Mind your own business," said Mary Ann quietly.

This polite reply, it must be admitted, was mainly due to surprise, for of all the people she would wish to avoid this morning, Sarah Flannagan came first.

"Pretending you're bad," said Sarah, "and playing in the street."

"I'm not."

"You are."

"Well, what you doing?" said Mary Ann, still quietly. "If you weren't out playing you wouldn't see me."

"I'm not out playing, so there, clever cuts. I've been about me teeth, to have a wire on. See?"

Sarah let Mary Ann see. She bared her teeth and pushed her face down to Mary Ann's level, and Mary Ann, after gazing wide-eyed at the row of large uneven teeth banded by wire, turned away and gave a vivid and audible imitation of vomiting, whereupon Sarah advanced upon her, crying, "You! get back to where you belong, the pigsties. Me ma says you won't be long there either, you're all going to get the push."

"What!" Mary Ann rounded on her, her old self flashing into life now that her family once more were being attacked. Her body stretched, her chin jutted, and she cried, "You! You and your ma! You know nothing. I wouldn't be found dead in the same back lane. You're jealous because of our fine house; and me da, fine and respected. . . . "

"Oh my good garden cabbage!" This was Sarah's equivalent, of "God in Heaven!" or "God Almighty!" exclamations which were strictly forbidden by Mrs. Flannagan. But Sarah put so much into the words that they took on the strength of blasphemy and enraged Mary Ann still further. She flew at Sarah, knocking the temporary mother of the twins on to her bottom in her rush, and standing so close to Sarah as almost to touch her, she barked up into her face, "You'll get the shock of your life, you will, you'll see! Me da's going to be a gentleman—a real one—a manager, and run a farm, and carry a stick and wear shiny leggings. And I'm going to be a lady, I am, a real lady, and talk nice. So stick that up your neb and blow your nose!"

Mr. Lord need not have mourned the loss of the battling intrepid fighter; she apparently had been merely sleeping. Mary Ann suddenly felt better, much better. Joined now to her yelling was the yelling of the twins, the shouts of the pretending mother and the four other accessories to the family tree. The noise having gone beyond the usual limit, the shop door was pulled open and two women appeared, one being the mother of the twins, the other Mrs. McBride.

"In the name of God," cried Fanny, "is it another war? Hallo, Mary Ann," she said in surprise, "what you up to?"

"It's her," Mary Ann's voice was drowned by the cries of the real mother and her offspring, but her finger, pointing at Sarah's now retreating figure, made everything clear to Fanny, who exclaimed, "Aye it would be."

The mother of the twins being totally blind to her children's smell, dirt and general ugliness, was now embracing them and bestowing on them such adjectives as beautiful and lovely. And as she trailed them away on one side of the street, Mary Ann and Fanny walked down the other, and as they went, Mary Ann, docile now, told Fanny she was playing truant.

"And why?" asked Fanny, definitely puzzled.

"I can't tell you outside," said Mary Ann.

Once inside Mrs. McBride's odourful kitchen, Mary Ann proceded to tell why she was off school. The telling of it was a little mixed, but this much was clear to Fanny, the child had the nerve of the devil. She may have had a shock over Mike's business, but it had deprived her of nothing, least of all her nerve, that she could see.

"You asked him to make your da manager?" she said. "Be God! you've got big ideas. No wonder he sent you packing. What made you think your da could do such a job; it takes Mike all the time to manage hissel'?"

"It doesn't. He could . . . he could do it fine; anything fine." Now her head was jerking and Fanny, her great hand making conciliatory motions in the air, said, "All right, all right. Don't shout. I'm not saying a word against your da. You know I wouldn't. I'm the best friend he's got, for that matter, but there's limits to all things. It was a miracle he got the job and you know it was, and now you're expecting not only a miracle but a visitation. Be God! child, don't you realise that old Lord's no fool, no yard owner is, and if he's taken a farm it's to make money. And although I know nothing of farms, even if me grannie did keep a pig and ten ducks in the back-yard until some delicate-nosed neighbour kicked up a stink. I know this much: the way they run farms these days takes a headpiece. You've only got to look at the milk bottles with their 'pasteurised' and their 'T.Ts' to know that behind the cow there's brains."

"Me da's got brains."

"He has, he has an' all, and I'd be the first to admit it, but there are brains and brains, and you need a special kind of brains on a farm. And what about this being a lady? Are you going to that school?"

"No, not now."

"Well, it's just as well as I see it. I can't see you settling in a place like that. You're not cut out for it, hinny," she patted Mary Ann's lowered head. "You're too like God made you, and I wouldn't like to see you spoilt. No, hinny, stay as you are; don't let them put any artificial manure on you, an' all."

"Mrs. McBride."

"Aye?"

"What's me da going to do?"

Fanny looked down on to the still bowed head, and after a moment she said, "I don't know, hinny. But do as I do, don't worry. Leave it to God, and He'll see you're all all right, as He has done me." She looked round her room; it was full of the remnants of furniture battered and torn by children's hands and feet. No one could have been persuaded to take the lot as a gift, yet their possession and the memories they stored were, to Fanny, gifts from God; and in these gifts she was happy.

"Let's have a sup of tea," she said. "Eh? It'll get your old spunk up. Come on, wash up me cups and don't worry no more about your da. He's like the cats, he'll fall on his feet."

"Why," asked Miss Thompson, "weren't you at school this morning?"

"I was sick."

"You weren't sick."

Mary Ann stared back at her teacher. Sarah had got her oar in.

"You'll get your mother to write me a note and bring it to me in the morning."

"Yes, Miss Thompson."

Mary Ann had expected much worse treatment than this, for Miss Thompson was a hard nut. The light sentence made her buoyant; and at play-time she boldly went up to

Sarah and said, "So, clever stick, you thought you'd get me wrong with Miss Thompson. Well, you didn't. She said it was all right. And she asked after me ma. You're so sharp you'll cut yersel' one of these days."

Mary Ann had completely recovered.

Sarah's retort was stifled by the appearance of the teacher, but her look said, "You wait," and Mary Ann, correctly interpreting the look, was not surprised when school was over to see a reception committee waiting for her outside the gate.

Accompanied by Cissie and Agnes, she was met by Sarah and four of her friends. They too had forgotten that only last week they had said, "Poor Mary Ann's da." Now Mary Ann Shaughnessy was once again a cheeky thing and a big liar, added to which she was getting swanky. They allowed the three of them to pass, then in a concerted chant they sang,

> *"Pig-sty Annie,*
> *Snout in trough,*
> *Tongue too long she'll bite it off."*

But this was not strong enough to turn Mary Ann about. What was more, she was remembering her mother's caution against fighting, a caution she had completely overlooked earlier in the day. So, with an exaggerated wobble of her small lips, she marched down the street flanked by her two aides. Not even when the chant became decidedly vulgar, dealing liberally with the anatomy of a cow, and comparing the same with Mary Ann's face, did she turn.

This aloofness was much too much for Sarah, and drove her to resort to the lethal weapon of Mike. After running to get closer to the tormentor of her dreams and flesh, Sarah yelled to her own cronies, "Do you know something? Me da's a grand man. He gets bottled up every Saturday night and dances in the street; and he's had the sack umteen times and he's going to get the push again."

Before she finished Sarah had gained her objective; Mary Ann had turned. But, against all procedure, she did not retaliate with her tongue—the cruelty of Sarah's words stilled her own but aroused such a protective passion in her for the maimed hero of her world that had Sarah been as large as an elephant she would still have attacked her.

In the mêlée that followed, when she found herself pinned against the lamp-post with her feet alone free, she used them, and for every blow she received across the face and head she gave Sarah one lower down, until her legs too were caught and held by one of the enemy.

"Now we'll see," cried Sarah, hopping on one leg and glaring into Mary Ann's flaming face. "I've got you now, and I'll give you something you won't forget . . . you and your da! the big, dirty, drunken lump . . . Manager indeed! There, take that! A gentleman with gaiters! And that and . . ."

"Stop it at once!"

The children all turned their eyes towards the kerb from where the harsh command had come.

"Get away, you hooligans!"

As they saw the old man make to get out of the car, Sarah and her army got away, leaving a stunned Mary Ann and two equally stunned followers.

Mr. Lord, on the pavement now and waving his arm towards the car, cried, "Get inside!" However much he may have been concerned for her it certainly did not show in his voice, or yet in his expression.

Mary Ann staggered into the car, but once on the seat she turned and looked at her dishevelled supporters, and in a small voice, she asked, "Can they come an' all? Will you drop them?"

"No!"

With a feeling of having deserted her wounded comrades Mary Ann was driven away, and not until the car had left Jarrow did Mr. Lord speak, and then only in the nature of a growl.

"You are a hooligan," he said.

Mary Ann did not attempt to defend herself. she was too concerned at the moment with the condition of her face, which seemed to be growing larger with every second. Her whole head pained and throbbed, and only strong control and the knowledge that Mr. Lord had no use for bubblyjocks stopped her from crying. But even the desire to cry was forgotten when Mr. Lord, pulling the car into the side of the road, stopped it, and turning to her said, "I want to talk to you."

She lifted her swelling eyes up to him. There was something wrong here, for that was what she always said.

"Are you listening?"

"Yes."

"Do you know what you asked me to do this morning?"

"Yes."

"Well, I'm going to do it."

Her eyes like pop-alleys devoured his face; then, "You are?" she whispered.

"Yes; but on my conditions."

She did not ask what these conditions were but waited without a blink of an eyelid for him to go on.

His brows beetling, his whole expression forbidding, he continued, "I'm going now to offer your father the post that you asked for him, but he's not to know that you suggested it, or that you offered to go away to school. Is that clear?"

Slowly she nodded.

"Is it quite clear?" he asked.

"Yes."

"What have you to do?"

"I . . . I haven't to let on to me da that I got him the job."

"Not ever," he said.

"Not ever," she repeated.

"And you haven't to mention going away to school. . . . But you are going away to school," he added with emphasis. "Don't forget that, mind."

"No," she said.

"But you are not to mention a word of it yet. In a few days time you can suddenly make up your mind that you want to go . . . you understand?"

"Yes."

"Are you quite sure now?"

"Yes, I'll suddenly say, 'I want to go to that school 'cos I want to learn French and things.' And I'll say it's—it's because I want to be like or better'n Lena Ratcliffe and show Sarah Flannagan a thing or two. That would do, wouldn't it?"

"Yes, I suppose so; something like that."

Mr. Lord mopped his brow and leaned back in his seat. All this business was very tiring; it had been a tiring day altogether. If anyone had told him first thing this morning that by this evening he would have come to the decision of offering Mike Shaughnessy the management of his farm he would, to say the very least, have termed that person mad. And here he was, not only proposing to offer Shaughnessy the job, but manoeuvring it so that he would be more likely to accept it, for he knew the man sufficiently by now to understand that were he to offer him the post because the child had asked it he would be just as likely to refuse it—he knew he had been given his present job solely for the child's sake, and in a man of his calibre, it had rankled. And now, should the stubborn, pig-headed red-head, through any pretext whatever, dare to turn down the offer he himself was mad enough to make, the refusal would take the form of a personal defeat, and at his age he felt he would not be able to stand such a defeat.

He was becoming vulnerable; he needed people; this child, the warmth of her; he needed the occupation that her future moulding would take. But it wasn't only his need that had brought about the present crazy state of affairs, it was the events following on each other from early this morning; those two fellows who had come after the post, one a nincompoop, the other knew too damn much . . . he was a walking encyclopaedia who would be out to renew every item of the farm starting from the chickens and the byres to the combiner and the bull; and then later the incident on the farm . . . the men coming and asking him to keep Shaughnessy on and they'd level out the work. He had put a flea in their ears and asked who said he was going to dismiss Shaughnessy at all, and they had gone off looking a bit silly, and leaving him feeling equally silly, for he had placed himself in a difficult position. . . . What was he to do with the man? And all the time in the back of his mind he knew. And he knew it would give him a kick to do it. He also knew that Shaughnessy would be his for life after such an offer. It had always been his policy in the yards to give a difficult man a little responsiblity. It had nearly always worked, and it would work again this time; that is, should Shaughnessy think the proposal came solely from him.

He looked down again on the gaping child.

"Do you understand that if your father thought I was giving him this job because you asked me, he would refuse it?"

After a moment she said, "Yes . . . yes, I do."

"And you'll never mention a word that you came to me about it?"

"No."

"If you ever did it would make him unhappy and he would leave. Do you understand that?"

"Yes; I do understand."

He looked into her eyes. Yes, she understood all right. There was little concerning the man and his reactions that she did not understand. Abruptly he turned to the wheel and started the car, and as they moved off Mary Ann moved up until she was close-pressed against his side. And there she remained until they reached the crossroads, where he said, "Don't go in looking so pleased with yourself. You're a bad girl, don't forget. And I found you fighting." He cast a sidelong glance at her, which was joined by a knowing gleam in his eye. She straightened up, shuffled on her bottom along the seat, and endeavoured by adopting a pained expression to subdue the bubbling excitement within her.

So they came to the back of the cottage and stopped opposite the kitchen window. . . .

"Here he comes," said Mike over his shoulder to Lizzie, "and he's got her with him. . . . I suppose this is it. He knows he can't keep dodging me for ever." He turned from the window, characteristically bracing his shoulders back. Lizzie said quietly, "Be careful, Mike."

The request irritated him. He wanted to go for the old fellow, to say, "Look here, tell me out what you mean to do, I want no more of this cat and mouse business." But there were so many things to curb his tongue . . . a roof over their heads; the look on Liz's face; the lad going back into that quiet, secretive way of his. He did not bring Mary Ann into his worrying, for he knew whatever his fate she would remain the same, loving him, believing in him, his alone . . . no matter what the old boy tried to do.

It was towards her he looked when the door opened, and his eyes narrowed.

"What you been up to?" he demanded.

But before Mary Ann could answer, Mr. Lord, using his most truculent manner, said, "Fighting . . . in the gutter . . . like a hooligan."

Mike and Lizzie stared at Mary Ann, and she stared back at them before lowering her head.

"You should do something." Mr. Lord was addressing Lizzie. "Never seen anything like it . . . fighting tooth and claw . . . like animals."

"I've warned you," said Mike quietly, "haven't I? Get up to bed."

"Wait a minute," said Lizzie; "look at her face. How did it get like this?" she asked Mary Ann as she bent over her and took off her coat.

"Sarah Flannagan, with her hand," muttered Mary Ann.

"I'm going to put a stop to this once and for all," said Mike. "Get up those stairs."

He was making a demonstration for the old man's benefit, Lizzie knew.

"I'll have to wash her," she said softly. "won't you sit down, sir?" She pulled a chair forward.

"No, no," said Mr. Lord. "I only want a word with your husband."

Lizzie, casting a swift pleading glance at Mike, took Mary Ann's arm and propelled her into the scullery, and after closing the door behind them she asked, "Where did all this happen?"

"Near the school, Dee Street end."

Lizzie turned in the collar of Mary Ann's dress.

"It's got to stop, as your da says."

Mary Ann could not assent to this, for the wet flannel was over her mouth.

"Did he say anything to you about your da?"

Mary Ann closed her eyes before the flannel reached them. She had to, so that she wouldn't see the anxiety in her mother's face, for with a word she could send it flying away. This event, she decided, was not going to be at all like the time her da got the job on the farm. Her da and ma had then acclaimed her, and she knew she was clever. But now, when she had to make on she knew nothing about it, all the fun would be gone. Well, nearly all; there still remained the fact that her da would be all right. . . .

Mary Ann, washed and dried, sat on the cracket, and Lizzie made a great to-do with the few dirty dishes, clattering them unnecessarily to deaden the sound of the voices from the kitchen, for the fear of what she would hear was heavy on her.

Mary Ann was not even bothering to listen, for quite suddenly she was feeling dizzy and a bit sick; but when the door was pulled open and her da stood there, she got to her feet. But Mike did not look at her, he looked at Lizzie, saying, "Come in here a minute."

Lizzie, drying her hands, went into the kitchen. She looked in open surprise at her husband's face, it was as if he had been reborn. The Mike she had left a few minutes earlier had been a dull, sullen man; here was a man with a light in his eye, such a light as she had not seen for many a long day. And his whole body had broadened again.

"Liz"—he spoke to her, but he looked towards Mr. Lord—"Mr. Lord's going to give me the chance. . . . " He stopped and ran his hand over his mouth. Then he turned to her: "He's going to let me run the farm as a trial for the next six months."

Lizzie, bereft of words, her mouth slowly dropping into a gape, stared at Mr. Lord. Then she whispered, "Oh sir! oh sir!"

"It isn't all it sounds," the old man growled. "It won't be easy, I promise you . . . in no way. There's the men. They might be willing to help you keep your job, but it'll be a different kettle of fish when you're giving them orders."

"I'll do me best with them, and I'll work . . . I'll work, sir."

Lizzie had never before heard that tone in Mike's voice.

"And I'll get books and things. I can do it if I like, I know I can. There's one thing I can promise on my oath . . . you won't regret it. I'll work as never before. . . ."

"And keep sober?"

It was a direct shot, and Mike looked back into the old man's eyes for a long moment before saying, "I'll do me best there an' all."

Into the embarrassing silence that fell on the three of them came a revolting sound from the scullery. Mary Ann was in the process of being actually sick, and once more came into the picture.

11

THE LAST WORD

The whole school was stunned, weighed under the magnificence that was surrounding her. At least this was the impression that Mary Ann got, for had not her ma been to see the headmistress and told her she was going away to a posh school? And at dinner time her ma had met her outside the gates for everybody to see, and they had gone together to Mrs. McBride's . And her ma had taken a point end of brisket along, for Mrs. McBride liked to make broth with brisket. And she'd also given her a dozen oranges. And Mrs. McBride had pretended that it was all news to her what her ma was saying.

Eeh! it was a good job, Mary Ann considered, that she had remembered telling Mrs. McBride about going to Mr. Lord's and gone to her and told her not to let on. For the first thing Mrs. McBride would have done on meeting her ma or da would have been to joke about the nerve of her asking for the job.

After having looked funnily surprised for a long while Mrs. McBride had laughed and laughed, then hugged her. And she herself had felt a little appeased, for it was nice to have credit from someone.

The past four days had been odd, queer days. Their happiness had been outside her, not inside, not the kind of happiness she felt when her da thought her wonderful. Her da was happy, and her ma was happy, so was their Michael; they were going to move into the farmhouse. This last should have filled her with pure joy; but it didn't, for she would be living in the farmhouse, only now and again. At night times she thought about it all, and to the time when she would be going away, away from her da for weeks on end, with only swanky people to speak to, very likely all the same as Lena Ratcliffe. She knew she would die when she got to that school; but she should have to go. Everything must be paid for, that's what Father Owen said.

Poor Father Owen; he was in bed with his cold. She'd braved Miss Honeysett and called at the house every day, but old Bumble Bee wouldn't let her inside the door. But as soon as school was over for the day she was going again, and if he was up she would ask to see him, for she had so much to tell him; not least her latest decision with regard to her future state, for she had decided quite finally that when she was finished with this school she was going on the pictures. This, she had concluded, would be quite easy for her to accomplish, for although with every breath she drew she acted, she had not consciously done so up to the last four days; and more so the day before yesterday when her da had spoken to her before she went to school, saying, "Mind, I'm telling you, any fighting in the street and you're for it."

She had stood with her back to him looking towards the scullery door, and in that moment she had decided that the time was right to do as Mr. Lord has bidden her. So turning to him, she said, "Da . . . you know that school Mr. Lord wanted me to go to?

Well, I want to go." She remembered the look that came over his face, but she could not say even now if it was a vexed look, or a nice look. She had no name in her mind to pin it down, because it was a different look.

Mike himself could not have interpreted his feelings on hearing Mary Ann make her request . . . irritation, disappointment, a touch of the old anger, and, covering all, a feeling of anticipated loneliness filled his mind. He thought, Something like this would have to happen.

He had said weakly, "But why do you want to go, we are going into the farmhouse?"

This alone he had felt should have been attraction enough, affording her something to brag about for months to come; but her answer was, "Yes, I know, but I . . . well, I want to go to school . . . and . . . and talk nice."

"And talk nice?" The old revolutionary in him was up in arms for the moment, and then he thought: It's a chance; who am I to deprive her of it? If I'd had it things might have been different. But as he looked at her he couldn't imagine any school being such an inducement that it could compete with himself.

His eyes narrowed and his head lifted, and he asked quietly, "Has Mr. Lord been talking to you?"

Her eyes had opened wide, and she had replied, "Mr. Lord talking to me? What about?"

"You know," he said, "going to school."

Now Mary Ann had lied for him all her life, but she had never been able to lie to him. Something in his eye always brought the truth out of her; it was as if she had no power to be other than what he demanded. But now, with the intuition born of her love, she knew from his odd quietness and the look on his face that Mr. Lord was right—if her da should guess she was going to school in exchange for his job he would get into a rage and everything would be spoilt. She could see him going to Mr. Lord and their fighting; and the result would be misery for them all again. So she cocked her head on one side and gave the first conscious acting performance of her life.

"Only when he was in the kitchen that day," she said, "and he mightn't send me now, but you could ask him. . . . Will you, da? 'Cos you're always on to me about fighting, and I can't stop fighting where Sarah Flannagan is. She's always at me. And I'd like to talk nice, and show her."

Mike's eyes were back to their normal roundness, and he turned towards the fire, saying, "Go on now, we'll see about it later."

She had gone out, but her ma had followed her to the gate, and there she had buttoned up her coat; then she had kissed her, a hard kiss, pressing her tightly. The kiss was not the usual morning peck, and it sent Mary Ann down the lane thinking, not of her da, and his reactions, because she knew that he had believed her, but of her ma.

Before telling her mother that her teacher required a note to say she had been sick on the particular morning she had played truant, Mary Ann informed her that she hadn't been to school but had gone to Mrs. McBride's the excuse she gave being that it was dictation morning and she couldn't do dictation, and also that she was afraid of Miss Thompson. As both these statements in a way were true, she had not felt so bad about lying to her mother, but Lizzie had looked at her long and hard and, to her surprise, had not reprimanded her in any way, only tucked her in bed and said good-night. She had put this lenient attitude down to her ma's joy at the turn of events. Yet now she wasn't sure, for her ma had said to her the next morning, "Mind, say nothing to your da about staying off school and going to Mrs. McBride's." And she had said "All right," and thought: Just as if I would.

All told, she was finding the whole business disappointing. There was no excitement about it, only the excitement of knowing she was acting, and that Mr. Lord knew she was acting. So the conclusion was reached that she was destined to become an actress, after first, of course, becoming a lady at that school.

Miss Thompson's voice exclaiming, "All you for Confession," brought the future bang into the present. She had forgotten about Confession . . . Bust! And it'd be Father Beaney. And if she talked too much, he'd blow her up. Well, she decided firmly, she wasn't going to him. She'd march with the rest, go in and pay a visit, say a "Hail Mary" for Father Owen, then go and see how he was.

But alas, there was still Miss Thompson to be reckoned with. Under that teacher's gimlet eye, it was quite impossible to carry out her plan and, in due course she found herself kneeling outside Father Beaney's box and wishing that she was miles away, or that he was. Her preparation for Confession was orthodox, but not her entry into the box; for she went in in a spirit of defiance. Yet she emerged, as one should, chastened; she had made so many promises she couldn't see then being fulfilled until she was an old woman. Oh, Father Beaney . . . he got on your nerves; he wasn't a bit like Father Owen. Fancy him saying she must stop ro . . . romancing . . . she didn't do that, she only made on about things. And she'd had to promise that she wouldn't fight any more, either with her tongue or hands, and that she would love her grannie . . . Well!

In a state of very mixed feelings she made her way to the altar of the Holy Family, and there she said her prescribed penance. It was no use, she knew, getting on about Father Beaney to them, for she could see by the look in their eyes they were on his side. She'd only get the worst of it. She next prayed for Father Owen. "Make his cough better," she asked them. "And let him come out again; or let me in, 'cos I want to talk to him and tell him all that's happened. And thank you, dear Holy Family, for making all these fine things happen to us, especially to me da." The gifts she had received from their hands made her contrite, and she added, "I'll try to be a better girl, like Father Beaney said, and not fight with Sarah Flannagan ever again, or swank to her; and if I do, may I be struck down dead." There! She felt that that spirit of sacrifice should please them. "And dear Holy Family, will you make Miss Honeysett let me in so as I can see Father Owen? Glory be to the Father and to the Son, and to the Holy Ghost. Amen. Oh"—she was almost off her knees—"there's just one more thing . . . me grannie. She won't come near us now 'cos she knows everything's all right. But will you make me ma send me down to her so's I can tell the old . . . her . . . me grannie, all about everything?" Here she paused, and, when by neither sign nor feeling an answer came to her, she concluded that they weren't in favour of this request.

As if before some gentle rebuke, her head drooped, and she said dejectedly, "But it's no use, I can't love her. You know yourself what she's like."

Was it the sound of a chuckle that brought her head up? Well, it was something; and there, lo and behold, the whole lot of them were smiling. They were laughing about her grannie—they knew what she was like all right, better'n Father Beaney.

She rose from her knees, genuflected deeply, smiled broadly at them; then, in reverent tip-toe, she went up the aisle and to the door leading to the porch. Here she stood for a moment, wallowing in her holy feeling and pulling on her woollen gloves. Then she straightened her hat, for she must be tidy if she were to meet Father Owen. Dusting down the front of her coat, she slowly made her way up the porch, but before she reached the door she was checked by a voice, low but audible, coming from the street outside, saying, "Eeh! it's a wonder God doesn't strike her down dead. Me ma says that one of these days the heat from the devil in her will set light to the confessional box and she'll go up in blue smoke. D'you know what she's saying now—she's saying her da's been made manager and that she's going to be sent to a posh school and be made into a lady. Did you ever! The voice rose: "Her! . . . Me ma says you can't make a silk purse out of a sow's ear, she says. . . ."

Mary Ann had heard enough. . . . Silk purse out of sow's ear! She wasn't exactly sure of the meaning of this saying, but that it reflected detrimentally on her she was sure. So she took three majestic steps out of the porch and confronted Sarah and her solitary listener, and startled them both by exclaiming, "You can tell your ma you can make a silk purse out of a sow's ear, so there! What does your ma know anyway?"

Sarah, casting one devotional glance down the church porch, hissed quietly, "You're starting again, and you're asking for it, and if we weren't near the church I'd give it to you."

"You'll give me nothing," said Mary Ann, "that I won't give you back. And I am going away to a posh school, me ma came the morning, you saw her."

"I saw her come because you got wrong for not bringing Miss Thompson a note, and you couldn't ask your ma for it, 'cos she didn't know you were playing truant."

"It wasn't, you see; I had brought the note. . . . Oh! . . ." Mary Ann's eyes slowly mounted the grey stone of the church and reached the heavens; then descending earthwards again and seeming to have received a celestial message, she said with aloof dignity, "It's no use talking to you. As me da says, some folks is born numbskulls and some fall on their heads."

With this parting shot Mary Ann marched off filled with a righteous feeling. She'd got the better of that do and she hadn't fought in the street.

Sarah's "Oh . . . Oh!" followed her, and she had not gone more than a few steps before Sarah's footsteps were behind her. Expecting at least a dig in the back and knowing that she would be forced to retaliate, she fled from temptation by spurting the few extra steps to the sanctuary of the priest's front-door step, and, without waiting to turn round, rang the bell.

This action alone stayed Sarah's hand—the daring this enemy of hers had at times the power to bring on a stillness akin to paralysis. She stood stock still, gaping at Mary Ann, who had the temerity to knock on the priest's front door, and him bad!

The door opened and Miss Honeysett, looking like a replica of the avenging angel, stood there.

"Well?" she said,

"Can I see Father Owen, please?" asked Mary Ann in a small voice.

"No," she said.

"Oh; is he worse then?"

"No," she said.

"Is he up then?"

"Yes," she said

"And is he out and about?"

"No, he's not, he's not out of his room. And I'm sick of answering this door."

"My name's Mary Ann Shaughnessy," said Mary Ann in her politest tones, "and if you told him it's me he'd let me in."

Now Miss Honeysett became the avenging angel himself; she swelled, and wrath emanated from her. "He would not! nor is he going to see anyone for days. You'd kill him, the lot of you. And don't come back botherin'."

The door banged. There was a loud snigger from behind, and Sara, her face wide with glee, said, "Can I see Father Owen, because I'm the great Mary Ann Shaughnessy? And I'm going to a fine school, and me da' as manager . . . poloney!"

Mary Ann, stumped for the moment, could only retort: "Aw, you! you think you're clever. I'll get me own back on you, you wait."

"Huh!" said Sarah, grinning from ear to ear. "The only way you'll get you own back is when you spit in the wind."

At this utter vulgarity, Mary Ann tossed her head and moved off until she came to the alleyway leading to the presbytery back yard. Here an idea struck her, and, turning to Sarah, she gave one emphatic bounce of her head, gathered up some gravel from the gutter, which action caused Sarah to duck, then marched disdainfully up the alleyway.

.   .   .   .   .

Father Owen had had a very trying day, during which the theory of loving his neighbour, in the person of his housekeeper, had been severely put to the test. For as many years as he could remember she had been trying to nurse him; in fact, he suspected her of praying illness on him. And now her prayer in some measure had been answered, and she had him where she wanted him. . . . But for very little longer; tomorrow he was out of this, if he had to shoot his way out. He smiled wryly at the picture of himself, two guns at his hips, shooting at Miss Honeysett. God forgive him, she was a good woman—if only she didn't fuss.

He looked towards the window. Well, he supposed he should be thankful. It was a grey day and the March wind had a nip in it, and here he was with a nice fire and a comfortable chair. What had he to grumble about? What? He lay back and closed his eyes, and was soon dozing. And now his dreams began to repay him for all the trials of the day and his life in general, for had he not here, in his very hand, an envelope with three thousand pounds in it, and not a word from whom it was from, except to say it was for the restoration of his church? And Jimmy Connolly, him who was known never to have put more than a penny on the plate, and not that if he could get off with it, Jimmy had left six ounces of the best baccy together with a bottle of the finest Scotch on the doorstep, with the written injunction to take a good stiff dose of the latter to ward off a cold. . . . Oh, the kindness of people. You'd never think, never dream. Under the skin they were all kind.

It was at this point of Father Owen's dream, and for no reason whatever that he could see, except perhaps for the unpredictability of human nature, that Jimmy Connolly fired a gun at him; from the vantage point of the outhouse roof, he fired at him, clean through the window.

"In the name of God!" Father Owen sat bolt upright in his chair. The noise of the gunshot was so realistic that it took some seconds for him to realise that he had been dreaming. He pushed his hands through his thinning strands of hair. He had been dreaming all right . . . six ounces of baccy and a bottle of Scotch! Not forgetting the three thousand, of course. With a muttered exclamation of impatience he made to lean back again, when he was almost brought clean out of the chair by a loud "Ping! ping!" on the window and as near resembling the crack of a gun as to be one.

"Glory be! Somebody throwing stones at the pane."

Pulling himself up, he went to the window and peered down into the yard. But he could see no sign of the culprit, until a waving arm, coming from the end of the passage a little to the right of him, brought his eyes to Mary Ann.

Oh, it was Mary Ann. The child had come to see him. Well, well. He smiled and waved to her. What was she saying? With a stealthy glance behind towards the bedroom door and pulling the neck of his dressing-gown well up about his chin, he opened the window.

"Hallo, there, Mary Ann."

"Hallo, Father. Are you better?"

"Right as rain."

"I've been trying to see you for ages, and she wouldn't let me in."

"She wouldn't?"

"No."

"Just wait till I see her, she'll get the length of me tongue." This whisper just reached Mary Ann, and that was all. She leant her head back now and whispered up hoarsely to him, "A lot's happened, Father; I've piles to tell you."

"Go on then, tell me."

"Well, you know what you said about me da being manager?"

"Yes, I do, well enough."

"Well he is. Mr. Lord's made him the manager."

Now Father Owen's surprise was genuine and his tone so full of awe that Mary Ann was filled with gratification.

"Yes, and we're moving into the farmhouse."

Father Owen stared down at the child. She was a modern miracle factory if ever there was one. . . . Old Lord to do that . . . And why not, at all? It was the power of God working in him. And not before time.

"And you know something else, Father?"

"No . . . tell me."

Before Mary Ann had told him she sent a swift glance down the alleyway and her voice became a number of tones higher. "He's sending me to a posh school."

"He's not!"

"He is . . . a convent."

"No!"

"Yes . . . And you know some more?"

"No . . . go on."

"I'm goin' to be a lady and go on the pictures."

"Glory be to God!" said Father Owen.

"And," went on Mary Ann, remembering Sarah's saying which coupled the farmyard and the bag industry with herself. "Sarah Flannagan says, Father, that I'll not, she says you can't make a silk purse out of a sow's ear."

"Nonsense!" cried the priest. And then again, "Nonsense! You tell her from me you can; for was not I meself modelled out of one?"

"You were, Father?"

"I was . . . I was indeed."

"There you are then," said Mary Ann loudly to the world at large. "And won't me da be a gentleman, Father?"

Father Owen was not called upon to sin his soul further, for a voice from behind him crying, "Father!" brought his head in, and with a hasty wave and a wink to her he was gone.

Glowing now in triumph Mary Ann sped down the alleyway, and just in time to stay Sarah's ignominious flight. With the width of the pavement between them they confronted one another. A swarm of cutting remarks were tumbling over each other in Mary Ann's mouth, some fancifully embellished, some flowery, and some just plain statements of fact, but something in Sarah's face checked their flow and they stuck between her teeth; and to her profound amazement and horror, she found herself actually feeling sorry for this dire enemy, so much so that she almost contemplated going off without a word. It was the most disconcerting feeling she had experienced in the whole of her life; and was not under any circumstances to be encouraged, for should she go off without some pithy remark Sarah would think she had gone soft and would yell after her. And nobody, least of all Sarah Flannagan, was going to think that she had gone soft. So gathering all the remarks, fancy, flowery and plain, she tied them together and delivered them as a bouquet:

"Spit against the wind yourself!" she said, and marched off . . . unmolested.

. . . . . .

Do you believe all about everything now? You don't?

Well, it'll serve you right if nothing nice ever happens to you; it will so.

The Devil and Mary Ann

1

From her bedroom window in the farmhouse Mary Ann was surveying her kingdom for almost the last time. Below her lay a part of the garden. Late wallflowers were blooming in patches of red and yellow glory; but it was to the lank and dropping leaves of the daffodils that her eyes were drawn now, for they symbolised her feelings. She too was dying . . . she knew she was dying. Tomorrow when she left the farm and her da and ma and their Michael she would die. How could she live without them? Well, without her da? The separation from her ma would be a dreadful wrench, but being parted from her da would drain from her all her desire to live. Her nose gave a series of rapid twitches, and she admonished herself, "You'd better not start bubbling, your ma'll be up in a minute." Her large, brown eyes, that seemed to take up most of her elfin face, blinked and she moved her gaze over her kingdom. The huddle of the farm buildings making three sides of the courtyard; the foundations of the big, new barn to the right; the two farm cottages, one of which her own family had so lately occupied, bordering the road that ran past the farm gates; and away up the hill, behind the cottages, Mr. Lord's new house, standing as guardian and owner over all. Even this came into the realm of her kingdom. And it was her kingdom, bought for her da with her sacrifice.

Mary Ann's thoughts may not have literally taken this shape, but her feelings told her more plainly than anything else she could have done that for love of her da she had sold herself to Mr. Lord, and the price he had demanded of her was—education, and that was to begin to-morrow. In return, her da had been made manager of the farm. But her da, of course, did not know of this deal. Eeh! no; and he must never know.

The fact that her da was now manager of the farm where, a month age, he had been just a farm-hand, still had the aura of a miracle around it. And the miracle enlarged itself a thousandfold, when she thought back to the time, just a few months previously, when they had lived in Jarrow in two attics at the top of Mulhattan's Hall and her da had worked in the shipyard and was forever on the booze! Eeh! fancy thinking that. She shook her head vigorously to throw off the memory. Her da never got drunk, not really; he got sick a bit but not drunk. Everybody knew he never got really drunk; it was Sarah Flannagan who had started that lie.

Oh, Sarah Flannagan! A little spark of joy forced itself into the gloom in her small chest. Today, when she went to Mulhattan's Hall to say goodbye to Mrs. McBride, she hoped that the big, lying, cheeky cat would be in the street and she'd show her. She'd be all got up in her new clothes—she wouldn't fight with her; no, that was strictly out now—but she'd go up to her and say, "So you see, Sarah Flannagan, every blessed thing I said has come true. Me da is a manager, and I'm going to be a lady and talk swanky. So get that out of your crop if you can." Yes, that's what she'd say to her, all swanky like. Then she'd walk away with her head in the air.

It was going to be a busy day. She must go and see Father Owen an' all and pay a last visit to the Holy Family. Sadness settled on her again on this thought, to be abruptly swept away at the sight of her da. He had just come out of the cowshed and was walking across the yard with Mr. Jones. Her heart swelled with pride. He looked grand did her da; even with only one hand he was better and bigger than any man in the world. The thought of his affliction brought a flame of tenderness into her body. But he was managing fine. She stressed this point to herself, for whenever she consciously thought of the accident that had taken off his hand a certain part of her mind was attacked by a fear, and this she would press away, making no effort to ask the reason for its presence. Mike Shaughnessy had done a very good job in taking the blame for his accident from her young shoulders and placing it at the door of his own carelessness; in doing so he had sealed off effectively the remorse that would surely have turned her brain.

When her da got the hook for the end, he said his hand would be worth ten of any other man's . He had said that to her only yesterday, when she had gone to his office—oh yes; it was his office now—to tell him that dinner was ready. And he had stopped what he was doing with the books and suddenly lifted her on to his knee and held her close for a long time. Then Mr. Lord had come in, and her da had put her down and his face had gone all red. Neither of them had said anything, and this had left her with a certain uneasiness. Yet she couldn't understand why she should feal uneasy. But she always did when Mr. Lord came on her when she was with her da. When she had Mr. Lord all to herself she never felt like that; she could talk to him twenty-to-the-dozen, and make him laugh. But not when her da was there.

Her da was now making his way to the house and Mr. Jones was going towards his cottage. Mr. Jones looked littler than ever. Mr. Jones didn't like her. He never spoke to her, not since the time she had thrown a One o'clock Gun under his bed on Guy Fawkes Day and he had run out of his house in his pants like a mad man. That was the day Mr. Lord had laughed and her da had got mad at her, madder than he had ever been and said she was to have a walloping and Mr. Lord said she wasn't. That was the first time she had felt that funny something between the two of them.

She knocked at the window now and waved to her da, and Mike waved back, a wide wave of his great arm. And he was almost at the side gate when round the outskirts of the house came Mrs. Polinski, and she called to him, "Good morning." And he said back to her, "Good morning." And he stopped at the gate as she hurried up, and Mary Ann looked down on them.

Mrs. Polinski was blonde, but her hair wasn't like her ma's in a great bun at the back of her head and of a lovely colour like looking into the sun; Mrs. Polinski's was—tousey, and she wore it cut like a lad's, all over the place. But she didn't look like a lad.

Mrs. Polinski was always very nice to her. Yet Mary Ann, as she somehow put it to herself, didn't know what was up with her; some part of the child wouldn't come to the fore and meet the new farm-hand's wife on the terms she so liberally offered . . . let's all be bairns together. Mary Ann sensed an unnaturalness in this attitude. Mrs. Polinski was old; she was over twenty, and therefore past the age of acting the goat, and this included hop-scotch. Her da laughed at Mrs. Polinski when she played with her, but her ma said, if she was to go in and mend Mr. Polinski's coat and get a good dinner ready for him it would fit her better. And her da had said, "She'll learn."

Her da liked Mr. Polinski. He said that although a puff of wind would blow him over he could do double what Mr. Jones did, and he'd have a farm of his own some day and good luck to him. Mr. Polinski was from Poland but Mrs. Polinski just came from Dover.

She watched her now, laughing up at her da and her da laughing in return. Oh, her da did look grand. His red hair wa rumpled and his shirt neck was open and she could see the curly hairs on the top of his chest.

"Haven't you got your things on yet?"

She swung round to the door, and there was Michael, his expression this morning without its usual brooding seriousness and his voice unusually kind. Up to yesterday his greeting would have taken the form of, "Get a move on, you, or else you'll catch it," to which her retort would have been of the quality, "Aw, you! . . . nuts!" But on this last day of life her reply even touched on sweetness as she said, "I won't be a tick, Michael."

And she wasn't a tick, for she flung herself into her clothes—not her good ones; these wouldn't be donned until after breakfast and her usual scamper around the farm—and she was downstairs in a matter of minutes.

As if she hadn't seen him for weeks she leapt from the doorway into Mike's arms. Mike had just turned from Lizzie, who was at the stove, and as Mary Ann pulled his face round to her he finished saying to his wife, "You could teach her a lot . . . Polinski has a thin time of it on the whole. Why don't you take her under your wing, Liz?"

"You know my views. Anyway, we'll talk of that later."

This hesitation on her mother's part to talk of Mrs. Polinski was, Mary Ann knew without any undue hurt to her feelings, because she was there. But from the little she had overheard, Mary Ann's opinion of her own judgement took on a heightened glow. Her mother didn't cotton on to Mrs. Polinski either.

"Sit up . . . come on." Lizzie turned from the stove and brought her hand in an affectionate slap on Mary Ann's bottom, and Mary Ann, grabbing at Mike's neck, yelled, "She's braying me, da, she's braying me."

This causing them all to laugh, even Michael, Mary Ann ascended into her seventh heaven, while tomorrow sprang into the far future, leaving her all the day. Her ma and da were happy and laughing, joined by a band of love that she could almost feel. Their Michael was nice, and there, with an egg on top of it, was a thick slice of Irish roll for her breakfast, not half a slice, as was usual, and that, too, only after she had pushed down a great bowl of porridge.

After they were all seated and the grace said, in which Mike did not join, and had started to eat, the chatter suddenly ceased, and Mary Ann, in the middle of chewing on and relishing the superb flavour of a mouthful of bacon, felt her mouth drop open as she watched her mother rise quickly from the table and go into the scullery. Was her ma crying? . . . And then her da, his eyes fixed on his plate, stopped eating. And then their Michael, his cheek full of fried bread, gulped down some tea, and her ma had told him, time without number, not to drink while he was eating. Then almost as quickly as she had gone Lizzie came back into the room bringing bread with her, and there, before Mary Ann's eyes, was a plateful not touched already on the table.

The silence shrieked in Mary Ann's ears, becoming almost unbearable, and her innate sense of requirement told her that a diversion was needed, and a strong on. And without further thought she heard herself saying, "When I see Sarah Flannagan again I won't half tell her something. I'll say, 'Your da can't buy you clothes like this'."

"And your da hasn't." Mike's tone was flat and held just a thread of bitterness.

Mary Ann looked across the table into Mike's eyes, then turned her gaze to her mother. Lizzie was busy eating and did not raise her head. She had said the wrong thing—her da hadn't bought her clothes, Mr. Lord had, boxes of them. Well, two big cases full, right from vests to one black felt school hat and one grey one for Sundays. and her name was on everything—Mary Ann Shaughnessy. Her ma had sewed and sewed at them for days. Everything she had had been given to her by Mr. Lord, and her da didn't like it. She was daft for saying such a thing . . . she was daft, she was. The lump, coming swiftly from nowhere, blocked her throat, but past it struggled the words: "I don't want to . . . I don't want t . . . to. Oh, Da!"

"There! See what you've started." Lizzie was on her feet, pulling Mary Ann to her and pressing her head into her waist.

Mike, rising from the table, went to the mantelpiece and grabbing at his pipe, growled, "I'm sorry." And Michael, making the greatest effort of his life in an attempt at small talk, put out his hand and stabbed gently at his sister's shoulders, and in a not at all steady voice said, "Now I'll be able to get my own back on you, you were always chipping me about the Grammar School. But a Convent's worse. You'll be so swanky when you come back we won't know a word you're saying. You'll be all South Country."

Mary Ann's crying ceased, and with a shuddering sob she turned from her mother and answered Michael: "I won't then . . . so! Nobody'll make me swanky . . . will they? Will they, Da?"

Her voice brought Mike round to her, and over the distance of the long shining kichen he smiled gently at her and moved his head slowly.

"No," he said. "No. Make up your mind finally on that, at any rate. Let nobody make you swanky. . . . You still want to go?" He asked this quietly, yet his voice filled the kitchen.

Now Lizzie's eyes darted between the two of them, and she brought Mary Ann's to hers. What Mary Ann saw there stilled the truth hovering on her lips and reminded her forcibly of the bargain with Mr. Lord, and she said, "Yes, Da."

"You sure?" said Mike.

"Yes, Da."

They looked at each other until Lizzie could bear it no longer, and grabbing up the dishes with a clatter and saying as she did so, "Well, this a breakfast spoilt, I must say," she went into the scullery, and after depositing the crockery in the sink she leant against the table for a moment, one hand gripping the front of her blouse. What if the child had said no! He would, and like a shot, have put his foot down. And then, as like as not, the whole situation would have exploded.

Lizzie knew that Mr. Lord, thwarted of his ambition to educate Mary Ann, was not likely to treat Mike as he was doing now, even though Mike was carrying out the difficult task of managing the farm much better than she had imagined he could do. Both Mr. Lord and Mary Ann, she knew, were under the impression that they, and they alone, knew of the bargain between them, the bargain being that, if Mary Ann agreed to going away to school, her father would be given the change to run the farm. How it had all come about she didn't know, but certain circumstances that led up to Mike's appointment showed only too plainly Mary Ann's finger guiding Mike's destiny. Any faint suspicion Mike might have felt had been lulled by Mary Ann herself. Mike did not know Mary Ann as she did. Somehow his very love for her blinded his vision, and should it ever come out that he owed all his present success not alone to his ability but to his child selling herself—and that is how he would put it—away would go the farm and their life of security. She could even see him making use of the six months' trial which he was now working to bring their life here to an end in order to keep his self-respect.

Tomorrow night, when she left the child all those miles away in the south, near St. Leonards, she would she knew, leave part of her own life behind her. But even so, she was longing now for the moment to arrive when Mary Ann would be safely installed, when the worst part of this business would be over and the future of them all secure . . . well, as secure as anybody's future could be allowing for fate, in the form of the bottle which had doged their married life. But, strangely enough, at this moment Mike's weakness was troubling her least. It was Mary Ann's strength that was worrying her. Would it carry the child through these final stages? After all, she was but a child, she was not yet nine. She had only recently, Lizzie thought fondly, been a baby. Wasn't it too much to expect of her that she should be parted from Mike, who was the very breath of her life, when she had only to make a sign and he would say, "To hell with education! She doesn't want to go and she's not going."

Lizzie let out a long painful breath. If only it was tomorrow morning and they were on their way. The thing to do was to keep her occupied today, and away from Mike as much as possible without arousing any comment from him. And so, going into the kitchen now, she said briskly, "Well, what are you going to do?"

"Who, me, Ma?"

"Yes, you. Who else? I generally know what the rest of my family are up to."

Lizzie laughed, and Mary Ann said, with just a touch of importance, "Eeh, well, I've got a lot of people to see. I must go and see Mrs. McBride, and say 'Tara' to Agnes and Mary. And, oh, I must go and see Father Owen and . . . and who else?" As she pondered with her head on one side, Mike and Michael looked from her to each other, and nodding they both said together, mimicking her voice and manner, "And, oh, that Sarah Flannagan."

Laughter filled the kitchen again, and Mary Ann dashed from her father to Michael, crying, "Oh, you! you! Go on, you cheeky things, you." and into Lizzie's worry came a thin thread of happiness. That little action of Michael in joining his father in this bit of teasing warmed her heart. Perhaps with Mary Ann gone Mike would turn more to the boy, and Michael's brooding nature would expand towards him, and he would forget the past and look up to this man whom he so closely resembled.

"Well, that's settled, at least." Lizzie bustled about, while Michael took up his bag and after making brief goodbyes went off to school—his term had already started. And Mike, after kissing Lizzie, lifted Mary Ann up and looked at her hard for a moment, then held her close for another brief moment before going quickly out, leaving behind him a strained silence, into which Lizzie poured her words with an attempt at lightness.

"You needn't help me with the dishes this morning. Go on, put your good things on and then you can get off. And, oh, by the way"—her voice stopped Mary Ann at the kitchen door—" wasn't there somebody else you forgot to put on your visiting list?"

"Who, Ma?"

"Mr. Lord."

"Oh, but I'll see him in the morning."

"But only on the way to the station, and we'll all be in the car then, I would call in on your way back and have a word with him. Are you going to stay and have something at Mrs. McBride's?"

"No, Ma. I was coming back for me dinner."

"Very well, you can go to Mr. Lord's this afternoon then."

"But Ma, he might come here—he's been nearly every afternoon."

Lizzie turned her back on Mary Ann and went to the stove and said slowly, "Well, in that case I wouldn't bother him. He'll likely want to talk to your da, and they can never do business with people about. You understand?"

"Yes, Ma."

Soberly Mary Ann went upstairs, a weight pressing on her shoulders. She understood she wasn't to chatter and jump round Mr. Lord in front of her da. She understood all right; her ma needn't have told her.

2

Again Mary Ann was telling herself something for the very last time; she was sitting in the bus on her way to Jarrow. With newly awakened eyes, she looked out of the window. Never had she seen a field of rhubarb running in scarlet and green waves, nor the long, flat patches of land stretching away into the distance aboil with molten yellow. Even the great chimneys, sticking up like pipe shanks on the horizon, looked beautiful; and the gigantic, gear-bespangled gantries that reared up from the river were like fairy tracery edging and hemming in this beautiful world she was leaving.

A rainbow, actually appearing in the sky at that moment, filled her small chest with wonder. And when it stretched its magnet ends over Jarrow, Hebburn and Pelaw and lifted them clean up from the earth to suspend them in dazzling light, it was too much for her. Her nose started to run; she sniffed and choked and groped for her hankie in the band of her knickers, forgetting that she had on her best clothes. Then, retrieving the neatly folded handkerchief, one which bore her name, from her pocket, she was in the act of desecrating it when the real pupose of its presence on her person at all today came back to her, and gently she pushed it into its folds again, name up, and carried out the operation on her nose with her thumb, but covertly, for this procedure was most strictly forbidden.

On raising her eyes, she saw they were now passing the gates of Mr. Lord's house, and her head swung round to catch one last glimpse of them. They seemed to be guarding the entry to celestial bliss. Never more would she go up that drive . . . oh well, she might this afternoon, but that would be the last time, for when she came back for the summer holidays Mr. Lord would be living in his new house up at the farm.

The bus was now skimming past the grounds, past the hedge and the barbed wire through which she had once forced her way. But that was a long time ago, years and years— in fact, last summer.

The bus was moving now among the close-packed houses, and when she alighted at Ferry Street it was raining, pelting down, yet the sun was still shining, and the conductor said, "You'll have to run, hinny, or you'll be soaked."

Running had not been laid down in her plans at all for today; she was to walk to the top of Burton Street and then slow down, taking her time, until she came to Mulhattan's Hall, for everybody in Burton Street knew her, and they would stop her and exclaim in tones of admiration, that is, all except Mrs. Flannagan. "Oh, Mary Ann," they would say, "you do look lovely and I hear you're going away to a posh school. And your da's somebody now, isn't he? . . . eh? Manager of the farm and gives orders. Well, well." And here it was, raining cats and dogs.

She dashed from the bus into a shop doorway for shelter. But inactivity never being her strong point, she was soon out again and, hugging the walls, she ran as quickly as her legs could carry her along the street. This procedure she even had to carry out in Burton Street, where, but for three toddlers blocking up the water in the gutter with their feet and freshly compounded mud, there wasn't a soul to be seen.

She galloped up the steps of Mulhattan's Hall to the testy exclamations of, "Hang and bust it!" and as she stood shaking the rain from herself Mrs. McBride's door was pulled open and the aperture was almost filled by the great bulk of Fanny herself.

"Hullo there, hinny. This is nice weather to bring. Come on in, don't stand there dripping like a cheap umbrella. Come inside."

"I'm all wet, Mrs. McBride."

"Aye. Well, you've been wet. . . . But by, what a shame, and them your new things. Let me have a look at you." Stooping, Fanny held her at arm's length. "By! you look bonny, real bonny."

Mary Ann's soul was soothed. "Do I, Mrs. McBride?"

"You do, hinny. But there, get them off. It's a good job I've a bit fire on, for sun or no sun it's cold. and then we'll have a sup tea, eh?"

Taking Mary Ann's coat, Fanny hung it over a chair, exclaiming of its colour as she did so, "Never seen a bonnier blue—never. And your hat matches an' all. . . . Sit down and tell me all your news. How's Mike?"

"He's grand."

"Ah, that's it. There's a miracle for you, if ever. . . . And now for a cup of tea. And there's some griddle cake, I made it last night. . . . What's he got to say 'bout you going away?"

"Oh, he says——" Mary Ann stopped and looked at the enormous rump of Mrs.

McBride as she bent over the fire, placing the kettle into its heart. There was no need to pretend here. Mrs. McBride was the only person in the world with whom she needn't pretend; that was, with the exception of Father Owen, yet he being a close relation of God's was not in the same category as Mrs. McBride. Like God, she felt, the priest had an unfair advantage; he knew what she was thinking and was going to say even before she started . . . at least, Father Owen had this power when in the confessional.

Fanny turned from the fire and, slowly straightening her creaking back, looked at Mary Ann.

"He doesn't want me to go."

"Well, that doesn't surprise me. It would only have surprised me if it had been t'other way round. What does he say?"

"Nothing much."

"That's bad. Always is with Mike. . . . And—and Mr. Lord. How does your da get on with him now?"

"All right. Fine . . . well. . . . "

"Aye. . . . Aye well, we'll leave it at that then, eh? And you're going away in the mornin'?"

"Yes."

Fanny sat down opposite to Mary Ann and, stretching her arm across the table, patted her young friend's hand. "I'll miss you, hinny. I missed you when you left here, but now it'll only be the holidays I'll see you."

A furious tickling came into Mary Ann's nose, worse than in the bus, and with unblinking eyes she looked at Fanny and whispered, "I don't want to go, Mrs. McBride."

After a moment of staring at her, Fanny's fat seemed to flow back and forward above the area of the table. Then with a hitch to her bust she brought it to a standstill, and stated the fact that was already sealed in Mary Ann's mind: "You've got to—remember there's your da, and you're doing it for him. And you're going to be educated like you never dreamed. Just think what'd happen if you backed out now. Think of the old boy . . . he'd give everybody up there a hell of a time, because he thinks he's God Almighty himself, does that one. And you know who'd come in for the brunt of it, don't you?"

Their eyes held; then Fanny, after a significant nod, raised her encumbering body and went to the now spluttering kettle.

Yes, she knew all right. Mr. Lord would give her da hell. Eeh! she was swearing . . . but not really, only thinking. And if her da got upset he might go on the . . . get sick again; and then her mother would look like she used to, all tightened up; and their Michael wouldn't laugh, like he did a bit now. No she knew her fate was sealed.

Fanny turned towards the table once again, the great brown teapot in her hand. And now her face was split by a wide beam and her voice sounded eager and full of interest as she said, "Is it true, what your ma was telling me? You're booked to learn languages?"

Mary Ann, quick to take the cue, forced a smile to match that of this virile old woman whose wisdom was tempered with the hard experience of life, and resurrecting herself from the abyss of despair into which she seemed bound to fall at any moment, she said, "Aye, I mean yes . . . French and German."

"French and German! My God! it's a scholar you're going to be. By, won't that be like a kick under the chin for our dear friends?" Fanny leant forward and thumbed the window indicating the Flannagans' house across the street, and Mary Ann, her face now springing into glee, poked her chin up and pursed her mouth as she articulated, "And el-e-cution an' all."

"El-e-cution?"

"Yes, talkin' properly you know."

"No!"

"Uh-huh!"

"My, wait till she hears that. That'll drive Nellie Flannagan up the lum."

"An' I'll be a lady." Now Mary Ann was getting warm. "A real one, and talk swanky, and look down me nose."

Principles were being swept away on a wave of pride when Fanny's finger suddenly took up an admonishing position. "Ah, now! now!" The finger wagged. "You've got to watch out . . . you don't want this school to change you altogether, do you? For then you won't only turn your nose up at the Flannagans, you'll turn it up at me and your——"

"No, no. Oh! I won't. Oh! Mrs. McBride, no I won't. I won't ever turn me nose up at you." Mary Ann was deeply hurt by the suggestion.

"Ah well, time will tell." Fanny sighed and the smile sank from her face. "You want treacle on your griddle cake?"

"Yes, please."

Mary Ann, now on her feet, watched Fanny go into the scullery, and her thoughts once again slipped into despondency. The only consolation this going away to school offered was that she would learn to be a lady and talk swanky. But now, apparently, there were dangers even in that.

The rain had stopped, the sun was shining brightly, but a cloud had settled on Mary Anne's chest, bringing a feeling of sickness with it. She sat down and waited for Mrs. McBride's appearance, wondering if she could say she didn't want any griddle cake now because she was feeling sick. But she knew she mustn't say this, she mustn't hurt Mrs. McBride. She must eat the griddle cake, even if it choked her.

     .   .   .   .   .

It was eleven o'clock when Mary Ann reached the church. She was "full up" in more ways that one. She wouldn't see Mrs. McBride again for ages and ages. Mrs. McBride had lifted her up and held her, and she had cried and pushed a whole half-crown in to her hand, with strict orders to spend it, the lot. Her fingers now blindly picked up the half-crown from the coppers in her pocket. Mrs. McBride was kind, she was; and she liked her da, she did. Oh, she was going to miss Mrs. McBride.

The church was empty except for two cleaners, women with long pinnies on and their hair tied up with scarves. They were washing the walls round behind St. Anthony's altar. Some feeling told Mary Ann that cleaners were out of place in a church; the church should need no cleaning by mortal hand, some act of God should keep the dust down and the floor clean. Slowly she approached the altar of the Holy Family; then knelt down and glued her eyes on the group of statuary. For as long as she could remember she had come to the Holy Family with her troubles, and even, at times, remembered to come with her joys. And now for the last time she knelt before them, and as they gazed down on her they looked as sad as she expected them to be . . . they knew she was going all right. The Infant moved in His Mother's arms, and Mary hitched Him up closer to her and said softly, "Well, Mary Ann?" And Mary Ann replied, "Oh, Blessed Mother Mary, I don't want to go. Make something happen to stop me."

The Infant screwed round and looked down on Mary Ann, and Saint Joseph looked down on her, and Mother Mary herself. And they didn't say a word between them, until the silence yelled in Mary Ann's ears and she dropped her head.

Then the Virgin said, "Look at me, Mary Ann." And Mary Ann said, "You have given your word. Moreover, Mr. Lord has paid you in advance for your word. Do not let the Devil tempt you to break it, nor ask me to show him the way."

Mary Ann's head dropped still further now. They weren't nice a bit, and this was her last visit an' all. Eeh! what was she saying? Eeh! she was sorry. Eeh! it was a wonder Our Lady didn't strike her down dead. . . . She'd light a candle.

Still with her head bowed, she moved to the half-moon of candles that stood to the side of the altar rail and groping at the coins in her pocket she pulled out two, and still with lowered eyes, dropped them into the box. But as the second one left her fingers a cry escaped her that rang through the empty church and brought the cleaners from behind the altar . . . she had put in her half-crown!

A long time ago she had done something similar, but that had been only a sixpence. This was a fortune, a whole half-crown. She turned her back on the cleaners and looked accusingly up at the group above her. They had let her go and do it, and they were laughing—Saint Joseph's beard was moving. It was nothing to laugh at; and she wasn't going to leave it in, she wasn't. She didn't care. No, she didn't! Candles were only twopence. She wanted her half-crown back, and then she'd light one—two perhaps—but she wanted her half-crown back first.

Her thoughts gabbled in her head as she looked back down the church. She could see no signs of the cleaners now, they were well behind the altar. There was nobody here but herself. She'd get her half-crown out of the box, she would.

The box, she saw, had only a little lock on the lid. Little or big, she knew she couldn't hope to open it, but she could . . . tip it up, couldn't she? Without further thought of the right or wrong of her actions and momentarily oblivious to the combined condemnation of the Holy Family, she lifted the box from its setting. And when she held it in her hand the cold iron burned her fingers. Anyway it set a spark to her conscience and she exclaimed, "Eeh!" And again, "Eeh!" but conscience or no conscience, and "Eeh" or no "Eeh!" she was going to get her half-crown out. She only had to turn it upside-down, like you did with a money box. But where would she do it?

She looked around her. If she went in out of the pews the women might hear her, even if they were behind the altar. This last brought a most helpful thought into her mind . . . why shouldn't she, too, go behind the altar? They wouldn't see her or hear her there. And she'd get her half-crown out and slip the box back and no one would be any the wiser, except herself. And it would learn her to look at her money in future. Her ma was always telling her.

But even with the decision determinedly taken, she found it needed a great deal of courage to walk up the steps and go behind the altar of the Holy Family. And, once there, the purpose for her presence was temporarily swept aside by the forbidding aspect of the place. The back of the altar looked mucky; and there was just enough room between it and the wall to allow for the movement of her elbows.

Cautiously she knelt down and attacked the box by turning it sharply on its side. The sound of the coins filled the space and ricocheted off the walls upwards, and she followed its flight with startled eyes—the roof of the church, seen from this angle, appeared as far away as the sky—the sound eventually died away, and tensely she listened, with her teeth clamped down hard on her lip. But there was no other sound, of voices or footsteps. And so she again returned to her operation, but turning the box gently this time upside-down on the floor. After giving it a little shake she looked beneath it. There was nothing there. Slowly she raised it above her eyes . . . and yes, there it was! her half-crown. She could see it lying partly across the slot, its shine outdoing that of the penny which blocked the other half. . . . What she wanted was a knife—when her ma emptied her Post Office Savings' tin she used a knife. But she hadn't a knife. . . . Perhaps if she just tilted it slightly it would slide out. She tried this at some length, but holding the box above her head made her arms ache.

"Bust!" The exclamation of exasperation was whispered, and she sat back on her heels with the box on her lap and asked herself what she was going to do next.

But she was never to know, for the voice of God hit her on the back of the neck, knocking her on her face and sending the box spinning into the air. And as it clattered down again, almost braining her, she screamed, and the voice came thundering over her, crying, "Get up! get up! Come out of that!"

Being unable to turn, slowly, with jangling limbs, she crawled backwards. Then God lifted her clean off the floor by the collar of her coat and swung her round to Him. And her hat fell off backwards and she was looking up into the startled face of Father Owen, whose mouth was agape and whose voice was so high that it came out of the top of his head as he cried, "For the love of God . . . Mary Ann!"

Mary Ann tried to swallow, but she found the process impossible, for here, one on each side of the priest, stood the cleaners. And it was the look in their eyes that was restricting her breath as much as the shock she had just experienced.

"I told you, Father, it was the way she came in. We watched her, didn't we?" one woman enquired of the other across Father Owen. "And all the bairns at school . . . we thought it was funny, didn't we?"

"Aye. And I said, 'Go and get Father Owen,' didn't I? Because if anything goes we'll get the blame, I've had some."

"Be quiet!" The priest held up his hand, silencing the women. Then still holding Mary Ann by the shoulder, he said, "Tell me, Mary Ann."

"Me . . . me. . . . " The lump moved but wouldn't go, and she gasped and coughed. And the priest, thumping her on the back, said, "There, there. Now tell me."

"Me half-crown, Father . . . I—I dropped it in—instead of a penny . . . I was only trying to get it out."

The priest's hold slackened and he straightened his long, thin length, looked almost furtively from one woman to the other, coughed and blew his nose so loudly that the noise re-echoed off the back of the alter and filled the church again before he said, "Why didn't you come and tell me?"

"I—I didn't know where to find you afore dinner time. You're always out."

"Yes, yes. Well, go in there and bring me that box, we'll get your half-crown out." He pushed her towards the back of the altar again, and as she disappeared he turned to the women and said, "You did quite right, quite right. But you see it has been explained."

The women, as if both worked by the same string, put their heads slightly on one side and surveyed the priest, as if seeing someone who called forth their pity. Then the same string turned them about and they went slowly up the church back to their work.

Father Owen sighing and looking once more down on Mary Ann where she stood, the picture of guilt, with the box in her hand, said, "You'll be the death of me one of these days, child. Of that I'm as sure as I am of being alive at this moment, and also of being taken as a dopey old imbecile by certain ladies I won't give a name to. Come along."

In the vestry Father Owen did not immediately open the box but, sitting himself down, he looked gravely on Mary Ann, which added much to her already heavy sense of sin.

"You realise, Mary Ann, you've done a very serious thing?"

"But Father . . . " It was a small protest.

"Never mind, 'But Father . . . ' " The priest's hand was raised now, his fingers spread wide, an action, Mary Ann recognised instantly, that was kept only for bad hats, them that broke windows in the schools and, deadly sickening thought, stole.

"Was it such a sacrifice to give half-a-crown to the Holy Family?" The priest stared hard at her. "If I'm to believe all I hear, they've done a lot for you. Just think of all the wonderful things that have happened in the past few months . . . think."

The last was a command, and Mary Ann thought. She thought hard. But the only thing that came to her mind was the event of her da losing his hand. They had let that happen, hadn't they? And then they had got her into this trouble now. Eeh! what was the matter with her . . . she'd go to hell. This thought, added to the misery of her impending departure, and the expression on the face of her beloved priest, was too much. She burst into a storm of tears.

Quickly, Father Owen brought her to his knee, all sternness gone. "There, there! Now, don't cry. Come on . . . come on."

But Mary Ann's head was pressed into his waistcoat, and it was some time, however, before he could induce her to stop. When finally, sniffing and sobbing, she drew away from him, he said, "Aw! look at your face now. Here, let me wipe it."

As he plied his handkerchief round her face Mary Ann gazed up at him and jerked out, on recurrent sobs, "I didn't mean it, Father. I didn't mean it."

"No, no, of course you didn't. It was the Devil tempting you and you weren't ready for him. That's how it was."

Yes, that's how it must have been. For Mary Ann, looking back, couldn't see herself doing anything so awful as to take the candle box behind the altar and try to empty it. Not for all the half-crowns in the world could she have done it on her own. It was the Devil all right that had pushed her into that.

"I don't want the half-crown, Father, not now."

"Oh, you'll have your half-crown. . . . The Holy Family would be the last to want to make on you. Come and sit down, child." He drew her up on to the bench and to his side. "There now." He looked her over. "I see you've got on your fine clothes already for tomorrow. But look at the bottom of your coat, it's all dust." He brushed it off; then, without looking at her, said, "You'll be starting a new life tomorrow, Mary Ann." He went on brushing lightly with his hand, and when there was no answer to his comment he added, "Are you excited?"

"No, Father."

"No?" He stopped his brushing.

"No, Father. I don't want to go."

Now the priest's head turned quickly, and they confronted each other. "Have you told your mother this . . . or . . . or you da?"

"No, Father."

The priest streched himself upwards before saying, "That's a good girl, because this time next week things'll look different altogether. Believe me, they will. And just think where you're going . . . one of the finest Convents in the country, and Mr. Lord's own sister Mother Superior. Why, you're a very lucky girl. Not many get your chance, Mary Ann."

"No, Father."

"And it will all work out beautifully."

"Yes, Father."

Would it? It was undoubtedly a chance of a lifetime, and would have very favourable results on ninety-nine children out of a hundred, but the priest had a fear in him that this child would be the hundredth. Old Lord had a bee in his bonnet where she was concerned, and if she pleased him her future was as sure as anything on this earth could be. But he was counting without Mike. . . . But no, that was wrong; it was because the old fellow had counted Mike and saw him as an opponent to his plans that he had picked on this convent so far away. The fact that it was run by his sister was merely an excuse, for he hadn't spoken to her since she had come over into the Faith thirty years ago. If it was eduction alone he was after for the child, there were fine schools and convents near that would have answered his purpose just as well. Father Owen shook his head at his thoughts. It was diabolical but he felt, nevertheless, true that old Lord's idea was to separate the child from her father for as long as possible, hoping that a different environment would estrange her from her present surroundings . . . and, through it, lift her affection and loyalty, not forgetting love, away from Mike and on to the higher plane of himself. Oh, he knew Peter Lord, and he knew that this was the substance of his scheme. Yet nothing could be done about it, for if the child didn't comply there would be a heap of trouble for the family again. And the awkward part was that the mite was fully aware of this. Oh, dear, yes . . . yes, she was aware of it all right.

"Well, Mary Ann—" Father Owen pulled down his slack waistcoat—"I envy you I do, going to the South of England. I was back there meself many years ago—at both Bexhill and Hastings I stayed—and, as I remember, the air was so fine it went to my head like wine and put me to sleep. I couldn't keep meself awake night or day . . . I was properly doped. I just couldn't keep awake."

"Couldn't you, Father?"

"No, I couldn't. And now, my child—" he took her two hands in his—"you won't forget us all in this fine school?"

"Oh no, Father—never." Her head moved slowly from side to side with the truth of this statement.

"Nor your ma, and, of course, your da."

"Forget me ma and da!" Her voice was full of incredulity, and a little smile that could have held pity touched her lips. "Forget me da!"

"Of course you won't!" The priest's voice was hearty. "But you mustn't understimate our friend." He bent above her with a thumb in each ear and his fingers played outwards as he said, "You know, old Nick. Not that he's any friend of mine although he's tried to take up with me for years." He laughed down on her now. "The devil, Mary Ann, let me tell you, has many guises . . . do you know that?"

"No, Father."

"Well, he has. He gets dressed up like so many different people that you don't know who he's gong to take off next. He's the unfairest specimen that ever walked. For instance. . . . " The priest looked up at the vestry ceiling as if searching for some case with which to demonstrate his point. "Well, for instance, should you ever meet a nice man whom you don't know and he offers you some sweets and asks you to go for a walk—" down dropped his eyes to Mary Ann, and his voice dropped too, as he ended—"Rest assured, Mary Ann, that will be the devil."

"It will, Father?"

"It will. . . . Or he may be driving a car and want to give you a ride. That will be him again. As sure as life that will be him. Or he may not be dressed as a man at all, he may be got up as a woman; or a girl even; but whatever guise he puts on, as soon as he opens his mouth and starts to tempt you to do something that your heart tells you isn't right you can be sure it's him, no matter what he's wearing."

Mary Ann's world suddenly became peopled with devils, with an easily recognised one right in the forefront, and she helped the priest in his illustration by saying somewhat eagerly, "I know, like Sarah Flannagan, Father."

"Not at all, not at all." the priest stood up quickly, his voice brusque now. "Sarah's got no more of the Devil in her than you have. There's fifty-fifty twixt you and her, believe me." He nodded sharply down at her.

This assualt, unfair as it surely was, obliterated even the candle-box incident and made her think, "Well, would you believe it!"

Father Owen's hand descended on her head, and at the look on her face his mirth rang out, and he cried, "Come along with you, or else I'll never get any work done today. and here—" he put his hand in his pocket—"here's your half-crown; I'll settle with the Holy Family later. How's that?"

"Oh, thank you, Father." She was slightly mollified.

"Come on then."

They went out of the vestry together, and after genuflecting side by side to the main altar they went up the aisle, Mary Ann keeping her eyes strictly turned from the altar of Saint Anthony where the women were. But when at the church door she looked up for the last time on her true friend the tears welled again.

Bending to her, the priest took her kiss on his cheek, and when, with her arms about his thin neck, she cried, "Father! Oh, Father!" he answered somewhat thickly, "There, there. Go on now, and may God bless you and take care of you."

With a push that was almost rough he thrust her away and quickly re-entered the church, and she was left with her world, for the moment, desolate.

The sun was shining with dazzling brightness on the wet pavement and made her eyes blink, and she stood sniffing and at a loss, considering the next step in the order of good-byes. It was nearly twelve o'clock by the big clock in Harry Siddon's, the watchmaker. Should she stay at the corner of Dee Street and wait for Agnes and Mary, or go right to the school gates? Her self-esteem at a very low ebb and crying out urgently for support immediately suggested the school gate, but also told her she'd have to run! So with no more debating she ran, and just reached the main gate as the bell rang.

Almost, it would seem, as if shot from both sides of the building there came two racing, widening streams of screaming children. Not being part of either, the noise to her seemed terrific, and it brought with it a feeling that puzzled her, for she could not recognise that she was envious of their rights of the moment for lung expansion.

The sight of her checked fragments of the avalanche, and they came to her side, crying "Hello, Mary Ann."

"Hello, Mary Ann."

"Eeh! Mary Ann. Hello."

"Hello," she said. "I've come to say good-bye to Agnes and Mary."

"Mary's off bad, she's got the mumps, and Agnes brought a note yesterday 'cos she's not coming' the day, she's goin' with her ma to Durham. Eeh! you do look nice, Mary Ann . . . doesn't she?"

The chorus of "Eehs!" applied a little salve to the acute feeling of disappointments at not seeing her friends for the last time, or to be more correct, that they were not having the pleasure of seeing her dressed in her splendour, nor the opportunity of pouring their ever-ready admiration over her head.

"When you goin', Mary Ann?"

"The morrer."

"Are you going in a train?"

"Yes, and in a car." She had brightened visibly; the pain of partings was forgotten; there was nothing but the present, for she had an audience. "Mr. Lord . . . he's coming for us at eight o'clock and takin' me ma and da and our Michael and me to Newcastle. Me ma's goin' with me all the way, and I've got dozens of boxes of clothes . . . cases, all new. And me name's on everything, full length—Mary Ann Shaughnessy."

"It would be, Milady Bug."

Mary Ann swung round, new clothes and prestige forgotten. There, standing not a foot from her and not apparently impressed in the slightest by her splendours, stood Sarah Flannagan.

They glared at each other, Mary Ann having to thrust her head back to keep her eyes fixed on the taller girl. This was the old battle ground.

"What do you want round here, anyway . . . showing off as usual? . . . I'm going in a big car!' " Sarah gave an impression of Mary Ann, which drew a titter from the fickle spectators. "and you'll come back, likely as not, in the Black Maria . . . or the muck cart."

Mary Ann's chin was out; her lips were out; and her eyes were popping. "You! . . . You're jealous . . . that's what you are"

"Huh! Listen to her. Jealous! What have I got to be jealous of? An upstart? For that's all you are. Me ma says you're nothing by an upstart. and what's more, my da hadn't to be dooled out with a job to keep him quiet. Me ma says if old Lord hadn't given your da the job on the farm, he would have had to fork out thousands and thousands for his lost hand. He's made a fool of him, and everybody knows it's only charity your da's on."

"You! . . . How dare you! Oh!" Mary Ann was lost for words. "You! You! and your ma," she managed to splutter. "You and your ma, there's a pair for you. And you'll end up in hell for the lies you tell. As for your da, he's so hen-pecked he can't wipe his nose afore he gets permission."

This last eloquent thrust was remembered from a little eavesdropping; it was a statement her father had laughingly made to her mother. Now it penetrated Sarah's superior guard, causing her fury to erupt. And this brought her even nearer to Mary Ann. Whereupon, Mary Ann, having no known supporter, retreated just the slightest, but not ignobly, for she brought to her face a tantalising sneer that seemed to make Sarah swell.

"You, you to talk about anybody . . . you've got some nerve with a da like yours, you have. A big drunken, fightin' no-good, and it's only a few weeks back that you had to come right up to our street and fetch him, and him singing with the street out. . . . Your da!" Sarah's scorn was searing, "Ten a penny."

The financial significance of the last remark subtly reduced Mike's standard, socially, morally and physically, to the lowest denomination. It was an insult not to be borne . . . it had to be repudiated, right away. Mary Ann needed words, fighting words, words of scorn and fire. They were all there, milling around inside of her but finding an outlet impossible owing to the barrier of indignation blocking their path somewhere in the region of her upper ribs. But there were no impending thoughts standing in the way of her right hand, and guided by, of course, nothing but right it raised itself and contacted Sarah's face full on with a resounding slap.

Sarah choked and gasped, and the "eehs" that filled the air told Mary Ann, if the pain in her hand had not done so, that that was a whopper. But Sarah's swift retaliation cut short the glow of conquest, all that Mary Ann was aware of in the next moment was that her head was ringing and that she was falling backward. Preservation of her new clothes forbade this indignity, and she told herself frantically that whatever she did she mustn't fall, so she reeled on her heels into the roadway, her arms waving in an endeavour to regain her balance. And she might have done so but for a shining puddle of water. It was just a small puddle, but one seeming to possess impish and magnetic qualities, for it drew her small buttocks towards it, and as they made contact with the muddy water, it flew away in sprays, that is, all that did not fall back on her.

Tears of fright and mortification ran from her eyes. Her one-time audience were now laughing their heads off, and Sarah's voice came to her, as if from a distance, crying, "Look at who's going to be a lady. I'm going to a posh school, I am, I'm going to be a lady. Lady Muck of Clarty Hall!"

Suddenly there was a scurrying of feet, and as Mary Ann turned herself tearfully over she saw them racing away in all directions. And when she was erect once more she was standing alone except for Miss Johnson, who was facing her from the gate.

"Oh, it's you."

"Yes, Miss."

Miss Johnson slowly advanced to the edge of the pavement, then vented her spleen on the child she had never liked.

"It doesn't look as if your glowing prospects have altered you much," she said. "Get yourself away home. I am sure your mother will be pleased to see you."

Turning slowly about, Mary Ann walked somewhat drunkenly away. She hated Miss Johnson, she did. And eeh! her clothes. Eeh! her ma would go mad. Eeh! what was the back like? Look at the front of her coat . . . and her hands and her cuffs. Eeh! what was she to do? . . . And all through her. At this moment she prayed through her feelings for every catastrophe, calamity, disaster, and mortification to fall on that—that . . . ! She could find no words as a fitting pseudonym for the hated name of Sarah Flannagan.

Her legs, without any directions from her, took her towards the bus stop, where, a bus arriving at the same moment, she was on it before her mind cried at her, "You should have gone back to Mrs. McBride, she would have cleaned you up."

The conductor stood over her, grinning, and his heartening remark, "By! your ma's goin' to be pleased to see you," seemed to endorse that of her teacher and suggested to her again that she should get off and go back to her friend, who had on many other occasions cleaned her up. But a deadness had descended on her, the result mostly of a morning that had not gone at all according to plan. It had been such a morning which her mother would have referred to as . . . something having got into it.

Father Owen's discourse on the Devil coming back to her mind, caused her head to move impatiently, a sure sign of her inward disbelief. According to him the Devil took up only half of Sarah Flannagan. Her critical faculty told her with authority that there were some things even a priest didn't know. But what was she to do now? These were her going away clothes, she just couldn't go home like this.

They were leaving the town, and it was the sight of the first tree that connected her harassed thoughts with Mr. Lord's house. He'd be out, at the farm, or in Newcastle or some place, and there'd only be old Ben in. Old Ben wasn't bad; in fact, he had been nice to her lately . . . well, not nice exactly but not awful, like on her first visit when he tried to throw her out of the house. She would go to him and ask him to clean her up.

The conductor's grin followed her when she alighted, but with as much defiant dignity as she could muster she ignored him and the departing bus, and, crossing the deserted road, made for the great open iron gates.

This position of the gates, even after some months, had failed to make them look at ease, for the burden of twenty years of locks and chains needed some throwing off, even by gates, and by their forbidding aspect it would seem that they did not thank their liberator as she ran past them and up the drive.

She hadn't even reached the turn of the drive before she heard the hum of the car. Unmistakably Mr. Lord's car, and if she had been able to think of anything it would have been that Father Owen was right after all—the Devil was certainly out this morning. Wildly she looked towards the hedges on each side of her, but, not being a ferret she saw there was no escape that way; she was trapped by the last person on earth she wished to meet at this moment. It wasn't fair, it wasn't . . . the last time she'd had a row with Sarah Flannagan he had to come on the scene, and she had a feeling that Mr. Lord got one up on her da when she was in this kind of a mess.

In another second they were face to face; Mr. Lord, with narrowed eyes beneath his white, bristling brows, was looking through the windscreen at her. Standing as if struck, in the middle of the drive she returned his scrutiny.

After suffering a long survey by Mr. Lord, during which he uttered no command of "Come here!" she walked slowly to the side of the car and, not with head bent in contrition, but with chin lifted to his scowling countenance, she muttered, "I fell down."

"You fell down?" The voice held neither anger nor pity, but what it did hold confirmed her earlier feelings.

"Yes."

"I don't suppose this could be the result of another fight, could it?"

She remained slient, and he went on, "And what are you doing here? Now—" he raised his finger—"don't tell me you've called to see how I am."

"I wasn't going to." Her chin jerked.

"Well?"

"I was going to ask Ben—Mr. Ben to clean me up."

"You were, were you! Well, Mr. Ben has something better to do . . . your mother will see to that. Get. in."

Dodging under his arm that held open the door, she climbed on to the seat. The door crashed closed, making her jump as it always did, and Mr. Lord, without looking at her and in the process of starting up the car, exclaimed, "I'm right, I imagine, when I think that you are wearing your new clothes, those in which you are to travel tomorrow?"

There was no need to answer this, and she sat upright on the edge of the seat, her eyes saddened by the unfair trials of the morning, but her pursed lips showing the spirit that still defied them.

The car leapt over the road, and almost, it would seem, within seconds the fields of the farm came into view, and with them retribution of some sort came nearer. . . . Mean, he was . . . that's what he was . . . mean. He could have let her go to Mr. Ben, he could. She hated him. . . . Eeh! no, she didn't. Well, he could have—

Her thoughts were checked by the car being turned up a side lane and brought to a stop. This, for the first time during the drive, brought her head round to him, and she looked up at the forbidding profile of "The Lord" as she thought of him. Only once before had he stopped the car like this, and that was when he told her he would give her da the farm manager's job if she would promise to go away to school and not let on that he had asked her. Perhaps he was going to say it didn't matter and she needn't go. No. Hope of such wholesale reprieve fled on the thought of "don't be daft", for he would, she felt, send her away to this school if she were dying. She had a swift mental picture of being carried on a stretcher to the train and being received at the convent by rows and rows of sympathetic nuns. Yet hope was never really dead in her, and it rose with its false voice and suggested that he might be going to say that she could go some place nearer, where she could come back at the weekends and see her da.

The car ceased its throbbing, and she watched him lean back, draw in a long breath, then let it out again, and as he did so he turned his head and looked at her. And then he smiled, just a little bit, with his mouth.

Quickly she responded to his mood. He could be nice . . . she liked him, she did. She would like making him laugh. But at the moment she didn't feel like laughing.

"Tomorrow morning there will be no time to talk, Mary Ann." His voice was kind, and he was looking at her as if he didn't mind the mess she was in . . . but, still, he was talking about tomorrow morning. "Now, child, listen to me." He had taken her hands into his long bony ones. "Now listen to what I'm saying. Tomorrow you begin a new life. From tomorrow you have the opportunity to become—well—" his shoulders moved; his moustache was pressed outwards and he released one hand and spread his fingers wide, and they seemed to encompass the world—"you can be anything you want to be, Mary Ann. Do you understand?"

Her eyes were fixed tight on his, and her head moved once.

"Anything. You must forget about—about all this." He waved his hand around the car, but the indication took in the farm and all it held.

The light in her eyes faded somewhat, and he was quick to add, "Until the holidays; they'll soon come round. And you must learn. Apply yourself to your lessons—think of nothing else but learning when you are there. And if you play your part at school, I'll play my part here. You understand?"

"Yes."

Yes, she understood the implications, and the knowledge of her understanding pressed like a weight on her heart.

"You have a head on your shoulders, Mary Ann." He nodded slowly at her. "You are older then your years . . . you can lap up knowledge quickly if you have the mind. Pay attention . . . above all things, pay attention to your English, then languages will follow as easily as—"He snapped his fingers. "I will know of your progress from your letters. . . . You will write to me?"

This last was not put as an order, but as a request, and she said, "Yes. Yes, I'll write to you."

After one look that took her in from her muddied hat to her shoes, he turned back to the wheel, and his next words tugged at and brought to the surface the affection she had for him. "You'll write . . . but you won't think of me until you have to do that irksome duty; you'll forget me."

Now she could respond, for below the brusqueness of his voice lay the buried loneliness that she had discovered on their first meeting. This was the part of him that she liked . . . loved. This was the part of him she used all her efforts to make laugh. All the benefits she and the family had received from his hands rushed before her, and she knew that but for him they would still be in Mulhattan's Hall . . . perhaps not even there, but some place worse.

She was kneeling on the seat now, close to his side, his bony, blue-veined hands gripped by her two small ones. "No, I won't! I won't forget you ever, I won't! And I'll try to learn for you, I will." She nearly added, "If you'll see to me da." But wisdom forbade this and prompted a more soothing balm to the old man's feelings, so swiftly she reached up, and, with her arms about his neck, she planted a kiss on the close-shaved wrinkled cheek. His eyes, now a few inches from hers, appeared pale and misty as they enveloped her, and with his hands cupping her small elfin face, he said, "Don't fail me, Mary Ann, will you?"

This softly spoken demand brought a damper to this nice part of the proceedings, and, after a somewhat doubtful sounding "No," she slid down to the seat. The car started and they were out on the main road again; then before you could say "Jack Robinson" they had turned into the lane which led to the farm, swept past the cottages where only a few weeks ago she had lived, right through the mud that the cattle made in the dip and into the actual farmyard.

Her eyes darted up at him. Why hadn't he put her off at their door, she'd only have to walk back? Then the sight of Mike, coming out of the cow byres at that moment gave her the reason. Yet again she couldn't fully explain it, she only knew that he wanted her da to see her all messed up. Oh! he was mean, he was.

Mike came swiftly towards the car, his eyes darting from one to the other, and he greeted Mr. Lord before he could alight. "Morning, Sir. Anything wrong?"

It was evident that Mike was surprised to see his master.

"No, nothing particularly." Mr. Lord eased himself out of the car. "When I phoned you to say I wouldn't be over until tomorrow morning, with this meeting coming up, I didn't know I was going to run into . . . this." He inclined his head slowly back into the car; then added, "Come on, get out." His voice certainly held no tone of endearment now, conveying only that Mary Ann and all her works were a source of annoyance to him.

Legs first, and with a good display of knickers, she slid from the seat and presented herself to her da, whereupon the wind was drawn in so thinly through Mike's teeth as to make a whistling sound, which spoke of exasperation and caused her heart to sink. He was mad at her; and it was her last day. Oh! it was mean of Mr. Lord, it was.

"Sarah Flannagan again." There was no sign of the laughter in Mike's voice that had accompanied the name earlier in the morning. "And your new things!"

From her eye level she was looking at the arm where it finished at the end of the sleeve. She wanted to grab it and cry, "Oh, Da! It was because she was saying nasty things . . . bad things about you that I hit her." But Mike's voice forbade any explanation whatever as he said, "Go on home, and see what your mother has to say."

Without looking at either of them she walked away to the sound of Mike's voice saying gruffly, "I'm sorry she put you out, Sir."

The world was all wrong; nothing was right, or ever would be again. Didn't they know it was her last day?

Dismally she took the path to the back door. The only consolation for her now was that things couldn't get worse, anyway not today, for whatever her ma said or did wouldn't be as bad as the way her da had looked at her.

But that there were differing degrees of trouble and that a large portion of the very worst kind awaited her was to be proved within the next minute, for she had hardly entered the scullery before the voice of her grannie hit her ear and brought to her face a wide-eyed look of incredulity. Not her grannie! Not the day, oh, no! She had never been near since they had come to live in the farmhouse, so she couldn't be here today. No, it couldn't be her grannie!

But it was her grannie. Only too true it was, and the sound of her told Mary Ann to escape, and quickly, for if her grannie saw her like this she would never hear the last of it.

Lifting her feet most cautiously now, she was about to turn and flee when the kitchen door, from being ajar, was pulled wide open, so that her grannie's voice came to her, saying, "Stone floors like these are a death trap. You'll be crippled with rheumatism afore you're here a——" The voice trailed off and Mrs. McMullen's eyes became fixed on Mary Ann's body caught in the stance of flight. "Well! So it's you. What are you up too?"

Mary Ann slumped; then closed her eyes as a gasp came from both her grannie and her mother, who, too, was now standing in the doorway.

"Oh! Mary Ann."

If her mother had gone for her it wouldn't have been so bad, but to sound sad like that, and in front of her grannie.

Mrs. McMullen's round, black eyes were moving over her grand-daughter with righteous satisfaction. "Well, you look a mess I must say. But it doesn't surprise me."

Mary Ann moved to her mother.

"How did it happen?"

"I fell, Ma."

"I fell, Ma!" As they stood looking at each other, Mrs. McMullen gave a "Huh!" of a laugh. "You fell all right; and, of course, you weren't fighting and acting the hooligan."

Lizzie's face became tight, as she turned her back on her mother. But her voice held no reprimand as she said to Mary Ann, "Get your things off and I'll see to them."

Mary Ann got her things off, watched silently by Mrs. McMullen, and when she turned to the sink to wash, her grannie went into the kitchen, but she sent her voice back into the scullery, saying, "If you expect any silk purses to be made out of sows' ears, then I'm afraid you're in for a disappointment. Money down the drain. The man must be in his dotage."

That there wasn't a hair's difference between her grannie and Sarah Flannagan, Mary Ann had always been sure, and now it was confirmed. Silk purses . . . that's what Sarah Flannagan had said.

She saw her mother's hands gripping her coat, and she knew it was because of her grannie. She turned from the sink and tiptoed to her, and with a most pained countenance whispered, "Oh, Ma!"

"Shush!" Lizzie's finger was on her lips, and when she wagged it warningly Mary Ann, with a hopeless sigh, went back to the sink again.

It was awful . . . awful. How long would her grannie stop? Hours and hours. . . . This was her day; everything should have been lovely; everybody should have been lovely to her; and what had happened? Something had got into it. . . . The Devil. She stopped rolling the soap between her hands. But why should he pick on her, and all at once? . . .

Mike's surprise equalled Mary Ann's when he came in and saw his mother-in-law already seated at the dinner table. There were no greetings exchanged between these two; enemies they had been from the beginning and enemies they would remain until the end.

A swift look that held pleading passed from Lizzie to Mike, for Mike's entry had not caused even a pause in Mrs. McMullen's discourse. He might have been a figment of Lizzie's and Mary Ann's imagination, so little impression did his presence apparently make on her.

That her grannie's cheap thrusts were now prodding her da, Mary Ann was well aware, and when Lizzie said to her, "Come and sit up,"she thought. And if she says any more, I'll say to her, "Shut up, you!" I will . . . I don't care.

"Chicken? Things are looking up!" Mrs. McMullen's fuzzy head was bent over her plate. "Ah, well, you can afford them when you get them for nothing, I suppose."

"We didn't get it for nothing; me ma bought it cos it's a special dinner the day, for——"

"Mary Ann!" Both Mike and Lizzie spoke together, and Mary Ann slowly drew her eyes away from her grandmother. And Mrs. McMullen, with her high, tight, neat bosom swelling, exclaimed, "You should've been a dog, you've got the bark of one!"

"That's enough." Mike's voice was deep and quiet; it rolled over Mary Ann's head like thunder. He was standing behind her chair and his hand slid to her shoulder. What was in his eyes she could not see, but whatever it was it quelled the retort on her grannie's lips, and at the same time narrowed her eyes and tightened her face. Yet it did not effectively still her tongue, for she continued to talk, addressing herself solely to her daughter, yet all the while aiming her darts at both her son-in-law and grand-daughter.

"Will I help you?" she called to Lizzie in the scullery. And when Lizzie's reply of, "No, thank you, I can manage," came back to her, she called again, "These floors will be the death of you . . . cold stone. Wait till the winter comes. And the distance you've got to walk! Frying pan into the fire, if you ask me. You were nearly killed by worry afore, now you'll be just as effectively polished off in this place. . . . Like a barracks."

"Start, will you?" Lizzie came hurrying into the kitchen. "Say your grace, Mary Ann. Don't wait for me, anyone, just start. Gravy, Mother?"

"When do you think you'll get all these rooms furnished?"

"Oh, gradually. Gravy, Mike?" Lizzie was seated now, a fixed smile on her face.

Silently Mike took the tureen, and Mary Ann said painfully, "You've given me sprouts, Ma, and you know I don't like them."

"Oh, have I? Well just leave them on the side of your plate."

"Huh! I never did."

There was no need to enquire as to what Mrs. McMullen never did, they all knew it was connected with sprouts and eating them whether you liked them or not. And from the look that the old lady bestowed on her grandchild, it was evident that it would have given her the greatest pleasure to ram the sprouts singly down Mary Ann's gullet.

"It's either all or nothing . . . eight rooms!" Mrs. McMullen had returned to the matter of furnishings. "You'll be ready for your old-age pension by the time you get them fixed."

"I don't think so." Lizzie's voice was even. "I'm going to the sales. . . . At sales you can often pick up bargains."

Mrs. McMullen's hands paused while conveying a piece of the breast of chicken to her mouth. "Bargains! Don't be silly; those auctioneer fellows are crooks and fakers. Just read what they are up to in the papers. Faking pictures and furniture."

"Well, as I won't be wanting that kind of thing, it won't trouble me." Lizzie still wore her smile. "Do you want some more stuffing, Mary Ann? And you can pick your bone up in your fingers."

Mary Ann picked up the chicken bone and proceeded to strip it. It was nice and sweet. She loved chicken wing, especially when the skin stuck to the bone at the end. She was dissecting the last piece of anatomy when she gave an unintential suck, loud enough to bring all eyes on her and, of course, her grannie's voice.

"Well, it's to be hoped they show you how to eat, if nothing else!"

Mike's eyes, like flashes of fire, darted to the old woman. But Mrs. McMullen's eyes were lowered to her plate and she continued her discourse regarding the furnishing of rooms. "Well, even if you get them furnished, what'll they be for, she's going?" This was accompanied by a bland nod towards Mary Ann. "And once she gets a taste of a fancy school, you needn't think this place'll hold her after a few years. And if I know Michael he'll be off as soon as he can, and there you'll be left, eight rooms for two of you. That's if you're here, of course."

As she spoke the last words Mike's chair scrapped loudly on the stone floor, and almost at the same time, Lizzie, the armour of her smile now gone, jumped to her feet, saying, hurriedly, "I'll bring the pudding in. Mike . . . Mike!" She had to repeat his name to draw his eyes away from her mother's bent head. "Mike, come and give me a hand . . . Mike!"

Slowly Mike turned from the table and went into the scullery, and Lizzie, close behind him, shut the door and, going to him, took him by the arm.

"Oh! Mike, why do you let her get at you? You know she's doing it on purpose. Why don't you laugh at her?"

"Laugh at her!" Mike's teeth ground each other, setting Lizzie's on edge, and his voice rumbled in his throat, "Strangle her, more like!"

"Mike! don't say that. Can't you see? She's mad because we're set and comfortable."

"Why didn't you tell me she was here?"

"I couldn't; she had just got in when Mary Ann came in, all mud and——"

"I know. He brought her back."

"Mr. Lord?"

"Aye."

"Oh! no." Lizzie's fingers went to her mouth. "And in her new things an' all!"

"Don't worry, he got a great deal of satisfaction out of it. I don't know whether he takes me for a complete fool or not where she's concerned, but he got a kick out of showing me just what he was taking her away from."

"Oh, Mike! don't look at it like that, he's not taking her away."

"Isn't he?" Mike reached for his coat, and as Lizzie moved to help his maimed arm into it, he thrust her aside almost roughly; then turning swiftly to her again, he grabbed her hand into his and, gripping it, he said, urgently, "Liz, I want to talk to you. I've been thinking all morning . . . and then that old——" His eyes flicked towards the kitchen door. "Liz, if we let her go we've lost her. I've never agreed with your mother in me life, but she's right there. This fancy place is bound to change her . . . it can't but help it. I'm frightened, Liz, frightened inside."

His hand was almost cracking her knuckles, and Lizzie was now filled with a feeling akin to terror. "Mike . . . she's got to go."

"Got to?"

"I mean she's—she wants to. She'll—she'll break her heart if she doesn't go."

"You really think so?" Mike's gaze was penetrating into her, and Lizzie willed her eyes not to fall before it. Then he ended rapidly, "Anyway, how does she know what she wants, she's only a bairn?"

"She's old for her years, you know she is, and it's a chance in a lifetime. You said yourself many a time you wished you'd had the chance of education."

His grip on her hand slackened and his head drooped. "It's sending her so damned far away that's getting me."

Lizzie looked at him with love and pity in her eyes, but she continued to press Mr. Lord's case. "He thought with his sister being Mother Superior she'd likely be better looked after there."

Her voice trailed off, and Mike turned away and picked up his cap. "I wonder. I wonder a lot of things. Sometimes I think . . . Oh!" he pulled the cap firmly on to his head and made for the door; but there he turned back quickly, and, coming to her again, he pulled her to him, and with his one arm about her, he kissed her roughly, "I'm sorry about the dinner, Liz, but you know how it is."

After holding him close for a moment, she let him go and, moving to the window, she watched him walk down the path and into the lane. And, as ever, pride of him rose in her, but it did not swamp the fear, and as she braced herself to go into the kitchen again the fear came flooding over her. But it was not of her mother—the feeling her mother aroused was simply acute irritation—no, the fear was of her daughter, and she prayed for tomorrow to come and be gone, and Mary Ann with it.

3

It was four o'clock and never had an afternoon seemed so long and empty to Mary Ann. After changing her clothes, right through, her mother had sent her out in her old things; and, glad to escape, she had immediately sought out her da. But to her surprise and inner hurt, Mike had said he was up to the eyes in work and that she must keep out of his way. He was a bit mad, she could see—that was her grannie. Oh, she hated her grannie, she did. But this was her last day; surely he hadn't forgotten that. Tomorrow she wouldn't be here, even if he had heaps of time to spare.

In the cowshed, Mr. Jones, too, had no use for her presence. He didn't even have to say so, he just looked. Len was up the long field mending a fence. Mr. Polinski only was available. But conversation was difficult at any time with him, and today doubly so, as he was working under a machine in the open barn. Not even the dogs were to be seen.

Completely at a loose end, she decided to go and say a lengthy goodbye to Mrs. Jones. But after three knocks on the cottage door she realised that even this doubtful pleasure was to be denied her. She was in the act of turning away when the back door of "their house"— she still thought of the next cottage as "their house"—was pulled open, and Mrs. Polinski stood there. She wasn't laughing now as she did when speaking to her da, her face was straight, and Mary Ann's discerning eyes told her that Mrs. Polinski had been crying, for in spite of her being all done up, her eyes were red and swollen.

When she saw Mary Ann the young woman's expression changed, and, smiling now, she said, "Hello there."

"Hello," said Mary Ann, politely. "I've come to say goodbye to Mrs. Jones, but I think she's out."

"Yes, she is. But aren't you going to say goodbye to me?" The young woman paused, waiting for Mary Ann to say, "Yes." And when she did so Mrs. Polinski stepped aside, saying, "Come in and see if I've got any sweets left. Come on."

Mary Ann went in, and was immediately arrested by the change in the cottage. She had known the kichen as a colourful place, all bright and shiny, but now it looked awful. There was a red carpet on the floor. Whoever heard of a carpet in the kitchen! No wonder it was mucky. And a red suite, all greasy at the back where the heads had been. And dust . . . the mantelpiece was thick with it. Even the ashes hadn't been taken out for days . . . anybody could see that.

"Look, have a chocolate, You're lucky, for they're nearly finished."

Mary Ann stared down at the box offered to her. You only had boxes of chocolates at Christmas. "O, ta . . . thank you." She took one, a silver-papered one.

"Take two."

"Oh, can I? Ta."

"You're going in the morning then?"

"Yes." The wonderful taste of the chocolate was taking even the sting out of this admission.

"You're lucky."

Mary Ann paused in her chewing, but remained mute to this.

"You don't know how lucky . . . with a man like Mr. Lord at your back." Mrs. Polinski shook her head slowly, as if at the wonder of it.

Again Mary Ann found nothing to say; so she ate the second chocolate.

"Do you know it's only four and a half years since I left school?"

Mary Ann stopped munching. "Only four and half?"

"Yes, and oh, how I wish I was back." Mrs. Polinski sat down heavily; then leant towards Mary Ann. "Make school last as long as possible."

Her voice sounded hard, and Mary Ann said, "I don't want to; I don't like school."

"No, not now you don't, no one ever does, but one day you'll look back and long for school again. How old do you think I am?" She pressed herself back against the coach, giving Mary Ann room for scrutiny.

Mary Ann looked at the round, smooth face, the blonde hair that wasn't like her ma's, and she thought, I don't know; but she's married so she must be old. "Twenty," she said.

"You're nearly right."

Mary Ann give no congratulatory exclamation at this, and Mrs. Polinski sighed and, pulling a bundle of sewing towards her, said somewhat dispiritedly, "I'm making myself a frock. Do you like the colour?" She held the dress up.

Politely Mary Ann looked at the dress, and politely she said, "Yes, it's nice." But in her head she was saying, quite distinctly, "I don't like it. Why does she have everything red?"

"Your mother's going to miss you."

"Yes," Mary Ann nodded. "So's me da."

"Your da." The hands became still on the material, and Mrs. Polinski looked at Mary Ann, a smile on her lips now. "You like your da, don't you?"

"Yes."

"Yes." Again Mrs. Polinski sighed; and her hands began to move once more. "Who'd blame you; he's a fine man is your father—your da." She laughed softly now, as if to herself.

As Mary Ann stared at the girl aimlessly fumbling with the material, she had a strong and urgent desire to get up from the couch and run away, to fly away. This was odd, for anyone who spoke highly of her da commanded her whole attention. Yet this feeling urged her not to listen to Mrs. Polinski, but to dash off and not to her da, but to her mother. And she knew what she'd say to her mother . . . she'd say, "I don't like Mrs Polinski, I don't." And if her mother asked why, she'd say, "'Cos she wants to go back to school." But she knew this wasn't really why she didn't like her. Then, why didn't she? She shook her head. Swiftly she rose now, saying, "Eeh! I've got to go, I forgot something. Thanks for the sweets."

"Oh." Mrs. Polinski pulled herself out of her reverie. "Oh, all right. . . . Well, goodbye, Mary Ann. Be a good girl, and remember what I told you."

There was no interest in her tone at all now, and its lack was expressed finally, when she added, "You can let yourself out. Bye-bye."

"Bye-bye."

Once outside, Mary Ann began to run, not caring very much where she was bound for; and her thoughts ran with her, jumping when she jumped. Mrs. Polinski was awful. The thought was high in her head. Look at her house, all red and dirty. She skipped over the grass verge. She didn't like her, she didn't. On and on she ran, her thoughts swirling around Mrs. Polinski until, when in sight of the main road, she was brought to a sudden stop by a stitch in her side.

She stood groaning. "Oh! . . . Oh! By gum . . . Ooh! Crikey Moses!" It was the worst of the many stitches she had experienced, it brought her over double. "Oh! Lordy! Lordy!"

"Are you hurt?"

She glanced up sideways at the young man bending above her.

"Oh! I've got a stitch. Oh! it's awful."

"Rub it." His face was serious and a little twisted, as if he, too, was feeling the stitch, and she did as he bid her, and rubbed her side vigorously.

Phew! As she straightened up she was actually sweating, and the young man's voice was sympathetic as he said, "Yes, I know what that is. It can be awful."

Mary Ann looked at him. "It's gone now."

"Good."

She continued to stare at the stranger as she rubbed her side. Who was he? He looked nice, and he talked swanky. Like Mr. Lord, only different. He was looking now across the field, to where stood the skeleton of the new barn.

"That barn," he said. "Whose is it?"

"Me da's."

When his eyes quickly came to hers, she added quickly and in a somewhat offended tone, "Well, he's manager, it's the same thing."

"I'm looking for Mr. Lord's farm."

She blinked twice, before saying, "That's it."

He was turning his gaze to the field again, when he hesitated and looked down at her once more, and there was the faintest trace of a smile on his sombre countenance, and it told Mary Ann that he understood things without a lot of explaining, and she thought again, He's nice.

"What's your name?"

"Mary Ann Shaughnessy; and me da's Mike Shaughnessy. He's a grand farmer, me da."

"Yes, I'm sure he is."

"He knows everything." She stressed this point, smiling broadly up at him.

"Does he? I'm glad of that."

"What's your name?"

"Tony. Tony Brown."

She didn't think much of Brown as a name, but he was nice, and not old—well, not very. She did not ask, "How old are you?" because her mother had said she hadn't to ask people that. But she tried to gain her information by putting her question on a more friendly basis: "I'm eight, goin' on for nine. Are you very old?"

"Yes, pretty old."

The admission was sad, and she said, comfortingly, "Well, it doesn't matter. Are you going to our farm?"

He nodded. "I suppose I'm going to see your father."

"Oh, are you?" Her smile spread into a great welcoming beam. "Oh, I'll take you."

"Thanks."

Tomorrow was again forgotten. Hopping and jumping over the puddles and on and off the grass verge, she led the way back to the farm, chattering to her new, sober-looking acquaintance all the while. But when, within a short distance of the yard, she found him standing staring towards the farmhouse, whereupon she offered proudly: "That's our house."

He looked at her, then asked slowly, "Doesn't . . . doesn't Mr. Lord live here?"

"No, not yet. His house isn't ready, but it soon will be. Look, there it is, on the hill . . . look!"

He followed her finger, and then said briefly, "Show me where I'll find your father."

"Come on then; he'll be here somewhere."

She went dashing off ahead now, crying loudly, "Da! Da . . . Oh, Mr. Polinski!" She pulled up as a short, dark man, in his late thirties, came from behind a rick, carrying a cart shaft on his shoulder. "Where's me da? Do you know?"

"In office—" he nodded towards the old dairy that the late manager had converted into an office—"wit old man."

Mr. Polinski's "old man" meant Mr. Lord. She hadn't known he was here again. He must have come by when she was in Mrs. Polinski's house. She turned round now and waited for the young man to come up.

"He's in his office," she said. "And Mr. Lord's there an' all, so I can't go in."

She saw the young man stop in his stride, and then he did a funny thing. He turned completely round towards the entrance to the farmyard, as if he was going back that way, and she said hastily, pointing, "The office is over there . . . that door."

Slowly he turned again, and then, without saying "Ta" or "Thanks", he went across the yard, and she stood watching him, standing with her finger-nail between her teeth, in sudden troubled perplexity. She knew she hadn't seen him before, and yet she felt she had. Perhaps she had seen him in Jarrow somewhere, or perhaps in church. And this feeling of recognition seemed to be connected with his walk, with his back?

Out of a million backs she could have picked her da's or her ma's, and somehow she knew she could have picked this young man's, too. It was funny. She bit on her finger as if trying to tear off the nail.

Before the young man reached the office the door opened and Mr. Lord came out, followed by Mike, and they both looked enquiringly at the young man, who had now come to a stop a few yards away from them.

Mary Ann now moved cautiously forward, and as she came up to them her da was saying, "Oh, yes, of course; you're Brown, aren't you?"

"Yes, sir." The young man was looking directly at her father, and Mary Ann's chest swelled with pride . . . he had called her da, "Sir."

"It's the young fellow from the Agricultural College, sir." Mike had turned to Mr. Lord, and when Mr. Lord did not answer, he added, "Remember? I told you he had written."

Mr. Lord's eyes, narrowed behind his beetling brows, were fixed on the visitor. And now the young man was returning his stare, hard, almost it seemed to Mary Ann with dislike, like she looked at Sarah Flannagan.

"Why do you particularly want to get experience here? It's only a small farm." Mr. Lord's mouth was at its grimmest.

"I don't." The words were shot out, and Mr. Brown bit his lip as if regretting them; then added, with slightly lowered head, "I mean, I don't mind, I would rather start on a small farm."

Mary Ann looked from one to the other, and she saw that the dislike was in Mr. Lord's eyes now, and she thought, Aw! he won't take him on; not when he looks like that he won't. Aw! And she felt a great sense of disappointment.

She saw her da give a hitch to his trousers, and his chin go up as he turned to Mr. Lord and said, "We'll have to have an extra hand, anyway, sir. What about a trial, we can't go far wrong in that?" He spoke as if the young man wasn't present. And Mr. Lord, moving his head restlessy, replied in much the same way, "I suppose it's up to you. But I'm warning you, we're carrying no dead-weight, Agricultural College or not, the milk comes out the same way; and they cannot alter the seasons."

Mr. Lord now walked away, but he had not gone far when he turned and called Mike to him. And when Mike, with a glance at the young fellow, went towards him, he said, "You've got a free hand as you know, but I'm not sure whether it would be wise to take him on; he looks all head and no hands, and you don't want that kind. It's labour you want."

For Mike's part, he had instinctively taken to the young fellow, but he was wise not to make this too evident. Moreover, he did no despise men with headpieces on a farm, for he was finding his self-imposed study at night more tiring than the work of the day. And so, hitching at his belt again, he sighed and said, "You're right there, sir, only too true. But what do you say if I give him a trial—that is, if it's all the same to you?"

Mr. Lord looked past Mike's head to the young man again and his eyes stayed on him for a moment before he said, "Well, don't start complaining to me about him, that's all." And on this he walked away.

Mike stood for a moment watching his master before turning and going back to the boy, and immediately he saw that the young fellow's back was up, and his sympathy went out to him, for he knew only too well how the old man could draw out a temper. The antagonism between the two had been the swiftest thing he had ever seen, except perhaps his own feelings for Ratcliffe, his late boss.

"Well, now—" he confronted the boy—"we'll have to talk, I suppose; but first of all, what about a cup of tea? Come on over to the house."

"Da." All this time Mary Ann had stood in the background, keeping her tongue quiet, but now she realised that her father had clearly forgotten about her grannie, for he was walking away towards the house, talking as he went. "Where are you living?" he was asking the young man.

"At present, in Newcastle. I have a room there."

"Da."

"Yes? Come on." Mike held out his hand, but went on, "You're not from these parts then?"

"No, sir." the young man did not seem of a communicative nature, and Mike said, "Well, you'll have to come nearer than Newcastle. Newcastle's a long way when the dawn rises early. Yes, we'll have to see about that."

"Da!" She tugged at his hand. He must be daft, she told herself, if he was going to take a stranger into their house, and her grannie there, for she would soon give him a picture of their life, and especially her da's, which would be awful, to say the very least. "Da!" she tugged again and whispered urgently, "Da! me grannie."

"Oh!" Mike stopped abruptly and looked down on her, and his colour rising just the slightest he said, "Yes, your grannie." But as he turned to his companion with a laughing apology on his lips, the need for it was taken away, for there, going along the road past the farm entrance were Lizzie and her mother, and Lizzie, looking in his direction, called, "Mary Ann!"

"Oh! bust."

"Go on." Her da was speaking under his breath, and reluctantly, with slow measured steps, she went towards the gate.

"Your grannie's just going . . . are you coming to the bus with us?"

The true and natural retort would have been "No!" but something in Lizzie's tone and the way she held out her hand asked for obedience, and so, taking her mother's hand, she walked reluctantly back along the road, trying to shut her ears to her grandmother's vicious chatter.

"Nothing ever stays put—get that into your head—we're here today and gone tomorrow, and that applies to worldly goods. And jobs an' all, a lot can happen in six months' trial, so don't bank your hopes on a golden future. You won't take to it kindly when you find yourself on the dung heap again."

Mary Ann felt her mother's fingers suddenly stiffen, and her voice came harsh when she demanded, "Who told you he was on a six months' trial?"

"Ah, I have me little birds."

Mary Ann saw them, hordes of them, fighting, screeching little birds, and she willed them to swoop down on her grannie and peck her eyes out. She even saw her grannie being borne to the ground by them, and with deep satisfaction she gazed down on her, pecked to death by her little birds.

Oh! her grannie. She wished she was dead, she did. Eeh! . . . well, she did.

"Well, you can tell your little birds that the six months' trial is only a figure of speech, he's set for life."

"Huh!" It was a small laugh that spoke volumes. "I'm glad you think so. But you were always one to fool yourself. You mark my words, if it isn't one thing it will be another."

"You hope it will be like that." Lizzie's voice was very low and came tightly from between her teeth.

"I've no need to hope. If I didn't know the man it'd be different. The first time you let him off the lead it'll be hi-ho for the pubs and 'Get the cans on John Michael'."

Mary Ann's fingers were hurting, so tightly crushed were they in her mother's hand. There was silence now, but as they neared the main road the sound of the approaching bus came to them, and Mrs. McMullen exclaimed in exasperation, "It's early, there's another five minutes yet."

Lizzie said nothing, not even when the bus stopped and she assisted her mother on to it.

From the platform, Mrs. McMullen turned, and now in a pathetic tone, that immediately caught the sympathy of the listeners in the bus, she said, "That's it, go and leave me in a huff. When are you coming down to see me?"

"I don't know."

"Well!"

The bus moved off, and Lizzie turned quickly away from the sight of her mother's pained countenance. But once in the shelter of the lane she stopped, and stood biting hard on her lip.

When Mary Ann edged close to her she put her arms about her and pressed her head into her waist for a moment, then easing her away again, she stooped and kissed her and looking deep into her eyes she spoke, not of her mother, or of what she had said, but to Mary Ann's surprise, she used the same words as Mr. Lord had done. "There won't be much time to talk tomorrow, Mary Ann," she said. "Now promise me you'll be a good girl at this school, and you'll learn and make us proud of you."

The weight of the world was on her again, and more heavily now.

"Promise . . . so much depends on you, Mary Ann."

Mary Ann stared up at her mother, and the look of anxiety she saw deep in Lizzie's eyes forced her to smile wistfully and promise, "All right, Ma, I will."

Lizzie kissed her again, and Mary Ann clung to her in an effort to stop the tears from spurting, and when, blinking rapidly, she looked up at her mother, Lizzie laughed and said, "That bus saved you, it was your turn next. You would have learned of all the things that aren't going to be in that school."

Mary Ann gave a sniffling, cackling, laugh, and Lizzie, catching hold of her hand again, cried, "Come on; let's go home."

So together, like two girls released from a tyrant, they sped down the road, laughing and shouting to each other as they leapt over the puddles.

It was over an extra wide puddle that it happened. Lizzie, with a lift of her arm, was assisting Mary Ann in a flying leap when she fell. Having been pulled down beside her mother, Mary Ann lay laughing into her hands for a moment. This was mainly to save herself from crying, for the stones had grazed both her legs and the palms of her hands. But she was brought quickly out of her simulated laughter by the sound of a groan from her mother. Lizzie was sitting on the road holding on to her ankle with both hands; her lips were apart, and her teeth were tightly pressed together.

"What's the matter, Ma? Oh! Ma."

"I—I've hurt my ankle. Help me up."

Mary Ann, with all her small strength, helped her mother on to her good foot; then watched the colour drain from her face. Terrified, she helped her to hop to the grass verge, and when Lizzie dropped down on it and gasped, "Go—go and get your da," she replied in a daze, "Me da?"

"Yes."

"Oh!" After one last look at her mother Mary Ann bounded away, calling, "Da! Da!"

She had reached the farmyard when she pulled herself up, and turning, made for the house. Her da would be in the house with the new man. But Mike wasn't in the house. Dashing back into the yard again she ran full tilt into Len, and to her garbled question of, "Where's me da?" he said, "In the new barn. But mind, the old boy's there. What's up with you?"

She was gone before he had finished, and when, still yelling, she rounded the outbuildings and came to the front of the new barn, she was confronted by three pairs of eyes and Mr. Lord's voice.

"Stop that noise this moment!"

For once, she took no notice whatever of him, or his orders, but flew to Mike, crying, "Oh, Da! Da!" The necessity to breathe checked her words, and Mike put in sharply, "Behave youself!"

"It's me ma . . . she's hurt herself . . . she's lying on the road and she's white!"

After just one second's pause while he stared down at her, Mike was away, and he was out of the gate before her flying legs had carried her half-way across the yard. When the young man caught up with her he called, "What is it?"

She was so out of puff that she didn't even try to answer. They were on the road now, and in the distance she saw her da raising her ma up with his one good arm. The young man sprinted ahead, and when, panting loudly, she reached the group, he was linking his hand to Mike's to make a seat for her mother.

Lizzie's face was drawn, and she was near tears, and when she exclaimed bitterly, "For this to happen!" Mary Ann felt, somehow, that she wasn't referring to the pain she was in but the accident's bearing on the morrow.

Walking now behind the two men, the meaning of what her mother's accident meant to her filled her with guilty-conscience-streaked joy: They wouldn't be able to send her the morrow. They couldn't if her ma couldn't walk, could they?

From its beginning, it had undoubtedly been a day during which the Devil had certainly been master. But once more he had been vanquished; her secret prayers had been answered. What was his power to compare with that of the Holy Family? Hadn't they even brought her grannie here to bring things about? Likely, her grannie had been in the middle of her washing, or some such, and they had said, "Get your things on and go and see Lizzie," because her mother would never have gone up the road if it hadn't been to see her grannie to the bus, would she?

Realising the advantage of possessing such allies as the Holy Family had unconsciously brought to Mary Ann's face an expression which was not in keeping with the events of the moment, and she was not aware that the relief she was feeling had slipped through, until her eyes met Mr. Lord's, where he stood by the gate.

The joy was wiped from her face; she even stopped dead for a moment, brought to a halt, it would seem, by the knowledge in the eyes regarding her. Then as she stared at him an odd thing happened, for out of his head sprouted two horns, and between his thin legs came flicking a tail, a forked tail. Her joy sank; she could feel it draining from her chest, right through her stomach and down her legs. Dread reality was on her again. It was as Father Owen said, the Devil had many guises. And now he had gone into . . . The Lord, and she knew that there was going to be a fight on between him and her amalgamated company of the Holy Family, and for the life of her at this moment she didn't know which side to back.

4

And now it was her da saying, "There won't be any time in the morning to talk." He was sitting on her bed and his voice was very low. He looked tired, weary.

"If you're not happy there, you'll tell me, won't you? You'll write? Very likely they'll read your letters. I think they do—but if you're not happy get a letter to me somehow. . . . Look . . . look at me." He brought her face to his again. "You really want to go to this school? Tell me the truth now."

No power of hers brought her head to a sharp nod, nor her voice to say, "Yes, Da"; it was the combined voices of her ma and Mr. Lord inside which did it. she could still hear Mr. Lord saying airily to her da, "She'll be all right. She'll be in the care of the guard to London, and a nun will meet the train. I've arranged everything. This is a very unfortunate happening. I would take her myself, but I hate trains and"—his voice had dropped to a note of regret—"and, of course, it's a pity you can't be spared." Then on again it had gone, lightly, airly, "Oh, she'll be all right. Anyway, she must be there for the beginning of term." And then her mother, holding her hand tightly until the bones hurt, and saying, "Mr. Lord has made all arrangements. And, darling, if your da should ask you if you still want to go, you'll say yes, won't you? You'll say yes."

She had said it.

Mike stared at her; then shook his head in a bewildered fashion. "Then why aren't you more happy about it?"

"Well. . . . Well, I don't want to leave you."

Pulling her to him, he held her tightly, and as he stroked her hair, he murmured, "Don't worry about me, I'll be all right."

Although he had not put it into definite words, she knew he was telling her he wouldn't get . . . sick. She clung to him silently, until, laying her down he pulled the clothes about her; then kissing her gently and saying, "Sleep now," he went swiftly out, forgetting to switch off the light.

She wanted to cry, a loud crying, that would bring him hurrying back, but instead, she lay staring up at the beam which started in the centre of the room and sloped down over her head, to disappear into the wall at the side of the bed. Methodically, she counted the holes in it, as many as she could see, and when she had reached seventy-two Michael came in. Awkward and shy, he stood at the foot of her bed and said, "Hello."

"Hello," she said.

This polite exchange was too much, and turning swiftly over she buried her head in the pillow, and Michael, moving quickly to her, whispered, "What is it?" He touched her shoulder, and when her sobs rose he went hastily and closed the door; then coming back to the bed, and going down on his hunkers, he whispered again, "What is it? Don't you want to go?"

Slowly she twisted round, and raising herself on her elbow and with the corner of the sheet pressed tightly over her mouth, she shook her head vigorously.

"Good Lord!" It was the lowest of whispers. But he did not ask, "Then why are you going?" This small sister who could madden him in so many ways had always remained outside his understanding. When he thought of the things she did and got off with, in his imagination they made her appear older than himself, quite grown-up in fact, different altogether from her appearance. Sometimes, looking at her in exasperation, he couldn't associate her doings with the look of her at all. She should have just been . . . his little sister, but "her!" "she!" and "that little beast!" as he sometimes was justifiably brought to think of her, never had any connection in his mind with her small and fragile make-up. Grudgingly, he was aware that she had powers which he himself was without. Cheek, he sometimes named them—he had not reached the stage where he could pin-point them simply as facets of character.

Now he looked into her eyes, all streaming with tears, and although he couldn't fathom it all out, he knew that she was not going to this school, as he had thought, partly to display her sense of showing off, but she was going solely to please Mr. Lord. And in pleasing Mr. Lord. . . . His thoughts would go no further; he would not allow himself to think. This is all mixed up with me da, for in that thought lay fear and insecurity. The wonder of his father being manager of a farm still lay on the surface of his mind—it had not yet weight enough to sink in—and made a reassuring pattern of life that held no fear . . . no fear of drink and unemployment and a broken home, and no fear of death that he had so nearly reached, when he put his head in the gas oven. . . . So, going so far as to take hold of her hand, which was a long way for him, he said, "You'll like it. And—and I'll write to you."

"Will—will you?" Unconsciously she blew her nose on the end of the sheet, and as he watched her he did not say, as he surely would have done under any other circumstances, "Stop that. Use your handkerchief, you dirty thing!" but "Yes, I will, and I'll tell you how things are going."

"You will?" She looked up, her face eager under her tears as she whispered, "Will you tell me about me da, and if everything's all right with him?"

They looked at each other in silence for a moment, and then he said, briefly, "Yes."

"Promise?"

"Yes."

"And of course about me ma and her foot . . . and the farm an' all. And everything."

"I promise I'll write you once a week."

In this moment, such a promise seemed a very small price to pay for what she was doing, and, quite suddenly, he knew that he didn't want her to go, and a fear came on him that with her going the bond that held them all together would be broken, and they would drift. The fear was not so much for his mother but for his father, yet he was only too well aware that what touched one touched the other.

Rising, he said, "Go on, get to sleep now, it's late. I'll put the light out for you. . . . I'm going to the station with you in the morning. Good-night."

The light went out and the door was gently closed, and slowly she slid down, and turning her face once more into the pillow she started to cry again, but softly, so that no one should hear.

.   .   .   .   .

It was the first time she had been "over the bridge", in Newcastle Central station, and never before had she seen a train as grand as this one, with places all set for breakfast and everything. And she was to have milk and biscuits at ten o'clock and her dinner at twelve—it was all arranged—and the guard was to look after her. She had four comics and a real box of chocolates, and a pile of money, one pound, seventeen and fourpence. The excitement of all this splendour and wealth had taken a slight edge off the coming wrench, until Michael said, "Just another five minutes."

This statement, while it sent her heart tumbling heavily into her shoes, seemed to arouse a nerve of energy in both her da and Mr. Lord. Mike moved quickly and went inside the compartment and looked up at the cases on the rack; then, turning to the elderly couple, the only other occupants of the carriage and interested spectators, he said thickly, "Would you—would you give an eye to her?"

The old man, hitching himself to the front of the seat, said, "Aye, lad, don't you worry—we're going right through. The missis and me'll see she comes to no harm."

The voice was thick Geordie, and, a little reassured, Mike nodded and said, "Thanks. Thanks very much. It's her first trip alone."

"Poor wee thing." The woman too, was sitting forward now, and she emphasised her statement by adding, "She looks so small."

"Aye—" Mike turned away and the words were lost in his throat—"she's small." Why the hell had he let this happen! Why had he stood for it! He should have put his foot down and said, "A school near, or none at all."

As he stepped down on to the platform, even his breathing was checked. Mr. Lord was bending over Mary Ann and tying a watch on her wrist. A flame of searing jealousy shot through him, making him fighting mad, as if he'd had a belly-full of booze. Buying her again . . . at the last minute like this . . . with a watch that looked all gold. And what had he himself given her? Some comics and a few chocolates. And now the old fellow was pushing an envelope into her pocket. God! he wished he could get over this feeling against him. He had tried, and he thought he had succeeded. Then last night when he had insisted on her going, he had hated him.

"Da! Da, look what Mr. Lord's given me. Isn't it lovely?" She was holding her wrist high.

The doors along the train began to bang, and Mr. Lord said quietly, "Come now." On this she turned from Mike and stared up at the face that seemed, in the last few minutes, to have suddenly become very, very old, and in her impetuous way she rushed at him and held up her arms and face.

Mike turned towards Michael, and he did not look round again until her voice cried, "Oh! Da . . . it's going!" Swiftly now he lifted her into his arms, and cupping her face with his good hand he held it still, drawing her on his mind.

"Oh! Mary Ann."

"Da . . . Da."

"Don't cry." His voice was unsteady, and he went on, low and hurriedly, "But remember what I told you last night—if you don't like it, tell me."

"Oh! Da."

"All aboard!"

"Oh! Da." Panic was now welling in her, and as Mike's arms crushed her close to him she became filled with terror, consumed by it, terror of the train . . . the school . . . the unknown.

"Da! Da! Oh! Da."

"There now. Ssh. There now. Say goodbye to Michael."

"Goodbye." There was no sound of the word, and when Michael put his lips to her cheek the tears spurted, and she was blind. She felt herself lifted into the carriage; she heard the door bang and the window pulled down; she felt her da's face close to hers again. Then Mr. Lord's voice, saying, "Goodbye, child. Learn—" was cut abruptly off. But the wheels took up his words and chanted, "Learn, learn, learn, learn—learny, learn, learny learn." Faster and faster they went, and her da was still beside the window, running with the train.

"Oh! Da."

"Be careful, hinny." The woman had hold of her.

"God bless you, my love."

"Careful! Oh! be careful."

He was gone, left standing alone on the very end of the platform, and she struggled from the woman's hands and tried to lean her head out of the window. But she couldn't reach, and so she put out both her hands and waved them frantically.

"There, there. Come on," coaxed the old woman.

Limply she sat down on the edge of the seat, and blinking through the rain of tears she stared dazedly at the blurred outline of the old couple.

"My! you're a clever lass to go all this way on your own. Come and sit aside, me and tell me your name."

The old man drew her over to his knee, and with a "Ups-a-daisy!" lifted her on to the seat. "There now," he said, "dry your eyes and tell me what they call you."

"Mary—Ann."

"Mary Ann." He smiled, and the old woman said, "That's a good old-fashioned name. And it's funny you know, we've got two grand-daughters, and one's called Mary Elizabeth, and the other's called Ann Elizabeth."

Mary Ann sniffed and rubbed at her eyes with her handkerchief. "Me ma's name's Elizabeth. She was c-coming with me, but she f-fell down last night and put her ankle out."

"Oh!" They nodded at each other, and the old man said, "By! he's a fine-looking fellow is your da. I've never seen a mass of red hair like he's got, not for years, I haven't."

Still emitting shivering sobs, she looked from one to the other. They were nice. The man was like Mrs. McBride, the way he talked, only he was a man; and the woman was very little, but she had a nice face.

She sobbed a great sob, and licked at her tears; then asked brokenly, "Would you like a sweet—a chocolate? They're real chocolates. It's a pound box—me da bought it for me."

Without waiting for their reply she slipped off the seat to fetch the chocolates, and when she was settled down again the old woman said, "My! what a grand box. . . . And who was the old man? Your granda?"

"No, he's Mr. Lord. He owns the farm; he's sending me to school."

"Oh." Over her head, the couple looked at each other again, and the old man said, "This school where you are going—where is it?"

"It's in the country, outside of a place called St. Leonards. It's the Convent of the Holy Child of Bethlehem."

"A convent?"

The horror in the old man's voice brought her attention sharply from the unwrapping of the Cellophane around the box, and she looked up at him. His brows were now gathered and his chin jutted as he repeated, "A convent?"

"Yes." Her voice was very small, as if she was admitting to some personal misdemeanour.

"God in heaven! all that way and to a convent. It isn't right."

"George!" The little woman's voice was stern now.

But George did not seem to hear it. "You a Catholic then?" he demanded.

"Yes."

"George!"

"Aren't there no schools near? Have you been in a convent afore?"

"George! Do you hear me?"

"No—I mean yes, there are some near." Mary Ann looked in bewilderment from one to the other. "But I haven't been in a convent afore."

"Come on, dear, open your chocolates." The old woman, greatly agitated, began to assist with the opening of the box, while the old man, leaning back against the seat with a soft thud, fumbled in his pocket for his pipe.

"Oh, they're lovely!" The woman gazed down on the top layer of chocolates, and Mary Ann said, "You have one."

"Thank you."

"Will you have one, Mi-mister?" Mary Ann turned to the old man. But once again he was obscured by the tears she could not stop.

"No, thanks, I'm having me pipe, hinny. . . . Ah well, all right, I will. There, I'll have that one." He picked a small chocolate from the corner of the box. "Our name's Wilson. How old are you?"

"Eight, nearly nine."

"Eight. My God!"

For no reason Mary Ann could see her age seemed to annoy the old man, for he stuffed the chocolate into his pocket, shook his head sharply, then glared at his wife. But Mrs. Wilson was occupied in extracting some knitting from her bag in the corner of the seat; so once again Mr. Wilson lay back. And as he filled his pipe he began to mutter to himself.

Mary Ann looked from one to the other questioningly, but neither of them looked at her, and she was puzzled. She liked them, they represented, through their voices and kindly manner, all the people she was leaving behind. If she hadn't felt so utterly miserable she would have talked to them and told them all about the farm and her da. They liked her da.

"Will you have another chocolate?"

"No, thanks, hinny," Mrs. Wilson smiled down at her. "You eat them, or save them for school; it's always nice to have some taffy or something as a stand-by at school."

Mary Ann sat staring down at the box on her lap. She had never seen such lovely chocolates, but she didn't want to eat them. Da. Oh! Da. Oh! Ma. Oh! Ma, I'm frightened. Panic was rising in her again when her attention was brought from herself by Mr. Wilson's mutterings becoming louder.

"Them places! . . . Traps . . . no schooling . . . I know what I know."

"George! That's enough." This was not said as a command but as a plea, and the gentle words seemed to have a strange power over Mr. Wilson, for they changed his attitude. After taking only one deep breath, he said brightly, "Would you like to go and sit in the corner, hinny, and look out of the window?"

"Yes, please."

"Go on then."

Heavily Mary Ann went across to the other seat and knelt up into the corner; then tucking her legs under her, she turned almost completely around so that in this position she could pretend she was looking out of the window and cry and they wouldn't know it.

The old people looked at each other; then Mrs. Wilson concentrated her attention on her knitting, while he gave himself up to his pipe and his mutterings, but kept the latter well below his breath.

.   .   .   .   .

The eternity of the journey was nearly over and Mary Ann was feeling tired—and different. The farm and all she loved seemed far away in time like last Christmas, and when she tried to think about them a funny thing happened—everything became blurred and ran into one; even her da's face wouldn't stay put, and she couldn't see what he looked like. But Mr. and Mrs. Wilson seemed to have been in her life for ever and she felt that she knew all about them, about Mary Elizabeth and Ann Elizabeth, and even about their other grand-daughter. But when Mr. Wilson started to talk of her, Mrs. Wilson had shut him up by saying, "George!" Yet at intervals during the endless journey he had kept coming back to her. Her name was Teresa. Teresa was in a convent, too, but they hadn't seen her for years, nor her father. Without being told, Mary Ann knew why this was . . . he had "turned". When people turned it did something, caused rows and things. She wished her da would turn. She prayed that he would, every night she prayed, because as everybody knew all Protestants were destined for hell. . . .

At times during the journey Father Owen's words came into her mind, and she wondered if Mr. Wilson was the Devil dressed up again. But then she had discarded that idea, for there was Mrs. Wilson, and she couldn't see the Devil being married.

But now she was having grave doubts as to Mr. Wilson's true identity, for after buttoning up his coat and adjusting his cap he sat down again on the edge of his seat and, leaning towards her, he said, solemnly, "Now, me bairn, listen to what I'm saying; you've a sensible head on your little shoulders." He paused before going on. "Now, if they do anything to frighten you at that place you write straight away to your da. They'll likely watch you like a prisoner, but you—"

"George!" Mrs. Wilson, gathering her belongings together, spoke urgently and sharply under her breath. "It's you who's doing the frightening. You'll have her scared to death."

"I'm only doing me duty." Mr. Wilson was on his feet again. "And if I'd only done it years ago and been firm with our Jimmy things wouldn't have been as they are today . . . family divided and—"

"Be quiet!"

Mary Ann looked quickly at Mrs. Wilson. She sounded just like her ma when her patience was being tried by her grannie.

"You're as much to blame as anybody. Talk about them being bigoted, they've got some way to go to catch up to you."

"Well!" Mr. Wilson's tone, beside being surprised, held all the hurt and misunderstanding in the world. He stared at his wife, then, stretching his scraggy neck out of his collar, he turned and looked out of the window, and Mary Ann yet once again divided her gaze between them. They were fighting, and about the convent. But why should they? Convents, although she had never been in one, held no terrors for her, rather the reverse. She had always wanted to go to one. The only terror lay in the distance that this one was from Newcastle—if it had been "round about", this first day would have been one of joy, for then she could have gone home for the night and told her da all about it.

"Are you all ready, my dear?" Mrs. Wilson was smiling now as if nothing had happened. "You've got all your things together? That's right, put your coat on. Can you feel the train slowing? Aye, it's been a long run, even it's tired."

After Mary Ann had put on her coat, her hands automatically went to her pockets, and coming in contact with the envelope for the first time, she drew it out and gasped her surprise. "Look!" she cried. "Look what I've found in me pocket!"

"Didn't you know it was there? We saw him put it in—the old man—didn't we, George?"

George, apparently forgiven, turned from the window, and said "Aye. Yes, we saw him. Go on, open it."

Mary Ann, opening the envlope drew out two sheets of paper. Between them was a folded pound note. Her eyes flicked up at the old people. Then slowly she read out the few words written on the paper:

"My dear child,
    If you want to please me pay great attention to your lessons and learn—learn everything you can. I know you won't disappoint me. You are a brave little girl, and when you think of me, think of me by the name you once called me—Your Granda."

There was a lump in her throat again. Oh! he was nice. Oh, he was. And to write her a letter. If her da, too, had thought of writing her a letter it would have been wonderful, better even than this. But he had bought her comics, hadn't he, and chocolates.

"By! some more money. By, you're lucky." Mrs Wilson was enthusiastic, but the sight of the pound note returned Mr. Wilson to his natural aversion which centred around anything Catholic. "If you want to keep it," he said, "you hide it. Have you any place to put it?"

"Me purse."

"Oh, they'll look through that."

"I've got me locket." From beneath her dress she pulled out a narrow chain, from which hung a locket, with a holy picture painted on each side, and when she sprung it open to reveal a small rosary Mr. Wilson made a sound in his throat which was too deep for interpretation. Then, with an evident effort towards calmness, he said, "Put them things in your bag, and put your note in there, and the other one an' all from your purse."

Not only did Mr. Wilson give her advice on the expedience of storage, but to his seeming satisfaction he also carried out the operation, and when the locket was once more reposing under cover on Mary Ann's chest, he said, "Well, that's that." Doubtless he felt he had gained a victory over all convents and their iron rules, and the Catholic Church in particular.

As the train come to a jolting stop, which nearly knocked Mary Ann off her seat, Mr. Wilson exclaimed, "Well, now, it's goodbye, me bairn, but we'll likely come across each other again; it's a small world when all's said and done. And when we go back at the end of the month I'll call and see your da, I will that."

"Oh, will you? Oh! ta."

"I will. Goodbye now, hinny, and be a good lass."

"Goodbye, me bairn."

"Goodbye, Mrs. Wilson." Mary Ann looked up at the old woman; then slowly turned her eyes to the old man. These were the very last links with home, and she was loath to let them go. Her voice shook slightly as she said, "I wish I was coming with you."

Mrs. Wilson tapped her cheek, then stooped and kissed her hastily, saying, "Well, you are in a way. We'll likely be on the same train all the way down, and when we get to St. Leonards, we'll look out for you getting off. There now. Now, now, you mustn't cry. Be a brave lass. Come on, let's get these things out, the guard'll be along in a minute."

Almost before Mrs. Wilson had finished speaking there appeared beyond the corridor window the guard, accompanied by two black-robed nuns.

"Go on, hinny, there they are. Go on. Goodbye. The porter will come and get your things."

Mrs. Wilson seemed suddenly anxious that Mary Ann should be gone, and so, manoeuvring herself to block her husband's exit into the corridor, she pushed her away, and Mary Ann, coming to the door, looked straight into the face of the nun and knew her first disappointment.

Nuns were merely angels walking the earth, they were young and beautiful and holy and always smiling. The face before her was youngish, but it was bespectacled and unsmiling and possessed the largest set of buck teeth that Mary Ann had ever seen.

.   .   .   .   .

On the journey from London to St. Leonards Mary Ann discovered only one pleasing thing about her escorts: the one that spoke to her spoke nice—swanky, but nice—but she never smiled. The other nun smiled but didn't speak, and Mary Ann sat looking out of the window lost and alone. Really alone now.

From time to time she fervently wished that Mr. Wilson was sitting opposite. She wouldn't even mind if he went on about the convent. She wasn't interested in the passing scenery—she had seen too much scenery today. Her only impression of it was that it was greener, and the hills went up and down, and on and on. Her mind became a confused maze, whirling round her da, Mr. Lord, Mr. Wilson, her watch, her ma, their Michael and, for some reason or other, the nice young man who had come to work on the farm. Then the rhythm of the wheels churned them altogether until only one filled her weary mind and tear-filled heart, and it went, "Diddle-de-da, diddle-de-da, diddle-de-da, diddle-de-da," then filed itself down into "Me da, me da . . . me da, me da . . . me da, me da . . . me da, me da . . . " and to this chant her head drooped sideways on to the nun's arm, and she went fast asleep.

When she awoke exactly an hour later she didn't know where she was. She looked up at the nun who was bending over her.

"Come along, we're there."

Drunkenly she got to her feet, and the nun, with deft fingers, straightened her hair and adjusted her hat, and then the train stopped, and she was on the platform. She had forgotten about Mr. and Mrs. Wilson until their bright faces and waving hands drew her attention, and she had only time to give one wave in return before the train ran into the tunnel.

"Hallo, there! well, you've arrived." She turned to face another nun who seemed to have descended from the roof, so quickly had she made her appearance. "You look tired. Are you tired?"

"Yes, Miss."

"Yes, Miss. Ha! ha!" The laugh ran down the empty platform. "Sister, child. I'm Sister Agnes Mary." The voice was deep, not unlike a man's.

"Sister." It was the escort speaking, and there was a strong breath of reprimand in the word.

Mary Ann, eyes slightly wider now, moved under the propulsion of the guiding hand of her escort towards the entrance, and ahead of them, carrying both her cases, strode Sister Agnes Mary. Fascinated, Mary Ann watched her make straight for a car, an old car, a very old car, and after dumping the cases into the boot pull open the door, squeeze herself in, and start up the engine.

Nothing at that moment could have surprised her more. Never had she seen a nun in a car, let alone driving one. All her preconceived ideas about nuns were being knocked to smithereens with sledge-hammer force.

"In you get." This was from Sister Agnes. "Push that box along, do it gently. You're not afraid of hamsters, are you?"

Mary Ann, in a stooped position on the step stood riveted, gazing at the wire box full of mice, as she thought of them.

"Oh, well, all right I'll bring them over here. . . . Here." She lifted the box over the back seat. "Hold it, Sister."

Sister Catherine took the box with no great show of pleasure, then putting Mary Ann into the back of the car, and indicating her silent companion to follow, she closed the door and without a word seated herself in the front next to Sister Agnes.

There was a grating somewhere under Mary Ann's seat, then, with a jerk that knocked her backwards, they were off. The young nun steadied her and smiled.

She had been in Mr. Lord's car when he drove fast, but it hadn't been this kind of fast, nor had it made all this noise and rattle. That the noise was even affecting the imperturbable driver was made evident when her voice , above the din, came to Mary Ann, crying, "Have to take His Eminence's inside out tonight."

"I thought you were going to do it this afternoon." Sister Catherine's voice, although loud, was still prim.

"Couldn't. Just got my Office in when I had to go to the laundry. Sister Teresa's got toothache. You'd think it would be rheumatics she'd get, not toothache, wouldn't you?" A pause. "She's small—what's her name?"

"Mary Ann Shaughnessy."

"Huh! 'Just a little bit of heaven'." The words were sung in a full contralto. "That should make the hearts of Sisters Alvis and Monica glad."

"Sister!" again the tone of reprimand, and then. . . . Could Mary Ann believe her ears, or was it the jingling of the car that made Sister Agnes Mary's reply sound like, "Oh, stow it!"

It must have been the jingling of the car, no nun could ever say such things, nuns couldn't know words like "stow it", they were angels. At this point, and so early in her acquaintance of the celestial beings, Mary Ann had to remind herself of this fact, which immediately placed her further acquaintance with the heavenly overflow on a very insecure footing. Matters such as nuns being angels, as everybody knew, should be accepted without question, like the sun coming up and the rain coming down.

The town was left behind now, and the car was rocketing through the narrow, high-hedged lanes. Then, with startling suddenness, that seemed to be the main facet of its character, or was it its driver, it was out of the narrow lane and thundering up a broad drive. And the next minute it had stopped, and Mary Ann was once again lying back in the seat with her legs in the air.

"Come on, out you get, Miss Mary Ann Shaughnessy."

Sister Agnes Mary was holding open the door and laughing. "It's a big name for such a little soul, eh?"

"Yes, Miss—Sister."

Mary Ann stepped out of the car, and recognised immediately that she had dropped, or been thrown, into a new world. Before her were wide steps leading up to a house which was so big that the wall on either side seemed to stretch endlessly away, and all about, in front of the house, people—girls of all ages and grown-ups, and nuns, and over all she felt the canopy of excitement.

Before Sister Catherine's hand descended on her she glimpsed behind her a balustrade and, through its grey stone pillars, terraces falling away in a glory of colour.

Sister Catherine's hand firmly on her head now, she was directed up the steps and through the wide-open doors into a huge hall, with broad oak stairs leading from its farthest end.

Only two impressions touched her whirling mind here. One was that the floor was so highly polished that she could see her white socks in it, and the other that the school was a funny place to have big pictures. In her ascent of the main staircase she glanced up in some awe at the gigantic old paintings covering the walls. But, arrived on the first floor, even these were thrust into the background by the maze of corridors branching from the long gallery. Like an appendage to the silent nun, she turned and twisted and dodged the scurrying figures of girls, and eventually arrived in a corridor away to the right, and at its end went through a door and into a dormitory full of beds. And the impression she had on arrival here was that nobody, nobody had taken the slightest notice of her. She could have been in her own school for all the curiosity she had aroused. And this, strangely enough, added to the weight of her loneliness.

Beside all the beds but one there were cases, and beside each case a child knelt or stood, and with the exception of two of them they were all chattering and laughing across to each other. Of the two, one was kneeling silently by her case and the other was crying by hers, and it was to the bed between these two that Sister Catherine took her. And from there she called imperiously to a girl at the end of the room: "Beatrice!"

Beatrice, a thin, lanky girl of about eleven, came running down the room. "Yes, Sister?"

"Must I remind you about running in the dormitory? Walk—I think we had all this out last term."

"Yes, Sister. I forgot."

To Mary Ann the voice sounded high, swanky and cheeky.

"This is Mary Ann Shaughnessy. Show her what is necessary, then take her down to tea."

"Yes, Sister."

Sister Catherine now turned to Mary Ann, saying, "When your cases come up Beatrice will show you what to do. After tea Reverend Mother wishes to see you; report to Mother St. Francis."

"Yes, Mi—Sister."

The Sister walked out, the door closed after her, and then to Mary Ann's open-mouthed horror, and it was horror, she saw Beatrice's face pucker up until her upper lip exposed in a half moon her top teeth, and her eyes screw up as if she were peering through glasses, and with her arms hanging like penguins' wings she took a few steps towards the door, saying, through her distorted mouth, "Catty Cathie! Catty Cathie!"

There were some apprehensive giggles, there were some laughs, there were also some murmurs of disapproval, but these were low, timid and covert.

"Did she bring you?" Beatrice was fronting Mary Ann now.

"Yes."

"Poor you; you should have had Aggie. Where are you from?"

"From Jarrow. No, I mean in the countryside outside—near Pelaw."

"Make up your mind."

Mary Ann stared at the girl. A moment ago she had stood in awe at her daring; a moment prior to that she had been made uneasy by her swanky voice and manner; now the voice and manner only annoyed her, and simply caused her to think, I don't like her, she's cheeky. Moreover, there was something familiar about the girl that puzzled her.

"What do you think you're doing?" Beatrice had turned from Mary Ann to the girl on her right who had lifted one of her cases on to the bed. "Get that off there—you know they haven't to be put on the bed."

The girl, who was nearly as tall as Beatrice, straightened her back and looked at her; then in a voice of a kind which Mary Ann had never heard before, she said, slowly, "Eef you do not like eet, then leeft it hoff, or go and run to teel Sister."

The two girls faced each other across the bed, then Beatrice nodding slowly, said, "All right, you wait until to-morrow when the marks start." With this she walked away, and an oppressive silence fell on the room for a few seconds. Then it was broken by the sound of a bell and a number of voices calling together excitedly, "Tea! tea! tea! Come on."

There was a scrambling round the cases, and Mary Ann watched the legs flying down the dormitory. The girls were all running now, but at the door Beatrice stopped for a moment and called back to Mary Ann, "Come on." But she did not wait for her, and as Mary Ann made to walk away from her bed the girl from the next bed said, "Take hoff your coat and hat."

The tone was kindly, and Mary Ann took her things off, then looked at the girl. And the girl held out her hand and said, "Come."

With her hand in the strange girl's Mary Ann walked up the empty dormitory, and she had the feeling she was with someone "grown-up". Before the girl opened the door she paused and said, "My name is Lola, and yours ees Mary Han?"

"Yes."

The girl nodded, and a little smile lighted up her grave face. Outside the door they surprised the girl from the other bed. She was rubbing vigorously at her face, and Lola said, off-handedly, "You make hit worse, Marian. You are not the honly one who cry today. Come on."

Marian, walking on the other side of Mary Ann, sniffed a number of times, then spoke across her to Lola. "I wasn't crying about coming back . . . I wasn't really. It was when Sister Alvis told me I was in Beatrice's dorm. She's awful. She's hateful. I wish I wasn't nine."

Mary Ann, perhaps in an effort to comfort someone who looked and sounded as sad as she felt, said, "I'm only eight."

Now she had the attention of them both.

"Height?" said Lola. "But you should be down in zee Lower School. Thees is Middle School, nine to thirteen."

"But I'll soon be nine—in August."

They did not remark on this, but turning in the opposite direction from the main staircase they joined a mass of girls hurrying, but not running now, towards a narrower stairway at the end of the gallery.

Mary Ann could see nothing but gym-slips and white blouses until, reaching level ground again, she had her first glimpse of the dining-hall. Tables jutted out from the walls all round a great room, except for a space at the bottom end, which was taken up by a long table running lengthwise. Still attached to Lola, she was guided to a table some way down the room and pushed into a seat. And there before her was a plate holding three slices of bread and butter, a square of cake and a dob of jam, and, leaning against it, a card which bore the words "Mary Ann Shaughnessy".

She was staring at the card when all shuffling was suddenly cut off. So quick did the silence fall that she turned round to see the cause, and just as she glimpsed it her head was brought to the front again by a shove from Lola. But by straining her eyes sideways she could see, filing through a side door and into the centre of the hall down towards the long table, a stream of nuns. She thought of them as a stream: she counted ten black-robed figures with white collars, and following these ten more in unrelieved black, and then, slightly behind, a small figure, so small that Mary Ann had the funny impression that the clothes were walking by themselves. She watched fascinated as they all filed into their seats, and towards the seat in the exact centre, facing the room, went the little black-encased figure.

"Bless us, O Lord, and these Thy gifts which we recive through Thy bounty. Through Jesus Christ, Our Lord. Amen."

"Amen."

The echo by the school to the Reverend Mother's voice seemed to be the signal for activity. Six of the white-collared Sisters left the table, and going, one after the other, to a lift in the wall, reached into the depths and brought out great enamel teapots and proceeded to supply the tables.

The grace that had just been said was at this moment giving Mary Ann a faint trace of comfort, for was it not the very same grace that she and their Michael said every day? After all, apart from its bigness, this school might be just like the one at Jarrow. That the grace was the only thing in common that the convent had with her late school was mercifully withheld from her.

"Eat your tea." A Sister was standing over her.

She looked up. "I'm not hungry, Sister."

"Nevertheless, eat your tea." The voice was low, thickened with an Irish twang, and the tone brooked no discussion.

Many of the plates about her were quickly emptied. Yet it was heartening to note that a number, like hers, still held a quantity of bread. So intriguing to her were the actions of the Sisters who were serving, and also the apparent immobility of all the black-robed figures at the top table, that when a little bell tinkled and the thin voice came again, saying grace, the fifteen minutes the tea had taken seemed like one to her.

In silence, the top table was vacated, but as soon as the last nun had disappeared through the side door the room became a hive of bustle, but, strangely, no chatter.

As Mary Ann went to move from her place, the Sister who had told her to eat her tea appeared again, but with a smile splitting her face now, and dropping to her hunkers which in itself was a surprise, as Mary Ann had always been in some indecision whether or not there really were real legs beneath the skirts of nuns, she took Mary Ann's hands and said in a voice gurgling with laughter, "Mary Ann Shaughnessy. What a name! Are you from Ireland, child?"

"No. No, Sister." Who, even with all the sadness of the world on their shoulders, could help but smile back into this round, beaming face.

"No? But your father was?"

"No, Well, yes. . . ." There had always been a doubt about this, but how could she say, "Me da was an orphan without any name and the name Shaughnessy was just given him. They took it from the porter who picked him up at the gate." She had never said, even to herself, "Workhouse gate."

"Ah, ha! Now don't try to tell me you're Welsh or something with a name like Shaughnessy . . . Shaughnessy. Oh! what a lovely mouthful. And what a North Country voice it is." She patted Mary Ann's cheek as she got to her fet. "Well, there, off you go. . . . Oh, you're with Lola? That's grand; Lola'll look after you."

The Sister patted Lola's cheek now, and for the first time Lola really smiled, and Mary Ann thought, She's nice, I like her, which could have meant, in this case, either or both of them.

"I'll take you to Mother St. Francis."

"Will you?" They were in the Lower Hall. "What do they call that Sister?"

"Sister Alvis."

"Oh." A question arose in Mary Ann's mind. "Why do they call some Mother and some Sister?" she asked.

"The Mothers har mostly teachers, the Sisters do the work. They har the ones who wear the white collars."

"Oh. . . . Is the Reverend Mother nice?"

"She ees all right. You weel not see much of her. Come this way."
More corridors.

"Will you wait for me? I'll get lost comin' back."

"Yes."

"And will you show me what to do? I don't want that Beatrice to show me."

"She wouldn't, hin any case."

"But the Sister told her." Mary Ann's eyes widened.

"Sister Catherine is always telling her. She tries to punish her by geeving her duties, but it makes no deeference. You will see has time goes on."

"Are you from a foreign country?"

"Yes." Lola now smiled down on her. "France and Germany."

"Two!"

"Yes, my mother is French and my father German. But you, too, are from a foreign country."

"Me!" Mary Ann stopped, slightly indignant. "Me! No, I'm not, I'm from England, Jarrow."

"Oh. Ha! ha!" It was a small laugh and did not annoy Mary Ann in the least, nor did the insult to her beloved North which followed. "It is, nevertheless, odd how you talk—very guttural. Some people in France speak like thees. You will soon mend it here. I am only three terms, and I am mending mine very much."

Mary Ann didn't know now whether she wanted her voice mended—mending it, she understood, would make it sound swanky. And yet, that's what she was here for, that's why Mr. Lord had sent her.

"Here is Mother St. Francis."

They were approaching a nun. She had a round, fat face and, not to be disguised by her habit, a round, fat body. She looked about sixty, but appeared like a hundred to Mary Ann.

"Mother, this is Mary Ann Shaughnessy. She ess to see Reverend Mother."

"Hallo, Sister—Mother."

"You are small. You're in Middle House, aren't you? Yes—I remember. I'm the bursar, I look after your money." She laughed. "And your letters and everything—and everything. You see? Come along this way. From the Tyne, are you? I know the Tyne. . . . Ah, yes, this way. You wait, Lola."

It was evident to Mary Ann that Mother St. Francis didn't need any answers, she gave them all to herself. She talked quickly as she waddled along.

"Now when Reverend Mother asks you a question, you answer 'Yes', or 'No, Reverend Mother', you see? And don't speak unless you are spoken to. You see? There now, here we are."

A tap on a door, to which a small voice replied, and they were inside the room. And there was the little woman, sitting behind a big desk. As Mary Ann was pressed nearer she could see less and less of her, until, standing right close up to the desk, there seemed only the head and shoulders left.

"And you are Mary Ann?"

"Yes, Sis—Reverend Mother."

"And you've come a long journey by yourself?"

"Yes, Reverend Mother."

"And do you think you will like being here?"

"No, Reverend Mother."

There, it had dropped out before she could stop it. And on its heels came a little gasp from herself and a loud one from somewhere behind her, but from across the table came a laugh, a little tinkling laugh that reminded her somehow of the bell that went just before you had Communion.

"Come here."

She followed the beckoning finger and went round the side of the desk, and there two small, dry hands took hers.

"Let me look at you."

The Reverend Mother looked at Mary Ann, and Mary Ann looked back at her, wondering that anybody so small could be in such a position of majesty—she didn't, at close quarters, seem much bigger than herself.

"Tell me, child, how is my brother?"

Her brother? Mary Ann's mouth fell open in perplexity, and then snapped quickly closed as she remembered that this person before her was Mr. Lord's sister. How this could be she didn't rightly know for Mr. Lord wasn't a Catholic and he didn't, she felt, like Catholics. She didn't connect "turning" with the woman before her—no one could "turn" into a Reverend Mother.

"He's all right."

"He's well?"

"He gets colds now and then, but that's because he lives in that big old house and he's only got Ben to see to him. When he comes to live at the farm, me ma. . . . "

"Ahem!"

The sound was right behind her again, and she finished lamely, "She'll see he's all right—Reverend Mother."

"He is very interested in you, my child."

She gave no answer to this, for didn't she know it. Look where it had landed her. She was forgetting where it had also landed her father and mother and Michael.

"And he desires that you learn, and learn well. Are you going to do that?"

"Yes—Reverend Mother."

"That's a good child. Now go with Mother St. Francis, and God bless you and make you happy here."

Her hands were released, she was turned about by her guide and the next minute she was in the corridor being handed over to Lola.

"There you are then. There you are, that's over. You see? Now, up to the dormitory. Get your necessary things put in your drawers, then bring all the rest down to the stores. Leave your case empty. Away now, then come to me and bring your money to be looked after. Off you go."

Not until they had reached the corridor leading to the dormitory did Mary Ann speak, and then she asked, "Do you really get your money back?"

"Yes, of course, when we go out on half-day, or to the beach."

Mary Ann was again silent—she didn't want to part with her money, any of it. She was glad now that Mr. Wilson had stuffed the notes in her locket. She touched her chest and felt a sense of comfort.

Her hand was still flat on her chest when she entered the dormitory, but it was immediately doubled into a fist as Beatrice's voice, which, at this moment, sounded strangely like her own, hit her, saying, "I'm from Jarr . . . aa . . . no, in the coun . . . tree. Pee . . . la."

Beatrice was standing in the middle of the dormitory and causing a great deal of amusement with her imitation, but as Mary Ann slowly advanced towards her the laughter died away leaving a strained silence.

By her own bed and within a yard of Beatrice, Mary Ann stopped. Her face screwed up to a button, she glared at Beatrice. She knew now who she reminded her of—it was Sarah Flannagan.

Schools may be housed in elaborate country mansions with extensive grounds and terraces and playing fields; awe-inspiring nuns and Sisters might float through their richly furnished interiors; rich men's daughters could be packed in dozens in air-conditioned dormitories; yet were these girls after all but exactly the same types that filled the schools in Jarrow and such like towns. The only difference was they talked swanky. This would have summed up Mary Ann's thoughts had she been able to define them, but all she was aware of at the moment was the feeling that was not uncommon to her, and now it was telling her that this Beatrice was a cheeky thing, a cheeky beast—even a cheeky bitch!

"Who are you makin' game of?"

Was there anything awe-inspiring or electrifying in that question? It would undoubtedly seem so, for never before had anything happened in the school lives of the ten spectators to call for such expressions as were now very much apparent on their faces. This new girl had dared to cheek a prefect, and such a prefect. She must be mad. The mouths were agape and hanging, the eyes stretched wide and bulging. Had Sister Alvis been present she would have supposed that nothing short of the second Pentecost, which alone she was for ever prophesying would be required to arouse them, had actually taken place. It is almost certain to say that to them something of equal importance had happened, for only a visitation by the Deity Himself could possibly have called forth the gasp that rose to the ceiling.

"You're a cheeky beast! And if you keep on I'll write and tell me da about you, so I will!"

The situation was quite beyond all recognized bounds. It was undoubtedly the first of such that had happened to Beatrice, and, as smart as she was, she could call up no move to counter it. All the unwritten rules on behaviour between prefects—although her real power could not begin until 6.45 a.m. tomorrow morning—and the crawling subservient sycophants known as pupils had been swept away by this—this— The word "common" leapt to Beatrice's rescue, and using it in a way that would turn defeat into victory, she lifted her nose as if detecting a vile smell, slowly raised her head on high, and turning away gave her authoritative sentence to the audience: "Common individual!"

The spring Mary Ann was about to make was abruptly checked by Lola's hand, and so painful was the grip on her arm that sanity returned to her, and with it deflation. Shrugging off the guiding hand of Lola she went to the bedside and, kneeling down with a thud beside her cases, she turned the key in the lock of the largest one and lifted up the lid. Then sitting back on her heels, she gazed through misted eye at the neatly folded clothes her mother had packed away only yesterday, and, her head drooping lower to hide her raining tears, she cried silently, "Oh! Ma, Ma, I want to come home. Oh! Ma."

5

Was it seven days or seven years or seven lifetimes that Mary Ann had been in the Convent of the Holy Child of Bethlehem? If you asked her she would have pondered, refusing to believe that all the many different things that had been pushed into her head had taken only seven days to accomplish.

This time last week she had been a small creature of another world, but now the doings of that world had become vague, and to remind her that it had ever existed there remained only a few people. Her da—always her da; her ma—when she was in bed at night; their Michael at odd times; Mr. Lord, when she was in class; Father Owen when she was in church; Mrs. McBride rather funnily enough when she saw Sister Alvis; and Sarah Flannagan whenever her eyes alighted on Beatrice, which unfortunately, even with the disparity in their ages, was often, for Beatrice was the allocator of marks—black ones. If nothing else had stuck in her mind the sources from which these were derived were firmly fixed. Dearly was she paying for cheeking a prefect. Although you acquired only one mark for being late, already her score in this section was four. But if you were skilfully manoeuvred to the last wash basin, and even there were the last to use it, what could you do? Only finish your dressing running along the corridor. Well, she had done that twice. The first time, encountering Mother St. Bede, she had been helped into her things, but the second time Mother St. Bede had not only sent her back to dress but had added two to her score. Then this same Mother St. Bede, who took English, a language quite different from any Mary Ann had previously listened to, had yesterday yelled at her, right at the top of her voice which was of some surprising height. "Child! child! child!" she had yelled, "it is not the BOO . . . CHER, it is the BUT . . . CHER. Say after me, the BUT-CHER, the BAYKER, the CANDLESTICK MAY-KER."

Dutifully she had repeated the butcher, the baker, the candlestick maker, and the laughter this oration in her own language had evoked had aroused her fighting spirit, yet at the same time made her want to cry. The whole place, in her estimation, was daft, with a daftness that went on in an intermittent never-ceasing whirl from seven-thirty a.m. till eight forty-five p.m.

On Mondays and Wednesdays the daftness was, if anything, intensified, for these were early Mass days when you were hoiked out of bed at a quarter to seven by Sister Monica, who slept behind a curtain at the end of the dormitory, and who brought you to life by slapping your bottom, and not just a little slap either, and at the same time calling, in a surprisingly cheerful voice at that unearthly hour, "Arise, arise. Arise to the glory of God. Come on now, up with yous."

Mary Ann was of the opinion that Sister Monica never slept. How could she, when even before that time she had said an hour's Office.

Having experienced as yet only one Monday and Wednesday, Mary Ann had already decided that she hated Mondays and Wednesdays. Back home she had liked going to Communion on a Friday and church at any time, but here church was different. It was inside the grounds, and the four houses, comprising children of seven to young ladies of seventeen, marched there in straggling, silent, crocodiles. If you dared to open your mouth it was ten-to-one that somebody would pounce on you and up would go your score. You wouldn't think they would have bothered at that time in the morning, but they did.

This scoring of marks was not an individual thing, either. Through them you apparently carried on your shoulders the honour of your house, for one girl's misdemeanours could prevent her house from getting the cup, and already Mary Ann knew just to what pitch of fervour each house could reach in their struggle to obtain this cup. Only yesterday it had been made clear to her by a spontaneous deputation, surrounding her on the playing field, that the attainment of the prize did not lie with her, but the loss of it did, and she had to stop getting black marks—or else.

For once in her life she had found nothing to say, but had stood near to tears in the corner of the field thinking, Oh! Da. Oh! Da. Then an odd thing had happened which took her mind off her troubles for a few moments. Over the railings in another field where the big girls were playing hockey she saw a strange sight. Her mind seemed to suggest that it was even a sacrilegious sight, for there, with her gown tucked up, was Mother St. Jude, and she was running, flying and shouting as she bashed out with a hockey stick as if she were throwing the hammer. Mary Ann knew very well now that nuns had legs, but this was the first time she had ever seen them, even a bit of them, and it didn't seem right. She was sure that none of the nuns in the North would ever run like that. Nuns should walk—and walk slowly.

Then there was Sister Agnes Mary. She couldn't get over Sister Agnes Mary. Sister Agnes Mary could take a car right to bits—she had seen her doing it yesterday in the yard—and she bred mice, called hamsters; and she laughed. She was laughing all the time, except when she said her Office; and when saying that she would go round muttering to herself with a very straight face, being sorry, Mary Ann supposed, for all the laughing she had done.

This saying of "the Office" business both interested and puzzled Mary Ann. In all odd places she would come across a nun saying this Office. Sister Alvis had really startled her one day, for when passing her, and she apparently deeply engrossed in her reading, she had suddenly heard her exclaim, and loudly, "Jesus!" It had sounded so like Mrs. McBride that she had looked at the Sister and exclaimed, "Eeh!" before being pushed in the back by Lola.

And then there was the timetable. Oh! the timetable. It was the axis of the daftness. Tuesdays, Thursdays, Fridays and Saturdays, you rose at seven-thirty, washed and dressed, and got down to breakfast, if no impediment, by eight o'cock, and not until after the meal were you allowed to open your mouth. This compulsory silence was a great trial to Mary Ann. Between eight-twenty and nine o'clock you were expected to do various things, which included making your bed, going to Mother St. Francis for your letters, toothpaste, soap, and salts if you couldn't go to the lavatory, and to Sister Catherine if you had buttons off or things like that. Then nine o'clock was upon you before you knew where you were. From nine o'clock till half-past you had religious instruction. It was like the Bible history she used to have in Jarrow, and she didn't mind that in the least. But from nine-thirty to ten it was science.

Now Mary Ann knew nothing whatever about science, and she didn't want to know, for science was all about frogs and tadpoles and she was repulsed by both, even before they were cut up. From frogs she went into French and Mother St. Matthew. Un, deux, trois, quatre. . . . The first four she could remember quite easily, for she resorted to a little unconscious Pelmanism and thought of the four figures as "under two cats". Le and la was another business entirely. Did it matter whether you knew they were males or females as long as you said Mr. or Mrs. That's all that mattered, surely. But apparently not to Mother St. Matthew.

Then followed milk; then gym. She liked gym—she could jump and skip better than some of the bigger girls, and "cowp her creels". This statement for turning a somersault had caused quite a diversion, but nobody was going to make her believe it should be "head over heels" . . . they were daft, all of them. Following gym, innocently arranged, was the visit to the infirmary and Matron who dealt with toothache, spots, and blisters. If you didn't have any of these things you had fifteen minutes to yourself.

From the infirmary you were pitchforked into history. Mary Ann thought of it as being pitchforked. She knew the word for her da used it a lot at one time. "I was pitchforked into the shipyard," he used to say, and now it seemed to describe the entry into the room where they took history. The room was at the end of a long corridor, and to Mary Ann that particular corridor was lined with prefects who pushed you along if you were speaking and pushed you along if if you weren't, and at the classroom door, a week's experience had taught Mary Ann, Mother St. Bede would be waiting—as if she didn't have enough of her in English—to fling you into your seats. The only consolation she felt was that here she wasn't the only one to experience the nun's treatment for tardiness.

Mother St. Bede was identified to Mary Ann by three things. She yelled in her English class, she pushed in her history class, and, thirdly, she was known privately as "Mother Fear-o'-God," for at the height of exasperation she was known to fling her arms wide and cry, "Nothing but the fear of God will knock it into you. It's past me, it's past me!"

The only thing to be remembered during history was that it would be followed by geography and Mother Mary Divine. Oh, Mother Mary Divine was nice . . . she was lovely. She loved Mother Mary Divine. Mother Mary Divine patted her cheek and called her "Dear child", and she had won Mary Ann's heart forever by asking, and in the proper voice, "And how is canny Jarrow?"

At twelve-fifteen she reluctantly left Mother Mary Divine and went tearing with the rest of her class in the scramble for letters. If you were lucky and there was one for you you took it into the General Study and there devoured it. If you weren't you went out into the playground or into the fields where Sister Agnes Mary usually was. But you couldn't get near her, everybody wanted to be with Sister Agnes Mary 'cos she made you laugh. If you liked you could go and feed the rabbits or the mice, or the budgerigars. These latter were bred by an old Sister so old that Mary Ann was fascinated by her wrinkles. She had little apples on her cheeks and her eyes were blue and sunk far into her head. Her name was Sister Prudence, but she was known, even to her face, as Sister Gran-Gran.

Dinner was a further trial to Mary Ann, for whether you liked it or not you had to eat it; if you didn't one of the Sisters stood over you until you did. Mary Ann didn't like cabbage. She hated cabbage and she had said so. This was another thing that had caused a diversion, and, indeed, even some smothered chortling from the servers.

The afternoons hadn't been too bad at first. There was art and botany and games, followed three times a week by a bath. And no fire to sit at after you were dry either.

Then yesterday she had been told that one lesson had to be missed every afternoon to be replaced by elocution. At first she had been excited and thought, Now I'll show Sarah Flannagan, but that was before the lesson. Bas—kets . . . bill—iards . . . bat—ter—ies, and bluebot—tles . . . Cas—kets, cam—els and castles, and sticking her tongue all over the place to try and talk swanky.

Following tea at four-fifteen there was twenty minutes' recreation, before the most trying part of the day. Whereas at home after school she could, and had, run wild, now she had to go and sit with her house in the study, and after the first ten minutes a bell would ring which meant "no talking". This was a foretaste of purgatory. It was no use trying to slip a word in, for at the high desk near the window sat first one study mistress and then another. Every half-hour they changed, and no matter who they were silence was the order of the day. The only diversion was the signal to leave the room, but even her courage failed at anything more than two requests.

From six-thirty to seven you could write your letter, that is if you had done all your homework, but they didn't call it homework. At seven o'clock you knelt and said the Angelus, and it was always wonderful to Mary Ann to hear the sound of her own voice again. Yet then, following this, they went to supper, she seemed to have very little to say to anyone—the inactivity of sitting always seemed to dry her up. After the meal, for one full hour the time was her own, to go out to play, weather permitting, or to write or read. The only thing you couldn't do was—moon. Nuns seemed to drop from the ceiling, appear through the walls, or up through the floorboards should you show the least suspicion of mooning.

Following on this hour was chapel for fifteen minutes. And here began another trial, because from the moment you stepped into line you were as good as gagged until breakfast the following morning. You could talk, oh! yes, if you were one of those people who were clever enough not to be caught, but Mary Ann had not yet learned the trick, so she was as good as dumb.

But tonight, the beginning of this particular trial was a good half-hour away. It was only eight o'clock and she was hugging three letters to her breast. They had all come at once, one each from her da, her ma and their Michael. This was only the second letter she'd had from her da, and it wasn't very long, but it was lovely, all about the farm. And then he said he missed her and was ticking off the days to the summer holiday. Her ma's letter was nice, but her ma's letters and everything about her ma were always nice. Her ma brought no worry to her mind, she could always be relied upon to be the same. She laughed at their Michael's letter. It was the first he'd written to her and it was funny, so different from when he talked. He said such things as "Up the school!" and "Miss La-de-da Mary Ann Shaughnessy". Then he had told her some bits of news that made her homesick in a different way. "You should have been home," he said, "on Wednesday. Mr. Polinski hit Mrs. Polinski and she came running to our house, and there was a to-do. And what do you know? The new hand is going to stay with us. I like him, so does me da—my father. Sorry, Miss Shaughnessy." Oh, their Michael was funny.

As it was raining the recreation room, if not crowded, was well filled and Mary Ann, lucky for once, had bagged a little table near the window and was busy, between chews at her pen and glances out of the window on to a view whose beauty was entirely lost on her, writing to her ma and da. Only the heading on the paper did no say "Ma and Da," it said, "Dear Mother and Father." Her first letter had been confiscated not only for beginning with "Ma and Da" but because she had gone on to give graphic details of meals, at which there was cabbage, marks, of which she was acquiring a burden, Mother St. Bede, who was awful, and last but by no means least Beatrice. Now her gazing out of the window was a concentrated effort to formulate her news in such a way that it would get through. As the time was beginning to ebb away and her mind would suggest nothing in the nature of a code, she continued her letter by saying, "I am lerning to talk proply every afternoon and say bas—kets, bil—li—ards, bat—ter—ies and bluebottles. Cas—kets, cam—els and castles. Tell Mr. Lord and I will write him the morr—tomorrow. I had a pain in me stomach this morning cos I had a pill, and oh it was awful, and then I had to eat——" She had been going to say cabbage, but remembering that this slip might mean the rewriting of the whole letter she substituted instead a kindness she had received from the very Sister who had stood over her and made her stuff the cabbage down her throat, thereby bringing censure on the poor woman who had been trained to show no discrimination among the children. She scratched out "I had to eat" and wrote "Sister Mary Martha slipped me three sweets cos I ate me dinner. I wish I could see you. I have got to go to bed now. I think of you in bed and say Hail Marys for you. The Holy Family in the church here isn't like ours in Jarrow, they are cut out of wood and haven't any colours on them, and haven't got nice faces. It's confession tomorrow, I wish Father Owen was here. Will our Michael tell him about me on Sunday? I've got to go, they're clearing up. Oh Ma. Goodnight Mother and Father and our Michael, and twenty million kisses, Mary Ann."

There, that was done. Just as she folded up the letter and placed it on top of the envelope ready for Mother St. Francis's inspection Marian came up and sat on the window seat.

"You writing again? You are always writing." She sounded slightly offended, and Mary

Ann said, "Well, I like to write to me ma and da."

"Why do you always say ma and da?"

"Well, cos they are."

"You're funny." This statement was given as a criticism, but Mary Ann took it in good part and looked at her new friend, whose face was very straight and whose mouth was tight and who, Mary Ann knew from a week's experience, could burst into tears at any moment.

"Why don't you write to your da . . . father?"

Marian turned away, breathed on the window and drew a pattern with the point of her finger. "He's always travelling, he'd never get my letters."

"Then why don't you write to your ma then?"

"I do, every week."

"But why don't you every day?"

"Oh, that would be silly." With a swift movement of her hand Marian wiped out the pattern. "What's your father like?"

This was the first time anyone had asked after her da. Mary Ann closed her eyes for a moment, then opened them wide as she began on the subject that forever filled her heart. "He's wonderful. He's big—oh, ever so big, and he's got a lovely face." At this point, before she had even got warmed up, her discourse was broken into by Marian's voice saying abruptly, "Oh, all right. What's your mother like?"

Mary Ann blinked. "Oh, me ma? She's lovely an' all. Her hair's like gold and she's got masses and masses of it." Then looking at Marian's tight face, she asked merely out of politeness and not because she wanted to know, "Is your ma nice?"

"Yes, she's lovely, she's wonderful." Quite lively now, Marian gave Mary Ann all her attention and described for her in glowing detail the wonder that went to make up her mother, and this description of a most glamorous being went on until Mother St. Francis's inspection interrupted it.

Mary Ann's letter having been passed with only her English at fault, which was nothing to worry about, at least in her opinion, the bell alone brought Marian's oration to a final stop. But she went to the chapel with face aglow, and even later when she was finishing her undressing under her nightie, as they all did, she smiled brightly across at Mary Ann. So it was surprising that some time later Mary Ann should wake in the faintly illuminated dark to hear the sound of muffled sobbing coming from Marian's bed. As she lay listening to it, it saddened her and made her want to join in, and she thought, Oh! Da. Oh! Ma.

When, after what seemed to her a long, long time, Marian was still crying, she raised herself up and peered towards her.

In the glow from the night-light at the end of the dormitory all she could make out was a contorted heap, and so it was the most natural thing in the world that she should get out of bed and creep over to Marian.

"Marian, what's the matter?"

Marian raised her head. "I—I want my—my Mummy and Daddy."

It was only a whisper, and Mary Ann whispered back, "So do I."

"Nobody loves me."

This statement stumped Mary Ann for a moment, then putting her arm around Marian's shoulder, she whispered, "Yes they do—I do, and Lola."

"Do you?" Their faces were close, their breaths fanned each other.

Mary Ann, shivering with the cold, at this point said, "Move over, and I'll come in with you."

Within a second she was well under the clothes and lying close to Marian, and, as if she were the elder, she put her arms about her and comforted her, saying, "Don't cry, Marian."

"I've no one to talk to," said Marian. "Lola won't listen, she says I'm to forget it."

Mary Ann did not enquire what she had to forget, but said, "Why don't you talk to the priest? I used to tell Father Owen everything."

"Did you?"

"Yes."

"I don't like to."

"Why not? They don't know who's telling them."

"They don't know?" There was a sound of amazed enquiry in Marian's voice; and after a couple of sniffs, she asked, "What do you mean?"

"Why, cos priests are blind when they are hearing confessions." Mary Ann spoke with authority. "I know cos Father Owen is in Jarrow; I used to tell him everything and he never knew it was me, cos God strikes them all blind once they get in the box. But they're all right when they come out again."

"That's silly!"

"'Tisn't, Marian, honest."

"Who told you?"

"I've always known."

"Is it the truth, honest? I've never heard it before."

"Yes, it's the truth. Honest. . . . You go and tell eveything to the priest—Father Hickey, he's not bad. But he's not like Father Owen. Oh, Father Owen was lovely. . . . Will you go and tell him what you're crying for?"

"Yes."

"Well, what are you crying for?" This was diplomacy at its worst.

There was a silence, during which Mary Ann became aware that she was being nearly smothered beneath the quilt, and she came up for air. And as she did so she had the terrifying impression that someone was moving about at the end of the dormitory. Then Marian said, "It's about my Mummy—my Mummy and Daddy don't live together."

"What!" Mary Ann brought her attention back to her bedmate.

"They're separated. . . . I—I've only seen Daddy once in—oh, once in a long, long time."

This admission threw everything else out of Mary Ann's mind, and bringing her head under the clothes again she whispered in deepest sympathy, "Oh, Marian." Her arms tightened around the bigger girl. "Oh, poor Marian! . . . Look—" she had an idea— "when I go back home you can come with me. You'll love me da, and he'll——"

What Mike was to do in the way of giving Marian comfort died in Mary Ann's mind almost in the act of its conception, for was it up from Hell or down from Heaven that the hands came. She didn't know, but come they did, two great powerful hands, and she was lifted sky high, swung through the air and plumped into her bed, and it stone cold. And a voice, which had certainly not been nurtured in Heaven, hissed over her, "Move out of there again if you dare! I'll see you in the morning, you wicked child!"

Terror filled the night. What had she done? Only got into Marian's bed cos she was crying. . . . Oh! Ma . . . Ma . . . . I want to come home. . . . Why was she a wicked child? and what would happen in the morning? She wished she was dead. This was a surprising thought, for up to now nothing but the trouble between her ma and da had power to evoke a wish for her own demise. Her feet were cold and she was shivering. She began to cry, and to the chant of "Oh! Ma. Oh! Da", which went round and round in her head, she went to sleep.

.   .   .   .   .

The outcome of the bed episode had an effect on the occupants of the dormitory equal in Mary Ann's opinion to that of someone swearing at a priest or hitting a teacher, or some such earth-shaking catastrophe. She was gaped at, talked at, talked about, and pushed around, and, what was more, she received five discipline marks and six more for discourtesy. This latter injustice because she had dared to speak back to Sister Mary

Martha, when all she had said was that she didn't know it was forbidden to get into another girl's bed. What was more, everybody in the house was laughing about priests being blind in confession, and this hadn't come about by Marian talking, but by Beatrice, who, seeing an opportunity to work for the cause of discipline marks, had risen stealthily and listened to the comforting advice Mary Ann was giving to Marian, and solely, let it be understood, in the cause of discipline had gone and informed the Sister.

And now Mary Ann was learning the deep science of comparative values of behaviour. Outside a convent you could sleep in a bed with somebody else, inside you couldn't. Sister Monica said so; Sister Agnes Mary said so; and Sister Catherine said so. Of course, Sister Catherine would! She said it a number of times, and in a number of different ways, as she took Mary Ann along to Mother St. Francis—who also said it. So, by ten o'clock, Mary Ann was left in no doubt as to the procedure of sleeping in a convent. And finally she awaited the order to appear before the Reverend Mother. But this threat did not materialise; instead, she was sent to Mother St. Bede—and English. And so unnerving had been the events of the morning that her stomach felt sick, and she wanted to go to the lavatory all the time; but such was the power of Mother St. Bede that her internal organs sympathetically understood the impossibility of a request to be relieved and did the only thing that was left to them, they swelled.

Half-way through the lesson Mother St. Bede banged the flat of her hand on the desk and called out loudly, "Mary Ann Shaughnessy! will you stop wriggling. Are you sitting on a pin?"

"No, Mother."

"Then don't act as if you were. Did you leave the room before you came in?"

This Irishism was fully understood by Mary Ann, and she said, "Yes, Mother," but had not the face to add, "but I want to leave again."

"Then sit still. Better still, stand up and read page fourteen."

Mary Ann turned the pages of her book, and to her relief she saw that the poem was one of Longfellow's. Oh, she could do him, she knew yards of Hiawatha—if only she didn't want to leave the room.

"What does it say?"

"Musins, by Longfellow."

"What does it say?"

"Musins. . . . "

"It does not say 'Musins', it says 'Musings'. Repeat . . . 'Musings.' . . . And who by?"

"Longfellow."

"It does not say Longfellow."

"Henry Wadsworth Longfellow."

"Begin."

> *"I sat by my window one night*
> *And watched how the stars grew bright.*
> *And the earth and the skies were a splendid sight*
> *To a sober and musin' eye."*

"Mus . . . inge . . . inge. Musing . . . eye."

"Musing eye." Oh dear! she felt sick.

"Go on."

> *"From Heaven the silver moon shone down,*
> *With gentle and mella ray . . . "*

"Stop! What's a mella ray? . . . Mellow, child."

" . . . *mellow ray,*
And beneath the crowded roofs of the town
In broad light and shadda lay."

Bang! bang! bang! Mother St. Bede's hand bounced on the desk.

"Shadda! shadda! shadda! . . . shad—ow—ow—ow—dow. . . . Shadow!"

Mother St. Bede's lips were so far out that her mouth resembled a snout, and her "ow—ow—ow" sounded like the wailing of a screech owl.

"Shadow."

It was hot, she felt sick, her stomach was bursting. . . . Oh! Ma. . . .

"Go on."

But Mary Ann did not go on. To the amazement and surprise of both Mother St. Bede and the whole class she sat down with a plop. As she saw the great black figure of the English mistress looming towards her all the self-control, of which she had shown a great deal, fled. She was sick, right over her desk and on to the back of the girl in front of her. This was disgusting enough, but, what was more disgusting to her, for it was happening for the first time in her life that she could remember, she wet her knickers. This act released a wave of homesickness, and it was set free on a flood of crying and gabbling, which mounted as she was led from the room, and the gist of it which fell on the tortured ears of Mother St. Bede was, "Oh! Ma, Oh! Da. . . . Aa wanna go hoom."

6

All trials have their end, and after five weeks of them Mary Ann was now sailing along in the stream of school life. She remembered to sound her g's and draw out her a's; she was even beginning to take an interest in English, so much so, that she talked swanky to herself in bed, and even, by mistake, did it once in class, which did not annoy Mother St. Bede, but on the contrary seemed to please her.

She could now count up to fifty in French, and also ask in that language, "Is that the pen of your sister, and the house of your brother?" and other such profound questions. She had also begun to learn German. But she hadn't any real fancy for German, because her mouth filled up with spit when she tried to say the words. She was good at catechism, and exceptionally good at P.T., and she was learning to swim.

This last feat had developed a joyful anticipation in her, and she lived for Monday afternoons and the visit to the baths. And when, as was happening this week, the Wednesday afternoon walk was to be turned into two hours on the beach, life, when she didn't think of her da, was bearable. At least it had been until she received a letter from Michael.

Michael had never missed writing to her once a week, and his letters were a source of constant surprise to her, for in them there was more news than in either her da's or her ma's letters. Michael told her about the farm, the new hand, whom Mr. Lord didn't like, Mr. Polinski and Mrs. Polinski. He told her a lot about Mrs. Polinski, and because of this, Mary Ann was puzzled. Sometimes, as she read, she would say to herself, "What's he got to keep on about her for?" and then last week he had said, "I don't like Mrs. Polinski, and don't blame Mr. Polinski for hitting her. And you know something? me ma doesn't like her either. She's never out of our house, and always comes at mealtimes. Me ma was stiff with her last week, and she hasn't been back since." And then he had finished quite abruptly, "I wish you were here."

Never before had Michael ever expressed a need of her. At home he had been wont to push her away from himself and his concerns, but now through his letters she felt him very close to her. It could be said that she looked for his letters even more than those of her da, for only through his letters did she sense the real feeling at present in her home. Her mother's letters were all about what she must do and be a good girl, and her father said mostly how he missed her, and Mr. Lord's—one arrived every Monday morning, as if to set the tone for the week—were, in their briefness, all about learning, her learning. So it was Michael's letters she really looked forward to.

What does our Michael mean? she had asked herself for nearly two whole days. Somehow it seemed mixed up with Mrs. Polinski. And then she had a funny letter from her da that made her laugh. They had got a new bull and it had chased Mr. Jones up a drainpipe. Her da had added a postscript that nearly made her roll up; he had said, briefly, "Outside the drainpipe."

She had laughed and laughed as she imagined Mr. Jones clinging on to the drainpipe. And so Mr. Jones and the bull dispelled the vague fear that Michael's letter had aroused. Until this morning, when she had received another one from him, and again he was on about Mrs. Polinski. After saying that Mr. Lord had gone for Tony in front of the men, he said, "It was all through that Mrs. Polinski; she was standing talking to him and making him waste his time. She's always talking to somebody. She's always waylaying me da. She's a brazen thing, paints and everything. There's only five more weeks to the holidays, but I wish you were here now."

Again Mary Ann experienced a disturbed feeling, and it over-shadowed the day. She had been so excited when she knew they were going to the beach this afternoon, even if it were all pebbles and not sandy like it was at home, but now all she could think of was, I wonder what's up with our Michael, keeping on about Mrs. Polinski. I wish I was home. She had consulted the picture calendar in the corridor on which days were marked off delegated to various causes, such as Our Lady of Calvary, Our Lady of Sorrows, Blessed Mother of Bethlehem, The Precious Blood, The Blessed Sacrament, The Sacred Heart, Blessed Michael the Archangel—and, of course, the Saints; it seemed to Mary Ann the whole lot of them. After she had mentally replaced them all by dates, she worked out that there were not only five whole weeks but also three more days before they broke up, and only then would she know what their Michael meant.

In the scramble after lunch for bathing customes, towels and their tent bags, under which they undressed, and then the arranging of herself in the crocodile so as to be next to Marian, she forgot, or at least pushed to the back of her mind, Michael and his letter.

The sun was fierce, the sky high and blue, and although she was wearing one of her outdoor dresses which was cool and light, she still felt hot and longed for the moment when the waves would splash over her.

The nuns in charge of the company of fifteen were Sister Alvis and Sister Agnes Mary, and no two Sisters could have been more suited for the job in hand, for they enjoyed the beach as much as did the children, and their broad smiles and rejoinders to the continual stream of questions flung at them on the bus journey caused surprised glances from the other passengers. When Sister Agnes Mary's hoarse laugh rang out there were raised eyebrows, and small, surprised smiles from various quarters, and when the company alighted before entering St. Leonards in order to take a short cut to the beach, the eyes of the passengers followed them. the Sisters in particular, as if they had witnessed for the first time two laughing bears.

Mary Ann had hold of Sister Alvis's hand. She liked Sister Alvis, for although she wasn't as old as Mrs. McBride, she was the nearest thing in looks and sound to her, particularly when she said, "Jesus", that could be found in this polite part of the world. And now Mary Ann, in an effort to draw the nun's attention, informed her of her prowess in swimming of which sister Alvis, having helped with her coaching, was already well aware. "I can swim six breast strokes, Sister."

"Can you, my child? Glory be to God."

"I'll soon be able to swim the length of the bath."

"You will, you will. With God's help, you will."

"I wish me da could see me."

Ah, we were on a very delicate subject here. Sister Alvis had had her instructions of how to deal with the da complex, and she now threw her attention to the front of the disordered ranks and found diversion as a small figure leaped away, in answer to the call of her first glimpse of water, and she cried, "Oh! Sweet Jesus in Heaven, there's Anna Maria off again. Come back here this instant. . . . Sister—" she turned to where Sister Agnes Mary was walking with the bigger girls—"look, Anna Maria has started again."

"Oh, she has—Anna Maria!" Sister Agnes Mary was after the enthusiast, running over the dunes, leaving the rest of them laughing. Everybody loved to see Sister Agnes Mary run, for she did so with a strong, almost masculine galloping gait, doubtless occasioned by the bulky habit, of which, as she watched the Sister running, Mary Ann became consciously aware for the first time. Oh! poor Sister Agnes Mary, she must be hot in all those clothes. And poor Sister Alvis—and all the Sisters and Mothers. She knew a sudden pity for them. Why couldn't they take some of them off? She had an overpowering desire to put this question to Sister Alvis, but already she had learnt one thing at the covent—painfully she had acquired a quality of restraint—so she turned her question into a statement. "Isn't it hot, Sister?" she said.

"It is, child—lovely. God be thanked for such a lovely day and may He send many more this summer."

Without asking, Mary Ann had been given her answer. Sisters and nuns didn't feel the heat.

The water was beautiful, even if you weren't allowed to go out past the sentries, the sentries being Lola and Beatrice and another girl. At first she lay at the edge and let the waves, which were gentle today, roll over her; then, enough of that, she kicked the water and yelled, and taking Marian by surprise, pushed her face forward into a wave, only to be concerned when Marian, having recovered herself, looked on the point of crying.

"Oh! Marian, I was only playing." Her contrition was equal to a misdeed of far greater magnitude. "Push me—come on, I'll let you. Come on!" Marian pushed, and Mary Ann, letting herself go, fell over backwards with a great deal of spluttering and not a bad performance of drowning, and then turning over she cried, "Look, watch me, I can swim seven now. Look!"

Marian watched her. She, after four years of learning, could swim about as much as Mary Ann was doing after as many weeks. But she didn't like the water; the baths were bad enough, but the sea was frightening to her.

Spluttering and squeezing the water down herself, Mary Ann stood beside her friend. . . . "Can't—can't I do it!"

"Yes, you're doing fine. But come on out; let's go and pick shells."

"But we've just come in; and, anyway, Sister won't let us."

"She will if we don't go far, just to where the rocks come out. If she'll let us, will you come?"

"Oh, all right."

This was indeed a sacrifice, and in case permission should be given, she plunged into the water again to make the most of her time, but almost before she had completed her six strokes, Marian was back, and pulling her up by the costume.

"She says we can, just as far as the rock, but not round it. We must keep in sight."

"Oh, all right." Mary Ann stood puffing and blowing. "But—but let's plodge along at the edge; we'll find a lot then."

So they paddled slowly to where the rock, jutting out, formed the cove, and when they reached it they sat down on one of the sandy patches and sorted out their shells.

At that point Mary Ann became aware of the voices from the other side of the rock she didn't know. She was lost for the moment in the wonder of the shells and her senses dulled somewhat by the heat, and perhaps she had forgotten she wasn't on the sands at Shields, and so the voices that came to her at intervals were not from another world but the everyday sounds she was used to. And then she was brought upright by a longdrawn sigh, and a voice saying, "Eeh by! it's hot."

She stared at Marian, but Marian was engrossed in grading her shells. And when the voice came again, saying, "Giz a drink, lass," she rose to her feet and carefully paddling to the point of the rock she craned round it and saw two people seated in the shade of the cliff. As she recognised them her mouth fell open and everything else was forgotten.

"Mr. Wilson!" She was scrambling round the small promontory and over the shingle to the couple who had now risen to their feet.

"Well! hinny." Mr. Wilson greeted her as if she were his own child. "Well! me bairn, where've you sprung from?"

"Hallo, hinny."

"Hallo, Mrs. Wilson." Mary Ann thrust out a hand to each of them, and they hung over her, exclaiming their wonder at her sudden appearance.

"I'm from round the bend . . . I'm with me house. It's Wednesday, we have it off, an' I was picking shells an' I heard you. . . . Oh!"

Her joy at being among her own kind again was something she as yet could not formulate into words, but Mr. Wilson did it for her. "An' you heard our voices, and it was like home again, eh?" he said laughing.

"Yes," she nodded.

"Well, come and sit doon—" he made his voice broader for her benefit—"and hev a drop tea. Well, hinny, we've often spoke of you. How you getting on?"

"Oh, all right, Mr. Wilson."

"You like it?"

Mary Ann did not answer immediately, but looked up at Mrs. Wilson who was handing her the top of the Thermos flask, brimful of milky tea.

"Ta." She slipped back as naturally as breathing into the old idiom. And then she answered Mr. Wilson. "Sometimes . . . but—" her face suddenly lost its brightness—"I wish I was at home, everything's different here."

"You're telling me, hinny; we've had 'bout enough an' all, haven't we, lass?" He looked at his wife, and Mrs. Wilson said, "Well, it isn't like home . . . though, mind, everybody's been more than kind. We came to stay for three months with me daughter, but we think we'll be making a move back soon. But it's a problem—we've let our house."

"Oh, we've been into that—" Mr. Wilson waved the house question aside—"we'll get fixed somewhere. But, hinny—" he took Mary Ann by the shoulders—"you're not as bonny as when I saw you last . . . thinner. Do they gi' ye enough to eat?"

"Oh, yes, heaps—and they make you stuff it down, cabbage an' all. And——"

"They treat you all right?" Mr. Wilson, finding nothing to get at in having too much food, altered his approach.

"Yes."

"Hit you or anything? Lock you up?"

Mary Ann's eyes widened. "No. No, they don't."

"Look, have a bit cake," Mrs. Wilson thrust a paper plate towards Mary Ann.

"Oh, ta, Mrs. Wilson."

"Mary Ann! Mary Ann!" The almost hysterical shouting coming from behind the rock startled them all, and Mary Ann, springing up and remembering that she wasn't on the sands, said, "Eeh! I'll catch it, I'm not supposed to be round here. That's Marian, my friend."

"Well, bring her round, hinny."

"It's out of bounds. Eeh! I'd better go."

"Mary Ann! Mary Ann! Oh Mary Ann!" Now Marian's screams were hysterical, and to her voice others were joined, a chorus of them.

"Eeh!" Mary Ann looked from one to the other, her eyes large and startled. "Eeh! Ta-ra, Mr. Wilson. Ta-ra, Mrs. Wilson; it was lovely seeing you."

She turned and ran down to the water's edge, and as she plodged wildly in she imagined somehow that the end of the rock had moved out into the water, for the shingle, sloping steeply at that point, brought the water round her waist. It was still calm and sunny water, but when three steps from the end of the rock it came up to her armpits, the world suddenly became a mass of water and she knew a tiny tremor of fear, and just as she heard Mr. Wilson's anxious voice, calling, "Come on back here, hinny!" around the bend rushed Sister Agnes Mary, with the bottom of her habit, although tucked up a little, trailing in the water.

"Child! you'll be punished for this. . . . You will! you will!"

Voice and manner were so unlike those of Sister Agnes Mary that all Mary Ann could do was to stare up at her, and when she was hoisted out of the water and into the Sister's arms, she saw that she was really flaming mad.

Sister Agnes Mary was flaming mad, but it was with fright. Like a distraught mother seeking relief from her fear in action and heedless of the shingle crippling Mary Ann's bare feet, she pulled her along the beach. At the assembling point from where, only ten minutes before, Mary Ann had departed, Sister Agnes Mary took her hands and slapped them; then did the same to her bottom, and sent her, crying now, to get dressed, while Marian stood by sniffling and saying, "I thought she was drowned when I didn't see her—I thought she was drowned."

During all this Mr. Wilson had been standing by the point of the rock, his trousers rolled up well above the knee, sending an angry commentary back to his wife.

"What did I tell you! Nun clouting her . . . and in the open. If they did that with folks lookin', what'll they do when they can't be seen. . . . It's as I've always said . . . for two pins I'd——"

"George! you'll do no such thing. Come on, it's none of your business. Perhaps the woman was worried."

"Worried? and belting her like that! She looks as big as a house and as mad as a hatter. . . . Convents! By, if I had my way."

He stood taking in the proceedings of the group, now being hustled into their clothes until the rising tide threatened to engulf him, when he retreated, telling his only listener what he thought about convents—as if she didn't already know—and that he'd give the bairn's da an earful of what went on when he saw him.

. . . . .

Dating from the beach incident, life became a problem to Mary Ann, one large, painful problem made up of lesser problems, one of which, the honour of her house, rated highly. Not that she cared too much for the honour of her house, but the ten black marks she had received for just going round the bend put her away ahead of the worst culprit in the convent, and was bound, she was assured from all sides, which included Lola, to place their house bottom in the running for the cup. She had lain awake at nights thinking along such entwined lines as "Bust the cup!" and "Oh! Da," and "What's out Michael mean? He's always keeping on"; then, during this particular week, fourteen days after the fateful Wednesday and still three weeks and three days from the holidays, she had asked herself each night not "What does our Michael mean?" but "Why didn't he write last week?" It was now eleven days altogether since she had heard from him, and during that time she'd had two letters from her da but only one from her ma, and all three letters had been short, telling her nothing, only to be a good girl and learn her lessons—as if Mr. Lord didn't tell her that every Monday morning.

Leaving out her home worries and returning to her school ones, there remained one ray of hope on her horizon, a ray that might be the means of her getting twenty-five whole marks and so erasing some of the blackness from her sheet. In each house, every year, was held a competition for the best written essay and the best sonnet. Now Mary Ann wasn't as yet much good at the essay, but as to sonnets—she knew them as poetry—she thought she was the tops. She was good at poetry, she told herself with conviction. Hadn't even Mother St. Bede praised her for her efforts—although she had added she must not misconstrue things, like the way she had when asked to write a twelve-line poem on "Flag Day", and she wrote:

> *It's washing day,*
> *It's washing day,*
> *My Py-jams are all soap.*
> *They'll shrink and shrink*
> *And shrink and shrink,*
> *Oh dear! there is no hope.*
>
> *It's washing day,*
> *It's washing day,*
> *The things are on the line.*
> *There's me ma's things,*
> *And me da's things,*
> *And next to them are mine.*

She couldn't have made it rhyme if she had stuck their Michael's name in, and she hadn't thought of turning "me ma's" to "my mother's", or "me da's" to "my father's", and this seemingly had detracted still further from the poem's merit; yet, in spite of this, Mother St. Bede had praised her, and apparently for the very thing that she had condemned which she called misconstruing.

She hadn't pointed out to Mother St. Bede that "Flag Day" was how her da referred to the washing in the back lanes; Mother St. Bede, she felt sure, wouldn't have understood if she had.

And now to write a poem, a beautiful poem, that would win not only the house prize but to be the top of the four houses and be set to music, as the winning poem always was. Just that morning they had all sung last year's winning song, which had been won by a girl not in the Upper House, but in the Middle one.

She hummed it to herself:

> *"Come fly out of doors and see the rain,*
> *Rain that won't come for a year again;*
> *Golden rain, brittle and brown*
> *Singing as it floats waverly down.*

Come, let joy sing in your veins,
For only once a year it rains
Leaves of Autumn
Yet promise of Spring.
Come fly out of doors and let your heart sing."

It was a lovely tune an' all. Oh, if only she could write a song like that. So filled did she become with her desire to write a song that the day was but a prelude to the recreation hour, and she waived all thought of letter-writing so that she could get down to it. Having bagged her favourite seat near the window she sat down to it when Marian made her appearance.

Marian, Mary Ann was finding, could be a bit of a nuisance. If she wasn't crying about her da she was talking about him. This side of her Mary Ann understood perfectly, and she always allowed her to go on for some time before butting in herself to continue the same theme, but, of course, with a very different da. When she spoke of Mike to her friend she continued to use the forbidden term, and through repetition Marian had come to think of Mary Ann's father as her da.

"What are you doing?" she asked now flatly.

"Writing some poetry, a poem." Mary Ann didn't look up.

"It's a waste of time, you won't get anything. Beatrice'll win it."

Mary Ann's head came up now, and quickly she retorted, "She won't! Mother St. Bede didn't take no—any notice of hers."

"Shush!" Marian looked slyly up and around. "She's over there. . . . You know what?" She sat down and brought her head near to Mary Ann's and, in a voice scarcely audible above the buzz in the room, she said, "She was going at Lola about you."

Mary Ann's attention was successfully brought away from her task. "She was?"

"Yes." Marian nodded and nuzzled nearer. "She said you were common, and this place would never alter you, and—and you were the biggest sow's ear she had ever known here. A sow's ear, that's what she called you."

Mary Ann had heard the first time. Sow's ear, she knew all about sows' ears. Mrs. Flannagan had said she was one, and Sarah Flannagan had shouted it after her, adding that you couldn't make a silk purse out of it. But Father Owen had told her that you could, for he had been a sow's ear himself once. But in this moment Mary Ann found no consolation in Father Owen's ancestry, which was apparently akin to her own. That Beatrice was a cheeky thing. She cast her eyes to the far corner of the room, where Beatrice was writing, surrounded by three of her cronies. For two pins she'd go over to her and say, "Who do you think you're calling a sow's ear! You're a brass-faced monkey. Take that!" She had a beautiful mental picture of delivering a ringing slap that would knock Beatrice clean off her feet.

"Don't look over there," begged Marian now in some fear, "she'll come over and then she'll give you more marks. Let me see what you've done."

"No." Mary Ann put her hand over the paper.

"Oh, well, all right, if you want to be huffy." Marian moved away a little and idly opened a book, and Mary Ann returned to her composing. But she had scarcely begun to think when Marian's voice came again, insinuatingly, "Aren't you going to write to your—da, tonight?"

"No."

"Oh."

Mary Ann's mouth went into a tight line. Why couldn't Marian do something? She was always "just asking". She wasn't going to take no notice of her, she was going to do her poetry. What went with . . . lawns of green? Bean . . . lean . . . sheen? Yes . . . sheen, lawns of green sheen . . . No. Glossy sheen. Yes, that was it: lawns of green and glossy sheen.

"I wish it was the holidays." There was a sigh from Marian, which elicited no response whatever from Mary Ann.

Falling like—like what? Mary Ann pictured the lawns outside below the terrace. What fell? . . . Waterfalls . . . oh yes, falling like waterfalls. But that wasn't long enough . . . and then there was something about de-da-de-da's that Mother St. Bede said you had to count to get the lines right. Oh, she couldn't bother about that, she would forget what she was making up. Lawns of green and glossy sheen, falling like waterfalls—to—to valleys . . . "

"Do you know that all the nuns—Sisters, too—were called to Mother Superior today? I wonder what for. Do you know?"

Mary Ann did not raise her eyes, but let out a long-drawn breath that sounded like the leak of a bicycle tyre. Bust Marian. And nuns and Sisters. . . . Oh, bums and blisters, she had lost it now. But her disappointment was suddenly turned to excitement by this last thought, which rhymed, nuns and Sisters, bums and blisters. Eeh! but you couldn't say bums, not here! A little laugh wriggled inside of her and found its way up to her lips and eyes. Eeh! but it could be funny. She liked doing funny ones, she was good at funny ones. Her pencil was now away ahead of her thoughts.

"Let's play needles and pins, Mary Ann." It was a whisper from Marian.

"No, not now, I'm working. Can't you see?" She would want to play needles and pins now. . . . Needles and pins, needles and pins, sit on them pronto for your sins. You see, she could write funny ones.

> *Needles and pins,*
> *Needles and pins,*
> *Sit on them pronto for your sins;*
> *If you don't eat your cabbage there'll be some fun*
> *And a whack on your bum by a Sister or a Nun.*

Eeh! it was funny. She could make a really funny one up out of that. But she'd have to take that "bum" out.

"What on earth are you writing?"

As the hated voice fell down on her a hand came over her shoulder, but before it could reach the paper Mary Ann's hands, aided by sheer terror and panic, had grabbed it up, and she had sprung from the table. And now both of these emotions were directing her self-preservation, for her hands, as she backed from her tormentor, endeavoured to tear up the paper.

"Give it to me!"

"No, I'll not!"

"Do as you're told."

"I'll not for you, so there!"

The whole attention of the recreation room was now turned on Mary Ann. And Beatrice, seeing that in a few more seconds there would be no evidence left of the self-convicting of this, to her, common individual, made a lunge towards her. But Mary Ann's riposte, owing to her slightness of form, was as quick as any foil in the hands of a master, and as she leapt to the side Beatrice, losing her balance, sprawled forward and aided by the glib surface of the floor, skidded some distance on her stomach being brought to a stop by a chair and Sister Alvis's thick Irish voice, crying, "Beatrice! get up out of that. Mother of God! what do you think you are playing at! Keep your hockey demonstrations for the fields, child."

Sister Alvis can be forgiven for lacking sympathy, for half the room had dared to burst into laughter at the result of Beatrice's attack; moreover, Sister Alvis had very little liking for Beatrice—a hoity-toity piece, and full of pride. Jesus forgive her for passing judgment—and so now, if she were under the impression that anything was amiss, she passed it over by crying loudly again, "Come on now! Come on now, all of yous, all of yous. And pick up those pieces, Mary Ann; you're spraying the floor with them. . . . Are you hurt, Beatrice? You're a big girl to go throwing yourself about like that. Away you go upstairs and tidy yourself; there's five minutes before supper. Now go on. Go on." She shook her head. "I can't listen to any chatter now."

Mary Ann could have flown to Sister Alvis and flung her arms about her. She was lovely, she was wonderful, she was holy, a saint—everything—the lot. A minute ago she had thought that the Devil didn't appear only in men who wanted you to go for rides in cars. She had seen him plainly advancing on her, dressed up as Beatrice. But Sister Alvis had come and saved her. Her faith in human nature, as supplied by convents, and justice, about which she had always had her doubts, were both revived and strengthened.

She picked up the pieces of paper with lightning speed, ran from the recreation room straight to the lavatory and pulled the chain on them. There! what would Beatrice do now.

Later, in the chapel, she looked across at the Holy Family. Wooden as they were, and without colour or feeling, tonight they seemed to be a little alive, warmer somehow, and for the first time since her coming here she addressed them as she would have the group back in Jarrow. "Thank you, dear Holy Family." Eeh! if she'd got hold of that paper I'd have been in for it. Oh, she's awful. . . . "Thank you for making Sister Alvis come in. She's lovely, like Mrs. McBride. I like her best next to Mother Mary Divine and Sister Agnes Mary, although she did clout me, Sister Agnes Mary, I mean. God bless me ma and da and our Michael, and make him write to me. And will you help me with me poetry, cos I want to get some marks. In the name of the Father and of the Son and the Holy Ghost. Amen." Eeh! where was she, they were giving the responses. She hadn't her mind on her prayers, on the real prayers. . . . "Spare us, O Lord—" she spoke up loud and clear. Then not being in her stride and over-excited by the preference God had so openly shown her tonight, she forgot that she should read the next line to herself and leave the verbal oration to the priest and so to her own horror she heard her voice, saying, still loud and clear and joined now solely with that of the priest: "AGNUS DEI QUI TOLLIS PECCATA MUNDI." Her Latin pronunciation was something akin to her English and "Paa—car—ta—Moon—day" trailed horribly away by the silence, and her head drooped to pew level, forced there by the quick glances of those about her. Eeh! Eeh! she had no words terrible enough to pour on her own head over this sacrilege, yet away behind a boarded-off section of her mind, the boards being constructed of convent veneer, the real Mary Ann was crying out in her own defence: What could you expect from a wooden Holy Family—they should have stopped her. It would never have happened in Jarrow.

.   .   .   .   .

Strange as it seemed to Mary Ann, she never got ticked off about the chapel incident, but it had its repercussions, one nice . . . lovely, and one horrible . . . beastly.

The first occurred the following morning. When bumping into Mother Mary Divine in a temporarily deserted corridor, the nun had bent above her and touched her cheek softly and whispered, "Agnus Dei, qui tollis peccata mundi . . . bless you. Indeed, bless you," and then had glided away. And Mary Ann had stopped for a moment to gaze after her, speechless but filled with a . . . lovely feeling . . . a holy feeling, and this feeling persisted right through the morning in spite of Mother St. Bede going at her again for the way she spoke. You never knew how you had Mother St. Bede. One minute she was praising you for your poetry, and the next she was going at you cos you said "cassel" instead of "carsal"; and then the blooming word was spelt castle—it wasn't fair. But the unfairness was not strong enough to force its way beyond her holy feeling. What completely shattered her celestial affinity, however, and brought her to mundane earth with a bump was when she ran into a group of four girls in a carefully prepared circle round by the side of the gym-house and all wearing mournfully long faces, behind which laughter was bubbling to escape. With eyes raised to heaven and with hands joined in prayer, they were groaning quietly, one after the other, in voices fitting their expressions:

"Agnus Dei qui tollis peccata mundi,
Spare Mary Ann Shaughnessy, O Lord."
"Agnus Dei qui tollis peccata mundi
Spare her da, O Lord."
"Agnus Dei qui tollis peccata mundi—and their Michael."
Now it was Beatrice's voice, groaning with emotion and strangled laughter:
"Agnus Dei qui tollis peccata mundi,
And her ma . . . and the farm and Mr. Lord—and—and the whole of Jarrow."

The last word was drowned in a concerted splutter, and their heads fell together. Then their arms flung round each other, their laughter burst high, crackling, almost hysterical.

Mary Ann stood as if glued to the spot, the whole of her body twitching, but especially her face. Her eyebrows jerked, her eyes blinked, her compressed lips rotated in a circle, and then she burst out, "You—you rotten cheeky beasts! I'll tell me—" She shut down on the word in time. But Beatrice supplied it for her. Stopping in her laughter, she cried, "Me da! You'll tell me da, won't you?"

Mary Ann stared up at her. The words on Beatrice's tongue sounded strange to her—she would not give them the stigma of "common" and she told herself that wasn't how she said them at all.

"I hate you!"

"Do you? Thank you very much, it is reciprocated." Beatrice was beginning to enjoy herself. She had at last got this foreign being on the raw.

"Mary Ann, there ees a letter for you."

Lola had come hurrying round the corner and she delivered her message while looking at the group facing Mary Ann. Now she pushed her hand out to Mary Ann and continued: "Go on, Mother St. Francis is waiting, go on." It was an order and for Mary Ann it carried more authority than if it had come from a prefect, for Lola had said it. And so she turned still raging with her anger, and went away, leaving someone much more capable of dealing with Beatrice than she was.

The letter was from Michael—she recognised that by the writing on the envelope—and the relief it brought soothed away the anger and humiliation, and hugging it to her, she went into the recreation room—empty on this blazing hot noon—to read it.

Swiftly she opened it, and when she saw three whole pages with writing on both sides, she said "Coo!" and wriggled with excited anticipation further on to the window sill. But after reading the first paragraph her body became still and her expression fixed. What was the matter with their Michael? what was the matter with their da and ma? What did Michael mean? What's he getting at? she thought.

She was up to page five before light began to dawn on her, and by the time she had reached page six she was thinking: Mrs. Polinski! and her old fears were back, swamping her in great waves. They were the fears that had filled her when her da thought her ma was going off with Mr. Quinton, and although Michael hadn't put the thing in actual writing, she was seeing it happen again, but with her da this time, and Mrs. Polinski.

Michael ended his letter again by saying, "I wish you were here."

As with the last trouble between her ma and da, Michael, in spite of his four extra years, was in no way fitted to deal with it—he could only be hurt by it. Mary Ann knew this, as she also knew that something was up, there was trouble. . . . That's why he hadn't written last week. And now, although this letter from his point of view, was actually giving nothing away,

Mother St. Bede snatched the piece of paper from Mary Ann's hand and looked at it.

mother was unhappy—that her da and her had had a row, and all over Mrs. Polinski, who, he said, was causing trouble on the farm an' all, for her da, as well as Mr. Lord, had gone for Tony for wasting time, and it wasn't his fault. Mrs. Polinski, when she couldn't talk to their da, would talk to Tony, and Mr. Lord didn't like Tony at all.

Back was the weight of the family on her shoulders. It brought a pinched look to her face and a wildness to her eyes. Folding the letter up, she went slowly out of the room and up the stairs and put it in the bottom drawer of the chest by her bed, forgetting that the dormitory was out of bounds except for ten minutes following prayers. Sister Catherine, finding her there and adding another black mark to her list, did not throw her into the depths of despair, for black marks had suddenly lost their potency. What did black marks matter anyway—there was something wrong at home, something drastically wrong. What could she do? If she wrote to their Michael and asked him, Mother St.Francis would have to see the letter, and then she'd want to see the letter she had received.

When she reached the hall again she was waylaid by Marian.

"What's the matter? I've been looking for you."

"Nothing."

Marian accepted this without comment; then after staring hard at her friend for a moment, she said, "Come on out and play and tell me about that hickaty-pickaty."

"Oh, I don't want to." Mary Ann shrugged her off.

Marian's face fell, and Mary Ann, seeing the suggestion of tears, tossed her head impatiently and went out and into the larger of the playing fields. And in a corner, with only a small portion of her mind applied to it, she began to instruct Marian further into the mysteries of North Country games.

Pointing first at herself and then at Marian, she began to chant half-heartedly,

> "Hickaty-pickaty, I-sill lickaty,
> Bumberrera jig;
> Every man that has no hair
> Generally wears a wig.
> One—two—three—
> Out goes she!"

Of course, as previously arranged, it meant that out went Marian, leaving Mary Ann the first to have a go with the ball. This she did in a most desultory fashion; and she was on the point of giving up altogether when she saw Lola. Although there were many girls playing she knew that Lola was running towards her. So sure was she of this that she stopped her play and went to meet her. Lola was out of breath from her running and could not for the moment speak. She stood over Mary Ann, gazing at her, her eyes wide. And Mary Ann, drawn out of her apathy, muttered, "What's up?"

"You leetle fool."

"What!"

"Why do you write such things?"

"Me?" Mary Ann's mouth fell open. "What have I writed—written?"

"What have you wrote? You know that. But do you know that Beatrice found eet and gave eet to Sister Catherine?"

"Give what? She couldn't—I tore it up." Mary Ann's now clear conscience was pointing to her particular effort of last night.

"You might have thought you tore eet up, but eet is now in the hands of Sister Catherine, and she wants you. Go on—go on." She pushed Mary Ann away with an angry gesture.

Mary Ann, no fear in her, for the same conscience told her she had done nothing, went towards the main door, up the steps, across the hall and to the office.

She had no need to knock on the door for it was open, and inside she saw standing round the table, and all looking at a piece of paper, Sister Catherine, Mother St. Bede and Sister Alvis.

Her presence made known by the diligent wiping of her feet, although perfectly dry, Mary Ann was not bidden to enter in the usual way; instead, Mother St. Bede, pointing a long finger at the floor, indicated what she should do, and Mary Ann, in spite of her clear conscience and feeling that here an' all something was up, walked slowly into the room.

The three nuns looked at her, but it was Sister Catherine who spoke first. "You are a wicked child," she said, "and you will go to Hell. There is no doubt about that."

"Wait a minute." Sister Alvis's thick voice interrupted her, and promised something of a reprieve from so final a destination as she said, "Let us go into this. . . . Mary Ann, you've been writing poetry lately?"

"Yes, Sister."

"Funny poetry?" These words of Sister Alvis's brought the heads of Sister Catherine and Mother St. Bede quickly upwards. But Sister Alvis went on, "When did you write your last funny poem?"

"Last night, Sister."

"Where is it?"

Mary Ann's eyes darted from one to the other. It was no use telling lies. Although all those pieces were now floating down some main sewer she felt that the three dark-robed figures would know all about them. "I tore it up."

"Not all of it—definitely." Sister Catherine's hand swept to the table, and taking up the piece of paper she thrust it before Mary Ann's eyes, so close that Mary Ann could see nothing but squiggles. "You recognize this piece of paper?"

Mary Ann's nose jerked up above the paper as she said, "No, Sister."

"You don't remember putting this in the back of your prep book?" It was now Mother St. Bede speaking.

"I never put any paper in the back of me homework book, Mother."

"I never put a paper—a—singular! Oh, what's the use!" Mother St. Bede's head drooped with her exasperation.

"You don't remember putting a paper in the back of your book? You don't remember, I suppose writing these words? Look at them. Read them."

Mary Ann's eyes now went to the paper and she read:

> *"You must not kiss, and you must not wink,*
> *You must not smoke and you must not drink,*
> *You must not gamble and you must not swear,*
> *Or wear high heels or curl your hair.*
> *Should you not follow this advice,*
> *You'll be taken to Hell by Sister Alvise."*

> *Signed by Catty Kath*
> *and Old Ma Bede.*

Mary Ann's lower jaw now hanging, her nose straining upwards and her eyes bulging, she again looked from one to the other. But she found she was unable to speak. They thought she had written this. Eeh! She had never written things like that . . . ever, Eeh! What made them think it was her?

"Well?"

Mary Ann swallowed. "It's not mine, Sister. I never did it."

Mother St. Bede snatched the piece of paper from Mary Ann's hand and looked at it.

"You say this is not yours? I couldn't mistake your writing, child, if I could overlook the context which points to your naughtiness. Your usual way of thinking . . . your—your—"

The latter part of Mother St. Bede's words were unintelligible to Mary Ann, she only knew she was being blamed for writing this poetry when she had never done it, and so she defended herself strongly , although her lips were trembling. "'Tisn't my writing, I never done it, I didn't. I don't know nothing about it, so there."

Grammar, delivery, attitude were passed over by Mother St. Bede, or did these things stun her, for with joined hands she turned way.

And now Sister Catherine took over. "You'll be punished for this, severely punished. Reverend Mother will be told about this. You forget where you are—we don't allow this kind of thing. . . . "

"Ssh! ssh!" Sister Alvis interrupted her and looked down on Mary Ann. "Now, my child, if you tell the truth you won't get into trouble. Why did you write this? It was a silly thing to do, wasn't it? Have you written any more like this?"

Mary Ann looked up at the Sister, so like Mrs. McBride in her manner, and her voice shook as she said, "I didn't write it, Sister, honest. I don't know nothing about it. Somebody's done it for spite, not me."

"Huh!" Sister Catherine was coming again to the fore, and her attack was just stopped by the sound of the bell, so that all she said was, "Get away! Get away to your class this minute."

Mary Ann got away. She went along the corridor and into the hall; and once round the corner she stood with four fingers in her mouth, biting at one after the other. But it was Sister Catherine she was biting, and it was to her that she silently spoke. "You! I didn't do it. Somebody's done it, it wasn't my writing! You're always at me. I hate you, I do! You're mean, you are. You! . . . I don't like you."

"What's the matter?" It was Marian again, excited and eager to know what the trouble was. "What did they want you for? I saw Sister Catherine. Oh, she looked wild."

Mary Ann, tears now welling into her eyes stammered, "They said I'd—I'd written some bad poetry, and I never did."

"Who?"

"Sister Catherine and Mother St. Bede and Sister Alvis. That Sister Catherine—she thinks she's Mrs. God!"

As this blasphemy was uttered the earth seemed to open, but not far enough to swallow Mary Ann, for there, not a few feet away at the entrance to the corridor, stood the three nuns in question.

Her eyes darting from one to the other of her contemporaries as if in confirmation of her opinion of this child, Sister Catherine, with foreboding quietness, said, "Go to the dormitory this minute, and don't move until I come."

Trembling as if with ague, Mary Ann squeezed past the three pairs of eyes and like someone drunk went up the broad, picture-laden stairs towards the dormitory.

.   .   .   .   .

Twenty-four hours had elapsed since Mary Ann had committed the heinous crime, of not writing cheeky poetry, but of insulting Sister Catherine. Each individual in the dormitory, with the exception of Lola, had given her own version of the affair as she had heard it—the different versions ranging from simply swearing at Sister Catherine to hitting, biting, and, lastly, spitting in her face. But Mary Ann heard none of these versions, for she was being ostracised. Marian, after her many accounts of the incident, had not the nerve to be seen openly talking to her; only the steadfast Lola still spoke to the culprit.

Mary Ann had spent all yesterday afternoon in the punishment room—a form of solitary confinement; no books, no paper or pencil, not even an underground comic to look at—and last evening, two full hours on her knees in the chapel, during which time the Holy Family had been less than useless; and this morning she had appeared before the Reverend Mother.

Had the Reverend Mother put her thoughts on this matter into words, it is probable that the whole of Mary Ann's life would have been changed, for the Reverend Mother did not believe that this child had written the words on the paper presented to her although the writing seemed to prove that she had. No, the Reverend Mother believed Mary Ann when she persisted in her denial of any knowledge of the paper but admitted frankly to having written cheeky poetry the previous night; and when with bowed head the child had repeated what she could remember of the rhyme, even to the mention of blisters on unmentionable anatomy, the wise woman realised that this child was confessing to something decidedly more vulgar than the words which were written on the paper. So she believed the child, but she didn't tell her so—that would never have done—she only dismissed her, with a caution to write nothing that she wouldn't want the whole world to see.

Following this, the Reverend Mother went to tell Sister Catherine her real opinion of the matter, which, from the many things reported to her, she linked with Beatrice. Her final word was that the child was to be punished no more, and if she misbehaved in future she was to be brought straight to her.

It was with some surprise then that Mary Ann received the order to get ready for the afternoon walk. Once again she found herself out in the sunshine, in the crocodile, walking with Marian. But now she was paying Marian back in her own coin, for she wuld have nothing to say to her—in her own words, "she wasn't kind to her".

The same two nuns were in charge of the walk, Sister Agnes Mary and Sister Alvis. Sister Alvis appeared to Mary Ann slightly aloof, and whenever Mary Ann's eyes caught hers she was made to feel her past sins by a gentle hurt look on the Sister's face.But not so Sister Agnes Mary—it would appear she had found favour in the eyes of Sister Agnes Mary. Forgotten was the beach episode. It could have been that this particular Sister had never lathered her behind, and when the hearty Sister took hold of her hand her love and gratitude rushed out to her.

On these walks each child was allowed sixpence to spend, and today when they touched on the town they were told off in threes to go into a sweetshop and spend their money. Mary Ann was one of the last three, and she was standing at the counter after giving her order for three-pennyworth of "Dolly Mixture" when a voice from behind her said, "Why, hallo, Mary Ann."

Mary Ann's eyes, as she stared at Mrs. Wilson, lighted up as if she was seeing her mother, and she turned from the counter and flung herself at the old woman. "Oh! hallo, Mrs. Wilson. Oh! hallo."

Mrs. Wilson, holding both of Mary Ann's hands, said feelingly, "I'm glad I've seen you, hinny, we're going back the night."

"Home?"

"Yes, my dear. Mr. Wilson can't stand it no longer here." She laughed. "He's lived too long in the North."

"The night?" There was a hungry longing in Mary Ann's voice and eyes.

"Yes, the night. Oh, I'm glad I saw you, hinny. I'll tell him—he often talks of you. Did you get wrong the other day?"

"No—well, yes, a little. Oh!" Mary Ann gripped the hands in hers. "Oh! I wish I was comin' with you and Mr. Wilson."

"The holidays will soon be here, hinny, and I promise you we'll come and see you when you come home."

"Thank you, Mrs. Wilson. Look," she reached eagerly and whispered, "will you go and see me da and ma when you get back, afore I come home?"

"Yes, we will, hinny, I promise you. And now I'll have to be going, I just slipped in to get a few sweets for the train. We're gettin' the four o'clock, we just live near here. Oh, Mr. Wilson will be glad I've seen you. Good-bye, hinny, and God bless you." Mrs. Wilson stooped and gently patted Mary Ann's face.

"Good-bye, Mrs. Wilson."

Then she was gone.

"Come on, the woman's got your sweets." One of the girls pushed Mary Ann, and she turned towards the counter, and took the bag and handed over her money. And when she got into the street she looked quickly up and down, but Mrs. Wilson had gone, and with her all comfort, all hope. Never before had she felt so alone in the world. She wanted just to stand and cry, but she was hustled into line and the march back to the convent started.

It was unfortunate that within five minutes of her entry into the convent two things happen to breathe life into the thought that at the moment was but a germ in her mind. The first was a letter from her mother, very short, telling her nothing, only as usual to be a good girl, to do her lessons, and that the holidays would soon come. But at the bottom Mary Ann noticed something that hadn't been on her previous letters—the cheap paper was raised in a blob where a drop of water had hit it.

Mary Ann recognized that blob. When she first came to the convent it had dotted her own letters—that blob was a dried tear. Her mother had been crying, and a longing to see her that would brook no cautionary advice such as "Eeh! but you know you can't, not till the holidays" assailed her. And then, as she folded the letter and went to move out of the recreation room, there was Beatrice standing in her way, laughter filling her eyes.

There was no retaliation left in Mary Ann at this moment with which to meet her enemy; she had not the power even to thrust out her chin. She knew that she could not fight Beatrice—she was not on her own ground, this was Beatrice's ground.

She could not realise that in a year or two this would be her own ground, too, and she could meet Beatrice as an equal; she knew only that Beatrice was the one who had written that bit of poetry in her book, Beatrice was the one who had caused her all this trouble, and there was no way of showing her up.

Like a small, fascinated rabbit, and very unlike herself, she watched Beatrice go out. Then she shivered, as if from a chilling wind, and waited, so as to give her enemy sufficient time to get well ahead before she followed her but not to the playing fields to join up with the rest of her form. There was a milling of girls in the corridor as the lessons changed, and she mixed with them; then made her way to the cloakroom. There she took up her gaberdine hat and mackintosh, stood for a moment swallowing hard, then, with the hat in her hand and the coat over her arm, she walked out of the cloakroom, across the great hall, down the steps and, unbelievingly, down the drive and out of the convent gate without a soul stopping to question her. Perhaps she had the appearance of a child who had come in from a walk and been sent quickly on some errand down to the lodge.

Only at the main gate did she pause, and that was when she had to make her way round a lorry that was unloading sand on to the side of the drive. She did not see the caretaker. If she had, some lie would have leapt to her lips that would have convinced him of her right to be there. And when once outside she did not pause in fright, nor start to run, but walked, with her heart pumping so hard that it made a knocking sound in her head, towards the main road where the buses ran.

She still had threepence left out of her sixpence and two pounds in her locket. She kept one hand over the locket as she waited for the bus, and when it came and she was firmly seated in it, she asked the conductor with a stammer that sounded natural, "How much is it to the station?" And when he said "Threepence half," she tendered the coppers with a feeling that God had started to direct the proceedings, for if the conductor had asked for more she would have had to get off and she didn't know where the station was.

As she alighted from the bus a clock confronted her and it said ten to four. She felt sick now and terrified, but it did not enter her head that she should return to the convent. She walked into the booking office, her eyes searching for the familiar faces of the Wilsons. And now the feeling that this whole business was out of her hands was confirmed, for there, among the numerous people standing in the hall, was Mr. Wilson, and he was alone. He was counting his change and looking at his tickets. When she pulled at his coat he looked at her as startled as if she had been an apparition.

"God in Heaven! hinny, where have you sprung from? Have you come to say us good-bye?"

"Mr. Wilson," the tears were now in her eyes and she choked on his name; then started again, "Mr. Wilson, I wanta go home."

Mr. Wilson straightened his back and pressed his head backwards as he said, "But, hinny you canna do that!"

"I want to, Mr. Wilson. Take me—oh, please!"

"Take you, hinny—home? Look, what's up with you? Is anything the matter? Have they been goin' for you?"

Now she nodded dumbly, and then added, "It's not only that, it's me ma—there's something wrong at home."

"What makes you think that, hinny?"

"I know by the letters me brother's sent—that's our Michael—he's always goin' on about me da and another. . . . "

When she stopped Mr. Wilson said angrily, "I knew from the beginning they should never have sent you this far. I've said all along to the missis. All this way for a bairn like you, I've said. You're North Country, you belong there like meself. This is no place for God nor man. I've found that out." He bent nearer to her as he delivered this last statement. "I'll be glad to see the Tyne again, hinny. Aye, by God! between you and me I will. But about taking you home." He straightened. "Aye, that's another kettle o' fish."

"Oh, Mr. Wilson, please." She lifted her face up. "Please. I've got the money, it's in me locket where you put it."

"'Tisn't the money, hinny, it's what's going to happen. And Mrs. Wilson, she'd never stand for it. No, hinny, it's out of the question."

Mary Ann's whole face crumpled, and then she whimpered, "I can't go back now, I'll get wrong and be put in the punishment room."

It was the last two words that did it.

"Punishment room!"

They altered Mr. Wilson's whole expression, for before his eyes he saw a cell, a convent cell, with high, grated windows, cold stone floor, and dry bread and water for sustenance.

His face was hard and flushed as he said, "Have you been in the punishment room, hinny, here?"

"Yes, yesterday. They said I wrote some bad poetry, and I didn't. And—"

The sound of a train passing through the station cut off her words, and Mr. Wilson looked round him, his thoughts written plainly on his face. He knew that if Mrs. Wilson caught sight of the child the game would be up, there would be no chance of getting her on the train, and now he was determined to get her on the train.

Mr. Wilson saw himself bringing his battle into the open—he was fighting a convent, all convents, because a convent had taken one of his grandchildren from him. "Look, hinny," he said in a strangely controlled voice, "stand aside, I'll get your ticket; we'll settle up later. Do as I tell you now," he said quickly, "the missis is in the main hall. When you come through the barrier after me make yerself scarce, for it'll be all up if she sees you." He nodded at her. "Keep out of the way—you understand?"

Mary Ann nodded quickly back at him and stood to one side, her eyes riveted on the old man. Mr. Wilson had now taken on the form of God—everything was in his hands and she trusted him implicitly. Father Owen's warning of the Devil and his many disguises was forgotten. Had she thought of it she would not have made it applicable to Mr. Wilson. Anyway, if Mr. Wilson had sprouted horns at this moment he would have had her vote of confidence. When, having bought the ticket, he turned from the booking office and did not look at her, but walked to Mrs. Wilson and pushed her ahead through the barrier, her heart began to race at an even faster pace. Close on his heels she followed him. But when the tickets were punched and they were through she kept her head down, and when she saw his legs going one way she turned and walked in the opposite direction, until in the distance she saw the very end of the platform. The emptiness this indicated brought yet another kind of fear to her; and so she stopped and glanced cautiously over her shoulder along the platform.But from where she stood there was no sign of the Wilsons, and in panic she scampered back between the groups of people. And just as she caught sight of them standing at the far end there came the train.

The panic in her head yelled, "Eeh! eeh! ee . . . eh!" and the second was much louder than the noise of the train. As the doors were flung open, Mr. Wilson marshalled his wife into a carriage, then furtively turned and thumbed Mary Ann towards another compartment. This action seemed to bring her out of her state of petrification, and she dashed towards the open door, scrambled up the high step and threw herself on to a seat opposite to two women, and there she endeavoured to compose herself to wait for Mr. Wilson.

She had no book, nothing to look at, so she looked at her hands, and the women from time to time looked at her and smiled. But she didn't smile back; instead she turned and fixed her gaze on the window, in case they should ask questions.

Ten minutes later, when the train had stopped and Mr. Wilson had not yet been along to her, she had a sudden desire to scream and jump out. But she put her fingers into her mouth and pressed her face closer to the window. The train moved again and she began to feel sick. And just when the sickness was about to get the better of her and she knew she would soon do something on the floor Mr. Wilson appeared in the corridor.

The old man's eyes moved swiftly between her and the two women, and then he smiled and said, airily, "Oh, there you are! Come on, hinny." Under the staring eyes of the women he held out his hand, and Mary Ann, grabbing it eagerly, left the compartment.

In the corridor, Mr. Wilson's smile vanished and he bent above her, saying, "Now, look. The missis is up in the air—she's not for having it, she wants to send you back. It's up to you, come on."

Mrs. Wilson looked a different person altogether from the one Mary Ann had seen only a short while ago in the sweetshop. Her face was white and strained and she didn't look at Mary Ann in a nice way, and on first sight she didn't even speak, her lips were pressed tight together. Then she sprang them apart, and began to talk as Mary Ann had never heard her talk. Much quicker than Mr. Wilson she talked . . . on and on.

"Look . . . you're a naughty girl . . . you shouldn't have gone and done it. You know you're a naughty girl, don't you?" Mary Ann just stared. "What d'you think's goin' to happen? We'll get into trouble, it's like kidnapping. Just think of the state they're in at the convent. They'll get the police, and then it'll be on the wireless and then you'll be found. You've got to go back . . . d'ye hear? As for you"—Mrs. Wilson now turned on her husband—"it's you who started all this, you and your talk about convents. You won't give credit that Teresa is the best off of all our grandbairns. Oh, no! it's because she's in a convent. And then you're the one to talk about bigotry—you started all this—you! But now I'm goin' to finish it—she's goin' back."

Mary Ann looked at Mr. Wilson. He wasn't the Mr. Wilson that she knew either, it was as if Mr. Wilson had become Mrs. Wilson, and Mrs. Wilson had become Mr. Wilson. He sat with his head bowed, his back stooped, and his hands dangling between his knees, and to her astonishment he didn't open his mouth. And she realised, as he had said, that it was now up to her. But what could she do against this force? Nothing.

Her heart was so heavy its weight was unbearable. She began to cry, silently, the tears in great blobs rolling down her cheeks. Mrs. Wilson watched her with her lips falling again into a hard line, and she seemed to draw them right into her mouth before emitting almost in a shout, "You're a bad lass! That's what you are, a bad lass. Why did you do it?"

"Me da . . . me—me ma. She—she must have been crying—it was on her letter—there's something up at home, it's Mrs. Polinski, she's after me da. Oh! Mrs. Wilson, I want to see me—me ma." In desperation she flung herself against the old woman's knee, and, throwing her arms around her waist, gave vent to a paroxysm of sobbing.

Mrs. Wilson hesitated only a second before gathering her up and saying, "There! there! All right, but something must be done." Then turning her eyes in the direction of her husband she spoke one word. "You!" she said.

The exclamation spoke of surrender, but Mr. Wilson's head did not lift but drooped lower. His hands came together in a tight clasp and he let out a long-drawn sigh.

7

With a rhythmic beat Lizzie hit the rough stone wall of the scullery with her clenched fist, while the mutterings from her lips sounded unintelligible even to herself; then turning with a swift movement she went and stood over the sink and retched. She retched as if she wanted to throw up her heart. Mary Ann! Mary Ann! Mary Ann! Even her pores seemed to ooze the name: Mary Ann! Mary Ann! Mary Ann! Since six o'clock this evening she had started. Was it the miss of her that had brought it about? the mirror she could not believe she was not looking at a very old woman. . . . Her child was lost, her child had been taken away by a man. And on the thought she cried, "Oh, my God . . . Oh, my God!"

All her life she had known worry, nothing but worry, worry; but during these last few months she had thought she was being repaid for all her tribulations, especially those of her married life. Hadn't Mike landed this grand job. After setbacks and trials he was now settled, and the child was away at a grand school receiving first-class education. And then the other trouble had started. Was it the miss of her that had brought it about? When had Mike first begun to notice Mrs. Polnski? She retched again and exlaimed, "Damn Mrs. Polinski! Damn everyone—everything! Mary Ann! Mary Ann! Mary Ann!" Where was she at this moment? Would nothing ever be heard of her again? It had happened to other bairns. Oh, my God! would she never hear anything? She raised her head and looked round the lighted scullery. Nearly midnight. Where was Mike? Where was Michael? Would they never come home and tell her.

She stumbled into the kitchen trying to shut down on the terrifying thoughts racing into her mind. But there was no power in her strong enough to keep them at bay, and she stopped dead to look at the picture presenting itself before her eyes. . . . Dead by now. Raped . . . raped!

"No! no! no!" She cried this denial aloud, then clapped her hands to her mouth. She would go mad, stark, staring, raving mad. And it was all her own fault. Why had she let her go? The child hadn't wanted to go. She had pushed her, pushed her to save Mike, pushed her to satisfy an old man's whim. She could have been educated at a school near here, just as well as all those miles away. It was as Mike had said, the old fellow had wanted to separate her from them. Damn him! Damn money and farms. Damn youth! Young girls, empty-headed with big breasts, flaunting them under a man's nose. Mike had laughed at her and said she was crazy. "I'm old enough to be her father!" he had said. "What! me take notice of that empty-headed piece when you are around? Don't be so damn silly, Liz! Be your age."

She had been her age and looked at Mrs. Polinski, a young sex-starved girl. Mike was missing Mary Ann. He wanted her laughter, her young hand in his, and so he talked to Mrs. Polinski. He just talked to Mrs. Polinski, that was all, but how she hated Mrs. Polinski. And then he had said, "You're jealous, Liz!" He enjoyed her being jealous. "Now you know what I felt like over Quinton. Now you know what it feels like, that feeling that somebody's stepped into your shoes. But you're mad, Liz, you're quite mad." She could hear his voice interrupting her thoughts that cried, Mary Ann! Mary Ann! Mary Ann! He had held her close in his arms one night and said, "We're missing her, that's what's the matter with us, that's what's the matter with all of us. The house isn't the same, nothing's the same. There's only one person happy out of all this, and that's the old boy. Damn and blast him—him and his money, him and his power." Oh, my God! She gazed about her wildly. What was she thinking? With a wave of her arm she swept everything from her mind but her child, and again she was crying aloud: "Please, please, Jesus, save my bairn. Oh, Holy Mother of God, do this for me. It doesn't matter if he loses his job, it doesn't matter if we go back to Mulhattan's Hall, nothing matters, security or nothing, only bring my child safely back to me. Don't let her come to any harm. Do you hear?" She raised her eyes to the ceiling: "Don't let her come to any harm!" She was shouting now. Then dropping into a chair, she buried her face in her hands and tore at her thick hair. She was going mad, stark staring mad—she couldn't bear it.

The latch of the door clicked, and she flung up her head, her eyes clutching at Mike's face. But when his eyes moved quickly away from hers she turned round and joined her hands together and pressed them into her chest.

Mike moved slowly across the stone floor, his steps ringing with the weight of his body, the weight that seemed to have increased in the past few hours. He was heavy all over, his head, his limbs, his mind. He was old; he, like Lizzie, knew he was old. Never again, he felt, would he find an urge towards life. The latest news was that she had been noticed leaving a Hastings train on Charing Cross Station. She had been in the company of an old man, he had had her by the hand. Her being with an old man had been confirmed earlier by the two women in the train who had rung up after the nine o'clock news.

He stood looking in the fire, his thumbs in his belt. He could see himself standing that way. He seemed to be outside of himself, and he saw himself possesed by an odd quietness, part of a terrifying quietness, a quietness full of calculated premeditation, and this part was talking to Mr. Lord. It was saying, "You're to blame for this, you and you only. You wanted to take her away from me, didn't you? Well, now you're going to pay for it." And as he watched this side of himself he knew that if she was not found by the morning he would make the old man pay, and pay thoroughly.

Then there was the other side. He both saw and felt this side—a tearing, raging, cursing side—wanting to run, to fly hither and thither; to search and kill; to turn men round in the street and stare in their faces and demand, "Have you seen her? Have you see her? Have you seen her?" He saw himself taking a man by the throat and bearing him to the ground and stamping on his face until there nothing left. . . .

The latch moved again, and now both swung round towards the door as Mr. Lord entered, accompanied by Michael. With a pitiable frailty the old man came into the room. Gone was his brusqueness and supercilious manner; he looked like any old man who had lost all he possessed, and when he spoke, even his voice sounded frail. He addressed himself to Mike, as he said haltingly, "I've just heard—there may be a chance she's on the North-bound train."

"What? Who? How did you hear?" Lizzie stood before him, standing close and peering into his face.

He put out his hand and patted her arm. "They phoned. I'm going to Newcastle now." He turned towards Mike, who said nothing but picked up his cap from the table and went out.

Mr. Lord now spoke to Michael, but without looking at him, as he made for the door. "Don't you come, you stay with your mother."

Michael stood watching him until he went out, and when the door was closed he turned and looked at his mother. Then throwing himself into a chair, he flung his arms across the table and, dropping his head on them, began to sob.

Lizzie, going swiftly to him, put her arms about him, and drew his head to her breast, saying, "There! there! She'll be all right. Very likely she'll be on the train. Yes, that's it. She wanted to come home." For a moment she tried to make herself believe this, until Michael, raising his head from her chest, muttered between gulps, "How—how could she?" Then again, "How could she? She couldn't come by herself." His head dropped, and Lizzie, her hands still on his hair and hope gone, murmured, "No, she couldn't come by herself."

.   .   .   .   .

It must have been three-quarters of an hour later when Lizzie, with her arms still around Michael but now sitting beside the fire in a form of stupor, heard the car come back. The sound seemed to inject them both with life again, and they sprang up and reached the door together, then stopped dead, peering into the night. The farm looked as if lit up for a gala. There were lights on outside the byres, there were lights in Mr. Lord's new house on the hill, which meant that Ben was also keeping vigil; the Jones's light was on to, but not the Polinskis'. The voice of Mr. Jones came to them from the farmyard. It was loud as if he was crying across a distance, and it asked, "You got her?"

When there was no answering voice, no scampering of feet, Lizzie's hand tightened on Michael's shoulder and they both turned slowly back into the house, leaving the door open.

Within a few minutes Mike came in. He looked wild, half mad, his hair was matted with sweat and falling into corkscrews, like a piccaninny's, about his brow. His eyes were sunk deep in his head, and he seemed to have lost his height. Lizzie looked at him across the table, and Michael looked at him, and he returned their glances with a wild stare.

Lizzie's voice sounded like a whimper when she said, "You heard nothing?"

"No." He beat his clenched fist on the corner of the table; then striding to the fireplace he leant his head again the mantelpiece.

Lizzie stared at his back. She could give him no relief—for a moment she was barren of everything but fear—it was left to Michael to offer a crumb of comfort.

"Tony's been in, Da. He's got the idea she'll make her way home somehow. He's gone back to Pelaw Station to the phone. He says——"

Mike swung round from the fire. "Make her way home! With an old man?" He was speaking to Michael now as one man to another, and Michael's eyes dropped before the knowledge his father was imparting to him.

"Oh, God in Heaven!" Now Mike's voice was high and rough, and he was shouting as Lizzie had been shouting, and using almost the same words. "She should never have left this house. But who's to blame for her going? Him! him!" He was still addressing Michael, but he was really speaking to Lizzie. "The old boy—the old boy who must be placated. Well, this is the end, I've had enough. I'm finished, but before I'm done I'll put paid to him. He wanted her away from me—I know, oh! I know, I wasn't blind—and now she's away—away! away! And he'll go away an' all. My God! he will."

Into Lizzie's misery came a terrible fear. The look on Mike's face was not sane, and his jealousy of the old man because of his love for Mary Ann was turning into something grim and gigantic. It was like a madness developing before her eyes, and what it would lead to she could see as plainly as if it was happening. By this time tomorrow tragedy could have been heaped upon tragedy.

She attempted to swing his thoughts away from his mad intent by saying angrily, "Yes, go on! Blame someone else, put the blame on anybody but yourself. Mr. Lord, what's he got to do with her going away? It was for you, you, she went away!"

"Me?" The demand filled the room.

"Yes, you—you who were never capable of doing anything on your own—you who had to be sustained by her. Why did she go away? Why? I'll tell you." In her effort to turn his mind from Mr. Lord she knew she was going too far, she was going to tell him things that in a saner moment she would have cut out her tongue rather than voice, she was going to make him plain to himself. "She was giving you security, she was buying you a job. Yes!" She screamed at him now, "Raise your eyebrows, open your mouth—she was buying you a job. She sold herself, if you like, to get you this job. Did the old man send her to school? Yes, but she only went because she knew that you owed him a debt and she was paying it. She was paying for your job, do you hear?"

Before her eyes Mike seemed to swell, and then up from the depths of his being, he dragged his voice, deep and terrible. "You're a bloody liar! Tell me you're a bloody liar!" He went a step nearer to her, just one, and he looked like a mountain shifting itself heavily. "Tell me!"

"I've told you the truth." Now Lizzie's voice was screaming, and her hands were pressed against each cheek, holding her face as if to give herself support for she had gone too far, she knew she had gone too far, but she could not stop herself and she went on yelling, "She's always borne your burdens, she's always directed your cause—you, the big fellow. And as soon as she was out of your sight what did you have to do? Laugh and lark on with a lazy, dirty, young——"

It was Michael's voice now, high-pitched, yelling, "Stop it! Stop it, Ma!" that checked hers. So hysterical was it that immediately it had a calming effect on them both, and when they turned from each other and looked at him he jumped with both feet from the ground, he jumped and stamped on the stone floor and yelled again. "Stop it! Stop it! Both of you." Then before they could react in any way he made a wild dash for the open door, and Lizzie, remembering another occasion when their fighting and the hopelessness of their lives had got the upper hand of him, rushed after him and caught him just on the threshold. But what words she would have said to him were checked, for there, coming up the path, was Mr. Lord.

Stepping back into the room and pulling the struggling boy with her, she made way for the old man to enter. When he had done so, he stood looking from one to the other. Nothing escaped him. Unasked and uninvited, he walked towards the table and slowly turning a chair round he sat down and, addressing Mike without looking at him, he said, "Sit down."

Mike did not move, and Mr. Lord, in a voice utterly unlike his own because of the touch of humility in it, said, "All right, I know how you feel, and I'm going to tell you now that I'm taking all responsibility. It was my fault the child went away." He raised his eyes to Mike's red-rimmed, staring gaze. "I wanted her to be different, I wanted to give her a chance that you hadn't it in your power to give her. I know I was wrong."

When Mike spoke, his own voice sounded calm, even normal: "Did you give me this job on condition that she went away to school?"

There was a long pause during which Lizzie's eyes were on Mr. Lord and Michael's were fixed on his father. Then Mr. Lord, his eyes dropping to his hands, said slowly, "Yes. . . . It was her idea in the first place. She came to me and told me you could manage this farm. I hadn't thought about it, it was the last thing that would have entered my mind, but I grant you that once it had entered I saw the possibility of it—of it being a good thing. And you've proved that, there is no doubt about it."

"Huh!" There was a smile on Mike's face, but a terrible smile, a smile devoid of pride, devoid of all the things that gave a man self-respect, and of all the qualities that any man needed Mike needed self-respect.

Lizzie had wanted to lift the blame from Mr. Lord's shoulders and put it on Mike's, and she had succeeded, but with an agony filling her she saw that the weight was too heavy for him. She need not now fear for what he might do to Mr. Lord, but she need fear, and fear terribly, what he might do to himself.

She moved towards him, until she was standing at his side, and she looked up into his face, all her love and tenderness returning, and just as she was about to put her hand on his sleeve it was arrested. Not only was her hand, but her whole body was stiffened into a stare of immobility. And not only hers, but Mr. Lord's and Michael's. Only Mike moved. His head jerked upwards on the sound of running steps, light, tripping, running steps. They all heard the gate bang; and the flying steps came up the path, accompanied now by short, sharp gasps of breath, and before their unbelieving gaze there stood the child, hat in hand, in the doorway, and it was evident in this moment that in spite of her audible breathing not one of them thought her to be real.

She stood, as it were, transfixed in the frame of the door, held there by their eyes. All the way from the cross-roads her mind had gabbled what she would say. "Oh! Ma," she'd say, "I'm sorry, but I had to come. Oh! Da," she'd say, "I missed you, I had to come. Oh! I did miss you. Oh! Ma," she'd say, "it was awful. . . . And Beatrice and Sister Catherine . . . and I can't go back. I don't care, I can't go back; I want to stay home." But now all that was pressed down by their eyes, and what she said was, "Hello." Just a small whisper, "Hello." The one word went to each of them, saying, "Hello." It made them all tremble in their combined relief at the memory of their fears of the past hours. It was Lizzie who spoke first.

"Child!" she said, "Child!" She flew towards the doorway, and Mary Ann, with a bound now, sprang towards her and flung her arms about her waist. And Lizzie, gazing stupidly down at her head, her hand smoothing her hair, repeated, "Child, child!" She did not ask, "How have you come? Where have you come from? Who have you been with?" but just kept saying, "Child! Child! Child!"

Mr. Lord was standing now by the table. He looked even older than he had done a moment ago, if that were possible. His wrinkled skin was moving in little tremors all over his face and his eyes were blinking as if he had just woken from sleep. Quite suddenly he sat down again. Nor did Michael rush to greet her, but groping behind him he felt for a chair, and he too sat down. This left only Mike.

Across the room Mike looked at Mary Ann, pressed hard against her mother, and a terrible feeling overcame him, a sort of hatred for this flesh of his flesh, this power embodied in the smallness of her, this power, without which, even his wife had said, he was lost. A wife was there to bolster a man, but when she told him the truth it was the truth, as he only too well knew now. He was nothing without his daughter. She had got him a job, a job as manager of a farm, a job beyond his wildest hopes and imaginings. He had imagined he had achieved this all by himself—him, the big, red-headed, burly, one-handed Mike Shaughnessy had secured a grand job with his own ability. But no, he had been given the job because of his child's power. She held the power to take hold of a heart—an old man's heart. And now, because of her, his whole life had been rent; he had been stripped naked, split open and presented to himself; it was as if he was gazing at his bowels and he could not bear the sight of them . . . and all because of her, because she had run away from school. He could see it now. She may have been with a man, but she had come to no harm, she had come in through the door just as if she had returned from school in Jarrow. Just as easy as that. But during the time she had left the convent and arrived in this room, his whole life had altered and he had became old. The first thing the news of her flight has done to him was to press the weight of years on to him. Never again, he felt, would he know what it was to feel young and virile; never would he be able to laugh, to bellow from his belly great sounds of mirth. And then the knowledge that she had bought him the job had stripped him even of his remaining manhood—he was nothing, only something that a child could buy. Inwardly, he had always resented the fact that it was because of her that Mr. Lord had first employed him, but his work on the farm, he felt, had proved his capabilities and carved his own niche. Now he knew that that was only a wishful thought in his mind—he had carved nothing. The old man had said, "Make your da a manager! Well, all right, I'll do it if you go away to school." He had carved nothing.

Mary Ann raised her wet face from her mother's body and looked through blurred vision across the room. There was her da, big as she remembered him. she could only see the outline of him, but now she rushed towards him, muttering, "Da! Oh, Da!" Her hands were outstretched and her body seemed to leap over the distance, but when she clutched at the remembered flesh something happened—she was thrust roughly back. She stood blinking up at him. Her vision cleared and she saw his face, and her mind told her that he was mad, flaming mad. He was vexed with her for running away, that was understandable, but nothing told her that she couldn't get round this. She thrust out her hand to grab his sleeve, and when the blow hit her, her thinking stopped and she became frozen inside. Her stunned mind did not even say, "Me da's hit me!" This was too big for even thought.

As Mike had raised his hand and struck at the fingers clutching at him, Lizzie had gasped and sprung forward. Michael too had gasped, only Mr. Lord remained still. And when Mary Ann, the tears flooding silently down her face, turned for an explanation and looked from one to the other, she saw that all eyes were not on her, but on her da. But no one spoke, no one said, "You shouldn't have done that."

Mr. Lord raised himself slowly from the chair. Not now did he say, "There's no need for that;" not now, as he once had done, did he check Mike from threatening to smack her bottom; instead he appeared indifferent to what might happen to her. His eyes looked at her but did not seem to see her; they rested on her as if he was making a conscious effort to blot her out of his mind, and when he turned from her, she found that for a moment the feeling of horror at the blow her father had given her was lost in a new feeling that made her want to rush to the old man and cry, "Oh! I'm sorry, I didn't mean to do it, but I wanted to come home. I'll tell you all about it and then you'll see." But she said none of these things. She knew Mr. Lord only too well, and her mind told her that he was finished with her, and this thought brought a pain into her body, surprising in its effect, because it was equal to that pain which her da had caused.

As Mr. Lord disappeared through the door Lizzie sank on to a chair. She, too, had felt something of what the old man was experiencing. She did not pay any attention for the moment to her daughter. Only Michael now turned his attention to her, and after staring at her for a moment his face screwed up, trying as it were to associate this small sister with the trouble and agony that had come upon the house, and finding it an impossibility. He turned from her and rushed upstairs, and when his door banged overhead, Mary Ann, shaking with sobs, walked slowly to her mother and put her hand tentatively on her knee, as if to question her welcome in this quarter, too. Lizzie's arms came out, slowly, but steadily, and pulled the child once again in to her embrace. And across her head she looked at Mike.

For the first time in his life Mike found he had nothing to say, good or bad, to his daughter. He had threatened to bray her often enough because of her escapades, because of her constant fighting with Sarah Flannagan; now, he hadn't brayed her as a child, but hit her a blow that he would have dealt to a grown-up.

He was standing staring into space, as if he were riveted to the spot on the hearth-rug, and the silence in the kitchen, apart from Mary Ann's sobs, was terrible. As always Lizzie's mind went out like that of a mother to him, and she asked herself over and over again, "What has she done to him? What has she done?" But not only the child was to blame, oh no, she must be fair, she herself had done a lot of damage tonight. Never in a thousand years would she have told him the truth, at least she had thought not, but the events of the night had rent tact and diplomacy from her, and deprived her of all wisdom, and although the relief of having her child back safely was now relieving the tension of her body, once again, as always, she was worrying, worrying about Mike and what would happen next.

Mary Ann's spluttering through her sobs, "I—I—I'm sorry, Ma, I'm sorry," told Lizzie that what she should do now was go for the child, spank her and send her to bed, but she knew that Mary Ann's entire world had dropped apart. Mike had thrust her off; Mr. Lord would have none of her; they weren't even interested in how she had got here—even she herself had forgotten to demand how she had come home, for from the first sight of her she knew that however she had come she was unharmed. She said gently to her, "How did you get here?"

Gulping and sobbing, Mary Ann said, "With Mr. Wilson."

"Mr. Wilson?" Lizzie's face screwed up.

"Yes. You know, the man me da met in the train and told to look after me." She cast her eyes hesitantly towards Mike's averted face. "They were coming back home, and I got into trouble at school and I got your letter, and——" Again her eyes flickered towards Mike, and she said, "I thought—I thought something was wrong. There were marks on it—I thought you were sick."

Puzzled, Lizzie muttered, "Marks on it?" Then rising angrily and almost upsetting Mary Ann off her feet, she exclaimed, "It's him that's at fault! He should be locked up for bringing you. He'd no right."

"He didn't want to, Ma, and Mrs. Wilson neither. She was frightened of the police."

Lizzie, her face set now, demanded, "How did you get here then?"

"He got my ticket, and we got off at Durham. Mrs. Wilson wouldn't come through in the train, and we got the workman's night bus from Durham. They put me off at the corner."

Just as simple as that. Mr. Wilson got her ticket; they got off at Durham; took the night bus and put her off at the corner, and in a few minutes here she was; and the agonies, the passions, the crucifixions of each of them were explained away in those few words. . . . But Mike?

Over Lizzie flooded an overwhelming sense of helplessness. Now she had another situation to cope with—Mike. Before, the situations concerning him had been mostly one-sided. She'd known their substance; Mary Ann had known their substance; and they both, as it were, had worked together for his good, leaving Mike happy in his male fantasy. But now the covers had been ripped off—Mike would be gulled no more, always he would be on his guard. His rejection of the child showed her the depth to which his hurt had gone. She didn't lay it all down to false pride, she knew that he himself had thought the worst had happened to her this night, and his relief in part had taken this form of rejection. And so, thinking that if he were left alone with the child it might help, she turned to Mary Ann and said, "Go on to the fire, I'll go up and get your bed ready."

When her mother had left the room, Mary Ann stood, her fingers in her mouth, loking towards the door through which Lizzie had disappeared. She did not turn to Mike; he still seemed frozen and unable to move, only the movement of his eyes showed his brain was working rapidly.

Mary Ann, never being able to bear silences at any time, was finding this one almost excruiating in its loudness. Her fingers still in her mouth, she turned slowly round and looked at her da's profile. Her da had hit her—and hard. Her hand hurt, her arm hurt. Some part of her told her that she deserved all she had got, and more, but she still could not get over the surprise that he had lifted his hand to her, for she had expected wide-open arms ready to greet her, she had imagined herself flinging herself against him, hanging on to his hair, kissing his face and watching his eyes moving over her features in the way she loved. Now, in spite of herself and the fear of another repulse, she moved towards him, and when she was at his side, with her first finger and thumb tentatively extended, she gently nipped the sleeve of his coat, and in a very, very, small voice, she muttered, "Da, I'm sorry." And then, as with her old apologies, she added, "I won't do it again."

The implied probability of a recurrence of this particular incident seemed to rouse Mike, and he moved his feet in a grating gesture. Her downcast eyes became fixed on them. She dare not look up into his face, but she waited for his hand to come on her head. And after a while, when it didn't, she slowly raised her eyes upwards. He was still mad, very mad, but it was a different kind from any she had ever witnessed before. He didn't look the same as she'd remembered him and, a trembling, terror-riddled feeling told her, he wasn't the same. This feeling urged her to cry out, and now she flung herself against his legs, with her arms round his thighs, crying, "Da! Oh, Da!"

He did not push her away, but he did not fondle her. What he might have done within the next minute cannot be known, for at that moment. Tony entered the room. On the sound of footsteps, Mike turned his head, and across the room his eyes met the young man's.

Tony's entry seemed now an excuse that he turn from her, and without a word he left the kitchen and went out into the night.

Tony stood looking across the table at the bowed head of Mary Ann. In the short time that he had been on the farm he had learned of this child's influence. He had only known her for a few hours, and thought her a taking—a fetching little mite. He liked these people—especially did he like Mike—and over the last few weeks it had hurt him to see the tenseness between him and his wife. Furthermore, since six o'clock last night their suffering had torn at his own heart, for, although he hadn't shown it, he, too, had thought only the worst could happen. And now apparently, from Mike's attitude, nothing of a very serious nature had happened, at least to her.

He had learned that she was a little devil for her escapades; he had taken it that she was an individualist of the first order; and now he had no doubt whatever about it, for after all the upset, here she was unscathed. Yet something about her touched him, she looked so forlorn, so very small, and however she had gone about the business of coming home, she had got here and that was an achievement for anyone of her size and age. So he went to her, and putting his hand on her head, he said, "There now, don't cry."

Snuffling she looked up at him, "Me da's mad at me."

He smiled a little smile. "Well, do you expect him to be anything else? You've had everybody very, very worried. . . . Do you know they were broadcasting on the wireless about you?"

Did a little bit of excitement flicker across her sorrow-laden face? Something very like it came over in her voice as she exclaimed quickly, "The wireless? Me?"

"Yes, the whole country's been looking for you."

Again she exclaimed, "Me?"

He nodded solemnly. "They thought you might have come to some harm." Not wishing to explain what he meant by harm he added, "It's a long way."

Blinking, sniffing and gulping, she looked away from him towards the fireplace, and said flatly, "I wouldn't come to no harm, I had a St. Christopher medal in me pocket."

This simple statement of faith caused his eyebrows to rise. . . . She would come to no harm because she was carrying on her person a piece of tin, depicting the saint who was supposedly a protector of travellers! The simplicity, the profundity of this small child's faith amazed him and caused the feeling of bitterness which he was rarely without, to rise and swamp him again in something like envy now, for never could he remember even as a child having faith.

When a fresh spasm of sobbing began to shake her and her head drooped once more, and she slipped her small hands between her knees and pressed them together, he bent swiftly down and lifted her up and placed her on his knee, saying, "Ssh! be quiet. There now. There now."

Desperately, she turned her face into his chest, as she had hoped to do in Mike's, but without any of the feeling of comfort she would have experienced from contact with her da. It was all so different from what she had expected; her da would have nothing to do with her; nor their Michael; and Mr. Lord was finished with her; even her ma, knowing she was feeling bad, had left her to go upstairs. . . . The fact that of all the people in the house only this boy had stayed with her added to her bottomless sadness, for, as she thought of it, he didn't belong to them. She liked him all right, she had liked him on the first day, but he wasn't her da, her ma, their Michael, or Mr. Lord.

Her crying mounting, she pressed her mouth hard against his shirt, and with his arms about her he sat stroking her head, until Lizzie, like someone sleep-walking, returned to the kitchen and, showing no surprise at finding Mike gone, carried her upstairs.

8

Twenty hours precisely had elapsed since Mary Ann's dramatic return, and they had been filled with everything contrary to what she had expected. She had talked to more policemen than ever she thought had existed. And not policemen as she knew them, but just in their ordinary clothes. And even men from newspapers. These men wouldn't believe that she didn't know Mr. Wilson's address. Had she known it and was trying to protect him she would surely have failed under their battery of questions. Mr. Wilson was going to get wrong, and she didn't want Mr. Wilson to get wrong. Mr. Wilson was nice, so was Mrs. Wilson, but it was Mr. Wilson, and he alone, who had brought her home. The day had been filled with talk, but no one had spoken to her personally, no one had spoken to her as if she was Mary Ann Shaughnessy. Her mother had said, "Eat your dinner," "Eat your tea"; their Michael had avoided her eyes; her da had not spoken at all; and she hadn't seen Mr. Lord. Only Tony had talked to her, or let her remain with him, but as yet in her mind he wasn't in the circle of the family, he was just "the hand".

And now she was lying in bed, wide awake, her eyes staring and blinking at the sloping ceiling, listening to her ma and da fighting, fighting quietly in the kitchen.

Like the wind at night, their voices rose and fell at intervals. From time to time she had strained to hear what they were saying, but couldn't; now, when her da's voice rose high for an instant and she heard him crying plainly, "I'll do what I bloody well like," she found herself out of bed and on the landing at the top of the stairs, listening, as was her old habit, feeling that she must know the torments of her parents and seeing their every move in her mind's eye.

Down in the kitchen, Lizzie sat by the table, automatically pushing her plate an inch first one way and then another, her eyes following its course as if it were something of deep interest. When Mike had yelled at her she hadn't answered, and now he was standing, his foot on the fender, his arms on the mantelpiece, his fingers beating a tattoo that seemed to fill the room with their angry, rebellious thumping.

Addressing her plate, she said quietly, "Whether you believe it or not, you've always done what you like."

"Aye, you've let me think I was doing what I like. You were very clever, Liz, but now all that's finished. I thought I was a man with a mind of me own and knew where I was going, but all the time you've been leading me—leading me through her. Well, that's over, I'm giving up. There are other jobs besides this, thank God, and I'll get one, but I'll get it on me own. Do you hear?" He turned round to her, his voice rising again, "I'll get it on me own, under me own steam. Under me own steam, d'you hear? Propelled by no woman or bairn." He paused, glaring at her downcast head. Then he flung out his hand at her, "Don't you realise—don't you see I've got to do things on me own?"

He watched her head sink lower towards the plate and his voice sank, too, as he said, "You used to understand—you knew me at one time better than I did meself. Perhaps that's what you did this for, manoeuvred her to manoeuvre me. You might have done it for the best, but. . . . "

Lizzie lifted her head. "I've never manoeuvred her. Whether you like to believe it or not the manoeuvring's been between the two of you. I couldn't come between you, not even if I'd wanted to. And now you're thrusting her off, not because of what she's done, but because of your own vanity. You always want to be the big fellow, don't you? Well, when you're thrusting her off you're thrusting yourself off because you're afraid to see yourself, because she's you, every bit of her. All her fighting, all her unthinking actions, the idea that she's only got to make her case plain and everything will be all right—that's you, you all over. And I'm telling you this, if you don't relent you'll be sorry. You always say you are like the elephant, well, so is she—she doesn't forget. She's likely to get over this if you drop it now, but if you keep it up, this silence, this putting her away, you'll live to regret it. I'm telling you, you'll live to regret it, for there are others, and I don't need to mention any names, who will be only too willing, even after what she's done, to step into your shoes."

Mike was in the act of turning away, and now he flung himself round at her and the words "Nobody can take her from me, the old boy nor nobody else" spurted into his mouth, but he didn't say them, he simply stared his anger at her. Since he had seen the child enter the door last night he had pulled down an iron shutter on his feelings for her and was refusing, even at this distance of hours, to recognize that they were beating for release against the barricade. But now the insinuation of the old man into the battle again brought his love bashing and crashing out of himself. He knew the agony of last night would leave an indelible stain on his mind, in fact it would alter the course of his life from now on; because of what had come to light through it he would be suspicious of every action of both Lizzie's and the child's for his welfare; he would fight to go his own road, fight for his right to support them all on his own merits, fight for the right to feel himself a man, his kind of man, his idea of a man, be what it may.

Instead of the words that were filling his mouth, he said, "And you think the old fellow will still have an interest in her after this, after all his high-falutin plans for her are brought low? Old Ma Flannagan said that you couldn't make a silk purse out of a sow's ear, and she's right. And you think the old fellow would be interested in the sow's ear? No, not if I know him. He had a prodigy in her, someone he thought he could mould, but he picked the wrong clay, she'll never be moulded by him or anybody else. . . . All right—if you like, she's like me. She'll remain herself, and to hell with the old man and his power, and his money, and his dictating, and that's what I'll tell him when I see him the morrow."

Lizzie's head jerked up and her eyes became startled, and seeing her fear he now became cruel and said, "Oh, don't worry; you won't starve, I'll get a job that will support you. I suppose you know Polinski's going? He's going as far as Dorset. Foreman he's going as. Told me only the day. And they're wanting a manager on that farm an' all." His eyes narrowed. "How would it be if I put in for it? I wouldn't be separated from her then would

I?" He paused. "That's another thing we've got to get straight, isn't it?"

Lizzie's eyes were stretched, very like Mary Ann's when surprised by pain, but she made no retort at all, she merely rose and with her hand pressed to her mouth went towards the door. She didn't reach it, however, for in a couple of strides Mike had her by the shoulders and had swung her round, and his arm pinning her to him, he was talking into her hair, crying, "Liz! Oh Liz! My God! what's come over us? Listen, Liz. Listen. Forget about the child! I'll deal with that. I'll deal with the old boy an' all—nothing can alter what I'm going to do. But about the Polinskis. My God! Liz, believe me on this; I would much sooner have thought of starting something with old Ma Jones than I would with that young, dirty piece. And I mean what I say, dirty in all ways . . . lazy, a lazy good-for-nowt. But Liz, she was the wife of one of the men, and I liked Polinski and was sorry for him. And, aye God! I was sorry for her. I knew what was the matter with her, Polinski didn't suit her. She wanted a man, any man who hadn't his whole mind as Polinski had on the farm and getting on. I laughed with her, cos I knew her game, and I laughed at her, that's all, Liz. Liz, where's your conceit—her against you. Oh no!" His arm tightened still further around her, and helplessly now she began to sob, and the sobs filled the house.

Mary Ann was leaning against the banister, all her fingers in her mouth. The tears slipping softly from her lashes were missing the wells of her eyes to drop on to the cheekbones and roll heavily to her chin. They were kind, they were kind to each other again. That's all that mattered, nothing else mattered, not the policemen, or the men from the newspapers, or which school she was going to, or her da leaving the farm and getting another job. They were kind, nothing mattered. She stumbled into the bedroom and into bed, and lying down she stuck the corner of the sheet into her mouth, and in a short while fell asleep.

.   .   .   .   .

The following morning Michael couldn't go to school, he had a fever. His body was hot, his hands were hot, and he wanted nothing to eat. Lizzie sat on the side of the bed and pushed his wet hair back from his brow. She knew that something was worrying him—she knew her son better than she did her daughter—and she said, "What is it? Tell me, what is it?"

She had asked this a number of times during the past few hours, but he had just tossed his head. And now he did it again. Then, when she did not persist in her enquiries, he swung himself round and burying his face in the pillow muttered something brokenly, and she bent her head to hear, and said, "Yes? Go on, tell me what's happened."

Slowly he turned his face so that he was looking into her eyes, and muttered, "I was to blame for her coming back like that."

"You?" Lizzie pressed her head away from him to see him better, and again repeated, "You?" as though she thought the fever was causing a slight delirium.

Snuffling, he nodded. "I wrote and told her." His eyes dropped. "I wrote and told her that I thought——" He paused again; then suddenly sitting up in bed and holding his knees tight and dropping his head on to them he ended, "I told her about Mrs. Polinski."

"Oh, Michael!" Lizzie was aghast. "Oh, you shouldn't have done that. Oh, Michael."

She was about to add, "But how did you know?" when she checked herself. How could he not know? How could anyone not know what went on in the house, they were all so closely knit together? She bent towards him and put her arm around him, saying, "You only did what you thought was right. You missed her, like all of us. And if she had been here there would never have been any mention of Mrs. Polinski. And I must tell you now, Michael"—she raised his head and looked into his eyes, demanding by her look that he believed her—"that was my fault, not your da's. It was my imagining things. I was longing for her an' all. Look"—she now put her hand under his chin and raised his face—"do something for me, will you? Go and tell your da what you've told me."

She felt him shrink from her, and she pleaded, "It'll be all right. You see, things have been said. I've said things I shouldn't have. It was all through the worry of this business—and I've upset him terribly. Do this for me, Michael. Tell him it was your fault . . . you wrote and told her about things that you shouldn't have. He won't blame her so much then."

She saw that he was making a great effort to conquer the fear of confessing to his father his share in the trouble.

"But will he wallop me?" he asked softly.

"Oh, no!" said Lizzie hastily. "Of course he won't wallop you. Anyway, I'll see he doesn't. He'll be only too pleased to know that all the blame isn't hers. Come on now, get up and go down to the farm.

Lizzie left him, and as he dressed he asked himself as he had done dozens of times since last night if he had really told her anything in his letters. Sometimes he thought he had and sometimes he defended himself flatly be saying, "I never said a thing about me da going with Mrs. Polinski."

Michael's bewilderment was caused by his failing to realize that he had the kind of sister who never read what was on the lines but the substance that lay between them. . . .

Mary Ann wandered aimlessly about for hours. She was home, she was on the farm. There were the cows, the bull, the young calves, the hens, the ducks, the geese, everything that she had longed to see again, yet now they held no interest for her. She had looked into the cowshed and met the cold stare of Mr. Jones. Mr. Jones had looked at her as if he could have walloped her, and Mrs. Jones, from the backyard, had not waved to her. Len had grinned at her and exclaimed, in awe-filled tones, "Eeh! by, you're not half a star!" Mrs. Polinski had looked at her coldly. Mrs. Polinski looked different, older than when she had last seen her, and she realized that she not only disliked Mrs. Polinski, she hated her. Another time she would have felt the strong desire to stick her tongue out at Mrs. Polinski, but today she just turned her head away and made for the barn.

Then she saw her da was in the barn—she saw his back bending over the bales—but she did not go to him. There was something high and unscalable between her and her da and she knew that she could do nothing herself to surmount it, so slowly and sadly she turned away and walked up the hill towards Mr. Lord's house. But only because she knew that Mr. Lord wasn't in. She had seen him depart for Newcastle in the car earlier on. Although Mr. Lord was now living in the house and the men had been and put up fine curtains at the windows, the house itself looked raw and unfinished. All round lay mounds of bricks and mortar and builders' refuse. Slowly, as if picking her way over new territory, she walked round to the back entrance, impressed, in spite of herself, by the grandeur she glimpsed through the long, low windows. She would have loved to go inside but she felt, in fact she knew at this moment, that she would never, never be asked inside Mr. Lord's house.

As she reached what was to be a walled courtyard with a pool in the middle, the place as yet merely roughly dug out, she saw Ben come out of the glass kitchen-door. Ben stopped when he saw her, and his grave and forbidding countenance, which had once frightened her to death, did not soften, nor even did it take on a sign of recognition. Ben was a reflection of his master, he was not seeing Mary Ann. Within a minute he had returned through the glass door, and Mary Ann hurried out of the yard and made her way down the hill again, her fingers now, one after the other in turn, being pressed into her mouth, and her mind crying at all these people in her own defence, "I wasn't to blame all the time . . . I wasn't. It was Mrs. Polinski and our Michael and that Beatrice, and Sister Catherine . . . I wasn't to blame, I wasn't. I don't care. Me ma's all right. Me ma's not like them. I don't care—I don't."

As she reached the gate near the farm, she saw across the yard a car draw up at the main gates, and she thought, "Them men again." This description covered policemen and newspaper reporters, but when she saw stepping from the car not only one of "them men" but also Mr. and Mrs. Wilson, she clapped both hands over her mouth. An urge bid her fly to her old friends but reason prevailed and she turned and dived behind the big barn, across an open space to the little barn, and dashed into its cool dimness and stood with her back to the wall, her whole body trembling. There would be a row, there was bound to be another row, and Mr. Wilson would get wrong. Eeh!

"And now what's the matter?"

She swung round, startled to see Tony. He was standing near a number of old, battered and belabelled trunks, and she went to him swiftly and said, "It's Mr. and Mrs. Wilson, they've just come." She stared at him for a moment then added, "There'll be a row."

"No there won't. It'll be all right. Stop trembling now." He took her hand and bent his face to hers and smiled, an unusually wide smile that momentarily took all the brooding sombreness from it. "What'll you bet that this time next week everybody's forgotten about the whole affair?"

She stared up at him. "They won't forget, cos nobody's speaking to me. But I don't care. . . . If only me——"

She didn't go on to say that she didn't care if nobody spoke to her again if only her da would, but Tony seemed to be able already to read her mind, and to understand Mike, and he said, "Don't worry, this time tomorrow you and your da'll be like—that." He crossed his long, lean fingers and held them up for her inspection and comfort. And she stared at them trying to see herself and her da joined again like them, but she couldn't and her head dropped and once again she started to cry.

"Come along, don't cry. Dry your eyes. You'll be back at your old school next week. You'll like that, won't you?"

Her tears stopped quite suddenly, cut off as it were by this small shock, and she jerked her head up towards him and repeated, "Old school?"

"Yes, don't you want to go back to your old school?"

She looked away from him around the barn, stocked with things that she had not noticed in it before. Old rubbish, she thought, from Mr. Lord's other house—trunks and cases and boxes. School . . . her old school. . . . Going back to her school in Jarrow, she found, did not bring her any comfort at all—it could be said she abhorred the thought. Sarah Flannagan and all them, jeering at her. For the first time she asked herself what she had done, and answered quite truthfully, "Eeh! I must have been daft," and the convent, from which up to a moment ago she was glad she had escaped, now appeared to her as something personal and valuable she had lost. And all through Mrs. Polinski and their Michael, and that Beatrice and Sister Catherine. But what school would she go to if she didn't go to Jarrow? She knew that Mr. Lord would send her to no other school. Mr. Lord was finished with her good and proper, there would be no forgiveness forthcoming from Mr. Lord. If he had been mad and stormed at her she would have had some hope, but no, Mr. Lord's silence was as final as death.

She was startled by Tony's next question. It was as if he had a looking-glass on her mind, for he said, musingly, "Do you like Mr. Lord?"

Her voice was very small and low, "I used to."

"He's been very good to you, hasn't he?"

Her conscience was heavy, and it weighed her head down as she murmured, "Yes."

"He's not good to many people, is he?"

She raised her eyes slantwise to him. "No, I don't think so; he's bad-tempered."

"And cold and hard as iron inside."

Now her eyes were wide and staring. Tony's face had taken on not only his solemn expression, but a hard, bitter look that made him suddenly appear old, and not a little frightening to her. She saw that his eyes were blazing, and she watched him lift his foot and savagely kick at one of the trunks. Then her eyes widened as she heard him swear under his breath, using bad words, as bad as any she had heard her da use, like "Damn him to blazes!" "Who the hell!" and "Blast him!" The only difference was he said them swanky.

Eeh! it was Mr. Lord he was at. He didn't like Mr. Lord. Mr. Lord had been at him, but to kick the boxes like that and to swear!

As if remembering her presence, he turned to her, his face still dark but his voice normal, saying, "I'm sorry, Mary Ann. Don't take any notice. I'm like you, I take the needle."

She slid off the box, and looking up at him, she asked as one sufferer to another, "Has he been getting at you?"

A smile that had no movement in it came into his eyes, and she thought, "He looks nice—sad-like, but I like him." And when he nodded, she said, as if in comfort, "Never mind, he's always getting at somebody." Yet as she said this she felt somehow that she was betraying a trust.

"Yes, he's always getting at somebody."

He turned away towards the door, and she fancied she heard him mutter, "He always has." And she thought, That's funny. What's he carrying on for? He hasn't been here very long. She felt that she had known Mr. Lord for ever, not just one year, while Tony, although he was "nice", was really a newcomer on the scene. She watched him walk away, then stop abruptly, grope in his pocket, then turn and come back to her.

"There's only three left. You like Buttered Brazils?"

"Yes. Oh, ta. Oh, Buttered Brazils!"

Buttered Brazils were far and away above her finances, and she said again, "Oh, ta." then it struck her that she shouldn't say "Ta" to him, because he didn't talk like she did, he talked like them back at the convent. She looked at him now with new interest in her eyes. And he was like them back at the convent. She had noticed something different about him at dinner time when she sat opposite him at the table. The way he sat, the way he ate, the way he talked to her ma. Yes, he was like them at the convent. She said now, "Thanks," in her politest tone, and he smiled down at her for a moment, before moving away. She thought again, He's nice, and not because he had given her some sweets. Mrs. Polinski gave her sweets, but she didn't think Mrs. Polinski was nice—but he was. She became very firm in her mind about this. She liked him—he was nice.

Thinking it policy to do so, she stayed in the barn for what seemed to her hours, not making a move to go outside until she heard from the distance the sound of the car starting up. And then, in spite of her relief, she felt a tinge of disappointment that nobody had come in search of her and a touch of curiosity as to why they hadn't.

When the fading *brr!* on the road told her the car was safely speeding away she walked into the yard again, around the big barn, and towards the house. There was no sign of her da or her ma, the whole place look deserted, as if everyone had gone away in the car. But as she neared the back door she heard her mother's voice, and the words that came to her told her she wasn't speaking to her da, and for a moment Mary Ann was riveted to the spot. Not her grannie, not today, she couldn't bear it if her grannie was here today.

"It wasn't really her fault," Lizzie was saying; "she should never have been sent in the first place."

Mary Ann, with her hand pressed tight to her chest, waited and when the thick North-Country twang came bouncing out to her, "Yer right there, Liz. Aa've said it all along, it was a mad thing to do, separating her from him," a feeling akin to a laugh swept over her, and she raced through the scullery and into the kitchen, crying, "Mrs. McBride! Oh, Mrs. McBride!"

Mrs. McBride's ox-like arms opened, and Mary Ann flung herself against her billowing bust, and the old woman cried, "Ah! hinny, it's good to see ye. Aw! it is, it is. Here, let me hev a look at ya. Stand away." She pushed Mary Ann to arm's length; then nodding her head and without a word of reprimand on her tongue, she said, "You're grown. You're grown up in the last few months."

"Have I, Mrs. McBride?"

"Ya have that, hasn't she, Liz?" The old woman looked up at Lizzie, and Lizzie, smiling for the first time in days, said, "Yes, I think she has, a little bit."

"When did you come, Mrs. McBride?"

"Just a minute ago, hinny."

"How?" Mary Ann was eager for details.

"By the bus, of course—me car isn't ready yet. But it will be soon, it's being made to measure!" She punched Mary Ann playfully, and Mary Ann laughed and grabbed at her hand and said, "Oh, Mrs. McBride!"

There was so much feeling in Mary Ann's tone as she spoke her old friend's name that Lizzie turned away and went into the scullery to fill the kettle, and Mrs. McBride said, with a tremor in her voice, "So you're back, me bairn?"

Mary Ann's face sobered, and she nodded solemnly.

The old woman touched her cheek and, shaking her head and with a smile spreading over her fat wrinkled face, she said, "Eeh! ye know what? it's a good job there are not two in the world like you, or else we would be in a state, wouldn't we?"

At this, Mary Ann moved into the comfort of the old woman's knees, and tracing her finger around Mrs. McBride's frayed and rusty coat sleeve, and with one eye cocked upwards that held just a trace of amusement in it, she said, "There was a nun like you in the convent, Mrs. McBride."

The shout that filled the kitchen brought Lizzie to the door, and Mrs. McBride, her hands in the air, bellowed to her, "Have you heard this 'un?"

Lizzie, smiling shook her head.

"There's a nun like me! Can you see that, Liz?"

Again Lizzie shook her head and her smile broadened, and Mary Ann, looking from one to the other the women, for the first time in days, laughed freely. "But there was, Ma. It was Sister Alvis; she talked like Mrs. McBride, and looked like her."

The roar filled the kitchen again, and Fanny cried, "Well, I've been likened to many things, and everything on the farm from a heifer to a cow in——" She rubbed her finger across her nose and did not finish her description, but cried, "And many more things I've been likened to. But a nun! Begod I'm going up in the world. What do you say, Liz, eh? A nun. Eeh! Oh, hinny!" She touched Mary Ann's cheek tenderly. "That's imagination for you. God help her, poor woman, if she was like me."

"She was, Mrs. McBride, and I liked her."

"Bless you, bairn."

"Mrs. McBride——" Mary Ann started playing with the buttons on the old woman's blouse as she said, "You know something? I can speak French and German."

"No! French and German?"

"Yes, I learnt it at the convent."

"Go on, let's hear you."

Mary Ann considered a moment, then said very slowly, as if each word was being dragged from as far away as the convent, "Nous avons—une grande maison—et—un beau jardin . . . Je vive—avec ma mère et mon père. That's me ma and da, that last bit."

"Your ma and da in French? God in Heaven! D'ye hear that, Liz? That's what education does for you. Makes you into a foreigner." She laughed. "Go on, tell us some more."

"German?"

"Aye, German. Oh my, can you speak German an' all?"

Mary Ann, all woes forgotten for the moment, and in an accent that was more Geordie than German, was telling her friend that this was her brother Hans, and Mrs. McBride's eyes were stretching to a complimentary width when an alarmed exclamation of, "Oh, no!" from Lizzie made them both look towards the window.

Lizzie was carrying a tray full of tea things which she now held stiffly suspended, and her gaze was fixed on something outside. Again she exclaimed, "Oh, no!" then quickly turning she looked across the room and said, "Your grannie!"

"Me grannie?" Mary Ann had pulled herself from Mrs. McBride, and Mrs. McBride exclaimed, "Oh, God in Heaven, not her! How did she get here, she wasn't on the bus?"

Lizzie wearily putting down the tray on the table said, "She's sported a taxi seemingly."

Mary Ann could say nothing. She looked from her mother to Mrs. McBride, then towards the door, but she did not attempt to make her usual escape. she was experiencing very much the same feeling as she had done when she had been confronted by Beatrice at the door of the recreation room. She felt tied to the room, to the spot. She turned towards a chair and sat down. She had no fight in her with which to combat what was surely coming from her grannie, and all for her, exclusively for her.

Within a minute, there came a sharp rat-tat on the front door, and walking heavily Lizzie went to open it, while Mrs. McBride arranged herself as if ready for battle. She opened her coat, smoothed down her skirt, hitched up her enormous bust, then folded her arms under it, while Mary Ann, from her chair, kept her eyes on the door.

As Mrs. McMullen's strident voice was heard from the hall, Fanny hissed across to Mary Ann, "Don't look like that, that's not you. Give her as good as she sends. Go on, up with that chin of yours."

With an effort Mary Ann lifted up her head, and as soon as her grannie entered the room she made herself look straight into her face. The look seemed to hold Mrs. McMullen, and she stopped and stared back at her grandchild. Then, with her eyes slowly drawing to slits, she gave a pregnant exclamation.

"Ah!" she said. Then looking towards Mrs. McBride, she added, "Huh!" and Fanny, her face and voice amiable, replied, "Aye, huh! We're all out the day, eh, like Flannagan's Fleas."

Mrs. McMullen, wearing a stately dignity, moved to the big chair near the fire. "You must speak for yourself, Mrs. McBride, I am visiting my daughter."

Now it was Fanny's turn to say, "Huh!"

"Will you have a cup of tea, Mother?" Lizzie stood near the tray, and Mrs. McMullen with raised eyebrows, said, "Well, I should think that goes without saying after this journey."

"Was your journey really necessary?" Fanny, trying to imitate a refined twang, muttered this under her breath, and it brought into Mary Ann's worried being a little gurgle of laughter. Oh, Mrs. McBride was funny. Oh, she was glad she was here. Her grannie wouldn't start on her surely, not in front of Mrs. McBride . . . she'd hold her tongue for a while.

But Mary Ann had misjudged her grannie's power of self-control, for no sooner had she received a cup of tea from Lizzie's slightly shaking hand then she turned her eyes on her grand-daughter and again gave her pregnant exclamation, then added, "So you're back!"

Mary Ann said nothing, she only looked at her grannie, and her grannie began to stir her tea while she peered down into the cup. Then without raising her eyes she said, "I suppose now that you've had the whole country on the alert for you you're feeling fine. Trust you to draw attention to yourself."

Mary Ann's eyes slid to her mother and Mrs. McBride and then back to her grannie. She had found no help in the sight of her ma's shoulders stooped over the tray, nor from Mrs. McBride's face which seemed to be expressionless—she had no one to rely on but herself. But the forced proximity to her grannie was restoring her fighting feeling. Her grannie's words were now stinging her all over, like hailstones.

"I suppose, as usual, you were greeted with open arms and patted on the head, and told what a clever girl you were, eh?"

There was a clatter of cups as Lizzie moved the tray, and there was a wriggle of Mrs.

McBride's hips as Mrs. McMullen went on, "And I suppose the big fellow said 'Well done'? Like father like daughter!"

"Mother, I'm having none of this. It's finished, it's all over. If you want to stay, please forget it."

Mrs. McMullen reared her head so high that it looked as if her hat was going to topple off the top of her abundant hair as she said, "Am I getting the door again?"

"There's no need to talk about the door, Mother. Only leave her be, she's been through enough."

"Huh! huh!" Mrs. McMullen sipped her tea then exclaimed bitterly, "You were always soft with her—like clarts."

There came a deep sigh from Fanny and she exclaimed quietly, "Well, in this case, it isn't like mother like daughter, is it? Eh?"

Mrs. McMullen turned her haughty gaze on Fanny, and replied icily, "I didn't think I was addressing you, Mrs. McBride."

"No," said Fanny, "neither did I. But tell me"—she leaned towards Mrs. McMullen— "tell me, what do you think of this fine job your son-in-law's landed? Isn't this one great, big, grand farm?"

"I am not in the habit of discussing my family's business with outsiders." Mrs. McMullen put down her cup and folded her hands.

"No. Only when you want to kick them in the backside, Mike in particular, with old Ma Flannagan." Fanny's voice was hard.

"Look," said Lizzie, her eyes darting between her mother and Mrs. McBride, "I want no more of this, one way or the other."

There was silence in the kitchen for a moment, during which Mrs. McMullen stood up and deliberately took off her coat and hat. Then sitting down again and unable to restrain her tongue or curiosity, she asked of Lizzie, "Well, and what's going to happen to her now? You can't tell me that the old boy will have any more interest in her after this. She's made him the laughing stock of the country." There was another tense pause, and Mrs. McMullen slowly turned around to meet Mary Ann's eyes. "Jarrow school, I suppose again, and serve you right. I hope you have a nice time when you meet Sarah Flannagan and the rest of them. I wouldn't like to be in your shoes when you go back there!"

"I'm not going back!" The words seemed squeezed out of Mary Ann's throat.

"Oh!" Mrs. McMullen's head bounced slowly. "And where are you going pray?"

"I'm going to another school—a better one." Mary Ann's nose was twitching, a sure sign of her inner agitation. "Bigger—nicer."

The wishful thinking was only all too plain to her grannie, and she laughed as she said, "You've got some hopes. If I heard aright, the old boy's washed his hands of you, and not you alone by all accounts. No, not you alone!"

Mary Ann knew instinctively who the "not you alone" meant. That meant her da. She was saying that Mr. Lord has washed his hands of her da. Her grannie was a liar. Her grannie was bad, wicked—the Devil. Yes, that's who her grannie was, the Devil dressed up! She wished she would have a fit and die in it.

And her grannie's next words caused Mary Ann to make an effort to bring her wishful thinking into operation. For just as Mrs. McMullen was placing her empty cup on the table she made a statement. "It's a case of the sow's ear all over again," she said.

No one was more startled than Mrs. McMullen as a sample of concentrated fury flung itself at her, and before her flabby hand could prevent it happening, her cheek was scratched in several places.

What followed was a good five minutes of sheer pandemonium, during which Mrs. McMullen poured her vitriolic venom into the air of the kitchen and Lizzie held the struggling and screaming child, while Mrs. McBride, yelling her loudest at Mrs. McMullen, and that was saying something, told her what she had thought of her, not only for the last year or so either, but from the time they had been girls together in the neighbourhood of Jarrow.

When at last Lizzie managed to quieten Mary Ann's screams, she picked her up in her arms and made for the stairs, and just as she reached them Mike came hurrying into the kitchen. He stood for a second on the threshold, taking in the whole situation, then growled, "What's going on here? You can hear you all over the farm!" His eyes moved swiftly from Mary Ann in her mother's arms to his mother-in-law's bleeding face, and he spoke directly to her, cutting off her own tirade just as she was about to flood him with it.

"We always get what we ask for. For my part I can say it's a pity it wasn't the other side an' all." Then moving across the room, he addressed Fanny briefly by saying, "Hello, there, Fan."

"Hello, Mike," said Fanny, just as briefly.

Then when he reached the door he gathered up Mary Ann from Lizzie's arms and went up the stairs.

9

Father Owen was very weary. He sat in the confessional box, his hand shading his eyes and only half listening, it must be confessed, to Jimmy Hathaway's confession. Jimmy had made the same confession for as many years as Father Owen cared to remember. It began, "Drunk, three times last week, Father . . . very sorry." Only the number of times he had erred ever varied. It could be as many as six or as few as one, but whatever the number his reactions to his lapse were always the same, and his way of confessing it never varied. "Knocked her about a bit, Father."

It was as well, Father Owen sometimes thought, that Peggy Hathaway could not become any dafter. Jimmy Hathaway was beyond hope, and, years before, the priest had given up any idea of earthly redemption for him, but this had not stopped him from trying to save his soul. But tonight he dismissed him without even the usual advice, with only a curt, "One Our Father and ten Hail Mary's," wondering as he did so, if they would ever be said.

Father Owen sighed as he heard Jimmy stumbling out of the box, and when next a thin whine came to him he repeated his sigh. It was a bad night, all the hopeless cases of the parish seemed to have got together at once. This penitent, he knew, was Mrs. Leggatt. Although he did not know what would be forthcoming in Mrs. Leggatt's confession, he knew her well enough to expect nothing but a tirade of petty spite and pilfering, and his mind said, "Oh dear, dear!" Altogether, it had been a trying day.

Father Beaney had been at his most pompous, his most patronising, his most overbearing. Of course he knew that his superior's attitude had been invoked by the young curate. The newcomer tested his own nerves, for what was more putting off to a man in his sixties than a warm-blooded enthusiast out to outdo even God Himself . . . out to reform all human nature in his own way . . . which was the best way, of course, being the latest way. Oh, yes, between Father Beaney and God's latest lieutenant, he'd been sorely tried this day. And not only today, but all the week. And this had brought about his own lapse. Only in extreme emergencies did he allow himself a double dose of his "cough mixture" before retiring. His weak will had tempted him to tell himself that the events of the week could be constituted an emergency. His patron saint, Miss Honeysett, his housekeeper, and the good God, together allowed him one glass, but at times he was apt to ignore all three and take a second helping of his comforter . . . his conscience didn't trouble him so much at night, for the flesh was warmed and weak then. But in the morning it was a different kettle of fish, for then it loomed at the side of his bed, looking at him, nodding its head and saying, "The LINO penance for you, me boy—the LINO penance for you." To an outsider the lino penance might seem so light as to be no penance at all, but when one of the things you have been unable to stand during the whole course of your life is your bare feet on cold linoleum, what more harsh treatement could a conscience extract from you but bid you get out of a warm bed and put your feet on to slabs of ice and to keep them there while you dressed— and the blood in your veins already like water. Oh, it had been a trying day. What was that? He pricked his ears up as Mrs. Leggatt's voice whimpered, "And it wasn't gold at all, Father, so I didn't feel so bad about it. Six shillings I got on it; that was all."

"Have you taken it back?"

"No, Father."

"And you come here expecting absolution?"

There was no answer from Mrs. Leggatt.

"Now away with you, and go and get that brooch out of pawn, and when you have returned it to its owner you can come back and we'll discuss the matter further. Away you go now."

Father Owen sounded angry. He was angry. Would they never learn?

He heard Mrs. Leggatt's heavy breathing and noticed, not without some satisfaction, that she tripped heavily on leaving the box. God had His ways.

His hand was again covering his eyes when the door opened and the usual shuffle to the kneeler was made, and he became slightly impatient when no voice started on the act of confession. He said, somewhat sharply, "Yes? Go on."

"Pray, Father, give me thy blessing, for I have sinned. It's been a week since my last confession . . . but not here."

Some feeling, not incomparable with the warmth of a good glass of whisky on a cold night, shot through Father Owen. It was Mary Ann. Well, he had been expecting her—it would be good to see the child again. Oh, my, yes, but he must not let her see this, he must give her a sound ticking off. She had really gone beyond all bounds this time. Stirred up the whole country for a few hours, and what was more had thrown over the chance of a lifetime. Wilful, wilfil. And that chance, if he knew anything, would not be repeated. Old Lord was not a man to give second chances, even to bewitchers like Mary Ann. He checked the eagerness in his voice and said flatly, "Go on."

Mary Ann's voice came to him clear and soft through the grill. I've never missed Mass, Father, or Communion, and I've said me morning and night prayers every day, but I've been bad, Father." There was a pause. "I run away from school." There came another pause which he did not break, and her voice when she went on was much more definite. "There was a girl there. She was really the Devil, like you said, so it wasn't my fault."

There was a gulp from the box and the priest muttered, "We won't go into whose fault it was. Get on with your confession."

The voice had a little tremor in it now as it came to him, saying, "I'm sorry, Father, I didn't mean to do it, but I was worried. Me ma was worried. It was all over me da."

Oh, that da! That child and her da! What had the man done now that had caused her to run away from school and throw up the chance of a lifetime? "What was the matter with your da?"

"Nothing, Father. Only there was a girl on our farm and our Michael told me about her. She was always running after me da, and me ma was worried, and I got a letter and she had been crying, and I wanted to come home."

Dear God! Drink, and now women. Would he never do anything right, that man? And having landed a job out of the blue like he had. And to jeopardise it by women now!

"Father?"

"Yes, my child?"

"Do you know it's me, Father? Mary Ann Shaughnessy?"

"Yes, I know it's you, Mary Ann."

Mary Ann sighed. The priest undoubtedly was blind but he wasn't deaf. She said again, "I'm sorry, Father, I didn't mean to do it. I'm very sorry."

The sincerity in her voice made Father Owen say, "Yes, I believe you are, child. But you committed a grave wrong, and now what's going to happen to you?"

"I don't know, Father."

"Mr. Lord won't give you a second chance."

"No, Father."

It was only a whisper, and Father Owen said, "No. At least I think we're agreed about that. . . . Well, it'll be back to school for you."

There was a long silence, and into the silence Father Owen read Mary Ann's reluctance to return to her old school. No matter what had made her run away some part of her had undoubtedly liked the taste of the convent, and now there'd be no more convents for her. Ah, it was a pity, a great pity. He'd had high hopes of her. Well, that was that. Perhaps God didn't want it that way. His ways were strange, and he himself mustn't be too harsh on her. No, no, he couldn't be too harsh with the child. Who could be harsh with someone that loved so much . . . she loved that great, big, red-headed lump of trouble with a heart that was as big as her body, if not bigger.

When he heard a slight snuffle his voice dropped to a tender tone, and he said, "Well, now, my child, don't worry any more. The thing is done, we can only look forward. Trust in God and pray. In the meantime, say a decade of the Rosary each night for a week. . . . On your knees mind, not in bed!"

"Yes, Father. . . . Father."

"Yes, what is it?"

"I've done something else bad, Father."

"And what was that?"

"I hit me grannie yesterday."

"You what?"

After a heavy silence, Mary Ann repeated, in a voice that was scarcely audible, "I hit me grannie, Father."

"Oh, that was very wicked of you, very wicked—an old woman. How could you, Mary Ann? That's the worst yet. I trust you're heartily sorry."

He waited, but no words of remorse came through the grid, and he repeated, "Did you hear what I said? I trust you are heartily sorry. Are you?"

After an extended pause the priest recieved the truth.

"No, Father."

This answer seemed to floor Father Owen and he made fluttering noises, and then demanded sternly but softly, "Did I hear aright? You're not sorry you struck your grannie?"

"I've tried to be, Father. I prayed to Our Lady last night that I would be, but I woke up this morning and I wasn't cos she said I'd always be a sow's ear. You remember, Father, you said you'd been made out of one, an' all, didn't you?"

Father Owen did no confirm this kinship, and in the heavy silence Mary Ann proceeded. "But it was what she said about me da that made me do it. She said——"

"I don't want to hear what she said. Say your act of contrition."

"O my God, I am very sorry that I have sinned against Thee, because Thou art so good, and by the help of Thy Holy Grace I will never sin again. Amen. . . . Good night, Father."

"Good night, my child, and—and God bless you. I'll be seeing you." The voice held no reprimand now, and Mary Ann said, "Yes, Father. Good night, Father."

The priest sighed heavily. God help her, for only He could now. No earthly persuasion that he could see would make old Lord fork out any more money on her behalf, and if he knew anything of the old man, Mike Shaughnessy would likely suffer because his plans for the child had gone awry. He must trip over there some day soon and see how things were shaping. . . . And she had hit old Mrs. McMullen! He rubbed his hands over his face. The day wasn't so far gone when he'd had the strong desire to do the self-same thing. But now he must pray for her—pray for them all. . . .

As Mary Ann said her penance at the side of the altar and gazed with moist eyes up at the Holy Family, she experienced the first semblance of peace since her arrival home. She did not go over the business of the journey with them—they knew all about it—nor did she mention her attack on her grannie—like Father Owen, she remembered, they did not always see eye to eye with her over her grannie, but she did cover the gamut of her errors over the past few days by saying, softly and contritely, "I'm sorry." This they accepted and looked at her kindly, but no word on the incense-laden air came to her, and she knew they would have little to say until she had proved her contrition. They were, she knew, biding their time—but they weren't vexed, and the sight of their beloved faces was a salve on her heart and had a steadying effect on the shivering anticipation that was filling every pore of her body, the anticipation of even a more serious nature than her being bundled back to Jarrow school, the anticipation of her da leaving the farm.

What happened after she had hit her grannie was hazy in her mind. She could remember very little until she found herself in bed and alone with her da. When her ma had left the room he had lifted her from the bed and on to his knee, and pressed her face into his neck, and without him saying a word she knew that everything between them was all right again. At least, that was how she had felt as she went to sleep, her hand in his. But this morning she wasn't sure, not really sure. He had smiled at her at breakfast time and put his hand on her head. But there was something still wrong, and as the endless morning had worn on she came to know what it was. It was the farm—her da's job, it was hanging in the balance. She saw it in the way he talked, his voice over-loud and cocksure. In all, she knew he didn't care any more whom he vexed or pleased.

Before leaving the Holy Family she stared hard up at them for a moment, and without her usual preliminary preamble she stated simply, "Please look after me da, will you? An' don't let him get vexed."

In this short plea she had said everything, for she felt that if her da kept his temper he'd keep his job.

She genuflected deeply to the alter, turned about and walked slowly up the church, past the grown-up penitents dotting the pews and out into the porch.

She had especially picked Saturday night to come to confession, for it wasn't usual for children to be there, having all been marshalled from school on the Thursday in an unrepentant horde, and so it wouldn't have been a matter of surprise to her to encounter Mrs. Flannagan, but to see Sarah startled her. There they both were on the edge of the pavement, right opposite the church door, and although Mrs. Flannagan had her back towards her and Sarah her profile, instinctively she knew they were waiting for her. A concealed tug by Sarah of her mother's sleeve told Mary Ann's sinking heart that this was a prepared attack.

"Oh!" Mrs. Flannagan turned casually round, and with well-simulated surprise confronted Mary Ann squarely. "Well!"

Only two words, but they halted Mary Ann as firmly as a weighty hand on her shoulder, and she looked, with almost a plea for leniency in her eyes, up at the tall woman. She was trapped in front of her enemy, Sarah, and her mother's enemy, Mrs. Flannagan, and even if she had wanted to fight she would have been unable to do so, for she dare not cheek a grown-up, even such an awful grown-up as Mrs. Flannagan.

"So you're back. Well! well! It's a short career you've had, isn't it? Not sufficiently long enough to turn you into a lady, I would say. You were going to be a lady, weren't you, Mary Ann?"

Mary Ann said not a word, humiliation was sweeping over her. The loud snigger from Sarah did for a moment stiffen her spine; but only for a moment, for Mrs. Flannagan took up the attack again.

"Well, have you lost your tongue? Aren't we going to hear your refined accents . . . or wasn't that wonderful convent used to dealing with sows' ears?"

No part of Mary Ann moved—except her eyes. For a second they fell away from the gimlet stare, but were brought back again to her tormentor as Mrs. Flannagan continued, "But, of course, they hadn't time to curb your craving for sensation. Rome wasn't built in a day, was it? But I doubt if that will ever be curbed. You went to town this time, didn't you . . . got on the wireless . . . nation-wide search. My! my!"

Another snigger from Sarah.

"Well, you must always remember, Mary Ann, the higher you climb the farther you fall. But I don't suppose there'll be another opportunity for you like that, will there?" Another pause, during which Sarah changed her balance from one foot to the other, then hung affectionately on to her mother's arm and looked up at her as she continued, "I saw your grandmother last night. She had a nasty mark on her face—it would take more than a convent to change YOU, wouldn't it?" In her last words Mrs. Flannagan had dropped her bantering tone, and her bitter feeling of enmity was stark as she went on, "She was telling me she had a long talk with Mrs. Jones on the bus back. You've shot all their bolts, haven't you? Your Fairy Godfather's got fed up, washed his hands of you, so if your da can't hold a farm job down by favour he certainly won't hold it down by experience, for he's had as much experience of a farm as I've had of ballet dancing. And unless you're well in favour with them that matter nobody's going to be fool enough to give a handicapped man such a responsible job. It stands to reason, doesn't it?"

The tears that Mary Ann would not allow to run from her eyes were blocking her throat and seemed to be forcing their way out through her pores, for she had broken into a heavy sweat and she stod helpless as Sarah, her voice filled with laughter, spoke for the first time. "She was going to learn French and German an' all, Ma."

"Yes, so I understand," said Mrs. Flannagan, bestowing a tight smile on her daughter. "You can learn French and German in Jarrow, but, of course, it wouldn't be the same French and German that you would learn in a posh convent, would it?"

Sarah giggled, and Mrs. Flannagan, hitching her coat up on to her shoulders preparatory to moving away, fired her last shot. "The attics in Mulhattan's Hall are empty again, tell your ma."

Even after they had moved off, Sarah joyfully skipping along by her mother, Mary Ann still stood where they had left her, and not until they disappeared round the corner did she stir, and then it was only to shudder. She stood for some long time staring down into the gutter, while she chewed on her fingers in an effort to suppress a tearing spasm of weeping.

Finally she moved away and to the bus stop, and when the bus came she mounted head down and made for the top end, where, there not being a seat, she stood, supposedly taking an interest in the driver through the glass partition. Not until she had alighted at the crossroads and was almost to the farm did she raise her head and her eyes from the contemplation of the ground and look about her and release some of the pain in her heart, by saying, "It's my fault. It's all my fault." She did not think now, "Oh, that Mrs.

Flannagan! Oh, that Sarah!" but, "Eeh! what have I done?"

For a moment, she had a wild idea of contacting, in some way, the Mother Superior, or Sister Alvis, and telling them she was sorry and wanted to come back. She saw herself leaving here as secretly as she had left the convent and arriving back in the south, and her presence there automatically wiping out the whole disastrous episode. But the picture quickly faded. Even if she could, she wouldn't want to go back—not all that way. She wanted to go to a nice school again, oh, yes, she wanted that, and with a desire the strength of which surprised her. But she wanted to be home, if not every day, at the week-ends. Above all, far, above all that, she wanted things back as they had been on the farm—her da settled and everything lovely. And now it would never be that way again. She felt this to be true, for as Mrs. Flannagan had said, she who had made everything lovely for her da and ma had "shot their bolts".

How true this was was proved as she neared the farm gates. The sound of a car coming out made her move off the road, and on to the grass verge, and when Mr. Lord, sitting at the wheel of his car, went by she glued her eyes on him, and in a flurry of prayers willed that he would look at her, just look—it wouldn't matter if he glared. But Mr. Lord never took his eyes from the road. It was impossible for him not to see her, but he didn't see her, he was blind to her.

Depressed beyond measure she went on and into the house, but here no comfort awaited her. Lizzie, with hard pats and thuds was busy cooking, but she was not drugged, as she usually was, into a cheerful calm placidity by the warmth and mixture of smells; instead she was immediately short with Mary Ann, telling her she had a half-hour before bed and no more. Michael was doing his homework on the table near the window, and he did look up at her for a moment, but he didn't smile as he had done this morning. His face had a familiar, funny look, and it brought fresh anxiety to her . . . something had happened. Had her da and Mr. Lord been at it? Oh no! no!

She left the kitchen, trying not to run, and when she reached the farmyard there was no sight of her da, or anyone else. The look on Michael's face had told her she must find her da, but he wasn't in the cowshed, nor yet in the big barn, nor in the loft. She shouted up, "Da! Da!" and when no answering call came to her, she ran towards the hill on which Mr. Lord's house stood. Half-way up was a stark gate-post, and if you climbed it and sat on the top you could see a number of fields around. But when she was perilously balancing on its foot square top, she still could not see her da.

On the ground once more, she stood, her forefinger between her teeth, again seeing the look on Michael's face. There had been a row . . . her da had gone out to—to Jarrow? No! No! She bit harder on her finger. . . . That was why her ma had been tossing about like that, thumping everything. Eeh! no, he wouldn't do it. After all this long time, he wouldn't go and get drunk again—anything but that. Suddenly her arms were round the post, and she was holding it tight. Her stomach gave a nervous heave, and she felt sick. Eeh! where was her da? He had gone out, but where? Perhaps he'd gone to the market about the cows. On a Saturday night? How long had he been out? Was he even now in The Long Bar or The Ben Lomond? She gazed about her in panic. She couldn't go back to Jarrow and look for him, her ma wouldn't let her, she'd only have to wait—wait and wait.

Then she saw Tony. He was crossing the yard. She saw him go round the big barn and make for the small one. He might know where her da was. Her da liked Tony, he liked him a lot—he might have told him.

On the thought, her legs carried her at a tearing pace down the hill! It was just when she left the grass and reached a section of the cinder track that she fell. She was used falling, and she usually recovered herself with a "Dash! hang! bust!" but this time she lay for quite some time, sprawled out, the tears flooding from her eyes into the dirt, before she raised herself. The palms of her hands and her knees were scraped and bleeding and covered with black ash, and at the sight of them her crying became very audible. But there was no one in sight to console her, so between sobs she picked off the largest pieces of the ash, and, spitting on her handkerchief, she dabbed at the blood, first one knee, then the other; then at her hands, exclaiming all the time, "Eeh! oh, it's bleeding all over. Eeh! Oh, oh, Ma."

She was telling herself that she would go home to her ma when she again thought of the reason for her running, and so, making a gallant effort, when she reached the yard she turned off and limped in the direction of the little barn. As she neared the corner of the big barn, the blood from one knee began to trickle down her leg and produced a feeling of panic, and the inward cry of, "Eeh! I'm bleeding."

She would bleed to death. To prevent this catastrophe she bent down and pressed her hanky to the spot, and as she did so her eye was caught again by the sight of Tony. He had come to the door of the little barn and was looking out, but from where she was he couldn't see her, and before she could call to him he had disappeared again.

Holding her hanky to her knee, she hobbled slowly towards the barn door, and just as she neared it and came in sight of his back she was stopped from calling out to him by the sight of what he was doing. She even forgot for the moment about her wounds, for Tony was opening up one of Mr. Lord's trunks.

There were six trunks in the barn. Four big ones, ends up, which stood higher than herself, with lots of labels on them, and two old black ones with rounded lids and brass bands. It was one of these that Tony opened, and his hands were now groping amongst the things inside. She watched him lift up and open a little box, and then slowly close it again. The next thing he lifted up was a blouse. She saw it was a bonny one, all lace and stuff, and cream coloured. He looked at it a long time before laying it down. Then she watched him bend further down, his arm thrusting towards the bottom of the trunk, and when he straightened himself he was holding three small-framed pictures. She saw him spread them out like her da did cards, then select one, and with his eyes still on it, lay the other two down.

It was at this point that she sniffed. It was a very loud sniff, for her nose was full of tears and she seemed to have been holding her breath for a very long time. The sound brought Tony round as if it had been the report of a gun. His hand was thrust behind him, the picture in it; his thin face was pinched tight and no longer looked nice, but dark and frightening. And as her eyes met his, she shivered and would have turned and run, but his voice came to her, belying his looks as he said in relief, "Oh, it's you, Mary Ann."

"Yes." She didn't move.

"What's the matter?"

"I fell."

"Let me have a look."

It was as if he had not been rummaging through Mr. Lord's boxes. She watched him turn and put the photograph back on top of the other two, and with his back to her, he said, "Come here and let me have a look."

Slowly she entered the barn, and he turned and came to meet her, then lifted her up on to the top of the other black trunk.

"My! you have had a toss. How did you do this?"

"Running down the hill." She kept her eyes on him while he wiped the dirt from her knees with his handkerchief. As he dabbed the blood with a clean corner of the handkerchief, he said, "You'd better go home, they need washing."

There followed a pause, during which he kept dabbing, even when there was no more blood to dab. Then quietly, without raising his eyes, he said, "I wasn't stealing anything, I was only looking for something."

Mary Ann said nothing, and now he brought his eyes up to hers. They were nice eyes again, not like they had been a moment ago. "Do you believe me?"

She did not say yes or no, and he said, "There's nothing to steal in these old trunks, there's only clothes and things."

Mary Ann's gaze slowly dropped sideways to the photographs, and quietly she murmured, "They're silver frames." She knew silver when she saw it because Mr. Lord had a lot.

She was surprised when Tony started to laugh, for it wasn't often he laughed, and more surprised when he sat on the box beside her and dropped his face on to his hand and his shoulders began to shake—she could see nothing to laugh at.

"Oh, Mary Ann!" He looked down on her and his eyes were wet. "I'm glad you're back; don't go away again."

She did not answer his laughter with her own, for her hands and knees were stinging—something awful. She really felt like crying again, and found it impossible to give this situation all the attention it deserved, for she sensed something funny was going on. There was something funny about Tony, yet not nasty funny, she told herself, although she had been frightened of the way he looked a few minutes ago. Then him talking like that, jumping from one thing to another, like what she herself did, which made her ma pull up and say, "Stick to the point," and her da would laugh and say——

At this point her mind was wrenched from thoughts of her da's sayings by the actual sound of his voice, which chilled her to the heart, for he was singing. Not loud and yelling as he did sometimes in the house in the morning, but just quietly. It was this quietness, this softness of his voice that made her close her eyes and want to die.

On the first sound of Mike, Tony had risen sharply. Going towards the trunk he hastily smoothed out the things and pulled down the lid. The lace of the blouse caught on the iron clasp as he did so and he had to raise the lid again in an attempt to extricate it.

With her eyes Mary Ann watched, but her mind did not take in anything he was doing. She did not make any attempt to move off her seat, it was as if the sickness in her heart had taken the life out of her body. Not even when Mike stood in the doorway, his hand on the stanchion, did she move. In boundless pity she gazed at him. He wasn't right drunk, just a little bit. He's only a bit sick, she told herself. But it was poor comfort; in fact no comfort at all. He had promised Mr. Lord . . . he had stood in the cottage kitchen and said, "I'll try me best, Sir." And he had tried his best, she knew that; but now he was back where he had started, and all through her. No it wasn't—she refused to take the sole responsibility for this terrible catastrophe—it was Mrs. Polinski, it was their Michael writing, it was Sister Catherine.

"Hello! hello! hello! what have we here, eh? Look at them knees." Mike pointed at her, laughing lightly. "By! wait until your ma sees you. . . . What have you been up to, eh?"

He moved towards her saying as he came, in an aside to Tony, "Hello, lad."

Tony didn't answer. His brows were drawn to a deep furrow between his eyes and his gaze was hard on Mike.

Mary Ann looked up at her father and said in a small voice, "I fell, Da."

"You fell?" He sat down heavily on the lid beside her; then continued ponderously, "You'll always fall, Mary Ann. Me and you, we're of the same kidney, we'll fall and fall. But we'll get up again, won't we?"

"Yes, Da."

"And start afresh, eh?" He bent over her.

"Yes, Da."

"In places where our fame hasn't gone afore us, eh?"

"Yes, Da."

"Aye, we will." He nodded at her, then looked towards Tony where he stood before the trunk, and again said, "Hello, there, lad."

"Hello, Sir."

Even in her misery Mary Ann could not help but be impressed by Tony's deference—she had never known anybody else call her da Sir even now, that was something—Tony liked her da, she liked Tony.

"You think us a funny crowd, lad, don't you? A lot of things puzzle you, eh? I puzzle you, don't I?" Mike did not wait for a reply but went on with a wave of his hand, "Oh, yes, I do. You've wondered how I could be running a farm when I know damn all; you with your book learning could buy and sell me. An' you've taught me a lot, lad. You've helped me to surprise me Lord and Master by glibly repeating some of the things you've said. Oh aye, I've played the learned boy. Johne's Disease, I've talked about. 'That pond in the bottom field wants filling in,' I said. 'Better be safe than sorry.' And Bloat—I even remembered you called it Tympanites—not that I didn't know about Bloat and have got rid of it with a twist of the knife in their hunkers afore now. But did I tell the old boy that? No, I spouted it from your book, word for word. 'The best method,' I said, 'is to insert a trocar and a canula into the rumen. The old methods are dead,' I said. He was impressed—an' you know something? So was I. I was impressed by all the things you knew out of books . . . not that they'll be any good to you without the experience." Mike paused and looked at Tony with his head on one side, then said slowly, "There's summat, lad, I've wanted to ask you, but in me sober senses wouldn't dream of doing it. But now I'm"—he paused and glanced derisively down on Mary Ann—"a bit sick . . . I'm a bit sick, aren't I, hinny? . . . Well, now I'm a bit sick I've the cheek of the devil. Your da always has courage when he's like this, hasn't he?"

Mary Ann had slid to the ground and was standing by his knee, and for answer she swallowed, and he turned to Tony again, his hand to his head now. "What was I saying, anyway?" He gripped the skin of his forehead tightly between his finger and thumb in an effort to clear his thinking. "Oh aye. You were wondering how I came by this job, how I could kid the old fellow. Well, I didn't kid him. He won me in a raffle sort of. S'fact. I was the penny that was tossed up between two gamblers and the old man won me. It's a fact. But you know, it's also a fact that gamblers always lose in the end, for what good does their winnings do them. The old boy won me and see how I've turned out. . . . And here's the loser." He put his hand on Mary Ann's head without looking at her. "She had to pay—pay the old boy—a child, he made her pay. What'd you think of that, eh? I'm talking rot, you say, I can see it in your eyes, but I'm not. . . . Or you didn't say anything. No, you wouldn't, you're a tight one all right. I know that much about you, lad, and I know you have as much love for the old boy as I have. Yet what has he done to you except growl? He hasn't stolen your bairn, he's done nowt to you—yet you hate his guts. That's why you and me get on together, isn't it? And that's what I was going to ask you. Aye, I knew it was something different to what I've been on about. Why did you pick this farm, you can learn nowt here that you don't already know? What you here for? That's what I've been wanting to ask you. . . . What's that?"

Tony had been supporting the lid of the trunk with the back of his leg—he had not been able to close it before Mike's entry—but on Mike's last words his body had seemed to jerk and the lid slipped into place with a click. Now showing up, almost white against the black leather work, was a piece of the blouse, just a couple of inches of lace, and it caught Mike's eye, and although his mind was fuddled it did not prevent him from associating the piece of lace with the click of the catch.

"Ah, ha! what's going on?" He rose as heavily as he had sat down and walked towards Tony, and when opposite to him he looked down at the age-seered lace, then up into the boy's face, and again repeated, "What's going on?" His voice was now no longer friendly. "I'm having none of that here, lad. I'm still manager, don't forget, and I've never pilfered in me life. I've done many things but I've never been for 'what's yours is mine'. That's the old boy's property. What've you taken?"

"Nothing, Mike, nothing. Honest. You don't understand."

Tony had called her da Mike, not Sir. Mary Ann stared at his white, strained face.

"Don't I! I understand you've opened this trunk, an' I want to know why. . . . Out of the way!" With a thrust of his arm, Mike pushed Tony violently towards the wall of the barn, almost knocking him off his feet. Then he lifted the lid and looked down on the jumbled contents of the trunk, and the first things that met his eye were the photographs. But his mind and his hand passed over these as not worthy of stealing. He was stirring up the contents as if he had his hand in a bran tub when Mary Ann let out a squeal. It was only a small squeal for it was strangled in her throat by the sight of Mr. Lord standing in the barn doorway. Only the Devil himself could have appeared so silently, and her turbulent, panic-stricken thoughts suggested that it was that very gentleman who was standing there, for never had she seen Mr. Lord look as he was doing now. He looked terrible, like, like——Her mind boggled for a description, and when the voice thundered, "Yes! and what may I ask, are you doing, Shaughnessy?" the whole barn seemed to become full of devils. She watched her da swing about with his eyes blazing and his jaw thrust out, and she saw on Tony's face, from where he stood in the shadow of the barn wall, the same look that had frightened her earlier. They all looked like devils.

"Well!"

The word seemed to splash into Mike's face, spurring him to retaliation. His head jerked upwards and he blinked once before saying, thickly, "It was knocked over, the catch broke. I was . . . putting things straight,"

If his pursed lips and slowly blinking eyes had not betrayed him, his voice would have done, and Mary Ann, in a sweat of fear, saw Mr. Lord's mouth become a thin grim line, and his eyes draw out into steely slits. Then whatever he might have said to her da was checked by Tony's voice crying, "I opened it." Her eyes sprang towards him as he moved quickly from the wall to the side of the trunk, one hand held behind him.

Mr. Lord's eyes swivelled slowly, as if reluctant to move away from Mike, and came to rest on the young man.

"It was me who opened it, do you hear—me!"

Mary Ann's blood and ash-smeared hand went to her mouth as she saw Tony take a step towards Mr. Lord, and a voice, loud within her, cried out to him, "Eeh! don't—don't you be cheeky or you'll get the sack an' all." Then the expression on Tony's face froze even her thinking. He looked as if he loathed Mr. Lord, as if he would hit him. She saw her da reach out and catch his arm. It was the arm that Tony was holding behind him, and when his hand was dragged forward he had in it one of the silver-framed photographs.

It was the sight of the picture that seemed to change Mr. Lord. From being like a dark, furious devil, ageless in his wrath, his entire body appeared to shrink; he became old, very old. For a moment his face moved into wrinkles of perplexity, then flushed into impotent rage, and he spluttered as he cried, "Wh-what are you doing with that! Stealing? . . . stealing? Who—who are you, anyway?"

Although Tony was still held in Mike's grip he leaned forward and strained his face towards Mr. Lord's, and with his eyes on the twitching mouth, and his words coming slow and bitter, he said, "Who am I? I've news for you, I'll tell you . . . I'm your grandson."

There was silence in the barn; the whole farm was silent, no mooing of cows, no cackling of birds, no barking from the dogs; no footsteps, no voices, not even the soft scrambling of one of the many barn cats disturbed the dreadful silence. Then Mr. Lord, in a voice high, almost like a scream, cried, "You're a liar! A liar! I had no son. Never had a son . . . never had a child . . . never . . . never." His voice stopped abruptly. He had the look of someone just awakening from sleep. His eyes became wide, his mouth stretched and his jaw hung slack, as if it wanted to fall off.

Distressed beyond measure, Mary Ann watched it, and her own mouth widened and dropped into a gape, for she was seeing what Mr. Lord was seeing, in fact what she had unconsciously noticed the first day this man and the boy had met, they were alike. She watched Mr. Lord's hands go first to his head and then to his throat, and he made a gurgling sound like the cows did when the grass went down the wrong way. Then she heard herself screaming as he fell. He went sideways, and although her da lumbered quickly forward, he couldn't save him.

The screaming was filling her head as on the day her da got his hand in the machine. Then it was silenced by a blow. Her da had hit her again, boxed her ears.

"Stop it! Stop it, d'you hear!" It was her da yelling at her and his voice was no longer fuddled. "Go and get your ma— tell her to go up to the house."

"Oh, Da! Da! Oh!—oh! he's . . . "

"Go on—do as I tell you. Go and get your ma."

She dragged her eyes from the crumpled form up to Tony, then muttering, "Yes. Yes, Da, yes," she ran out of the barn, carrying with her not so much the impression of the prostrate figure of the old man but of Tony standing stiff and white and frightened.

"Ma! Ma!" She went screaming across the yard, "Ma! Ma!" out into the road and to the gate, through it and up the path. "Ma! Ma! Oh, Ma!"

Before she reached the door Lizzie was there, fear on her face. "What is it?" She stopped Mary Ann's mad-long rush.

"Oh, Ma, it's, it's——"

"Calm yourself. Is it your da?"

Mary Ann could have said yes to this, but she shook her head and gasped, "Mr. Lord. He fell—he's bad—in the barn. Come on. Me da says come on."

Lizzie was now running down the path, Mary Ann beside her, and when they entered the farmyard it was to see Mike crossing it, carrying Mr. Lord in his arms. And supporting the old man's head to stop it from dangling was Tony.

As Lizzie came up, Mike said briefly, "Go and warn Ben. Phone a doctor."

Without comment Lizzie ran ahead, but Mary Ann did not run with her, she stayed where she was. She did not even attempt to follow the trio up to the house. She was feeling sick, Mr. Lord was dying. She was experiencing a great depthless sense of loss; if only they had been kind. If he died and they weren't kind what would she do? Love for the old man blotted out everything at this moment, it even smothered the worry over her da and the latest trouble—his lapse.

She stood tearless, her head bowed on her chest thinking. She had a theory that you could never ask God for two important things at the same time. Five minutes ago she had wanted only one thing in the world—the well-being of her da—and, as on other occasions she had bargained with God to bring this about, now she was willing that if only one request could be asked of Him, it should be for Mr. Lord's life, and if it could only be paid for by neglect of her da, and such neglect she imagined would mean his complete fall, then let it be so.

She turned slowly and went towards the little barn again, and kneeling down by the open trunk, for somehow she felt close to him here, she began to entreat the Holy Family for Mr. Lord's life, offering them, in exchange, her own blameless and lieless life in the future.

10

Mary Ann lay on the kitchen couch with her face turned to the wall. Her hands were smarting, her knees were smarting, and her heart was sad. Moreover, the place was alive with excitement, and she was shut out of it—or, to be more correct, shut in from it.

After she had said her prayers in the barn she had intended going to the house, for then Mr. Lord would be in bed and looking, if her prayers had been answered, all right again, but she had hardly finished blessing herself when their Michael had come running in to say their ma said she hadn't to go near the house but was to go indoors and stay there. She had protested, as was only natural, even going so far as to emphasise her protests with a number of pushes, but Michael was adamant and she found herself hauled to the kitchen where he none too gently washed the grazes on her hands and knees, then applied Dettol—raw. When she bawled loudly at this torture, he liberally applied more, whereupon he received just payment by a good hard kick on the shins.

Following on this, her plans to slip out, when he was gone, did not materialise, for he didn't go out but settled himself down to his homework. His lack of feeling and refusal to be drawn into a discussion as to what was happening nearly drove her frantic, until at last she flung herself on to the couch and suffered agonies of frustration when she heard, at intervals, the sound of cars coming into the yard. By this time she wasn't speaking to their Michael, and as Michael had the only view of the yard from the window and she wouldn't demean herself to go near him, she had to remain in ignorance as to the identity of the visitors.

It seemed years later when the kitchen door opened and her da appeared and brought her from the point of sleep. She swung her legs dazedly off the couch, but had to sit for a moment to collect herself, and in that moment she saw that her da was in no talking mood, for his face was tense, his expression closed, and he was now quite sober.

"Your mother wants you. Go on up to the house." He was looking and speaking to Michael, and Mary Ann thought, "It isn't fair, it should be me, I want to know how he is." She looked up at Mike, but couldn't say, "Is he better?" in case he wasn't. She felt sick, her head was aching, her hands and knees hurting, but it was the pain in her chest which centred around Mr. Lord that felt the worst.

Michael, after one hard look at his father, went out, and Mary Ann rose from the couch and went towards Mike.

"Da."

"Yes?"

"Da—is he——?"

"He's all right." Mike turned his back on her and stared down into the fire. "Go on up to bed."

"I don't want to go to bed, Da."

"Then go on the couch."

Mary Ann looked up the broad expanse of Mike's back, then turned slowly about and went back to the couch. Her da wanted to be quiet, she knew the signs, he would only get mad if she kept on. She lay down, her eyes on him for a time until the sound of his knuckles beating on the mantelpiece made her throw herself round and face the wall again.

Her da was worried—upset . . . perhaps Mr. Lord was dying. Eeh! no, he mustn't die. If he died Tony would be to blame. What had Tony said? Eeh! yes, that Mr. Lord was his granda. Eeh! . . . Well, she had said the same thing herself. But she had only been making on; Tony hadn't been making on, he had meant it. And she had a feeling that he didn't like it . . . didn't like Mr. Lord being his granda.

Her mind puzzled itself about this new problem, and when some time later she awoke to the sound of Tony's voice she couldn't believe she had been asleep and wondered how he had come in without her hearing him. He was talking softly to her da, and she couldn't make out what he was saying, for she was lying on one ear. When she did move her da was speaking.

"Why didn't you come openly and tell him? This was no way to do the thing, sneaking about."

It was some time before Tony's voice came to her, and then she could only just hear it. "I had no intention of telling him at all. I was paying him out because of my grandmother's life. . . . "

"She did her own paying, I would think, to go off like that and not let on she was having a child. I don't hold much to her."

"You didn't know her."

"I know the old fellow, and I know this much, if he'd had a child, son or daughter, he'd have been a different man. He's the loneliest creature on God's earth, that's why he tried to take her."

Mary Ann felt their eyes on her back, but she didn't move, for if her da knew she was awake they would stop talking.

"You don't know what a life my grandmother had."

"By the accounts I've heard of it, it was a pretty good one. It nearly broke him, anyway."

"A woman will spend money if she can't get anything else. He had no more feeling than an iceberg, and he was old enough to be her father."

"She knew that in the first place. What happened to the fellow she went off with?"

"He left her when my mother was six."

There was silence now in the kitchen, and Mary Ann waited, trying not to turn round to see what they were doing, and just when her curiosity was about to get the better of her, Mike's voice said, "Well, she's not the first woman that's had to work to bring up a child, and she won't be the last."

"But it was different for her, she had never worked in her life, she was made for pleasant things." Tony's voice held sorrow.

"Aren't we all!" Mike's tone was mocking.

"You don't understand."

"I understand all right. I understand you've been brought up by a woman who had the knack of making you see things and people exactly as she wanted you to see them. It's my idea that your grandmother knew that she had wronged the old man and that made her keep talking about him—her conscience was at work. Were you brought up with her all the time?"

"Yes, my mother and father had to travel about, they were in Rep. I was only ten when they died. They both went together . . . they were trapped in a fire in an old theatre."

Again there was silence, and now Mary Ann was saying to herself. "Eeh! poor things."

"If your grandmother was hard up why didn't she write to him?"

"Write to him? You say that you know him! Wouldn't it have given him a kick to know she was begging!"

"I wonder . . . I wonder. Anyway, I think she did him a great wrong. If he'd known he had a child. . . . My God! When you come to think of it, it was wicked, damn well wicked. I could say evil. . . . It's no use your rearing up like that, Tony. You're a young lad, you've got all your life afore you. Just imagine someone withholding the fact that you had a child. But you've never been married, you don't know how it'd feel . . . you don't understand."

Mary Ann heard her da pacing the mat, and then his steps stopped and his voice demanded, "If she had such a struggle to bring you up how did you manage the money to go to college?"

"I didn't have to have much money, I passed for the Grammar School. Left when I was sixteen and got a grant to the agricultural college. The little money that I did need had to be borrowed. I've still got to pay that back." his voice was bitter.

"What's happened to your grandmother?"

Mary Ann waited for quite a while before she heard Tony mutter, "She died, a year ago."

"Damn good job, I should say."

Mike's words had been quick, and Tony's response was even quicker. "Shut up! Don't you dare say that. I'll have none of it. As I've said, you didn't know her."

Mary Ann held her breath in the silence that followed. Her body was nerve-stiff, they were nearly fighting.

"I'm sorry, it's none of my business." It was Mike speaking. Then after a moment Tony said, as if struggling with his emotion, "You didn't know my grandmother, I repeat that, she was a wonderful person, but you know him, and yet you're taking his part."

"Aye, I am in this. I know he's a hard man, and I know if he sets his heart on anything he doesn't care who he tramples on while getting it. But there's another side to him, and I've had to admit this, as much as it's irked me. Up to a point he's just, and sometimes beyond the point. And you must remember this, lad, a man isn't born hard—something makes him hard. Anyway, what I'd like to know is, why, if you hated him so much, did you seek him out?"

"I didn't seek him out. I came this way looking for a job. Oh, I know it looks like it. Perhaps I really did come this way to see him, I can't tell exactly what my feelings were, but at the time I was looking for a job and was given three farms to go to. I didn't know he had a farm. It was the name, Lord, that first suggested that this one might be his. Even the day I walked along the road I still didn't know if I was on the right track, but as soon as I saw him in the yard, then I knew."

"If he dies, what about it then? Will you claim?"

Mary Ann stiffened—they thought he was going to die.

"I don't know."

"You'll have some job proving your case. Your grandmother gone, your parents gone. Anyway, if he survives what's to stop the old boy saying that you're a fraud? How can you prove your mother was his daughter, couldn't she have been the other fellow's?"

"What do you think?"

Mary Ann could feel them looking at each other.

"I think you're his grandson all right. Something puzzled me about you from the first. I couldn't quite place it. It was your temper, your manner when vexed—it's just like his." Mike gave a soft, consoling sort of laugh, and then he said, "Well, whichever way things go there's going to be an upheaval."

"Do you think I had better go?"

"Go? What in the hell are you talking about! How can you go now?" Mike's voice was harsh. "Don't you realise that it's the fact that the old boy recognised you as his that brought the attack on? What's going to happen if he comes round and you're not here? You wait a minute—" Mary Ann could see her da in her mind's eye, holding up his hand—"let me have me say. You've got to face him. And what's more, and I say this, you've got to hear his side of the affair. You needn't go black in the face. Anyway, you knew there'd got to be a showdown some day. I feel that's what you came here for."

"I didn't!" The protest was vehement.

"Well, why the hell were you messing about with the trunk?"

"Because my grandmother used to talk about when she was first married, and how, in her lonely hours, she would wander about that great house waiting for him coming home, and likely as not, ending up in the attics. She happened to mention the old black trunks with the quaint brass bands, and it was because I thought I might find something of hers that I looked in them."

"I'm sorry to keep harping on about this—" Mike's voice was plainly sarcastic—"but from what I've heard she wasn't the kind of girl that would spend her time sitting in an attic waiting."

"Do you know how old she was when she married him? Seventeen. After the honeymoon she sat at home like a good wife for nearly a year, and then she realised that she could go on sitting like that for the rest of her life. There were times she didn't see him for days—he would sleep at the office—but when he came home he'd expect to find her there."

"Couldn't she understand what he was going through? He was trying to save his business."

"Get a beautiful woman in her twenties to understand that when a man won't go near her for days on end. You say I have no experience—I know this much of human nature. Five years is a long time when you're young. She had nothing to do but spend money."

"And not caring a damn that she was taking it out of a swiftly sinking ship." Such was the tone of Mike's voice that Mary Ann's muscles jerked and she would have turned round and spoken in order to break up their conversation, but at that moment she heard the door burst open and Michael's voice say quickly, "Da! me ma wants you to go into Newcastle with the doctor."

There were no more words between Tony and Mike, and a moment later she heard the door close again and she knew that Michael had gone back with her da. She had the desire to turn round and look at Tony, but something kept her with her face to the wall, and then she heard an odd sound, mixed with the scraping of the chair on the stone floor. Then came the very faint but recognisable sound of crying, the smothered difficult crying like their Michael did. . . . Tony was crying! He was a grown up, like her da, and he was crying! Her ma could cry; their Michael could cry; but not their da, not men; and Tony was a man. The situation had become such that she felt she was unable to deal with it, so she lay stiffly staring at the wall while the quietly muffled sound went on.

11

The school holidays had started, as was evident in the back streets of Jarrow. Tumbling, gambolling, squatting groups covered the pavements, and the roads, and as Mary Ann threaded her way amongst them, often being pushed or jabbed and returning the thrusts with interest, she thought: I wish I was home. She had been sent on errands to the butcher's the chemist's, and the Home and Colonial, and in all three she'd had to wait. Waiting always irked her, and now she gladly saw the bus stop ahead. In another minute or so she'd be on the bus and back home—and be experiencing once again the waiting feeling. She was thinking about this waiting feeling that was permeating the farm, when her mind was swept clear of the sombre issues by being brought swiftly to a personal one, and one that set her mouth agape. There, coming towards her, was none other than Sarah Flannagan, but not accompanied by her mother or her cronies, but by—two lads.

Mary Ann's eyes widened; her mouth contracted again and slowly formed an "O" and her eyebrows went up even farther. In this moment she did not know what to expect. Would

Sarah Flannagan stop and attack her, aided by her male escort? If so, she was lost. Reluctantly she kept walking, every step bringing her nearer to the trio, until they were almost abreast. And not till then did she realize that something was wrong with Sarah Flannagan. She knew Sarah wasn't blind—she had second sight where she herself was concerned—but she wasn't seeing her! She was looking straight ahead. One of the boys was talking to her while the other moved silently along, his head down and his hand in his pockets, yet seemingly, and this was evident to Mary Ann, seemingly pleased to be where he was.

How anyone could want to be with Sarah Flannagan was quite beyond the powers of Mary Ann to understand. These two lads must be daft.

The three were abreast of her now, and she stared pop-eyed at them. Could it be that Sarah Flannagan was sick, ill, or had she really been struck blind, for she was going past without a word, without even a look? The only sign that could be taken for recognition, Mary Ann's hypnotised stare told her, was the slight lift of Sarah's chin. They were past, and Mary Ann was brought to a stop and forced round to stare at the three receding backs, walking all very decorously along the street. And then it dawned on her. . . . Eeh! Sarah Flannagan had a lad. Eeh! Sarah Flannagan was going with a lad. Eeh! two lads.

This astounding knowledge seemed to press heavily on her, and her steps, as she approached the bus stop, were weighed down. She couldn't get over it. For the first time in their lives she and Sarah had passed each other without a blow or a word, and all because Sarah Flannagan had a lad. There was something here that needed strong concentration and, of course, some condemnation. You shouldn't have lads, not when you were only nine or ten. But then Sarah was eleven. Perhaps when you were eleven you could have a lad. Suddenly she remembered Sammy Walker. Sammy Walker had been in her class last year in Jarrow, and he would sometimes give her a sweet. But there were times when he didn't and pinched her bottom. She didn't like Sammy Walker. Yet she did like Bobby Denver. But Bobby Denver never looked the side she was on.

The bus came, and it was a very puzzled Mary Ann who took a seat, as was her wont, near the front, so she could think by herself. If Sarah Flannagan had a lad, why shouldn't she have a lad? If she went back to Jarrow School next term and Bobby Denver was in the same class. . . . Her thoughts came to an abrupt stop. She didn't want to go back to Jarrow School next term, even if she did want to see Bobby Denver and he should take it into his head to slip her sweets. Perhaps she could get another lad. If Sarah Flannagan could have two, then why not her? Why not! She'd ask her ma when she got home. She would say to her, "Ma, how old have I to be afore I can have a lad?"

For the rest of the journey her mind was taken up, apart from Bobby Denver, in selecting a lad. Fat ones, thin ones, dirty ones, and clean ones, she went over all the boys she knew, but somehow she didn't fancy any one of them, and by the time she approached the farm, even Bobby Denver no longer appeared desirable.

She was coming under the influence of the waiting feeling again.

She had just reached the cottages when she saw her mother. She was some way down the road from their gate and was waving frantically to her. On the sight of her Mary Ann sprinted forward, her mind saying, "Eeh! what's up now?" As she neared her, Lizzie's hand came out and grabbed at the basket. This she put down straightaway on the road, then automatically began to straighten Mary Ann up as she talked, her words low and rapid. "Now listen: you're to go to the house, he wants to see you. And mind——"

"Me? Mr. Lord . . . he wants to see me?"

"Yes . . . what am I telling you! By! you've been some time. Where have you been? It's over an hour since he asked for you."

"I had to wait in the chemist and the Home and Colonial, Ma."

"Let me have a look at your hands. . . . Here!" Lizzie wetted her apron and rubbed at a mark on Mary Ann's palm. "Now there you are, you're all right. Now mind listen to what I'm saying. Mind your p's and q's and be careful what you say."

Mary Ann made no reply to this, she only stared wide-eyed at her mother, but she did ask, "Is he all right?"

"As right as he'll be for some time. Don't be cheeky, don't fidget, just speak when you're spoken to, you understand?"

"Yes, Ma."

Mary Ann made to move hastily off when Lizzie grabbed at her, and stooping down and pulling her foot up, she quickly dusted her shoes, one after the other, gave another tug to her coat, another touch to her hat, another push, and said, "Go on. And mind, be civil to Ben."

Mary Ann had no time to think, no time to wonder what she was going to say. As if she had been dropped from the wind she found herself at the back door of the house, and it would seem that Ben had been standing behind the door waiting for her knock, for immediately he opened it and looked down on her. His face was the same as ever, grim as the grave, yet now, it seemed to Mary Ann as if it was older. How that had come about she didn't know, for to her mind Ben could get no older, he was as old as old. Without a word she stepped into the kitchen. She hadn't been in the house since the furniture came in, and now she scarcely recognised it. It was like one of them kitchens in a magazine, all colour and light, and the woman in her said that such a kitchen as this would be lost on such a man as old Ben. Now if her ma had it. . . .

Ben, too, like her mother, was looking at her clothes. He pushed her to one side, in the opposite direction to that which Lizzie had placed it; he pulled her coat straight; and he, like Lizzie, looked at her hands. Then he spoke. "Come along," he said.

Mary Ann came along through the hall, splendid with its antique furniture. There were no big bits from the other house, only little bits, she noticed, tables with curved legs, chests against the walls, with brass standing on them. Then up the stairs, deep and soft to her feet, the colour startling to her eyes, cherry red, and this against startling white walls, with bits of gold here and there.

Such was the change in the house that the furniture and decorations had made that for a moment or two her mind forgot why she was here. Then they were on the landing, big, too, as big as the kitchen and again all white and yellow and cherry. Then a pause before a door, and Ben's wrinkled face coming close to hers, his breath hot on her cheek as he muttered, "Mind you be careful. Don't upset him."

She did not give an answer but gave the slightest shake of her head. Then Ben tapped on the door and they were in the room.

The first thing Mary Ann saw was not Mr. Lord but a nurse, a great big nurse, nearly as big as her da, and when she smiled, her smile was big, too, cheerily big, and when she spoke her voice matched everything about her.

"Ah! there you are," she said. "Now you mustn't stay long, ten minutes, that's a good girl. Go on."

Before Mary Ann moved towards the bed, over the foot of which she had not yet raised her eyes, she looked back at Ben. But Ben was looking at the nurse and it was evident to Mary Ann that he disliked her as much as he had, at one time, disliked herself. It wasn't until the door closed on them both that she looked over the bottom of the high bed to the propped-up figure, and such was her relief that she nearly blurted out her thoughts: Eeh! he didn't look much different, only thinner, perhaps, and whiter. But that, likely was his nightshirt that was buttoned up to his chin. The look in his eyes was as she remembered it, penetrating and hard. But she didn't mind this for he was seeing her; he was not pretending that she wasn't there. Slowly she walked round the bed and to the head, and there they were, close together again, his hand only a few inches from hers.

His eyes had never left her face, and although she remembered that she hadn't to talk, the silence between them was really unbearable and she said, very softly, "Hello."

Mr. Lord did not speak, but lifting his hand slowly from the coverlet, he pointed to a chair, and Mary Ann, realizing that if she sat on it she would be unable to see him, gently and with some effort, lifted it round. Then, getting on to it, she sat up straight. But even so he seemed miles away.

"Sit here."

Mary Ann stared in surprise. "On the bed?"

He did not reply, but pointed to the chair, indicating that she could stand on it to reach the bed. This she did and when she let herself down very gently, near his legs and with her face now almost on a level with his, only with an effort did she stop herself from laughing and saying, "Eeh! what if Ben comes in."

"How are you?" His voice was very low and thin not a bit like she remembered it.

To this polite enquiry she blinked her eyes. That's what she should have asked him.

"I'm all right, thank you. How are you?"

"I'm all right, too."

He didn't look it, not now, for though he didn't look as bad as she had expected him to look, close to, like this, he looked awful. The silence fell heavily between them again, and she became a little embarrassed under his stare and sought in her mind for a topic of conversation which they both could share. Then a brainwave, as she put it, made her remember the nurse, and she asked, but very quietly, "Is she nice?"

"Nice? Who?" His brow puckered.

"The nurse."

It was evident immediately that she had said the wrong thing—the nurse mustn't be nice—for she felt his legs jerk to one side and his head moved impatiently on the pillow. Then he said, "I didn't send for you to talk about the nurse."

"No? Oh."

"No. I want an explanation."

"An explanation?"

"You heard what I said." He took a few short breaths. "Are you sorry for your escapade?"

Mary Ann's head drooped and she started to pluck at the bed cover with her fingers, pulling at the threads of a hand design. "Yes, I'm very sorry—very."

"You didn't like the school?"

Her head was still lowered as she answered, "It wasn't that, I did like the school except Sister Catherine and a girl there, but——" She stopped. She'd better not tell him about her da and Mrs. Polinski, that would make him mad, so she finished, "I missed everybody. I wanted to be home."

"That wasn't the only reason, was it?"

She raised her eyes to his and was forced to say, "No."

He did not press her any further, but moved again with some impatience, then said, "They'll push you out in a few minutes. I want to ask you something. And mind—" he stopped again and took some breaths—" I want a truthful answer."

She looked up and watched him strain his neck out of his nightshirt, then her eyes dropped to his hands, for very much as her own had done, his were plucking at the bed cover. "That boy——" There was a pause, and he started again, his voice rasping, "That boy on the farm, do you like him?"

Her face must have shown her surprise, for he demanded, in a voice that was much stronger, "Well?"

"You mean Tony?" She waited; then went on, "Yes I like Tony very much."

"Why?"

"Cos he's nice."

"Do you like Mr. Jones?"

"No."

"Why?"

"Cos I think he's silly, he tries to make rows. He tells me da about this one and that one."

"And Len?"

"Len's all right."

"Just all right?"

"Well." Mary Ann being unable to explain Len's dimness shook her head. "He's all right, he's nice enough, but he's not nice like Tony. Tony's different somehow. Me da likes Tony." Immediately after saying this she bit her lip. Had she said the wrong thing again? His eyes were fixed hard on her now, but he showed no reaction whatever to her words.

"What do you know about him?"

She blinked at him. "Eeh? I mean, what? Tony?"

"I said, what do you know about him?"

"Nothing." She wasn't going to give Tony away.

He seemed to sink down into his pillows now. His disappointment was evident, and his voice sounded tired as he said, "That's very unusual for you. As I remember you, you made it your business to know something about everybody."

"Well, I said he was nice, and he is nice—in spite of having a nasty gran——"

She closed her eyes tight against herself as Mr. Lord's body came slowly up in the bed. She dared not look at him. Eeh! now she had done it. What had she said? She was unable immediately to form the connection between Tony's grannie and Mr. Lord, but there was a connection, a strong connection, and something that she should not, under any circumstances, have referred to.

"Open your eyes."

Slowly she opened her eyes. Their faces were close now. "What do you know about his——" There was a considerable pause and a number of laboured breaths before Mr. Lord added the word "grannie?"

"Only that she wasn't nice, she was a bit of a tartar."

"Who said she wasn't nice?"

"Me da."

Now Mr. Lord's bewilderment was evident in his face, for it was screwed up as she repeated, "Your da?"

"Yes. Me da went for Tony when he was talking about his grannie and saying how nice she was, and me da said she wasn't."

"Why did he say that . . . your father?"

Mary Ann's eyes seemed to do a revolving stunt before she added, softly, "Cos she ran away from you."

Mr. Lord swallowed, the blue veins on his temples stood out, his chin dropped down to his chest, and he swallowed again before raising his head. But now his eyes were not on Mary Ann, they had moved beyond her to the end of the room, and beyond that, down into the past. And when he spoke his voice seemed far away. "How did you come to know all this?"

"I was lying on the couch and I heard me da and him talking. They thought I was asleep. It was the night you were took bad. Me ma wouldn't let me come up here, nor our Michael, and I woke up and me da and Tony were nearly fighting. And then when me da went out, Tony began to——" She stopped. She wouldn't say what Tony had begun to do.

Mr. Lord's gaze came back to the room, and to her, and he questioned softly, "Yes? What did he do?"

The jerking of her head increased and the thread between her fingers puckered up tne material. "Nothing."

"Look at me."

Reluctantly she raised her eyes, and when he said again, softly, almost in a pleading tone, "Tell me," she muttered, "He was crying, with his head on the table."

After giving Tony away, her own head dropped again, and she felt the old man sink slowly back on to his pillows.

His silence once more weighed hard upon her, and she could find no word of her own to break it, so steathily she began to take in her surroundings. She found them very pleasing to the eye, and a section of her mind which was always open to appreciation said, "Eeh! isn't it a lovely room."

"Mary Ann."

"Yes?" She brought her attention quickly back to him.

"I want you to come here every day until I'm up again, even if they only let you stay a short time. I want you to keep your eyes and ears open, and tell me all you see and hear."

"But what about?"

"Everything, everybody."

Something about this request, or was it a demand, hurt her. She felt that she could jabber about people but not tell tales, and what she was being asked to do was a form of tale-telling, and she imagined that if her da knew he would raise the roof. Well, her good sense told her, her da mustn't know. She wasn't going to carry tales about Tony, but she'd tell Mr. Lord little things, just to keep him quiet.

Once again she was coming into her own, her mind was working along the old lines. The fact that they were friends was smoothing away all her fears. Now, without reasoning, she could see a way out. She did not give way to the old bargaining thought, "If I do this for him, he'll do something for me da," but it was there in her mind, making her alert once more. But the feeling was separate from the protective once that was filling her now. She smiled at the old man and very gently put out her hand, and with the tips of her fingers touched the raised blue veins on his.

The hand had scarcely touched the old man's before it was buried within his palms, and he had once more edged himself up from the pillow. And now there was a deep note of urgency in his voice as he whispered, "Listen, Mary Ann, I want you to——"

The door opened and the big, smiling nurse stalked in.

"Ah, there you are. You've had your nice little talk. And on the bed! Well, well. But come along now."

Eeh! Mary Ann's attention was drawn from the nurse back to Mr. Lord. Eeh! he had sworn worse than her da. It was the first time she had ever heard Mr. Lord swear. His face looked black again, as if he was in one of his old tempers, but strangely enough he didn't go for the nurse as she had expected him to, he just lay back on his pillows and when she said, "Ta-ra." and did not even amend it quickly by saying, "Goodbye," he made no effort to check her by word or look.

She was escorted out of the room as if her visit had just been an ordinary one, and she knew, oh, she knew very positively that her visit had been no ordinary one.

Her legs had wings, and they took her out of the house and down the hill, into the road and up the farm path in a jiffy, and as she hurled herself into the farm kitchen crying, "Ma! Ma!" she was brought to a dead stop, for there, and as if they were all waiting for her, was not only her ma, but her da, their Michael—and Tony. Never had she seen them altogether in the house except at meal-times and at night. It was her ma who stepped towards her and, quickly voicing her anxiety, asked, "How did you get on?"

Mary Ann's eyes left her mother and touched over the other three. They did not rest on her da particularly, although of them all she felt most his keenness to know what had happened. And the look on his face told her than this was the time for real diplomacy, or as she put it, keeping her mouth shut. If she wasn't to make any slips she had to be careful, so looking at her mother again she answered, "All right," then walked past them all to the table.

Lizzie turned and followed her, and sitting down opposite to her pressed her face forward and said, "But what did he say, child? Tell us."

Once again she looked at the faces about her, and after stretching her nose, and searching assiduously for her hankie, remarked, "Oh, nothing."

Lizzie sat back tight against the chair back and repeated, "Nothing?"

Mary Ann now moved her finger around a little bundle of crumbs on the table, then exclaimed, "Well, just about the farm and things."

Into the hush that followed this evident lie burst Mike's laugh. It was deep and loud, but not his nice laugh, and it startled them all. Mary Ann looked sharply at him, then back to her mother, who was looking at him, too. Then, much to Mary Ann's surprise, she heard her ma's laugh join her da's, but it was an uneasy laugh, and even their Michael's face was showing signs of a laugh. Only Tony's countenance remained the same.

Then her da, taking no notice of anybody, not even herself, and with his laugh still ringing, buttoned up his coat and marched out of the kichen. It was as if he had gone daft, as if they had all gone daft—except Tony.

Mary Ann had made seven visits to the sick-room. At eleven o'clock every morning she had been ushered in and exactly ten minutes later she was ushered out. She always returned straight home, and after her third visit Lizzie ceased to question her but would say something like, "Do you want a drink?" or "Have you had anything?" to which the answer was invariably, "Yes, please," or "No, I've had nothing."

Her da, after his queer, laughing bout, had started to look at her funnily, and after her second visit he had stood at the farthest point of the kitchen and, staring at her while making small movements with his head, had said, softly, and did she detect with bitterness, "So it's starting again. After all this, it's starting again." Her ma had said sharply, "Mike!" and he had gone into the scullery saying, "No, by God! It won't, not if I know it. No more bargaining for this bloke."

She had not been able to understand fully the gist of his remarks, but she knew that it had to do with herself and Mr. Lord. And now, preparing herself for her morning visit, she wished from the bottom of her heart that she wasn't going. Not that she didn't like visiting Mr. Lord—she admitted to herself, she loved it—but her da didn't like her going. She knew that, yet she also knew that it was for his good that she was going . . . for all their goods.

As she crossed the yard she saw her da and Tony up in the loft. She did not hail them, but walked sedately up the hill to the house. As usual Ben let her in, and as usual took her up to the door, where, as on every occasion, he cautioned her with the same words, "Mind, you be careful." The nurse, too, nearly always greeted her in the same way and informed her as to the length of her visit. But following on these the visit did not follow its usual pattern, for hardly had the door closed on her this morning, and even before she had time to say, "Hello," Mr. Lord, sitting up much straighter today, said, "Go and get your father."

Her brows shot up as she exclaimed, "Eh?"

Mr. Lord's eyes closed, and he muttered, "If you use that term again. . . . We went into that yesterday, remember?"

"I'm sorry."

"You heard what I said, go and get him."

Mary Ann did not linger. She passed the astonished nurse at the bottom of the stairs and Ben in the kitchen, and was out of the door before he could check her flight. And such was her haste that the poor old man was positively sure in his mind that she had at last achieved the death of his master, which, owing to her capers, he had from time to time foretold to himself.

Yelling at the top of her voice she raced across the yard: "Da! Da!" Then coming to a halt at the ladder leading to the loft, she stared up into Mike's questioning face and amswered his abrupt "What is it?" with "You're wanted."

"Who wants me?"

"Mr. Lord."

She saw him turn his face away, and she knew he was looking at Tony. Then through the aperture she saw Tony's legs. They had turned away from her da. The next minute Mike was standing by her side, and he looked down at her and said abruptly, "What did he say?"

"That's all. I just got into the room and he said, 'Go and get your da.' That's all."

Mike turned from her, saying sharply, "You stay where you are." He dusted down his trousers, lifted his coat from a nail, gave it a brief shake and put it on while crossing the yard. His mouth was grim and his body tight, as he showed himself to Ben and briefly explained his presence there.

Without any questioning, for he had a respect for this big, one-handed fellow, Ben led the way upstairs. But before they reached the landing their glances met sharply as Mr. Lord's voice came to them, crying, "Get out woman and leave me alone! I'll see who I like, and when I like. Get out!"

The door opened before they reached it and the nurse flounced out, no longer smiling. She paused for a moment to say something to Mike, then, changing her mind, passed him with only a jerk of her head.

Mike entered the room and slowly closed the door, his eye on the knob as he did so. Then he turned, and across the room looked straight at Mr. Lord.

Mr. Lord said nothing, but with a gesture indicated that he take a seat. Heavily, Mike covered the distance to the bed, then swivelling a chair round he sat down and faced the old man and waited for him to speak.

"Well, Shaughnessy?"

"Well, Sir?" Mike's voice was not harsh, for in spite of himself he was touched by the frailty of the old man. He saw that he was much changed, better of course than when he had last beheld him, but he could not see him ever again as he was once, a virile, steely, strong old man. He had a sapped look that touched Mike and forced him to say, "I hope you are feeling better, Sir."

"I'm well enough." Mr. Lord examined his hands now as they lay palms down on the cover, as if he was looking at them for confirmation of his own remark. Then he surprised Mike utterly with his next words. "Loneliness is a dreadful thing, Shaughnessy. I don't suppose you've ever experienced loneliness?"

After a moment of staring at the white, downcast head, Mike moved his hand hard down one side of his face, then said, "I've had me share, Sir. I was brought up in a workhouse. Perhaps you didn't know that."

Mr. Lord raised his eyes without moving his head. "No, I didn't know. I'm sorry. And yet because of that I feel you'll understand me a little now. You may not have done so before. You thought I would like to take the child, didn't you, to estrange her from you? Well"—his eyes dropped again, and now both his hands began to move in a sliding movement back and forward over the cover—"perhaps you were right, perhaps I was doing just that, but she was the only person I ever met who wasn't afraid of me. She talked to me." He made a little sound in this throat that could have been the shadow of a laugh, as he added, "At times I found her more than my equal, even my superior. But I am beating about the bush, I'm misleading you. I didn't bring you here to talk about her. She's yours, and she'll always remain yours—money and possessions cannot buy her. I've always envied you, I suppose I always will, but that's finished. I want your advice about another matter."

Into Mike's heart had come a great feeling of easement. He did not speak, but waited for the old man to go on. He watched him lie back, join his hands together, the fingers linked tightly; he watched his thin, blue lips move in and out with the mobility of the aged; but when his eyes came up there was no weakness and their penetrating stare, and his voice, too, was strong as he asked, "Do you believe he is my grandson?"

Without hesitation Mike replied, "Yes, Sir, I do."

"Give me a reason."

Mike now gave a little quirk of a smile, and he replied, "Well, his temper for one thing."

Mr. Lord's eyelids drooped and he asked, "Is that the only thing?"

"No, Sir; he's got the look of you. I knew there was something about him from the first, and I couldn't place it. It puzzled me. I suppose I would have noticed it if you both hadn't——" He stopped.

Mr. Lord's eyes were on him again, tight, and he demanded, "Yes, if we both hadn't what?"

Mike moved restlessly on the chair before saying, "Well, you know how things were, Sir, you both went for each other, from the start.

"Yes, we did." It was a softly-spoken admission. "What's your opinion of him? Now don't make excuses for him in any way. This is a private conversation, nothing that you say will be referred to again. I want your honest opinion of him."

"He's a good boy." Mike said this without any hesitation. "I liked him from the start. But he was brought up by a woman and it's twisted his outlook. It'll take some changing."

"Why did he come here in the first place?"

"I think you'd better ask him that yourself, Sir; he can give you a better answer than I can."

The old man moved from side to side in the bed. He pulled at the cover, tugged at the buttons of his nightshirt, then reached to a side-table and took a drink from a glass. When he had replaced the glass he said, "It's my money he's after, not the farm. That's small fry—it's the shipyard."

Mike's lips pursed and he shook his head. "I don't think so, Sir. He can fend for himself all right, and he's as independent as they come. No, I don't think it's that. Perhaps he's got your own complaint, perhaps that's what brought him here—loneliness, wanting to belong to somebody. He won't admit it, who would? but I think that's the real reason, I do."

"What am I going to do, Shaughnessy?"

Perhaps for the first time in his life Mike was at a loss. The old man, the old devil, was appealing to him, Mike Shaughnessy, asking him what he should do, waiting for his advice. He found himself leaning forward, and his feeling came over in his voice as he said, "Do what you want to do, Sir, in your heart. Recognize him."

This suggestion seemed to agitate the old man, and he muttered, "But it could all be a fluke, this resemblance. He could have belonged to——" He shook his head. "Don't you think that she would have told me if she knew she was bearing my child?"

Before Mike could answer the old man pressed himself back amongst the pillows, and, raising his hand as if to check any comment, went on, "No, no, she wouldn't. She would have done it to spite me. She did it to spite me. Yes. Yes, she was capable of that." His eyes looked into Mike's now. "Women are cruel—cruel."

The room was quiet. Mr. Lord was lying now as if he was dozing, and Mike did nothing to disturb him. He felt that the old man had momentarily gone back into the past, and as the silence went on he thought: "God! what a life he's had. Give me mine any day, workhouse an' all. And I had Liz, I've got Liz, and the other one." It was strange, but he knew that in his mind he did not think of Michael, he did not think of his son, yet the old man before him had craved, he knew, all his life for a son.

He was startled by Mr. Lord's voice, and his sudden change in manner, almost an alertness, as he sat up and said, "What's he paying you?"

"Paying me?" Mike was puzzled.

"For board?"

Now Mike did smile. "I think he pays Lizzie three pounds a week."

"Three pounds! Not enough—not enough these days. I'll charge him four, perhaps five, he's got to know the value of money."

It was all Mike could do not to give vent to a roar. He wanted to put out his hand and touch the old man's shoulder. He had come into this room thinking that it was his job that would be the topic of conversation and feeling already a dismissed man, not, he had told himself, that he cared a damn, for he had already applied for two other jobs. And now the matter of his work had not been mentioned, the matter of his lapse had not been mentioned and he couldn't see even a heart attack blotting that out from the old man's mind. He stood up and said, softly, "Would you like to see him, Sir?"

"No, no!" Mr. Lord became agitated. "I don't want to see him. I don't want him here. I was only thinking, that's all, just thinking. You're to say nothing about this whatever, do you hear— I wouldn't have brought you here. . . . "

"It's quite all right, Sir, don't worry." Mike's voice was soothing. "I won't say a word. I just thought——"

"Say nothing, nothing. I don't want to see him."

"But what if he should go, he's talking about it, Sir?"

For a moment the old man looked startled, then with a return of his old, truculent manner, he exclaimed. "Then let him go. Let him go. There's nobody stopping him." Mr. Lord now waved his hand as if in dismissal.

"Goodbye, Sir." Mike turned and made for the door, but before he opened it, Mr. Lord's voice stopped him "Shaughnessy!" Mike turned again towards the bed.

"About the farm, and your work. The accounts, I mean. The buying and selling, I've found it too much—too much. You'll have to take that on." The pale blue eyes peered at Mike across the distance, and he demanded, "All right?"

On a great sigh of relief that Mike could hardly suppress, he nodded his head once, and said firmly, "All right, Sir." And without another word he went out, down the stairs, across the hall, through the kitchen—with a nod to Ben, and out on to the hill almost as quickly as Mary Ann had done a short time earlier. Below him the farm lay bathed in sunshine. The accounts—the buying and selling. He was manager now without a doubt. He had not, until this moment, realized just how fearful he had been of losing this job, the job on which he was merely a probationer, and now, with a few words, the old man had passed the management, the complete management, to him. Even if he acknowledged Tony to be his grandson that would make no difference—the old man was always as good as his word, give him his due. His shoulders back, he marched down the hill, across the yard and up to his house, and going into the kitchen he went straight to Lizzie and to her astonishment grabbed her with his one arm and kissed her on the lips. So fierce was the kiss, yet so full of relief, that Lizzie, without a word, began to cry. Whatever had happened, everything was all right with her man.

.   .   .   .   .

Three weeks had passed since her da had gone to see Mr. Lord, and everything was lovely, or nearly so. Anyway, joy of joys, the farm was her da's, or as nearly so as made no odds. Her da did all the books, he sat in the office at nights and he went to the market and sold the cows, and if anybody came to the farm on any business whatever it was to see Mr. Shaughnessy—Mr. Shaughnessy, Sir. Yes, that's how they addressed her da now, Mr. Shaughnessy, Sir. And joy on top of joy, she wasn't going back to Jarrow school. That humiliation had been lifted from her life the day after her da's visit to Mr. Lord, for her da picked her up in his arm and pushed her onto his shoulder and galloped her round the kitchen, then had set her on the table and said, "You're going to a good school, me girl. Do you hear that?" He had pushed his finger into her chest. "And it's me that's sending you there. Do you hear that?" She had wanted to jump and yell her joy, but her ma had gone into the scullery, and she saw that she was crying. So now, in a very short time she'd be going to this posh school. But she'd travel home every night. She'd been to see it only last week, it had been closed for the holidays but had, nevertheless, been very impressive. She had told Mr. Lord all about it as he sat before the big window in his drawing-room, smothered up with rugs.

Mr. Lord was a lot better, but he was still very weak. She had tried to make him laugh, but she hadn't succeeded. Each day, as he had commanded her, she gave him an account of the doings of Tony, and she saw that all she said was to Tony's merit. But even this didn't make him ask to see Tony. She had never said to him "Why don't you let him come in?" for, after his visit, her da had taken her aside and warned her to keep off the subject of Tony when with Mr. Lord. "Least said, soonest mended," he had said. "The old man will make his decisions in his own time. So mind, be careful what you say and don't mention his name." She hadn't told him that Tony was the only thing that she talked about, and the only thing Mr. Lord wanted her to talk about; but even so she had been wise enough to refrain from saying, "Why don't you let him in?" But now things had come a cropper. Tony was saying he was going away. He had said it only that morning. She had heard her da arguing with him in the scullery, and saying, "Now hold your horses, I'm telling you I know what I'm talking about." But Tony had said, "It's no use, Mike, I'm going before he gets on his feet and starts playing cat and mouse with me. I couldn't stand that. If he wanted to see me, he would have made a move before now."

This news had put a blight on Mary Ann's day. She knew that Mr. Lord would find it nearly impossible to send for Tony, but she also knew that he would be very sorry if Tony went away. Moreover, she was only too well aware that Tony would on no account present himself to the old man without being asked. She liked Tony. Last night she had put a question to her mother, as she tucked her up in bed. She had said, "Ma. How old must I be before I can have a lad?" Her ma had burst out laughing, then playfully smacked her bottom and said, "A good many years, yet, me girl. Sixteen you'll have to be."

"Sixteen!" She had sat up in bed, all her shyness over asking the question gone, as she explained, "But Sarah Flannagan's got one . . . two!" Her mother had made a long face, then exclaimed, "Oh, has she, indeed! So that's what put it into your head." She had been strong in her denials, saying that she didn't mind Sarah Flannagan having a lad, but anyway she couldn't understand what any lad could see in Sarah Flannagan. Yet on the other hand, if Sarah Flannagan had a lad, why couldn't she? Her mother had smacked her bottom again and said, "Sarah Flannagan's a good deal older than you."

"Sixteen," she had said from the door, nodding her head; then added, with a laugh, "Fifteen, if you grow up quickly."

Fifteen, and she was just turned nine! . . . How old was Tony? Nineteen. He was a man, yet her da always talked of him as if he was a lad. And she thought of him as a lad. But when she was nineteen Tony would be twenty-nine. Would she know Tony when she was nineteen? Her quick mind told her she wouldn't if he once left the farm. Once gone, Tony would go out of her life, and out of Mr. Lord's life, and as much as she didn't want him to go out of her life it was much more necessary, she knew, that he should not go out of Mr. Lord's life. Mr. Lord needed him.

She reached the back door, passed through the kitchen, saying, "Hallo," to Mrs. Quigley, who was now helping out, then on through the hall and into the drawing-room. It was so beautiful, it almost took her breath away. Mr. Lord was by the window, but not wrapped up so much this morning. He was pushing at Ben's wavering hands, and crying, "Give over, man! You're like an old hen. You and she are a good pair."

Mary Ann knew he was referring to the nurse, and when she said, "Hello," both Ben and he answered her. "Hello," they said. Then Mr. Lord, turning on the faithful Ben as if he hated the sight of him, cried, "Go on, get out and leave me alone."

Quite unruffled, Ben finished his patting and straightening before leaving his master, and Mary Ann, taking her usual seat on a padded footstool, remarked, "It's a lovely morning."

"I don't want to hear about the morning. I can see it."

He was in a bad temper. Her da said it was a good sign when he was in a bad temper; it showed he was getting better. "Well, what have you got to say?"

"Nothing." Mary Ann looked up at him. His fierce gaze did not disturb her. Her mind was working rapidly, telling her something had to be done. She would likely, she knew, catch it from her da and ma if she carried out the hazy plan in her mind. Moreover, if Mr. Lord started to yell and got excited and brought on another heart attack she would get all the blame. But as her da said, the worse his temper the better he was. So, looking at him now, she deduced that he must be feeling pretty well this morning.

"What do you mean—nothing!"

She faced him squarely and moved her head from side to side just a little bit cheekily, as she said, "Well, you want to hear about Tony and there's nothing more to tell you, because he's going away." She saw the hand resting on the arm of the chair suddenly contract, until the knuckles became shiny.

"When?"

She did not really know when—it could be the end of the week or next week—but she felt that the greater the urgency she could give to this matter the greater its success, so she said flatly, "The day."

"Today?"

She watched his face twitch, then his hands, then his feet. She watched them kick off the rug that Ben had placed around him, and with an effort and the aid of his stick, draw himself to his feet, then with faltering steps walk towards the open window.

He stood there for so long and so quietly that she was forced to cough to remind him that she was still there. The cough apparently did the trick, for he returned to his seat, but much to her surprise did not question her further. She wanted to say to him, "Will I fetch him?" but she knew what his answer would be. It would be a bark of "No!"

Some time elapsed before he spoke, and then it was not to her but to himself that he said, "Let him go."

Mary Ann rose and stood looking at him. Then she said softly, "I'm going. Bye-bye."

He brought his eyes to her, opened his mouth to speak, then shook his head at himself and said briefly, "Goodbye."

She went out quietly and closed the door. In the hall she stood biting at her thumb nail. He would never ask anybody to bring Tony here, and if Tony did not leave the farm and Mr. Lord met him when he got about they would surely fight like cat and dog, and then Tony would go off in a huff. It seemed as broad as it was long. Somehow, she felt that Tony had to come into this house—he had to meet Mr. Lord when he was bad, but not too bad that he would collapse, yet not too strong that he would say "Go!" and mean it.

Suddenly she gave a little skip that was soundless on the thick carpet. She knew what she would do. She would likely get wrong off everybody, but she was always getting wrong, so once more wouldn't make any difference, would it? Two things only were in her mind now. One was that Mr. Lord was very unhappy and she wanted above all things to make him happy; the other was, she didn't want Tony to leave the farm. Outside the house she began to run, but cautioned herself when she reached the cinder track. She'd had enough of running on that to last her a lifetime, her hands and knees still had scars on them. In the farmyard she met Len leading the bull with a pole and made hastily for cover in one of the byres, from where she shouted, "Len, where's Tony?"

"Top field," replied Len, with a backward movement of his head.

When the bull was well past she ran across the yard, through a gate and over a field, and from there, in the far distance, she saw Tony. Long before reaching him she drew his attention with her voice and waving arms, and he came towards the field gate to meet her.

Her running stood her in good stead, for her gasping was the real thing as she brought out, "You're to come. . . . You're to come, he wants you."

She saw his face lose its colour, and he asked, "Who?"

She knew well enough that he knew to whom she was referring—he knew she wouldn't have run like that if her da had wanted him.

"Mr. Lord, of course."

She rested her hands on the bar of the gate and let her small chest heave like a miniature sea as she looked up at him. She could not see how the name actually affected him, for his lids covered his eyes as if he had dropped asleep while standing, and so she put her head through the bars of the gate and demanded, "What's up with you, didn't you hear me?"

"What did he say?"

For a moment she was stuck and looked across the half-mown field to where the corn stood as high as herself; and then she remarked, "He just said, 'Go and fetch him'." The lie slipped convincingly from her lips, so much so that when his eyes looked down on her through narrowed slits she did not flinch but asked, "Are you coming?"

She saw him turn away, hiding his face from her knowing gaze, and she was aware of the conflict that was raging inside him. Also, she was not unaware of his feeling of fear which she, herself, had felt in the past when about to confront the Lord.

When he came through the gate and held out his hand to her she took it, but as he made to go down the lane and through the farm she altered his course by saying, "You could cut across by the bull's field." Then added, "The bull isn't there, Len's got him." He said nothing to this, but turned right, lifted her over some barbed wire, pressed the wire down as he flung each leg over, then taking her hand again skirted the field, and then another that led them to the back of the house.

Not until they reached the courtyard did any feeling of apprehension touch her, and then with something like panic she thought; "Eeh! what if he dies. What if he has a fit and dies." Cold feet almost forced her to give her scheme away be telling Tony the truth, but he himself prevented this by stopping. He stood staring across the yard towards the back door, his teeth pressing tightly down into his lip. The sight of him standing there dispelled her own fear, and very much as Mike would have done, she said to herself, "Well, get on with it, it's now or never." So tugging at his hand she pulled him forward.

When Ben opened the door both his astonishment and resentment were evident to Mary Ann. She had not questioned whether Ben knew about Tony, but now from his looks she knew that anything there was to know Ben was already aware of.

"What do you want?"

It was Mary Ann who said, "He's got to come in. He wants to see him." She left Ben to sort out the "He's", and with another tug on his hand drew Tony over the threshold and without hesitation, and now ignoring the snorts from Ben, passed out of the kitchen, across the hall and to the drawing-room door. Here she paused and glanced up at Tony's stiff, white face, and her mind cried at her: "Eeh! what've you done now? Eeh! you'll get into trouble. Eeh! there'll be a row. . . ." Mr. Lord would be mad. They would both be mad. And she'd not half get it from her da. Eeh! But before the last "Eeh!" had slithered over the surface of her mind, she had opened the door.

Mr. Lord was sitting staring straight ahead out of the window, and it was some seconds before he turned to find out who had entered the room. From the slow movement of his head his neck suddenly jerked to take in the pair of them standing silently just within the door. Colour like a blood-red sunset enveloped his entire face. The fit that she had feared seemed imminent. She saw his bony Adam's apple jerk up and down his scraggy neck like a piston in an engine. When it stopped for a moment he gulped and swallowed as if it was choking him. Then, as she watched, the colour faded from his face and he leaned his shoulder against the chair as if for support.

Mr. Lord had not taken his eyes from Tony for a second, and she knew Tony was all—"het up", for he was hurting her hand, crushing her fingers so much that she wanted to cry out.

Then the pain was forgotten as she received the greatest surprise of her nine years. "Get out!"

She pulled her hand from Tony's and slowly pointing her forefinger at her breast said in astonishment, "Me?"

Mr. Lord was not looking any longer at Tony, he was looking at her, and there was not really any necessity to confirm his order, but he did.

"Get out of here, before I take my stick to you!" he cried.

Swiftly she glanced up at Tony, then back to Mr. Lord again. It was evident that Tony was not included in the dismissal. Well, that was all right, but why should he turn on her—she wanted to know what was going to happen, if they were going to be kind. Anyway, hadn't she arranged all this?

A movement from the chair and an unintelligible babble of words, followed by a bellow, flung her round out of the door, and there she was, standing in the hall, staring at the flat, shiny surface of the drawing-room door.

It wasn't fair, it wasn't. He was a nasty, bad-tempered old thing, he was. But there was one consolation left to her: if he wouldn't let her see, he couldn't stop her from hearing.

She took a step towards the door and leant her head down to the keyhole, which unfortunately had a flap over it. No sound came to her from the room, but as she waited she heard the soft pad of footsteps on the carpet and she knew that Tony was moving forward. And then she could hardly believe her ears as Mr. Lord's voice came to her, shaky but nice, even kind, as it said, "Sit down. No, not there, sit where I can see you."

So strange was this that she felt she must see what was going on and was on the point of kneeling down before moving the keyhole flap, when for the second time in a matter of minutes she received another shock. She had no warning, heard no sound of footsteps, felt no presence, until a hand gripped her collar and she was swung up and on to her toes and pushed across the hall and into the kitchen. She was too startled for the moment to make protest. Still held at arm's length and unable to turn her head to see which one was doing this to her, her surprise was increased a thousandfold to behold Ben and Mrs. Quigley in the kitchen. She was shot past their gaping mouths, and not until she was in the yard and pulled round did she realize that the evictor was her da.

When in her transit through the kitchen she had been given proof that she was in the hands of neither Ben nor Mrs. Quigley, her old adversary, the Devil, had suggested himself as being the only other person who could do this to her. Now as she stared up at her da she saw that he had taken on the guise of Mike and she became afraid.

"What've you been up to?"

"Nothing," she whimpered. Then qualified this by adding, "I didn't mean anything."

She saw Mike stretch himself upwards and inhale deeply, then bring his lips tightly together before saying, "My God! child, if any harm come of this. . . . " He seemed unable to go on and shook his head. Then demanded, "The old man didn't send for Tony, did he?"

"No."

They stared at each other. Then Mike, thrusting out his hand, pushed her roughly and said, "Go on, get home."

She turned and ran from him, her tears spurting from her eyes, and when she reached the kitchen door so great had been Mike's strides that he was close behind her.

Lizzie turned a startled face from the dresser, saying, "What is it?"

Mary Ann made straight for the armchair and throwing herself into it she buried her face in the corner and gave way to her crying. There was no restraint in her weeping now, for she bellowed loudly, while Lizzie, gazing at Mike, cried, "What is it? What's happened?"

"She's taken Tony into the old man, and he never sent for him."

"Dear God!" Lizzie's hand went to her mouth. "What if it should——" She stopped. "Mary Ann!" Her voice was angry, and Mary Ann did not lift her head but bellowed more loudly. Then once again she was whirled up and about, and she found herself across the room and standing at her mother's knee.

"You've gone too far this time, me lady. Do you know what might happen? What if Mr. Lord dies?"

For a moment Mary Ann's bellowing increased, then of sudden it stopped, and, looking with streaming eyes at her mother, she said, "He won't."

"What makes you think that?"

"Cos—cos—" a number of sniffs—"he bellowed at me."

There was a quick exchange of glances between Mike and Lizzie, then Lizzie said, "What if they row, and he has another heart attack? Did you think of that?"

"He won't . . . they won't."

Again the swift exchange of glances, then Mike's voice demanded, "Why are you so sure of that?"

After her rough treatment May Ann felt disinclined to enlighten them. They deserved to be kept in the dark. She would have liked to have flounced round and sat in the chair and sulked and kept her mouth shut, but the latter being an impossibility she found herself saying, "Mr. Lord was nice to him, he asked him to sit down, where he could look at him. He was nice and kind."

After a long, thoughtful moment Mike gave a great sigh, wiped the sweat from his forehead, walked to the fire, put his forearm on the high mantelpiece and, resting his head against it, muttered, "Is there any tea going—strong?"

Lizzie rose and went out into the scullery, and Mary Ann returned to her chair, miserable and misunderstood. She hated everybody. Yes, everybody, right down from her da and ma through Mr. Lord, and Father Owen, right down to Sarah Flannagan, not forgetting their Michael, Ben and Mrs. Quigley. She watched her da drink his tea—he never even offered her a sup. She was only allowed to drink tea at breakfast and tea-time, but sometimes her da gave her a drop in his saucer, but not today. He had three big cupfuls, one after the other, with piles of sugar, yet after he had drained the last cup he did not go out, but remained in the kichen by the table, rubbing his hand over it every now and again. Her mother, too, remained in the kitchen. She busied herself at nothing, and when this had gone on for what appeared to Mary Ann a lifetime, but which was merely half an hour, she felt she could stand it no longer, and made a move to rise, only to sit back with a plop as her da barked at her, "You stay put. Don't move out of here till I tell you."

Her lips trembled again. What was the matter with him, keeping on. You'd think she had committed a crime. He was going on nearly as bad as he did the night she came back from the convent, when all she had done was to please Mr. Lord—and she knew she had pleased him. It didn't matter what he said about not wanting to see Tony, he had wanted to see him. She knew.

The present monotony was broken by the appearance of Michael who enquired somewhat anxiously, "What's up?"

Mike answered him briefly, saying, "You'll know soon enough." But Lizzie went on to explain the situation, nodding while she did so at Mary Ann's bowed head.

When Michael, whom she knew was looking at her said, "My hat! What will she do next!" Mary Ann found great difficulty in restraining herself from barking, "Something that you wouldn't think of, anyway, you big softie." And she might have said this within the next second, but the kitchen door opened again, and the attention of them all was directed towards it.

Tony was standing there, and he wasn't looking at her da or ma or their Michael, but straight at her. He looked different somehow. She watched him come into the room, and when she realized he was making for her, she pressed herself back in the chair. Fear rushed upon her and her mind gabbled, "Eeh! what have I done. Eeh!"

Tony's face was giving nothing away, on he came until he towered over her. When his hand came out and grabbed her she let out a terrified squeak, and as she was once again lifted from the chair her cry of "Da!" turned into an astonished gulp when she felt his lips brush her cheek, and when he muttered, "You little devil you," she looked into his eyes, which were close to hers, and a little giggle started to work up from her stomach. But before it reached her lips she stopped it. Over Tony's shoulder she looked at her da's relieved face, and her own took on a primness which said plainly to him, "You see, what did I tell you? All that fuss and bother!" She wriggled from Tony's arms and walked over to the table where Lizzie was standing leaning heavily on it, her relief also evident, and she looked up at her mother and, with the injustice she had received at the hands of her family made plain in her voice, she asked, "Can I have a drop of tea now?"

12

What was the matter with everybody? Mary Ann had no way as yet of describing to herself that flat feeling that follows on too much excitement. During the past two weeks the excitement about the farm had been intense. People coming and going, two men all the way from London. And Mr. Lord's solicitor from Newcastle came nearly every day for a week. And men from the works, all going in and out of the big house—and Tony there nearly all the time. When he wasn't there he was with her da, talking. They talked and talked and talked, her da and Tony, of things she could find no interest in at all—about herds and buying more land and building a stockyard, whatever that was.

The day following her final piece of stategy she had not of course gone to Mr. Lord at her usual time, for that, she told herself, would have been daft. She was not out to court trouble, she'd had enough of it. So instead she had gone up on to a half-levelled rick to play, only to be dragged down by her mother, her hair and clothes straightened, and yet again she was sent up the hill at a run. Yet there had been no quiet reconciliation awaiting her. When she went into the drawing-room Mr. Lord barked her head off as she knew he would, and she said to herself that it wasn't fair, he could be nice to Tony whom he had been going on about all the time, and now because she had made things right for him he was going for her! It wasn't fair. When, the unfairness getting the better of her, she began to snivel, he suddenly became nice and pulled her to him, but bewildered her still further by saying, in his rare and kind voice, "Don't ever let anyone change you, Mary Ann. Always act on your heart."

She could understand the first bit all right, but not the second. Whatever way she acted, she thought, she always got wrong.

Then there was the excitement of Tony moving up to the house. He hadn't really wanted to go; he had said things could go on just as they were. It was her da who had said he must go. But anyway, it hadn't made much difference, for he was always in and out of their kitchen, having scones and things. Her ma liked Tony. So did their Michael.

In some way the entire farm seemed to have changed. The Polinskis had gone and in their place was a new man, a Mr. Johnston, and there was a Mrs. Johnston and a big girl called Lorna. Lorna was sixteen and worked in Newcastle. Mary Ann didn't quite know if she liked Lorna or not. But Lorna was not sufficiently on her horizon as yet to warrant any mind searching.

Last week Mr. Lord had sat outside and watched the men make his garden. There were umpteen of them, and he had yelled at one, which proved he was a lot better. Yesterday, he was yelling at everbody, that is, everybody except Tony. This peculiar attitude of his towards Tony intrigued her. He never yelled at Tony; every time he spoke to him his voice was quiet, even, she could not believe the word herself but it seemed, gentle. With regards to Tony Mr. Lord was not acting to pattern, and she asked herself from time to time when she saw them together, "What's up with him?"

Now, after fourteen days of excitement and school looming up on Monday, life had became suddenly stale. There was nothing to talk about any more. Everybody on the farm knew everything, of course—there was no one of her own age to brag to. She had seen Sarah Flannagan once in the past two days, and again with an escort, a single one this time. It was the lad who had walked with his head down. Sarah Flannagan seemed to have moved into another sphere, an enviable sphere. Although Mary Ann would have died rather than admit this, there were times now when she gave this matter much thought, for Sarah Flannagan's life seemed full of excitement compared with her own.

She had taken heart when her mother had informed her last night that she was to go to Mrs. McBride's today, taking with her a chicken all ready for the oven and a dozen eggs. She had seen this as an opportunity to tell Tony's story, with embellishments of course, to her friend. Moreover, while in Burton Street, there might present itself the opportunity to throw into Sarah Flannagan's face the glory of the new school. In any case, she knew that if she failed to encounter Sarah, Mrs. McBride would soon impart the news to Mrs. Flannagan and take joy in doing so.

Excitedly she had started out with the chicken and eggs and reached Mulhattan's Hall in a glow of benevolence, only to find Mrs. McBride out and her grandson in charge. The grandson's name was Corney, and she didn't like Corney very much, he was bigger than her and always pulled her hair. Yet at this meeting she found herself viewing him in a different light: was he eligible for—a lad? No. His rough, red face and moist nose turned her sensitive feelings away from such a proposition, and reluctant as she was to leave without seeing Mrs. McBride she could not risk staying in the same room with him, unless she was prepared to have a rough and tumble. And she knew who would get the better of that. So leaving her gifts and a message, she had retreated hastily from Mrs. McBride's kitchen and Mulhattan's Hall.

Burton Street was practically empty, which was very unusual. She looked across to the Flannagan's house. The windows were prim and neat as ever, but there was no sign of Sarah or Mrs. Flannagan. So, in a very depressed state, she left the neighbourhood and made her way to church, to pay a visit before embarking on the bus for home.

The church too, with everything else, had changed. The Holy Family were of little or no comfort at all. She told them all about everything, but they looked as if they couldn't care less. It was funny about them, she thought. Sometimes they were all over you and other times they didn't let on you were there.

The Holy Family having taken on the ways of the world, Mary Ann had looked about her in the hope that she would see Father Owen and have a talk with him about something—the Devil or anything, it wouldn't matter as long as she could talk. Of course, it wouldn't be any good talking to him about the affairs of the farm, for he knew as much about them as she did, if not more. He had been at the farm twice in the past week, and closeted with Mr. Lord. She hadn't known up till then that when he was a lad he had been friends with Mr. Lord, for she couldn't imagine Mr. Lord ever being a lad. Also that Father Owen had known Tony's grannie. So to talk of the business of the farm would be covering old ground. Yet at the present moment she would have willingly covered any ground just to be able to talk to him. But he wasn't to be seen. Nor did any rustling or noise come the vestry to indicate his presence there. She did think for a moment of going and knocking at his house door, but then what excuse could she made to Miss Honeysett, because he wasn't bad or anything and had to be visited. Life was very dull, so dull that had she encountered Mrs. Flannagan and Sarah as she left the church she would have welcomed the sight of them. She thought of the morrow, the new school and strange girls. Well, they couldn't be more snooty than the girls at the convent. She had no qualms about her status in the new school. It might be posh, it was posh, and nuns taught there, but it couldn't be posher than the convent. Already she was looking down her nose a little at this new school.

She crossed the road and was walking slowly towards the bus stop when a honk-honk of a motor-horn brought her around with face abeam. And there drawing up to the kerb on the other side of the road was Mr. Lord's car, but with Tony at the wheel.

Taking no heed of the traffic, she dashed across to it, and hanging on to the window exclaimed, "Eeh! what are you doin' here?"

For answer Tony said firmly, "Don't you run across the road without looking where you're going."

As she dived round the back of the car she thought, "He's like Mr. Lord, always on." When she was seated beside him, she asked excitedly again, "What you doing here? Where you going?"

"Home, of course." He pressed his foot on the pedal.

"But what have you been in Jarrow for?"

"I just came down for some hinges for the stockyard gate."

"Oh." The stockyard gate. . . . Her da and him and Len were making a stockyard for the bullocks. They could talk of nothing else, and they wouldn't play or lark on. She was sick of the stockyard, and in less than fifteen minutes she would be home and confronted by it all again. This at the moment seemed unbearable. She wanted to go for a ride in the car—somewhere . . . anywhere.

A wonderful idea suddenly hit her. She wriggled round on the seat and said excitedly, "Me ma sent me with a chicken and some eggs to Mrs. McBride and she wasn't in and I left them there, but I've got to go back and see if she's got them. Will you take me round?"

"Where does she live?"

"Oh, it won't take you a tick. It's just four streets and a bit away, at the end of Burton Street."

"Very well." He smiled sideways at her. "But mind, I'm not staying, I've got to get back. Mike—your father's waiting for me."

She wriggled herself straight again and looked out of the window. "There won't be any need to stay, I've just got to tell her."

If Mary Ann ever harboured any doubts about endeavour having its just reward they were put to flight as the car swung into the top of Burton Street, for whereas she had left it only half an hour earlier almost deserted now it was full with people. Immediately she sensed the cause of the change—there was a row going on. Twisting herself round and kneeling quickly up on the seat she discerned in the far distance Mrs. McBride. Dressed in her outdoor things, she was standing at the top of the steps of Mulhattan's Hall, with her fists dug into her sides and her head bouncing in the direction of the road, where stood Mrs. Flannagan with Sarah behind her.

The street was alive. People were at their doors and windows, children thronged the gutter, while a group of the more courageous formed a barrier across the road to get a close-up of the scene.

"It's a row." Mary Ann passed this information to Tony without looking at him, and Tony, without interest, asked, "Where do you want to go?"

"Right to the top, where it is—where the row's going on. It's Mrs. McBride, she's going for Mrs. Flannagan."

This information caused Tony quickly to brake the car, much to Mary Ann's consternation, and she turned round on him and demanded, "You're not going to stop here! Go to the top."

"The road's full, I can't get up there. Anyway, you don't want to go into that row, do you?" His face and voice showed concern, and she looked at him in amazement as she said quickly, "It's Mrs. McBride. Ah, Tony." She paused a moment, then changed her tone into a coaxing wheedle as she realised that it was a chip of Mr. Lord she was dealing with and not just Tony, for the set look on his face told her that he was not going to drive into the row. "Aw! come on, take me up. Aw! come on, Tony. I won't ask you to do anything else . . . ever, honest I won't. Just this once. Aw! come on."

Tony looked at her, shook his head slowly, drew in a breath, and accelerated just the slightest. The car moved slowly up to the outskirts of the crowd, and as he shut off the engine Mrs. McBride's voice came booming to them, yelling,

"Kicked her in the shins, did he. Well, she's lucky he didn't kick in the backside an' all! I would've done, and you an' all, me fine lady. And let me tell you, you lay a finger on him and begod! you'll wake up and find yourself a corpse. And it's me that's tellin' you."

Tony found himself with a ringside view of the fight. He saw a thin woman standing in the roadway, her face contorted with temper. He did not know her, but he did recognize the fat old woman on the steps. And so angry and flaming was her countenance that he warned Mary Ann sternly as she made to get out, "Stay where you are."

What! She turned quickly and looked at him. Stay where she was and a row going on. She sensed that he was afraid for her, and she laughed within herself at anyone being afraid of mixing up in a row, especially in Burton Street, and more especially when one of the combatants was Mrs. McBride. No harm could ever come to her if she was under the banner of Mrs. McBride.

"I've told you, you're not getting out. At least not yet." His hand was firmly holding her arm.

"Aw! man, nothing'll happen to me. It's Mrs. McBride—she's at Mrs. Flannagan. Her there." She pointed. "Mrs. McBride always beats her. Aw! Tony, leave go, it'll be over in a minute."

"It's over now. Look, she's seen you, she's coming down." He nodded to where Mrs. McBride was descending the steps, her chin up in the air, and shouting to the children as she reached the pavement, "Out of me way! Out of me way! Out of me way to the lot of you."

"You see." The look Mary Ann bestowed on Tony was not without satisfaction; it told him he deserved all he was likely to get, for now the car was encircled with children and all crying, "It's Mary Ann."

"Hullo, Mary Ann."

"Hullo, Mary Ann."

"It's Mary Ann."

"Eeh! Mary Ann. Is this your car?"

"Eeh! by, Mary Ann."

"Oo . . . ooh! Mary Ann. Ooh!"

"Out of me way." Mrs. McBride's face filled the open window, her smile breaking up her anger. "Why, hullo there, hinny. What's brought you this way?"

"Hullo, Mrs. McBride." Mary Ann smiled widely back at Fanny. "I came before. I brought you a chicken from me ma and some eggs."

"A chicken did you say? and eggs. Well!"

"Did you hear that?" Fanny withdrew her head from the car, and looking over the top of it sent her piercing gaze towards her enemy, repeating, "A chicken and eggs. Did you hear that? Sent to me from me friend."

Her head popping into the window again, she now addressed Tony, nodding to him and saying, "Hullo, there, lad."

"Hello," said Tony.

Both in his manner and voice it was evident that Tony was slightly nervous and somewhat at a loss. Quantities like Mrs. McBride needed getting used to, especially when they were in their battling form.

"Aren't you coming in for a drop of tea, the pair of you?"

Mary Ann looked swiftly at Tony, and her disappointment was great as he said, with some slight emphasis, "No, thank you. You see I'm on an errand." And aiming to temper his refusal, he added, "It's for Mike—some hinges."

"Oh!" The exclamation swept over the street, which Mrs. McBride now addressed, rather than Tony. "Grand news I've been hearing about Mike. Running the whole show he is now. Well, haven't I always said he had it in him? Aye, the just shall be rewarded." Her head was bouncing over the top of the car towards Mrs. Flannagan again, and the prim lady, not being able to stand any more either of her enemy or of the other thorn in her flesh, now preening herself in the car, turned away, marched through her front door and banged it after her. It was evident that she had, for the moment, forgotten about Sarah, who made no move to follow her mother but stared fascinated at the car, and at Mary Ann seated on the far side of the nice-looking young lad.

Acutely embarrassed, Tony was telling himself that he must get out of this, for now converging on the car from all sides, slowly, and somewhat tentatively but nevertheless insistently, were the neighbours, all apparently anxious to hear Mary Ann's news. So when Fanny put her head once again through the window he said quickly, "If you'll excuse us, I must get back."

"Certainly, certainly, lad. I understand. And give my very best to Mike. And——" Mrs. McBride's podgy and none too clean hand came in and grabbed at Mary Ann's and she muttered, somewhat softly now, "And thank your ma, hinny, for me. Tell her God bless her."

"I will, Mrs. McBride." Mary Ann's face was agleam. she was the benevolent lady bestowing chickens and eggs right and left. At this moment she would have loved to have a lorry piled high with chickens and eggs, the former, of course, inert, to distribute among the entire population of Burton Street—with one exception, naturally, the Flannagans.

"Goodbye, hinny."

"Goodbye, Mrs. McBride."

As Tony started the car and was edging it forward, Mary Ann made a plain statement. "You can't get out at the top, you'll have to turn here," she said.

With an intake of breath, he slowly turned the nose and backed, under shouted directions from Mary Ann inside the car and from Mrs. McBride outside, and he was openly sighing his relief and about to take the car swiftly forward when Mary Ann's grip on his hand almost turned the wheels into the kerb.

"What are you doing! Be careful!" He braked, looking and sounding angry as he did so.

"Stop a minute . . . oh, just a minute. Just a tick, Tony."

"Look here, Mary Ann!" He was talking to her back, for she was now hanging out of the window addressing a grim-faced, tallish girl.

There was no lad now with Sarah Flannagan and no mother; she stood unprotected, her face not now tranquilly lost in the throes of first love, nor yet grinning under the protection of her mother . . . she was alone—Mary Ann did not count the other children gathered on the pavement. And as once before she had addressed her enemy from out of the window of this very same car, she now repeated the process. Her tongue going twenty-five to the dozen in an effort to get it all in before he started up, she cried, "You thought I was coming back to your school, didn't you, you and your ma! Well, I'm not, see—I'm going to another posh school, a bigger one. And me da's taking me, see! Sending me on his own, see!"

This news made no impression whatever on Sarah's countenance. Her mouth remained tight, her eyes narrow, her face overall very grim. Mary Ann was naturally, therefore, forced to do something to break this indifference. So quickly she resorted to a subject that had been very much in her mind of late—lads.

"And you're not the only one who can have a lad, see!" This was accompanied by a deep bounce of her head. "I've got one, and a better one than you'll ever have, see!" Covertly, she thumbed in the direction of Tony, and not only did she indicate him with her thumb, but with her eyes, too.

Sarah's widening gaze as she took in the young man was like a draught of heady wine to Mary Ann, and stimulated by it nothing could prevent her from going the whole hog.

"And me ma says I can go out when I'm fifteen and be married when I'm nineteen, so there!"

From its expression of amazement Sarah's face now turned to one of open scorn and disbelief, and this had a sudden dampening effect on Mary Ann. She knew she had gone beyond the bounds even of fantasy, and nothing could prove her right but a declaration from the horse's mouth itself. So quickly she turned her face to Tony. He was looking at her with very much the same expression that Sarah had been wearing, which filled her with irritation, and if she'd had time to think about it she would have thought along the lines of Mike and would have said, "He's not quick off the mark about some things." And when a person isn't quick off the mark, he has to be prompted.

"Aren't I going to be married when I'm nineteen?"

That her advanced thinking had definitely stunned Tony for the moment was plain to be seen, for he made no response, until a jab of her blocked and, therefore, quite hard toecap in his ankle brought him to his senses, and he explained over-loudly, "Yes, yes—that's so——"

The rest of his mumbled words was lost on her for she was now half-way out of the window. It seemed that she couldn't get near enough to Sarah as she spurted the remainder of the fantasy at her. "So you see. And he buys me——" she was going to say bullets, but her mind quickly rejected this as common and changed it to sweets. But even this word in a split second was discarded for something more glamorous, and she ended, "Chocolates. Big 'uns, in a box, like you have at Christmas. So there . . . you see!"

There was a sharp burr as Tony's foot struck the pedal, and her words were whipped away on a gasp as she was pulled inside the car, plumped on to the seat, and for a second held within the circle of his arm as he pressed her to his side, He was laughing now, laughing so much that she could not hear the sound of her own voice as she cried, "Give over. Aw! give over, man. What you laughing at?"

When they reached the main road Tony was still laughing so much that the tears were running down his face, and she was becoming a little irritated. Perhaps it had been funny, but why was he keeping on? And she said again, "Aw! give over." She didn't like being laughed at so much. She liked to make people laugh but not them to laugh at her and keep on. Now he was looking down at her, his face more bright and alive than she had ever seen it, even after the morning he had come from Mr. Lord's, and in an imitation of her own voice, he demanded, "Can't a lad laugh at his lass?"

Her head slowly drooped from his gaze, and she moved primly on the seat, trying to suppress a smile. He had said she was his lass. Suddenly, she had visions of herself being escorted back down Burton Street by him, but on their feet—cars, for the purpose she had in mind, moved too quickly—and they would be walking, of course, under the wilting gaze of Sarah Flannagan. And still with the eyes of her enemy upon her and bulging with envy, she saw herself walking up the aisle of the crowded church in her best clothes followed by her escort . . . and, finally, going to the pictures. But on this thought her reason leapt at her and said flatly, "Don't be daft. You won't be able to do that for ages and ages."

She slanted her eyes and glanced at Tony. He was still smiling, but he had returned to normal and was driving with his whole attention on the wheel. A feeling of ownership took hold of her, as strong as any feeling she'd had for Mr. Lord.

She was only nine and she had a lad!

Love and Mary Ann

To Sarah and Jack

1

A RIVAL

He stands at the corner
And whistles me out,
With his hands in his pockets
And his shirt hanging out.
But still I love him—
Can't deny it—
I'll be with him
Wherever he goes.

Mary Ann hitched and skipped as she sang. It would seem that she was entertaining the field of sheep, but all except one, a weak-kneed lamb, appeared oblivious to her prancing. Coming to the end of her ditty, she began again as she had done at least ten times already, and she waved the empty feeding-bottle high above her head as she continued her capering, and the lamb, thinking this was but a prelude to another feed from this two-legged mother of his, gambolled with her.

She had reached the elevating line which ended, "And his shirt hanging out", when she gave an extraordinarily high leap and swung round in mid-air as a voice bellowed above her, "Stop that!"

When she reached the ground she stared wide-eyed for a second at the old man standing beyond the gate, and then she exclaimed in high glee, "Why, you're back."

She scampered the few yards to the gate and climbed on to the bottom rung and looked up into the thin, wrinkled face of Mr. Lord, and again she exclaimed, "Why, you're back." And then she added, "They're not expecting you afore next week. Me mother was going up to the house the night to see Ben about the spring cleaning. . . ."

"TO . . . NIGHT."

She swallowed but kept her eyes unblinkingly on him as she repeated dutifully, "Tonight." Oh, lordy, he wasn't going to start already, was he?

She smiled broadly at him now, a smile of welcome, for she was truly pleased to see him, and to take his mind off the obsession for good grammar she held up the empty feeding-bottle and, thumbing down towards the lamb which was now nibbling at the wire-netting covering the gate, she said, "I feed Penelope. He thinks I'm his ma . . . mother. His mother died and me da said if I fed him . . . I mean fed it . . . her—it's a her—he would let me keep her and not send her away."

She continued to look up at him, waiting for him to make some comment. She knew that she had said da instead of father, but it was no use, she couldn't call her da her father; she'd had that out with Mr. Lord a long time ago.

"What were you singing?"

"Eh?"

"Eh!"

"I'm sorry, I mean pardon." She dropped her eyes away from him now. Oh, he was ratty. And just come back from a month's holiday. She had missed him, but she'd also missed his chastising.

"I asked you a question."

"I don't know what it's called really, I think it might be 'Whistle an' I'll come to ye, me lad', but it goes, 'He stands at the corner and whistles me out. . . .' "

"I heard how it went. Do they teach you that at school?"

"No."

"Where did you hear it then?"

Her head moved around as if she were casually observing the flock of sheep. She knew if she spoke the truth and said "From Corny, Mrs. McBride's grandson" he would know she had been going to Burton Street and Mulhattan's Hall and she had told her mother that she shouldn't be allowed to go there, that all those old associations should be dropped. Her mother had tactfully refrained from stating her opinion on this matter, but later on, when her da had found out, he had said, "She's going to Fanny's when she wants to," to which her mother had replied, "He didn't really mean Fanny in particular. I suppose he was thinking that if she went there she would meet up with Sarah Flannagan and there would be the usual fighting in the street. It was that he was likely thinking about." But her da had said flatly again, "She can go to Mulhattan's Hall whenever the fancy takes her." And then he had added, "Don't you start trying to alter her, Liz; there's enough working along that line with the old boy; he's an educational establishment in himself."

So, knowing the way the wind blew, Mary Ann was forced to fib. "I heard a comic on the wireless singing it." She turned her head to look at him to see if he believed her. . . .He didn't.

"Come along."

She went to climb over the gate when his bark hit her again. "Mary Ann!"

She got slowly down from the third bar of the gate, lifted the heavy latch, pushed the lamb away from following her, closed the gate again, then looked at him.

"You're a big girl now, you shouldn't have to be told to walk through a gate instead of over it."

She continued to look at him. You didn't know how to take the things he said. He had called her a big girl, when just before he went on his holidays he had said to her mother, "We must get her to do special exercises, she's not growing as she should." She did not point out to him that she was always doing exercises to make herself taller, such as hanging from the lower boughs of trees and fixing her feet in the rails of the bed and trying from there to reach the window-sill, which even at the nearest remained two feet away. One day she had been over the moon when the distance had cut itself in half, only to find after some observation that it was the bed that had moved. She knew she was little; she didn't like being little, but she would rather be little than do any more exercises—Mr. Lord's kind of exercises, anyway, for they were sure to turn out to be some form of motion that she didn't like. He usually made her do things that she didn't like.

"Where's everybody?"

They were walking along the road now towards the farm, and Mary Ann realised that this question at least was not out of order, for there was not a soul to be seen. She could see the farm-house, which was their house, along the road to the left, and there was no sign of anyone near it. And still to the left, away up the hill, nearly at the top, opulent in its newness and dominating in its position, was Mr. Lord's house. And there wasn't a soul to be seen near that either. The sloping garden was all ablaze with daffodils, tulips and the first azaleas, and presented a magnificent sight, and she drew his attention to it, saying, "Look, isn't the garden bonnie? They weren't out when you left."

Mr. Lord cast his eyes up the hill and he let them rest there for a moment before he said, "Where's Tony?"

The house and the garden had reminded him of his grandson, if he needed reminding, and she realised, if she hadn't done so before, that he was in a paddy. He was always in a paddy when he spoke Tony's name like that, sharp, as if Tony was committing a crime for not being within sight. It was just over three years ago that Mr. Lord discovered he had a grandson at all, and her da had said then, and often since, that he wouldn't be in Tony's shoes for all the tea in China, for Tony now couldn't call his soul his own, and it was as well for him that he was learning to run the managing side of the shipyard, for if he had remained on the farm, as he had really wanted to do, he wouldn't have been able to get out of the old man's sight to draw breath. That's what her da said. She liked Tony . . . oh, she did. When she grew up she was going to marry him and have three boys and three girls. The boys were going to be called Peter, James and John like the Apostles, and the girls were going to be called Mary, Martha and Elizabeth like those in the Bible history, and they would all live in Mr. Lord's house on the hill, and they would have a television.

There was no television on the farm at all. It was one of the few things that her da and Mr. Lord seemed to agree about. Mr. Lord said it was . . . What was the word? A long word . . . like mortal sin . . . demoralising. Yes, that was it—he thought it was demoralising. And her father wouldn't hear of television in the house because of Michael and her having to do their homework. And he, too, did homework—well, sort of, for he was always reading up books about cows and bullocks and all the things they could catch. Her mother said that if she had known that animals could catch so many diseases she would never have eaten meat in the first place, but now she supposed it was too late to bother.

"Has everybody been wiped out by a plague or something? . . . Shaughnessy!"

They were standing in the yard now.

"It's no use shouting for me da, he's not there. He's gone into Jarrow, to the wharf, about some timber. Him and Tony. Tony's driving the lorry because he hadn't to go into the office this morning, and our Michael went with them to help load."

Mr. Lord looked down on her. He stared down on her, and she did not know if it was because she had said him and Tony went, instead of Tony and he, or that he was vexed at her da and Tony going off together. She knew he didn't like Tony spending so much time in their house and talking to her da.

Three years ago, when Mr. Lord had been very ill and unable to do much shouting, everything on the farm had been lovely. But since he had got better he had gone around looking for trouble. You always knew he was well when he shouted; he only talked quietly if he was bad or very angry about something. In a way she preferred his shouting. And now he shouted at Mr. Johnson, who was coming out of the cowshed.

"Is everybody asleep around here?"

Mr. Johnson came quickly towards him. He was a biggish man, and thick with it, and he was always smiling, and Mary Ann didn't like him. Her mother said Mr. Johnson's smile was smarmy, and she supposed that was why she didn't like him. She didn't like any of the Johnsons—Mr. Johnson, Mrs. Johnson or their Lorna. Lorna worked in Newcastle in an office and thought herself the last word. She was always wearing something different and whenever she could she talked to Tony. . . .This was the main reason why she didn't like Lorna. The reason why she didn't like Mrs. Johnson was because her ma didn't care for Mrs. Johnson. Every time Mrs. Johnson talked to her ma she was always telling her what a wonderful worker Mr. Johnson was and how clever he was with animals, and how highly everybody thought of her daughter. Her mother said she talked as if Lorna had just to raise her finger and all the men in Newcastle would fall on their knees.

"Oh, it is nice to see you back, sir. And how're you feeling? Have you enjoyed your holiday?"

Mr. Lord did not return Mr. Johnson's beaming smile, nor answer his kind enquiries, but asked abruptly, "Where's everybody? Jones? Len?"

"Well now, well now." Mr. Johnson pursed his mouth and made a motion with his fingers as if to pluck his lips off his face. "Jones . . . well, Jones is down in the bottom meadow, Mr. Lord; he went down there half an hour gone. And Len . . . Len is mixing meal in the store-room at this minute. As for the boss——" Here Mr. Johnson paused. "Well, he's taken a trip, as far as I know, into Newcastle."

"He hasn't. He's gone to Jarrow to see about some timber."

Mary Ann looked up into Mr. Johnson's now unsmiling face, and, turning her gaze on Mr. Lord, she said, "He hasn't gone into Newcastle. He's gone to Jarrow, as I told you."

Mr. Lord did not answer her, nor Mr. Johnson, he just looked at the man before turning away. And Mary Ann looked at Mr. Johnson before she, too, turned away. That's the kind of thing Mr. Johnson did. . . . A trip in to Newcastle. It was just as if her da had gone off on a jaunt. Oh, she didn't like the Johnsons.

Mr. Lord was now striding towards the farm-house, and Mary Ann hoped fervently that her mother would have some coffee ready and would ask Mr. Lord to sit down and have a cup and he would get over his temper. As she made her wish she drew a quick pattern of the Sacred Heart on the flat chest. And, as often before when she had made this magic sign, her wish was granted, for her mother had just made some fresh coffee, and it was in the new percolator her da had bought at Christmas.

Her mother's face was flushed because she had been at the oven turning some scones. She always looked bonnier when her face was flushed; it set off her blonde hair and made her look like a young girl again. Her ma had got bonnier and bonnier this last three years. And she had some nice clothes an' all, not like Lorna Johnson's flashy things, but nice.

Lizzie Shaughnessy turned to her husband's employer with a sincere warm greeting, saying, "Oh, Mr. Lord, I'm glad to see you. Come in and sit down." And when he was sitting by the kitchen table she said tactfully, "We weren't expecting you so soon, but," she added quickly, "nevertheless it's good to see you. I didn't hear the car."

"No, I had a puncture coming out of Pellet's Lane. I left it there." And now his thin shoulder went back and he looked at her as if she was in some way responsible for the farm appearing deserted, for his voice was harsh as he said, "And here I come home and not a soul to be seen."

"Mike's gone for some timber, Mr. Lord. The others are about at their work."

"Yes, yes, so I understand." He flapped his hand at her. "But that's not all. . . .I'm annoyed, Mrs. Shaughnessy, not so much about the place being deserted, but about this one here." He put out his arm and indicated Mary Ann.

Lizzie looked at her daughter, her own face expressionless. What had she done now? Mary Ann's indignant countenance was telling her quite plainly that in her own opinion she had done nothing, nothing to merit Mr. Lord's censure. Lizzie knew that Mr. Lord's censure was always for Mary Ann's own good, but, oh, it could be trying to everybody. He had this bee firmly fixed in his bonnet about moulding her into a little lady. Well, everything was being done to this end. Her daughter was attending the best convent school in the county, she was mixing with the better-class children of Newcastle and Durham and thereabouts, but . . . Lizzie paused on the but. Was there any noticeable impression of all this on Mary Ann? Her school reports said that she was making good progress in all subjects, particularly English. At school Mary Ann evidently proved to the teachers that she was making good progress, and when in company and on her best behaviour Lizzie herself had evidence of it, but once she was on the farm and running loose she seemed to revert back to the child she had always been. English and grammar had become the bugbear of their lives—she wished she could take Mike's view and laugh at it. Mike was all for Mary Ann being educated; he was paying for her school fees himself, not allowing Mr. Lord to spend a penny on her, yet at the same time she knew that her husband took a covert delight in that the convent polish was not adhering to his daughter. Mary Ann, like her father, was an individual. She wished at times she wasn't so much of an individual. Yet she knew that if it hadn't been for her daughter's character she wouldn't at this moment be in this kitchen, happy as she had never been in her life before, nor would Mike be in the position of manager of a farm, with a bank-book behind him and a settled future before him. Everything they had they owed to this child and her individuality. Had she been other than she was Mr. Lord would have passed her by. It was because they had one particular trait in common that he was attracted to her; the trait of tenacity. Mary Ann's tenacity had taken the form of working towards her father's security, and because of her tenacity in this direction she had captivated Mr. Lord. The Lord as she had called him until recently.

Never was a man, Lizzie thought, so well named, for he was not only lord of all he surveyed, he was lord of all their lives; particularly was he lord of her daughter's life. Deep within her she was aware that Mary Ann's destiny lay in his hands. She did not express this view to Mike, for it would have aroused his anger. Three years ago, when Mr. Lord had acquired a grandson, he had on the surface relinquished his deep interest in Mary Ann, but Lizzie knew the letting go was only on the surface; he was as determined as ever to shape her life. She said quietly, "What has she done?"

"She was entertaining the cattle with a bawdy song."

"A bawdy song?" Lizzie looked at Mary Ann, and Mary Ann, her small mouth drawn into a tight line, turned cold, accusing eyes on Mr. Lord. Bawdy meant nasty. Well, whatever it meant, "He stands at the corner" wasn't that kind of song. She snapped her eyes from him up to her mother and said primly, "It wasn't. I was only singing 'He stands at the corner'."

Lizzie lowered her eyes for a moment before looking at Mr. Lord. She knew "He stands at the corner," she knew it as a child, but she had never heard Mary Ann singing it and she didn't know where she had picked it up. Certainly not from anyone in the house.

"Do you know this song?"

"I . . ." Lizzie hesitated. "I heard it years ago. It's a very old song."

"And in my opinion most unsuitable for a child."

There followed an uncomfortable silence until Lizzie asked, "Can I get you a cup of coffee, I've just made it?"

"Yes. Yes, thank you."

Mary Ann sat on the wooden chair near the fender looking into the fire. She was filled once again with a feeling of being the sole recipient of injustice. This feeling was not new, oh no. And she said to herself, "If it isn't one thing with him, it's another." The last time, just before he went away, he had been on about "Those are they." She had been invited to tea with him and before she could eat a bite he had made her say twenty times "Those are they" instead of "Those are them." It had happened because when he had asked her what she would like she had said, "A squiggle." "A squiggle?" he had repeated. "What are they?" And she had pointed to the thinly rolled slices of brown bread and butter and stated, "Those are them." So there had followed "Those are they" twenty times. And then there was the day she had said "was you." She thought he had been going to have a fit that time. She had known well enough that it was "were you," but when you didn't have time to think it just came out. Oh, she was fed up with grammar and everybody who talked grammar, so there! On this thought her mind was lifted to her two best friends, Beatrice Willoughby and Janice Schofield. They had lovely voices and talked ever so nice, and when she was with them she talked ever so nice too, and this afternoon, when she went to Beatrice's party, she would talk ever so nice. . . . But who wanted to talk ever so nice on a farm? Her mind was suddenly brought from the uselessness of grammar on a farm to something Mr. Lord was saying. He was asking her mother what she knew about Lorna Johnson. Why was he wanting to know about Lorna Johnson? She looked towards him now and her mother, turning sharply to her, said, "You can go out to play again, Mary Ann."

She slid off the chair. She knew the technique. Her mother did not want her to hear what Mr. Lord was going to say about Lorna Johnson. But why should he want to talk about Lorna Johnson, anyway?

She was going through the scullery when she decided to wash her hands. The kitchen door was open, and if she were to hear anything while washing her hands, well, she couldn't help it. The kitchen door closed abruptly, and as she dried her hands she sighed.

She had just reached the back door when everything unpleasant was forgotten in a loud whoop of joy, for there was the lorry stacked high with timber turning into the farm-yard gate. Tony was at the wheel and next to him sat her da and their Michael. She raced down the path, along the road and into the yard, and greeted them all as they climbed down from the cab.

'Hullo, Da. You'll never guess who's back." And before any of them had time to comment she went on, "Mr. Lord, and he's in a tear."

"He's back? But he wasn't expected until next week." This comment came from Tony, and Mary Ann watched him and her da exchange quick glances. But they had no time to do anything more because Michael, speaking under his breath, said, "Here he is now."

They all turned and watched the old man approach them, and when he reached them his manner suggested that he had seen them all not longer than that morning, for he did not even stop to speak but addressed his grandson as he passed, "The car's in Pellet's Lane; there's a puncture; see to it, will you, and then come up to the house." His voice was quiet.

He was away out of the far gate and going up the hill towards his house before they looked at each other again, and then Mike, using the hook that replaced his lost hand, scratched at his thick, vigorous red hair and said under his breath, "Well, that speaks for itself. What's happened now?" Slowly he turned his eyes down on his daughter. "You been up to something again?"

Mary Ann blinked, her head bowed slightly, as she said in an offended tone, "Well, I was only singin'."

"Singin'?" Three pairs of eyes were levelled at her, and Mike repeated, "Singin'? What were you singin' to put him in that mood?"

Mary Ann's head went lower. " 'He stands at the corner and whistles me out.' I was just singing it to meself as I fed Penelope, and I was dancin' a bit, and then he barked at me from the gate."

When the silence around her held, Mary Ann, looking up into the face of this beloved man, saw to her joy that his countenance was cracking. First his lids drooped and then his mouth moved from one side to the other. Then his big, straight nose twitched at the end, and to her immense delight he flung back his head and let out a bellow of a laugh that surely must have carried up the hill to Mr. Lord before he managed to stifle it.

Mary Ann, her face wreathed now in one wide grin, clapped her hands over her mouth, and when Michael asked, "What song is that, Dad?" Mike said in mock surprise, "You don't know 'He stands at the corner'? Where've you lived all these years? Listen . . . it goes like this." And placing his hooked hand on Michael's shoulder and his good arm around Mary Ann he walked them out of the yard singing under his breath, "He stands at the corner and whistles me out, with his hands in his pockets and his shirt hanging out." But when he came to "Still I love him" he changed it to "Still I love her," and the lift of his arm brought Mary Ann's feet from the ground and her laugh bubbling out again.

But before they reached the road Mike stopped and, looking round, seemed surprised not to see Tony following them. Tony was still standing looking in the direction his grandfather had taken, and Mike, calling to him, said, "Come away in for a minute and have a drink of something." And they stood waiting until he came up.

Tony, a young man of twenty-three, was, outwardly at least, a very good copy of his grandfather. He had the same leanness of body, the same thin features; he also, like Mr. Lord, carried his chin at an angle, and also, like his grandfather, he had a temper, but strangely he had shown very little of it in the last three years. His one concern seemed to be to please his grandfather, and, as Mike was not above saying, the old boy took advantage of this. Tony looked at Mike now and said in a voice which denied any connection with the Tyneside, "I can't understand it. Why has he come back? I had a letter from him just this morning saying to expect him next Friday. There's something wrong somewhere; it can't just be her singing." He looked down on Mary Ann now and smiled, and Mike said, "You worry too much. I've told you afore, take him in you stride. He nearly had my hair white the first year I was here. I've got more sense now, and, anyway, he doesn't mean half he says. . . . Come on, come in and have a cup of something and listen to this, what she was singing, it's a grand ditty . . . edifying." Mike laughed. Then, nodding his head slowly towards his daughter and raising his index finger, he beat time and counted, "One, two, three," and on the word three she joined her voice to his and, grabbing his hand, went singing and swinging into the road and towards the house, with Michael and Tony coming up in the rear laughing.

"Well!" Lizzie exclaimed as she looked at her husband and daughter as they marched into the house still singing, and before she could voice any further opinion of the display, Mike, his deep and musical voice ringing out the words "Still I love her," swung her around the kitchen floor.

"Stop it! Stop it this minute. Oh, Mike, don't be so daft, leave go." When at last Lizzie had disentangled herself from Mike's arms she looked with disapproval on him and said sternly, "It's all right you playing games and laughing, you should have been here a few minutes ago."

"Well, all I can say is, if he was upset by a thing like that, then God help him. And don't look at me in that way, Liz, you can't lay it at my door. I never learned her that one."

"Perhaps she learned it from . . . my friend Beatrice." Michael was mimicking what he called Mary Ann's Sunday voice, and she turned on him in wrath, crying, "Oh you! our Michael. Beatrice never learned me . . . taught me!" She bounced her head at him to emphasise her use of the correct grammar. "Beatrice doesn't know songs like that."

Michael, throwing his head back in a similar attitude to that used by his father, laughed, "You're telling me . . . dear Beatrice is too dumb to know anything like that."

"I'll smack your face if you call Beatrice . . ."

"That's enough! That's enough!" It was Lizzie speaking. "Stop it, Michael. And you Mary Ann, not so much of the smacking faces or we might finish up with the other end being smacked. And, anyway, who did you hear it from?"

In deep indignation Mary Ann looked at her mother, and in a voice and manner that once again spoke of the indignities of her life she said primly, "Corny."

"Corny?" Lizzie's eyes were screwed up in questioning perplexity when Mike put in, "Don't be so dim, Liz. . . . Corny. You know Corny . . . Corny Boyle. That's who you mean, isn't it?" He turned and looked towards Mary Ann. "Mrs. McBride's Corny."

Lizzie's face was no longer screwed up but stretched wide now as she looked at her daughter and demanded, "When did you see him?"

"When I was at Mrs. McBride's a week or so ago."

Lizzie, continuing to look at Mary Ann, sighed deeply but said nothing. She remembered Corny Boyle and her memory made her shudder slightly. If ever a child went to the extreme to gather her friends it was her daughter. Corny Boyle on one hand and Beatrice Willoughby on the other. The poles were nearer than these two. She did not ask Mary Ann how long she spent in the company of Corny Boyle; she only had to use her imagination. Mary Ann had learned "He stands at the corner" from him. But there was another matter Lizzie had to attend to at the moment, and its importance outweighed the doings of Mary

Ann, and so she said to her, "Go on upstairs now and get your things out for this afternoon. I've ironed the ribbon to slot through your frock; leave the ends loose and I'll do the bow."

Mary Ann looked hard at her mother for a moment. It was only eleven o'clock; she wasn't due at the party until four. As for slotting the ribbon through her frock, she wasn't going to put that one on; she was going to wear her nylon, her blue nylon. There was something up and her mother wanted rid of her.

She did not waste her still indignant glance on any other member of the family, but walked out of the room and up the stairs. And she was quick to notice that no voices reached her from the kitchen until she was across the landing, and then it was her mother's voice she heard and it brought Mary Ann to a stop. It also brought her head on one side and caused her ear to cock itself upwards, and what she heard her mother say was, "You might as well know. It wasn't about her and the song that he was mad. He didn't like it, naturally and he came in here and told me so, but it needs very little thought to realise that neither her nor the song had anything to do with him coming back unexpectedly like this."

"You know what brought him?"

It was her father's voice, and now Mary Ann, retracing a number of her steps, was back at the head of the stairs when her mother's voice came again, saying, "I've a good idea." There followed a pause before Lizzie's voice, softer now and speaking to Tony, asked, "Have you been going out with Lorna Johnson, Tony?"

Mary Ann's mouth dropped into a gape.

"Good God!" That was Tony saying that. He said it again. "Good God! How could he know about that?"

"Aw, lad, don't tell me you've been so daft." This was her father's voice, and it was unusually quiet and sort of sad, and Tony answered sharply, "It was all so simple, it only happened the once. I was going into the cinema, there was a queue and I had to wait, and Lorna was standing not a yard from me. What could I do, pretend I didn't know her?"

"Did you come home together?"

"Yes." Another pause. "After we'd had supper. What was wrong in that? But it's as I thought, and I've had the idea for a long time, he's been having me watched. . . . By damn! I won't stand for it. Oh no! I'm not standing for that."

"Hold your hand a minute." Her da's voice was lower still now. "Don't jump to conclusions. He could have heard about it by accident."

"What! In Naples?"

"Yes . . . well, you've got something there. But don't be rash. And I maintain what I said a minute ago. You were a fool to take her out, and to make it a supper an' all."

"I couldn't get out of it, Mike; the situation was impossible. I see her every day."

"You mean she sees you every day." This was Michael speaking with unusual audacity, and he was promptly silenced by Mike saying, "That's enough, quite enough."

"Was it just that once, or are you seeing her again?"

Her da, Mary Ann realised, was talking as if he were Tony's da an' all, and when, after a short silence, Tony's voice came to her saying, "Oh, what of it? I've made a date, but there's nothing in it," her da said, "You're mad."

"All right, I may be, but I swear that if he keeps on I'll go the whole hog, I will. I've stood his iron hand for as long as I can, but this is a bit much . . . spying on me, setting someone to spy on me. I'm going to have it out with him right away."

She heard the scuffling of feet and her father's voice fading away, saying, "Here, hold on a minute. Steady up. Let's talk this over."

Her hand across her mouth, Mary Ann went softly into her room and closed the door. Tony had taken Lorna Johnson to the pictures, and not only to the pictures but out to supper. A cloud had passed over the sun. Tony had taken Lorna Johnson to the pictures. Tony was her property; he had always been hers. Always . . . all her life.

Tony was her . . . her lad. He had said so himself, a long, long time ago.

She found that her face was twitching and she wanted to cry. But she mustn't cry, for her ma would want to know why. And then there was the party this afternoon. Bust the party; she didn't want to go to the party. Tony had taken Lorna Johnson to the pictures. She hated Tony . . . yes, she did. She hoped Mr. Lord would go for him. Oh no, she didn't. She didn't want them to fight because Tony might lose his temper and go away. She could never hate Tony, but she hated Lorna Johnson. Oh yes, she hated Lorna Johnson. She hated all the Johnsons. Oh, she wished . . . she wished that they would die, all of them, especially Lorna. She went to the window and stood looking across the farm buildings in the direction of the two cottages, one of which was the home of the Johnsons.

A picture now filled the whole space of the farmyard. It was of a table. At one side sat Tony and at the other Lorna Johnson. She could see Lorna's high pencil-slim heels and short skirt. She could see her sheer nyloned knees. Her eyes travelled upwards over Lorna's close-fitting suit to her bold, dark eyes and black hair. She saw Tony looking at her across the table. Tony had that clean, washed look that was peculiar to him, and he was wearing his grey suit, the new one that he had bought last month and looked smart in. She saw him handing Lorna Johnson a plate, and on the plate were fish and chips. She watched Lorna nibbling at the fish and then . . . a wave of triumph passed through Mary Ann's slight body when she observed the smartly clad Lorna Johnson rolling on the unsubstantial ground in agony. . . . She had been poisoned and she would die and it served her right.

2

"GOOD AFTERNOON, MRS. WILLOUGHBY"

"Now mind your manners," said Lizzie, as she buttoned the coat carefully over Mary Ann's blue nylon dress. "Say 'Good afternoon, Mrs. Willoughby', and when you are leaving don't forget to say 'Thank you very much for having me, Mrs. Willoughby. I've enjoyed it so much.' And don't forget to say 'Mrs. Willoughby'; it's always nicer when you say the person's name. Do you hear?" She gave her daughter a slight shake.

"Yes . . . yes, ma."

"What's the matter with you? Don't you want to go to the party?"

"Yes . . . yes, ma."

In some bewilderment Lizzie looked down on Mary Ann. Then, giving her a slight push, she said, "Go on then, there's Tony waiting for you. And mind what I've told you and behave yourself."

Mary Ann made no rejoinder to this. She walked sedately down the path, through the gate and on to the road where Tony was in the act of turning the car round. And when she was seated next to him she gave him no welcoming "Hullo" as was usual. Nor did he speak to her. He looked mad, in a temper. He had likely got it in the neck from Mr. Lord, and serve him right. Yet again she thought that it wasn't him she really wanted to get it in the neck, it was Lorna Johnson.

It wasn't until they were actually entering Newcastle that he spoke to her.

"What's the name of the street again you're going to?"

She turned to him and said coolly, "It isn't a street, it's a drive . . . The Drive, Gosforth. Me ma told you. Number fifty-eight." And then she added, in a further dignified effort to point out the difference between a street and a drive. "It's a lovely drive, and a lovely house, beautiful, and they call it Walney Lodge. And Beatrice's father is a superintendent of ships, and her mother launches them." She gave a little jerk to her head to add to this impressive statement, and for a flashing second Tony's eyes rested upon her, and there was a semblance of a smile on his face, but all the response she got out of him was, "My! my!" and she didn't like the tone in which he said that.

When they finally reached Fifty-eight, The Drive, Mary Ann was quick to notice that while she was gushingly welcomed by her best friend Beatrice, Mrs. Willoughby and Tony were talking in the same kind of voices, high up in the head, sort of swanky. So it was with some bewilderment that Mary Ann received her hostesses' welcome of "Hullo, Mary Ann." According to orders she answered, "Good afternoon, Mrs. Willoughby," and in her best voice which, no matter how hard she tried, would not come out of the top of her head.

When she entered the hall hand in hand with Beatrice she recognised immediately the nice smell that had attacked her nostrils on her previous and first visit. It was a lovely smell and was all over the house. Not that—she now defended the smells of her own home—not that their house didn't smell nice, but theirs had a different smell, a bready smell, things-out-of-the-oven smell. This smell was scented, like flowers. Perhaps the smell was from flowers, for there, in front of the huge electric fire that Beatrice said burned imitation logs, there was heaped a wonderful array of flowers. They all sprang out of a low dish on the hearth. It was like a shallow baking bowl, not like the vases her ma put flowers in and stood on the window-sill.

She went up the beautiful staircase that had a wrought-iron balcony at the top through which you could look down into the hall below, but her mind was lifted from the beauty and unusualness of the house by her name being cried, and she turned round to see coming across the landing Janice Schofield, her other best friend.

"Oh, Mary Ann, isn't it lovely?"

Mary Ann did not know exactly to what Janice was referring, whether it was the house, or the party, or the meeting with herself after the long separation of a whole day, but she nodded brightly, and in the admiring and superior company of her two best friends she forgot for a moment about Tony and his cruel desertion. She was at the party and, oh, she was going to have a lovely time.

And Mary Ann did have a lovely time, for of all the fifteen guests she found herself prominently to the fore. Only one thing disappointed her: they did not have the television on. Between games and tea, and then more games and ice-cream, she glanced longingly towards the big white square eye of the world that stood on its pedestal in the corner of the large drawing-room. At one period towards the end of the wonderful party a fellow guest, a boy and another apparent television-yearning soul, suggested that they should switch on and see "Bronco Layne." Mary Ann seconded this by joining her hands under her chin and exclaiming, "Yes! Oh yes!" but the young hostess squashed the plea immediately. Yet turned her refusal into a compliment by saying, "Oh no, we don't want the silly television. You do one of your funny rhymes, Mary Ann."

"What! Me?"

"Yes, go on."

Mary Ann looked round now at the momentarily silent company and just for the smallest accountable fraction that one could measure in a second she felt shy. It was one thing to entertain her friends behind Sister Catherine's back and make them giggle by leaning towards them and whispering such things as, "Isn't it a pity that skitty Kitty can't be

really witty." This was considered excrutiatingly funny because Sister Catherine's weakness
was sarcasm. But it was quite another thing to . . . do some poetry . . . before a company.

"Do about the bluebottle," cried Janice. "Go on, Mary Ann, do about the bluebottle."

"Yes, do." Beatrice turned to where a smart young woman was leaning over the head of
the couch watching the proceedings and cried, "She makes them up, Aunt Connie. Oh,
they're funny."

"Come on, Mary Ann, do the bluebottle."

So Mary Ann, standing with her back towards another arrangement of flowers that
entirely covered the drawing-room fireplace, did the bluebottle. With a twinkle in her eye
she began:

> "He said it was a bluebottle,
> I said it was a fly.
> He said it was a bluebottle,
> And then I asked him why.
>
> Jus 'cos, he said,
> Just 'cos that's all.
> Wasn't any answer,
> Was it,
> At all?"

The amusement came from the way Mary Ann delivered this more than from the words
themselves, and there was much laughter and cries for more.

"Now do 'The Spuggy.' "

The slang term for a sparrow did not sound uncouth when coming from Beatrice's lips,
but Mary Ann was apparently not quite happy at the suggestion she should do "The
Spuggy"—"The Bloomin' Spuggy," to be correct. And, anyway, it wasn't one of her own.
But the requests heaping on one another, she once again stood with her back to the
flowers and began, in a north-country accent you could have cut with a knife, "The
Bloomin' Spuggy."

> "There was a bloomin' spuggy
> Went up a bloomin' spout,
> And then the bloomin' rain came doon
> And washed the bloomin' spuggy oot.
> Up came the bloomin' sun
> And dried up the bloomin' rain,
> And then the bloomin' spuggy
> Wentupthebloominspoutagain."

This effort was greeted enthusiastically and with much laughter, especially by the
young males of the party, and when Beatrice, basking in the limelight of her dear friend
Mary Ann, cried, "Now do . . ." she was abruptly cut off by her mother's polite tones,
saying, "No more, dear, now; the time's getting on. You've just time for one more
game. Now what is it going to be?"

There were a lot of "ahs" and "ohs," and then it was decided the wonderful party
would finish with hide-and-seek.

The choice seemed rather a young one for these ten-to-twelve-year-olds and Mrs.
Willoughby raised her eyebrows to her cousin, the smart young woman, who was still
leaning over the head of the couch.

Mary Ann, now very excited by her triumph, was determined to find some place to hide where she would never be found—well, not for a long time, anyway, she wanted this party to go on for ever. The majority of the guests were scampering on tiptoe through the hall and up the stairs, but Mary Ann made for the kitchen. It was a big kitchen; she had noticed this when she had helped to carry some of the plates from the dining-room. It was surrounded by tall cupboards, and one was a broom cupboard. It was the last cupboard, nearest to the back door. She knew this because she had seen Mrs. Willoughby opening it to get a cloth because somebody had spilt jelly on the floor.

The kitchen was empty and within seconds she had inserted her slight figure into a space between the standing and hanging brushes, and there she stood shivering with excitement, hoping and praying that this would be the last place that Beatrice, who was the seeker, would look for her.

When she heard the footsteps coming into the kitchen she bit on her lip and hunched her shoulders up over her neck. It was Mrs. Willoughby who had come into the kitchen and she was talking to Beatrice's Aunt Connie. She could hear the voices just as easily as if she was standing by their sides. Mrs. Willoughby was saying in her high, swanky voice, "Hide-and-seek. It's a cover-up for Sardines, I suppose. Were we ever as goofy over boys as they are? I suppose we were, but it's really embarrassing to watch them at times. Well, it's nearly over and thank goodness."

"I don't know how you stand it, Jane. They've left the house in a frightful mess."

"Oh, that will soon be cleared up, but I'll leave most of it until Mrs. Stace comes in in the morning. She's very good like that after a party, she doesn't mind coming in on the Sunday."

"What did you think about . . . 'The Spuggy?' "

"Oh yes." There came a little laugh. "I was dreading what she would follow up with."

"She's a quaint little thing, isn't she?"

"My dear, Beatrice adores her." There was another laugh. "She's got a pash on her, as has Janice. I think it's because they're such opposites. You couldn't find two more opposite than Beatrice and her, now could you? . . . or Janice."

"No, I suppose not, but she's rather taking, I think."

"Oh yes, I grant you that, but there was a time when the sound of her name could make me scream. When she first came to the convent three years ago I got Mary Ann Shaughnessy for breakfast, dinner and tea."

"What did you say her name was?"

"Shaughnessy."

"Shaughnessy?"

"Yes. What's the matter?"

"Is her father a farmer, or a manager or some such?"

"Yes, he manages old Lord's farm. You know Peter Lord, the shipyard man. He's got a pet hobby of farming, I hear. But what's the matter, do you know them?"

Mary Ann, standing in her secret place, waited and the smart young woman's next words brought the thought to her mind that life could go on smoothly for months, even years, and then of a sudden everything happened together. Like today, Mr. Lord going for her, then finding out about Tony, and now the woman was saying in a low, pained tone, "My dear, it's that child's mother that is the cause of Bob and me breaking up."

"No, that's impossible. She must be just an ordinary woman."

"Ordinary woman or not, she's the woman."

"You must be dreaming, Connie."

"I wish I were."

"But I didn't know it was a woman that had caused the trouble. I thought it was . . . well . . ."

"Well, what?"

"Oh, I don't know—the growing pains of marriage, I suppose."

"The growing pains of marriage don't usually cause separation, it's nearly always another woman, and in my case it's Elizabeth Shaughnessy."

"But how do you know? Wait a minute until I close this door."

Mary Ann, from within the darkness of the cupboard and the darkness that was now filling her small body, heard the footsteps go towards the kitchen door, and when they returned the smart young woman said, "Just by chance, I suppose you would call it, or fate or some such . . . You remember when I went to open the sale-of-work in Shields last Christmas?"

"Yes, I remember."

"Well, after it was over an awful old woman came up to me and made herself known. She said she had known Bob for years, and then she went on, with what she imagined to be deep subtlety, to tell me that she had nearly been Bob's mother-in-law. That for years he had courted her daughter but that in a moment of madness the girl had gone and married a big, red-headed good-for-nothing with the name of Shaughnessy, and she knew the marriage wouldn't last, as did Bob, and for a further number of years they apparently both hung on waiting for it to break up. And when it didn't and the man got this position as farm manager the old hag suggested to Bob that it was now time he stopped waiting. . . . In her own words, a man needs companionship and has to marry some time."

"No, Connie!"

"Yes, my dear, it's a fact. I think I could have killed her. And guess how I felt when later Bob came to pick me up and in a few words verified all this woman had said, for he asked most kindly after Elizabeth, most kindly. And that's putting it mildly."

"Oh, but that was no proof. Now, don't be silly, Connie."

"I'm not being silly; you don't know Bob as I do. You only see him as the charming, quiet individual. He had been morose and difficult for months, and I thought it was because I didn't want to start a family, but from that night I knew what the trouble was. He couldn't forget this woman."

"Did you tackle him with it?"

"Yes . . . yes, I did. We had a few words about something, nothing to do with this. Then, as it goes, one thing led to another and I brought up this woman's name, this Elizabeth Shaughnessy. My dear, the guilt was written all over him; the very mention of her name made him jump as if he had been shot."

"What did he say?"

"What do they all say? He denied it, of course. He didn't deny that he had at one time hoped to marry her, but he wanted me to believe that once she had married this fellow Shaughnessy all he wanted was her happiness. At the end, I asked him was he telling me that he hadn't hoped these two would split up and he bawled at me then and said, no, he wasn't telling me any such thing, and yes, he had hoped they would split up and he would have her, and that he would have her tomorrow if he could. And on that he packed his case and went."

"Oh, Connie! It all sounds so silly. . . . And I know you, Connie. Ever since we were children you would keep on and on about a thing until the other person admitted you were right. Now you know you did."

"I had no need to keep on about this, Jane. Anyway, the matter's finished. But it seems strange that that child should be this particular Elizabeth's daughter . . ."

At this moment both the women jumped round with exclamations of fright and astonishment as the brush cupboard door was burst open and a tiny figure flew across the kitchen in the direction of the sink, and there, putting her head over the porcelain basin, vomited in no refined fashion.

Whereas Mary Ann just imagined that the three years she had known Tony constituted the whole of her life, she had no need to bring her imagination into play when the name of Bob Quinton was mentioned, for one of her first memories was of hearing her Grannie speak his name and of the trouble that followed. It seemed to her that this man's name just had to be whispered and the harmony in her life was cut through as if by a sword's thrust. And she remembered the time when her mother had nearly left her da. If it hadn't been solely through Mr. Quinton, he, in the first place, had been the cause of the trouble, her da's trouble. Not even at the advanced age of twelve would she term it . . . drinking. Even though she no longer thought of him when in drink as just being sick, she nevertheless refused to look upon his lapses as getting drunk . . . Anyway, it was all because of this Bob Quinton that her da had had a number of lapses in the past.

She had prayed and prayed for years for something to happen to Mr. Quinton and God had got him married, which act had taken on the form of a miracle, but now the miracle had turned a somersault and they were back to the beginning. And this beginning was worse than the original one, for if Mr. Quinton could not like a smart, beautiful girl like Beatrice's aunt, then . . . then . . . It was at this point that her stomach had turned over and she had had to erupt herself from the brush cupboard.

The voices of Mrs. Willoughby and her cousin were passing back and forward over her head now. "What a thing to happen. I wouldn't for the world have opened my mouth."

"Well, how were we to know? It was this game they were playing. . . . But in the brush cupboard! None of the others would have thought of going there. It's because she's so small. There, there, my dear, don't strain any more. Let me wipe your face."

"Mrs. Willoughby was taking a flannel gently round Mary Ann's face when the door burst open and Beatrice cried, "Oh, here's Mary Ann."

"Go away and close the door . . . do you hear me, Beatrice? It's time for things to finish now, anyway. Close the door, I say. Mary Ann's not well; she's having a bilious attack."

The voices from the hall floated dimly to Mary Ann, saying, "Poor Mary Ann."

"Mary Ann's having a bilious attack."

"Mary Ann's sick."

"Poor Mary Ann."

But their sympathy did not bring any easement to Mary Ann's tight breast.

"I'll get them into the drawing-room preparatory to packing them off, and then you can take her upstairs."

When Mrs. Willoughby had hastily left the kitchen the young woman sat down and drew Mary Ann gently towards her knee, and then she said, "Oh, my dear, what can I say?"

When Mary Ann made no response, she added, "Did you hear everything?"

Mary Ann, her head cast down, gave it a small bounce and the young woman said, "I—I didn't mean it, not all of it. Mr. Quinton and I have just had a little disagreement."

Now Mary Ann's head came up and, looking straight into the smooth and beautiful face of Mrs. Quinton, she made a statement. "My Grannie's a pig," she said.

Mrs. Quinton's eyebrows gave a quick jerk and Mary Ann exclaimed again, "She is. She's a pig. Me da used to say she was pig, hog, guts and artful, and she is."

Mrs. Quinton's mouth was slightly open and her eyes were wide, but she could not find any words with which to answer this outburst, and Mary Ann went on, "And me ma loves me da. Me da's a fine man. Everybody says so. Mr. Lord says so and he should know." This latter was accomplished by a number of jerks from her head. "And me ma thinks the world of me da, and she wouldn't leave him for anybody, not anybody."

"I know she wouldn't, my dear. Don't upset yourself. There, there, please don't cry. Look at me."

As Mary Ann looked into the deep brown eyes before her she was, in spite of her own grief, slightly surprised to see that they were blurred with tears, and again it was to her surprise when she found that this sight checked her own emotion and aroused in her a feeling . . . even a nice feeling . . . towards this person who had brought trouble back into her life, and she asked her now, very quietly, "Do you like him?"

"Him? You mean Bo . . . Mr. Quinton?"

Mary Ann nodded.

The lids were lowered, shutting the brown eyes away from Mary Ann's gaze for a second, and then they were opened wide again. And then Mary Ann got her answer. "Yes, I like him, I like him very much, better than anyone else in the world."

They looked at each other for a long time, then Mary Ann turned her head away and gazed at the floor. Her feelings at this moment could she have transcribed them into words, would have been a profound reflection on the stupidity of men, men as a whole, but of Bob Quinton in particular. For Mary Ann's opinion was that Mrs. Quinton was nice, she was very nice, and lovely to look at, and Mr. Quinton must be mad to still want her ma. Not that her ma wasn't beautiful, there was no one more beautiful than her ma, but it was a different kind of beauty to that of Mrs. Quinton. So her profound thinking was summed up in three words: he was daft.

There came the sound of voices from outside the house, which suggested that the leave-takings were in progress. Some minutes later the kitchen door opened and Mrs. Willoughby appeared, but she did not enter, she merely beckoned to her cousin and at the same time said gently to Mary Ann, "Stay there a minute, my dear . . . just a minute."

It was a long minute. It stretched itself into five, and then ten. Mary Ann could hear voices in the hall outside the kitchen door. She knew they were those of Mrs. Willoughby and Mrs. Quinton. And once she thought she heard Tony's voice. Then she knew she hadn't been mistaken when the door opened at last and into the kitchen came Tony, accompanied by the two women. He looked gently at her for a moment before saying, "Are you feeling better, Mary Ann?"

"Yes, thank you." As she looked at Tony she knew he had learned about Mr. Bob Quinton and her ma.

Her clothes were brought downstairs, and everybody helped to put them on her, and she was led from the house to the car like some sick personage. And into that particular section of her mind that was kept for such observations there slid the thought that you always got attention like this when you couldn't enjoy it.

It was only when she was seated in the car that she remembered that she hadn't thanked Mrs. Willoughby in the correct manner—in fact she hadn't thanked her at all. So, looking out of the window at her hostess, she said dismally, "Thank you very much for having me, Mrs. Willoughby. I've had a lovely time."

She was further surprised at the result of her good manners, for both Mrs. Willoughby and Mrs. Quinton bit on their lips and lowered their gaze from hers before turning away.

The car jerked forward and she was on her way home.

It was when the journey was more than half over that Tony stopped the car and, looking at her with his kindest glance, he said, "You won't say anything at home about what you heard this afternoon, will you, Mary Ann?"

She stared at him blankly. What did he take her for? Did he think she was daft an' all?

Misinterpreting her silence, Tony added quickly, "You know it would only cause trouble, and you know how fond your mother is of——"

"I know, I know." Her chin was thrust upwards. "I'm not going to say anything . . . I never say anything . . . I didn't afore."

Tony's face was thoughtful as he looked down at this elfin, lovable, but unpredictable child. He still thought of her as a child. The tenseness of her face indicated to him just how she felt, but he guessed that her feelings concerning her parents' happiness wouldn't be those of a girl of twelve. Mary Ann's capacity for loving and hating was of an adult quality, and so it was with the pain she suffered. He said no more, but smiled at her tenderly before starting the car again. . . .

"I told you to have bread and butter and not a lot of cake." Lizzie looked sternly down on her daughter.

"There was no bread and butter, Ma. They don't have bread and butter, just sandwiches."

"That's what you get for stuffing your kite." Michael, seated at the table, was surveying her with a broad grin on his face, and she turned on him, but without vigour now, saying, "I didn't stuff me kite, our Michael."

"What made you sick then?"

She looked at her mother, and then at Tony, before turning towards her father where he stood with his back to the fireplace, and she said, "It was likely the jumping and running about."

"They were very pleased with her." Tony spoke directly to Lizzie. "They tell me she did quite a bit of entertaining."

"Oh."

The gaze of all her family was upon her now, and there was a touch of pride in Lizzie's voice as she asked, "Did you recite . . . some of *Hiawatha*?"

"No, Ma."

"Then what did you do?"

"I did the Bluebottle and I said——"

"Yes, what else did you say?"

Her answer was some time in coming, because she knew what reception it would invoke.

" 'The Spuggy.' " Her voice was very small.

"No! Mary Ann!" On Elizabeth's shocked tones there came a combined bellow from Mike and Michael, and Michael cried, "She did 'The Spuggy' before the Willoughbys! Oh, I wish I'd been there."

Mike was now on his hunkers facing his daughter, his laughter rippling as he said, "You should have gone one better, hinnie, and done 'He stands at the corner.' That would have shaken them, an' no mistake."

"Yes, Da." It was a quiet, dead response.

The laughter slid quickly from Mike's face. Michael's strident young bellow faded away. Elizabeth stood gazing down at her daughter. Then she watched her turn away from Mike and walk out of the kitchen and towards the stairs.

Now Lizzie looked at Mike, and Mike looked at her and then towards Michael, and lastly they all looked at Tony. And Mike asked, "Were they all right to her?" And Tony answered, "More than all right, I should say. They were all very taken with her, saw her to the car, gave her the honours, the lot." He looked straight back into Mike's face as he spoke, and when Mike, although reassured, shook his head in perplexity, Lizzie said, "Well, there's something wrong. She's not herself, and if I know her it isn't only a bilious attack."

3

CORNY

The situation called for a prayer, not just a gabbled "Our Father" and a "Hail Mary"; nor being a participant at Mass. It needed a session to itself.

She had just sat through the Mass, but it hadn't left her with any feeling of comfort, so she had decided to wait behind until the church was clear and then go to the altar of the Holy Family. At one time she had been a frequency visitor at this altar. The troubles of her life had driven her to the steps of the Holy Family to beg, beseech and entreat them to make things better for her own family. And they had done so, though not without some little trouble on her own part. Nevertheless, her prayers had been answered. But Mary Ann, like the rest of humanity when things are going smoothly, forgot about the hard times, and the help she had received during them. So it was rather a shame-faced Mary Ann who now genuflected deeply to the altar of the Holy Family before kneeling down and bowing her head. It must be said for her that she felt a little uneasy as she realised that although she had viewed them from the centre aisle week in week out for years she had never thought to come near them. And now when she was wanting something, here she was back again in the old position.

"Jesus, Mary and Joseph."

She got no further. A long, long time ago when she had knelt here with her petitions she had thought that the Holy Family talked to her. Now she didn't imagine they were talking, but she knew without a doubt that their expressions were speaking louder than any words. The look on St. Joseph's face said plainly, "Well, what are you after now?" and Mary's expression, even in a gentle way, was saying, "So you've come back?" and Jesus, who was not looking like a baby at all, His expression was saying the most, and it hurt the most, for it said, "Even Sarah Flannagan would have come back and said thank you for all the good things that had happened to her."

She bowed her head away from their reproachful glances wondering why Sarah Flannagan had to be brought into it. She couldn't pray to them, she couldn't ask them to do anything for her. After a long silence, during which she got a cramp in her legs, she fell back on St. Michael and the set prayer to him seemed to be quite in order with her own wishes.

> "Blessed Michael the Archangel,
> Defend us in the Day of Battle.
> Be our safeguard against the wickedness and snares of the Devil.
> Rebuke him, we humbly pray,
> And do Thou, Prince of the Heavenly Host,
> By the Power of God,
> Send down to Hell Satan and all the wicked spirits
> Who wander through the world for the ruination of souls."

Ruination was her own word.

In the darkness behind her closed lids she saw St. Michael brandishing his sword, and falling under the brandishment . . . was Mr. Quinton. And she was watching with satisfaction his quick descent into Hell, when she felt the tap on her shoulder. She gave a mighty start, followed by a gasp, as she opened her eyes to a white-surpliced figure standing at her side.

He was tall and grim-visaged, and not until he spoke did she realise that it was the head altar boy, who in actuality was no longer a boy.

"Father Owen wants to see you."

She did not speak. She was still trembling from the shock of having imagined that the power of her prayer had called forth the saint.

She did not look at the Holy Family as she left their altar, but she was conscious of their eyes following her until she reached the vestry door and there she saw Father Owen waiting for her. He was sitting on a wooden bench with one leg stretched stiffly out, and this he was rubbing vigorously. On the sight of her he stopped for a moment, saying "Hullo, Mary Ann, come away in. I've got a touch of me rheumatics. It's the spring, I always get it in the spring. Sit down," he added, then continued with his rubbing until the last altar boy had said goodbye to be answered with, "Don't be late for Benediction, mind."

The outer door closed, and, the vestry to themselves, the circular movement of Father Owen's hand came to a halt. Without any preamble he turned his head sharply to Mary Ann and said, "Well, what's the trouble now?"

"Trouble, Father?" Mary Ann's eyes widened.

"Yes, I said trouble." Father Owen's long head now drooped towards Mary Ann; and his eyeballs slowly disappearing backwards in his skull, he asked, "What's wrong with your da?"

"Me da?" Mary Ann's whole face stretched with her amazement. "Nothing's wrong with me da, Father; he's fine."

Father Owen's head moved slowly to the front again and up, and his eyeballs returned to their natural position. "Well, is your mother all right?"

"Yes, Father, me ma's fine an' all. We're all fine. And our Michael's going to sit for his G.C.E., and if he passes me da says he can stay on and later he'll go to college."

Michael would have been astonished if he had heard with what pride she reported his progress.

"Yes, yes, Michael's doing fine. I know all about Michael. How is Mr. Lord? . . . Oh, but he's away."

"No he's not, Father, he came back yesterday. He's all right an all . . . but he's in a bit of a temper."

Father Owen's head turned quickly again towards her as he asked, "With you?"

"Just a little bit, Father."

"What about?"

"Me grammar."

The priest's head bobbed and he laughed now as he repeated, "Me grammar."

"My grammar, Father."

"That's better. Well now, it would seem that you're all in very good health and spirits on the farm. . . . I forgot about Tony—how's he?"

"He's all right, Father."

"Ah well, you've everything to thank God for, you're all all right." The priest now turned himself completely round and placing his palms on his knees with his elbows sticking outwards, he bent towards her and enquired softly, "Well now, will you tell me, Mary Ann, why the Holy Family has had the honour of a visit from you?"

She stared back unblinking into the pale-blue eyes and she made no answer.

There was a quirk to the priest's lips now as he said, and still in a very soft voice, "Would I be right in thinking that you went to enlist their assistance again in polishing somebody off?"

Mary Ann blinked once; it was a quick blink. All her life she had been under the impression that there was a close affinity between God and Father Owen, the only difference being that God was supposed to know everything whereas Father Owen actually did, at least concerning her.

"Were you praying for your grannie to die?"

She had her head down now. "No, Father."

That was the truth, anyway; she hadn't in those past few minutes when kneeling before the Holy Family asked them to polish off her grannie. But had her grannie come to mind when kneeling there the thought would have been accompanied, voluntarily or involuntarily, by the desire for her demise.

"Look at me, Mary Ann." Father Owen's finger came under her chin and lifted her face towards him. "Tell me, what's the trouble."

"Nothing, Father." Her lids were blinking rapidly now and the priest stared at her for a long moment before patting her cheek and saying, "Ah well, come to confession Thursday night. Go along now and give my love to your mother and them all. Tell her I'll be running in to see her one of these days soon, and I'll want a big tea. Tell her that, mind."

"Yes, Father, I'll tell her." Mary Ann smiled. "Goodbye, Father."

"Goodbye, my child. Thursday night, mind."

"Yes, Father."

As Mary Ann walked up the aisle she knew for an absolute certainty now that there was not even a gossamer thread between God and Father Owen. No one but God himself would have realised that she couldn't talk about this matter in any other place but the confessional box. For years she had poured out her secrets to Father Owen in the confessional and they were safe with him. She could come out of the box and within a few minutes look the priest in the face knowing that all she had told him had been obliterated from his mind. It was as if he labelled her sins individually and sent them post haste to their different departments in heaven, there to be dealt with expertly. And once they were gone they were forgotten. . . .

Always during her short life when danger had threatened Mary Ann's loved ones she had sought the solution to her problems and solace for the hurt from three sources: the Holy Family, Father Owen, and lastly Mrs. McBride. The Holy Family were there to listen to her problems, Father Owen to give her advice about them, and Fanny McBride to bring an untranslatable feeling to her, untranslatable because it was a mixture of so many things—easement, laughter, hope and pride. Oh yes, one main ingredient could definitely be picked out as pride, because in Fanny McBride her da had a great advocate. Fanny always made her feel proud of her da and today she wanted to feel extra proud of him, to hear that he was so wonderful that it was unthinkable even to suggest that anyone . . . anyone could take her ma from him. So now she did not make her way to the bus and home, but, ignoring the fact that she hadn't told her mother she was going to Mulhattan's Hall, and should her visit become known to Mr. Lord it would make him mad, she turned in that direction and walked towards Burton Street.

Although she hadn't lived in Burton Street for years, Mary Ann was always instantly recaptured by the feeling of the place. Today it had the Sunday feeling, it was empty. Or almost. The front doors were closed and here and there a blind hadn't been drawn—those were the ones who didn't go to Mass, or chapel or church. The sight of these windows created in her a slight feeling of condemnation.

Before she reached Mulhattan's Hall she cast her eyes across the road in the direction of the Flannagan's freshly painted house, and her interest at this moment in the Flannagans was almost dormant. It was over a year since Sarah and she had met, and on that occasion they had passed each other without doing battle, for the simple reason that Sarah, being accompanied by . . . a lad, had refused to look at Mary Ann. Mary Ann did not wish to remember at this moment that the ignoring of herself by her enemy had cut her as deep as any slight and had been as provocative as an open challenge.

But now there was no sign of Sarah Flannagan, and this morning Burton Street was quiet. That was until she reached Mrs. McBride's window. Even before she came near it she knew that Mrs. McBride was . . . on; and when she had walked up the steps and across the fusty hall and knocked on her door, she had to repeat the knock twice before Fanny's strident voice yelled, "Come away in then!"

"Hullo, Mrs. McBride."

"Oh, hullo, hinnie. It's you. Come in, Mary Ann, come in. Come in and sit down. I'm just going at this one."

This one was no other than Corny, Mrs. McBride's grandson and the only one of her many grandchildren for whom she had a strong liking. Corny was a tall boy of fifteen, a gangling, loose-limbed lad, with a face out of kindness one would call plain. It had one good feature: the shape of his mouth. Detached from its particular fixture Corny's mouth could have been termed beautiful, but in its present position its assets were outweighed by the other accompanying features. Again that was, until he smiled, or was deeply amused by something, and then his eyes, looking through his almost closed lids, held an infectious merriment that made the onlooker wonder about this gamin plainness. But at the present moment the plainness was very much in evidence, as was the look of frustration and irritation.

"Hullo, Corny." Mary Ann was pleased to see Corny.

"Hullo." His voice was rough.

"Aw, you wouldn't open your mouth to him, Mary Ann, if you knew what he was up to. He makes me wild, he does." Fanny was covering the distance between the oven and the table, and after banging on to the table a blackened meat dish holding a more than well done point-end of brisket, she cried, "Look at that! Almost gone to a cinder, that's him." She looked at Mary Ann while indicating her grandson with her thumb over her shoulder. "You'll never guess what he's up to now, not in a month of Sundays you won't."

"Aw, Gran."

"Now shut your mouth, you; you've said enough already you have!"

Her fat body had turned swiftly towards her grandson, and now, turning as swiftly back again towards Mary Ann, she said, "You know the trouble, lass, I've had with one and another, now don't you?" She did not wait for Mary Ann's reply but went on, "It's all past so they say, all over and done with, but when my Jack married a Hallelujah, hell broke loose, and now, God in Heaven, you wouldn't credit it, not two in me own family, but this one here's goin' the same road." Again she thumbed her grandson, and Corny broke in, "Aw, Gran, divint be daft. Aa'm not gannin the same road, it isn't the Salvation Army."

"It's not a kick in the backside off it." Fanny was now standing face to face addressing her grandson, and she brandished a long, black, double-pronged meat fork in her hand as she did so. "What's the Church Army or Boys' Brigade, or somethin', but a first cousin to them?"

"But, Gran, Aa'm not joinin' them."

"No, not yet, but wait a week or so an' be God they'll have you in, as soon as you learn to blow that blasted cornet to their satisfaction. Then they'll have you in. Do you think they're goin' to learn you to play the thing as you said for nowt. Oh no, not if I know them Willies. If you had told me he was goin' to charge you a bob a lesson, then I would have thought nowt of it, but a bandmaster in the Boys' Brigade goin' to do something for nowt . . . Oh, away." She flapped her hand at him, and he protested vehemently.

"Mr. Bradley's a nice man, he is, Gran. He doesn't want nowt off me, he just said Aa'd it in me to be a good player, if Aa'd some lessons. An' Aa only told you 'cos I thought you'd be pleased. . . ."

"Pleased—of course I'm pleased. You've made me Sunday." Thrusting her arm right out, she pointed a podgy finger at him and, wagging it in front of his nose, she stated her ultimatum, "I'm so damned pleased I'll tell you this. You go to that fella for lessons an' you don't come back here. And mind I'm tellin' you, you don't put your nose in this door. Now that's finished . . . ended, that's enough." Fanny emphasised the end by showing her grandson the palms of her hands with her fingers spread wide, and he looked through them up into her face but said nothing. He just put his lips firmly together and moved his head from side to side and said nothing.

And now Fanny turned to Mary Ann and cried, "Well now, sit down, me dear, and let's hear your crack. How's everything up yonder?"

"Oh fine, Mrs. McBride."

"Mike?"

"Oh, me da's grand." And then Mary Ann added, "I didn't tell me ma I was coming or else she would have sent you something, Mrs. McBride."

"Oh, yer ma brought me a pile of stuff in last Wednesday, eggs, butter, the lot, and a chicken the week afore. Your ma keeps me supplied . . . Lizzie's a good friend."

Mary Ann looked at Mrs. McBride and her mouth dropped open to repeat, "Me ma here last Wednesday?" Her ma hadn't said she came to Mrs. McBride's every week. A soft understanding smile spread over Mary Ann's face. Her ma didn't want her to come too often to Mrs. McBride in case it upset Mr. Lord, but she was seeing to it that Mrs. McBride didn't go short of titbits. Her ma was nice; oh, her ma was nice.

"Will you have a bit dip and bread. Look, it's nice and fat." Fanny indicated the grease in which the brisket was swimming, and Mary Ann, looking towards the fat, felt her stomach give a little heave. But she managed to smile as she said, "No, thank you, Mrs. McBride; it would put me off me dinner and then me ma will go for me."

"Aye, perhaps your right. What about you?" Her countenance was disgruntled as she addressed her grandson, and the substance of Corny's answer was the same as Mary Ann's. "Aa'm not hungry," he said.

"That's a change; something's going to happen. My God, you not hungry . . . world catastrophe imminent."

On this statement they all, after a second's hesitation, simultaneously burst out laughing, and Fanny sat down, crying, "Oh, I'm not the woman I was. I can't laugh as long or as loud. I have no puff now."

Mrs. McBride had been very ill; they had thought she was going to die. But Mary Ann couldn't see her friend dying. Mrs. McBride was Mrs. McBride and would go on forever.

Mary Ann regaled her now with her own particular news of the farm and listened yet once again to Mrs. McBride telling her she had always known that Mike had it in him to be a grand farmer. The conversation was most satisfying, and when half an hour later she went to take her leave she was not displeased that Corny, who had been mute since his battle with his grannie, now made it evident, and without words, that he, too, was about to take his leave. And this called forth comment from Fanny.

"You not stayin' for your dinner?"

"No, Gran; me ma wants me across home."

"You didn't say that afore."

"Ya didn't give me a chance, Gran."

"Have you got somethin' special?"

"No, nowt that I know of."

"Well, why do you want to go skiting off?" Whether it was an unusual thought had struck Fanny or whether she was checked by the expressive hunch of her grandson's shoulders, she stopped her cross-questioning and, looking at Mary Ann, she smiled broadly, saying now, "All right, get yersels along and my love to your ma and da, hinnie."

"Bye-bye, Mrs. McBride."

"Bye-bye, hinnie. And thanks for comin'; it does me good to see you. . . . So long, you."
She accompanied this last terse farewell with a dig from her thick fist in her grandson's
back, and he, bestowing on her now an affectionate grin, replied, "So long, Gran; be seein'
ya."

"Aye, be seein' ya."

She led them out of the door and watched them walk side by side down the steps. "So
long," she called again. And they answered her, "So long."

As Mary Ann walked down the street with Corny she began to experience an odd
sensation. She was pleased to be with Corny . . . yet she was ashamed, and she was
ashamed of being ashamed. It was rather confusing.

She glanced sideways at him . . . up at him, for he was almost twice her height. His
clothes looked funny, not a bit like the boys' who were at Beatrice's party. Both the ends of
his trouser legs and the cuffs of his jacket seemed to be moving farther and farther from their
appointed places with each step he took. She realised that he had outgrown his suit, and she
felt slightly indignant that his mother hadn't done something about it.

He now turned and, catching her eye on him, he smiled as he said, "Me grannie's a
tartar, isn't she?"

"She's nice."

"Aye, she's aal reet is me grannie. Aa divint knaa what Aa'd dee if Aa hadn't her."

This seemed an unusual remark for Corny to make, at least Mary Ann thought so.
If three weeks ago, before their first meeting for some time, she had given a thought to
Corny Boyle her mental picture would have presented her with a dirty-nosed, dirty-
faced teasing lump of a lad, of whom, had she been truthful with herself, she was afraid,
but these two brief meetings had shown her a different Corny altogether. She was at
this moment wishing that she hadn't to take the bus and he could walk all the way
home with her, yet at the same time there was this feeling of being ashamed to be seen
with him in such clothes. And, moreover, she was finding that she was criticising his
way of speaking. Mrs. McBride talked broad and she liked to hear her, and she herself
could talk a bit broad, but now, alone with Corny, she had an urge to talk proper, even
to talk out of the top of her head like Beatrice. She also became more confused by her
feelings when she realised why she wanted to do this . . . it was in the hope that he
would try to copy her . . . and talk, well, if not proper, a bit different from what he did.

The hope was strangled even as it struggled for birth by the sound of Corny's voice
saying in his rich Geordie accent, "Hev ya heard Eddie Calvert?"

"Heard Eddie Calvert?" Her words were precise. "Who is he?" Even to herself she
didn't sound like herself.

"He's a cornet player. Why . . . the best. By lad, he can myek her taalk. Mr. Bradley
says if Aa stuck at it Aa could myek a go of it an' be as good as him . . . Eddie
Calvert . . . But there"—the gangling limbs seemed to fold up at this point—"Aa've
got neewhere to play. Neebody wants to hear yer practisin' the cornet."

Mary Ann forgot for the moment about talking properly, she forgot about being
ashamed of his suit or the broadness of his twang; she seemed to forget everything,
even the revelations by Mrs. Quinton yesterday, the revelations that could shatter the
harmony of her home. Everything at this moment was forgotten but the desire to
comfort and please Corny. The sudden shyness that was accompanying this desire
forced her to look straight ahead as she said, and in her ordinary voice now, "I like
hearing you practising. You played nice that morning. An me da knows the song you
were playing. If you want to practise there's plenty of space on our farm, and me da
wouldn't mind you comin', I know he wouldn't. . . . Nor me ma." She ignored a pause

in her thinking at this point which seemed to check her tongue, and went on in a gabble now and looking at him as she walked. "It's my birthay on June the first. You can come to me party—that's on the Saturday—if you like, and you can play . . ."

He had stopped and was looking at her, his face straight and his voice unusually quiet now as he said, "Yu mean that? Yu're not just kiddin'?"

"No. No, I'm not. Yes, I mean it."

And she did mean it. Every fibre of her meant it. As she looked into his now gently smiling face, she meant it. As they turned and walked silently now towards the bus stop, she meant it. As he stood looking at her through the window of the bus, she meant it. She meant it more than ever as she went along the road towards the farm. She meant is until she looked up the hill towards Mr. Lord's house, and then she stopped, and with her gaze fixed on the imposing structure she said defiantly, "Well, it's just his suit." Yet before she reached home she knew it wasn't just Corny's suit; and as she entered the house she could see Mr. Lord and Corny confronting each other and she exclaimed to herself, "He'll have a fit."

And there was no need to explain to whom she referred.

4

MIKE PASSES HIMSELF

Monday morning, as is generally understood, sets the main pattern for the week, and the scene in the kitchen before Mary Ann departed for school indicated a stormy time ahead.

In bed last night Mary Ann had realised that if she had told her ma of the extended invitation to Corny immediately on entering the house it would have been over and done with, but she hadn't, and so following a night of weird dreams dominated by Corny, dressed in a smaller suit still, blowing his cornet into Mr. Lord's face, she decided she must tell her ma before she went to school. Strategically she left the telling until almost the last minute. And now the place was in an uproar.

"Whatever possessed you, Mary Ann? After asking Beatrice and Janice and the rest!"

"Not forgetting Roy Connor." This last remark was an almost unintelligible exclamation from Michael.

Roy Connor, the product of a private school, had last year entered the grammar school and was, in Michael's estimation, a pie-eyed cissy.

Mary Ann could give no attention to her brother, for her whole mind was on her mother and the temper she was in. Even her da was not coming to her assistance; he was apparently indifferent to the situation and was standing filling his pipe as if nothing was happening.

But here Mary Ann was wrong, for following Lizzie's next remark Mike joined in the fray.

"You'll just have to tell him you can only have a certain number and you've already asked them. . . . Anyway, I don't care what you tell him, the boy cannot come. You've got yourself into——"

"Hold your hand a minute, Liz; hold your hand a minute." Mike closed the lid of his tobacco tin and placed it in his pocket before adding, "She's asked him. The thing's done.

and she can't back out of it now."

"You keep out of this, Mike. . . . Have you seen Corny Boyle in this last year or two?"

"No, I haven't, but I remember the lad."

"Well"—Lizzie drew herself up—"that should be a reference for an invitation to her party."

"She says he's changed." A jerk of his head indicated Mary Ann. "He must have, for as I remember, she was scared of him."

"Yes, he's changed all right and not for the better . . . at least in looks. You should see him and the way he's turned out."

"Well, that's likely his mother's fault. Anyway, she can't get out of it now."

"Do you know what the result would be if he came down?" A jerk of Lizzie's head indicated the house on the hill and its master, and on this Mike turned swiftly and said angrily, "If he comes he's welcome, and if he doesn't like the people in the house, then he knows what to do. Corny Boyle's been asked and Corny Boyle's coming and that's that."

Mary Ann watched her da stalk out of the room; and watched her mother put her hand to her throat and close her eyes; she watched their Michael draw in his lips and shake his head at her, and she wished she was dead.

"Don't you ever think, child?" Lizzie was looking at her with reproach-laden eyes.

"He had nowhere to play his cornet and . . ."

"Oh, my God!" Lizzie now put her hand over her eyes. It was very rarely she used such an expression, and it indicated to Mary Ann the depth of her feelings on this matter.

"He's not playing that cornet here. I'll throw the thing in the pond."

Mary Ann turned her glance on Michael now. Under other circumstances her retort would have been, "You try it on and it'll be you who'll land in the pond." Although there was a year's difference between Corny and Michael, Corny could already give inches to her brother. But she held her peace. Michael, being another boy, could make it tougher for Corny than her mother could . . . that's if he ever reached the party.

"Go on." Lizzie's voice had a low, hopeless note now. "You'll miss your bus; we'll sort this out later."

"Bye-bye, Ma." Mary Ann's voice, too, sounded hopeless.

"Bye-bye."

It seemed an effort for Lizzie to stoop and kiss her daughter, and Mary Ann left the house with the weight of the world on her shoulders. But as she passed the farm gates her da came from behind the open byre and, looking down on her, he said quietly, "Don't worry, everything will be all right. Corny'll come. Go on now." And again he repeated, "Don't worry."

So the week began.

On the Monday afternoon Sister Catherine gave Mary Ann a hundred lines for not paying attention. It was odd that she had "not paid attention a hundred times before." She had entertained her friends at the sister's expense, she had done a number of things for which she could have been given lines, but today, because she had done nothing, and literally that, she got a hundred lines. It was all so unfair.

On the way home she lost her bus pass. Added to this, a very strained welcome from Lizzie when she reached home completed the Monday.

On Tuesday, on her return from school, she heard that there had been trouble on the farm with the new bull whose name was Neptune. He had kicked out at Len when he was being groomed; and Len said his rightful place was at the bottom of the sea, and if he had his own way . . . etc.

Mary Ann was not surprised to hear Neptune had kicked out; she didn't like Neptune and never went near him. Great William, the old bull, was her favourite. He was known as Bill and would let you rub his nose.

Also on this Tuesday she learned that Mr. Lord and Tony had been at it, because Tony, she understood, would not cancel his date with Lorna Johnson. Tony, to her mind now, deserved everything he had evidently got from Mr. Lord. She saw no similar situation in the fact that she could not cancel her invitation to Corny.

But Monday and Tuesday were nothing to Wednesday. The trouble on Wednesday started early with the arrival of the postman. Before Lizzie opened the letter everyone knew who it was from; and when with her breakfast half finished she read it, then laid it by the side of her plate without making any comment, the silence at the table was a waiting silence. It wasn't until the meal was finished that Lizzie, with the air of making a casual remark, said, "My mother's looking in on Saturday."

Oh no! The protest was loud inside Mary Ann's head. Saturday, the only day she hadn't to go to school, the only day she could romp on the farm from early morning till late evening, and her grannie had to come on Saturday. That her grannie has to come at any time was something in the shape of a catastrophe, but on a Saturday!

It wasn't until Mike was putting his coat on preparatory to leaving the house that he made his remark, also in a casual tone, "I'll change me day off," he said. "I've got things to do in Newcastle; I'll make it Saturday."

"Oh, Mike!" Lizzie sounded hurt, all pretence gone now. "You know she'll hang on and hang on waiting for you to come in."

"She won't unless she stays the night, and she'll not stay the night under my roof, you know that, Liz."

"It'll only make things worse."

"Now look here, Liz." Mike turned and confronted his wife. "It's months since she was here, I know, and months before that when she paid us a visit, but does she ever change? That woman's got the devil in her and she'll never let up on me until I'm dead, and not even then. I know her, Liz, I know her. The only thing I don't know and don't understand is how she comes to be you mother."

"Oh, Mike!"

"It's no good, Liz. I'm takin' me day off on Saturday. Perhaps I'll take me daughter into Newcastle with me, eh?" He put his head on one side and caught Mary Ann's glance, and brought from her the only joyful note of the week so far, "Oh yes, Da; that would be lovely."

And this is how Mike and Mary Ann happened to be in Newcastle on a Saturday morning and, of all places, in Durrant's.

Mike had done his business at the bank, he had been to the corn-chandler's, he had been to the garage about spare parts for the tractor, he had ben to an office and talked with a man about the show in Castle Douglas, and then he had said, "What about a drink?"

It was at this point that they were passing Durrant's. Mary Ann had heard of Durrant's. Beatrice and her mother sometimes went there, as did Janice and her mother, and so with daring she put her suggestion saying, "Da, Durrant's is nice; you can get coffee and cakes there."

Coffee and cakes, she knew, held no attraction for Mike, who by this time of the morning and on his one visit a week to Newcastle would have a thirst for a drink . . . a real drink, but a limited drink. For three years now he had never broken his solemn vow not to go over two pints and a double. This treat only once a week might for him be near the line of total abstinence, yet it was enough to make him feel that he could still take it if he wanted it. Although he knew he should never go beyond this line, for his own self-respect he did not look upon it as a compulsory line.

Mike now, looking down on Mary Ann with a deep twinkle in his eye, repeated, "Coffee and cakes in Durrant's? And why not? We've been let out." He squeezed her hand and then, with a lift to his broad shoulders and a tilt to his head, he pushed his daughter before him and entered Durrant's.

There were big tables and small tables and people dotted all round, and Mary Ann's proud gaze swept over them, and in its sweeping it was checked and brought back to a near point and focused on a high white, gauze-trimmed hat, and beneath it two large brown eyes that were looking at her. The owner of the hat was not a couple of arm's lengths away from her and, smiling, she said, "Hullo, Mary Ann."

Mary Ann had stopped, causing Mike to stop behind her, and now she cast a swift glance upwards at her da before looking again towards Mrs. Quinton.

"The lady's speaking to you, Mary Ann."

"Hullo."

"I'm waiting for Beatrice." After making this statement Mrs. Quinton's eyes lifted from Mary Ann to the big red-headed man standing at her side and she said, "You're Mary Ann's father?"

"Yes. Yes, I'm Mary Ann's father." The two adults smiled at each other.

"Are you looking for a table?" Won't you sit down here? Beatrice will be delighted to see you." Mrs. Quinton addressed the latter part of her remark to Mary Ann, and Mary Ann, looking once again up at her da, waited.

"Thanks. Come along, sit down." It seemed that Mike had to press Mary Ann into the seat before he took his own opposite Mrs. Quinton.

"Mary Ann hasn't introduced us but I'm Mrs. Quinton."

"Mrs. Quinton!" Mike's voice showed pleased surprise. "Well, well."

"You know my husband, of course?"

"Yes . . . yes, I know your husband. Yes, I know Bob."

Mary Ann could gather nothing from her father's remark. What she did gather was that he seemed quite at ease in this posh café and quite at ease talking to Mrs. Quinton, and she was posh an' all. And she noticed something else: Mrs. Quinton kept her eyes fixed on her da as if she found him nice. Slowly the tension began to seep out of her body. In some inexplicable way she felt that this meeting did not worsen the situation, and that the menace of Mr. Quinton was in some way lessened by it.

"How is Bob? I haven't seen him in years."

"Oh." The brown eyes were hidden for a moment by a flickering of the lids, and then Mrs. Quinton said brightly, "Oh, he's very well . . . very well."

Mary Ann noticed that her da made no further remark on the subject of Mr. Quinton's health but that he kept his eyes on Mrs. Quinton and asked, "What's he doing now?"

"Oh, building . . . building as usual."

"Anything in particular?"

"Well . . . er . . . he's doing some houses up Low Fell way . . . Did you hear about the party on Saturday?" Mrs. Quinton, jumping from one subject to another, now looked at Mary Ann and there was a question in her eyes, but it wasn't answered by Mary Ann, for Mike replied, "I hear you gave her a grand time."

"Yes, yes . . . Ah, here's the waitress."

"Let me see to it."

Mrs. Quinton made no protest and Mary Ann listened to her da giving the order for coffee for four. He did it as if he came to Durrant's every day and ordered coffee; and when he turned again to Mrs. Quinton and began to talk, Mary Ann sat looking at him, her mouth slightly agape. He never talked like this to her ma, nor had she heard him talk like this to anybody else. Not that he was putting it on, but he was talking nice and . . . passing himself. If she didn't know he was her da she would have taken him for a man like Mr. Willoughby, a gentleman, or her own Mr. Lord, who never dirtied his hands and always wore a blue suit and collar and tie. She had seen her da in all kinds of moods, drunk and sober. She had, to her deep shame, seen him singing in the street when he was as full as a gun. She had seen him crying with shame. She had seen him standing up to Mr. Lord. But never before had she seen him entertaining a lady to coffee. It was a revelation to her, a joyful revelation. Oh, she was so proud . . . her da could pass himself.

It was more than twenty minutes before Beatrice put in an appearance and she gushed over Mary Ann, and Mary Ann, relieved for the moment of all worry and responsibility and basking in the gentlemanly glory of her father, returned Beatrice's effusion, and over yet another cup of coffee and some more cake Mary Ann let herself go and jabbered to her friend and forgot to feel responsible for her da.

It was fifteen minutes later when they all parted company and Mary Ann watched her da shaking Mrs. Quinton by the hand and saying, "Now remember me to Bob. And don't forget what I told you: you look us up. We're always at home, and Lizzie would be delighted to see you."

Mrs. Quinton assured him that she would do as he asked, and added to this the unnecessary remark that she hoped they would meet again.

"You didn't tell us that you had met Mrs. Quinton at the party."

Mike was striding along looking ahead as he spoke, and Mary Ann, after a moment's pause said, "I forgot, Da."

"Did you see Mr. Quinton on Saturday?"

"No, Da."

There was a break in the conversation as they became divided by a trio of prams, and when they came together again Mike went on, but more so now as if he were asking himself a question and not her: "Why did she say he was on houses up Low Fell? They were finished more than a month gone. I passed through there over three weeks ago and the place was all tidied up."

Mary Ann now put in quickly, "We mustn't forget me ma wants that ribbon for binding the blankets, Da."

Mike looked at his daughter for a moment and then he laughed. She couldn't make out why he was laughing, but when he grabbed her hand and pulled her to him she did not search to know. The tone of the day was set.

They did more shopping. Then Mary Ann waited while Mike went in and had his drink. She did not have to wait long, for he seemed to be in and out in no time. Then around one o'clock they had a good dinner. And afterwards went to the pictures.

It was a glorious day, and when towards evening they made their way home in the bus Mary Ann was bursting with the events of it. So many things had happened, nice things, but the crowning one was that her da had passed himself. He had talked to Mrs. Quinton, and Mrs. Quinton had liked him talking to her.

As always when filled with joy she wanted to hitch and skip, to throw off her exuberance, and she started, as soon as they left the bus, by hitching along the grass verge. It wasn't until they reached the farm gate that she stopped, as Mike, with a critical eye on her, remarked, "We're in for a dampener if she hasn't left yet."

Oh . . . her grannie! She hadn't thought about coming home and finding her grannie. It certainly would put the tin hat on everything if her grannie was still in the house.

Being of the same mind and not wanting to confirm their suspicions, they did not go straight to the farm-house. Mike, turning into the yard, went towards the office, there to deposit some samples he had with him. Mary Ann, still bubbling with excitement, skipped towards the cow byre just to have a . . . peep in, until her da made his appearance again.

But between Mike's office and the cowshed was the bull-pen, Bill's bull-pen. The pen had two doors, one leading into the open section and one into a covered part that had at one time been a small byre but which had been given over to make a very comfortable house for Bill. Bill had his own doorless aperture which led from the byre into his private yard. The gate leading from the open section into the farmyard proper had a slip catch which could only be opened from the outside, as also had the door leading into the byre part. Mary Ann had been warned never to lift the latch of the open pen gate, but this warning was not extended to the byre door because even when the byre door was open there was a barricade about a yard's distance from the door. This was the back structure of what had at one time been the feeding bins and had been left as an added security against the bull getting out. It had an opening at the end big enough for a man to enter but not big enough for the bull to come through.

Mary Ann, after lifting the wooden latch from the door, entered the byre and, looking over the partition into the dim region beyond, she said, "Hullo there, Billy boy . . . Come on, scratchy noses." When this soft endearment was answered by a low rumbling roar she laughed and said, "You in a bad temper, Bill? Come on, and I'll scratch your nose."

Apparently Bill was in a bad temper, for he pawed at the straw under his feet and emitted a dull roar.

As she was once again about to tempt him with endearments a voice from behind her in the yard said, "Oh, hullo there, what you up to?"

She turned her head to take in at a glance the, to her mind, under-dressed figure of Lorna Johnson, and she answered briefly, "I'm talking to Bill."

"No accounting for tastes." Lorna had taken a step nearer and was now standing in the doorway of the byre.

"Come on, Bill, come on." Mary Ann, her voice low and wheedling, was still persisting with her coaxing, and as she did so she wondered what had got into Bill and at the same time what Lorna Johnson was doing in the farmyard, because it was no secret that Lorna didn't like animals; she was even afraid of cows.

In the next moment Lorna made it clear why she was in the yard, for taking a very wary step to Mary Ann's side she said in a lowered tone, "Have you seen Tony about?"

Mary Ann's eyes flickered sharply upwards to the heavily made-up face, and her tone was flat and curt as she answered, "No, I haven't."

Lorna gazed steadily down on Mary Ann and then, with a twisted smile breaking the painted moulding of her lips, she said, "And you wouldn't tell me if you had, would you?"

"No, I wouldn't."

"No, I thought you wouldn't . . . you're a blasted little cat."

Mary Ann's face widened with indignation. She did not like Lorna Johnson, she had never questioned Lorna Johnson's feelings towards her, but now she knew them without any doubt. Then Lorna Johnson said something that Mary Ann could not quite take in. She said, "Well, my little madam, your days are running out, and if I can do anything about it I'll help them along, you damned little upstart, you."

All this was delivered in a low tone. The tone even suggested that Lorna could have been saying something quite pleasant, and although Mary Ann could only half understand the implication of the words she realised full well that they were derogatory and she was mad at Lorna Johnson, and she knew that if she didn't get away from her she would cheek her, with the result that she would get walloped. So without more ado she swung away from the girl and, leaving the byre, pushed the door closed after her. This action was merely an off-shoot of her anger combined with the habit of always closing the door when coming out of the byre. It had no premeditation whatever about it. It did cross her mind at this moment that she was leaving Lorna Johnson in there with the bull, and Lorna was afraid of the animal. But she had taken no more than three steps from the byre door when a combination of sounds turned her about so swiftly that she almost leapt from the ground.

She could not tell which she heard first, whether it was the heavy wooden latch dropping into the slot as the door banged, or the ear-piercing screech of Lorna, or the terrible bellow of the bull, but in the next instant she found herself frantically trying to unlatch the door. At other times it had always been quite easy. Though the slot where the wooden latch fell into was deep, the sides were smooth and lifting the latch was a simple matter of a second, or it had been until this moment. Whether the latch had actually stuck or it was the terrifying sound of Lorna and the bull apparently trying to out-yell each other, Mary Ann found that she couldn't get the latch out of its socket.

Then, on the point of screaming herself, she felt her body lifted from the ground, and as she hung dangling from a great hand she saw the latch being swung up and the door pulled open. And as her feet touched the ground again she saw Lorna staggering into the yard, her mouth wide and the screams still issuing from it.

"It's all right, it's all right. There, you're all right." It was Mr. Johnson's voice shouting above his daughter.

"Sh . . . sh . . . she lo . . . locked me in. Sh . . . sh . . . she . . . lo . . . lo . . . locked . . ."

"All right, you're all right. . . . She did, did she? You . . . you blasted little swine!"

It was Mary Ann who now screamed. She screamed as Mr. Johnson's hands gripped her shoulders. Then for the next second or so she did not know where she was, she only knew she was being shaken and thought her head would fly off at any minute. She was gasping and choking so much that she couldn't get her yells out. And then she felt as if she was being pulled in two. Her feet touched the ground and she fell on to her bottom with a plop. Before her bouncing vision she now saw her da facing Mr. Johnson.

She saw her da's fist go out and Mr. Johnson's arms flaying, then Mr. Johnson fell down, and as he hit the ground he gave an awful cry. It was this last cry, with its high screeching quality, that outdid both Lorna's and her own screams and the bull's roaring and caused a blackness to surround Mary Ann. Although she could see nothing she could still hear voices, and before she fainted away she was aware that the yard was full of voices, among them her mother's and Tony's. . . .

She rose struggling out of the thick blackness to find herself on the couch in the kitchen, with her mother bending over her, saying, "Drink this." But she couldn't make herself drink. As her da was wont to say when he was very tired, "I haven't got the list to lift a hand," so she felt now. She could scarcely lift her eyelids to look at her mother, but even the little she saw of her was enough to convey dimly to her that her mother was vexed, even angry, and she had the feeling for a moment that she wanted to pass out again, to escape from the look. But the sensation of fainting was still so near to her that she rejected this idea and lay still. With the passing moments she became more aware of what was taking place about her, and when her mother said again, "Drink this," she drank from the cup, then lay back and closed her eyes.

She was aware from time to time of her mother and Michael and Tony whispering, but she was too tired to make an attempt to listen. That was, until she heard Mr. Lord speaking. She didn't know if his voice was coming from the far end of the kitchen or outside the house, but she heard him say plainly, "Nice state of affairs, Shaughnessy. The man's ankle is broken as clean as if you had cut it with an axe."

"Should have been his neck."

"Well, he has his own opinion on that. He tells me you struck at him first."

"Who's denying it? He was shaking her like a rat."

"It's understandable when you give it a little thought. The man was upset about his daughter. I myself would not like to have been locked in that place with Neptune."

Neptune? It was William. Or was it? Faintly she remembered the unusual roar of William. Eeh! It couldn't have been Neptune. She herself would never go near Neptune. . . . And then another thought, weak yet gathering strength of conviction; she hadn't locked her in . . . she hadn't locked Lorna Johnson in, that was a lie.

Then Mr. Lord's voice came again, "There will be an outcome of this business; that man'll make trouble."

"Let him."

"What are you going to do for someone in his place?"

"I'll manage."

A few minutes later she felt forced to open her eyes, and there above her she saw the thin, wrinkled face of Mr. Lord, and in an odd intuitive way she realised that for all his stiffness and the sound of his voice he wasn't mad about the business, not really mad. But her da was mad, as was her ma.

"Are you feeling better?"

"Yes."

"Do you think you're able to talk?"

"Yes."

"What induced you to lock that girl in the bull-pen?"

"I didn't." She would have liked to take her denial further but she hadn't . . . got the list.

"They say you did."

"I pushed the door as I was going out . . . the latch must have dropped . . . it was stuck."

"Why was that girl in the bull-pen, anyway?"

Mary Ann was aware for the first time that Tony was standing at the bottom of the couch, and she looked at him and back to Mr. Lord and then towards where her ma and da were standing, and she closed her eyes and her mother's voice said, "Don't make her talk any more just now, Mr. Lord. Please. We'll go into this tomorrow."

It was a short time later, when upstairs in her bedroom Lizzie was undressing Mary Ann, that she uttered a sharp exclamation and, going to the door, she called softly, "Mike, here a minute."

When her da came into the room her mother was standing behind her but she knew she was pointing to her shoulders. She did not know if there were any marks on her shoulders, she only knew that they were paining her, and her neck was so stiff that she could hardly turn her head. Her da's words came on a deep, low tone, as he said, "What did I tell you? He was shaking her as if he was going to throttle her, and it looks as if he almost done it." His face came down to hers and he said gently now, "Does your back hurt, hinnie?"

"Me neck does, Da."

"Aye." he patted her cheek. "Your ma'll rub it for you and it'll be all right in the mornin'." And now he turned to Lizzie and said, "And you go off the deep end because I hit him."

"Well"—Lizzie was speaking quietly now—"all this to happen after a day like I've had . . . waiting . . . waiting."

"Your mother didn't turn up?"

"No."

"Any word why she didn't?"

"No."

"Huh! Then that's a pleasure we've to look forward to."

"And your day off wasted." Lizzie was pulling the clothes up under Mary Ann's chin as she made this statement, and Mary Ann saw a touch of lightness come to her da's face as he looked at her and said, "Well, I wouldn't say that, not entirely. We had a nice time, didn't we, Mary Ann?"

She tried to nod her head but it was too painful, so she gave him a little smile. She had looked forward all the way home in the bus to telling her mother about the meeting with Mrs. Quinton, but that would have to wait until another time.

5

MRS. McMULLEN

Sunday morning found Mary Ann back on the couch in the kitchen; her neck was so stiff that she could hardly move it, and her shoulders were very painful . . . and all black and blue. She had managed to turn her head sufficiently to see a little of the result of Mr. Johnson's big hands. Her mother had been for her staying in bed, but she felt too shut out from everything up there and had begged to be allowed to lie on the couch in the kitchen. But up to now it hadn't proved very pleasant, she was not being treated in the light of an invalid. Their Michael had started things off just before he took his departure for Mass by remarking with a wide shake of his head, "By! I wonder what you'll trigger off next. You're the limit, the outside limit. You've got more power for trouble in you than ten atom bombs."

"I didn't do anything, our Michael; it wasn't me. I told me ma; didn't I, Ma?" She appealed to Lizzie's unresponsive back. "Lorna Johnson was looking for Tony, and because I couldn't tell her where he was she swore at me and I went out and banged the door." She paused. "And the latch dropped and got stuck. It wasn't me."

"She had a different story. She says you called her in to see the bull, then ran out and shut the door on her."

"Oh, the big liar!"

"That's enough of that talk, Mary Ann."

"But, Ma . . ."

"Enough, I said."

Then Michael had gone to Mass and her mother had gone about the business of preparing the Sunday dinner in a silence which indicated her worried state. Mary Ann sat until nearly dinner-time getting more and more bored, unable to concentrate on reading, and fed-up with the pain in her neck. She wished somebody would come in . . . anybody. Although she hadn't outlined the Sacred Heart on her breast her wish was granted within a matter of minutes. And it brought her upright with such a painful jerk that she brought out, "Ooh! Oh, Ma!" and her voice trailed away on a sound akin to a groan as her grannie's voice came from the back-door saying, "Anybody at home?"

Lizzie was at the oven with her back bent and she seemed to hold the position for a long time although she had closed the oven door, and then she straightened up and looked across the room to where her mother stood in the kitchen doorway, dressed in her Sunday best.

"Well, the place looks as lively as a morgue; not a soul to be seen, only that lad Len. Where's everybody?"

"Oh . . . oh, come in, Mother. Oh, they're about. Michael's gone to Mass." Lizzie pulled a chair from under the table and said, "Sit down. Let me have your hat."

Mrs. McMullen, placing her handbag on the table and slowly taking the pins from her high, black, satin-draped hat, looked towards the couch and Mary Ann and made a cryptic remark. "Aye! aye!" she said.

"I was expecting you yesterday, Mother. I thought you might be ill."

"No, I'm all right, never been fitter. Somebody came in and I couldn't get away. What's wrong with that one?" She nodded towards the couch as if Mary Ann was a deaf-and-dumb

mute who had to be alluded to objectively, and without waiting for Lizzie to reply she
handed her her hat and coat and, ignoring the chair that Lizzie had offered, took the one
nearest the fire, Mike's particular chair, and sat down.

Lizzie, going towards the hall to deposit her mother's clothes, remarked, "She had a fall."

"Aye, I heard about it."

Lizzie must have thrown the clothes on to the hall table, for she was back in the kitchen
within a second, saying, "You've heard about it? You've been quick, haven't you?" Her
voice was curt.

"No, not that you'd notice. I came along the road with that Len. He told me there'd been
the devil's figgarties on here last night. He said she'd . . ." there was a bouncing of the head
in Mary Ann's direction, "that she'd locked a lass in with a savage bull and the girl's nearly
gone off her rocker, and her father and the noble Mike went at it. And now her father's in
hospital with a broken leg and his face all bashed in."

"Nonsense; he hasn't got a broken leg, it's just his ankle. And his face isn't bashed in."

"Well, that's what I heard. I'm only repeating what I heard. And don't shout at me,
Lizzie. I've only just got in; don't let us start right away."

As Mrs. McMullen took a neatly folded handkerchief from the pocket of her skirt and,
shaking it out, wiped the end of her nose, Lizzie turned towards the table, raising her eyes
ceilingwards as she did so. Then, muttering under her breath, "I won't be a minute," she left
the kitchen and Mary Ann at the mercy of her grannie . . . Or was it the other way about?

The combat would have been equal had Mary Ann been feeling fit, but she was
feeling . . . bad. She knew that her mother had gone out to warn her da about the visitor,
and she guessed, and rightly, that her grannie had said she was coming yesterday to
hoodwink her da, knowing that he would dodge her if he could. She looked now to where
her grannie was sitting, her gimlet eyes sending their light across the room, a light which held
no trace whatever of affection, and like a young wounded polecat she waited for the old,
healthy, wily, ageless cobra to strike. It did.

"Quite a while since you had your name in the papers, isn't it?"

Mary Ann said nothing.

"Must be on three years ago since the country heard of your exploits, when you ran away
from that convent. Sussex it was, wasn't it? You got your name on the wireless that
time. . . . You've been quiet for a long spell. Most unnatural. . . . Do you know, if the bull
had killed that girl they could have hung you?"

On occasions such as this, and there had been a number, and with the same opponent,
Mary Ann became vividly aware that she possessed bowels and that there were a lot of
them, for the feeling her grannie engendered in her would run up and down and back and
forwards all over her stomach. It was an almost indescribable feeling, being a mixture of
sickness, aggressiveness, loathing, and desire. It was the ingredient of desire which was at
the forefront of her mind at the moment, and she was wishing the old wish yet once again.
Oh, if only her grannie would drop down dead. Remembering what Father Owen had said
to her on Thursday night about wishes always coming home to roost, she turned her eyes
quickly from her grannie's face, and the movement caused a momentary excruciating pain
in her neck, and she was reminded of her grannie's words about hanging. But she did not
put her hands to her neck, she clapped them on her stomach.

"I shouldn't worry about getting into the paper though, for you'll be in soon enough by
the sound of things. That Len said that the man is going to take an action against yer father
so he'll have to go to court and you along with him. You'll be in print once more, and that
should satisfy you."

For once Mary Ann could make no rejoinder, she was feeling awful; her stomach felt as if
it was doing somersaults.

"Cat got yer tongue? Or have you realised you've gone too far with this latest escapade and this'll be the finish of you? I wouldn't be surprised if the man claims so much damages that it'll be the finish of him an' all."

Him did not refer to Mr. Johnson, Mary Ann knew; *him* was her da, and she was stung to retort, "It wasn't me da's fault. And it wasn't mine either. So there. Len wasn't there and he knows nothing about it. You're always on and trying to make————"

"Mary Ann!" It was her mother speaking as she came into the kitchen. And her grannie's hurt and indignant tone followed up with, "Oh, don't stop her, she's just showing me her convent manners. But as I told you in the first place, it would take more than a convent to refine her. As for making her talk properly, you have a vain hope there. She's me'ing this and me'ing that as much as ever she did. It's money he's putting down the drain all right in this case. He might as well drink it—he'd have some satisfaction out of it, any rate, then."

"Now look here, Mother." Lizzie was standing in front of her mother. "I've told you before, you're welcome to come to my house at any time, but I won't have you here if you're going to create mischief."

Mrs. McMullen looked up at her daughter with a pained, hurt expression, and her voice had almost a break in it as she said, "Well, I like that. I haven't darkened your door for months, and I'm not inside it fifteen minutes and you accuse me of making trouble. Well, I can go the same way as I come; get me my hat and coat. . . ."

As she half rose from the chair Lizzie said, "Don't be silly, I'm only telling you. I don't want any trouble one way or the other."

"Well, who's making it? I just open my mouth and make a statement and somebody jumps down my throat." She did not name the someone but flickered her eyes towards the couch. "And if there's any complaining to do I can do my share of it. Here I've come all this way and you've never offered me a cup of tea."

Lizzie sighed. "The dinner'll be on the table in a few minutes, Mother. . . . All right, I'll make you a cup of tea. Or would you rather have a glass of cider or ginger beer?"

"I'll have a cup of tea if you don't mind, please." The tone was definite.

Mary Ann watched her mother walk with quick steps to the kitchen. She watched her grannie, after meeting her glance, turn her eyes haughtily away and, leaning her head against the high back of the chair, close her lids as if intending to sleep. Mary Ann, too, lay back against the head of the couch and waited. As she knew her grannie was waiting, waiting until Mike should come in before she started again.

It was nearly half an hour later when they all sat down to dinner, for Lizzie had had to go for Mike at least three times, and when he eventually entered the kitchen he looked towards Mrs. McMullen and his voice was airy and his glance held nothing out of the ordinary when he said, "Hullo there."

Mrs. McMullen did not return the greeting, not verbally at any rate, but inclined her head stiffly towards him.

The first part of the meal was passed over in deceptive friendliness. Mrs. McMullen addressed her remarks to Michael. Mrs. McMullen liked her grandson, and at one time he had liked her, but not so much now, and his answers to her questions about his school career were of such a nature as to have little personal touch in them at all. So the conversation was kept moving mainly between Michael and his grandmother.

It was at the point where Lizzie was asking "Does anyone want any more meat?" that Mrs. McMullen brought up the subject of horses. It was as if the roast sirloin had in some way reminded her of horses, for she said, "I suppose you know you've got riding stables opened up not far away?"

"Oh yes." Lizzie nodded at her mother. "They've been going about three months now. It's a young fellow that's running them. I hear he's doing well."

"Yes, he is." Mrs. McMullen had attacked her fresh supply of sirloin and she kept her eyes directed towards her plate as she made the remark, and it brought the eyes of the others on her as she knew it would.

"Do you know him?" Lizzie's fork was poised halfway to her mouth.

"Yes, yes, I know him. He's young Eddie Travers, Mrs. Flannagan's youngest brother."

"Oh no." Lizzie's voice sounded most dismal at this news and Mary Ann, looking at her mother, wondered why she should be so affected by it. She herself was always in some way affected by the name of Flannagan, especially if it had Sarah before it, but why her mother should sound like that she didn't know. That was, not until her da's head went back and he made huh-ing sounds before dropping his head forward again and looking directly at her, saying, "Well, that's exploded your birthday surprise."

"Oh, Mike, be quiet!"

"What's the use? Can you see her going taking riding lessons there alongside Miss Sarah Flannagan? They fought in the gutter afore, and there's no reason to think they'll stop if they're on horses. We don't want any horse combats and one or the other breaking their necks."

Mary Ann was looking at Lizzie now and her eyes were full of disappointment. This then had been the big surprise for her birthday that her mother had hinted at, to take riding lessons. And now it was all nipped in the bud because the man was Sarah Flannagan's uncle. Yet it wasn't against Sarah Flannagan she felt embittered at this moment, but against her grannie. If her grannie hadn't said anything she would likely have gone to the stables and started, and once having started she would have kept on. But now with the knowledge that she was almost sure to run into Sarah, who might already be a horsewoman of some repute—she had a mental vision of Sarah mounted on a large bay, leaping over all the farm gates—she couldn't run that risk! Oh! Her grannie! Her teeth went straight through the crust top of a baked potato . . . her grannie!

But her grannie had only just begun, she did not show the real reason for her visit until they reached the applie pie and custard. Then her remark-cum-question brought Mary Ann head up so swiftly that she winced at the pain of her neck as her grannie said, apropos of nothing that had gone before, "Have you heard the latest about Bob Quinton?"

"Bob?" Lizzie looked full at her mother. "No, what is it? Has he retired out of the fortune he's made from building?"

"No, it's nothing to do with building. But he's retired all right . . . from his wife." Mrs. McMullen's round eyes rested now on her daughter and she added, "It shouldn't surprise you; it didn't me. I've been waitin' for it practically since the day he married."

"Yes, I can understand that." Mike's words were slow and definite and brought his mother-in-law's gaze not on to him but directed towards her plate again.

"I don't believe it. Where did you hear that?" There was a worried note in Lizzie's voice. "It's just gossip. People will say anything, especially when a couple are happy."

"What makes you think they were happy?" Mrs. McMullen's small eyes seemed to spring open and upwards towards her daughter. "They never struck me like that. As for any truth in it, it's true all right because he told me himself."

"But why?" Lizzie's hands were resting on the table now.

"Because she's a piece, that's why. He could never be happy with a woman like that. Her, a painted————"

"She's not! She's a nice woman, she's beautiful."

"Mary Ann! Stop that!" Although Lizzie's tone was sharp there was also bewilderment expressed in it. And her bewilderment grew as she looked at Mike as he said, "Leave her alone, Liz." Mike's voice was low and even. "She's only speaking the truth. It's as she says. Connie Quinton's a nice woman, a beautiful woman, and personally I would say that's an understatement."

"What do you know about her?" Mrs. McMullen's tone was scathing, but Mike answered her with irritating calmness. There was even a touch of laughter in his voice as he replied, "Well, dear Mother-in-law, more than you think. For your information we had coffee together yesterday morning."

"Ha! ha! ha!" The ha-ha's were merely an imitation of mirth and Mrs. McMullen followed them up with, "That's the laugh of the week, that is. You havin' coffee with Connie Quinton. My! my! That'll be the day."

"He did then. We both had coffee with her and me da and her talked a long time. And she liked him, and she's going to call . . . see!"

"There now, what d'you make of that, eh?" Mike had risen to his feet and had pushed his chair back and was standing looking down at Mrs. McMullen, with a superior smile twisting his lips. "That's something for you to set the town on fire with, eh? Connie Quinton likes me. Me, Mike Shaughnessy. And she's going to call. Now what d'you make of that, eh? You'd better get on your hat and coat as quick as you can and tell Bob that bit. Go on now. But before you go don't forget to tell Liz"—he lifted his eyes to his wife's amazed face—"don't forget to tell Liz that you knew this was going to happen and that I'd go off with another woman; in fact you've known I've been carrying on for years, in fact that's why Bob and her split up."

"I'll not stay in this house and be insulted."

"No, I wouldn't. And if you hurry you'll just catch the bus at the corner. And, anyway, you'll be quite happy to go, won't you, for you've said all you came to say. Only it didn't have the reaction you hoped for, did it? Ah, well, knowing you, you'll think up something else before very long." Mike turned from the infuriated glance of his mother-in-law, to turn back leisurely again, adding, "Oh, and when you're talking to Bob, tell him it's Durrant's we go to."

Without even casting a glance in Lizzie's direction, Mike now walked out of the kitchen and through the scullery, and they all listened as the back door closed, not with a bang, but just in the ordinary way.

The kitchen was left in a deep, numbing silence. Mary Ann's mind was as full of bewilderment as her mother's face. Her da had called Mrs. Quinton Connie. He had only known her name was Connie because Beatrice had said Aunty Connie, but he had spoken as if he had known her for a long time and had been to Durrant's with her every Saturday. What was the matter with her da? As for her grannie . . . She looked towards the disciple of the devil, who, the picture of offended dignity now, was getting into her coat. Oh, if only something would happen to her grannie, something swift, sure and final.

When a few minutes later Mrs. McMullen, putting the finishing touches to the lapels of her coat and adjusting her hat on a dead straight level, addressed her daughter saying, "Well, Liz, it'll be a long time afore I darken your door again, you mark my words on that." Lizzie, standing on the hearth-rug, looked at her mother, and all she said was, "Goodbye, Mother."

"Goodbye."

Mrs. McMullen took three steps across the room towards the door, then turned and asked, "Aren't you comin' to the bus with me?"

"No, Mother, I'm not."

"Well, now I know where I stand. That's a daughter for you. You can work and slave for years, and what do you get? . . . 'No, Mother, I'm not. . . .' What about you, Michael?"

Michael glared at his grannie but his voice was quiet as he said, "I'm sorry, but I'm going out with Tony in the car at two o'clock and it's nearly that now."

"That's a family for you. My God! What is the world coming to? Well, as I said——" She swung round to her daughter and, emphasising her words now with a wag of her finger, she cried, "It'll be a long time afore you'll see me again."

She was gone. Lizzie sat down in the chair by the fire but she didn't speak. The table was littered with dishes, but she made no attempt to clear them away, which in itself was unusual for immediately a meal was finished everything on the table was taken into the scullery.

Mary Ann watched Michael go and stand near her mother and put a tentative hand on her shoulder, saying, "Don't worry, Mother. Anyway, she won't come back for some time now; you've got that to be thankful for. Come on . . ." He gave her shoulder a little shake, then added, "I'll dry up for you before I go."

There were times when Mary Ann liked their Michael, when she liked him very much. She was going to say, "You go and I'll dry up," even knowing that it had come as anything but a pleasant surprise when he had said he was going out with Tony . . . and in the car. But Lizzie, getting to her feet now, said, "I'm all right. Get yourself away and don't be late."

Five minutes later there was only Mary Ann and Lizzie left in the kitchen and the dishes were still on the table, and Lizzie was touching something on the mantelpiece when she said in an off-hand kind of way, "You did have coffee with Mrs. Quinton yesterday morning, then?"

"Yes, Ma."

"Why didn't you tell me before?"

"Well, Ma . . ." Mary Ann paused. "I meant to when I came in, but then . . . then that other thing happened, and this morning my neck was paining and I forgot."

"Yes, yes, I can see that." Lizzie started to move the dishes now and Mary Ann watched her face. It had an odd look on it, a look that she had never seen on her mother's face before, not even when she was worried over her da taking a drop.

The true nature of the look on Lizzie's face was not made clear to Mary Ann until that same night when she was in bed and her ma and da were downstairs together waiting for Michael coming in.

She had strained her ears to the low drone of their voices for the past half-hour but had not been able to make anything out, until her mother's voice, rising suddenly, seemed to force its way up through the floorboards below the bed. It brought her into an upright position.

"Well, you could have mentioned it when we got into bed. Or even this morning."

The words came muffled, and Mary Ann had to bend floorwards to hear them. But there was no need to strain to hear her da's swift reply. "All right, all right, I'm holding something back. I wasn't just turning the tables on you mother. Have it your own way. I'm starting an affair with her. And why not? Why not indeed?" His voice was higher now. "I went through hell for years through you and Bob. And now they're splitting up why shouldn't I chance my arm? And don't be like your mother and say I'll be steppin' out of me class, because that doesn't hold in this day and age. And, what's more, the lass is lonely and I wouldn't have to work very hard to get her to accept some comfort. Now, there you've asked for it and you've got it. Are you satisfied now?"

There followed an awe-filled silence when no words came up through the floor, and Mary Ann, with her face cupped in her hands, stared down towards it, waiting. Her body was once more filled with fear and anxiety and she kept saying to herself, "Oh, Da! Oh, Da!" She knew that her da was being cruel and in a way he was making things up about Mrs. Quinton, and yet there seemed some semblance of truth in what he said. This was brought to her by the picture of her da and Mrs. Quinton sitting looking at each other across the café table. . . . But her da loved her ma; she knew he loved her ma. Then how could he say such awful things? How could he hurt ma by suggesting that he would go off with Mrs. Quinton? The whole situation had turned topsy-turvy. It was Mr. Quinton she had been afraid of coming after her ma again.

Thoughts of Mr. Quinton and her ma led her back to what she had overheard while standing in the brush cupboard last Saturday afternoon, and there seemed a similarity between what Mrs. Quinton had said about the row she had had with her husband and her da and ma going at it in the kitchen now. Or was it what Mrs. Willoughby had said? Mrs. Willoughby had said, "I know you, Connie; you keep on and on." And that's what her ma had been doing, keeping on and on.

And when she heard the back-door bang Mary Ann knew that her da was doing what Mr. Quinton had done, walking out. But her da would go no farther than the farm. Or would he go walking round thinking of Mrs. Quinton and then . . .

She was out of bed and down the stairs within a matter of seconds.

Lizzie was sitting at the kitchen table, her face buried in the crook of her elbow, and though she made no sound Mary Ann knew that she was crying bitterly.

"Ma. Oh, Ma!"

Lizzie's head came up with a start, but she did not look at her daughter; she kept her face turned away as she said, "Now what do you want? You should be in bed."

"Ma, Mrs. Quinton doesn't want . . ."

Lizzie was on her feet glowering now. "Get back to bed. You'll keep your ears open once too often, milady. Go on upstairs this minute with you. And don't let me hear you mention Mrs. Quinton's name in this house again. Do you hear?"

Mary Ann, her head drooped, turned away and walked slowly upstairs. She had been going to tell her ma that Mrs. Quinton didn't want her da, she only wanted Mr. Quinton. She had been going to tell her what she had heard from the brush cupboard, but Lizzie's manner had indicated to her plainly that she had taken a dislike to Mrs. Quinton and that being so it was not likely that she would believe anything nice about her.

As Mary Ann stood at her bedroom window and looked out on to the dark shape of the farmyard, screwing up her eyes in the hope of catching a glimpse of her da, she knew that the three years of peace had suddenly slid out of life as if they had never been, and the old pattern had returned. It only wanted her da to go and get . . . she halted her mind on the thought. She would not even think that it only wanted Mike to go and get drunk for life to be as it was.

Her eyes lifted from the yard to the sky and in a vague way she realised she was changing, and the realisation was forced upon her by the clarity with which she was seeing the position between her parents and the Quintons. And she was saddened by the knowledge that the more people loved, the more intensely could they hurt and be hurt, and as she turned from the window and groped her way to the bed she wished with a deep solemn wish that she need never grow up.

6

MR. LORD LOOKS AHEAD

On the following morning Mary Ann came downstairs feeling like nothing on earth. When she was in bed her ma had asked her how she felt and she said, "All right," but now she was up her neck was paining her and, what was most unusual, she didn't want to go to school.

On entering the kitchen she was going to tell her mother this when she was stopped by the sight of Tony. He was already dressed for the office, and he was talking to her da and did not pause to look at her when she entered the room but went on saying, "And the latest is,

I've got to promise I won't marry for five years . . . or else. I have no intention of marrying yet awhile, but to make such a promise is another thing."

"Oh, it's all on account of this Lorna business. I wouldn't lay too much stock on what he says at the moment."

Mary Ann noticed that this morning her da did not sound as interested as usual in Tony's problems, from which she gathered that her ma and him hadn't made it up. But her ma's voice was kind, even gentle, when, looking at her, she asked, "Is your neck paining you now?"

"Yes, Ma, It's very sore."

"Well, you'd better not go to school this morning."

"All right, Ma."

Tony caught her attention again but not very strongly as he said to Mike, "And when I said to him, 'And I suppose you'll want to pick who I'm to marry?' he said quite flatly, 'Yes, you can rest assured that'll be more than likely.' " She found she couldn't work up the interest the situation between Tony and Mr. Lord warranted. The pain in her neck was making her feel a bit sick and there was the business of her ma and da.

Lizzie bent over Mary Ann now, saying, "Aren't you going to eat your cereal?"

"No, Ma. I don't want anything."

On this Mike spoke to Lizzie without looking at her. "You'd better get her to the doctor's," he said.

"Yes, that would be a wise move at this point." On Tony's words Mike looked at him enquiringly but did not speak, and Tony, taking his glance from Mike for a moment, said, "That's really why I popped in, to warn you. They're going to take the matter to court."

"What!" The exclamation came from Lizzie.

"Yes," said Tony. "They are going to make it assault and loss of work for both of them." His voice was very low as he gave this information, and Lizzie, perhaps for the first time that morning, looked at her husband. Mike did not return the look, but his head went up and he said, "Let them. Let them do their damndest. I've got a case to put an' all." Then his chin coming in, he turned his head sharply to Tony and demanded, "You still seeing that one?"

"No I'm not, Mike." Tony spoke definitely. "She made it her business last night to waylay me and she gave me this information, hoping, I think, that I'd try to persuade her father not to take any measures against you. But you know what that would mean, don't you, and I thought you'd rather have things as they stand now."

"Aye, damn, yes. Don't you go putting your head into a noose because of me. You did right there. And take my advice and give her a clear road."

"Well, once they've left the place it won't be difficult, but at the moment I seem to stumble over her at every step I take. I'm sorry about all this, Mike; it's really my fault, as you said, taking her out in the first place."

Mary Ann felt no relief at Tony's changed attitude towards Lorna Johnson. Even the prospect of being taken to court did not reach the gigantic proportions of the situation that was now in existence between her parents. The situation that spread its atmosphere through the kitchen and which could be felt by everybody, Tony and Michael included, for Tony now took his leave without the usual cheery goodbye, and Michael ate his breakfast in a questioning silence that caused his eyes to flicker every now and again between his parents.

From the window of his office Mike saw Mary Ann and Lizzie pass the gate. Mary Ann looked into the farmyard but not Lizzie, her gaze was directed straight ahead, and Mike said, "Blast, damn and blast." What he wanted to do was dash after them, pull Lizzie round to him, look into her eyes and say, "Aw lass, come on, come on. Now ask yourself, now ask yourself, is there anybody on God's earth for me but you?" He had said similar words to her three years ago when she had got worked up over the Polinski girl. It was odd, but he had never given her cause to be jealous. That was one thing he hadn't got on his conscience. Now he himself had had cause to be jealous, for at one time Bob Quinton was never off the doorstep, waiting for the moment she was going to walk out. He rubbed his hand roughly around his face. He supposed he shouldn't have said what he did to the old girl yesterday, it must have sounded a bit odd. But the chance to get one over on that old devil had been too much for him. He realised he had made more out of his acquaintance with Mrs. Quinton than was necessary, and he wouldn't for the world have done it if he had thought Liz was going to take it the way she had. He expected her to laugh over it. But then he should have had the sense to know that women don't laugh at the same things as men. The trouble was that once this kind of rift got hold you never knew where it would end. In some cases it split the lives in two with the shock of an earthquake, in others it just spread unobtrusively like a malignant disease, until one morning you woke up petrified with what had hit you.

His elbows on the desk, he brought his head on to his good hand, and it was in this position that Mr. Lord came upon him and said abruptly, "Hullo, what's the matter? Under the weather?"

Mike got hastily to his feet, answering as he did so, "No, sir. I just happened to be thinking for a minute."

The old man stared into Mike's big face, his eyes narrowed and penetrating. He stared until Mike, moving uneasily, asked, "Anything up, sir?"

"That's what I would like to hear from you."

"Me? I don't know what you're getting at. Are you referring to Saturday night's business?"

"No, I'm not referring to Saturday night's business. I happen to be referring to the situation between you and your wife."

Every feature in Mike's face became stiff, but before he could make any retort Mr. Lord put in, "And don't tell me it isn't any of my business. If you shout your business loud enough for people coming to your door to hear what is being said, it is no longer your own business."

"What are you talking about?" Mike's expression was now one of bewilderment.

"I happened to call on you last evening for the purpose of enquiring if Tony had returned home. You were going at it so hard that I heard every word you said when I was yards away from the door. . . . This woman Connie Quinton, what about her?"

Mike seemed to reach half his height again and there was quite an interval before he spoke, and then his words came low and dangerously deep as he said, "Now look you here, sir, I'm not unaware of what I owe you, and I repay you with my work from dawn, many days until dusk. Aye and later. And I repay you with my loyalty and with trying to save every shilling I can for you. But there you have all my life you have any right to; the rest is my concern. Do you hear me sir? What happens behind them walls over there——" He now worked his thumb vigorously over his shoulder. "——what happens within them walls concerns me and my wife."

Mr. Lord was staring fixedly at Mike all the time he was speaking, and now his gaze dropped away for a moment as he said in an extraordinarily calm tone, "I've always admired you for one thing, Shaughnessy: you speak your mind. And I had found that you speak the truth. But you can't intimidate me with this manner of yours about the sanctity of your married life. Your wife is troubled. I like your wife, she's a very fine woman, and I don't want to see you playing ducks and drakes——"

"Look, sir." Mike was trying to keep his temper under control. "This is all a mountain out of a mole-hill."

"It didn't sound like that to me. Nor would it have done so to anyone else who was passing your house last night. It sounded as if you were having an affair with this woman and your wife had found out. Is she, by any chance, the wife of Quinton the builder . . . my builder?" He motioned his head in the direction of his house.

"Yes, she is. And I'm not having an affair with her." Mike paused to draw in breath through his teeth. "God in Heaven, I met the woman on Saturday morning in a café when Mary Ann and I went in for a cup of coffee. I'd never clapped eyes on her before. She happens to be the aunt of Mary Ann's school pal. We spoke for ten minutes or so, and that's the beginning and end of it as far as I'm concerned. Look, sir"—Mike's voice became slow and patient sounding—"it was like this . . ."

For the next few minutes Mike explained what had occurred on Mrs. McMullen's visit yesterday, and the explanation seemed to satisfy Mr. Lord. It even seemed to give him some slight amusement, for the muscles of his face twitched as he listened. And when Mike had finished he said, "Well, if that's the case you must make it up with Mrs. Shaughnessy and let's have no more of this. We've enough trouble on our hands without domestic ones. Now about Johnson." He jerked his head in a bird-like fashion before going on. "The wife has just been up to me. She means to make the most out of it. They're taking the matter to a solicitor. That means court, unless you come to some arrangement and pay what they ask. Have you any money saved?"

"About ninety pounds."

"Huh! Well, that won't go far. If it reaches court those sharks'll have that in the first lick if you lose; and let me tell you, as I see things you are likely to. Blast the man! And his family!" Mr. Lord's face now became stiff, as did his voice, as he went on, "I never liked him from the day he came. . . . Now don't say it. Don't say it. I know I engaged him myself, but I still maintain I've never liked him, and the sooner he's gone the better. The sooner they're all gone the better. As things stand I think it's just as well he's taking the matter to court because if he didn't he would expect to carry on here as usual, and I don't want him here. I want them gone as soon as possible. You understand?"

"Yes, sir, I understand?"

Mr. Lord turned and looked away from Mike and out of the office window, and now he said, "You seem to do a lot of talking to Tony, and him to you. What does he think about this girl?" The last two words were rapped out.

"I don't think you need worry in that direction—that is, if you don't pull the reins too tight. He's a man, he's not a lad any longer, and you've got to recognise this and let him go his own road."

Mr. Lord swung his gaze from the window on to Mike, repeating as he did so, "Own road? That's just what I won't let him do, and finish at a dead end. That's where young men finish who are let go their own road. Dead ends. Look, Shaughnessy, I'm going to speak frankly to you. There are very few people whom I can say that to, but you're concerned in this particular matter as much as I am. . . . Yes, you can look surprised, but whatever tight rein I hold on him will ultimately be for your benefit as well as my own, you and yours. Do you follow me?"

Mike's eyes were screwed up as he peered at the old man and he said quietly now, "No, sir, I'm afraid I don't. I can't very well see what Tony's future has got to do with me."

"I said you and yours." The two men were staring at each other, and in the silence that fell on them could be heard the lowing of the cows in the byre and the purring of a tractor in a far field. And then Mr. Lord said, "Little girls grow up. In five years' time Mary Ann will be seventeen. Now do you understand me?"

Yes. Yes, Mike understood and he was shocked with his understanding. The shock was overlaying his surprise and was so great that for a moment he couldn't speak. And Mr. Lord said, "My life went wrong. I've had very few interests in my time, that is until I met your child, and from then things seemed to happen to me—I built a house where I had never intended building a house, then Tony came and everything was completely changed. I'm old, but not too old still to have desires and dreams, and my main desire, my one dream, is to see that my grandson gets the right woman. You should take it as a compliment, Shaughnessy, that I'm picking on your daughter, for, after all, she's two-thirds you. But I see that it isn't affecting you that way. Now, now"—he raised his hand firmly in front of Mike's face—"don't say it. Not now, for you'll likely tell me you'd see me in hell first before you would let me have my own way. Well, that is what I'd expect you to say, but I don't want to hear it. The only thing I'm asking you is to remember that I trust you, and as yet Tony must know nothing of this. I'll tell him when the time is ripe. Now I must away." He looked at his watch, and without any word of goodbye he left Mike with a face as red as his hair. . . .

Mike slowly sat down on the office stool. He couldn't find words, not even strong ones, to use as an exclamation to fit the old man's audacity. After a moment he said to himself: "What can you say?" A few minutes ago he had been worrying about the state of affairs between him and Liz, and now here it had been told to him, and by no other than the old boy himself, who was worth God knows what, that he proposed keeping his grandson and heir free until Mary Ann was of an age to marry. It was fantastic. But even "fantastic" didn't seem to fit the situation. It was somehow . . . shocking, even indecent in a way. Mary Ann, a child of twelve, well, near thirteen, and Tony already twenty-three. How would Tony take it when he found out what was in the old man's mind? Pack up and go off—and likely marry the first girl that came his way just to show the old boy who was master of his fate. And who could blame him?

And then there was Mary Ann. How would she react in five years' time? Would she be a different Mary Ann? Of one thing he was certain: she wouldn't be so changed that if she wanted Tony and he was still available there would be no obstacle she wouldn't remove to have him. But, on the other hand, if she didn't want Tony nobody on God's earth would be able to make her take him. The odds seemed to lie with Mary Ann.

Mike raised his head and looked out of the open doorway to where in the far distance a cloud of dust coming down the hill indicated that Mr. Lord was on his way to town. Yet it wasn't of the old man that Mike thought as he watched the car disappear, but strangely it was of Corny Boyle. Mary Ann, used as she was now to Tony, and acquainted with the gracious living that was the daily routine in the house on the hill, also mixing daily with the class that she met in the convent, had asked to her party Corny Boyle. Yes, the decision would lie with Mary Ann.

This was a very relieving thought, and it pushed Mike's head back and he smiled and gave a relieved ha-ha of a laugh before getting up from the stool and going about his work.

No bones broken, was the doctor's report on Mary Ann. The pain in her neck was from the bruises, about which he remarked that it looked as if she had been clutched by a gorilla.

Mary Ann repeated the doctor's remark to Mike at dinner-time and he said, "We must remember that."

Mary Ann was puzzled by Mike's attitude when she returned home. He wasn't mad any more and he was making an effort to get her ma round. But this appeared to be fruitless. At odd times during their dinner she found him looking at her, not the way he did when he was vexed or yet pleased, but in a way she couldn't make out.

During the afternoon she felt better, and because of this the time began to drag. She was reluctant to go round the farmyard after Saturday night's business. She had a greater reluctance about paying a visit to Mr. Lord. She did think that she might wander up and talk to Ben. But then she didn't know if Mr. Lord was in or out. So by four o'clock she was wishing heartily for the morrow when she would be back at school again, and thinking of school she decided to go to the main road and meet Michael coming off the bus. This would undoubtedly surprise him, but she was thinking less of that than of the excursion giving her something to do.

She had just gone a short way along the road when she heard the wireless playing. She knew it was the Johnsons' wireless and they would be sitting in the garden with the window open. She hadn't seen any of the Johnsons since Saturday night and she was afraid of meeting them now, yet at the same time she was glad they were in the garden, for she had something to say to Lorna Johnson.

Mrs. Johnson and her daughter were sitting in deck-chairs on the tiny square of lawn below the cottage window. Mrs. Johnson was knitting and Lorna was reclining with her hands behind her head. That was, until she caught sight of Mary Ann, when she sat bolt upright. Mrs. Johnson, too, sat upright, and putting the knitting on the grass, she rose to her feet and walked a few steps to the railings that separated her from Mary Ann, and over them she greeted her with, "You! You damned little bitch! You know what I'd like to do with you?"

Mary Ann stopped in the middle of the road and looked at Mrs. Johnson. You weren't supposed to answer grown-ups back, so, taking her eyes from Mrs. Johnson's angry dark face, she looked to where Lorna was still sitting in the chair and she said quietly, "I didn't lock you in with the bull, and I never asked you into the byre. You know I didn't. You came in yourself, you know you did. You were looking for——"

"Shut up your mouth and get yourself on your way before I forget meself and slap the face off you." Mrs. Johnson looked as if she could carry out her threat any minute, and Mary Ann, who was backing away and looking at Mrs. Johnson now, said, "Well, I didn't lock her in; it's all lies."

"Yes, you did." Lorna had joined her mother. "Ooh! You little rat, when I think what you've done!" Lorna's lips were wide apart and her teeth were tightly clenched, and it looked for the moment as if she were going to have another screaming fit, when her mother commanded sharply, "That's enough. Say no more, keep it for the court. Go on, get yourself away, you." Mrs. Johnson flung her arm wide as if to swipe Mary Ann from the face of the earth, and Mary Ann turned and got herself away and in a hurry. She was trembling and more than a little afraid. The viciousness of the Johnson woman was something that she hadn't encountered before.

When she came within sight of the main road but still some way off she recognised the boy standing on the verge near the main road as their Michael, for his future was similar to that of her da, only in smaller proportions. But what brought her almost to a stop was the fact that Michael was not alone. He was standing talking to a girl, and the girl was sitting on a pony with her back to Mary Ann.

Mary Ann had never seen Michael talking to a girl; Michael didn't like girls. Her step became slower, her curiosity deepened. Their Michael knew a girl with a horse. His prestige mounted . . . until she came silently within a few yards of them and they, still intent with each other, did not hear her coming. Even before Mary Ann halted, the amazing revelation was working its way with furious indignation up through her body. The girl on the horse was not in jodhpurs but in jeans, and topping the jeans was a red sweater, and lying down the back of the red sweater was a long black pony-tail of hair. It was the hair style that had decieved her; she would have known that back in a million if it hadn't been for the hair style.

The ferocity of her feelings must have reached the pair in front of her, for as Michael turned his head sharply in Mary Ann's direction Sarah Flannagan swung her slim waist round in the saddle.

In three years Sarah Flannagan had changed mightily. She was a tall, slim girl with attractive dark looks and appeared much older than fourteen. The manner in which she handled the meeting with her life-long enemy bore this out, for with a wry smile on her face she looked down on the diminutive figure and said with disarming casualness, "Hullo, Mary Ann."

It was an approach that would have taken a strong wind out of a galleon's sails and it stumped Mary Ann. Never before had she heard Sarah Flannagan speak in a voice like that to her, or anyone else for that matter. Mary Ann was quick to recognise immediately that gone was the girl who used to taunt her and walk behind her chanting:

> "Swanky Shaughnessy—there she goes:
> Two boss eyes and turned-in toes;
> She cannot even wipe her nose,
> Swanky Shaughnessy—there she goes."

Or the edifying rhyme which went:

> "Pig's belly,
> Wobble Jelly;
> Pig's fat,
> Dirty cat.
> Pig's skin,
> Double chin;
> Pig's cheek,
> Shiny beak.
> Pig's lug,
> Ugly mug—
> And that's Mary Ann Shaughnessy."

But Mary Ann remembered. Yet not because of the insults hurled at herself. Those didn't matter. What did matter was that this girl had been the main taunt of her life where her da was concerned. Had she not written up on the wall for all to see:

MARY ANN SHAUGHNESSY IS A BIG LIAR AND HER DA'S A DRUNKEN NO-GOOD AND EVERYBODY KNOWS IT.

So to Sarah's greeting she answered not at all, but, turning her stiff, indignant glance on her brother, she said, "Our Michael!" and in those two words was conveyed all the recrimination that his disloyalty warranted.

Michael, his face one large blush now, demanded, "What's up with you?"

What could Mary Ann answer to this but, "I'll tell me ma."

"Go on, tell her. Go on, nobody's stopping you."

Mary Ann, floundering now in a situation of which she hadn't time to get the measure, turned her eyes upwards again towards Sarah and with something like the flavour from the old battle-field she demanded, "What you doing here, anyway? This is our place."

"Oh, be your age." This scathing and cool remark brought Mary Ann's chin rearing upwards, but before she could say anything Sarah in a changed tone added, "We are not kids in Burton Street any more; why can't you forget about them days?"

It was as if an adult was chastising her. It was most unsettling and it would have deflated her entirely had she not grasped at one flaw in the seemingly superior poise of her old enemy. Sarah Flannagan had said "them" instead of "those"; she didn't speak properly. Slowly now and with Sister Catherine's tuition well to the fore, she looked directly up into Sarah's face and ejaculated—"said" could never describe her next words—"I-am-bee-ing-my-age, and-no-matter-how-old-I-grow-I-shall-never-forget-what-you-have-said-about . . . my father."

It was as surprising to herself as to her listeners to hear her refer to Mike as "my father." "Me da" was synonymous with her feelings and claim to Mike as a parent; "my father" was a word used by other children for other men.

Sarah, without raising her voice, said, "All right, I'm not denying it."

"Well then!"

"Well then, what about it?"

"You were always a liar."

On this statement a change came over Sarah's face and she looked more recognisable to Mary Ann. In another minute they would have been back on their old footing had not Sarah's desire for peace, instigated, it must be confessed, by her acquaintance with Michael and her hopes for its continuance, made her turn what could have been a damning remark merely into an offensive one by saying, "Well, you could do your share. And, anyway, what I said was true, wasn't it?"

"It wasn't!" The denial was definite.

"Oh, come off it, Mary Ann; you can't hoodwink yourself any more. And what is it, anyway, getting drunk?"

"He didn't. He never got drunk."

"Shut up and don't be so stupid." Michael's indignant tone brought Mary Ann round to him, and Michael, towering over her now, his voice nearly as deep as Mike's, said, "Sarah's right. Be your age. You know he drank like a fish, and would now if it wasn't for——"

"Shut up, you! I'll slap your face, our Michael, if you don't shut up."

Michael shut up, and he boiled with rage as he shut up. It wasn't the knowledge that she had a sore neck and shoulders that kept his hands off her, but he didn't want to make a spectacle of himself in front of Sarah. And now Sarah, from her superior height, poured warm oil on the troubled waters, for she said quickly, "What does it matter about your da drinking; mine drinks like three dry Scotsmen. He has from that Coronation night when he went out with your da. . . . Oh yes"—she laughed down on Mary Ann now—"if you're holding things against people, I should hold that against you, for it was from that night he started drinking, and heavily. But there"—her head wagged—"I don't hold drinking against me da, because he's able to hold his own against me mother now more than he ever did afore and that's a good thing. Me mother's not half the tartar she was."

Mary Ann's face was undergoing alterations, she was staring up at this Sarah Flannagan, at this new Sarah Flannagan, who was saying she didn't mind her da drinking, and was saying that she knew her mother was a tartar. Then Sarah brought Mary Ann's mouth into an even bigger gape when she said, "I'm getting away from home as soon as I can. When I leave school at the end of the summer Burton Street won't see me. I'm coming out here to work in the stables for my uncle—I love horses." She turned her eyes now on the the pony's neck and stroked its mane for a moment before looking down, not on to Mary Ann now, but on to Michael, and saying without any preamble, "I've had 'flu. I'm off school for a week and me uncle lets me exercise the horses if they haven't been out during the day. You can come over any night and help if you like." Then without waiting for Michael's answer she said, "So long now." Flicking her gaze next to Mary Ann, she said, "So long, Mary Ann." With a tap of her heels into the pony's flanks she was off, leaving two strangely disturbed people behind her.

Well, to talk to their Michael like that, to ask him to come and see her like that, pretending that it was to take the horses out. Well! Mary Ann had to find something to dislike this new Sarah Flannagan for. She couldn't, not all in one go, turn the enemy of her life into a friend. Friend! That would be the day. Tolerable acquaintance would be more fitting the mark. And their Michael to talk to her . . . to even want to talk to Sarah Flannagan. And he did—she could tell by his face that he wanted to talk to her. She turned and looked now at her brother, but her brother was looking at the heels of the pony and its rider who was disappearing round the bend of the road, and from his expression Mary Ann knew to her shocked amazement that their Michael was "gone on Sarah Flannagan." Wait until her ma heard that.

It would seem that Michael had heard her thoughts, for he turned on her violently now, saying, "Go on, what's stopping you now; get home and spill the beans. And let me tell you something." He stooped from his height and dug his finger into her narrow chest. "If you were as sensible as Sarah Flannagan you would do; and, what's more, there wouldn't be half the trouble going on—see?"

She had come to meet their Michael off the bus—it had been a nice thought in its origin—and now she had met him, and all she wanted to do was lash out and kick his shins. But, as last night, she realised she was growing older. And now as she watched Michael's indignant back moving swiftly away from her she realised, too, that lashing out and kicking shins as a form of retaliation was also gone. Gone with the years of "Pig's belly: Wobble jelly," with "Swanky Shaughnessy, There she goes," with

> "Boxy, boxy,
> Push it down your socksy;
> Umper, umper, push it up your jumper."

The world was changing, her world was changing, she didn't feel like herself any more. Slowly, and keeping a good distance behind Michael, she made her way home.

What impression Michael's news had on their mother Mary Ann did not know because she hadn't been present when he told her. That he had told her she was positively sure because it was confirmed as soon as her da entered the kitchen, for turning to his father, Michael said, "Da, I've been talking to Sarah Flannagan at the end of the road; is there anything wrong in that?"

Mike looked at his son for a moment, then repeated, "Sarah Flannagan? Here? What's she after?"

"She was exercising one of the ponies—her uncle's ponies."

"Ooh." Mike flicked his eyes in Mary Ann's direction. She was waiting for his glance but could make nothing of it. And then Michael said, "And she's asked me to go along there and help if I want to."

"Do you want to?"

Michael's eyelids flickered before he said, "Well, yes, yes I do."

"Well, there's no reason why you shouldn't, is there? That is if you get your homework done."

Mike and his son looked at each other for a space, and then Mike, with a wry smile to his lips, said, "Enjoy yourself. And it's a good way to start—with horses."

With horses! Her da had said nothing about Sarah Flannagan, nothing that he should say. And her mother had said nothing. People were funny. Everything was very funny at the present time, and it wasn't funny ha-ha either.

7

DIPLOMACY

Almost invariably Mike's mail consisted of bills in thin brown envelopes or of catalogues. The latter he would peruse during breakfast, commenting on their nature to Lizzie with such remarks as: "They are on about immunizing the calves against husk. Better be safe than sorry, I suppose," or "I think I'll try these Conder people for seeds for the barley." But never had Mary Ann known him to read a letter then put it in his pocket, which was what he had just done. The envelope had been typed, she had noticed this as she watched him slit it open, and some change in his expression as he looked at the letter caused her to keep her eyes on him. And when he had finished it she watched him slowly fold it up and place it in his back trouser pocket, for he hadn't a coat on. Her mother, too, had noticed this, and under ordinary circumstances would have said, "What's that about?" But Mary Ann knew that although her mother spoke to her da in front of them she was still . . . not kind with him, and this prevented her from asking about the letter.

Then at the end of breakfast Mike said something that chilled Mary Ann's heart, and her mother's too, for she saw her mother's face turn a greyish colour when her da said, "I'll have to be slipping out this mornin'. I'll go and see to Len and Jonesy and then I'll be off." With this, he pulled on his working coat and left the kitchen.

Mary Ann looked at their Michael, but Michael was looking at their mother, and Lizzie was looking out of the kitchen window watching her husband stride down the path towards the gate.

This was Saturday. Her da had taken his day off yesterday as usual. What had he to go out for . . . into Newcastle for? She felt that Newcastle was his destination. Was he going to see . . .? She would not even say the name to herself, but she saw the face of Mrs. Quinton smiling under her smart white hat and, as always when anxiety hit her, it registered in her stomach and for a moment she felt sick. And her mother felt sick, too. She could tell by her face that she felt sick.

But Lizzie's expression now was nothing compared to the look on her face when, half an hour later, Mike came downstairs dressed in his best suit. He glanced in the mirror and pulled his tie straight before saying, "I'll be off now."

Her face was half turned from him and her voice was low as she asked, "Will you be long?"

"No, I don't suppose so." He bent his head and kissed her cheek and she never moved.

Mary Ann had not asked, "Can I go with you, Da?" It was Saturday morning and she had nothing to do, but she hadn't asked a question that she knew would be useless. And when he went out without bidding her a goodbye she felt as if her world had come to an end. The feeling she was experiencing was even worse than at those times in the past when he had gone out to get full. In a way she knew how to cope with drink, experience had taught her so much, but a woman was different. Mrs. Quinton had said she loved her husband. Then why was she going after her da? Perhaps she wasn't, perhaps the letter wasn't from her. The feeling in Mary Ann's breast held out no hope that she was mistaken. She sat in the kitchen, her face the picture of misery, until some time later Lizzie, turning on her sharply, said, "Don't sit there looking like that, get yourself out to play."

"I don't want to play, Ma. And, anyway, there's nobody to play with."

"Well, go and do something. Do your homework or anything, but don't sit there looking like that."

When Mary Ann got to her feet and stood hesitating whether to go outside or upstairs Lizzie said suddenly, "You can get your things on and go to Mrs. McBride's and take her some eggs and things."

Another time she would have jumped for joy at being allowed to go to Mrs. McBride's, particularly as her mother had been doing her best to keep her away from Mulhattan's Hall and the district. But this morning it brought her no joy. Silently she went upstairs and put on her coat, brushed her hair and was about to tie it back with a ribbon when she remembered the pony-tail hanging down Sarah Flannagan's back. So she left it swinging loose. Then returning to the kitchen, she took the basket from the table and her bus fare from her mother, and without any other word but a dull "Bye-bye, Ma," she left the house.

Coming dolefully to the main road, Mary Ann discovered she had lost the bus she usually took into Jarrow, so she caught the next one. The route was a little longer but would get her there just the same.

She had been travelling in the bus for about fifteen minutes and was passing an open space where a factory was under construction when her interest was quickened by seeing in large letters the name that was actually filling her mind at the moment. It was heading a hoarding which said simply: ROBERT QUINTON—BUILDER AND CONTRACTOR. The hoarding drew her eyes like a magnet and she twisted around in her seat to catch a last glimpse of it.

When she alighted at the next stop she did not remember having made the decision, the advisability of which she questioned by saying to herself, "It's Saturday, there'll be nobody about." The glimpse she had had of the place had shown her no one at work. But as she walked back up the road towards the main entrance she said to herself, "There'll be a watchman or someone and he'll tell me when he'll be there." The last "he" referred to Mr. Robert Quinton, Builder and Contractor. Had she been asked she would have been unable to tell you when the thought of going to see Bob had entered her mind. Now that it was in and firmly fixed, see him she must.

The enclosure was a mass of bricks, girders, and machinery surrounding the skeleton of a large factory, with a row of prefab. buildings to the side of it. There was no sign of a watchman. In fact, there was no sign of a living soul about the place. A notice which had the single word "Office" and an arrow on it led her around a pile of rubble, under the arm of a gigantic grab, and behind a cement-mixer, and there she saw the building. It was the last of the line of prefab. structures. It had one window and this was almost taken up by a man's back—likely the watchman's.

Making hastily for the door and not looking where she was placing her feet, she tripped and almost fell. She just saved the basket from scattering its contents, but sent an empty tin drum, which she had grabbed in an effort to save herself, clattering amongst a heap of iron. When she was upright once again and facing the window the back had disappeared, and before she had reached the office door it was opened. And there stood Bob Quinton himself.

"Well, well, Mary Ann. What . . . what are you doing here?"

She saw that Mr. Quinton was surprised to see her, and also that he was slightly agitated.

"I wanted to see you and I was looking for the watchman to ask him . . . I didn't think you'd be here when they're not working."

"Oh, I'm usually around when there's no work to do." He laughed as if he had made a great joke, then stopped abruptly. Looking down on her, he said, "It's a long time since we met, Mary Ann—you haven't changed much."

This was a way of telling her that she hadn't grown. She said, "I'll be thirteen on the first of June."

"Will you indeed? Time does fly, doesn't it?" He moved from one foot to the other, and rubbed his hands together. His actions spoke of his unease, and this somehow strengthened Mary Ann's courage and she said quietly but quite firmly, "I would like to talk to you, Mr. Quinton."

"You would?"

"Yes . . . yes, please."

"Oh." Now his unease mounted to almost agitation and he said, "Well now, well now, I'm—I'm rather full up with work, clerical work, you know."

"I won't keep you, if I could come in just for a minute?"

There were two reasons why she wanted to enter the office: first, to be able to put the basket down some place safely, preferably on a level floor; second, her legs were beginning to shake and she wanted to sit down.

But her request seemed to throw Mr. Quinton into a dither, and if Mary Ann hadn't known she had left her mother safely at home, she would have thought Mr. Quinton had her in his office, and so did not want to let her go in. But when after a minute or so and a big intake of breath Mr. Quinton stood aside and without speaking allowed her to enter the office, she found it quite empty.

Thankfully she placed the basket on the floor, and without waiting for a formal invitation she sat down. Then, without any preamble as was her way when dealing with important things, she came straight to the point, saying, "I was at Beatrice Willoughby's party a week past Saturday and I met your—I met Mrs. Quinton."

Mr. Quinton, knowing something of Mary Ann's past history, remained quiet, but seemingly even more agitated, for his eyes ranged round the room, and at one time Mary Ann was surprised to see him biting on the side of his forefinger. He had turned his gaze completely away from her when she said, "We were playing hide-and-seek. I was in the brush cupboard in the kitchen and I heard Mrs. . . . Mrs. Quinton and Mrs. Willoughby talking. They were talking about you and . . . and me ma, Mr. Quinton."

Bob's head jerked round towards her even while his body was turned from her. And, looking at him standing in this strained position, she went on, "And I felt sick and had to come out of the cupboard. And Mrs. Quinton held my head, and after we got talking and she told me something."

Bob was facing Mary Ann now and he had his eyes closed, and he said, weakly, even pleadingly, "Mary Ann." Her name spoken in such a tone was a plea for her to stop, but she didn't stop, she hadn't reached the important point of her mission yet, she was coming to it. Ignoring the plea, she went on with quiet resolution. "She said she liked you . . . she liked you very much, the same way as me ma likes me da."

Bob Quinton now put his hand out backwards and, grabbing at a seat, swung it round. Then, dropping on to it, he faced Mary Ann. But all he said was, "Oh, Mary Ann," in a tone one would say, "My dear, my dear." And encouraged, she went on more quickly now, and, sensing an advantage, she let her imagination have full play by adding, "Mrs. Quinton was crying"—this at least was true—"and she said that she was silly and jealous and she couldn't help going on and on about a thing and it got on your nerves. But that she still liked you—and she would always like you, forever."

Bob Quinton's head was bowed and his lids lowered and his face had a sad look and Mary Ann found that she was liking him. She refrained from referring to the other point of the triangle, that of Mike and his supposed infatuation for Mrs. Quinton, for reason told her that if Mr. Quinton went back to his wife that would put paid to her da. Mr. Quinton couldn't know anything about this part and what you didn't know couldn't do you any harm. That was Mrs. McBride's saying. Even as bad as she knew her grannie to be, she didn't think she was bad enough to go and tell him what had taken place on Sunday. So surely it was better to let some sleeping dogs lie while rousing others, so she said, "Me ma's so proud of me da because he's got such a fine job and Mr. Lord thinks the world of him, and he's steady now and everything's going fine, and——"

"Mary Ann." Bob was holding her hands tightly. "Say no more. I understand, and everything is going to go as you want it with your . . . your ma and da. You take that from me."

She stared into his face for a moment before filling her narrow chest with air, and then she smiled and said soberly, "You won't tell me ma that I've been, will you?"

"Don't worry, Mary Ann, no one shall know about this visit, only you and me." He touched her cheek now, saying gently, "Don't worry your head any more, everything's going to be all right."

There was no need to stay any longer. She rose from the chair and, picking up her basket, she made her way to the door. When Bob had opened it for her he put his hand into his inside pocket and, taking out his wallet and extracting a pound note, he handed it to her, saying, "That's for your birthday, buy something."

"Eeh, no! No, thank you, Mr. Quinton."

"Go on, don't be silly."

"But where would I say I got it?" She was staring up into his face now, wide-eyed. "I would have to tell me ma who I'd got it from."

The pound note fluttering in his fingers, Bob smiled wryly as he said, "You think of everything, Mary Ann."

Mary Ann now returned his wry smile; then after a moment of quick thinking she extended him a tentative invitation, saying, "But if you came to my party it would be all right for me to have it then. You could just drop in as if . . . well, as if . . ."

His smile widened and his eyes twinkled as he said, "As if I was just passing. All right, I'll accept that invitation. June the first, was it you said?"

"Well, no, it's going to be on the Saturday because we're off school then. That's a fortnight today."

"It's a date. I'll be there and with the pound note."

"Oh, well, it isn't just 'cos of the pound note." She had to put that in because it was, she knew, the polite thing to say. But she added to it, "You won't let on that I asked you?"

"No not on your life."

She smiled her farewell now, then turned away. But she hadn't gone a few steps when she turned towards him again and said, in a low tone, "You will go and see . . .?"

Her voice was cut off abruptly with, "Yes, yes, I promise you. Go on now and don't worry." His voice pressed on her reassuringly, and she turned about and left the building site with her heart lighter than it had been for days.

Bob Quinton had hardly closed the office door on Mary Ann when another door at the other end of the room opened and Mike walked slowly into the room, and the two men stood looking across the space in silence for a moment. Then Mike, characteristically rubbing his face with the palm of his hand, muttered, "It makes you sort of humble. My God! It isn't right for a child to have such a capacity for feeling."

"Do you think she knew you were coming here?"

"No, no." Mike shook his head emphatically. "They had no idea where I was coming. Or perhaps they had their own ideas, but they would certainly not think of me coming to see you. No, things have been going over in her mind and she saw this as a solution to her own problem."

"And to mine," said Bob. "But really, Mike, I didn't know where to put myself. And you behind that door and not knowing what she would come out with next. Not that there is anything in my past that you don't know. Still, that didn't make things easier. But it's odd that she should turn up at this time and you here. Isn't it? Any other time and it would have been strange enough, but at this very minute. Well"—he jerked his head—"there are more things in heaven and earth than are dreamt of in philosophy. And now, Mike, to get back to business." Bob went back to his desk and, lifting a blotter, took from beneath it a letter and, looking at it, he went on, "If I follow Mary Ann's advice it will give her the lie, won't it?"

As Bob sat on the edge of the desk Mike lowered himself heavily into a chair and, nipping his lower lip between his teeth, he said, "It's really unbelievable. Mind you, Bob, as I said, I told her to get on the bus pronto and come and tell you. But you know how you say these things and never expect a person to take you at your word. By God, she's a wicked old bitch, if ever there was one."

"I've always known she was a trying old girl, Mike, and you may not believe it, there were times when I didn't envy you your position as son-in-law although, as you know, and you don't need me to tell you, I would gladly have been in your shoes at one time. But that's over and done with. And I always tried to be nice to the old girl because, you see, I was brought up next door and didn't want her to get the idea that because I had got on a bit it had gone to my head. Moreover, she had always liked me, and you know, say what you like, it is difficult to dislike anyone who likes you and shows it. But this"—he flicked the letter—"that finishes me with her."

Mike said now, "You believe me, don't you?, that I'd never clapped eyes on your wife before last Saturday morning?"

"Yes, of course I do."

"Mind you"—Mike lowered his head now—"I suppose I'm to blame in a way because she was so damned insistent that nobody of your wife's standard would look the side I was on, that I wanted to prove her in the wrong, but even that didn't justify her writing such a letter as that. . . . My God, I have the urge now to take the quickest transport into Shields and throttle the old bitch. . . . The trouble that old woman's caused in my life, you wouldn't believe it."

"Oh yes I do."

"What are you going to do about it, Bob?"

Bob looked down at the letter in his hand, which started, 'It's because I've got your interests at heart, Bob, that I'm telling you this. . . .' "Ignore it, I think," he said, "It isn't written with any idea of helping me, and not wholly to get her own back on Connie for snubbing her. Its vitriolic aim is set mainly at you."

"It's incredible, but that woman means to part Liz and me or die in the attempt. . . . Well, I swear this, if she ever managed it she wouldn't live to enjoy it."

"I know how you feel, Mike, and I can tell you I'm not comfortable about my share in your troubles." He gave Mike a little shame-faced look after making this statement. "At times lately I've even thought: Without lifting a hand Mike's getting his own back."

"No. No, man, I wouldn't want my own back on anybody. All I want to do is carry on with my job and live in peace with Liz and the two youngsters. And for the past few years it's been like that. But as is always the case, trouble never comes alone, it has hangers-on. I've always found that let one thing happen to me and there'll be three. And I already know what the third is to be." He did not inform Bob of the nature of the coming trouble but he knew it would be the court case with Johnson. Instead, he added, with a grin, "It's funny, you know, but the old devil's really done me a good turn. We've never been able to talk, us two, have we? There's always been Liz atween us."

"Yes, I suppose you're right there, Mike, at least up until I met Connie. The odd thing is that I know Connie's right for me and me for her, yet I fight with her like I know I never would have with Lizzie."

Mike laughed at this. "I know what you mean there all right; it must be that fightin' and lovin' go together. Well now"—Mike straightened his back and pulled his waistcoat down—"what are you going to do? Are you going to make it up again pronto?"

"Oh." Bob flexed his chin and rubbed at it. "It was me who walked out, so it's me who'll have to walk back, and that's going to take some doing. You know how it is. How does one start? And there's always the fear of a rebuff. Connie can be as aloof as an owl in a tree."

"Aye, making it up can be a skin-stripping business. I've had some. It all depends on the time and place. It can be over in a minute or it takes days. Well now, I'll be off." He got to his feet. "She's had time to get the bus."

Bob turned his head to one side and laughed. "Mary Ann. You know, Mike, I used to envy you Mary Ann, and I still do." He rose and walked towards the door, and as he passed Mike he said, "That's the trouble, not having a Mary Ann of one's own."

"Well, you can rectify that."

"Well, we'll see." He laughed self-consciously. "Goodbye now, and thanks for coming, Mike. I feel better."

"Goodbye, Bob. And let me know how things go, won't you?"

"Yes, yes, I'll do that."

"Goodbye then."

"Goodbye, Mike."

"Oh." Mike turned after taking a few steps from the door. "Don't forget you've got an invitation to the party."

"Oh, the party. No, I won't forget. I'll be there, Mike."

"Good. So long."

"So long."

Bob watched Mike go, liking now, with a warm understanding liking, the man he had always despised.

8

WHEN EXTREMES MEET

In the meantime Mary Ann had made her way to Mulhattan's Hall and Mrs. McBride's kitchen, only to find that Mrs. McBride was out. But that didn't matter so much today because Corny was in. He grinned at her when he opened the door and saw her standing there, and exclaimed without any greeting, "Funny, I didn't see you comin'. I've just got in. Me grannie's out, likely at the store." Then he turned round and walked into the room, and Mary Ann followed him and placed her basket on the table next to the shining cornet.

Seeing her eyes on the instrument, he exclaimed, "Aa went to Mr. Bradley's. By, he was good. He plays like nobody's business. Coo! You should hear 'im. An' you know what?" He bent slightly towards her, his eyes twinkling. "Me grannie was right; he is after me t' join, but for God's sake don't let on, else she'll make it so hot for me Aa'll jump off the ferry landin'. Aa told him Aa was a Catholic and he was decent and said——" Now Corny broke off and, his mouth stretching across his face, he laughed. "You knaa what he said? He's funny—he said it didn't matter how Aa blow meself to God as long as Aa blows mesel there. Funny, wasn't it? Still"—his face became serious—"Aa'm larnin' and that's aal that matters. It's aal to do with the breath. Look." Before her admiring gaze he picked up the cornet and, without making any sound, demonstrated the art of breathing in order to play the instrument.

"Go on, play something." Mary Ann, seated now by the table, looked at him in wide-eyed admiration.

"Aa dorrsn't. They"—he indicated the other dwellers in Mulhattan's Hall by a circular movement of his head—"they played war 'cos of the other time."

Mary Ann knew he was referring to the morning when he had played "He stands at the corner" and she sympathised with him by saying, "Spoil sports."

Corny, seating himself now at the opposite side of the table from her, suddenly changed the conversation from cornets to farming by asking abruptly, "What've you got on yore place?"

"Got? You mean on our farm?"

"Aye."

"Oh." Mary Ann wriggled her bottom on the seat, and placed her elbows on the table in order to rest her face on her hands. "Oh, we've got cows—fifteen cows and calves—seven lovely little calves—and two bulls, Bill and Neptune. Bill's nice, like a lamb." The comparison was neither correct nor even desirable from a bull's point of view. And then, "We've got sheep and lambs—oh, dozens of lambs, they're all over the place. And pigs—I don't like pigs, nor hens, very much. We haven't got many hens, just enough for eggs for us and Mr. Lord. And you know something?" Her head moved in the cup of her hands. "Me da's goin' up to Scotland at the back end; he's going to buy some Galloways."

"What d'ye want pit ponies for?"

Mary Ann gave a superior laugh. "Galloways are not pit ponies—they're cattle, special cattle. Me da's going to start breeding them. I know it's a funny name for cattle."

He grinned at her, then asked, "Hev ya any horses?"

There was a pause before Mary Ann made the admission that they had no horses on the farm. Then without seemingly drawing breath she said, "You know Sarah Flannagan, her across the road?" She swung her head up. "Well, she's gone all hoity-toity and thinks she's the cat's pyjamas because her uncle's started a riding school near us and she can ride. And you know something?" She leant further towards him now. "She's after our Michael."

"He goes to the Grammar School, disn't he?"

Corny was ignoring the main issue, and Mary Ann brought it back into focus by saying, "She asked him to go and meet her; I heard her, I was there. She said, 'Come along to our place any evening and you can help with the horses.' It's only because she wants him for her lad."

"What's yore Michael goner be?"

Mary Ann lifted her face from her hands. Corny was refusing to take the cue. As she rose from her chair she said off-handedly, "Oh, I don't know. He'll go to college, I expect, if he passes his exams."

Corny, too, rose, and now, picking up his cornet from the table, he looked at it as he said, "Aa'll get on an' all. I'm goin' in a garage as soon as Aa leave school. There's piles o' money to be made oot o' cars, but Aa'm only goin' to stay there till Aa larn this properly"—he patted the cornet—"and then Aa'll show 'em." He turned and looked down on her now, his face solemn and plain in the extreme, and he repeated, "Aye, Aa'll show 'em."

"Will you tell Mrs. McBride that I've been?" Mary Ann took the things out of the basket and placed them on the table, adding, "I'll have to be going."

He laughed now as he looked at the eggs, butter and bacon on the table. "Well, she won't think Mrs. Flannagan's left 'em will she?"

They both laughed, and as he went through the door with her she enquired, "Are you going home?"

"No. Aa'm just goin' oot for a bit."

Mary Ann looked down at the cornet in his hand and asked, "Well, why don't you leave that in the house?"

"Oh." He grinned good-naturedly now. "Me grannie's gettin' as bad as me ma; she's threatened to smash it to smithereens if she gets her hands on it. Not that she would though, mind, but Aa'm tyeking nee chances. If she comes back in a bad temper, God knaas what she'll de."

Mary Ann smiled and nodded in sympathy, and as they went out of the house she knew that Corny was going to see her to the bus as he had done the other day, and she felt happy and sort of excited.

But the journey to the bus took much longer today than it had done previously, for they talked, and as they talked they wandered off the usual route, neither knowing who was the leader in the manoeuvre. They laughed when they finally came out at the top of Ormond Street and on to the main road, but they made no remark on the length of the detour or the long walk facing them back to the bus stop.

Mary Ann liked Corny. The more she was with him, the more she was finding that she liked to be with him. And when he suddenly asked her in his abrupt "no nonsense" fashion whether the invitation to the party still held good, she turned on him wide astonished eyes, saying "Why, of course! Of course you must come, Corny," at the same time knowing that she had missed the opportunity of following her mother's advice—express command would be a better statement—in putting Corny off. But she comforted herself with the memory of her da saying, "You've asked him, you can't get out of it now."

After this they walked on in a silence that lasted so long that Mary Ann, casting her eyes upwards to see how he was looking after being reassured about the invitation, experienced a most odd sensation. It wasn't weird and it wasn't frightening, but it was odd . . . lovely . . . odd. She was finding that she couldn't clearly see Corny for between them floated a silver mist that had nothing to do with the atmosphere of Jarrow. The silver mist slowly enveloped Corny. She knew he was still by her side, she knew that his suit was awful and his face wasn't much to look at, yet she knew at the same time and with a certainty that he was beautiful. The sensation was becoming more and more odd. Although the silver mist separated them, and Corny seemed to be floating away on it, she felt that he was standing close to her, very close, closer than he had stood yet, so close that she felt a heat radiating from him and into herself. It was . . . like getting into a hot bath when you are very cold. Then the mist, the beautiful silver mist, was wrenched away by no other cause than her name being spoken. But not by Corny.

Blinking as if coming out of a dream, she turned her face towards the road and the car that was pulling to a stop at the kerb. At the wheel of the car was Tony, but on the near-side, and with his face now only a few inches from her, was Mr. Lord. If she had awakened in hell and been confronted by the devil she couldn't have looked more surprised.

"What is the matter with you, child? Stop blinking your eyes like that. Who is this?"

"Oh." Mary Ann, still blinking, turned her demisted gaze now on Corny, and she gulped and said, "He's Corny, Corny Boyle." She gave Corny a tentative little smile as she made the introduction. Then turning her face towards Mr. Lord again, she added, "Mrs. McBride—you know Mrs. McBride—well she's his grandmother."

Mr. Lord was staring past her to Corny, and Corny, with a face that could not be straighter, was returning the old man's scrutiny. And Mr. Lord, without looking at Mary Ann, said, "Get in."

Mary Ann did not obey Mr. Lord. She didn't like the tone of his voice. She knew what it portended: a lecture. She also knew that Mr. Lord didn't like Corny, and instinct told her that she could disobey Mr. Lord without losing him, but should she reject Corny at this moment he would be gone from her for ever.

"I'm going to bus it home," she said.

Mr. Lord's eyes seemed to take a high jump from Corny to land on her, and his beetling brows drew together until they formed a bushy line across his wrinkled forehead. "You heard what I said." His voice was very quiet now.

"I'm——"

"Get in Mary Ann." It was Tony speaking; his request was calm, with no implied insult to her companion threading it, and in the moment that she hesitated before also rejecting Tony's command Corny spoke with his voice and his hand. Pushing her roughly in the back he cried, "Go on, get in when they tell you." And then, lowering his head down to the window and Mr. Lord's face, he stared at the old man for a moment before declaring with deep, painful emphasis, "Aa'm as good as you lot any day. Aye, Aa am. And Aa'll show you. By God, Aa will that."

Mary Ann shivered. Deep within her she shivered. The shiver spread to every vein of her body. She closed her eyes against it. She could have understood Corny swearing, but to take our Lord's name in vain like that, that was dreadful. It would have been dreadful if Mr. Lord hadn't heard it, but Corny had almost spat it in his face. Slowly she opened the car door, got in, and sat down. She could not bear to look at Corny; she could not bear to look at anybody; she hung her head, and when the car jerked away there was only the sound of the engine. When the silence held all the way to the farm Mary Ann realised that the situation was serious and that there would be a dust-up when she reached the house.

Mary Ann's surmise was right. Mr. Lord ordered Tony to take the main road and not turn up the hill. When Tony stopped the car outside the farm-house Mr. Lord, getting out and ignoring Mary Ann completely, strode through the gate and up the path to the house.

Tony, turning now and leaning over the back of his seat, opened the door for Mary Ann, and as she went to get out, her head still bowed, he stopped her with his hand and, lifting her face upwards, he said softly, "Do you like Corny?"

Near to tears and with drooping lids, she said, in an indifferent tone, "He's all right."

"I like him."

Her lids came up and she stared at him as he asked, "Where does he work?"

"He doesn't work, he's still at school." She saw that this surprised Tony.

"He's a big fella to be still at school."

She nodded dismally. "That's why he's growing out of his clothes. There's a lot of them and his mother can't buy him things. He has jeans, but they look worse."

Tony nodded without speaking for a moment, then asked, "Where do they live? In Burton Street?"

"No, he only came there to see Mrs. McBride; he lives across the water in Howden, but I don't know where."

Tony nodded again. Then, leaning farther towards her, he asked quietly, "What were you talking about when we came up?"

Mary Ann blinked as she tried to remember what Corny and she had been saying before Mr. Lord barked her name, and she couldn't remember; she could only recall, and faintly now, the weird sensation about the mist, and she said to Tony, "We weren't talking, at least I don't think we were. Why d'you want to know?"

"Oh, no reason." Tony couldn't say that the look that the big gangling boy and the diminutive Mary Ann had been exchanging as they stood stock still on the pavement in the middle of a busy thoroughfare had even astonished him, so the effect on his grandfather must have been electric. He patted Mary Ann's head now, saying, "Go on, face it. There'll be high jinks, but stick to your guns and no matter what he says you pick your own friends." He emphasised this with two taps on her head as he added, "I'm with you."

She smiled at him sweetly now. Tony was nice; she liked Tony, oh, she did. Nearer tears than ever, she climbed out of the car and made her way to the kitchen and the battle.

"Look, Mike"—Lizzie's face was as stiff as her voice—"she cannot bring that boy to her party."

"Now, Liz, you look here." Mike's tone was cool, it even suggested indifference to the seriousness of the situation. "I don't care what the old boy said or what he didn't say, she asked him and he's comin'—that's if he wants to. But very likely after this morning's business he'll think twice about it."

Lizzie pressed her lips together and moved her head slowly before saying, "It's all very well you taking this 'don't forget your class' stand, but who will have to bear the brunt of it? He expects you to put your foot down." Lizzie laid emphasis on the "you."

"Well, let him tell me that, Liz, and I'll give him his answer."

Lizzie stared at him. She couldn't make him out. Oh, she was fed-up, tired and weary, sick to the heart, and she asked herself why she was worrying about the outcome of Mary Ann's invitation to this lad. If Mike got it in the neck, then serve him right. Yes, serve him right. He was asking for it. He was asking for more than that. On any other occasion he would have been up in the air about the old man leading off over things that didn't concern him, over one person who didn't concern him. On other occasions he would have been shouting about his right of ownership. But since he had come in, from wherever he had been he had looked so pleased with himself that nothing could upset him.

"Come here." She felt herself swung round by his one big hand, but she would not look at him, and when he said softly, "Don't you want to hear what I've got to say?" she answered tartly, "All I want to hear is you telling her that she can't have that boy to her party." The hand lifted from her shoulder and as it did so she chided herself, saying, "Oh, you fool." And when he turned from her, his voice no longer pleasant, he said, "Well, you'll have to wait a long time afore you'll hear me tell her that, Liz, so there you have it. And don't keep on, because it won't be any use."

When the door closed on him Lizzie turned towards her daughter who had been sitting unusually quiet in the big high-backed chair, and she cried at her, "You're the cause of all this."

"Oh, Ma." It was so small as to be almost a whimper.

"The trouble you start. You never have any sense. Mr. Lord is right. Your three years at convent might never have been; you've no idea of the fitness of things, and you nearly thirteen. And if you haven't the sense now you never will have."

Lizzie turned from the round, bright eyes, and, placing her hands on the table, she bent forward and took a number of deep breaths, and when in the next moment she felt Mary Ann's hands on her arms she shrugged them off, saying, "Don't come near me."

"I'll tell him, Ma. I . . . I'll tell him."

Mary Ann's voice was breaking, but Lizzie took no notice of it, and without looking at her she said, "The trouble's caused now; get yourself away from me."

Mary Ann got away, she got away at a run, her hand tightly pressed over her mouth. She ran down the path into the road, hesitated for a moment and turned into the empty farmyard, her blurred vision searching wildly for some place quiet. Her eyes picked out the great barn with the steps leading to the loft. She had never been in the loft since the day she nearly fell through the trap-door into the combine harvester and her da had got hurt, so hurt. The hook on the end of his hand showed to what extent. But now at a run she made for the stairs. The door at the top was closed, indicating that no one was inside, and when she entered the dim loft and was enveloped in the sweet, dry smell of hay she gave vent to her pent-up crying. Stumbling to the farthest corner, she flung herself down on some straw behind a bale of hay and cried unrestrainedly into her arms.

She cried until she could cry no more, and then for a long time she lay shuddering at intervals.

All afternoon she lay enveloped in the dim light and the quietness. Up here the familiar farm sounds seemed a long distance away; cushioned by the bales of hay, all sound was muted. After a while she sat up, and with her back against a bale began slowly to plait some long straws. After she had made a number of plaits she then plaited them together and by the time she had finished the thick braids her fingers were moving very slowly. When as from far off she heard Len calling his particular call that brought in the cows she knew it was tea-time. But this knowledge did not arouse her hunger; she only wanted a drink.

Some time after this the light in the barn, she noticed, began to change and she thought she had better get out before it got too dark. But she didn't move; it was as if she was drugged with a mixture of the subdued light, warmth and the sweet smell that pervaded the barn. Coupled to this the feeling of exhaustion brought about by her long, violent weeping produced a form of inertia, and when she knew she was falling asleep she did nothing to try to prevent it because, as she knew, when you were asleep you didn't think about things. . . .

Some hours later Mary Ann slowly awoke from a long, deep, refreshing sleep to the sound of her mother's voice. For a moment she thought that her mother was speaking from the landing until the light flashed on to the great beams above her head, and as she dimly realised she was still in the loft she heard Lizzie's voice saying, "It's no use looking along there, she would never come up here. She's never been near the place for years." She did not say "Since you lost your hand."

As she lifted herself dazedly up on to her elbow she heard her da's heavy footsteps ringing on the boards. The light from his lantern swung over the bale and would have missed her had she not pulled herself to her feet and said dreamily, "Da, is that you, Da?"

The next minute they were both standing in front of her, not saying a word. She blinked at them, her eyes full of sleep. She saw her ma take the lantern, then her da, stooping, hoisted her up to him with his one arm and she laid her head against his neck. And still nobody spoke.

Mike carried her down the ladder, across the yard and into the house, and even when Michael came running after them, his mouth open to ask where and when, and how, he was silenced by some sign from Lizzie.

Mike went on into the house, straight up the stairs and into her bedroom, and when he had lowered Mary Ann on to the side of the bed he stroked her head for a moment before turning away and leaving her alone with her mother. And still he hadn't spoken.

Mary Ann, coming more awake now, looked at her mother, and Lizzie, her face white and her lips trembling, put out her arms and drew her into a tight, relieved embrace, whispering as she did so, "Oh, I'm so sorry, my dear, I'm sorry."

At this moment Mary Ann had to recall what her ma had to be sorry for, and as she remembered she said hastily, "It's all right, Ma; it's all right." And then, "Don't cry, Ma . . . oh, don't cry."

When Lizzie stopped crying and released Mary Ann she helped her to undress and seemed reluctant to leave her. As she was tucking her up in bed she said, "Do you want a drink?"

"Please, Ma; I'm very thirsty. What time is it?"

"About half-past ten."

"Half-past ten? Oh, I slept up there a long time. Did . . . did you think I was lost?"

It was some time before Lizzie answered, "Yes . . . yes, we thought you were lost."

"I didn't do it on purpose, Ma."

"No, I know you didn't, my dear. Don't worry. I'll get you a drink. There now, lie down."

Mary Ann was now wide awake, and, getting more so every moment, she waited for her mother's return. Without doing much thinking about it she knew that her ma and her were . . . kind again . . . very kind again; but she also realised that the same feeling was not in existence between her parents. It wasn't because her da hadn't spoken; she knew that was the result of him being upset because he couldn't find her, and it wasn't an angry silence.

Mike, she sensed, was amenable and would make it up any time, but it was her ma who was still holding out. Mary Ann felt that she knew the reason, and as she lay looking towards the door she sensed there would never be an opportunity like the present to talk to her ma. Tomorrow her ma might still be nice to her, but tonight would be in the past, and the feelings that were high now, tomorrow they, too, would be in the past, and should she attempt to mention Mrs. Quinton's name her ma would shut her up. But tonight she held an advantage. Lizzie would not go for her tonight.

So when her mother came into the room with the drink and placed in on top of the book-case by the head of the bed she hitched herself up into a sitting position and whispered, "Ma, can I talk to you?"

This was the second time in one day that she had said that.

Lizzie, her back stooped, turned her face towards her daughter and said, "It's late. And don't you want to go to sleep?"

"No, Ma, I'm not tired now. Sit down, Ma." She pulled at Lizzie's skirt, and Lizzie sat down and Mary Ann, taking her hand and looking into her face, said, "I want to tell you something, Ma, and I want you to promise on the Sacred Heart"—she drew the diagram of the Sacred Heart on her breast—"not to open your mouth for . . . well, five minutes. Will you promise?"

Lizzie lowered her eyes, gave a little sigh, made the sign of the Sacred Heart on her breast and said softly, "I promise. Go on."

Mary Ann, too, gave a little sigh and then started quietly, but rapidly with, "Well, Ma, it was like this. You know the Saturday I went to Beatrice's party? Well, when it was nearly over we played a game of hide-and-seek and I remembered that there were some fine big cupboards in the kitchen and when I was waiting to be found Mrs. Willoughby and Mrs.—Mrs. Quinton came into the kitchen and they began to talk." Mary Ann's voice became slower and steadier and she tried to remember faithfully the conversation that she heard between the two women. If she embellished it here and there it only eased Lizzie's mind the more and made Mrs. Quinton out to be, as had already been stated, a nice woman. And she finished up, looking now at her mother's bowed head, "And she's in love with him, Ma." It was about the first time Mary Ann had used that term; she had always substituted the word "like" for the word "love." "Love" had always semed a word belonging to the conversation of grown-ups and had a slight indecency about it, but now she said quite firmly, "She loves him, Ma, very much, and she's lonely. And she looked lonely that time we went into Durrant's and saw her. And you see, Ma, she thinks it's you that . . . that. . . ." Mary Ann could not go on and say "that you are the cause of her trouble". And there was no need now, for Lizzie's hands were gripping hers tightly and she saw that her ma was crying again, but it was a different kind of crying from what she had done at the kitchen table.

When Lizzie lifted her eyes to her daughter she stared at her for a moment through blurred vision before suddenly pulling her for the second time that evening to her breast and hugging her tightly. Then she rose from the bed and, pressing Mary Ann gently back on to the pillow, she said softly, "Go to sleep now."

"Ma."

"Yes, what is it?"

"You'll be all right with me da?"

Lizzie tucked the clothes around her shoulders, she straightened the covers and she stroked the tuft of hair back from Mary Ann's forehead before she said, "Don't worry any more; everything will be all right now. God bless." Her lips stayed longer than usual on Mary Ann's cheek and then she was gone. The door was closed, the light was out, and Mary Ann, breathing deeply, followed this by letting out a great quantity of air from her lungs before turning her head into the pillow. She was sleepy again. Everything was all right, everything—she had forgotten for the moment about Corny, Mr. Lord, the looming court case with the Johnsons and the minor trouble, but still irritating one, of their Michael and Sarah Flannagan.

9

GETTING KIND

On Sunday Mary Ann found that, contrary to what she had expected, her mother was still in the same mood in which she had been in the emotion-filled hours of the previous night—she was nice. Not that her mother was ever anything else, but her manner this morning held a special kind of niceness. Yet in spite of this she was quick to realise that things weren't back on the old footing again between her parents. Her ma, she saw, was nice to her da but it was a polite niceness. Her manner left no room for chaff or that imperative sharpness which all mothers use to keep order both with husband and children and which is recognised merely as a facade. And it was because there were none of these elements present in Lizzie's dealings with Mike and Michael and herself that Mary Ann knew that, although her mother wasn't vexed any more, she still wasn't kind with her da. Perhaps it was her da's fault and he hadn't given her the chance. Her da was like that; he'd go inside himself for days and you couldn't get near him. And yet Mary Ann had to admit to herself that he seemed pleasant enough this morning, even happy, for hadn't he walked with her to the bus when she was going to Mass and jollied her along with great lifts of his arm. And at the end of the road he had dusted her shoes with a hankie because she had got them messed up with the jumping. She would have said he was in very good fettle. And yet they weren't kind.

Everybody was nice to her all day, and Tony came to tea. It was a smashing tea. Her mother had made eight different kinds of cakes. During tea Tony asked Michael if he would like a run out in the car, and Michael, brightening visibly, answered, "Rather," then caused a general laugh by adding, "You know he's only asking me so's he can get past the Johnsons under escort. Once he's passed he drops me at the end of the road."

Mary Ann kept her eyes on Tony, hoping he would include her in the invitation, and she felt slightly piqued when he didn't. He never took her out in the car, he never took her anywhere, not like he did their Michael. But later she had at least evidence that Tony thought of her and her concerns, for after he had talked quietly to her mother in the kitchen, so quietly that she couldn't hear a word, he went up to the house and returned some time later with a great parcel. And when her mother unrolled the paper and displayed to her eyes a conglomeration of clothes she asked quickly, and in surprise, "Who's them for?"

"Who's them for?" Tony's look and voice were a laughable imitation of his grandfather, and, shaking herself, she said, "Oh, you, Tony, you know what I mean. Who-are-they-for? There, will that suit you?"

"At least it's better. They are for your friend."

"My friend? You mean Corny?"

"Yes, Master Corny."

"Oh, Tony. Oh, thanks, Tony." She grabbed his hand. Then her head on one side, she looked up at her mother and said with sudden caution, "Isn't it nice of Tony, Ma?"

When Lizzie seemed too occupied to answer she turned to Tony again, saying, "Oh, Corny will love them, Tony."

"Well, I don't know." Tony jerked his head. "It all depends if they'll fit him—he's a great lump of a fellow. I'd like to bet that already he's got a bigger chest measurement than me. He'll be as big as you, Mike, before long." Tony cast a laughing glance over towards Mike, where he sat smoking at the side of the fireplace, and Mike replied, "I haven't seen the lad in years."

"But isn't it nice of Tony, Da?" Mary Ann went and stood by the side of Mike's chair, and Mike, nodding at her, replied, "Very nice, very nice." But he did not sound enthusiastic and he did not look at Mary Ann as he spoke but at Lizzie's back where she was standing at the table. Then, bringing his gaze on to Mary Ann again, he stared at her before giving her an almost imperceptible nod.

Mary Ann, reading the message, turned about and went over to the table and, fingering the clothes that Lizzie was folding, asked softly, "Can he come then, Ma?"

Lizzie went on putting the seams of a pair of trousers together and her voice was low when at last she replied, "Well, it would be a shame to waste all these things, wouldn't it?"

Mary Ann's arms went swiftly round Lizzie's waist and she laid her head against her side for a moment. Then, lifting up a pair of almost new brown shoes from the assortment, she asked, "When can we take them, Ma?"

"Oh, I don't know; I'd better drop Mrs. McBride a card. Corny will have to come across—the suit might need a little altering."

Mary Ann nodded in approval. Her mother was a dab hand at altering, she had been a dab hand at trouser making—she had made Michael's for years.

Suddenly Mary Ann felt warm and happy. Everybody was nice. It was her birthday on Wednesday, but the great day would be Saturday when she had her party. And Corny could come. For some reason she couldn't fathom, Corny's presence at her party promised it an aura of glamour, which quality had not been suggested by the persons of any of her posh friends, male or female. It was a very odd situation, which, although she did not know it, had to do with natural, very natural in her case, selection.

Mary Ann retained the nice feeling until Monday morning, when, sitting at breakfast, she watched Mike open another sealed letter. It was a longish envelope and the paper was thick and stiff and she felt a fleeting return of anxiety as she watched him reading it. But the anxiety fled when he did not place it in his pocket but, putting it on the table, laid his hand flat on it and stared down at it as he asked grimly, "Who do they think they're trying to frighten?"

"What is it?" The apprehension Lizzie was feeling came over in her voice and Mike answered without looking at her, "A solicitor's letter."

"Let me see it here." Lizzie held out her hand, and Mike, after a moment, passed her the letter.

The letter was headed: Ringmore Chambers, Purley Street, Newcastle-on-Tyne, and at the left side were the names Bristow, Yates and MacFarlace, Solicitors, and the letter began:

Dear Sir,

Our Client, Mr. Henry Johnson of Moor Farm, has acquainted us with the events which took place at Moor Farm, Fellhurst, on Saturday, May 20th.

We are instructed that at the time and place you seriously assaulted our Client, knocking him to the ground and occasioning him to sustain a broken ankle in addition to bruisings and shock, as a result of which he has had to seek and receive medical attention.

We are writing, therefore, on his behalf to inform you that he proposes to seek redress in the courts for what has occurred.

It is not possible for us at this stage accurately to quantify his claim until it is seen how he recovers from the injuries which he sustained and whether or not there is likely to be any permanent disability, and it therefore will be a little time before the proceedings which we have instructions to commence are served upon you.

In the meantime if you have any proposals to make concerning the matter you may care to communicate with us, and if you wish to take legal advice before doing so no doubt you will do so.

Yours faithfully,
Charles Bristow.

Mary Ann watched her mother put the letter slowly down on the table and, almost as if she was copying Mike's attitude, lay her hand on it and with a notable tremor in her voice ask, "What will be the outcome of it?"

Mike did not answer for a moment but rose from the table and, going to the mantelpiece, he took his pipe from the rack and prepared to fill it. Not until it was almost fui. did he speak. "They'll take me to court," he said. "And if I lose the case I'll have to stump up, that's all."

He came to the table, picked up the letter, then took his coat from the head of the couch, but before making his way to the door he paused for a moment by Lizzie's chair and said quietly, "Don't worry, things'll pan out."

Mary Ann watched them looking at each other. It seemed as if they looked at each other for a long time before her mother's eyes dropped away and her da left the kitchen.

"If he loses, how much would they make him pay?" Michael was looking earnestly at Lizzie, who, rising from the table now, said, "Oh, I don't know. Anyway, why should he lose? He's got a good case. Come along, get ready for school."

Michael did not pursue the subject as Mary Ann would have done, but in his thoughtful, serious way he got his things together and after saying goodbye to Lizzie left the house.

Mary Ann hadn't to leave for another fifteen minutes and she made up her mind to go and find her da—he hadn't said goodbye to her. But she was forestalled in this by Lizzie saying, "You've got time to run up with these eggs to Ben. They've never had any since Friday, they must be out."

Mary Ann made no protest, she might see see her da on the way. She followed her mother into the stone larder and took the wire basket in which lay a dozen eggs, and, hurrying almost at a run but carefully so she wouldn't trip, she went up the hill, through the side gate, round the courtyard and towards the back door. But long before she reached the door she heard Mr. Lord's voice, and she knew he was going at it, and likely at Tony. Her last surmise was confirmed when, with finger on the bell, she was about to press it—she never dared to enter Ben's kitchen without permission; she could walk straight into the drawing-room through the french windows, but never into the kitchen—when the door was wrenched open and Tony marched past her, only to draw up quickly and turn an anger-suffused face towards her.

Looking at him in amazement, she saw that he was right mad about something, and then she sensed that the anger in his look seemed to be directed towards her, and there was not only anger in the look. What it was she couldn't put a name to, but she found she wanted to turn her face away from it, it was as if Tony hated her. But she had done nothing, nothing at all. After a swift searching of her mind and finding her conscience clear over the last few hours she went to speak about a quite irrelevant matter, the eggs. Her mouth open and the wire basket held up, she was about to draw his attention to them when he swung away from her and strode towards the gate.

What was up with him? He needn't take it out on her because Mr. Lord had gone for him. "Give them here."

She turned to find Ben's hand extended towards her, and was further amazed to find that his expression bore some resemblance to Tony's. When he grabbed the basket from her she curbed her natural reaction to demand, "What's up with you all?" and asked, "Can I have the cage back?" and her face stretched in indignation when she heard his reply.

"You should be in a cage, along with the rest of them. . . . All women should be in cages."

She watched the old man shamble into his kitchen. What was the matter with him, saying she should be in a cage? Ben and her were usually all right; he was nicer to her than he was to anybody on the farm. Of course that wasn't saying much, not for Ben. But still, to say that she should be in a cage . . .

When he returned with the empty basket she demanded stoutly, "What's up? I haven't done anything."

"You'll be doin' things till the day you die. Go on. Go on now." He flung his arm widely over her head.

And Mary Ann went. She went backwards for a number of steps, for her amazement was unbounded. She hadn't done anything, she knew she hadn't done anything, and she told herself all the way down the hill that she hadn't done anything. She was so disturbed she even forgot to look for her da.

When she reached the kitchen she said to her mother, "Has Tony been in, Ma?"

"No." Lizzie turned her head and looked at Mary Ann, her eyes narrowed as she asked, "Why, what's the matter? Why are you looking like that?"

"I don't know, Ma." And she didn't know "They were going at it up there, Mr. Lord and Tony, and Tony passed me without speaking. And then Ben went for me. I've done nothing, have I, Ma?"

Lizzie stared at her daughter and then she asked softly, "Well, only you know that. Have you?"

"No, Ma, honest. Look, on the Sacred Heart." She made the sign on her chest again. "I swear, Ma. Well, I've never been out, have I?"

"No. No, you haven't, not since tea-time yesterday, anyway." Lizzie stood thoughtful for a moment and then said briskly, "Well, if you haven't done anything there's nothing to worry about. Go along and get your coat on and get off."

A few minutes later Mary Ann left the house and she turned into the farmyard determined to say goodbye to her da and, incidentally, to see if he could throw any light on the matter of Tony. But this solace was denied her, for on nearing the office she heard Mr. Lord's voice. He was talking to her da and what amazed her now still further was that he wasn't shouting, his voice was quiet. Although she couldn't catch what he was saying, she seemed to detect a sympathetic note in it which was even more puzzling still.

But as nothing would induce her to face Mr. Lord this morning, even in spite of his quiet-sounding tone, she turned about and made her way to the bus and school. It was Monday again and the pattern of the week was set . . . at least for her.

The day seemed interminable to Mary Ann, although during break and lunch hour she was hovered over and made much of by her friends who wanted to talk of nothing but the party and those who were likely to be present—Roy Connor for instance and Alec Moore. Oh, Alec Moore was the tops. Janice hugged herself at the mere mention of Alec Moore.

Mary Ann simulated interest; she did her best because a certain standard of enthusiasm was expected of her, but all the time her mind was back at the farm and the incident of this morning.

For a short space Beatrice did catch her attention; it was when she said that her Aunt Connie had been enquiring after her.

Mary Ann had thought quite a bit on and off about Mr. Quinton since Saturday, and she had come to the conclusion that if his coming to her party only resulted in her being able to accept the pound note, then somehow his visit would be wasted. To settle this matter once and for all, Mrs. Quinton should be there. But she didn't know where Mrs. Quinton lived and she was averse, somehow, to asking Beatrice for this information, and should she tell her to bring her Aunt Connie to the party Beatrice would laugh. Aunt Connie was all right, but she was grown-up and Beatrice had voiced the opinion more than once that all grown-ups were stuffy. Mary Ann had always agreed with her, so you could hardly ask anybody who was stuffy to a party. Yet unless she came and . . . got kind with Mr. Quinton, things in a way would remain as they were, and Mr. Quinton at large without a wife was, even after the reassurance of Saturday morning, still a potential danger to her da.

It was a chance remark of Beatrice's that gave Mary Ann the solution. "I was on the phone to Aunt Connie on Saturday night," she said, "and it was then she asked about you." If Beatrice could phone her Auntie Connie, why shouldn't she? The only snag was she had never used a phone in her life. There was one in her da's office, and when occasionally she would put her hand on it her da would say, "Now, now, leave that alone," as if it was alive and would bite. But now the time had come, she told herself, when she must try it.

This matter settled as far as she could take it at the moment, her mind returned to the farm again and the question, What had happened up at the house this morning? And when school was over and the usual gushing farewells exchanged she couldn't get home quickly enough to ascertain if her ma had found out anything.

Apparently Lizzie was no wiser than when Mary Ann had left her, for to her immediate enquiry, "Have you seen anybody?" Lizzie replied, "No, not a soul today. Only your da, of course."

Mary Ann looked at her mother and was able to see right away that things between her ma and da were also as she'd left them this morning. They hadn't made it up.

It was Michael who brought Tony's name up at tea-time, saying, "What's the matter with Tony?" He looked towards Mike as he spoke. "He went along the road in the car as if the devil was after him."

"Didn't he stop?" asked Lizzie.

"Well, he didn't actually pass me; I saw him turning up the lane. He took the hill as if he was in the races."

When Michael's gaze turned slowly on to his sister and he asked gruffly, "Have you been up to something?" she flared round on him. That was after banging her cup on to her saucer and gulping a mouthful of tea. "No, I haven't, our Michael. Why should I get the blame for everything?"

"Now, now, that's enough of that."

"Well, Ma, he blames me for everything."

Michael turned again to his father. "Do you know what's up with him, Da?"

Mike's eyebrows went up and his gaze went down and, shaking his head, he said slowly, "No, I don't; I'm in the dark as much as you. I've never clapped eyes on him the day and that's unusual. I don't think that's happened all the time he's been here except when he was on holiday. But the night's young, he'll likely look in later."

But Tony did not look in later. And when it was time for bed and Mike had locked up for the night he stood in the middle of the kitchen winding his watch, and after a time, during which he contemplated the banked-down fire, he remarked, "There's something fishy about this. I don't like it."

"Do you think it's to do with Lorna Johnson?"

"I just don't know, I haven't a clue."

"Did he . . . Mr. Lord say anything?"

"Not about Tony, but he was as smooth as butter with me. I always feel he's up to somethin' when he's smooth. When I showed him that letter this mornin' he said, 'Oh, not to worry.' He says he knows Bristow personally and will have a talk with him; the matter might be dealt with out of court . . . for a stated amount. He seemed sure that I'd lose the case if it came up, and if I let it go on I'll be up to my neck, he says. He's very likely right an' all. Hell!" Mike abruptly walked towards the fireplace now and, putting his foot on the fender and gripping the rod under the mantelpiece, went on grimly, "I hate to think of Johnson getting a penny of mine. I've never saved in me life until now and it's to go on him. My God!"

"Mike." Lizzie's voice came from close behind him and he turned slowly and confronted her. "I've got a little put by. I saved it out of the housekeeping and the presents you give me. It's about thirty pounds. You know it's there for you if you want it."

After a short while, during which they gazed fixedly at each other, Mike exclaimed thickly, "Liz." His arm came out and around her neck and pulled her close to him. When her face was hidden from him he put his mouth into her hair and muttered, "I don't care a damn really about Johnson, or his courts, or the old boy. It's us. Let's talk this out, Liz . . . now, for I can't stand much more of that angelic acceptance of yours, it wears me down. You think I went off on a personal spree on Saturday, don't you . . . that's what's worrying you, isn't it?"

When Lizzie's head moved against him but she made no comment, he said, "Look at me," and when he had pulled her face level with his she felt a stab of pain go through her as he said, "I don't want to tell you this at all because it's going to hurt," but when he added, "but not so much as if I'd gone off to meet Mrs. Connie Quinton," the pain subsided and her lips parted questioningly. "But I went to see a Quinton all right—Bob."

"Bob! You went to see Bob on Saturday?" Lizzie's face was screwed up now.

"Aye, I did. That letter I got was from him. Your mother had written to him about . . . about his wife and me. . . . There now, there, don't look like that; I told you it wouldn't be pleasant."

"Oh, Mike!"

"Don't worry, Liz; she's done her worst and failed. It didn't upset me; nothing really upsets me but you and me not being at one."

"Oh, Mike!" Lizzie seemed incapable of saying anything else at the moment. She was really horrified that once again her mother had tried to harm this man, and she closed her eyes and bent her head into Mike's neck as he said, "She did me a good turn in a way; I never thought I'd get on with Bob Quinton, but I'd like to bet we're friends for life now. And I've got another little surprise for you. You'd better sit down." He led her to the couch, and when they were seated he looked at her with a wry smile on his face as he said, "Bob had another visitor the time I was there—your daughter."

"Mary Ann!"

"Aye, Mary Ann. None other. I skedaddled into the lavatory when I saw her coming."

"What on earth was she doing there? Was it at his house?"

"No, in the works' office. She told him she'd been hiding in a cupboard at that party the other Saturday and overheard Connie and her cousin talking about you."

"Oh no, not that." Lizzie put her hand over her mouth.

"Did you know about the cupboard episode, Liz?"

"Yes"—Lizzie's voice was just a whisper—"she told me on Saturday night. She tried to tell me before but I wouldn't listen to her. Oh, my goodness, what does he think?"

Mike's eyes were soft now as he looked at Lizzie and said quietly, "He'll think just what she told him, that his wife loves him. Yes, she told him that, and also that her ma loves her da and thinks the world of him . . . oh, the world of him." There was a tremor of laughter in Mike's voice now.

"Oh, Mike!" Although the tears were gushing from Lizzie's eyes her lips were smiling. "She's right, she's right."

They were locked hard together and Mike's kiss had been long on her lips when his glance was drawn upwards and towards the door leading into the hall, there to see Mary Ann standing in her nightgown. Slowly he withdrew his mouth from Lizzie's and, pressing her arm tight as a warning, said as casually as he could, "Come in. What are you up for at this hour?"

With slow, measured steps Mary Ann came into the kitchen and looked at her mother. Lizzie was not looking at her daughter, but was busily straightening her hair, and when she went to rise from the couch Mike's hand prevented her, and he spoke again to his daughter, saying, "Come here."

Mary Ann now went and stood before them and she looked from one to the other, blinking her eyes rapidly the while. It did not and never had embarrassed her to see her parents loving; rather she was filled with the joy that came to her at only rare times, like the morning she was dancing with the lambs or when in some stage at benediction she would be carried away out of herself.

She fell against them now, her arms round their necks, bringing their three heads together, and she started to laugh. And Mike laughed, and Lizzie laughed, and for a space this large section of Mary Ann's world became wonderful.

10

NEVER JUDGE A MAN BY THE FIT OF HIS CLOTHES

Her ma and da were kind again. Except for the court business and Tony's oddness, most of the sky was rosy. It only required that Mr. Quinton should meet Mrs. Quinton and everything would be fine. She pulled open the heavy door of the telephone kiosk.

When some seconds later it swung heavily to behind her she wondered for a moment if she'd ever have the strength to open it again—well, somebody would be sure to come along and help her. Gingerly she put down her school satchel on the cleanest part of the floor, then reached up for the top-most of the three great books.

From tacit enquiries of Beatrice and Janice she had learned that you had only to look in the telephone directory and there was the name and number of everybody in Newcastle. It had sounded so easy. She looked and looked, but she couldn't find any sign of Newcastle. People in Carlisle by the hundreds, Penrith too, every place seemingly but Newcastle.

When at last she raised her eyes from the book she realised there were three people standing in a row outside the kiosk and they were all looking at her. They were two women and a man, and as she returned their gaze the man pulled the door open and asked, "Can I help you, hinnie?"

"I'm looking for Newcastle."

He looked down at the book. "Well, you won't find it in that one; here's the one you want." He reached in and pulled the bottom book forward. "Who do you want in Newcastle?"

She looked at him for a moment before saying, "Quinton. The name's Quinton."

"What's the initial?"

"What? Oh, you mean his . . . Mr. Quinton's?"

"Well, whoever pays for the phone." He laughed, and the women joined in, and she said, "His name's Bob . . . Robert."

"Robert . . . R. Quinton." He thumbed down the page, then asked, "R. J. Quinton, Burley House, Thyme Crescent, is that it?"

"I think so."

The man and she stared at each other, and then she said, "You just think so, you're not sure?"

When she didn't answer he added, "Well, the number's Newcastle 4343601. Can you think of that, or will I get it?"

When she still did not answer, the man picked up the phone and got the exchange and stood with the receiver to his ear and his eyes fixed quizzically on her. He stood for some time in this attitude, and just as his eyes jerked towards the mouthpiece Mary Ann put in hastily, "I want Mrs. Quinton, Mrs. Connie Quinton."

"Oh, aye. . . . Hullo there, is that Mrs. Quinton, Mrs. Connie Quinton?"

Mary Ann watched him listening, she watched him nod his head. Then passing the instrument down to her he said, "There you are, go ahead."

But she did not immediately go ahead, she did not go ahead until the man, with a laugh and some remark to the women, left the box and closed the door behind him. And then she said:

"Hullo."

The voice that came to her over the wire didn't sound like Mrs. Quinton's but she knew that it was, and when the voice said, "Who is it?" she replied immediately, "Mary Ann . . . Mary Ann Shaughnessy."

"Oh . . . Mary Ann!" The voice sounded high and surprised. And then it said, "How are you, Mary Ann?"

"Very well, thank you."

"And your mother and father?"

"They're all right." She was stumped for a moment. How did you talk to somebody when you weren't looking at them? It was an experience new to her. Then the voice over the wire helped her out. After a pause it said, "Were you wanting to tell me something Mary Ann?"

"No, no, I was only going to ask you if you'd come to my party . . . my birthday party, on Saturday, about four o'clock."

There followed another pause, so long that she held the receiver farther away from her for a moment and looked at it, then stuck it quickly back against her ear again as the voice said, "I would love that, Mary Ann. Thank you very much for asking me. Beatrice and Janice are coming, aren't they? I'll run them over."

"No, no, don't do that. Well, what I mean is, I haven't told Beatrice I was asking you. Could you not . . . well, could you not just make it that you were popping in?"

Another pause, even longer this time, then the voice said, "Does your mother know that you have asked me to your party, Mary Ann?"

There was no time to think about lying and the consequences of lying, for she knew instinctively that if her mother was not supposed to be in on this invitation Mrs. Quinton wouldn't just drop in, although her da had invited her, so she said hastily, "Yes. Yes, she does, but I wanted to ask you. I wanted to . . . to phone." And then to give a valid reason for the way the invitation was being given she said, "I've never phoned before. This is the first time and I wanted to do it. And I never told Beatrice because it's a girls' party and she'd . . . she'd . . ."

She heard Mrs. Quinton laugh gently before saying, "All right, Mary Ann; it'll be as you wish—I'll just drop in."

"Thank you, Mrs. Quinton, thank you. Goodbye."

"Goodbye, Mary Ann. Goodbye."

Mary Ann heard a click on the wire and she took the receiver away from her ear and again looked at it. It was difficult to know how Mrs. Quinton felt when she couldn't see her face—her voice had sounded a bit odd when she had said, "Goodbye, Mary Ann."

"Well, you've got it over?" The man had pulled open the door, and she turned to him and said, "Will I put it back now?"

"Yes, that's the procedure, put it back."

She put the receiver back on the stand, and as she went from the box the man and the two women laughed, which caused her to feel indignant—she could see nothing funny in phoning. Anyway, she had done it, and she had also done her best to put things right between the Quintons. She could do no more. Only it was a long time till Saturday to see the results of her strategy.

On Wednesday morning everybody was jolly at breakfast; at one point even Lizzie was rolling helplessly with her laughter. This was when Mary Ann, her face straight but her eyes wide with suppressed merriment, read aloud a card, the blood-connection duty card which she received each year from Mrs. McMullen. And this one, under the circumstances even more farcical than previous ones, read:

> TO MY DEAREST GRANDDAUGHTER
> The sweetest day in all the year
> Is when I send you this.
> May all your life be free from care
> And overflowing with bliss.
>   From
>   Your Grandmother.

"Oh!" said Mike, wiping his eyes. "Thank God we can see the funny side of it."

But now Lizzie said nothing, until Michael, saying as if to himself, "The sweetest day in all the year," caused a fresh outbreak of laughter, when she cried, "Enough! enough! Come on, get you breakfasts, you'll all be late."

It was a pity, Mary Ann thought, that she had to go to school on her birthday. She would like to have browsed over her cards, of which she had fifteen, and try on the dress her mother had bought her. Then there was the lovely encyclopaedia from her da to be perused, not forgetting the book from Michael by Nancy Martin called *Young Farmers in Scotland*. She was even generous enough on this particular morning not to question his choice, for he had also bought her a brooch with her birthday stone in it. Oh yes, everything was wonderful, even if she did have to scatter to school.

But as she finished golloping her breakfast she did remark to herself that no one had brought up the matter of the riding lessons. Well, she didn't want to go, anyway. Not where Sarah Flannagan was, that she didn't.

Then into the joy of the morning intruded another thought, and she knew she was not alone with this particular thought, for although neither her ma and da nor their Michael had mentioned Tony they were all thinking about him—he hadn't been near the house since Sunday. She knew also that they had thought, as she had, that her birthday would bring him in. Last year he hadn't waited until breakfast but had come diving upstairs before she was up. He had given her a lovely present of a camera and a box of candies. She had the box yet and it still had the big bow on it.

She couldn't see why a row with Mr. Lord should prevent him from coming in. He'd had rows before and far from keeping him away they had kept him longer in the kitchen talking. Her da, she knew, was getting a bit worried about the business. He had said last night that short of waylaying him and asking him outright it looked as if they'd remain in the dark. But the job was how to waylay him, for he hadn't clapped eyes on him. And then he had turned to her and asked quietly, "Sure you haven't been up to anything?" And she had vowed as she made the sign of the Sacred Heart. "No, Da. On the Sacred Heart, no."

The arrangements for the day were set by a card to Lizzie from Mrs. McBride, which said she would have Corny at Mulhattan's Hall that evening at five o'clock and Lizzie knew she would always be more than pleased to see her. And so it was arranged that Mary Ann, who did not want to miss the look of wonder on Corny's face when he received this bundle of fine clothes, would go straight to Burton Street from school and meet up with her mother.

A meeting with Mrs. McBride and Corny in the middle of the week she looked upon as an unexpected treat, and its anticipation coloured her birthday to a rosy glow. At ten minutes to five she jumped off the bus and made her way hastily to Burton Street.

She couldn't explain the feeling to herself other than that she seemed to become different when she was in this part of the town. People spoke to her. They hailed her: "Hullo there, Mary Ann!" "How you doing, Mary Ann?" "How's yer da, Mary Ann?" "By! Mary Ann, yer lookin' grand." She always felt as if she was somebody when she came to Burton Street.

Wanting to get there quickly, she took a short cut and was turning the corner round by Tullis's, the outdoor beer shop, when she bumped slap into Mrs. Flannagan. She had said, "Pardon. Oh, I'm sorry!" before looking up into the thin, peevish face of Mrs. McBride's—and her own—enemy.

She drew back from the contact as if she had been stung by an enormous wasp. Then her face showed blank amazement as Mrs. Flannagan spoke. It was as if the wasp by a magic touch had turned into a harmless bumble-bee, for Mrs. Flannagan was smiling her thin smile, and it was very hard to believe that in her refeened voice which Mary Ann knew she kept for special occasions she was speaking to her. "Oh, it's you, Mary Ann. And how are you?"

Mary Ann backed into the gutter, making a wide circle around this alarming Mrs. Flannagan, and she mumbled as she did so, "All right, thank you."

"And how is everyone?"

Everyone meant her ma and da. Mrs. Flannagan was asking after her ma and da! She gulped, and still retreating backwards she said again, "All right, thank you."

"That's right. That's right."

What was right Mary Ann couldn't make out, but she nodded before turning swiftly about and making for Mrs. McBride's.

Mrs. Flannagan had spoken to her . . . civilly. The world would surely come to an end. And then she began to giggle inside, seeing a picture of herself when she got home mimicking Mrs. Flannagan to her da. And she would tell Mrs. McBride. Yes, she would make her ma and Mrs. McBride split their sides telling them how Mrs. Flannagan had spoken to her. "And how is everyone?"

She ran the rest of the way up the street to Mulhattan's Hall. But when she reached the steps her run dropped to a walk, and then she stopped. Mrs. McBride was leading off, she was leading off something awful. For a moment she thought her ma had not arrived. But it was Lizzie, wearing her keep-your-tongue-quiet look, who opened the door to her.

When she entered the room there was Mrs. McBride standing at one side of the table, her fists dug into her great hips, and at the other side stood Corny, a plain, furious-faced Corny, and between them, on the table, were the clothes her ma had brought—the suit, the shoes, the two shirts, the pullover, the socks, and the three ties. That the matter was serious Mary Ann knew immediately, for Mrs. McBride did not turn to welcome her but went on yelling at her grandson.

"Who the hell d'you think you are to turn your nose up at things like this!" Mrs. McBride's fist came off her hip and she lifted a shirt high in the air with a flick of her finger. "Stuff you'll never be able to afford in all your born days, for you'll end up playing that blasted cornet in the back streets. That'll be your end, me lad. You'll take those things and

you'll say thank you very much and you'll put them on. Aye, you'll put them on if I have to
strip you and dress you meself."

"Aa won't . . . Aa won't hev 'em. Aa've towld ye, Gran." Corny's voice was not loud,
and because it was not loud it carried more weight and power than his Grannie's. "Aa din't
want his things. If me ma can't buy me new clothes Aa've towld ya Aa'll wait till Aa can buy
'em mesel'. But Aa divn't want them!" He flicked his hand across the table as if swiping
away something repulsive.

"In the name of God!" Fanny closed her eyes for a moment before opening them wide
again and turning them on Lizzie. And now her voice was a tone lower as she said, "Lizzie,
would you believe it if you weren't seeing with your own eyes and hearing with your own
ears? Would you believe it? Here's this walking scarecrow——" Fanny now flung her head
round towards Corny. "—that's all you are, a walking scarecrow, a laughing-stock, a big
gowk. You're fond of singing 'He stands at the corner and whistles me out, With his hands
in his pockets and his shirt hanging out,' but that's a respectable figure compared with you,
for you're hanging out from all points, north, south, east, and west. Your arms are hanging
out of your coat, your legs are hanging out of your trousers, and your neck's craning a mile
up out of your shirt. Have you seen yerself lately?"

"Aye. And them that doesn't like me they knaa what they can dee. An' ye can taalk
yerself sky-blue-pink, Gran, but Aa'm not takin' that aald bloke's things."

"They're not Mr. Lord's things, Corny." Lizzie's voice was soothing. "They belong to
Tony. He's the young fellow, and very nice, you would like——"

"Aye, Aa've seen him. He was in the car the other day. Aa divn't want his things."
Corny's voice was getting lower now and quieter, and his head drooped as he added,
"Thanks, aall the same, Mrs. Shaughnessy, but ye see, Aa divn't want them things."

"All right, Corny, I under——"

"Well now, you don't want them things?" Fanny had started again. "Well now, listen to
me, me lad, and I'm tellin' you: this is an ultimatum as good as you'll hear comin' over the
wireless. I said an ultimatum, and that's what I mean. You take them things and you wear
them or else you never put your nose in this door again."

Corny raised his head and looked at his grannie, and his grannie looked at him. They
stood thus for a long time, or so it seemed to Mary Ann, an unbearably long time, and she
felt an awful ache pass through her chest when Corny, still looking at his grannie, said
simply, "Fair enough, Gran, fair enough."

Mary Ann's eyes, wide with apprehension, followed him as he walked round the table,
past his grannie, past her ma and out of the door. They were letting him go.

She looked swiftly to where Mrs. McBride stood, her arms akimbo once again, her face
purple hued, and from there to her mother, who looked terribly troubled. Then without a
word to either of them she turned swiftly about and ran out of the room.

When she reached the bottom of the steps Corny was halfway down the street. She
scampered after him and, pulling up breathlessly by his side, exclaimed, "Oh, Corny! Oh,
you didn't mean that, did you?"

Corny did not answer. He was striding along, his arms moving as if he was on a route
march.

Mary Ann tried again. Walking and running alternately, she looked up at him and said,
"You'll have to go and see her . . . your grannie. She's in a bad temper, that's why she said
you hadn't to go back. Will you go and see her? Will you, Corny?"

When there was still no answer to her plea, she said with a touch of indignation,
"Everybody was doing everything for the best, and, as Mrs. McBride said, they were lovely
clothes, and it will be a long time before you can buy things like them, and——"

He had stopped so abruptly that she went on for a few steps before she realised he had
come to a halt. When she went back to him he looked down on her and with his mouth

grim, yet trembling slightly, he said, "Then if Aa can't buy 'em Aa'll hev to dee withoot, won't Aa? An' that's just what Aa'll dee. An' Aa'll tell ya somethin' else when Aa'm on. She didn't want me to hev 'em no more'n Aa did mesel."

"What! Your grannie?"

"Aye, me grannie. That was aall a put-on show cos she didn't want to upset yer ma. Aa knaa, Aa knaa me grannie, Aa knaa her inside oot. An' Aa knaa she knaas how Aa felt, for aall her life she's never had nowt else but second-hand, aye, an' third-hand things. Me ma says she's never had a new rag since the day she was born. . . . Well, that's not gonna happen to me. If Aa can't buy 'em new, than Aa'll dee withoot. Ye can tell that to yer Mister God-Almighty. Ye can an' aall."

As Mary Ann stared up into the tight, angry face she wanted to cry. She wanted to cry for Mrs. McBride, who had never had a new thing in her life; she wanted to cry for Corny, who was determined not to start on the same road. She wanted to cry because of the feeling she had for Corny. It wasn't like the feeling she had had the other day, all vague and misty, it was a firm feeling, solid, and it was taking up a large space dead-centre of her chest, and it made her say very quietly, "Well, I don't care what you wear."

Corny stared at her for some time before swinging away and saying, "Aw! Go on back home."

But Mary Ann didn't go back home, she continued to walk by Corny's side in the direction of the ferry. It was she who was setting him home now. It was a silent journey until just before they came to the ferry landing, when Corny, looking straight ahead and as if he was continuing the conversation, said, "Ye divn't mind round here, round these quarters, but ye'd soon turn yer nose up if Aa showed up at your place like this."

"I wouldn't. No, I wouldn't."

"Aw well, yer needn't worry." He moved his head in a flinging motion from side to side.

"I'm not worrying at all. But I wouldn't mind, I wouldn't." She felt that she had to convince him that she wouldn't mind, yet somewhere in the back regions of her head she knew that she would mind. Not for herself—if there was only to be Corny and herself she wouldn't mind—but she would mind others seeing him.

The first time she had walked in the street with him she knew she was ashamed of people seeing him with her, but now she was only ashamed of people seeing him so poorly put on.

"Ye can't come any farther."

She realised this, as they had reached the ticket office, and she looked up at him sadly, waiting for him to say something. But all he said was a muttered, "So long." Yet the quiet, subdued tone told her that in a way he was thanking her for her championship.

When he got his ticket and moved away from the box-office without again looking at her, she cried after him loudly, "Corny! I'll . . . I'll expect you on Saturday."

Corny did not pause in his walk, he went on towards the ferry where it was waiting to cross the Tyne, and the waters of the river were not so deep and wide as the gulf between them. Mary Ann became acutely aware of this as she watched his gangling figure disappear, and for a moment she hated the circumstances that separated them. She wished, oh, she wished with a deep longing, that she lived once more again in the attic in Mulhattan's Hall, and then it wouldn't have mattered what Corny wore, she could have talked to him every day in the streets and nobody would have raised an eyebrow.

When she could no longer see him she turned away and walked slowly back to Burton Street. She was sad with a new kind of sadness. It was a different sadness to that which she experienced when her ma and da weren't all right; this sadness was a more private feeling, she couldn't work it out with herself. She did not know that she was paying the first instalment on the price that is attached to rising socially. Not only were you expected to say mother and father instead of ma and da. Not only were you expected to speak grammatically in everything you said. Not only were you expected to say you were going to the bathroom when you were really going to the lavatory. But there were the big issues, like forgetting the people you once knew just because they dressed differently and talked differently. Dimly Mary Ann became aware that of all the things entailed by a rise in position the one that concerned people affected her most, and in the depth of her subconscious, unknown to herself, a revolt began, a revolt against everything and everybody who would try to turn her from . . . her ain folk.

11

THE NIGHT BEFORE THE PARTY

It had been a hectic week for Lizzie. Cleaning and polishing from the top to the bottom of the house and baking in preparation for the great day, her hands and feet had been busy from morning until night. Her mind, too, had been busy, and it was not completely at rest.

Mike and she were all right again—she thanked God for that, oh she did—but there had been the rather distressing business of Corny and the clothes on Wednesday which had upset her more than a little. She had felt ashamed of her attitude towards the boy, yet at the same time being glad that he wouldn't be turning up at the party, with or without the clothes. He was over-big and too near to being what Lizzie considered a youth for Mary Ann to shower her first out-going affection on; besides, he was a rough kind of lad. Yet in spite of all this, some part of Lizzie's heart was drawn to the boy, for she recognised in him traits that were in Mike, pride and stubbornness, and she had thought that he could be her son more than Michael was. Then, too, there was the business of the looming court case. Like Mike she was sick at heart to think that their little bit of savings might have to go to people like the Johnsons. And last, but certainly not least, was the business of Tony. She just could not understand Tony. And as she stood at the table filling the boat-shaped tins with spoonfuls of cake mixture, she brought the subject up again with Mike.

Mary Ann, almost sick with excitement—at least Lizzie imagined it was excitement that had caused the tummy upset—was in bed and asleep, and Michael was in the front room doing his homework. They had the kitchen to themselves. Pausing with the spoon in her hand, Lizzie looked at Mike, where he sat by the fire reading a farming journal, and asked, "Haven't you any idea at all about Tony?"

"No. . . . No," said Mike again. But he did not lift his eyes from the magazine as he spoke. Most of the day a thought had troubled Mike, and he said to himself again now, "Oh, away, he would have more sense than to take umbrage at that."

"Well, I think his attitude is very odd and I think, Mike, it's your business to find out what the trouble is."

"Hold your hand a minute, Liz. Who am I to go barging up to him and ask why he hasn't been in? The door's open for him; if he doesn't want to come in that's his business."

As Lizzie was about to make further comment Mike held up his hand and said, "Sh! Somebody's coming up the yard."

"Good gracious!" Lizzie had leaned towards the window, and now, turning her head swiftly, she whispered, "It's Ben."

"Ben?" Mike was on his feet. Ben had never been to the farm-house door since they came here. Ben's world centred around the house on the hill and its master. Mike went quicky to the back door and a few minutes later he re-entered the kitchen with Ben at his side.

Looking kindly at the old man and trying to hide the surprise she felt at his visit, Lizzie said, "Come away in, Ben. It is nice to see you."

"Surprised?" Ben's voice held its usual gruff note.

Before Lizzie could attempt to lie pleasantly Mike said, "Here, take a seat, Ben."

"Thank you all the same, Mr. Shaughnessy, but I won't be staying more than a minute." Ben always addressed Mike as Mister Shaughnessy and so drew from Mike in return a definite respect and liking.

"Well, even if you're only going to stay a minute, now that you're here you can take a seat. And perhaps a glass of cider or home-made wine? Lizzie's a dab hand at making home-made wine. I'm sorry I've nothing in the way of a drop of hard to offer you." Mike smiled ruefully at the old man, attempting to put him at his ease, and Ben, in return, moved his parchment skin in what was for him a smile as he answered, "Thank you all the same. It's very kind of you but I'll have to be getting back. I just wanted to have a word with you." He looked from one to the other of them, then added, "A word with you both."

When he paused, Mike put in quietly, "Go ahead then. Go ahead, Ben."

"It's about Master Tony. He's aiming to leave. He could do it any minute, just go off. He's been getting his things together in a quiet way all this week, and if he goes"—Lizzie watched the muscles of the old man's face twitch as he finished—"it'll break the master."

"But why?" Lizzie sat down, and then she repeated, "But why? Why should he want to leave? What's happened, Ben?"

Ben now seemed reluctant to go on. He lowered his head and moved it from side to side before saying, "The master and he had a few words the other morning. It was from then."

"What was it over, Ben?" Mike's voice was quiet.

Ben raised his eyes now and looked at Mike, and his lips trembled and his words came stumbling as he said, "It's a . . . it's a very delicate subject, Mr. Shaughnessy."

"Let's hear it, Ben."

"Well, it's this way." Ben was turning his gaze towards Lizzie at the moment her eyes were being attracted by a dark form entering the court-yard. She was on her feet in a second and, stepping away from the view of the window, whispered hoarsely, "It's him . . . Mr. Lord."

At the mention of his master's name Ben started as if he had been shot, and Mike said quickly, "You can slip out the front way—he'll never know you've been here. Come on."

As Ben moved across the kitchen there came a sharp rap on the back door. The sound seemed to halt him and, looking at Mike, he said flatly, "I'm too old to scurry and I don't like running away, not even from him." He again gave Mike what he considered a smile, and Mike, nodding in approval, said, "I'll let him in."

When Mr. Lord entered the kitchen Ben was supporting himself with his hand on the edge of the table, and on the sight of his servant his head went up and he exclaimed in a high, disapproving tone, "Well! You've strayed haven't you? What are you doing here?"

Ben's tone was as curt as his master's as he replied, "I'm visiting . . . I'm visiting my friends. Find fault with that if you can."

"Since when did you start going out visiting?"

"Since I decided it was high time I took a bit of regular leave. I've hardly been across the door for years and I'm tired of my own company."

"You're lying. Go on, get up to the house and I'll talk to you later."

Ben moved slowly across the kitchen, and when he was level with Mr. Lord he straightened his bent shoulders and looked him full in the face, but what remark he was about to make was checked by his master barking at him, "And you mind your own business. You're an interfering old busybody, as fussy as an old fish-wife. You cause more trouble than enough. Go on, get yourself up to the house."

Ben's face tightened and his wrinkled chin became a knobbly mat as he declared stoutly, "You'll go too far one of these days and you'll get a surprise. I'll not only go up, I'll go out . . . I'll clear out."

"Huh! I wish to heaven you would carry out your threat. Go on, you're only wasting time." This last was accompanied by a deprecating wave of the hand.

Lizzie listened to this angry exchange between the two old men with her hand on her throat. She felt consumed with sorrow for Ben . . . poor, faithful Ben. On the other hand the exchange almost made Mike laugh. These two had been together so long that they would be like limbless men if the one lost the other. He moved now towards Ben, saying quietly, "I'll let you out, Ben. Look us up any night, you're always welcome."

The huh! that escaped from Mr. Lord on hearing this invitation sent them on their way to the back door, where Mike took leave of Ben by patting him on the back and whispering, "I'll slip in in the morning, Ben, and have a word with you."

The old man nodded and seemed thankful for the suggestion, and for a moment Mike watched him shambling across the yard before returning to the kitchen.

Mr. Lord was seated on a stiff-backed chair, which seemed to suit his present attitude, for no sooner had Mike entered the room than he demanded, "Well, what was he after?"

"After? What would he be after? As he said, he had just dropped in to see us."

"Don't stall, Shaughnessy. He had come down here to talk about Tony, hadn't he? Well, hadn't he?" He now turned his gaze on Lizzie and went on, "He had come to tell you that the boy was making plans to go off without letting me know, and he must be stopped. Well now, I'll tell you something." His eyes were on Mike again. "Let him go, do nothing to stop him. I don't care if I never set eyes on him again."

His voice had risen and was so full of anger that Lizzie, remembering what his fury had done to him three years ago and the disastrous heart attack that followed, cried, "Stop now. You don't mean that, Mr. Lord. . . . Let me make you a drink."

"I do mean it, Mrs. Shaughnessy. That boy is a fool. I should have recognised it in the beginning. He's his grandmother over again—empty-headed, stupid, wilful. . . ."

"Now, sir"—this was Mike speaking quietly—"you know that isn't true. If it's true of him, then it's true of you, for you're as alike as two peas."

"Don't start that again, Shaughnessy. He's got no more of me in him than you have. And I'm telling you"—his voice was even higher now—"he'll not get a farthing, not one brass farthing of mine. I'll leave it to a dog's home . . . cat's home . . . rest home for old horses, anything but people . . . never a penny to him. I swear it. I do . . . I do."

"Mr. Lord. . . ." Lizzie was standing close by the old man's side as she said, "I'm going to get you a drink. Will you have a cup of strong coffee?"

Looking up at her, Mr. Lord swallowed twice, then took in a shivering breath before saying in an absolutely changed tone, "Thank you, Mrs. Shaughnessy, yes, I'd like a cup of coffee." He glanced towards Mike now and in the form of a polite request he asked him, "Would you mind going to the car? There's a flask in the right-hand pocket. I always carry a little . . . a little brandy with me."

After one quick glance at his master Mike hurried out, and Mr. Lord, with his hand pressed tightly under his ribs, looked at Lizzie again and asked quietly, "Did your husband tell you of the conversation we had the other morning regarding . . . regarding Mary Ann's future?"

Lizzie's eyes widened just a fraction and she shook her head.

"Well, that's what all the trouble is about."

"Trouble?" As Lizzie repeated the word a wave of fear sped through her. Somehow she had known all the time that this business was wrapped up with Mary Ann. But she couldn't understand Mike knowing about it and not mentioning it to her, or, as was usual when the old man showed more than a little interest in Mary Ann's future, going off the deep end about it.

Mr. Lord took in another deep breath before he said, and softer still now, "I thought he might have told you."

At that moment Mike came hurrying into the kitchen, a flask in his hand, and going straight to the dresser and taking a glass from the rack he poured out a generous measure of the brandy and handed it to his master, who took it without a word and sipped at it slowly for a few moments. "You didn't tell your wife," he said, "what we discussed the other morning, Shaughnessy?"

Mike flashed a quick look at Lizzie's back, "No, sir," he replied, "I didn't think there was any need."

"Well, she had better know as it concerns her. It concerns us all. As I've just told her, it's the cause of all the trouble." He took another sip of the brandy and, looking down into the glass where he had rested it on the corner of the table, he said, "Perhaps I was a bit too hasty after all, but I thought the boy still had an interest in that Johnson girl. I told him I was going down that morning to tell them they must vacate the cottage as soon as possible to make way for another man coming in, and he told me I couldn't do it, it was cold-blooded."

"And so it would have been." Mike's voice was stiff.

Mr. Lord continued to look down into the remains of the brandy in the glass as he went on, "Johnson was engaged weekly, I owe him nothing but a week's wages. I was going to be generous and give him a month's pay in lieu of notice, but even that didn't suit my socialistic-minded grandson, and one word led to another. And then, I'm afraid, I lost my temper and told him that if he saw that girl again I would put the family out on the road. I also told him what I told you that particular morning."

"Oh Lord!" Mike was not addressing Mr. Lord, he was groaning aloud, and, looking at his employer squarely, he said bluntly, "Well, sir, I thought you would have had more sense."

Lizzie clutched the front of her dress and waited for Mr. Lord's response, and when it came it surprised her, for there was no lightning change of tone. "Yes, Shaughnessy, I should have thought so myself. But there, it was done, and if I had told him he mustn't marry for five years because I had a rich widow lined up for him he could not have reacted in a worse manner."

"And I don't blame him."

"Would you mind telling me what all this is about?"

Lizzie looked from one to the other, and Mr. Lord, after returning her enquiring glance, had the grace to bow his head and leave the telling to Mike.

"It's just like this, Liz." Mike paused, and his face was tight and his brows meeting as he went on, "Mr. Lord proposes that Tony doesn't marry for the next five years, in fact until Mary Ann is seventeen. I leave the rest to your imagination."

Lizzie's hand moved up from the front of her dress to her mouth. Mary Ann had inherited her squeamish stomach from her mother, and now Lizzie felt her whole inside heave. For the moment she saw the suggestion as something nasty . . . dirty . . . even obscene. Mary Ann was still a child. But no, Mary Ann had been thirteen on Wednesday, she was a young girl. Yet she was still only a child—of course she was a child—and there he was planning for her to marry a man nearly ten years older than herself. It was . . . it was shocking . . . like the things you read about, like they did in foreign countries, marrying children in the cradles.

The voice of sensibility again intruded into Lizzie's mind, saying, Mary Ann is thirteen, and girls are mothers at sixteen and before.

"You don't take kindly to the idea, Mrs. Shaughnessy?"

"No, sir, I don't. I think . . . I think . . ." Lizzie's lips trembled and she couldn't tell the old man what she thought. And when Mike put her thoughts into words for her she was more amazed still by the calmness of his manner.

"She's a bit shocked, sir," he said.

"I'll have that cup of coffee now, Mrs. Shaughnessy, if I may."

Silently Lizzie poured out the coffee and placed it at his elbow, and as she watched him drink she wondered, among other things, how he could swallow it so hot. When the cup was empty and not one of them had spoken for some moments, Mr. Lord rose slowly to his feet and, looking from Mike to Lizzie, he said quietly, "You're nice people. Others would have looked upon the proposition as a good thing, for if I don't disinherit my grandson part of his assets should be around two hundred thousand pounds when I die. Thank you for the coffee, Mrs. Shaughnessy."

"You're welcome, sir." Lizzie's voice was very small.

Mr. Lord took three steps towards the door before turning to them both again, saying, "I'd better tell you my other bit of news while I'm at it. I had a talk with Bristow and he tells me Johnson is determined to make quite a bit out of this affair. By the way, his ankle is fractured, which makes the case against you blacker. He can be off work from anything up to a month or more, you can never tell with a fracture. If he goes to the County Court and wins you might get off with a couple of hundred—anyway, he can't get more than four hundred there—but if he goes to the Sessions there's no knowing what you'll be run in for. . . . Now don't say anything, Shaughnessy——" Mr. Lord lifted his hand in a gesture now as if he was tired, and Mike refrained from making any comment. "Bristow says the best thing to do will be to settle out of court, and I agree with him. I took it upon myself, Shaughnessy, to ask him to probe the matter and find out how much Johnson will settle for. And whatever it is I'll see to it; the quicker this thing is done the better. Once a case like this starts to drag on there's no knowing where it'll end. Now please"—he again made a gesture—"let me do this. I owe it to you, anyway. I would have paid much more than they are likely to ask to get that girl away from the place. Really it's Mary Ann who should be paid a lump sum and a studded collar given to Neptune." He gave a weary smile. Then his head drooped forward and, in a voice that had a muttering quality, he said, "There's one thing I would ask of you, and you'll think I'm in my dotage after what I said previously this evening, but if you could talk to the boy and make him see sense I'd be obliged, Shaughnessy."

He remained for a moment longer, with his eyes downcast. Then, raising them to Lizzie, he said, "Good night, Mrs. Shaughnessy."

"Good night, sir."

"It's all right, Shaughnessy, I can see myself out."

"If it's all the same to you, sir, I'll walk with you as far as the house. I've got to do the round in any case."

Again Mr. Lord turned to Lizzie, and again he said, "Good night."

"Good night, sir."

Slowly Lizzie sat down by the side of the table. The mixture in the boat-shaped tins had gone flat and lost its rising quality. She stared at it, her fingers across her mouth. Was there ever such a strange man? Planning to marry Mary Ann to Tony. No wonder Tony had kept away from them. . . . And Mike taking it all so calmly, she couldn't understand that. And then the old man going to pay that sum of money, which, by the sound of it, wouldn't be small. She couldn't make him out, he did the most contrary things. . . . But planning to marry Mary Ann off at her age . . . well really!

As she sat pondering over the matter the door leading from the hall opened and Michael came in, a stack of books in his arms.

"Did I hear Mr. Lord come in?" he asked.

Lizzie looked up at him, and then smiled tenderly at her son as she said, "Yes, he's been in, talking to your father."

Michael did not ask what Mr. Lord had wanted, nor had Michael been listening. Michael was not Mary Ann.

He placed the books on the couch and, stretching his arms above his head, he exclaimed, "Oh, I'm tired."

"I'll get you a drink. What would you like, cocoa or Horlicks?"

Michael did not answer Lizzie's question but bent over the couch again and sorted his books into a neat pile before saying quietly, "I saw Sarah Flannagan tonight, Ma."

"Did you? Where was she?"

"On a pony along the road. . . . Ma——"

"Yes?" Lizzie stood at the stove.

"Can I bring her over to tea tomorrow?"

"Michael!" Lizzie had swung round as if she had been scalded.

"All right. All right. I only asked."

There was his father speaking and Lizzie, looking at his bent, flushed face, said, "You know, Michael, I wouldn't mind in the least, but just think how she'll take on. And you know it's her party."

"Has she always to have her own way?"

"Oh, now, that's unfair!"

"It isn't, Ma, and you know it. If she sets out to get her own way she gets it in the end, or there's hell to pay."

"Michael! Now don't you use words like that. Really!"

"I'm sorry, Ma, but you see——" He ran his hand through his hair. "Well, I want Sarah to come here. I want her to see you. I want her to see us all in this house." He spread his arms wide and kept them there during the moment of silence that followed. Then letting them flap to his sides, he exclaimed, "And that's not all . . . I . . . I like her, Ma"

Lizzie looked hard at her son. Michael had never bothered with girls. He was a sensible, level-headed boy, but she knew that if he said he liked Sarah Flannagan, then he liked her and he wouldn't be put off her. Yet why had it to be Sarah Flannagan? Oh dear, oh dear, the emotional upsets in the family during these last two weeks were beyond belief. Hadn't she enough to think about with this business of Mary Ann and Tony without Michael starting on about Sarah Flannagan? What was happening to everybody?

Her mind swung back to Wednesday and the memory of Mary Ann coming back to Mrs. McBride's crying her eyes out. Well, at any rate that business of the clothes had been a blessing in disguise . . . she wouldn't have to worry about Corny Boyle turning up with people like Mrs. Willoughby rolling to the door in her car to deposit her daughter, and Mrs. Schofield bringing her Janice, not to mention the other four. . . . She said now to Michael, out of the blue, "Is she presentable?"

"Presentable, Ma? She's smashing. She's the best-looking girl going."

"Sarah Flannagan?"

"Yes, Ma, Sarah Flannagan. It's years since you saw her. She's different, with lovely black hair, and she's nearly as tall as me."

"Well, all that isn't going to placate Mary Ann any. Whether you realise it or not, your sister's touchy about her height, and if Miss Flannagan"—now Lizzie's tone was slightly sarcastic—"and if Miss Flannagan's as tall as you, then Mary Ann is going to be at a still greater disadvantage, isn't she?"

"Look, Ma. Don't take it like that, please." His voice sounded hurt.

"Oh, I'm sorry, son, I'm tired. But I still don't think it'll be wise to bring Sarah Flannagan tomorrow."

"If you think Mary Ann will be put to a disadvantage by Sarah, think again, Ma. Have you ever known her to be at a disadvantage with anybody? If she is it only makes her show off the more."

"All right, all right, don't keep on. Look, it's late, get yourself off to bed, we'll talk about it in the morning. Good night."

"Good night, Ma." He kissed her gently and went out. Lizzie sat down again. She was tired. Oh, she was tired; she would just like to go upstairs this minute and go to bed. That batch of mixture was no good now. Well, there'd be piles of stuff for everybody; she had baked enough to serve at a wedding. She wished Mike would hurry up and come in.

As if in answer to her wish she heard him coming in the back-door, but she closed her eyes wearily when she realised that he wasn't alone.

"Hullo, Lizzie." Tony was standing just inside the kitchen door.

"Hullo, Tony. Come and sit down." Lizzie blinked her tiredness away. "Will you have a cup of something? The coffee's still hot . . . a cup of coffee?"

"As you like." Tony's voice was subdued.

Mike was striding about the room now and she could not make out whether his annoyance was real or simulated when he said, "Sit yourself down there, you're not moving out of here until we get things straight. Pour me one out, Liz, when you're on. Make it black, I've got a lot of talking to do."

Lizzie poured out not only two cups of coffee but three. And having handed the two men theirs, she sat by the table listening, not to Tony, for he still hadn't spoken, but to Mike, and she soon found that without the aid of coffee she was wide awake, for Mike was talking as she had never heard him talk before, at least when he was discussing his daughter.

"As I told the old man the other morning, Tony, if Mary Ann wants you she'll have you, and if she doesn't want you the devil in hell won't make her take you, not if you were hung around with the two hundred thousand the old man says you're likely to get."

"He told you that?"

"Yes, and don't go off the deep end again."

"Oh, but, Mike, it's nothing but that all the time, holding out bait. Look, I would stay and gladly and I don't need any bait. I hadn't thought about leaving him, not until the other morning."

"Well, you can forget that," Mike put in quickly. "And I'm telling you something that the old man is blind to: he's blind to the fact that all the grooming in the world, all the grammar learning, all the mixing with the right people"—Mike gave this particular word great stress—"cannot change the blood in your veins. If Mary Ann lives to be eighty and she marries into the top drawer, let me tell you this, Tony: she will remain a child of the Tyne. I don't know much about psychology and that sort of clatter, but I do know the first ten years of your life counts. I know that from experience. I know that from what I've seen in others. Have you ever thought of some of the pitmen and dockers from around these quarters who have risen and become Members of Parliament. Some of them come back and live on their old door-steps. The others that don't and live in their big houses, what do they talk about among their friends? They talk about the past, their boyhood in the pits or in the shipyard. I tell you, Tony, a man or a woman are their first ten years. Look at me. I've got a good job now, a wife second to none, a good home and two children that I'm proud of. My dreams should be pleasant. Yet I wake up in the night and I'm back in the bare, stone-walled dormitory in the workhouse. And mind, that memory goes back to well before I was five because I was in the Cottage Homes from I was five."

"Oh, Mike." Tony moved his head and, his voice filled with concern, he murmured, "I didn't mean to make you talk. . . ."

"Look here, don't get me wrong," Mike interrupted him. "I'm not plugging any sob line, I'm just trying to explain to you that Mary Ann is not going to be the product of the old boy. I realised this three years ago when she ran away from the convent, and it's helped my peace of mind since. Why, lad, I can laugh at his schemings, and you've got to an' all. The thing is you've got to play up to him. He's an old autocrat of the first water; if you let him get you rattled you're done. I know that from experience an' all. But if you play him, things'll run along slowly. So there, I've told you. And if you leave here don't let it be on account of the child. If you stay, let the old man have his dream. Only remember, his awakening lies with Mary Ann."

"I wish I could see things your way, Mike." Tony sighed. "But the snag is I'm with him most of the time and he'll keep on about it, alluding to it. I don't think I could stand it. I might tell you I've never had such a shock in my life as when he blurted it out the other morning." He turned now and looked at Lizzie, then added by way of explanation, "It all started because he had seen me bringing the parcel down on Sunday, he wanted to know what was in it. By the way, did the things fit him?"

It was Lizzie's turn to drop her head. "He wouldn't accept them, Tony."

"No?"

"It was nothing personal. . . ."

"That's just what it was, Liz," Mike put in abruptly. "Don't try to paint the situation. It was like this, Tony. The lad saw you and the old man as the boys with the money, and as I understand it the old man didn't hide how he felt about him. It got under the lad's skin, and I can understand that very well an' all. So he wouldn't accept your charity. Apparently he's a lad who thinks for himself, and he thinks along the lines that whatever he's going to wear it's not coming off somebody else's back. I don't expect you to understand that, Tony."

"Oh, but I do, Mike, I do. And I like the boy all the more for it. Still, it's a pity in a way, as it'll be one less at her party." It was the first time he had alluded directly to Mary Ann, and he smiled now as he went on, "And I somehow think he would have been the guest of honour."

Mike laughed at this, but Lizzie's face remained straight, and Tony, looking at her, said, "You've no idea how I've missed coming in." Then getting abruptly to his feet he added, "Well, I must be off; he'll be waiting up for me. That's another thing that gets under my skin—he never goes to bed until I come in."

Lizzie now walked over to Tony and, standing in front of him, looked at him keenly as she said, "I don't think you realise, Tony, just how much you mean to him. Since you came into his life it's as if he had been reborn again. In fact he said as much to me in this very kitchen. I'm going to say this, Tony, and it mightn't please you, but I don't think you really understand him. You don't try. You're still carrying the handicap of being brought up by someone who didn't like him." Lizzie's voice dropped low at this stage as she added, "And in our own family we know the damage a grandmother can do. It would be a good thing if you would try to see his side of you."

"But I do, Lizzie, I do. Mike knows——" he turned his eyes towards Mike, "—he knows the things I put up with from him."

Lizzie shook her head impatiently. "Those are external things, his shouting, his bossing, all the things he uses as a cover-up for his real feelings. But you haven't given him anything of yourself, Tony. Don't ask me how I know this, but I do, and if you search your conscience you'll admit I'm right. You are tolerant with him but you've never shown him any love, never. Now have you?"

Tony's eyes moved downwards and then across the darkening room to the window, and there was a long pause before he answered, "It's difficult; he pushes you off."

"That's just his manner, his armour, a protection he has built about himself against people over the last forty years. He was hurt so badly that even at this late stage he's terrified of it being repeated. Why do you think he's planning for you and Mary Ann? It's just to keep you near him in case you should marry somebody who will whisk you away. He knows something of Mary Ann and her love and loyalty, and he knows that he holds a share in that loyalty, and if for no other reason than that Mary Ann would keep you with him to the end. . . . Try to understand."

Slowly Tony brought his eyes back to Lizzie, and after a moment of staring at her he turned away, saying quietly, "Good night, Lizzie." Then looking towards Mike, he said, "Good night, Mike . . . and thanks."

As the door closed on him they looked at each other and almost at the same time they both sighed. Then Lizzie, watching Mike make for his chair, said with startling abruptness, "Don't sit yourself down, for I'm not going to talk about her, or Tony, or the old man, or anything else tonight. I'm dropping on my feet. And I've all this place to clean up and tomorrow facing me, and I can tell you I'm not looking forward to it."

Answering not a word, Mike, with his one hand, lifted the laden tray from the table and balancing it expertly, carried it into the scullery. Could you get over women, or understand their reactions. Just a matter of minutes ago Liz had heard that the old man was planning to marry her daughter off to his heir, and she didn't want to talk about it . . . she wanted to clear away. Could you beat it?

12

THE PARTY

The sun was shining, the house was shining, and the table now stretching across the farm kitchen was shining with its white cloth and best china laden with food. The sitting-room door was wide open, its windows were wide open, and there were flowers in the fireplace. Mary Ann had personally seen to this touch. Michael was wearing his best suit, and Lizzie was wearing a new dress which made Mike think to himself, as he was wont to do at times, "She's beautiful, is Liz."

Lizzie was moving up and down the table, adjusting a plate here, a napkin there. And after she had made the round of the table three times and was now at the side table going through the same process with the dishes of trifle and fruit, Mike exclaimed, on a laugh, "Let up, Liz, or you'll snap! What you tensed up about, anyway—the young 'uns, or those who'll be bringing 'em?"

When Lizzie did not answer, he went on, "Just you remember, my girl, you can hold your own with the best. It's me who should be worrying about meeting the gentry, not you. But perhaps you're worrying because of me, eh?"

"Oh, don't be silly, Mike." Lizzie turned about and faced him and then laughed as she admitted, "I don't know what's the matter with me, I'm all on edge. And she's not making me any better; it's as if she didn't want the party. She's not herself, hasn't been all day. Other time she'd be bouncing about the place and you couldn't knock her down if you tried."

"Where is she?"

It was Michael who answered his father, saying, "She's at the gate waiting."

As Mike went out of the kitchen and through the hall towards the front door Michael turned to Lizzie and asked, "Did you say anything to her about what I said last night?"

"No I didn't, Michael."

"Well, I'm bringing her, Ma."

"Now, Michael. . . ."

"Well, I can't get out of it now, I've asked her."

"Oh!" It was a loud exclamation of impatience. "You're another one lashing out with invitations without thinking. You made game and criticised her for inviting Corny, and now you go and do something similar yourself."

"Oh, Ma, hold on, you can't compare Sarah with Corny Boyle. Good Lord!"

"That's just a matter of opinion. Now be quiet, listen! Is that a car?"

As Lizzie made her way quickly to the hall Michael cried after her, "Well mind, Ma, I'm going to risk it and bring her. If our Mary Ann shows off and causes a scene that'll be her look-out."

Michael's voice trailed away from Lizzie's hearing as she reached the front door. When she caught sight of the car drawing to a stop at the gate her heart began to pound nervously.

"Oh, Mary Ann."

"Oh, hullo, Beatrice. I am pleased to see you." Mary Ann was doing the honours. "How do you do, Mrs. Willoughby? Mrs. Willoughby, this is my mother."

"How do you do?" said Lizzie, inclining her head forward.

"I'm very pleased to meet you," said Mrs. Willoughby.

That was funny. . . . This thought nipped into the proceedings and presented itself to Mary Ann. It was funny that it should be her ma who should say "How do you do?" and Mrs. Willoughby who should say "I'm pleased to meet you"; the correct greeting should have been "How do you do?"—she had learned that much long ago in Sister Catherine's social sessions.

"This is my husband."

Mrs. Willoughby was shaking hands with Mike, and if her expression was anything to go by she was quite impressed with the big red-headed man.

"Oh, isn't it lovely here? Oh, what a pretty house you have, Mary Ann." Beatrice was gushing aloud, and she turned to her mother and said, "Isn't it lovely, Mummy?"

"Yes, delightful."

"Won't you stay and have a cup of tea?" Lizzie was smiling. The ice was broken and she was feeling just a little more at ease.

"Thank you, but no, I have an appointment in town this afternoon. But some other time I would love to, if I may."

Mrs. Willoughby sounded as if she meant what she said, and as Lizzie looked at the expensively dressed woman her nervousness left her completely. What was she, after all, but just another woman, just another ma. She became calm inside and rather proud, because now Mike was opening the door of the car for Mrs. Willoughby and there was a natural heir about him that many a man in a better position would have envied.

"I'm afraid you'll have to back down here and turn in at the farm gate, the road's rather narrow and a bit rough."

Mike was bending down to Mrs. Willoughby, and she smiled widely at him as she replied, "Oh, that's all right, I'll manage, Mrs. Shaughnessy." She put the gears into reverse and then added, "Goodbye for the present, I'll see you later."

But Mrs. Willoughby hadn't backed the car as far as the farm gate when another car, coming at a tearing rate, made its appearance round the bend, and it was followed by yet another one.

In a low aside to Lizzie Mike now exclaimed in thick dialect, "Aalltegither like the folks o' Shields."

"Mike!" It was a warning from Lizzie, and Mike laughed and went forward to the traffic jam that was building up outside the farm gate.

"Why couldn't you stay up on the broad part of the road, Lettice?" Mrs. Willoughby was leaning out of her car and calling to Janice's mother now, and this gaily attired individual, thrusting her head out of the window, cried, "Swing her round, darling, you'll take the gate-post up in a minute. Give me a couple of inches and I'll get by. . . ."

"Oh, you are a fool, Lettice!" Mrs. Willoughby sounded more than a little annoyed, until Mike, coming to her side, guided her clear of the heavy gate-post with the iron latch protruding from it, saying, "Over a bit. A little more left. That's it, that's it, you're through now." He bent down towards her and advised, "I'd stay put for a second or so until the others get past."

The third car was being driven by an extremely fat lady with a replica of herself sitting at her side, and Mrs. Willoughby, looking up at Mike, asked, "Who is that?"

"I haven't the foggiest notion." Mike's eyes were twinkling. "But the child's likely another . . . dear friend of Mary Ann's."

Returning Mike's twinkle, Mrs. Willoughby laughed softly now. Connie hadn't exaggerated when she said that the Shaughnessy man had points, he certainly had. She wished she'd been able to accept the invitation to tea. She could also see where the attraction lay for Bob—the child's mother was a most arresting woman, and without any artificial aid at that.

"There you are, all clear now." Mike guided Mrs. Willoughby's car into the road again and waved her goodbye before walking back towards the house gate.

"This is my husband, Mrs. Schofield."

"Oh . . . hullo, Mr. Shaughnessy, I've heard such a lot about you. Janice talks about Mary Ann from morning till night, and Mary Ann talks about you. You see, it's like jungle telegraph . . . you're just like I pictured you. And you, too, Mrs. Shaughnessy. I knew before I clapped eyes on you that you had marvellous blonde hair and were beautiful."

"Oh, Mrs. Schofield." Lizzie was definitely embarrassed, but she had to laugh—they all laughed. She could see that Mrs. Schofield was a sort of character—a cross between a Mrs. Feather and a Blondie. "Will you stay and have a cup of tea, Mrs. Schofield?"

"Yes, of course I'll stay to tea, and thank you, Mrs. Shaughnessy."

"Oh, Mammy, you don't have to stay——" This was Janice addressing her mother in horrified tones. "It's a girls' party."

"Away with you! I'm still a girl . . . aren't I, Mr. Shaughnessy?" She spoke as if she had known Mike all her life, and Mike replied gallantly, "And you will be all you life, Mrs. Schofield."

The laughter filled the front garden. It surrounded Mary Ann and should have made her heart glad: everything was going like a house afire, everyone was so nice.

"What did you say, Beatrice?" She turned to Beatrice who had whispered something to her.

"Where's Michael?" Beatrice was looking quite coy, and Mary Ann, in a manner more off-hand than she should have used to a guest, and to her best friend into the bargain, said, "Oh, he's about somewhere."

"I've brought you this, Mary Ann. I hope you'll like it." The fat girl was now holding out a long, gaily-covered box to Mary Ann, and Mary Ann, taking it, gushed, "Oh, thank you, Betty. Oh, that is sweet of you. Oh, I'll love it." Later she wondered why Betty had to give her a bath puff with a long handle when you could sprinkle talcum all over you from any fancy container.

"Here's another car. Oh, it's Alec Moore." Janice, definitely excited, forgot about her mother's intrusion and joined Mary Ann at the gate.

The car not only held Alec Moore but Roy Connor and a boy little bigger than Mary Ann, called Dennis Braton. They were all smartly dressed, bright-eyed, and they all carried parcels which in turn they dutifully handed to Mary Ann.

"Oh, thank you, thank you. Oh, that is kind of you. Look, Mother—look what the boys have given me." Not only Mike and Lizzie looked, but everyone crowded around to admire the presents. No one had moved from the vicinity of the gate, but the party had certainly begun.

It was in full swing when Tony arrived. He came round the front of the house where the deck-chairs were scattered on the lawn. He stopped near Mike and was introduced by him to Mrs. Schofield, who immediately invited him to take a seat near her. After a courtly bow, which would have pleased his grandfather, and with words to the effect that he would defer the pleasure until he had seen Mary Ann, he went in search of her.

"Isn't he lovely? Who is he? Oh, he's charming."

As Mike looked down on Mrs. Schofield and gave her the necessary information he wondered to himself how such women as this ever came to be married, and, further still, how they managed to be mothers. And yet, he concluded with a quiet laugh, rabbits managed that function all right.

"Do you know, I used to dream about being a farmer's wife, Mr. Shaughnessy?"

"Really?"

"Yes, really and truly. Honest. Honest, I'm not joking. But perhaps I'm not quite the type. What do you think?"

Mike, chuckling inwardly, was taking the bait when Mary Ann, rushing from the house cried excitedly, "Father! Father!" For the moment he did not realise that the title was meant for him, and when he did it was as much as he could do to stop himself from bellowing aloud, "Father, indeed!" It was the first time she had ever called him that.

"Look . . . look what Tony has given me." She lifted up from the front of her dress a gold cross on a thin gold chain. "Isn't it lovely?"

"Yes. . . . By, it's beautiful! Did you thank him?"

"Oh yes. Yes, of course." She looked from Mike to Mrs. Schofield for a moment, then back to Mike again. She wanted to say, "Tony's all right now," but this wasn't the place, and Mrs. Schofield was such a funny woman that she would likely want to know if he had been bad or something. She hadn't imagined Janice having such a funny mother; she didn't think she would like a mother like Mrs. Schofield.

"Well, well, we're all excitement."

Mike, Mary Ann and Mrs. Schofield turned towards the deep voice of Mr. Lord, and Mike, pulling a straight garden chair forward, said, "Good afternoon, sir. Will you have a seat? This is Mrs. Schofield. Mr. Lord, Mrs. Schofield."

"How do you do?"

Mrs. Schofield was reminded of the young man through the way this old one inclined his thin body towards her.

"I'm very well, very well. Do sit down, I've heard such a lot about you. My father-in-law used to be connected with Redheads."

"Did he? No, I won't take a seat yet awhile. . . . Hullo, Mary Ann."

"Hullo, Mr. Lord."

"A happy birthday to you, Mary Ann."

"Thank you, Mr. Lord." She smiled at him a welcoming smile, for she was genuinely pleased to see him. Tony and he must be all right or he wouldn't have come. She watched him look towards the road. Then when he looked back at her he asked, "Have you had a lot of nice birthday presents?"

"Oh yes, some lovely ones. Look, Tony gave me this cross." She held the cross up to him.

"Yes, very nice, very nice." He nodded at her and she smiled at him again. He hadn't given her a present, but that didn't matter, he spent lots of money in other ways. She had, she knew, much to be grateful to him for, and when he was nice, as now, she was grateful. She didn't want a present from him.

He looked to where the boys and girls were searching among the bushes, and Mary Ann explained, "We're having a treasure hunt."

He nodded, then said, "You have a lot of nice friends, Mary Ann."

She did not smile at him now, for she was seeing the picture of Corny standing on the pavement saying, "I'll get on. By God, I'll get on!" and she shuddered a little as in thought she took the Lord's name in vain.

Mr. Lord now looked at his watch, and then from Mary Ann to Mike before he said, "I'm expecting someone."

"Yes, sir?" Mike looked enquiringly at the old man.

"They should be here any minute."

Mary Ann looked slightly startled, for she too was expecting someone, in fact two someones. It was this fact that contributed to her nervousness all day.

She was uneasy about a number of things; she wasn't happy although she was trying her hardest to pretend to be. On the surface she had every reason to be happy, for her party was going with a swing and promised to be an enormous success and the subject of conversation for many days to come. And she had proof of this as she looked at her young guests dashing uninhibited about the garden and the house. Even their Michael had joined in, Beatrice had seen to that. A thought intruded at this point to ask what was up with their Michael? He had been looking at her funnily all day. But she couldn't waste time at this stage on Michael and what was up with him, for Mr. Lord was saying and in an odd way, "Any minute. Any minute now."

Her attention was lifted from him to the road once again by the arrival of yet another car and her da exclaiming, "Not another! I thought we'd had the lot."

When the car stopped at the gate and Bob Quinton alighted Mike assumed the right reactions towards this visitor. He remained quiet and kept his face straight, and this was rather difficult to do when he saw his daughter's agitation. At the same time he kept his glance on Lizzie as she greeted Bob, wondering in spite of all he knew to the contrary if she would be affected at the sight of him, and if this perhaps had been the actual cause of her nervousness all day. But he could see nothing in her attitude but feigned surprise.

"Why, hullo, Bob. Well, what's brought you up here today?"

"Oh, hullo there, Lizzie. Hullo, Mike. Hullo, Mary Ann." Bob made the greetings before he gave Lizzie an answer and then he added with a side-long glance at Mary Ann, "I just happened to be passing along the top of the road and I thought: I haven't seen the Shaughnessys for years." He spread his eyes now around the garden and said, "I'm sorry, I've butted in at the wrong time. I didn't know you were having a party."

"It's Mary Ann's birthday, Bob, but you're welcome, and you must stay and have a cup of tea."

"I'd like that, Lizzie, thanks." He was turning to Mike when a voice from the garden exclaimed in high excited tones, "Why, Bob, what a delight!"

Mike heard the groan that Bob gave as he walked towards Mrs. Schofield's chair, saying, "Hullo there, Lettice. Well, well, fancy seeing you out in the country."

As Mary Ann watched Mrs. Schofield hanging on to Mr. Quinton's arm and listened to her high, laughing, jocular remarks, it crossed her mind that if Mrs. Quinton did come she wouldn't get much chance to make it up with Mrs. Quinton if Mrs. Schofield was still about, and her sympathy deepened for Janice. No wonder Janice said her mother was a drip. The term had rather horrified Mary Ann, but she could see Janice's point.

"Hullo there, Quinton; you lost?" Mr. Lord's voice was terse.

"No, no, sir; just paying a visit to old friends. How are you?"

"I'm well, thank you."

Mary Ann was puzzled by Mr. Lord's attitude, for all the time he talked to Mr. Quinton he kept glancing up the road. And, moreover, he wouldn't let her away but told her to wait a moment, for he wanted her. Then even as she was wondering what on earth he could be wanting her for—he couldn't possibly be about to go for her in front of everybody—he gave a loud "Aah!" and crossed the lawn to the gate, saying as he did so, "Mary Ann...Mary Ann, come here."

When Mary Ann stood by his side in the middle of the road and looked along it, she was looking into the sun and all she could see for the moment was the outline of a horse. And when the horse came into the first shadow of the farm buildings, sharp indignation ran through her. It was not only a horse she was seeing but, of all people ... Sarah Flannagan! The cheek. What did she want here?

Sarah was not riding the horse—pony would be the more correct term—she was leading it. It was small and a piebald, and even at a distance looked a beauty. But Mary Ann was not concerned with the horse. What was Sarah Flannagan doing here? They were not alone now on the road; all the grown-ups were standing around the gate, and some of the younger guests, out of curiosity, had joined them. But Mary Ann had eyes for no one but Sarah Flannagan. Daring to come to her party and bring her horse!

Then her indignation was supplanted by stark surprise, threaded with not a little fear, for as the two unexpected guests advanced nearer Mr. Lord greeted Sarah in a kind voice, saying, "There you are. You got here, and on time. Good girl."

Mr. Lord knew Sarah Flannagan, he was talking to her as if he liked her. For a second Mary Ann was consumed by a blinding feeling of jealousy, a feeling that only a year ago would have prompted her arms and legs into battle.

Everyone about her was exclaiming on the beauty of the pony until Mr. Lord silenced them with uplifted hand. Then, taking the bridle from Sarah, he turned about and, looking at Mary Ann, who was at the moment not wearing her best face, said, "This, Mary Ann, is your birthday present."

"Eh?" The ejaculation was shot out of her in surprise. "For me? Mine? ... Oh no!" She shook her head.

"You don't like him? You don't want him?"

Her gaping mouth closed and her eyes lifted in amazement from the pony to Mr. Lord's face, and she cried, "Yes, oh yes. But a horse! I never ... never ..." She turned her head first one way and saw her mother, and then the other way and saw Mike, exclaiming now, "Oh, Ma! Oh, Da!" at the same time knowing that the use of such familiar terms was no way to repay Mr. Lord for his kindness. And as she could think of no words which would express her feelings she just flung herself impetuously at him and reached her arms up round his neck.

"There now, there now, that's enough." Although he blustered, she knew he was pleased. And as she held on to the pony's bridle with one hand she held on to him with the other.

They were surrounded now by the company, and Sarah was in the middle of the circle standing close to Mary Ann. Discovering herself looking straight into the eyes of her old enemy, there seemed nothing for it at this particular moment but to smile, and she heard herself saying as if she was talking to one of her best friends, "Oh, he's lovely, and thanks for bringing him. I'll have to learn to ride. What's his name?"

"He hasn't got one, we just called him Nip 'cos he's nippy on his legs; but Mr. Lord said you'd give him a name yourself."

"Yes, yes." She did not know what to say next to this new Sarah Flannagan, but she knew what she should have said to show her complete magnanimity when she heard her mother say, "You must stay to tea, Sarah."

"Thanks, Mrs. Shaughnessy, I'd like to."

"There you are, you never told me." It was their Michael speaking to Sarah now, and everybody listening. "I was going to the bus for you. Why didn't you tell me?"

"I wasn't supposed to."

Michael was looking at Sarah with unveiled admiration; and as Mary Ann thought, Our

Michael's clean gone on her, she found to her surprise that this no longer made her angry.

Whereas Mary Ann was no longer feeling angry, Mike was now having difficulty in suppressing this emotion. For as much as Mr. Lord's gift had delighted Mary Ann it had angered him, and for two reasons. The first being that he always resented the old man giving her lavish presents; the second one was that the old man had forestalled him. For some time now, since Lizzie had first suggested it would be nice if Mary Ann learned to ride at the new school that had opened, an idea had been growing in his mind that it would be nicer still if she had her own pony, and he had thought, "I'll get her one; as soon as she can ride I'll get her one." And now the old man had stepped in before him. . . .

"Remember what you told me last night, Mike?"

Mike turned his head sharply to look at Tony. The young man was smiling quizzically at him, and now with his voice very low he said, "You must practise what you preach, you know."

On a sudden Mike laughed. He put out his fist and punched Tony, and Tony, looking over Mike's shoulder, said under his breath, "He's wanting you."

When Mike turned and looked at Mr. Lord over the heads of the crowd the old man, making unusual deference to Mike's position, said, "Will the top field behind the house be all right to put him in, Shaughnessy?"

"Yes. Yes, that will be quite all right."

"Well, you put her up then." Mr. Lord looked at Mike as if he were asking a favour. He had never been as soft-toned before, to Mike's knowledge.

Mr. Lord was indeed in a good frame of mind this afternoon. The boy had seen sense, and he had just given Mary Ann the present he had been considering for some time and which would give her the opportunity to enjoy the pastime of a young lady. Moreover, he had, by a word to Shaughnessy, got the animal housed in the field behind his house, which would ensure that he saw the child daily; for although she visited him often there were days when he didn't see her at all. Yes, he was in a very good frame of mind.

With a swing of his arm Mike lifted Mary Ann into the saddle, and when she was seated on what appeared to her the top of the world, so high was she from the ground, she did not look at the pony but straight into Mike's eyes, and she whispered, "Oh, Da!"

Aw well—Mike smiled reassuredly to himself—as he was always saying, it would take a lot to change her. In spite of all her fancy friends it took just a little real emotion to turn him into her da again. With a pat on her knee and directions to Michael, who was at one side of the pony's head for the sole reason that Sarah was at the other, he sent his daughter on her perilous but triumphant ride down the road and through into the farm-yard, which was the shortest way to the field at the top of the hill, and the whole company followed.

Mike was now walking with Mrs. Schofield, and Lizzie was a few steps behind accompanied by Bob Quinton. Being the last of the procession, they were just turning into the farmyard when Lizzie stopped, her glance caught by a solitary figure walking along the road. Seeing her hesitate, Bob too turned his gaze along the road, and then his steps jerked to a halt and he stood staring.

Lizzie's mind was in a whirl. The woman coming towards her was a stranger, she had never seen her in her life before and yet she knew her. She saw immediately that she was extremely smart, one of those women who could afford to dress with the utmost simplicity, in fact the type that was made outstanding by simplicity. Her dress and hat were grey and her shoes were navy. They were nothing in themselves, there was nothing much about them, and yet it looked as though she had stepped out of a plate-glass window.

"Hullo, Connie." Bob's voice was low and his face was flushed.

"Hullo, Bob." Connie's voice was equally low but her face was not flushed, it was extremely white.

"This——" Bob's hand went out to indicate Lizzie and in the second before he said,

"This is Elizabeth," he thought, My God, what a situation! Her to come here and find me with Lizzie of all people. But in the next second he was in a measure relieved, for Connie, turning towards Lizzie and offering her hand, said, "I've heard quite a lot about you," and there was no double meaning in the remark.

"I'm glad to meet you." Lizzie's voice was level and showed nothing of the agitation inside of her, but she swallowed and, looking towards the back of the retreating column, said hastily, "I'll call Mike—he's just gone on with Mrs. Schofield."

"Schofield? Lettice?" Now Connie turned to Bob and asked, "Is it Lettice? Is she here?"

The red was fading somewhat from Bob's face and he gave a little smile now as he said, "Yes, I'm afraid so."

Lizzie, looking from one to the other, put in apologetically, "She brought her daughter, she's one of Mary Ann's friends . . . it's Mary Ann's birthday party."

"Yes, yes, I know." Connie was now looking hard at Lizzie, and after a moment's hesitation she added, "You . . . you were expecting me?"

There was just a fraction of a pause before Lizzie said, "Yes, oh yes . . . yes, of course." Her voice was slightly too loud and she went on now, too rapidly, "Will you excuse me just a minute, I'll have to dash back to the house. I've just remembered I've left the kettle on for the tea—it'll be boiled dry." Then just as she was about to hurry away she added, "If you don't want to follow the cavalcade come back into the house. I'll run on, I'll—I'll see you in a minute."

As Lizzie hurried back along the road to a kettle that didn't need seeing to she felt hot to the roots of her hair. Wait until she got hold of Mary Ann, she would skin her alive, she would; this was too much. And yet—she paused as she pushed open the garden gate and restrained herself from looking back along the road—you never knew what an unexpected meeting like this could bring about. But she shouldn't have done it; no, she shouldn't have done it. And now this would mean another one for tea and she hadn't enough cups. There were already two more than she had bargained for—she had to be prepared for Mr. Lord staying to tea, and then there was that Mrs. Schofield. She'd have to slip out the back way up to Ben's and ask him for the loan of some cups. . . .

Connie and Bob were standing exactly where Lizzie had left them. Connie's head was turned to one side and her eyes moved nervously about as she said in a low, strained voice, "It's dreadful, she didn't expect me."

"She didn't expect me, either."

"No?" Connie's eyes came round to her husband's.

"No." Bob wasn't sure of this, but he knew that if Connie thought he was in the same boat as herself she wouldn't feel so badly about it. He said now, "Who gave you the invitation . . . Mary Ann?" His eyebrows moved up as he said the name.

"Yes, Mary Ann."

"She gave me mine, too." The corner of his mouth was pulled in. "She's a terrible child is Mary Ann."

The wary smile was wiped from Bob's lips as he saw Connie's eyes close tightly for a second and her hand press across her lips, and when turning quickly from him she muttered, "I can't stay, make my apologies. Tell them I've had to . . .", he said rapidly and softly, "Connie . . . Connie, don't go." His hand was on her arm.

"I . . . I must; I can't stay here. It's . . . it's so embarrassing."

"It needn't be, Connie. Connie, look at me." His hand slipped down her arm until it reached her fingers, and as he clasped them her head fell forward and, the tears streaming down her face, she stammered, "This . . . this is dreadful! I'll have to go, I must go."

"Well, go this way." He turned her about and led her in the direction of the house, and when they reached the hall he said softly, "Come in here, there's no one in here."

In the front room she dried her eyes while he stood close to her watching the process, and when she murmured, "I feel dreadful, barging in like this," he knew that she was feeling dreadful not because she had barged in, but because of her meeting with him. He, too, was feeling dreadful . . . ghastly. He said softly, "Forget it. Lizzie won't give it another thought; she's used to people coming and going."

"She's nice . . . she's so nice, Bob." Connie was now looking at him. "Different from what I expected, and—and she is rather beautiful."

"Oh, damn Lizzie, look!" There was a moment during which they stood gazing at each other before his arms went round her and she fell against him, silent, and so, so thankful. . . .

Mike, just within the door of the kitchen, placed the three cups and saucers quietly on the dresser and, turning to Lizzie with wide twinkling eyes and exaggeratingly miming the words he had just heard, he said, "Oh, damn Lizzie."

Lizzie gave him an anything but gentle push before she went silently to the door leading into the hall and quietly closed it. Then, ignoring Bob's comment on her, she whispered, "I'll skin that one alive."

"Why?" Mike was whispering also.

"She planned all this, asking them both here today."

"Well, hasn't it worked out? Damn Lizzie. Isn't that enough for you?"

"Oh, you!"

Mike grabbed at her arm and she said hastily, "Now, now, Mike, stop it. Don't start any carry-on here, they're all coming back. And don't forget Mrs. Schofield, she expects you to give her all the attention."

"Meow!" said Mike. Then, aiming at an impression of Bob's voice, he said, "Damn, Mrs. Schofield!" whereupon they both laughed softly.

"I'll make the tea now," said Lizzie, "and we'll get that over. Go and get them in. No, not that way." She turned him about and pushed him in the direction of the back door, saying "You haven't much sense really." And to this Mike replied, "Well now, you couldn't expect me to, Liz, havin' passed it all on to me daughter."

They were all seated at the table and it was proving a tight squeeze. Connie, now appearing as her suave, cool self, was seated between Mike and Bob, and across the table sat Mrs. Schofield between Mr. Lord and Tony. Mary Ann, on Mr. Lord's right, had the place of honour at the head of the table, and as she looked down its length over the colourful array of cakes and pyramids of sandwiches mounted with little flags to indicate what they were made of—an idea her mother had got out of a magazine—past the single-tiered birthday cake that dominated the centre of the table and with her name on it, right down the length of the board to where sat their Michael and Sarah Flannagan at the bottom, she thought that in a way it was fitting Sarah Flannagan should be here today to witness her wonderful party. She was seeing her surrounded by all her friends, her posh friends, for they were posh, you only had to listen to their voices; even when they were gabbling as they were doing now, talking and laughing all at once, they still sounded posh. Yes, it was fitting that Sarah had been allowed to witness this triumph. Yet it was strange but Mary Ann knew that she hadn't the feeling that should accompany this triumph. She knew how one should feel when they were triumphant, she had experienced triumph a number of times in her life, and today she should be over the moon with everything that had happened, because wasn't everything all right with everybody? With her ma and da. Oh yes, you only had to look at her ma and da to realise they were all right. And hadn't it worked out all right for Mr Quinton and Mrs. Quinton? And Mr. Lord and Tony were all right again—that was a very good thing. And then there was that lovely, lovely pony. Oh, that pony. And their Michae was happy and she wasn't feeling nasty because it was Sarah Flannagan who had brought this about. But in spite of everything there was something missing. It was something that she would not think about, it was pushed to the back of her mind. She could, she knew, tell herself the one thing that was needed to make this day a day of light and wonder, to make this day a really outstanding, happy day, but she wouldn't say it. She became immersed in the babble of voices, the passing of cups, the handing of plates, the laughter. There was a lot of laughter; even Mr. Lord was laughing with his head back and his mouth open. Mrs. Schofield had achieved this. Tony was leaning across the table saying something funny to her da because her da's eyes were twinkling and he was wagging his hand at Tony. Mr. Quinton was talking and laughing with Mrs. Quinton, and Mrs. Quinton was looking at him with a look that told Mary Ann that it had been true what she had said, she liked him very much.

When the babble was at its highest, Roy Connor bent over the table and, looking up to the head of it, shouted, "There's someone at the front door, someone knocking." He must have had excellent hearing, for no one else seemed to have heard the knocking. And Mike called back, "Well, let them come in then," and, raising his voice further, he cried, "Come away in there. . . ."

When his grannie wanted anyone to enter her house she cried, "Come away in there," and so Corny, hearing the remembered voice of Mike Shaughnessy calling above the noise of the room, "Come away in there," pushed his trembling limbs forward and obeyed it. He walked from the front door, across the hall to the slightly open door of the kitchen and tentatively pushed it wide before taking one step inside the room.

It would be hard to imagine a more effective means of ensuring silence than Corny's appearance in the farm kitchen. No one could have looked more out of place and no one could have felt more out of place than he did. He had not known what to expect, he hadn't been able to visualise the party, Mary Ann's party. The parties they had at Christmas in their house consisted of a sing-song which got louder as the bottles of beer became fewer and which usually ended up in a fight if the whisky flowed too freely. So Corny had not been able to imagine anything like this room, or rather this table and the people seated round it, all without exception, with their eyes fixed on him. It would be true to say that not one person at the table had been able to veil his surprise.

Lizzie was groaning to herself, "Dear God. Oh, no . . . oh, what am I to do?" But she knew what she had to do, for in the next instance, when Mary Ann cried out on that high joy-filled note, she put her hand out swiftly and stopped her daughter from rising and dashing from the table.

As Lizzie's hand caught Mary Ann's arm Mr. Lord's came out on the other side of her, and she glanced from one to the other in surprise and startled indignation, and then looking towards the door she let out an agonised "Oh!" for Corny was no longer there.

Then the eyes of Mary Ann, and not only Mary Ann but the whole company, turned to Mike, for, pushing his chair back briskly and rising to his feet, he strode swiftly towards the hall.

When Mike got on to the road Corny was well past the farm gate, and he hailed him, calling, "Here a minute. Hi there!" But Corny took no notice, and when Mike saw the boy's step was on the verge of a run he sprinted over the distance between them. Coming up to the lad's side, he smiled easily as he asked, "What's your hurry? Corny, isn't it, Corny Boyle? You remember me?"

Corny stood confronting Mike now, and after looking at him squarely for a moment his eyes swished away and he said, "Aye, Aa remember you, Mr. Shaughnessy."

"Well then, come on, come on back to the house."

"No . . . no, Aa shouldn't a' come. . . . Aa knew Aa shouldn't a' come."

"Why shouldn't you come? Mary Ann asked you, didn't she?"

"Aye she did, but Aa didn't think—Aa didn't think there'd be aall them there, them lads and lasses. An' that old bloke." With a defiant glint in them now Corny brought his eyes back to Mike, and Mike, laughing, said, "Oh, the old fellow . . . Mr. Lord. Oh, you don't want to be afraid of him—his bark's much worse than his bite."

"Aa'm not afraid of 'im. . . . Aa'm not afraid of neebody." The shoulders went back and the chin out, and Mike, putting out his hand, touched the shoulder that was not much below his own and said quietly, "That's the ticket, lad. As long as you speak the truth and owe no man nowt you needn't be afraid to face the Queen herself."

Mike was now answering Corny in the own thick dialect, and when he said in an off-hand easy way as if Corny's visit was an ordinary one, "Come on, let's get in to tea," Corny did not move. But his head dropped and his voice was not so arrogant now as he said, "No thanks aall the same, but Aa wouldn't get by with them lot. Aa knew Aa shouldn't a' come in the forst place, not in these togs anyhow. If it hadda been next week." He stopped and his head moved slightly before saying, "Me ma's gettin' me a new suit next week. She's gettin' a thirty pund club and havin' wor Bob, Harry and me aall rigged oot."

There was something about this last statement that brought an odd feeling into Mike's throat: it was the feeling that had at times, when he was a lad, made him either hit out with his fists or seek some corner where he could cry unashamedly. He put out his one arm and, gripping Corny by the shoulder, said roughly, "Let's hear no more about clothes; it isn' clothes that make the chap. And one of these days you'll have more suits than you'll have pegs to put 'em on."

Corny's head shot up and his eyes were bright and there was a look of amazement on his face as if he had heard a prophet speaking, and he said softly, "Aye, Aa know, Aa've aallways told meself that. One day Aa'll have ten suits and everythin' Aa want. Funny you sayin' that." A smile touched his face now and Mike laughed and turned him slowly about as he lied, or let it be said, as he told a tale, for was he not Mary Ann's father. "I'm a bit of a fortune-teller meself," he said. "A better name for it would be character-reader. I can generally tell what a bloke is made of and what he's coming to."

"Can ya?" Corny was relaxed for a moment; he was looking up admiringly at Mr Shaughnessy—Mike Shaughnessy—whom he remembered having seen rolling drunk and dancing in the street and who now looked . . . well, like as if he was rich.

"Aye," said Mike—he was walking slowly and casually towards the gate. "You remember the fellow you saw driving the car the other day with the old 'un?" As he felt Corny's shoulder stiffen he added, "Oh, he's all right. That's Tony; he's the old fellow's grandson. They didn't discover the relationship until three years ago. The old man hasn' had the chance to alter him. Tony's all right, you'll like Tony."

"He sent me some things." Corny's voice was low now and he looked at his feet as he walked. "And I wouldn't hev 'em."

"Oh, I don't blame you." Mike's voice was airy. "But mind you——" He paused slightly in his step. "Tony would mean no offence, his only aim was to give you a hand."

"Aye, p'raps. But, aall the same, Aa'm not startin' on second-hand togs, Aa swore Aa wouldn't. Ye see, me ma's always told me about me grannie and . . . ."

"Aah!" Mike cut in. "There's a woman, your grannie. You know, Fanny's the best friend I've got. Ah, here we are. Get yourself in there." He pushed Corny slightly forward, and kept pressing him until they entered the kitchen. And with his voice on a high airy note he cried, "Is there any room up at the top there? Ah, yes, move along, Mary Ann. Is there a chair, Liz? . . . By the way, this is a friend of mine." He put his arm around Corny's shoulder as he surveyed the company. "We can't go into individual introductions at the moment, there's too many of us, but you just call him Corny, short for Cornelius . . . eh?" He gave Corny a little hug, then added, "You'll get to know everybody by and by. Come on, let's get on with this tea."

Mary Ann's heart was thumping under her ribs, and for the first time today she had that jumping, joyous feeling inside of her. She ignored the subdued quietness that had settled on the table; she ignored the terrible look on Mr. Lord's face; she ignored her mother's stiff countenance; she ignored the polite, surprised look on the faces of her two best friends and was about to smooth matters in her own way when her da caused the silence to break on tentative laughter when he exclaimed loudly, "Put you bugle down, lad. You're not going to drink you tea through that, are you?"

Mary Ann, eagerly taking the instrument from Corny's hand and laughing high in her head, cried, "Oh, Da! It isn't a bugle, it's a cornet, and Corny's a smashing player." There was more laughter, a little louder this time, but still lacking the unrestrained quality that had pervaded the party before Corny's arrival. For the moment the company seemed to be dominated by the feelings of both Lizzie and Mr. Lord, which were vividly expressed in their faces. And then Mrs. Schofield spoke and she addressed herself directly to Corny. "I have a brother who plays the cornet," she said.

"Hev ya?"

On the sound of "Hev ya?" Lizzie lowered her eyes. Up to this moment she would have said of herself that she was no upstart, but now she admitted quite frankly that all her feelings were those of an upstart, for she was ashamed that she or anyone belonging to her had ever been in such circumstances as would oblige them to make even the acquaintance of anyone like Corny Boyle. Oh, she wished him far away, anywhere but here . . . "Hev ya?" Oh, Mary Ann! What was to be done with her? It was true what Mr. Lord said, she had no sense of correct behaviour, she would never have mixed her invitations to this drastic extent if she had. Of all the children she could have invited from the district round Mulhattan's Hall, Corny Boyle was the roughest customer. It wouldn't have been so bad if he had come at any other time, but now, when she was surrounded by . . . these others. Lizzie refrained from giving Mary Ann's posh friends any class status. And there was Mr. Lord; he was livid. Oh, what would the outcome of this be? The party was spoiled, couldn't Mary Ann realise that—for doubtless "hev ya?" was just the beginning.

She looked at her daughter, but Mary Ann was engrossed at the moment in what Mrs. Schofield was saying to Corny.

"Yes, and he drove us nearly round the bend; in fact, as the saying goes, up the wall and over the other side. And I was the first one over." Mrs. Schofield cast her deep blue eyes round the table now and caught the laughter to her, then went on, "Of course, that was when he was learning, but now when he can play, well he hardly ever touches it. It'll be the same with you." She looked back to Corny.

"Noo . . . noo, it won't. Aa'm gonna larn it proper. A man near us is larning me now."

"Well, good for you. You'll have to play something to us after tea, eh?"

"Aye . . . aye, Aa will." Corny was looking directly at Mrs. Schofield, and to do this he had to cut his glance from Mr. Lord who was at her elbow.

"Perhaps you'll give me a lesson," said Mrs. Schofield, still talking to Corny. "I feel I've missed something in not taking advantage of our Robert. It mustn't sound so bad when you're doing the blowing and not just listening. What do you say?" She turned her eyes for the fraction of a second on Mr. Lord, and before he had time to make any caustic comment she flashed her laughing gaze round the table again, crying, "We'll have a percussion band. You, Mary Ann, you can play the comb. And you, Beatrice, we'll give you a tray. And Janice, you can bang two loaf tins. And Tony there can . . ."

Mike looked across the table at this woman who was allotting household instruments to everyone at the table, and the smile deepened on his face as he thought to himself: I made a mistake; now I know why men marry such women. She's no fool, that one, and she's kind with it for all her dithery lah-de-dah. Aye, she is that. He took up the ball she had set rolling and cried, "What would you give me?"

"Oh, now let's see." She appealed to the whole table. "What shall we give him?"

There were cries of this and that, and when Connie to the side of him said, "I'd give him a wash-board," he turned to her, laughing. "All right," he said, "and wait till you hear me; a wash-board it will be."

Everybody had made a suggestion for the percussion band with the exception of Lizzie and Mr. Lord. Lizzie now handed Corny a cup of tea for which, after looking hard at her, he said "Ta," and then almost before he had laid the cup on the table he made an impatient exclamation to himself and, putting his hand in his pocket, he pulled out what appeared to be a stick of thumb thickness, about nine inches in length, wrapped in newspaper, and for the first time since coming to the table and sitting next to Mary Ann he turned and looked at her and spoke. "That's for yer borthday," he said.

"Oh . . . oh, thanks, Corny." She hadn't the foggiest notion what was under the paper, and for a moment she hesitated to open it in fear that it would be something that might bring derision on the giver. Slowly she unfolded the wrapping, and when the thing lay across her hand there was a gasp of surprise from those nearest to her, for Corny's present was a small flute cut out of black ebony and inlaid between the stops with mother-of-pearl. It was of exquisite workmanship and delicate beauty, and that it should have been given by this rough lump of a lad seemed to add to its lustre.

"Oh, isn't it beautiful!" Connie was leaning forward across the table, and Mrs. Schofield, bending forward too, exclaimed, "Oh, that is lovely."

Speaking to Corny for the first time, Tony asked quietly, "Where did you come across that?"

"Aa picked it up in a junk shop."

He picked it up in a junk shop. Mike was repeating the words to himself. This unprepossessing lump of humanity—for even Mike couldn't in any way glamorise Corny, this lad who had been brought up in the low end of Howden, who had never experienced any of the niceties of life—had . . . picked out from among junk this instrument of beauty. He himself was no musician. He could dig away at the piano by ear and he could sing a bit, but he knew nothing about musical instruments, yet he did know that the flute, or whatever is was, was a little miracle of workmanship.

"Oh, Corny!" Mary Ann's lips were trembling, perhaps a little with relief but mostly with happiness. Of all the presents she had had today, and she'd had a lot, this was the best. Nor had she forgotten the pony. She looked up at Corny, and although her voice was low it brought a hush to the table. "I'll learn to play it, Corny. Yes, I will. I promise I'll learn to play it."

"Between homework and riding lessons?"

She flashed a quick look over her shoulder towards Mr. Lord. His voice was even and controlled but it did not deceive her; she knew he was vexed, even mad, but that did not stop her from saying, "Yes, yes, I'll fit it in some way, but I'll learn it." She flashed her laughing face up at her mother now and said, "I'll play it in bed, Ma." In her excitement she had forgotten that for today her ma also was not her ma but her mother.

Mr. Lord looked down at his plate and applied himself to crumbling up a piece of cake. He was hurt, deeply hurt, and angry. Angry at himself for being angry, for allowing this child to retain the power to hurt him. He had given her the pony for her birthday present, for he knew that nobody else would be able to give her such a present, even if they had thought of it, and she had been overjoyed with the pony, but neither the animal nor himself had elicited from her the feeling which she was bestowing on this . . . penny-whistle, gormless, uncouth individual. What had he said to him? "By God! I'll get on." He glanced at the boy now. He was drinking his tea, likely with loud sucking sounds if it was possible to hear him.

Just as Mr. Lord was twitching his eye back to his plate again, Corny, from over the rim of his cup, looked at the old man and, catching his disparaging glance on himself, returned it unblinkingly. It was Mr. Lord who looked away first.

If that boy had entry into this house, and there was every likelihood that he would, following on Shaughnessy's attitude, then the child would be influenced by him. How old was he . . . sixteen or so? He would have to do some thinking about this and step warily. It was a pity, he thought now, that he had already exchanged words with him; he could do much more to nip this thing in the bud had he approached the youth from a different angle. There was one thing for sure: he must make it his business to get this boy away from the vicinity by some means, either fair or foul. He was certainly not going to have his schemes brought to nothing by a lump of a lout like this. No, he certainly was not. He more than surprised Tony by turning to him at this juncture and saying, in a tone which by a stretch could be termed jocular, "Why haven't you learned some musical instrument?"

"What! Me?" Tony's eyes were wide as he looked at his grandfather, but he was not deceived by the old man's change of front, for he knew he was furious at the boy's intrusion, but he replied with a laugh, "I'm tone deaf, you know I am; I can't even sing in the bath. Don't forget you've complained of the noise more than once."

After this exchange, Tony's and Mike's glances, meeting quietly across the table, said: "The old boy's not going to lie down under this."

The tea lasted much longer than Lizzie had anticipated, and although she herself was not feeling at ease she was glad to see that the company had apparently forgotten Corny's presence—that is, all except Mary Ann. She would have to talk to Mary Ann later tonight or perhaps tomorrow. She would have to tell her, in a quiet way, that you didn't look at people as she was doing at Corny, even if you liked the person, and that if she wanted to keep anybody's affection—and God forbid that she would ever want to keep this boy's—she must hide her feelings, and for a long, long time. There were lots of things she must talk to her about—she was thirteen now. Oh dear! dear! Why had this boy put his nose in the door today, today of all days, when everything was going so beautifully?

Lizzie now gave Mary Ann a slight dig in the side which had the two-fold purpose of drawing her attention away from Corny and giving her the signal that she and the younger members could leave the table. But apparently the older members wanted to leave the table too, and there was a general outpouring into the sunshine and on to the lawn again. But not with the instruments of the percussion band. The talk about that had served the purpose Mrs. Schofield had intended.

Corny kept very much in the rear of the company and for the short time she was allowed Mary Ann stayed by his side. She was happy. This was the most wonderful party she had ever had and, oh, she was going to learn to play the flute. It was a beautiful flute, everybody thought so. It was the nicest present she had received today—or at any other time. Well, there was the pony. But that was different somehow. Mr. Lord had been mad at Corny coming. That was at the beginning; he didn't seem so bad now, he was with Mrs. Schofield. Mrs. Schofield was a funny woman, but she did make people laugh. She was making them laugh now. On the sound of the laughter she deluded herself that everybody was enjoying themselves and there was no need for her to bother and she could spend the rest of the time with Corny.

Looking up at him now, she said with bald diplomacy, "You needn't go when the others do, need you, because you came late. If you'll stay I'll show you round the farm and take you up to see my pony. Oh, he's lovely."

"Did ya da gie you it?"

"No . . ." She paused before the admission. "It was Mr. Lord."

"Oh, him. He doossn't like me."

"Oh, but he will in a little while; he's like that with everybody to start with. Oh"—it was a loud "oh"—"he was worse than that with me. He even told Ben, that's his servant, to throw me out of his house."

"He did?"

"Yes, he did."

"Mary Ann!"

Mary Ann turned to find her mother looking at her.

"You must see to your guests and play some games." As Lizzie said this she gave Corny a weak smile, and Corny, understanding, stood stock still.

"I won't be a minute." Mary Ann reassured Corny before reluctantly leaving him to join Beatrice and the rest. She did not say, "Come along and join in"—she couldn't imagine Corny playing, not at their games, anyway.

As Corny found himself looking at Lizzie he felt as he had done when he first entered the kitchen, and once again he said, but under his breath, "Aa shouldn't a' come, should Aa?"

"Don't be silly, Corny, of course you should; you're very welcome." Lizzie was surprised at the enthusiasm she put into this comforting but untrue statement.

He said now, "Me Gran will go off the deep end when she knaws."

"Why should she?" Lizzie found she was saying all the things she didn't mean, for were she in Fanny's place she'd find more than enough to go off the deep end about.

She was wondering in her mind what to say to him next when the situation was saved by Mrs. Schofield crying, "Oh, there you are. Now come on, play that cornet, and something jolly, mind, nothing highfalutin."

"Aw, Aa couldn't play anythin' high flootin' if Aa tried."

Corny was laughing now, and Lizzie found herself being amazed at the fact that this dizzy woman could put this lump of a lad at his ease, whereas she herself, who was, she felt, an understanding, sensible type, put him on edge. But then, wasn't she Mary Ann's mother? Mrs. Schofield had nothing to lose with Corny.

"Ya reely want ta hear it?"

"Of course I do, everybody does. Listen, everybody." She stopped and flung her arm upwards as if she was mistress of ceremonies. "Squat a minute, Corny's going to play."

"Oh, Lord!" It was the boy Roy Connor speaking from where he stood at the bottom of the lawn among his friends. "This'll be Corny by name and Corny by cornet." The witticisim brought sniggers from the girls and guffaws from the boys, until a voice said, "Connor!" It was the voice of the fifth-former speaking to a second-form grub, and the grub reacted without remembering that he wasn't at school and said humbly, "Yes, Shaughnessy?"

"We'll have none of that."

"No, Shaughnessy."

In this moment Mary Ann loved their Michael and she told herself that she would never, never, never be nasty to him again. It was in this moment, too, that the first stirrings of love flickered in Sarah Flannagan's breast for Michael Shaughnessy. She had liked Michael, she had always like him, she had always been attracted by him, mostly it must be said, because of the halo of the Grammar School. But it was now that the liking changed to the first small spark of rare love, and thereby Michael Shaughnessy's and Sarah Flannagan's destinies were entwined, painfully entwined. But as yet they did not know this and were ecstatically happy on this afternoon of the party.

"Quiet now . . . quiet." Mrs. Schofield was now flapping her hands wildly, and her daughter, in shamed tones, whispered to Mary Ann, "Oh, Mary Ann, I'm sorry. Oh, I hate it when Mummy takes control and acts the goat; oh, I am sorry."

Mary Ann, glancing for a moment at Janice, suddenly realised that you could be ashamed of your people for other things beside drink. It was a very comforting thought, a very comforting thought indeed. Anyway, she couldn't now see much about Mrs. Schofield to be ashamed of, but nevertheless Janice was ashamed and deeply. Remembering the technique of Mrs. McBride in praising her da when she herself needed comfort on his behalf, she turned to her friend and said, "I think your mother's lovely."

"You do?"

"Yes . . . yes, I do. And she's a sport. And I think you're awful for saying that."

"Quiet, you grown-ups." Mrs. Schofield was now silencing Connie and Bob and Mike with more flaps of her hands. She disregarded the fact that they were speaking to Mr. Lord. "Now, there you are, they've all stopped talking. Now play, Corny."

Before Corny lifted the cornet to his mouth he looked at Mrs. Schofield and smiled. It was a broad smile and changed his face completely.

Nobody seemed to recognise the piece Corny was playing, but what the elders did recognise was that the notes were true and unblurred and that the boy, holding the cornet pointing skywards, had completely lost his self-consciousness and become an entirely new being. His coat sleeves had slid down almost to his elbows, but this did not make him appear ludicrous; it was the player who was to the fore now. Mike, as he listened, thought, "Aye, and he might an' all have more suits than pegs to put them on—this is the age of the cornet and such noises. He might have been born at the right time, who knows?"

When Corny stopped there was loud clapping, and when it ceased he said, "That was me own piece, Aa made it up." And then with an unselfconscious twinkle, said, "D'ya know this?" And he had reached only the third note when there were scornful cries and laughs of, "Oh, Blaydon Races!" but before he had finished it there was only one person on the lawn who wasn't singing, and that was Mr. Lord.

Lizzie was in the kitchen clearing away and she was not a little amazed when she heard the singing, and perhaps a little relieved, but a few minutes later, when she came into the hall and looked on to the back of the player where he stood in front of the open doorway, she once again closed her eyes and lowered her head, for the tune he had started was being picked up by Mike and his clear deep tones were ringing across the lawn, accompanied by the laughing treble of Mary Ann. They were singing, "He stands at the corner and whistles me out." And the climax came with a great roar of laughter when a cow in the byre set up a loud moo-ing. Then everybody was singing, "He stands at the corner and whistles me out, With his hands in his pockets, and his shirt hanging out."

Again it was only Mr. Lord who didn't join in; again it was only his face that wasn't cracking with laughter. He stands at the corner and whistles me out! He could see Mary Ann singing and gambolling with the lamb as she sang this song, and there she was now yelling her head off, sanctioned this time by her father. Well, he mustn't worry, things had worked out for him in the past; he hadn't the slightest doubt but they would work his way again. Undoubtedly, it would need greater effor, but then all things worth while needed effort.

And he began right away on the effort when Corny finished playing. In clear tones he spoke to him across the space that divided them, saying, "I think, young man, that you'll make something of that instrument before you're finished."

Corny stared at the old man, not able to believe that he was speaking to him, and in a tone of praise. But he was wary, on his guard, and he made no reply. When a few minutes later the old man walked casually to his side and said, "Tell me, what do you intend to make of yourself?" he looked at him for a long while before answering, and then his tone was gruff and dull, "Aa'm gonna be a cornet player."

"How are you going to eat until you become a professional cornet player?"

It was a sensible question and Corny gave it a sensible answer. "Aa'm goin' in a garrage forst," he said.

"Ah, a garage. You're interested in cars, then?"

"Aye, Aa am." Corny's tone could have been interpreted as: make what you like of that.

At this point Mike stopped Mary Ann from going to Corny and claiming his attention, and as he watched the old man and the lad talking he thought, The old boy's up to something; but, anyway, if the lad gets talking he'll find he's no fool and he'll forget his suit and see the makings of him.

But Tony, looking at his grandfather talking to the boy, just thought, Poor devil. What chance does he stand? . . .

It was about seven-thirty when the cars began to arrive. The party was at an end. Of all the farewells the high peak was the waving away of Mrs. Schofield, and the last words Mike said to her were, "Bless you," and she laughed up into his face from the car wheel and said, "Bless you, too, Mike. And don't think you've seen the last of me, for I'm coming again, invitation or no." Lizzie, too, laughed at this woman. In spite of her dizziness she felt that she liked her. Anyway, she had certainly eased a nasty situation.

There was more laughter when Mrs. Schofield's car once again got into a tangle with Jane Willoughby's outside the front gate. Jane was in a bad temper, for on the sight of her cousin Connie all compatible again with Bob, she felt she must have missed a great deal by not making an effort and staying to tea.

Bob had already helped his wife into his car before going round to take his seat at the wheel, and now there was Lizzie on his side and Mike and Mary Ann on Connie's to say goodbye. Connie's last words were for Mary Ann. "I wouldn't have missed your party for anything, Mary Ann," she said.

Mary Ann could say nothing, she could only smile from one to the other in turn as she hung on to her da's hand—the Quintons were kind again and were no longer a menace to her family, so that was that.

It was when the last car had gone, the last farewell had been said, that Tony, touching Mike's arm and drawing him slightly aside, motioned with his head to where Mr. Lord was still sitting talking to Corny, an apparently enraptured Corny now. And Tony with a quizzical smile on his face said, under his breath, "You'd never believe that he could get going so quickly but he has already disposed of the boy."

"Disposed? What do you mean?"

"He's got him interested in America and cars."

"But what's that got to do with disposing of him?"

"Can't you see, Mike? Oh, but perhaps you don't know. He's got connections who have a car business in America and he holds more than a few shares in the concern. I've been listening to him working." Tony laughed. "He's told the lad he can get him set on there."

"But why? What does he want to do that for? He looked as if he hated the lad's guts when he came into the kitchen."

"Oh, be yourself, Mike," Tony laughed. "Where are your wits? Can't you see he's making my path clear by removing an obstacle. And from you daughter's show of interest in our musician he's definitely going to be an obstacle. Don't you get it?"

Mike looked at Tony in silence for a moment. He was relieved and glad that he was seeing the business now with an amusing slant and he shook his head as he murmured, "Well, well. Can you beat it? He's simply amazing. But look . . ." He nodded over his shoulder. "Look there. Somehow I don't think we need concern ourselves overmuch about Corny being drafted to America, do you?"

Mary Ann was running up the garden towards Corny and Mr. Lord. Everybody had gone now; she could have Corny to herself; she was going to take him round the farm and Mr. Lord wouldn't mind. For Mr. Lord liked Corny, he had talked to him for the last hour—she wouldn't have believed it, not after what happened in the street that day. She came to a stop at Mr. Lord's knee and cried, "Hasn't it been a lovely party, Mr. Lord? Hasn't it been wonderful?" Then before Mr. Lord could say anything she grabbed Corny's arm and cried, "Come and see my pony. Mr. Lord gave it to me for my birthday present—

didn't you?" She leant towards the old man and put her hand affectionately on his lapel, and for an instant he placed his own wrinkled, blue-veined one on top of it, but he said nothing; he just watched her hurry away, with the gangling boy at her side. As the ill-assorted pair passed Mike and Tony at the gate Mike stretched out his hand and said to Corny, "You'd better leave that with me. If you start blowing that up in the fields you'll scare the wits out of the cattle." Corny, without hesitation, handed his beloved cornet to Mike, then with his head not bowed and his limbs not so gangling he looked ahead and strode out down the road, Mary Ann at his side.

But now she was not hitching and skipping as was usual with her when she was happy, for like an unexpected blow it had come to her that her hitching days were over. It was at the moment that Corny had handed the instrument to Mike that it happened. It was as if her da had recognised that Corny was to be her lad, and approved. In this moment of awakening she also realised, and fully, that he was the only one who did approve. She knew, too, that she had been daft to imagine that Mr. Lord was talking to Corny because he liked him. She asked now in a sober tone: "What were you and Mr. Lord talking about?"

"Cars."

"Cars?"

"Aye, cars." Corny cast a sidelong glance down on her, and she saw that he was amused and that he was surprisingly at his ease. He was no longer on the defensive. "American ones."

"Oh!"

"He's got a say in some works oot there."

"In America?"

"Aye." He walked steadily on, looking ahead. "He's for hevin' me set on."

"In America!" Her voice was high.

They had just turned into the farmyard gate. They stopped and looked at each other.

"But . . . but you can get work in a garage here—in England."

"Aye . . . aye, Aa knows that, but he wants ta pack me off to America."

"But why?"

"To get rid of me cos'."

As they continued to stare at each other Mary Ann's feelings became a mixture of fear, misery, and disappointment. Then these emotions were swiftly engulfed by a surge of indignation . . . That was why Mr. Lord had been kind to Corny. Oh! . . . Oh!

"Are you going?"

"Well——" Corny pulled on his ear and, as he did so, he turned his head and looked about the farm-yard, saying quietly, "There's one thing sartin: Aa'll nivver git a chance like this agen. It could set me up. This could be it. Aa aallways knew Aa'd git be chance one day."

"Oh, but, Corny . . ."

The wonder of the day had vanished and Corny did not seem to hear her appeal, for he went on looking about him and talking. "Aa could take it 'cos he doesn't knaw Aa'm on ta him—he thinks Aa swallowed it. He's not very bright up top or he wouldn't uv changed his tune so quickly an' laid it on see thick."

With a sudden pull on his arm she drew his attention back to her. "I know why he wants to send you to America."

"Aye, so div Aa."

Her eyes became so large that her face looked even smaller in contrast.

"It's to stop me an' you dunchin' inta each other. Me grannie told me a while since what he's got on the cards for you, an' he's got the idea Aa might muck it up." There followed a pause, then, "De ya want me ta gan t'America?"

"No, oh no. No, I don't." In the look on her face and the intensity of her words, she was exposing her vital weakness to Corny. A weakness that amounted almost to a flaw in her character, for where she loved she could not lie. Her feelings would always present her as a target. She was fortunate that Corny's interior was in direct contrast to his outward appearance, for there was neither arrogance nor roughness in his manner as he said, "Well then, Aa won't."

The heaviness left her body and for a second she had a desire to jump, but she checked it, and found she had to take three quick steps, for Corny had resumed his walk again.

"Yer da's fer me."

Mary Ann's whole face was bright; her great eyes were shining as with triumph as she answered, "Yes, yes. I know."

"Yer ma's not though."

"She will be."

"No, no, she won't. Aa divvn't taalk nice enough for hor."

"Oh, Corny, I'll learn . . . teach you. I will." She half stopped, but he carried on, his big feet hitting the ground flatly with each step. "Divint knaw as Aa want ta talk different. Any road, Aa won't hev time, workin' an' arl that."

When she made no comment he glanced sideways at her and remarked, "Not less Aa come oot here a night or so a week."

"Yes, yes, you could do that." She was eager again.

"Aye." He seemed to consider. "Aye, Aa could de that."

"Yes, yes, I could do that."

"What?"

"Just what you said: 'Aye, aye, Aa could de' that.' " She smiled gently at him. "Say 'Yes, yes, I could do that.' That's your first lesson."

"Aw!" He put his head back and laughed.

"Go on, say it."

"Aw, no man."

"Go on."

"Aw well! . . . Yes, yes, Aa could do that."

The translation was too much for them both, for they began to laugh. They laughed and they laughed. Then Mary Ann, grabbing at his hand, compelled him to run with her. And he suited his step to hers as he was always to do.

When the sound of laughter floated down over the garden it carried no indication that a boy's life had been taken in hand, or that Mary Ann's destiny was already cut to a complicated pattern, and certainly not that the owner of the deep laugh had just managed a translation from thick Geordie into northern accented English.

Then the laughter was abruptly cut off and replaced by the strains of a song.

As he listened Mike's face widened into a smile, but Lizzie's face had a neutral look. The effect of the sound on Mr. Lord was to make him close his eyes.

The breeze, seeming to catch Mary Ann's voice and separate it from her partner's, bore it down to the garden, and the words hung on the air:

> "Still I love him, can't deny it.
> I'll be with him, wherever he goes."

Life and Mary Ann

PART ONE

Growing Pains

1

I wish I'd never clapped eyes on him. I wish he had left us alone.

What! In Mulhattan's Hall?

Mary Ann hunched her shoulders as indication that she was ignoring the voice of gratitude that usually played no small part as a component of her character. Well, he made you sick, he did. Who did he think he was, anyway? Playing God. Directing all their lives. He certainly tried to live up to his name. . . . Mr. Lord, indeed! Well, he could think he was the Lord, and act like him, but he wasn't going to get the better of her in this latest fight. . . . But he had, he had already got the better of her, hadn't he?

Mary Ann unclenched her hands and rose slowly from the side of the bed and walked towards the window. There had been a black frost in the night, there would soon be snow. The cutting air came from the window-pane and chilled her nose and lips. So cold was her mouth that she did not feel her teeth biting into the flesh. But she felt the trembling of her chin in its fight, not against the cold, but against the rising storm of tears.

Although she was gazing across the farmyard towards the house on the hill, Mr. Lord's house, she was seeing none of these things. The width of the farmyard had taken on the shape of a face. The buildings at each side were cheeks, high-boned, prominent cheeks, and Mr. Lord's house on the hill was a deep brow, half covered with tumbled black hair, Somewhere, in the distance between the farm and the house on the hill, were the eyes of Corny. They were deep-set, and dark. She couldn't see if they were merry, or sad, or held that spark of fighting fire that made him stand up to people. . . . Stand up to Mr. Lord.

For over three years Corny had stood up to Mr. Lord. From the very day he had come to her thirteenth birthday party, a belated, awkward, aggressive grotesquely dressed guest, he had stood up to him. His appearance on that day had thrown the whole party out of joint. But he had made an impression on Mr. Lord, for the old man had recognised in the gangling fifteen-year-old a worthy opponent, worthy to fight, worthy of many things . . . in fact, of anything in the world, but herself. Corny, in a subtle, even cunning way, had stood firm against all Mr. Lord's tactics, and had got the better of him time and time again where she herself was concerned. And in the end he would have won. She knew this, she felt it. But what does he do? What does Corny do? Of a startling sudden, he gives in to Mr. Lord. He accepts the offer that the old man has been dangling like a golden carrot under his nose for years.

When she had gone for him last night, almost reaching five feet in her wild indignation, he had remained utterly calm. The only time he had raised his voice was when he said, "Look, I'm tellin' you, he's got nowt to do with it."

She knew that he had used nowt to vex her, because he could speak as anybody now, even as good as their Michael. Had she not coached him month after month from that thirteenth birthday when she had given him his first lesson in English?Northern English, for although her grammar was correct, the inflexion of the dialect was still thick on her. But so convincing had been his denial that Mr. Lord had any hand in his decision to go to America, that she had asked, with pain-touched docility, "Is it because they are always ragging you about me being so little?" He gave a scornful, hard laugh before saying quietly, "Don't be daft." And then he had added, with a touch of the quiet, sly humour that she loved. "It's just as well you're no bigger, else you'd aim to wear the pants all the time. Not that you don't have a go, even now."

She had not laughed for her mind was looking at the saying literally. The waist of his trousers would reach up to her bust, and her head came far below his thick shoulder. Over the last few years she had done everything possible to put on inches. During one period, she had measured herself every day for three months, until the disheartening result had begun to affect her. Her mother had said, "If you worry, it will stop you growing." Her da had said, comfortingly, "You'll sprout all at once, you'll see. One of these mornings you'll wake up and find your feet sticking through the bed rails. Anyway," he had added, with his arm about her shoulder, "you've got more in your little finger than most people have got in their great boast bodies." But that comfort did not make up for such silly remarks as, "You two are like Mutt and Jeff," or, "Here comes the long and the short of it."

She had tried wearing very high heels. The first pair of stiletto shoes she had worn had caused her da and Corny to fall against each other with laughing. Somehow she didn't suit high heels, and so she had been unable to take advantage of such helpful accessories. But what did it matter? High heels, the long and the short of it, Mutt and Jeff, that wasn't the reason he was going. He was going because Mr. Lord had won.

At this point in her thinking the bedroom door clicked and her mother came in. At thirty-eight Elizabeth Shaughnessy appeared like a woman bordering on thirty. Her face was without lines, her long blonde hair resting in a bun on the nape of her neck still retained its natural sheen. Her bearing was dignified. During the last three years, with the lessening of worry, life had seemed to stand still for her. Only during these last years had she taken the comfort of the farmhouse and the security of Mike's position as a natural sequence of events. Mike no longer drank—at least he no longer got drunk—and this fact alone would have spelt security no matter where they had lived. But in the comparative opulence of the farm-house—comparative when thinking of their early beginnings, in the slum in Burton Street, known as Mulhattan's Hall—the fact that he was steady had paid dividends far surpassing anything she had ever dreamed of. Not that she had been entirely free from worry over the last three years; she experienced the usual worries of a mother concerning her son and daughter. But, as from the very beginning, it was the daughter who gave her cause for most concern. Somehow, Michael's life had always seemed cut and dried. Right from when he was a child, even before he ever saw a farm, he had wanted, like his father, to be a farmer. In times past she had thought this was the only thing father and son had in common. Now, all that was changed. But with Mary Ann it had been different. Perhaps it was the fact of Mr. Lord coming into her life that had made Mary Ann more of a trial. And yet she knew she shouldn't think of her daughter in that sense. Mary Ann had been the saviour of them all. But for Mary Ann they would be rotting in Mulhattan's Hall at this moment. She had no illusion about the strength of her husband. Without this environment, brought about by his daughter's strategy, Mike would still be fighting a losing battle with the drink and the shipyard.

Lizzie knew that everything in life must be paid for, and Mary Ann was expected to pay Mr. Lord in the kind of payment he most desired. By becoming the wife of his grandson she would be tied to him for life. He would then have claims on her far outreaching those of the present. And it was a glorious prospect, Lizzie knew, when looked at unemotionally: Mary Ann Shaughnessy, a child from the slums of Jarrow, lifted into the family, the élite family of the Lords, where money and power went hand in hand.

Three years ago, when the old man's plans had been made known to her, Lizzie's first reaction had been one of shock and disgust. Mary Ann was only a child, a child of thirteen . . . not thirteen. And Mr. Lord was actually voicing his plans to marry her to Tony, his grandson. Tony was then twenty-four and seemed already a very adult man. But the shock and disgust had not lasted long, for when Lizzie thought about it calmly she became excited, even elated, almost overcome with the idea of this wonderful future for her child. That was until she realised that Mary Ann's interest in Corny Boyle was no passing childish fancy. Her daughter, she knew, took strong likes and dislikes, and where she liked she almost nearly loved. She loved her father more than she did God. She loved, yes, she loved the old man, there was no doubt about that. She loved him, she stood up to him, she fought with him but she loved him. And she also loved Corny Boyle. That was the trouble, that was the worry now in Lizzie's life. Or it had been up till yesterday when Corny had sprung his decision on them all. He had walked into the kitchen unannounced, and with a coolness that set Lizzie wondering, he had told them he was going to America. She wondered if this big, raw-boned fellow was calculating the benefits to be derived from submitting to Mr. Lord, or if he was being super-humanly unselfish and leaving the road clear for her daughter. Whichever way it was, she thanked God from the bottom of her heart that Corny Boyle had decided to go to America. But now before her lay the task of comforting Mary Ann.

"Come on downstairs, lass, you're froze up here."

Mary Ann remained gazing out of the window. And her voice was flat-sounding as she replied, "I'm all right. I'm not cold." Her mother had called her "lass". She only called her that when she was deeply touched. She usually called her Mary Ann or "My dear", and she had insisted some time ago that she be called "Mother" and not "Ma". Mary Ann's lips moved tightly over one another. That was Mr. Lord again. She could hear his voice now, saying to her mother, "You must make her drop this 'Ma' way of addressing you, Mrs. Shaughnessy. Make her adopt Mother. It is a much nicer term, don't you think?" When her da had found out about this—and he had found out, because her mother kept insisting that she did not call her "Ma"—he had cried indignantly, "To hell! If you are Ma to her, then you are Ma to her. . . . And let me tell you this. You'll lose something by being more Mother than Ma. I'm tellin' you! As for the old boy. If he approaches me with the idea of turning me into Father, I'll spit in his eye. So help me God, I will."

Her mother had had to do a lot of talking to calm her father down that time.

"Come on down." Lizzie's voice was soft and coaxing. "The tea's all set, and Michael and Sarah will be here any minute. Come on."

Mary Ann turned and looked at her mother, and her voice held no bitterness as she said, "You're glad he's going, aren't you?"

"Oh no, I'm not. What makes you say that? Oh no, I'm not." Lizzie's reply was too quick. There was too much emphasis on her words. Mary Ann lowered her lids, covering her great brown eyes from her mother's gaze. Her mother couldn't lie very well. She turned her head away and looked out of the window again before saying, "Why is it you have always minded me and Corny?"

Lizzie could find no words, no false words with which to answer this statement. If she had spoken the truth she would have said, "It's a man's position that matters. Michael's future is set. At the end of this year, when he finishes his probation on the farm, he will go to the Agricultural College. His future is mapped out. He'll be a farmer. If there wasn't a job waiting for him here, he could get set on anywhere. Perhaps I would have liked someone better than Sarah Flannagan for him, because, as you know, none of us can stand her mother. But I admit that Sarah's turned out to be a nice lass. And moreover she's Michael's choice." Perhaps her son had one more thing in common with his father. There'd only ever be one woman for him. There were men like that. They were few and far between, God knew, but there were still some left; and she had the feeling in her heart that Sarah Flannagan was the only one for Michael and he for her, strange as it seemed, for only a few years ago Sarah hated the sight of Mary Ann, and Michael into the bargain. But then, like a child, she was taking the pattern from her mother.

Mary Ann said into the silence, "You're supposed to like Mrs. McBride, and she's his grandmother."

"Of course, I like Fanny. I could almost say I love her. But there's a great difference between a woman and her grandson. Not that I don't like Corny. I've told you, I do like Corny. Why do you keep on?"

Mary Ann nodded to the icy window-pane. "But you don't like him for me, because there's Tony, isn't there? And Mr. Lord. Mr. Lord's little plan. Oh, I know all about it. But listen to me, Mother." She pulled herself away from Lizzie's side. She even stepped back a pace to widen the distance between them, before saying, "I'll never marry Tony. Not to please you, or him, or anybody else."

"Who's talking about Tony?"

"You are. You're thinking about him all the time. That's why you've never been able to take to Corny. Corny hadn't a big house. He hadn't a splendid job. He hadn't a grandfather rolling in the money. But let me tell you, Mother, Corny will make his name with either one thing or the other. With either cars or his cornet. Oh, yes. That's been a laugh in the house for a long time now. Corny, with his cars and his cornet. The three C's. Well! you wait and see. . . ."

As Mary Ann's head drooped forward and the tears began to roll down her cheeks, Lizzie cried, "Aw! lass, lass. Aw! don't cry like that." And she enfolded her daughter in her arms and rocked her gently back and forwards as if she were still the little elfin-faced child. The endearing, maddening, precocious, beguiling child. And she was still a child. She would always remain a child to Lizzie. And she wanted her child to be looked after; and like every mother, she felt that half the battle would be won if there was money at hand to help with the looking after.

Saturday tea was still a function, a time when Lizzie had her family all around her. It was usually a meal of leisure with no one dashing to catch a bus to the secretarial school in Newcastle—that was Mary Ann; or golloping the meal to attend to this, that, or the other on the farm—that was Mike; or, if not following his father's pattern and dashing outside, reading, reading, reading—that was Michael, always reading, and not eating. There were more books in the house concerning the diseases that animals were prone to than in the Public Library, so Lizzie thought. But Saturday was different.

All Saturday morning Lizzie baked for the tea. Besides the old standbys, egg-and-bacon pie, fruit tarts and scones, there was always something new. She liked to try a new recipe each week. On Tuesday she would look forward to the coming of her magazine. Not for the stories, but for the recipes, and each Saturday they would tease her, "What's it the day, another stomach binder? By! I'll sue that paper afore long." Mike would generally start in this way, and the others would follow suit. However, they nearly always ate the last crumb of her new recipe. But to-day things hadn't gone according to plan. Mike made no reference whatever to the table. His large, heavy, handsome face looked dark as he took his seat at the head, and immediately he gave signs of his inward mood by running his hands through his thick red hair, and this after combing it only a few minutes earlier.

Lizzie felt a rising irritation in her as she gauged her husband's mood. He wasn't going to start and take up the cudgels again. Talk about like father, like son. It had never been like that in this family, it had always been like father, like daughter. Mike was also, she knew, blaming Mr. Lord for Corny's decision. Although the boy had stated flatly that no one had influenced him, Mike was as furious at this moment against the old man as was Mary Ann herself. It was quite some time now since any major issue had occurred to make Mike take sides against Mr. Lord. As Lizzie looked sharply between her husband and her daugher, she thought she could almost feel the emotions flowing between them, as if they were linked by actual blood vessels. Talk about Siamese twins. As was her wont when worried, she muttered a little prayer to herself. It was, as usual, in the nature of a demanding plea, and in this particular case she asked that Mike might not lose his temper with the old man. "Let him go for anyone else, but not for Mr. Lord, dear God."

Trying to bring normality into the proceedings, Lizzie now addressed herself to Sarah. "How's business been this week, Sarah?" she asked with a smile.

"Oh, not too good at all. The roads have been so slippery. It's hard enough to exercise them. And nobody seems inclined to ride. I don't blame them. I nearly stuck to the saddle yesterday morning."

"I don't know how you do it. I think you're wonderful."

Sarah Flannagan remained smiling across the table at Lizzie. But she made no answer. She would have been glad had this woman thought she was wonderful, but she felt it was merely a phase. She knew there was tension in the house and that Elizabeth Shaughnessy was trying to smooth things over. Some day she hoped, and from the depth of her being, that this woman would be her mother-in-law, and yet she was a little afraid of her. Yes, the truth was, she was a little afraid of her. She thought she wasn't quite good enough for Michael. All mothers felt like that about daughters-in-law, so she understood, and so she felt sure that Elizabeth Shaughnessy would finally accept her into the family, whereas she would never reconcile herself to accept Corny Boyle. This thought brought her eyes flicking towards Mary Ann. It was hard at this moment to think that Mary Ann and herself had been bitter enemies from the day they first met until just a short while ago. She did not delude herself that the first day she came to this house, when she led the dapple, Mary Ann's thirteenth birthday present from Mr. Lord, up the road, and was asked to stay to tea, that it was from that day that she and Mary Ann had become friends. No, on that day Mary Ann had tolerated her because her mind was taken up with other important things. Corny Boyle, for instance, and her pony, and her posh friends from Newcastle, to mention a few. Even in the days that followed Mary Ann's acceptance was touched with condescension, although she gave her back with good measure everything she dealt out. . . . In a way, they had still been at war. It was only in the last few months Mary Ann had been different. But then she herself had been different. They both seemed to have grown up over night, and recognising this they had come together and talked. They had talked about Michael and they had talked about Corny. So now at this moment she could understand what Mary Ann was going through. She also knew that because his daughter was unhappy Mr. Shaughnessy was in a tearing rage. She never had seen him look so thundery. She could remember back to the times when he used to come home roaring drunk to Mulhattan's Hall. She could remember the day he had danced and sang in the road; and Mary Ann had come and taken him home and she had gibed at her: "Your da is a no-good drunk," she had shouted. And mimicked Mary Ann's oft-repeated phrase, "Me da's a grand man." And yet now there was nothing more she wanted in life than to be a member of this family, and to call Mike Shaughnessy "Da". In a way, although she loved her own father, there was something greatly attractive, greatly endearing about Mike Shaughnessy. And it would be an added happiness the day he became her father-in-law.

"What are you dreaming about?" The gentle dig in the ribs from Michael turned her face towards him, and she laughed and said, "Horses."

Michael let his eyes rest on her. He loved to look at her. He knew she hadn't been thinking of horses; he had come to know all the flowing movement and expression of her vivacious dark face. Sarah was beautiful, she was more than beautiful. To him she was everything a fellow could dream of. She had a lot of sense in her, which was strange when he thought of her father and mother, though he must say he liked Mr. Flannagan; he liked him much better than he liked her mother. But Sarah was like neither of them. She had a sort of deep wisdom about her. If he was going off the deep end about this, that, or the other, she would come out with something that astounded him with its profundity. He who had attended the Grammar School up to a year ago could not think to the depth that Sarah's mind took her. He wondered how his mother would take it if he wanted to get married before he started college. Likely she would go mad.

"Michael, you're not eating anything." Lizzie brought his eyes from Sarah, and he said, "Well, what do you expect after all that dinner?"

"I've never known your dinner stop you eating your Saturday tea." Lizzie now turned to Mary Ann and said, quietly, "Shall I fill your cup again?"

"No, Mother, no, thanks. I've had enough." As she turned her glance from her mother, she met the full penetrating force of Mike's eyes on her. They were looking into her, probing the hurt, and feeling it almost as much as herself. In his eyes was a reflection of her own anger, and she thought in the idiom that no convent-school training, no English mistress who had selected her for personal torture while dealing with clauses had been able to erase: "Eee! there'll be ructions if I don't stop him. But he's not to go for Mr. Lord. I'll tell him what I think, meself." She knew she could tell Mr. Lord what she thought, she knew that she could show her temper to him, answer his own arrogant manner with what her mother would term "cheek" and get away with it, but, not so, her da. Mr. Lord liked her da. She felt that although she in the first place had to point out to Mr. Lord, and emphatically, the qualities that made up her father, he had come to respect and like him from his own judgment. But that wan't saying that he would stand her father accusing him of sending Corny off to America, and that is what Mike would do if she didn't stop him. She was thankful that Mr. Lord wouldn't be back on the farm until Tuesday. In the meantime she must get at her da. But she knew she wouldn't have much weight with him unless she could prove to him that she wasn't all that much affected. This would be nigh impossible if she continued to go around looking as if the end of the world had come. But it had for her. Her world seemed to have been sliced in two, so that she was faced with a gulf over which she must either jump or remain in a state of pain for ever. She made an attempt at the jump by looking at Sarah and asking in a voice which she strove with great effort to make ordinary, "What are you wearing for the wedding?"

Sarah, looking back at her with the threaded intuition of youth, immediately played up by raising a laugh. "If this weather keeps up, black stockings, woollen undies, and a wind-cheater."

Lizzie laughed, louder than she would have done on another occasion. Michael laughed, his head back in the same attitude that his father used when his laughter was running free. Mike only allowed a quirk to appear at the corner of his mouth, but he nodded towards Sarah as he said, "Sensible idea."

"Fancy having a white wedding at this time of the year. And those two, with a nuptial mass!" Michael bowed his head and shook it from side to side as he chuckled to himself, and then added, "I shouldn't have been surprised if Len had said he was going up to the altar in tails."

Mary Ann too wanted to laugh at the thought of Len, the cowman, going up to the altar in tails. Len was dim—they all knew that Len was dim—and Cissie, his girl, was even lower down in the mental grade. She was round and placid, and ever smiling; and she had a stock phrase, with which she punctuated every question and answer. She could hear her now, "Well now, Mrs. Shaughnessy, I've always wanted a white weddin'." "And well now, with Mr Lord showing his appreciation of Len so, standing the spread for us, and givin' Len a rise and all that, well now, I thought we should do things fittin' like." Part of Mary Ann felt sorry for Cissie but she didn't really know why. Sometimes she thought it was because, as she said to herself, Cissie had never had a chance, there had never been a Mr. Lord in Cissie's life. Yet at the same time she recognised that all the Mr. Lords in the world couldn't have made much difference to Cissie. Cissie, like Len, was dim. But that didn't say they shouldn't have a nuptial mass. . . .

This point was as good as any other on which to start an argument with Michael. She knew she had to do something, and quickly, to switch her thoughts from weddings in general to a wedding in particular, which of late had been finding a prominent place in her thinking. So, as she had done from as far back as she could remember, she attacked Michael in her usual way. "What's funny about a nuptial mass, about their having a nuptial mass? They've as much right to have a nuptial mass as you or anybody else!"

"Oh! here we go again!" Michael rolled his eyes towards the ceiling before bringing his head down and bouncing it towards Mary Ann, emphasising each word as he said, "I didn't say they hadn't the right to have a nuptial mass. But those two won't have a clue what it's all about. They'll sit through the service without a clue. Do you think they will be affected by the spirituality of the whole thing? Can you imagine Len thinking?"

"How do you know if they'll be affected spiritually or not? Because Len has never been to a grammar school it doesn't say that his spiritual awareness isn't as alive as yours!"

"Aw. . . . Bulls, heifers, cows and calves!" Michael always managed to impregnate this saying with the same quality that another would give to strident blasphemy and it affected Lizzie in this way; she often thought she would rather hear Michael swear than say that. It wasn't the words themselves but the stringing of them together, and the inflexion of his voice as he said them. "Now, that's enough, Michael. And you too, Mary Ann! The pair of you stop it."

"Well, Mother, I ask you." Michael knew he was being pulled up, and why. But he smiled at Lizzie and said pityingly, "Well, I ask you. Len and Cissie in a nuptial mass! If one of them had been a little different, a bit bright, it mightn't have appeared so bad, but they are a pair . . ."

"Yes, you've said it there, they're a pair." Mike was speaking now and they all looked towards him. But he was looking at Michael only. "And they're paired properly. What do you think Len's life would be like if he was marrying a more intelligent girl? . . . Hell, that's what it would be. There's something in nature, if let alone, that helps us with our picking. We're not always aware of it at the time, sometimes not for years. Len's marriage won't break up, because he's picked according to the level of his mind. He doesn't know it, he never will, and he'll be all the more content. It sometimes comes about that you don't get the one to fit both your mind and your body, then things happen. . . . Take it on a lower plane, so to speak. Take it in the breeding of stock. . . ."

"Mike!" Lizzie's back was very straight; and Mike turned his face full to her and lifted his hands in a flapping motion, as if wiping away his name, before saying, "Look, Liz. There's neither of them at school any more. They're no longer bairns! And all right, Sarah's here, but Sarah deals with animals."

"Well, it's no conversation for the tea-table, and I'm not having it. I know where it will lead. We'll have the stockyard on our plates before many more minutes are over. Likening people to animals!"

"There's not a lot of difference that I can see." Mike's voice was suddenly quiet; and there was a tinge of sadness in his tone as he went on, "I've a sick cow in the barn now. Nobody will have it, nobody will believe that it's because Brewster's gone. But from the day she watched him mounting the ramp into that van, she's gone back. . . . Cows are women. . . ."

"Mike!" Lizzie had risen to her feet.

"All right, you won't have it." Mike had scraped his chair back on the floor and was looking up at her. "You won't have it, but nevertheless it's true. . . . You know, your mother did everything under God's sun to prevent you and me coming together, didn't she? Well, if she had succeeded it would have been a bad thing, a loss to both of us, and you know it. The same thing is happening now and you're glad. You're glad, Liz. That's what hurts me, you're glad."

Mike was on his feet now glaring at Lizzie, and she put her fingers to her lips as she stared back at him, muttering, "It isn't true, it isn't true. You know it isn't true."

"Aw, I know you, Liz. I can read you like a book. Only remember this, you can't push big houses and money into a heart. A heart's only made for feeling."

Mike's voice had come from deep in his chest on the last words, and they all watched him walking down the long farm kitchen towards the door. And when it closed on him Lizzie turned towards Mary Ann, her voice breaking as she said, "He's blaming me. He's blaming me for it all! What had I to do with Corny going to America? I had nothing to do with it." She was appealing to Mary Ann, seeming to have forgotten Michael and Sarah. "You believe that, don't you?"

Mary Ann got to her feet. She too seemed to have forgotten the couple sitting opposite, their heads bent in embarrassment; and she put her arms about Lizzie as she said, "Don't cry, Mother. Don't cry. Yes, I believe you. There, there, don't cry." She pressed her mother into her chair again, and going to the teapot, poured her out a fresh cup of tea; and as she handed it to her she said again, "There, now, don't worry. I know you had nothing to do with it."

But even as she said this, she was thinking along the lines of Mike. She knew her mother was glad and relieved, even happy, at the way things had turned out. She also knew that she must talk to her da before he met Mr. Lord, or the place would blow up.

2

"How d'you think it's gone, Mary Ann?"

"Wonderfully, wonderfully, Len. It was a wonderful wedding."

"Aye. Aa feel it was."

Mary Ann smiled at Len, and her smile was as sincere as her words had been. For to her mind it had been a wonderful wedding, surprisingly wonderful. The nuptial mass had not been ludicrous, as Michael had foretold. In fact, as she had looked at the white-robed Cissie and the unusually spruce Len, she had felt that they were deeply threaded with the spirituality of the moment, as very likely they were. Cissie had even looked pretty. She was detached from all dimness in this moment. Cissie was a bride, and Mary Ann had wanted to cry.

She said to Len, "You'll like Harrogate." At the same time she wondered why on earth they had chosen Harrogate. Harrogate was stuffy—snobbish and stuffy. Cissie had said it was because there were things to do; it had a winter season. That was funny, if you came to think about it. The Spanish City in Whitley Bay would be more in their line.

"You know, Aa wish we weren't goin' away. . . . Well, you know what Aa mean." Len laughed. "Aa mean not so soon like. Aa would uv liked to stay for the dance later on. Aa bet it's the first time there's ever been a dance in this old barn. Anyway, for many a long year." Len looked along the length of the barn to where Lizzie was supervising the clearing of the tables and added, "By, your mother made a splendid turn-out, didn't she? With Cissie's folk not being up to anything like this, it's made her feel . . . well, you know what I mean."

Mary Ann nodded. Yes, she knew what he meant. As well as all the bought cakes, her mother had cooked nearly all the week for the wedding spread. Hams, tongues . . . the lot.

"And the old man's all right at bottom; curses you up hill and down dale one minute, then stands your weddin' expenses. He's all right, he is, if you understand him like. Look, there he is now. He's laughin'. Look, he's laughin' with that Mrs. Schofield. By, she's a nice woman that. She's got no side, has she?" He looked at Mary Ann. And she, looking to where Mr. Lord was being entertained by Mrs. Schofield, nodded before saying, "Yes, she's nice."

Lettice Schofield was the mother of Mary Ann's school friend. She had first come to the farm on Mary Ann's thirteenth birthday, and had since then not infrequently looked them up. Everybody liked Mrs. Schofield, but everybody thought her a bit dizzy. Perhaps they liked her for that reason. At least everybody but Mike. Mike didn't think Mrs. Schofield was dizzy, he never had. From that birthday party he had said, "There's depth in that one. All this Mrs. Feathering is just a barricade against something." And over the past three years there had been times when Mary Ann thought her father was right, and others, when she listened to Mrs. Schofield's little brittle chatter and her high tinkling laugh, when she had been inclined to think with Janice that her mother acted silly, like a girl . . . and she nearly thirty-four years old. Another thing that made Mary Ann wonder at times about Mrs. Schofield was the fact that Mr. Lord was always entertained by her, and she knew only too well that Mr. Lord could not suffer fools gladly. So, on the whole she was inclined to think that her da's opinion of Mrs. Schofield was correct. But whether she was thinking along the lines of her da, or her friend Janice, there always remained in her a liking for Mrs. Schofield, a funny kind of liking, a sort of protective liking. It was a bit crazy when she came to analyse it, for it made her feel as if she were older than the mother of her friend. But the main trend of her thinking at this moment was not on Mrs. Schofield, but on Mr. Lord, and she thought bitterly as she looked at him, "Yes, he can laugh and be amused. He's got his own way again."

"Come on, me lad." Mary Ann turned her head to where Mike was pushing his way through the crowd of guests towards Len. Her da stood head and shoulders above everybody in the barn. Dressed in his best, he brought a thrill of pride to Mary Ann, that for a moment obliterated thoughts of Mr. Lord.

"Come on, lad. Do you want to miss that train?" He beckoned with his one arm above the heads of the gathering, and Len, laughingly jostled from all sides, pushed towards him.

Mary Ann, left alone for a moment in a little island of space, watched Mrs. Schofield leave Mr. Lord to go and say goodbye to the bride. Then to her consternation she saw Mr. Lord rise slowly and come towards her.

It was the first time they had met face to face since his return, which had not been on Tuesday as expected, but yesterday morning, which was Friday, and since then he had, she felt sure, kept out of her way. In fact, out of everybody's way, until two hours ago when the wedding party had returned from the church. From which time he had allowed himself to be entertained by Mrs. Schofield.

Mr. Lord was standing close to her now and he looked at her for a long moment before speaking, and then he took the wind completely out of her sails by saying, "You're wrong, you know, Mary Ann."

As always when stumped, she blinked, but she continued to stare up at him.

"You have been blaming me for Cornelius's decision regarding America." He always gave Corny his full name when speaking of him. "Well, I want you to know I had nothing whatever to do with making up his mind. Oh, yes." He raised his hand. "I'm not going to deny that I have pointed out the advantages that would attend his taking up a position in America, and I have gone as far as to tell him I could secure him a post. Oh yes, I have done all that. But that was some time ago. More recently, I gave up the idea of trying to persuade him because I realised he was a very determined young man and would not be influenced by me, or anyone else, but would go his way. So I was surprised, as no doubt you were, when his decision was made known to me. He was the last person I expected to see in my office, and our meeting was brief, for in accordance with his character he came straight to the point. He told me what he wanted, and asked some questions. . . . Usually I am the one who asks the questions, and I don't take kindly to cross examinations." He smiled his tight smile down on her. Then finished abruptly. "Cornelius Boyle knows exactly what he wants. I should say he will go far. . . ."

"Now, now, now, Mary Ann, don't be silly. You're not going to cry. This is a wedding, remember." He took her arm in a firm grip and she allowed him to walk her towards the barn door.

She hated him, she did. Well, he could make all the excuses he liked, but she would never marry Tony just to please him. That was what he was after. . . . Oh, she knew, she knew what his subtle game was. And played so smoothly, you couldn't get at him.

"If you start crying everyone will blame me."

"I'm not crying."

"Very well, you're not crying, not yet. But if you do start I will get the blame. Especially from your father, because he, too, thinks like you, doesn't he?"

They had reached the left side corner of the barn when he pulled her to a stop. And looking at her with a gentleness that always managed to break her down, he said softly, "Whether you believe it or not, Mary Ann, anything I do, I do for your own good. Out of the essence of knowledge garnered through a long and trying life, I can see what is right for you . . . I know what is right for you . . . I know what is right for you, and I want you to have what is right for you. . . . You believe me?"

She was not crying, but her large brown eyes were so misted she couldn't see his face as she gazed up at him. He had done it again. She hated him no longer. What he said was right. Whatever he did was for her good. If only he would do something for Corny to stop him from going away. Her love gave her courage to say, "I like Corny, Mr. Lord."

"Yes." He nodded at her. "Yes, of course, you like Cornelius. I know you like Cornelius. Anyone would be blind, or stupid, if he didn't realise you like him. And go on liking him, there's no reason why you shouldn't. And you should be proud that he wants to go to America and make a position for himself, so that when . . . when the time comes, he will have something to offer you. He would have nothing to offer you if he stayed in England."

"He was getting on well at the garage. He's had a rise."

Mr. Lord turned his head with a quick jerk to the side as if he was straining to look up into the sky, and it was into the sky that he sent his words: "Had a rise!" The scorn in them made Mary Ann stiffen, and she made to pull her hand from his grasp when he brought his gaze once more to bear on her and again softened his scathing comment by saying, "What is a rise in that work? A few shillings a week! You give Cornelius a year in America and he will be making twice as much as the manager of that garage. Believe me. . . . Well. Well, now." He had turned his head quickly towards the gate of the farmhouse, where a car was backing in, and he ended abruptly, "No more of this now. Here's Tony."

Mr. Lord did not go towards his grandson but waited for him to come up to them. And although he kept his gaze fixed on the approaching figure, the expression in his eyes, which could have been taken for pride, was veiled with a mask of impatient arrogance.

Tony was tall and thin. A faint replica of Mr. Lord himself. Perhaps he was better looking than Mr. Lord had been at his age. His skin, even in the winter, kept a bronzed tinge as if he had just returned from a southern beach. In some measure, too, he had about him a touch of his grandfather's aloofness, which at the age of twenty-seven added to his attractiveness.

From a child Mary Ann had been conscious of this attractiveness, and in a childish way had looked upon Tony as hers. She had begun by liking him, then she had loved him. . . . That was until she met Corny. But she still liked Tony very, very much, and was aware of his attraction, as were most of the girls who came into contact with him. His charm and natural ease of manner were part and parcel of his character. But he also had a vile temper, which could rip the charm off him like a skin, to disclose a stubbornness and cold arrogance for which one hadn't to look far to find the source. And it was mainly when he was fighting with that source that these two facets came into evidence.

As Mary Ann watched him approach them now, she said to herself, "He's wild about something." She knew Tony as well as she did her da, or ma, or Mr. Lord.

"Hello, there, you're late. The wedding's nearly over." Mr. Lord's tone was clipped.

"Yes, I'm sorry. I couldn't make it. I told you I might be late." Tony nodded to his grandfather while looking him straight in the face. He did not look at Mary Ann, although he asked, "Where's Mike?"

Was he mad at her? Why was he pointedly ignoring her? She had done nothing. She said to him, "My father's gone to the house with Len." She always gave Mike the title of father when speaking of him in front of Mr. Lord.

"Thanks." Still Tony did not turn his gaze on her, not even in a sweeping glance.

As she watched him stride away, she looked up sharply at Mr. Lord, saying, "He's wild about something."

The old man dusted his hands as if they had been soiled, and then he said, "Young men are always wild about something. That's why they are young men. Once they stop being wild they are no longer young men."

Mary Ann, looking at him for a moment longer, saw that he was not worried about Tony being wild. He was not coldly questioning why his grandson's manner was so abrupt, and this was unusual. And why he was not questioning was because he already knew.

She looked hard at the old man, who was looking to where Tony was now hurrying across the yard, not towards the farmhouse, but towards the gate that led up to the house on the hill. And she realised, as she had done so many times in the past, that this old man was clever, clever and cunning. He was like the devil himself. He could make you believe in him, in the goodness of his intentions, even while he plotted against you. And, as she had done in the past, she knew that she would hate him at intervals, but during the longer periods, and in spite of everything, she would always love him. And then she asked herself: What could he have done to upset Tony?

Corny arrived at six o'clock in Bert Stanhope's old car. Bert Stanhope was the chief mechanic in the garage. He was also the leader of the "Light Fantastics", a suitably fantastic name for the four members of his band. For Bert himself was short and stubby, while Joe Ridley was as thin as a rake, and possessed a club-foot. Arthur Hunt, on the other hand, was of middle height with muscles straining from his coat sleeves. He had come by these, he proclaimed, through playing the mandoline. Topping them all by a clear head and shoulders was Corny.

Corny now eased his long legs out of the front seat of the car, and after raising his hand quickly in a salute to Mike, who was coming out of the barn, he turned his head in the direction of Bert, to ask, "What did you say?"

"Aa said, 'Is that the place we're doin' it?' "

"Yes, that's the barn."

"Coo, lor! It'll be like the Albert Hall, only barer."

Joe Ridley, surrounded by what looked like an entire band of wind instruments, remarked caustically, "We'll have to blow wor brains oot to put anything ower in there. The sound'll all come oot through them slats up top."

"You'll get them blown oot if we don't put it over, me lad."

They were all laughing at their leader's reply when Mike reached them.

"Hello, there. You all set." He looked around the four young men, but addressed himself to Corny.

"Aye. Yes, Mr. Shaughnessy." Corny had always given Mike his full title, and perhaps this was another reason why Mike was wholeheartedly for him. "This is Bert Stanhope. It's his band. And this is Joe Ridley; and Arthur Hunt."

Mike nodded with each introduction, then looking at the paraphernalia spread round their feet, he asked seriously, "Where are the others?"

"The others?" Bert flicked an enquiring and puzzled glance towards Corny before finishing, "What others?"

"Well, with this lot, I thought it must be the Hallé Orchestra that had come!"

There was more laughter, louder now, as the young fellows picked up the instruments and made for the barn. Corny, about to follow them, was stopped by a light touch on his arm, and Mike, his face serious now, said, "I want a word with you."

"Now?" Corny was looking straight at Mike. Their eyes were on a level.

"No, it needn't be now. Perhaps when you have an interval."

"All right." As Corny turned away, Mike said quietly, "Mary Ann's just gone over to the house, if you want to see her?"

Corny did not turn to meet Mike's gaze now, but answered evenly, "They want to start right away. We're a bit late. I'll see her later."

Mike said nothing to this but watched Corny stride towards the barn, before turning and making his way to the house.

And there he banged the back door after him as he went into the scullery. But when he entered the kitchen he stopped just inside the door and looked across to the fireplace where Tony was standing, one foot on the fender, his elbow resting on the mantelpiece and his face set in a stiffness that spoke of inner turmoil.

"Oh, you all alone?" Mike attempted to be casual.

Tony moved from the fireplace and stood on the edge of the mat, rubbing his left shoulder with his right hand, a characteristic action of his when worked up about anything.

"Where's Mary Ann?"

"I think she's upstairs. I've heard someone moving about, and Lizzie's still in the barn. Look, Mike, I didn't intend to say anything to her. I was going to ignore the whole affair, but I've just got to tell her that I'm not in on this business of Corny's deportation."

"Deportation is right!" Mike nodded at him. "That's the most suitable word I've heard for it yet. But don't worry, I don't think she would believe for a moment you had a hand in it."

"Oh, I don't know so much, Mike. She said the other day, over some little thing that I did, she said I was as wily as my grandfather. She might be thinking that, although I'm opposing the old man on the surface, I'm glad that Corny is going."

"And are you?" The question was flat sounding.

"Aw, Mike, no. No."

"But you like her?"

"Yes, of course I do. You know that, Mike."

"Do you more than like her? I've got the right to ask this, Tony. Do you more than like her? Do you love her?"

Tony turned his head quickly and looked towards the fire, then bringing his eyes back to Mike he said slowly, "Yes. Yes, Mike, in a way, I suppose I do. I always have done. But it's an odd kind of love. I don't understand it quite myself. I'm always fighting against her inside myself. I suppose this is the result of the Old Man's plans. If he hadn't pushed it but let it take a natural course, things might have been different; at least on my side. But no matter what I had felt it wouldn't have made very much difference as long as Corny was in the picture. And you know, Mike——"

"And when he's out of the picture?" Mike cut in. "What then? On your side, I mean."

"I don't know, Mike. I've got to wait and see. The odd thing is I've never met anyone I like better. I was brought up, so to speak, on her personality." He smiled now, before adding, "And as you know, it'll take some beating."

Mike turned from Tony and, pulling a chair from under the table, straddled it. And with his one hand he thumped the top with his closed fist as he said, "I'm mad over this business, Tony, flaming mad. I know the old boy, he's worked on that lad for years." He looked up at Tony. "You know this is the kind of situation that always makes me want to get drunk." He gave a little jerk to his head. "I'd better not let Lizzie hear me say that. But at this moment I'd like to get blind drunk. You see, all my early married life, and occasionally even now, I've had to fight against Lizzie's mother. You know the old girl. Well, I see in the old man a male replica of Madam McMullen. He's aiming to direct and ruin Mary Ann's life as surely as Lizzie's mother tried to ruin ours. And I tell you, Tony, it boils me up inside. . . . Ssh!" Mike got to his feet quickly. "Here she's coming. Look, Tony. I wouldn't say anything now. Let is pass off, for the night at any rate. Talk to her later. Let her dance the night and have a bit of carry on, and forget it if she can. Although she'll be hard put to it with Corny up there blowing his heart out through that cornet, and nothing will convince me but he'll go on doing that where she's concerned, America or no. . . . Ssh!"

Although it was Mike who had been doing the talking he admonished Tony to silence with his last Ssh! and when the door opened and Mary Ann came into the kitchen he flung his arm up over his eyes and cried, "Oh, Lord, what a dazzle!"

"Don't be silly, Da." Although Mary Ann's voice was chiding, she smiled at Mike but did not look towards Tony, until he said, "A new dress, is it?"

"Yes." She nodded her head once.

"It's nice. Red suits you."

"It's not red, it's cyclamen."

"Oh . . . oh. Cyclamen, is it? Well, anyway, it's very charming. Although, mind, I think it makes you look older."

The last was a covered compliment and would have at any other time pleased Mary Ann, for next to wishing to be taller she longed to appear older. Although she would soon be seventeen, she sometimes, because of her height, looked no more than fifteen years old.

"The band's come," said Mike, his back half towards her now. "Listen, they've started. Come on, wrap yourself well up. Wait, I'll get my bit coat and put around you; your top looks half-naked, you'll catch your death."

When Mike went out into the hall, Tony, moving towards Mary Ann, said, "May I have the first dance, Miss Shaughnessy?" His smile was kind, and she returned it. But she did not enter into his playful mood.

Mike, coming into the room again, put his coat about her and they all laughed at the picture she presented; then, one on each side of her, they went out of the house down the road to the farm gate, and across the yard to the barn. And when they were inside the doorway, Mike took his coat from her, and she turned to Tony, and they danced. . . .

Lizzie was standing in the far corner of the barn behind the refreshment table, which also served as the bar. And it was the bar at this moment that was worrying Lizzie. Mr. Coot was attending to the bar and also to himself. In her estimation he'd already had too much, and the night was young yet. The bride's father had not been satisfied with the amount of wine and beer Mr. Lord had provided, but had had to bring his own quota. Instead of spending so much on drink, Lizzie thought to herself, they could have bought something different for the young couple instead of that clarty cheap tea-set. Or provided some of the eatables. Thriftless lot. She had better see Mike and tell him to keep an eye on Mr. Coot and his personal friends.

She was looking here and there in between the dancers for Mike when she saw Mary Ann and Tony dancing together. At the sight of her daughter's dress, all thought of Mr. Coot left her mind for the moment. Oh, that dress! Why on earth had she picked a red dress? It wasn't her colour and the style was all wrong. It was the first dress she had let her buy on her own, and she had to pick red! It looked cheap, and it didn't suit her; it made her look older. She could be eighteen . . . nineteen. She kept her eye on her daughter as she waltzed nearer. And as the couple passed the table, Lizzie smiled at them. Anyway, Mary Ann was dancing nicely. It was the first time she had seen her dance except in the kitchen at the Christmas do's. Her steps and Tony's seemed to match. Somehow, she didn't look out of place with Tony, not like she did with . . . Lizzie's eyes flicked towards the temporary platform where the band was arrayed. Corny, his legs apart, his elbows level with his shoulders, his head back, was blowing his heart into his cornet. She could see the full meaning of Mike's phrase now. He was cornet mad, that boy. And, yes, yes, from the bottom of her heart she was glad he was glad he was going to America. And she prayed God that he would go soon and Mary Ann would have a chance to settle down with . . . She turned her eyes to Tony and Mary Ann again. Then she brought her gaze to the right of her, where Mr. Lord was sitting, once again being entertained by Mrs. Schofield. Let him scheme, let him plan, she was with him every inch of the way. Although she would not be able to open her mouth to him about the matter, she knew that the day her daughter married his grandson would be one of the happiest in both their lives.

She saw Mike now and she came round from behind the table and threaded her way towards him, and when she reached him she turned and stood by his side, letting her gaze follow his as he looked at the merry-making. But under her breath she said, "You'd better keep your eye on that Mr. Coot. He's going it some with the bottle."

When Mike did not answer or turn his eyes towards her she was forced to look at him, and she said, still in a whisper, but with an edge to it, "I'm saying something, did you hear me?"

"Yes, I heard you, Liz, but it happens to be a weddin'."

"But you don't want it broken up, do you, with a drunken brawl?"

"Who says there's going to be a drunken brawl?"

"The night's young, and I'm telling you he's pretty well loaded now."

"And he mightn't be the only one afore the night's out."

Something jumped within Lizzie's chest. It was a frightening feeling. But one that was familiar—at least had been familiar up to these last few years. And now the feeling attacked the muscles of her stomach, bringing with it a slight nausea and she was back in the past, when each week-end had been a dread, and she didn't know from one day to another how they were going to get by. She was staring through glazed sight at the dancers while she cried out wildly inside herself, "It's not fair, it's not fair, he's taking it out on me." Then her vision clearing, she turned her eyes without moving her head towards the seat of state, in which Mr. Lord still sat; and she ended her thinking with, "Well, far better he take it out on me than on the old man. But if he gets one too many himself it will be on both of us." On this she was swamped with apprehensive fear, and the fear made her bold. With her eyes still directed towards the swirling couples, and her voice almost drowned by the noise and laughter, she said, "If you do anything to spoil this night, Mike, I'll walk out . . . I'm telling you, I'll walk out."

"Will you, Liz?" Mike too had his eyes fixed on the dancers, and his tone was deceptively even as he went on, "I should have thought you knew better than that, Liz. Threats have always been as effective on me as water on a duck's back."

The band stopped. The dancers clapped and called for more. The band started again and Mike, without any further words, walked from Lizzie's side and along to where Mr. Lord was seated. As Lizzie watched him go her hand went instinctively to her lips. Then slowly it dropped away and her shoulders went back, and her chin moved up just a little as she watched her husband bending over Mrs. Schofield. She watched him put his arm around Mrs. Schofield's slender waist while she rested both her hands on his shoulders. She watched for a moment longer as he laughed down into Mrs. Schofield's pretty face, and she watched Mrs. Schofield laugh up at him; and then she turned abruptly away.

She had, up to this minute, liked Mrs. Schofield, even though she thought her a bit dizzy.

Yet Mike had never thought her dizzy. He had always maintained there was another side to her. . . . Oh, she wished it was tomorrow and the wedding well behind them. She wished it was next week or the week after, or whenever it was Corny Boyle was leaving. Once he was gone Mary Ann would settle down. She would do everything in her power to see that she did settle down. But, oh, she did wish this night was over, and she wished that Mrs. Schofield hadn't come.

When the band stopped for a break, Mary Ann was standing waiting to the side of the platform for Corny. She had no pride left. During the hour and a half the band had been playing, Corny hadn't looked at her; at least, when she was looking at him. It was as if she didn't exist for him; or, once having existed, he had decided to forget her. She knew that her father would try to get at him during the interval. And if not, her mother would insist that he had something to eat. Or Mr. Lord would raise an authoritative finger to beckon him to his side. And then the interval would be over, and when the dance finished he would pack up and go back with the other lads, and she didn't know whether he was coming tomorrow or not. She just had to talk to him.

As he stepped down off the wobbling planks, she looked up into his big face, which was redeemed from ugliness only by the mould of the mouth. This feature, taken separately, could be described as beautiful, yet it almost went unnoticed in the ruggedness of the whole. "Hello," she said. It was as if they had just encountered each other.

"Hello." After looking down at her for a moment he thrust his head upwards, and gazing towards the refreshment table he exclaimed, "Lord, but I'm starvin'."

"I'll get you some sandwiches . . . stay here, and I'll get them. Look, there's a seat." Her voice was rushed, eager, and he looked down on her again. Then jerking his head, he said abruptly, "I can get it."

"Corny, I've got to talk to you."

"Aw, Mary Ann. . . ."

"You'll go with the others as soon as the dance is finished, won't you?"

"Aye, it's the only way of gettin' back. I can't do anything else."

"Well, I've got to talk to you now."

"Leave it till the morrer."

"Are you coming tomorrow?" Her eyes were wide and fixed hard on him now.

He looked anywhere but at her as he said, "No. No, I wasn't. I promised to take our Stan's motor-bike to bits."

As she stood gazing up at him she made a great effort to use the pride that was in her and turn from this gangling individual and march away, her head in the air and her step firm. But, as with her da, she could bring no pride to her aid when dealing with Corny, at least not as yet. In the past she had sold her soul to the devil over and over again in her own small way to defend her father. And she would do the same for this boy. She did not question why she should love Corny, she only knew that she did. And it was a love that could not be killed by ridicule or parting. Or even a statement from his own lips to the fact that he did not love her. That was a strange thing. And she had dwelt upon it quite a bit these past few hours. Corny had never said in words that he loved her; but in every possible way his actions had spoken for him. He had never even paid her a compliment that she could remember, and he had certainly never said, "Oh, Mary Ann, I love you." And his desertion now was not to be verbal either. He spoke, as usual, in actions, and his actions, like the proverb, spoke louder than his words.

"Comin' for some grub?" Bert was calling him from the far side of the stage. And Corny, looking over his shoulder, answered in an over-loud voice, "Be with you in a tick," and then, walking towards the seat that Mary Ann had proffered, he said quietly now, "Sit down, I'll get you something."

She remained standing looking at him. "I don't want anything. . . . When are you going away?"

"Aw, Mary Ann, man." He tossed his big head from side to side. "Let's forget it."

"When are you going away?"

"All right, all right, if that's how you want it." Again his head was tossing. But it had ceased its moving before he said, "The fourteenth." His voice had dropped and his head with it. His eyes were not looking at her, but were shaded by the wide lids, and they flickered once when her voice, cracking with surprise, cried, "The fourteenth! That's just over a week. . . . Oh, Corny!"

"Look, Mary Ann, don't go on. I'll come over the morrer. . . . Yes, I will, and talk about it. . . . Look, I'll go and get something to eat. Sit there, I'll be back."

He did not wait for more protestations but hurried from her and threaded his way towards the far corner and the refreshment table.

Mary Ann sat down. She felt lost, sick, and she wanted above all things to lay her head on her arms and cry.

Up to a moment ago this corner of the barn had been comparatively empty, but now people were making their way back to the forms that lined the walls, carrying plates balanced on the tops of cups of coffee or glasses of beer. And as she was forced to answer, and even smile when she was spoken to, she was thinking, "There's no place for him to sit now. And it's too cold outside, and he won't come over to the house." She looked around now, not for Corny, but for Mike. Just to stand near her da would be a comfort. Moreover, she realised that she should be sitting close to her father from now on; because when she last saw him there had been a glint in his eye that told her he was well past his restricted number of whiskies.

Corny had pushed his way to her with a dinner-sized plate full of food, but his attention was not on her, for he kept looking towards the stage. And then he brought out under his breath, "Lordy, I hope they don't play about with the instruments. Bert will go crackers if anything's busted up."

Mary Ann, following his perturbed gaze, saw Mrs. Schofield, her head back, her mouth wide with laughter, holding a trombone, and Tony, who was sitting at the piano—which incidentally had been brought down from the house but had not so far been played—calling to her: "One . . . Two . . . Three."

The sound that issued from the stage now caught the whole attention of the barn. And everybody was laughing as they looked towards Mrs. Schofield. It was evident that she had some knowledge of the trombone but was laughing so much herself that she could not keep in time with Tony, but the guests, catching the theme of "The Old Bull and Bush", began to sing.

Mary Ann didn't join in, nor did Corny, but he whispered to her in reluctant admiration. "She could play that, you know. With a little practice she could be good."

Mary Ann looked at Mrs. Schofield, who was consumed with laughter and only intermittently keeping in time, and thought, "That is what Janice means when she says her mother is dizzy." And she felt a little ashamed of Mrs. Schofield. Ashamed of her, and ashamed for her. She was too old to act the goat like that. Mary Ann at this moment gave thanks that her mother would never do anything like that.

But it would appear that Mary Ann was alone with her feeling concerning Mrs. Schofield, for the rest of the company were enjoying her with high delight. And when one song was finished there was a call for another, and another.

Then Mike was on the stage, standing by Tony, and he let his deep rich voice soar through the barn as he led the singing. That was all right; Mary Ann liked to hear her da sing. And as long as he was singing he wouldn't be drinking. Yes, it was all right until Mrs. Schofield went and joined him. And then Mary Ann watched her da put his arm around

Mrs. Schofield's shoulder and lead her to the front of the stage, and with their heads together they sang duets to the great amusement of the company, with the exception of herself and her mother. For Mary Ann caught sight of her mother's face, and she knew that she was upset. She also knew that her da was letting rip like this on purpose because he was vexed, not only with Mr. Lord but with her ma. And it was all on account of her and Corny. As Lizzie had said a short while ago, now Mary Ann also said to herself, "Oh, I wish this night was well over."

There was just one other person who was not pleased with the spectacle. And that was Mr. Lord. He had found Mrs. Schofield a very entertaining companion; when you got past the frivolity of her veneer there was a serious side to the woman. He had found her intelligent and observant, and possessed of a quality that, in his opinion, was rare in most women—wit. Many of them had a sense of humour, but humour and wit were on two different planes. Yes, indeed, he had liked Mrs. Schofield and he did not relish seeing her making a spectacle of herself with Shaughnessy, and his grandson. Shaughnessy, too, he noted, had taken on more than was good for him, and in a very short while his good humour would turn to surliness, and from that . . . Well, he wasn't going to be present when Shaughnessy brought up the subject of why young Cornelius Boyle had decided to go to America. He was well aware of Shaughnessy's championship of the boy. And it was not only because of Mary Ann's affection for the fellow, but because Shaughnessy saw in the big, bony, unlovely Cornelius a replica of himself as he was at that age. And in championing his daughter's choice, he was also pandering to the vanity in himself. Oh, he knew Shaughnessy, he could read Shaughnessy.

"Well, I must be making my way up the hill, Mrs. Shaughnessy." Mr. Lord was facing Lizzie now, bending towards her to make himself heard. And she only just managed to keep the relief out of her voice as she answered, "You must be tired, it's been a long day. . . . Thank you very much, indeed, for all you have done."

The old man raised his bushy brows into his white hair, and brought his chin into his neck as he said with a rare twinkle in his eye, "We're never thanked for the right things by the right people, Mrs. Shaughnessy. The ones who should be thanking me are past thinking of anything at this moment but the next drink. I have done nothing to deserve your thanks, but there it is. That is life." He nodded his head slowly. "And I am grateful for your thanks, Mrs. Shaughnessy."

They looked at each other for a long moment.

"Good night, Mr. Lord."

"Good night, Mrs. Shaughnessy. And don't worry. Everything will turn out all right." He did not explain to what he was referring; there was no need. Lizzie looked back into his pale eyes as she said, "I'm sure it will, Mr. Lord. I sincerely hope so from the bottom of my heart." The last words were merely a whisper.

Again he nodded. "We understand each other, Mrs. Shaughnessy. It's a very good thing when two people understand each other. Good night, Mrs. Shaughnessy."

"Good night, Mr. Lord. Good night, Mr. Lord. You'll be able to manage?" She pulled the barn door open for him.

"Yes, quite well, Mrs. Shaughnessy, quite well; there's a moon."

He paused for a moment and looked up into the sky, then turning his head towards Lizzie he said, "Don't let her stay up too late. Young girls should get their rest."

Lizzie did not answer but inclined her head towards him, and stood for a moment watching him walk across the moonlit farmyard. He was telling her to protect Mary Ann from the moonlight, the moonlight and Corny. For a moment, just for a fleeting moment, Lizzie experienced a feeling that she thought could be akin to that which was eating up Mike. Why should Mary Ann be kept from the moonlight and Corny? The moon was made for the young. But as she closed the barn door again, the feeling passed. He was right;

moonlight was dangerous. A dose of it created a madness that some people had to pay for all their lives. She was not going to stand by and see Mary Ann paying such a price. . . .

The dance ended at eleven o'clock, but long before this time Tony and Mrs. Schofield were running a shuttle service taking people home. Tony's first car-load had contained the prostrate form of Mr. Coot, who, true to Lizzie's prophecy, had become blind drunk early in the evening. But not aggressively so as she had feared. Whereas Mike, who was not as drunk as he could have been, was tinder dry for a row. Mr. Lord's disappearance had brought forth his caustic comments, and Mr. Coot's recumbency had aroused his scorn. Tony he frowned on more and more as the evening advanced, and it would appear the only person who pleased him was Mrs. Schofield. But it seemed that as Mike's boisterousness increased, Mrs. Schofield's merriment went the other way, until, towards the end of the evening, although still smiling, her gaiety had diminished. Perhaps this was because Mrs. Schofield did not drink. Even a natural gaiety is hard to sustain hour after hour on lemonade. Or perhaps it was because Mrs. Schofield was really a nice woman, an understanding woman.

Yet Lizzie's liking for Mrs. Schofield did not return, not even when she witnessed her persuading Mike from getting in the car and accompanying her in her taxi-ing. You can't like a woman who is trying to prevent your husband from making a fool of himself even when you know that she is in sympathy with you. . . .

The barn was almost deserted when the band finally packed up. And Mike, swaying just the slightest, stood with his arm around Corny's shoulder, and he grinned widely at him as he muttered thickly, "Cum on, me young buck, cum on. You and me 'ave got some talkin' to do."

"I've got to go, Mr. Shaughnessy. They're waitin'."

"Waitin'? What for? Let them get themselves away, you're comin' in with me. Why, the night's young, lad."

"I'll come in the morrer."

"You'll cum in the night!"

"Da!"

Mike turned to look at his daughter, saying, "Ah, there you are. I was just tellin' Corny here the night's young."

"Da. Come on indoors, please."

"We're all goin' indoors, me dear."

"Listen, Da." Mary Ann gave a rough tug at Mike's arm, pulling him to attention. "Listen. Corny wants to go home; they're waiting for him." She inclined her head backwards. "Let him go! Do you hear me, Da? Let him go!"

Not only did the tone of her voice catch Mike's attention, but it brought Corny's eyes hard on her. His neck jerked up out of his collar as if he had been suddenly prodded with a sharp instrument, and he looked down on her with a wide, startled expression as she went on, "You go now, Corny." Her words were spaced, her voice level. "Go on. And don't come back tomorrow, or any other time. Go to America, and I wish you luck. . . . Come on, Da."

As she had done so often in her young life, she tugged at Mike's arm and guided him away, and this time unprotestingly away, leaving Corny in a wilderness of words he could not voice. And as she went, she clung on desperately to the fringe of her old courage, which she had dragged from its retreat to save her from utter desolation after an evening of torment, an evening of being rejected, overlooked by the only one that mattered. Just a short while ago she had rehearsed a plea she would make to Corny when she had him to herself. For somehow she would get him to herself, at least that is what she had thought.

Mary Ann had never yet in her life recognised total defeat. Her agile mind had always supplied her with a plan. But in this telling moment if it had presented her with a plan that would keep Corny at her feet for life, she would have rejected it.

As they entered the garden Mike's docility vanished and he pulled them to a stop, exclaiming, "Why the hell! I'm not havin' this. Where is he?" He flung round, only to be dragged back again by Mary Ann, and, her voice as stern as Lizzie's ever could be, she said to him, "Look, Da, listen to me. I'm telling you, I don't want to see him."

"Aa . . . ah! So you're playing the old fellow's game, eh?" he swayed slightly towards her.

"I'm playing nobody's game. Come on in." Suddenly her tone changed and she was the little girl again, pleading with him. "Aw, Da. Come on. Come on to bed . . . I've had enough for one night."

He peered at her through the moonlight, and then without further words he put his arm about her, and together they went up into the house.

3

"What are you goin' to be when you leave your typin' school . . . a secretary?"

"Yes, I suppose so, Mrs. McBride."

"Do you want to be a secretary?"

"No, not really."

"Then what did you go in for it for?"

"Oh, well." Mary Ann gave a faint smile and, looking down, said, "I fancy I'll be able to write."

"Write?"

"Yes, stories and things, you know. I've always been able to make up poetry."

"Well! well!" Fanny stopped basting the joint and gazed down on Mary Ann where she sat at the corner of the kitchen table. "Now, that's an idea, a good idea, for you were always the one for tellin' a tale. Oh, you were that. . . . Remember the things you used to spin around, about all the cars, and the horses your da had, and the big house you lived in?"

Mary Ann nodded, and she kept smiling up at this old friend of hers as she listened to her recalling the escapades she got up to in the days when they lived in the attics at the top of this grim house. But she knew, as Mrs. McBride kept prattling on in her loud, strident voice, that they were both just marking time, waiting for the moment when Corny's name would be mentioned. She was bitter in her heart against Corny. Although she had dismissed him with a cold finality the night of the wedding, she hadn't imagined for a single moment that would be the last she would see of him. When he hadn't come on the Sunday, she had known he would turn up one night during the week. But as the days ticked off towards the fourteenth of November, her pride sank into oblivion once more, and she paid earnest, even frantic, attention to her praying, beseeching Our Lady to bring him before he sailed. But her prayers weren't answered. And the day of his departure came without a word or a note from him.

Her da was still mad, and part of his temper now was directed towards Corny himself. Even her mother was annoyed at Corny's cavalier treatment. And she had overheard her saying to Michael in the kitchen, "After the way he's been welcomed in this house. Every week-end for years he's been here. And never once was she invited back!"

Michael had answered, "Well, you can understand that. The fellow wouldn't want to take her to the set-up in Howdon."

"Well," her mother said, "I hope it shows her she's well rid of him."

When their Michael had answered, "I wouldn't count on it doing that, Ma," she had wanted to fly into the kitchen and cry, "Well, it has! Me ma's right. Me ma's right. I never want to set eyes on him again."

That was a week ago. And now here she was, drawn to Mrs. McBride's, waiting, as each minute passed—glossed over with topics that didn't matter—for her to speak about her grandson.

Fanny pushed the dripping-tin back into the oven, and threw the coarse sacking oven-towel on to a chair. Then going back to the table, she sat down opposite Mary Ann. Heaving a sign that hardly disturbed the huge sagging mountain of her breasts, she put her head on one side and looked at Mary Ann with compassion in her glance. "Well!" she said abruptly.

Mary Ann, staring at her old friend, bit on her lip, looked downwards, then back into the wrinkled face, and muttered, "Oh, Mrs. McBride, I feel awful."

"You do, hinny?"

Mary Ann nodded and blinked, but the blinking could not check her crying, and the tears welled from her eyes.

"Aw! there now, there now, don't cry. It had to be like this, lass. It had to be like this."

"He . . . he went off and never even said good-bye to me. He needn't have gone off like that and . . . and after him coming to us every week. He . . . he never missed, and then to go off . . ."

"Now wait a minute." Fanny held up her hand. "There was a reason for him goin' off like that. And you know it."

"I don't, Mrs. McBride. I don't." She was shaking her head desperately.

"Aw, come on, come on. Face up to facts. If he had come to say good-bye to you, he would have never seen America."

Mary Ann's mouth was open and she moved her head in a slow painful motion, her tears still running down her face.

"It's a fact," said Fanny. "He stood in this kitchen . . . Stood? No, I'm tellin' you a damned lie. Stand, he didn't do, he raged about the room until I threatened to hit him with the frying-pan if he didn't let up. And talk. I never heard that lad talk so much in all me born days. All mixed up, seemingly without sense or reason, until I shouted at him. 'If you don't want to go, don't go,' I said. 'Blast Mr. Lord. You'll get other chances.' 'Where?' he said. 'If I was even managing that garage I wouldn't be able to make much more than fifteen quid a week, and what can you do on that?' 'What can you do on that?' I said to him. 'I wish to God I had the half of it, that's all.' "

Fanny paused now, and after nodding towards Mary Ann she went on more slowly. "It was after I said that, that he held his head in his hands and said, quiet like, in a way that made him sound like a settled man. 'Gran, you don't know what you're talkin' about. I'm not askin' her until I have enough to start off decent, and if I don't get goin' now, it'll be too late. Unless I start doing things on the side with the cars to make a bit like the rest of them. And I don't want to get mixed up in anything, I've seen where that can lead. . . .' "

"Oh! Mrs. McBride. If he had only told me . . ."

"Wait a minute, wait a minute. I haven't finished yet," said Fanny. "You know how I like your mother, don't you? I think of Liz with more affection than any of me own. But apparently she doesn't see me grandson in the same light. She's got ideas for you, Mary Ann, and——" Fanny spread her arms wide. "It's natural, isn't it? She's your mother. But my Corny is no fool. Perhaps I say it as shouldn't, but he's a big chip, a great big chip of meself, and he read through Liz right from the beginnin'. The same as he knew what old Lord was up to all the time. Old Lord wants you for Mr. Tony, lass, and you know, I can see his point an' all. And I'm not blaming your mother for wantin' to fall in with his little scheme. For it would be a wondeful thing if her daughter, her Mary Ann, could marry the old man's grandson. . . . Now, now, don't take on so, I'm just statin' facts, and there's no hard feelin's atween Liz and me, and never atween you and me. We know each other too well, don't we now?" She reached forward and patted Mary Ann's hand.

It was all too much for Mary Ann. Turning on a loud sob, she buried her face in her arms on the table, and Mrs. McBride, pulling herself to her feet, stood over her, tapping her shoulder and saying, "Come on, now. Come on." Then after a moment she said, "Stop now, an' I'll give you somethin'. He left it to me for to do with what I thought best. 'If you think she needs it, Gran, let her have it,' he said. 'If you don't, put it in the fire'."

Mary Ann raised her tear-stained face and watched Fanny take her wobbling body to the fireplace, where she reached up and extracted a letter from behind the clock. When she placed it in her hand, Mary Ann looked down on it. There was no name on the envelope, no writing of any kind; and when automatically she turned it over, she knew from the condition of the flap that it had been steamed open. This did not affect her, it did not bring any feeling of resentment against her friend. Fanny had likely wanted to know what her grandson had said, and whether she should pass it on or not.

Slowly Mary Ann slit open the envelope and read the very short letter it contained.

If you read this it'll be because you have been upset at me going and you didn't really mean what you said the other night. I'm going to stay in America for a year. If I know I can make a go of it I'll come back then and tell you. If I feel I can't—that is make a go of it—then don't wait but do what they want you to. Perhaps in a year's time you'll want to do that anyway because you always liked him.

Corny.

Would you come and see me Gran now and again? She gets lonely for a bit of a crack.

"Oh! why couldn't he tell me this?" Mary Ann shook the letter in her hand as she looked up into Mrs. McBride's face.

"Why couldn't he say it?"

"Well, he was never very ready with his tongue, especially when it was about anything that really mattered."

"I'll wait. Oh, I'll wait, Mrs. McBride."

"Well, now, hinny. " Fanny put her hand heavily on Mary Ann's shoulder. "Make no rash promises. You're only sixteen, you know. You're very young yet."

"I'm getting on seventeen, Mrs. McBride."

"Well, aye, you might be, but you know you still look such a bairn. And a lot of things can happen in a year, God knows that."

"Nothing will ever happen to change me, Mrs. McBride."

"Aw, well, we'll wait and see. But now you feel a bit better, don't you?"

Mary Ann nodded.

"Would you like a bit of dinner?"

"No thanks, Mrs. McBride."

"A bit of bread dipped in the gravy?"

Mary Ann gave an involuntary shudder when she thought of the black fat surrounding the meat. But she smiled and said, "Thanks, all the same, but I'll have to be off. You know what me ma is if I'm not there on time. . . . Good-bye, Mrs. McBride, and thanks." Impulsively she reached up and kissed the wrinkled cheek. And Fanny held her tightly for a moment, and as she did so she whispered, "You're not the only who'll miss him, you know, lass."

"I know that, Mrs. McBride . . . and, and I'll come and see you more often."

"Do that. Do that, hinny. You're always more than welcome."

"Good-bye, Mrs. McBride."

"Good-bye, lass. Give me love to Lizzie, and don't forget Mike. Tell them I'll drop in one of these days."

"Oh, do, do, they'd love to see you."

After more repeated good-byes, Mary Ann went down the steps of Mulhattan's Hall with a lighter tread than she had ascended them, and as she hurried through the quiet Sunday-stripped streets towards the bus stop, she gripped the letter in her hand inside her coat pocket. She had no experience of love letters with which to judge this, her first one; but even so she knew it was lacking in the niceties that went to make up such a letter. Yet every line had brought Corny closer to her. The terse, taciturn, blunt individual was near her once again. There had been no sign in the letter of his lessons in English. Corny could, she knew, speak all right when there was nothing to deflect his attention from the rocks and pitfalls of grammar. But when he was angry, or disturbed in any way, he fell immediately back into the natural idiom. But what did she care how he talked? He could talk broad Geordie for the remainder of his life if only he was here with her now. But she had his letter, and his promise, and to this she would hang on for the coming year. And longer, yes, longer, if necessary. As long as ever he wanted.

4

The farm had fallen under a spell of peace. It was like an enchanted place because everybody was happy. Mike sang and joked once more. Lizzie bustled about her house. She cooked more than ever. She took an interest in books that went in for pictures of big houses, and she laughed quite a bit. And Mr. Lord seemed to be very pleased with himself these days. He appeared to be floating on a firm cloud of achievement. As for Tony, Tony smiled and laughed and teased Mary Ann; and on occasions took her out for a run in the car. This was a new departure and might account for Mr. Lord's cloud of achievement. . . . Then Michael and Sarah; they were living in a world of their own and enjoying a separate happiness—they were not involved with Corny Boyle.

This change in the atmosphere as far as Mary Ann and Mike were concerned had been brought about simply by Corny's letter. Mary Ann had, on the quiet, shown the letter to her da, and Mike had grinned widely and said, "Stick to your guns. Don't let on. Let them go on thinking and planning what they like." He had not intimated who "they" were, but she knew he was referring to her mother and Mr. Lord. He had added, with a warning lift of his finger, "Don't show that to your mother, mind." And looking back at him she had said, "As if I would." And they had laughed together. But some time later Mike had said to her, "I would show that letter to Tony if I was you."

"To Tony?"

"Yes. It would put things straight in his mind, and he won't start walking up any garden path."

So she had shown the letter to Tony, with the result that after a long moment of looking down at her, with perhaps just a trace of sadness in his expression, he had suddenly punched her playfully, saying, "What do you say to playing them at their own game?" And she knew that here, too, Tony was referring not only to his grandfather but also to her mother, Lizzie, with whom he was on very good terms. But she had asked, "What do you mean?" He didn't explain fully what he did mean, but said, "Well, we needn't fight, need we, and give them cause for worry? I'll have to take you out for a run now and again, and to a show. It'll make the year pass quicker. What about it?" she had laughed freely for the first time in weeks. Her da was happy again, so was her mother. What did it matter if it was for different reasons. And Tony was nice. She had always liked Tony. As Corny had said, she had always liked Tony. But that wasn't loving. There was all the difference in the world.

So everyone, with the exception of Michael and Sarah, began putting on an act.

It was on the Thursday morning that Mary Ann received a letter from Janice Schofield, asking if she could come up and see her on the Friday evening. During working hours Mary Ann, escaping the keen eye of Miss Thompson and wishing to show off her typing prowess, wrote Janice a sketchy reply, the gist of which was: Of course, she could come up on the Friday evening.

Mary Ann had been rather surprised to receive a letter from Janice. At one time during her school days, they had been good friends; but Janice had never been close to her like Beatrice Willoughby. Beatrice, to use schoolgirl jargon, was her best friend, and Janice was her second best. Janice was nine months older than Mary Ann and had left school more than a year ago, while Mary Ann had just finished in the summer term. Beatrice on the other hand, was still at school making her way to college. . . . Years ago Mary Ann had thought she, too, would like to go to college, but Corny had changed her mind about this matter, and strangely, when she had put forward her idea of taking up shorthand and typing, there had been little or no objection from any quarter. This she had reasoned, was because her da had Corny in mind and further education was going to serve no purpose. In fact, it might do Corny a disservice. Her mother's reaction, she knew, was patterned on Mr. Lord's, and this is where the word "strangely" applied most. For Mr. Lord had not gone off the deep end about her proposal to become a secretary.

Two more years at school and three at college would not have helped Mr. Lord's scheme at all. Five years is a long time when a man is over seventy.

Mary Ann wondered what Janice wanted to see her about, and she hurried home on the Friday night and changed into her new loose sweater and pleated skirt so as to look her best when Janice arrived. For Mary Ann knew that she would come all dressed up—"killingly smart", as their Michael termed it, "and smellin' like a poke of devils". Janice worked on the cosmetic counter in a large store in Newcastle, and undoubtedly this had a lot to do with her choice of perfume.

Lizzie had lit the fire in the sitting-room, and at ten minutes to seven, Mary Ann and Michael went down the road to the bus stop. Michael to meet Sarah, and Mary Ann to meet Janice. But only Sarah alighted from the bus.

At eight o'clock Mary Ann, accompanied this time by Mike, met the bus again, but still there was no sign of Janice.

"You'd better phone her up," said Mike, "and find out why she hasn't put in an appearance."

They now had an extension of the phone in the house, and the operator, after trying several times to get Janice's number, informed Mary Ann that there was no reply. So there was nothing for it but to wait until the next morning and see if there was a letter from her.

But on the Saturday morning there was no letter from Janice. As always, Mary Ann was in a tear to get to the bus, and she did not phone the Schofield's house until she returned at lunch time, when once again she was told there was no reply.

Lizzie said now, "Likely their phone's out of order; you should take a trip over there this afternoon and see her. It's a lovely day, it will do you good."

"But it's such a long way. It's right outside the town, Mother."

"Well, it's just as long for her to come here. . . . Why don't you ask Tony to run you over? He's nearly sure to be going into Newcastle this afternoon."

Lizzie had her face turned from Mary Ann when she made this proposal, and Mary Ann allowed herself the reaction of raising her eyebrows slightly, but that was all.

Not for a long time had she asked Tony to take her anywhere, even from the night he had proposed that they, too, should put on an act she had left the invitations to him. But today, when she did ask him, he expressed delight at the opportunity of running her into Newcastle. He would do more than that, he said. He would take her to the Schofields. He would very much like to see his theatrical partner again. Oh, yes, Mrs. S. and he should team up.

He repeated much of this when he called for her, and Mike and Lizzie and he all laughed together, but Mary Ann thought he was overdoing it a bit.

Lizzie smiled warmly down on Mary Ann as she watched Tony reach over and tuck the car rug around her; she even waved them off as if it was a special occasion.

They were out on the road going past the cottages when Tony gave Mary Ann a sidelong quizzical glance as he remarked, "Everybody's happy . . . everybody. For the Lord himself gave his blessing on our excursion before I came out."

Tony was referring to his grandfather. And now her laughter joined his. Oh, Tony was nice, he was. He was good fun. She liked him ever so much. For a fleeting second she even wished that she didn't know Corny. But it was just for a second.

Mary Ann had not been to the Schofields more than three times during her acquaintance with Janice. But Mrs. Schofield had been to the farm many times; in fact, Mary Ann had lost count of Mrs. Schofield's visits during the past few years. The Schofield's residence, one would be right in calling it that, was an imposing house standing on a piece of land unusually large even for such houses in that select district. You entered the grounds through a long drive, which was bordered by larches. Although the trees were bare they were entwined with the dark, shining green of canes. These, in turn, were laced with dead bramble. The effect was the same as entering a tunnel, although not quite so dark. The gravel of the drive was covered with matted grass and, except for two deep car ruts, appeared like a field track. The front of the house, too, when they came upon it, had the appearance of being buried under masses of undergrowth. It looked as if it was fighting the clematis, climbing roses, and virginia creeper hanging in dead profusion, even from its tile.

Perhaps it was the unexpected condition of the house that made Tony bring the car to a stop before he reached the front door. He sat with his head bent forward, staring upwards through the windscreen for a moment, before saying, "Great Scott! There hasn't been much work done here for some time, I should say."

"It wasn't as bad as this the last time I was here." Mary Ann was speaking in a whisper. "But that's nearly two years ago. It was rather nice then. It was summer. Mrs. Schofield used to do the garden herself. There's a beautiful rose garden at the back. . . . Will you wait until I see if they're in?"

"Of course, of course." Tony brought his gaze round to her. "I'll come in with you for a moment. I meant what I said, I'd like to see her . . . not Janice." He nipped his nose, and they both laughed. Then he added, "She's not a patch on her mother."

"She's all right." Mary Ann felt bound to defend her friend. "You've just got to know her."

"I don't want to, thank you very much."

They were out of the car now and walking towards the front door, which was covered by a glass porch, quite a large porch. They stood for a moment, as people do, hesitating just that second before ringing the bell, and it was as Tony's hand was uplifted that the yell came to them. Bawl would be more appropriate in describing the sound of the man's voice. It came from the right, from inside the room to the right of the front door. This room had a large high window, which protruded into the drive with squared sides. Looking through the glass of the porch they were right opposite one side of the window, which was a pane wide but half-covered by a twist of dead stems. The bawl had been in the form of a curse. It was a word that Mary Ann hadn't heard before, although Mike at times swore freely. And its effect on Tony was to make him bring his startled glance down on her, and then to take her arm and move her quickly back towards the drive. But before they reached the entrance to the porch they had stopped again, and were once more looking towards the window. And there to be seen quite plainly was Mrs. Schofield. She was walking backwards into the far corner of the recess, and advancing on her was a man. When Mrs. Schofield could go no further the man, too, stopped, and his voice came clear and penetrating to them. "You would bloody well put up with it and like it, and if you make any more of your highfalutin shows I'll bring her here. . . . You're always on about needing help, aren't you?"

"You can't do this to me, I'll . . . I'll leave you."

The man threw his head back and laughed. "That's what I've been wanting you to do for years, but you won't, will you? You're afraid of what your dear, dear friends would say. That wonderful, charming Lettice couldn't hold her man! You wouldn't like that, would you? Oh, no!"

"I'll go when I'm ready." Mrs. Schofield's voice came to them in trembling tones like those of an old woman; and immediately there followed the man's voice, saying, "You'll go when . . . I'm . . . ready. You'll stay here until Jan is married. And then I'll have the great pleasure of escorting you to the door with my foot in your backside. . . . You stuck-up bitch, you!"

Mary Ann was standing with her hand pressed tightly to her mouth, and as he saw the man's arm come up she closed her eyes and turned her face towards Tony's chest. Automatically Tony's arms went round her shoulders, but he did not look at her, and when the sound of the second blow came to Mary Ann she felt his body jerking as if the man's fist was hitting him.

There were footsteps sounding inside the house now, and Tony, loosing his hold on Mary Ann, turned and faced the front door.

Her fingers still tightly pressed to her mouth, Mary Ann stood looking apprehensively at Tony. She had often seen him in tempers, but she had never seen him look like this. There was not a vestige of colour in his face, it had a bleached look. Even his eyes appeared to be drained of all pigment. She was as frightened at this moment for Tony as ever she had been for Mike. There was going to be a fight. She knew there was going to be a fight; and it would be a terrible fight. Mr. Schofield was a big man, as big as her da. She had only met him once and she hadn't liked him. Tony was tall, but he had no bulk with which to match Mr. Schofield. Yet he had something else that perhaps might kill Mr. Schofield; it stemmed from the livid passion showing on his face.

The footsteps had gone, and the door hadn't opened. A full minute passed before Tony turned his neck stiffly and looked towards her. Then his gaze lifted almost reluctantly towards the window again.

Mary Ann, too, looked through the window. Mrs. Schofield was now sitting in a chair, her face turned into the corner, and she was crying, but no sound reached them. What they did hear was the whirr of a car engine starting up. The next second there shot from the side of the house a Humber Snipe with Mr. Schofield at the wheel.

If Tony's car had been opposite the front door the man must surely have seen it, but from where it was standing on the far side of the drive underneath the overhanging trees, it must have escaped his notice, for he did not stop. Within seconds, the loud grinding of changing gears told them that he was on the main road.

Mary Ann was feeling sick. She always felt sick when there was fighting. But this was a different kind of sickness. She was puzzled, bewildered, and absolutely out of her depth. Mrs. Schofield was bright and gay, and had a lovely life. That's what people thought about Mrs. Schofield. She was light as thistledown, she was amusing . . . she amused Mr. Lord. This couldn't be Mrs. Schofield; this woman who had backed away across the room and almost whimpered when she talked. Mary Ann had lived in the slums of Jarrow and yet she had never seen a man actually strike a woman. She had heard of Mr. and Mrs. So-and-So having rows and going for each other, but she had never actually seen them fight; and never once in her life had she seen her da raise his hand to her ma, not even when he was paralytic drunk.

"What are we going to do?" She was whispering up to Tony. "Oh, poor Mrs. Schofield." She shook her head and swallowed against the threatening tears.

When Tony did not answer but kept staring through the window, she asked softly, "Shall I ring?"

"No." His voice was sharp. "She won't answer." He moved from her, out of the porch, on to the drive; and she followed him. And when he stood on the overgrown flower-bed before the window and tapped gently on the pane, she herself was startled, so quick was the jump Mrs. Schofield gave from the chair. She watched her stand for some minutes staring in painful amazement through the window at Tony, before screwing her face up, and then burying it in her hands.

"Open the door." Tony's voice was quiet. And when Mrs. Schofield only shook her head slowly from side to side, he called louder, "Open the door."

A few seconds later the front door opened, and Mary Ann, following Tony, saw Mrs. Schofield's back disappearing down the dim hall.

They were in the room now, and Mrs. Schofield was standing looking through the window, and Tony was standing behind her talking to her back. Quietly he said, "We saw what happened, so it doesn't matter. Let me look at your face."

"No, no, please . . . and please go away."

"I'm not going away."

Mary Ann noticed he did not say we. And then he went on, "How long have you put up with this?"

"Oh, please." It was a low, beseeching cry. And when Mrs. Schofield's head dropped, Tony took her gently by the shoulders and turned her around.

Mary Ann gave a sharp gasp before going to the side of this woman who to her had been the personification of frivolity and lightness. "Oh! Mrs. Schofield. . . . Oh! I'm sorry. Your poor mouth. Will . . . shall I get some water?"

Mrs. Schofield's head was held level now, and although the tears were running down her swelling cheekbone and over her bruised lip, she managed a faint smile as she said, "Don't worry, Mary Ann. It's all right, it's all right. Come and sit down."

Tony, with his fingers just touching her elbow, led Mrs. Schofield to the couch, and when he had seated himself on the edge beside her, with his body turned fully to her, he asked pointedly, "Why do you stand it?"

As Mary Ann watched Mrs. Schofield's mouth quiver she wanted to say to Tony, "Don't ask any questions. Can't you see she's upset enough," but she continued to look at this surprising woman as she moved her eyes slowly about her drawing-room. It was as if she were looking at the articles about her with surprise, as if seeing them after a long time. And then she answered him absently with, "Why? Yes, why?" Her head continued to make small pathetic jerks until her eyes came to rest on Tony, and then she said, in that voice that held a peculiar charm for all who heard it, "I suppose it's because I was born here. I was brought up in this house. My whole life has been spent here."

"Is it worth it?"

"No! No! Oh, no."

There was vehemence in the tone now, and as Mrs. Schofield went to cover her face once again with her hands, she stopped, and seeming to be becoming fully aware of Mary Ann's presence, she swallowed and drew in a deep breath, before turning and looking at her and saying, "You've come to see Janice, I suppose, Mary Ann?"

"Yes, Mrs. Schofield. She was going to come last night, and she didn't, and I couldn't get through. I tried several times."

"No, you wouldn't. The line's broken." She didn't go on to explain how the line was broken, but added, "Janice is upstairs."

Before Mary Ann could make any reply to this, Tony brought out in an amazed tone, "Upstairs! and all this going on?"

Mrs. Schofield did not answer Tony, but, turning to Mary Ann, asked, "Would you like to go up to her, Mary Ann? It's the second door at the top of the landing, on the right-hand side."

"Yes. Yes, Mrs. Schofield." Mary Ann glanced towards Tony, but Tony was looking at Mrs. Schofield.

Out in the hall she stood for a moment gazing about her. The house inside was clean, tidy and clean, not bright like their house was bright, but not dirty. She did not go immediately up the stairs, for she was overwhelmed with pity not untouched with shock. She had just experienced the first great surprise of her life. She had been shown in one swift swoop the meaning of . . . putting a face on it. Mrs. Schofield must have spent all her married life putting a face on it. She could see her now on the night of Len's wedding, standing on the platform playing the trombone when she could not stop herself laughing. And later that night she would have gone home to perhaps a similar scene to that which had just taken place. . . . Ee! it was awful. Poor Mrs. Schofield. She went slowly up the stairs and knocked on the second door to the right. And when it was opened, Janice said, "Oh, you." Then looking past her and towards the stairs, she asked, "How long have you been here?"

"Not very long. I tried to phone you, but couldn't get through. I thought something was wrong when you didn't come last night, after saying you would." Janice turned her back completely on Mary Ann and walked back into the bedroom; then after she had sat down on the side of the bed, she said, "Well, come in, don't stand there."

Mary Ann went into the room, closing the door behind her. She felt rather gauche in Janice's presence, and very, very young. Janice was sitting with her hands nipped between her knees, and she looked at her hands as she asked, "Did you hear anything going on?"

"Yes, we did."

"We?" Janice's head came up.

"Tony's with me."

"Oh, my God! Although Janice said this in a very swanky tone, it sounded much more of a blasphemy than if, say, Mrs. McBride had said it.

"Well, he would get an earful."

"I think you should come down. Your mother's lip's all swollen."

Janice looked down at her hands once more and began to rock herself, before she said, "Oh, it won't be the first time. And anyway, she asks for it."

"Asks for it?" Mary Ann's voice was high and sharp. "She's nice. I've always said that."

"If that's the kind of niceness you want, yes. But she's always got on his nerves. She should never have married him. She should have taken someone polished, and re-feened. Someone who liked to go to concerts, yet someone who would laugh at her jokes when she was being funny ha-ha. But most of all somebody who would keep up this damn mausoleum." She released her hands from between her knees and flung them sidewards. "Oh, she gets on my goat too."

"But he hit her, Janice . . . twice!"

"He was drunk and worried about me."

"About you?"

"Yes. It all came out last night. That is what I wanted to see you about. I was in a blue funk yesterday, but now all the beans are spilt it doesn't matter. . . . I'm going to have a baby."

Mary Ann's mouth dropped into a large "O", before she brought her lips together again, saying, "Janice!"

"Oh! For God's sake, don't look like that, Mary Ann. You look like the Virgin Mary, only more damned good."

Although Janice had attended the Convent she wasn't a Catholic, and Mary Ann had always resented her digs at the Virgin Mary. But now all she could say was, "Are you . . . are you married?"

"Oh, be your age. . . . Why I thought of coming to see you I don't know. Of course I'm not married. What do you think all this hoo-ha is about? And I'm telling you, I don't care much if I do or I don't. But Father's going to play the gigantic square and make him do . . . the right thing. Oh, my God!" Janice jerked herself from the bed. "The right thing! And live a life like theirs! I wouldn't have believed it, but Daddy's taken it worse than she has. You get surprises if you've got anything left to feel surprise with. She didn't blink an eyelid, yet Daddy, he nearly went through the roof. And him running one in Newcastle and another in Pelaw."

It must have been Mary Ann's puckered expression that made Janice close her eyes and fling her head back as she cried defiantly, by way of exclamation. "A woman . . . he's always had a woman, but now he's got two."

Mary Ann knew that she should sit down. She had a frightened feeling. It was like the time she had thought that Mr. Quinton wanted her mother. She wasn't as green as Janice thought she was. It wasn't Janice's knowledge that was shocking her, but the open flaunting of it. She herself would rather have died than talk like this about her parents. Then Janice surprised her still further by turning on the bed and flinging herself face downwards.

"Oh, don't, Janice, don't." Mary Ann grasped Janice's hand which was pounding into the pillow, and when she began to cry with a hard, tearing sound, Mary Ann knelt on the floor and put her arms around her and her face on the pillow as she murmured over and over, "Oh, don't Janice, don't. Don't cry, don't cry so."

When Janice finally stopped crying she seemed to have washed away the hard covering of her personality, for, sitting once again on the side of the bed, one hand only now nipped between her knees, she looked at Mary Ann and said quietly, "I won't have a life like theirs, I'd rather take something and finish it."

"Oh, Janice! Don't say such things, don't. And you needn't have a life like theirs. . . . Is . . . is this boy nice?"

"No. No, he's not. He's as far removed from me as Daddy is from . . . from her." Janice now turned her head to the side and said, "I've got a lot of my father in me so that's why I know that if I marry Freddie I won't be able to stick it. I think that's why I grew to dislike her . . . my mother. Because she had the power to stick it. To put a face on it. She should have left him years ago. And she might have, too, if it hadn't been for Grandpa. He died only three years ago. They were both barmy about this house and garden. There's something to be said on both sides, because it was Daddy's money that was keeping it going. That is until he turned nasty . . . and he can be nasty, hellish. He cut out the gardner, and the maids . . . and, oh . . . oh, lots of things. And the more things he did the more face she put on, and that drove him almost round the bend. . . . But I won't marry Freddie, I won't."

"He can't make you if you don't want to." Mary Ann was holding Janice's hands tightly between hers now. "Look, come and stay with us for a while."

Janice turned and stared into Mary Ann's face. "Would your mother let me?"

"Yes. Yes, of course she would." Mary Ann hadn't stopped to consider whether Lizzie would fall in with this arrangement or not. She only knew she wanted to help Janice.

"I'd be glad to get away from here. If only for a few days. But I'm beginning to show . . . and there's your Michael!"

Yes, there was Michael, and Sarah. But Mary Ann, overriding this as well, said casually, "What does it matter? They're not to know."

"Oh, they'll know. Everybody will know shortly. It would be better in the long run, I suppose, to do what I'm told."

"Does he . . . Freddie, want . . . want to get married?"

"Oh, yes. He would jump in feet first at the idea. He's only in the dock office and he'll know when he's on a good thing; Daddy would set him up. Oh, I know exactly what'll happen. He'll set him up, and he'll buy us a house and a car. He's rotten with money, and he'll spend it on anything or anybody outside of this house."

The bitterness was creeping back into Janice's tone, and Mary Ann shook her hand and said, "Well, wait and see. And think about coming to us. You needn't worry about phoning or anything, just come. My mother will love to have you."

Janice, now looking down into Mary Ann's upturned face, smiled and said, "You're sweet, you know, Mary Ann. I used to be jealous of you and Beatrice being close pals. I always wanted you for a friend, a complete friend. Because you were different somehow. I suppose it was because you had nothing in your family life to hide."

"Oh . . . oh!" Mary Ann's head went back on a little laugh now. "Oh, Janice, you don't know the half of it. I'm beginning to think we all have something to hide. I've been fighting for me da since . . . oh, I can't remember the time when I wasn't putting him over as somebody wonderful; when I wasn't covering up his drinking bouts. It isn't like that now, but things still happen and I always seem to be covering up for him. You do things like that when you love someone. . . . Nothing to hide! Do you know, I've always envied you."

"Envied me? God! Envied me? The times I've been going to run away, or commit suicide; or throw myself over the banisters to stop them havin' a row. . . . Envy me!"

The two girls sat looking at each other on the side of the bed. And their hands held tightly for a moment, before Mary Ann said through a break in her voice, "I'd better be going down now, Janice; Tony will want to be getting away. But remember what I said. Come any time . . . any time. Goodbye, now."

"Good-bye, Mary Ann, and thanks. But I'll let you know if I'm coming. I'll drop you a line, or phone. Good-bye. I feel better now. Good-bye."

In the drawing-room Tony was no longer sitting on the couch but on a chair some distance from Mrs. Schofield, and as Mary Ann entered the room it did not seem as if she had interrupted their talking, it was as if they had been sitting quiet for some time. She stood in front of Mrs. Schofield when she said, "I've asked Janice to come and stay with us for a while, Mrs. Schofield."

Mrs. Schofield did not speak, she only moved her head slightly. And then Mary Ann added, "I'll have to be going now." She turned sharply and looked towards Tony, and he rose from the chair but made no comment.

Mrs. Schofield, too, rose to her feet, but she did not accompany them from the room, rose from the chair but made no comment.

Mrs. Schoffield, too, rose to her feet, but she did not accompany them from the room, and Mary Ann was slightly puzzled when Tony took leave of her with just a single good-bye; a rather curt-sounding good-bye.

As the car went through the tunnel of the drive, Mary Ann said softly, "It's awful, awful."

Tony made no response to this. He slowed the car up as he neared the end of the drive, then, when he had swung into the main road, he quickly changed gears and they went roaring towards the city.

Mary Ann realised that Tony was quiet because, like her, he was upset. He, too, must have seen Mrs. Schofield as a gay creature. And she supposed that men could be shocked as much about things as women could. She said now, as if they were continuing a conversation, "I hope she doesn't marry that Freddie."

"Who? Who are you taling about?"

"Janice."

"Is she going to be married?"

"Well." She glanced at him. Did he, or didn't he know? She said softly, "Well, you know she's going to have a baby."

"Good God!" The car almost jerked to a stop, then went on again. "So that's it." He was not speaking to her but answering some question of his own. She did not take it up for he did not look in the mood to talk. He looked like her da did at times, but more so like Mr. Lord when he was very angry inside. So they didn't speak again until they reached the farmyard. And there he turned the car before stopping. Then reaching over to open the door for her, he said, "Are you going to tell your mother?"

"Yes." Mary Ann hesitated. "I'll have to if Janice is coming."

"Yes." He nodded his head without looking at her, and said again, "Yes."

She closed the car door,then watched him speeding back along the road down which they had just come.

Mike had been going in the direction of the byres, and he turned on the sound of the car leaving the yard again and, coming to her, said, "My! you're soon back. Where's he gone?"

Mary Ann, looking up at Mike, meant to say "I don't know," but instead she bowed her head and burst out crying.

"What's the matter? What's happened?" Mike's voice was deep.

"Nothing. Nothing."

"Tony said somethin' to you?"

"Oh, no, no. Come in a minute, will you? I've . . . I've got to tell me ma."

In the kitchen, with Mike sitting at her side and Lizzie sitting in front of her, she held their silence with her story. And when it was finished she looked from one to the other, and they returned her gaze, still without speaking. Then Mike, getting up and walking to the pipe rack, lifted a wire cleaner from the top of it and rammed it down the stem of his pipe before shaking his head and saying, "I think this is one of the biggest surprises of me life."

"Yes, that's how I felt, Da. I couldn't take it in."

"Poor soul! Poor soul! Look at her the night of the wedding. Who could have been more full of fun?" Lizzie had forgotten her irritation towards Mrs. Schofield on that particular night, and her sympathy at this moment was very genuine. "Did you actually see him hit her?"

"Yes Ma." Mary Ann reverted to the old form of address. At moments such as this Ma seemed more fitting, for the three of them were joined in their pity. "I didn't see him do it the second time; I hid my face."

"You never know, do you?" They both looked towards Mike as he went on pushing the cleaner down the stem of the pipe. "I would have staked me last shilling that she was the happiest woman alive. Mind you"—he wagged the pipe towards Lizzie—"I've said, haven't I, that she wasn't as dizzy as she made out. I knew from the minute I first clapped eyes on her there was a depth there. But it never struck me that all this light fantastic was just a cover . . . did it you? Did you ever have an inkling?"

"No. No. Like you, I would have sworn she was happy." Again Lizzie added, "Poor soul."

"You don't mind me asking Janice here?" Mary Ann now asked of Lizzie.

"No, no. It will be better if she's away from that set-up for a time. But with a man like that, it looks as if he'll get his own way, and make her marry the fellow. Which, I suppose,

will be for the best. At least best for the child. . . . Oh, dear God, it's awful, when you think
of it. I've never liked Janice very much, but now I'm sorry to the heart for her. And not a bit
of wonder she's gone wrong, not a bit."

"Oh, I'm not as sorry for her as I am for the mother." Mike put the pipe into his mouth.
"That young un's got a tough core, she'll get by. . . . But you see, don't you, Liz, money
isn't everything." Mike now thrust out his arm and wagged his finger at Lizzie. It was as if
money, and its value, had been under discussion. "Schofield's rotten with money. I
understand he's got his fingers in all sorts of pies. Real estate, shipping, the lot. He's as bad
as the old man. And where's his money got him? What has it done for him? Except help him
to run three homes!"

"Mike!"

"Oh, don't get on your high horse, Liz. She's told us all about it, hasn't she? It's herself
that's told us." He flapped his hand towards Mary Ann. "Her education's been advanced
this afternoon. But as I was sayin' about money . . . see what it does?" Mike bounced his
head once, then turning on his heel, went out, and Lizzie, sitting straight in her chair,
remarked in hurt tones, "Why has he to go off the deep end like that?" Who was talking
about money?" She looked at Mary Ann and shook her head. Mary Ann said nothing. She
knew that her da had been pointing out to her ma that people who married for money were
not always happy. And she knew that her mother was being purposely blind to the parable.

The sound of Michael coming in the back way at this moment brought Mary Ann to her
feet, and she said hastily, "I'll go upstairs and do my face. Don't tell him about Janice, will
you not? He doesn't like her very much and if she's comin' here it will make things
awkward."

"Go along. All right. Don't worry."

Mary Ann had not reached the hall door when Michael entered from the scullery, and as
he watched her disappearing back he remarked, in a brotherly fashion, "What's up with
her? Has she been crying? Why did they come back so quickly?"

"Oh . . . Janice wasn't very well."

"What's she been crying for?"

"She's upset. Just a little upset about something."

"What?"

"Oh, Michael, don't ask so many questions."

"Oh, all right, if it's private. Only if I started to howl my eyes out, there'd be a reason for
it."

Lizzie turned and looked at her son and smiled fondly at him as she said, "There would, if
you howled your eyes out; that would be the day when you howled your eyes out."

Lizzie was to remember these words and to think, "Isn't it strange the things we say? It's
as if we have a premonition of what's going to happen." But at this moment she had no
feeling of premonition. She just said to her son, "It's time you were getting yourself
changed as Sarah will be here and you not ready."

"Mother."

"Yes, what is it?" Lizzie had gone to the sideboard and taken out the teacloth.

"I want to ask you something."

She turned and glanced at him. "Well, I'm listening, go on."

"It's about my holiday."

"Your holiday? It's late in the year to start talking of holidays."

"Father owes me a week. He said I could have it at any time. You remember?"

"Yes. But we'll soon be on Christmas. And you don't want your holiday with snow on
the ground, surely?"

"Yes, that's just it, I do."

"Where are you going?"

Michael turned from her penetrating gaze and walked towards the fire. "I want to go to Switzerland."

"Switzerland?"

He swung round sharply to her. "Yes, Mother, Switzerland."

"But that'll cost a penny, won't it?"

"Well, I've never had a real holiday in my life. South Shields, Whitley Bay, Sea Houses. But now I want to go abroad. It will only be for a week."

"Well, well. If you want to go, I suppose you'll go. What does Sarah say to this?"

Michael now looked down towards the mat. Then without raising his head, he cast his eyes up towards Lizzie as he said, "That's it. We want to go together."

Lizzie's lips closed with a light pressure; the line in between her brows deepened, and then she said quietly, "Together? You and Sarah away in Switzerland?"

"I'm nearly twenty, Mother."

"Yes, I know that. And don't tell me now that Sarah's eighteen. I know that too, and I'm going to tell you right away I don't hold with young people going away on holiday together. And there's your father. Just think what he'll say to this."

"I've asked him."

"You've asked him . . . well! . . . What did he say then?"

"Do you want to know word for word?"

Lizzie made no reply. But her shoulders went back a little, and she drew her chin in.

"He said it's my own life; nobody can answer my conscience but myself. He said, 'If you ever intend to marry a girl never take her down first if you can help it. . . .' "

"Michael!" Lizzie's voice seemed to hit the back of her throat and check her breathing. Twice in the matter of minutes life in the raw had been let loose in her kitchen.

"Well, I'm only telling you what he said, and I know he's right. And I'm just repeating it to put your mind at rest. . . . You understand?"

Lizzie understood all right; but it didn't alter the fact that she didn't want her son to go on holiday alone with Sarah Flannagan or any other girl. She knew men, even the best of them were what she called human. Well, he'd certainly had his say. Lizzie wiped her lips. "Is there anything more you have to tell me?"

"What father said? Well, he said there were worse things than a man getting drunk; and I'm beginning to believe him. . . ."

"No, I didn't mean I wanted to hear anything more your father said. He's said enough, I should imagine. As for worse things than getting drunk, there's two opinions on that point. And I should have thought you knew that."

"Yes, I do, Mother." Michael's tone was soft now and he came towards her, and putting his arm about her shoulders he said, "Don't worry, we'll do nothing we shouldn't do, let me tell you." He smiled at her now. "Sarah will see to that."

Lizzie pulled herself away from Michael's hold. She didn't like this kind of talk; not from her son, her Michael. She knew that one day, and not in the far distant future, she would have to give up this boy of hers, but until that day came he would remain her boy. Not someone who discussed the possibilities of intimacy on holiday. What were young people coming to! She knew that young people went away on holidays together even when they weren't engaged, and she was also well aware of what happened; but she didn't want that kind of thing in her family. And Michael having a good deal of his father in him was bound to be . . . human. Oh dear, oh dear, one thing on top of another. She had thought she would have no more worries when she left Mulhattan's Hall. It just showed you. The word Mulhattan's Hall conjured up first Mrs. McBride, and then Mrs. Flannagan, and she turned swiftly towards Michael and said, "What about her mother? What does she say to this?"

"I don't know." Michael held out his hand with a sort of hopeless gesture. "I won't know until Sarah comes. She's asking her this afternoon."

They continued to look at each other for a moment longer, then Lizzie, with a deep flick, spread the cloth over the table, and Michael, with an equally deep sigh, went upstairs to change.

It was after dinner on the Sunday and the family were relaxing in the front room. Mike was asleep in the deep chair, his long legs stretched out towards the fire. Lizzie sat opposite to him at the other side of the hearth. She was pursuing her favourite hobby of looking at antique furniture and big houses. Michael was sitting at one end of the couch reading *The Farmers' Weekly*; and Mary Ann, with her legs tucked under her, was sitting at the other end. She had two books on her lap. One was *The Art of the Short Story* and the other was Fowler's *Modern English Usage*. But she was reading neither at present. She was staring across the hearth rug into the fire. Her thoughts darting from Corny to Mrs. Schofield then back to Corny again, then on to Janice and back to Corny again. Then to Tony, and strangely not to Corny now but to Mrs. Schofield. For she was seeing them wrapped in that strange silence when she entered the drawing-room of that unhappy house yesterday. Then once again she was thinking of Corny; hearing Mrs. McBride talk of him; seeing Mrs. McBride give her his letter. Her mind dwelt on the letter. She had read it countless times in the past few weeks. She could, without any exaggeration, have quoted it word for word backwards. But the thought of it at this moment brought her legs from under her, and in order not to disturb her da nor yet her mother nor Michael, she went quietly out of the room and upstairs to her bedroom.

After the heat of the sitting-room the chill of the bedroom made her shiver, and she swiftly went to the top drawer of the dressing chest, and there, from the box in which she kept her handkerchiefs and the flute which Corny had given her for her thirteenth birthday, and which, in spite of her promise, she had never learnt to play, she took out the letter. To read it she had to stand by the window, for the sky was dark with coming snow, and her heart quickened as it always did when she came to . . . "If I know I can make a go of it, I'll come back then and tell you." There was a statue of Our Lady on a little shelf above the head of her bed and she turned her eyes up to it as she did night and morning, and now she prayed: "Make the time go quickly, dear Mother . . . please."

When she folded the letter again she held it to her cheek for a moment as she looked out of the window. One minute her eyes were dreamy, lost in the promise of a year ahead. The next minute she was bending forward towards the window pane, her mouth open and her eyes screwed up. It couldn't be! But it was; yes, it was. She stared one moment longer at the figure walking primly towards the house gate, and then she thrust the letter into her handkerchief box, banged the drawer closed, and went belting down the stairs. As she thrust the sitting-room door open, all concern for her father's afternoon nap was gone as she cried, "Mrs. Flannagan! . . . It's Mrs. . . . It's Mrs. Flannagan . . . Mrs. Flannagan's coming."

"What! Who?" Lizzie and Michael had turned towards her, and Mike, shaking his head and blinking rapidly, pulled himself into a sitting position. "Good God! Flannagan? The old 'un? You said her . . . Mrs?"

Before Mary Ann could make any further retort, Michael cried, "Oh Lord!" And Lizzie, turning on him, hissed under her breath, "This is you and this Switzerland business. Good gracious, on a Sunday afternoon, and me looking like this!"

"Let me get out."

As the knock came on the front door, Mike, buttoning up his shirt neck, pushed past Mary Ann and made for the stairs. And Michael, about to follow, was checked when Lizzie hissed, "Now, Michael, you're not going to leave this to me, you've got to face it."

"Oh, Mother! . . . Well, let her get in, I'll come back in a minute . . . it mightn't be about that at all."

"Michael!" Lizzie was whispering hoarsely to Michael's disappearing back as Mary Ann, on the second knock, went towards the door.

"Oh, hello, Mrs. Flannagan." The feigned surprise, and even pleasure, in Mary Ann's voice, said a lot for her advancement from the days when, next to the justifiable hate she had for Sarah, she considered Mrs. Flannagan not only an enemy of her . . . ma and da, but someone in close association with the devil himself.

Mrs. Flannagan was dressed very nicely. She had always attended to her person with the same meticulous care she gave to her house. These qualities of cleanliness were considered by Mrs. Flannagan offsprings of virtue and as such had been enough to arouse Fanny McBride's hate, and Mary Ann, always a staunch ally of Mrs. McBride, would have hated Mrs. Flannagan if for no other reason but that Mrs. McBride couldn't stand . . . the upstart.

"I hope you don't mind me comin' like this, Mary Ann?" Mrs. Flannagan's tone held none of the old condescension.

"No, no. Come in, Mrs. Flannagan. You must be frozen. Isn't it cold?" Mary Ann closed the door behind the visitor. "Will I take your hat and coat?" She was playing for time to allow her mother to compose herself, and perhaps tidy her hair; but at this moment Lizzie came to the sitting-room door.

Lizzie couldn't be blamed for the slight tilt to her chin as she looked at this woman who for many years had been the bane of her existence. Life was strange. But she had no time to delve into this deep problem now, she would keep that for when she lay in bed awake to-night. She was glad, oh she was, that she had insisted on having the new square carpet for the hall. In spite of Mike's saying "It's madness, lass. It's madness, with all the feet tramping in and out". But she had always wanted a proper carpet in the hall, with a matching colour going up the stairs. Mike had said, "Why pick on a mustard colour" And she had informed him that dark mustard would go with the old furniture, the pieces that her flair had guided her to bid for at the auction sales. And now on one of these pieces, a small hall table, stood a wrought-iron basket showing off a beautiful plant of pink cyclamen. Oh, she was glad her hall looked nice. If only she'd had a chance to change into something decent. But her skirt and blouse were really all right, and what was more, oh, of much more significance, she was mistress of this fine home. . . . Yes, life was funny.

Lizzie fell into the part of hostess. With only a slight touch of reserve to her manner she held out her hand to Mrs. Flannagan, saying, "If I'd known you were coming, I would have had Michael meet the bus." The censure wasn't too tactfully covered, it wasn't meant to be. But Mrs. Flannagan was, to-day, out to placate, and she answered, "Well, I know I should have phoned, Mrs. Shaughnessy. But it was the way Sarah sprung it on me. And it made me rather vexed." She smiled. "So I said, 'Well, I'll go myself and see what Mr. and Mrs. Shaughnessy have to say about it.' . . . But very likely you don't know what I'm talking about?"

"Yes. Yes, I think I do." Lizzie inclined her head. "But come in and sit down; it is so cold to-day, isn't it?"

Mary Ann followed Mrs. Flannagan into the sitting-room. She had a great desire to laugh. Laugh loudly. . . . Go and see Mr. and Mrs. Shaughnessy. Oh! Mr. Shaughnessy would have a laugh about this for weeks ahead. The times Mrs. Flannagan had called her da a drunken no-good. . . . All of a sudden she was glad Mrs. Flannagan had made this unexpected visit. After yesterday, she needed light relief, she felt they were all in need of a little relief. She sat down opposite Mrs. Flannagan and watched her look around the sitting-room with open amazement. And she found herself even liking her when she said generously, "What a beautiful room, Mrs. Shaughnessy, what a beautiful room. Did you do it yourself?"

"We all helped, Mrs. Flannagan. Mike's very good at papering and painting." Lizzie's chin, still high, moved a little to the side.

"But my mother chose the furniture," Mary Ann put in. "She's always picking up nice pieces." She looked with pride towards Lizzie, and Lizzie smiled back at her. And then inclining her head towards her guest, she said, "Would you like a cup of tea?"

"That's very kind of you, Mrs. Shaughnessy. . . . Yes, I would. I'd be obliged."

"I'll make it, Mother."

Mary Ann jumped up and left the room. And as she went laughing into the kitchen, Michael, standing to the side of the door, pulled at her arm.

"What has she said?"

"Nothing, nothing. We've only reached the polite exchange stage so far. You've got all that to come, me lad." She dug her brother in the chest.

"Oh! They get you down." Michael put his hand to his head.

"Who?"

"Oh, mothers. The lot of them."

"Me ma's all right about this." Mary Ann's face took on a straight pattern as she nodded solemnly at Michael. She had only heard that morning about the proposed holiday in Switzerland, and her first reaction had been one of shock. And then she had thought . . . well, it would be all right, they were Catholics. But this statement had been countered by a cynical voice that was making itself heard in her mind quite a lot of late, and it said, with a little smear of a laugh, "What difference will that make when it comes to . . ." She had shut the door of her mind on the voice before it had dared to go into forbidden topics. But she found now that she was vexed with Michael's attitude towards her ma, because her ma, she knew, put Michael first, and always had done, the same as her da had put her first and would always do so. And Michael knew this, and up to now he and her ma had been very close. If she hadn't had her da's unstinted love she would have at times been jealous of Michael. She said again, "Me ma's right." And he turned on her, whispering fiercely, "What do you know about it? Your ideas are so infantile, you should still be in white socks."

"Well!" She drew herself up. Then with sisterly affection she finished, "I hope you get it in the neck."

At this moment the kitchen door opened quietly and Mike entered, and at the sight of him both Mary Ann and Michael were forced to laugh.

"Oh, Da! She must have you frightened at last." Mary Ann was spluttering through her fingers.

Mike, unloosening the button on the coat of his best suit, and hunching his shoulders upwards, said, "All right, laugh. I'm on me own ground; but I still feel I need some armour against that one." Then looking at Michael he said kindly, "I've always had the idea that Sarah was adopted."

"I don't think I'll hang anything on to that hope." Michael returned his father's grin. "She takes after her mother in some ways . . . she's finicky about her clothes."

"Well, I wouldn't stand there, both of you," Mary Ann thrust at them. "I'd go on in and get it over."

"After you." Michael held out his hand with an exaggerated gesture to his father. And Mike, following suit, replied, "No, after you. This visit, don't forget, is for the benefit of your soul."

"Ha!" On this telling exclamation Michael led the way out of the kitchen, and Mary Ann, in case she missed much, flung the things on to the tea-tray and only a few minutes later carried it into the sitting-room, there to see her da ensconced in the big armchair with his legs crossed, his pipe in his mouth and his whole attitude proclaiming the master of the house, and to hear Mrs. Flannagan repeat an earlier statement, "It's a beautiful room, Mr. Shaughnessy."

"My wife has taste, Mrs. Flannagan."

Mrs. Flannagan lifted her watery smile up to Lizzie's face, and Lizzie, slightly embarrassed, and praying inwardly that Mike was not all set to have his own back on this she-cat-turned-dove, said, in a smooth tone that tempered the abrupt plunge into essentials, "It's about Sarah and the holiday you've come, Mrs. Flannagan?"

"Yes, yes, Mrs. Shaughnessy, you're right. You see, I would never have dreamed of coming without an invitation." She flicked her eyes around the company asking them all to bear witness to her knowledge of propriety. "But this, I felt, was an emergency. You know what I mean." She eased herself to the edge of the chair. And as she did so Michael coughed, and Mike made a funny sound down the stem of his pipe that brought Lizzie's sharp warning glance on him. "Now as I said to Sarah, this thing has got to be talked over; not that I don't trust you, Michael." Mrs. Flannagan's head now went into a deep abeyance. She had lost her nervousness; she had forgotten for the moment that she was in the enemy's camp, so to speak. For Mrs. Flannagan, at rock bottom, was no fool; she knew that Mike Shaughnessy's memory was long. And although she didn't want to do anything to put a spanner in the works of the match, she wasn't going to let her daughter appear as a . . . light piece, her own phraseology for any female who gave to a man her company in the first hours of the day. "I do trust you, I do, Michael, but . . ." Mrs. Flannagan seemed to be stumped for words with which to make her meaning plain, but this obstacle was overcome for her by Mike.

"But taking into account human nature, Mrs. Flannagan?"

Was Mike Shaughnessy laughing at her? Mrs. Flannagan stared back into the straight countenance of the big red-headed man. There was no sign of laughter on his face, but that was nothing to go by when dealing with him. She knew this from experience, but now she clutched at his explanation, which was really what she had wanted to say but had found a little indelicate. Now, however, she affirmed, "Yes. Yes, you're right, Mr. Shaughnessy. Human nature has got to be taken into account. And . . . and the look of the thing, it's the look of the thing, and what people will say. And once give a dog a bad name, you know. . . ."

"Yer . . . ss, I know. I know, Mrs. Flannagan." Mike was nodding at their guest. "Don't I know, Mrs. Flannagan."

Oh my. Mary Ann had a little uneasy fluttering inside her chest. This could lead to anything. Her da was going to rib Mrs. Flannagan. He was going to lead her on, and on, and then knock her flat. She knew the tactics. In the hope that it might divert the topic, she put in quickly, "You haven't drunk your tea, Mrs Flannagan."

"No. Oh, no." Mrs. Flannagan smiled at Mary Ann and took two very ladylike sips from her cup. It was as she took the second sip that she gulped slightly, for Michael was speaking, and with no prelude.

"I hope some day to marry Sarah, Mrs. Flannagan." His voice was quiet, his tone very level, and his air not that of a boy not yet twenty, but of a man who knew his own mind.

Mrs. Flannagan's head made a half-moon turn as she took them, one by one, into her glance again. Then after a gulp that had nothing ladylike about it whatever, she addressed Michael pointedly. "There, that's what I said to her. I said, 'It would be different altogether if you were engaged or something.' That's what I pointed out to her. I said, 'If there was an understanding or something.' "

Oh, Lord. Mary Ann's head dropped. This was enough to break up any romance. Poor Michael. Poor Sarah.

"Michael will do what he thinks is right in his own time, Mrs. Flannagan."

"Yes, yes, I'm sure he will, Mrs. Shaughnessy."

"You might as well know I don't hold with this business of holidaying together any more than you do."

"Oh, it isn't that, Mrs. Shaughnessy."

"No, no, it isn't that." Mike's voice was a deep bass as he repeated Mrs. Flannagan's words. And it was evident he meant to go on, when Michael cut in sharply on them all, and he was on his feet when he spoke. "Leave this to me, Father . . . and you, Mother." And now he looked straight at Mrs. Flannagan while he said, "Sarah and I have the same ideas about an engagement. We've talked it over. In the meantime we want to go away together. . . . We don't intend to sleep together. . . ."

"Michael!" Lizzie, too, was on her feet, and Mike, sitting up straight in his chair, said quietly, "It's all right, it's all right. It happens, don't be so shocked. Nor you, Mrs. Flannagan. Go on, son."

Michael swallowed before saying, "What we do want is to go away for a time and enjoy ourselves, and be together all day. And see different places . . . together. On our own. And you know"—he was now not looking at Mrs. Flannagan but casting his glance sideways at Lizzie as he went on—"It's not held as a sin any longer when a fellow and a girl go off holidaying together. It might be frowned on but——"

At this point Michael stopped and jerked his head round towards the sitting-room door. Mary Ann, too, was looking towards the door. Her attention had been drawn to it before Michael had stopped talking, and now Lizzie said, "What is it?" and following Mary Ann's gaze she asked abruptly, "See if anyone's there. It might be Tony."

Mary Ann was at the door before her mother had finished speaking, and when, pulling it open with a quick tug, she almost fell on to the high breast of her granny, she let out a scream.

Her granny. Of all days her granny had to come to-day. Of all times her granny had to come precisely at this time, when Mrs. Flannagan was here. She had always considered her granny a form of witch who went round smelling out mischief for the sole purpose of enlarging it. As far back as she could remember she had hated her granny. There was no alteration in her feelings at this moment. In the presence of her granny she lost all her girlish charm. Mrs. McMullen had the power to bring out the very worst in Mary Ann, and she always put this power into motion as soon as her eyes alighted on her grand-daughter.

"Well, knock me over. That's it, knock me over."

"Oh, no!" Mary Ann heard her mother's stifled murmur, and above it came Michael's audible groan. Mike alone made no sound. But Mary Ann knew that of all of them her father would be most affected by her granny's visit. Whereas he would only have chipped Mrs. Flannagan, and revelled, no doubt, in the superiority of his family's position now that the tables were almost completely turned, the afternoon, nevertheless, would have gone off with a veneer of smoothness, but when her da came up against her granny veneers were useless. For her granny hated her da, and would do until the last breath was dragged from her.

"What are you gaping at? Standing there looking like a mental defective."

"I'm not then. . . ." Whether Mary Ann was denying that she was standing gaping, or that she was a mental defective was not plain. The only thing that was plain was the aggressive note in her voice.

"Well, there's one thing I can always be sure of when I visit my daughter, and that's an all-round welcome."

Mrs. McMullen was now in the room, and her chin went up and her abundantly covered head, both of hair and hat, went slightly to the side as she feigned surprise at the sight of Mrs. Flannagan.

"Well! Well! And who would have expected to see you here! . . . Good afternoon, Mrs. Flannagan."

"Good afternoon, Mrs. McMullen." Mrs. Flannagan was smiling her thin smile, but it was evident that she was more uneasy now than she had been before Mrs. McMullen's entry.

"Well, Lizzie." Mrs. McMullen looked at her daughter.

"Hello, Mother. . . . I wasn't expecting you."

"Are you ever?"

"Well, you rarely come on a Sunday. I've never known———"

"All right! All right! I rarely come on a Sunday. But I live alone, don't forget, and people do forget that old people are living alone and without company. So I felt that I would visit my daughter, and have a look at my grandchildren." She made no mention of her son-in-law who was now sitting, legs uncrossed, his spine tightly pressed against the back of the chair.

"Sit down. Give me your hat. . . . Will you have a cup of tea?"

"Well, I won't say no. I'm practically frozen to the bone."

"Pour your granny out a cup of tea, Mary Ann."

"Why does she have to look so gormless?" Mrs McMullen had turned her gimlet eyes on her grand-daughter, and Mary Ann, rearing up now well above the side table and Mrs. McMullen's seated figure, spat out, "Do you make a list of all the sweet things you're going to say before you———"

"That's enough!" Lizzie was not only speaking to Mary Ann as she extended her one hand towards her, but was already addressing Mike with a warning look, for Mike had pulled himself to the edge of the chair, his face dark with temper.

It was at this point that Mrs. Flannagan, seeing herself in the light of peacemaker, turned to Mrs. McMullen and remarked, "I was just saying to Mr. Shaughnessy, what a delightful room this is."

Mrs. McMullen's head moved in a series of short waves as she calmly and aggravatingly surveyed the room; then her verdict came. "It's too light." There followed a pause when no one spoke, and then she went on, "Never put good pieces of dark furniture against light wallpaper. I've told her." She looked towards Lizzie. "I was picking up things in antique shops long before she was born and I've always said dark paper, dark furniture . . . haven't I?"

Lizzie did not answer her mother. And Mrs. McMullen took a sip from her tea, only to comment, "No sugar."

"I did sugar it."

"Well, I should say that in this case the sugar is about as sweet as the donor."

It was evident to all that Mrs. McMullen was in a temper. She was usually in a temper. It seemed to be her natural state. But she generally waited until she could diplomatically fire her darts. Unfortunately, whatever had upset her to-day had robbed her of her finesse. And then she gave evidence of the source of her annoyance by turning to Michael for the first time.

"What you want is a visit from the priest."

"WHAT!"

"You heard what I said."

There was a wrinkled query spreading over the faces of them all as they looked towards the old woman, ageless in her vitality. "You heard what I said. A priest . . . going away with a young lass for a week!"

The comments to this remark seemed to come simultaneously from all directions of the room.

"Mother!" This was Lizzie.

"Look here, Gran." This was Michael.

"Really, Mrs. McMullen!" This was Mrs. Flannagan.

"Well, I'll be damned! Your cuddy's lugs got working quick, didn't they? Did you find it draughty standing in the hall?" This from her beloved son-in-law.

Only Mary Ann made no comment, for she was thinking rapidly. She would have to get her da away out of here else there would be a row. This would have to happen when Mrs. Flannagan was here, wouldn't it?

Mrs. McMullen, it would appear, had not heard her son-in-law's remarks, for she turned now to Mrs. Flannagan, and her tone was sympathetic as she said, "I can well understand how you feel, I would be the same in your shoes. And you're right to put your foot down and forbid such a carry on. . . ."

"But . . . Mrs. McMullen, it . . . it isn't like that." Mrs. Flannagan was definitely floundering. She held out a wavering hand towards Mike, who looked livid enough to explode, and he cut in on her in deep, deep tones.

"If my son wants to take Sarah away, then he has my permission and my blessing on the trip. . . . Are you listening?"

"Mike. . . . Look, wait a moment."

"I'm not waitin' any moment, Liz. I'm making this clear once and for all. My son is not a boy, he's a man." This was the second time Mike had spoken of Michael as my son, not our son, and he had stressed the "my" this time.

"You know my opinion, Mrs. Flannagan." Mrs. McMullen was entirely ignoring Mike, and doing it in such a way that a saint would have been forgiven for springing on her and putting a finish to her mischief-making existence. "You must be very worried, and you're quite right to put a stop to it. . . ."

"But, Mrs. McMullen, wait. . . ." Mrs. Flannagan was leaning towards the old woman now with her hands raised in an agitated flutter. "You've got me slightly wrong. I trust Michael with Sarah." She glanced with her thin smile towards Michael's stiff countenance. "Mr. Flannagan and myself think very highly of Michael, and now that, well . . . they're going to be engaged, I can't, as I was saying to Mr. Shaughnessy a moment ago, see any harm in them having a holiday together, now they're going to be engaged. . . . You see, Mrs. McMullen?"

Mary Ann had never liked Mrs. Flannagan, and she had imagined that she never could, but at this minute she had a strong desire to fling her arms around her neck and hug her. True, she had precipitated an engagement, but that's what she had come for. Still, no matter how she had accomplished it she had got one over on her granny. But, what was much more significant, she had sided with her da against her granny. This was indeed a change of front and a blow to her granny, because Mrs. Flannagan and her granny had been on very polite speaking terms simply because they both had a joint enemy in her da. And now Mrs. Flannagan had blatantly left her granny's ranks and come over to their side. Oh, if only her da would use this turn in the situation and play up. And her da, being her da, did just that.

Undoubtedly Mrs. Flannagan's statement came as a surprise to Mike, and that is putting it mildly. Perhaps before the end of her visit she might have indicated that if the couple were engaged, they would have her blessing to take a trip together. Whether she had cunningly grasped at the situation to use a little motherly blackmail didn't matter. She, Mrs. Flannagan, the thorn that had been in Mike's other side for years, had openly flouted his mother-in-law, and had openly agreed with him. Whatever he had thought of her in the past, this afternoon he would be for her. He reached for his pipe and once more lay back in his chair and crossed his legs, before saying with a smile, which he directed entirely upon Mrs. Flannagan, "Yes, you're right. An engagement makes all the difference. You can trust your daughter as I can trust my son. And I don't think there'll be any need for a priest. Do you, Mrs. Flannagan?"

Mrs. Flannagan blinked, she preened, she returned Mike's smile in the face of Mrs. McMullen's thunderous countenance as she replied banteringly, "Well, not just yet awhile, Mr. Shaughnessy." And she continued to smile across the hearth-rug towards this big rugged, red-headed man, who had more than once threatened to throw her down the stairs if she didn't mind her own so-and-so business. But those things were in the past. For now she was delighted that Sarah would marry into such a family. Into a family that would soon be connected with Mr. Lord, and him owning a shipyard. She knew why Corny Boyle had been sent packing. She couldn't get much out of Sarah these days, but some time ago she had let slip that old Lord had his grandson all lined up for Mary Ann.

"What do you say to this?" Mrs. McMullen had turned her whole body towards Lizzie, and her attitude would have intimidated anyone less strong. From anyone less used to the subtleties of this woman it would have brought forth the truth. And if Lizzie had spoken the truth at this moment she would have said, "I'm as against it as you are." But she could never desert Mike openly in the face of her mother. Nor could she stand on one side while Mike was taking sides with Mrs. Flannagan. Where Mike stood in this she must be also. She looked down into her mother's face and said, with just a little side dig of censure at Mrs. Flannagan, "I think we are all concerning ourselves far too much about something which isn't entirely our business. Michael and Sarah will do what they want in the long run, with or without our consent."

"You've gone soft, me girl."

A silence followed this remark, and Mrs. McMullen moved her body slowly round again and surveyed the company. And when her eyes came to rest on Michael, his dropped away, and he tried his best at this juncture not to laugh. . . . Talk about manoeuvring and counter-manoeuvring. They had settled his life between them. He was already engaged; if they only but knew it, he had been engaged to Sarah from the first moment he set eyes on her, and she to him. But let them have their say, let them think they were fixing everything. There would be no harm done.

He looked towards his father, and Mike, catching his eye, gave the faintest of winks. As Michael grew older he found he liked his father more and more. It hadn't always been like that. He knew now that Mike was enjoying the situation, he had got one up on the old girl, even if it meant joining forces with Mrs. F. It was as good as a play, the whole set-up.

Lizzie broke the awkward silence now by saying, "I think I'd better set the tea."

"I'll help you, Mother." Mary Ann, glad of the chance to escape, was about to move from behind the table when Mrs. McMullen, turning her cold fish eyes on her, remarked, "Nice goings on among your friends, eh?"

"What?"

"Is that all you two can say?" Mrs. McMullen flicked her eyes between Michael and Mary Ann: "WHAT!"

"No, it isn't all I can say." Mary Ann defended herself, standing squarely in front of her grandmother now. "And what do you mean about my friends?"

"That Schofield piece, no better than should be expected."

At the name of Schofield, a swift glance passed between Lizzie, Mike and Mary Ann. Then Mary Ann's eyes came to rest on her granny again. It was true what she had always maintained, her granny was in league with the devil. Father Owen had told her years ago that the devil walked the earth in different guises, and for a certainty, she would maintain, he had taken on the guise of a bitter, envious, hateful, cantankerous old woman. How else would her granny know of Janice's trouble? But now Mrs. McMullen gave her the answer.

"A come-down for the Schofields, I'd say, wouldn't you, them having their daughter tied up compulsorily with the Smyths?"

"Which Smyths are you talking about?" Lizzie, now, not Mary Ann, snapped the enquiry at her mother.

"The Smyths above me, you know them well enough. Two doors up. It's their Freddie she's got mixed up with. And there was her dear papa yesterday afternoon in his car as big as a house, and May Smyth in tears after. But they weren't too salt, for there's money there."

"What do you know about it?" Mike's voice was harsh. "You're just surmising, as always. Putting two and two together, a putrid two and two."

Mrs. McMullen did not turn her superior expression on her son-in-law, but looked up at her daughter as she said, "Mrs. Smyth told me the whole story after Mass this morning."

"She's a blasted fool then."

Mrs. McMullen continued to ignore Mike as she went on, still looking at Lizzie. "Of course it didn't surprise me, with a mother like she's got gallivanting here, there, and everywhere. Never in, I should say. Every bazaar and flower opening, there she is, with that Mrs. Willoughby and Bob Quinton's wife. They have nothing better to do, the three of them, but going around showing themselves off on platforms and not attending to their families. It will be the Willoughby one next . . . and you, me gel." Now Mrs. McMullen brought her face sharply round to Mary Ann's dark countenance. "You should go on your bended knees every night and thank God you haven't got a mother who gallivants——"

"When I go on my bended knees every night, it isn't to thank God but to ask Him——"

"Mary Ann!" Lizzie had to shake Mary Ann by the arm to bring her riveted attention from her granny.

"Oh, leave her alone, leave her alone." Mrs. McMullen flapped her hand at her daughter. "I suppose it shows some good quality when she tries to defend her friends. And they need some defending is all I can say. . . . With the girl in a packet of trouble, and the mother joy-riding up the country lanes with that young fellow."

Mrs. McMullen did not go on to give the name of the young fellow, but she looked around her silent audience, waiting for one of them to prompt her disclosure. But when no one spoke, she wagged her head before ending, "I wonder what the almighty Mr. Lord will say to his grandson running round with a married woman?"

"Oh, you! you wicked old . . .! You always were a wicked creature, you . . .!"

"Stop that." It was Mike speaking now, his voice low and steely. "Let your granny go on, she came to give this news. She won't rest until she tells us."

But Mary Ann didn't allow her grandmother to go on. She was quivering with rage as she blurted out, "You're lying. Tony never saw Mrs. Schofield until yesterday."

Mrs. McMullen's eyebrows went up just the slightest at this new piece of information and she replied coolly, "Yesterday? I'm not talking about yesterday. I'm talking about to-day, not an hour gone. The police were holding the traffic up, there'd been an accident, and as I sat in the bus I happened, like any ordinary person, to look at the passing cars. He was letting them pass one by one as the lorries were half over the road, and there, sitting side by side, was your Mr. Tony and the Schofield woman. And something else I'll tell you, she had her head down, but that didn't prevent me from seeing one of the best black eyes I've spied for a long time."

"It's a pity someone hadn't the guts to give you——"

"Please, Mike, please!" As Lizzie appealed to Mike she had her eyes closed, and looking up into his white face he obeyed her plea. But, pulling himself to his feet, he remarked, "Let me out of this. I'm in need of fresh air."

As Mike reached the sitting-room door, Mary Ann was behind him, and as they went into the hall Michael came on their heels.

All three stood in the kitchen and looked at each other, and then Michael asked quietly, "Is it true, do you think, about . . . about Janice Schofield?"

"Yes, it's true enough, more's the pity." Mike took in a deep breath.

"And about . . . Tony?"

"No, it isn't. That part isn't true. Mr. Schofield hit Mrs. Schofield yesterday, and Tony and I saw him. Tony was taking me to see Janice. That's all there was to it." Mary Ann stopped gabbling and again they looked from one to the other, but not one of them said, "Why is he with her to-day though?" Yet Mary Ann knew that both Michael and her father were asking themselves this same question. She sensed Michael's bewilderment at the situation, but she more than sensed her father's real reaction to this latest piece of news. He would welcome the idea of Tony having an affair. . . . And she herself, how did she feel about it? If Corny had been here, perhaps she would have just shown a friendly interest, mixed with a little wonder that Tony should take out a woman so much older than himself, for Mrs. Schofield must be nearly thirty-five. . . . But Corny wasn't here. And she was amazed at the feeling of resentment that had whirled up in her quite suddenly against Mrs. Schofield. She liked Mrs. Schofield. Yesterday, she had loved her. If pity is akin to love, then she had loved her. But this afternoon she was out with Tony!

She turned her eyes from her father's penetrating gaze and said aloud, with the fervour of the younger Mary Ann who had cared nothing about self-discipline, decorum, and putting a face on things, "I could kill me granny! And you know, one of these days I feel sure I will, I won't be able to help it."

5

Janice neither wrote nor phoned during the following week to say that she was coming, and Lizzie, her sympathy now ebbing, said testily, "She might have at least let us know. I suppose she doesn't think there's a room to be got ready, and other things." She had gone to some pains to make the spare room attractive, and she had added, "Only three weeks to Christmas and everything to do. People don't seem to have any consideration at all these days."

Mary Ann did not in her usual way make any defensive retort. She understood how her mother felt. She was feeling slightly annoyed herself. Janice might have phoned. Moreover, she was curious to know what was happening. She had been tempted twice already this week to bring up the subject with Tony, but strangely enough she had found herself shy of broaching it! For Tony, from the time he had said, "Are you going to tell your mother?" had, it would seem, dismissed the Schofields from his mind, for he had made no reference whatever to them. This would have seemed strange enough if Mary Ann had not known he had met Mrs. Schofield since the incident at the house, but now that she knew he had taken Mrs. Schofield out on the Sunday it was more than odd. His silence, she felt, put upon the situation a cloak of secrecy that wasn't . . . nice. And it was this cloak that prevented her from enquiring about Janice.

Yet when he called into the house he laughed and talked with her ma and da, and seemed in very good spirits. And she asked herself on these occasions, didn't he himself think it was odd, knowing that she had told them about Mrs. Schofield, that he shouldn't mention the matter?

Then there was her mother's attitude towards this business. The fact that Lizzie hadn't referred to her granny's denouncement added another cloak of secrecy to the affair, and strengthened this feeling of the situation being beyond the pale of . . . nice.

Her mother had said last night that everything happened around Christmas time and that she wished it was over. She knew that her mother was worried about Michael going to Switzerland with Sarah, for it was now settled that they would have their holiday together. And in bed last night she herself had felt a keen jealousy against the two of them. It did not last long and she went to sleep on the thought:"When Corny comes back I shall have my holiday with him. Me ma won't be able to say anything, she can't after this. . . ."

When yet another week had passed and still no word had come from Janice, Lizzie dismissed the subject with the emphatic statement, "That's the last bottle I'm putting up in that bed."

It was a week before Christmas and on a Friday night that Mary Ann brought home news of Janice. Lizzie was in the kitchen and anxiously looking towards the clock—Mary Ann was half an hour late, which was unusual. Lizzie got worried when she was five minutes late—you heard of such dreadful things happening to girls these days.

The sound of Mike scraping his boots on the scraper outside the scullery door brought her hurrying through the kitchen, and as he opened the door she said, "She's not in yet."

"No! What's keeping her, I wonder? She phoned or anything?"

"No." Lizzie shook her head. "Would I be like this if she had? Hadn't you better go down and meet the next bus?"

"Aye. Yes, I'll do that." He rebuttoned the top of his greatcoat, saying as he did so, "The buses will likely be late, the roads are icy." Then as he was about to turn from her he laughed as he cocked his head upwards. "Listen, that's her running. All your worry for nothing again." He pushed past her and, taking off his coat, sat down on the cracket in the scullery. He was unlacing his big boots when Mary Ann came in.

"What's kept you?" Lizzie's tone was sharp and indicative of her anxiety.

"I lost my bus. I came on the one on the top road."

"What's the matter?" Mike lifted his head from its bent position, and his fingers came to a halt where they were entwined in his laces. Mary Ann stood looking down at him for a moment, and her voice shook just the slightest as she said, "Janice phoned just after I'd finished."

"Oh? Well . . . go into the kitchen, you look froze. Get something to eat before you go any further."

Mary Ann went into the kitchen, and she turned her white, peaked face towards her mother as she said, "I don't want anything to eat, not yet, just a drink."

"What's the matter?" Lizzie's voice was now quiet.

"It's Janice. She's married."

"Married? Oh." Mike, coming into the room, picked up her words. "Well, she could have let you know sooner, couldn't she?" He sat down in his chair, and Mary Ann, looking from him to her mother, said, "No."

"You're upset about something." Lizzie put her hand around her daughter's shoulders. "Sit down and I'll get you a cup of tea."

Mary Ann sat down, but immediately turned her face into her mother's waist. It was an action that she had not indulged in for a long time. But at this moment she had a frightened feeling. Life could be terrible. Life, she knew, was hard and painful. She had been educated in that kind of life all during her early childhood, but there were other things in life, terrifying things. She drew her head from the shelter of her mother's flesh and looked up at her as she whispered, "She tried to kill herself!"

"Oh, my God!"

"Did she tell you this?" Mike was leaning towards her now, his hand outstretched holding hers.

"Yes, Da. I had just finished work and Miss Thompson told me I was wanted on the phone. It was Janice. She sounded just as if . . . well, as if she was drunk. She was laughing most of the time, except at the end. She kept talking and talking. She said she was married last Friday and her father was going to set Freddie up in a business. He had bought them a car and a bungalow on the Fells Road. And then she stopped laughing and carrying on and said she was sorry about not letting me know she wasn't coming, but she hadn't expected to go anywhere for she had taken some stuff and locked herself in her room." Mary Ann's lips began to tremble. "From what she said I think she would have died but her mother climbed up the trellis and got in through the window—the house is covered with creeper—and after her doing that she . . . she said, Ma, Janice said that she hated her mother, that she should have left her alone. . . . Poor Janice. She must have been in an awful state."

"Poor mother, I should say." Mike now hitched himself up to Mary Ann and, patting her hand, said, "Don't be upset, lass. Madam Janice will come through all right, you'll see. I wish I could say the same for her mother."

"Where was she married?" asked Lizzie. "Newcastle or Shields?"

"Newcastle, Ma. At the Registry Office."

"But she couldn't . . . he's a Catholic."

"Oh my God! Liz." Mike shook his head.

"All right, all right. There's no need to use that tone."

Mary Ann rose from her chair, saying now, "I'll get washed, Ma."

"Will I set your tea on a tray and have it in the front room? Michael and Sarah are there."

"No, Ma. I'll have it here."

Almost before she had closed the door behind her, she heard her da speak. It was the bitterness of his tone that made her pause for a second to listen, as he said, "If the old man gets his way, what about it then? Tony's no Catholic and I'm damned sure you'll not get him to turn. He's as stubborn as they come, and no blame to him."

"I'll meet that obstacle when it arises. And what's the matter with you going for me like this?"

"Because it makes me flaming mad, Liz, when you put a second-class label on people who aren't Catholics."

"Oh! How can you say such a thing? What about us, eh?"

"I'd be a better man in your eyes if I changed me coat."

"Oh, that's unfair, Mike. That's unfair. Oh, it is."

As her mother's voice trailed away in sadness, Mary Ann went slowly up the stairs. Why was it that nothing was going right inside or outside of the house lately?

Some minutes later when Mary Ann descended the stairs into the hall again, she approached the sitting-room door with a discreet cough. She would say Hello before she had her tea. But when she opened the door—without knocking, of course—such action would have slapped diplomacy in the face—she did not find Michael and Sarah sitting on the couch, but Michael sitting on his hunkers in front of Sarah, and he looked up quickly at Mary Ann, saying, "She's off colour."

"Are you feeling bad?" Mary Ann bent over the back of the couch.

"No, not really bad. I just can't explain it." Sarah dropped her head backwards and looked up into Mary Ann's face. "A bit head-achey, a bit sick . . . achey. Just like when you're going to get the flu; but I don't feel as if I've got a cold. Oh!" She smiled up at Mary Ann. "I think the real truth is I'm after a few days in bed. As much as I love those horses, it's been pretty stiff going in more ways than one these last few mornings. I had to break the ice on the trough with a hammer this morning."

"I know," said Mary Ann. "Prince's water was the same. Me da's kept him inside for days, he doesn't like the cold And I haven't ridden him for nearly three weeks."

"But look here," Michael drew Sarah's attention to him again with a tug at her hand, "you don't want to take this lightly. And don't try to be brave and laugh it off. I think it's as you said, you want a few days in bed, you're under the weather."

"Yes, sir." Sarah's voice was demure, and she laughed now, and Michael, getting to his feet, his face straight, passed off his concern by saying, "Now look, don't you go and get anything serious. After all the schemozle there's been about our holiday, you're going to go on it if I have to take you in a box!"

Twenty-four hours later, Michael, remembering these words, was to droop his head and press his chin into his neck with the horror of them. But he now looked at Mary Ann and said, "She hasn't had a bit of anything to eat all day."

"Does me ma know?"

"No, but I'm going to tell her. You stay there." He dug his fingers down towards Sarah, and added, "You'll eat what I fetch in."

When the door had closed behind him, Sarah, looking at Mary Ann, who was sitting beside her on the couch now, said, "I won't, you know, I just couldn't."

"Perhaps your stomach is upset." Mary Ann nodded knowingly. "Whenever there is trouble of any kind it always goes to my stomach." She laughed. "Even if I get into a temper, I'm sick. Oh! Last Sunday night I felt like death after dear grandmam's visit. . . . Oh, Sarah, I do hate that woman."

Sarah, nodding sympathetically, said, "I'm not very fond of her myself. Never was."

"That needn't worry you, for she's no relation of yours, but she's my granny, and the only one I've got. And oh, I hate the thought of her being my granny. Do you know, I felt so hateful on Sunday that I could have killed her. I could, I'm not just kidding, I could. I've always prayed, as far back as I can remember, that she would die. But on Sunday I actually felt that I could have killed her. It was a dreadful feeling, Sarah. I felt awful after and, as I said, I was sick."

"Talking of killing"—Sarah's head fell back on to the couch again—"it doesn't seem so very long ago since I felt that way about you, and you about me, remember?"

Mary Ann, her face straight now, nodded her head, and bit on her lip before she said, "Seems daft now, doesn't it?"

Sarah did not answer this, but staring up towards the ceiling, she said slowly and quietly, "I'll die if anything separates me from Michael . . . I'll die."

"Oh, Sarah, don't talk like that. Why are you talking like that? Don't be silly, what can separate you from Michael?" As Mary Ann looked at Sarah's face, her eyes staring upwards, she was amazed to see two large tears roll down in the direction of her nose. Leaning swiftly forwards she touched Sarah's cheek saying under her breath, "What is it? What is it, Sarah?"

"Nothing." Sarah lifted her head with a heavy movement from the back of the couch, and groping for her handkerchief, she remarked, "I feel altogether odd, I can't remember ever feeling like this before, sort of depressed." Then after blowing her nose, she lifted her eyes to Mary Ann, saying, "I know how you feel about Corny, and I think you've been marvellous. I should have gone round looking like . . . well, as your da would say, a sick cow. Do you still miss him?"

The conversation wasn't keeping to pattern, but Mary Ann said, "Yes, awfully. I just seem to be passing the time towards the end of the year . . . not this year but what I think of as his year. I get terrified when I think he won't come back."

"You could never like Tony?"

"Not that way."

"He'd be a catch."

"Could you give up Michael for someone similar to Tony . . . a catch?"

Sarah shook her head, and then clapped her hands swiftly over her mouth and muttered through her fingers, "I'm—I'm going to be sick."

Mary Ann, leading Sarah into the kitchen, exclaimed to her mother and Michael, "Sarah's sick . . . she wants to be sick."

"Oh! my dear." Lizzie, taking up a position on the other side of Sarah, hurried her towards the scullery. And that was the first of a number of trips between the front room and the scullery during the next hour. At half-past eight, Lizzie, standing in the kitchen looking at Mike, said, "She's in no fit state to go home. We'll have to get word to her mother in some way."

"I'll phone the house and see if Tony's in."

Tony was in, but on the point of going out, and when, a few minutes later, he came into the farm kitchen after a brief word with Sarah, who was now lying on the sitting-room couch, he looked from Lizzie to Mike and said, "I would get a doctor."

"What are you thinking it is?" Mike narrowed his eyes towards Tony. And when Tony said what he thought might be the matter with Sarah, Lizzie cried out, "Oh no! no! Not that."

"I hope it isn't. I may be wrong. But those symptoms look pretty familiar, I've seen someone with them before. I'd phone the doctor if I were you, and I'll slip into Jarrow and take a message to her mother."

The kitchen became very quiet, the house became very quiet, and the quietness was heavy with fear.

Mike phoned the doctor. He came within half an hour, and within a few minutes of his arrival the life of the house changed.

It was suspected that Sarah had polio.

The waiting-room was quiet. It had coloured pictures on the wall, and modern low tables and comfortable chairs. Michael, sitting on the edge of a chair, had his elbows on his knees, his hands clasped between them, and he kept his gaze fixed on his hands, except when the waiting-room door opened. It hadn't opened for some time now. Mary Ann sat next to him. She kept going round the edge of her handkerchief with the finger and thumb of her right hand, while she smoothed the small piece of cambric material with the other. Opposite to them, across the low table, sat her mother and Mrs. Flannagan. They had all ceased to talk. From time to time her da would push the waiting-room door open. Or Mr. Flannagan, or Tony. And then they would go out again and sit in the car.

At a quarter to twelve a grey-uniformed sister entered the waiting-room, followed by a doctor. The sister remained silent as the doctor talked. He was very, very sorry, yes, the young girl had polio. How serious it was, was yet to be seen. He advised them to go home. They'd be kept informed. No, it wasn't advisable for any of them to see her. Perhaps tomorrow. Everything that possibly could be done would be done, they could be sure of that.

"I'm staying," said Michael.

"I wouldn't," said the doctor. "You can do no good. Come in first thing in the morning and see how things are going then."

"I'm staying," said Michael again.

The doctor nodded.

The doctor now looked at Mrs. Flannagan and said, "You are the mother?"

"Yes." Mrs. Flannagan had lost her spruceness. For the first time that she could remember, Mary Ann saw her other than neat. Her face was tear-stained; her hair, like thin wire, stuck out from each side of her hat. She seemed to have shrunk and was now no bigger than Mr. Flannagan. It seemed odd, too, to see her sitting there with one hand clasped in the tight grip of her mother's hand.

Mike and Mr. Flannagan came into the room, and the doctor said again, "It would be better if you all went home, for you can do nothing, nothing at all."

He was passing Mary Ann now, and he put his hand on her head as if she was a child, as indeed she looked at this moment. And he seemed to be addressing her solely when he said, "The only thing now is to pray and leave the rest to God. . . ." And it was with a sort of gentle enquiry that he added "Eh?" to his words.

Michael, not to be deterred, stayed in the waiting-room and Mr. Flannagan stayed with him. Mrs. Flannagan went back to the farm with Lizzie and the rest. . . .

Three days later Sarah was fighting for her life, kept alive only by the miracle of the iron lung. On the seventh day it was known that she would live, but without the use of her legs, and Michael sat at the kitchen table, his head buried in his arms and cried. And Lizzie cried, and Mary Ann cried, and Mike went out to the cowshed.

Lizzie stood by Michael's side, her hand on his head, but she could say nothing. She could not find words adequate for comfort, until some minutes elapsed, and Michael, lifting his head slowly from his arms and shaking it from side to side in a despairing movement, muttered, "And I said I would take her on that holiday if I had to take her in a box. . . . Oh! God." And Lizzie, remembering the time not long ago when she herself had said, "That'll be the day when you howl your eyes out," whispered brokenly, "We say things in joke, take no notice of that. She's alive, and they can do wonderful things these days."

Mary Ann's throat was swollen with the pressure of tears as she stood at the other side of the table and looked towards Michael. Poor Michael. But more so, poor Sarah. She was feeling for Sarah, at this moment, anguish equal to that which she would have felt if they had been sisters. It was impossible to remember that they had ever been enemies. She thought, "Her poor legs, and she loved to ride. Oh, what will she do?"

It was as if Michael had heard her thinking, for he stood up and, brushing the back of his hand across his eyes and around his face, he said, "As soon as she comes out we'll get married."

"Michael."

Lizzie had just spoken his name, there was no indication of shock or censure, but he turned on her sharply, saying, "You can do what you like, Mother, say what you like, put all the obstacles on earth up, but as soon as she's out of that place we're getting married."

"Yes, yes. All right, Michael, all right."

"Don't say it like that, Mother." He was yelling at her. "As if I'd get over it and change my mind, and by the time she's out I'll be seeing things differently. I won't, I won't ever."

"Don't shout, Michael." Lizzie's voice was very low. "I understand all you feel at this minute, believe me. . . ."

"But you wouldn't want me to marry Sarah, crippled like that, would you? She would handicap me, wouldn't she? What would happen to my career?"

"Now, now, now." This was neither Lizzie nor Mary Ann, and they all turned to see Mike standing in the kitchen doorway. His face looked pale-ish, his eyes very bright, and his voice and manner were quiet. How much he had heard of the conversation Mary Ann didn't know. But little or much, she knew he had got the gist of it, for looking at Michael, he said, "Don't worry at this stage. Just go on praying that she'll get better quickly, and then do what your heart tells you you've got to do."

Mary Ann watched Michael looking towards her da. She watched their eyes holding for a long while before Michael turned away and went out of the kitchen and up the stairs. It was strange, she thought, Michael was her ma's, her ma and Michael were like that—metaphorically, she crossed her fingers—yet lately it had been her da who had seen eye to eye with him, while her mother seemed to cross him at every point. Perhaps, like all mothers, she was afraid of losing him, and he knew it, and this was bringing a slight rift between them.

Lizzie had the palms of her hands pressed tightly together. If her fingers had been lifted upwards, they would have indicated her praying, but they were pointing towards the floor, and she rasped her palms together as she said under breath, "He says they're going to be married as soon as she comes out."

"I heard." Mike nodded his head. "Well, you'll have to face that, Liz."

"But how will he manage? He's just starting out, Mike." Lizzie's voice was soft. There was no tone of opposition in it, just helpless enquiry.

"People have managed like that afore, they're shown a way."

"But if she can't walk. If she's in a chair. . . ."

"Liz!" Mike walked over to her and put his arm around her shoulder. "Listen to me. Things'll pan out. Just remember that. Whatever you think or do, things'll pan out one way or the other. But this much I think you'd better get into your head and accept it. Whatever condition Sarah comes out in, she'll be the only one for him. . . . Now it's no use saying he'd get over it. Don't start to think along those lines, because I know this . . . he'd rather have his life a hell of a grind with Sarah than be on velvet with anybody else. . . . Now don't cry."

But Lizzie did cry. She turned her head into Mike's shoulder, and as he held her and spoke softly to her, he looked across the room towards Mary Ann, but she herself could hardly see him, her vision was so blurred. She felt a weight of sadness on her that she had never before experienced. It sprung, she supposed, from Sarah's condition. Yet she knew that not all her feelings were due to Sarah. Vaguely she realised that life was opening her eyes wide, stretching them with knowledge, painful knowledge, such as the fact that her mother was crying, not so much because Sarah was crippled for life, but because her son was determined to take on a burden that to her mind would cripple him too.

It was the worst Christmas Mary Ann had ever known. No one felt like jollification. Presents were given and received without much enthusiasm. Mr. Lord bought Mary Ann a portable typewriter for her Christmas box, and although she was pleased with the gift, she simulated delight that she didn't altogether feel. But Mr. Lord was very thoughtful and kind during this period. And she wanted to please him.

The old man had shown great concern over Sarah. Twice a week he sent her gifts of flowers and fruit, and once, when he had stood in the kitchen, he had looked at Lizzie and said, "There's no need to enquire if the boy will stand by Sarah. I feel that Michael knows his own mind, and it's a very good thing. Perhaps it will be very good for both of them. And he can rely on all the help he needs when the time comes."

Lizzie had said nothing, but Mary Ann had wanted to fling her arms about the old man's neck, as she had done years ago, by way of thanks.

Corny did not send Mary Ann a Christmas box, but he sent her a letter which was of much more value in her eyes. Although the letter was brief, she read volumes between the lines. He liked it in America. He liked the people he was staying with, they were very good to him. He liked his job. The boss was very good to him. He had been put into another department which meant more money. He could get a car if he liked, but he wasn't going to. He was saving. It was funny not being at home for Christmas but everybody was so nice to him. Mary Ann felt a stir of jealousy against this oft-repeated niceness. But she told herself he hadn't known what to say, he was no hand at letter-writing. his writing was as terse as his speech. Her Corny was a doer, not a sayer. She liked that idea, and she told herself a number of times: Corny was a doer not a sayer. The letter ended with the same request as had his first one: Would she go and see his granny?

The only other thing of note that happened over the Christmas was an announcement in the paper to the effect that Mrs. Lettice Schofield of The Burrows, Woodlea End, Newcastle, was seeking a divorce from her husband.

PART TWO

The Year Passes

6

"Look," said Mike, as he leant towards Michael across the little table in his office, "I know the old fellow means well, at least I want to keep on thinking that. But I'd rather you didn't start your life, your real life along with Sarah, beholden to him."

Michael, with one elbow raised high resting on the top of the small window, tapped his ear with his fingers as he stared out across the farmyard towards the chimneys of the house, where they reared up above the roof of the byres. "I know, I know what you mean." His voice was deep and very similar to Mike's now, except for the inflexion garnered from the Grammar School. "I don't want to take the place, for the very reason you've just stated, but another reason is that Sarah's cut off enough where she is now. Although she's with her mother, she's cut off. She feels lost, they don't speak the same language. She's closer to her father, but he's out all day. And then there's not a blade of grass to be seen, looking out from that window on to the street. It drives me mad when I'm sitting with her. I can't imagine that we ever lived opposite. The only good thing in taking the bungalow is that she would see a tree or two, and the fields. But then it's a good two miles away, and although there's houses round about, Sarah doesn't want other people." He brought his eyes from the window towards his father. "She's already one of us. She's always seemed to have been one of us. She hasn't said this, but I know that she looks upon us as . . . her people. As I said, she likes her da, but I can tell you this, she likes you ten times more."

Mike dropped his eyes away from his son as he said, "That's good to hear, anyway."

There was silence in the little office until Mike said, "There's a way out of this." He cast his eyes on the open ledger as he spoke, and Michael kept his eyes on the view across the farmyard as he replied, "Yes, I know. But who's going to put it to her?"

He did not say put to Mother . . . but to "her", and this phrase hurt Mike. Although it meant that he and this boy were closer than ever before in their lives, it also meant that Michael had moved farther away from Lizzie during the last few months. Somehow, he would rather that the situation were the same as it had been years ago . . . yet not quite. He did not want his son to hate him and he had, at one time, done just that. No, he didn't want that again, and please God he would never deserve it, but he didn't want Lizzie to be hurt. Michael was Lizzie's; at least she had always considered him so. It was as if years ago she had said to him, "You have got Mary Ann, Michael is mine."

At this moment the door was pushed open and Mary Ann, coming round it, said, "Oh, there you are." She looked at Michael. "I'm going in to Sarah's, Tony's running me down. Is there anything you want to go?"

"No." He shook his head. "Tell her I'll be there round about six."

"What's the matter?" Mary Ann looked from one to the other. "Anything wrong?"

"No, no." Mike got to his feet. "We're just talking about the bungalow."

"Oh, the bungalow." Mary Ann nodded her head, and looking again at Michael she said, "Are you going to take it?"

"I don't want to."

Again she nodded her head. "Then why don't you ask her?"

Again, the "her" was referring to Lizzie, and Michael, moving out into the yard, said, "I couldn't stand a row. And if she did consent, having Sarah on sufferance would be worse than anything so far."

Mike and Mary Ann, left together, looked at each other, and when Mike's eyes dropped from hers she said to him under her breath, "Something should be done, Da. What's going to happen to Sarah up there by herself all day? It won't work. He just couldn't take that place." She looked at Michael's broadening back as he went across the yard, then her gaze lifted up the hill towards Mr. Lord's house, and her tone indignant now, she commented, "If he's going to advance him the money for a bungalow why couldn't he have one built here? He's got piles of land."

"There's such a thing as laws about building on agricultural ground."

"Poloney!"

"Not so much poloney as you think." Mike nodded solemnly at her. "Once you start that, it's like a bush fire, one house goes up and then the place is covered."

Mary Ann looked her disbelief, then after sighing she remarked, "Well, I'm off, Da. See you later. . . . Good-bye."

His good-bye followed her as she went across the yard towards the road that led up to Mr. Lord's house. She knew that he was standing watching her.

In the far distance she could see the hood of Tony's car. She glanced at her watch. He had said half-past two on the dot, and now it was twenty-five to three. She walked slowly up the hill, through the gate, over the back courtyard to where the car was standing. There was no sign of Tony and, going to the back door, she knocked as she opened it, a courtesy she still afforded Ben.

"Hello, there." The old man's tone was gruff, and he hardly raised his eyes from the occupation of silver cleaning to look at her. But Mary Ann, over the years, had come to know Ben, and a "Hello there" she had come to consider a very affectionate term.

"Lovely day, isn't it, Ben? How's your hip?"

"Same as afore."

"Well, it's your own fault." She stubbed her finger at him. "You should have taken it easy these last few weeks while Mr. Lord was away. It's your own fault."

"And have him come back finding fault in every corner, like an old fish woman."

"You should let Mrs. Rouse do it."

"Ugh! Ugh! I have to go behind her all the time now."

Mary Ann smiled, then said, "Is Tony upstairs?"

"No. In the study . . . on the phone."

"Oh." Mary Ann went out of the kitchen and across the large hall towards the study. There was no sound of anyone speaking on the phone, and she stood outside the door for a second before saying, "Are you there, Tony?"

"Yes. Come in."

When she entered the room she saw him sitting at the desk, and he turned his head towards her, saying quickly, "I won't be a minute, I want to get this off."

She sat down in the hide chair to the side of the fireplace, and her small frame seemed lost in its vastness. She liked this room: the brown of the suite, the soft blue of the deep carpet; the low, ranging bookcases set against the panelled walls. She looked towards Tony, his head bent over the letter. He looked nice . . . he always looked nice, but to-day she seemed to be seeing him in a different light. She realised with a kind of pleasant shock that he was very handsome, in a thin, chiselled kind of way. She supposed Mr. Lord had once looked like this. Her gaze was intent on him when he turned his head quickly and looked at her. "I'm glad you came up," he said. "I hoped you would, I want to talk to you."

As she watched him turn to the desk again and quickly push the letter into an envelope, she experienced a quiver of apprehension. It went through her body like a slight electric shock, and felt as unpleasant. Tony and she had exchanged nothing but polite pleasantries for months. He had continued to take her into town on a Saturday, and sometimes he picked her up later, but where he went in the meantime he did not say. Nor did he ask where she spent her time. He no longer seemed interested in anything she did, but she knew that Mr. Lord was under the impression that they were together during these Saturday afternoon jaunts. She had an idea now, in fact she knew, what he was going to talk about. And when he came towards her, and pulled a small chair close to the big one before sitting down and leaning forward, she could not meet his eyes.

"Mary Ann."

"Yes." She still did not raise her eyes.

"If Corny had not come on the scene, would you have liked me enough to have married me?"

She lifted her head with a jerk, and her eyes flicked over his face for a moment before she looked away towards the window beyond the desk. And she seemed to consider for quite a while before she answered.

"I don't know . . . I suppose I might, and yet I don't know." She paused again. "There might have been someone else. You just don't know, do you?" Now she was looking at him full in the face.

"No, you just don't know. But as things stand you want Corny, don't you? Tell me . . . please."

"Yes . . . yes, I want Corny." She felt she was blushing right into the depths of her stomach.

"Yes, I knew you did. But I wanted to hear you say it. I didn't want you on my conscience. I have enough to face up to without that. . . . I'm going to marry Mrs. Schofield, Mary Ann."

Although Mary Ann had known that he had wanted to talk about Mrs. Schofield, that he might say to her, "I'm friendly with Mrs. Schofield . . . I like Mrs. Schofield," she had not expected him to say, slap bang, that he was going to marry her. This statement suggested an intimacy between him and Mrs. Schofield that deepened the blush. She could have said she was going to marry Corny, and Michael could say he was going to marry Sarah, but in either case it would not have been the same as Tony marrying Mrs. Schofield. Mrs. Schofield was a married woman. And then there was Mr. Lord. Mr. Lord would go mad, she knew he would go mad. She said as much.

"What will he say? He'll go for you, he won't stand for it. He'll go mad."

"I know that. But whether he will or no, I'm marrying Lettice as soon as the decree nisi is through."

Mary Ann put her fingers over her lips and swayed a little. She felt some part of her was in pain, and it was for Mr. Lord. At this moment she would gladly have fallen in with his wishes and married Tony if that had been possible, just to save him the pain that she knew the failure of his cherished plans would bring him. And the pain would not be alone. There would be with it anger and bitterness. Once before she had seen what extreme anger and bitterness did to him. That was the time when he had discovered that Tony was his grandson. And what had been the result? He had a heart attack and nearly died. She clasped her hands tightly now between her knees and asked, "How are you going to tell him?"

"I don't know. Lettice wanted to come and tell him herself. But I wouldn't have that."

It was funny hearing him speak of Mrs. Schofield as Lettice. She hated Mrs. Schofield at this moment, yet remembering back to the time when she liked her, she also remembered that Mr. Lord liked her too. Here was a ray of hope. She said to Tony, "You should have let her come. He liked her. She could get it over better than you, I'm sure of that. There'll only be a row if you tell him, and that's putting it mildly. Don't forget what happens when he gets worked up." She leant further forward. "Do you realise this might . . . it might kill him."

"I've thought of all that. It's been hellish this last few months. In fact since that day . . . you remember, that Saturday when I saw him hit her, I knew then what was going to happen to me. I think I knew before. You see, Mary Ann"—his voice dropped almost to a whisper—"I was attracted to her long before that day. When she used to come up here, to your house, I always made a point of being there. Perhaps no one noticed. They wouldn't, would they?" He smiled a sad smile at her. "But that day when I saw that pig of a man—and he is a pig of a man, Mary Ann, and that's putting it mildly—when I saw him hit her, I knew it was all up with me. It was as if the blow that struck her had sprung my mind wide open, and I saw the fix I was in. And I'm not going to say at this juncture that I tried to fight it and make a brave stand against it. Oh, no. Although I knew what it would mean to the old man in the end I went ahead, and I still count myself lucky that I did. She is a grand person, Mary Ann. A very, very sweet person."

Mary Ann dismissed the unique qualities of Mrs. Schofield, and said, "He'll cut you off?"

"Yes, I expect that. But I've got quarter shares in Turnbulls. He signed those over to me two years ago. They'll give me a start somewhere, and Lettice doesn't want much. . . . It seems odd though to think that those very shares were the first thing he allowed me to put my name to, although I was supposed to be his heir. And he only gave them to me as an inducement to fall in with his plans concerning his . . . protégée." Tony's hand came out and grasped Mary Ann's. "I could wish at this moment for him that his plan had worked out, because, you know, I like his protégée very much." He squeezed her fingers.

Mary Ann swallowed and blinked her eyes, the tears were welling in her throat, and as she pulled her hands from his she said with a touch of the cheeky asperity he knew so well, "I'm not crying because of you, don't think that."

"I wouldn't for a moment, Mary Ann."

"I just don't know what's going to happen to him when he finds this out." She sniffed twice, blew her noise, then asked, "When is he coming back? It was next Tuesday, wasn't it?"

"As always he's changed his plans. You know his old trick of dropping in when he thinks nobody is expecting him, that's likely what will happen this time. I had a wire this morning to say he was staying on another week. But I shouldn't be surprised if he came in tonight, or tomorrow night, or then, on the other hand, not for another month. We should know by now, shouldn't we?"

"But he'll come." She bounced her head at him. "And you'll have to tell him. . . . When are you——" she paused and her voice sunk again as she ended, "getting married?"

"It could be in three weeks' time."

"But if he shouldn't be back by then you won't leave, will you? You won't leave and get married before he gets back?"

"No, Mary Ann, I won't do that."

She turned her eyes from him, and feeling again that she was going to give way to tears, she jumped up from the chair, saying, "It's awful, I think it's awful. He'll die."

"No, he won't." Tony had his arm around her shoulders now. "He's tougher than you think."

"If he gets into a paddy, he'll have a heart attack, you'll see."

"Oh, Mary Ann, don't make it worse for me, please."

"I don't want to." Her voice was soft now. "But I'm frightened for him, Tony." She looked up. "And you won't make matters any better because you'll lose your temper and there'll be a pair of you. You know you can't keep your temper with him. I don't think you should tell him. I think you should leave a letter for him, something like that. . . . Oh, I don't know what to suggest."

"I won't leave a letter for him, Mary Ann. What I've got to say, I'll say to him."

"And kill him!"

"Don't!" He swung away from her. "Don't keep suggesting that. It's got to be done." His voice had risen now. "And I'll have to stand the consequences, but don't keep saying that."

They stared at each other in hostility, and then Tony, taking his breath in on a deep sigh, said, "Come on. We had better be going. Sufficient unto the day." He opened the door for her and she went past him, through the hall and into the kitchen. And she did not say good-bye to Ben, where he sat still rubbing away with his rheumaticky hands at the silver, and this caused him to stop work, and even rise to his feet and go towards the door from where he watched her getting into the car.

When a few minutes later Ben returned to the table, he looked at his work for a moment before touching it, and remarked, "What now, eh?"

Mrs. Flannagan's front room was fourteen feet by twelve feet. In it was a three-piece suite, a small sideboard, a corner cabinet, besides two small tables and an ornamental coal scuttle. The floor was covered by a small carpet and a surround of highly polished check-patterned linoleum.

Sarah was sitting on the couch, her legs painfully immobile beneath the rug. Her back appeared bent as if she was leaning towards them, and her complexion, which had been a thick cream tan, had now a bleached look. The only thing about her appearance that remained untouched by her illness was hair. It was still black and shiny. She held out a half-finished nylon petticoat towards Mary Ann, saying rather hopelessly, "Look at those stitches, I'll never be able to sew."

Mary Ann looked at the stitches. "You're doing fine; they're only half an inch long now, they were an inch on Wednesday."

They both laughed, and Sarah moved her shoulders into the cushion. Then the smile disappeared from her face when, looking at Mary Ann, she said below her breath, "Oh, I wish I had that chair. I want to get out. I want to get out. I'll go mad with much more of this."

"They said next week, didn't they?" Mary Ann's voice was low also. "But Tony would come and take you out tomorrow. He's offered time and time again. Why won't you go?"

"Oh." Sarah moved her head wearily on the pillow. "To be carried into a car and all the street out. It's bad enough in the ambulance going to the hospital. I don't want to be carried and lifted for the rest of my life. And I'm not going to." She pulled her body forward now until her face was close to Mary Ann's, and then she whispered fiercely, "I've been praying and praying and praying. I'm going to use my legs again, I am. I don't care how long it takes—ten years, twenty years." Her voice was becoming louder now, and Mary Ann, getting up and putting her arms around her, said, "That's the spirit. You feel like that and you will. Oh, I'm glad to hear you say that. It's like an answer to my prayers. In fact, I'm sure it is. Every night after I've left work I slip into church and say a decade of the rosary for you, just for that, that you'd get the urge to use your legs. . . . Isn't it funny?" Her voice was high with excitement.

"Oh, Mary Ann." Sarah leant her head wearily between Mary Ann's small firm breasts. "You've been so good, always coming in. People stop after a while, you know. They used to come in a lot at first, but not now. And I'm seeing too much of me mother. Oh, I know I shouldn't say this because she's been so good, but she keeps on, she keeps on, finicking about, polishing, dusting, tidying up, all the time, all the time. . . . Mary Ann?" It was a question.

And Mary Ann said, "Yes, Sarah?"

"Do you think that Michael really wants to marry me?"

Mary Ann drew away from Sarah and actually gaped at her as she repeated, "Really wants to marry you. He'll go round the bend if he doesn't. What's put that into your head?"

"Oh, I think people are saying things. I know they are. I hear that Mrs. Foster in the kitchen with me mother. It's not what she says, it's what she leaves unsaid . . . the pauses. They don't think it right that I should marry Michael, not like this, I know they don't. But if

I don't, Mary Ann"—she looked into Mary Ann's eyes now and repeated—"If I don't, I'll do meself in, I will."

Another one talking about doing herself in. Janice, and now Sarah. Was this what sorrow did to you, took away all desire for life. She couldn't see anything bad enough happening to her to take away the desire for living. She loved life, she loved breathing. She used to stop sometimes, on the road from the bus to the farm, and say to herself, "I'm breathing." It wasn't silly for she knew within herself, deep within herself, that it meant a great deal, something she couldn't as yet explain. She was breathing, she was alive. She felt at times that no matter what happened she wanted to live. . . . To know all about living and then write about it. She dreamed of writing about living. Yet two girls that she had known intimately talked about dying, about killing themselves, and one had already tried. She shuddered and grasped hold of Sarah's hands as she said, "Don't say such things, Sarah. And now get this into your head, there's only one person in the world for Michael and that's you. And if you don't know it by now, you never will. He's driving us all crazy about you."

Sarah's smile spread across her face. It was a sweet smile, and it made her beautiful, more beautiful than when she had been the outdoor, hard-riding, youth-filled girl. But the smile faded, and on its going she said, "Your mother's not pleased, and I can't blame her. I can understand how she feels."

"What's got into you all of a sudden? Don't be silly. Of course mother's pleased, she'd rather have you for Michael than anybody else."

"Has she said so?"

"No, there's no need. I know."

"You're just being kind as usual, Mary Ann. You're always trying to fix people's lives. I used to laugh about it at one time, but I give you leave to fix mine right now." She shook her head. "But if your mother wanted me for Michael she would have asked me to go there, to live with you. I wouldn't have been a burden, I wouldn't. I feel that if I could go and live with you all I would get better. When I was in hospital, Michael sort of said that we'd have . . . the front room. It was like a dream that I hung on to. I thought your mother must have suggested that we could, and I thought it was wonderful of her, because it's a beautiful front room, and you can see the farm from the window. I dreamed of that front room. Then when I came home Michael said Mr. Lord was going to put up the money for the bungalow. There was no more mention of the front room, and I knew somehow that your mother had never said anything about it. . . . I don't want that bungalow, Mary Ann. I don't want to go and live all that way off. I want to live close to Michael, where his work is. And with your da near abouts. Your da infuses strength into people, Mary Ann. It's funny that, isn't it? For me to say that, I mean. But he does. I always feel that I could get up and walk when he's talking to me. Not that I don't like your mother, I do. I think she's a fine woman . . . sort of a lady. I've always thought of her as a lady. . . ."

"Oh, Sarah, Sarah! Look, don't worry. Everything'll come out all right. And you will live with us, I promise you will."

Sarah smiled through very bright eyes now at Mary Ann, and it was doubtful if she was seeing her as she said, "You've always made rash promises, you're the Holy Family rolled into one, not that they make rash promises. . . . You know what I mean. You were always going to the side altar praying to them, weren't you?" She laughed now, a sharp loud laugh to stop herself from crying as she said, "I remember I stopped going to their altar because I didn't want to do the same thing as you."

"Oh, Sarah." Mary Ann could not cap this with any amusing reply. She felt she couldn't bear much more to-day. There had been Tony just an hour ago, and now Sarah in this state. It was awful, awful. Everything was awful.

She stood up and looked towards the window merely to turn her face from Sarah's for a moment, and as she did so she saw coming down the steps of Mulhattan's Hall, right opposite, the great wobbling figure of Fanny McBride. The sight of her old friend brought a smile to her face and she turned round to Sarah and explained excitedly, "Look, bend over, there's Mrs. McBride coming down the steps. I'll pull the curtain and you can wave to her."

Mary Ann dared to pull Mrs. Flannagan's stiffly arranged curtains to one side, and she went even further, she dared to tap gently on the pane to attract Fanny's attention. And when Fanny, her eyes darting across the road, caught sight of Mary Ann, she waved her great arm in the air. Mary Ann now acting on the assumption "In for a penny, in for a pound", ran to the couch and pushed the head towards the window . . . and now Sarah waved. The two girls watched Fanny hesitate a moment at the bottom of the steps, undecided to risk the journey across the road to the portals of her enemy. But the habit of years was too strong. Mary Ann knew that Fanny was indeed sorry for Sarah, but she also knew that she still held Mrs. Flannagan in lip-curling disdain. But the sight of the old woman did them both good, for they laughed as they watched her wobbling away down the street to the corner shop. And when her figure had disappeared, Mary Ann said, "Well, there's one thing you should be thankful for: you're in this room and not in Fanny's." Yet as she said this she wondered if Sarah would not be better, in both health and spirits, were she in the untidy, smelly, lumber-filled room on the ground floor of Mulhattan's Hall.

Later that evening, as Mary Ann neared home, her depression deepened, which was unusual, for the mere sight of the farm had the power to bring a feeling of security to her and to lessen the day-to-day irritations, which were multiplying, she was finding, as she was growing older. But this evening she didn't want to reach home, she didn't want to face her mother, for she knew that she wouldn't be able to resist bringing up the question of . . . the front room. It was funny about the front room. Her da had thought the front room was a grand idea for Michael and Sarah. Michael had thought the front room was a grand idea for himself and Sarah. She had thought the front room was a grand idea for the pair of them. Yet to her knowledge not one of them had mentioned the subject to her mother, and yet she knew that her mother was well aware of what they were all after. She also knew that the front room was her mother's pride. It was the only room in the house in which she had been able to let her ideas have scope. The front room was really hers. A place where she could invite people without making excuses about the upset, or the untidiness. None of them left magazines, or books, or sweet papers lying about in the front room. It was an unspoken agreement that they cleared up their stuff each night before they left the room. The kitchen could look—as Lizzie sometimes said—like a paddencan, but never her front room.

And now Mary Ann knew the time had come when the room must be brought into the open. Not only to relieve the tension in the house, but the tension in Sarah. She was very worried about Sarah.

She had hardly got in the door before Lizzie said, "How is she?" and she answered, "Oh, she's very depressed, Ma. I'm worried."

"Why? What is she depressed over? I mean more than usual."

Mary Ann looked at her mother. She was sitting in the easy chair in her front room. She fitted into the room. The subdued colour of her dress, the calmness of her face—she had her eyes cast down—all seemed to be part of the atmosphere of the room. She was busy copying some recipes from a weekly magazine into her cookery book.

Mary Ann stood in front of her, their knees were so close they almost touched. She knew it was no use leading up to this subject. She was feeling so keenly about the matter at the moment that she would only make a mess of any strategic approach, so she said, straight out, "Ma?"

Lizzie gave a little lift to her head and said, "Well?"

"Sarah doesn't want to go and live in the bungalow."

"No?" There was a sound running through the syllable as sharp and hard as the point end of a carving knife.

"It would be as bad there as it is in Burton Street. And she's nearly going off her head there. . . . Ma . . . Ma. . . . She wants to come and live with us."

As Lizzie stared back into her daughter's face she had the strong desire to lift her hand and slap it. It would have to be her who would bring this thing into the open, this thing that had hung around them for weeks. Hidden under quick tempers and sharp retorts. Under sullen silences and pathetic looks. She had resisted them all. Because it wasn't as if Sarah was homeless, she was going to have a lovely bungalow built. She was going to marry Michael; yes, she was going to marry Michael. Was she not having her son? Wasn't that enough? But no . . . she wanted . . . they all wanted to take this room from her. There had been no suggestion of Sarah having one of the rooms upstairs, because that was an impossibility. No, the idea, which she knew was a flame behind the asbestos curtain of all their minds, was that she should give up this room to Sarah and Michael.

"Get out of my way."

"But, Ma."

"I said, get out of my way, I want to get up."

When Mary Ann was slow in obeying, Lizzie jerking herself to her feet, almost thrust her on to her back. The little table to the side of the chair, which had held the magazine and her notebook, jumped from the floor as if it had a life of its own. Lizzie put out no hand to steady it. She marched towards the door. But before opening it, she turned to Mary Ann and demanded, "Did they pick you as spokesman for them all?"

"No! No, Ma. I haven't talked about it with anyone. It was just what Sarah said."

"Are you sure?"

"Yes, Ma."

Mary Ann was speaking the truth, she hadn't discussed it openly with her da and Michael, but she knew that from the time Michael had heartened Sarah with the thought that she was coming to live here, the idea had been prominent in all their minds.

Lizzie, turning from the door, made one step back into the room, and, looking intently at her daughter, she said in an almost threatening tone, "Well, if it hasn't been discussed, don't you start now, do you hear me? I forbid you to say anything about it."

"All right, Ma." Mary Ann's voice was very low.

"And furthermore . . . listen to me."

"I'm listening, Ma." Her voice was still low.

"Well, do then. And remember what I'm saying. Don't you tell either your father, or Michael, that you mentioned this to me. . . . Do you understand?"

Yes, Mary Ann understood. If the matter wasn't brought into the open by either Michael or her da, the room was safe. In as quickly as it takes lightning to strike, a strange feeling assailed her, a fearful feeling. Out of nowhere came a hate for this room, and, more terrible still, a dislike of her mother. As she looked at Lizzie's tight, straight countenance, she knew she disliked her. "Oh . . .!" She groaned aloud with the fear of this feeling, and turning away she cupped her face in her hands. Then, sitting down, she dropped her head into the corner of the chair. But she did not cry, she was too frozen with fear of this dreadful thing that had come upon her—she didn't like her mother.

After one long look at the back of Mary Ann's head, Lizzie turned sharply away and went out of the room and up the stairs. When she entered her own room she stood in the darkness with her back to the door. She knew that she had reached a crisis in her life, not a crisis brought about by the desertion of her husband for another woman, not a crisis brought about by Mike's drinking, as had often happened during the early years of their marriage, or yet by her son walking out on her and picking a girl that she did not like. Nor yet a crisis where her daughter had got herself into trouble, but a crisis caused by the fact that she wanted to hang on to her way of life. And her way of life was personified by her sitting-room. The sitting-room that everyone remarked on. The sitting-room that she loved, that she had made part of herself. For months now she had been warding off this moment, daring them by her silence to approach her and mention this room. And now she knew that the matter could no longer be shelved, because Mary Ann had dared, with her usual foolhardiness, to bring it into the open. If Sarah came here to live, the life of the house would be changed. It wasn't that she disliked Sarah; she liked her. She liked the girl very much, she could even say she liked her next to Mary Ann. She could say in all truth that she liked her better than any of the friends Mary Ann had picked up for herself at school, much better. And she knew, crippled though she was, that she was the right one for Michael. She also knew something else. . . . She stared into the blackness of the room, and in its depths she faced up to a fact that she had not permitted herself to look at these past weeks, although it had been thrusting itself at her almost daily from the direction of her son and her husband, and within the last few minutes it had stared out of the face of her daughter, the fact was that if she kept her room she would lose them all. She might live with them for years and years, but things would never be the same again. If Michael took Sarah to the bungalow he would never come back into this house as her son . . . her Michael. She had felt him drifting away from her lately, but she knew now that by making this sacrifice she could pin him to her for life. But there was another reason why she hadn't wanted Michael and Sarah to start their married life in this house. She must be fair to herself, it wasn't only the room. As much as she liked Sarah, she knew she could not bear to see another woman—a girl, in this case—ruling his life. Being all in all to him. Filling her place entirely. Only if she hadn't to witness it, would it be bearable. This had been more than half the reason for her conduct. But now the decision had to be faced. Did she want to lose Mike, too, through this business? Not that he would ever leave her. But he could go from her without leaving the house. . . . And, Mary Ann? . . . Yes, and Mary Ann. Look how she had glared at her before she had turned her face away into the chair. She had never seen her daughter look at her like that before . . . never.

Lizzie groped in the darkness towards the bed. She did not switch on the light, nor turn down the cover. But flinging herself on to the bed she thrust her face in the pillow and cried. . . .

An hour later, when Mike came in, he found Mary Ann in the kitchen. "All alone?" he said.

"No, Da."

"Where's your mother? In the front room?"

"No, she's upstairs, Da."

Mike looked intently at his daughter before asking quietly, "What's the matter?"

"Nothing, Da. I think she's got a bad head. I think she's lying down."

"You think, you're not sure. Haven't you been up?"

"No, Da."

"What's happened?" He took her by the shoulder and turned her towards him. As she looked back at him she said, "Nothing, Da."

"How long has your mother been upstairs?" Mike's voice was quiet and even.

"Just over an hour, I think."

"And there's nothing the matter?"

"No, Da. . . . Do you want a drink?"

"Yes. Yes, I want a drink. But it isn't tea or cocoa."

The old anxiety leapt within her to join the fear that had sprung on her in the front room. If her da went out in this mood he would likely come back drunk, and he hadn't been drunk for a long time. She said to him, in the little-girl voice she had used to coax him years ago, "You're not going out now, Da, are you?"

"What do you think?"

"I wouldn't. I would have some tea, strong tea."

"Aye . . . well." He sat on the edge of the chair undecided. And as she stood before him the anxiety made her tremble, and he thrust out his arm and pulled her towards him, saying, "All right, all right, come on, don't worry. Stop that." He punched her gently in the chest. "Where's that tea?"

Mary Ann made him a strong pot of tea. She cut him a shive of meat pie. She watched him as he ate, and when a few minutes later she watched him settle himself in the big chair towards the side of the stove, she felt sick. He wasn't showing any signs of going upstairs to see what was wrong with her mother. This in a way was worse than him getting drunk and coming back roaring out all the things that were troubling him. Her ma, she knew, would suffer more from this attitude than from the drink. She felt, as she had done years ago in Mulhattan's Hall, torn asunder with anguish for them. She could stand anything, anything as long as they were close. The feeling of dislike for her mother had fled as swiftly as it had come. All she wanted now was to see her ma and her da close once again, laughing and chaffing, and that meant loving. And they hadn't been like that for weeks.

7

During the week-end that followed the tense atmosphere of the house did not lessen, and at the beginning of the week Lizzie began to behave peculiarly. Rain, hail or snow, she washed on a Monday, but not this Monday. On this Monday she declared to her family that she was going to do no more heavy washing. She was going to send all the sheets, towels and pillow-cases to the bag-wash. She'd had enough of heavy washing to last a lifetime. It was as she served breakfast that she made this revolutionary statement.

Under ordinary circumstances there is no doubt that the family would have shot comments at her: Why? Hadn't she said, time and time again, that the laundries poisoned the clothes, they were never the same again if sent to the laundry? But this morning they did not bombard her with whys, and if she thought their reactions were peculiar she made no comment.

There was really very little she could comment on, for neither Mary Ann nor Michael said anything. And Mike, merely raising his glance from his plate, remarked, "You feeling like that? Well, it's Monday mornin'."

That was all.

On Monday evening, when she stated she was going into Newcastle the following day to do some shopping, Mary Ann was the only one who reacted. Without a great deal of enthusiasm she said, "Do you want me to meet you?"

"No, I don't think so," said Lizzie, in a tone that could be considered airy. "I'll see how I feel, but I might go to the pictures in the afternoon."

Mike was doing his accounts at the edge of the kitchen table—it was warmer in the kitchen than in the office—and he brought his head round to look at Lizzie, but Lizzie was bending over the stove. And as his eyes returned to his work they met Mary Ann's for a second, and widened slightly. Still he did not say anything.

But Mary Ann knew that, like herself, he had been surprised. Her mother never went to the pictures, she didn't care for the pictures. They had talked about getting television ages ago, but she had said, "I don't care for the pictures, so I don't suppose I'll care for that." And now she had stated she was going to spend the afternoon at the pictures. . . .

By Friday of that week Lizzie had been out on her own three times, and it came as a surprise to no one except perhaps herself, when Mike stated, in a casual, even off-hand manner, which however did not disguise that his statement was one of retaliation, "I think I'll have a day out the morrow meself. I'm long overdue for a trip."

Michael's eyes darted towards his father, but Mary Ann did not look at him. She knew what the trip forbode, and she thought sadly to herself, "Well, me ma has asked for it this time. She may never have done before, but she's asked for it this time."

Lizzie had been on her way to the scullery with a tray of dishes as Mike spoke, and when she reached the table she slowly put the tray down, but without releasing her hold on it she bent forward over it and bit tightly on her lip. That was all for the moment.

Mike went out to do his round, and Michael, as usual after changing, got on his bike and rode to Jarrow and Sarah, and no sooner had the door closed on him than Lizzie's cold, calm front dropped away. Coming to Mary Ann, where she sat before the fire, working assiduously at her shorthand, she said quickly, "Leave that a minute and listen to me. Your da will be back at any time. . . . Put it down, I say." She flicked the book from Mary Ann's hand, and this caused Mary Ann's face to tighten.

"Don't look like that. I'm telling you don't look at me like that. And listen to me. . . . If your father goes out tomorrow you must go with him."

"He won't want me with him."

"I don't care if he wants you with him or not. . . . Look." Suddenly Lizzie knelt down by Mary Ann's side, and as she caught hold of her daughter's hand her whole expression changed. Mary Ann was now looking at her old ma, the ma she knew and loved. And when she saw the tears come into Lizzie's eyes her face and body relaxed, and the resentment she was feeling at the moment against her mother died away. She asked under her breath, "What is it, Ma? What's the matter?"

"Nothing, nothing. I only want you to do this for me. Please do this for me, keep with him to-morrow. He mustn't get anything into him to-morrow. Will you do it? You can. You know you can."

"But if he says I haven't got to go with him. If he says no, what about it then?"

Lizzie turned her eyes away and looked towards the fire, and after a moment she pulled herself to her feet and said in a dead tone, "Well, if he won't let you go with him, I'll . . ." Her voice trailed away. "I'll only have to tell him. . . ."

"Tell him what?" Mary Ann was on her feet.

Lizzie shook her head. "Oh, it doesn't matter . . . it doesn't matter. I just didn't want him to break out to-morrow, that's all. Go on, get on with your work, it doesn't matter."

Mary Ann stared at Lizzie as she went towards the scullery again. What was the matter with her mother? What was up anyway? Where had she been those other times this week? On Monday she had gone to the pictures. But she was out on Wednesday, and yesterday again. And she looked all worked up, and she sounded worked up. Mary Ann went back to her seat, and as she picked up her notebook she looked down at the last words she had written in shorthand. They read, "Me da says he's going out to-morrow. He sounds just like he used to years ago when he was going on the beer. . . . Will things never straighten out?" She looked up from the book. Would things never straighten out?

There was a wind blowing over the fields. It was like a gigantic scythe whipping across the frozen earth. It bit into Mary Ann's ankles causing her to comment, "I wish I'd put my boots on."

Mike, walking by her side up the road towards the bus stop, did not pick up her remark, and it was the third such she had made about the weather since leaving the house. But when she slipped on an icy patch in the road his hand came out swiftly and steadied her, and as he released her he said, "Your mother told you to come along of me, didn't she?"

"No, Da."

"All right, don't tell me if you don't want to. But I know me own know. After last night she was frightened I was goin' to get bottled, and she had reason, for that's just what I intended to do."

"No, Da."

Mary Ann was looking up at him, but Mike kept his eyes ahead as he asked abruptly, "Do you know where your ma's been this week?"

"No, Da."

His eyes were hard on her and there was a sharpness in his tone as he said, "Now look, Mary Ann. This could be serious. I might do just what she fears, and in spite of you go and get a skin full. I feel like it. By God! I do at this minute. So if you know what she's been up to on these jaunts, tell me."

"But I don't Da." Of one accord they drew to a halt, and Mary Ann looked at him as she went on, "I only know she's upset about something, sort of worked up." Her eyes flicked away. "She did say to me to come with you to-day. For some reason or other . . . well, she doesn't want you to do anything. . . ." Her voice trailed off.

Mike continued to look down on her for a moment, then with a deep intake of breath he walked on, and she had to hurry her step to keep up with him.

Mike did not speak again until they reached the crossroads and then he said, as if to himself, "If the old fellow were here I'd feel there was something hatching, but I can't blame him for this."

Mary Ann, picking up his words, said, "No, Da, you can't. And talking of him, I'm scared of him coming back an' all, for there's going to be trouble."

A moment ago she'd had no intention of telling him about Tony, but it now appeared like a heaven-sent diversion, a subject that would interest him and keep him, at least for a while, from thinking, and not kindly, of her mother.

"Trouble?"

"Yes, about Tony. . . . He told me yesterday that he's going . . ." She lowered her head and finished in a soft-toned rush, "He's going to marry Mrs. Schofield, Da."

Mike was silent so long that she looked up at him.

"He told you that himself?"

"Well, my God!" Mike pushed his trilby back from his brow. "That'll be news that'll knock the old man over. Although it's really no surprise, not to me, it isn't, but it will be to him, because he hasn't got the vestige of an inkling. I know that. . . . And what about you?" His head came down to her. "How did you feel when he shot that at you?"

Mary Ann raised her eyebrows, then turned he gaze away over the fields as she said, "A bit odd for a moment."

"You're still keen on Corny though?"

"Yes, Da."

"If there hadn't been Corny would you've had Tony?"

She brought her eyes back to him again. "That's what Tony asked me. How can I say? I don't know. I like Tony, I always have."

"Do you think your mother knows and this is what's been upsetting her?"

"No, Da. No. He told me first, I feel sure of that."

"Well, there's one thing certain." Mike drew in another long breath. "When your mother does know it's not going to make her any happier. She didn't take much notice of that tale your grannie brought that Sunday, about seeing them together. She remarked at the time on Mrs. Schofield being so much older than him and she dismissed the idea as ridiculous, because she wanted to go on thinking about the nice cushy future all planned out for you. For, like the old fellow, she had set her heart on this business and believed in the tag that time would tell. But you know, when he first mentioned it she went off the deep end. Can you believe that? She was actually shocked. Ah well, time has told, hasn't it?" He put his hand out and touched her cheek. "Life's funny. But don't worry. Tony wasn't for you. He's a fine fellow, but not for you. He's not your type of man . . . don't worry."

"But I'm not worrying about that, Da. Not about Tony and me, but I am worrying about Mr. Lord coming back. You remember the last time him and Tony went at it?"

Again Mike took in a deep breath before saying, "We'll wait until he does come and see what happens then. I think the best thing that you and me can do is to both get drunk . . . eh?" He was bending down towards her, and they both laughed now. With a sudden impulsive movement she tucked her hand into his arm, and for no other reason but that she was with her da and he wasn't going to go on the beer, she felt a momentary wave of happiness.

As was usual on his visits to the city, Mike did some business for the farm. Then he and Mary Ann had lunch together. Following this, he pleased her mightily by taking her to the pictures.

It was turned four o'clock and nearly dark when the bus dropped them at the crossroads again. They were quiet now as they went down the road, and neither of them spoke until, through the dusk, the farm came in sight, when Mary Ann exclaimed, "Look, Da. Is that our Michael on the road?"

Mike screwed up his eyes. "Aye, it is. I wonder what's up. He's waitin' . . . he seems as if he's on the look-out for us. . . ."

Before Mike had finished speaking, Michael came towards them at a run, and Mary Ann's heart began to pound with painful intensity. Something had happened to her ma. she knew it had. That was the feeling that had been with her all day. In spite of the joy of her father's company, and the brief happiness she had experienced this morning, there had been a heaviness around her, and Mike endorsed this feeling in himself when he muttered under his breath, "I've been waitin' for this."

But when Michael's face loomed up through the dusk and he came panting to their side, both their expressions took on a similar glint to his own, for Mary Ann was smiling, and Mike's eyebrows were raised in pleasant enquiry.

It was Mike who spoke first, saying, "It can't be the sweep, the results won't be through yet. . . . What are you looking so happy about?"

"It's me ma." Michael, in this moment of high excitement, had dropped what was to him the familiar use of mother. "You'll never believe it. But come on . . . come on, hurry up. I've been on the look-out for you on and off for the last couple of hours. Where've you been?"

"To the pictures. But what is it?" Mary Ann tried to catch hold of his coat as they now hurried on. "What's me ma done?"

"Wait and see." Michael was one step ahead of them, practically at at trot.

"Here, hold your hand a minute." Mike gripped his son's arm. "What's happened? It's something nice for a change anyway to make you look like that."

"Just you wait and see . . . just wait and see. No, don't go in the back way." He turned and pulled at Mary Ann as she was about to enter the farm gate. "Come on in the front."

"With our slushy boots on? Do you want us to get murdered?" Mike was still following Michael, and Michael threw over his shoulder, "You won't get murdered this time."

When they reached the front door, he stopped and, looking from one to the other, he said, "Shut your eyes."

"Shut me eyes!" Mike pulled his chin into the side of his neck, and slanted his eyes at his son. "What's the game?"

"Go on, Da. Shut your eyes."

Mary Ann didn't need a double bidding to shut her eyes. She screwed them up, anticipating as she did so a happiness streaked with wonder. It must be something wonderful that Michael had to show them because his face was portraying a look that she had never seen on it before. It radiated a feeling of deep, deep happiness.

After opening the door she felt Michael grip her hands, and her da joggled her as they tried to get through the framework together. She wanted to giggle, but it was not the moment for giggling, she knew that. When she felt Michael turning them in the direction of the front room she sensed immediately what she would see. Yet the surprise was so great that she was for the moment struck speechless. She was looking at what had been her ma's room. Now, as if a giant hand had swept the house, mixing up the furniture, she was gazing wide-eyed at a complete bed-sitting-room, and there, sitting propped up in bed, looking like her old self, was Sarah.

Michael, standing near the head of the bed gripping Sarah's hand, looked at them, saying softly, "Would you believe it?"

"No, no, I wouldn't." Mike came slowly across the room, and when he was standing at the foot of the bed he looked down at Sarah and said, with what might have been a break in his voice, "Hello, lass . . . you got here then." It sounded as if he knew she had been coming. So much so that Michael exclaimed in a surprised whisper, "You didn't know, did you, Father?"

"No, I didn't know. Not an inkling."

"Nor me." Michael gave a series of quick shakes to his head. "It's amazing."

Mary Ann came and stood by Michael's side, and putting her hand out she touched Sarah's face, and there was no disguising the cracking of her voice as she said, "This is what me ma's been up to all week, isn't it?"

Sarah nodded. She was unable to speak.

Mike now said, "I'll be seeing you, lass," and turning quietly from the bed, went out of the room.

Sarah, looking from Michael towards Mary Ann, brought out brokenly, "I'll love her all me life."

It was too much emotion for Mary Ann to cope with without openly breaking down, and she too went hastily from the room, thinking as she made her way towards the kitchen, "An' I will an' all." In moments of great stress she always dropped into the old vernacular.

As she pushed open the kitchen door it was to see her mother held tight in her da's arm, and to hear him saying over and over again, "Oh! Liz. Liz." And as her mother raised her head quickly from his shoulder, he finished, "You won't regret it, we'll all see to that."

Lizzie braced herself against Mary Ann's rushing onslaught. It was indeed as if they had all slipped back three or four years. And as Lizzie's arms went round her daughter, she said, "There now, there now, stop it, and let me get on."

"Oh, Ma, I think you're wonderful."

Lizzie made no open comment on this but a section of her mind, speaking with a touch of sadness, said: "All my married life I've done what one or the other wanted and they never thought to say I was wonderful, until now." The feeling she thought she had conquered during the early part of the week returned, and for a moment she felt the bitterness rise in her again. She had created a beautiful room—it was the symbol of her personal success—worthy in its taste of the finest house, and then they had succeeded, with their innuendoes of silence and suggestion, to bulldoze the ultimatum at her . . . the room or us. . . . Either you let Sarah have the room or you keep it . . . just to yourself, for we'll have none of it.

"But how did you manage it?" Mike was following her round like a kitten—a better description would have been a huge cat—purring on her, and when his arm, coming swiftly out and round her waist, almost lifted her off her feet as he pulled her to him again, the action seemed to slam the door shut on her self-pity. She had been right. Oh, yes, she knew she had been right. Sarah was happy and would like to get better much quicker here. And although she had only been in the house a matter of three hours, her gratitude had been so touching that it didn't seem to matter any more about the room. There would be times, she told herself, being a level-headed woman, when she would want her room to herself, but they would be few and far between. The main thing was she had her family with her again going her way. How, she wondered now, had she ever let them go so far from her? She must have been mad. She pushed off Mike's arm, saying, "And you stop it, an' all. I've got to think of the tea, nobody else seems to be going to bother."

"But how did you do it, Liz? I want to hear."

"I went out three times this week, didn't I?"

"You did, Mrs. Shaughnessy!" He nodded his head deeply at her.

"I went off jaunting to the pictures!"

"You did, Mrs. Shaughnessy." His head was moving slower and deeper now, and Mary Ann began to laugh. The laugh was high and thin. It spun upwards in a spiral of sound ending almost on a squeak, and the next minute Mary Ann had her head resting in the crook of her elbow on top of the sideboard and Mike was saying, "Ah, there now, there now, give over. It's no time for crying." With his one good arm he swung her up and carried her like a child towards the chair, then, sitting down, dumped her on his knee, and as he stroked the back of her head he muttered into her hair, "You're always the one for enjoyment, aren't you? It's like old times; when anything nice happened you always had to bubble." Mike looked to where Lizzie was now flicking the cloth across the table and their gaze met and held. They were both thinking back to the ending of many of their rows and disagreements, and they couldn't think of one where Mary Ann had not howled her eyes out with happiness. Or was it just relief?

"Now that's all right, Mr. Flannagan." Mike laid his heavy hand on the small man's shoulder. "She would have been coming into the family soon in any case."

"Yes, yes, I know that. They would have got married, yes, I know that, Mr. Shaughnessy." Mr. Flannagan had always addressed Mike as Mr. Shaughnessy. From that far-away day of the peace tea, when the little man had rebelled openly against his wife's tyranny and had marched down the street with Mike to get blind drunk for the first time in many years. From that day, whenever he had spoken to him since, he had always given Mike his full title, and Mike had returned the compliment.

Mike liked the little bloke, and in a way admired him, for he had showed his missus he was no worm, although she had treated him as one for years.

"That room was so pokey." Mr. Flannagan moved his head from side to side. "I'd think about her at odd times of the day stuck in there and her loving the open air, but here it's so wide looking, so free. And the view from that window does your heart good. I'm not being hoodwinked by what you're sayin', Mr. Shaughnessy. It's the goodness of yourself and your wife's heart that have brought this about. And if she gets better, I mean if she gets her legs back, then it'll be thanks to the pair of you."

"Now, now, let's forget it. What about a little wet on the side . . . I've no hard." He winked at the smaller man. "It's not allowed in the house, except at Christmas, and births and deaths, and we haven't had any of them for a long while." They both laughed. "Of course, beer's a different thing. Liz tells me that the beer hasn't been brewed yet that could make me drunk!" Their laughter rose, then Mike, jerking his head towards the front room, said, "Hark to 'em. They're going at it in there, aren't they?"

"It sounds like a party. It does that, Mr. Shaughnessy. And listen there a minute . . . I believe I can hear her laughing above the rest." The *her* referred to his wife, and Mr. Flannagan's face was definitely stretched with amazement. There came a deep twinkle into his eye now as he looked up at Mike. "The age of miracles isn't passed, is it, Mr. Shaughnessy?" Mike's head was going back to let out a bellow of laughter when he checked it, saying, "I think that's someone knocking, but I can't hear for the noise."

He handed Mr. Flannagan a glass of beer, then went hurriedly through the scullery towards the back door, and when he opened it he exclaimed in almost startled surprise, "Good God!"

"No, just me, Shaughnessy. I always turn up like the proverbial bad penny."

"You're . . . you're welcome, sir."

"Yes, but you didn't expect me, you never do. May I come in?"

"Yes, sir. By all means." Mike pulled the door wide.

"Oh, you've got company?" The sound of the laughter penetrated to the scullery, and Mike answered, "Only the family, and Sarah and her parents."

"Sarah?" Mr. Lord nodded at Mike. "She's here then? Oh, that's good, she's getting out and about, I'm very pleased to hear that."

Mike did not at this moment go into any particulars. The old boy wasn't going to like it when he heard that Michael was turning down the bungalow. He mightn't be greatly distressed about it, but nevertheless he didn't like any of his suggestions to be flaunted, and it would be in that light he would take this business.

In the kitchen, Mike said, "This is Sarah's father. This is Mr. Lord, Mr. Flannagan."

"Good evening."

"Good evening, sir."

Mr. Lord did not know Mr. Flannagan, but Mr. Flannagan knew Mr. Lord. He received his pay packet from him every week, for he worked in his yard. It was funny when you came to think about it, Mr. Flannagan's mind told him, but if things worked out the way Mrs. Flannagan said they were going to, Mr. Lord here and himself would, in a way, be connected. . . . Very distantly, admitted, but still connected. Life was indeed funny, Mr. Flannagan commented.

"You're Sarah's father?"

"Yes, I am, sir; I am that sir."

"Very nice girl, very nice. A great pity about this business. But still, wonderful things are done these days. . . . We'll see, we'll see."

"Did you have a good trip, sir?" Mike was speaking now.

"Yes, Shaughnessy. A very, very good trip. I enjoyed every moment of it. I only wish I could have made it longer."

Mike was thinking . . . "Well, why didn't you then, things go on just the same," when Mr. Lord said, "Is Tony here?"

"Tony? No, sir."

"Do you know where he is?"

"No. No, I don't, sir. He doesn't usually tell me where he's going." Mike gave a small smile.

"He hasn't been out with Mary Ann to-day?"

Mike's eyes dropped away. "No, no, not to-day. I took Mary Ann into Newcastle. . . . Won't you sit down a minute?" He turned the chair towards the old man, then added generously, "I'll tell Mary Ann you're here. She'll be pleased to see you."

"Thank you, Shaughnessy. I'll be pleased to see her, too. Yes, yes, I will indeed. Thank you."

Mike left the kitchen and went into the front room, and held up a sharp warning finger to stop the laughter and chattering. Making sure that the door was closed behind him before he spoke, he said under his breath, "He's come home. The old boy."

"What, Mr. Lord?" He looked towards Lizzie, who had risen to her feet.

"But I thought Tony said another week or so," Michael put in.

Mike now nodded at Michael as he whispered, "Well, you know him."

Mary Ann hadn't moved from her position on the side of the bed near Sarah. Part of her wanted to dash into the kitchen and throw her arms around the old man's neck in welcome, but there was a larger part that was filled with anxious fear. it was just like him, as Tony said, to do the unpredictable. They had all been so happy . . . happy and laughing. It had been like old times. She had felt during the last hour or so that life was going to run smoothly again. She had forgotten for the moment what Tony had told her about him and Mrs. Schofield. She had forgotten what that would mean to the old man who had just come back. Her da was looking at her and speaking again, still in a whisper, "Come on. Get off that." He pointed to the bed. "He wants to see you."

"What's the matter with you?" Lizzie's voice was soft but sharp. "Don't go in looking like that. He'll think he's as welcome as a snake in paradise."

Lizzie did not often make these quips, and there was a low rumble of suppressed laughter. Mary Ann did not laugh. She pulled herself off the bed and went slowly round the foot, excusing herself as she stepped over Mrs. Flannagan's feet, and made her way towards her da who was now opening the door. There was nothing to laugh about, nothing to smile about any more. They weren't to know that perhaps in a short time—the distance was determined on how long it would take Mr. Lord and Tony to come together—he would be dead. He could not stand shocks, great shocks, at his age, with his heart in the bad state it was already.

When she reached Mike, he stopped her passing him by saying quickly, "Hold your hand a minute till I bring Mr. Flannagan in here, it'll be better that way. . . . Stay a minute."

Within a matter of seconds Mike came from the kitchen accompanied by Mr. Flannagan, and nodding to Mary Ann he held the kitchen door open for her, and she went in to greet Mr. Lord.

"What's the matter with you?" said Lizzie some time later, as they piled sandwiches on to plates ready for transporting into the front room.

"Nothing," said Mary Ann.

"Now don't be silly . . . nothing. You know there is something. You were all right until Mr. Lord put in an appearance." She stopped her arranging of the sandwiches, and, turning Mary Ann towards her, she said, "You haven't been up to anything, have you?"

"Me, Ma?"

"Yes, you. And don't look so wide-eyed." Lizzie was smiling now. Smiling down on her daughter. She was relaxed and happy; it was as if she'd had a drink, like at Christmas. But the strongest drink she had taken tonight was coffee.

Mary Ann could have told her mother what was troubling her, but she did not want to spoil this night, and if she said to her, "Tony is going to marry Mrs. Schofield," the night would indeed be spoilt for her. She would have to know sooner or later, but not tonight, because she was happy in the sacrifice she had made. Everybody was full of praise for her, and all their gratitude flowed round her in a heart-warming wave. She could not spoil it.

"Well then, if you've been up to nothing"—Lizzie moved her head gently—"stop looking like that. To say the least, you don't seem very glad to see him back. And as usual he's been more than kind. Fancy him thinking about a camera for Michael, and such a camera. And a projector to go with it. The two must have cost sixty pounds if they cost a penny. And he's going to get a television for Sarah. You know, he couldn't be kinder."

She lifted up three plates now, and balancing two on one hand and one in the other, she went towards the hall, saying, "I'm looking forward to seeing his American pictures. You know he's a marvellous old man really, going around taking pictures at his age. You remember the ones from his last holiday. . . . Oh, that's them now." She half turned. "They've got back. Bring the coffee."

Mary Ann picked up the tray with the percolator and milk jug, and turned from the sound of her father's and Mr. Lord's voices coming from the scullery.

Mary Ann, at this moment, was not interested in seeing the pictures of where Mr. Lord had been. She was feeling very down and apprehensive. She wished that Mr. and Mrs. Flannagan would go home, and the house was quiet and they were all in bed. She wanted to think, and you couldn't think in this chattering racket. . . .

The big chair was pulled up to the side of Sarah's bed and Mr. Lord directed to it.

Michael had arranged a portable screen at the far end of the room and fixed the table for the projector. This took a little time as he had to arrange a number of books to bring it to the required height. And then all was ready.

"We'll have the lights out now," said Mr. Lord. Then with a little lightness that for him amounted to high gaiety, he said, "The show is about to begin." There was a murmur of laughter before silence took over in the room. Silence but for the warm burr of the projector.

There were six magazines of slides, and Michael, after slipping in the first set, worked the handle that clicked each picture into focus on the screen, and on each one Mr. Lord commented. This was the aeroplane with which he did the trip to New York. That was the hotel in which he stayed. . . . Oh, yes, that Negro had been a porter in the hotel and had proved himself very helpful. On and on it went, thirty-six pictures in the first magazine, thirty-six pictures in the second magazine. And when Michael was about to slip in the third set, Mr. Lord stopped him by saying "We won't have that one as arranged, Michael, let me have the end one next. . . . Yes, the end one."

There were a few minutes of anticipatory silence while Michael made the changeover, then came the first click. Hardly had the picture lit up the screen but there burst from everyone in the room, perhaps with the exception of Mrs. Flannagan and Mr. Lord, one name . . . Corny! For it was Corny. A full-length picture of Corny in a red sweater, tight cream jeans, and a grin on his face that almost split it in two.

Mary Ann's hands were cupping her face, pressing her cheeks in and her lips out. Her eyes were riveted on the screen. Corny was looking straight at her, smiling his wide grin. Michael did not click away Corny's face for some minutes. When he did, she recovered her breath and turned with the sound of a laugh in her voice as she cried to the old man, "You said you wouldn't be able to see him. . . . You said it was too far . . . thousands of miles down the country. . . . Oh, Mr. Lord! . . ."

"Wait a moment, wait a moment." He checked her impetuous thanks with a quick pat on her knee. "There are many, many more. Wait a moment."

The click came again, and there was Corny once more. His figure was shorter now. He was in a sort of gigantic showroom, where cars stretched, it appeared, for miles. It seemed to hold all the cars in the world, and there was Corny standing by one of them, pointing out something to a man.

Mr. Lord's voice penetrated Mary Ann's mind now saying, "He sold that car to that client. He's doing very well in that department, although he's only been there a month. Yes, he's doing very well indeed. We'll have the next one, Michael."

They had the next one, and the next, and the next. Corny with this car, and that car. Corny in a great glass office. Corny sitting at the wheel of a car. Then the pictures changed abruptly. First, there was a picture of a house. It was a beautiful house with an open garden. There were two cars standing in the roadway, each looked as big as two English cars put together. There were a number of people sitting on the lawn of the house having tea, and Corny was one of them.

The next picture was of a tennis court. Corny was playing tennis. Mary Ann's eyes narrowed at the stationary figure on the screen, the racket held ready for a back-hand drive. She had never imagined Corny playing tennis. The picture changed again. And there was the blue sea, it was very, very blue, and the edge was trimmed with a high frothy breaker. On the beach there were a number of people, and Corny was among them. They were having a picnic.

"They are a great family for picnics." Mr. Lord's voice broke in on Mary Ann's thoughts again. "They're always eating out of doors. They have taken to Cornelius and like him very much. America has done him good. He seems to have opened out quite a lot . . . not so tongue-tied as I remember him . . . at least, that's a mistake, I wouldn't say tongue-tied, brusque would be a better term. Yes . . . he is not so brusque as he used to be."

Mary Ann's fingers were holding the neck of her jumper now. She was looking at Corny in the water. His head was close to that of a girl, the girl she had seen in the front garden of the house. And also on the same side of the net on the tennis court. Although then she had her back to the camera, Mary Ann knew it was the same girl, for she had blonde hair, and although it was tied back it still reached below her waist. Suddenly she hated that hair. Her own hair, although a lovely dark chestnut with a deep shine, only came below her shoulders. She not only hated the fair hair, she hated its owner, but more so in this moment she hated Corny Boyle. And she thought of him as Corny Boyle, not just the familiar Corny.

"He seems to be having the time of his life." This was Mrs. Flannagan's voice coming out of the darkness.

"Yes, I think he is." Mr. Lord's voice was pleasant, and he seemed to be speaking to Mrs. Flannagan alone. "At least he is getting a broader view of life. His years in America will certainly not be wasted."

His years. . . . Mary Ann gulped and tried to make it noiseless.

The machine clicked again, and there was Corny playing his beloved instrument. Elbows up, head back, it was as if he was standing in the room before them. But he wasn't in the room, he was standing on the steps of that house, and there, squatting all round, were that family again. Only there seemed to be more of them this time, for protruding from the edge of the picture were numerous arms and legs. It looked like another party.

"This was one of their usual get-togethers. Corny and his playing are in great demand." There was no answer to Mr. Lord's remark.

The machine clicked yet again, sharply this time, and there was Corny in a close-up, sitting on the top of a gate, and next to him was the girl with the long fair hair. She was very bonny, beautiful they would call her out there . . . and Corny and her had their arms round each other.

It was the end of that particular magazine and no one made any comment whatever until Mr. Lord spoke, and directly to Sarah now. "Would you like to see more pictures, Sarah?"

It was a few seconds before Sarah said, "Yes. Yes, I would . . . please." But there was no enthusiasm in her voice. Sarah was now one of the family and through her own feelings for Michael she could gauge at this moment how Mary Ann felt, and she knew, as surely as did Mary Ann, that the pictures of Corny had been shown for a purpose.

The set of pictures now flicking on and off the screen were dealing with the scenery, and as Mr. Flannagan said in a respectful tone, "Aye, it's a grand-lookin' country. I've always had an idea I'd like to go there," Mary Ann slid quietly from her chair and went out of the room, and no one said, "Where are you going?"

But it was only a matter of minutes before Mike joined her in the kitchen. He came straight to her where she was standing looking down into the fire. She wasn't crying, but she nearly did when Mike put his arm around her shoulders and, pulling her tightly to his side, said, "The old swine. He's a bloody scheming old swine, and I've got to say it."

Mary Ann said nothing. And Mike went on, "Take no notice of pictures like that. Ten to one he was told to pose for them. Things are done like that, you know. Come on, they'll say. Come on, huddle up together there, I'm going to take your picture. . . . You know what it's like, don't you? We've done it ourselves in the garden. You remember when Michael took me and Mrs. Schofield and we were laughing our heads off, remember that tea-time? Well, anybody seeing that would get the wrong idea, wouldn't they?"

Still Mary Ann did not answer. She had been hating Mr. Lord, she was still hating him. She knew, and her da knew, that he had deliberately brought these snaps to show her that Corny was no longer remembering the North or anyone in it . . . was no longer remembering her. And the name of Mrs. Schofield did not soften her feelings towards the old man. But as though Mike had picked up her thinking, he said after a moment's silence, "I could have one great big bloody row with him at this minute if it wasn't for the fact that he'll have enough to think about in a very short while when Tony spills the beans. . . . Look." He turned her round, gripping her with his one hand. "I tell you, take no notice of them pictures. You know the old fellow's always scheming. When he took them he didn't know that his plans were already down the drain. And if I know Corny Boyle, and I think I know him, he's not the kind of lad to be swept off his feet by a bunch of golden locks and two goo-goo eyes." Mike gave a little laugh. "She had goo-goo eyes, hadn't she? Not forgetting a big sloppy mouth. Come on . . . come on, laugh at it. What do you bet? I bet Corny's back here within the next few months."

Within the next few months, her da had said. Within the next few months, not this month, or next. The year was nearly up, and next month it would be Christmas again, and Corny had said he would give it a year. But when he said that he hadn't realised the temptation of promotion, of big money, of a car . . . if he wanted one . . . of a girl with long blonde hair whose eyes weren't goo-goo, nor whose mouth was not big and sloppy. Mary Ann didn't hide the fact from herself that the girl with the long blonde hair was beautiful, by any standards she was beautiful.

"Look, come on back into the room, and don't let him see it's affected you. Keep the old boy guessing, that's the best way with him. Come on . . . laugh, smile." He stretched her mouth gently with his middle finger and thumb, and when she didn't respond, he said urgently, "Listen to me. Apart from what you feel, what we both feel about this, for it's made me as mad as a hatter, we don't want to spoil this day for your mother, do we? . . . and Sarah. Because Sarah is as near content now as she'll get until she's on her legs again. We don't want to do anything to bust up this day, eh? Come on."

Side by side they went out of the kitchen, across the hall and quietly into the room again to hear the end of Mrs. Flannagan's comment, "He's a very lucky young mn." Which told them that there had been more pictures of Corny.

"I'll have to put the light on a minute, this one's stuck," said Michael.

As the light went up in the room, and caused them all to blink, Mary Ann found that Mr. Lord was looking at her, but his eyes were not blinking. With their penetrating blueness they peered out at her from the wrinkled lids, and there was a question in their depth and Mary Ann, looking back at him, found she could not play up to her father's request and smile. And the old man, reading the hurt he had dealt her, looked sad for a moment. But only for a moment.

They were all late going to bed. Mary Ann heard the clock strike twelve as her father came up the stairs and made his way to his room. She had been lying for the last half-hour staring at the sloping ceiling, her eyes dry and burning. She hadn't cried and she told herself she wasn't going to. She was angry not only with Mr. Lord, she was angry with Corny Boyle. She did not believe what her da had said, that Corny had been pushed into posing for these pictures. He might have been the first time, but there had been a dozen or more of him with those people . . . and that girl was always near him. If he wanted to stay in America then he could; nothing apparently she could say or do could stop him now. He was too far away for her to have any impression on him. But she hated him for wanting to stay in America.

As the muttered, companionable sound of her da, talking to her ma, came to her from their room across the landing, she was enveloped in a wave of self-pity. Of a sudden she felt utterly alone, quite lost, friendless. She had neither Corny Boyle nor Tony. The term "falling between two stools" was certainly right in her case. The burning in her eyes became moist, and now she no longer tried to prevent the hot tears flooding down her face. Turning swiftly, she buried her head in the pillow.

She must have cried for about half an hour, for she felt weary and sick when she turned on to her back again, and continued, through blinking wet lids, to look towards the ceiling. It was at the point where sleep was about to carry her away from her misery that the sound of the telephone bell jangled through the house.

Mary Ann brought her head up from the pillow and listened. She expected to hear the door of her parents' room being pulled open. After some seconds, when the telephone bell, ringing again, seeming determined to disturb the quiet of the house, she threw back the bedclothes and, getting out of bed, pulled on her dressing-gown. She was on the landing when Michael's door opened, and she whispered across to him, "It's the phone."

As they went softly, and hurriedly, down the stairs together Michael whispered back to her, "I'll bet something's happened to me grannie."

Mary Ann felt not a trace of sympathy at the thought of anything happening to her grannie, and whispered back, "She would pick this time of the night. It's just like her."

So sure were they both that they would hear some news of Mrs. McMullen that, after switching on the hall light, they exchanged knowing glances as Michael lifted the mouthpiece from the stand on the hall table.

"Hello?"

The voice that came over the phone was no stranger's telling them that their grannie had been taken ill, but the voice of Mr. Lord. He was saying, "Oh, is that you, Michael? I thought it might be your father."

Again they exchanged glances.

"Is anything the matter, Mr. Lord?"

"No, no, nothing I hope . . . I just wanted to enquire if your father knew where Tony was going this evening . . . or last evening. It is now after one o'clock and he's not in."

Again the exchange of glances.

"Your father is not awake, I suppose?"

"No, no, Mr. Lord, or he would have been down. I suppose he's in a deep sleep, and my mother too, they had rather a hectic day." Michael said nothing about his own hectic day, and the excitement that was still depriving him of sleep. He said now, "Very likely Tony's gone to a dance."

"To my knowledge, he doesn't go to dances."

Michael's eyebrows went up as his eyes slanted towards Mary Ann's again, and his lips pressed themselves into a tight line and his expression interpreted the words coming over the wire.

"Would Mary Ann know where he was likely to be?"

Mary Ann bit on her lip and shook her head at Michael.

"I don't think so, Mr. Lord."

"Haven't they been going out on a Saturday as usual?"

Again Mary Ann motioned towards Michael, nodding her head this time.

"Yes . . . yes, I think so, Mr. Lord."

"You think so? You're not sure?" The voice was loud and the words clipped, and Mary Ann took more of her lower lip into her mouth.

"Did Tony not tell Ben how late he might be, Mr. Lord?"

"As far as I can gather, no. From the information I have screwed from Ben, it would appear that he hasn't even seen my grandson since I left the house three weeks ago. I have long suspected Ben to be an idiot, now I have proof of it."

From this heated remark, Mary Ann knew that Ben was within ear-shot of the old man. Poor Ben. He'd likely got it in the neck because he hadn't been able to tell Mr. Lord where Tony was. Very likely if he knew about Mrs. Schofield he still wouldn't have told on Tony. The main reason being not so much to protect Tony from the old man's wrath, but to protect his master from the consequences of that wrath.

"I shouldn't worry, Mr. Lord. He's likely gone to a dinner or something."

There followed a pause so long it would have indicated that Mr. Lord had left the phone but for the fact that there hadn't been the usual click at the other end of the line. The old man's voice came now, thick and muffled, saying curtly, "Thank you. I'm sorry to have got you out of bed. Thank you." Now came the click. And Michael put the receiver back on to its rest.

"Lord! There'll be a shindy. I wonder what Tony's up to. He doesn't dance, does he?"

Mary Ann did not give a reply to this but said, "We'd better look in on Sarah and tell her it's all right." Michael nodded and moved towards the front-room door, and after opening it gently and putting his head round, he said, "You awake, Sarah?"

He closed the door quietly before turning to Mary Ann. "She's dead to the world. Relief, I suppose." And going towards the stairs again he whispered, "I wonder what Tony's up to. Likely he's got in at a party or something. But I didn't think parties were in his line."

"He's with Mrs. Schofield."

"What!" Michael stopped dead on the stairs. "How do you make that out?"

"They're going to be married." There was a trace of bitterness in Mary Ann's tone.

"Him and Mrs. Schofield. You're kiddin'?"

"No, I'm not kidding."

"How long have you known this?"

"Since Friday."

"I didn't even know he was seeing her."

"Well, you and me ma and Mr. Lord must be the only three people on the Tyne who didn't know about it."

Michael watched Mary Ann ascent the stairs in front of him. Then, moving slowly, he followed her. For a moment he felt a deep brotherly concern for her. She was a tantalising, aggravating little madam at times, but she was also an engaging little madam. And she was kind. Look at her with Sarah. And she had indeed been given enough to-night to try the temper of the best, with those pictures of Corny and that blonde. And this, on top of knowing that Tony was going to marry Mrs. Schofield. . . . Mrs. Schofield, of all people. She seemed old enough to be his mother. Well, perhaps not quite, but too old for him.

On the landing he paused as Mary Ann's door closed on her, then his eyes were drawn towards his mother's room. Lord, this was going to be a blow for her. She had set her heart on Tony for Mary Ann as much as the old man had done. There was a balloon going to burst shortly.

Mary Ann, sitting on the edge of her bed, tried not to think of where Tony was at this present moment. He could not have married Mrs. Schofield, as the decree had not yet been made absolute, but there was no other place she could think of where he could be, except with her. The young Mary Ann told herself he was wicked, wicked. And she was answered by the Mary Ann against whom life had been thrust wholesalely these past few months, saying, "Be your age, it happens . . . it happens every day. Is he any different?"

Yes, Tony was diffferent. He should be different. Like Corny. Corny was different. . . . He should be different. It appeared to her that because she liked both Corny and Tony, they should be different. When her mind, still clinging to the black and white theory of her upbringing, asked her why people did bad things, she said to herself, and impatiently now, "Oh, go to sleep and forget it."

But she couldn't go to sleep and forget it. It must have been around four o'clock in the morning that her fitful dozing overbalanced into sleep. Then it seemed as if she was only in this beautiful oblivion for a matter of seconds when a hand dragged her upwards out of it. She woke to her father's voice, saying, "Mary Ann!" and his hand gently rocking her shoulder.

"Yes, Da?" She was sitting straight up blinking at him.

"Don't look so worried, it's all right. There's nothing wrong." He bent towards her. "I had to get up a short while ago, I heard Prudence bellowing her head off. She got her horns fixed in between those boards again, and when I was out I saw the light on up in the house, downstairs, and I was just wondering what was wrong when I caught sight of the old man walking up the hill. I could see him plainly . . . the moon's full."

"What time is it?"

"About twenty past five now, but this before five, I've just had a word with Michael. He's had a sleepless night it appears, too much excitement over Sarah I think in that quarter, but he tells me that the old man rang about one o'clock. Tony wasn't in then, and it looks as if he's still not in. I've got a feeling that I should go up and have a word with him. What do you think?"

"You mean tell him about Tony and—Mrs. Schofield?"

"What do you think?"

Mary Ann looked down at the rumpled bedclothes, and she pulled her legs up under her and shook her head before answering, "I don't know. When Tony does come in there'll be a dreadful row, because now, having to explain . . . well, he'll likely blurt it out."

"Yes, that's what I was thinking. I was thinking an' all it wouldn't be a bad idea if it was to come from you."

"Me, Da! Me tell him about them?"

"Yes. I don't think the shock would be half as great. You see, Tony will lose his temper, but you won't, not on this occasion." He smiled at her. "And although the old man will be worked up he won't be aggravated, and by the time Tony does get in he'll likely have got the matter settled in his own mind. He won't be less furious. I'm not looking forward to seeing him when he hears the news from either you or Tony, but I think it's likely to have less of a bad effect if you tell him."

Mary Ann looked towards the window as she said, "When, Da.?"

"Well, what about now? Do you feel like getting up?"

"Yes, Da. I'll be down in five minutes."

"Don't make a noise. I don't want your mother disturbed. She won't take this matter much lighter than the old man, you know."

"I know, Da."

Bending swiftly, Mike kissed Mary Ann on the side of the cheek. It was an unusual gesture. Their deep love and understanding for each other did not show itself in demonstration, other than the clasping of hands. And when the door had closed on her father, Mary Ann had a desire to start to cry all over again, even more heart-brokenly than she had done last night, but instead she grabbed angrily at each garment as she got into her clothes. . . .

Ben let them in, it was as if he had been waiting for them. "He's in the drawing-room," he said.

If the business of coming to the house at this hour wasn't odd enough, Mr. Lord too seemed to be expecting them, for he showed not the least surprise when Mike, gently pushing Mary Ann before him, went past Ben, who was holding open the door, and into the room.

Mary Ann looked towards Mr. Lord sitting in a chair to the side of the big open fireplace, with the fire roaring away up the chimney. And for all the heat of the room, she felt as cold as Mr. Lord looked.

"Sit down, Shaughnessy."

Mr. Lord did not appear to notice Mary Ann as he addressed himself to Mike. "Do you happen to know where my grandson spent the night? Don't tell me, please." The old man lifted up a tired-looking hand. "Don't tell me that you think he has been to a party, or a dance. He is no dancer, and not given to all-night parties. I happen to know the friends he has do not go in for all-night parties."

"It's a pity, sir. Perhaps it would have been better if he had picked friends who did go in for all-night parties." Mike did not end as he was thinking, "You've made a rod for your own back."

"What are you telling me, Shaughnessy? That he has gone off the rails and that it is my fault? . . . And I think it would have been better had you come alone." Mr. Lord was still ignoring Mary Ann's presence even as he spoke of her.

"I don't think so, sir. Mary Ann, we all seem to forget, is no longer a little girl, and this business concerns her more than any of us. Next to you, she, I should imagine, is the most concerned." Mike knew he wasn't actually speaking the truth here. Next to the old man it would be Lizzie who would be most concerned about the failure of the plans for Mary Ann's future. And he ended, "And as she's known what has been going on while all the rest of us were in the dark, I think it had better come from her."

For the first time since she came into the room, Mr. Lord looked at Mary Ann. He looked so frail, so tired, that pity for him mounting in her obliterated all other feeling at the moment. Only his eyes indicated the vitality still in him.

"Well! What have you to tell me, Mary Ann?"

She did not know how to start. There seemed no way to lead up to this business. Even as she searched frantically in her mind, none came to her.

Mike gave her arm a gentle squeeze, saying, "Go on, tell it in your own way."

Someone began to talk. Mary Ann didn't feel it was her voice. It had a cracked sound, yet was unhesitant, and she heard it say, "You like Mrs. Schofield, Mr. Lord?"

"Mrs. Schofield? Yes. Yes, I like Mrs. Schofield. What about her?"

"Only that Tony and Mrs. Schofield have been seeing a lot of each other this past year."

Mr. Lord's face seemed to close. It had looked tight and drawn before, but now the wrinkled flesh converged towards the point of his nose and became white. The whiteness spread over the nostrils and around the blue-lipped mouth.

The voice, that still didn't sound like her own, went on, "It was one Saturday when I went to see Janice . . . Janice Schofield, and as we knocked on the door there was shouting, and we saw through the window Mr. Schofield hitting Mrs. Schofield. . . . It was from then."

She watched the tremor pass over the old man's body, right from the lips, over his shoulders, down the legs right into the hand-made shoes. But whatever emotion Mr. Lord was feeling he was going to great lengths at this moment to control it. Now his lower jaw began to move slowly back and forward, and she could hear the sound of his dentures grinding against each other in passing. Her father's voice broke in quietly, "These things happen, sir, unavoidably . . . unaccountably . . . for no reason whatever. People don't want them to happen, but they happen. . . . Mrs. Schofield's a nice woman."

"Mrs. Schofield is a married woman."

The words came from Mr. Lord's lips as if they were indented on a thin strip of steel.

"She got her divorce a few weeks ago, sir."

"She is still a married woman."

My God! Mike closed his eyes for a moment. The old man wasn't speaking from any religious bias. He had no God, not to Mike's knowledge anyway, yet in this day and age he could be narrow enough to discredit divorce.

"Moreover she is a woman years his senior."

"She doesn't look it, sir."

"He won't marry her, I'll see to that." With what seemed a great effort the old man pulled himself up in the chair until his spine was pressed tightly against the back.

"You can't stop him." It was Mary Ann speaking now. "He loves her. He loves her very much."

"What are you talking about, child? What do you know about love?"

"I know that Tony loves Mrs. Schofield." Mary Ann had stepped a small step away from Mike and towards Mr. Lord as she spoke. She could recognise her own voice now. She felt that the worst was over, he wasn't going to have a heart atack, not yet anyway. "Mrs. Schofield's a nice woman. She'll be better for him than I would have been. Tony never loved me and I didn't love him, not in that way."

"She's a silly, feather-brained woman."

"Now, sir." Mike was smiling. "You know that isn't true. You know yourself you found a depth in her that couldn't be hidden by that airy-fairy manner. If I might suggest, sir, it would be a good thing if you would accept the situa——"

"Be quiet, Shaughnessy! I will accept no such situation." Now Mr. Lord did look as if he could be on the point of a heart attack. His turkey-like neck was stretching out of his collar and his head was wagging with such a speed that it looked as if it could spiral itself up and off. "Accept the situation! I will tell you this much. He will come into this house just once more, and that to get the little that belongs to him, and that will be the end. I want to see him, or hear of him, no more. . . . Accept the situation! What do you think I am? He has been out all night. . . ." Mr. Lord flicked his eyes towards Mary Ann then back to Mike. "I want to speak to you alone for a few minutes."

Mary Ann looked at her da, and when he gave a nod of his head she went slowly from the room and into the hall, there to see Ben standing.

"He's all right? He's not bad?"

"No."

"He didn't have an attack of any sort?"

"Only temper, Ben." Mary Ann touched Ben's sleeve. "Don't worry, he's all right. At least until Tony comes. What will happen then. . . ." She shook her head.

"Is it true what you said in there about Master Tony and Mrs. Schofield?"

"Yes, Ben."

"God above! I knew there was something on. I felt once or twice that he wanted to speak to me but was afraid to in case I told the Master. He needn't have worried. . . . I wouldn't be the one to kill him off."

"Well, it hasn't killed him off, Ben. We can be thankful for that."

"Yes, but as you said, not yet. Wait until the young one comes in. . . . I'll make some strong coffee and lace it."

He turned like a busy old woman and shambled towards the kitchen, and Mary Ann went towards the long window that looked on to the garden. The curtains had not been drawn and she looked up into the still dark, deep, frost-laden sky. Well, part of it was over. She knew why Mr. Lord wanted her out of the room, he wanted to talk about Tony, and where he had been all night. He needn't have worried about shocking her. She knew Tony had been with Mrs. Schofield. Married or not, they had been together. As she turned from the window and walked across the hall towards the kitchen she felt old, very old. She seemed in this moment to know all about life, and it wasn't a nice feeling. She had thought that no matter what happened to her in her life, whatever sadness came into it, she would still have the desire to go on breathing . . . living. And oddly enough it wasn't the fact that she had lost Corny . . . and Tony, that made her for a moment lose this desire but the cause of her having been sent out of the room. This was what momentarily dampened the desire for existence. This thing that wasn't nice. This thing that you read about in the papers. This thing that the girls at the Typing School nattered over, and giggled over. This thing that made you turn on yourself at times and say, "Be your age. Remember Janice Schofield had to get married because she was going to have a baby. And there are girls at the school who don't go home until four o'clock in the morning. And another is going with a man nearly fifty; and people think nothing of it."

In the kitchen Ben was pouring a glass of brandy into a cup of black coffee. It was as he picked the cup up that they heard the car come into the courtyard, and at the moment Tony entered the kitchen Mike came in from the hallway.

Tony stood with the door in his hand looking from one to the other. Then in a voice that sounded remarkably like Mr. Lord's when about to mount his high horse, he said, "He's back then?"

This wasn't a question, it was a statement, but Mike answered, "Yes, last night, early evening."

"Trust him. . . . And now I'm to be chastised like a naughty little boy for being out all night. Is that it, eh?"

"I think it's a bit more than that, Tony." Mike's voice was low. "Mary Ann, on my advice I might say, broke the news to him. I thought it would come easier on him from her than from you."

Now there was a strong resemblance to Mr. Lord as Tony looked at Mike and said, "You shouldn't have done that, Mike, that was my business."

"Aye, it might have been, but I know what the pair of you are like when you get going. I didn't want you to have anything more on your conscience." Mike's voice too had taken on a cold note. "If he had collapsed on you I doubt whether you would have felt so determined to go through with this business of yours."

"Nothing would have stopped me going through with . . . this business of mine, as you call it. And it's because it happens to be my own business that I prefer to look after it."

Mary Ann's eyes, dark and large, were flicking now between her father and Tony. Things were taking a tangent she had never imagined possible. Her da and Tony were on the verge of a row. Her da liked Tony, and Tony liked her da, but there was a bitterness between them now, she could feel it. Her da might subdue himself to Mr. Lord out of respect for the old man's age and because, deep down, he was grateful to him, but she was sure he did not have the same feeling towards Tony. Tony had come to the farm as a boy, a student, out to learn. That he was Mr. Lord's grandson made no difference, he was still an ordinary young fellow in her da's eyes. There were very few people whom her da would knuckle under to, and Tony was taking the wrong tack if he was going to try to put her da in his place. To deflect their attention from each other, she said sharply, "I had made up my mind, Tony, to tell him in any case, because, what you seem to forget at the moment is that I am concerned in this affair. Not that I want to be. And I don't think I was minding anyone else's business but my own when I explained to him that his plans hadn't worked out. What's more, I didn't want to see him drop down dead when you blurted this——"

"Don't worry, Mary Ann." The voice came from the half-closed door in front of which Mike was standing, and they all swung round as Mr. Lord came through into the kitchen. ". . . don't worry, I've no intention of dropping down dead."

Mary Ann looked at the tight face. The skin had that awful bluish hue, right from the white hair line to where his neck disappeared into his collar.

The old man turned his gaze now from Mary Ann, and although his eyes were directed towards his grandson they did not look at him, but at some point above the top of his head, as he said, "I'm not expecting any explanation from you, nor have I any intention of listening to one. I would be obliged if you would make your departure as quick as possible."

Tony's chin was up and out, but nevertheless it was trembling. "You needn't worry, this is one time I'll be pleased to obey you. But whether you want any explanation or not, I'm going to tell you that I haven't spent the night with Mrs. Schofield. She happens to be in London. You can confirm that if you like."

"I'm not interested in your activities, nor in the people you choose to share them with." Mr. Lord's eyes came down from the space above Tony's head, and looking at Ben he said, "As soon as our visitors have gone you might lock up. I think we need a little rest."

As his thin body turned stiffly towards the hall door again, his glance came to rest on Mike. His expression did not alter, nor his tone, as he said, "Thank you, Shaughnessy." He did not look at Mary Ann.

When the door had closed on him, Mary Ann, Mike and Ben turned towards Tony. Whereas Mr. Lord's face had been of a blue hue, Tony's was scarlet. He was shaking, and this was evident to them all when he turned to Mary Ann and there was deep bitterness in his voice as he said, "You see, it'll take a lot to make him drop down dead. He's tough, and he glories in it. You have to live with him just to know how tough he is. He's——"

Ben's quivering lips were open to make a protest when Mike put in sharply, "Don't say anything you'll be sorry for later, Tony, because then you'll remember he's always been good to you . . . I would say more than good. You can't blame him for wanting his own way. We all do. You particularly. And you've gone your way, so don't blame him."

"You definitely know which side you're on, don't you?" Tony's voice was as furious as his glance.

Mike's tone threatened fire too, with the retort, "Look you here! I'm only being fair. You know my feelings about the old fellow, and I toady to no one, so be careful. But if you want my opinion—and you don't—I'll say you've got off pretty lightly with this business. What did you expect him to do? Greet you and her with open arms?"

For a moment longer Tony returned Mike's glare, then with a swift movement his head drooped sideways and, his teeth digging into his lower lip, he stared at the floor. Then with a muttered, "Oh, hell!" he thrust himself out of the room.

Mike walked to where Mary Ann stood near the table, and turning her about, he led her to the door, saying grimly, "So long, Ben."

"Good-bye, Mr. Shaughnessy."

Mary Ann did not speak. She did not speak as they went down the hill and across the farmyard. Nor did she speak when she entered the kitchen, but she flung herself into a chair, and, burying her face in her arms, burst into a storm of weeping.

As the sound of Tony's car breaknecking down the lane into the main road came to them, Lizzie pushed open the kitchen door, her eyes blinking with sleep, as she exclaimed, "What on earth's the matter?"

"You'll know soon enough," said Mike. "But I think we'd all better have a strong cup of tea first." On this, he lifted up the kettle from the hob and went into the scullery. And Lizzie, bending over Mary Ann, said, "Stop it, stop that crying and tell me what's the matter now, and at this time in the morning. What is it?"

"Tony . . . Tony's lea . . . ving. He's going to marry Mrs. Schofield."

Lizzie straightened her back. Her mouth was open and her gaze directed to where Mike was coming in from the scullery, but she could only stare at him, she could not speak.

8

The Typing School term had ended and Mary Ann had received a diploma for her speed at typing and a certificate for her shorthand. Moreover, she had written her first short story, but she knew that no magazine would print it, because it was much too sad, and too long. Also she realised, from what she had read about short-story writing, that it lacked two main essentials: a plot and a twist. Her story was just about people and the sad things they did. She could not write about the reverse side of life, for at the moment she could not see it.

There had been no word at all from Corny since Mr. Lord had come back. Mrs. McBride would undoubtedly have heard from him. But in spite of her promise to go and visit his grannie, Mary Ann had not been near Burton Street for some weeks. Mrs. McBride, she knew, would have been kind. She would likely have laughed the whole thing off, and the louder she laughed the more awful, Mary Ann knew, it would have been. She couldn't risk it. Nor had Lizzie been near her old friend, but she had sent a parcel now and again and had received a card in Fanny's almost illegible handwriting to say, thank you. Neither of the women mentioned Corny . . . or Mary Ann.

So many things were adding to the sadness of life for Mary Ann at the present moment. Her mother, for instance. Her mother had taken the news of Tony much better than she had expected. At least, that was, at the time, that early morning in the kitchen. But as the days went on there seemed to settle on her the lassitude of defeat, and this quietness spoke of her disappointment louder than any words. Mary Ann thought that if it hadn't been for Sarah's presence in the house, which strangely enough had a brightening effect on them all, the place would have been more dismal than a cemetery.

If Mary Ann could have measured her own feelings, she would have found that her sadness, which was balanced between Corny and Mr. Lord, tipped not a little towards Mr. Lord. Although the shindy on that particular early morning had not caused him to have a heart attack, it seemed to have brought him up-to-date with his age, for suddenly he was a very old man. The vitality that had suggested youthful vigour was gone. So much so, that he had been into town only twice during the last month. As Mike had said macabrely, "The house was like an open grave, with him lying in it just waiting to be covered up."

Mary Ann left the warmth of the kitchen and the Christmas smell. She left Sarah sitting in her wheel-chair close up to the table, happily helping Lizzie with the Christmas cooking. Getting her hand in, as she laughingly said, for when she would have to do it herself. Sarah had become very close to Lizzie during these past few weeks and this had aroused just a tiny bit of jealousy in Mary Ann, although she saw that the urge to be close came from Sarah. Lizzie made no effusive return of affection, but Mary Ann knew that her mother was pleased with Sarah's gratitude; moreover, she liked Sarah. With the wisdom that was an integral part of her, Mary Ann realised, despite her own feelings, that this state of affairs was really all to the good, because Sarah was going to need her mother in the future, more than she herself would.

She pulled the coat collar around her ears as she went up the hill towards the house. It would snow before the morning, she could feel it. Like most northerners, she could smell snow coming.

Her breath was rising before her face in clouds when she entered Ben's kitchen. Ben was setting the tea-tray with old-fashioned silver that was polished to reflection standard. Mary

Ann smiled at him as she took off her coat, saying, "There'll be snow before morning."

"We don't want that."

Mary Ann looked towards the Aga cooker and said, "Is the tea made? I'll take it in."

"You'll do no such thing." Ben hadn't even looked at her. He was going about his duties as if she wasn't there. But that didn't affect her, for she knew he was always glad when she came up. One day lately she hadn't paid her usual visit and he had trudged all the way down the hill to find out why. He hadn't seemed satisfied that having a tooth out was sufficient reason for her not coming up to see his master. Ben, too, seemed to have aged in the past few weeks. He had always appeared to Mary Ann as a very old man, half as old again as Mr. Lord, but now the word ancient was more appropriate to him. She said impetuously, "Don't be silly. I'll carry it in."

"When I'm not able to carry the tea-tray in, then you can do so with pleasure. And I won't mind, for I won't be here."

She gave in and said, "How is he?"

"Just the same. Very cold. I doubt if that coal will see us over the holidays. We should have had another ton in."

"Oh, there's plenty of wood down in the shed. I'll get Len to bring some up."

She tapped on the drawing-room door and without waiting for an answer went into the room. In contrast to the outside atmosphere the room was stifling. There, before the fire, almost lost in the huge armchair, sat Mr. Lord. He turned his face towards her as she came across the room, but did not speak. She sat down in the chair at the other side of the fireplace. She did not say "How are you?" or "We'll have snow by the morning," but she sighed and leant back in the depth of the chair. Then after a few moments she said, "I've just finished a short story."

He nodded his head at her. "What about?" His voice was just a mumble.

"Oh, I don't know. . . ."

For a moment he seemed to come out of his cocoon, and a tiny spark of the old irritability was visible as he said, "Don't say such silly things. You say you have written a story, so you are bound to know what it is about."

She said, "Well, I meant to say that it wasn't the right way to write a short story, there are too many people in it doing too many things."

He said now with a show of interest that caused her to move in the chair, "You must bring it and read it to me."

"Oh, I couldn't do that."

"Why? . . . Is it about me?"

"No. Oh, no." Her denial was too emphatic, and he lifted his hand wearily as if to check any further protest. Now leaning his head back against the wing of the chair and closing his eyes he said, "What would you like for Christmas?"

What would she like! She knew what she would like. He had taken from her the person she had liked best in the world, apart from her da, and he could give him back to her. For it was in his power to bring Corny tearing across the Atlantic. But she wouldn't want Corny that way, she wouldn't want Corny as a gift from Mr. Lord. She didn't want anyone who hadn't a mind of his own. She was going to answer him, "I don't know," when Ben entered the room following a tap on the door. But he was not carrying a tea-tray. He came right up to the side of his master's chair and, bending his already stooped back further down, he said gently, "There's someone to see you, sir."

"Who is it?" Mr. Lord had not opened his eyes.

"It's a lady, sir."

"A lady! Which lady? What's her name?"

"She did not give me her name, sir." This had been quite correct, there was no need for the visitor to give Ben her name. If he hadn't already known it, he would have surely guessed it.

Mr. Lord now opened his eyes, and his wrinkled lids flickered as he said, "I don't have to tell you that I'm not seeing anyone, lady or gentleman. Why have you . . .?"

There was a movement in the room, and as Mary Ann brought her head from the cover of the wing, she almost gasped to see Mrs. Schofield standing well inside the drawing-room. With a wriggle and a lift, she was on her feet, apprehension showing in every part of her.

Mr. Lord had his eyes on Mary Ann, and now he slowly moved his body in the chair, bringing it round so that he was looking squarely at Ben. Then his eyes, flicking to the side, came to rest on Mrs. Schofield, where they stayed a moment before returning to Ben. His voice was louder than Mary Ann had heard it for a long time when he said, "I have no desire to see this lady, Ben. Kindly show her out."

"I know you don't want to see me, Mr. Lord, but I must see you." Mrs. Schofield's voice was low but her words came slow and distinct.

"You heard what I said, Ben."

Ben turned away, but he did not go to the door and hold it open for Mrs. Schofield. He passed her and went out and closed the door after him. And the action brought a flow of blood to Mr. Lord's deathly complexion.

Mary Ann now brought a chair towards Mrs. Schofield, and Mrs. Schofield looked at her, and thanked her, as if she had brought her some precious gift.

"I do not wish you to sit down, madam." Mr. Lord was not looking at Mrs. Schofield but directly ahead, and now Mary Ann, coming to the side of the chair, surprised even herself, with not only her tone, but her words as she said, "Don't be so silly."

Mr. Lord's Adam's apple moved up into the hollow under his chin, stayed there for a second, then slid down to the deeper hollow at the base of his neck.

Mary Ann said, "I'm going now. . . . Listen to her . . . listen to Mrs. Schofield. There can be no harm in listening."

"Sit down."

"But I'm——"

"I said sit down."

Mary Ann, turning from the chair, sent an apologetic glance towards Mrs. Schofield, then sat down.

After a moment of an uneasy silence she looked towards the older woman, and her first thought was, "By, she's beautiful!" and then, "She's not old."

Mrs. Schofield was staring at the averted profile of the old man, and her lip was trembling just the slightest as she began to speak.

"I—I haven't come to plead my cause. I am not going to marry your grandson, Mr. Lord."

Mary Ann's eyebrows sprang upwards, drawing the contours of her face with them. She transferred her wide gaze to Mr. Lord, but his expression had not altered in the slightest.

"I—I intended to marry him when my divorce was made absolute, but since he left you I have realised that should I marry him I would have to combat you for the remainder of my life."

Now there was a movement in the old man's face. For a moment Mary Ann felt he was going to turn his glance on Mrs. Schofield and it would have been one of enquiry. But when his nostrils stopped twitching he remained immobile.

"My married history will, I am sure, be of no concern to you, but I have been combating forces, seen and unseen, for the past seventeen years. And I am tired, Mr. Lord, very tired. I am tired of putting on a front. I have acquired a deep feeling for Tony, but it isn't strong enough to enable me to take up my life with him, knowing that you will be always there in the background of his mind, and whether he would believe it or not, he would be blaming me for having separated him from you. I have started by telling you this, but it isn't the only reason for my visit. Nor is it, I think, the real reason, for I didn't come with any hope that you would relent and give us your blessing. I came . . . I came because Tony has had an offer from Brent and Hapwood. Since they heard about his break with you they have been after him. They have even offered him a place on the board, so badly do they want him."

Even before Mrs. Schofield had finished speaking, Mr. Lord's body had turned towards her. Slowly, as if on an oiled pivot, he brought himself round to face her. And then he spoke. "Hapwood," he said under his breath. "Hapwood? Why do you think they want him? Do you know why they want him? . . . They want him because they imagine I will relent and leave him everything. There is nobody else I can leave the yard to, is there? And so I will relent. . . . Old Lord wouldn't leave his money to a Dogs' Home or Spastic Children. No, of course he wouldn't. He's only got one kin and he's too fond of him not to relent. That's the idea, isn't it? And when I'm gone—which won't be long they hope—they will be able to amalgamate Lord's yard with their fiddling, little-finger-in-every-pie industry. Well, you can tell him and them that I have no intention whatever of relenting. So if they are going to employ him it better be for his work alone."

There was a pause before Mrs. Schofield said, "It may be difficult for you to believe, Mr. Lord, but I am convinced that Tony does not want your money. But he must live, he must work. He doesn't want to go to Brents, he—he wants to come back to you."

Her voice had sunk to a whisper and Mr. Lord continued to stare at her for a long moment before saying, "Then why, madam, may I ask, had he to send you as his advocate?"

"He didn't send me. He doesn't know I'm here. Nor would he admit to me that he wanted to come back. But I happen to know him."

"You acquaintance has ripened in a very short time."

"I think you can live with some people for twenty years and know nothing at all about them. Well, there it is, Mr. Lord, if I drop out of his life will you have him back? Make—make the first gesture."

"Make the first gesture!" Mr. Lord's eyes looked like small pale-blue beads. "No, madam, I will make no gestures whatever. I didn't bring about this state of affairs, it was he who did that. Whatever gestures are to take place they must come from him. If he is sorry for deceiving me, and is man enough to say so, then I hope I will be man enough to listen."

On this pompous statement Mary Ann closed her eyes. Tony was too much of his grandfather ever to admit openly that he was in the wrong. She could not envisage him coming to this house and saying, "I am sorry, please forgive me." But it was not so much Tony she was concerned about at the moment, it was Mrs. Schofield. She wanted to cry for Mrs. Schofield. With the impetuousness of her emotional make-up she wanted to fly the few steps to her, and comfort her, to put her arms around her, and bring her head down to rest on her shoulder. She felt that if anyone needed comfort at this moment it was Mrs. Schofield. She was sitting there, looking so humble, sad, sweet and painfully humble. If she went to her she knew she would say, "Oh, don't look like that, he won't thank you for it. He knows nothing of humility, you've got to stand up to him."

In the next moment Mr. Lord brought her attention away from Mrs. Schofield, and, listening to him, it seemed that he had regained a spark of his old self, for picking up a point that Mrs. Schofield had made earlier he said, "You decided before you came here that you weren't going to marry my grandson?"

"Yes. Yes, I came to that decision."

"Because you thought his conscience would be an irritant to you?"

"If you like to put it like that." Her voice was so low her words were scarcely audible.

"Taking the supposition that he might some day return, what then?"

"I'll give you my word, I won't marry him."

Mary Ann was sitting right on the edge of the chair. With intent concentration she was watching Mr. Lord. She could almost see his mind at work. Tony back in the fold, Mrs. Schofield's promise to which she would hold, making the way clear—Tony would be in the market for herself again. "No. No." The protest was so loud in her head that it burst from her mouth, startling both Mr. Lord and Mrs. Schofield. But it was to the old man that she addressed herself, and without any finesse. "I'll never marry Tony. Don't think that if he were to come back things would go as you want, because if there had never been Corny I wouldn't have married Tony, because I don't like him enough to marry him. Nor he me. He never wanted to marry me, so don't get that into your head."

"Mary Ann!"

Definitely it was the tone of the old Mr. Lord, the Mr. Lord who would brook little or no interference. But for the moment she was past caring. She was standing up now and their heads were on a level. She had regained her breath and her next words caused him to close his eyes, for she was speaking in the idiom that was natural to her, and claimed no connection with her convent education. "Now look here, an' I'm tellin' you, if Tony comes back an' he doesn't marry Mrs. Schofield, then I'll leave home. I can, you know . . . if I made up me mind. If there's a good enough reason me ma or da wouldn't stop me, I know that. Not if I went to live with Mrs. McBride, an' that's where I would go, an' . . ."

"Be quiet!" Mr. Lord still had his eyes closed, and he repeated in what was nearly a growl, "Be quiet!"

Mary Ann became quiet. The room became quiet. There was no sound, not even of hissing from the fire, until a knock came on the door and, following it, Ben entered, pushing a trolley noiselessley over the thick carpet. As Mary Ann turned towards him she knew that he had been standing outside the door listening, and must have felt that this was the strategical point at which to make his entry.

Mr. Lord looked towards Ben and the moving trolley, but he made no comment. Slowly he turned his body away from both Mary Ann and Mrs. Schofield, and sinking back into the big chair he directed his gaze towards the fire.

Ben now moved the trolley close to the side of Mrs. Schofield's chair, and his action, and he arranged the cups to Mrs. Schofield's hand, also said clearly that she was a woman he wouldn't mind having about the house. Mrs. Schofield might not be able to read this from the old man's attentiveness but she could, and, what was more, Mr. Lord could.

When the door had closed on Ben, Mrs. Schofield looked appealingly at Mary Ann, master heard it, and in hearing, would know his servant's opinion on this delicate matter.

And Ben's opinion, Mary Ann knew, was conveyed to Mr. Lord as clearly as if he had shouted "I'm for her." And not only that, Mary Ann saw that Ben's deferential attitude, as he arranged the cups to Mrs. Schoffield's hand, also said clearly that she was a woman he wouldn't mind having about the house. Mrs. Schoffield might not be able to read this from the old man's attentiveness but she could, and, what was more, Mr. Lord could.

When the door had closed on Ben, Mrs. Schoffield looked appealingly at Mary Ann, then flicked her eyes towards the figure in the big wing chair. All Mary Ann did was to nod. It was an encouraging nod which said, Get on with it.

The cups rattled slightly as Mrs. Schofield poured out the tea. Mary Ann took Mr. Lord's cup, putting in the required amount of sugar, before placing it on the little table to the side of him.

It could not be said that any one of them enjoyed the tea, and no one partook of the hot buttered scones.

Mrs. Schofield had scarcely finished her tea before she gathered her gloves and bag towards her and, standing up abruptly, said, "Good-bye, Mr. Lord."

It was evident to Mary Ann that her quick departure had nonplussed him, for she saw his lower jaw working agitatedly. But he did not answer Mrs. Schofield until he heard the door open, and then moving only his head, he said, "Madam."

"Yes?" She had the door in her hand and she turned and looked at him.

"Thank you for coming."

Mrs. Schofield made no answer to this, she merely inclined her head just the slightest, then went out and closed the door softly behind her.

Mary Ann could not see the door because the tears were full in her eyes. She could not even see Mr. Lord, but she spoke to him, saying quietly, "She's nice. Tony will never get anyone nicer than her. You're being very wrong in stopping them."

"I am not stopping them."

"You can say that, but you know you are. She'll make Tony come back, she'll promise him this, that, and the other, so that he'll come back. As soon as he does, she'll go off where he can't find her."

The tears cleared from her blinking eyes for a second as his voice came to her with the old cutting quality, saying, "I would keep your romantic fiction for the books you intend to write." For a moment she could have laughed, but only for a moment.

He said now, "Stop crying and come here."

She went to him and stood by the arm of his chair, and his thin, mottled-skinned, bony fingers touched hers lightly as he said, "Were you telling me the truth when you said that you didn't care enough for Tony to marry him?"

"Yes, the absolute truth. Nothing would make me marry Tony. You sent Corny away because you thought if I didn't see him, I would turn to Tony, didn't you?" She didn't wait for an answer but went on, "You see, you cannot make people like people . . . or love people, or turn liking into love. Tony and I . . . well, we like each other, but that's all, we'd never be able to love each other. But he loves Mrs. Schofield, and if you don't let him have her, he'll likely marry somebody eventually who's entirely opposite to him and who'll drive him round the bend." She just restrained herself from adding, "Like you were when you married somebody who didn't suit you."

"Mary Ann." His voice cut in on her.

"Yes?"

"I'm very tired." He withdrew his hand from hers and slumped back into the chair. Then looking at her, he said, "Would you like to tell Ben I want him?"

This was dismissal, and she nodded at him. Then bending forward she laid her lips against the blue cheek. When she straightened up his eyes were closed again, and she put her fingers gently on to his brow and lifted to the side a wisp of thin white hair, saying, "You'll sleep better to-night. I'll be over first thing in the morning."

When she reached the hall Ben was waiting, and she said to him, "He's tired, Ben."

"I guess he would be." He moved past her towards the drawing-room door, then turning his bent shoulders round towards her, and beckoning her with a finger as bony as his master's, he whispered, "Here, a minute." And when she came to his side his head nodded with each word, as he muttered, "If you see Master Tony tell him Ben says he likes madam." And then he gave her the reason for his swift and open championing of Mrs. Schofield. "There's no telling, I might go before he does, and what then?"

"Oh, Ben! You're going to live a long time yet." She smiled at him. "But I'll tell him what you said, Ben. I know it will please him."

But as she went out of the house she thought dully, "How can I? I don't even know where he is, or even where Mrs. Schofield is staying." And as she went down the hill she chided herself for her lack of inquisitiveness in this particular case by saying, "You are a mutt. Why didn't you go after her and ask her?"

9

Early in the morning of Christmas Eve Mary Ann brought her mother to a dead stop as she was crossing the kitchen. She said to her, "Ma, what am I going to do with me life?"

"What?" Lizzie had heard what her daughter had said. But this was Christmas Eve, and a mountain of work staring her in the face. It was no time to discuss life, particularly Mary - Ann's life.

Mary Ann, aware that her mother had heard her remark, went on, "I'll never be able to write, not to make anything of it. Everything I do reads like rubbish, and I don't want to go into an office . . . not stuck indoors all day."

"Look," said Lizzie slowly, "it's Christmas, and me up to me eyes."

"Well, I don't feel it's Christmas," said Mary Ann bluntly.

"You mightn't" said Lizzie. "It may surprise you that I don't feel it's Christmas either. But there are other people to consider; and when you are grumbling about your future life just remember you've still got the use of your legs."

"Oh, Ma, that isn't fair."

Lizzie, coming towards her daughter, now said softly, "Look, Mary Ann, you've got to snap out of this; what can't be cured must be endured."

"It isn't only me, Ma." Mary Ann was looking at her feet. "It's everybody. Nobody seems right."

"That's life, and you'll find you've got to accept it. You never used to go on like this. What's really the matter with you?"

Mary Ann lifted her head and stared back at her mother, until Lizzie turned away sharply, saying, "Well, I've just got no time to bother with you and your fads." But as she neared the hall door she looked over her shoulder, and said quietly and patiently, "Why don't you go down and see Mrs. McBride. We can't get decorating until after tea, and Sarah is going to help with the last bit of baking this afternoon."

"I'm not going to Mrs. McBride's."

"Very well." Lizzie closed her eyes and lowered her head in a deep abeyance, and the irritation was back in her voice as she said, "Do what you want to, only don't go round with a face like that, because when you're like that, he's not far behind."

Mary Ann looked at the closed door. It was true what her mother said. Her da too wasn't particularly joyful these days. Although he didn't say so, she felt that he was concerned about Mr. Lord, and not only him, but Tony. He had parted in anger from Tony, and her da wasn't the one to hold his anger. But he had been unable to do anything about it, because from the morning Tony left the house no one had seen or heard of him since.

With what she felt was righteous indignation, Mary Ann asked herself now how her mother expected her to go about grinning from ear to ear when everybody was at sixes and sevens. And anyway, if the rest of the family were falling on each other's necks, she would still feel the same. She had not had the scribe of a pen from Corny, and threaded through her longing, and hurt, was a strong feeling of bitterness against him. He could have written her, couldn't he, and told her he wasn't coming back, not left it to those pictures, which he knew Mr. Lord would show her. It was a cowardly way out, and she had no use for cowards of any sort. . . . But oh! oh, she wished. . . .

She heard the telephone ringing in the hall and her mother answering it. Then the kitchen door opened and Lizzie, her tone lowered and slightly puzzled, said, "It's Ben, he says Mr. Lord's asking for you. . . . But you've just come down, haven't you?"

"Asking for me? Yes, Ma. I've just come down because he wasn't awake. Ben said he was dozing. He had been on the prowl about the house half the night again."

"Well, he wants you, so you'd better go right away."

"Did he say he was bad or anything?"

"No. No, he didn't sound worried. He just said that Mr. Lord wanted you." Lizzie smiled now. "Very likely he's going to give you your Christmas box."

Mary Ann raised her eyebrows and widened her eyes as she shook her head. It was as if she had never heard of Christmas boxes. And truth to tell, she was not interested in Christmas boxes, not the ordinary ones anyway. She pulled on her coat and went out, and she didn't slide on the thin patches of ice covering the flagstones, along the path, nor yet scrape the sprinkling of frosted snow into a ball and pelt it into the air. The joy of breathing, of being alive, had slipped its hold; she felt very old. And she had once imagined that nothing could happen to her to make her want to die. How wrong could you get.

Ben said, "Go up. He's still in bed."

"Is he all right?"

"No different from what he was yesterday, or the day before, as I can see."

She mounted the thick carpeted stairs, crossed the wide landing, and tapped on Mr. Lord's bedroom door, and was immediately bidden to enter. He was sitting, as she had so often seen him before, propped up in bed, his white nightshirt buttoned up to his chin, his face, like a blue-pencilled etching, above it.

She said immediately, "Are you all right?"

"Yes. Yes, I'm all right. Sit down."

"Did you have a good night?"

"I have had some sleep."

"I think we'll have more snow, it's enough to freeze you."

"We won't waste words talking about the weather. You're wondering why I sent for you."

"Yes, I am." She could be as blunt as himself.

"I'm very tired, Mary Ann."

Although she was looking at him she jerked her body now more squarely to him. "You're not feeling . . . bad, or anything?"

"I'm no worse, or no better, than usual. I've just said that I am very tired. Tired of fighting, tired of wanting, tired of desiring, tired of hoping. I am very tired of life, Mary Ann."

"Oh." It was a small sound and again it came, "Oh." She knew how he felt but she said, "Don't say that." She reached out and grasped his hand between her own, and he looked down at them, and placing the long thin fingers of his right hand on top of hers he actually smiled as he asked, "Are you happy, Mary Ann?"

She stared into the pale-blue eyes for a moment before saying, "Not very."

"I have been rather cruel to you. What I did, I did with the best intention in the world. . . . Selfish men always use that phrase, and I can't think of a better one to replace it. . . . Yes, I have been cruel to you." His fingers tapped hers. "And now I doubt whether I shall be able to rectify my mistake. You know what I mean?"

She knew what he meant. He had sent Corny to America. He had had him housed with a charming family, and the charming family had a daughter. Oh, she knew what he meant. But she said now soothingly, "It's all right, it's all right. Don't worry."

His fingers patted her hand again and he lay back on his pillows and closed his eyes, and after a space he said, "You have a big heart, Mary Ann. It was bigger than your body when you were a child. It hasn't grown any less, that is why I love you."

She nipped at her lip and blinked her eyes but kept looking at him. Never before had he said outright that he loved her. She had the desire to drop her head on to his knees, but she refrained because he wasn't finished, there was something more he wanted to say. And after a short space, during which he kept moistening his lips, he said it.

"I want to see my grandson, Mary Ann. I have waited for him coming, forgetting that he is so much a part of me he won't give in. If there had been only himself to consider perhaps he might have come back. . . . But there . . . there. . . . Will you tell him, Mary Ann?"

"Yes, oh yes." The words had to leap over the lump wedging her gullet, and now she dared to say, "And Mrs. Schofield?"

"With or without her."

The words were so low she could scarcely catch them, but she squeezed his hand tightly, and getting immediately to her feet she bent towards him, saying, "I'll bring him."

He did not open his eyes. She felt he dare not. He was not Mr. Lord at this moment, not THE MR. LORD. He was just an old man, a lonely old man, and he was weak as old men are weak.

She managed to pause in her rush through the kitchen and cry to Ben, "He wants me to get Tony."

"Thanks be to God."

"Yes . . . yes, thanks be to God." She was out of the door and running down the hill—she actually slid on a stretch of ice—and her running did not stop until she came to the cowshed and heard Mike's voice calling to Michael at the far end. And then she herself called, "Da! Da!"

"What is it?" Mike turned about and, seeing her bright face, added, "Hello, what's happened this time?"

"He . . . he wants to see Tony. He told me to fetch him . . . and Mrs. Schofield . . . and Mrs. Schofield, Da."

"No!"

"Yes, yes, it's a fact. He said, Da"—she shook her head—"he said he was tired."

"Poor old boy."

"What's this?" Michael came up and joined them, and Mary Ann said, "He wants to see Tony. He wants me to go and fetch him. And Mrs. Schofield an' all."

"No kidding?"

"No kidding, that's what he said."

"Well, what's holding you?"

Mary Ann didn't move, the smile slid from her face. She looked from Mike to Michael then back to Mike again. Her first finger and thumb were jointly tapping at her teeth as she exclaimed on a high note, "But, Da, where will I look? I've no idea where he is."

"You've hit something now." Mike nodded his head at her.

"You could try phoning places, that would be a start," Michael said. "Try some of the yards first, he's bound to have a job of some sort."

"Can I use the office phone, Da?"

"Go ahead."

Mike pushed her, and she ran out of the byre.

It could be a Dickens Christmas Eve. She did not like to think of Mr. Lord as a Scrooge, but part of her mind was commenting, "It's funny what Christmas does to people."

By five o'clock Mary Ann had not only made thirteen phone calls, she had been into Newcastle as well. Michael had been going in to pick up some goods from the station, and he had run her out to Mrs. Schofield's old home, only to find it completely empty. So empty that it looked as if it hadn't been inhabited for years. They even visited Mr. Lord's yard, but the chief clerk in the office could give them no help. He hadn't seen Mr. Brown for weeks, but he said that Mr. Connelly might be able to help them. Mr. Connelly was works manager, and they went out to his house, but without success. . . .

And now Mary Ann was tired, and Lizzie said to her, "Sit down there and get your tea, you're not going out again unless you have something to eat. The next thing I know I'll have you in bed."

It was Sarah who said, "Have you thought of going to Father Owen?"

"Father Owen?" Mike screwed up his face. "It isn't likely that Tony would go to the priest; he's not a Catholic, you know, Sarah."

"I know that, but you did say that Mr. Lord and Father Owen used to be friends in their young days. It was just a thought, and Mary Ann seems to have been every place else."

Mary Ann, jumping at this pleasant possibility, gulped at her tea and said, "It's an idea, Sarah, there are very few people around that Father Owen doesn't know."

"That might be in Jarrow and thereabouts"—Lizzie moved her head slowly—"but don't forget Tony is more likely to be living in Newcastle." She did not add "because Mrs. Schofield will be there."

"And don't you think Father Owen would have said something when he was up to see Mr. Lord last week?" Lizzie again was using her reason.

"No, Liz. I don't think he would have," Mike put in. "He knew how the old boy felt, and he wasn't likely to talk about Tony, not even to mention his name. He knew that one thing might lead to another, and before you could say Jack Robinson something would be said that would be better unsaid. For he's not without his share of temper, is Father Owen, and whatever some people might imagine to be the reverse, priests are not infallible."

On this remark Lizzie's expression became prim, and she was just about to make some sharp comment when Mary Ann startled her by jumping up from the table, saying, "Well, look, I'm going to see him anyway."

"Sit down and have your tea first."

"Oh, Ma, the time's getting on and he's been waiting all day. . . . Will you run me in, Michael?"

"Okay."

"It will be a wild-goose chase, if you ask me." Lizzie looked around at the tea—hardly anything had been touched—and Mike, following her gaze, leant towards her and, patting her on the shoulder, said, "Don't worry, it'll all have disappeared afore the night's out. . . . Go on." He turned towards Mary Ann and Michael, and pushed at them with his hand, saying, "Get yourselves away. And don't come back without him."

As Mary Ann ran to the hall once again to scramble into her coat, Lizzie exclaimed on an indignant sigh, "I get sick to death of this family and the things they get up to . . . always something happening, Christmas Eve and everybody going mad."

"You want the old boy to go on living, don't you? Or do you?"

"Mike! The things you say."

"Well then, hold your whist."

Michael with head reverently bowed, spoke out of the corner of his mouth, saying, "We'll be here all night, there's half Jarrow waiting to go in."

Mary Ann turned her head slightly on her clasped hands and answered in a whisper, "I'll go to confession and ask him there."

Michael made no comment on this. Trust her to do something that other people wouldn't even dream about. Using the corner of his mouth again, he said, "You'll be a good hour, I'll slip home and come in again."

She made a slight motion of assent with her head, and when Michael left her side she too rose, and crossing over from the aisle that fronted the altar of the Holy Family, she went and joined the sombre throng waiting to go into Confession.

Father Owen sat in the candlelit gloom of his section of the confessional and waited. Mrs. Weir had bad feet, it always took her a long time to shuffle out of the box, and once outside she always meticulously closed the door after her. That it would be pulled open almost instantly seemingly did not occur to her, she must finish the job properly. So she obstructed the next penitent with her overflowing hips. As Father Owen listened to her fumbling with the door, he wondered, rather wearily, how many more were out there. He would like a little quiet and rest before midnight mass, and he was feeling cold. Either that boiler chimney was blocked up or Jimmy Snell had gone off again without banking down properly. It was either one or the other. Or perhaps it wasn't, it was more likely the system. He had felt the church cold more than once lately, and it wasn't all due to his old bones. He rested his head on the palm of his hand and wondered if in the beginning of the year he could encourage somebody to start off a subscription jaunt to get a new water system in. If only Father Bailey would come off his high horse about tombola, the thing would be as good as done. But there, he had a very pious bee in his bonnet. If only the bee didn't split hairs. What was the difference in tombola and running raffles at every function he could. . . . Oh there, what was the use. Anyway, sooner or later there would be a burst, and if it took place in the pipes under the grid the consequences could be both disastrous and amusing. He had an irreverent picture of one of a number of his more tiresome parishioners being sent heavenwards on a spurting jet of hot water.

"Please, Father, give me your blessing for I have sinned. It is three days since my last confession."

In the name of God it was Mary Ann. Well! well! well! It was some time since she had been to him for confession. She took herself to Newcastle or Gateshead more often than not now, because they were nearer. Well! well! Christmas Eve and Mary Ann. He felt a spark of gaiety ascending up his cold body, but this was followed immediately by what could only be described as a long question mark which covered him from head to toe, and the question mark said, "What's brought her in? Something's wrong." Three days since her last confession and here she was again! She was after something . . . oh, he knew Mary Ann.

"Is that you, Mary Ann?"

"Yes, Father." It was a haloed whisper.

"How are you?"

"I'm not too bad, Father."

Not too bad. He knew it, he knew there was something wrong. "How's your da?"

"Oh, he's fine, Father."

Well, that was the biggest obstacle out of the way. It was usually her da who brought her helter-skelter to the church. At least in the past it was Mike who could have been given the credit for her ardent piety. "And your mother?"

"She's very well, Father."

That disposed of the two main factors in her life. Michael and Sarah were all right, at least they were up to a few days ago when he had visited the farm. He hadn't seen Mary Ann on that occasion, in fact, he hadn't seen her for quite this long while. Was it her grannie? He now said, "Don't tell me, Mary Ann, that you've come to confess to murdering your grannie." Aw, it was Christmas Eve and the good Lord would forgive him for a joke even in the confessional.

On her side of the box Mary Ann suppressed a giggle. And her lips were quite near the wire mesh as she whispered, "No, Father, but it's very likely that some day I will."

There was many a true word spoken in jest. He metaphorically crossed himself and said, "Go on, my child. I will hear your confession."

And Mary Ann had enough sins on her mind to make a confession, even though her conscience had been cleared three days previously. She laid aside her main reason for coming to see Father Owen and said, "My heart is full of bitterness, Father, against someone, and I don't want it to be like that—I want to forgive. And there is Sarah, Father. There are times when I give way to jealousy. I like Sarah, Father, I like her very much. But my mother has become very fond of her and I get jealous. It is wrong of me but I can't help it. It would be different if——" She stopped, she couldn't go on and say, "If I had anyone of my own." Because she had someone of her own. Hadn't she her da? But that wasn't what she meant.

"Go on, my child."

"I miss my morning prayers very often, Father, and I have started . . ." There followed another long pause, and the priest prompted her, saying, "Yes? yes?" "I have started to criticise my religion, Father."

There was silence behind the grid. She'd had no intention in the world of confessing that sin, it had just slipped out. And she didn't really criticise, she only tried to work things out in her own mind.

On the other side of the grid Father Owen suddenly knew he was an old man. He had known Mary Ann since she had first toddled up to the side altar and made her bargains with the Holy Family, and now she had reached the age when she was thinking for herself, and when you started thinking for yourself you couldn't help but criticise. It was a phase of life. He said to her gently, "You are growing up, Mary Ann. Don't worry. Your religion will bear your criticism. A thing that cannot bear criticism is built on sand and will soon be washed away by the tongues of men. Come and have a talk with me sometime and tell me what you think. We'll have a long crack on the subject, eh?"

Oh, he was lovely was Father Owen, he was always lovely. He made things so easy.

"Make a good act of contrition."

"Oh, my God, I am very sorry that I have sinned against thee, because thou art so good, and by the help of thy Holy Grace, I will not sin again."

He said the absolution.

"Amen."

"A happy Christmas, Mary Ann."

"A happy Christmas, Father."

"Father." She could, in this moment have cast off nine or ten years and be hissing her petitions through the grid one more.

"Yes, Mary Ann?"

"Do you remember Tony?"

"Do I remember Tony? Of course, I remember Tony, Why?"

"Do you know where he is?"

Ah, so that was it. He said, "No, I don't, Mary Ann. Why? Do you want to find him?"

"Mr. Lord has been asking for him."

"Oh!" So he had been asking for him. When he saw him the other day the name of Tony was not mentioned between them. He had hoped it would be because he felt that Peter Lord's burden needed lightening if he were to go on living. He was a man without hope. He whispered now, "I wish I could help you, Mary Ann, but I can't."

"Thank you Father."

"Wait a minute." Father Owen took his hand away from the side of his face that sheltered it from the penitent, and he brought his fingers over his lips as he thought, Young Lettice Schofield! He had known her father, Brian Trenchard, as a young man, and many were the times that Brian had dined him well. It was hard to think that she, whose life story had been filling the papers of late, was the same young Lettice he had teased when he was a guest in her father's house. He had seen little of her since her marriage, and it had come as shocking news to him the life she had led. For he felt she must have suffered nothing less than refined torture to keep up the facade of respectability. God knew that she was to be pitied, yet it was she who had caused the rift between Peter Lord and his grandson. Unintentionally perhaps, for he could not imagine there being any vice in Lettice. He had run into her quite unexpectedly about three weeks ago and they had talked about this and that without touching on anything personal. But he did remember now that she had mentioned that she was staying with her uncle, and if he remembered rightly Brian Trenchard had only one brother, and his name was Harold. He said now, "Mrs. Schofield might help you. She was staying with her uncle. His name is Harold Trenchard. Look in the telephone directory and go on from there."

"Thank you, Father. . . . Oh, thank you, Father."

"God bless you, my child."

"Good night, Father."

"Good night. . . . A minute, Mary Ann. How many do you think are waiting?"

"I should say over twenty, Father."

Father Owen closed his eyes. Over twenty! "And at Father Bailey's box?"

"About ten, Father."

Father Owen sighed. "Thank you. Good night."

"Good night, Father."

Self-consciously Mary Ann went down the aisle, past the patient penitents. They would, she thought, be thinking that she hadn't been to confession for a year, she had been in so long.

Kneeling before the crib she said her penance, one Our Father, and three Hail Marys. It was a stock penance of Father Owen's. She didn't know what other people got, but she had never got anything worse than that. Even when she had tried to empty the candle money box behind the altar. She looked at the Holy Family, not the real Holy Family that stood up on the altar, larger than life size, but the little Holy Family staged among the straw with the animals around them. And she prayed for each member of her family, and for Father Owen. And then, still being Mary Ann, she had to ask for something. She said, "This being Christmas Eve, please help me to find Tony, and I'll——" She just stopped herself from making some outrageous promise in return for their guidance. In the past she had always promised them stop hating her grannie, or to tell no more lies, or to resist getting one over on her enemy, Sarah Flannagan. This thought coming into her mind made her smile, and, looking up from the small statues towards the group that had been focal point of her spiritual life, she knew that the power of God was wonderful, for there was in her heart now not the smallest trace of jealousy towards Sarah. In this moment when the sacrament of penance was washing her conscience she could even see the funny side of her grannie. This feeling wouldn't last, she knew it wouldn't, but while it did she thanked God. She did not mention the name of Corny Boyle to them. It would have been too difficult to explain about the part of her that didn't care, and the part of her that cared too much. And then about the part of her that was bitter and full of resentment. Oh, she couldn't go into all that.

And now she went out of the church, and there was Michael waiting in the sloping passage to greet her, as he had done once many years ago. He said, "Where on earth have you been?"

"You know where I've been."

"Well, you've taken long enough about it. I've nearly froze waiting for you. What did he say?"

"He doesn't know where Tony is, but he thinks Mrs. Schofield's staying with her uncle. . . . I want a telephone directory."

"Where for?"

"It'll be in Newcastle."

"Oh, good lord. We're not going tearing off there now, are we?"

"If there's a Harold Trenchard, we are." She looked at him and smiled, and then with an unusual gesture she tucked her arm in his.

Mr. Harold Trenchard's name was in the telephone directory. Michael suggested, before dashing off to Newcastle, why not phone and find out if Mr. Trenchard was there. And this she did.

It was a woman's voice who answered the phone, and she said she was Mrs Trenchard. Mary Ann politely made her enquiries, and the woman at the other end said, "Who's speaking?"

"My name is Mary Ann Shaughnessy."

"Oh, Mary Ann Shaughnessy. Oh yes, I've heard of you. . . . Well, Lettice . . . Mrs. Schofield is not with us now."

"Oh."

"But I can give you her address."

"Thank you. Thank you very much." Mary Ann repeated the address and Michael wrote it down in his pocket book. And then Mary Ann said, "Good-bye and thank you." And she added, "A Merry Christmas."

Mary Ann had hardly put down the phone before she started to gabble. "Look, it's not in Newcastle, it's in Shields. She's in Shields, Sunderland Road!"

"Well, come on, don't stand gaping." With brotherly courtesy Michael pushed her out of the box, and when she almost slipped on the frost on the pavement he grabbed at her, saying, "That's it, break your neck. We only want that now." They were both laughing when they got into the van.

Within a quarter of an hour they had reached Sunderland Road, and after some searching they found the house. There was a plate to the side of the door that held three cards, and the bottom one which said Flat 3 had the name Lettice Trenchard written on it. They rang the bell twice before there was any response, and then a man opened the door. Without waiting to question them he said, "I thought I heard someone there. Is it the top flat you want, because the bell's out of order? But just go on up."

"Thank you." They went past him and up the two flights of stairs. And when the came opposite the door they exchanged glances before Mary Ann tapped gently.

When the door opened there stood Mrs. Schofield, her lips apart with surprise. No one spoke until Mary Ann, after what seemed a long moment, said quietly, "Hello, Mrs. Schofield."

Mrs. Schofield, after wetting her lips and looking from one to the other, smiled and said, "Mary Ann!" Then she half-turned her head over her shoulder and looked behind her, before saying, "Won't you come in?"

Mary Ann walked slowly past Mrs. Schofield into a tiny hall, and Mrs. Schofield said, "Will I take your coat?"

"We won't be staying, Mrs. Schofield. We just came to . . . to ask you something."

"Well, you'll sit down for a while. Let me have your coat . . . and yours, Michael."

She took their coats and hung them on the hallstand. Then going towards one of the three doors leading out of the hall, she opened it. And when they entered the room, there, standing on the hearth-rug before a small fireplace, was Tony.

The sight of him was as much a surprise to Mary Ann as her and Michael's arrival had been to Mrs. Schofield. She hadn't really expected to find Tony here. Somehow, she thought Mrs. Schofield would have cut adrift from him in order to make it easier for him to return to Mr. Lord.

Mrs. Schofield must have sensed something of what Mary Ann was thinking, for after she had seated them she looked at her and said, "You may not believe it but Tony has only been here a short while; a matter of minutes, in fact. I'm being discovered all in a bunch it

Life and Mary Ann

would seem."

Tony had not spoken to Mary Ann, and his greeting to Michael had been merely an abrupt nod of the head. Now all his attention was on Mrs. Schofield, and Mary Ann's attention was on him. He did not, she noticed, look his usual spruce self, anything but, in fact—he looked rather ill. Her sympathy aroused, she said now, "Well, hello, Tony." And when he turned towards her he gave her a smile as he answered, "Hello, Mary Ann." Then looking towards Michael he added hastily, "How's it going, Michael?"

"Oh, not so bad, Tony. How's it with you?"

"Oh, fine. . . ."

"It isn't fine, don't tell lies." Both Mrs. Schofield's glance and voice were soft as she looked at Tony. Then glancing between Mary Ann and Michael, she said, "He's been ill, he's had flu. I knew nothing about it."

"Have you been on your own?" Mary Ann's tone was full of concern as she gazed at him, and now he replied in a slightly mocking tone, "Yes, entirely, but I don't want you to cry about it."

"Who's going to cry about it?" Mary Ann's chin jerked up, and on this they all laughed. The tension was broken, and Mary Ann, becoming her natural self, exclaimed as she looked him straight in the eye, "You're a fool."

"I wouldn't for the moment dream of contradicting you. Now tell me, what have you come for? What are you after?"

"Well, if you're going to use that tone, I've a good mind not to open my mouth."

"That'll be the day."

This retort came almost simultaneously from Tony and Michael, and again there was laughter.

"Take no notice of them, Mary Ann. . . . Come here." Mrs. Schofield was holding out her hand to Tony. "Come here." Mrs. Schofield was holding out her hand to Tony. "Come and sit down."

As Mary Ann watched Tony, with willing docility do as he was bid, she thought, and not without a slight pang, "She could do anything with him, anything."

"Tell us what brought you, Mary Ann." Mrs. Schofield was now looking at her, and Mary Ann answered her as if Tony was not sitting beside her, saying, "Mr. Lord wants him back. He asked me to fetch him. . . ."

"On conditions that I——"

Mary Ann, turning sharply on Tony, cut him off with, "On no conditions attached whatever! You don't give me time to finish." Her voice dropped. "He's very low and tired . . . and lonely, and he said to tell you to come back, with or without. . . ." She turned her eyes from him now to Mrs. Schofield as she ended, "With or without you. But I do believe he would rather it were with you."

There followed an embarrassing silence, during which they all seemed to be staring at each other, until Mrs. Schofield whispered, "Oh, Mary Ann." Her face began to twitch and she lowered her head and bit hard on her lip.

When Tony's arms went about her and he drew her tightly into his embrace as if quite oblivious of either Michael or herself, Mary Ann experienced embarrassment that brought her to her feet, and she blurted to no one in particular, "We'd better be getting back. If you like, we can all go together."

Again Mrs. Schofield said, "Oh, Mary Ann." Then pulling herself away from Tony's clasp and looking up through wet eyes, she exclaimed on a broken laugh, "That's all I seem able to say . . . Oh, Mary Ann. But I must add: Thank you. Thank you, my dear."

"And me too, Mary Ann. That's all I can say too: Thank you." Tony was on his feet now looking down on her. "You were always the one for getting things done, for getting your own way. And from the bottom of my heart I can say at this moment, I'm glad you're made like that. Because—because I want to see him. It's been pretty awful these last few weeks. . . ." When Mary Ann, finding it impossible for once to say anything, remained mute, Tony turned abruptly from her and, looking at Michael, said in a lighter tone, "How's Mike?"

"Oh, the same as usual, you know."

"Yes. But I don't suppose he'll be the same with me though. . . . I'll have to do a bit of apologizing in that quarter."

"Oh, forget it. I'm sure he has, he's not the one to remember rows, he's had too many of them."

"Well, come on, get your coat on." Tony had turned to Mrs. Schofield, but now she looked back at him and shook her head, saying, "No, you go alone. I'll come to-morrow. You can come and fetch me."

"I'm not going without you."

"Now don't be silly, Tony."

"He's right, it's Christmas Eve and we're not going to leave you here." Mary Ann bounced her head. "And if you won't come now we'll just sit down and wait until you change your mind, won't we, Michael?"

"We will that."

Mrs. Schofield looked from one to the other, then she turned swiftly from them and went into the bedroom.

Tony went into the hall and collected their coats, and as he handed Mary Ann hers, he said under his breath, "I woke up this morning feeling like death and wishing it would come quickly. I was in digs, awful digs, and I thought: Oh, my God, Christmas Eve. . . . But I never dreamt it would turn out like this." A quiet smile spread over his white features as he ended, "It wouldn't take much to make me believe that your . . . Holy Family had been at work, Mary Ann."

"You can laugh." Her voice was prim. "But if it hadn't been for Father Owen, we wouldn't be here, would we, Michael? So you can say that the Holy Family had a hand in it."

"I'm not laughing, Mary Ann, far from it. I don't feel like it at this moment. Oh, no, I'm not laughing—not when I've just been handed two good reasons for living. And the Holy Family apart . . . thank you, Mary Ann."

When Tony put out his hand and gently touched her cheek she had a sudden desire to howl her eyes out there and then, for the excitement was over, the good deed had been accomplished. Tony had Mrs. Schofield, Mr. Lord would have Tony. Sarah had Michael, and her ma had her da. And who was there for her? Nobody. She hated Corny Boyle.

10

"Well!" Mike let out a long-drawn breath that expanded his chest and pressed his ribs against his shirt. "It's been a night and a half."

Lizzie, making no pretence to stifle the yawn, said, "Night? It's day again. It's half-past one on Christmas Morning. Come on, let's get upstairs or I'll sleep until dinner-time tomorrow." She turned towards Mike who was now standing staring pensively at the two bulging stockings hanging from the brass rail. On Christmas Eve two stockings had always hung in front of the fireplace, no matter where they lived or how little money they had. But this year they were not Mary Ann's and Michael's, they were Mary Ann's and Sarah's, Michael having thankfully relinquished the childish habit kept up by Lizzie.

Mike had his hand in his pocket and his shoulders were hunched, and after looking at him for a moment longer in silence she said softly, "What is it now?"

"Oh, I was just thinking." He raised his head and looked across the high mantelpiece which was covered with a galaxy of Christmas cards, then up to the strings looped to the picture rail which were carrying the overflow, and he remarked, "Everybody happy but her."

"Now, now. Oh, don't let's start that, not at this time."

Mike turned slowly towards her, and putting his hand out he softly lifted her chin, and his voice held a deep and gentle note as he said, "You're the best in the world, Liz, and I know it, but there are times when I think you've got a hard spot in you towards her."

"Oh, Mike, that isn't right, and it's unfair of you to say it. Just because I don't go around dribbling, it doesn't say that I don't feel for her. I do."

"Yes, perhaps you do. I'm sorry." His fingers rubbed against her soft flesh.

Lizzie was very tired. Her eyes began to smart and her voice broke as she said, "You shouldn't have said that to me, Mike. Not at this time. Bringing up things like that at an hour when we should all be in bed."

"Well, it was in me mind, and you know me. I said I'm sorry, and I am. But I'd mortgage me life at this minute to see her happy. She's run off her feet all day to put things right for the old man and Tony, and she's as happy about Mrs. Schofield as if she was you. And then the night, at supper did you see her face when Sarah named the wedding day?" He now slipped his arm around Lizzie's shoulder as he said, "Our girl is very human, Liz. She's all emotion, all feelings, and she's seventeen and a half and she hasn't got a lad. You know, I feel in two minds about Corny Boyle at this minute. If he was standing afore me now, I don't know whether I'd punch him on the jaw or shake him by the hand. . . . What would you do, Liz?"

Mike had shot the last question at Lizzie, and he felt her start under his hand. And then she said, "You think I didn't like Corny. It wasn't that at all. Corny was a nice enough lad. Being part of Fanny he was bound to have good in him. I had nothing against Corny, not as a lad. But somehow I wanted somebody different for her, somebody who could give her things. It is understandable, isn't it?" She turned her head and looked up at him.

"Aye, Liz, I suppose it is. Her mother didn't do very well for herself, did she?"

"Aw, Mike." She dropped her head now against the strong muscles of his neck. "What do you want me to say?"

"Nothing, nothing."

"Well, I can tell you this." Her voice was smothered against him. "If I had to pick again this minute I would make the same choice." As his arm pressed her tighter to him she straightened up, saying, "Come on, we'd better get up, and quietly, or we'll be wakening the house."

When he released her she did not move away from him, but looking into his weathered, ruggedly handsome face, she said simply, "I love you, Mike."

"An' I love you." Slowly now their heads came together, and the kiss they exchanged was gentle.

"Happy Christmas, Liz."

"Happy Christmas, Mike."

Their arms around each other, they went out of the room, Lizzie switching off the light as they went through the door.

It was as they went, still linked together, to mount the stairs, that the unmistakable sound of a motor-bike being pulled up in the road outside the house brought them to a halt.

"That's a motor-bike, and stopping here." Lizzie was whispering.

Mike's ear was cocked. "Likely somebody looking for Len and didn't see the cottages."

"They're not having a do, are they?"

"I didn't think so, not till the New Year."

Simultaneously, they turned from the foot of the stairs and went into the hall again. And although they were both expecting a knock, they were visibly startled when the rat-tat came on the door.

Mike went forward, leaving Lizzie in the centre of the hall, and when he opened the door the exclamation he let out was high. "Well, my God!"

Lizzie repeated this phrase to herself when Mike, moving aside, said, "Look, Liz. Look what the wind's blown in."

As Corny Boyle stepped slowly into the hall, Lizzie gaped at him with open mouth, and her gaping was caused by a number of reasons, not the least was that here stood a different Corny Boyle from the lad she knew. Here, enveloped in a great coat, his big head actually on a level with Mike's, was a man, not the boy she remembered.

Corny Boyle cast his glance between them as he said quietly, "I'm sorry I'm so late, but I'm glad I caught you up, I thought I might. I was held up here and there, or I'd have been over sooner."

"Well! well! well!" Mike was gazing at Corny. He too was surprised at the change he saw in him. It was only a few minutes since he had said that if he were confronted by this lad he wouldn't know whether to shake him by the hand or punch him on the jaw. But he knew what to do, for his hand went out as he said airily, "Don't worry your head about the time, the day's young. I'm right glad to see you, Corny. You're a better sight than Santa Claus. . . . Mary Ann!" This last was a bellow up the stairs.

"Mike! You'll have the house awake." Lizzie's lids were blinking rapidly.

"And why not?"

"MARY ANN! Do you hear? MARY ANN!" His voice was even louder this time.

"Are they all in bed?" Corny looked at Lizzie, and Lizzie, not quite sure of her feelings at this moment, almost answered, "What do you expect, going on two o'clock in the morning?" But she managed to be gracious and say, "Well, they haven't been up all that long, but we have Mrs. Schofield with us. You remember Mrs. Schofield?"

Corny's smile was the old wide remembered grin, and he nodded his head as he said, "I should say I do. Is she staying over Christmas?"

"Yes." Lizzie paused and then added, "Yes, she's staying with us over Christmas." It was evident that Corny knew nothing about Mrs. Schofield's affair. Lizzie still thought of the situation as an affair but Corny disillusioned her the next moment by saying, "Is Tony with her?"

Lizzie's eyebrows moved just the slightest. "No, not here, he's up at the house with Mr. Lord."

"Mary Ann! . . ." Mike was at the beginning of another bellow when Michael appeared at the top of the stairs. He was pulling his dressing-gown on as he exclaimed, "What is it? What are you bawling for?"

"I'm not bawling for you, anyway. Give a rap on her door or else I'll be up there."

But there was no need now to give a rap on Mary Ann's door, for even as Mike spoke she came on to the landing, and looking down the stairs, she too asked, "What is it?"

"What do you think?" Mike had pushed Corny towards the wall out of her line of sight, and his face was one large grin as he looked up at her saying, "What would you like in your stockin'?"

If Mary Ann hadn't been sure that she had left her da solid and sober in the kitchen somewhere about an hour ago, she would have sworn he was tight.

Michael had gone down the stairs, and was now standing in the hall under the pressure of

Mike's hand, which warned him to make no comment on what his eyes were seeing, and then Mary Ann came within three stairs of the bottom and she looked from her da to Michael standing side by side, then behind them to her mother. Following this her eyes lifted to the side and saw, standing near the wall between the kitchen door and the sitting room, a man who looked like Corny Boyle. Her fingers went to the top button of her dressing-gown and pulled on it so sharply that she gulped.

"Hello." The man that looked like Corny Boyle had stepped away from the wall and was speaking to her. She felt slightly dizzy. All the faces rolled together, and before they separated her da's voice came to her saying, "Well, open your mouth. Here he's come all the way from America on a motor-bike." Mike laughed at his own joke and went on, "And you can only stand and stare. Didn't you ask Santa for something in your stockin'? . . . Well . . ."

"Be quiet, Mike." Lizzie now took the situation in hand. "Come on into Sarah's room. She's bound to be awake and it's warmer in there." Lizzie pushed open the door exclaiming, "Are you awake, Sarah?"

"I'd have to be dead, Mam, not to hear the cafupple."

"It's Corny." Lizzie was talking into the room.

"Yes, I've guessed as much."

During this Michael had moved past his mother into the sitting-room, and Mary Ann had moved down the stairs and was now standing opposite Corny Boyle.

Corny Boyle . . . Corny Boyle. . . . But a different Corny Boyle. This was not the boy she remembered, he was almost a stranger. So much so that she felt she didn't know him.

"Well, this is a nice welcome. What's the matter, have you lost your tongue?"

Mary Ann jerked her head from Corny and looked at her da. She stared at him for a moment before turning towards Corny again. And now she did speak. "Did Mr. Lord send for you?" she said.

"No, he didn't. Nobody sent for me. I COME on me own."

The answer had come so quickly it startled her, and for the first time in the last surprise-filled minutes she recognised in this unfamiliar man the boy she knew.

A laugh now came from the sitting-room, and Michael's voice cried, "They've started."

At this Corny too laughed and, turning completely away from Mary Ann, said to Mike, "It's as if I'd never been away, isn't it? Oh, Mr. Shaughnessy, you don't know what it's like, this feeling being back."

Mary Ann, still looking at him, but at his back now, was thinking two things. He had come on his own after all. That was one. And the other, that although he looked different, and sounded different, for he didn't talk like he used to, he still called her da Mr. Shaughnessy. As she allowed her da to push her into the sitting-room, she remembered that for years she had tried to make Corny speak differently, with little success. Yet here he had been gone just over a year, and besides looking like anybody else but Corny Boyle, he was speaking like anybody else but Corny Boyle. There was explanation . . . somebody had worked on him. This thought pulled her round to look at him as he went across to Sarah and took hold of her outstretched hands. Nothing could make him beautiful, nor handsome, yet he looked . . . She searched for a word, and might have found it, but Mike's voice cut across her thinking as he yelled up the stairs again, "Mrs. Schofield!"

"Oh, Mike, have you took leave of your senses?" Lizzie was dashing out of the room, and Mike answered her, "We can't leave her up there and all this going on."

It seemed a matter of seconds before Mrs. Schofield's voice came from the landing, saying, "Nothing could stop me coming down. I heard who it was. Oh, I am glad."

In the sitting-room, Mary Ann, seeming to stand apart as if watching a play being acted, saw Mrs. Schofield and Corny greeting each other, holding hands and laughing as if they had been lifelong friends.

"Where is it?" Mrs. Schofield made a pretence of looking behind him.

"Where's what? . . . Oh, I've left it in me grip, but I'll bring it over to-morrow and serenade you."

Indeed here was a different Corny. His grip . . . and would serenade Mrs. Schofield. The other Corny would never have talked like that. If this time yesterday someone had said to her, "How would you feel if Corny were suddenly to drop out of the sky and into the house, now would you feel?" she would have drawn a long breath and clasped her hands together, and answered truthfully, "Oh, wonderful. It would be the most wonderful thing on earth that could happen." And now here he was, larger than life, and she was quite numb. She was even asking herself at this point: Had she ever been mad about Corny Boyle? The Corny Boyle that she had known . . . and loved . . . was a reticent person; brusque, Mr. Lord had said. But Mr. Lord had also said that America was bringing him out. . . . America had certainly brought him out, you could say that again. Sarah turned Mary Ann's attention away from her questioning thoughts by saying, "Oh, Mary Ann, isn't this wonderful! I'm so happy for you."

She was holding Sarah's hand now, and looking down into her great dark eyes. She was envying her again, jealous of her in a funny way. Sarah was happy . . . she loved Michael, and Michael adored her. Somehow it didn't seem to matter about her legs. Sarah had said, "Oh, I'm happy for you." For what? Why was she feeling like this? Things weren't right.

Mike's eyes were tight on his daughter now, and the tie between them that had always been stronger than any umbilical cord transferred to him in some measure what the effect of Corny's appearance was having on her, and so he cried, "Look! We want something to celebrate with. It's got to be tea, or beer."

"We'll make it tea." This was Lizzie.

"Good enough. Hi! there, Mary Ann, get yourself into the kitchen and get busy."

"I'll——"

The pressure of Mike's hand on Lizzie's arm cut off her words, and he cried again, "Did you hear what I said? Get that kettle on, me girl. The sooner you get your hand in the better."

Mary Ann, relinquishing her hold on Sarah's hand, went round the bed and out of the room, without once looking in the direction of Corny. And she closed the kitchen door behind her, she stood with her back to it and with the fingers of both her hands pressed over her mouth. She stood in this way for some seconds gazing, but unseeingly, at the stockings hanging from the rod, before going to the fire. The kettle was on the hob, but the fire had been banked down and would take too long to bring up again, so she took the kettle into the scullery and put it on the gas stove. Then she returned to the kitchen and put the cups on the tray, and after picking up the teapot she went into the scullery again. She was measuring out the tea when she heard the kitchen door open, and her hand became still as the footsteps came nearer. Then there he was, as she knew her da had planned. And when he spoke there was a faint resemblance to the old Corny by his straightforward approach to the subject.

"You don't seem overjoyed to see me."

She turned and looked at him. "Should I be?"

"Well, what do you think I'm here for?" His face was straight. "It isn't like getting a bus from Jarrow, popping over from America!"

"No, no, it isn't."

"Why didn't you go and see me grannie?"

"Why should I?" She rounded on him now, her tone sharp. "You know, Corny Boyle, you've got a cheek. I never hear a word from you for months, and you expect me to be sitting waiting for you coming . . . to drop in, as me da says, like Santa Claus!"

"You know that I don't like writin' letters, I'm no hand at them."

"There's lots of things I don't like doing that I've got to do. . . . Anyway, you were going to come back when the year was up, but you didn't. And you didn't even write to tell me that. No . . . you had to send some fancy photographs through Mr. Lord."

"I didn't send any fancy photographs through Mr. Lord. What are you gettin' at?"

"Well"—she shook her head slowly as she gazed at him—"surely you haven't got a double in America, and Mr. Lord was taking the wrong Corny Boyle at picnics, parties, swimming and tennis."

"No. It wasn't a double. I'm the same bloke. People live like that out there. Everybody mixes up together, it's a different world. It took me some time to get used to it, but——"

"But when you did, you lapped it up, didn't you?"

Corny's head had dropped slightly to the side, and now the corner of his mouth came up and there spread across his face the grin she remembered. But she could have slapped it off when in the next moment he said, "I was beginning to worry, I thought you had stopped likin' me . . . coo! I was sweatin'."

"You needn't start any of your glib American chat here. Not on me. You can keep that for—for——"

"Good-looking girls with blonde hair?"

Her lips came together, her chin went up, and her eyes flashed danger at him. But apparently he was not unduly disturbed, for his grin widened, and he dared to go on and say in a voice that was almost a drawl, "They called her Priscilla, but she wasn't a bit like her name. And she was tall, taller than most girls, five foot eight, and one of the best lookers over there, I should say. . . . But it was no use. . . ." The smile suddenly slid from his face and he went on, rapidly now, "Everybody was nice, more than nice. They had my life planned until I was ninety, and the more cushions they kept padding around me, the more I was seeing you. I told meself that I could live with you until I was ninety; even if we fought every day I could still live with you. . . . But those over there. . . ." He shook his head slowly. "I couldn't make them out. I couldn't explain if I tried, I only know why they have two or three wives. But even then I might have stayed because although I told you I'd be back when the year was up, I'd no intention of comin'. I knew what your mother wanted for you, I knew what Mr. Lord wanted for you. I could never, not in a month of Sundays, hope to compete against Tony and what he stood for. And as me grannie said, it was better to leave the way open to you, there'd be less recrimination in later years if it was your own choice. Then she wrote me a letter, me grannie, not a fortnight since. She said that you hadn't been near the door but she had heard that there was an affair going on between Tony and"—his voice dropped—"Mrs. Schofield. That Mrs. Schofield was divorced, and Tony had left old Mr. Lord. Well, that decided me. I couldn't come on the minute, I had to work a bit of notice. But I finished yesterday, or was it the day afore. Anyway, I didn't arrive in Howden until ten o'clock last night. Well, there it is, Miss Mary Ann Shaughnessy, so what about it? Your mother isn't pleased I've come back, I know that, but what about you?"

"Oh, Corny! . . . Corny!"

As his arms came out and lifted her off her feet she cried again, "Oh, Corny!"

They had kissed before, fumbling, shy, self-conscious kissing. This was different. Corny was no longer a gauche lad, and Mary Ann was no longer a little girl. When he released her they stood, their arms holding tight, staring into each other's eyes for a long while. And then he said thickly, in a voice that sounded oddly like Mike's, "I've fetched you a Christmas box." And putting his hand into his pocket he brought out a small box and handed it to her.

She knew before she opened it what to expect. But the sight of her first ring swamped her with joy. He said, "Do you like it? I got it through the Customs. It was Christmas Eve and they were kind to me." She raised her eyes from the ring. "It's wonderful, Corny, wonderful." Swiftly she put her arms round his neck again and once more they were lost in each other.

When she looked at the ring she started to sniff, and said, "I'd better make this tea.

They're all waiting."

"There's no hurry. Your da's a very astute man, Mary Ann."

"Me da's a lovely man." She looked up at him. "I'm glad you like him, and he likes you."

"I feel he does. I wish your ma did though." He was once again speaking in the tongue of the old Corny, and as he ran his fingers though her hair she replied in the idiom of the real Mary Ann, "Ee! I must mash the tea, leave over." And they both laughed together.

In the kitchen she pointed to the tray of cups saying, "Fetch it in." And then she went before him into the room.

The conversation stopped as soon as the door opened. All eyes were turned on her, and as Corny put down the tray next to Lizzie, Mary Ann held out the box before her mother and said, "Look. Corny's brought me a Christmas box."

"Oh, isn't that beautiful!" The exclamations came from both Mrs. Schofield and Sarah. Michael said nothing, nor did Mike. And Lizzie just looked at the ring that Mary Ann was holding in front of her. Then she almost ricked her back, so quickly did she twist about when Corny made a casual-sounding remark, as he turned from the table. "We're going to be married next year," was what he had said.

"Well, my God!" said Mike, on a deep note.

"Fast work," said Michael.

"Oh, how lovely, Mary Ann," said Sarah.

"Congratulations, my dear." This was Mrs. Schofield.

Lizzie said nothing, she just gaped. And Mary Ann gaped too, she gaped at the audacity of this big fellow who was again behaving unlike Corny Boyle. And without thinking about the rest of them she cried at him, "What do you mean, next year? You haven't even asked me."

"No?" Corny was looking straight at her, the quizzical lift was at the corner of his mouth again. "I'm just tellin' you now. I'll ask you the morrow, or later on the day, that is."

The bellow that Mike let out filled the room, and set them all off laughing, all except Lizzie. Lizzie was still gaping. Married next year, indeed! Married! Mary Ann? She was still. . . . The word child was ripped from her mind. No, she would never be a child again. She would soon be eighteen. In another year she would be nineteen. . . . But married. She turned again, as Corny spoke and directly to her now, looking her straight in the eye as he said, "If her mother will have me in the family?"

What could she say? What could she do? There was only one thing she was thankful for at present: this Corny Boyle was different from the Corny Boyle that went to America. Certainly the year abroad had not been wasted. And after all, she supposed, the main thing was that Mary Ann should be happy. She must remember the hell on earth her own mother had caused her when she married Mike. She mustn't be a pattern of her mother. She'd faced up to the problem of Sarah and that had turned out a hundred per cent to the good. Well, if this worked out properly, perhaps it would have the same result. She prayed to God it would anyway. She smiled now at Corny as she answered him, "I can't see that you've left me much say in the matter, Corny. But there's one thing very evident. You would never have learnt to be such a fast worker had you stayed in England."

"I don't know so much about being a fast worker." Corny was slightly red in the face now, but showing a relieved grin. "It was that way or going on shilly-shallying for weeks. It's no use talking to her." He thumbed in the direction of Mary Ann. "She'd only argue, you know what she's like."

In her own mind Lizzie confirmed her previous statement. Yes, indeed, Corny Boyle had learned a lot in America. The person whom it was no use talking to and who would argue, had not been Mary Ann . . . but herself. She had to admire him for his adroitness. In a way she felt pleased.

Mike was roaring, and as he hugged Mary Ann to him he cried down at her, "Well, me lass, you've met your match this time." And then he turned to Mrs. Schofield, who was seated at his side, and drawing her into the family, said, "What's your opinion of all this?"

Mrs. Schofield, looking between Corny and Mary Ann, said softly, "I think it will be a wonderful match. I hope they have all the happiness they both deserve." She looked at Mary Ann and said, "Do you remember your thirteenth birthday?"

Mary Ann nodded. Tears were misting her vision and she had no words to fit this occasion. Mrs. Schofield now looked towards Corny and said, "Do you remember it?"

"Could I ever forget it? Me and me shrunken suit!" He extended his long arms to demonstrate how his coat cuffs had at one time receded.

"Oh, I don't mean that. Don't be silly. I meant you and your cornet. You remember how you played, and we all sat on the lawn and sang. Oh, I've thought about that day often, and often. And that song: 'He stands at the corner'."

"Oh, aye." Mike's head went back. "He stands at the corner and whistles me out. By! It's a long time since we sang that one. Come on . . . come on, all of you. Come on, all together. Come on, Liz." He grabbed her hand and held it in a comforting grip. "Come on now. One, two, three.

> He stands at the corner
> And whistles me out,
> With his hands in his pockets
> And his shirt hanging out.
> But still I love him—
> Can't deny it—
> I'll be with him
> Wherever he goes."

Mary Ann was singing. She was looking at Corny and his eyes were hard on her. There were only the two of them in the entire world, and they were singing to each other. And when the chorus was finished for a second time the last line echoed loud in the large territory of her heart.

> I'll be with him wherever he goes,
> I'll be with him wherever he goes,
> I'll be with him wherever he goes,
> I'll be with him . . . WHEREVER HE GOES.

Yes, Corny was the one for her and she would be with him—come hail or shine.

Marriage and Mary Ann

To Muriel Baker

*An unusual friend, who from the beginning
not only liked my books, but bought them*

1

"And all this has come about because they went on a holiday." Fanny McBride thrust out her thick arm and pulled the blue sugar bag towards her, and after ladling three spoonfuls into an outsize cup of tea she added, "But you're sure you're not enlargin' on everything, Mary Ann?"

"No, Mrs. McBride. I wish I was. But it isn't imagination, it isn't."

"Well, I was just thinkin' you have a lot on your mind at the present moment, with Michael and Sarah's wedding in the offing, and your own looming up ahead. By the way, I must tell you, I was glad when you and Corny decided not to make it a double-do. I think you want your own glory on a day like that." Fanny smiled broadly at Mary Ann. "Aw"—she shook her head—"the day I see you and Corny married I think my heart'll burst for joy. I've known you since you were that high"—she measured a short distance with her hand—"and I've watched you grow up to great things."

"Aw, Mrs. McBride." Mary Ann was shaking her head as she stared down towards the table. "I've done nothing with me life, nothing as yet."

"Not for yourself you haven't, me dear, except to take me grandson for your husband, but you've done it for others. Where would your da be the day without you and your schemes, eh?" She poked her broad face towards that of the heart-shaped, elfin face of Mary Ann. "Would Mike be managing a farm with a grand house, an' be the right hand of Mr. Lord, if it be his only hand?"

"It was through me he lost his hand, don't forget that, Mrs. McBride."

"Do I forget that God works in strange ways, child? If Mike hadn't lost his hand he wouldn't be where he is the day."

"I know that."

"Well then, you've no need to bother your head about the things you haven't done, for to my mind you've achieved almost the impossible where your da's concerned. As you know, I'm very fond of Mike, an' I know him inside out, his strength and his one weakness, an' that being the drink. But he's conquered that, thanks be to God. Well, knowing him as I do, I wouldn't have said that he had a weakness for the women, although I could say that some women might have a weakness for himself, for the older he gets the more fetchin' he gets."

"That's the trouble."

Mary Ann was looking solemnly at this big, voluptuous old woman, who, as she had said, had known her from a small child. And from a small child Mary Ann had looked upon Fanny McBride as her friend and comforter. From the day they had first come to live in the attic of Mulhattan's Hall—which place her mother had considered the very end of the downward trail—from that day she had been comforted and helped by the tenant on the first floor, Mrs. Fanny McBride. There was no one else in the world she could talk to freely about her da, except to this woman, because, as Fanny had also stated, she knew Mike Shaughnessy inside out.

Mary Ann said now, "It seems sad to think that it was mother's first real holiday, and she had been looking forward to it so much; and we all had fun and carry-on before they went saying what would happen to them at a holiday camp. The awful thing is that it was herself who plumped to go to a holiday camp; me da wasn't for it at all, he just went to please her."

"How old did you say the girl was?"

"Nineteen."

"And she has red hair?"

"Yes, and my mother says that's how it started. They were at the same table and her mother—the girl's mother, Mrs. Radley—pointed out that me da's hair was almost the same shade as her daughter's. Then he danced with her, and after that they were in the swimming pool together. My mother can't swim and she just had to sit and look on. At first she didn't think anything about it, until Mrs. Radley and her—Yvonne, they call her—tacked on to them everywhere they went . . . and me da seemed to like it."

"And your mother told you all this?"

"Yes."

Fanny shook her head again. "Lizzie must be upset in her mind to speak of it so plainly, because she was ever so close about some things was Lizzie, reserved like, about the private things in her life, even when she was upstairs here. She must be taking this very badly, and it's hitting her at the wrong time of life. But then, that always happens; these things always hit women at the wrong time of life. I think men were built to cause it to be so, just to make things harder for us."

"She can't set her mind to the wedding because they're coming."

"Who was it asked them?"

"It must have been me da because she says that she never did."

"Well, it needn't have been him, you know, Mary Ann. People, clever people, have a way of gettin' themselves invited—aye! begod, even into me house here." She laughed. "They put you on a spot. Perhaps your da was put on a spot; I wouldn't lay that at his door."

Mary Ann rose from the table and walked to the window, and, looking out through the narrow aperture of the curtains down into the dull, sunless street, she turned her gaze towards the top end from where she hoped to see Corny coming, and then she fingered the curtains before saying, "He must have known that if she came to the wedding me mother would be upset, and if he didn't ask them outright he could have done something to put them off. That's what's in me mind all the time. I have to think of him deliberately hurting me mother."

Fanny, pulling herself to her feet by gripping the worn, wooden arms of her chair, shambled towards the open fire, and there, lifting up the long rake, she pulled some pieces of coal from the back of the grate down into the dulling embers. Then, placing the rake back on the fender, she said, "Tell me, was he pleased to see them when they came on the hop last Sunday?"

"Yes . . . yes, he was. He seemed a bit taken aback at first, but then he started to act like a young lad, skittish. I . . . oh, Mrs. McBride. . . ." Mary Ann turned from the window and looked across the cluttered, dusty room to the old woman, and she bit her lip before she ended, "He made me so ashamed. I . . . I never thought I would feel like that about him . . . ashamed of him. It was . . . it was a different kind of feeling to when he used to get roaring drunk. I wasn't really ashamed of him then, only sorry for him, pitying him, sort of; but last Sunday I . . . I knew I was ashamed of him. Oh . . . oh, Mrs. McBride, it was awful. I . . . I can say this to you, can't I, because I've always been able to talk to you, haven't I?"

"Aye, hinny, you have that," said Fanny in a low tone. "It's another thing I've thanked God for. Go on."

Mary Ann came and took her seat at the table again, and, moving the spoon round in the empty cup, she concentrated her gaze on it as she said, "Well, there was a time when I began to dislike me mother for certain things she did, for her attitude towards the front room. . . . Remember, when she didn't want Sarah to have it. And then the way she used to go for me da at times. But I could never imagine me ever disliking me da, because you know . . ." She lifted her eyes to those of Mrs. McBride and said very softly, "I worship him, I really do. At least I did. He was like God to me, but when I saw him actually put his arm round that beastly, scheming cat's waist"—her lips were now squared from her teeth—"I felt that I hated him."

"Where did this happen?"

"It was in the kitchen, but me mother was there."

"Aw well, that's not so bad. It would have meant something much worse if she hadn't been there."

"I don't see it like that, Mrs. McBride, for if he'll do that in front of her what'll he do when she isn't there? That's how I see it. And . . . and he's started sprucing up. He never used to get changed in the evening unless he was going out, because sometimes he's got to see to the cattle late on, but now after tea he goes upstairs and gets into a good suit, collar and tie and everything."

"Does he take himself out?"

"One night last week he did."

"Did you know where he went?"

"No. He didn't say, and me mother didn't ask him, and I wouldn't. But on other nights he just strolled round the fields all dressed up like that."

Returning to her chair, Fanny lowered herself slowly down, her head wagging the while. She sucked in her lips, closed her eyes, and joining her hands together, moved these too in a wagging movement; then simultaneously all these actions ceased and she looked straight ahead towards the fire as she said, "Within a few months you'll be married, Mary Ann, an' life will open out for you, an' you'll learn lots of things. But they all won't come at once, an' let's thank God for it, but it'll be some time afore you come really aware of the fact that there comes a period in life when women are not themselves. You'll have likely heard without understanding much about it that the middle years are very trying to a woman, but nobody's likely told you, for nobody seems to think along the same lines regarding men, but . . ." Now Fanny swung her head round towards Mary Ann, and, pointing her finger at her, she said solemnly, "But now, let me tell you, because I know, havin' reared a number of the specimens, that men are tested much more sorely than women during the middle years, maybe not along the same lines, but nevertheless they are tested. There's something stirs in them, aggravatin' them, seeming to say 'Come on, lad, you're not dead yet. Show them that you're as young as ever you were.' An' there, Mary Ann, you've got the core of the whole matter . . . as young as ever they were. Now a woman doesn't like growin' old, it hurts her vanity; even if she's ugly as sin it hurts her vanity. But, begod, a man likes growin' old less, for it not only hurts his vanity, it threatens his manhood. He is torn to shreds in that way much more than a woman is. Men, you know, Mary Ann, are merely grown-up lads. They may look old, and act old, but under their skins they're just lads, an', as I've said, there comes a time when they want to prove to the world they're still lads, so what do they do? Well, they take up with a lass young enough to be their daughter, some young enough to be a granddaughter. Now as I see it, this is what's happening to your da, an' your mother should know all about this. There's no doubt she does, but she's troubled in herself, an' in me own opinion Lizzie's no fit person to handle this situation at all. No, as I see it she's not; but you, Mary Ann, you with all your experience of your da, you're the one best able to talk to him."

"Oh no. Oh no." Mary Ann was again on her feet. "I couldn't, Mrs. McBride, not about this."

"But you've done it on other occasions, you've talked him round from other things than drink."

"Yes, well . . . but I haven't so much talked to him as did things. . . . Oh, I can't explain."

"There's no need to, I know. As I've said afore, you've schemed and manoeuvred. . . . Well, why not use the same tactics now?"

"I couldn't, Mrs. McBride; I tell you, I just couldn't over this. Him going mad over this girl, this young girl. I've thought about it but I just couldn't. I . . . I can't even speak to him ordinarily."

"You mean you're not speaking to Mike at all?"

"No, I haven't for the past three weeks."

"Aw, God in heaven! Now you are askin' for trouble."

"Well, I can't help it."

"Well now, Mary Ann"—the fat, not too clean, finger was wagging at her again—"you'll just have to help it, for that's the worst thing you could do, not be speakin' to him. . . . Tell me, how's Lizzie treatin' him?"

"She hardly speaks to him either."

"Name of God! I thought you both had more sense, at least you. If you want to drive him away that's the way to do it. Go on not speakin' to him, push him out, and that girl, with the help of her mother, will have him in her arms afore you can say Jimmy McGregor. Now look. . . . Aw"—Fanny turned her head towards the door—"if I know that step, this is the Lado himself, so we'll take this mater up another time. But think on what I've said."

Mary Ann, too, was looking towards the door, and when it opened she managed a smile for the young man entering.

Corny Boyle was now six foot two and broad with it. He had a fine physique, and if he'd had a matching face he might have been billed as a modern Apollo, but Corny could lay no claim to good looks. His best feature were his eyes; for the rest, his face gave the impression of a piece of granite that had been hacked by a would-be sculptor. He looked older than his twenty-three years, in fact he could at times have passed for thirty; this was when his face was in repose, for when he smiled he looked youthful. It could be said that to Corny's one good feature you could add his smile, for it was an impish, irresistible smile, and it infected those it fell upon; it even at times gave some people the impression that he was handsome. It had this latter effect on Mary Ann.

"Hello, Gran." He took three strides across the room to Fanny's side, and, bending over her, he kissed her cheek, while she placed her hand on his thick hair. Then, looking towards Mary Ann, he said, "Hello, you."

"Hello yourself. You've been some time. You said four o'clock."

"I know I did but I'm only half-an-hour out and I knew you'd be here, sitting gossiping"—he glanced towards Fanny—"and so . . ."

At this point Mary Ann, bouncing her head, took up his words, and together they chanted, "And so I went and had a look at Meyer's garage."

Fanny's head was back now and her laugh was filling the room. "Aw, begod, you're startin' early! Well, as long as he wasn't in Flanagan's bar, or at the bettin' shop waitin' the result of the last race, it isn't too bad, eh?" She put her hand out towards Mary Ann, and Mary Ann, laughing, replied, "That's all he can talk about, cars, cars, cars."

"Well, as I'll have to support you on cars for the rest of your life what better subject could I talk about?" Corny bent his long length above her and they stared at each other for a moment, their faces becoming solemn; then, doubling his fist, he twice punched her gently on the side of the chin before saying, "Well, if you want to go to that dance and go home first, you'll have to get a move on."

"Oh! A move on! We're now all bustle and hurry." Mary Ann inclined her head towards Fanny's broadly smiling face, and as Corny exclaimed, "Who is it wants to go to the dance, anyway?" she put on her coat and hat and, turning to Fanny, said softly, "Bye-bye, Mrs. McBride, and thanks . . . for the tea and everything."

"Thank you, hinny, for comin' in."

"Bye-bye, Gran." Again Corny kissed the networked skin, but before he straightened up he cast his glance towards Mary Ann, saying, "Don't you think it's time you called this old faggot Gran, instead of Mrs. McBride?"

Fanny and Mary Ann looked at each other, then with a small smile Mary Ann said, "I suppose so, but somehow . . . well, I always think of you as Mrs. McBride and it's got the same feeling as me saying ma, or da. . . . You understand?"

"I understand, hinny, an' I'll remain Mrs. McBride. An', you know, I like it that way; it's got a dignified ring, don't you think . . . Mrs. McBride?"

"Dignified!" Corny now took the flat of his hand and pushed the big broad face to one side, exclaiming, "You, dignified! . . . You're in your dotage, woman."

"Get out of it, an' this minute, or I'll let you see who's in their dotage . . . or an old faggot at that."

Fanny pulled herself up and brandished her fist at him, and Corny, pushing Mary Ann into the passage and about to follow her, looked back into the room and said softly, "Go on with you, fat old Fan. Dignified, indeed!"

Her grandson's words could have been a compliment, for they brought a warm tender smile to Fanny's face, and when the door closed on him she sat down again, and the smile remained with her as she looked about her with eyes that did not take in the muddle and dust amidst which she sat; for what was muddle, she would have said if she thought about it, and what was dust when your heart was happy knowing that your favourite grandson had had the good sense to pick himself the nicest little lass in the world?

In the street, the nicest little lass walked sedately by Corny's side. She always felt slightly self-conscious when with him in the street, for she remembered experiences when children had shouted after them, "De ya want a step-ladder, miss?" and, "Aa'll bunk you up to him for thrup-pence." Then there was the day when the woman behind them in the bus said, "That's the long an' the short of it, isn't it?" And so she resisted her desire to link arms with him, for in her mind's eye she could see how ludicrous it would look. Even when they held hands it must appear to other people as if he was taking a child for a walk. She was five foot tall and, try as she might, she couldn't add a fraction of an inch to this. Her height wasn't noticeable when she was on her own, only when she was with Corny, for besides being small she was slightly built, and this didn't help matters.

"You're quiet," he said; "what's the matter?"

"Nothing."

"Well, it couldn't be much less, could it?" They turned their eyes towards each other and smiled, and the smiles brought a humorous twist to their faces.

"Want to go to that dance?"

Mary Ann moved one shoulder, "I'm not really particular, I'd just as soon go to the pictures or the bowling alley. What about you?"

"Anything'll suit me. I tell you what though. . . ." He moved nearer to her and, his voice dropping to a whisper, he went on, "I've got some new car catalogues. We could have a smashing time just sitting looking at them."

Forcing herself not to laugh, she pushed at him with her elbow as she replied, "That would be wonderful. You wouldn't like us to sit on that seat outside Meyer's garage, would you?"

"Aw." He moved his head as if in wonder. "Aw, that would be simply marvellous, just to sit all the night looking at Meyer's garage and them cars."

"You're barmy. Cars, cars, cars."

Now her tone had an edge to it, and he mimicked it, saying, "Cars, cars, cars." Then went on, "Yes, I'm barmy about them all right, an' before you're finished you'll be glad I'm barmy about them, because cars, cars, cars, are going to get you all you want. . . . In the end they will, anyway."

"How do you know what I want? For all you know I might want you to go round the streets playing your cornet."

He slanted his eyes down at her for a moment, then said quietly, "Look, what's up with you? You're ratty about something. Anything happened in me grannie's?"

"Of course not. What could happen in there?"

"Only talk. . . . What were you talking about?"

"Oh, nothing. Look, there's the bus." She pointed. "If we miss it, it'll be another half-an-hour."

Grabbing her arm, he ran with her, almost lifting her off the ground, and he actually hoisted her on to the platform of the bus just as it was about to move away.

Half-an-hour later they were in the country, walking up the lane towards the farm. Although it was a dull day the field to the right of them seemed lit by sunshine, for, with the breeze passing over them, the full heads of barley were making waves of light and shade.

Mary Ann's eyes, following the waves, were lifted into the far distance to the big house on the hill, Mr. Lord's house . . . and now Tony's house . . . and Lettice's house. It was strange to think of Tony married to Lettice and them both living with Mr. Lord . . . and he liking it. Why was it, she asked herself now, that in spite of her good intentions she always felt the slightest bit of jealousy when she thought of Mr. Lord liking Lettice living with him? Although she herself had had a hand in Mr. Lord's acceptance of his grandson's wife, she still couldn't help the feeling that she didn't want him to be too happy about it. . . . But she really knew what caused this feeling. It was the fear that if he became too engrossed in Tony and his wife he would forget all about her.

"You're not listening to me."

"What? What did you say?"

Pulling her to a stop, Corny placed his hands on her shoulders and surveyed her through narrowed eyes before saying, "I said, if they make that branch road off the Newcastle road and come up by Meyer's garage, and if we get the garage, we're made. That's what I said. I've been talking since we got off the bus and you haven't heard a word."

"You're always talking." She smiled tenderly up at him. "But you don't talk to the right people."

"Oh, don't I?" He raised his brows. "Well, I'll have to find the right people, won't I? But for the present I'll keep practising on you, to get me fit for the real thing. . . . And that's another thing, I was talking about the real thing a minute ago, but you weren't with me. We are going to have a wedding, aren't we?"

"Yes." She blinked her eyes. The smile was still on her face, but when he snapped his body upwards away from her, exclaiming harshly, "You're as interested in what I'm saying as if I was talking about a Methodist Sunday School treat," she cried: "All right! All right! Don't go on like that." She swung away, her voice cracking now. "I might as well tell you I can't think of the wedding . . . so there. I can't think of anything but me da at the present moment."

"God in Heaven!" Corny put his fist to his brow. "Don't start on that again—it'll work out. Men go through these phases. . . . It'll work out."

As she stared at him she thought, That's what Mrs. McBride said. It's a phase and it'll work out. But what if it doesn't work out?

"How do you know it'll work out?" she demanded now. "Have you been through the phase?"

"I don't happen to be in me forties." The impatient note in his voice caused her to respond with, "Oh, it happens in the forties, does it? Then you've got something to look forward to, haven't you?"

"Aye, yes." He put on a false smile and his tone was harsh now as he went on, "I hadn't thought about it in that way. You've got a point there. And, by lad, by the time I've lived with you until I'm forty I imagine I'll be damned glad of a little variety . . . that is, if I manage to stick it out that long."

"Manage-to-stick-it-out-that-long!" She spaced his words. "Well, I can tell you here and now, Mr. Cornelius Boyle, there'll be no need to endure any purgatory through me."

They were off again. Their association had always taken this pattern: sunshine, then sudden storm, then sunshine again.

"Good . . . good." He was towering over her, glaring down at her. "So we're breaking up. That's it, isn't it?"

"Yes, that's it."

They stood for a long moment exchanging their momentary animosity, then with a swiftness that startled her his hands were under her oxters and he had lifted her off her feet, and he was kissing her, a hard, rough kiss. Then still holding her to him, he said softly, "I had to have that for the road, seeing that I'll be on my own for the next forty years." Now both their bodies began to shake and melt into each other. Her arms were around his neck as she repeated, "Oh, Corny! Corny! I'm daft I am. I'm daft."

"I know you are."

"I mean about me da."

"That's what I mean an' all; but I tell you he'll get over it."

"But me mother's worried sick, Corny. And it's the disgrace, and with a young girl. Do you know she's months younger than me?"

"She looks ten years older, and I'm not kiddin'."

"That's as may be, but she's younger, and when I see her with me da . . . oh, it makes me sick, and I just can't believe it. I can't believe he can be so silly, so nauseatingly silly."

"Has it happened like this afore?"

They were walking slowly up the lane now, their arms about each other.

"No, not like this, but there have been women who have fallen for him. But then, as I say, they were women, not girls."

"Did he have affairs with them—I mean the women?"

"No, no, never; he just laughed at them, and laughed about them to me ma. Not that she wasn't worried once or twice, like the time she thought he was gone on Mrs. Quinton."

"Mrs. Quinton? Bob Quinton's wife? She's a smasher."

"There you go . . . smasher. Well, perhaps she is a smasher but she liked me da." She nodded her head up at him. "But this present business is different; it's—it's nasty, and it's keeping on."

"It's just because he's flattered. Look, do as I say, let things rest and take their course."

"I can't, Corny, because I'm frightened, really I am. I know it's as you say, it's because she flatters him. And her mother and all, she's as bad, and he laps it up. . . . All the more so now because me mother doesn't let on he's there. . . . Well, you know what I mean? But she hasn't made much of him for a long time, because she hasn't been feeling too good herself." She stopped in the road and, twisting round, looked up at him, saying, "Do you know, I can see both their minds working, both that sly cat's and her mother's. They've got it all set between them. I'll be out of the way when I get married; Michael and Sarah will be in the bungalow; so there will be only me mother and me da left, and now that it's open knowledge that the farm will be me da's one day they think they're on to a good thing. Miss Yvonne's just got to have an affair with me da . . . get herself a baby, and then me mother's out. . . ."

"Mary Ann!" As Corny loosened his hold on her he drew his chin into his neck, and the action seemed to pull his voice up from deep down in his chest. "Don't talk like that," he said. "I'm tellin' you, don't talk like that."

Mary Ann stared at him. Both in voice and manner he could have been her da at this moment. Her lips trembled; she felt alone, lost. Mr. Lord no longer required her company, and her da had gone from her, and now Corny turning on her. Well, she wasn't going to put up with it, she wasn't. She cried at him, "Why shouldn't I talk like that? It's the truth."

"It may be, but I don't like to hear you taking that tack."

"You don't, do you? . . . Well, for your information, I'd better remind you we're in nineteen-sixty-four, and I would also remind you that you're supposed to have been around a bit . . . America and all over the . . ."

"I don't care if it's twenty-and-sixty-four." His voice had a rasping edge to it. "And yes, I've been around a bit, scoff as much as you like, but I've been around more than you have, and when I was . . . around America I didn't hear the girls, at least not the ones I mixed with, saying things like that. If you were still living in Mulhattan's Hall, or over our way in Howden, and you hadn't had your fancy education, it would be understandable."

Mary Ann's neck and face were scarlet. Her wide eyes were smarting, and her trembling lips moved with soundless words a number of times before she whimpered, "You can think what you like about me, I don't care, I don't care, only I know it's true what I've said; it could happen. As for the girls in America not talking like that, don't . . . don't make me la . . . laugh." Choking on the last words, she gave a demonstration of laughter by bursting into tears. And when he caught her close, crying, "There! There! Give over. I'm sorry," she gabbled, "I'm worried. I'm frightened. I know it could happen. I do, I do. And you . . . you going for me and making me out to be something nasty just because I said what . . . what I know she's trying to . . ."

"There! There! All right, all right. Come on, don't cry. And you're right. Listen . . . listen to me." He lifted her face upwards. "I know you're right, but somehow . . . well"—he moved his head slowly—"I hate to hear you talk like that. Let everybody else in the world say what they want to say, and how they want to say it, but you . . . aw." He hunched his shoulders. "Here, dry your face."

Clumsily he wiped the tears from her face, then said, "Come on, smile. You don't want to go in and give your mother something else to worry about, do you? She's got enough on her plate at present. Come on." His mouth twisted sideways as he ended, sanctimoniously, "Let us be a comfort to her in her old age, anyway."

Mary Ann hiccoughed; the tears were still rolling from her eyes but she wanted to laugh, and she actually did laugh when, bending down to her, he whispered, "About the American girls, that was a pack of lies. Coo! The things that some of them used to say, they made you sizzle, like water on a hot frying pan."

"Oh, Corny, Corny, you're daft. Oh, you are daft."

They were hurrying up the road now, close once again, and as they neared the farm the dull clouds parted and the sun shone, picking out the newly pink-cement-dashed farmhouse, with its two ornamental red-bricked chimneys straining upwards towards an overhanging branch of a mighty oak tree whose base boarded the road some yards away. It picked out the farm building, white-washed and neat, forming three sides of a square. It showed two farm cottages with their long gardens patterned with vegetables and early chrysanthemums.

As they entered the farm gates there was a murmuring of cattle from the byres, the sharp bark of the dog, and the distant thud of a galloping horse sporting in the field beyond the buildings.

This, her home, had always been a form of heaven to Mary Ann, but now she was experiencing the knowledge that surroundings only become significant when the people close to you are at peace. But there was no peace either in or between those close to her, and the reason for that state was now coming across the courtyard.

Mary Ann did not call to Mike or hurry to greet him, or he to her. As she took in the fact that he was hesitating in the middle of the yard she felt Corny's swift decision, almost as if he had said aloud, "Well, somebody's got to stand by him." "I'll be with you in a minute," was what he said to her, and as he went towards her father she made her way slowly towards the house.

2

Mary Ann woke up with the sun streaming on to her face, and she blinked into it; then, turning completely over on to her stomach, she stretched one leg after the other and lay supine for some moments. Her mind not yet disturbed by thoughts, she felt relaxed and warm . . . and nice; but the more she tried to hold the feeling the faster she was becoming awake. As she wondered what time it was, she raised her head and looked at the bedside clock. Half-past seven. She twisted round and pulled herself upwards by putting her hands behind her head and gripping the bed rail, then, leaning back and staring into the sun once more, she began to pick up the sounds from below her. She heard the even note of her mother's voice, then the deeper tone of Michael's; then came a short, thick spray of words, the tone of which she had not heard before rising from the kitchen at this time of the morning. It brought her upright in the bed; she had forgotten for the moment that Corny had slept here last night. They had all, except her father, stayed up late talking about the wedding, and when Corny was ready to go it was blowing a gale. It was her mother who had said, "You can't go out in this, you'll get soaked." As usual, Corny had his motor-bike with him but he hadn't a cape. He hadn't taken much persuading to stay and he had phoned a fish-and-chip shop that was three doors away from his home and asked a neighbour to tell his mother that he was staying the night.

Mary Ann smiled to herself; it would be funny going down and seeing Corny at breakfast. She had better get up. She threw the clothes back and sat on the edge of the bed and again she stretched—she hadn't to go to the office today. She had taken the day off to help get things ready for the morrow, and Sarah's wedding. That's why she had felt so nice, she supposed, when she woke up, not having to go into work. But the niceness hadn't lasted very long, had it, because now she was feeling as she had done for weeks, worried. Well, she sighed, she wasn't the only one, everyone in the house was worried. . . . And yet that wasn't true. Michael wasn't really worried about what was going on; nor was Sarah. They both seemed already to be living separate lives, a joint separate life. And they were discussing the business of her da and Yvonne Radley. Sarah, because she had become very fond of Mike, and Michael, Mary Ann knew, because he wanted to preserve the picture of her da that he had built up around him these last few years. He didn't want to go back to his childhood and the feeling of hate he'd had for the man who couldn't stop drinking. Michael and her da had become very close during the last few years, and now he was shutting his eyes to anything that would show up her da in an unfavourable light. . . . She wished that she, too, could shut her eyes to it.

A few minutes later, when she went into the bathroom, she found all the towels wet. That was their Michael; he not only used his own towel but everybody else's. She felt she wanted to rush to the stair-head and cry, as she sometimes did, "Not a dry towel again! You leave my towel alone, our Michael." But as she looked in the mirror she said to herself, "Stop it, there's enough trouble." Yet she still asked her reflection, "But why does he want to use so many towels?"

Ten minutes later, as she descended the stairs, she paused for a second when she saw Mike crossing the hall. He was going out the front way and he had his big boots on. . . . He was just doing it to aggravate her mother, for her mother took pride in the hall and it always looked lovely.

When she reached the bottom stair Mike had pulled the front door open, and he turned towards her, and after a second, during which he looked hard at her, he said, "Mornin'."

"Good morning, Da."

"Mary Ann." His voice was low.

"Yes, Da?"

He jerked his head and beckoned her to him, and when she stood before him he looked straight at her as he said, "I should be down in the bottom field around ten, do you think you could spare me a few minutes?"

Her eyes dropped from his. "I . . . I don't know; me mother's got so many things she wants doing and——"

"All right, all right." He stood stiffly, holding up his hand in a checking movement. "Don't come if you don't want to; I understand it's a very busy day for everybody." His tone was sarcastic. "But just suppose you have a minute or so to spare, I would—" he paused, "I would be grateful for a word with you."

She looked up at him. Her da had never talked like this to her in his life, sarcastically, nor had he ever had to ask her to go and have a word with him. He'd always had to push her from him, stop her from having too many words with him. "I'll be there," she said.

"Thank you." The sarcasm was heavy in his tone.

She turned away and went into the kitchen, there to meet her mother's enquiring glance. It was just the flick of Lizzie's eye but it said plainly, "What did he say? What did he want?"

Mary Ann answered it with, "I don't want any bacon, Mother, just some cereal."

"You'd better get a breakfast into you."

"I don't feel like it."

Mary Ann now turned her head towards the table and looked at Corny. His eyes were waiting for her. "Hello," she said. "Did you sleep all right?"

Corny grinned as he replied, "Like a man with a clear conscience."

"Huh! Aren't we self-righteous." She sat down opposite to him, and Corny, looking now at Lizzie and his grin widening, said, "This is the first time I've seen her first thing in the mornin'. Lord, doesn't she look miserable!"

Lizzie smiled faintly at this boy, at this young man, at this big fellow whom she had tried so hard to dislike—this boy who was the last person on earth she would have wanted Mary Ann to marry; this young man who was too big altogether for Mary Ann and whose prospects, on the other hand, were too small for what she wanted for her daughter; this big fellow who was the cause of Mary Ann not marrying Tony. For years she had set her heart on her daughter becoming the wife of Mr. Lord's grandson and having all things that that marriage would entail. But apparently it wasn't to be. How many more disappointments in life could she put up with? How much more could she stand and keep sane? Her mind on the last thought had moved away from Mary Ann, and now she was saying to herself, What were they talking about at the front door? . . . And fancy him going out the front way in his dirty boots. He just did that to work me up after last night. As she picked up the teapot she thought, Perhaps I should have let him talk. Yet listening to him making excuses and giving reasons for his madness would only have made things worse. I couldn't have bore it.

Mary Ann's raised voice brought her attention to the table. "What's the matter now?" she asked.

"Well, I'm just saying I'm right." Mary Ann looked up at Lizzie as she pointed a finger of toast across the table in the direction of Corny. "He said, why do I want to cut up the toast like this and put finicky bits of marmalade on it, and I said it was the right way. And it is, isn't it? Not to butter and marmalade a slice all at once, I mean."

"Oh, Mary Ann!" Lizzie shook her head at her daughter with a despairing movement. "Why must you start on such things?"

"But I didn't, Mother, it was him." She nodded at Corny.

"Huh!" said Corny. "She was talking as if I didn't know the right way to eat. I know all about fingers of toast and dabbing bits of this, that, and the other on it, but you only do that when you're in hotels, or out with posh company, don't you, Mam?" He addressed Lizzie with the familiar term he had always used since he had become engaged to Mary Ann; and his attitude now towards her was as if she was his mother and arbitrator in a family dispute.

And now Lizzie smiled at him. You couldn't help but like Corny; however much you tried not to, you couldn't help but like him. She nodded at him saying, "Yes, you're right, Corny."

"He's not, Mother. And don't stick up for him about such things, it only makes him worse . . . big-headed."

"Whose going to stick up for whose big head?" The door from the scullery opened and Michael came in. He looked a younger edition of his father, and as he walked down the long room to the table he could have been Mike himself twenty years earlier. When he picked up a slice of toast from the rack and started to butter it, Lizzie said, "You've had your breakfast not half-an-hour ago."

"Was it only half-an-hour? It seems I've never had a bite since yesterday."

"Well, tomorrow's not affecting your appetite, that's something." Lizzie smiled tenderly at her son, and Michael, reaching out for the marmalade, stopped with his hand in mid air and enquired of Corny, "What's the matter?"

"Nothing . . . nothing." Corny's voice was rapid. "Go on, marmalade your bread."

"Aw you!" Mary Ann, her lips tight now, was shaking her head at the aggravating individual, and when Michael had finished spreading his slice of toast thickly with marmalade, Corny looked at her and gave one wide grin as he let out a deep chest full of air and said, "There now."

"There now, what? What's this all about? What's the matter with you two first thing in the morning?"

"She says it ain't—" Corny stressed the ain't, "she says it ain't refeened to eat toast like that, Michael. We should cut it into refeened little fingers, like so." He demonstrated.

"Oh, we should, should we?" Michael was returning Corny's grin. "Oh, what it is to be a lady; it must be painful." And leaning towards Corny, Michael pityingly added, "Boy, I don't envy you. . . . Poor blighter. . . ."

"Aw, there's a pair of you." Mary Ann tossed her head disdainfully. "You eat like pigs, clagging everything up. . . ."

"HA!" A high derisive hoot came from Michael. "Listen to her. Listen to her. Listen to her. Ooh! Miss Shaughnessy, how can you let yourself down to such a low level? Did you hear what she said, Corny?" He turned wide eyes in Corny's direction again. "Clag, she said. Did you hear her? . . . Clag."

"Now, now, stop it, or it'll end up in words, hot words, if not in tears." Lizzie, addressing the two young men and bringing their eyes towards her, motioned with a jerk of her head towards Mary Ann's back.

"Tears." Mary Ann rounded on her mother. "They won't reduce me to tears, not that pair."

As she bounced up from the table, Lizzie placed a hand on her shoulder and said, "Sit down and have something to eat. Now you're not going to start doing anything until you have your breakfast." As she pressed her daughter into the chair again she could have added, as she might have done some weeks earlier, "What's put you in this tear so early in the morning?" But she had no need to question her daughter's state of mind, she knew the reason only too well.

Although Lizzie's own nerves were near to breaking point, and her heart was sore, and her feelings towards her husband were almost verging on hate at this moment, she wished Mary Ann had not taken a stand against her father, for her attitude towards the man she had always adored seemed to Lizzie to put a finality on the whole thing. Nothing Mike had ever done in his life had made Mary Ann stop speaking to him, until now, and Lizzie found her feelings entwining round her daughter, loving her as she had not done for some time, in fact, since she was a baby, because since Mary Ann had come to the use of reason she had always taken her father's part. Be he in the right or wrong—and he was more often in the wrong than not—Mary Ann had always stood valiantly by him. But Mary Ann was no longer a child, she was almost twenty and she was soon to be married, and in her father's present madness she was seeing him for the first time as he really was. Yet in spite of all this Lizzie wanted to say to her: "Go and talk to him; be kind to him, because I can't." And, knowing her husband, she knew that he needed somebody . . . he always needed somebody to be kind to him.

At this moment there came the sound of fumbling with the handle of the door leading from the hall, and although all their eyes turned in the direction of the door no one got up to open it, and it was seconds later before it was pushed wide, and there entered Sarah Flanagan.

Sarah was supporting herself on two elbow crutches, and while her right foot tentatively touched the ground she dragged the whole of her left leg from the hip downwards as if it was part of a dead carcass that had been tied to her. From the waist up she was well formed, and above the long neck was a radiant face.

This was the Sarah Flannagan who had lived opposite to Mary Ann in Mulhattan's Hall for years. This was the girl who had been Mary Ann's enemy, who had fought with her daily, playing on her weak point, her affection for her drunken father. This was the girl who had written things about Mike Shaughnessy on walls and had driven Mary Ann to a frenzy of retaliation. This was the girl who had found, at an early age, that she loved horses and wanted to work with them, and had worked with them until two years ago when she had been struck with polio. But above all, this was the girl who loved Michael Shaughnessy and whom Michael Shaughnessy adored. There was no resemblance between this wise, tender, beautiful cripple, and the girl who had been brought up in Burton Street.

No one in the room moved to help her until she almost reached the table; then Michael went quietly to her side and pulled out a chair for her, and when she was seated they looked at each other for a moment. It was the look that always brought an odd feeling into Mary Ann's body. Mary Ann, it could be said now, also loved Sarah as much as she had once hated her. And although they had scrapped all their lives, she also loved Michael. Yet when she saw Sarah and Michael together there emanated a feeling from them that created in her a sense of want, and of loss. For what exactly, she didn't know; she told herself it was because they never fought, but seemed always at peace in each other's company, whereas she and Corny rarely met unless they went for each other in some way.

"Sleep well?" Michael was asking Sarah; and she answered with a shake of her head. "No, hardly at all. . . ." She paused, then asked, "Did you?"

Michael, bowing his head as if in shame, tried to suppress a smile as he confessed, "Like a top."

"They have no finer feelings, that's why they can sleep." Mary Ann was looking at Sarah, and Sarah answered, "Perhaps you're right. Or no nerves." She cast a swift glance again towards Michael, and he, bending and kissing her quite unselfconsciously, said softly, "I'll move my coarse presence from you to the cow sheds."

As Michael went to leave the kitchen Corny asked, "Give you a hand or anything,

Michael?" And Michael, turning from the doorway, answered, "We never say no to an extra hand, Corny, but I thought you'd have to be at the garage."

"No, I took a couple of days off," said Corny. "And for no other reason, mind you"—he was nodding his head now at Michael—"but that Miss Shaughnessy had done the same and she'd be lonely without me. . . . Wouldn't know what to do with herself, in fact."

Michael was laughing, Sarah was laughing, but Mary Ann, refusing to smile, was giving Corny a straight stare as he, rising from the table, bent towards her and chucked her under the chin, saying with tenderness that was more real than make-believe, "Good-bye, sugar."

When the door had closed on the two young men Mary Ann let her face slide into a smile, and when she looked at Sarah they both began to laugh.

Lizzie sat down at the table, poured herself out a cup of tea, and, looking at her daughter, remarked, "Your breakfasts, in the future, should be very entertaining."

"Well, he's so aggravating."

"And you're not, of course." Lizzie's remark was softened by the tilt of her lips. "In some ways I think he's very patient with you."

"Patient! Huh!" Mary Ann tossed her head, while at the same time feeling pleased that her mother was taking Corny's part. She wanted her mother to like Corny, for she felt that even after all this long time of knowing him, and accepting him as her future son-in-law, she was still in two minds about him.

But her attention was drawn to Sarah, who was saying, "Breakfasts in the future are going to be different for me; I'll miss all this . . . the talk . . . the bustle." She looked at Lizzie as she spoke, and Lizzie replied softly, "I'll miss you, too. It won't be the same without you, Sarah."

As her mother and her future sister-in-law exchanged warm glances there was wafted to Mary Ann again that feeling of want, of loss. Her mother liked Sarah, and this fact alone said a great deal, because Lizzie adored her son, and Sarah was marrying that son . . . taking him away.

Sarah was now saying, "It's funny how your opinions change. A year ago I was dead against going into the bungalow, wasn't I? And so was Michael, although his reasons were different from mine. He didn't want to be beholden to Mr. Lord, whereas I didn't want to be stuck helpless in a house away from you all. But now—" her smile widened and lit up the whole of her face, "now I can get about, it's different. . . . And fancy me being able to drive a car. You would never have believed it a year ago, would you?"

"No," said Lizzie, "You never would, Sarah. It's like a miracle."

Yes, thought Mary Ann, what had happened to Sarah was like a miracle. When she came to take up the front room here it was with the idea of her and Michael marrying almost straight away, and then one day she announced, and quite calmly, that she wasn't going to marry Michael until she could walk. Her decision had caused a bit of an upheaval at the time and a great number of shaking heads. But tomorrow Sarah would achieve the goal she had aimed at, she would go up to the altar rails on her feet. In a white wedding gown that would cover her trailing limb, she would stand by Michael's side while they were married.

Remembering the work, the patience, yes, and the tears that Sarah had endured to achieve her object, there now attached itself to that odd feeling in Mary Ann one of inadequacy. She felt useless, utterly useless. She had never done anything. When Mrs. McBride's words of yesterday came to her, she said to herself, Aw, what's that? Mrs. McBride was just trying to be nice. And as she rose abruptly from the table she wished that something awful would happen so that she could prove herself like Sarah had.

"Where you off to in a rush?" Lizzie looked at her sharply.

"Nowhere. I just wanted to make a start. . . . Shall I do the dishes and clear the scullery?"

"Yes. Yes, you could do that."

As she stood at the sink washing the dishes and the murmur of her mother's and Sarah's voices came to her, she thought, Why don't they get up and get going? She said there was so much to do—that's why I stayed off the day. . . . When her hands became still in the soapy water she looked down at them and said to herself, I don't feel nice inside, I don't. . . . It's awful, awful feeling like this.

At half-past nine Mary Ann was wondering what excuse she could make in order to leave the house and go down to the bottom field. And then her mother made it plain sailing for her by saying, "Will you take the tea out to them?" She did not say to your da. "They're in the bottom field, I think."

Taking the basket loaded with three lidded cans of tea and a cellophane bag of substantial cheese sandwiches, she left the house by the back door, then cut across the farmyard, calling to Simon as she did so. She touched the Labrador's head as he took up his position close to her side, and when they went through the gate and on to the field path a long-haired black cat jumped from a low hayrick and joined them. The cat mewed and she stooped and patted it, saying, "All right, Tigger." Then they moved on, the dog close to her side and the cat trotting behind them.

When they reached the low wall that bordered the south meadow Sarah's horse—which she was determined to ride one day—threw up its head and came galloping towards them, and when, neighing as it went, it trotted at the other side of the wall, Mary Ann called to him, "When I come back, Dusty, when I come back." When they reached the end of the wall the horse, unable to go further, neighed loudly as they went down a steep cart track towards a large field, where, in the far distance, she could see the binder, driven by Michael, turning in the direction of Corny, who was at the other end of the line. But she couldn't see her da. She walked towards where the ground rose before dropping into a miniature valley, and as she neared it Mike came into view.

On the sight of him the dog gave one staccato bark, and Mike turned his head, then straightened his back, and as they approached the dog left Mary Ann's side and went quietly forward and nuzzled him.

"I've brought your break." She was looking down into the basket.

"I'm ready for it." He held out his hand, and she handed him one of the cans.

"Come and sit down a minute." He pointed to a hillock of ground, but she answered quickly, "I've got to take theirs; it'll . . . it'll get cold."

"It can wait a few minutes." His gaze, fixed on her face, brought her eyes up to his and she went and sat down.

When Mike lowered himself to the ground, but not too near her, the dog lay down against his side, while the cat, thinking it was about time to show some remnants of her independence, strolled, delicate-pawed, over the stubbly grass along the hedgerow.

Taking the lid off the can, Mike drank thirstily. After replacing the lid and setting the can on the ground, he wiped his broad mouth with the pad of his thumb; then, pulling up his knees, he rested his forearm on them, and, his head going slightly back, he looked up into the wide, high sky before saying gruffly, "What's come over you and me, Mary Ann?"

When she made no answer, except to lower her head, he, with his eyes still turned skywards, went on, "I thought nothin' on God's earth could come atween us. I would have sworn that if I'd committed a murder you would have stood by me."

"And I would." Her words were scarcely audible to him. "You know I would. . . . But this isn't a murder, it's something different . . . something . . ." She paused for a long while before adding in a thin whisper, "Nasty."

"Aw, my God, Mary Ann!" He was no longer looking skywards; his head had drooped and his brow was resting on his clenched fist, and his face became contorted as he ground his strong teeth. Then, raising his head slightly from his hands, he muttered, "You don't know. And how should you? You can't understand; things happen. You don't ask for them to happen, you don't want them to happen, they happen in little episodes. Aye, that's how they happen, in little episodes. And I can tell you this. . . ." He turned his head slightly in her direction. "They would stay little episodes if people would leave them alone, if they would stop making issues out of them; stop keeping on, if they would forget them, or just take them as part and parcel of life. Then they wouldn't grow. You understand what I'm saying now?" His head was fully turned towards her, waiting for her answer, and she turned hers and looked at him. She understood what he was saying. The people he was referring to were simply her mother; but she didn't blame her mother for the attitude she had taken, how could she? Very likely she would react in the same way herself if Corny were to carry on with another girl. . . . Oh, she would go on worse than her mother, she knew that. Her mother could be cool, and distant, staving off words. . . . She paused here in her thinking. Perhaps that attitude was worse than having it out, having a row. Yes, she knew it was.

"Look, Mary Ann, I've done nothing wrong." Mike's voice was quiet and level now. "You understand what I mean, don't you?"

"Yes, Da." She gave a small nod. "Yes, I understand. But how long will you be able to say that?" She was amazed at herself for asking such a question, of her da of all people.

"Mary Ann." Mike closed his eyes now and rocked his big head in wide, slow movements. "It's a passing phase, it'll blow over."

"Why did you start it?"

"Why does a man breathe? You don't know . . . it's one of those things." He turned and looked over the wide field to where the binder was now coming towards them, and he said, as if to himself, "Life gallops on, and the quicker it gallops the more set it gets. And sometimes in the night you get frightened—aye, frightened; you're done for, finished, you're old. And then along comes somebody who makes you feel a lad again, and you like it. You get a new lease of life, it's like a drug. And you've got enough sense in the back of your mind to recognise it as just that, an' you know damn well that its effects will wear off. But for the time being you're living like you thought you would never live again. . . . Aw, it's all too complicated. . . ."

Mary Ann, her own hands clasped tightly now, was thinking, Mrs. McBride, that's what Mrs. McBride had said. At least, her words had meant the same thing. She was wise, was Mrs. McBride. But then she was very old; whereas her mother wasn't old enough to be wise in that way yet, and her da was being cruel to her. He was indulging in a second childhood. Well, anyway, a second youth, and not thinking about the effects on her mother . . . or the effect on herself. This thought forced from her mouth the words, "She's younger than me, Da."

As Mike began to beat his brow with his clenched fist, Mary Ann rose slowly to her feet, and when she went to pass him his hand shot out and pulled her close to him. Her face just above his, they stared at each other. Looking at him, Mary Ann did not think as she had done from a child, He's handsome, me da, and there's something about him. Years ago she had been flattered when women like Mrs. Quinton had liked her da, but not any more. Her eyes now took in his neck. It was thick, and brown, and had lines on it; and there was hair sprouting from within his ears. Her da was no longer a young man, he was in his forties. Never before had she thought like this about him, she had always seen him young.

"Are you listening to me?"

She blinked twice. "Yes, Da."

"I said, it would be over the morrow."

"What?"

"You weren't listening . . . I said it'll be finished the morrow."

"Oh, Da." Slowly she smiled at him. "You'll tell them . . .?" She did not think of the girl alone in this matter; her mother was a force to be contended with also, and she was fully aware of this. "When they come to the wedding, you'll tell them?"

"Well. . . ." He moved his full lips one over the other and lowered his gaze for a moment, before saying, "There . . . there won't be any need to tell them, but it'll be finished, you'll see."

"But, Da. . . ."

"Believe me." He cupped her cheek with his hand. "Don't worry any more; it'll be over the morrow night, you'll see. I promise you that."

She believed him. She knew he meant it. She wanted to burst into tears and fall against him, burying her head in the beloved neck. She gulped and, lowering her head, turned from him, saying, "All right, Da, all right."

Mike made no further move to detain her, but as she hurried across the field Corny's voice hailed her, shouting, "Hie there!" But it did not turn her round. For answer, she began to run, the tears raining unchecked now down her face. Her feet slipping on the stubbles, she ran until she reached the cart track, and it was as she was crossing this that another voice came to her from where the track joined the road leading to the farm. And there she saw Tony's car, and Tony himself waving to her.

Aw, what was she to do? If she didn't go down to him he would turn back to the house and find out what was wrong with her. She rubbed her face hastily with her handkerchief and, walking slowly now, went down the slope towards the car.

As Tony came to meet her she could see Lettice leaning from the car window, and as she answered Lettice's salute with a lift of her hand, Tony came up to her, saying, "What's the matter? What are you crying for?"

"Leave me alone." She could talk like this to Tony.

"Well—" he smiled ruefully, "to use your own phraseology, Miss, nobody's touching you."

"Aw, don't be clever or facetious, I can't stand it this morning." She had for a long while now stopped thinking, with regard to Tony, I could have married him if I'd liked, because she knew that Tony wasn't for her, or she for him. Lettice was the right one for Tony. She might be a bit older but she was what he needed.

"Hello, Mary Ann." Lettice opened the door and stepped into the road.

"Hello, Lettice."

Lettice now bent towards her, saying softly, "What's the matter?"

"Oh . . ." Mary Ann shook her head. "You know what it is."

As Lettice remained silent, Tony put in, "You're still worrying about Mike?"

"Wouldn't you? If you were in my place . . . or me mother's?"

As Tony raised his brows, Lettice put in, "Of course he would, but at the same time, Mary Ann, I can't imagine your father doing anything really stupid. He's flattered by the girl; men are made like that."

If anybody had experience about men being flattered by girls it was Lettice. She had suffered from it for years, putting a face on things to keep her first marriage together, and what had happened in the end?

"Some men," went on Lettice, with a knowing quality in her voice, "would let it go to their heads, but not Mike."

In the pause that followed, Tony put in, lightly, "I saw Michael earlier on this morning. He appeared as calm as a cucumber, quite unconcerned."

Mary Ann gave a little smile at this, saying, "Our Michael doesn't give much away. I heard him moving about in his room at two o'clock this morning. Yet he told Sarah he slept like a top, and made her believe it."

Lettice and Tony laughed, then Tony said, "I've got a message for you . . . he wants to see you."

There was no need for Mary Ann to question the "he"; there was only one he . . . Mr. Lord. "What does he want?" she asked.

Tony shook his head. "I don't know."

Mary Ann stared up into the thin face that was so like Mr. Lord's, and she said, "Of course you know; there's nothing you don't know. . . . He does know, doesn't he, Lettice?"

Confronted with the question, the older woman said, "Leave me out of this, Mary Ann. But I can tell you this, he's in good spirits this morning."

"That's a change," said Mary Ann. "What's brought it on?"

"Oh . . ." Lettice looked from Mary Ann to her husband, then back to Mary Ann as she said, "He had a bit of news last night that seemed to please him. He's . . . hoping for a great-grandson."

Mary Ann's mouth dropped open as she turned her gaze towards Tony, but Tony was looking at Lettice. Lettice was going to have a baby, but she was old. . . . Oh well, not really . . . but old to have a baby. She was over thirty-six. Well, people had babies up to forty and after, didn't they? She supposed so, but somehow . . . well, it didn't seem quite right. Lettice herself was a grandmother. Her only daughter, whom she rarely saw, had had a baby last year.

Both Lettice and Tony were looking at her now, and she made her smile broad as she said, "Oh, that'll be lovely for you. Fancy you going to have a baby. . . . Do you want a baby?"

Lettice's attractive face puckered as if in doubt; and then she said, "Not . . . not particularly, Mary Ann, but I have two men to please, and both of them seem bent on it. The old one more than the young one, I must confess." She now lent her head gently towards Tony, and he put his arm around her and pressed her to him. And Mary Ann thought, I wish they wouldn't do that. And this was strange, because never had she witnessed affection between her da and her mother without finding joy in it. When they were happy she wanted the whole world to be happy, but when, as now, they weren't happy she supposed she resented other people's happiness. And yet she'd had a large hand in bringing happiness to Tony and Lettice, so she shouldn't feel like this.

She said quickly, "Eeh! I'll have to be going, there's so much to do. . . . But I'm glad for you, I am, I am. . . . Will you call it Mary Ann if it's a girl?"

"Not on your life. Fancy another like you!" Tony pushed at her with the flat of his hand as he laughed, then added seriously, "You will go up, won't you?"

"Yes, I'll go up. . . . Imagine what would happen if I disobeyed the order."

"Yes, imagine."

"And you won't tell me what it's about?"

"I told you, I don't know." He was grinning at her now.

"Oh, go on." She turned from him, then turned back again, saying swiftly, "Bye-bye, Lettice."

"Bye-bye, Mary Ann."

Mary Ann did not give her mother Lettice's news, because she felt that Lizzie would consider it should be her to whom this news should apply, and so would cry. What she did say to Lizzie was, "I saw Tony and Lettice going out in the car. Tony said Mr. Lord wants me."

"What for? Did he say?"

"He said he didn't know, but I'm sure he does."

"Well, you'd better get yourself off, hadn't you?"

"But there's all those cakes to ice."

"Never mind about them, get yourself away up."

Her mother always saw to it that Mr. Lord's orders were obeyed, at least as far as it lay within her power, and she added now, "Don't dawdle, you don't know what he might want to see you about."

"Well, it can't be anything that's going to go bad for an hour or so, can it?"

"Mary Ann!"

"All right, all right, I'll go now."

Once again Mary Ann went through the farmyard, but this time she turned up the hill towards the big house that stood on the brow. She went through the paved courtyard, with its ornamental urns of flowers, to the back door, and, after knocking, she opened the door and entered the kitchen.

A middle-aged woman, turning from the Aga stove, said brightly, "Good morning, miss."

"Good morning, Eva . . . Ben about?"

"I think he's with the master, miss."

The advent of a woman servant in Mr. Lord's house, and in Ben's kitchen, in itself spoke volumes for Lettice's power.

As she left the kitchen, Ben, his old head sunk into his hollowed shoulders, came shambling across the hall. He had a small tray in his hand, on which was an empty glass and plate, and on the sight of Mary Ann he put the tray on the side table and, turning to her, said in a hoarse whisper, "He's waiting for you. He's in high fettle this morning." His wrinkled face moved into what for him was a smile, and Mary Ann, bending towards him, whispered, "What does he want, do you know, Ben?"

It wasn't strange that Mary Ann should ask Ben this question, because Ben knew everything. Ben had lived with the taciturn Mr. Lord for as far back as he cared to remember, and although his master treated him at times as a numbskull, to Ben he was God, all the God he needed.

The small smile still on his face, Ben said, "You'll know soon enough. Go on, don't keep him waiting."

When Mary Ann entered the drawing-room, Mr. Lord was sitting in his favourite position before the tall windows, looking out on to the terraced gardens. He was a tall man, thin as a rake, with skin wizened almost as much as that of his servant, but his pale-blue eyes held a brightness and vitality that denied his age.

"You've taken your time." The voice was stern, the face unsmiling, and to this greeting Mary Ann said, "Well, Tony only told me not more than fifteen minutes ago; I can't fly."

A quiver passed over the wrinkled skin, and the eyes, from under lowered lids, looked keenly at her as he said, "In a bad mood this morning, aren't you?"

"Me in a bad mood?" Her eyes stretched wide, and on this he held up his hand, saying, "All right, all right, we won't go into it. . . . Everybody very busy, I suppose?" His voice held a quiet note now.

"Yes." She sat down in front of him. He always demanded that she sit in front of him, where he could look fully at her.

"And everybody on edge?"

She nodded at him, then said, "All except Sarah and Michael."

He smiled, and the wrinkles on his face converged together. And then his head nodding slowly, he said, "They'll be happy, those two. Although he's taken on a burden, it'll become lighter, not heavier, with the years, and as she works at her miracle she'll weave wonder into their lives. . . . Don't you think so?"

The pale, steely gaze was tight on her face, and she answered abruptly, "I don't know." And she didn't know, because she wasn't thinking of Michael or Sarah. But she knew this old man, she knew that his mind was really not on Sarah and Michael's future, but was working in another direction.

His eyes still hard on her, his lips moving as if he were sucking on a sweet, he stared at her for a full minute before enquiring, "What's the matter with you? You're upset."

If Mary Ann knew her Mr. Lord, Mr. Lord knew his Mary Ann.

"I'm not. What makes you think that?"

"You always were a big liar, my dear, but you were also a bad liar. What's troubling you? I ask you, what's troubling you?"

"I tell you, nothing. But we're all in a rush down there." She motioned her head backwards towards the window, indicating the farmhouse. "We . . . we don't have a wedding every day."

Again the pale-blue eyes were holding hers. And now Mr. Lord said, "It's Mike, isn't it? . . . Oh! oh! don't get on your high horse." He now bent his stiff body towards her and said softly, "I know that look in your face, and only your father can put it there. He's done so before and he's doing it now, and I've no doubt he'll do it again many times before you die."

"I tell you . . ."

"You can go on telling me, but what I want to hear is what he has been up to now."

"Nothing, nothing." That would be the last straw if Mr. Lord heard about Yvonne Radley. Oh, Holy Mother—a section of her mind was praying now—don't let him find out about that.

"If you don't tell me I can find out. I have my ways and means." He was nodding quickly at her. "Tony and Lettice just tell me what they think is good for me, but if I want to know anything I have my ways and means." His head was moving slower now, and Mary Ann thought, Yes, he has his ways and means. Ben was his ways and means. She liked Ben, and Ben, she knew, liked her; surprisingly, because Ben had no thought but for this old man here, and that his days should be spent in peace and free from worry. But to achieve this she knew that Ben, even in his doddering old age, would take on the task of the C.I.D. to find out anything his master needed to know. But Mary Ann thought none the less of Ben for this, she only feared what his probing might do to her da, because, besides trying to rule her life, Mr. Lord had also tried to rule Mike's, and her father wasn't as easy under the reins as she was. Not that she was really easy.

"Well, have it your own way." Mr. Lord leaned back and rested his head against the wing of the chair, and, after drawing in a long thin breath and placing his bony fingertips together, he said, "How would you like me to do something for that big fellow of yours?"

Mary Ann's eyes were completely round now, and, knowing the other thing he had done for Corny, which had transported him to the other side of the world, she was wary in her answer. "It all depends on what it is," she said.

"Yes, that's a good answer: it all depends what it is. Well . . . how would you like to see him set up in a garage, a real garage?"

"But . . . but he's after the one in Moor Lane."

Mr. Lord jerked his head disdainfully. "That isn't a garage, that's a broken-down repair shop, and on a side road at that. What business can he expect there?"

"They're thinking of opening it up, making it a main . . ."

"Yes, yes, in twenty years' time. I know all about that. . . . But there's a place going now, at least shortly, on the main road . . . Baxter's."

"Baxter's!" Her mouth now formed an elongated O, and when she closed it she swallowed before repeating, "Baxter's! But it's a show place."

"I grant you it's a show place. But it also does a very good business."

"Oh." She was smiling. "You'd really set him up in that?"

He nodded. "Yes, I would. I feel I owe him something for that little trip he made on my suggestion. Baxter's will be in the market in three months' time. I intend to buy it and lease it to him, and if he shows progress I'll give him a share in it, say in a year or so. I think that is a fair enough deal, don't you?"

"Oh, yes . . . yes." Her words were slow. It was wonderful. She said now, "He's got quite a bit of his own saved up, over four hundred."

"Four hundred! Huh!" Mr. Lord's tone was now derisive. "What do you think can be done with four hundred, Mary Ann, when you want to buy a business of this kind? Baxter's will go for nothing less than thirty thousand . . . thirty thousand pounds!"

Her face was straight. She couldn't visualize the enormous sum of thirty thousand pounds and the potentialities therein, but she could see the great achievement, and what could be done with four hundred pounds because she had helped in the gathering of it. When Corny would say on a Saturday night, "Shall we go down to the bowling alley in Jarrow?" she would think for a moment: if they went to the bowling alley it would mean anything up to two pounds spent in the evening. So time and time again she had said, "Oh, let's go for a run on the bike." And sitting on the pillion, clinging tightly to him, she had spent wind-torn, chilling hours, to enable them to add to the growing sum on which their future was to be built.

"You must be realistic, Mary Ann. Businesses are not bought in hundreds today, it takes thousands, tens of thousands to get a start, that is if you want to make real money and not peddle your life away in a backwater."

The backwater he was referring to was, she knew, Meyer's garage in Moor Lane.

"You're pleased, aren't you?" It was a question, and she forced herself to smile as she answered, "Oh, yes, yes. And it's kind of you."

"Don't be a hypocrite." He was sitting upright again. "You don't think it's kind of me at all. You don't like the idea that your Cornelius can't buy a motor concern with his four hundred. . . . Am I right?"

She did not reply for a moment, but her head wagged just the slightest. And then, getting to her feet, she said, "Yes, you are right, because he's worked hard to save it and——"

"Doubtless, doubtless. And I like to hear it, it's a promising trait in him; it could get him far, the saving trait, but not four hundred, not in the car business, not in this day and age. The days of the Morris miracles are over. But your future husband, Mary Ann, has, I think a head on his shoulders and he won't be so foolish as to look a gift horse in the mouth. . . . Now will you go and tell him that I would like to see him? I understand he is on the farm, and"—he raised a finger to her—"I would like to think that his reception of my offer will be a little more enthusiastic than yours."

"I'm sorry . . . I know it's good of you and I'm grateful, I really am." She moved towards the chair and placed her hand on his, to find it immediately gripped, and she was almost brought to tears for the second time that morning when, his face softening, he said, "I want to do things for you, Mary Ann. I want to see you settled with all the comforts and amenities which would have been yours if you had come into this house I have grown very fond of Lettice . . . yes, I have, which is just as well, for it helps to oil the wheels of living together, but Lettice will never be you, my dear. . . . I've thought recently that you might have imagined that you were being shut out, but no, no. And I thought I must do something to prove to you that that'll never happen. And then, when I learned yesterday that I may in the near future be presented with a great-grandchild, I was pleased, and when one is pleased one thinks about other people, and as you, my dear, are never very far from my mind, I thought, I'll celebrate." He squeezed her hand. "And what better way to celebrate than by acquiring a garage."

There was a lump wedged tightly in her gullet. Oh, he was good, good, he always had been; aggravating, dominating, an old devil at times, but good. Swiftly, she bent forward and pressed her face to his while holding his other cheek with her hand. When, turning quickly from him, she went to leave the room, he checked her quietly, saying, "Tell Cornelius I want to see him."

She hurried through the kitchen with her face averted from both Ben and Eva, and then she was running down the hill. When she came to the low stone wall she mounted its broad top and, looking over the fields to where, in the far distance, she saw the figures of Michael and Corny, and her da, she put her fingers into her mouth and blew a sharp high whistle that could have been the envy of many a boy, and when she saw the faces turn towards her she cupped her mouth in her hands and called, "Cor-NY! Here . . . here!" When she felt she had his attention, she beckoned him with a wide wave of her arm.

She saw Corny break away at a trot and take the field in long, loping strides. She saw him jump the other end of the stone wall, and then he was coming up the steep incline, still running, towards her.

When he reached her he stood for a moment, panting; then exclaimed, laughingly, "Coo! That would get you in training. . . . you want me?" His face wore a broad grin, and before she had time to reply, he added, "A whistling woman and a crowing hen is neither good for God nor man . . . that's what me mother says."

"Perhaps your mother's right."

He narrowed his eyes at her as he stooped down and, looking searchingly into her face, asked, "What's up? You been crying?"

"No." She jerked her chin to the side. "You've got to go and see Mr. Lord."

"Who, me? What for?"

"Because he wants you to . . . that's all." The downward movement of her chin now lent emphasis to the words.

"When he wants me it doesn't mean good. I don't trust that old boy, and never will." He straightened up and pushed his shoulders back.

"Now, Corny, stop it. It is for your good . . . for our good."

"Ah . . . ah. Here we go. . . . Well, what is it?" His expression changed.

As she stared up into his stiff, straight face she decided that if he was to obey Mr. Lord's command she'd better keep Mr. Lord's proposal to herself. She knew her Corny. His mind was full of odd values, odd ideas. You never knew but that he might turn down the offer if it wasn't put to him right. She lied unblinkingly as she said, "If I knew what he wanted you for wouldn't I tell you? He just said he wanted to see you."

Corny wrinkled his big nose. "I don't like it. He's hardly spoken to me since I came back from America."

"Can you blame him? You shut him up before he started by telling him that you wanted help from nobody and that you were going to join the band."

"Aye, yes, I did." At the memory, a smile twisted Corny's lips. "And I remember he said that all I'd have to live on would be the hot air that was left over from blowing my cornet. He's sharp, is the old boy."

"And he was right. That's all you would have had to live on if you'd taken up with the band again. They went flat . . . in more ways than one."

"That's because they hadn't me with them." As he brought his fist along the point of her chin, she said softly, "Go on, Corny. And don't aggravate him." She caught at his hand. "He's old."

"All right." He gripped both her hands now and went to pull her towards him, but Mary Ann, noting the deep, tender look in his eyes, protested swiftly, "Eeh! no, Corny. Now stop it, there's Jonesy down in that field."

"He won't mind."

"Don't be daft. . . . Now give over. Ooh!"

She tried vainly to push off his long arms as they went around her, but when her feet left the ground and she was held tightly to him, and his mouth touched hers, she relaxed against him for a moment. And she still leant against him when he released her and she was on her feet again. Then, as was often the case, they turned from each other without a word, for words would only have diminished the depths of feeling between them.

"You're mad . . . daft . . . up the pole." Mary Ann seemed to grow as she stood facing

Corny; and now she twisted her head around and addressed her mother, where Lizzie was toying with her half-finished dinner. "Isn't he, Ma? Tell him, isn't he mad?"

Lizzie was vitally aware of Mike sitting at the far end of the table, his head bowed over his plate, eating solidly as if all that was going on was no concern of his. But Mary Ann had asked her a question—she had not, as usual, asked it of her da, she had asked her. She turned her head slowly to where Corny stood, seemingly isolated on the edge of the hearth rug, and she forced herself to say what was in her mind, yet the translation of her thoughts were mild, for all she said was, "I think you're being very foolish, Corny; it's a wonderful offer."

"Wonderful offer be damned!"

Mike had risen from the table, almost overturning the chair as he did so, and although he had taken up, and repeated, Lizzie's words, it was to Mary Ann that he looked as he barked, "He's right. And he's told you why he's right; the old man is not doing this for him, he's doing it for you so that when you're married he can still keep the reins on you. . . . You're being foolish!" He was again quoting Lizzie's words, and it was her he was yelling at, her he was getting at, not at Mary Ann, although he levelled his spleen towards her. "Let him go his own road, make his own decisions. He's made one the day; instead of going for him stand by him. You mightn't have so much jam on it but what you do have will be what he's earned and worked for, it won't come from the backhander that's buying your affections."

As Mike grabbled up his pipe from the mantelpiece and stalked from the room Lizzie rose slowly from her seat, and she stood, her hands gripping the edge of the table, looking to where Sarah sat with bowed head, and Michael opposite to her chewed on his lower lip.

"See what you've done?" Mary Ann's voice, cracking with temper, turned on Corny, and before he could answer her Michael's clear tone cut in, "He's done what he thinks is right."

Michael was also on his feet now, and, looking towards Corny, he said, "I know how you feel. I felt the same when he first offered us the bungalow. . . ."

"But you took the bungalow, didn't you?" Mary Ann bent her body aggressively towards her brother, and he, his voice rising now, shouted back at her, "But only on my own terms, not as a gift."

There was a moment of tense silence when no one moved, but in it Mary Ann noticed the slight quiver attacking Sarah's shoulders, and, contrition swamping her, she bowed her head and murmured, "I'm sorry . . . I'm sorry, Sarah, I . . . I didn't mean anything."

"I know, I know." Sarah's hand moved out in Mary Ann's direction, and Mary Ann, going towards her, said, "All this carry-on and your wedding the morrow."

"That makes no difference. . . . Would you hold the chair?"

Mary Ann held the back of the chair firmly while Sarah gripped the table and pulled herself to her feet; then looking towards Michael, she said soiftly, "Have you a minute? I've packed that case but I can't close it."

Without a word Michael went towards the door leading into the hall, and, holding it open, waited until Sarah had passed, before following her into the front room.

And now Lizzie gathered up an armful of dishes and went into the scullery; a minute later the door clicked shut, and Corny and Mary Ann were alone together. Mary Ann stood with her back to him, a stiff, defiant, angry back, and she almost thought it was her da speaking when Corny's voice came at her, saying too quietly, "You've got to make up your mind, and soon, if it's me you want or a big house and a lush life, because I can tell you here and now it'll have to be one or the other for a good many years because I can't see me getting rich quick, I'm not built that way. If I was I would have jumped at his offer and become a yes man, and I would have risen to manager, but the business would never have been mine. . . . Oh, aye. . . ." Although Mary Ann wasn't looking at him she knew he was wagging his head in wide sweeps. "Oh, I know I was to be given a share, enough to enable me wife to live as he thinks she should live, as she would have lived if she had married

Tony. . . ." She swung round on him now but she didn't get a chance to speak, for his look stilled her tongue. Slowly he turned his gaze from her, and, picking up his cap from the chair, he went towards the scullery door, saying, still quietly, "There it is. I'll give you time to think it over one way or the other. I'm going home now, but tell Michael I'll be back in the morning in plenty of time."

As the door closed on him she put out her hand towards it, but she didn't move from where she was. Then, as if her legs had suddenly become tired with running, she found she had to sit down. She didn't want to cry; nor was she in a temper any longer; but filling her small body now was a feeling of fear. It said to her, "You'd better go careful, you could lose him. You can't please both of them. And if you lose him you'll never get anybody to love you as he does, for in a way he loves you like your da does." This was true, she knew, and the ingredients in her love for him were similar to those in her love for her father. She had loved Corny from when he was a gangling boy, but she loved him more deeply when she recognized traits in him similar to those in Mike. She had a desire now to fly after him, and fling her arms about him, and cry, "Corny . . . Corny, have it any way you like, your way will suit me."

At this moment Lizzie re-entered the kitchen. she did not look at Mary Ann as she gathered up the remainder of the dishes, but just as she was about to return to the scullery she said, "He said he told you you've got to think about what you want, he's going to give you time."

Mary Ann, looking up into Lizzie's face, knew that deep down in her, her mother would be glad if Corny and she were to break up. "I won't need any time, I've done all the thinking I'm going to," she said under her breath.

Lizzie paused as she was turning from the table, and her eyes asked, "Well, and what are you going to do?"

"Whatever he wants will suit me in the long run."

Lizzie did not immediately turn away, and when she did she sighed, and her lids drooped, and as she crossed the kitchen she remarked, as it to herself, "That's the way it always works out."

3

Taking up the two front pews at the left-hand side of the church were Sarah's people—her aunts, her uncles, her cousins, but dominating them, the figure of her mother. Mrs. Flannagan was seated near the aisle. Her back was straight, her head was high; her thin face—which, to use Mrs. McBride's description, was snipy—was at this moment aglow with satisfaction. God was just. She had demanded that He would be so to her, for hadn't she struggled all her life against the environment of Burton Stret, and what help had she got? . . . for he—meaning her husband—had done nothing in his life but disappoint her. And then for her only child to be afflicted with polio; she had thought that would be the end. But God's ways were strange; He had used the affliction as an instrument, and he had given her daughter courage to fight, and this had not gone unnoticed by Mr. Lord. Mrs. Flannagan did not think of Michael at this moment. Michael was just another one of God's instruments placed in Sarah's path to bring her to the notice of the influential owner of a shipping firm, a dock—even if it was only a small one—a farm, and a splendid house. Mary Ann Shaughnessy was not now alone the recipient of all good things.

The thought of Mary Ann brought Mrs. Flannagan's eyes to where Mary Ann herself was kneeling behind the bride and bridegroom, and if Mrs. Flannagan had ever given way to the weakness of gratitude she did so now, for she was thankful, she told herself, that Mary Ann had decided against making this a double wedding, for this was her daughter's day . . . and her own day, the day she would shine as the mother of the bride, the beautiful bride, for her daughter did look beautiful in spite of everything; but it would have been difficult to shine if she had been one of the mothers of the brides, the other mother being Lizzie Shaughnessy. Yes . . . yes, she was grateful to Mary Ann for this.

At the other side of the aisle there sat in stronger force the friends and relations of the bridegroom, and Lizzie Shaughnessy was thinking much the same thing. Oh, she was glad that Mary Ann had decided against a double wedding, for with her heart so sore the strain of Mary Ann going at this particular time would have been too much—Mary Ann, she knew, was on her side, wholly and completely. The thought in itself was of some comfort, for she was a good ally to have, was Mary Ann; that was why, she supposed, she had at times been jealous of her whole-hearted affection for her da. At this point Lizzie became conscious of Mike standing by her side, almost touching her, yet they were poles apart; all that closeness that had been between them was gone, never to return. Nothing would ever be the same again. She wondered what he was thinking as he watched his only son being married. Was he remembering his own wedding day and the starvation years that followed, she wondered.

Mike wasn't remembering his own wedding day, or the starvation years that followed, but as he stared at the straight back of his son he thought, It'll pass him by, the torment, the hell; he'll hold to her through life, and if his love ever fades there'll be compassion. But he doubted if his love would fade. Sarah had a habit of working at things; because of her handicap she would work at marriage, not just accept it. No, there was no need to worry about that pair. And they were starting off well, with a fine little house, and Michael with a sure job ahead of him for the rest of his life. And what was more, people all around him were kindly and sympathetic to them both. . . . And what had he himself started with? Kindness and sympathy? No. Censure all his life; right from his upbringing in the cottage home which was part of the workhouse, until he met Liz. Then there were a couple of golden years, poor but golden, and although the gold dimmed as time went on it had never really tarnished, until these last few weeks. Mike's head moved downwards and his glance took in the black-gloved hand of his mother-in-law and the thought that took the feeling of guilt away was, And that's another thing Michael won't be handicapped with, and old fiend like this. He'll manage Mrs. F., but the devil in hell couldn't cope with this one. His head was immediately brought up by yet another thought: God in heaven! What if she gets wind of this? He took his handkerchief and wiped the sweat away from around his face.

He's sweating, Mrs. McMullen commented to herself, and he's a right to, it's his sins oozing out of him. He's got a nerve to put his face in the church door. There should be some law about Protestants being allowed in the church; they should be made to sit separate like. She looked towards the altar. She wished the priest would put a move on, he was talking too much. They would find out what it was all about before long, especially her grandson. That poor lad had taken on a packet, he must be mad. If she had had anything to say in the matter it would never have come about . . . a cripple like her. Well, God worked in strange ways. There had been that talk of them going off on a holiday together, hadn't there, when they weren't even engaged; and people knew what happened on holidays. Well, Sarah Flannagan had paid in advance for that sinful thinking. . . . Aw, would the priest never finish? She was dying for a cup of tea and a drop of something in it—her legs were playing her up, like cramp she had, from the back of her heels up to her buttocks. . . . Aw, there they were coming from the altar, and not afore time. It was a disgrace it was, dressed in white and walking like that, like some drunk. It was a wonder Michael wasn't ashamed to be seen with her. Aye, she supposed, her face was all right, but that didn't make up for that dot-and-carry-one gait of hers. . . . Aw, and look at those two behind, the long and the short of it. Well, we get what we deserve, God sees to that. And she's going to get Fanny McBride's grandson, and good luck to her, she deserves no better. But of the two it's him that should be pitied, for if ever there was a little upstart it's that one. Look at her now walking down there as pious-looking as a saint, and mealy-mouthed into the bargain. If ever there was a creature with a mask on it's her. The damned little spitfire. Well, he's big enough, and I hope begod he takes it out of her. . . . And look at Old Flannagan there, grinning like a Cheshire cat. He's no man is that one, as soft as clarts. . . . And now there was the big fellow, Mike himself, leaving her side and the pew and not giving her a hand up. Aw, well, his day would come, and it wasn't very far ahead if all rumours were right. For years she had told her daughter what he was, and what thanks had she got? Told to mind her own business. Well, it was her business. She pulled herself to her feet . . . she couldn't wait to get back to the house to get on with that particular business. There was never smoke without fire, and, as she said to herself as she walked up the aisle amid the crowd leaving the church, If I can bring a glow to the fire that's under him, God guide me.

Sarah was ready to go. She sat in the front room dressed in a smart grey costume and a cherry-coloured hat. She looked quiet and utterly happy, and as Mary Ann stood holding her hand within her own two, she said softly, "You look so serene."

"I feel it . . . as if I was sort of filled with wonder."

"Oh, I wish I was like you, Sarah."

On this they both laughed, and Sarah said, "Fancy saying that. Remember the fights, the rows? But it seems to me now as if they never happened, or they happened in a different life. You know what I mean?"

Mary Ann nodded her head. "I wish you all the happiness in the world, Sarah; you know that, don't you?"

"Yes, Mary Ann."

"And you know, Sarah?" Mary Ann squeezed her hand. "I can say this to you now. You know, I've been a bit green about you, and I still am, because . . . well, I can see you going down the years supremely happy, no skull and hair flying between you and Michael, whereas us—" she spread out her free hand significantly, "we're like two wild animals at times. You see, even to-day, on this very special day, we're not speaking." She smiled wistfully. And Sarah could not help but laugh, as she replied, "Well, you know something . . . as confessions seem the order of the day I might as well tell you that I'm not such a reformed individual as you think, for I've done my share of turning green. While you've been envying Michael and me for our placidness, for that's what it really is, well, I've been jealous of you and Corny many a time when you've been going at one another."

"What!"

"It's a fact. You see, you're both so boisterous, so full of life. That's how it should be when you're young. For myself, I feel I've been pushed into something that I shouldn't have realized for years and years, some kind of acceptance that only comes with age, if you know what I mean."

"Aw, Sarah, don't think like that. Aw, you've been wonderful, wonderful. But"—she pulled a long face—"I'm glad you've been jealous of me, it's a sort of comfort in a way. . . ."

They were both laughing again, loudly now, their two heads together. They were like this when Lizzie found them, and she paused for a moment in the doorway before saying, "Come on, come on, stop your carry-on the pair of you, everybody's waiting. They've all gone to the barn."

Lizzie bustled around, gathering up Sarah's handbag, her case, her silk scarf, talking all the while to cover her feelings, to cover the fact that at this moment her son was leaving her for ever. There was no real thought for Sarah in her mind now, no affection; what was filling her mind and body was an agony that cried, Oh, Michael! . . . Michael! She had lost her husband—she felt sure of this—and she was losing her son; in a different way perhaps, but more irrevocably, she was losing her son.

"Come on, come on." she bustled them into the hall and to Michael, where he was standing waiting for his wife, and out of the front door and down the garden path towards the car and the crowd outside the barn.

Amid the confusion and good-byes, Michael now detached himself for a moment and, going to Mary Ann, to her utter surprise, he took her face between his hands and shyly kissed her, saying hastily, "It's been fun knowing you."

It was too much. Before the car was out of sight she was back in the front room, standing with her face to the wall very much as she had done when a child, and as she had often said when standing in such a position, Oh, our Michael! Our Michael! She said his name again, but in a different way, he had said, "It's been fun knowing you." He had said that . . . their Michael. Oh, our Michael! Our Michael!

"What's the matter with you?" Lizzie had come quietly into the room. She had not expected to see Mary Ann there.

"Oh, nothing. I just feel I've lost our Michael."

"You feel you've lost our Michael?" Lizzie closed her eyes and, biting on her lip, hurried from the room.

It was eight o'clock and the jollification was going with a swing in the barn . . . too much with a swing. There was too much noise, too much raucous laughter. Lizzie wished it was over. Oh God! How she wished it was over. To Lizzie's feelings now was added one of fear. She feared what she might do if she let herself go. For two solid hours she had watched that girl ogling Mike, she had watched them dance together. True it was in the lancers, and he had danced with others as well, but when he put his arm around her Lizzie felt it was with a difference. And there were others who were aware of it too. Her mother, hawk-eyed, waiting. She did not know how she hadn't sunk to the ground and dissolved in shame and tears as she watched them. That was until this feeling took possession of her, the feeling that urged her to get the girl outside, somewhere quiet, and thrash her with her hands, a stick, anything, anything.

Lizzie moved away from the barn doorway. Where was she now? She looked about her, her eyes searching the thronged floor. . . . There she was. The bitch. Lizzie made no apology for the title. There she was dancing with Corny. . . . But Corny didn't like her. Was he doing it to upset Mary Ann because of what happened yesterday? Oh! . . . Like a gleam of light coming into the darkness of her mind came the thought, if only she would turn to Corny. Mary Ann was young; she would get over it; it was different when you were young. But now the gleam of light faded. This dance was the ladies' choice. It was she who had asked Corny. . . . Then where was Mike? She remembered now that she hadn't seen him for quite some time.

"Ma." Lizzie turned and looked at Mary Ann. In times of stress Mary Ann nearly always substituted ma for mother. "Yes," she said.

"Have you seen me da?"

Lizzie shook her head. "No; why do you ask?"

"I haven't seen him for nearly an hour."

"Have you looked?"

"Yes, in the house and all over."

"Is the car in the garage?"

"Yes; I looked there."

They stood close together now, their eyes scanning the room. "Mrs. Radley's talking to me grannie," said Mary Ann.

"I see that."

"Ma."

"Yes?"

They were still looking ahead.

"Me grannie's got wind of something."

"How do you know?" The words came as a groan from Lizzie.

"She was at me, trying to stir me up, when they were dancing together. She caught hold of me as I was passing, and dug me in the ribs and said, 'Look at that. How does that look to you, eh?' "

"What did you say?"

"I pretended I didn't know what she meant."

"I . . . I don't think I can stand much more." Lizzie's hand was encircling her throat and she strained her neck upwards as if she was choking.

"But, Ma"—— Mary Ann caught hold of her arm and said softly and rapidly, "You won't have to. He . . . he promised me yesterday it's going to be over the night."

Lizzie's eyes darted to Mary Ann's. "What did he say?"

"Only that . . . that it'll be finished the night."

Lizzie now moved her head in a bewildered way, and as Mary Ann was about to say something further there was a fuddled movement in the doorway to the right of them, a gurgle of a laugh, deep and well remembered, and they both swung round to see Mike smiling at them, and to see him as drunk as they had ever seen him for years.

"Oh, no, no." Mary Ann put her hand to her mouth. She knew her da had disposed of a good many glasses since he returned from the church, but then he could stand a good many glasses of both beer and whisky. It took a lot to make him shake on his feet. Before she had time even to think anything further Mike had shambled the few steps towards them, and, gripping Lizzie roughly by the shoulder, he cried, "Come on, Lizzie Shaughnessy, let's trip a measure. Come on."

"Leave go of me." Lizzie hissed the words at him. "Stop it! Stop showing yourself up, and leave go of me."

"Come on, it's a weddin', girl, it's a weddin'."

Mary Ann watched her da reel and stumble almost on to his back as her mother thrust him forcibly from her. She knew that her da was what is termed rotten drunk, which meant fighting drunk. Anything could happen now. And after he had promised, promised faithfully to finish it. Oh. . . .

Mike was rocketing through the couples now, knocking them right and left with his swaying gait, causing laughter here, surprise there, and not a little uneasiness generally. And now he was thrusting Corny from Yvonne. Gripping her round the waist, he swung her into a staggering quick step. The next moment the inevitable had happened: they were both on the floor, as were the next two couples. Again the laughter was high, but only in some quarters.

When they got Yvonne to her feet her face was white. It could have been with shock or with anger, but no one was to know, for her mother quickly took charge and, guiding her to a seat, consoled her, while Mike lay with his legs spread-eagled and his one arm flaying the air.

As Lizzie rushed from the barn into the night Mary Ann followed her, but more slowly. it was the first time that she had turned from her da when he was in drink. Before, this fact had always drawn her irresistibly to him to protect him from people's censure, and always the following morning from what was even worse, censure of himself.

As she saw the pale blur of her mother running towards the road, making for the house, she stopped; she couldn't follow her, she couldn't witness her pain. She stood with her knuckles pressed tightly to her teeth and her feelings in this moment took her beyond tears . . . she felt ashamed, degraded.

The door of the barn was wrenched open and Corny came running, making for the house. And then he saw her. Last night was forgotten. Immediately he put his arms about her and pressed her head gently to his shoulder, and they stood silent for some minutes, until Mary Ann's voice, in almost a whimper, said, "Oh, Corny, how could he do it? And he promised to finish with her the night, and just look at him. . . ."

"What did you say about him finishing it?" Corny was now holding her from him, peering down into her face. "He told you he was going to finish it?"

"Yes, he promised faithfully."

"Well then." His voice was high and his grip tightened on her shoulders and her body jerked under the movement of his hand. "Don't you see? This is how he's doing it . . . getting blind drunk to put her off, to . . . well, to show her his other side as it were. . . . Can't you see?"

Mary Ann brought her eyes from the dim outline of Corny's face to the door of the barn. Then she whispered, "You think that's why he's doing it?"

"Certain, because I've never seen him as blotto as this, and you know I've seen him when he's been pretty far gone and razing Burton Street."

"Perhaps you're right. Now I come to think of it you are. . . . Oh, let's get him out." She tugged at his arm now.

"Oh, no, leave him to it—for a time, anyway. Let's walk quietly round the buildings."

"But what if he's still carrying on when Tony and Lettice come back?"

"Well, they'll understand. But the old man . . . it's him I'll be worrying about . . . I wouldn't have him upset for anything, you know that."

Although she couldn't see his face she knew from the tone of his voice that he was grinning at her, and she said softly, "You. . . . Oh, Corny." Then she added, "About yesterday, you're right, I know you're right."

Again he had his arms around her and again they were silent, until a great whoop of drunken laughter came from the barn and tore them apart, and Mary Ann cried, "I've got to get him out, Corny." And as she turned to go towards the door she stopped and, looking up at the dim figure at her side, exclaimed, almost in horror, "Me grannie's in there. Aw, dear Lord, she only needed this to set her up for the rest of her life. Now he'll never live this down, never."

When they opened the barn door there were no dancers on the floor, the band was having a rest and being entertained by the sight of the big one-armed red-headed bloke making a pass at a young girl up in the corner.

Mike's antics had drawn the attention of the whole room towards him. He had his arm around Yvonne's shoulders and he was slobbering and grimacing and yammering as only a drunken man can. Mary Ann's eyes jerked to where her grannie was sitting. Her eyes riveted on her son-in-law, she looked like a female god, a self-satisfied female god. It was as if all her prophecies were being enacted before her eyes, and not only her own eyes but also those of a large audience.

Mary Ann groaned audibly and was about to make her way across the room when Corny's hand gently stayed her, and he whispered down to her, "Hold on a tick, just a minute or so."

It was at this moment that Mr. Flannagan, self-appointed M.C., declared that they would now give the young-uns a chance to show their capers and have a twist.

As the band struck up Mike pulled himself to his feet with the obvious intention that Yvonne should partner him in the twist, but apparently the proceedings were becoming too much for Miss Radley's nerves, for now and in no gentle manner she tore her hand from his, pushed him upwards away from her to allow herself to rise, and as he reeled to the side she hurried as quickly as her stilt heels could carry her around the outskirts of the dancers and made for the door, there to be joined by her flurried mother and to be confronted by Mary Ann.

"You going?" As Mary Ann, with a great effort, forced an ordinary enquiring lightness into her tone, Yvonne Radley looked down at this interfering, tonguey little upstart, as she thought of her, and she had the desire to take her hand and slap her mouth for her. She cast her glance towards Corny and her instinct told her that here was the one she would have gone after if he'd had any prospects, her mother or no mother. As if her mother had heard her thinking and decided right away to make clear their future policy she listened to her voice saying to Mary Ann with that calmness she both envied and hated, "Well, we'll be going now, but we'll look in tomorrow perhaps." There followed a pause before she added, "your father's in high fettle, isn't he, but that always happens at weddings. The soberest of men always let go at weddings, don't you think?"

Before Mary Ann could answer, "But me da's not a sober man at any time," Mrs. Radley put in quickly, "Well come on, dear, we'll just go to the house and get our things . . . and say good-bye to your mother." She nodded at Mary Ann, her long thin face and granite jaw pushed into a smile. "She'll be glad when it's over, weddings mean nothing but hard work. Good night. We'll be seeing you soon."

When the door closed on them, Mary Ann looked sadly up at Corny. "It didn't work, they'll be back."

"No, they won't; that was a face-saver." He nodded quickly down at her. "You'll see. As your da said he was going to, he's put an end to it."

"You think so?"

"Sure of it. Come on, let's go out."

"No. Look." She made a small movement with her hand.

Mike was no longer standing where the Radleys had left him. He was now, to Mary Ann's horror, confronting her grannie. Swaying before her, he was telling her exactly how she was feeling.

"Bustin', aren't you? Bustin' at the seams with righteousness. Haven't . . . haven't you told Liz all these years what to expect eh? An' haven't your words come true? Aye, an' with interest. You're gloatin', aren't you? Your black beady li'l eyes are full of divilish delight. . . . Will I help you up now an' . . . an' push your creakin' bones over to Liz so's you can tell her once again how right you are . . . 'He's no good. Aa've told you afore an' Aa tell you now.' Come on, you rat-faced old divil; come on, an' I'll help you on your way, an' you can tell her. . . ."

"Da! Da!" Mary Ann was pulling on his arm, with Corny at his other side, saying, "Mike. Mike, come on, man . . . come on away."

"Aw." Mike was allowing himself to be turned from the unblinking eyes and tight-lipped face of his mother-in-law when Mrs. McMullen spoke. Addressing herself solely to Mary Ann now, she said, "You should feel at home now you've got your old job back again. And it looks as if it might be permanent. . . ."

Mike almost swung Mary Ann off her feet, so quickly did he jerk around, but Corny's bulk and young strength restrained him from returning to the attack, perhaps now with more than words.

On their erratic journey towards the door they passed Mrs. Flannagan. Her look held a mixture of disdain, patronising pity, and self-glorification, and the glorification covered her family. But she made no comment. Perhaps because Mr. Flannagan was standing close to her side, his hand hidden in the fold of her dress. Mr. Flannagan was no longer the worm that she had created in the early years of her marriage. Mr. Flannagan was now a person to be contended with, so much so that when he nipped her leg she did not even turn on him, she just kept her mouth shut.

They were outside when Mike, jerking his body from right left, freed himself from their clutching hands and cried loudly, and angrily, "Leave over, leave me go, I'm not a child you're playin' with, I'm a man an' I make me own decisions. Do you hear that?" He was leaning towards Mary Ann, peering at the outline of her that seemed to have grown even smaller. "I do things in me own way. You see. Well, it's over. I promised you, didn't I? But in me own way, I said an' with no words. . . . No, begod! No words on . . . either side, 'cos you can't end with words somethin' that's never been started with words, can you now?"

As Mary Ann gazed unseeing up at Mike and felt the gust of his breath fall on her she realized that, although he was drunk, he wasn't half as drunk as he had made out to be in the barn.

"Well now, back to normal, eh? Back to normal and everybody happy. Aw God, yes, everybody happy." There was such sadness in his tone now that she wanted to fling her arms around him and comfort him, but he was moving away, and although he was still swaying his step was much steadier than it had been.

When Mary Ann heard the little wicker gate bang shut, she knew that he had not gone to the house but into the fields. And as she felt Corny's hand groping for hers, she said sadly, "Let's go to me ma."

Lizzie was in the kitchen. She had been standing looking down at the fire, but she turned her head swiftly as they entered the room.

Mary Ann went to her side while Corny stood at the table.

"They came over for their clothes. Have they gone?"

Lizzie made no answer but turned her eyes towards the fire again.

"Ma." Mary Ann was clasping Lizzie's arm with her two hands. "Sit down for a minute. Come on, sit down, I've got something to tell you."

"I don't want to hear anything more." Lizzie's head drooped, yet she turned from the fire and sat down on the chair that Corny brought forward. Then raising her weary face to Mary Ann, who was now standing in front of her, she said, "Where is he?"

"Outside."

"Going to take them home in his condition?" Her voice was bitter.

"No, Ma, no." Mary Ann shook her head. "He's gone into the fields. Ma—" she stood close beside her mother, holding her hand tightly, "he did it on purpose, it was his way of breaking it off, to show . . . well, what he was like—in drink I mean . . . you see?"

Lizzie saw, and she lowered her head. Then raising it again she looked at Corny and, asking for confirmation, said, "You really think so?"

It was as he nodded that Mary Ann put in, "It was Corny who realized it first. He saw why he was doing it, and I know now it's true, because knowing how our Michael hated me da when in drink he would have done anything rather than get drunk the day. You can see that, can't you? . . ." Mary Ann now lifted Lizzie's hand up towards her breast and asked pleadingly, "Be nice to him. Talk to him, he'll feel awful the morrow . . . will you?"

"I'll see . . ." said Lizzie slowly. Then sighing, she added, "Your grannie'll be here until tomorrow night. After that perhaps . . . perhaps things might get back to normal. . . . They might."

"I've always wished she'd never set foot in the house, but tonight, of all nights, I wish it. And he's been for her already."

"What! In the barn?" Lizzie's tone was sharp.

"Yes."

"I'd better go over. You're sure he's not there?"

"No, Ma, no; he went through the bottom gate."

As Lizzie moved across the room, she said, "The electric blanket's on in the front-room bed——" She no longer called it Sarah's bed. "Will you see to the bottles for upstairs?"

"All right, Ma, I'll see to them."

When they were alone together, Corny sat down in Mike's chair to the side of the fireplace and, holding out his hand, said softly, "Come here."

When Mary Ann went to him he lifted her as lightly as if she had been a child and sat her on his knee, and, looking at her, he said briefly, "Let's make our day as soon as possible, eh?"

"Our wedding? . . . But . . . but we said December."

"I know, but there's no need to wait that long, the date wasn't fixed. We could do it in November, say about the middle."

She waited a moment; then moving her head slowly, she said "All right. I'll . . . I'll go and see Father Owen and make arrangements for us to see him together. Will I?"

"Yes . . . yes, do that."

His arms slid over one another as they pressed her to him, and she lay against him, not joyful but sad and quiet; and when his voice, close to her ear, said, "We'll make a big go of it, us two together; we'll show 'em how it really should be done," she turned her face into the opening of his coat and began to cry.

4

"It's not right for an old woman to be on her own. I could be taken ill or drop down dead and who would know but God himself." Mrs. McMullen shook her abundantly haired head at the sadness of it all. "I'd be in nobody's way in the front room there. If you could put up with strangers for two years, and after all what was Sarah but a stranger to you, then you should consider the nearest of your kith and kin, and who's nearer your kith and kin than your own mother?"

"I want my front room for myself." Lizzie was mixing a batter as she stood at the long table, her gaze concentrated on her moving hand.

"I've never heard anything so selfish in me life."

"Perhaps not."

"I'm nearing eighty."

"I'm aware of that."

There followed a pause, and it added significance and emphasis to Mrs. McMullen's next words. "Aw, well, you never know but that you'll be offering it to me in a very short time. With them all gone and you on your own you might be glad of company."

As Lizzie's hands became still Mary Ann came in from the hall. Her face looked small and pinched, and she glared at her grannie as she cried, "The day me ma'll be entirely on her own won't matter to you very much because you'll be dead."

"Mary Ann!" Lizzie turned sharply towards her.

"Nice, isn't it?" Mrs. McMullen's head drooped downwards as she spoke. "All ready to go to mass she is and she comes out with things like that. If any girl has taken advantage of her convent education I would say it was your daughter, Lizzie."

"Aw, I don't care what you say about me, Grannie, you've never said a good word about me in you life and I don't expect you to start now, but let me tell you. . . ." As Mary Ann advanced across the room, Mrs. McMullen brought her head up sharply to meet the onslaught. "The only way me mother would be left alone is if you come to live here. And the Lord himself knows, when that happens——"

"Mary Ann!" Lizzie had her daughter by the shoulders now, and, swinging her about, propelled her forcibly back towards the hall, and when she had her there she pushed the kitchen door closed with her foot, saying under her breath, "As she said, you're going to mass and this is no way to——"

"Look, Ma, the old devil won't rest until she's in that room." Mary Ann thumbed violently towards the front-room door. "And if you want to drive me da away you let that happen."

"She's not coming here, now or at any other time."

"Honest?"

"Honest." Lizzie closed her eyes. "Don't you think I've had enough to put up with without asking for more. Be sensible, girl."

"Yes, yes, I know." Mary Ann took in a deep breath, then added, "But I also know her. She'll keep on till she wears you——"

"She won't wear me down, never."

"But what would happen if, as she says, she took bad?"

"Then she'll go to hospital, or I'd travel all the way down to Shields every day to see her, but I won't let her come here."

Mary Ann's tight gaze dropped from Lizzie's; then her head sank down towards her chest as she asked, quietly, "Have . . . have you spoken to me da?"

Her mother's silence brought her head up again, and when their eyes met they held for a moment before Lizzie answered, "It'll take a little time, but don't worry." She put out her hand and touched Mary Ann's arm gently with her finger. "It'll come all right now, so don't worry any more."

"And you'll stop worrying?"

"Yes . . . yes." Lizzie sighed. "It takes two to make a quarrel and two to mend it, you understand?"

"Yes, Mother."

"Go on, get yourself off or you'll miss the bus."

Before Mary Ann turned away she asked, "Can I bring Corny back to dinner?"

"Yes, of course. . . . But I thought he went to Mrs. McBride's?"

"Not every Sunday, he sometimes has it at home."

"Well, please yourself; he's welcome, as you know."

When Lizzie closed the door on Mary Ann she stood with her back to it for a few minutes, as if fortifying herself before returning to the kitchen.

As she entered the room she saw that her mother was sitting stiff and straight in her chair, with her index finger tapping out a slow rhythm on the wooden arm; this was always a bad sign. Lizzie picked up the bowl of batter, went into the scullery and put it in the fridge; then, returning to the kitchen, she was in the act of clearing a small side-table when her mother said, "How long has it been going on?"

Again Lizzie's hands became still, before she answered, "What do you mean?"

"Now, don't try to pull the wool over my eyes, because even if you did I could still see, I'm not blind. If he had humiliated me as he's done you I would send him flying. A young piece like that! Brash as they come. But he picked his own colour . . . like to like."

"Be quiet!" Lizzie had swung round from the table but was pressing her hips into its edge, and she stood twisting her hands as if aiming to wrench them from the wrists, as she cried, "There's nothing in it, nothing, I tell you. It's in your mind, your bad mind. You would like it to happen, wouldn't you? You've been waiting for it for years. Well, I tell you it won't happen, it's finished. . . . It never started, it was nothing. . . . And I should know, who better? If I was worried about it I would have done something about it, wouldn't I? Well, I've done nothing, not lifted a finger. That's just how much I was worried. Some girls are all mixed up inside and this causes them to make a dead set at older men, but it doesn't say that the older man makes anything of it other than something to laugh at, and that's how it is. For your information, that's how it is." She bent her body from the table while still keeping her buttocks pressed against it. "That's what happened in this case, so make out of it what you like."

As her mother and she exchanged glances, one sceptical, the other defiant, Lizzie became aware of a movement in the scullery. She had been shouting so hard, she hadn't heard anyone come in, but as she turned away from her mother she saw from the window who it was who was going quietly out. Mike was making his exit towards the back gate, not on the paved path, but on the grass verge. Lizzie pressed her lips tightly together and her face puckered painfully. How much had he heard? Enough, she supposed, to make him creep out like that. The breath that she took into her body lifted her breasts upwards. Well, as she had said to Mary Ann, it took two to mend a quarrel. She had done her part, now the rest was up to him. He knew where he stood with her, and now she could await his reaction.

The almost silent dinner was drawing to a close when the front door bell rang. Lizzie raised her head, Mary Ann raised her head, Mrs. McMullen went on scraping the remains of her pudding from her plate, and Corny, rising from the table, said, "I'm nearest, I'll see who it is."

Mike pushed his chair back and went to the fireplace and took his pipe from the mantelpiece. He was standing with his back to the fire, scraping the bowl, when the muffled but recognizable voices came to him, and he stared, or rather gaped, towards the door to where Corny was standing aside to allow Mrs. Radley and her daughter to enter the room.

"We were on our way to Newcastle to my cousin's for tea, but we thought we could drop in to see how you're all faring after the excitement of yesterday."

Lizzie, her eyes wide, her mouth tight, stared at the woman. Then her gaze slowly moved to Yvonne, but the girl was not looking at her; she was looking across the room at Mike, and her brown eyes soft and moist were forgiving him for his misdemeanour of last night. Lizzie's head now moved to take in her husband's face. There was a white line around his mouth, standing out against the ruggedness of his weather-beaten complexion, and there was a look on his face she had never seen before. She likened it to that of a shipwrecked man who, sighting the shore, felt the tide turning beneath him and knew that he was helpless against it. Deep from within her there arose the familiar prayer, but in the form of a cry, "Holy Mary, Mother of God, pray for us sinners now and at the hour of our death!"

5

"It's good of you to see me, Father."

"It's good to see you, Mary Ann." The priest put out his hand tentatively and touched her cheek. "You're looking a bit pale. Are you all right?"

"Yes, Father."

"And everybody at home?"

"Yes, Father."

"Ah, sit down, Mary Ann, and let's have a crack. . . . It's a long time since we had a wee crack, isn't it?" The priest leant his long length towards her, and she smiled widely at him. Oh, Father Owen was nice, wasn't he? Comforting; like Mrs. McBride in a way, only different. She had always been able to talk to these two people without reserve. Well, not quite without reserve to Father Owen. Whereas she could openly discuss her da's weakness with Mrs. McBride, she had always tried to hide it from the priest. Not that her efforts accomplished anything in the long run, for he always got to the bottom of things.

"It was a lovely wedding, Sarah and Michael's, wasn't it?"

"Yes, Father, lovely."

"They should be very happy. . . . Have you seen them since?"

"Yes, Father. They both came over on Monday night . . . they made on they felt lonely" She laughed. "Michael said he missed the farm, and Sarah said she missed the house and me ma and me, but nobody believed them."

"And I don't blame them." They were both laughing now. "And if I know anything, Sarah will be at the farm as much as Michael when he gets back to work. That car is a godsend. . . . You know, Mr. Lord is a very good man, Mary Ann."

"I know that, Father." She nodded at him. "I can't imagine where we would have been without him. But yes I can . . . still in Burton Street."

"Yes, perhaps . . . perhaps you're right, Mary Ann." The priest paused. Then putting his head on one side, he went on, "He's an old man, set in his ways, and the only pleasure he's got in his life is doing little things for other people. Of course, it depends on what you call little. But he likes to help, Mary Ann, you know that?"

"Yes, Father." She sat stiffly now, knowing what was coming.

"His intentions are always good, I'm sure of that, no matter how things appear, and you know, Mary Ann, I think it's very foolish of Corny to have turned down this offer."

Mary Ann did not ask the priest how this piece of news had come to his knowledge. Years ago she had likened Father Owen to God, and the impression at times still held. She looked straight at him as she said, "It's no use, Father, he won't be persuaded; he's got his own ideas about what he wants to do . . . and . . . and I'm going along with him."

The priest's head went back now and he let out a high laugh. "Aw, it's funny it is to hear you say you're going along with anybody, Mary Ann. The individualist of individualists following a leader. Aw, well, perhaps it's a good thing."

After her laughter had died down, the priest waited a moment, giving her the chance to state the reason for her visit, but when she sat looking at her hands he prompted gently, "And what were you wanting to see me about, Mary Ann?"

She raises her eyes to his without lifting her head. "We . . . we wanted to bring our wedding forward, Father. We . . . we thought about the beginning of November instead of December."

Father Owen stared at her, and although his eyes didn't leave her face, Mary Ann knew that he was seeing her as a whole, and the thought this prompted brought a rush of blood to her face and caused her to bring out in fluttering protest, "No, Father . . . no, there's no reason, Father. I mean we just want to get married sooner."

She watched the shadow pass from the priest's face and his eyes light up, and the lightness came over in his voice as he cried, "And why not? Why not indeed!" Mary Ann did not return his smile but said soberly, "You were going to see us one or two evenings before. . . ."

"Yes, yes, that can be arranged at any time. . . . Tell me, have you discussed the future between yourselves?"

"Yes, Father; a bit."

"You've talked about children?"

"Yes, Father."

"And you yourself want children, Mary Ann . . . sincerely want them?"

"Oh, yes, Father, yes." Now she did smile at him, her eyes and mouth stretching with the achievement she would in time accomplish. "I'm going to have three, Father," she said "two girls and a boy."

"Oh?" The priest's long face took on a comic serious expression. His eyebrows formed points directed towards his white hair, and his voice was flat as he said, "Three?" Then again "Three! You've got it all cut and dried, Mary Ann, like the rest of them. Tell me, why stop at three? That is, if the good God means you have any at all. But if He does, I ask you, why stop at three? . . . You know something?" He bent towards her again and poked out his long turkey neck as he stated firmly, "I'm one of thirteen."

"You are, Father? Thirteen!"

"Ah-ah. Ah-ah. Thirteen, and there wasn't a happier family living, although mind, it was a bit hectic at times."

"Oh, your poor mother!" Mary Ann shook her head, and her lips were now pressed together to stop her laughter.

"Aw, you needn't pity her, for she was in her element. It was her vocation to have children, and she reared every one of those thirteen children with the sole help of Hannah Anne."

"Hannah Anne?"

"Yes, Hannah Anne." The priest looked across at the sparsely furnished room to where, on the wall, hung a large portrait of Our Lady, and he seemed to be talking to the picture rather than to Mary Ann as he went on, "Out of all the millions of impressions that a child takes in . . . that a youth takes in, only a few come over with him into manhood, only a few remain clear-cut, the rest are vague and have to be grabbed at and pulled into the light, but a few remain clear. . . . Hannah Anne remained clear."

Mary Ann was no longer smiling, she was looking up at this old priest who she felt at this moment had gone from her; although he was talking to her, he was no longer with her, and she said no word, made no sound to prompt him onwards, but waited, and then he said, "Mondays and Fridays, those are the days I always connect with Hannah Anne, Mondays and Fridays." He turned his face now towards Mary Ann, but his eyes still looked unseeing as he went on, "You see, she washed all day on Monday, and she baked all day on a Friday. She baked yuledoos on a Friday; you know what I mean, bits of dough with currants in. There were nine of use when she first came to the house, and she made nine separate yuledoos, all different sizes according to our ages. I was fourteen then and Hannah Anne fifteen. She was paid one and sixpence a week and she slept under the roof." His head drooped slightly, and so quiet did he become that it almost seemed as if he was dozing. But Mary Ann knew he wasn't dozing. He was back in his boyhood standing in the kitchen waiting for his yuledoo from Hannah Anne, who was just a year older than himself. Then with a quick movement that almost startled her he was back with her again, and from the look on his face she knew that he was going to speak no more of Hannah Anne. But she wanted to hear more, so she said quickly, "Did you lose sight of her, Father?"

"Lose sight of her?" There was surprise in his tone. "No, no, she's in Felling to this day, and every time I'm that way I call." He screwed up his face at her. "I try to make it on a Friday for she still bakes on a Friday, but tea cakes now, and she's generous with the butter." His chin moved outwards. "No, Hannah Anne is still going strong. And you know something? She was twenty-seven when she married. She waited until we were all up, so to speak, and then she married, and I, Mary Ann . . . I performed the ceremony. It was my first wedding. People laugh, you know, when they hear of folks crying at weddings." He had once again turned his eyes from her, and once again they were on the picture on the wall, and Mary Ann's heart became sore for something intangible, something that could not be spoken of, something that might have been if God had willed it; something between Hannah Anne who washed on a Monday and baked on a Friday and was just a year older than a boy of fourteen. Hannah Anne who had shown the priest how easy it was to cry at a wedding. Quite suddenly she decided to let God, and of course Corny, settle as to the size of her coming family. She put her thoughts into words by saying gently, "I'll let things take their course, Father."

"That's it, that's it, Mary Ann, let things take their course. It's a wise decision. Now when do I see you and Corny? Say on Tuesday evening at half-past seven, how's that?"

"That will be fine, Father."

She rose from the chair, and Father Owen, getting to his feet, said, "Now will you have a cup of tea before you go? Miss Neilson always has the pot on the hob."

"Thanks all the same, Father, but I've got to go to Mrs. McBride's; Corny's meeting me there." She had no desire to meet the priest's housekeeper, for she still had memories of that gaunt lady's reception of her in the past.

"Aw, you're going to Fanny's. Well, give her my regards, although it's not over two days since I last saw her. She keeps fine, doesn't she? In spite of everything, she keeps fine." He bent his long length down towards her and grinned as he said, "She'll take some killing that one, what do you think?"

"I think like you, she'll take some killing, Father. And I'm glad."

"That makes two of us."

"Good-bye, Father."

"Good-bye, Mary Ann. Don't forget, half-past seven on Tuesday night the pair of you. God bless you. Good-bye now."

She walked up the street, crossed the road in the direction of Burton Street, and as she went her mind reiterated: Thirteen children . . . I don't think I'd want thirteen; it would wear you out, wouldn't it, thirteen. And they'd all have to be fed and clothed . . . and if the garage didn't go all right . . . Aw—she literally shook herself—what was she going on about? Thirteen children. . . . But what if she did have . . .? Aw, she was mad, daft, thinking this way. As she had said to Father Owen, let things take their course.

In a few weeks she would be married. Her step became slower. She couldn't quite take it in, but she was glad they weren't waiting until December. When the true reason for this came to her she tried to turn away from it, to bang a door in her mind shut on it, but the fact still remained clear before her, she wanted to get away from home. She wanted to get away from the sight of her da. The da who had become weak, the da who had lost his power to create wonder in her. Nothing had apparently changed since the Radleys' visit last Sunday afternoon; an onlooker might imagine that Mike Shaughnessy had made his stand last Saturday night and was abiding by it, but she knew differently. She was too close to Mike not to gauge his feelings, and she knew that before him lay a course from which he was shying. She knew, and he knew, that the only way to treat this matter was with decisive action, to openly tell the pair of them not to come back to the house again. But she also knew that it was almost impossible for her da to take such action towards a girl who was being charming to him, for he wouldn't want to be confronted with the look of feigned incredulity and the consequent reply of, "You've got ideas about yourself, haven't you? Fancy you thinking like that; why, you're old enough to be my father." And Mary Ann knew that was the kind of retort he would get from a girl like Yvonne Radley once she was made aware that she was wasting her time, and he wasn't strong enough to face being made to look an old fool.

She should be happy and joyful because she was to be married—she loved Corny with all her heart—yet here she was, sad to the soul of her. For the first time in her life she felt dislike and bitterness well up in her against her da; and she said to herself, If it keeps up I won't own him, I won't, I won't!

It was Sunday afternoon again and Lizzie had all her family around her. This, she knew, should have made her the happiest woman on earth: there was Michael and Sarah looking so radiant that it brought a soft pain to her heart; there was Mary Ann, a quieter, more subdued Mary Ann these days, and Lizzie felt she liked her daughter better this way, she seemed more predictable. Yet one never knew with Mary Ann. And there was Corny, talking, talking, talking. She should be thankful for Corny, grateful to him, for she knew why he was talking. He was, in his own way, aiming to bring a lightness to the atmosphere, and she really was grateful to him. There were sides to Corny that she could not help but admire, sides that she could trace back to his grannie; one side, in particular, that made him wise . . . heart wise. . . . And then there was Mike. Her husband was sitting to the side of the fireplace, smoking. He might appear at ease, but she knew that, like herself, he was on tenterhooks, he was waiting. . . . If they had been on the two-o'clock bus they would have been here before now, but there was always the three-o'clock, and the four-o'clock. How many times, she wondered, had he seen her since last Saturday? During the past week he had been out only once in the evening, and then for not more than two hours. But a lot could happen in two hours. She had wanted to tackle him on his return and say "Well?" but she had thought better of it, there might just be the chance that he hadn't been with her. Sometimes she told herself she was making a mountain out of a molehill, that there was nothing in it, only what her imagination put there. She explained the situation to herself; Mrs. Radley and her daughter were two people they had met at a holiday camp, wasn't it natural that they should pop in and see them now and again? But the answer that burst from her tortured mind was, "Natural that they come every Sunday and her looking like that? Contriving always to expose herself in some way: showing off her bust with her low, square necklines; sitting with her legs crossed so that her skirt rode almost to her thighs." No, she was no fool. That girl meant business . . . and her mother meant business. Once during the last few days she had said to herself, "I'll walk out and leave him." But then her reason told her that that was what they were waiting for. Like a double-headed cobra, they were waiting their time to strike. For a moment she saw them ensconced in her front room, which, since Sarah's departure, had become "her" room again.

Lizzie's mind was brought from herself by Corny speaking to her, and she turned to him and said, "What was that, I didn't get what you said?"

"I was just sayin'," said Corny, "that she should send this one to one of the magazines, the ones that sell round the North-East."

"Which one is that?"

"The one called 'The Northerner'."

"Oh, give over." Mary Ann reached out to grab the sheet of paper from Corny's hand. "Me mother hasn't heard it."

"She hasn't?" Corny looked at Lizzie again. "Well, it's about time she did," he said. "Listen to this."

Lizzie listened as she looked at the big fellow, standing in a set pose, his arm extended as he read what was apparently Mary Ann's latest effort at poetry.

"The Northerner," announced Corny in the grandiose manner:

> "I longed for spring after winter gales,
> And sleet and snow and muddy feet,
> But when it came it quickly passed,
> And summer followed, and that was fleet.
> Then autumn brought me thoughts of wind,
> Of raging, tearing, swirling air.
> And, as a dreamer, I awoke
> To beauty of trees dark and bare,

Of branches lashed with sleet and rain,
Of racing cloud and raging sea,
And I was bidden to rise and greet
The winter which is part of me.

"There now. Isn't it good?"

Sarah was the first to answer. "I think it's grand," she said; "it says what it means."

"Yes, it's quite good." Michael pulled on his cigarette as he lay back in the corner of the couch; then with a brother's prerogative he added, "But I think it's a bit too simple, I mean to get into a magazine or anything."

"Simple, you say? Of course it's not too simple." Corny was on the defensive. "Anyway, that's how people want things written, so's that they can understand them."

"There is simple and . . . simple, old fellow. There's the simplicity of things like 'Milk Wood' . . ."

"Aw, you and 'Milk Wood'. We had this out afore, remember?" Corny now threw himself into a chair opposite Michael. "Because you went on about it, I read it. And you know what? It's snob stuff. He mightn't have meant it that way when he wrote it, but I'd like to bet me bottom dolar that seventy-five per cent of people who read it do so because they think it's the thing to do, sort of slumming in literature. . . ."

"Slumming! 'Milk Wood'? Go on, man, you don't know what you're talking about." Michael laughed derisively.

"Don't I?" Corny pulled himself to the edge of the chair, and he spread his glance over Mary Ann, Sarah, Lizzie and Mike, who were all sitting now like people waiting to be entertained, and he went on, "I'm tellin' you: half the people that read that kind of stuff neither understand nor like it, but they're afraid to say they don't because they'll be looked upon as unintelligent nitwits."

"What do you know about it, Corny?" Michael was smiling with a quiet, superior smile now, a smile that was meant to draw Corny on still further. "Have you joined a literary society or something?"

"No, I haven't, and I wouldn't if they paid me, but I read; I read what I like, not what they tell me to read in the reviews, 'cos what happens then? Some bloke quotes two lines of something out of a book and they sound wonderful and you break your bloomin' neck to go and get the book, and before you're half-way through the damn stuff you realize you're being had. All the fellow wrote in that book was those two lines, all the rest is what you or anybody else could think of. But some bloke, I mean a reviewer, for one of a dozen reasons picks on those two lines, and when you can't like the book you get the feeling there is something wrong with you up here." He prodded his head with his forefinger. "And you start to ask why."

"Very good question, Corny, a very good question to ask yourself, and it's about time you did, too."

"Give over, Michael, stop teasing." Sarah pushed at her husband, and they both laughed and looked at Mary Ann. And Mary Ann laughed, and Lizzie smiled faintly, but Mike . . . he just kept looking at Corny, his countenance giving nothing away, not of amusement or interest, and Corny, going back into the attack, demanded of Michael, "Come on, let's know what you've read. Have you read Steinbeck, John Steinbeck?"

"Oh, years ago."

"What? What did you read of his?"

"Oh, I've forgotten."

"If you had read Steinbeck, man, you wouldn't have forgotten a word of it. An' I bet you've never heard of Salinger, eh, have you?"

"Of course I've heard of him."

"Have you read him? Have you read *The Catcher in the Rye?* . . . No, you haven't. Well, it's a marvellous book. He's a marvellous writer . . . an American."

"You don't say!" Michael was now shaking with laughter and Corny, suddenly thrusting his hands out, gripped him by the collar and pulled him off the couch and on to the floor. At this Lizzie cried, "Give over! Give over, the pair of you. Corny, get up. Michael, do you hear me? Stop acting like children."

Still laughing, they broke apart, and Michael, taking his seat again beside Sarah, looked at her as he straightened his tie and remarked in a mock serious tone, "Her a poetess and him a literary critic . . . coo! Won't we have something to brag about? . . . 'Cos neither of them can spell!"

"Now stop it, Corny!" Lizzie clamped down on yet another attack, and Corny, putting his coat to rights, cried, "There's many a true word said in a joke." He was now nodding his big head at Michael, and Michael, returning the same gesture, answered solemnly, "True, true, Victor Ludorum of the literary field. True, true. Ah! How true."

Corny, now screwing up his eyes questioningly, asked, "Victor Lu . . . who? Who's he? Never heard of him."

"He was in a band, blew a cornet before he started . . ."

"Stop it, our Michael!" Mary Ann thrust out her hand towards her brother. "Don't be so clever."

"Well, I'm only telling him." Michael was shaking with laughter again.

"O.K., I'm willing to learn, who is he? I can't know them all, can I, and if you don't ask you never know."

"You want your ears boxed, our Michael. Box his ears, Sarah." Mary Ann was on her feet, and thrusting out her hand and grabbing hold of Corny, said, "Come on, I want to go for a walk."

"But I want to get to the bottom. . . ."

Michael was now rolling helplessly on the couch, and he clutched at Sarah as he tried to speak, and Mary Ann cast a withering glance at him and cried again, "Come on. Do you hear, Corny?"

Corny, grinning, and scratching his head with one hand, allowed himself to be tugged across the room, and as he passed Mike's chair Mike touched him on the sleeve, and, looking up into his face, said, with strange gentleness, "You'll be Victor Ludorum in anything you take up; you'll master all that comes, Corny, never you fear."

As they exchanged glances the grin slid from Corny's face. Then, still being led by Mary Ann, he went out into the hall and on into the kitchen, and there, pulling her to a stop, he said under his breath, "What's this Victor Ludorum lark? Who is he, anyway?"

Mary Ann dropped her lids for a moment before looking up at him, saying, "It's just a term, Corny. It's for whoever comes top of the sports at school, it's a Latin term meaning victor of the games."

"Aah." He stared at her for a long moment, and again he said, "Aah." Then rubbing his hand across his wide mouth, he remarked, "That's what comes of not going to a grammar school. . . . Still—" his eyebrows moved up, "we live and learn, don't we?"

"Michael didn't mean anything, you know that. He wasn't trying to be clever or anything. It's just that he's too slap-happy he doesn't know what he's saying half the time."

"Aw, I don't take any notice of Michael." He turned from her and walked slowly down the length of the long kitchen, and as he went he muttered, "Victor Ludorum. Your da says I'll be Victor Ludorum in anything I take up." He turned his head slightly and glanced down at her. "Victor of the games, you said; master of anything, Mike said. Well! Well!"

They went out through the scullery and down the garden path that led to the road, and although he had hold of her hand and they were walking close together, she knew that he wasn't with her. This silly business had put a bee in his bonnet. She almost felt it taking shape: Victor Ludorum . . . Victor of the literary game! She wanted to go back and slap their Michael's face for him. Showing up Corny's ignorance like that. And yet . . . and yet Corny wasn't ignorant. Corny had read more than their Michael, much more.

When he turned his head towards her and said abruptly, "I am the captain of my soul, I am the master of my fate. It's the same thing, isn't it, as this Victor Ludorum?" She remained silent. It wasn't really; one was physical, the other was mental and spiritual. . . . Or was it? Was conquering your fate physical? Oh, she didn't know, it was the kind of thing that took thinking out. But Corny was waiting for an answer and he wanted her to say, yes, it was the same thing, because he intended to be master of his fate, did Corny. And so she smiled softly as she replied, "Yes, Corny, it's the same thing exactly."

With a sudden jerk he pulled her hand up through his arm, and with a step to which she had to trot he marched her down the road.

Already, she knew, he was Victor Ludorum.

6

The weeks that followed went with different speeds for different members of the family. For Lizzie, each day dragged, yet, overall, they seemed to move too fast and ominously towards Sundays, when the visitors would call, sometimes to stay only for an hour, sometimes to stay for as long as four or five. It all depended if they had to wait to see Mike or not. But if their visits were long or short, during them Lizzie tortured herself all the while as she watched for some signal, some look to pass between Mike and the girl which might mean the arranging of a meeting or a change of plan. Now he went out twice a week in the evenings, and with the coldness forming into ice between them, she could not break through and enquire, even in anger, where he'd spent his time.

For Mary Ann the days were moving too fast. It was only just over a fortnight before she would be married, and nothing settled yet about the garage. But perhaps Corny would clinch it this afternoon. She hoped so. Oh, she did, she did, because she didn't want to start her married life living at home. A few months ago she wouldn't have minded a jot, but not now.

She came down the stairs and into the kitchen, and Lizzie, turning and looking at her, said flatly, "You're off then?"

"Yes, I'm meeting Corny at the garage; it might be settled this afternoon."

"I hope so," said Lizzie kindly.

"Thanks, Mother. . . . You wouldn't like to come along with me? It's a nice day, the outing would do you good."

"No, thanks, lass. Michael and Sarah might pop over and I wouldn't like to be out if they came."

"All right." She nodded. "But don't wait tea for us, you never know how long it will take . . . that's if the business gets going."

"Will he move out straight away if it's settled?" asked Lizzie.

"He said he would . . . he said he's going to live with his daughter. He's got nothing much left in the flat upstairs anyway, she's already seen to that . . . the daughter I mean. . . . Well, I'll be off." She kissed Lizzie's cheek. "Bye-bye, Mother."

"Bye-bye, dear." Lizzie now looked Mary Ann up and down before saying, "I like you in that coat; that particular blue suits you and it adds to your height."

Mary Ann leaned forward and again kissed Lizzie, then hurried out without making any comment. It hurt her when her mother was kind, because she knew the effort it must take to say nice things, feeling as she did, desolate and lost, and . . . spurned. Yes, that was the word, for her da was spurning her ma openly now.

As she went up the lane towards the main road she glanced about her. Her da would likely be walking the fields, she had heard him whistle Simon earlier on. Not that she wanted to see him; this looking for him was only a habit. As she rounded the bend of the lane she heard Simon bark, but she could not see the dog, or Mike. Likely they were in the old barn. She looked towards the building that stood somewhere off the road on the edge of a field path, and then her gaze darted to the further end of the lane to where two people were walking with their backs to her. They were Yvonne and Mrs. Radley. Her heart gave a double sickening beat and she thought bitterly, Oh, me da, having her here on the sly. It didn't lighten the accusation that the mother was with Yvonne. She was always with her; she'd be with her until something was definitely settled. That seemed the mother's self-appointed role.

When she came level with the barn she looked deliberately towards it, and there standing outside was Mike, and his gaze was brought sharply from the distance by the sight of her. She would have kept walking on but his voice, sharp and commanding, said, "Mary Ann! Wait . . . wait."

When he came up to her he looked down into her face before speaking, and then he said quietly, "Again it's not what you think, they just happened to be passing and saw me."

She returned his penetrating look as she answered derisively, "Da, don't be so silly." She watched the colour deepen in his face, and now he growled, "I'll have you remember who you're talkin' to; you seem to have forgotten lately."

His angry tone did not upset her as it once would have done, and she replied defiantly, "Well, whose fault is that? You said they were just passing. We're miles off the beaten track. Why would they be coming this way if it was not to see you? Don't tell me they were taking a walk right from Pelaw."

"I don't know what they were doing, but they told me just that, that they were out for a walk. . . . You don't believe me?" His voice was quiet now and she hesitated a moment before replying. "No, Da, I can't. . . ." Then, her voice almost gabbling, she rushed on, "How can I believe anything you say when you're out two nights a week or more and you never used to go, and me ma nearly demented, and you not opening your mouth to her, except to talk at her. . . . Don't you see what you're doing to her? Don't you?"

"I'm doing nothing to her; it's her imagination that's doing it to her . . . and yours."

"And mine? Then why did you say on the night of the wedding that you'd finish it if there was nothing to it? Why?"

"You can't finish what hasn't started, can you?"

"But you admitted it then . . . you did."

Mike dropped his head and raised his hand to it, and, moving his finger across his wide brow, said tensely, "Mary Ann, don't make me lose my temper. I've told you, I've told you more than once, there's nothing in it; but I'll be damned if I'm going to insult two nice people just to please you an' your mother and make meself out a bloody fool into the bargain. And what makes me more determined on this point is that neither of them has ever said a wrong word against you, or Lizzie. Just the reverse; they've had nothing but praise for the whole family. . . ."

"Oh, be quiet, Da, be quiet." Mary Ann was now cupping her ears with her hands, pushing her hat awry as she did so. "You're talking like a young lad. Even Corny would laugh at that. And me . . . I'm not very old but I know that's one of the oldest of women's

tricks in the world. They're clever, both of them . . . clever, and you're a fool, Da, a fool."
She stepped back from the angry glare in his eyes and the pressure of his voice as he cried,
"Mary Ann!"

"I don't care, I don't care, somebody's got to tell you. Do you know what they are?" She
pressed her lips tightly together before she gave vent to the word, "Bitches! That's what they
are, a pair of bitches." She didn't wait for his reply to this, but, turning from him, ran up the
road. And it wasn't until she neared the main road that she drew to a walk. Her body was
smouldering with her temper, and when, leaving the lane, she saw Yvonne and Mrs. Radley
waiting for the bus, it needed only this to ignite it into flame.

What would have been the outcome of the meeting had the bus not arrived at that
moment is left to surmise, but the look that Mary Ann bestowed on both of them as they
turned smiling faces towards her must have warned them that their tactics and polite
conversation were going to be lost on this particular member of the Shaughnessy family.
They mounted the bus before her and took their seats together on the right-hand side. There
was a double empty seat in front of them, but she ignored this and sat next to a woman on
the opposite side. The woman alighted at the next stop and Mary Ann moved up to the
window and sat looking out, telling herself that if they didn't get off before her she would
pass them without as much as a glance.

But they did leave the bus before her; they alighted on the outskirts of Pelaw, and for a
moment she saw them standing on the pavement, from where they looked straight at her
and she back at them before snapping her gaze away as the bus moved forwards.

And apparently she wasn't the only one who had looked at them through the window,
for almost immediately she became aware of the voice of one of the women sitting behind
her, saying, "Did you see who that was?"

"Yes," answered the other. "Ma Radley and her insurance policy." At this the two
women laughed, and Mary Ann said to herself, "Insurance policy?" They were referring to
Yvonne, but insurance policy . . . she just couldn't get it. She strained her ears now to hear
their conversation, but because of the noise of the bus only isolated words came to her, and
these didn't make sense and could have referred to anything. But it was at the next stop that
she heard something that brought her sitting upright in her seat. The woman who had first
spoken said, "Two she's had; the second's in a home, and they tell me the other has an old
bloke lined up now."

"Two she's had." Mary Ann repeated. That could have meant men, but the words "the
second's in a home" didn't apply to men, it applied to children, babies. She turned round
quickly and looked at the women, and they brought their eyes from each other and looked
back at her. She noticed that they were very nicely dressed, very respectable-looking. One of
them flushed and glanced quickly at her companion; then, looking out of the window, she
said, "We're here," and on this they both rose to their feet and left the bus.

And Mary Ann left it also. Almost as it was about to move off she jumped from the step.
"Excuse me." She was breathless when she came to their side. "Please"—she moved her
head now—"I know it's awful, but I was listening. I heard what you said about . . . about
Mrs. Radley and her daughter. . . ."

"Now look here." The taller woman pulled in her chin—an indignant motion. "We were
merely discussing something private."

"I know, I know, but this is important to me. I wonder if you could tell me anything. . . ."

"No! It's none of our business what other people do." The indignation was righteous
now. "And you shouldn't listen to people's conversation."

"Then you shouldn't talk about them, should you?" Mary Ann thrust her chin up at the
woman. Then, reminding herself that this attitude would get her nowhere, she said in a
softer one, "I just wanted to know if——"

"You'll get no information out of me. If you want to know anything about Mrs. Radley or her daughter why don't you go and ask them?"

On this the taller woman turned away and, after a quick glance at Mary Ann, her companion joined her.

Mary Ann stood on the pavement. She stood biting her thumbnail and watching the women walking away. She watched them cross the road, pass three streets and then pause before the taller woman went up a side street while the other woman continued along the main road.

Intuition was Mary Ann's second nature, and now once again she was running. And when she came abreast of the woman she crossed over the road in front of her and waited for her approach.

"I'm sorry," she began immediately, "but . . . but will you help me? It's important. You see . . ." She paused, and, looking at the straight face of the other woman, she realized that only stark truth would get her anywhere, so she went on rapidly, "Well, the old man you friend referred to is . . . is me father."

The woman's face softened and she nipped at her lip before saying, "Oh, lass, I'm sorry, but it's no business of mine. An' you were right, we shouldn't have said anything."

"Oh, please, please, don't mind that. I'm so glad you did. But the Radleys . . . well, you see they are causing trouble; me ma's in a state."

The woman shook her head in sympathy. "I bet she is, poor soul. Look"—her voice dropped to a whisper now—"don't stand here. I just live round the corner; come in for a minute." But before she moved away the woman glanced surreptitiously over her shoulder as if she expected to see her friend appear again. Then, as if by way of explanation, she said, "I . . . I wouldn't like her to think I'm doing anything behind her back. You understand?"

"I understand," said Mary Ann, nodding her head quickly. Again the woman felt there was need for explanation, and as she walked quickly up the street she went on, "She's my friend and she has a lot to say, but when it comes to the push she'll never stand by it. I know more about the Radleys than she does, but I don't let on, I just let her have her say. . . . Well, here we are." She fumbled in her bag for her key, and after opening the door she stood aside to allow Mary Ann to enter.

It was a nice house, Mary Ann decided at once, clean, spanking clean, and orderly.

"Sit down," said the woman as she herself took off her hat and coat. "Well now." She took a seat opposite to Mary Ann and she poked her chin out as she said, "You look so young, hinny, for your da to be such an old man."

"But he's not old, not really, he's just turned forty."

The woman now screwed up her eyes. Then, her lips pressing together, her face expressed a knowing smile. "Forty?" she said, on a high note. "Well, that puts a different side to it, for the man that goes to the Radleys, well, he'll never see sixty again, not by a long chalk, although, mind, he's pretty spruce. You see. . . ." She wriggled her buttocks to the edge of the chair. "How I know all this is because me daughter lives two doors from them. I get all the news from her, but I don't let on to me friend." She nodded towards the door now as if to indicate her friend. "I always say Peggy tells me nothing—that's me daughter—but this old boy has been going to the Radleys, as far as I understand, for the last three months or so. You see, Ma Radley wants to get her married off . . . Yvonne I mean. I always said the French name went to her head, because she was like a march hare when she left school. Our Peggy was at the same school but she was a bit older. And then she had the bairn afore she was sixteen . . . I don't mean our Peggy, I mean Yvonne, you understand?" She was smiling at Mary Ann, but Mary Ann did not return the smile, for her face was set in a blank, fixed stare, and her mouth opened twice before she repeated, "A baby! She had a baby?"

"Oh, aye, two and by different fellows. That's why Ma Radley won't let her out of her sight. I've got no room for her at all . . . I mean Ma Radley, but I must admit she's had a handful with that girl." The woman, warming to the theme, was becoming colloquial, her speech thickening with the northern inflexion as she went on, "Then the second one she had last year. The man was married and he was made to pay for the bairn. And that one's in a home, sort of, because Ma Radley wouldn't have it in the house. But her first one was to a lad no older than herself, in fact not as old, and they couldn't do much about that. Anyway, he's skedaddled. But that one was adopted. Oh, she's been the talk of the neighbourhood, has that madam. But now I think this second business has scared her a bit because she's letting her mother hold the reins, so to speak. There's no coffee bars for her now an' coming home at two in the morning. And, of course, now it's pretty hard on her because none of the lads around here or in the factory wants her . . . except for one thing, and perhaps she's realized that twice is enough; anyway, everybody's just been waiting to see if she snaffles the old boy. Mrs. Radley gave it out that he was her uncle, but it's funny that nobody round the doors heard of her uncle up till a few months ago. As for the old boy, well, he must be barmy thinking he can hold a young girl like her. But then all men of that age are barmy, aren't they?" She waited for an answer, and when none was forthcoming she made an enquiring movement with her head and said, "And your da, hinny, he's gone on her, is he?"

"No." Mary Ann denied firmly what she knew to be true. "No, but she keeps . . . they keep coming to the house. My mother and father met them at a holiday camp, you see, and as far as I gather she made a set at me da. . . ."

"Oh, aye, she would that, anything with trousers on. And you don't think he knows about the bairns?"

"Oh no." Mary Ann shook her head. "I'm sure of that." And she was sure of that. Her da, she would swear, had no knowledge of this wonderful piece of news, and to her at the moment it was a wonderful piece of news. If he had known about her having a baby . . . in fact two babies and getting rid of them as it were, that would have finished anything before it had begun, because he himself had been brought up . . . not in a home, but in the workhouse, left at the gate when only a few weeks old, without even a name pinned on him, and had been christened after the porter who had found him, Mike Shaughnessy. . . . Oh no, there would have been no affair if Mike had known about the babies. Although she did not raise her eyes towards the ceiling, her whole being was looking upwards in thanksgiving. This, she considered, was the answer to her daily prayers over the past months.

She smiled now, saying, "It's been good of you telling me this. You don't know what it means to me, what it'll mean to me ma."

"Oh yes I do." The woman nodded knowingly. "And you tell your ma, it'll stop her worrying. He won't be such a fool when he knows the truth."

Mary Ann rose to her feet, and although she said, "Yes, yes, I'll do that again," she was already in two minds about passing her information on to her mother; she would have to think about it, talk it over with Corny. Yes, that reminded her, she was late already, she must hurry.

As she followed the woman along the passage to the front door she said again, "You don't know how thankful I am." And the woman, on opening the door, said, "I can give a good guess, lass. Anyway, I hope everything turns out all right for you." She dropped her head to one side now. "If you're passing this way any time I'd like to hear how things turn out. Will you call in? Oh, except on Friday." She laughed self-consciously. "My friend comes round on a Friday; we have tea and go to the pictures."

"Yes, all right. Yes, I will. Thank you." Mary Ann was now in the street, and she looked at the woman where she stood above her on the step and said again, "Yes, I'll drop in and tell you. Good-bye."

"Good-bye," said the woman; then added quickly, "oh, by the way, what's your name?"

Mary Ann hesitated. She realised now she had hoped to get away without revealing her name. "Shaughnessy," she said.

"Oh," said the woman; "Shaughnessy. It's an unusual name. . . . Well, bye-bye and good luck."

"Bye-bye," said Mary Ann.

By the time she had waited for another bus she was half-an-hour late when she reached the garage and she fully expected Corny to explode before she had time to explain what had delayed her. But Corny, standing in the wide doorway of the barn-like structure, greeted her with a smile. He did not even say "You're late"; what he did say was, "It's done, clinched." He was breathing fast.

"No!" said Mary Ann, forgetting her own news in this moment.

"Aye, it all happened like that." He snapped his fingers. "When I came along this morning he was still for holding out, saying the road might come through this way next year; he'd had a hint of it, he said." And now Corny's voice fell to a whisper and he pulled her further into the garage as he went on: "When I got here this afternoon, his daughter was on the scene and had been arguing with him like mad. It appears that they are moving to Doncaster and she told him that if he didn't give up the place, then he would just have to get somebody in to look after him because they'd be gone within a fortnight. She told him to sell when he'd the chance, because if he was coming with them the place would be left empty and go to rot—she's like a good many more, she doesn't even believe the road will come this way. But, anyway"—he let out a long breath—"he's put his name to the paper at last, and it'll all be fixed good and proper on Monday."

"Did he come down?" Mary Ann asked him eagerly.

At this Corny lowered his head and kicked his toe gently against an oil cask as he said, "No, just the reverse, he pushed me up another couple of hundred."

"Aw, Corny."

His head came up quickly. "Look, I'm telling you, even at that it's a clinch. Just you wait, give me a couple of years."

"But that'll make it four thousand."

"I know, but I can manage it . . . I mean I've got just about enough to put down. And look, Mary Ann, it's worth it." He pulled her now from the shelter of the garage and on to the rough, gravelled front, where stood two petrol pumps, and beyond into the road, and pointing to the side of the main garage he said proudly, "There, look at it, our house."

It was as if he was showing her something she hadn't seen before; and she was looking at it now as if it wasn't a place she had seen before. There it stood, a red brick building, the lower part given over to what appeared like a shop window, with a space behind it big enough to hold a car, and about the same amount of space to the side which was blocked now by two garage doors looking badly in need of a coat of paint. Above this was the house, their future home. She knew it had four rooms, a bathroom and a lavatory, but she had never seen them. She slipped her hand through his arm and, squeezing it, said, "When can we go up?"

Corny looked down at her and said softly, "He'll be out by Wednesday—his daughter's insisted on that—so we can get the place done up, at least as much as we can do in a week. But it'll be enough to start with, eh?" His voice has dropped to a whisper and she nodded back at him and answered as quietly, "Yes, yes, it'll be enought to start with." Their arms pressed close together, he said, "Come on, I want to go and tell me grannie, and then we'll go home and tell Mike and your ma, eh?"

It was as they rode into Jarrow on the bus that she told him about the episode with the woman, and the knowledge she had come by.

Corny was wide-eyed as he looked down at her, and there was almost a touch of awe in his voice as he said, "You were right about her, what she meant to do, I mean. If she's done it twice she could do it again, and with a fellow like Mike and how he feels about bairns . . . well. But now this'll clinch it, he'll get her measure now. But how are you going to tell him?"

"I don't know," Mary Ann said, and she didn't. "But," she went on, "I don't think I'll tell me ma yet, for somehow I imagine she would feel worse about it than ever. She'd likely get frightened that he might be more sympathetic towards her simply because she's had the two babies. I don't think he would, but me ma doesn't think like me, I know that."

"Why not tell me grannie?" said Corny. "She might come up with some idea of how to use it, I mean the information. She's wise, is me grannie, about these things; she's had a lot of experience you know."

"I know," said Mary Ann. And yes, she thought, if anybody could tell me how to go about this it would be Mrs. McBride.

"Name of God!" said Fanny. "That should put the kibosh on it. Two bairns you say? God Almighty! She's got a nerve has that one, whoever she is. But I should say it was more the mother to be feared than the girl, although she couldn't do any damage without the daughter. Well now." She looked across the table to where sat Mary Ann and Corny, side by side, and she said, "It takes some thinking about, this. You ask me what you should do. Well, as I see it at the moment it's this way, and I'm speaking now with my knowledge of Mike. Now were you to put this to him gently, and give him time to think, begod, it might have the opposite effect altogether and put him in sympathy with her. You never know men . . . oh no, you never know men, even the best of them. And another thing: if she's given time she'll likely explain the whole thing away with a wet eye; there's nothing like tears for turning a man's opinion, even against himself and his better judgment." She moved her big head on her thick neck. "No, as I see it, you've got to use surprise tactics . . . drop it like a thunderbolt when they're both there."

"Both there!" Mary Ann, her eyebrows raised, glanced at Corny. "You mean tell her, or tell me da, in front of her?"

"Nothing short of it, as I see it. You've got to blow the lid off it with no lead up. An' you can do it in an easy, diplomatic sort of way."

"I can?" Mary Ann again glanced at Corny before looking back at Mrs. McBride.

"Aye . . . aye, when they're there together you can just sort of enquire how the bairns are. You see?"

Mary Ann saw—oh, she saw—but she also saw she wasn't up to this task, and she said rapidly, "Oh no, Mrs. McBride, not in front of them both, I couldn't. I could tell me da or . . . or I think I could go to her and tell her what I know, but . . . but to say it in front of them both . . . I . . . I couldn't"

"Well now, please yourself. You've asked for my advice and I've given it to you. But do whatever you think is best."

"She's right." Corny was nodding down at Mary Ann. "You go to Mike and tell him and give him time to think and he'll soften; in spite of him being brought up in a home—in fact that's what'll make him soften towards her, the very thing, and the Lord knows what the offshot will be. Then if you go to the girl she might call your bluff, and as me grannie says"—he nodded in Fanny's direction without looking at her—"tears can have a knock-out effect especially if they're from a V.P. like she is. . . . V.P. has nothing to do with important persons, in this case it stands for voluptuous piece." He grinned at her, but she wasn't to be drawn into smiling at his quip.

"But . . . but, Corny, I just couldn't."

"There's another way," said Fanny. "You could tell your mother and perhaps she would do it. . . . Aw"—she screwed up her face dismissing the idea—"but then it might look like spite comin' from Lizzie, and Mike being a man might hold it against her, you never know. They keep worms in their minds for years, men do."

Mary Ann looked from one to the other now, her face wearing a sadness, and her voice matching her expression, she said, "It's me wedding day a week come Saturday, and now

I've got this to tackle."

Corny made no comment, he just continued to look at her tenderly, but Fanny, pulling herself up from the table, stated flatly, "That's life, Mary Ann, that's life." And going to the hob, she picked up a huge brown teapot, from which she refilled their cups, but in silence now, and in silence they drank.

7

It was again Sunday, and judging from Mary Ann's feelings it could have been the day of doom. She was still doubting very much whether the bombshell method, suggested by Mrs. McBride, was the right course to take. Yet the alternative ways in which she could use her information all seemed to have loopholes that could lead to further complications.

She should be highly delighted about Corny's deal and the fact that she would now have a home to go to when she was married, but this big event in her life was being overshadowed and pushed into the background by the weight of the knowledge she carried.

Her preoccupied manner had not been lost on her mother either, for Lizzie had said to her, "Are you having second thoughts about the garage?" and although she had answered immediately, "No, no, I'm over the moon," she knew her mother hadn't believed her.

Then there was Corny's mother and father. They had said to her last night, "How do you feel about it?" whereas, if her manner had been normal, there would have been no need to put this question. Not that she minded very much what Corny's parents thought, because she hadn't taken to either of them, Mr. Boyle least of all. And she knew she wasn't alone in her attitude, for Corny didn't like his father either, although he had never put his feelings into words. And with his mother he was impatient; and Mary Ann thought he had every right to be, for she never kept the house clean or her pantry well stocked, her excuse being that it was no use trying to keep a place clean where there were eight children, which also make it hopeless trying to keep any food in the house. Although Corny's mother was Mrs. McBride's own daughter, they had nothing in common, except perhaps their untidiness, because that, too, was Mrs. McBride's failing. But of one thing Mary Ann was sure: Corny loved his grannie. He had always shown this by spending more time in her two rooms in Mulhattan's Hall than across the water in his own home in Howden, where, incidentally, he didn't often take her. But because he was excited about getting the garage they had gone over last night.

And then this morning, her mother, pushing her own trouble aside, had taken her into the front room and said gently to her, "Don't worry, everybody is like this before their wedding, you're up and down. At times you don't know if you should go on with it." She wouldn't have been surprised had her mother added, "And it would be a good thing if some of us didn't." But what she said was, "This time next week it'll be over and"—she had smiled wryly—"just beginning."

Mary Ann had wanted to take her mother's hand in hers and say, "But, Ma, it's not that I'm worrying about, it's you, and me da and . . . and what I've got to do this afternoon, because I still don't know if it's the right way to tackle this thing." But she hadn't spoken and Lizzie had said, "Go up and see Tony and Lettice." And then she added, "It's a pity you went to first mass; if you had gone to eleven o'clock that would have filled the morning and made the time pass until he came. You always need to be reassured by the sight of them at this time."

Mary Ann had stared at her mother in silence; she couldn't tell her that she was barking up the wrong tree. . . .

But now the waiting was nearly over. It was close on three o'clock, and if they had caught the two-fifteen bus they should be here at any time. She looked around the room. All the family were present, and as her glance passed from one to the other she thought, It's getting like a play every Sunday afternoon, the stage all set waiting for the first act to begin . . . or perhaps, to-day, the last act.

It was raining heavily outside and blowing a bit of a gale, and the big fire in the open grate was doubly welcome. If she hadn't known how he was feeling it might have appeared that her da was enjoying the blaze, at least from the way he was sitting with his legs stretched out towards the tiled hearth, his pipe in his mouth, and his head in the corner of the winged chair. She could not see his expression, but she had no need to look at his face to know that it would be tight . . . he was waiting.

Her mother was sitting back from the fire, more towards the window. She was knitting. She did not usually knit on a Sunday afternoon, she generally read. Not once did she turn her eyes towards the window, but Mary Ann knew that she, too, was waiting.

Then there was Michael and Sarah, seated as usual on the couch, their hands joined as naturally as if they were children. Looking at them, Mary Ann thought, Our Michael's changed, in this short time he's changed. He's bubbly inside, yet in this short time he's changed. He's all bubbly inside, yet relaxed. His main job, she felt, was to keep his happiness under cover, to stop himself from being too hearty. As for Sarah, her happiness formed a radiance round her. Mary Ann could almost see the light, and at the present moment it aroused just the slightest bit of envy in her. Sarah could be happy, she had nothing on her mind, nothing to worry her. . . . Aw, Mary Ann Shaughnessy! Mary Ann now reprimanded herself sternly. Sarah nothing on her mind? With that handicap? Aw, well—she mentally shook her head at herself—what I meant was, her da's not in trouble, and she hasn't facing her what I have in the next hour or so.

At this moment Sarah, looking across at her, caught her eye. Michael's gaze also joined his wife's, and Mary Ann, gazing back at them, realized that they, too, were waiting, and that below their evident happiness there was anxiety.

And there was Corny. Corny was holding the floor again. Like a master of ceremonies, he was to the forefront of the stage, and as if he knew there was a bad play to be put over he was doing his best to entertain the audience beforehand.

"Anybody can write pop songs: Lyrics they call them. Godfathers! They've got a nerve. It's a racket, 'cos they can pinch the tune from the classics. But they daren't go pinching some bloke's verse, they've got to pay for that. So what do they do, the smart lads? Well, they hash up these so-called lyrics." Corny now threw himself into a pose and sang in an exaggerated but tuneful tenor voice, "I ain't loved nobody since I loved you, and, 'coo Liza, you ain't half got me in a stew."

Even Lizzie laughed, at least she laughed with her mouth; Michael and Sarah rocked together; and Mike, turning his head, cast a quizzical glance up at the big clown. As for Mary Ann, she held her hands tightly across her mouth, and as she laughed she thought, Oh, Corny, you're sweet. It wasn't the right adjective to describe her future husband, but it described his intention, the intention of his clowning.

Corny was demanding of the entire room now, "I'm right, though . . . it is all tripe, isn't it?"

"Oh, I wouldn't say all." Michael came back at him. "There are some good lyrics."

"Tell me them then. Go on, just one."

"Oh, I can't think of any off-hand."

" 'Trees', for instance," said Sarah.

" 'Trees'!" Corny's voice was high. "But that's as old as the hills; it was written over thirty years ago, it's got whiskers."

Corny's eyes were now brought round to Mike's face where Mike was once again slanting his eyes towards him, and he pushed his hand in the direction of his future father-in-law, laughing heartily as he cried, "You know what I mean, Mike. Anyway, you haven't got whiskers." He turned once again to Michael. "I'm meaning the modern stuff. Granted there are plenty of decent writers, but they don't get the chance. I tell you, it's a racket. As for writing lyrics, I've made up umpteen tunes on me cornet but do you think they'd ever be taken?"

"Have you written them down?" asked Michael.

"No, I haven't."

"Then how do you expect them to be taken? Put them down and send them up, and then if they're rejected you'll be speaking from experience; as it is you're just hearing from hearsay."

Corny turned his gaze upwards now as he scratched the back of his head, and his mood changing with mercurial swiftness, he said seriously, "Aye, perhaps you're right. If I could put them down . . . if. But"—he now looked at Michael—"I can't read music." He was grinning in a derogatory way at himself. "I can make tunes up—I've got umpteen in me head—and can bring them through the wind, but that's as far as it gets. But anyway"—he moved his body impatiently—"we weren't talking about tunes, we were talking about the words. Now Mary Ann there: do you think they would put any of her stuff to music?"

Michael now cast a glance in his sister's direction, and with brotherly appreciation he said, "There's a chance, that's if she ever did anything good enough."

"Oh!" Mary Ann's voice sounded indignant. "Don't praise me, Michael."

"Don't worry," said Michael, "I won't." But he laughed gently at her as he spoke.

And then Corny came back at him, crying, "She's done some good stuff. If she had any sense she'd keep sending it off, but she doesn't." He bounced his head at her, and for a second they exchanged glaces, and then he went on, "Some of her prose is like poetry."

"You don't say," said Michael, with mock awe now.

"Aye, I do. It's always the same in families, it takes an outsider to see what's going on."

"Well, that's soon going to be rectified," said Michael. "And then you'll be blind to all our good points, especially your wife's. . . ."

As the door-bell rang and cut off Michael's voice they all looked startled. It would seem that Corny had succeeded in his efforts during the last few minutes and had made them forget what they were waiting for, but now he stopped his fooling; his part for the present was finished, but he said "Will I go?" And Lizzie nodded to him without raising her head. Sarah pulled herself further up into a straighter position on the couch, as did Michael, while Mike, leaning forward, knocked the doddle from the bowl of his pipe. Only Mary Ann made to move. She sat farthest from the door and to the side of her mother, and as the sound of footsteps came across the hall her heart began to race. She hardly saw the mother and daughter enter the room, for there was a mist before her eyes, and she was afraid for the moment she was going to faint, or do something equally silly. That was until she saw Corny's face. His expression soft, his eyes were looking at her over the heads of the others, saying, "It's all right, it'll soon be over."

"What a day!" said Mrs. Radley. "And how are you, Lizzie?"

Lizzie had not risen to greet the guests, but she raised her eyes and, looking at Mrs. Radley, answered, "Quite well, thank you . . . I wonder that you ventured out in such weather."

"Oh"—Mrs. Radley swung her permed, bluey-grey head from side to side, dismissing the weather—"we like to get out. We must get out." She leaned towards Lizzie now. "We're not like you all here, we're not so fortunate as to have open land all round us; and when one loves the country, it's a great strain on the nerves being hemmed in by brick walls."

Yvonne Radley was standing to the side of her mother; she had not addressed anyone in the room as yet. Her eyes had gone straight to Mike as soon as she came through the door. He'd had his back towards her, but now, when he turned to her, there was a defeated look about him; yet at the same time his eyes spoke of the anger he was feeling, anger at the combined attitude of his family and the obvious hostility filling the room. Getting to his feet, he said, "Sit down."

"Thanks . . . Mike."

Yvonne's hesitation in saying Mike's name suggested to Mary Ann's disturbed mind an endearing familiarity. She watched her father pointing to the couch and saying to Mrs. Radley, "Sit down, won't you?" And as he spoke his angry glance was directed towards his son, for Michael, although he had risen reluctantly to his feet on their entry, had not offered his seat to the visitors.

"We are not going to stay long. We merely come with an invitation."

Mary Ann's gaze, which had been directed towards her hands, snapped upwards now to Yvonne Radley, but the girl, a simpering expression on her face, was still looking at Mike and holding his attention as she went on, "You see, it's my birthday on Wednesday and we'd like you to come along in the evening. We're having a little party." She paused; then, her eyes flitting to Lizzie, she added with a girlish laugh, "All of you I mean, of course, that's understood. . . . Will you?"

Lizzie now laid down her knitting and looked across the room at this girl for a full minute before answering her. She took in once again her long legs, her high bust, her round blue eyes, her simpering expression, her hair hanging like burnished bronze on to her shoulders, and as she looked she had the fearsome urge to spring on her, grip her by the throat and bang her head against the wall. The thought was terrifying in itself and it affected her voice as she answered, "I'm . . . I'm sorry, but I have an engagement for next Wednesday evening."

The word engagement seemed so out of place, the excuse so evidently an excuse that it actually created a wave of embarrassment among all those present, with the exception perhaps of the Radleys themselves.

"How old will you be?" It was Corny speaking now. His voice rough-edged, his face straight, he looked directly at the girl, and she, returning his look with a searching one of her own, answered, "Nineteen."

"Oh, Mary Ann's got a couple of months up on you."

"Yes . . . yes." Yvonne smiled now across the room at Mary Ann, and Mrs. Radley, following her own reasoning, put in quickly, "Yvonne's got an aunt who is only sixteen. That's funny, isn't it? Yvonne nineteen, with an aunt of sixteen." She beamed from one to the other.

"Would you like a cup of tea?" Although Mike's voice sounded ordinary, his whole body looked stiff and defiant as he asked the question.

"Oh, no, Mike, don't bother; we won't stay," said Mrs. Radley. "We set out to have a nice long walk and we'll carry on. The weather doesn't deter us . . . does it, Yvonne?"

"What?" Yvonne brought her gaze from Mike's averted face, then said, "No, no. No, we love tramping. I love open spaces."

As Corny, the devil in him, began to whistle softly, "Oh give me a home where the buffalo roam," Mike turned a fiery glance on him, and Corny allowed the tune to fade slowly away, but not too slowly, then went and stood beside Mary Ann and imperceivably nudged her with his arm.

Mary Ann did not need any nudging to be reminded of what she had to do. But how? How was she to start? She became panicky when she saw Mrs. Radley rise to her feet, followed by Yvonne. She had never expected them to go so soon, they had only just arrived. She couldn't do it—not in a hurry like this, anyway. She glanced at Lizzie sitting frozen-faced beside her, and it was the sight of her mother's patent unhappiness that loosened her tongue.

"Are you having many to the party?" Her voice was high and unnatural sounding, and she was conscious of everyone turning their eyes towards her, for never had she addressed either of the Radleys since their first visit.

"Well, no." Again the simpering attitude from Yvonne. "Only friends, close friends."

Mary Ann gathered saliva into her dry mouth and swallowed deeply before she said, "But you'll be having the children . . . the babies?"

There, it was done. The fuse was lit.

From the time the match is put to a fuse until the actual explosion takes place there is a period of comparative silence. This silence now filled the room; and as all eyes were once more turned towards her she had the desire to scream and break it. She saw the mother and daughter exchange a startled glance; then they were looking at her again, their eyes seeming to be spurting red lights towards her. The knowledge of exposure had been in their flicking glance, and it brought trembling power to her, and she said now, addressing Yvonne pointedly, "Oh, of course, you mightn't be able to bring your eldest, him being adopted, but the baby you could; they'll let you have him from the home for the day, won't they?"

"Yo-u! . . . yo-u!" Yvonne took two rapid steps forward, but was checked from advancing farther by her mother crying, "Stop it, Yvonne!" Mrs. Radley had gripped her daughter's arm and now, turning her white-strained face towards Mary Ann, she said, "I don't know what you mean?"

"I think you do," said Mary Ann, her voice more normal sounding now; "and so does she. Or would you like me to explain further?"

Yvonne Radley, pulling herself from her mother's grasp, gripped the head of the couch and, leaning forward over Sarah towards Mary Ann, hissed, "You swine! You prying, sneaky little swine." And now her tone was no longer recognizable, nor yet her expression. "You think you're smart, don't you? You pampered, undersized little brat you. For two pins I'd. . . ."

"You'd what?" said Corny.

"Yvonne! Yvonne! Stop it." Mrs. Radley was now pulling at her daughter's arm, and the girl, angered with frustration and disappointment, burst into tears. Her wide, heavily painted mouth agape, she spluttered, "I'll get me own back on you, you'll see, you little upstart you. I hated you from the minute I clapped eyes on you . . . you . . ."

"Come away, come on." Mrs. Radley's voice, piercing now, seemed to verge on hysteria, as she cried to Mary Ann, "You haven't heard the last of this, miss, oh no. Oh no, not by a long chalk. You'll hear more of this; up for defamation of character, you'll see. You'll see, you nasty-minded little ——" Mrs. Radley used a term which no one, judging from her previous refined manner, would have dreamt she ever knew—"That's what you are, nothing else, a nasty minded little —— Come on. Come on. You'll not stay here another minute." She pulled her daughter through the doorway into the hall, and nobody in the room made a move to follow them and let them out of the house.

The feeling of apprehension and worry which had filled Mary Ann since hearing Mrs. McBride's suggested method on how best to deal with the information concerning the Radleys was nothing compared with the terror filling her as she looked at her da. She was unaware of the others looking at her, their expressions all different. There was admiration in Michael's and Sarah's eyes; there was love and concern in Corny's; there was a look of amazement, mixed with pity and incredulity on her mother's face; but she saw none of these, she only saw Mike's face filled with black anger; it seemed to ooze from him. She fancied she could smell it, and her mind gabbled: He must have been in love with her. It was serious then. Oh dear Lord. As she watched him coming slowly and heavily towards her, she trembled with this new fear, fear of her da and what he was going to do to her. Now he was towering over her, his body stretched, his muscles hard and his one fist clenched. His jaw moved a number of times before his mouth opened to speak; then he said in a terrible tone, terrible because it was quiet, "You think you've done something clever, don't you, Little Miss Fix-it? You've torn out somebody's innards and held them up for inspection. She had sinned, hadn't she? not once, but twice, so you, the good Catholic little miss, must——"

"Mike!" It was Lizzie's voice, commanding, loud, and it brought Mike's head swinging towards her, and, his voice no longer quiet now, he barked, "You! . . . you! I'm warning you. You be quiet. It's you who started this, you and your fancies. And you see what you've brought her to, because she did it for you. She's turned into a sneaking little righteous ferret. So do what you've been doing for many a week, keep your mouth shut."

And Lizzie kept her mouth shut, tight now, in a proud, bitter line.

Mike was again looking at Mary Ann, and, his tone dropping once more, he addressed her, saying, "You're not out of the wood yet, me girl; marriage won't make you immune from emotions. Well, now"—he pushed his shoulders back even further—"you intended to fix it for her, didn't you? Well, perhaps you have. Perhaps you've done just that . . . the lot of you, among you." He flicked his eyes around the room before again levelling them on Mary Ann and going on: "There's an emotion you know very little about as yet, me girl. It's called compassion, an' it can do very odd things, especially with an . . . old . . . man"—he stressed the old—"an' a young lass saddled with two bairns." He paused now, and into the pause Mary Ann whimpered, "You wouldn't, Da, you wouldn't. Oh, I'm sorry, for what I did, but you wouldn't, you wouldn't."

"Wouldn't I? Well, just you wait and see, me girl. I'm going to finish what you and your mother started. It's always good policy to finish a job, isn't it?"

Mary Ann, still staring at Mike, heard her mother's sharp intake of breath, and it was as if she had leapt inside Lizzie's body and was retaliating for her, because now, of a sudden, she cried up at Mike, "Well then, go on, go on, what's stopping you? Everybody wants to laugh out loud; they've been smothering it for weeks, so go on, and they can let it rip. You with your neck all creasy"—she pointed up at him—"and big brown freckles on the back of your hand, which are not freckles at all, but the first signs of age coming on they say; and there's grey in you hair, but you can't see it at the back of you head, the same as you won't be able to see yourself as a doddery old man when you're left home here with the bairns while she goes . . ."

As the hand came across her face she thought that her head had left her body. She was conscious of herself screaming as she toppled backwards over something hard, then there was noise and yelling all about her.

As she felt her mother's hands raise her head from the floor the mist cleared from her eyes and she saw, standing like two giants within the open doorway, Corny and her da. They stood close together. Corny had hold of Mike's lapels, and Mike, his good arm sticking out at an angle from his body, was saying in that terrible voice again, "Take your hands off me, boy."

"YOU . . . You shouldn't have done that." Corny's voice, too, was deep and unnaturally quiet, but his anger was causing him to stammer. "If . . . if you were . . . weren't . . ."

"I told you . . . take your hands off me."

"Corny! Corny!" Michael was now tugging at Corny's arms. "Leave go. . . . Do you hear?" With a quick, strong pull he wrenched one of Corny's hands from Mike's coat and slowly Corny relinquished the other.

Mike now, taking a step backwards, lifted his hand and straightened his collar and tie while straining his neck upwards, and as he did so he looked at the two young men confronting him, both faces, that of his son and his future son-in-law, full of dark hostility. With a movement that seemed to lift his body completely from the floor he swung round, and the next sound that came to them was the banging of the front door.

Corny shook his head as if coming out of a dream; then, turning swiftly, he went across the room to where Mary Ann was being supported by Lizzie, with Sarah in an unwieldy position on the floor at her other side.

"Don't cr . . . cry. Don't cry." He was still stammering.

"Lift her on to the couch," said Lizzie in a toneless voice. "She's hurt her hip on the side of the chair."

Corny lifted Mary Ann from the floor as if she were a child, and, seating her on the couch and still with his arms about her, he pressed her head into his shoulder, and it was the warm comfort, the understanding pressure of his arms, that released, in full flood, the agony in her mind—the agony of the knowledge that her da had hit her. Her da! . . . Corny, Mr. Lord, Mrs. McBride, or even Father Owen could have struck out at her—fantastic as the assumption was, she could have stretched her imagination to see it happening—but never, never her da.

"Don't, don't cry like that. Mary Ann, do you hear me?" Lizzie's hands had turned her face from Corny's shoulder and were cupping it. "Stop it now."

"Oh, Ma! M . . . ma!" She was spluttering and jabbering incoherently as she had done at times when a child and her world had broken apart. But now she was no longer a child, and things, some things, were more difficult to say; the words were sticking in her gullet, "He . . . he . . . Ma."

"Give over, child, give over." It was as if Lizzie, too, was seeing her as a child again; and now she said to Corny, "Carry her up to bed, will you?"

As Corny picked her up in his arms she turned her head towards Lizzie, crying, "Ma, he . . . he didn't mean it."

"There now, don't fret yourself any more, go on." Lizzie pressed Corny forward.

"He didn't, Ma, he didn't, I te . . . tell you. . . . Where's he gone? Our Michael . . . our Michael, go and find him. Go on, Michael."

"All right," said Michael. "Don't worry, I'll go and find him."

From somewhere behind Mary Ann now her mother's voice, no longer toneless, said quickly, quietly and bitterly, "You'll do no such thing, Michael. Stay where you are. He's gone. Let him go, and I hope I never see him again."

As Corny lowered Mary Ann on to the bed she held on to him, crying hysterically now, "See . . . see, I shouldn't have done it. She said it would be all right; your grannie, she said it'd be all right, and now, look. A bombshell, she said. Fancy Mrs. McBride saying that. . . . A bombshell, a bombshell. . . ."

8

Lizzie didn't know how much past midnight it was; she couldn't recall whether it was Saturday, Sunday or Monday; she was only aware that she had reached the crisis of her life, and she was living in that crisis. Years ago she had almost walked out on Mike and gone to her mother's, but now he hadn't almost walked out on her . . . he had walked out, he had gone completely. Why had this happened? Was she to blame? If she had laughed at the whole thing, would it ever have reached this point of torment? But she wasn't made to laugh when the vital issues of life were being undermined. She was not one of those who could follow the advice given by the wise sages in the women's magazines; these wisdom-filled females who had never touched on the experiences on which, each week, they poured out their advice; and such advice: "Your best plan is to ignore the whole situation"; "Welcome her to the house, treat her as if she were your daughter." Were there woman anywhere who could follow such advice?

Well, it was over, he had gone. She looked at the clock. No one had wound it up and it had stopped at twenty-five past twelve. If he had been coming back he would have been here long before now. Yes, it was over. Then she should go up to bed, shouldn't she?

She couldn't face that bed. She didn't think she would ever lie in it again; happy or otherwise, they had shared that bed for close on twenty-five years. No, to-night of all nights she couldn't face that bed. She would stay where she was, by the fire. She leant her head back in the corner of the high chair and looked across to where Mike's chair, startlingly bare, faced her. "Oh, Mike, Mike." It was a wail, coming as it were from far back in the beginning of time, spiralling up through her being, choking her, strangling her with the agony of things past, good things past.

"Are you all right?" Michael's hand on her shoulder brought her upright in the chair, her own hands gripping her throat.

"I'm sorry; did I wake you?"

"No, no, I wasn't asleep."

He was on his hunkers before her now, his eyes soft on her face. "Go on up to bed, Mother, go on."

"I couldn't Michael. I'm all right here. Don't worry. You go on in to Sarah."

"She can't sleep either."

"It's the couch, it isn't long enough."

"No, it isn't that."

"Where's Corny?"

"Outside somewhere."

Lizzie's eyes stretched slightly. "Outside in this?" She listened for a moment to the howling of the wind and the steel-rapping of the rain on the windows. "What's he doing out there?"

"I don't know, he just feels like that. He's upstairs one minute and outside the next. He's been like that for hours."

"What time is it?" she asked.

"It's after one, nearly half-past I should say. . . . How is she?"

"She was still asleep a short while ago."

"That tablet has done the trick. It'll likely put her out until the morning. . . . Michael." Although Lizzie spoke her son's name she turned her face from him, and it was some seconds before she went on, "Will . . . will you carry on the farm?"

And it was some seconds before Michael answered, "Aw, Mother, you know I will . . . but . . . but it won't come to that. . . ."

"It'll come to it all right, Michael, let's face it. This is the end."

"He'll come to his senses. You've got to give him a chance. He was mad at the way it happened."

"I don't want him, Michael, when he comes to his senses. Once he has spent a night with that girl nothing on God's earth could make me take him back. I can't help it, that's how I'm made. I've never wanted anybody but him in my life, and up to now it's been the same with him. But . . . but it wouldn't be any use him crawling back when his madness has cooled off. No use at all."

Her voice was so level and conveyed such finality that Michael knew that no persuasion would make any impress on his mother's attitude. As he pulled himself up straight a noise in the yard brought him sharply round, his face to the kitchen door. And Lizzie's head came up, too, at the sound of running steps. The next minute they heard the back door open, and within seconds Corny appeared in the doorway. The water was running from his plastered hair down on to his black plastic mack. He stood gasping for a moment, wiping the rain from his face with his hand before coming farther into the room; then looking from Michael to Lizzie, he brought out, "He's back."

"Me father?" It was a soft question from Michael, but Lizzie made no movement.

"Where?" said Michael now.

"I saw him going up into the loft. All night I had a feeling he was somewhere round the place. I looked everywhere, but no sign of him, yet I couldn't get rid of it, the feeling. And then it was Simon who gave me the tip. You know that little bark he gives when he sees him, or smells him. Well, I heard him come out from the lower barn growling and then there was this little bark, and I stood in the shelter of the byres, and I saw the outline of him. He . . . he was swaying a bit. It could be that he's got a load on, yet I don't know. But I didn't go near him." He jerked his head to the side. "After what happened he wouldn't welcome the sight of me."

"I'll get the lantern." Michael was running across the room; then at the door he turned and said to Corny, who was about to follow him, "Don't come. Stay with me mother." And he cast a glance in Lizzie's direction before hurrying out of the room.

Getting to her feet, Lizzie went and stood before the fire, with her hand lifted to the mantelpiece and her head bowed. It was a stance she often took up when deeply troubled.

After some minutes of silence Corny approached the fire, but not too near to her; and holding his hand out to the warmth, he said softly, "I feel that I'm to blame as much as anybody for what has happened, Mam. You see, when Mary Ann told me and said she didn't know what to do, I mean about letting on about what she knew, I told her that the best one to go to for advice was me grannie, and it was me grannie who suggested that she make her information into a bombshell. I can see now it was wrong, but . . . but you can always be wise after the event, can't you?" He waited a moment, and when no answer came to him he lowered his head and muttered, "I'm sorry."

Lizzie turned towards him now and, putting out her hand, touched his arm. "Don't blame yourself, Corny," she said. "If you want to know something, I think it's just as well it hapened like this. It had to come to a head sooner or later. It had to burst."

"What'll happen now?" he asked softly. "You'll not take it out of . . .?"

Turning from him, Lizzie said abruptly, "We'll just have to wait and see, Corny, won't we? We'll just have to wait and see. . . ."

They were standing in silence, finding nothing more to say, when Michael came hurrying back into the kitchen. It seemed that he could not have been as far as the big barn in so short a time. He, too, was gasping with his running against the wind, but he came straight to Lizzie, where she stood on the hearthrug waiting, and straight to the point, saying, "He's in a bad way, Mother, he's——" He shook his head slowly. "He's never been out of the fields. He's covered with mud from head to foot and wet to the skin; the things are sticking to him. He must have been headlong in the dyke down by Fuller's Cut. He's shivering as if he had ague." He put his wet hand on hers. "He's never been away, you understand, not farther than the fields."

Michael watched as his words slowly brought the colour back into his mother's face. He seemed to watch the years drop away from her. Her voice had a slight tremble in it as she said to him, "Give me my coat, will you?" Then when Michael had brought her coat from the hall and helped her into it, she asked, "Is the lamp outside?" And when he nodded, she said, "Don't come with me." Then, looking from him to Corny, she added, "Go to bed,

Corny—the spare bed is ready."

Corny said nothing, and Michael said no more, but they both watched her as she swiftly pulled the hood of her coat over her head and went out of the room.

Having picked up the lantern at the back door, Lizzie battled her way across the farmyard towards the barn. When she reached the great doors she stood for a moment to regain her breath; then, pushing open the small hatch door, she bent down and entered the barn. As she walked unsteadily towards the ladder that led to the loft, the light from the lantern, and her steps, caused a scurrying of small creatures. Then she was on the ladder, mounting it slowly, and when she reached the top Simon's wet nose greeted her before he turned and ran to the far end of the loft, where a bale of straw had been broken and on which lay a huge, huddled figure.

As the light of the lantern fell on Mike, Lizzie paused. Her body still stiff and erect, her face still set, she looked down on her husband, and with the exception of the empty sleeve no part of him was recognizable to her, but she was made immediately aware that the mud-covered shape was shivering from head to foot. Bending slowly over him, she touched his shoulder, and after a moment he turned his face towards her, only to turn it quickly away again. Evidently he had not expected to see her.

It was the unguarded look in his eyes that softened the ice round Lizzie's heart, for the look reminded her of the dog they had found in Weybridge's cottage three years ago. The Weybridges were a no-good family who had lived off the beaten track about two miles over the fields, and whose debts had caused them to do a moonlight flit one night, and they had left their dog chained up in an outhouse. He was there a fortnight before Michael had found him and brought him home, and the poor creature had crawled on his belly across the length of the kitchen and laid his head across her feet. He was an old dog, and partly blind. Apparently he had been used to a woman and had immediately given to her his allegiance, and in return she had looked after him lovingly until he had died last year.

"Come on, get up," she said softly. But Mike did not move. "Do you hear me?" she said. "Get on your feet."

For answer he buried his face in the straw and muttered something which she could not hear.

Placing the lantern at a safe distance, she bent over him again, and, gripping him by the shoulder and using all her strength, she jerked him from his prone position. And now, with his head hanging, he muttered through his chattering teeth, "Leave me be for the night, will you?"

"I'll do no such thing; get on your feet."

"I . . . I can't. I'm finished for the time being. I'll . . . I'll be all right in the mornin'. Go on in, go on in." He went to lie down again but her hands prevented him. "Get up," she said. "Come on, get up." Her voice was soft, pleading now, and after a moment he turned on all fours and raised himself up on to his knees, and then up to his feet.

She was appalled at the sight of him. As Michael had said, he must have fallen headlong into the muddy ditch at Fuller's Cut.

She guided his shaking form to the ladder, then on to it, and held the light aloft until he had reached the floor of the barn. Then descending quickly, once again she guided him, and when they were in the yard she put her arm about him to steady him against the wind, and with the docility of a child he allowed himself to be helped by her until they reached the back door, and there, stopping and pulling himself slowly from her grasp, he muttered, "Are they in?"

"No, no," she whispered hurriedly, "they're all in bed."

In the scullery he stopped again, and, looking down at the condition of himself, he brought out, his words rattling like pebbles against his teeth, "I'll . . . I'll change here."

For answer she pulled off her coat, saying briskly, "You're going straight upstairs into a bath."

She led the way now, quietly through the kitchen, into the hall and up the stairs; and he followed, stepping gingerly, his limbs shaking with every step he took. But when they entered the bathroom and she had turned on the bath and pulled some warm towels from the rail, he said, without looking at her, "Leave me be now, I can manage."

When he felt her hesitation he added, in a tone that was more like his natural one, "I'll be down when I'm tidied, leave me be."

When Lizzie returned to the kitchen her own legs were shaking so she felt she must sit down before she dropped. But as she neared a chair she stopped, saying to herself, "No, no, keep going, keep going." She knew it would be fatal at this moment to sit down and think. If she sat down she would break down, and she didn't want that. He would need something hot, piping hot, if there wasn't to be repercussions to this state he was in. How long had he been wet through to the skin? Eight . . . nine hours? And in this wind that was enough to cut through you like a sword! Hot bread and milk, she said, that will act like a poultice and. . . . She looked towards the store cupboard, seeing at the back of it, hidden among the bottles of sauces, mayonnaise and pickles, a flask of whisky. It had stood there a long, long time, waiting for an emergency; and this was the emergency. She had put her foot down on Mike having whisky in the house, yet she had always kept that flask hidden there. It was strange, she thought, as her hand groped knowingly over the shelf and brought out the bottle of Johnnie Walker, strange that she herself should give him a whisky. . . .

It was half-an-hour later when Mike came downstairs. When she heard his soft, padded approach her body began to tremble and she went hurriedly into the scullery and brought the pan of bread and milk from the stove, and she was pouring it into a basin when he entered the room. She did not look towards him; nor did Mike look at her, but, pulling the cord of his dressing-gown tighter about him, he walked to the fire and stood, very much as she had done earlier, looking down into it, his one hand gripping the edge of the mantelpiece.

Lizzie now opened the flask of whisky and poured a generous measure into a beaker, and after adding brown sugar to it she went to the fire and, bending sideways so that no part of her touched Mike, this seemingly back-to-normal Mike, she lifted the boiling kettle from the hob and, returning to the table with it, filled the beaker. Then, the kettle in one hand, the beaker in the other, she went once again to the fireplace, placed the kettle on the hob and, with her eyes fixed on the beaker as she stirred the hot whisky and sugar, said softly, "Drink this."

Without moving his body Mike brought his head round and looked at her, then at the beaker. The smell that came from it was of whisky, the liquor that was forbidden in the house, forbidden because of his weakness. The hot stinging aroma swept up his nostrils and down into his body. It was too much, too much. He took his hand from the mantelpiece and pressed it over his face, digging his fingers into his scalp as if he would tear the whole facade of his features from their base, and his body crouched forward and writhed in agony as he brought out her name, "Liz. Oh, Liz."

As she swiftly laid her hand on his bent head she had the feeling she was touching him for the first time. She could not see her hand or his head now; the ice fast melting round her heart was flowing from her eyes, bathing her face, and refreshing her soul like spring floods on a parched land. She put her arms about him and he clung to her fiercely while a torrent was released from him, too—a torrent which checked his speech and choked him yet could not stop him repeating her name over and over. And he asked forgiveness and said what he had to say with his hand as it moved in tight pressure over her head, her shoulders and her back. How long they stood like this they didn't know, but presently Lizzie muttered chokingly, "It'll . . . it'll be cold." Blindly she put out her hand to the side and lifted the glass from the mantelpiece and put it to his lips; and over the brim of it they looked at each other. Once again they were survivors, once again they had swum ashore. And with this rescue Lizzie was sure of only one thing: never again would Mike sail so near the wind, and never would he sign on, so to speak, in a vessel similar to the one that he had just escaped from.

That voyage was over.

As the late dawn broke Mary Ann came out of her drugged sleep. She lay for a moment quite still, staring towards the dim lines of objects in the room. She felt awful, her head ached; and as she thought of her head aching, she realized that her face was aching too, as if she'd had toothache, and her leg felt stiff. As she put her one hand to her face and another to her hip the reason for her aches and pains crept slowly into her mind and she groaned as she turned round and half buried her face in the pillows. Closing her eyes, she went over the scene of last night. She remembered crying and shouting after her da had hit her. She remembered that she couldn't stop, and that she had kept blaming Mrs. McBride for it all. That was just before her mother gave her that tablet; it must have been a sleeping tablet.

She turned on to her back again and looked towards the window. Mrs. McBride wasn't to blame, she herself was to blame. When she had found out about Yvonne Radley she should have gone to her mother with the news, or, failing that, she could have got her da on the quiet and risked the consequences. She felt a wave of sickness creep over her as she thought that, whatever she had done, the result couldn't have been any worse.

But what had happened since last night? Her mother left all alone. In this moment she had not doubt but that her mother had been alone all night, for remembering the look in her da's face she knew it meant defiance and going his own road. She must get up and see her mother.

As she pulled herself into a sitting position she thought, Oh dear, I feel awful, awful, and she lay back again, her head against the bed-head, listening for a moment to the usual household sounds that the dawn brought: the muffled steps rising from the kitchen below, a door closing, Simon barking, the lowing of the cattle . . . the cattle. She lifted up her head from its resting position. . . . Who'd look after the cattle, the farm as a whole? Michael, of course. . . . Yes, there was Michael. Her head dropped back yet again. She must get up and find out what was going on, but oh, she felt awful.

She was pushing the bedclothes off her when there came the sound of footsteps on the landing; they were quiet, heavy and slow. Recognition of these steps brought her face round to the door. She paused with the bedclothes in her hand, one leg hanging over the side of the bed, and when the gentle almost imperceptible tap came on the door she pulled her leg back into the bed and the clothes about her and waited.

When the door opened and she saw her da enter, and he in his night things with his dressing-gown on, a cup of tea in his hand and a look on his face that she hadn't seen there for many a day, she wondered for a moment if she had died in the night, or if she was still dreaming? Or, if she was awake, was she being affected still by the sleeping tablet? She kept her eyes on him as he walked slowly to the bed. She watched him put the cup of tea on the table, then lower himself down on to the bed side. As she stared into his face the years slipped from her; she was seven again, or nine, or eleven, or thirteen, and she knew that in all the world there was no one like her da. There had never been anyone anywhere on earth like him before and there would never be again; yet in all their past comings together she had never seen a look on his face like now. She would have said her da knew nothing about humility; her da could never be humble, but within this big-framed, virile individual who was sitting before her now was a humble man, a shamed man, who was half afraid of how his gesture might be received. She watched him bring his hand to her face, to the painful side, and when she felt his fingers touch her cheek she hunched her shoulders and cradled his hand while her arms went swiftly up around his neck.

"I'll never forgive meself."

"Forget it, oh forget it, Da. It was nothing. I asked for it."

"I'll never forget it to me dying day."

She pressed him from her and she looked at him, but she couldn't see him. And she asked him a question. It didn't seem necessary but she had to ask it. She had to hear him answer it. She said, "Is everything all right, Da?" Dimly she saw the movement of his head, and then he held her again before he answered, in a thick murmur, "Aye, thanks be to God."

Thanks be to God, he had said, and her da didn't believe in God—well, not the recognized God anyway. . . . But thanks be to God. And she, too, from the bottom of her heart, from the core of her being to which he had given life, she, too, said, "Thanks be to God." But aloud she responded in her usual way. "Oh, Da! Oh, Da!" she said.

9

"You had better go on up," said Lizzie, "Mr. Lord will be waiting for you."

"I will in a minute, Ma," Mary Ann answered as she dashed through the kitchen and into the hall, calling from there, "I just want to see the weather report."

Lizzie smiled at Sarah where she sat in a chair to the side of the fire busily stitching, and she whispered down to her as she passed her, "The weather report. The weather report for the third time today." They laughed softly, exchanging glances, and then Lizzie went on into the front room, there to hear the announcer, who was seemingly talking solely to Mary Ann from the screen, telling her she had no need to worry, for he and God had conspired on her behalf to still the elements, and all would be bright and serene on the morrow.

Mary Ann turned and smiled at Lizzie as she came to her side, and she leant against her mother's shoulder, and Lizzie put her arm around her and squeezed her gently for a moment. Then, pressing her hastily away, she went and closed the front-room door and came quietly back; and, looking down at her daughter for a moment before dropping her gaze to the side, she said hesitantly, "I've . . . I've never spoken about last Sunday, and there mightn't be any more time before tomorrow, I mean . . . I mean when we can be alone, but I want you to know"—she raised her eyes slowly—"I want you to know how I feel. . . ."

"Oh, Ma, don't talk about it, it's over."

"I've got to talk about it, just this once; I've got to put into words that I'm grateful." With her raised hand she hushed Mary Ann's attempt to speak, and went on, "Perhaps it's the last thing you need ever do, in that way, for your da. I know now what it must have cost you to go through with it, because if it had gone wrong, as it could well have done, you would have blamed yourself to the end of your days. But as usual, where he is concerned, you took the right tack."

"It wasn't me, it was Mrs. Mc . . ."

"I know all about that, my dear. But Mrs. McBride didn't do it. And you know something! I've got a feeling that all this just had to happen. . . ." She paused, and her expression softened still further before she went on, "I can say this to you because to-morrow you're going to be married. You've got a lot to learn, and as the years go on it'll get harder, not easier, but somehow I think you already know that . . . you've had enough experience." She smiled a small smile that Mary Ann returned. "But this business has opened your da out . . . I mean towards me, because he's never been the one to talk and try and get to the bottom of things; he's been afraid to, inside. And I know now that I haven't helped him much in that way; I close up like a clam. It's my nature, I suppose, and I've always told myself that I couldn't help it, but now I know it would have been better for both of us if I'd tried. Anyway"—she jerked her head—"to cut a long story short, we've talked the last few days as we've never done in our lives before. We've gone deep into things, and the deeper we've gone the closer we've become; and as I see it, we've got you to thank for it."

"Oh, Ma, no. No. Don't, don't go on."

Lizzie leant forward now and kissed her daughter and they held each other tightly for a moment. Then pushing Mary Ann towards the door, Lizzie said in a voice that was not quite steady, "Go on now, go on up. You don't want him to get annoyed, do you?"

Mary Ann made no answer to this, but, going swiftly into the hall, she grabbed up her coat from the hall-stand and went out by the front way.

The light from the cow-sheds was illuminating the yard as she hurried towards the far gate. She heard her da chastise Primrose, saying, "Behave now, behave yourself." Primrose was a milk chocolate, dappled, wide-eyed Jersey cow, and, unlike her eight sisters, she had a temper. Their Michael used to say that she herself was like Primrose both inside and out. She saw Michael now, his silhouette outlined against the window. He could be mistaken at a distance for her da. She made her way more slowly now, up the hill towards the brightly lit house standing on the brow, and when she entered the kitchen Lettice, wearing a large apron over her smart dress, turned to greet her. Ben was sitting to the side of the Aga stove, a small table at his hand, on which stood articles of silver that he was busily cleaning. She had never seen Ben with his hands idle. He gave her his tight smile, and Lettice, coming round the table and taking off her apron, said softly, "Oh, I'm glad you've come, he's getting fidgety. Tony's with him now. He's had poor Ben here run off his feet all afternoon."

"But it was only about an hour ago I got the message . . . I was coming up, anyway."

"Well, you know what he is." They smiled at each other, and then Lettice, leading the way into the hall, asked softly, "Excited?" She turned and looked at Mary Ann. And Mary Ann, looking squarely back at her, said, "No. I don't feel anything at all. It's as if I've had an injection, like after getting a tooth out, you know, just like that."

Lettice laughed softly. "It's the usual reaction."

"I suppose so." Mary Ann gave a little hick of a laugh. "The only thing I've been concerned about to-day is to-morrow's weather."

"Well, that's a good sign." They were laughing quietly together as they entered the drawing-room.

"Oh, hello there." Tony rose to his feet. "Well, how goes it?"

Before Mary Ann could answer him Mr. Lord turned his steely gaze on her and remarked caustically, "Taken your time, haven't you, miss?"

"I've been busy."

"What about a drink?" said Tony. "A glass of sherry or something?"

"No, no thanks, Tony." Mary Ann shook her head. "I'm not long after having my tea."

"Don't encourage her to drink." Mr. Lord now glared at his grandson. "Sherry, sherry, sherry . . . I don't believe in this constant imbibing, and don't encourage her to start; she'll acquire enough bad habits after to-morrow." Mr. Lord was staring towards the blazing fire as he spoke, and Lettice, Mary Ann and Tony exchanged glances.

Looking at Mary Ann but speaking to Mr. Lord, Tony said teasingly, "I grant you she's very young, but we aren't and we need a drink." And on this diplomatic reply he took Lettice by the hand and they went from the room, Tony winking at Mary Ann knowingly.

And now Mary Ann sat down facing Mr. Lord. They looked at each other in silence for some minutes, and as she stared at her benefactor—and benefactor he had been—the odd numbness that had been filling her all day quietly dispersed and she was filled, in fact overcome, by a feeling that could be described by no other name but love. She loved this old man, really loved him. Her feelings stretched out her hands to him, and when he grasped them they still remained in silence looking at each other. When at last she spoke, she said something that was quite unrehearsed, something she had never dared to say before. She said, "I've never had a granda . . . I mean I've never known one, either me mother's or me da's, and so inside I've always thought of you as me granda."

The sagging muscles twitched, the lips moved, the creasy lids dropped over the eyes, then gently he drew her up from her chair and towards him, and then for only the second time in their acquaintance she found herself sitting on his knee. And as she lay with her head buried in his shoulder he talked to her. His voice no longer harsh or cutting, he said, "You have not only been to me as a granddaughter, Mary Ann, you have also been a source of life. The day you came on to my horizon I was merely existing. . . . You remember that day?" She made a slight movement but did not speak. "And with your coming you restored my faith in human beings. Moreover, you brought me a family, because, you know, I look upon your mother and father, and Michael—and Sarah now—as my family. You brought me Tony, and through Tony you brought me Lettice, which, contrary to my first opinion, has turned out to be a good thing after all. . . . You've brought me all this and now you are going. To-morrow, I could say, I am going to lose you. But no . . . no"—the bony frame moved in the chair—"I'm not going to say that, Mary Ann, because I'll never lose you, will I?"

Her voice was cracked and high as she said, "No, no, never."

"There now, there now. Don't cry." He blew his own nose violently, then added, "I don't want to be browbeaten by Mr. Cornelius Boyle for upsetting you." This was intended to be funny, and Mary Ann smiled at him as she sat up and wiped her face. Mr. Cornelius Boyle! Would he never call him Corny? No, never. That would be too much to ask. He was saying now, "That reminds me. Look, there on the desk." He pointed. "There are two envelopes, go and get them."

She slid from his knee and brought the envelopes to him, and when she put them into his hand he looked at them, then, handing one to her, he said, "That is for you. I haven't bought you a wedding present, get what you want with it." The envelope was addressed simply: "To Mary Ann." Then he handed her the other envelope, on which was written "Mr. Cornelius Boyle", saying, "This is for Cornelius. I always believe that a man and woman should share everything, happiness, money, and troubles, so I have made you both alike. I would have given this to him himself if he had honoured me with a visit, but one must make allowances, for he is a very busy man at the moment . . . a very busy man."

Again he was attempting to be amusing, and now Mary Ann, flinging her arms around his neck, hugged him almost boisterously, and as she hugged him she whispered softly, "I love you, I love you." And she did.

"Go on. Go on." He pressed her up from him; his head was lowered, and once again he was blowing his nose; and now through his handkerchief he said, "I'll see you to-morrow." And then he added softly, as he lifted his misted eyes towards her, "Look beautiful for me, Mary Ann. Look beautiful for me."

She could say no more, she could only stare at him for a moment longer before hurrying from the room.

In the hall she stopped and wiped her face and blew her nose; and while she was busy doing this, out of the morning room came Lettice and Tony. Apparently they had been waiting for her, and without speaking they took up a position on either side of her and walked with her into the kitchen and to the back door.

And now Tony took her face in his hands, and, bending solemnly towards her, kissed her, saying, "Be happy, Mary Ann. And you will be, you deserve it. God bless you." And as he turned away from her, Lettice put her arms about her and muttered something like, "Thank you, Mary Ann; I hope you'll be as happy as you've made it possible for me to be."

She was running quite blindly down the hill, completely choked with happiness. Everybody was nice. Everybody was being kind to her. Everybody was lovely. Look what her ma had said, and Tony and Lettice. But look what Mr. Lord had said. Oh, she loved him. she did, she did. . . .

She went headlong into the gate and winced with pain, and as she rubbed her leg, which was still sore from contact with the chair on Sunday, she said to herself, "Wipe your face; don't do in like that. If our Michael sees you looking like that you know what'll happen, he'll give you a lecture on the feebleness of sentiment. Even when he's wallowing in it, he won't spare you. You know our Michael."

As she entered the scullery she heard Corny's voice coming from the kitchen, saying, "Lord, I'll never get through, and I've got to go to confession, I promised Father Owen I would."

"You should have gone with me last night, I told you."

He turned to her, his eyes merry, his face bright. "Stop nagging," he said. And now he looked at Mike, who was standing with his back to the fire. "Coo! What it's going to be like after, man. You know, I've got cold feet." And now his merry tone changed and he added flatly, "And no kiddin'." As he finished speaking he held out his hand towards Mary Ann—the action in itself had an endearment about it—then, looking at her more closely, he asked, "What's up?"

"Nothing, nothing." She put her hand in her pocket. "I've been up to the house. Mr. Lord's given us our wedding present, one each." She handed him the envelope, and Corny, looking down at it, read aloud, "Mr. Cornelius Boyle", then asked quietly, "What's on yours?" She turned the envelope towards him and he read, "To Mary Ann".

"Funny, isn't it?" He glanced at Mike, and Mike nodded, saying, "It's one of the things you'll have to get used to, Corny. We've all been through it." And half in fun and whole in earnest, he said, "She's been . . . ours"—he had almost said "mine"—"only after she's been his, and the situation will remain the same after to-morrow. You'll have to get used to taking second place, lad."

"Oh, Da." Mary Ann chided him with her look; then she slit open the envelope. Inside was a cheque, nothing else, and the sum on it brought her mouth agape. She looked from the cheque to Corny and back to the cheque, and she whispered, "It's for a thousand pounds." Then, casting her eyes first to Lizzie, and then to Mike, she repeated again, "A thousand pounds. Ma, look . . . look, Da." She held the cheque out stiffly to them, and they looked at it. Then Mike, raising his eyes to Corny, where he stood slightly apart, his face wearing a blank look, said, "Open yours, Corny."

Slowly Corny opened the envelope and he, too, drew a cheque from it, and his amazement and mystification when he saw the same sum written on it elicited the exclamation of "God Almighty!" before he added below his breath, "Why, he's givin' me the same, the same as you."

Mary Ann nodded at him.

"A thousand." Corny, his eyebrows pushing towards his hairline, shook his head; then on a higher note: "A thousand pounds!" His head moved wider. "Mike! Man! A thousand pounds! Two thousand atween us! Struth, I can't take it in." He brought his eyes down to Mary Ann. Then his tone changing, he asked, "Is it something he's up to?"

"No. No." Mary Ann's voice sounded like a bark. "Stop being suspicious of him. It's his kindness; he's done it out of kindness and understanding. He . . . he said that a"—she could not bring herself at the moment to say husband and wife so substituted a couple—"couple should always start off equal, that's what he said, and you go putting the wrong construction on it as usual." Her voice was rising and was only checked by Corny lifting his hand in a very good imitation of Mike, saying, "Enough. Enough." As they all laughed, Mary Ann bowed her head and tried to suppress a grin. Then swiftly she raised it, and looking at Corny again she said quietly, "But it's wonderful, isn't it?"

"Wonderful? That isn't the word. I'm simply floored." He looked at the cheque once again. "I've never seen a cheque for a thousand pounds, but, what's more, I just can't get over him givin' it to me. Why, you should have heard him when I was up there last time, I almost crawled out of the room. I mean I would have if I'd let myself be intimidated by him, for he went for me left, right and centre. And now—" he waved the cheque, "and now this. . . . It's way . . . way beyond me."

"You'll have to go up and thank him," said Lizzie.

"Yes, yes," Mary Ann nodded emphatically.

"Aye. Yes, of course," said Corny. "Yet"—his mouth twisted into a wry grin—"I'll need some practice. I don't know how I'll go about it. Anyway, I can't go now, as I said I've got to go into church, so I'll do it when I come back."

"He'll be in bed then," said Mike.

"Well, I won't be able to do it until to-morrow after . . ." He paused and looked softly towards Mary Ann; then asked her, "Will that be all right then?"

"Yes. He doesn't know I'm seeing you to-night, anyway. You needn't have received it until to-morrow. But look, before you go"—she held out her hand—"come and see what the girls in the office bought us."

Corny allowed himself to be led into the front room, which had taken on the appearance of a combined linen and china shop, and there she pointed out to him an addition to the presents; it was a fireside chair.

"Coo! That's nice." He sat in it and stretched out his long legs. "It was decent of them, wasn't it, and you not being there long."

"Yes, it was. They got it at cost from the firm; it's a very good one." She patted the back near his shoulder, and Corny, looking at her, his eyes almost on a level with hers, turned the subject by asking her quietly, "How do you feel?"

"Aw, well. You know. . . ." She gave a sheepish grin, shrugged one shoulder, then lowered her head a little. "I don't believe it's happening to me. It's as if all this"—she waved her arm about the room—"was for somebody else. One thing I can't take in is that it's . . . it's my last night here . . . in this house."

"You're going to miss it." He was staring straight-faced at her now. "Our place is nothing like this. Even when we get it all fixed up it still won't be like this; we'll be looking out on to a main road . . . at least I hope it will be a main road. And if that comes about the fields at the back will be built on. It'll never be like this. That's what we've got to face up to."

"I can face up to anything as long as you're there." They stared at each other, and the time passed and neither of them made a move until Corny, putting his joined hands, which looked like one large fist, between his knees, concentrated his gaze on them as he said, "There's something I want to say to you. I don't suppose I'll ever mention it again after we're married, and . . . and I find it difficult to say it now. And that's funny because all the time inside it's what I'm feeling. . . . It's just this. I . . . I want to say thanks for having me, Mary Ann."

"Aw. Aw, Corny." The sound was like a painful whimper, a surprised whimper.

"I mean it." He had raised his eyes to her again. "All the time, inside, I'm grateful. It started a long time ago. I think it was when we walked together through Jarrow for the first time. You remember? And when his lordship"—he motioned his head towards the house on the hill—"when he stopped the car and ordered you inside and I yelled at him. I remember the very words I used: 'Aa'm as good as you lot any day. Aye, Aa am. An' Aa'll show you. By God! Aa will that.' That's what I said. . . . Well, I haven't shown him very much, only that I don't look upon him as God Almighty. But it was on that day that I became grateful to you inside, for you didn't want to leave me. And then you asked me to your party and we went walking after and you tried to teach me grammar"—his hand moved slowly up and gripped hers—"and with your mother and the old fellow openly against me, and your school friends horrified at me accent, me clothes, and me scruffy look, you faced them all and stood up for me. It was that I remembered when I was in America. All the time I kept saying to meself. Who among all those fine pieces——" His mouth again gave a small, wry twist, but there was no laughter on his face as he went on—"I said to meself, which one of them would have championed me, me as I was as a lad, for what I lacked in looks I didn't make up in charm, and I was too well aware of it. So my weapon was defiance, open defiance. Your da believed in me and that helped, but it was you, Mary Ann, you who brought me up out of the mire."

"Oh, Corny!" The tears were once again raining down her cheeks. She had no voice with which to protest.

He rose to his feet and drew her gently into his arms, and as he bent his head and buried his face in her hair he muttered, "So thanks, Mary Ann."

It was too much, really too much. She wasn't used to people thanking her, and all day everybody had been thanking her: her mother, Mr. Lord, Lettice, and now Corny. And what was more, she hadn't done anything, she hadn't. She knew she hadn't really done anything in her life to help anybody; she just did what she wanted to do, what pleased her. She was selfish she was. Recrimination, self-denigration, was attacking her on all sides when Corny, pushing her from him and gripping her by the shoulders, and in his now recognizable voice hissed down at her, "But mind, I'm tellin' you, I'm not keeping this up. I've said it and that's the finish, understand?" He shook her gently, and as she laughed through her tears and he pulled her fiercely towards him again the front door bell rang.

As the sound pierced the house it also pierced Mary Ann's memory, and, clapping her hand over her mouth, she whispered between her fingers, "Me grannie! We forgot about the bus. Oh! Oh, heavens above! Nobody thought to meet the bus." She scampered from him into the hall, there to meet Lizzie coming out of the kitchen. Pushing her mother back into the room, she gabbled in a whisper, "It'll be me grannie."

It was now Lizzie's turn to put her hand to her mouth, and she turned her head over her shoulder and looked towards Mike, saying under her breath, "I clean forgot. Oh, there'll be murder."

"Is the room ready?" said Mike, coming forward.

"Oh, yes, that's all right. But how could I forget about her coming to stay?"

"Well," said Mike with a grin, "that's to be understood; it'll be the first time she'll have slept under our roof."

As the bell sounded again, a continued ring now, Corny said, "Will I go and open it?" and Lizzie answered, "No, no, I'll go and get it over."

"Now don't tell me that you've been so very busy and occupied that you forgot." The avalanche hit Lizzie as she opened the door. "There I was in the dark, out in no-man's-land. You could fall in the ditch and not be found until you're dead. Talk about thoughtlessness!" She was in the hall now and the very hairs of her head seemed to be quivering, and as her hold-all hit the floor it was as if she had thrown it from a great height. "Froze I am. Talk about a reception. You could be murdered on these roads. An' would that have mattered, says you."

"Give me your coat, Gran."

"What!" Mrs. McMullen turned on her granddaughter and glared at her; then she put her head on one side as if she hadn't heard aright. And perhaps she hadn't, because never before had she heard Mary Ann speak to her in this gentle, quiet way, nor offer to relieve her of her outdoor things. Her head straight once again, she replied, "I'm still able to take me own coat off, thank you. And don't come all smarmy with me, for it's past the eleventh hour. It's too late now."

Mary Ann, her face tight now, left the hall and went into the kitchen, there expecting to have a sympathetic exchange of glances with her da, and Corny. But the room was empty, until Sarah came hobbling from the scullery and towards her, saying softly, "Corny says to tell you he's going straight back to the house after church, and Mike says to tell you"—her smile broadened here—"that he and his son are going to the house now. . . . Pronto, and they hope to get the sitting-room done to-night."

"Oh." Mary Ann shook her head helplessly. Then motioning it backwards, she whispered, "She's her old self, only worse. It's going to be a lovely evening."

"We'll go in the front room, there's plenty to do."

"I'd forgotten clean about her coming."

"I hadn't," said Sarah. "But I didn't think it was so late. Ssh! . . ." she moved forward, hoping to reach a chair before the visitor should enter the room. But this she did not accomplish, and Mrs. McMullen stood surveying her erratic progress with a cold eye in a flaming face; then herself moving towards the fire, she looked at Sarah as she passed her, saying, "Why don't you use you wheel-chair, girl?"

The question and all it implied caused Sarah's head to droop and the sight of this was too much for Mary Ann. She had prayed last night to Our Lady to give her the strength to be nice to her grannie, at least until the wedding was over, and she had started off well. She had spoken nicely to her and what had she got? Well, if she wanted it that way she could have it, wedding or no wedding. How she spoke to her was one thing, but to tell Sarah that she looked awful when she was walking, and that's what she had meant, was another. Looking boldly now at the bane of her life, she declared, "Sarah doesn't need a chair, she's walking fine, she's getting better every day. Anyway, who would have thought this time last year that she would have been on her feet at all; and, what's more, driving a car. She. . . ."

"All right, all right, madam. I thought it wouldn't be long before you started. It's well I know you and can't be taken in. Your good intentions are about as strong as a May Day wind. You're still the . . ."

"Are you ready for a cup of tea, Ma?" Lizzie was looking towards the old woman, the tight, defensive look back on her face again, for although this woman was her mother she held thoughts akin to her daugher's concerning her.

"Well, as I haven't broken my fast since dinner-time I supose I am ready for a cup of tea . . . and a bite of something. But if you're busy, don't stop what you're doing, for of course you must have been very busy to forget that I was coming."

"I didn't forget you were coming, only I didn't think it was as late as it was."

"You still have clocks." The terrible old woman turned her gaze up to the mantelpiece; then she sighed and lay back in the chair. It was as if the first onslaught was over.

Lizzie turned to the table and began preparing her mother a meal, and Sarah, looking towards Mary Ann where she stood in a somewhat undecided manner near the door, said, "If you'll bring me the box with your veil in, Mary Ann, I'll fix the wreath—it'll save us doing it in the morning—and now that there's nobody in you can try it on."

"Veil? Wreath? I didn't know you were going to be married in white."

"You did, Mother." Lizzie spoke without turning round. "We told you a while back."

"You didn't tell me. You talked about it over my head, and as far as I could gather you decided against it. And it would have been wiser if you had stuck to that, for she's not big enough for white. . . . And as for those two sisters of his being bridesmaids. . . . Huh!"

Lizzie signalled across the room to Mary Ann now, warning her with a look not to take any notice, and as she watched her daughter swelling visibly with indignation she put in quickly, "The girls look bonny enough when they're dressed. As for Mary Ann's frock, it's lovely, and she looks lovely in it." And on this she nodded to Mary Ann as if to stress the truth of her statement.

"Huh!" Mrs. McMullen looked up at one corner of the ceiling, and then to the other, as if searching for inspiration for her invective; then turning her gaze in the direction of Sarah, she said in a conversational tone, "White weddings and no honeymoons don't go together. What do you say? You managed a honeymoon, and under the circumstances you should have been the last one to tackle it. . . . You know what I mean?"

Sarah knew what she meant only too well, and in this moment she fully understood Mary Ann's hate of her grannie, for she was a dreadful old woman, cruel.

"We don't want a honeymoon." Mary Ann's voice, in spite of Lizzie's silent, imploring gaze, came barking across the kitchen now. "I could have a honeymoon, as you call it, if I'd wanted it, but I don't want to waste money staying in some strange hotel. We'll have a honeymoon all right, but we'll have it in our own home."

"All right, all right, madam, stop your bawling; I can make a remark, can't I? But no, I should have learned by now I can't open me mouth in this house. My God!" Mrs. McMullen shook her head sadly. "If you can't act like a human being the night afore your wedding you never will be able to. . . . I hold out no hope for your future happiness if this is how you mean to start off. Anyway, truth to tell, now that we're on, I might as well say that I've never held much hope for you in that direction, so you have it, not with the partner you've picked. Bairns and a scrubbing brush, that's your future. As I can read anything I can read that."

"Mother! Now look"—Lizzie was standing above the old lady, her face white and strained, her forefinger wagging violently—"if you're going to stay the night, and I hope you are, you've got to keep a civil tongue in you head."

"Me! A civil——"

"You, yes. A civil tongue in your head. There's nobody starts these things only you. Now I'm warning you."

"Oh, I only needed this . . ." Mrs. McMullen closed her eyes. "That's all I needed, you to start on me. Anyway, I hope I've got it in me to understand, 'cos I saw the minute I entered the door you were all het up. And is it any wonder? If everything I hear is true . . . if only half I hear is true, it's understandable that your nerves are all of a frazzle. . . . Tell me. Are you still being visited by the Radleys, or are the visits going the other way now? For by what I hear . . ."

Mary Ann seemed to shoot across the room to her mother's side, and from there she glared at her grannie and, leaning threateningly towards the old woman, cried at her, "You know what I wish? You know what I wish?" Her voice dropping suddenly, she added through her clenched teeth, "I wish you would drop down dead, you old——"

"Mary Ann!" Lizzie, seizing her by the shoulders, pushed her towards the hall, then into the front room, and there she put her arms round her and held her as once more she burst into tears, angry tears now, bitter tears; and looking up at her mother, Mary Ann stammered, "On . . . on the night be . . . before me wedding she's made me say a thing like th . . . that. It was awful, I know, but it's true, Ma, it's true. But f . . . fancy me saying it." She was crying loudly now, and Lizzie hushed her and rocked her as if she was a little girl, the little girl who had many, many times wished her grannie dead. And now Mary Ann, raising her head again, spluttered, "Scrub . . . scrubbing brushes and b . . . bairns, that's what she said, that's all Corny can give me, scrubbing brushes and b . . . bairns."

"One scrubbing brush," said Lizzie with a faint smile.

"What, Ma?" She was sniffing loudly now.

"Bairns, and a scrubbing brush," Lizzie explained, "just one scrubbing brush."

"Oh." Mary Ann slowly began to glean the funny side of it all, and weakly she returned Lizzie's smile. And Lizzie, stroking her hair back from her wet brow, said softly, "There's worse things than bairns and a scrubbing brush, if you're happy with the man that provides both."

10

"But, Mrs. McBride, you've just got to come to the church; Corny would go mad."

"Now look, me lass, I proffered to come over here so that I could see to things when you had all gone, and have everything nice and ready when you come back."

"But everything is ready, and Jonesy and his wife are staying behind, it's all arranged. What's got into you?" Mary Ann's high tone droped. "It won't be me wedding if you're not there. And I'm telling you, he'll go mad."

"Huh! He'll know nothing about it. He'll be so taken up wondering if you're going to come or not. They're all like that at the last minute."

"But why? It's always been understood you'd be there."

Fanny turned from Mary Ann and walked down the length of the large barn, and as she walked she moved her head to the right, and the left, looking at the tables set as yet with only crockery and flowers, and, going to the top table, she gazed at the two chairs, bigger than the rest, like two thrones awaiting their occupants. Then turning and facing Mary Ann, who had followed her, she said, on a deep sigh, "Well, knowing you, you won't stop till you get to the bottom of it, so it's like this, plain and simple, I'm not going to go into the church and disgrace you both in me old togs."

Mary Ann's mouth opened and shut like that of a dying fish, and then she brought out, "But, you've got new clothes . . . you were getting new clothes."

"Aye, so I thought." Mrs. McBride examined the skin on the back of her large, wrinkled hands. Then she repeated quietly, "Aye, so I thought, right until until just a week ago when it was too late to do anything about it. You see"—she lifted her eyes to Mary Ann—"our Florrie said she would get me a couple of clubs, enough to get me a coat and hat and be shod decent, and I waited and waited, never thinking but that she would get them for me. And then over she comes at the last minute, on Wednesday night it was, saying she can't get any more, for the whole crowd of them want so much of this and that, and she had gone over her credit, far over. . . . Aw, I suppose it wasn't too late even then. If I had dropped a word to our Phil he would have been down from Newcastle like a shot and rigged me out—he's wanted to do it time and time again—but as I said, what do I want new clothes for, I'm never out of the door except to go to early mass on a Sunday, and along to the shop. If I got new clothes, I've always said to him, what would I do with them? They'd just hang there and rot."

"But Corny would have . . . he would have seen to everything."

"I know, lass. Don't I know he would have seen to everything . . . and beggared himself still further. I've had to put me foot down afore where that un's concerned, and I'm keeping it down from now on that he's a married man, for, refuse how I may, he's left me something every week; come back and pushed it under the door he has after we've gone for each other hell for leather. Oh, I know Corny would have me rigged out like a duchess, but, Mary Ann"—she moved her head slowly—"I'm an independent spirit, I've never asked any body for anythin' in me life. Why don't you get supplementary? they say. You've earned it, they say; it isn't charity, it's yours by rights, they say. Huh! . . . I know what's mine by rights, so I'm not goin' after any supplementary an' havin' a man comin' to me house checking on what I've got and sayin' to me, 'With all those children scattered all over the country you shouldn't be wantin' supplementary, now should you?' Aw, I know. No, Mary

Ann, what I can't have I've always made it a point of doin' without. And so there you have it. So you just keep quiet, me dear, and no one will be any the wiser but that I was in church. I can say to them here that I'm comin' in the last car, an' at that time I won't be around."

"No. No." Mary Ann shook not only her head but her whole body. "You're coming, and not in the last car. I tell you Corny'll go mad. And don't think he won't miss you; he'll be standing in the front of the church and he'll see everybody, and it'll upset him if he doesn't catch sight of you."

"Nonsense, nonsense. There's only one thing that would upset him this day and that would be if you didn't arrive. Why . . . do you think he'll say, 'Hold your hand a minute, hold everything, I must go and find me grannie'?" Fanny let out a bellow of a laugh at her own joke, and Mary Ann laughed too. Then stopping abruptly, she said, "You're coming, clothes or no clothes," and, turning from her, she ran down the barn, out across the sunlit farmyard, up the path and into the back door, where the buzz of noise came at her like a blow. The house was full. She had never seen so many people in it. Sarah met her, saying, "Where have you been? Mam's looking all over for you. It's time you were getting ready."

"Where's me da?"

"With my dad in the front room, I think. And Corny's father and the lads are there. . . . What's the matter?"

"I'll tell you in a minute." Mary Ann made her way through the kitchen which was packed to capacity. People were standing, and sitting, and talking, and she heard the tail end of Mrs. Flannagan's voice saying in high, refined tones. "And he thinks the world of her. He must do, mustn't he, to buy her a car after setting her up in a bungalow."

Some section of her mind told Mary Ann that Mrs. Flannagan had heard of Mr. Lord's generous wedding present to herself and Corny and was proving to somebody that it was nothing compared with what he had given to Sarah. She could smile at this.

The front room seemed full of men of all ages.

"Da . . . Da." She tugged at his arm.

"Aren't you away upstairs getting ready?" Mike looked tenderly down at her, and she answered, "I want you a minute."

As she went into the hall, followed by Mike, Mrs. McMullen came out of the kitchen and made her way to the front room, remarking in passing, to no one in particular, "Common as muck, the whole lot of them."

Her grannie, Mary Ann knew, was referring to Corny's mother and father and the squad of children, and although she would have died rather than agree with anything her grannie said, she did think they could behave a bit better than they did. Corny's father was useless with regards to keeping his tribe in order, and his mother wasn't much better; she just shouted and the lads laughed at her.

"What is it?" asked Mike.

"Come outside a minute." She took his hand and drew him through the front door and round the corner of the house. And there she said hastily, "It's Mrs. McBride. You know what, she's not coming to the wedding because she has no new clothes."

"Not comin'. . . . No new clothes! But didn't they see to that?"

She told him briefly what had happened, and when she had finished he stood looking down at her with his face screwed up. "Hell for a tale that," he said. "Well, to my mind she must be at your weddin'. What do you think?"

"I think the same, Da. She's always been in my life. . . . I mean she's closer . . . well, than most people. But apart from that, Corny . . . he'll go mad if she's not there. You know, Da"—her voice sank to a whisper and she glanced about her in case any of Corny's family should be within hearing distance—"Corny doesn't care two hoots for any of them except her. He loves her."

"Aye, aye, I think you're right. In fact, I know you are. . . . What time is it?" He looked at his watch. "Ten past eleven. . . . You leave this to me. Where is she?"

"In the barn, Da." Her eyes were bright as she whispered, "You'll take her in . . . get her a coat and things?"

"Yes, just that. . . ." Pausing, he patted her playfully on the cheek. "You knew I would, didn't you?"

"I hoped so, Da. But . . . you'll be back in time?"

"I'll be back, never fear. You go upstairs and get dressed, that's the main thing. It won't take me two shakes of a lamb's tail to get into me togs, so go on now an' leave it to me."

"Thanks, Da." She reached up and kissed him; then added, "You might have a job getting her to agree."

"She'll agree . . . go on now."

She turned from him and ran into the house, and Lizzie, meeting her in the hall, said, "Where've you been? Look at the time. Go on up, it's time you were starting. . . . Where's your da?"

"Here a minute." Mary Ann took her mother by the hand and led her upstairs, and briefly she put her in the picture. And Lizzie said, "Oh dear. But yes, I see she's got to be there, but . . . but will he have time, will he be back in time? He's got to put a new suit on and you know what he's like with a new suit."

"It'll be all right, Ma."

"Well I hope so. . . . Come on, off with your things and let's get started."

As Mary Ann went to pull her jumper over her head there came a tap on the door, and when Lizzie, her tongue clicking impatiently, opened it, she gave a cry of surprise that turned Mary Ann about, and, her arms still in her jumper, she, too, exclaimed aloud, for there stood Sarah; at one side of her was her father, at the other, Mr. Boyle.

"She's made it," said Mr. Flannagan proudly. "We wanted to carry her up, but no. 'One at a time,' she said, and she's made all sixteen of them."

Sarah, her face flushed to a deep pink with the exertion of her effort and the triumph over herself, shambled into the room and, flopping into the chair, looked at Mary Ann and laughed as she said, "I always intended to do it . . . to help you dress like you did me."

"Aw, Sarah." Mary Ann put her hand gently on Sarah's head, and as she did so Lizzie exclaimed, "Well now, well now, we want to get started." This remark was directed towards the men, and as she was about to close the door on them Mr. Boyle turned a red-faced grin on her, and under his breath he said, "No disrespect, Lizzie, but——" He paused here and his eyes flashed to Mr. Flannagan, then on to Mary Ann, who had turned towards him, then back to Lizzie before he added, "Has anybody thought of shooting your mother?"

Lizzie forcibly prevented herself from laughing, but from Mary Ann there came a high, gleeful sound and she cried in no small voice, "Oh, I have, Mr. Boyle." She had always addressed him as Mr. Boyle and couldn't see herself ever calling him anything else. She had never liked him; in fact if she had asked herself the question she would have answered that she disliked him, but now in a flash she saw him in a different light. He might booze, swear, and not bring his money home, but there, beneath the skin, she saw Corny.

Lizzie prevented him from taking a step into the room as Mary Ann cried, "We'll get together later and fix up something, eh?"

"Right. Right, Mary Ann, that's a deal."

"And count me in." It was little Mr. Flannagan now piping up, his face alight with merriment.

Lizzie slammed the door on the two men and, turning to the laughing girls, she said indignantly, "Really! Really!" But in spite of the reprimand, Mary Ann saw that her mother had her work cut out to stop herself laughing aloud.

"And you!" said Lizzie. "Standing there with no jumper on."

"Eeh!" Mary Ann looked down at herself. "So I was. What are things coming to?" The two girls giggled. Then Mary Ann, about to divest herself further, turned to Lizzie and exclaimed, "Queenie and Nancy. Who's seeing to them?"

"Their mother. She'll put them right."

"But will she?" Mary Ann's eyebrows moved up. "If she sees to them as she does every day I'm going to have two beautiful bridesmaids."

"She can do things all right when she puts her mind to it, and I've seen them and they're very sweet. Now don't bother about them; get your things off and let's get started."

As Lizzie moved towards the wardrobe she had to pass the window, and Mary Ann's bedroom window overlooked the farmyard. Lizzie looked at the farmyard so many times a day that now she didn't see it, and she had glanced through the window and reached the wardrobe before she dived back to the window again and there a long-drawn-out "Ooh!" escaped her.

"What is it?" asked Mary Ann and Sarah together.

"The boys, they're on the silage in their new clothes and their father and your grannie are going at it."

Mary Ann came to the window and looked down on Corny's two youngest brothers, the nine-year-old twins, who had evidently been enjoying themselves. The silage was kept in a yard apart from the main one, and the boys with long pronged forks in their hands stood now in the opening between the two yards, and even from this distance she could see that their boots were filthy and their clothes bespattered. They had only once before been at the farm and everybody remembered their visit. The open spaces seemed to have a maddening effect on them, for they had raced like wild horses from one place to the other. She brought her eyes from them to their father. She could see that he was smiling, but she could also see that he was wagging a large forefinger in her grannie's face and the forefinger, denying the smile, spelled out to Mary Ann, "Now look here, old lady, you mind your business and I'll mind mine."

As Lizzie opened the window and called down to her mother, Mrs. McMullen's voice came high and clear on the crisp, sun-filled air, saying, "Disgrace, that's what they are; like young pigs on the wrong side of the fence."

"Oh, look!" As the exclamation was drawn from Mary Ann she pulled her mother back from the windows and whispered urgently, "Mr. Lord, Tony and Lettice . . . coming down the hill."

"Oh no!" Lizzie lifted her hand to her head. "They'll run into that, and if my mother corners Mr. Lord. . . . Oh, why isn't Mike here! And where's Michael in all this?" She turned and looked at Sarah as if she were responsible for Michael's non-appearance in the yard. Then Mary Ann put in, "Look, Ma, you go on down, I'll manage. And I've got Sarah. Go on, see to things. Don't let me grannie meet him, not out there. And if he sees the twins like that, he'll be so wild, and . . . it'll look bad for Corny. Oh, go on, Ma."

"Aw. Dear, dear." Lizzie hesitated only for a moment then hurried from the room, and Mary Ann and Sarah looked at each other. Then Mary Ann, going to her dressing-table, sat down and through the mirror said to Sarah, "Me wedding day. I just can't believe it's me wedding day." She gave a wry smile. "All these little things happening, just like any other day, or more so, and yet I don't feel the same as on other days. I've . . . I've got a racing feeling inside. . . . You know what I mean?"

Sarah nodded through the mirror.

"I don't know whether I want to race to the church or race away from it." They both giggled at this, then Mary Ann went on, but seriously now, "For a while last night I felt wonderful, not a bit afraid or anything. When we stood outside, just before he went, and the moon was shining and everything was so quiet, it was then I felt wonderful, happier than I'd ever been in my life. I had a sort of safe feeling with it. I felt as long as I was with Corny everything would always be all right. . . . You know?"

Again Sarah nodded through the mirror. "Yes, I know. And it's the right feeling. If you feel like that nothing much can touch you."

"You think so?"

"I know so."

Mary Ann, staring hard at Sarah now, saw that she was looking at a woman, that Sarah had grown up, leaving her still a child. She said thoughtfully, "But the feeling didn't stay, for as soon as I woke this morning I felt frightened, in fact I wished it wasn't going to happen, and I wanted to be some place quiet and think and try to get a nice feeling inside." She spread out her hands. "But look at it. Everything's happened that could. And people coming far too early; his mother was to bring the girls at half-past ten and what did she do but bring the whole bang lot of them with her . . . and at ten o'clock. Of course there was one person delighted . . . me grannie, for she was running out of targets."

As if in answer to this jibe Mrs. McMullen's voice came penetratingly through the floor, and Mary Ann put her hands over her ears and, swinging round and facing Sarah, her eyes dancing, whispered, "What do you bet, when Father Owen says 'If anyone knows of any impediment, etc.,' she doesn't get to her feet and shout, 'Any impediment! I can give you a round dozen. . . . Now you just listen to me'." Mary Ann had mimicked her grannie's voice, and now the two girls, hands clasped, threw back their heads and laughed, high, gleeful laughter. But in Mary Ann's case it spoke plainly of nervous strain and tension.

It was here, this was the moment. This was the joyous moment. . . . At least, it should have been joyous but she still felt frightened. She was too young to be married. She should never have said she would do it. Her legs would give way when she was walking down the aisle. And all those people behind her outside the church door, how had they known? . . . Mrs. McBride. Yes, Mrs. McBride. They couldn't get the car near the kerb, and the voices from all over the crowd shouting, "Eeh! Look, Mary Ann. Hello, Mary Ann. Mary Ann. Oo! Oo!" She had kept her head down but had lifted it to look at a woman as she entered the church door, for the woman had said and somewhat sadly, "Aw, hinny, you won't be Mary Ann Shaughnessy for much longer now."

And she wouldn't be Mary Ann Shaughnessy for much longer. She hadn't thought about that before, she was going to lose her name. She liked her name. MARY ANN SHAUGHNESSY. In a short while she would be Mary Ann Boyle. It sounded awful . . . Mary Ann Boyle. Oh no, she didn't want to be Mary Ann Boyle.

"Are you all right?" Mike was looking down at her, gently drawing her hand through his arm. She looked up at him blinking. She was hot and sweating; her make-up must look awful, and she wanted to cry. . . . Don't be so silly. She blinked rapidly and saw Mike's face, then all of him. He looked grand, did her da. His new suit fitted him to a 'T'. They stared at each other oblivious for the moment of the bustle about them. Somebody was whispering to the bridesmaids, "Hold them like this, don't let them droop." That would be the posies. The organ was rumbling overhead, waiting for the signal, and in this moment there came to Mary Ann the strange idea that she was inside her da, right inside of him, thinking his thoughts, feeling his feelings, and he, too, wanted to cry. She turned her eyes from him. It was awful. She was going to be married, she should be joyful. What was the matter with her anyway? MARY ANN BOYLE. Oh, she didn't like that name. She would never be Mary Ann Boyle whatever happened, she wouldn't. Inside herself she would always be Mary Ann Shaughnessy. She would remain Mary Ann Shaughnessy for ever. She wanted to tell her da that she would never be anybody but Mary Ann Shaughnessy. She would always keep his name. . . . But . . . but what was she talking about, for Shaughnessy wasn't his name, not really. . . . Anyway, what was in a name?

Mike squeezed her hand and, bending his head sideways down to her, whispered, "You'll be all right. Don't worry. Do you know something?" He waited.

"What, Da?" Her lips were trembling and she spoke without turning her head.

"You look very beautiful."

"Oh, Da." She pressed his arm to her.

"And . . . and I'll love you till the day I die. Never forget that."

Ooh! Oh, he shouldn't have said that, he shouldn't, it was too much. She would burst, she would cry.

There was a movement in front of them; someone said, "Ready?"

There was bustle behind; a second later the organ swelled into loud chords and she was walking forward out of the dim vestibule, round by the holy water font, in which she had dipped her fingers from the time she could reach it, to the top of the central aisle. The wish was strong in her now that they could go down the side aisle and that she could be married at the altar of the Holy Family, for they had always been part of her family. . . . Where had all the people come from? The church was almost full. Her high-heeled shoes slipped just the tiniest bit on the grating and she felt the heat from the pipes coming up under her dress. She had loved to stand over the grating in the cold weather and get her legs warm. Sometimes the boiler went wrong and the church was as cold as death, but today the boiler was all right, Father Owen had seen to that. The church was warm, the atmosphere was warm, the people's faces, those turned towards her, were warm. She didn't look at them but she could feel their warmth. But when she approached her own people she looked at them. Her mother, oh, her mother looked bonny, lovely, young, even though her eyes were sad; and there was Sarah, bright-faced, happy-looking Sarah; and Lettice and Tony. Tony was looking full at her and she exchanged a direct glance with him, which said something, which meant something, but which in this moment she couldn't decipher. Then there was Mrs. Flannagan, proud, pinched-faced, but smiling Mrs. Flannagan, kind at last; and now the face of her grannie. . . . Oh! Why had she to look at her grannie, why at this moment had she to look at her grannie, for belated maternal love and benevolence had not touched her grannie's countenance. It was the same as she had always seen it. But there was another face, a face really showing love and benevolence . . . and pride: the face of Mr. Lord. His eyes were on her, pale-blue misty eyes, but piercing into her, sending her a message, and she answered it, sending him her love and gratitude for as long as he might need it.

Then on the other side of the aisle were Corny's people. His mother and father, their faces full of smiling good-will. . . . Why had she never liked them?—because they were really likeable. What did it matter if she didn't keep her house clean? And there was all Corny's relations filling three pews . . . Corny had said they would fill three pews. But in the very first seat of the first pew was a face whose beam spread itself over all of them. It was topped by a blue velour hat of unspotted newness, it was the wrinkled, battered face, the wise face of her friend, Fanny McBride, and the knowledgeable eyes held Mary Ann's for more than a second until they seemed to usher her gaze to the front, to where, on the altar steps, stood Father Owen, kind, loving, understanding Father Owen. . . . They had said to her, "Why do you want to be married in Jarrow Church? You're nearer to Pelaw." But Jarrow had always been her church, and Father Owen was her priest. Father Owen knew all about her, everything, the good and the bad. Now Father Owen's gaze drew her eyes with his and they travelled past their Michael, tall and handsome, a young edition of her father, to someone else, tall . . . and handsome. For Corny in this moment looked handsome to her. His red hair was lying for once in well-brushed order, his deep-set dark eyes were warm and shining, his wide-lipped mouth was gentle. She wished he wasn't so tall, she wished she wasn't so small, she wished . . . she wished. . . .

"MARY ANN . . . MARY ANN."

It was as if he was calling her name.

"MARY ANN, OH, MARY ANN."

Mike let her go. She felt the moment of release as if he had thrust her from him. She was by herself, getting nearer to Corny. She was close to him now, and as she looked at him for a moment his eyes blotted out everything about her. Gently their message sank into her and she felt it lift her round to face the priest.

GOOD-BYE, MARY ANN SHAUGHNESSY.

Good-bye, Mary Ann Shaughnessy.

Good-bye, Mary Ann.

Good-bye.

Good-bye.

"Wilt thou take this woman . . .?"

Mary Ann's Angels

To Mam
My Mother-in-Law

1

"If he can talk, why doesn't he, Rose Mary Boyle?"

"'Cos he doesn't want to, Annabel Morton."

The two six-year-olds stared at each other, eyes wide, nostrils dilated. Their lips spread away from their teeth, they had all the appearance of two caged circus animals dressed up in human guise for the occasion.

"My mam says he's dumb."

"Your mam's barmy."

Again, wide eyes, quivering nostrils and stretched lips, and a waiting period, during which the subject of their conversation, one hand held firmly in that of his twin, gazed alternately at the two combatants. He was fair-haired, round-faced, with dark blue eyes, and his expression was puzzling, for it could have been described as vacant, yet again it could have been described as calculating.

"He spoke the day, an' if your ears hadn't been full of muck, you'd have heard him."

The fray was reopened. Rose Mary turned to her brother and bounced her head towards him, whereupon he stared back at her for a moment, then looked towards their opponent again.

"He made a funny sound, that's all he did, when he was eating his dinner."

"He didn't make a funny sound, he said 'HOT'."

"He didn't, he said 'ugh!' Like a pig makes."

Rose Mary's right, and working arm, throwing itself instinctively outwards, almost lifted David from the ground, and by the time he had relinquished his hold of her hand and regained his balance, with her help, Annabel Morton had put a considerable distance between them. And from this distance she made a stand. "Dumb David!" she called. Then added, "And Rose Mary, pain-in-the-neck, Boyle." And if this wasn't enough she went as far as to mis-spell boyle. "B-O-I-L!" she screamed at the limit of her lungs.

"Now, now, now." There loomed over Annabel the tall, thin figure of her teacher, Miss Plum.

Rose Mary, her hand again holding David's, watched Miss Plum as she reprimanded that awful Annabel Morton. Oh, she hoped she got kept in the morow. Oh, she did. And Miss Plum was nice, after all she was nice. Oh, she was.

Now Miss Plum was advancing towards her, and Rose Mary greeted her with uplifted face, over which was spread a smile, the like that had in the past been called angelic . . . by people viewing it for the first time. Miss Plum had never made that mistake. She looked down on Rose Mary now and, her finger wagging near her nose, she said, "I don't want to hear, Rose Mary, I don't want to hear. And you should be on your way home."

"But Miss Pl——"

"No, not another word. Away with you now."

Rose Mary turned round abruptly, and her twin had his eyes wrenched from Miss Plum and was jerked into step by his sister's side, and only because she was grasping his hand firmly could he keep up with her. His legs were plump, and although he was older than his sister by five minutes his speed was geared to about half hers. But of necessity, perhaps out of an instinctive urge for preservation, he had learned to put on a brake against her speed. He did it now by throwing himself backwards and resting on his heels.

Rose Mary came to a stop. She looked at him and said, "Miss Plum! Four-eyed, goggle-mug Plum. Her head's like Lees's clock." Whereupon David laughed a high appreciative laugh, for as everybody in Felling knew, even the works in Lees's clock were made of wood.

Rose Mary now joined her laugh to her brother's. Then pulling him to her side, she walked at a slower pace down Stewart Terrace, and as she walked, her whole mien sober now, she thought, "It must be made of wood else she'd be able to make him talk. There must be something that would make him talk, more than one—unintelligible to others—word at a time. Yes, there must be something. But what?"

When she felt a sharp tug on her hand she realized she had almost passed the point where they crossed over to get the bus, but David hadn't. She looked at him in admiration, a grin splitting her pert face. "There, you see," she addressed an adversary known only to herself. "He's all right, you see. I nearly didn't cross over, but he was all there." She jerked her head at the adversary, then gripping David's hand more tightly, she crossed over the road and went towards the bus stop.

The bus conductor, assisting them upwards with a hand on each of their shoulders, said, "Come on, you Siamese twins you. And don't you have so much to say, young fellow-me-lad." He pushed David playfully in the back. "And now I want none of your cheek," he admonished him with a very thick index finger as David hoisted himself on to a seat.

David grinned broadly at the conductor, and Rose Mary, handing their passes, said, "You back then?"

"Well, if I'm not," said the conductor, straightening up, "somebody's havin' a fine game." Then bending down to her again, he asked under his breath, "No talkie-talkie?"

Rose Mary shook her head.

"Shame."

They both now looked at David.

"Aw well." The conductor ruffled David's hair. "Don't you worry, young chap, you're all there."

When the conductor had passed down the bus Rose Mary and David exchanged glances, and to her glance Rose Mary added a small inclination of the head. The bus conductor was a nice man, he knew that their David was all there.

The bus stopped on the long, bare, main road, bare that is except for traffic, and right at the top end of their side road. Rose Mary and David stood gazing at the conductor where he stood on the platform until he was lost to their sight, then hand in hand they ran up the land that lay between two fields, and to home.

The first sight they got of home was of two petrol pumps, around which lay a curved line of whitewashed stones. The line was terminated at each end by green tubs which were now full of wallflowers, and to the right-hand side of the pumps and some distance behind them, there stood their home. Their wonderful, wonderful home. At least it was to Rose Mary; David, as yet, had not expressed any views about it.

The house itself was perched on top of what looked like a shop, because the front of the ground floor was taken up by a large plate-glass window and was actually the showroom to the garage. But at present it was empty. Next to the house was a low building with a door and one window, and above the door was a board which read simply: FELL GARAGE: C. BOYLE, Proprietor. Below this, above the door frame, was another slim board with the single word "OFFICE" written on it. To the side of the office was a large barn-like structure, the garage itself, and inside, and leaving it looking almost empty, were three cars. One car stood on its own, a 1950 Rover, which was polished to a gleaming sheen. The other cars were undergoing repairs, and under each of them someone was at work.

"Hello, Dad." Rose Mary, still pulling David with her, dashed up to the man who was lying on his back half underneath the first car, and for answer, Corny kicked one leg in the air, and when they knelt down on the ground by his side to get a better look at him his muffled yell came at them, "Get up out of that, you'll be all oil. Get up with you."

By the time he had edged himself from underneath the car, they were on their feet, grinning at him.

"Hello there." He looked down on them. "Had a nice day?"

"Ah-ha." Rose Mary jerked her chin up at him, then brought her head down to a level position and a soberness to her face, before adding, "Well, except for Annabel Morton. She's a pig."

"Oh. What's she done now?" Corny was wiping his greasy hands with a mutton cloth.

"Here." His daughter beckoned his distant head down to hers, and when his ear was level with her mouth, she whispered, "She said he couldn't talk."

As Corny straightened himself up and looked down at his daughter, who was his wife in miniature, he wanted to say, "Well she's right, isn't she?" but that would never do, so he said, "She doesn't know what she's talking about."

"An' I told her, an' I told her that."

"And what did she say?"

Rose Mary, picking up David's hand, now turned him about, and glancing over her shoulder at her father, said flatly, "She called me pain-in-the-neck Boyle."

There came a great roar of laughter, but not from her dad. It came from behind the other car, and she yelled at it, "Aw, you Jimmy!" before dashing out of the garage, along the cement walk, around the back of the house—no going in the front way, except for company—and up the stairs, still dragging David with her. And from here she shouted, "Mam. Mam. We're here, Mam."

"Is that my angels?"

As they burst on to the top landing, Mary Ann came out of the kitchen and, stooping over them, enfolded them in her arms, hugging them to her.

"Oh, Mam." Rose Mary sniffed. "You been bakin'? What you been bakin'?"

"Apple tarts, scones, tea-cakes."

"Ooh! Mam. Coo, I'm hungry, starvin'. So's David."

Mary Ann, still on her hunkers, looked at her son, and, a smile seeping from her face, she said to him quietly, "Are you hungry, David?"

The light in the depths of David's eyes deepened, his round, button-shaped mouth spread wide as he stared back at his mother.

"Say, 'Yes, Mam'."

For answer David made a sound in his throat and fell against her, and, putting her hand on the back of his head she pressed it to her, and over it she looked at her daughter. And Rose Mary returned her glance, soft with understanding.

Now Mary Ann, pushing them both before her, said, "Go and get your playthings on. Hang your coats up. And Rose Mary. . . ." When her daughter turned towards her she said slowly, "Rose Mary, let David take his own things off and put his playthings on."

"But Mam . . ."

"Rose Mary, now do as I say, that's a good girl. Go on now, and I'll butter a tea-cake to keep you going until teatime."

When they had gone into their room Mary Ann stood looking down at her hands. They were working one against the other, making a harsh sound; the action made her separate them as if she was throwing something off.

She was in the kitchen again when her daughter's voice came to her from the little room across the landing, saying, "I hate Miss Plum, Mam."

"I thought you liked Miss Plum, I thought she was your favourite teacher?"

"She's not, I hate her. She's a pig."

"Now I've told you about calling people pigs, haven't I?"

"Well, she is, Mam."

"What did she do?"

"She wouldn't let me talk."

Mary Ann, about to lay the tea cloth over the table under the window, put her hand over her mouth to suppress her laughter. It was as if she had gone back down the years and was listening to herself.

"Mam."

"Yes?"

"David drew a lovely donkey the day, with me on its back."

"Oh, that's wonderful. Have you brought it home?"

"No. Miss Plum said it was good, and she pinned it on the wall."

"Oh, that's marvellous." Mary Ann swung the cloth across the table, then paused and looked down, over the garden behind the garage, on to the waste land, and she thought, "I'm blessed. I'm doubly blessed. He'll talk one day. Please God, he'll talk one day."

"We're ready." They were standing in the doorway when she turned round to them.

"Come and have your tea-cakes."

"Can't we take them out with us?"

"Yes, if you like. . . . Did David change himself?"

Rose Mary's brows went upwards, and her eyelids came down slowly twice before she said, "I helped button him up, that's all."

Mary Ann handed them the tea-cakes, and they turned from her and ran across the landing and down the back stairs, and as she listened to Rose Mary, her voice high now, talking to her brother telling him what games they were going to play, she was back in the surgery this time last week looking at the doctor across the desk. He was smiling complacently and telling her in effect to do the same. "Not to worry, not to worry," he said. "Half his trouble, I think, is his sister. He doesn't talk because there's no real necessity, she's always done it for him. But don't worry, he's not mental, or anything like that. He'll likely start all of a sudden, and then you won't be able to keep him quiet." And he added that he didn't see much point at present in separating them.

Separate them? As if she would ever dream of separating them; it would be like cutting off one of their arms. Separate them, indeed. If David's power of speech would come only by separating them, then he would remain dumb. On that point she was firm. No matter what Corny said. . . .

It was half-past five when Corny came upstairs. The seven years during which he had been the owner of a garage, a married man, and the father of two children had aged him. The boy, Corny, was no more. The man, Corny, was a six-foot-two, tough-looking individual, with a pair of fine, deep blue eyes in an otherwise plain face. But his plain features were given a particular charm when he smiled or grinned. To Mary Ann he was still irresistible, yet there were times when even their Creator could not have been blamed for having his doubts as to their love for each other.

"Anything new?" She mashed the tea as she spoke.

"Thompson's satisfied with the repairs."

"Did he pay you?"

"Yes, in cash, and gave me ten bob extra."

"Oh, good." She turned and smiled at him.

"Hungry?"

"So, so."

"Give them a shout."

Corny went to the window and, opening it, called, "Tea up."

The thin voice of Rose Mary came back to him, crying, "Wait a minute, Dad, he's nearly finished."

"What are they up to over there?"

"They were digging a hole when I last looked," said Mary Ann.

"Digging a hole?" said Corny, screwing up his eyes. "They're piling up stones on top of something. . . . Come along this minute. Do you hear me?"

"Comin', comin'."

A few minutes later, as they came scampering up the stairs, Mary Ann called to them, "Go and wash your hands first, and take your coats off."

Tea was poured out and Corny was seated at the head of the little table when the children entered the room. "What were you up to over there?" He smiled at Rose Mary as he spoke.

"David made a grave," she said, hitching herself on to her seat.

Mary Ann turned swiftly from the stove and looked at her daughter. "A grave?" she said. "What for?"

"To bury Annabel Morton and Miss Plum in."

"Rose Mary!" There was a strong reprimand in Mary Ann's voice. "How could you."

"But I didn't, Mam, he did it hisself."

"He couldn't do it himself, child." Mary Ann leaned across the table and addressed her daughter pointedly, and Rose Mary, her lips now trembling, said, "But he did, Mam." Then turning to David, she said, "Didn't you, David?"

David smiled at her; he smiled at his mother; then smiled at his father. And Corny, holding his son's gaze, said quietly, "You dug a grave, David?"

David remained staring, unblinking.

"You dug a grave, David, and put Miss Plum and Annabel Morton in?"

Still the unblinking stare, which left Corny baffled and not a little annoyed. Turning to his daughter, he now asked her quietly, "How do you know it was Miss Plum and this Annabel Morton?"

"'Cos he took a picture out of my book, the Bantam family, where the mammy wears glasses like Miss Plum."

"And he put that in the hole?" asked Corny, still quietly.

Rose Mary nodded.

"And what did he put in for . . . for Annabel Morton?"

"A bit out of the funnies, 'The One Tooth Terror', 'cos Annabel Morton's got stick-out teeth with a band on."

Corny put his elbow on the table and rubbed his hand hard over his face before again looking at his daughter and saying, "And who told him to dig the grave and bury the pictures in it?"

"I didn't, Dad."

"Rose Mary!" The name was a threat now, and Rose Mary's lips trembled visibly, and she said again in a tiny squeaking voice, "I didn't, Dad, I'm tellin' the truth I am. He thought it all up for hisself, he did."

"You're going to instruction for confession on Thursday, Rose Mary; what will you tell Father Carey?"

"Not that, Dad, not that, 'cos I didn't."

"Well, how did you know it was a grave?"

"I don't know, Dad, I don't know." The tears were on her lashes now.

"Corny." Mary Ann's voice was low, and it, too, was trembling, but Corny, without looking at her, waved her to silence and went on, "Did he tell you it was Miss Plum and Annabel Morton?"

"No, Dad."

"You just knew?"

"Yes, Dad."

"How?"

"'Cos he dug a long hole and put the pictures in the bottom and covered them up, like when they put people in the ground in Longfields."

"Have you ever seen anyone being put in the ground in Longfields?"

"Corny." Mary Ann's voice was high now, but still he waved her to silence.

"Yes, and everbody was cryin'. . . ."

Corny lowered his eyes, then said, "And you didn't tell David to do this?"

"No, Dad. I was diggin' my garden, putting in the seeds you gave me, when I saw him diggin' a long hole. Then he ran back to the shed where all our old books an' things are and he came back with the pictures."

Once more Corny and David were looking at each other. David's lips were closed, gently closed, his eyes were dark and bright, and if he hadn't been a six-year-old child, a retarded six-year-old child, a supposedly retarded six-year-old child to Corny's mind, he would have sworn that there was a twinkle of amusement in the eyes gazing innocently into his. He rose from the table, pushing his chair back, and went out of the room, and Mary Ann, looking from one to the other of the children, said quickly, "Get on with your teas. No chatter now, get on with your teas." And then she followed her husband.

Corny was expecting her, for when she went into the bedroom he rounded on her immediately, and with his arm extended down towards her he wagged his hand in her face, saying. "It's as I've said before, that little bloke's laughing at us, he's having us on a string."

"Stop talking about your son as that bloke, will you, Corny; it's as if he didn't belong to you."

"Look, I'm not going to be made a fool of by a nipper of six, no matter what you say. As I said before, if he was on his own for a time he would talk all right. Send him to the farm for a few weeks and he'll come back yelling his head off."

"No, no; they can't be separated, they mustn't be separated. And the doctor said so. It's inhuman. I don't know how you can stand there and say such a thing. He's your son, but the way you talk you'd imagine he didn't belong to you."

"He's my son all right, and I want him as a son, and not as the shadow of Rose Mary. If he can think up that grave business and put the teacher and the Morton child into it because they had upset Rose Mary, he's got it up top all right. The only reason he's not talking is because he finds it easier not to. And mark you this." His finger was jabbing at her again. "He thinks it funnier not to. . . . That bloke. . . . All right, all right, all right, THAT CHILD. Well, that child is laughing up his sleeve at us, let me tell you."

"Don't be so silly. A child of six. . . . Huh!"

"Six, you say. Sometimes I think he's sixty. I believe he's an old soul in a young body."

"Oh, Corny." Mary Ann's voice was derisive now, and she closed her eyes giving emphasis to her opinion on this particular subject. "You've been reading again."

"Never mind about reading, I mean what I say, and as I've said before, if those two are separated that boy'll talk, and that's just what I'm . . ."

"Well, you try it." Mary Ann drew herself up to the limit of her five feet as she interrupted him, and, her face now red and straight, she said under her breath, "You separate them and you know what I'll do . . . I'll go home."

As soon as it was out she knew she had made a grave mistake. In her husband were a number of sensitive spots, which she had learnt it was better to by-pass, and now she had jumped on one with both feet, and she watched the pain she had caused, tightening his muscles and bringing his mouth to that hard line which she hated.

"This is your home, Mary Ann, I've told you before. These four rooms are your home. You chose them with your eyes open. The place that you've just referred to is the house where your parents live, the home of your children's grandparents, but this . . ." He took his fist and brought it down with a bang on the corner post of the wooden bed. "This is your home."

"Oh, Corny." It was a faint whisper. "I'm sorry. You know I didn't mean it."

"You've said it before."

"But I didn't mean it. I never mean it." She moved close to him and leant her head against his unyielding chest, and, putting her arms about him, she said, "I'm sorry. Hold . . . hold me tight."

It was a few minutes before Corny responded to the plea in her voice. Then, his arms going about her, he said stiffly, "I'll get you a better house, never you fear. One of these days I'll build you a house, and right here. But in the meantime, don't look down on this . . ."

"Oh, Corny." She had her head strained back gazing up at him and protesting, "I don't, I don't. Oh that's not fair, you know I don't."

"I don't know you don't, I know nothing of the sort, because you're always breaking your neck to visit the farm."

"Well, so are you. Look at the Sundays I've wanted to stay put, but it's been you who's said, 'Let's go over. If we don't they'll wonder. And they want to see the bairns!' You've said that time and again."

"I've said it because I knew you wanted to go. All right, let's forget it." He took her elfin face between his two big hands, and after gazing at it for a moment he said below his breath, "Oh, Mary Ann." Then pulling her close to him, he moved his hand over her hair saying, "Aw, I want to give you things . . . the lot, and it irks me when I go to the farm and everybody looks prosperous. Your da and ma, Michael and Sarah, Tony and Lettice."

"Aw, now, Corny, that's not fair." She was bristling again. "It isn't all clover for Tony and Lettice living with Mr. Lord. As for me ma and da looking prosperous. Well, after the way they've struggled. And as for our Michael and Sarah, we could have had a better place than them if . . ." Mary Ann suddenly found her words cut off by Corny's hand being placed firmly but gently across her mouth.

"I'll say it for you." Corny was speaking slowly. "If I'd taken the old man's offer and let him set me up with the Baxter garage, we'd have been on easy street. That's what you were getting at, isn't it? But I've told you before I'd rather eat bread and dripping and be me own boss. I'm daft I know, do-lally-tap, up the pole, the lot, I know, but that's the way I'm made. And again I say, you knew what you were taking on, didn't you?"

He took his hand slowly away from her mouth, and with his arms by his sides now he stood looking at her, and she at him. Then she smiled up at him, a loving little smile, as she said, "And I've told you this afore, Corny Boyle. You're a big pig-headed, stubborn, conceited lump of . . ."

"You forgot the bumptious. . . ."

Suddenly they were laughing, and he grabbed her up and swung her round as if she, too, was a child.

"Eeh! stop it, man, you'll have the things over." She thumped him on the chest, and as he plonked her down on the side of the bed there came to them from directly below the wailing note of a trombone.

The sound seemed to prevent Mary Ann from overbalancing. Looking up at Corny, she screwed her face up as she exclaimed, "Oh, no! No!"

"Look." He bent his long length down to her. "It's only for half-an-hour. I told him he could after he had finished the job and before the bairns had gone to bed. And think back, Mary Ann, think back. Remember when I hadn't any place to practice me cornet, who took pity on me?" He flicked her chin with his forefinger and thumb.

"But that's a dreadful sound, he knows nothing about it."

"So was my cornet."

"Aw, it wasn't." She pushed him aside as she got to her feet. "You could always play, you were a natural. But Jimmy. Why doesn't he stick to his guitar, he isn't bad at that?"

"They're trying to make the group different, introducing a trombone and a flute into it."

"Well, why didn't he pick the flute?" She put her fingers in her ears as a shrill wobbling note penetrated the floor-boards. "Oh, let's get into the other room. Not that it will be much better there."

As they entered the kitchen Rose Mary turned excitedly from the table, crying, "Jimmy's playing his horn, Mam."

"Yes, dear, I can hear. Have you finished your tea?"

"Nearly, Mam. David wants some cheese."

"David can't have any cheese, I've told you it upset his stomach before. He's got an egg and . . ." She bent over her son and looked down into the empty egg-cup, saying, "Oh, you've eaten your egg, that's a good boy. But where's the shell?" She turned her eyes to her daughter, and Rose Mary, looking down at her plate, said quietly, "I think he threw it in the fire, he sometimes does. But he'd like some cheese, he's still hungry."

"Now, Rose Mary, don't keep it up. I've told you he can't have any cheese."

"I've had some cheese."

"Oh." Mary Ann closed her eyes and, refusing to be drawn into a fruitless argument, took her seat at the table, only to bring her shoulders hunching up and her head down as an extra long wail from the trombone filled the room.

When it died away and she straightened herself up it was to see her daughter convulsed with laughter. David, too, was laughing, his deep, throaty, infectious chuckle. She was feigning annoyance, saying, "It's all right for you to laugh," when she saw Corny standing behind David's chair. He was motioning to her with his head, and so, quietly, she rose from the table and walked to his side and stood behind the children, and following her husband's eyes her gaze was directed to the pocket in her son's corduroy breeches. The pocket was distended, showing the top of a brown egg.

As they exchanged glances, she wanted to laugh, but it was no laughing matter. This wasn't the first time that food had been stuffed into her son's pockets, or up his jumper; it had even found its way into the chest of drawers. She was about to lift her hand to touch David when a warning movement from Corny stopped her. The movement said, leave this to me. Quietly she walked to her seat and Corny, taking his seat, drew his son's attention to him by saying, "David."

David turned his laughing face towards his father.

"Did you eat the egg that Mam give you for your tea?"

The smile slid from David's face, the eyes widened into innocence, the moist lips parted, and he bestowed on his father a look which said he didn't understand.

"Dad. Dad, he tried . . ."

"Rose Mary!" Without moving a muscle of his face Corny's eyes slid to his daughter. "Remember what I told you about telling lies. Now be quiet." The eyes turned on his son once again. "Where's the egg you had for your tea, David?"

Still no movement from David. Still the innocent look. Now Corny held out his hand. He laid it on the table in front of his son and said quietly, "Give it to me."

David's eyelids didn't flicker, but his small hand moved down towards his trouser pocket, then came upwards again, holding the egg. It took up a position about eight inches above Corny's hand, and there remained absolutely still.

"Give me the egg, David." Corny's voice was quiet and level.

And David gave his father the egg, his little fist pressed into the softly-boiled egg crushing the shell. As the yoke dripped on to Corny's fingers he smacked at his son's hand, knocking the crushed egg flying across the table, to splatter itself over the stove. Then almost in one movement he had David dangling by the breeches as if he was a hold-all, and with his free hand he lathered his behind.

David's screams now rent the air and vied with the screeches of the trombone and the crying of Rose Mary as she yelled, "Oh, Dad, don't. Oh don't hit David. Don't. Don't."

Mary Ann wanted to say the same thing, "Don't hit David. Don't," but David had to be smacked. Quickly, she thrust Rose Mary from the room, saying, "Stay there. . . . Now stay." And turning to Corny, she cried, "That's enough. That's enough."

After the first slap of anger she knew that Corny hadn't belaboured David as he could have done. It was only during these past few months that he had smacked his son, and although she knew it had to be done and the boy deserved it the process tore her to shreds.

She wanted to go to David now and gather him up from the big chair where he was crouched and into her arms, and pet him and mother him, but that would never do. She took him by the hand and drew him to his feet, saying, "Go into the bathroom and get your things off."

Outside the door, Rose Mary was waiting. She exchanged a look with her mother; then, putting her arms about her brother, she almost carried him, still sobbing, to the bathroom.

When Mary Ann returned to the room Corny said immediately, "Now don't say to me that I shouldn't have done that." She looked at him and saw that his face was white and strained, she saw that he was upset more than usual, and she could understand this. The defiance of his son, the indignity of the egg being squashed on to his fingers, and having to thrash the child had upset him, for he loved the boy. About his feelings for his son, she had once analysed them to herself by saying that he was crazy about Rose Mary but he loved David.

Everything seemed to have changed this last year, to have got worse over the past few months. At times she thought it was as Corny said, David had it all up top and he was trying something on. And this was borne out by the incident just now, for even she had to admit it appeared calculated.

Another blast from the trombone penetrating the room, she flew to the window, thrust it open and, leaning out, she cried, "Jimmy! Jimmy, will you stop that racket!"

"What, Mrs. Boyle. . . . Eh?"

She was now looking down on the long lugubrious face of Corny's young assistant, Jimmy McFarlane. Jimmy was seventeen. He was car mad, motor-cycle mad and group mad, in fact Mary Ann would say Jimmy was mad altogether, but he was a hard worker, likeable and good tempered. Apart from all that, he was all they could afford in the way of help.

"Sorry, Mrs. Boyle, is it disturbin' you? Is the bairns abed?"

"They're just going, Jimmy, but . . . but give it a rest for to-night at any rate, will you?"

"O.K., Mrs. Boyle." Jimmy's voice did not show his disappointment, and he added, "The boss there?"

"What is it?" Mary Ann had moved aside and Corny was hanging out of the window now.

"Had an American in a few minutes ago. Great big whopper of a car. . . . A Chevrolet. Twelve gallons of petrol and shots and oil, an' he gave me half-a-crown. Could do with some of those every hour, couldn't we, boss?"

"I'll say."

"He was tickled to death by me trombone, he laughed like a looney. He laughed all the time, even when I wasn't playing it. He must have thought I looked funny or summat, eh?"

"Well, as long as he gave you a tip, that's everything," said Corny. "I'll be down in a minute."

"O.K., boss."

After he had closed the window, Corny went straight into the scullery and returned with a floor cloth with which he began to wipe the mess from the stove.

"Corny. Please. Leave it, I'll see to it."

Abruptly he stopped rubbing with the cloth, and without turning his head said, "I want to clean this up.."

Standing back from him, Mary Ann looked at his ham-fisted actions with the cloth. There were depths in this husband of hers she couldn't fathom, there were facets of his thinking that she couldn't follow at times. There were things he did that wouldn't make sense to other people, like him wanting to clean up the mess his son had made. She said gently, "I'm going to wash them; will you come in?"

He went on rubbing for a moment. Then nodding towards the stove, he said, "I'll be in."

When he had the room to himself, and the egg and shell gathered on to the floor cloth, he stood with it in his hand looking down at it for a long moment. Life was odd, painful, and frightening at times.

2

Mary Ann liked Sundays. There were two kinds in her life, the winter Sundays and the summer Sundays. She didn't know which she liked best. Perhaps the winter Sundays, when Corny lay in bed until eight o'clock and she snuggled up in his arms and they talked about things they never got round to during the week. Then before the clock had finished striking eight, the twins would burst into the room—Rose Mary had her orders that they weren't to come in before eight o'clock on a Sunday, on a winter Sunday, because Dad liked a lie in.

On the summer Sundays, Corny rose at six and brought her a cup of tea before he went off to early Mass in Felling, and as soon as the door had closed on him the children would scamper into the bed and snuggle down, one each side of her, at least for a while. Eight o'clock on a summer Sunday morning usually found the bed turned into a rough house, and on such mornings Mary Ann became a little girl again, a child, as she laughed and tumbled and giggled with her children. Sometimes she was up and had the breakfast ready for Corny's return, but more often she was struggling to bring herself back to the point of being a mother, with a mother's responsibility, when he returned.

But this summer Sunday morning Mary Ann was up and had Corny's breakfast ready on his return. Moreover, the children were dressed and both standing to the side of the breakfast table, straining their faces against the window-pane to catch a sight of the car coming along the road.

"He's a long time," Rose Mary commented, then added, "can I start on a piece of toast, Mam?"

"No, you can't. You'll wait till your dad comes in."

"I'm hungry, I could eat a horse. David's hungry an' all."

"Rose Mary!"

Rose Mary gave her shoulders a little shake, then turned from the window, and, moving the spoon that was set near her cereal bowl, she said, "I hope old Father Doughty doesn't take our Mass this mornin', 'cos he keeps on and on. He yammers."

"Rose Mary, you're not to talk like that."

"Well, Mam, he does."

"Well, if he does, it's for your own good. And you should listen and pay heed to what he says."

"I pay heed to Father Carey. I like Father Carey. Father Carey never frightens me."

Mary Ann turned from the sideboard and looked at her daughter; then asked quietly, "Are you frightened of Father Doughty?"

Rose Mary now took up her spoon and whirled it round her empty bowl before saying,

"Sometimes. He was on about the Holy Ghost last Sunday and the sin of pride. Annabel Morton said he was gettin' at me 'cos I'm stuck up. I'm not stuck up, am I Mam?"

"I should hope not. What have you to be stuck up about?"

"Well, it's because we've got a garage and it's me dad's."

"Oh." Mary Ann nodded and turned her head back to the cutlery drawer. "But I thought you said you weren't stuck up."

"Well, just a little bit. About me dad I am." The spoon whirled more quickly now. Then it stopped abruptly, and Rose Mary, turning to her mother, said, "What's the Holy Ghost like, Mam?"

"What?"

"I mean, what's he like? Is he like God? Or is he like Jesus?"

Mary Ann made a great play of separating the knives and forks in the drawer. Then, turning her head slightly towards her daughter but not looking at her, she said, "God and Jesus and the Holy Ghost are all the same, they all look alike."

"Oh no they don't."

Mary Ann's eyes were now brought sharply towards her daughter, to see a face that was almost a replica of her own, except for the eyes that were like Corny's, tilted pointedly upwards towards her. "Jesus is Jesus, and I know what Jesus looks like 'cos I have pictures of him. An' I know who God looks like. But not the Holy Ghost."

Mary Ann's voice was very small when, looking down at her daughter, she said, "You know who God looks like? Who?"

"Me granda Shaughnessy. He's big like him, and nice and kind."

Mary Ann turned towards the drawer again before closing her eyes and putting her hand over her brow. Her da like God. Oh, she wanted to laugh. She wished Corny was here . . . he would have enjoyed that. Big, and nice, and kind. Well, and wasn't he all three? But for her da to take on the resemblance of God, Oh dear! Oh dear!

"Aha!" The sound came from David who was still looking out of the window, and Rose Mary turned towards him, crying, "It's me dad."

Both the children now waved frantically out of the window, and Corny waved back to them.

The minute he entered the room they flew to him, and he lifted one up in each arm, to be admonished by Mary Ann, crying, "Now don't crush their clothes, they're all ready for Mass."

"Dad. Dad, who said seven o'clock?"

"Father Doughty."

"Oh, then Father Carey will say eight, and Father Doughty will say nine, and Father Carey will say ten. Oh goodie!" She flung her arms around his neck and pressed her face against his, and David, following suit, entwined his arms on top of hers and pressed his cheek against the other side of his father's face.

The business of Friday night was a thing of the past; it was Sunday and "family day". Although the pattern of Sunday differed from winter to summer it had only been what Mary Ann thought of as "family day" since Jimmy had been taken on, because Jimmy came at eight o'clock on the summer Sunday mornings and stayed till ten, and, if required, he would come back again at two and stay as long as Corny wanted him. Jimmy was saving up for a motor-bike and Sunday work being time and a half he didn't mind how long he stayed. And when he was kept on on Sunday afternoon it meant they could all go to the farm together.

"Sit yourselves up," Mary Ann said, "and make a start. I'll take Jimmy's down."

Before she left the room they had all started on their cereal. When David had emptied his bowl he pushed it away from him, and Corny, looking down on his son, asked quietly, "Would you like some more, David?"

David looked brightly back into Corny's face and gave a small shake of his head, and Corny, putting his spoon gently down on the table, took hold of his son's hand and said quietly, "Say . . . no . . . thank . . . you . . . Dad." He spaced the words.

David looked back at his father, and Rose Mary, her spoon poised halfway to her mouth, looked at David.

"Go on, say it," urged Corny, still softly. "No thank you. Just say it. No . . . thank . . . you."

David's eyes darkened. The mischievous smile lurked in the back of them. He slanted his eyes now to Rose Mary, and Rose Mary, looking quickly at her father, said, "He wants to say no thank you, Dad. He means, no thank you, don't you, David?" She pushed her face close against his, and David smiled widely at her and nodded his head briskly, and Corny, picking up his spoon again, started eating.

Rose Mary stood with one hand in Mary Ann's while with the other she clutched at David's. She wasn't feeling very happy; it wasn't going to be a very nice Sunday. It hadn't been a very nice Sunday from the beginning, because her mother had got out of bed early, and then her dad had been vexed at breakfast time because David wouldn't say No thank you, and now they were going into Felling by bus.

Her mam had snapped at her when she asked her why her dad couldn't run them in in the car. She couldn't see why he couldn't close up the garage for a little while, just a little while, it didn't take long to get into Felling by car. And what was worse, worse for her mam anyway, was that she had to go all the way to Jarrow by bus. She didn't like it when her mam went to Jarrow Church, but she only went to Jarrow Church when she was visiting Greatgran McBride, killing two birds with one stone, she called it. She herself liked to visit Greatgran McBride, and so did David. They loved going to Greatgran McBride's. They didn't mind the smell.

"Mam, couldn't you leave going to Greatgran McBride's until this afternoon?"

"Don't you want to go to the farm this afternoon?"

"Yes, but I'd like to go to Greatgran McBride's an' all. Dad could run us there afore we went to the farm."

"Dad can't do any such thing, so stop it. And don't you start on that when we get home. I'm going to see Greatgran McBride because she isn't well and she can't be bothered with children around."

"She always says she loves to——"

"You're not going to-day."

There was a short silence before Rose Mary suggested, "Couldn't we come on after Mass? We could meet you an' we could all come back together. I could get the bus; I've done it afore."

"Do you want me to get annoyed with you, Rose Mary?"

"No, Mam." The voice was very small.

"Well, then, do as you're told. What's the matter with you this morning?"

"I think it might be Father Doughty an' I don't like——"

"You know it'll be Father Carey. And not another word now, here's the bus, and behave yourself."

Twenty minutes later, Rose Mary, still holding David by the hand, entered St. Patrick's Church. Inside the doorway she reached up and dipped her fingers in the holy-water font, and David followed suit; then one after the other they genuflected to the main altar. This done, they walked down the aisle until they came to the fifth pew from the front. This was one of the pews allotted to their class. Again they genuflected one after the other, then Rose Mary entered the pew first. One foot on the wooden kneeler, one on the floor, she was making her way to where sat her school pals, Jane Leonard and Katie Eastman, when she became aware that she was alone, at least, in-as-much as the other half of her was not immediately behind her. She turned swiftly, to see David standing in the aisle looking up at Miss Plum. Miss Plum had David by one hand and David was hanging on to the end of the pew with the other. Swiftly, Rose Mary made the return journey to the aisle, and Miss Plum, bending down to her and answering her look, which said plainly, "Now what are you up to with our David?" whispered, "I'm putting David with the boys on the other side."

"But, Miss Plum, he won't go."

A low hissing whisper now from Miss Plum. "He'll go if you tell him to, Rose Mary."

A whisper now from Rose Mary. "But I've told him afore, Miss Plum."

"Go and sit down, Rose Mary, and leave David to me."

Rose Mary stared up into Miss Plum's face. Then she looked at David, and David looked at her. Whereupon David, after a moment, turned his gaze towards Miss Plum again and made a sound that was much too loud for church. The sound might have been interpreted as, "Gert yer!" But, of course, David never said any such thing. He just made a sound of protest, but it was enough to put Miss Plum into action. In one swift movement she unloosened his fingers from the end of the pew and, inserting both her hands under his armpits, she whisked him across the aisle, plonked him none too gently on the wooden pew, then sat down beside him.

David made no more protesting sounds. He gazed up at the straight profile of his teacher, stared at her for a moment with his mouth open, then bent forward, to see beyond her waist, to find out what Rose Mary was up to in all this. He was now further surprised to see his sister, miles away from him, kneeling, with her chin on the pew rail staring towards the high altar. His brows gathered, the corners of his eyes puckered up. He was very puzzled. Rose Mary wasn't doing anything. He gave a wriggle with his bottom to bring him further forward, when a hand, that almost covered the whole of his chest, pushed him backwards on the seat, making him over-balance and bump his head and bring his legs abruptly up to his eye level.

When Rose Mary, from the corner of her eye, saw Miss Plum push their David and knock his head against the pew, she almost jumped up and shouted out loud, but, being in church, she had to restrain her actions and content herself with her thoughts. She hated Miss Plum, she did, she did. And David wouldn't know anything about the Mass. He wouldn't understand what Father Carey was saying, and he wouldn't be able to sing the hymn inside hisself like he did when he was with her. . . . Wait till she got home, she would tell her dad about Miss Plum. Just wait. She would get him to come to the school the morrow and let her have it. Plum, Plum, Plum. She hoped a big plum stone would stick in her gullet and she would die. She did, she did. In the name of the Father, and of the Son, and of the Holy Ghost. Amen.

Father Carey was kneeling on the altar steps. "Our Father Who art in heaven, hallowed be Thy name." She had taken their David across there all because of Annabel Morton, 'cos last Sunday when Annabel Morton had punched their David under her coat so nobody could see, David had kicked her and made her shout out. . . . "An' forgive us our trespasses, as we forgive them that trespass against us." Miss Plum had blamed her and she wouldn't believe about Annabel Morton punching David and she had been nasty all the week. Oh, she did hate Miss Plum. Their poor David havin' to sit there all by hisself, all through the Mass, and it would go on for hours and hours. Father Carey was talking slow, he was taking his time, he always did. "I believe in God the Father Almighty, Creator of Heaven and Earth." If her dad wouldn't come down and go for Miss Plum the morrow she knew who would. Her Grandad Shaughnessy would. He would soon tell her where she got off. Yes, that's who would give it to her, her Grandad Shaughnessy. "I believe in the Holy Ghost, the Holy Catholic Church." And Father Carey would likely go on about the Holy Ghost and the Trinity this morning; when he started his sermon he forgot to stop, although he made you laugh at times. Oh, she wished the Mass was over. She slanted her eyes to the left, but she couldn't see anything, only the bowed heads of the other three girls who were filling up the pew now. If she raised her chin and stuck it on the arm rest she had a view of Miss Plum, but there was no sign of David. Poor David was somewhere down on the kneeler yon side of Miss Plum. Well, it would serve Miss Plum right if he started to scream.

Rose Mary brought her head slowly forward and she looked to where the priest was mounting the steps towards the altar. But she wasn't interested at all in what Father Carey was doing, for forming a big question mark in her mind was the word WHY? . . . WHY? . . . hadn't he screamed? Why wasn't their David screaming? He always screamed when he was separated from her? Perhaps Miss Plum was holding his mouth. She jerked round so quickly in the direction of her teacher that she overbalanced and fell across the calves of the girl next to her.

When a hand came down and righted her more quickly than she had fallen, she caught a fleeting glimpse of its owner, and now, staring wide-eyed towards the altar again, she wondered how on earth Miss Watson had got behind her. Miss Watson was the headmistress. Miss Watson usually sat at the back of the church in solitary state.

As the Mass went on the awful thought of Miss Watson behind her kept Rose Mary's gaze fixed on the altar, except when she was getting on or off her seat to stand or kneel, when her head would accidentally turn to the left. But she might as well have kept it straight, for all she could see past the bodies of her schoolmates was the tall, full figure of Miss Plum. No sight, and what was more puzzling still, no sound of their David. . . .

The Mass over at last, Rose Mary came out of the pew in line with the others, genuflected deeply, then looked towards Miss Plum. But Miss Plum's profile was cast in marble, in fact her whole body seemed stone-like. A push from behind and Rose Mary was forced to go up the aisle, and she daren't look round, for there at the top stood Miss Watson. She bowed her head as she passed Miss Watson as if she, too, demanded adoration.

Outside, she waited, her eyes glued on the church door. All the girls had come out first, and now came the boys . . . but not their David, and not Miss Plum. The grown-ups appeared in a long straggling line, and among them was Miss Watson, but still no sign of Miss Plum. Rose Mary could stand it no longer. Sidling back into the church, she looked down the aisle, and there, standing next to Miss Plum and opposite Father Carey, was their David, looking as if nothing had happened. The priest was smiling, and Miss Plum was smiling, and they were talking in whispers. When they turned, David turned, and they all came up the aisle towards her. And when they reached her Miss Plum looked down on her and said, "David's been a very good boy, and he's going to sit with me every sunday."

Rose Mary sent a sweeping glance from Miss Plum to David, then from David to Father Carey, and back to Miss Plum. She was opening her mouth to protest when the priest said, "Isn't that a great favour, David, eh?" He had his hand on David's head. "Sitting next to your teacher. My My. Everybody else in the class will be jealous." He now looked at Miss Plum, and Miss Plum at him, and they smiled at each other. And then Miss Plum said, "Good-bye, Father." She said it like Annabel Morton said things when she was sucking up to somebody. Then she went out of the church.

Rose Mary, now grasping David's hand, looked at the priest, and said softly, "Father."

"Yes, Rose Mary." He bent his head towards her.

"Father, our David doesn't like being by hisself."

"But he hasn't been by his—himself, he's been sitting next to Miss Plum, and liked it."

"He doesn't like it, Father."

"Now, now, Rose Mary. David's getting a big boy and he must sit with the big boys, mustn't you, David?" The young priest turned towards David, and David grinned at him.

Rose Mary contemplated the priest. She liked Father Carey, she did, he was lovely, but he just didn't understand the situation. She now jerked her chin towards him, and whispered,

"Father." The word was in the form of a request that he should lend her his ear, and this he did, literally putting it near her mouth, and what he heard was, "He can't talk without me, Father."

Now it was Rose Mary's turn to lend him her ear and into it he whispered, "But he doesn't talk now, Rose Mary."

Now the exchange was made again, and what he heard this time was, "He does to me, Father."

Again a movement of heads and a whisper, "But we want him to talk to everybody, don't we, Rose Mary?"

"Yes, Father . . . oh, yes, Father. But . . ."

The priest whisked his ear away, straightened up and said, "We'll have to pray to our Lady about it."

"But I have, Father, an' she hasn't done anything. . . . Perhaps if you asked her, Father."

"Yes, yes, I'll ask her." Father Carey drew his fingers down his nose.

"When?" She could talk now quite openly because their David didn't know what it was all about.

"Oh, at Mass in the morning."

"The first Mass, Father?"

Father Carey's eyebrows moved slightly upwards and he hesitated slightly before saying, "Yes. Yes, the first Mass."

"Could you make it in the half-past eight one, Father?"

The priest's eyebrows rose farther; then his head dropped forward as if he was tired, and he looked at Rose Mary for a moment before saying slowly, "Well, if you would like it that way, all right. Yes, I'll do it at the second Mass."

"Thank you, Father." She bestowed on him her nice smile, the one that had earned the unwarranted title of angelic, then she finished: "An' now we'd better get home, 'cos me mam worries if we're late. We'll have to run, I think."

"That's it, run along. Good-bye, David." The priest patted David's head. "Good-bye, Rose Mary." He chucked her under the chin; then with a hand on each of them he pressed them towards the church door, and then for a moment he watched them running down the street, and he shook his head as he thought, Dear, dear. It was as Miss Plum said, she had her work cut out with that little lady. It was also true that the boy would make little progress as long as he had a mouthpiece in his sister. And what a mouthpiece, she'd talk the hind leg off a donkey. He re-entered the church, laughing.

Rose Mary walked down the street and away from the church in silence, and the unusualness of this procedure caused David to trip over his feet as he gazed at his sister instead of looking where he was going. Then of a sudden, he was pulled to a stop, and Rose Mary, bending towards him, said under her breath, "Father Carey's going to tell Our Lady to ask God to make you speak the morrow mornin', he's goin' to tell her at the half-past eight. And you will, won't you, David?"

David's eyes darkened, and shone, his smile widened and he nodded his head once.

Rose Mary sighed. Then she, too, smiled. That was that then. Everything was taken care of. If things went right he should be talking just when they reached their classroom.

Getting on the bus, Rose Mary reminded David, in no small voice now, that it being Sunday they'd have Yorkshire pudding and if he liked he could have his with milk and sugar before his dinner; then she went on to explain what there would be for the dinner, not forgetting to pay stress on the delectability of the pudding. Following this she gave him a description of what there was likely to be for tea at Gran Shaughnessy's. By the time they alighted from the bus the other occupants had no doubt in their minds but that Rose Mary and David Boyle had a mother who was a wonderful cook, a father who could supply unstintingly the necessities to further his wife's art, and grandparents who apparently lived like lords. And this was as it should be, otherwise she would have indeed wasted her breath.

3

Lizzie Shaughnessy looked at her daughter from under her lowered lids. When they were alone like this it was always hard to believe that her Mary Ann was a married woman and the mother of twins, for she still looked so young and childlike herself. It was her small stature that tended towards this impression, she thought.

Lizzie knew that her daughter was worried and she was waiting for her to unburden herself, and she knew the substance of her worry: it was the child. She joined on another ounce of wool to her knitting, then said, "Do you know what they're going to do with Peter?"

"Send him to boarding school," Mary Ann said.

Lizzie slowly put her knitting on to her lap and, turning her head right round to Mary Ann, said, "Who told you?"

"Nobody, but I guessed it would come. I remember years ago Tony saying that Mr. Lord had a school all mapped out for the boy."

"But neither Tony nor Lettice wants to send him away to school."

"I know that, but he'll go all the same; they'll send him because that's what Mr. Lord wants. He always gets what he wants."

"Not always," said Lizzie quietly. And to this Mary Ann made no rejoinder, for she knew that one of the great disappointments in her mother's life, and Mr. Lord's, was when his grandson and herself hadn't made a match of it.

"The old man will be the one who will miss him most," Lizzie went on. "But it amazes me that he can put up with the boy; he's so noisy and boisterous and he never stops talking. . . ."

Mary Ann got up from her chair and walked to the sitting-room window, and Lizzie said softly, "I'm sorry, I wasn't meaning to make comparisons. You know that, oh you know that."

"Of course I do, Ma." Mary Ann looked at her mother over her shoulder. "It's all right. Don't be silly; I didn't take it to myself, it's just that . . ." She spread out her hands, and then came back to her seat and sat down before ending, "I just can't understand it. He's not deaf, he's certainly not dim, and yet he can't talk."

"He will. Be patient, he will. . . . You . . . you wouldn't consider leaving him with us?"

"Corny's been at you, hasn't he?"

"No. No." Lizzie shook her head vigorously.

"Oh, don't tell me, Ma. I bet my bottom dollar he has. He thinks that if they were separated, even for a short time, it would make David talk. It wouldn't. And Rose Mary wouldn't be able to bear it. Neither would David, they're inseparable. At any rate, the doctor himself said it wouldn't be any use separating them."

"You could give it a trial." Lizzie had her eyes fixed on her knitting now.

"No, Ma, no. I wouldn't have one worry then, I'd have two, for I just don't know what the effect would be on Rose Mary, because she just lives and breathes for that boy."

"Yes, that's your trouble." Lizzie was now looking straight at her daughter. "That's the trouble, she lives and breathes for him."

"Oh, Ma, don't you start."

"All right, all right. We'll say no more. Anyway, here they come. . . . And don't look like that else they'll know something has happened. Come on, cheer up." She rose from her seat and put her hand on Mary Ann's shoulder, adding under her breath, "It'll be all right; it'll come out all right, you'll see."

"Gran, Gran, Peter's got new riding breeches. Look!" Rose Mary dashed into the room, followed by a dark-haired, dark-eyed, pale-faced boy of seven.

"Have you all wiped your feet?" was Lizzie's greeting to them.

"Yes, Granma," cried Rose Mary. "An' David has, an' all."

"An' I have too, Granshan."

Their quaint combination of the beginning of her name with the courtesy title of Gran attached had been given to her by Tony's son from the time he could talk. To him she had become Granshan, and now it was an accepted title and no one laughed at it any more.

Following Peter, Sarah hobbled into the room. She was still on sticks, still crippled with polio as she would be all her days, but moving more agilely than she had done nearly seven years ago, when she had stood for the first time since her illness at the altar to be married. Behind her came Michael, refraining, as always, from helping her except by his love, which still seemed to hallow them both, and behind Michael, and looking just an older edition of him, came Mike.

Mike's red hair was now liberally streaked with grey. He had put on a little more weight, but he still looked a fine strapping figure of a man, and the hook, which for a long time had been a substitute for his left hand, was now replaced by thin steel fingers that seemed to move of their own volition.

Mike, now turning a laughing face over his shoulder, asked of Corny who was in the hall, "You wiped your feet?"

"No," said Corny, coming to the room door. "I never wipe my feet; it's a stand I've made against all house-proud women, never to wipe my feet."

"You know better," said Lizzie, nodding across the room at him. Then she cried at the throng about her, "I don't know what you all want in here when the tea's laid and you should be sitting down."

"Am I to stay to tea, Granshan?"

Lizzie looked down on the boy and said, "Of course, Peter, but you'd better tell your mother, hadn't you?"

"Oh, she knows." He wagged his head at her. "I told her you'd likely invite me."

In his disarming way he joined in the roar that followed, and when Michael cuffed him playfully on the head the boy turned on him with doubled-up fists, and there ensured a sparring match, which David and Rose Mary applauded, jumping and shouting around them. It was the fact of David shouting that brought Corny's and Mary Ann's hands together, because the boy was actually making an intelligible sound which could almost be interpreted as "Go on, Peter. Go on, Peter."

Mary Ann's head drooped slightly and she made a small groaning sound as her mother's voice brought the sparring to an end with a sharp command of, "Now give over. Do you hear me, Michael, stop it. If you want any rough-house stuff, get you outside, the lot of you. Come on now."

Michael collapsed on the couch, and this was the signal for the three children to storm over him, and Lizzie, turning to the rest, commanded, "Get yourselves into the other room and seated . . . I'll see to these."

Five minutes later they were seated round the well-laden tea table. There had been a little confusion over the seating in the first place as Rose Mary wanted to sit next to Peter, and

Peter evidently wanted to sit next to Rose Mary, but David not only wanted to sit next to Rose Mary, he also wanted to sit next to Peter, so in the end David sat between Peter and Rose Mary and the tea got under way.

It was in the middle of tea, when Corny and Mary Ann between them were giving their version of Jimmy's trombone playing, that Peter suddenly said, "I'd jolly well like to hear him. They've got a band at school, but it's just whistles and things. Perhaps Father will bring me over to-morrow when he comes to see you, and I'll hear him play then, eh, Uncle Corny?"

"Tony . . . your father's coming to see me to-morrow, Peter?" Corny looked down the table towards the boy, and Peter, his head cocked on one side, said, "Yes, he said he was. He wants a new car, and you're going to buy it for him."

"Oh?"

All eyes were on Corny. This was a good bit of news, it meant business, yet the elders at table knew that Corny wasn't taking it like that. To get an order from Tony, who was the grandson of Mr. Lord, Mr. Lord who had for so long been Mary Ann's mentor and who was still finding ways and means of handing out help to her, would not meet with Corny's approval, even if it meant badly needed business.

Mike's voice broke the immediate silence at the table, saying, "You've spilt the beans, young fellow, haven't you?"

Peter looked towards the man, whom, in his own mind, he considered one of his family, and said, with something less than his usual exuberance, "Yes, Granpa Shan, I have . . . Father will be vexed." He now turned his gaze down the table towards Corny and said, "I'm sorry, Uncle Corny. I wasn't supposed to know, I just overheard Father telling Mother . . . I'll get it in the neck now, I suppose." The last statement, said in such a polite tone, was too much even for Corny. He laughed, and the tension was broken as he said, "And you deserve to get it in the neck too, me lad."

"You won't give me away to Father?" Peter was leaning over his plate as he looked down towards Corny, and Corny, narrowing his eyes at the young culprit, said, "What's it worth?"

This remark brought Peter upright. He looked first towards Rose Mary's bright face, then towards David's penetrating stare, and, his agile mind working overtime, he returned his gaze to Corny and said, "Let's say I'll help to clean one of your cars for you during the holidays . . . that's if I can stay to dinner."

They were all laughing and all talking at once, and Sarah, leaning across the corner of the table towards Mary Ann, said, "He'll either grow up to be Foreign Minister, or a confidence trickster," whereupon they both laughed louder still.

But behind her laughter a little nagging voice was saying to Mary Ann: If only David had said that; and he could have, he could be as cute as Peter any day, if only he could break through the skin that was covering his speech.

If only. If only. If only there was some way. . . . But not separating them as Corny wanted, and now her mother. No, not that way.

4

It was half-past ten in the morning and a beautiful day; cars were spinning thick and fast over all the roads in England, and the North had more than its share of traffic. There were people going on their holidays to the Lake District, to Scotland, to Wales. There were foreigners in cars who were discovering that the North of England had more to show than pits and docks. Yet Corny, who had been in the garage since half-past six that morning, had sold exactly four gallons of petrol.

It couldn't go on, he had just told himself as he sat in his little office looking at his ledger. Last week he had cleared seventeen pounds, and he'd had Jimmy to pay out of that, and then there had been the building society repayments, insurance, and the usual sum to be put by for rates, and what did that leave for living? They had dipped into their savings so often, the money they had banked from Mr. Lord's generous wedding present to them both, until it was now very near the bottom of the barrel. Mary Ann worked miracles, but at times there was a fear in him that she would get tired of working miracles. She was young, they were both young, and they weren't seeing much of life, only hard work and struggling. This was what both his parents and hers had had in their young days, but the young of to-day were supposed to be having it easy, making so much money in fact that they didn't know what to do with it, or themselves. And it was a fact in some cases. There was his brother, Dan, twenty-four years old, not a thought in his head but beer and women, and yet he never picked up less than thirty quid from his lorry driving; forty-five quid some weeks he had told him, and just for dumping clay, not even stepping a foot out of his cab.

Life at this moment appeared very unfair. Why, Corny asked himself, couldn't he get a break? Nobody worked harder, tried harder. It was funny how your life could be altered by one man's vote in a committee room. When he had bought the garage seven years ago he had been sure that the council would widen the lane and make it into a main connecting road between Felling and Turnstile point, but one man's vote had potched the whole thing. . . . But not quite. It was the "not quite" that had kept him hanging on, for there had been rumours that the council had ideas for this little bottle-neck. Some said they were going to buy the land near the old turnstile for a building estate. Another rumour was that they were going to build a comprehensive school just across the road in what was known as Weaver's field.

During the first couple of years he had sustained himself on the rumours. He seemed to have been very young then, even gullible, now he knew he was no longer young inside, and certainly not gullible. No rumour affected him any more; yet at the same time he kept hanging on, and hoping.

He rose from the stool and walked out into the bright sunshine. Everything looked neat and tidy. Nobody, he assured himself, had a prettier garage. The red flowers against the white stones, the cement drive-in all scrubbed clean, not a spot of oil to be seen—perhaps that was a bad sign, he should leave the oily patches, it would bear out the saying: where there was dirt there was money. He turned and looked into the big garage. It, too, was too tidy, too bare. He hadn't a thing in for repairs. The garage held nothing now but his old Rover and some cardboard adverts for tyres.

As he stared down the long, empty space Jimmy came from out of the shadows with a broom in his hand, and, leaning on it and looking towards Corny, he said quizzically,

"Well, that's that. What next, boss? . . . There's a bird's nest in the chimney, I could go and tidy that up. . . ."

"Now I'm having none of that . . . an' you mind." Corny's voice came as a growl, and Jimmy, the smile sliding from his face, said, "I was only kiddin', boss. I meant nowt, honest."

"Well, let's hope you didn't. I've told you afore, if you don't like it here there's plenty of other jobs you can get. I'm not stopping you. You knew the terms when you started."

"Aye. Aye, I know. An' it's all right with me. I like it here, I've told you, 'cos I've learned more with you than I would have done in a big garage, stuck on one job. . . . It's only, well. . . ." Jimmy didn't go on to explain that he got bored when there were no jobs in but said, with a touch of excitement, "Look, what about me takin' that monstrosity out there to bits and buryin' it, eh?"

He walked past Corny, and Corny slowly followed him to the edge of the garage, and they looked towards his piece of spare land that bordered the garden and where stood a car. Three nights ago someone had driven a car there and left it. The first indication Corny had of this was when he opened up the next morning, and the sight of the dumped car almost brought his temper to boiling point. They just wanted to start that; let that get round and before he knew where he was he'd be swamped. They had started that game up near the cemetery, and there were two graveyards up there now. He couldn't understand how he'd slept through someone driving a car down the side of the building, because a car had only to pass down the road in the night and it would wake him, and he would say to himself, "It couldn't come down in the daytime, could it."

He had been on the point of taking a hammer and doing what Jimmy suggested they should do now, break the thing up and bury it, but the twins had caused him to change his mind, at least temporarily, for Rose Mary had begged him to let them have it to play with, and strangely, Mary Ann had backed her up, saying, "It would give them something to do now that they were on holiday, and might stop her pestering to be taken to the sands at Whitley Bay or Shields. So Corny had been persuaded against his will to leave the car as it was. He had siphoned out what petrol there remained in the tank, cleared the water and oil out, and left the children with a gigantic toy, hoping that their interest might lag within a few days and he would then dispose of it. But the few days had passed and their interest, far from waning, had increased.

From where he stood he could see the pair of them, Rose Mary in the driving seat with David bobbing up and down beside her, driving to far-off places he had no doubt, places as far away as their Greatgran McBride's in Jarrow. He smiled quietly to himself as he thought they were like him in that way, he had always wanted to go to his Grannie McBride, for his grannie's cluttered untidy house had been more of home to him than his real home; and it had been her dominant, loud, yet wise personality that had kept him steady. . . . Yes, undoubtedly, the pair of them would be off in the car to their Greatgran McBride's.

"No go, boss?"

Corny gave a huh! of a laugh as he turned to Jimmy and said, "What do you think? Go down there and tell them you're going to smash it up and there'll be blue murder."

"Well, what'll I do?" Jimmy was looking straight up into Corny's face, and Corny surveyed him for a full minute before answering, "Well now, what would you like to do?"

On this question the corner of Jimmy's mouth was drawn in, and he looked downwards at his feet as if considering. Then, his eyes flicking upwards again, he glanced at Corny and they both laughed.

"Well, mind, just until the missus comes in. I'll give you the tip when I see her coming up the road, for she's threatened to leave me if she hears any more of your efforts."

Jimmy's mouth split his face, and on a loud laugh, he said, "Aw! I can see her doing that, boss. But ta, I'll stop the minute you give me the nod."

Less than a minute later the too quiet air of the garage and the immediate vicinity was broken by the anguished, hesitant wails of the trombone.

The sound had no effect on Corny one way or the other. He had practised his cornet so much as a lad that he now seemed immune to the awful wailing wind practice evoked. Although when he stopped to think about it the boy was learning, and fast, in spite of the quivering screeches and wrong notes.

He was in the office again when he heard a car approaching the garage and almost instantly he was outside, rubbing his hands with a cloth as if he had just come off a grimy job. The car might pass, yet again it might stop. He had noticed before that the sight of someone about the place induced people to stop, but apparently this car needed no inducement, for it swirled on to the drive and braked almost at his feet.

Jimmy's American.

Corny recognized the Chevrolet and the driver, inasmuch as the latter's nationality was indicated by his dress, particularly his hat.

"Hello, there." The man was getting out of the car.

"Good morning, sir."

The man was tall, as tall as Corny himself, and broad with it. Like most Americans, he looked well dressed and, as Corny thought, finished off. He was a man who could have been forty, or fifty, there was no telling. He was clean-shaven, with deep brown eyes and a straight-lipped mouth. His face had an all-over pleasantness, and his manner was decidedly so. Without moving his feet he leaned his body back and looked up through the empty garage, and, his face slipping into a wide grin, he said, "The youngster's at it again?"

"Oh yes. He's gone on the trombone. I let him have a go at it. . . ." He just stopped himself from adding "when we're not busy". Instead he said, "They're forming a new group and he's mad to learn."

"He's not your boy?"

"Oh no. No." Corny turned his head to one side, but his eyes still held those of the American. "Give us a chance."

"Of course, of course." The American's hand came out and pushed him familiarly in the shoulder. "You in your middle twenties I should say, and him nearing his twenties." His laugh was deep now. "You would have to have started early."

"You're saying!"

"Well now." He looked towards his car. "I want it filled, and do you think you could give her a wash?"

"Certainly, sir."

"Not very busy this morning?"

"No, not yet; it's early in the day. A lot of my customers work on a Saturday morning, you know, and they . . . they bring them in later."

"Yes, yes."

As Corny filled the tank with petrol the American walked to one end of the building, then to the other. He stood looking for a moment at the children climbing over the car. Then coming back, he walked into the empty garage, and when he came out again he stood at Corny's side and said, "Happen you don't have a car for hire, do you?"

"No. No, sir. I'm sorry, I don't run hire cars."

"It's a pity. I wanted this one looked over, I've been running her hard for weeks and I've got the idea she's blown a gasket. I'm staying in Newcastle, but I want a car to get me back and forwards until this one is put right. . . . You've a car of your own, of course?"

"Only the old Rover, sir."

"Oh, that one in there? She looks in spanking condition." He walked away from Corny again and into the garage, and Corny, getting the hose to wash the Chevrolet down, thought, "That's what I want, a car for hire. I've said it afore. Look what I'm losing now, and it isn't the first time."

"Do you mind if I try her?"

"What's that, sir?" Corny went to the opening of the garage. The American had the Rover's door open and was bending forward examining her inside, and, straightening up, he called again, "Do you mind if I try her?"

"Not in the least, sir. But she's an old car and everything will be different."

The American had his back bent again, and he swung his head round to Corny and his mouth twisted as he said, "I was in England during the war, and after, I bet I've driven her mother."

They exchanged smiles, and then the American seated himself behind the wheel. "Can I take her along the road?"

"Do as you like, sir." Corny stood aside and looked at the man in the car as he handled the gear lever and moved his feet, getting the feel of her.

"O.K.?" He nodded towards Corny, and Corny nodded back to him, saying, "O.K., sir," and the next minute Fanny, as Mary Ann had christened the car after Mrs McBride, moved quietly out of the garage, and Corny watched the back of her disappearing down the road.

He would have to take her right to the end before he turned, he thought, but that bloke knew what he was doing, he was driving her as if along a white line. She looked good from the back, as she did from the front, dignified, solid. He wasn't ashamed of Fanny, not for himself he wasn't.

Well, he'd better get on cleaning this one down. He was a nice chap was the American. No big talk. Well, not as yet, but you could usually tell from the start. . . . Lord, this was a car . . . and look at the boot, nearly as big as a Mini.

He had almost finished hosing the car down before the American returned. He brought the Rover on to the drive and, getting out, came towards Corny and said, "You wouldn't think of letting her out for a day or two?"

"The Rover? To you?" Corny's mouth was slightly agape.

"Yes, she's a fine old girl. You wouldn't mind?"

"Mind? Why should I mind, when you are leaving this one?" He thumbed toward the Chevrolet.

"Yes, I see what you mean, but, you know, I consider that many a wreck of a Rover is a sight more reliable than some of the new models that are going about now."

"You're right there, sir; you're right there."

"Well then, if you would hire her to me you could go over this one." He pointed towards his car.

"If it suits you, sir, it suits me."

"That's settled then."

An extra loud wail from Jimmy's trombone reverberated round the garage at this moment. It went high and shrill, then on a succession of stumbling notes fell away and left the American with his head back, his mouth wide open, and laughing heartily, very like, Corny thought, Mike laughed.

"You know." He began to dry his eyes. "I've thought a lot about that young chappie since I saw him last, and I always couple his face with the trombone. . . . No offence meant. It's a kind of face that goes with a trombone, don't you think, long an' lugubrious."

"Yes, I suppose so, looking at it like that." Corny, too, was laughing.

"Will you stop that noise, Jimmy!"

The voice not only hit Jimmy, but startled the two men, and they turned and looked to where Mary Ann was standing at the far end of the garage. She had come in by the back door and the children were with her.

"Coo, Mrs. Boyle, I thought you was out."

"Which means I suppose that every time I leave the house you play that thing. Now I'm warning you, Jimmy, if I hear it again I'll take it from you and I'll put a hammer to it. . . . Mind, I mean it."

"Aw, Mrs. Boyle. . . ."

Mary Ann turned hastily away, taking the children with her, and Jimmy came slowly down the garage, the trombone dangling from his hand. The American began to chuckle. Then, looking at Corny, he said softly, "That was Mrs. Boyle?"

"You're right; that was Mrs. Boyle," said Corny, below his breath.

The American shook his head. "She looks like a young girl, a young teenager, no more. But there's one thing sure; no matter what she looks like, she acts like a woman."

"And you're right there, too, sir." Corny jerked his head at the American. "She acts like a woman all right, and all the time."

The American laughed again; then said, "Well now, about you letting me have your old girl. Oh, make no mistake about it, I'm referring to the car." His head went back and again he was laughing, and Corny with him, while Jimmy stood looking at them both from inside the garage.

"It's up to you, sir."

"All right, it's up to me, and I'll settle for a charge when I pick up my car. You won't be out of pocket, don't you worry. You won't know at this stage how long it's going to take you to do her; but I'll look in to-morrow, eh?"

"Do that, sir. If there's nothing very serious I should have her ready by then."

"Oh, there's no hurry. I'll enjoy driving the old lady."

"Corny."

The American now looked over Corny's shoulder to where a petite young girl—this was how he saw Mary Ann—was standing at the door of the house. Corny, following the American's gaze, turned to see Mary Ann, and Mary Ann, her head drooping slightly, said quickly, "Oh, I'm sorry, I didn't know you were busy. I just came to tell you. . . ." Her voice trailed off.

The American was smiling towards Mary Ann, and Corny, motioning towards her with his hand, said, "This is my wife, sir." Whereupon, with characteristic friendliness, the American held out his hand as he walked towards her, saying, "The name's Blenkinsop."

"How do you do, Mr. Blenkinsop." Mary Ann smiled up at the American and liked what she saw. And now Corny said, "Mr. Blenkinsop's taking our car for a day or so while I do his."

"Our c . . . car?" Her mouth opened wide and she looked towards the Chevrolet. Then she turned her gaze towards Corny, and he said, "Mr. Blenkinsop knows she's an oldun but he's driven Rovers before."

"Oh." Mary Ann gave a small smile, but she still couldn't see how a man who drove this great chrome and cream machine could even bear to get into their old Rover.

At this moment Rose Mary and David put in an appearance. They came tearing out of the garage, and when they reached Mary Ann, Rose Mary didn't take in the presence of the American for a moment before she said, "You wouldn't break up Jimmy's trombone, would you, Mam? I told him you were only funnin'."

Mary Ann looked at the American; she looked at Corny; then, shaking her head, she looked at her daughter and said, "I'm not funning, and you go back and tell Jimmy that I'm not funning."

There was a pause before she added, "He's practising the trombone and he makes a dreadful racket." She was addressing the American now, and she was surprised when he let out a deep rumbling laugh as he said, "I know." Then, the smile slipping from his face, he asked her in all seriousness, "You don't think he's funny?"

"Funny! Making that noise?" Mary Ann screwed up her face. "No, I don't."

"Well! Well! Well! It just goes to show. You know, Mrs. Boyle, he's the only thing that's given me a belly laugh since I came to England. Plays, musical comedies, the lot, I've seen them all and I've never had a good laugh until I saw that boy's face as he sat blowing that trombone. As I was just saying to your husband, he's got a face for the trombone."

Mary Ann smiled. She smiled with her mouth closed, and she looked at Corny as she did so. Then looking back at the American, she said, "The difference is, you don't have to live above the racket."

"I wouldn't mind."

"You wouldn't?"

"No."

"Well, there's a pair of you." She nodded to Corny. "He doesn't mind it at all, but I really can't stand it, it gets on my nerves."

The American now lowered his head and moved it from side to side, looking at Corny as he remarked, "It's as I said, she acts like a woman. They're unpredictable." He turned his head now towards Mary Ann and smiled broadly, then added, "Well now, I must be off. I've got a lunch appointment for one o'clock. . . . Here." He beckoned to the children. Then, putting his hand in his pocket and pulling out his wallet, he flicked a pound note from a bundle and handed it to Rose Mary, saying, "Split that betweeen you and get some pop and candy."

"Oh, thank you."

Before Rose Mary had finished speaking, Mary Ann said, "Oh, sir, no; that's too much." She took the note from Rose Mary, whose fingers were reluctant to release it, and she handed it back to Mr. Blenkinsop, and he, his face looking blank, now asked rather sharply, "What's the matter? Don't they have ice creams or candies or such?"

"Yes, yes, but this is too——"

"Nonsense." His tone was sharp, and he turned abruptly from her and, speaking to Corny in the same manner, he said, "Well, I'll be off. See you to-morrow."

Mr. Blenkinsop got in the Rover and started her up; then, leaning out of the window, he said, "How's she off for petrol?"

"She's full."

"That's good. See you."

"Yes. See you, sir." Corny smiled at Mr. Blenkinsop, then raised his hand and stood watching the car going down the road before turning to Mary Ann.

Mary Ann, with the pound note still in her hand, held it towards him, saying, "He must be rolling, and he must be bats or a bit eccentric to go off in ours."

"What do you mean, bats or a bit eccentric, there's nothing wrong with our car?"

"No, I'm not saying there is, but you know what I mean. Look at it compared with that." She pointed to the Chevrolet.

"You're just going by externals. Let me tell you that the engine in the Rover will still be going when this one's on the scrap heap."

"Yes, yes, I suppose so, but it's the looks of the thing. Anyway," she sighed, "he seems a nice enough man."

"Nice enough?" said Corny, walking towards the car. "He's a godsend."

"I wonder what he's doing round these parts," said Mary Ann.

"I don't know," said Corny, "but I hope he stays."

"Can we keep it, Mam?"

"What?" Mary Ann looked down at her daughter, then said, "Oh yes. Yes, you may, but you're not going to spend it all, either of you. You can have half-a-crown each, and the rest goes in your boxes."

"Oh, splash! said Rose Mary. "I know what I'm going to buy. Can we go into Felling this afternoon, Mam?"

"I suppose so." Mary Ann turned abruptly towards Corny, saying, "By the way, what did he mean, I act like a woman?"

Corny brought his head from under the bonnet of the car and, laughing towards her, said, "He took you for a young girl, and then when he heard you going for Jimmy he said you acted like a woman."

"Well, I should hope I do act like a woman. What did he expect me to act like, a chimpanzee?"

There was a splutter of a laugh from the garage doorway, and Mary Ann turned her head towards Jimmy. But she had to turn it away again quickly before she, too, laughed. It would never do to let Jimmy think she was softening up.

"Don't stand there with your mouth open." Corny was shouting towards Jimmy now. "We've got a job in."

"That!" said Jimmy, moving slowly towards the big cream car. "The American's?"

"Yes, the American's."

"An' she's in for repair?"

"She's in for repair," said Corny.

"And it all happened when you were concentrating on your trombone, Jimmy." This last, said quietly, but with telling emphasis, was from Mary Ann, as she stood at the corner of the building, and, making a deep obeisance with her head, she moved slowly from their view.

Corny and Jimmy exchanged glances; then Jimmy, jerking his head upwards, muttered under his breath, "It's as that American says, she acts like a woman, boss."

"Go on, get on with it."

And Jimmy got on with it. But after a while he said, "You know what, boss? That has something."

"What has?" asked Corny from where he was sitting in the pit under the car. "What you talking about?"

"What the American said: she acts like a woman. It's a punch line, boss. Could make a pop Da-da-da-da-da-daa. She acts like a woo . . . man." He sang the words, and Corny, stopping in the process of unscrewing a nut, closed his eyes, bit on his lip and grinned before bawling, "I'll act like a man if I come up there to you. Get on with it."

5

Mary Ann was sitting at the corner of her dressing-table. She had a pencil in her hand and a sheet of paper in front of her, and she sat looking through the curtains over the road in front of the garage, over the fence and to the far side of Weaver's field, where four men had been moving up and down for a long time, at least all the time she had been sitting here. The far side of Weaver's field was a long way off and she couldn't see what they were doing. But she wasn't very interested; they were only a focal point in her eyes, for her mind was on composing a song.

Last week, after the American had been and left his car, Corny had come upstairs and said, "You know, Jimmy's all there, in this music line, I mean." And she had turned on him scornfully, saying, "Music line! You don't put the word music to the sounds he makes."

And to this he had replied, "Well, he's got ideas. Things strike him that wouldn't strike me."

"I should hope so," she had said indignantly; then had added, "He's a nice enough lad, but he's a nit-wit in some ways."

"He's no nit-wit," Corny had protested. "You've got him scared, and that's how he acts with you. You don't know Jimmy. I tell you he's a nice lad, and he's got it up top."

"All right," she had said. "He's a nice lad, but what's struck him that's so brilliant?"

"The title of a song," Corny had said. "The Amer . . . Mr. Blenkinsop said you acted like a woman, you remember? Well, Jimmy said it was a good title for a song, and the more I've been thinking about it the more I agree with him. She acts like a woman. It's like the titles they're having now, the things that are catching on and get into the Top Twenty. So why don't you have a shot at writing the lyrics?"

"What! Write lyrics to, She acts like a woman? Don't be silly."

"Oh, all right, all right. It was only a suggestion. You're always talking about wishing you had something to do, something to occupy your mind at times. And I've told you you should take up your writing again now that you've got time on your hands, with them both away at school. Anyway it was just an idea. Take it or leave it."

He had turned from her and stalked out, and she had looked at the door and exclaimed, "She acts like a woman!" But the words had stuck with her and she had begun to think less scornfully about them when, following Mr. Blenkinsop's return and his generous payment for the hire of the car and the repairs Corny had done, there had been no further work in of any sort for four days.

This morning, their Michael had brought the tractor over and ordered some spares, but they couldn't keep going on family support. It was this that prompted the thought, yet again: if only she could earn some money at home.

Years ago when Corny's hopes were sinking with regard to the prospect of the road, she had started to write furiously, sending off short stories and poems here and there, but they all found their way back to her with "The editor regrets". At the end of a year of hard trying she had to face up to the fact that they would have been better off if she hadn't tried at all, for she had spent much-needed money on postage, paper and a second-hand typewriter.

But this idea of writing ballads, not that she thought the words to some of the pop songs deserved the name of ballad, might have something in it. She had always been good at jingles. But that wasn't enough these days. For a song to really catch on it had to be, well, off-beat.

She had thought that if she could get the tune first she could put the words to it, so she had hummed herself dry for a couple of mornings until she realized that she wasn't any good at original tune building, because most of the songs she was singing in her head were snatches and mixtures of those she heard on the radio and television. So she decided that she would have to stick to the words, and for the last three days she had written hundreds of words, all unknown to Corny. Oh, she wasn't going to let him in on this, although he had given her the lead. She had her own ideas about what she was going to do.

She knew what she wanted. She wanted something with a meaning, something appertaining to life as it was lived to-day, something a bit larger than life, nothing milk and water, or soppy-doppy; that would never go down to-day. It must be virile and about love, and understandable to the teenager, and to her mother and grandmother.

She had almost beaten her head against the wall and given up the whole thing, and then this morning, lying in bed, the words "She acts like a woman" going over and over in her mind, there came to her an idea. But she couldn't do anything about it until she got Corny downstairs and the children out to play. Now she had conveyed her idea in rough rhyme, and it read like this:

SHE ACTS LIKE A WOMAN

SHE ACTS LIKE A WOMAN.
Man, I'm telling you,
SHE ACTS LIKE A WOMAN.
She pelted me with everything,
And then she tore her hair.

SHE ACTS LIKE A WOMAN.
I'd given her my lot,
I was finished, broke,
And then she spoke of love,

SHE ACTS LIKE A WOMAN.
Me, she said,
Me, she wanted,
Not diamonds, mink, or drink,
SHE ACTS LIKE A WOMAN.

I just spread my hands,
What was I to do?
You tell me.
SHE ACTS LIKE A WOMAN.

Early morning, there she stood,
No make-up, face like mud,
And her big eyes raining tears,
And fears.
SHE ACTS LIKE A WOMAN.

Then something moved in here,
Like daylight,
And I could see,
She only wanted me.
SHE ACTS LIKE A WOMAN.

The lead singer would sing the verse, then the rest of the group would come in with "She acts like a woman", and do those falsetto bits. Again she read the words aloud. As it stood, and for what it was, it wasn't bad, she decided. But then, it must have a tune and she wasn't going to send it away to one of those music companies; they might pinch the idea. These things happened. No, it must be set to a tune first, and the only person she could approach who dealt in tunes was . . . Jimmy.

She didn't relish the idea of putting her plan to Jimmy. Still, he was in a group and perhaps one of them could knock up a tune. Of course, if they made the tune up they'd have to share the profits. Well, she supposed half a loaf was better than no bread, and the way things were going down below they'd be lucky if they got half a loaf.

She got slowly to her feet, still staring across the field. She could see her song in the Top Twenty. Young housewife makes the Pop grade, Mary Ann Boyle—she wished it could have been Shaughnessy—jumps from number 19 to number 4. . . . No, number 2, with her "She acts like a woman".

What were they doing over there, those men? Ploughing? Oh no; they could never grow anything in that field, it was full of boulders and outcrops of rock. Her mind, coming down from the heights of fame, concentrated now on the moving figures. What were they doing going up and down? Then screwing her eyes up and peering hard, she realized they were measuring something, measuring the ground.

She took the stairs two at a time.

"Corny! Corny!" She dashed into the office, only to find it empty, then ran into the garage, still calling, and Corny, from the top end, came towards her hurriedly, saying, "What's up? What's up? The bairns?"

"No, no." She shook her head vigorously. "There's something going on in Weaver's field."

"Going on? What?"

"I don't know. I saw them out of the bedroom window, men with a theodolite. They looked like surveyors measuring the ground."

He stared down at her for a moment, then repeated her words again, "Measuring the ground?"

"Yes. Come up and have a look."

They both ran upstairs now and stood at the bedroom window, and after a moment Corny said, "Aye, that's what they're doing all right. But it's yon side, and what for?"

"Perhaps they've been round this side and we haven't heard them. They could have been at yon side of the hedge and we wouldn't have seen or heard them."

"They could that," said Corny. "But why? . . . Anyway, whatever they're going to do, you bet your life they'll do at yon side, they wouldn't come over here."

"Aw, don't sound like that." She sought his hand and gripped it.

"Well, it always happens, doesn't it? Look at Riley. He's made a little packet out of the buildings going up at yon side, and he's got a new lot of pumps set up now. I actually see my hands turning green when I pass the place."

She leant her head against him and remained quiet. She, too, turned green when she passed Riley's garage. His garage had been no better than theirs when he started, at least not as good—Riley never kept the place like Corny did—but because of a new estate over there and the factories sprouting up, he had got on like a house on fire. And now Riley acted as if he had been born to the purple; his wife had her own car, and the ordinary schools weren't good enough for the children; two of them were at the Convent, and the young one at a private school. . . . Would they ever be able to send Rose Mary to the Convent and David . . . ? Her thinking stopped as to where they would send David, and, straightening herself abruptly, she said, "Why don't you take a run round that way and make a few enquiries?"

"It's not a bad idea. But no matter what I find out it won't be that they're going to build this end of the field, for this part's so rock-strewn it even frightens off the speculators."

"Well, go and see."

"Aye, yes, there's no harm in having a look."

He was on the point of turning away from her when he paused, and, gripping her chin in his big hand, he bent down and kissed her, then hurried out of the room.

Mary Ann didn't follow him. There had been a sadness about the kiss and she wanted to cry. The kiss had said, "I'm sorry for the way things have turned out, that my dream was a bubble. I'm sorry for all the things I've deprived you of, I'm sorry for you having to put on that don't-care attitude, and this is the way I want it, when you go to the farm."

"Bust! blast!" The ghost of the old impatient, demanding, I'll-fix-it Mary Ann, came surging up, and she beat the flat of her hand on the dressing-table. Why? Why? He worked like a nigger, he tried every avenue, he was honest . . . perhaps too honest. But could you be too honest? There was more fiddling in cars than there was in the Hallé Orchestra, and he could have been in on that lucrative racket. Three times he had been approached last year, and from different sources, but he would have none of it. You're a mug, they had said. He had nearly hit one of them who wanted to rent "this forgotten dump", as he had called it, for a place to transform his stolen cars.

Slowly now, she picked up the paper on which she had been writing from the dressing-table. In the excitement of the moment she had forgotten about it. It was a wonder Corny hadn't seen it. At one time he always picked up the pieces of paper lying around, knowing that she had been scribbling.

She heard the Rover start up and saw Corny driving into the lane. After the car had disappeared from view she looked at the sheet of paper in her hand. This would be a good opportunity to tackle Jimmy and see what he thought about the idea.

She was halfway across the room when she stopped. Would he think she was daft? Well, the only way to find out would be to show him what she had written, and she'd better do it now, for Corny wouldn't be long away.

She ran down the back stairs, and when she reached the yard she saw, over the low wall, the children playing in the old car. She waved to them, but they were too engrossed to notice her. She went through the gate, down the path between the beans and potatoes, over a piece of rough ground, to the small door that led into the garage.

"Jimmy!"

Jimmy was sitting on an upturned drum, stranding a length of wire. He raised his head and looked towards her, and said, "Aye, Mrs. Boyle." Then he threw down the wire and came hurrying to her. He liked the boss's wife, although at times when she had her dander up she scared him a bit, but they got on fine. That was until he started practising. Still, he understood, 'cos his mother was the same. She was good-hearted, was the boss's wife, not stingy on the grub. He wished his mother cooked like she did. Cor, the stuff his mother hashed up. . . .

"Aye, Mrs. Boyle, you want me?" He smiled broadly at her.

Mary Ann smiled back at him, and she swallowed twice before she said, "I'd like your advice on something, Jimmy."

". . . .My advice, Mrs. . . . ."

"Yes. Yes." She shook her head, and her smile widened. "And don't look so surprised." They both laughed sheepishly now, and Mary Ann, taking the folded sheet of paper from her apron pocket, said, in a voice that held a warning, "Now, don't you make game, Jimmy, at what I'm going to tell you, but . . . but I've written some words for a song."

She watched Jimmy's long face stretch to an even longer length, and, perhaps because of the tone of her voice, all he said was, "Aye." He knew she wrote things, the boss had told him, the boss said she was good at it, but a song. He never imagined her writing a song. He thought she was against pop. He said quickly now, "Pop? Pop, is it?"

"Well, sort of. I wondered what you would think of it. Whether you would think it was worth setting to a tune. You know what I mean."

"Aye, aye." He nodded, then held out his hand, and she placed the sheet of paper in it.

"She acts like a woman. Coo! 'cos I said that?" He dug his finger towards the paper. "'Cos I said that was a good title you've made this up?" He sounded excited; he looked excited; his large mouth was showing all his uneven teeth.

"Yes." She nodded at him. "Mr. Boyle"—she always gave Corny his title when speaking of him to his employee—"Mr. Boyle thought it was a very good title."

"Aye, I think it is an' all . . . but you know, it wasn't me who said it in the first place, it was that American, and it just struck me like. . . ."

Time was going on and she didn't want Corny to come back while they were talking. "Read it," she said. She watched Jimmy's eyebrows move upwards as his eyes flicked over the lines, and at one stage he flashed her a look and a wide grin.

When his eyes reached the bottom of the page he took them to the top again and said slowly, "She acts like a woman."

"Well, what do you think?"

"Ee! I think it's great. It's got it, you know, the kind they want. Could I take it and show it to Duke? He's the one that got our group up. He's good at tunes. He can read music an' all; he learned the piano from when he was six. I'll swear he'll like this, 'cos it's got the bull-itch."

Mary Ann opened her mouth and closed it again before she repeated, "Bull-itch? What do you mean, bull-itch?"

"Well, you know." Jimmy tossed his head. "A girl after a fellow."

"Oh, Jimmy."

"Well, that's what they say, Mrs. Boyle. When it's t'other way round they call it the bitchy-itch, an' this 'as really got both."

"Oh, Jimmy. And you think that the words give that impression?"

"Oh, aye. An' they're great. But I didn't know you wrote this stuff, Mrs. Boyle. I bet Duke'll make somethin' of it."

"Oh, if only he could, Jimmy. And then we'll get together and see about getting it recorded and trying for the Top Twenty."

She could have sworn that Jimmy's face dropped half its length again. "Top Twenty?" His voice was high in his head. "But, Mrs. Boyle, you don't get into the Top Twenty unless you've got a manager and things, like the Beatles, and we're just startin' so to speak. Well, I mean, I am; I'm the worst, among the players, that is." He lowered his head.

"What do the others do?" asked Mary Ann, flatly now.

"Well, Duke can play most things a bit; Barny, he plays the drums; and Poodle, he's best on the cornet. But he's on the flute now, and Dave has the guitar."

"What do you call yourselves?" asked Mary Ann.

"Oh, nowt yet. We've been thinkin' about it, but we've not come up with anythin' yet, not anythin' catchy. You want somethin' different, you do, don't you?"

"Yes," said Mary Ann. "I'll think up something."

"Aw." Jimmy's face was straight now. "Duke'll want to see to that; he's good on thinkin' up titles and things."

There was a pause; then Mary Ann said, "You'll have to bring Duke along to see me."

"Aye, I will," said Jimmy. "He'll be tickled, I think."

"Jimmy."

"Aye, Mrs. Boyle."

"I don't want you to say anything to Mr. Boyle about this."

"No?"

"No. It might come to nothing, you see."

Jimmy looked puzzled, then said, "Well, even if it doesn't, it'll still be a bit of fun."

Mary Ann wanted to say that at this stage she wasn't out for fun, she was out for money, but she was afraid Jimmy wouldn't understand, so all she said was, "Don't speak of it to Mr. Boyle till I tell you, will you not?"

"O.K., Mrs. Boyle, just as you say."

"And when you bring Duke along, tell him not to say anything either."

"Will do, Mrs. Boyle, will do."

"Thanks, Jimmy." She smiled at him. And he smiled at her; then watched her go out through the little door.

Well, would you believe that, her writin' things like that. He looked down at the paper and read under his breath: "I'd given her my lot. I was finished, broke and then she spoke of love. She acts like a woman." He lifted his head and looked towards the door again. It was as Duke was always sayin', you never could tell. . . .

6

Rose Mary, from her position on top of the car, saw her mother come out of the garage and go into their back yard, and she called to her "O-Oo, Mam!" but her mother didn't turn round. Perhaps she hadn't called loud enough.

Oh, it was hot. She clambered down from the roof, saying to David, "I'm going to lie in the grass, it's too hot. Come on."

When they were both lying in the grass, she said, "I wish we could go to the sands at Shields. If Greatgran McBride lived in Shields instead of Greatgran McMullen we would go more often. I don't like Greatgran McMullen, do you?" She turned her head and looked at David, and David, looking skywards, shook his head.

She wished it wasn't so hot; she wished she had an ice-cream. She wished they could go on a holiday. Peter had gone on a holiday. He was going to come and play with them when he came back, but that would be a long time, nearly three weeks. he had said the other day that he would rather stay here and play on the car. He liked playing with them. . . . Oh, it was hot. They had only broken up for the holidays three days ago and she wished she was back at school. . . . No, she didn't, 'cos last week had been awful. Miss Plum had been awful right from the Monday following the Sunday when she had taken their David to sit beside her. Nothing had gone right from then. And Father Carey had messed things up an' all. She had gone to school on the Monday knowing that something would happen because Father Carey was a good pray-er. And things did happen, but not the way she wanted them to, because they had hardly got into the classroom before Miss Plum collared their David and put him in the front seat right under her nose, and David didn't let a squeak out of him. He usually squawked when anybody took him away from her, but he didn't squawk at Miss Plum. She waited all morning for him to squawk, or do something. It was nearly dinnertime before she realized that Miss Plum had got at Father Carey before she had, and that he was doing it her way.

Oh, it was hot. Oh, it was. And she hated Miss Plum, oh, she did. And she didn't like Father Carey very much either. Ee! She would get wrong for thinking like that. Well, she couldn't help it. She had thought it without thinkin'. And she hadn't made her first confession yet, so she wouldn't have to tell it, so that was all right.

Her mam said when she was a little girl she took all her troubles to Father Owen and he sorted them out for her. She wished she could go and see Father Owen, but he lived far away in Jarrow.

Aw, it was hot.

"Come on." She pulled herself up and put out her hand. "I'm goin' in for a drink."

She was too hot to do any shouting on the back stairs, and she was in the kitchen before she opened her mouth. And then she closed it quickly because her ma and da were talking, dark talking. She knew she hadn't to interrupt when they were dark talking. They dark talked at night-time when she was in bed, and if she tried hard enough she could hear what they said. Usually, it made her sad, or just sorry like. And now the tones of their voices told her they were dark talking again. Her ma looked sad and her da's face was straight, and her da was saying, "Sort of winded me like, to see him sitting there talking to Riley and the car standing near the pumps. I thought he liked what I did to the car and I just charged him the minimum. I didn't put a penny extra on because he was an American, and he seemed over the moon at the time. But that's over a week ago; and when he didn't show up this week I thought he had gone on. But there he was, at Riley's garage."

Rose Mary watched her mother look down towards her feet, and she wanted to say to her, "Can I have a drink, Mam?" But she didn't, 'cos her mam was taking no notice of her.

"What's he doing in these parts, anyway?" said Mary Ann now.

"I don't know, I didn't like to probe. And a funny thing, unless I'm vastly mistaken, the car he had to-day, although it was a cream one, wasn't the same one as he brought here the other day."

"But he can't have two cars like that?"

"A fellow like him could have three, or half-a-dozen."

"But how could you tell the difference when you were just passing?"

"Oh, you notice things quick when you're dealing with cars. This one hadn't so much chrome on, but it was as big. I noticed, too, that the boot was open a bit and the end of a long, narrow case was sticking out, like the end of a golf bag, only it couldn't have been a golf bag 'cos that boot would take ten golf bags. Anyway, it looked chock-a-block, as if he was all packed up to go . . . so, that's that."

"And you didn't find out about the men in the field?"

"No, I stopped before I got to Riley's and tried to find a place over the hedge to look through, but it's a tangled mess down there. But I did ask a scavenger, but he could tell me nothing. And well, after I passed the garage I didn't bother, the wind seemed knocked out of me. It was a funny feeling. I mean about the American. I really thought as long as he was in these parts he would come here."

The silence that fell on the kitchen was too much for Rose Mary, and besides she had that sorry feeling seeing her dad and her mam with their heads bent and she wanted to cry. She said softly, "We're dry, Mam; can we have a fizzy drink? Lemon?"

"What? Oh, yes. Just a minute." Mary Ann turned away and went into the scullery, and Rose Mary went and stood close against her father's leg, and, taking his limp fingers in hers, she looked up at him, and said, "I hate that American."

"Rose Mary!" His voice was sharp now. "You're not to say such things. Mr. Blenkinsop was very kind to you."

"Well, I don't want him to be kind, I hate him. An' David hates him an' all. Don't you, David?" She looked to where David was stretched out on the floor, and David turned his head lazily towards her and moved it downwards.

"Stop it!" Corny now bent down, and, his face close to hers, he said, "Now look, Rose Mary. You don't have to hate everybody that doesn't do what you want them to do, understand? And David doesn't hate the . . . Mr. Blenkinsop. Who bought you the ice-cream and lollies last week? Mr. Blenkinsop gave you that money, and don't forget it."

There came to them now a distant tingling sound, and Mary Ann called from the scullery, "That's the phone, I think." And when she came into the kitchen with the two glasses of fizzy lemon water, Corny was gone. As she handed one glass to Rose Mary and one to David, Rose Mary said, "I do hate that American."

"You heard what your father said to you, didn't you?"

"Well, he's buying his petrol from Riley's."

"He can buy his petrol anywhere he likes."

"Our petrol's better than Riley's."

Mary Ann closed her eyes and turned away.

"It is."

"Rose Mary!"

"If I had that pound note I'd give it him back."

"Rose Mary!"

"Mary Ann!"

Hearing Corny's voice calling up the front stairs, Mary Ann hurried out of the room and on to the landing, and, looking down at him, she said, "What is it?"

"Prepare yourself."

"What's happened? What's the matter now?"

"Michael's just phoned. Your grannie's on her way here."

"Me grannie coming here!"

"So Michael thinks."

"But why? Is she at the farm?"

"No, she was there on Sunday. But Michael was driving back from Jarrow and at the traffic lights he happened to glance up at the bus, and there she was sitting, and, as he said, you couldn't mistake the old girl. Busby an' all."

"But how does he know she's coming here?"

"Well, she was on the Gateshead bus, and she doesn't get that one to go to the farm, so he put two and two together and got off at the first telephone box and broke the news. He thought you would like to be prepared."

"Oh, no. I only wanted this. . . . But why is she coming, and at this time in the day? It must be two years since she was here."

"Well, get the bairns changed." Corny's voice was soft now, soothing. "And put your armour on, and smile."

"Aw, Corny." Mary Ann's voice, too, was low, but it had a desperate sound. Her grannie. The last person she wanted to see at any time. "Corny look." Her voice was rapid. "What about me taking them out for the day? You could tell her we've gone to the sands."

"It's no use. From the time Michael phoned, the bus could be at the bottom of the road by now, and you could just run into her, even if you were ready. . . . Stick it out; you're a match for her."

"Not any longer, I haven't got the energy."

"Wait till you see her, it'll inject you with new life." He smiled up at her, then turned away, and she stood for a moment looking down the stairs, before moving swiftly back in the room.

"Hurry up and finish your drinks," she said, "and come on into the bathroom."

"We goin' to have a bath again, Mam? We had one last——"

"I only want you to wash your face and hands and put on your blue print, the one with the smocking."

"We going to the sands?"

"No." Mary Ann called now from the landing. "Your great-gran's coming."

"Me great-gran?" Rose Mary was running out of the room on to the landing, and David was behind her now. "Which one?"

"McMullen."

"Aw, not her, Mam."

"Yes, her. Come on now." Mary Ann pulled them both into the bathroom. "Get your things off and you wash your face and hands, I'll see to David."

David had never been washed and changed so rapidly in his life. When he was attired in clean pants and tee-shirt he stood watching his mother jumping out of one dress and into another, and then, with Rose Mary, he was hustled back into the living-room and ordered to sit. He sat, and Rose Mary sat, and while they waited they watched their mother flying round the room, pushing their toys into the bottom of the cupboard, tidying up the magazines, putting a bit of polish on the table, even rubbing a wash leather over the lower panes of the window, and she had only cleaned the window yesterday. At last Rose Mary was forced to volunteer, "Perhaps she's fallen down, Mam?"

Oh, if only she had. Mary Ann groaned inside. If only she had fallen into the ditch and broken her leg. How gladly she would call the ambulance and see her whisked away. But her grannie wouldn't fall into a ditch and break her leg. Nothing adverse would happen to her grannie; her grannie would live to torment her family until she was a hundred, perhaps a hundred and ten. She could never see her grannie dying. Her grannie was like all the evil in the world. As long as there were people there would be evil. As long as there was a Shaughnessy left there would be Grannie McMullen to torment them.

"Mary Ann! You've got a visitor." It was Corny's voice from the bottom of the stairs, and Mary Ann, turning about, walked across the room. But she paused near Rose Mary's chair to say, "Now mind, behave yourself. I don't want any repeat of that Sunday at the farm. You remember?"

Her words were like an echo from the past, like an echo of Lizzie saying to her, "Now mind yourself, don't cheek your grannie, I'm warning you." She opened the door and went on to the landing and said, "Who is it?" Then she made a suitable pause before adding, "Oh, hello, Gran."

Mrs. McMullen was coming unassisted up the steep stairs, and when she reached the top she stood panting slightly, looking at Mary Ann, and Mary Ann looked at her.

Ever since she first remembered seeing her grannie she hadn't seemed to change by one wrinkle or hair. Her hair was still black and abundant, and as always supported a large hat, a black straw to-day. Her small, dark eyes still held their calculating devilish gleam. The skin of her face was covered with the tracery of lines not detectable unless under close scrutiny, so she looked much younger than her seventy-six years. She was wearing this morning an up-to-date light-weight grey check coat which yelled aloud in comparison to the hair style and hat adorning it.

"It's warm to-day," said Mary Ann.

"Warm! It's bakin', if you ask me. And the walk from the bus doesn't make it any better. I would have thought that after being stuck miles from civilization afore you married you would have plumped for some place nearer the town. But I suppose beggars can't be choosers. . . . Aw, let me sit down, off me feet."

"Let your grannie sit down." Mary Ann was nodding towards Rose Mary, and Rose Mary, sliding off the dining-room chair, stood to one side, and as Mary Ann watched her grannie seat herself she thought, "Beggars can't be choosers. Oh, what I'd like to say to her."

"I'll get you a cup of tea." Mary Ann moved towards the scullery now, and Mrs. McMullen, without turning her head, said, "There's time enough for that; I'll have something cold if it's not too much trouble. . . . Well now." Mrs. McMullen put her hands up slowly to her hat and withdrew the pin, and as she did so she looked at the children. First at Rose Mary, then at David, then to Rose Mary again, and she said, "You underweight?"

"What?"

Rose Mary screwed up her face at her great-grandmother.

"I said are you underweight? And don't say 'What?' Say, 'What, Great-gran?' Do you get weighed at school?"

"Yes."

"Didn't they tell you you were underweight?"

"No . . . no, Great-gran."

"Well, if my eyes don't deceive me, that's what they should have done."

"I've brought you a lemon drink."

"Oh . . . thanks. I was just saying to her"—Mrs. McMullen nodded to her great-grandchild—"she looks underweight. Anything wrong with her?"

"No, no, nothing. She's as healthy as an ox." Mary Ann was determined that nothing that this old devil said would make her rise.

She watched the old woman take a long drink from the glass, then put her hand in her pocket and bring out a folded white handkerchief with which she wiped her mouth. And then she watched her turn her attention to David. "Hello there," she said.

David looked back at this funny old woman. He looked deep into her eyes, and his own darkened and he grinned. He grinned widely at her.

"He not talking yet?"

Mary Ann hesitated for a long moment before saying, "He's making progress."

"Is he talking or isn't he?"

Steady, steady. Metaphorically speaking, Mary Ann gripped her own shoulder. "He can say certain words. The teacher's very pleased with him, isn't she, Rose Mary?"

"Yes, yes, he's Miss Plum's favourite. She takes him to the front of the class and she pins up his drawings."

"They only have to do that with idiots."

The words had been muttered below her breath but they were clear to Mary Ann, if not to the children. As Rose Mary asked, "What did you say, Great-gran?" Mary Ann had to turn away. She went into the scullery, and as her mother had done many many times in her life, and for the same reason, she stood leaning against the draining-board gripping its edge. She longed, in this moment, for Lizzie's support, and she realized that this was only the second time that she had battled with her grannie on her own; there had always been someone to check her tongue, or even her hand. On her grannie's only other visit here two years ago, she'd had the support of their Michael and Sarah, but now she was on her own, and she didn't trust herself. How long would she stay? Would she stay for dinner? Very likely. But Corny would be here then, and Corny could manage her somehow. She had found she couldn't rile him, consequently she didn't get at him. She was even pleasant to him; the nasty things she had to say she said behind his back.

She almost jumped back into the kitchen as she heard her grannie say, "Be quiet, child. Give him a chance, let him answer for himself."

"I was only sayin'——"

"I know what you were saying." Mrs. McMullen now turned her head up towards Mary Ann. "This one"—she thumbed Rose Mary—"is the spit of you, you know, she doesn't know when to stop. I don't think you'll get him talkin' as long as he's got the answers ready made for him."

Mary Ann forced herself not to bow her head, and not to lower her eyes from her grannie's. It was galling to think that this dreadful old woman was advocating the same remedy for David's impediment as Corny and her mother. Mrs. McMullen now turned her eyes away from Mary Ann, saying with a sigh, "Aw well, it's your own business. And you'd never take advice, as long as I can remember . . . I think I'll take me coat off, it's enough to roast you in here. I'd open the window."

"The window's open." Mary Ann took her grannie's coat and went out of the room with it, and laid it on the bed in the bedroom. And now she stood leaning against the bed-rail trying to calm herself before returning to the room. The old devil, the wicked old devil. And she was wicked—vicious and wicked. On the bedroom chimney-breast hung a portrait of Corny and her on their wedding day, and her mind was lifted to the moment when they were walking down from the altar and her grannie stole the picture by falling into the aisle in a faint; and in that moment, that wonderful, wonderful moment when all her feelings should have been good, and her thoughts even holy, she had wished, as she saw them carrying her grannie away down the aisle, that she'd peg out. Yes, such was the effect her grannie had on her that on the altar steps she had wished a thing like that.

When she returned to the kitchen it was to hear Mrs. McMullen saying to Rose Mary, "But how many in a week, how many cars does he work on in a week?" and Rose Mary replying, "Oh, lots, dozens."

"Does he get much work in?" Mrs. McMullen's gimlet eyes met Mary Ann's as she came across the room.

"Who? Corny?" Her voice was high, airy. "Oh, yes, he gets plenty of work in."

"Well!" The word was said on a long, exhaling breath. "It must be his off time, for what I could see when I passed the garage was space, empty space, and the floor as clean as a whistle. . . . Why doesn't he sell up? I heard your father on about him having an offer."

"Oh, yes, yes, he's had offers, but he doesn't want to sell up, we're quite content here."

Her da on about them having an offer. Her grannie must have been saying something to her mother and her da had made it up on the spur of the moment about them having an offer. That's what he would do. Good for her da.

Mary Ann said now, as she brought the tray to the delf-rack and took down some cups and saucers, "We did consider one offer we had, but then it's so good for the children out here, plenty of fresh air and space, and the house is comfortable."

"You can't live on fresh air and space. As for comfort . . ." Mrs. McMullen looked around the room. "You want something bigger than this with them growing, you couldn't swing a cat in it."

"Well, we don't happen to have a . . ." Mary Ann abruptly checked her words, and so hard did she grip the cup in her hand that she wouldn't have been surprised if it had splintered into fragments. There, her grannie had won. She put the sugar basin and milk jug quietly on to the tray and took it to the table under the window before saying, "It suits us. I'm happy here. We're all happy here."

"Your mother doesn't seem to think so."

"What!" Mary Ann swung round and looked at the back of her grannie's head. "My mother would never say I was unhappy. She couldn't say it, because I'm not unhappy."

"She doesn't have to say it. She happens to be my daughter, I know what she's thinking, I know how she views the set-up."

Mary Ann again went into the scullery and again she was holding the draining-board, and she bit on her lip now, almost drawing blood. It was at this moment that Rose Mary joined her and, clutching her dress at the waist, she looked up at her. Her ma was upset, her ma was nearly crying. She hated her great-gran, she was an awful great-gran. She whispered now, brokenly, "Don't cry, Mam. Aw, don't cry, Mam."

"I'm not crying." Mary Ann had brought her face down to her daughter's as she whispered. "Go back into the room and be nice. Go on. Go on now for me."

"Aw, but Mam."

"Go on."

Rose Mary dutifully went into the room and took her seat again, but she did not look at her great-grandmother.

"What are you doing at school?"

When silence greeted Mrs. McMullen's question, David turned his bright gaze on his sister, and when she didn't answer he moved quickly to her and shook her arm, and for the first time in her life she pushed off his hand, and Mrs. McMullen, quick to notice the action, said, "You needn't be nasty to him, he was only telling you to answer in the only way he knew."

Now Rose Mary was looking at her great-grandmother and, the spirit of her mother rising in her, she said, "I don't like you."

"Ah-ha! Here we go again, another generation of 'em. So you don't like me? Well, I'll not lose any sleep over that."

"I like me Great-gran McBride."

Mrs. McMullen's face darkened visibly. "Oh, you do, do you? And I hope you like her beautiful house, and her smell."

"Yes, yes, I do. And David does an' all. We like goin' there, I'd go there all the time. I like me Great-gran McBride."

"Rose Mary!" Mary Ann was speaking quietly from the scullery door, and Rose Mary, now unable to control her tears, slid to her feet, crying, "Well, I do like me Great-gran McBride, I do, Mam. You know I do."

"Yes, I know, but now be quiet. Behave yourself, and stop it."

"I don't like her, I don't, Mam." Rose Mary, her arm outstretched, was pointing at Mrs. McMullen.

"Rose Mary!" As Mary Ann advanced towards her, Rose Mary backed towards the door, staring at her great-grandmother all the while, and as she groped behind her and found the handle she bounced her head towards the old lady, saying, "I'll never like you 'cos you're nasty." Then, turning about, she ran out of the room and down the stairs.

She'd find her dad, she would, and tell him. Her great-gran was awful, she was a pig, she'd made her mam cry, she'd tell her dad and he would go up and give her one for making her mam cry.

She ran to the garage, but she couldn't see her dad. But through her tears she saw a big car standing in the mouth of the garage and another car at the top end with Jimmy working on it. She ran out of the garage again and went towards the office, but she stopped just outside the door. Somebody was talking to her dad, and she recognized his voice. It was that nasty American who bought his petrol from Riley's.

"Rose Mary!" It was her mother's voice coming from the stairs. She looked round before running again. She wasn't going to go upstairs and sit with her great-gran, she wasn't. She hated her great-gran. She would hide. Yes, that's what she would do, she would hide. She looked wildly round her. And then she saw a good hiding place and darted towards it. . . .

7

In the office, Corny leant against his desk, mostly for support, as he stared down at the American sitting in the one seat provided. "I can't quite take it in," he said.

Mr. Blenkinsop smiled with one corner of his mouth higher than the other. "Give yourself time," he replied. "Give yourself time."

"May I ask what made you change your mind, I mean to build your factory at this side instead of yon side?"

"You may, and I'll tell you. But it won't do you any good. I mean it won't help you any further, for you've already reached the stage when you know that it's best in the long run to play fair."

Corny screwed up his eyes as he surveyed Mr. Blenkinsop. He had always played fair in business, but he wondered where he came in in the American's plan in this line, but he waited.

"As I told you my father built up Blenkinsop's from making boxes in a house yard, with my three brothers and six sisters all rounded up to help in the process, cutting, nailing, getting orders, delivering. It was before the last war and things were bad. I was just a youngster, but my father thought I had what it took to sell, and so I was put on to do the rounds going from door to door in the better-class neighbourhood of our town, showing them samples of our fancy-made boxes to put their Christmas presents in, the kind of presents that we kids only dreamed of. From the beginning it was, as our father said, small profit and quick return. 'Put into your work,' he said, 'more than you expect to get back in clear cash and the profits will mount up for you.' You know, that took a bit of working out to us boys whose only thought was to make money, and fast, but after a time we understood that if you make your product good enough it will sell itself a thousandfold, and in the end your profits will be high. . . . Well, after the war the business went like a house on fire. We were all in it, those of us who were left. Three died in the war, my three brothers, but the girls and their husbands still carry on their end of it, and our father's maxim still holds good."

Corny shook his head, but he still did not quite follow, and the American knew this, and he lit a cigarette and offered Corny one before he went on, "It's like this. I have two cars. I brought one to you, and I took one to Mr. Riley. I knew exactly what was wrong with each; in fact, the same was wrong in both cases. Mr. Riley charged me almost fifty per cent more than you did, and he bodged the job, at least his mechanics did. I guessed he'd put on twenty per cent in any case, me being an American and rolling. They think we are all rolling. But to pile on fifty per cent . . . Oh no. No. So I made a call on Mr. Riley this morning and told him I thought he had slightly overcharged me. He was, what you call, I think, shirty. In any case, Mr. Riley thought he'd got it all in the pan. He knew I had bought this whole piece of land a month ago, and as he said, only a fool would think of building this end, for just look at the stuff they would have to move, rock going deep. Well, he got a little surprise this morning when I told him it was on this end I had decided to put my factory, at least the main gates of it. My storehouses will now back on to the far road, there will be main gates leading to the main road, and another at the far end of this road leading to your Gateshead, but I'm putting my main building towards the end of your road, here. . . . Oh no"—he raised his hand and waved it back and forward—"not entirely to help you, but because it is advantageous, as I see it, to my plan. As I've told you, seeing the material we're dealing with I don't want petrol stores too near to the works, but I want them near enough to be convenient for the lorries and cars, and from the first I saw I had the choice of two petrol stations, and I've made it. The fifty per cent supercharge finally decided me which of the two men I preferred to deal with. That's how I do business. I look over the ground first—panning for gold dust my father used to call it. Always look for the gold and the dirt will drop through the riddle, he would say. . . . Well." Mr. Blenkinsop surveyed Corny. "There it is."

"Well, sir, I'm . . . I'm flabbergasted."

"Oh." The American put his head back. "That's a wonderful word, flabbergasted." He rose to his feet. "We'll do business together, young man." He put his hand on Corny's shoulder, much as a father would, and said quietly, "You leave this to me now. You'll need money for more pumps; we'll want a lot of petrol because our fleet of lorries won't be small. There'll be a great many private cars, too, as nearly all the workers in England have cars now; it isn't an American prerogative any longer." He smiled. "How much land did you say you had to the side of you, I mean your own?"

"Just over three-quarters of an acre. It runs back for about four hundred feet though; it's a narrow strip."

"Good, you'll need every bit of it. You'll want workshops and a place for garaging cars. That's a good idea." He made for the door now. Then, turning abruptly, he said, "What's kept you here for seven years, in this dead end?"

"Hope. Hoping for the road going through; hoping for a day like this . . . someone like you, sir."

"Well, all I can say is that I admire your tenacity; it would have daunted many a stronger man. You know, you with your knowledge of cars would likely have made a much better living working in one of the big garages."

"I know that sir, but I've always wanted to be my own boss."

The American surveyed him with a long, penetrating glance, then, punching him gently in the shoulder, he said, "You'll always be your own boss, son. Never you fear that. But now . . ." He stepped out of the door, saying, "I've got a mixed week-end before me, business and pleasure. I'm off to Doncaster to see a cousin of mine, who'll be on the board of the new concern. Also, I hope to persuade him to be my general manager. I should be back on Monday, and then we will get round the table and talk about ways and means." He took two steps forward and half-glanced over his shoulder and said, "You wouldn't like me to buy you out?"

Corny stopped behind him. He could see only a part of the American's profile; he didn't know what expression was on his face, whether this was a test or not; but he said immediately, "No, sir, I wouldn't like you to buy me out. I don't want anybody to buy me out; I want to work my business up."

"Good." Mr. Blenkinsop moved on again towards the garage, saying, "And I haven't the slightest doubt that our arrangement will go well."

"Nor me, sir. I've always liked working with Americans."

Mr. Blenkinsop stopped and turned fully round now. "You've worked with Americans before?"

"Yes, I was in America for close on a year, just outside New York."

"Well, I'll be jiggered. And you never opened your mouth about it?"

"Well, sir, I didn't think it would be of any interest to you; you must meet thousands of people who have been in America."

"Yes, and they always start by telling me just that. What were you doing over there?"

"Oh, I first of all worked on the ground floor in Flavors."

"Flavors! The car people?"

"Yes. And I did a bit in the office, and got into the showrooms."

"All in under a year?" Mr. Blenkinsop's eyes were now slits of disbelief, and Corny, lowering his head, said, "It was influence, sir."

"Ah! Ah! I see. But why didn't you stay on?"

"Well, just as I said a minute ago, I wanted to be me own boss, go on my own road. I wouldn't turn down help, but I didn't want to be carried, and in this particular case I wasn't being carried for meself; it was . . . well, it's a long story, sir, but it was because of my wife. There's an old gentleman—he's the owner of the farm her father manages. He's very fond of her, and between you and me he wanted to get me out of her way; he had other ideas for her."

The American's head went back and he let out a bellow of a laugh. "And you beat him to it by coming back. Good for you. You know"—his chin was forward once more—"I wouldn't like to come up against you in a fight, business or otherwise. I've an idea I'd lose."

"Aw, sir." Corny, laughing too, now, moved his head from side to side.

"Well, anyway, I'm glad to know you've been to America. But tell me, did you like it there?"

"Oh, yes, sir. I liked it, and the people, but I was missing Mary Ann . . . my wife."

"The one that acts like a woman?" Again there was laughter. "Well, you did right to come back. Now I'd better be off. And you go and tell your wife the good news. . . . Well, I hope you consider it good news."

Corny opened the car door for Mr. Blenkinsop. Then, closing it, and bending down, he said, "Quite truthfully, sir, I'm dazed."

"You won't remain in that state long. I'm speaking from experience. You'll take the breaks good and bad, in your stride. You'll see." They smiled at each other. Corny straightened up, then watched the car backing out of the garage. He followed it as it turned out of the drive, and he answered Mr. Blenkinsop's wave with a lift of his big arm.

Lord! Lord! Could he believe it? Could he? That his luck had changed at last? He had the desire to drop down on his knees and give thanks, but, instead, he turned round and pelted back across the drive, through the house door and up the stairs, and, bursting into the room, he came to a dead stop. Aw, lor, he'd forgotten about old bitterguts! But why not spill the good news into her lap as way of repayment for all she had put Mary Ann through for marrying him, and before that? "Mary Ann!" He shouted as if she were on a fell top, and she came to the scullery door wide-eyed, saying, "What's wrong?"

It was funny, he thought, that whenever they shouted at each other they always thought there was something wrong. In a few strides he was across the little kitchen, and, his arms under her armpits, he hoisted her upwards as if she was a child, and before the amazed gaze of her grannie he swung her around, then set her to the floor. But, still holding her with one hand, he bent and lifted David on to his shoulders, and, like this, he looked down at Mrs. McMullen and cried, "Behold! You see a successful man, Gran."

"You gone barmy?"

"Yes, I've gone barmy."

"Well, it's either that or you're drunk."

"I'm both. I'm barmy and I'm drunk." He pressed Mary Ann to his side until she almost cried out with the pressure on her ribs. Something has happened, something good. But what? The road? She looked up at him and said in awe-filled tones, "Corny. The road . . . the road's going through?"

He looked down at her, and, still shouting, he said, "No, not the road . . . the American."

She tried to pull away from him. "The American? What you talking about?"

"He's building a factory right at our door, this side of the field, and Bob Quinton's got the job. But he's contracting me to supply all the petrol, and much more, oh, much more, cars, garaging, repairs . . . the lot . . . the lot. What do you think of that?" He was not looking at Mary Ann now but bending towards Mrs. McMullen, and that undauntable dame looked back at him and said, "I wouldn't count me chickens afore they are hatched; there's many a hen sat on a nest of pot eggs."

"Oh, you're the world's little hopeful, aren't you, Gran?" He was still bending towards her, with David holding on to his hair with his fists to save himself from slipping, and Mary Ann, now pulling away from him, stood with her hands joined under her chin, and, forgetting about her grannie, forgetting about everything but Corny and the American, she said, "Oh, Corny! Oh, Corny! Thank God. Thank God."

"Humility. Humility. Thanking God. You must be cracking up."

"Gran!" Mary Ann looked towards the set-faced old woman. "You couldn't upset me if you tried. Go on. Think up the worst that's in you, and I'll fling my arms around you and hug you."

Mary Ann was surprised at her own words, as was Mrs. McMullen. The old lady was evidently taken aback for a moment, but only for a moment, before she said, "I wouldn't do any such thing. I'm an old woman and the shock might be the finish of me; for you to show me any affection would be more than me heart could stand, the last straw in fact."

Corny and Mary Ann looked at each other; then they laughed, and Corny, reaching out an arm, pulled Mary once more into his embrace, and said, "I would like to take you out this minute and give you a slap-up meal. What've you got in? What's for dinner? All of a sudden, I'm ravenous."

"Some ham and salad and a steamed pud, that's all. But we'll have a drink, eh? Go on. Put him down." She laughed up at David, who laughed back at her. Then, pulling herself from Corny, she ran towards the scullery, but paused at the door to call over her shoulder, "Go and bring Rose Mary."

"Rose Mary? Aw, where is she?" Corny looked about him.

"Oh, she went downstairs a little while ago, about ten minutes ago. She'll likely be in the old car."

Corny took his son from his shoulder and put him on the floor, and he didn't enquire why Rose Mary had gone out without David, for he fancied he knew the reason. The old girl had likely upset her, as she had done her mother so many times in the years gone by.

He ran down the back stairs and looked towards the old car and called, "Rose Mary! Rose Mary!" And when he didn't receive an answer he went into the garage and there saw Jimmy at the far end. Oh, he would have to tell Jimmy the news. Oh, yes, he must tell Jimmy.

It took a full five minutes to tell Jimmy, and all the time Jimmy, bashing one fist against the other, could only say, "Ee, boss! Coo, boss! No, boss! You don't say, boss!"

Then as Corny bent his long length to go out of the top door to the back of the garage again, Jimmy called to him, "Does that mean I'll get a rise, boss?"

Twisting round, Corny grinned at him. "It could," he said. "It just could."

"Good-oh, boss."

Corny now ran across the field towards the old car. He wanted to hold his daughter, to throw her sky high and cry, "We're going places, my Rose Mary, we're going places. And you're going to a good school, me girl." He wanted to get into his car and fly to the farm and yell to Mike, "I've done it, Mike. It's come, Mike." And Mike would understand, and he would thump him on the back. And Michael would thump him on the back, and Sarah would hold his hands and say, "I'm glad for you both." . . . But what would Lizzie say? Perhaps Lizzie wouldn't be so pleased, because her eyes had always said to her daughter, "Well, I told you so." And then there was Mr. Lord. Mr. Lord, who had offered him the bribe of Baxter's up-to-date garage, not to help him personally but so that he would be able to afford to keep his wife in the way that Mr. Lord thought she should be kept, the way she would have been kept if she had married his grandson, the way Lettice was kept now. Aw, he would go to him and say. . . . What would he say? He stopped at the end of the field. He would say nothing; he would just let time speak for him; he had a long way to go yet but the road was going through. Oh boy, yes. A different road to what he thought, but, nevertheless, a road.

"Rose Mary!" he shouted towards the car; and again "Rose Mary!" She was hiding from him, the little monkey.

When he got to the car he saw at a glance she wasn't there. He returned to the garage, calling all the way, "Rose Mary! Rose Mary!"

"Jimmy."

"Yes, boss?"

"You seen Rose Mary?"

"No, boss, not since the pair of them were on the old car."

Corny stood at the opening to the garage, looking about him, and spoke over his shoulder to Jimmy, saying, "That was some time ago. She's been upstairs since, and came down."

"Where's David?" Jimmy had come to his side now.

"Oh, he's upstairs; their great-grandmother's come. She upset Rose Mary and she came downstairs. She must be hiding somewhere."

"But where could she be hiding, boss?"

Corny looked at Jimmy. He looked at him for about ten seconds before swinging round. Yes, where could she be hiding? He now ran round to the back of the house and opened the coal-house door, and the doors of the two store-houses; then, dashing up the back stairs, he burst into the kitchen, saying, "Has she come in?"

"Rose Mary?" Mary Ann turned from the table. "No, I told you, she's out."

"She's not about anywhere."

"But she must be somewhere." Mary Ann moved slowly towards Corny and stared up into his face as he said, "I've looked everywhere."

"Perhaps . . . perhaps she's gone for a walk up the road." Her voice was small.

She'd never go up the road without him. Corny slowly drooped his head in the direction of David, who was standing stiffly staring at them, his eyes wide, his mouth slightly open.

"Take the car," said Mary Ann quietly, "and go to both ends of the road."

"Yes, yes." Corny nodded quickly, and as quickly turned about and went out of the room and down the stairs.

As Mary Ann looked towards her grannie, thinking, "It's her fault; she's to blame; she scared her, as she did me for years," David made a sound. It was high, and it sounded like Romary. Mary Ann, moving swiftly towards him, caught him to her, and he clutched at her dress, crying again, higher this time, on the verge of a scream, "Romary!"

"It's all right, darling." Mary Ann lifted him up into her arms. "Daddy's gone to fetch Rose Mary. It's all right; it's all right."

"Romary."

Mary Ann stared into the eyes of her son, glistening now with tears. Romary he had said. It wasn't a far cry to Rose Mary. She pressed him closer to her.

"She wants her backside smacked."

Mary Ann hitched David to one side in her arms so that she could confront her grannie squarely. "She doesn't want her backside smacked, and she's not going to get her backside smacked, wherever she is."

"That's right, break her neck with softness. It's been done before." The old woman's gimlet eyes raked Mary Ann up and down.

"How I bring up my children is my business. . . ."

"Oh, now, don't start. You were acting like an angel coming down by parachute a minute ago, and now you're getting back to normal."

"Look, Gran. I don't want to fight with you."

"Who's fightin', I ask you? Who starts the fights?"

"As far back as I remember, you have."

"Well, I like that. I come here, all this way in the baking heat, and that's what I get. Well, I should have known. I've had so much experience, I should have known." The big, bushy head was moving in wide sweeps now, and Mrs. McMullen, pulling herself to her feet, said, "Get me me coat."

Mary Ann didn't say, "Aw, Gran, don't be silly. Stay and have a bite of dinner." No. She put David down and marched out of the room, and returned a minute later with the coat in her hand. She did not attempt to help her grannie on with it; she just handed it to her, for she couldn't bear to touch her.

"There." Mrs. McMullen pulled on the coat. "Wonderful, isn't it? The kindness of people. I'm going out the way I come, without bite or sup, except for a drop of watery lemonade. I've got a long journey ahead of me afore I reach home, and I could collapse on the way. . . . But that would suit you, wouldn't it? Wouldn't that suit you, if I collapsed on the way?"

"You won't collapse on the way, not you, Gran. If I know you, you'll stop at some café and fill your kite."

Mrs. McMullen stared at her grand-daughter. Begod, if she had the power she would strike her dead this moment. God forgive her for the thought, but she would. But on second thoughts, perhaps not dead, but dumb. She would have her dumb, like her son, so that she could talk at her and watch her burning herself up with frustration. If there was anybody in this world she hated more than another, it was this flesh of her own flesh. But there was little or none of her in this madam; she was all Shaughnessy; from her toes to the top of her head, she was all Shaughnessy . . . Mike Shaughnessy.

Mrs. McMullen now passed her grand-daughter in silence. Her head held high, her body erect, she went out of the room and, unaided, down the dim stairs.

Mary Ann sat down and drooped her face into her hands for a moment. Why was it that her grannie could make her feel so bad, so wicked? She felt capable of saying the most dreadful things when her grannie started on her. And everything had been lovely for those few minutes, with Corny's great news. Well, she straightened up, she wasn't going to let the old cat dampen this day. No, she wasn't. When they found Rose Mary they would celebrate; in some way they would celebrate, even with only ham and steamed pudding.

"Come on," she said, rising and holding out her hand to David, who had been standing strangely still on the middle of the hearth rug. His stillness now got through to her, and she bent to him swiftly, saying, "It's all right. Rose Mary's only hiding. Come on, we'll find her."

Ten minutes later, with David still by the hand, she was standing on the drive-way when Corny brought the car back, and she looked at him, and he looked at her and shook his head. And it was a moment before he said, "Not a sign of her anywhere. I . . . I met the old girl half-way down the road and gave her a lift to the bus. She's black in the face with temper. You go for her?"

"Me go for her? You should have heard what she said. But don't bother about her, what's happened to Rose Mary?"

"You tell me. Why did she run out?"

"Because me grannie was at her an' all. She was saying . . . Oh. . . ." She put her fingers to her lips. "I know where she is." She pressed her head back into her shoulders as she stared at Corny. "She's gone to your grannie's."

"Me grannie's?"

"Yes, I bet that's where she's gone. That's how it started. Me grannie was needling her, and I heard her say she liked her Great-gran McBride, and me grannie said did she like her house and the smell an' all? Then Rose Mary said she didn't like her, and she ran out."

"But how would she get there, all that way?"

"She'd go on the bus, of course; she knows her way."

"Had she any money?"

"She could have taken it out of her pig, the bottom's loose."

"Well, did she?"

"I don't know, Corny; I haven't looked." Mary Ann's voice was high now, and agitated.

"Well, we'd better look, hadn't we?" He dashed from her and up the stairs, and when Mary Ann caught up with him he had the pig in his hand and the bottom was intact.

"She might have had some coppers in her pocket," Mary Ann said as she started down at the pig. Then she added, "Oh, why had this to happen on such a day, too? Oh, Corny, suppose she's not at your grannie's."

He gripped her hand. "She's bound to be there. Look, I'll slip down; it won't take long. If she went by bus she'd just be there by now."

"Roo Marry!"

The scream startled them both. Then it came again "Roo Marry!" Not Romary but two distinct words now, Roo Marry.

They flew down the stairs, and there stood David on the drive, his body stiff, his mouth wide, ejecting the two words "Roo Marry!"

Corny hoisted him up into his arms, saying, "All right, all right. It's all right, David. Rose Mary will soon be here."

"Roo Marry! Roo Marry!"

Corny turned his strained face towards Mary Ann. "Rose Mary. He's saying Rose Mary."

"Yes, yes." She put her hands up to her son's face and cupped it, saying, "Don't cry, David. Don't cry. Rose Mary's only gone for a walk."

"Roo Marry! Roo Marry!" Now there followed some syllables in quick succession, unintelligible. Then again "Roo Marry!"

"Put him down and get to your grannie's."

Corny put David down, and Mary Ann took hold of the child's hand. Then, as Corny strode towards the car, he was stopped in his stride by a yell that said "Da-ad! Da-ad!" And he turned to see his son tugging his hand from Mary Ann's and stretching out his arm to him. Retracing his steps, he took the child's outstretched hand, saying, "I'll take him with me."

Long after the car had disappeared from her view, Mary Ann stood on the drive. She was possessed of a strange feeling, as if she had lost everybody belonging to her. David had wanted to go with his dad. And he had said dad. In his own way he had said dad. He was talking. The wonder of it did not touch her in this moment, because Rose Mary was lost, really lost. . . . Don't be silly. She actually shook herself, and swung round and went into the house. But in a moment she was downstairs again and sitting in the office with the phone in her hand.

It was Mike who answered her. "Hello there," he said.

"It's me, Da. Tell me. Has Rose Mary come over there?"

"Rose Mary?" She could almost see her father's puckered brows. "No. What's happened?"

"Oh, so much, I don't know where to begin. Only we can't find Rose Mary. Corny's gone down to Gran McBride's. You see, me grannie came this morning. . . ."

"Oh, my God!"

"Yes, as you say, oh, my God! She was in fine fettle, and she taunted Rose Mary about something, and Rose Mary told her she didn't like her and she liked Grannie McBride, and then she ran out, and we think she may have made her way down there."

"God above! What mischief will that bloody woman cause next? Somebody should shoot her. Look, I'll come over. Have you looked everywhere round the place?"

"Yes, Da, we've looked everywhere. And don't come over yet; wait until Corny comes back. I'll ring you then; he might have found her."

"But what if he doesn't? What will you do then?"

"I don't know."

"Now look. If when Corny comes back he hasn't got her, you get on to the police straight-away."

"The police! But she might just be round about. . . ."

"Listen to me, girl. If Corny hasn't got her, get on to the police, and don't waste a minute. Look, I think I'll come over."

"All right, Da."

Mary Ann rang off, then sat looking out of the window to the side of her. This should have been a wonderful day, a marvellous day, but her grannie had to turn up, that evil genie, her grannie. Corny had made it at last; they should be rejoicing. And look what had happened. But she didn't really care about anything, about the garage, or the factory, or anything . . . if only Rose Mary would come back.

"Would you like a cigarette, Mrs. Boyle?" Jimmy was standing in the doorway, a grubby packet extended in his hand, and, shaking her head, she said softly, "No thanks, Jimmy."

"She'll turn up, never you fear, Mrs. Boyle. She's cute, and she's got a tongue in her head all right."

"Yes, Jimmy, she's got a tongue in her head. And she'll talk to anyone. That's what I'm afraid of." It had come upon her suddenly, this fear; as she had said to Jimmy, she'd talk to anyone. Oh, my God! She got off the seat and pushed past Jimmy; she wanted air. You heard of such dreadful things happening. That child, just a few months ago, taken away by that dreadful man. Oh, God in Heaven! Holy Mary, Mother of God, pray for us sinners now and at the hour of our death. Amen. Protect her. Oh, please, please. It won't matter about the garage, or money or anything, only protect her. . . . Here she was back to her childhood again, bargaining with the denizens of heaven. It was ridiculous, ridiculous. God helped those who helped themselves. She had learned that. . . . She must do something, but what? She had got to stay here until Corny returned. And then her da might come any minute. But she just couldn't stand about. She turned swiftly to Jimmy, saying, "I'm going up the road, to the crossroads. Tell Mr. Boyle if he comes back, I won't be long."

She was gone about twenty minutes, and when she returned there was the car on the drive and Corny standing at the office door with David by his side. Some part of her mind registered the fact in this moment that her son didn't rush to her, and she was hurt. The secret core in her was already crying. She stood in front of Corny and again he shook his head, then said, "She's never seen hilt nor hair of her, and I've stopped the car about twenty times and asked here and there."

"I phoned the farm; me da's coming."

"I phoned an' all, from Jarrow."

Corny, his face bleached-looking, turned from her and went into the office and picked up the phone, and coming on his heels, she stood close to him and whispered, "What are you going to do?"

"Phone the police."

A few minutes later he put the phone down, saying, "They'll be here shortly." Then, rubbing his hand over his drained face, he walked out on to the drive, and he looked about him before he said, "I didn't think about it at the time when I was taking her to the bus, but now I wonder why I didn't throttle that old girl. Somebody's going to one of these days. I never really understood how you felt about her." He looked down at Mary Ann. "But I do now. My God! I do now."

8

The search was organised; the police cars were roaming the district. Mary Ann was walking the streets of Felling; Michael was doing Jarrow; Jimmy was stopping odd cars on the main road to enquire if anyone had seen a little girl in a blue dress, while Corny traversed the fields and ditches, and the by-lanes right to the old stone quarry four miles away and back to the garage, all the while humping David with him. As he came at a trot into the driveway carrying David on one arm, he heard the phone ring, but when he reached the office and lifted up the receiver the operator asked for his number.

He went out on to the drive again, David still by his side, and rubbed his sweating face with his hand. Where was Mike? Mike was supposed to stay put. "Mike!" he called. "Mike!" Then, going round to the back, he saw Mike's unmistakable figure in the far distance walking by the side of the deep drain.

Corny shook his head; they had done all that. He should have stayed here and waited for the phone. He had asked him to do just that because Jimmy was better on the road, and he himself was quicker on his pins over the fields, even handicapped as he was with the child. "Mike!" he shouted. "Mike!"

Mike was breathing hard when he reached the old car, and he called from there, "You've got news?"

Corny shook his head, and Mike's pace slowed.

Corny shook his head, and Mike's pace slowed.

"The phone's been ringing," said Corny when Mike reached him.

"Oh! Oh well, I was about for ages, I just couldn't stay put, man. I thought of the ditch over there. It's covered with ferns in places."

"We've been all round there, I've told you." Corny turned away and Mike's chin went upwards at the tone of his voice, and then he lowered it again. This wasn't the time to take umbrage at a man's tone, not the state he must be in. For himself he was back to the time when Mary Ann had run away from the convent in the south and had been reported seen in the company of an old man. Those hours had nearly driven him to complete madness.

Around to the front of the garage again they went, David still hanging on to his father's hand. There, Corny stood, leaning for a moment against the wall. He felt exhausted both in mind and body; too much had happened too quickly in the last few hours. He couldn't ever remember feeling like this in his life before, weak, trembling all over inside.

"Da-ad."

David repeated the word and tugged twice at Corny's hand, before Corny looked at him, saying, "Yes. yes, what is it, David?"

"Roo Marry . . . Lost?" The word lost was quite distinct.

Corny continued to look at his son for a moment. Then, lifting his eyes to Mike, he said, wearily, "I've always said part them and he'd talk. But God, I'd rather he remained dumb for life than this had to happen before he did it."

Mike said nothing but looked down at his grandson, to the little face swollen with crying. Lizzie, like Corny, had always maintained that the boy would talk if he hadn't Rose Mary to do it for him, and they had been right. He could talk all right, stumbling as yet, but, nevertheless, he had been shocked into speech.

Corny, now pulling himself from the wall, said, "If only that damned old witch hadn't put in an appearance this morning. With the news Mr. Blenkinsop brought me I should be on top of the world. I was for about five minutes."

"You will be again," said Mike. "Never you fear."

"That depends." Corny looked his father-in-law straight in the eye.

Again Mike made no answer, but he thought, "Aye, that depends."

Corny slowly moved towards the office with David at his side, and Mike, walking on his other side, looked towards the ground as he said, "I don't think there's a woman anywhere who's caused as much havoc as that one. You know . . . and this is the truth . . . twice . . . twice I've thought seriously of doing her in." He turned his head to the side and met Corny's full gaze. "It's a fact. When I think, and I've often thought that I could have been hung for her, I get frightened, but not like I used to, because she can't make me rise now as she could a few years ago. And I'm positive that's why she came here to-day, just to get Mary Ann on the raw, because when she came to us on Sunday she got no satisfaction. Peter was at the tea-table, and Peter in his polite, gentlemanly way is a match for her. And we were all laughing our heads off and not taking a pennorth of notice of her. She didn't like it. She couldn't make anybody rise. Everybody was too happy for her. But she couldn't go a week without finding a target, so she came back to the old firm. Who better than her grand-daughter? God, I wish she had dropped down dead on the way."

"I endorse that. By, I do!" Corny shook his head. Then, drawing in a deep breath and looking down at David, he said, "Are you hungry?"

"NO-t."

"You're not hungry?"

"No-t, Da-ad."

"Would you like some milk?"

"No-t."

"Say, no, David."

"No-oo."

"That's a good boy." Corny turned and looked at Mike, and their glances said, "Would you believe it?"

Now David, crossing his legs, pulled at Corny's hand and said quite distinctly, "Lav, Da-ad."

"Well, you know where it is, don't you? You can go by yourself. . . . Go on."

David went, and as Corny and Mike watched him running round the corner of the building, the phone rang. Within a second Corny was in the office and had the receiver to his ear.

"Mr. Boyle?"

"Yes, Mr. Boyle here."

"It's Blenkinsop."

"Oh, hello, Mr. Blenkinsop."

"I don't know how to begin, for I suppose you're nearly all mad at that end. . . . You'd never believe it, but . . . but I've got her here."

Corny closed his eyes and, gripping Mike's arm tightly, he wetted his lips, then said, "You did say you've got her there, Mr. Blenkinsop?"

"Yes. Yes, I've got her here all right. She gave me the shock of my life. I stopped at an hotel for a drink and when I came out, there she was, sitting as calm as you like in the front of the car."

"In the front of the car?" Corny repeated slowly as he cast his eyes towards Mike. "How did she get there?"

"Well, as far as I can gather she was hiding from someone, great-grandmother or someone, so she says, and she climbed into the boot, as the lid was partly open. At this moment I feel I should pray to somebody in thanks that the lid was open and wouldn't close tight because of some gear I had in there. She says she fell asleep because it was hot, but woke up once the car got going and did a lot of knocking, and, by the look of her face, a lot of crying, and then she fell asleep again. Apparently she found no difficulty in lifting the lid up once the car had stopped. One thing I can't understand and that is how she slept in there at all, especially when the car was moving."

"Oh, she's been used to sleeping on journeys since she was a baby. They both have, her and David."

"Well, boy, am I dazed. But you . . . you must be frantic."

"You can say that again. The whole place is alerted. The police, the lot. But I never thought of you, not once."

"Well, who would? I tell you, she gave me a scare sitting there; I thought I was seeing things. Look. Here she is; have a word with her."

Corny bowed his head and closed his eyes and listened. "It's me, Dad."

"Hello, Rose Mary." His voice was trembling.

"I didn't mean to do it, Dad, but I wanted to hide from Great-gran. I didn't want to go back upstairs, 'cos she was horrible, and so I climbed into the boot, like it was the old car. The lid was open a bit but it was hot. When the car started going I tried to push the lid up, and I shouted, but it was noisy. Are you all right, Dad?"

"Yes, yes, I'm all right, Rose Mary. We only wondered where you were."

"And David? Is he wanting me?"

"David's all right, too."

"And me ma. Did she cry?"

"Yes, yes, because she couldn't find you, but she'll be all right now."

"I'm sorry, Dad."

"It's all right. It's all right, Rose Mary."

"Mr. Blenkinsop has been trying to get on the phone a lot."

"Has he? We've been out and about."

"I'm going to have some dinner now and then I'm coming back. . . . You're not mad at me, Dad, are you?"

"No, no, I'm not mad at you."

"You sound funny."

"And so do you."

He heard her give a little laugh. Then he said, "Let me speak to Mr. Blenkinsop again."

"Tahrah, Dad."

"Bye-bye, Rose Mary."

"Well now." It was Mr. Blenkinsop speaking again. "If it's all right with you, as she says she'll have some dinner, and then I'll make the return journey as quickly as possible."

"I'm sorry, sir, if this has spoiled your trip."

"Oh, don't be sorry about that. I'm sorry for scaring the daylights out of you. And if I know anything you're still in a state of shock; I know how I would feel. . . . I tell you what though. We're just about twenty miles out of Doncaster; I wonder if you'd mind if I ran in and told my cousin . . . I was going to spend the night with him and his family—I think I told you—and if I explain things they'll understand, because I won't make the return journey back to them until to-morrow."

"Yes, yes, you go ahead and do that. I'm sorry it's putting you out."

"Oh, not at all. Just that being so near, it would be better to explain in person, rather than phoning."

Mr. Blenkinsop laughed his merry laugh. "What a day! What a day! I'm just thinking; I brought you a bit of good news and then I took all the good out of it."

"It wasn't your fault, sir."

"Well, I'm glad you look at it like that. I'll be back as quickly as I can, and that should be shortly after six."

"Right, sir."

"Here she is to say another good-bye."

Corny heard Rose Mary take a number of sharp breaths. "Bye-bye again, Dad. Tell David I won't be long. And me mam."

"Bye-bye, dear."

He listened until the receiver clicked, then put the phone down and turned and looked at Mike. Mike was leaning against the stanchion of the door, wiping his face and neck with a coloured handkerchief. Corny sat staring at him. He felt very weak as if he had just got over a bout of flu or some such thing.

"Well!" said Mike, still rubbing at his face.

"Aye, well," said Corny. "I just can't take it in. I feel so sick with relief I could vomit."

The corner of Mike's mouth turned up as he said, "Well, before you give yourself that pleasure you'd better get on to the police."

"Aye, yes." Corny picked up the phone again.

"Aw, I'm glad to hear that," said the officer-in-charge. "Right glad."

"I'm sorry to have put you to so much trouble."

"Oh, don't bother about that. As long as she's O.K., that's everything. I'll start calling them off now."

"Thank you very much. Good-bye."

Corny walked past Mike and looked up at the sky. He still felt bewildered.

"What are yoiu going to do now?"

"Go and find Mary Ann," said Corny. "She seemed to think she might have gone to some of her playmates. I'll go round Felling, and when I pick her up I'll go and find

Michael. That's if the police haven't contacted him beforehand. . . . You'll stay here?"

"Oh, aye, I'll stay here. I feel like yourself, a bit sick with relief."

"Da-ad be-en."

The two men turned to where David was running across the cement towards them, and when the boy threw himself against Corny's legs, Corny looked down at him but didn't speak, and Mike, after a moment, said softly, "Aren't you going to tell him?"

Corny looked at Mike now and he said slowly, "I've only got till six o'clock."

"What do you mean?"

Corny, now speaking under his breath, muttered, "The minute she comes back he'll close up like a clam; she hasn't been away long enough."

"Aw man, my God, be thankful." Mike's voice was indignant.

"I am, I am, Mike. Thankful! You just don't know how thankful, but this"—he motioned his head down to the side of him—"I wanted to hear him. . . . You know what?" He moved his lips soundlessly. "More than anything in life I wanted to hear him. . . . I wanted this garage to be successful as you know. For seven years I've hung on, but if I had to choose, well, I know what I would have chosen. . . . His state has come between me and sleep for months now. I've told Mary Ann that if . . ." He looked down at David again, at the wide eyes staring up at him, and, looking back to Mike, he began to speak enigmatically, saying, "If what has happened the day could have been made to happen, you know what I mean, one one place, one the other, just for a short time, it would have worked. I've told her till I'm sick, but she wouldn't have it. But I've been proved right, haven't I? You see for yourself."

"Yes, I see. And Lizzie's always said the same thing. But be thankful, lad, be thankful. He won't close up."

"I wish I could bet on that. She'll be so full of talk that he'll just stand and gape."

"Ssh, man! Ssh!" Mike turned away with a jerk of his head towards David, and Corny, now looking down at his son's strained face and trembling lips, said, "Rose Mary is coming back, David."

"Ro-se Ma-ry," the child's lips stretched wide, and then he again said, on a high note, "Ro-se Ma-ry." The name was clear-cut now.

"Yes, Rose Mary is coming back. You remember the American man, Mr. Blenkinsop?"

David nodded his head, and Corny repeated, "You remember the American man, Mr. Blenkinsop?"

"Ya."

"Yes," said Corny.

"Ye-as," said David.

"Well, Rose Mary was hiding in the boot of his car, and he drove away and she couldn't get out. . . . What do you think of that?"

The light in David's eyes deepened, his mouth stretched wider, and then he laughed.

"I'm going to pick up Mam now. Do you want to come?"

"Ye-as," said David.

"Go on, then, get into the car." Now Corny, turning to Mike, said, "If she should phone in tell her I'll wait outside the school. That's the best place."

"Good enough," said Mike. "Get yourself off."

Corny brought the car out of the garage and stopped it when he neared Mike, and, looking at David sitting on the seat beside him, he said, "Say good-bye to Granda."

"Bye, Gran . . . da."

"Good-bye, son."

Corny, with his face close to Mike, looked him in the eyes and said, softly, "You know, it's in me to wish that she wasn't coming back to-night or to-morrow."

"Corny! Corny, don't be like that!" Mike's voice was harsh.

"She's safe so I'm content. And I say again, give me another day, perhaps two, and I'd have no fears after that. But just you wait until to-night, it'll be a clam again, you'll see."

"Aw, go on now. Go on and stop thinking such nonsense." Mike stepped back and waved Corny away, and as he watched him driving into the road he thought, "That's a nice attitude to take! There'll be skull and hair flying if he talks like that to her." But after a moment of considering he turned in the direction of the office, asking himself what he would have felt like if Michael had, to all intents and purposes, been dumb? Pretty much like Corny was feeling now, because he knew, in a strange sort of way, that he and Corny were built on similar lines and that their reactions, in the main, were very much alike.

"Look, have a drop of brandy." Corny was on his hunkers before Mary Ann, where she sat in a straight-backed chair in the kitchen.

"No, I'm all right. I'm all right; it's just the reaction; it's just that I can't stop shaking."

"I'll get you a drop of brandy. . . . You keep it in as a medicine, and this is a time when medicine is needed." Corny went to the cupboard and, reaching to the back of the top shelf, brought out a half-bottle of brandy, and, pouring a measure into a cup, he took it to her. Placing it in her hand, he said gently, "There now, sup it up."

"I don't like brandy."

"It doesn't matter what you like, get it down you. Come on." He guided the cup to her lips, and when she sipped at it she shuddered. Then, looking at him, she said, "What time did he say he'd be back?"

"Something after six."

"And it's just on five." She raised her eyes to the clock. Then, stretching out her hand, she put the cup on the table near where David was standing looking out of the window, waiting for a glimpse of the car that would bring Rose Mary back, but the movement of her hand caught his attention and he turned from the window and, looking from the cup to Mary Ann, he said distinctly, "Sup?"

There was a quick exchange of glances between Corny and Mary Ann, and, smiling now, she said, "No, David, it's nasty." Then again, she was looking at Corny, the smile gone, as she said, "I can't believe it. I just can't believe it. I won't be able to really take it in until I see her."

Corny made no answer to this. He was looking towards David, where the boy was again gazing out of the window, and he said softly, "I always told you, didn't I? Get them apart for a while. . . ."

"It wasn't that, it wasn't that." Mary Ann was on her feet. "It was the shock."

"Aye, you're right. But if she had come back right away there would have been no chit-chat, not like now. . . . As it is, I'm a bit afraid that as soon as she puts her face in the door he'll close. . . ."

At this moment they heard a knocking on the staircase door and Jimmy's voice calling, "The phone's going, boss. You're wanted on the phone."

As Corny made swiftly for the door Mary Ann was on his heels, and she was still close behind him when he entered the office, and when, with his hand on the phone, he turned and looked at her, he said quietly, "It's all right, it's all right, there's nothing to worry about now."

She shook her head as she watched him lift the phone to his ear. "Hello. Oh, it's you, Mr. Blenkinsop. Hello there, everything all right?" Although he wasn't looking at Mary Ann he felt her body stiffen, and when Mr. Blenkinsop's voice came to him, saying, "Oh yes, as right as rain," he cast a quick glance at her and smiled reassuringly, then listened to Mr. Blenkinsop going on, "It's just that I thought I'd better phone you as I've not been able to get away from my cousin's yet. You see he has four sons and there was quite a drought of female company around her, and they've got her up in the train-room. I've had two unsuccessful attempts at getting her away; not that she seems very eager to leave them. They've gone right overboard for her. Their verdict is she's cute. This is quite unanimous, from Ian who is three, to Donald who is ten. So, as it is, it's going to be nearer nine when I arrive . . . I hope you're not mad."

"No, Mr. Blenkinsop. That's O.K., as long as she's all right."

"All right? I'll say she's all right. Can you hear that hullabaloo?" He stopped speaking, and Corny hadn't to strain his ears to hear the excited shrieks and the sound of running feet. Then Mr. Blenkinsop's voice came again, saying, "They've just come in like a herd of buffalo."

Corny turned his eyes to Mary Ann again. There was an anxious look on her face, but he smiled at her and wrinkled his nose before turning his attention to the phone again as Mr. Blenkinsop's voice said, "Just a minute. There's a conclave going on, they want to ask you something. Just a minute, will you?"

As Corny waited he put his hand over the mouthpiece and said under his breath, "She's having the time of her life."

"He hasn't left there yet?"

"No, there's four children, boys, and apparently they've got a train set. They're kicking up a racket." As he looked at her strained face he said, "It's all right, it's all right, there's nothing to worry about."

"Hello. Yes . . . yes, I'm here."

"Look, I don't know how to put this but they're all around me here, the four of them . . . and their mother and the father an' all. Well . . . well, it's like this, they want me to say will you let Rose Mary stay the night?"

". . . Stay the night?" Corny put his hand out quickly to stop Mary Ann grabbing the phone, and he shook his head vigorously at her and pressed the receiver closer to his ear to hear Mr. Blenkinsop say, "You know, if you could agree to this it would save me a return journey to-morrow because Dave, my cousin here, and me, well we could get through our business to-night and I'd make an early start in the morning. But that's up to you. I know that you and your lady are bound to want her back, but there it is." There was a pause which Corny did not fill, and then Mr. Blenkinsop's voice came again, saying, "Would you like to speak to her? Here she is."

"Hello, Dad."

"Hello, Rose Mary. Are you all right?"

"Oh yes, Dad. It's lovely here. They've got a big house and garden, an' a train-room, and they're all boys." Her next words were drowned in the high laughter of children.

"Don't you want to come back to David?" As Corny listened to her answer he held out his free arm, stiffly holding Mary Ann at a distance from the phone.

"Oh yes, Dad. Yes, I wish David was here. And you, and me mam. Is me mam all right?"

"Yes, she's fine. And would you like to stay there until the morrow?"

"No! no!" Mary Ann's voice hissed at him as he heard Rose Mary say, "Yes, Dad, if it's all right with you and me mam."

"Yes, it's all right with us, dear. You have a good time and enjoy yourself, and then you can tell us all about it to-morrow. Well, good-bye now."

"Bye-bye, Dad. Bye-bye."

As Mary Ann rushed out of the office he listened to Mr. Blenkinsop saying, "We'll take great care of her. She's made a great impression here. I think you'd better prepare yourself for the visit of four stalwart youths in the future.

Corny gave a weak laugh, then said, "Well, until to-morrow morning, Mr. Blenkinsop."

"Yes, until to-morrow morning. I'll bring her back safe and sound, never fear. Good-bye now."

"Good-bye." Corny put down the phone and tried to tell himself that he was disappointed that she wasn't coming back to-night. And then Mary Ann appeared in the doorway again.

"You shouldn't have done it."

"What could I have done?"

"You could have told him that I was nearly out of my mind and I wanted her back."

"Well, she's coming back. It's only a few more hours, and the man asked me as a favour."

"Oh yes, you'd have to grant him a favour, knowing how I felt, knowing that I was waiting every minute. You know. . . ." She strained her face up to him. "You're glad, aren't you, you're glad that she's not coming back to-night because it'll keep them apart a little longer. You're glad."

"Now don't go on like that. Don't be silly."

"I'm not being silly. I know what's in your mind; you've been preening yourself, ever since I got in, about him talking, that it would never have happened if they hadn't been separated. You were frightened of her coming back in case he wouldn't keep up the effort."

"All right, all right." He was shouting now. "Yes I was, and I still am. And yes, I'm glad that she's not coming back until to-morrow morning. It'll give him a chance, for he damn well hadn't a chance before. She not only talked for him, she thought for him, and lived for him; she lived his life, he hadn't any of his own. . . . I'll tell you this. He's been a new being this afternoon. And I'll tell you something else, I wish they had invited her for a week."

There was a long, long silence, during which they stared at each other. Then Mary Ann her voice low and bitter, said, "I hate you. Oh, how I hate you!" Then she turned slowly from him, leaving him leaning against the little desk, his head back, his eyes closed, his teeth grating the skin on his lip.

I hate you! Mary Ann had said that to him. Oh, how I hate you!

"Da-ad." Corny opened his eyes and looked down to where David was standing in the open doorway, his face troubled, and he said, "Yes, son. What is it?"

"Ma-am." There followed a pause before David, his mouth wide open now, emitted the word, "Cry."

Corny considered his son. The child had seen his mother cry, yet he hadn't gone to her, he had come to him. He reached out and took his hand. Then, hoisting him up on to the desk, he looked straight at him and he said, "Mam's crying because Rose Mary is not coming back until to-morrow."

David's eyes remained unblinking.

"You're not going to cry because Rose Mary isn't coming back until to-morrow, are you?"

The eyes still unblinking, the expression didn't change, and then David slowly shook his head.

"Say, No, Dad."

"No, Da-ad."

"That's a good boy. I'm going to mend a car. Are you coming to help me?"

Again David moved his head, nodding now, and again Corny prompted him. "Say, Yes, Dad."

"Yes, Da-ad."

"Come on then." He lifted him down, and they walked out of the office side by side and into the garage, and as he went Corny thought, "I'll give her a little while to cool off and then I'll go up."

9

If Corny hadn't heard the car slow up and thought it was someone wanting petrol he would never have gone on to the drive at that moment and seen her going.

The occupants of the car decided not to stop after all, and it was speeding away to the right of the garage. But, going down the road to the left, Corny stared at the back of Mary Ann. Mary Ann carrying a case. He stood petrified for a moment, one hand raised in mid-air in an appealing gesture. God Almighty! She wouldn't. No, she wouldn't do that without saying a word. She was near the bend of the road when he sprang forward and yelled, "Mary Ann!" When there was no pause in her step he stopped at the end of the line of white bricks edging the roadway, and now, his voice high and angry, he yelled, "Do you hear? Mary Ann!"

Taking great loping strides, he raced towards her, and again he shouted, "Mary Ann! Wait a minute, Mary Ann!" It wasn't until he saw her hasten her step that he stopped again, and after a moment of grim silence he yelled, "If you go, you go. Only remember this. You come back on your own, I'll not fetch you. I'm telling you." Her step didn't falter, and the next minute she was lost to his sight round the bend.

The anger seeped out of him. He felt as if his life was seeping out of him, draining down from his veins into the ground. How long he stood still he didn't know, and he wasn't conscious of turning about and walking back to the garage. He didn't come to himself until he saw David standing with his back to the petrol pump. She hadn't even come to see the child. She was bats about the boy, she was bats about them both. Why hadn't she taken him with her? Perhaps because she knew that he wouldn't have let him go. And she was right there. He wouldn't have let the boy go with her.

"Ma-am. . . ."

Corny looked down at the small, trembling lips, and he forced himself to speak calmly, saying, "Mam's gone to Gran's."

"Gra-an's?"

"Your Grannie Shaughnessy has got a bad head, she's not very well. Can you go upstairs and set the tray for your supper, do you think? Your bunny tray with the mug and the plate. Then wash yourself."

The boy was looking up at him, his eyes wide and deep, with that knowing look in their depths. Then he said, "Yes, Da-ad," and went slowly towards the house. And Corny turned about and went into the office and dropped into his chair. He felt weak again and, something more, he felt frightened; this kind of thing happened to other fellows, to other couples, but it couldn't happen to them. He had loved her since he was a boy, and she had loved him from when she was ten. She had loved and championed him since he could remember. She had stood by him through all the hard times. And there had been hard times; there had been weeks when they both had to pull their belts in in order that their children got their full share of food, and during these times both had resisted gobbling up food when they went to the farm on a Sunday and sat down to the laden table. No one must know how things really stood. They would get by. It was she who had always said that. "We'll get by," she'd said. "We'll have a break, you'll see. It'll come. . . ." And it had come; it had come to-day, like a bolt from the blue. And with it the break in his family had come too.

But it just couldn't happen to him and Mary Ann. They had made a pact at the beginning, never to go to sleep on a row, and they never had. Well, there was always a first time, and by the looks of things that first time was now, because she had no intention of coming back to-day; she had taken a case with her. He dropped his head on to his hands. And all because he hadn't said the word that would bring Rose Mary back to-night. What were a few more hours of separation if it was going to loosen her son's tongue? Couldn't she see it? No; because she didn't want to see it. She didn't want them separated for a minute from each other, or from her. She had once said they were as close as the Blessed Trinity, and on that occasion he had asked where he came in in the divine scheme of things, and she had laughingly replied, "We'll make you Joseph." But he was no Joseph, he was no foster-father. David was his son, and he carried a deep secret ache, a yearning to hear his voice. And now he was hearing it, but he was going to pay dearly apparently for that pleasure.

He heard a car come on to the drive and it brought him to his feet, and when he reached the office door, there, scrambling out from a dilapidated Austin, was Jimmy and his pals. Corny had never seen this lot before. He had seen other pals of Jimmy's, but they hadn't been so freakish as the boys now confronting him. These looked like a combination of The Rolling Stones and The Pretty Things, and Jimmy looked the odd man out, because he appeared the only male thing among them. At any other time Corny would have hooted inside, he would have chipped this lot and stood being chipped in return, but not to-night. His face was straight as he looked at Jimmy and asked, "Well?"

"I just popped in, Boss—we was passing like—just to see if Rose Mary was back."

"No, she's not back. She's staying with Mr. Blenkinsop's friends until the morning. He's bringing her back then."

"Oh." Jimmy now turned and nodded towards his four long-haired companions, who were all surveying Corny with a blank, scrutinising stare.

"The missus all right?" Jimmy glanced up at the house-window as he spoke, and Corny, after a moment, said, "Yes. Yes, she's all right."

"Busy, is she?"

"No." Corny screwed up his eyes in enquiry. "She's got a headache; she's lying down. Do you want something?"

"No, no, boss. I was just wondering, after all the excitement of the day, how she was farin'. And we was just passing like I said. Well, fellas," he turned towards the four, "let's get crackin'."

The four boys piled back into the car. Not one of them had spoken, but Jimmy, now taking his seat beside the driver, put his hand out of the window and passed it over the rust-encrusted chrome framing the door and, smiling broadly, said, "She goes."

"You're lucky." Corny nodded to him but did not grin, as he would have done at another time when making a scathing remark, even if it was justified, and Jimmy's long face lengthened ever further, his mouth dropped, and his eyebrows twitched. He sensed there was something not quite right. The boss was off-hand, summat was up. "Be seeing you in the mornin'," he said.

For answer, Corny merely nodded his head, and as the car swung out of the driveway he went into the office. . . .

Again he was sitting with his head in his hands when the phone rang. He stared at it for a moment. He knew who it would be . . . Mike. Slowly he reached out and, lifting up the receiver, said, "Yes."

"Corny."

He had been wrong; it wasn't her da, it was her ma.

Lizzie's voice sounded very low, as if she didn't want to be overheard. "I'm sorry about this, Corny."

He didn't speak. What was there to say?

"Are you there?"

"Yes, I'm here, Mam."

"I want you to know that I'm with you in this."

He widened his eyes at the phone.

"I've always said if they were separated, even for a short time, it would give him a chance. I've told her I think you're right. But . . . but, on the other hand, she's been worried nearly out of her mind and it mightn't have been the right time to have done it."

"What other chance would I have had? You tell me."

"I don't know, but, as I said, I'm with you. I can't tell her that, you understand, not at present. She's in an awful state, Corny. . . . What are you going to do?"

"Me?"

"Yes, you. Who else?"

"I'm going to do nothing, Mam. She walked out on me, she didn't even come and see the boy. I ran down the road after her, yelling me head off, but she wouldn't stop. I wouldn't even have known she had gone, it was just by chance I saw her. So what am I going to do? I'm going to do nothing."

"Oh dear. Corny. Corny. You know what she is; she's as stubborn as a mule."

"Well, there's more than one mule."

"That's going to get neither of you anywhere. And you've got to think of the children."

"It strikes me you can think of the children too much. In one way I mean. The children shouldn't come before each other. Whatever has got to be done with the children should be a combined effort."

"Well, you didn't make it much of a combined effort from what I hear, Corny. You told that man that Rose Mary could stay until to-morrow morning, and didn't give her the chance to say a word."

"Well, what harm was there in it? Just a few more hours. And if she had been unhappy then I would have whisked her back like a shot; I would have gone out there for her myself; but by the sound of her she was having the time of her life. And at this end David wasn't worrying. That is what really upset madam, David wasn't really worrying. What was more, he was talking."

"He'll worry if she doesn't come back soon. . . . I mean Mary Ann not Rose Mary."

"I think he's worrying already, he's trying not to cry." Corny's voice was flat now.

"Would Mike come over and get him?"

"No, Mam, no thank you." His voice was no longer flat. "The boy stays with me. If she wants him she's got to come back home. . . . Home I said, Mam. This is her home, Mam."

"I know that, I know that well enough, Corny. And don't shout."

"Where is she?"

"She's gone down to the bottom field to see Mike."

There followed a short silence. And then Lizzie spoke again, saying, "It seems terrible for this to happen, and on a day when you've got such wonderful news."

"Oh, she told you that, did she?"

"Yes, she told me. I'm so glad, Corny, I'm delighted for you. If only this business was cleared up."

"Well, there's a way to end it. She knows what to do. She walked down the road, she can walk up it again."

"Don't be so stubborn, Corny. Get in the car and come over."

"Not on your life."

"Very well, there's no use talking any more, is there?" Lizzie's voice was cut off abruptly, and Corny, taking the phone from his ear, stared at it for a moment before putting it on the stand.

Go over there. Beg her to come back. Say he was sorry. For what? For acting rationally, sensibly?

He marched upstairs and into the kitchen. David had put his mug and plate on the tray but was now standing looking out of the window. He turned an eager face to Corny on his entry, then looked towards the table and the tray, and Corny said, "By, that's clever of you! Are you hungry?"

David nodded his head; then before Corny had time to prompt him, he said, "Yes, Da-ad."

"You'd like some cheese, wouldn't you?"

David now grinned at him and nodded as he said, "Yes, Da-da, cheese." He thrust his lips out on the word and Corny was forced to smile. Cheese upset his stomach; it brought him out in a rash; but that was before he could say cheese. He would see what effect it had on him now.

He was cutting a thin slice of cheese from the three-cornered piece when he heard the distant tinkle of the phone ringing again. "You eat that," he said quickly, placing the cheese on a piece of bread. Then he patted David on the head and hurried out.

This time it was Mike on the phone, and without any preamble he began, "Now what in the name of God is all this about? What do you think the pair of you are up to?"

Corny, staring out of the little office-window, passed his teeth tightly over each other before saying, with forced calmness, "Well, I'm glad you said the pair of us and didn't just put the lot on me."

"That's as it may be." Mike's voice was rough. "But this I'm going to say to you, and you alone. What the hell were you at to let her come away?"

"Now look you here, Mike. I don't happen to have sentries posted at each corner of the house to let me know her movements; I didn't even know she was going until I saw the back of her going down the road. . . ."

"Well, why didn't you bring her back?"

"Look, I shouted and shouted to her, and the harder I shouted the quicker she walked."

"You had legs, hadn't you? You could have run after her."

There was a long pause following this. Then Corny, his voice low, very low now, said, "Yes, I had legs, and I could have run. And I could have picked her up bodily and carried her back. That's what you mean, isn't it? Well, now, you put yourself in my position, Mike. Liz walks out on you; you run after her; you call to her, and she takes not a damned bit of notice of you. What would you have done? She's got a case in her hand; she's leaving you and her son . . . and, this is the point, Mike, she's going home."

"Oh, I get your point all right. But what do you mean, home? That's her home."

"Aye, it should be, but she's never looked on this as home; she's always looked on your place, the farm, as home. And there she was, case in hand . . . going home. Think a minute. What would you have done, eh?"

"Well." Mike's voice faltered now. "Most girls look upon their parents' place as home. Look at Michael here. Never away, even when he's finished work. That's nothing."

"It mightn't be nothing to you, but it's something to me. She knew what she was taking on when she married me. This was the only home I could give her until I could get a better, and now, when the prospects of doing just that are looking large, this happens."

"You're a pair of hot-headed fools." Mike's voice was calmer now. "Look, get into the car and come over."

"No, not on your life, Mike. If there's any coming over she's going to do it. She can get cool in the stew she got hot in."

"Man!" Mike's voice was rising again. "She's upset. More that upset, she looks awful. You know for a fact yourself she just lives for those bairns."

"Yes," shouted Corny now. "I know for a fact she just lives for those bairns. She's lived for them so much she's almost forgotten that I've got a share in them. If she'd done what I'd asked months ago and let you have David for a few days this would never have happened. But no. No, she couldn't bear either of them out of her sight. She made on it because she didn't want them separated, they mustn't be separated, but the real truth of the matter is that she couldn't bear to let one of them go, not even for a night. All this could have been avoided if she had acted sensibly."

"It's all right saying if . . . if . . . the thing's done. But you can't stick all the blame for what's happened to-day on her. The one to blame is that blasted old she-devil. If she hadn't come along Rose Mary would have been home this minute and nothing like this would have happened. The trouble that old bitch causes stuns me when I think about it."

There was silence again between them. Then Mike's voice, coming very low, with a plea in it, said, "When you shut up the garage come on over. Come on, man. Drop in as if nothing had happened."

Slowly Corny put the receiver back on to its stand. Then looking at it, he muttered, "Aw no, Mike. Aw no. You don't get me going crawling, not in this way, you don't. I've just to start that and I'm finished."

10

Mary Ann stood at the window of the room that had been hers from a child. She had never thought she would spend a night here again, at least not alone, unless something had happened to Corny. Well, something had happened to Corny.

She stood with her arms crossed over her breast, her hands on her shoulders, hugging herself in her misery. There was a moon shining somewhere. The light was picking out the farm buildings; the whole landscape looked peaceful, and beautiful, but she did not feel the peace, nor see the beauty. She was looking back to the eternity that she had lived through, from the minute she had come back home yesterday.

She had never for a moment thought that he would let her go. Although she had been flaming with temper against him, the sensible, reasonable part of her was waiting for him to convince her that he was right. When she heard his voice calling to her along the road she had felt a wave of relief pass over her; she wouldn't have to go through with it. He would come dashing up and grip her by the shoulders and shake her, and go for her hell for leather. He would say, "Did you mean what you said about hating me?" And after a time she would say, "How could I? How could I ever hate you, whatever you did?"

All this had been going on in the reasonable, sensible part of her, but on the surface she was still seething, still going to show him. After he had called her name for a second time and she heard his footsteps pounding along the road behind her she quickened her stride and told herself she wasn't going to make this easy for him. Then she was near the bend and his footsteps stopped, and his voice came to her again, saying, "If you go, you go. Only remember this, you come back on your own, I'll not fetch you." That forced her pride up and she couldn't stop walking, not even when she was round the bend, although her step was much slower.

When she was on the bus she just couldn't believe that she was doing this thing, that she was walking out on him, walking out on David. But David wasn't hers any more, he was his. He had claimed David as something apart from Rose Mary.

Her temper had disappeared and she was almost in a state of collapse when she reached the farm. The shock of Rose Mary's disappearance was telling in full force and it had been some time before she had given her mother a coherent picture of what had happened. And then, later, she was further bemused and hurt when Lizzie, of all people, took Corny's side in the matter, because her mother had always had reservations about Corny, but in this case she seemed wholeheartedly for him.

It was only her da's reactions that had soothed her. He didn't blame her, he understood. After talking to Corny on the phone he had put his arm about her and said, "Don't you worry, he'll be along later," and she hadn't answered, "I don't want him to come along later. I don't care if I never see him again," which would have been the expected reaction to a quarrel such as theirs. She had said nothing, she had just waited. She had waited, and waited, and when ten o'clock came, her mother had said, "Go to bed; things will clear themselves to-morrow."

The clock on the landing struck three. She wondered if he was asleep, or was he, too, looking out into the night. She remembered their pact, never to go to sleep on a quarrel. She had the urge to get dressed and fly across the fields, cutting the main roads, by-passing Felling, and running up the lane to the house and hammering on the door. But no, no, if she did that, that would be the end of her, he'd be top dog for life.

By eleven o'clock the following morning the bitterness was high in Mary Ann again. Her da, Michael, and her mother were in the kitchen. It was coffee time, and their Michael, forgetting that she was no longer an impulsive child but the mother of two six-year-old children, was leading off at her, "You know yourself you were always ram-stam, pell-mell, you never stopped to think. Now I know Corny as well as anybody, and if you're going to sit here waiting till he comes crawling back you're going to have corns on your backside."

"Oh, shut up, our Michael. What do you know about it?"

"I know this much. I think Corny's right. I also know that you haven't changed very much over the years. Oppose you in anything and whoof! The balloon goes up."

"That's enough," Mike said sharply, his hand raised. He looked towards Michael as he spoke and made a warning motion with his head.

During the heated conversation Lizzie had said nothing; she just sat sipping her coffee. And so it was she who first heard the car draw up in the roadway. This was nothing unusual, but the next moment a faint and high-pitched cry of "Mam! Mam!" brought her eyes wide, and her head turned to the others, and she cried to Mike, who was now consoling Mary Ann with the theory that Corny was waiting for Rose Mary to arrive and then he'd bring them both across, "Quiet a minute! Listen!" And as they listened there came the call again, nearer now, and the next minute the back door burst open and Rose Mary came flying through the scullery and into the kitchen, and as she threw herself at Mary Ann, Mike cried, "Well, what did I tell you? It was as I said." His face was beaming. Then breaking in on his granddaughter's babbling, he cried, "Where's your dad? Has he gone on the farm?"

"Me dad?" Rose Mary turned her face over her shoulder. "No, Grandad; me dad's back home. Mr. Blenkinsop brought me. He's looking in the cow byres, waitin'."

Mary Ann rose to her feet, and, looking down at Rose Mary, she said quietly, "Mr. Blenkinsop? Why did he bring you here, not home?"

"Me dad asked him, Mam. He did take me home, and me dad said would he drop me over." Rose Mary now glanced about her quickly, and added, "Where's David? Where is he, Mam?"

"David?" There was a quick exchange of glances among the elders, and then Mary Ann said, "Didn't you see David when you went home?"

Rose Mary screwed up her face as she looked up at her mother, and her voice dropped to a low pitch when she said, "No, Mam. David wasn't there. I just got out of the car and me dad said hello and . . . and kissed me; then he asked Mr. Blenkinsop to bring me over 'cos you were here, and I thought David was with you. . . . Isn't he, Mam?"

Mary Ann stood with her head back for a moment, looking over the heads of the others. Her fists were pressed between her breasts, trying to stop this new pain from going deep into the core of her. He had split them up, deliberately split them up, giving her Rose Mary and keeping David; he had not only split the twins, he had split her and him apart, he had rent the family in two. Oh God! She drooped her head slowly now as she heard Mike say, "I'd better go and see this man."

"No. . . . No, leave this to me." She walked stiffly towards the door, and when Rose Mary made to accompany her she said, "Stay with your grannie, I'll be with you in a minute."

She found the American, as she thought of him, talking to Jonesy in the middle of the yard. When she came up to them Jonesy moved away and she said, "Mr. Blenkinsop?"

"Yes, ma'am. Well." He moved his head from side to side. "I don't know how to start my apologies. You must have been worried stiff yesterday."

"Yes, yes I was, Mr. Blenkinsop."

"Well, she's back safe and sound and she's had the time of her life. She floored them all, they went overboard for her, hook, line, and sinker. . . ." His voice trailed away as he stared down at this pocket-sized young woman. There was something here he couldn't get straight. He was quick to sum people up; he had summed her husband up and found him an honest, straightforward young fellow, and also a man who had, you could say, taken to him, but she was a different kettle of fish. She wasn't for him in some ways. The antipathy came to him even though her voice was polite. And there was something else he couldn't get straightened out; the young fellow's attitude had been very strained this morning, he hadn't greeted his daughter with the reception due to her, in fact he had been slightly off-hand. He bent his long length towards Mary Ann and asked her quietly, "Did you mind me keeping the child overnight?"

Mary Ann took a long breath. This man was to be a benefactor, he could make Corny or leave him standing where he was. She should be careful how she answered him about this. But no, she would tell him the truth. "Yes, I did mind, Mr. Blenkinsop. I was nearly demented when Rose Mary was lost and . . . and naturally I wanted her back, but . . . but my husband saw it otherwise. You see, my son hasn't been able to talk, and it's been my husband's theory that he would talk if he was separated from his sister. I've always been against it. Well . . ." She swallowed again. "My husband saw your invitation as a means of keeping them separated for a longer period to . . . to give the boy a chance, as he said. I didn't see it that way. I . . . I was very upset."

Mr. Blenkinsop straightened up and his face was very solemn as he said, "Yes, ma'am. Yes, I can see your point. I can see that you'd be upset. Oh yes." He did not add that he could also see her husband's side of it. It was not use upsetting her still further. "I'm very sorry that I've been the instigator of your worries. I can assure you I wouldn't have enlarged upon them for the world. If only I had known I would have whipped her back here like greased lightning."

Mary Ann's face softened, and she said now, "Thanks. I feel you would have, too."

"I would that. Yes, I would that."

They stood looking at each other for a moment. Then Mr. Blenkinsop said, "Well, I must be on my way, but I'll be seeing you shortly."

"Would you like to stay and have a cup of coffee?"

"No, no thank you, not at the moment. But in the future we'll have odd cups of coffee together no doubt, when the work gets under way." As he turned towards the car he stopped and said, "You're pleased about the factory going up?"

"Yes, oh yes, Mr. Blenkinsop; I'm very pleased."

"Good, good." When he reached the car, he looked over it and said, "Nice little farm you've got here."

"Yes, it's a very nice farm."

"I'd like to come and have a look round some time."

"You'd be very welcome."

"Good-bye, Mrs. Boyle. Please accept my apologies for all this trouble."

"It's quite all right, Mr. Blenkinsop." They nodded to each other, and then she watched him drive away, before slowly walking out of the yard and through the garden to the farmhouse again. As she entered the house Rose Mary's voice came to her, laughter-filled and excited, saying, "Yes, Grandma, I'd have liked to have stayed if David had been there, but I couldn't without David, could I?"

Mary Ann paused in the scullery. She leant against the table and looked down at it. How was she going to explain the situation to Rose Mary? How to tell her that she had to stay here while David remained at home? How? She could put her off for a few hours, but in the end, come this evening, when she knew she wasn't going home she'd have to explain to her in some way. . . . Oh God! Why had this to happen to her, to them all?

11

But before Mary Ann was called upon to explain the situation to Rose Mary she had to explain it to someone else—to Mr. Lord.

It happened round teatime that Rose Mary came running into the house calling, "Mam! Mam!"

"What is it?" Mary Ann came out of the front room, where she had been sitting alone, leaving Lizzie busy in the kitchen. Lizzie had refused her offer of help, and this, more than anything else since she had come home yesterday, had made her feel, and for the first time in her life, a stranger, a visitor in her home. She had gone into the front room and made a valiant effort not to cry. She met Rose Mary in the hall, and again she said, "What is it?"

Rose Mary was gasping with her running. "It's Mr. Lord, Mam. He says you've got to go up."

"Didn't I tell you not to go anywhere near the house? I told you, didn't I? I told you to keep in the yard."

"But I was in the yard, in the far yard, and Mr. Ben, he waved me up the hill. And when I went up he took me in to Mr. Lord, and Mr. Lord asked if you were still here."

Mary Ann lowered her head, then walked slowly into the kitchen and spoke to her mother.

Lizzie was setting the table. She had her back to Mary Ann, and she kept it like that as Mary Ann said, "He knows I'm here; he wants me to go up."

"You should know by now that you can't keep much from him, and you'd better not try to hide anything from him when you see him."

"It's none of his business."

Now Lizzie did turn round, and her look was hard on her daughter as she said, "Your life has always been his business, and I'm surprised you have forgotten that."

Again Mary Ann hung her head, and as she did so she became aware of Rose Mary standing to the side of her, her face troubled, her eyes darting between them.

As she turned away, walking slowly towards the door, Rose Mary said, "Can I come with you, Mam?"

"No, stay where you are."

"Are we going home when you come back?"

Mary Ann didn't answer, but as she went out of the back door she heard her mother's voice speaking soothingly to Rose Mary.

Mary Ann entered Mr. Lord's house by the back door, as she always did, and found Ben sitting at the table, preparing his master's tea, buttering thin slices of brown bread, which he would proceed to roll into little pipes. His veined, bony hands had a perpetual shake about them now; he was the same age as his master but he appeared much older; Ben was running down fast. Mary Ann was quick to notice this, and for a moment she forgot her own troubles and the interview that lay before her, and she spoke softly as she said, "Hello, Ben. How are you?"

"Middling, just middling."

"Is Mrs. Rice off to-day?"

"They're always off. Time off, time off, that's all they think of."

"Shall I take the tray in for you?"

"No, no, I can manage." He looked up at her and, his voice dropping, he said, "He's waitin'."

"Very well." She paused a moment longer and added, "You should stop all this; there's no need for it." She waved her hand over the tray. "There's plenty of others to do this; you should have a rest."

"I'll have all the rest I need shortly."

"Oh, Ben, don't say that."

"Go on, go on. I told you, he's waitin'."

As she went through the hall, with its deep-piled red carpet hushing her step, she wondered what he would do without Ben. Ben had been his right arm, also his whipping post, and his outlet; he'd pine without Ben.

She knocked gently on the drawing-room door, and when she was bidden to enter, the scene was as it always remained in her mind. This room never changed; this was Mr. Lord's room. Tony and Lettice had their own sitting-room. It was modernly furnished and very nice, but this room . . . this room had beauty, and dignity, and it was a setting for the figure sitting in the high-backed chair. There was not beauty about Mr. Lord, except that which accompanies age, but there was dignity. It was in his every moment, every look, every glance, whether harsh or soft.

He turned his head towards Mary Ann. Giving her no greeting, he said, without preamble, "You have to be sent for now?"

She did not answer, but walked to the seat opposite to him and, sitting down, said quietly, "How are you?"

"I'm very well. How are you?"

"All right."

"Then if you're all right you should make your face match your mood."

She stared at him; she had never been able to hide anything from him. She turned her gaze to the side now and looked out of the window; then looking back at him, she said, "Have you heard from Tony and Lettice?"

"Yes, I had a letter this morning. They're enjoying their holiday very much."

"And Peter?"

"I understand that he, too, is enjoying himself."

"You will miss him."

"You have to get used to missing people."

"Yes . . . yes, I suppose so." You have to get used to missing people. Would she ever get used to missing Corny? How was it going to end? What was she going to do? . . .

"Well. Now, you've made all the polite enquiries that are necessary to this meeting, you can tell me why you came yesterday and spent the night alone, without either your husband or children?"

She kept her gaze lowered. It was no use saying who told you I came yesterday. Ben was also Mr. Lord's scout; nothing escaped Ben. He might be old and doddery, but his mind was as alert as his master's. From his kitchen window he looked down on to the farm, and on to the road that led to the farm. Few people came or went without Ben's knowledge.

"Have you and Cornelius quarrelled?"

She still kept her head lowered; she still made no sound.

"Look at me!" Mr. Lord's voice was now harsh and commanding. "Tell me what this is all about?"

She did not look at him, but, as she used to do when a child, she pressed her joined hands between her knees and rocked herself slightly as she said, "Rose Mary got lost yesterday. Me grannie came to visit us and upset her. She hid in the boot of a car belonging to an American, a Mr. Blenkinsop. He didn't discover she was there for a long time. We were all searching when Mr. Blenkinsop phoned to say he had found her and he took her to some friends of his. They live in Doncaster. Then, later, he phoned to ask if she could stay the night." She paused here before going on. "I wanted her brought back straightaway, but Corny said it was all right and she could stay."

"Well, well, go on. He said it was all right; he wouldn't have said that if it wasn't all right. Did he know this man?"

"Yes."

"Well then, there would seem little to worry about. But I take it that you didn't like the fact that Rose Mary wasn't coming back right away and so you got into a paddy."

"It isn't as simple as that. You see . . ." She now looked him full in the face. "Corny has always said that David would talk if they were separated. I have always been against it, and when I came home yesterday, I mean after searching for Rose Mary, he was full of the fact that the boy was talking. It must have been the shock of Rose Mary being lost, and Corny said he would have a better chance if they were kept apart a little longer. I thought it was cruel; I still think it is cruel."

Mr. Lord pressed his head back against the chair and screwed his pale-blue eyes up to pin-points. His lips moved from his teeth and he kept his mouth open awhile before he said, "You mean to say that is the reason you left Cornelius?"

"It sounds so simple saying it, but it wasn't like that."

"Stick to the point, child." He still thought of her as a child. "Your husband wants his son to talk; he feels that if he is separated from his sister he will talk. The opportunity presents itself, and no one is going to be any the worse for the experiment, and you mean to say that you took umbrage at this and came home, and stayed the night away from him, purposely. . . . You mean to tell me that this is what it was all about?"

"I tell you it isn't as simple as all that. . . ."

"It is as simple as all that." He leant towards her. Then, moving his index finger slowly at her, he said, "Now, if you know what's good for you, you will get down to the farm quickly, get your things on and make for home."

Mary Ann straightened herself up. "No, no, I can't."

"You mean you're going to remain stubborn."

"I mean I can't; he saw me coming away and he didn't stop me."

"Well, I should say that is something in his favour. I uphold his action. . . . But tell me. How did Rose Mary come here? Did she come by herself?"

"No, he . . . he sent her with . . . with the American. When Mr. Blenkinsop took her home he asked him to bring her here."

Mr. Lord leant back in his chair again, and after a moment he said, "Do you realize, Mary Ann, that this is serious? Situations like this lead to explosions. Now, you do as I tell you." He did not say take my advice; this was an order. "Get yourself away home this very minute, and try to remember that you're not dealing with a silly boy, but a strong-willed man. I've reason to know the strength of Mr. Cornelius Boyle. Twice in my life I've come up against it. Because he cares for you deeply you might bend his will, but don't try to bend it too far. For, if you do, you'll break yourself and your little family. . . . Come here." He held out his hand and she rose slowly and went to him, and when she stood by his side he took hold of her arm, and, looking up at her, he said, "Don't destroy something good. And you have something good in your marriage. As you know, he wasn't the one I wanted for you, but one learns that one is sometimes wrong. Cornelius is the man for you. Now promise me," he said, "you'll go home."

Mary Ann moved her head from side to side. She pulled in her bottom lip, then muttered under her breath, "I can't, I can't."

With a surprisingly strong and swift movement she was thrust aside, and, his voice angry now, he cried at her, "You're a little fool! Now, I'm warning you. Start learning now before it's too late. If you make him swallow his pride you'll regret it to your dying day, but you'll gain if you swallow yours. Have sense. . . . Go on, get away, get out of my sight."

She got out of his sight. Slowly she closed the door after her and walked through the hall and to the kitchen. There Ben raised his eyes but not his head, and neither of them spoke.

She did not immediately return to the farmhouse but went up a by-lane and stood leaning against the five-barred gate that led into the long field. Her whole being ached. She wanted to cry and cry and cry; she felt lonely, lost and frightened. But she couldn't go back. He had let her come away when he could easily have stopped her if he had wanted to. If he had cared enough he could have stopped her. She had been in paddies before and he had talked her out of them, coaxed her out of them. He had always brought her round, sometimes none too gently. Once he had slapped her behind, as he would a child, because he said she was acting like one. That had made her more wild still. They hadn't spoken for a whole day then, but come night time and in bed his hand had sought hers and she had left it there within his big palm.

But she couldn't go back, she couldn't, because what he had done to her was cruel. She had nearly been demented when Rose Mary was missing, and no matter how much stock he had put on his theory of David talking if they were separated, he should have forgone that, knowing the state she was in, knowing how she longed to see Rose Mary again and to feel that she was really safe. But all he could think about was that he had been right, and David was talking. She was glad, oh yes, she was glad that David was talking; and now once he had started he would go on. There had been no need to keep them apart; no matter what he said there had been no need to do what he had done. He had been cruel, cruel, and she couldn't go back, not . . . not unless he came for her.

12

But Corny did not come for her, and now it was Tuesday and the situation had become terrifying. Her da had been over to the house; Michael had been over to the house; and when they had come back neither of them had said a word, and she had been too proud to ask what had transpired.

Then to-day her mother had been over. She hadn't known she was going; it was the last thing on earth she thought her mother would do, to go and talk to Corny. Now Lizzie was sitting with a cup of tea in her hand and she looked down at it as she said, "You'll have to make the first move."

"What if I don't?"

"Well, that's up to you; it's your life."

"Why should I be the one to make the first move?"

"Because you're in the wrong."

"Oh, Ma!" Mary Ann was on her feet. "You're another one. Everybody's taken his part, everybody. It's fantastic. Nobody sees my side of it and what I went through, what agony I went through when Rose Mary was lost."

"We know all about that." Lizzie took a sip from her cup. "But that's beside the point now; the whole issue, to my mind, is the fact that you've always been against the twins being separated even for a few hours. Now, if you'd only been sensible about that, this whole business would never have happened. And another thing, Corny was absolutely right, the child's really talking. Four days they've been separated and he's chattering away like a magpie." Lizzie now leaned towards Mary Ann and repeated, "Chattering. It's like a small miracle to hear him. And that alone should make you realize that you've been in the wrong, girl."

"All right, all right." Mary Ann flung her arm wide. "He's proved his point, he's right. But that's just the outside of things; there was the way this was done, and the time it was done, and how I felt. Isn't that to be taken into consideration?"

"You're not the only one who's felt like this; I nearly went mad when you were lost, remember. All mothers feel like this."

"Aw, you're twisting it, you won't go deeper. And another thing." Mary Ann bounced her head towards Lizzie now. "You don't want me here. Oh I know, I can tell, but don't worry, you won't have to put up with me much longer, I can get a job anytime."

Lizzie, ignoring the first part of Mary Ann's small tirade, said quietly, "And you'll let Rose Mary go back home?"

"No, I won't."

"Who's keeping them separated now? And that child's fretting. She's hardly eaten a peck in two days; she's got to go back to that boy, not because of him but for her own sake. David's not worrying so much. He asked for her, but that's all. He's as bright as a cricket. Do you know where he was when I got there? Under a car with Corny, and thick with oil, and as happy as a sandboy."

Mary Ann walked towards the window. She wanted to say sarcastically: was Corny as happy as a sandboy too? But she couldn't mention his name. Her mother hadn't said anything about Corny. She was acting like her da, and their Michael, in this. They were all for him. Yes, even her da now. It was fantastic; everybody was for Corny and against her.

She swung round from the window, saying, "Well, I'm not crawling back, Ma, no matter what you say or any of you. As I said, I'll get a job."

As she stumped past her mother on her way across the room to the hall, Lizzie said quietly, "Don't be such a fool, girl. The trouble with you is that you have done the manoeuvring and fixing all your life, so much so, until you've come to think that things have to be done your way or not at all."

"Oh, Ma!" Mary Ann turned an accusing face on Lizzie.

"You can say Oh, Ma! like that, but it's true. Now you've come up against something you can't have fixed on your terms. Corny's a man; he's not your da, or Mr. Lord, or Tony, he's your husband; and he has his rights, and I'm warning you. You try to make him crawl and you'll regret it all your days."

Mary Ann banged the door after her. Her ma had said practically the same words as Mr. Lord. What was the matter with everybody? They were treating her like someone who had committed a crime. She had rights too. Or hadn't she any right to rights? The equality of the sexes. That made you laugh. . . . Bunkum! It was all right on paper, but when it was put into action, look what happened. Everybody took the man's side, even her mother. . . . She couldn't get over that. She could understand her da in a way, him being a man, but her mother! She was for him, up to the neck and beyond. Everybody was for him and against her.

Then the next morning Fanny came.

Mike ushered her in, unexpectedly, through the back door, crying, "Liz! Liz! Look at this stupid, fat old bitch walking all the way up from the bus. Hadn't the sense to let us know she was coming, and we could have picked her up. . . . Get in there with you."

Mary Ann was entering the kitchen from the hall, and she saw her mother rush down the long room and greet Fanny at the scullery door, saying, "Oh, hello there, Fan. Why didn't you tell us?"

"Now, why should I, Lizzie? I've a pair of pins on me yet; and when the doctor said it would do me good to lose some of me fat, do a bit more walking, I said to him, 'Now where the hell do you think I'm going to walk . . . round and round the block?' 'No,' he said; 'get yourself out for a day or so. Take a dander into the country, a bus ride, and then a wee stroll.' I thought to meself at the time that's Mike and Liz getting at him . . . did you get at him?"

Lizzie and Mike were laughing loudly, and they both shook their heads, and Mike said, "No, we didn't get at him. But we wish we had thought of it, if it would have brought you out more often. There, sit yourself down."

He helped her to lower her great fat body into a chair while saying to Rose Mary, "Let her be now. Let her get puff."

Rose Mary, moving aside, looked towards her mother and cried, "Me Great-gran!"

Fanny turned her eyes and looked across the room now towards Mary Ann and said, "That's just in case you can't see me, Mary Ann, just in case."

Mary Ann smiled and came forward and, standing by her friend's side, she said simply, "Hello."

"Hello, hinny." Fanny patted her hand; then asked, "How are you keepin'?"

"All right."

"Good, good." Fanny nodded her head.

Her questions and attitude as yet gave Mary Ann no indication that she knew anything about . . . the trouble, yet it took an event of importance to get Fanny away from the fortress of her home in Mulhattan's Hall, that almost derelict, smelly dark house, divided into flats, one consisting of two rooms in which Fanny had lived since she was married, in which she had brought into the world twelve children, all of whom had gone from her now, some not to return, although they were still living. Jarrow Council had not got down yet to demolishing Burton Street and Mulhattan's Hall, but they would surely come to it before they finished the new Jarrow, and Mary Ann often hoped that Fanny would die before that day, for surely if she didn't she would go when Mulhattan's Hall went.

"Here," said Lizzie; "drink that up."

"And what's this?"

"Don't ask the road you know, get it down you," said Lizzie, speaking brusquely to this old friend of hers; and Fanny, sniffing at the glass, smiled and, looking sideways at Lizzie, said, "Brandy, I'm glad I came." Then, putting the glass to her lips, she threw off the drink at one go, gave a slight shudder, then placed the glass back in Lizzie's hand, saying, "Thanks, lass."

"Look," put in Mike. "Now that you've got this far and we're in this lovely weather why don't you stay for a day or two?"

"Mike, I'm getting the four o'clock bus back. I've said it and that's what I'm going to do. But thanks all the same for the invitation."

"You're a cantankerous old bitch still." He pushed her head none too gently with the flat of his hand, and she retaliated by bringing her hand across his thigh with a resounding wallop. "There," she said. "An' there's more where that comes from. Now get yourself away about your business with your female family, go on."

All except Mary Ann were laughing now, and as Mike made for the door he replied, "Me family's not all females; there's a definite male element in it, and I'm expecting two results of his efforts at any minute now."

"Aw, the poor animals, they don't get away with much, like ourselves. What do you say, Lizzie?"

Lizzie smiled gently as she said, "I'd say, give me your hat and coat now that you've got your breath and get yourself settled in the big chair there." She pointed to Mike's leather chair at the side of the fireplace. "Then you'll have a cup of tea and a bite that'll put you over till dinner time."

If Mary Ann at first had wondered what had brought her friend to the farm, half-an-hour later she was in no doubt whatever, because, of all the topics touched upon, Corny's name or that of David had not been mentioned, and when her mother, holding her hand out towards Rose Mary, said, "I'm going to the dairy, I want some cream. Come along with me," Mary Ann knew that Mrs. McBride was being given the opportunity to voice the real reason for her visit.

Mary Ann was standing at the long kitchen table in the centre of the room preparing a salad, and Fanny was looking at her from out of the depths of the leather chair, and for a full minute after being left alone neither of them spoke, until Fanny said abruptly, "I don't blame you, lass. Don't think that."

Mary Ann turned her head swiftly over her shoulder and looked at this fat, kindly, wise, bigoted, obstinate, and sometimes harsh old woman, and after a pause she asked, "How did you find out?"

"Oh, bad news has the speed of light. I read that somewhere, and it's true. It was last night, comin' out of confession, I met Jimmy's mother. She's got a mouth on her like a whale. She didn't know the real rights of the case, she said, but she said you were gone to your mother's because she was ill, and you had taken the girl with you leavin' the boy behind you. She thought it was a funny thing to do as Jimmy had said you couldn't separate the two with a pair of pliers. What did I think of it, she said. Was it all right between them; they weren't splitting up or anything? I said to her, when I heard that the Holy family was splitting up then I'd know for sure that my grandson and his wife were following suit. . . . But I was worried sick, lass, sick to the soul of me. I knew that something must have happened for you to separate the children, an' so I went along this mornin'."

Mary Ann was standing with her buttocks pressed against the back of the table. She moved her head in small jerks before she said, "You've been home already to-day?"

"Aye, I got there around half-past nine, and, when I got to the bottom of things, let him take what I gave him."

Mary Ann stared at Mrs. McBride, her lower lip hanging loose. Corny was the pride and joy of this old woman's heart. In Mrs. McBride's eyes Corny was all that a man should be, physically, mentally and morally. Her standards might not be those of Olympus but they were high, and she knew what went to make a good man, and she had always considered that her grandson, Corny, had all the ingredients for the pattern in her mind. Yet here she was, against Corny, and the first one to be so.

Everybody had been against her. They had said: You're a fool. It's your temper. It's your stubbornness. You can't have everything your own way, and you've got to realize that. But nobody, up till now, had said that Corny was at fault. Yet here was his grannie shouting him down.

"I told him he was a big empty-headed nowt, and he didn't know which side his bread was buttered, and that if you never went back to him he was only gettin' what he deserved."

"Oh, Mrs. McBride!" It was a mere whisper, and Mary Ann's head drooped as she spoke.

"Well!" Fanny was sitting upright now, as upright as her fat would allow. "When he told me what it was all about I nearly went straight through the roof. A man! I said. You call yourself a man, and you take the pip at a thing like that. Just because she expresses her opinion you go off the deep end?"

Mary Ann raised her head slightly. "I . . . I said things I shouldn't have, Mrs. McBride; he's . . . he's not altogether to blame. I . . . I said I hated him."

"Aw!" Mrs. McBride pushed her fat round in the chair until she was half-turned away from Mary Ann, and, looking into the empty fireplace, she thrust her arm out and flapped her hand towards Mary Ann as she cried, "Aw, if a man is going to let his wife walk out on him because she says she hates him, then every other house in the land would be empty. I've never heard anything so childish in me life. Hate him! I'd like a penny for every time I've said I hated McBride. And mind . . ." She twisted herself round again in Mary Ann's direction, and, her arm again extended and her fingers wagging, she said, "I always accompanied me words with something concrete, the frying pan, the flat iron, a bottle, anything that came to hand. You know me big black broth pan, the one I can hardly lift off the hob when it's full? I can just about manage it when it's empty. Well, I remember the day as if it was yesterday that I hurled it at his head, and I used those very words to give it God speed: I hate you. And I didn't say them plain and unadorned, if you get what I mean; I always made me remarks to McBride a bit flowery. Be god!" She moved her triple chins from one shoulder to the other. "If that pan had found its target that particular day it would have been good-bye to McBride twenty years earlier. Aw! Me aim was poor that time. An' it was likely because I was carryin'. I gave birth to me twins three days later. One of them died, the other one is Georgie, you know."

Mary Ann wanted to smile; she wanted to laugh; she wanted to cry; oh, how she wanted to cry.

"Come here," said Fanny gently. "Come here." And Mary Ann went to her, and Fanny put her arms round her waist and said, "I'm upset to me very soul. He's as near to me as the blood pumping out of me heart, but at the same time I'm not for him. No, begod! The way I see it is, he was given a pot of gold and he's acted as if it was a holey bucket picked up off a midden. He let you walk away . . . just like that." She made a slow gliding movement with her hand.

"B . . . b . . . but, Mrs. McBride. . . ."

"Oh, I don't blame you for walkin' out, I don't blame you, not a jot, lass. You've got to make a stand with them or your life's simply hell. Even when you do make a stand it isn't easy, but if you let them walk over you you might as well go straight to the priest and arrange for a requiem to be said, because your time's short. You can bank on that."

Mary Ann stood quietly now, fondling the creased and not over-clean hand as she asked, "How was he? And David?"

"Oh, a bit peakish-looking about the gills. They all get very sorry for themselves. He'd been having his work cut out getting the breakfast ready; the place was strewn with dishes. Hell's cure to you, I said. You're just gettin' what you deserve. But David, he was sprightly. He speaks now. I got the gliff of me life."

Mary Ann's hand stopped moving over Mrs. McBride. "It was about that that all the trouble started."

"About David talkin', you mean?"

"Yes, Corny had said that if they were separated David would talk. . . . Well he's been proved right, hasn't he?"

"Nonsense, nonsense. It was the scare he got when Rose Mary was lost that made him talk, not the separation."

"Yes, I know. But Corny thought that if they came together too quickly that David wouldn't make any more effort. And I can see his point, I can, Mrs. McBride, but——"

"Now don't you go soft, girl. No matter what points you see, don't you go soft, because you'll have to pay for it in the end. He's a big, ignorant, empty-headed nowt, as I told him, an' I should know because he's inherited a lot of meself." She nodded at Mary Ann, and Mary Ann was forced to smile just the slightest.

It was funny about people. They never acted as you expected them to. She had really been afraid of Mrs. McBride finding out and going for her, and yet here she was taking her part. She bent down swiftly and kissed the flabby, wrinkled face, and Fanny held her and said, "There now. There now. Now don't cry, he's not worth it. Although it's meself that's sayin' it, he's not worth it."

At the same time, deep in her heart, Fanny was praying, "God forgive me. God forgive me for every word I've uttered against him in these last few minutes."

It was the evening of the same day, when Mary Ann was in the bathroom bathing Rose Mary, when she heard the car stop in the lane outside the front door. Rose Mary, too, heard it, and she looked up at her mother and said, "There's a car, Mam."

Mary Ann's heart began to pound and she had trouble in controlling her voice as she said, "Come on, get out and get dried."

"Mam." Rose Mary hugged the towel around her. "Do you think it'll be me . . . ?"

"Get dried and put your nightie on. Come on. Here, sit on the cracket and give me your feet." She rubbed Rose Mary's feet vigorously; she rubbed her back, and her chest. She had put her nightdress on and combed her hair when the bathroom door was pushed open and Lizzie stood there, saying, "You'd better come down; there's an assortment down there wanting to see you."

Mary Ann's eyes widened. "An assortment? Who? What?"

"Well, come and see for yourself. Five of them, headed by that Jimmy from the garage."

A cold wave of disappointment swept through her, making her shiver.

"What do they want?" she said.

"You, apparently."

"Me! What do they want with me?"

"You'd better come down and see."

"Can I come, Mam?"

"No, stay where you are. Go and get into bed."

"But, Mam."

"Get into bed, Rose Mary."

She turned from her daughter and passed her mother; then ran down the stairs and to the front door. And it was as Lizzie had said, it was an assortment that stood on the front lawn facing her.

She knew for certain that Jimmy was a boy, but she had first of all to guess at the sex of the other four. True they were wearing trousers, but there ended any indication of their maleness, for they were also wearing an assortment of blouses, one with a ruffle at the neck; their hair was long and ranged from starling blond to tow colour, from dead brown to a horrible ginger. There wasn't a hair to be seen on their faces, nor yet on what skin was showing of their arms. The sight of them repulsed Mary Ann and made her stomach heave. She turned her attention pointedly to Jimmy, and noticed in this moment that although his hair, too, was longish, his maleness stood out from that of his pals like a sore finger.

Jimmy grinned at her. "Hello, Mrs. Boyle," he said.

"What do you want, Jimmy?" Mary Ann's tone was curt.

"Aw, I just thought I'd pop along and see you. You know, about . . . about the lines you did. You know."

"Oh!" Mary Ann closed her eyes for a moment and wet her lips. She had forgotten about the lines. She wanted to say, "Look, I'm not interested any more," but Jimmy's bright expression prevented her from flattening him with such a remark.

"These are me pals . . . the Group. This is Duke." He thumbed towards the repulsive, red-haired individual. "He runs us and he's good at tunes. I was tellin' you." He nodded twice, then thumbed towards the next boy. "This is Barney. He's on the drums." Barney was the tow-haired one. He was also the one with the ruffle. He opened his mouth wide and smiled at Mary Ann. She had never seen such a big mouth on a boy before. It seemed to split his face in two. She turned her eyes to the next boy as Jimmy said, "This is Poodle Patter. We call him that 'cos he's good at ad lib, small talk you know, keeping things goin'. Aren't you, Poodle?"

Poodle jerked his head at Mary Ann, and a ripple passed over his face. It was an expression of self-satisfaction and had no connection whatever with a pleased-to-meet-you expression.

Mary Ann stared at Poodle, at his startlingly blond hair, and she had to stop her nose from wrinkling in this case.

"And he's Dave." Jimmy thumbed towards the back of the group, where stood the brown-haired individual. He had small merry eyes and a thin mouth, and he nodded to Mary Ann and said, "Wat-cher!"

"Dave plays the guitar, and he can do the mouth-organ."

Jimmy jerked his head towards Dave, and Dave jerked his head back at him, and they exchanged grins.

Mary Ann was tired; she was weary with worry; she was sick at this moment with disappointment; she had thought, oh, she had thought that Corny had come for her; and now she was sick in another way as she looked at these four boys. Jimmy didn't make her sick, he only irritated her. She said to him, "Look, Jimmy, I'm very busy. What do you want?"

Jimmy's long face lengthened; his eyebrows went up and his lower lip went down, and he said, "Well, like I said, about your lyrics. Duke's put a tune to them."

"Oh!"

"Haven't you, Duke?"

Duke now stepped forward. He had an insolent walk; he had an insolent look; and he spread his look all over Mary Ann before he said, "It was ropey in parts."

"What was?"

"Well, that stuff you did. The title's all right, and the punch line, 'She acts like a woman,' but the bit about not wantin' diamonds and mink, well, that isn't with it, not the day. They don't expect them things. A drink, aye, but not the other jollop."

"No?" The syllable sounded aggressive, even to Mary Ann herself.

"No! Not the teenagers don't. Who's going to buy them furs an' rings and things, eh? Unless a fellow hits the jackpot he can just scramble by by hisself." Duke now wrinkled his nose as if from a bad smell. "Aw, it's old fashioned. Ten years, even twenty behind the times. But I've left it in about the rings. But they don't talk like you wrote it any more; still the way I've worked it, it'll come over."

"Thank you."

"The pleasure's mine."

Mary Ann's jaw tightened. They don't talk like you wrote it any more. How old did he think she was, forty?

"Well, how do they talk?" The aggressive note was still there.

"Huh!" Duke laughed, then slanted his eyes around his mates, and they all joined in, with the exception of Jimmy, for Jimmy was looking at the bad weather signs coming from Mrs Boyle. He knew Mrs. Boyle's bad weather signs.

"Want me to tell you?"

Before Mary Ann could answer Jimmy put in, "Aw, give over, Duke. You know you like it; you said it had it, especially that line."

"Oh aye, I've just said, that's a punch line: 'She acts like a woman.' But the rest . . . aw it's old men's stuff . . . Bob Hope, Bing Crosby."

"Well, there's nothing more to be said, is there?" Mary Ann had a great desire to reach out and slap his face. She turned quickly away. But as she did so Jimmy put his hand out towards her, saying, "Aw, Mrs. Boyle, that's just him. Don't take any notice; he's always like this. But he likes it, he does." He turned his head over his shoulder and said to Duke "Come off it, Duke, an' tell her you think it's good. We all think it's good." He swung his gaze over the rest of them, and the other three boys nodded and spoke together, and the gist was that they thought the lyrics fine and with it, just a word had needed altering here and there.

"You see." Jimmy nodded at Mary Ann. "Would you like to hear it?"

"No, Jimmy." Mary Ann's tone was modified now, and she added swiftly, "I'm . . . I'm busy."

"Aw, come on, Mrs. Boyle; that's what we've come out for, to let you hear it. And then if you think it's all right we was goin' to try it out at 'The Well' on Saturday night. An' you never know, there's always scouts hanging round an' they might pick it up."

Mary Ann looked from Jimmy to Duke, and back to Jimmy, and she said, stiffly now "That wasn't my idea; I thought it could be sent away to——"

"You do what you like, missus," Duke put in, shaking his head vigorously, "but if you send it away that's the last you'll hear of it, until you recognize snatches of the tune on the telly and hear your words all mixed up. You send it away if you like, but it's as Jimmy says there are scouts kickin' around, on the look-out for punch lines, an' you've got one here, 'She acts like a woman'. It's got a two-fold attraction; it'll appeal to the old dames over twenty, and make the young 'uns think they're grown up. See what I mean?" Duke was speaking ordinarily now, and Mary Ann nodded and said, flatly, "Yes, I suppose you're right." But she wished they would get themselves away. She was still feeling sick with disappointment. She wanted to be alone and cry. Oh, how she wanted to cry at this minute. What was she standing here for anyway? As long as she remained they wouldn't budge. She was turning round when Jimmy pleaded, "Will you listen to it, then?" His face was one big appeal, and before Mary Ann could answer, and without taking his eyes off her, he said, "Get the kit out."

The four boys stared at Mary Ann for a minute, then turned nonchalantly about and went towards the car, and Mary Ann, looking helplessly at Jimmy, said, "Where are they going to do it?"

"Why, here." Jimmy spread his hands. "We can play anywhere."

Mary Ann cast a glance over her shoulder. There was only her mother in the house; her da and their Michael were still on the farm; they were having a bit of trouble getting a cow to calve. If they had been indoors she would have said a firm no to any demonstration, but now she just stood and looked at Jimmy, then from him to where the boys were hauling their instruments out of the car.

Jimmy brought his attention back to her when he said, softly, "I miss you back at the house, Mrs. Boyle."

She looked at his straight face and it was all she could do not to burst into tears right there.

"It isn't the same."

"Be quiet, Jimmy."

It was no use trying to hoodwink Jimmy by telling him she was staying with her mother because she was sick, or some such tale, for behind Jimmy's comic expression Mary Ann now felt, as Corny had always pointed out, there was a serious side, a knowing side. Jimmy wasn't as soppy as he made himself out to be. Even a few minutes ago, when he had pointed to Duke as the leader of the group, she felt that whatever brains were needed to guide this odd assortment it was he who supplied them.

The boys came back up the path, and one of them handed a guitar to Jimmy; then, grouping themselves, they faced her and, seemingly picking up an invisible sign, they all started together. There followed a blast of sound, a combination of instruments and voices that was deafening.

SHE ACTS LIKE A WOMAN
SHE ACTS LIKE A WOMAN

Mary Ann screwed up her face against the noise. She watched the fair-haired boy, Poodle Patter as Jimmy had called him, his head back, wobbling on the last word: WOOMA . . . AN. This was followed by a number of chords, and then they all started again.

MAN, I'M TELLING YOU.
SHE ACTS LIKE A WOMAN.

SHE PELTED ME WITH THINGS,
AND THEN SHE TORE HER HAIR.

SHE ACTS LIKE A WOMAN.

I'VE GIVEN HER MY LOT,
NOW I WAS FINISHED, BROKE,
AND THEN SHE SPOKE OF LOVE.

SHE ACTS LIKE A WOMAN.

ME, SHE SAID, SHE WANTED,
NOT RINGS OR THINGS.

SHE ACTS LIKE A WOMAN.

MAN, I JUST SPREAD MY HANDS.
WHAT WAS I TO DO?
YOU TELL ME,
WHAT WAS I TO DO?
EARLY MORNING THERE SHE STOOD,
NO MAKE-UP FACE LIKE MUD,
BIG EYES RAINING TEARS AND FEARS.

SHE ACTS LIKE A WOMAN.

THEN, MAN, SOMETHING MOVED IN HERE,
LIKE DAYLIGHT,
AND I COULD SEE SHE ONLY WANTED M-EE.

SHE ACTS LIKE A WOOO-MA-AN.

As the voices trailed off the last word and all the hands crashed out the last note, Mary Ann gaped at the five boys, and they stood in silence waiting. For a brief second she forgot her misery. It had sounded grand, excellent, as good as anything that was on the pops. He was clever. She looked directly at Duke and said what she thought.

"I think you've made a splendid job of it, the way you've arranged the words and brought out that line. I think it's grand."

All the faces before her were expanding now into wide, pleased grins. Even Duke's cockiness was lost under the outward sign of his pleasure, when, at that moment, round the corner of the house, came Mike. He came like a bolt of thunder.

"What the hell do you think you're up to! What's this?"

After the words had crashed about them they all turned and looked at the big fellow who was coming towards them, his step slower now, his face showing an expression of sheer incredulity. They stood silent as he eyed them from head to toe, one after the other. Then, his voice exploding again, he cried, "What the hell are you lot doing here? Who's dug you up?"

"Da . . . Da, this is Jimmy. You know Jimmy."

Mike turned his eyes towards Jimmy; then returned them slowly back to the other four as Mary Ann went on hastily, "They are Jimmy's Group; they've . . ." She paused. How to say they had set some of her words to music; this wasn't the time. "They had a tune they thought I . . . I would like to hear."

"THEY . . . HAD . . . A . . . TUNE they thought you'd like to hear? Have you gone barmy, girl? You call that noise a tune? It's nearly put the finishing touches to Freda."

"Then Freda isn't with it, is she, Mister?" This was Duke speaking. His tone was insolent and brought Mike swinging round to him. "Freda's more with it than you, young fellow, if that is what you are, which I doubt very much. Freda's only a cow, a sick cow at the present moment, but I wouldn't swap her for the lot of you."

The four boys stared back at Mike, their faces expressionless. It was a tense moment, until the fair-haired boy, Poodle Patter, asked quietly, "What she sick with, Mister?"

"She's trying to calve, but you lot wouldn't understand anything about that, being neither one thing nor the other."

Again there was a silence, during which Mary Ann's hand went out towards Mike. But she didn't touch him; she was afraid she might explode something here, for she could see him tearing his one arm from her grasp and knocking them down like ninepins.

"You'd be surprised." This calm rejoinder came from Duke. "As me dad says, ministers wear frocks but they still manage to be fathers."

Mike and Duke surveyed each other for a moment. Then Mike, his lips hardly moving, said, "Get yourselves out! An' quick."

For answer, Duke lifted one shoulder and turned about, and the others followed suit, Jimmy coming up in the rear. As they neared the gate Poodle stopped, swung round, and, his face wearing a most innocent expression, addressed Mike, calling up the path to him, "Can you tell me, Mister, if the caps are put on the milk bottles after the cows lay them, or do they all come through sealed up?"

Mary Ann's two hands now flashed out and caught Mike's sleeve, and she begged softly under her breath, "Da! Da! Don't, please."

Outside the gate and standing near the car, Duke turned again and looked up towards Mike, and he called in a loud voice now, "If you'd started anything, old 'un, you'd have come off second best, an' if you hadn't been a cripple with only one hand I wouldn't have let you get away with half what you did. But don't try it on again."

Mary Ann leant back and hung on to Mike now, and as she did so Lizzie and Michael appeared at the other side of him, and Lizzie said, tersely, "Let them go. Let them go. Come on, get yourself inside." They pulled him around and almost dragged him indoors.

Neither of them had said a word to Mary Ann, and she stood leaning against the stanchion of the door, looking at the car, waiting for it to go, and as she watched she saw Jimmy spring out and come up to the path again. And this brought her agitatedly from the doorway and hastily towards him, crying under her breath, "Get yourself away; get them out of this."

"All right, all right, Mrs. Boyle; they'll do nothin'. I'm sorry about all this, but you see I didn't only come about the tune, there . . . there was something else. It was . . . well, I won't be seeing you again, I don't suppose. That's what I meant to say first of all."

Mary Ann shook her head, and the boy went on, "You see, I'm leavin'."

Mary Ann forced herself to say, "I'm sorry," and was about to add yet again, "Get yourself and that crowd away," when Jimmy put in, "So am I, but with the boss s . . . sellin' up. . . ."

"What! What did you say?" She put her hand out towards him as if she was going to grab the lapel of his coat. Then she closed her fist and pressed it into her other hand and almost whimpered, "Selling up. What do you mean?"

"Well, that's what I came about. You see, I think the boss is goner sell out to Mr. Blenkinsop. He wouldn't sell out to Riley, 'cos he doesn't like Mr. Riley, does he? But . . . but I think he'll sell out to the American. And I wouldn't want to stay if the boss wasn't there, so I'm lookin' out for another job. . . ."

"Who . . . who told you this?"

"Oh. Well, you know me; I keep me ears open, Mrs. Boyle." He stared at her, his long face unsmiling. "It's awful back there without you. An' I don't think the boss can stick it, that's why he's goin' I suppose."

There was a loud concerted call from the car now, and Jimmy said, "I'll have to be off, but . . . but that's really what I came about. Bye, Mrs. Boyle."

She nodded at him and then said under her breath, "Good-bye, Jimmy."

She watched the car move away in a cloud of black smoke from the exhaust, and when it was out of sight she still stood where Jimmy had left her. It was many, many years since she had experienced the feeling of utter despair, and then it had been her da who had evoked that feeling in her. Yet she could recall that her despair in the past had always been threaded with hope, hope that something nice would happen to her da. And nice things had happened to her da. Bad things had also happened to him, but in the main they were nice things that had happened. He stood where he was to-day because of the nice things she had wished and prayed would happen to him. She had always worked at her wishing and her praying—she had never let God get on with it alone—and so her da had made good.

But now she had reached a point in her existence where the main issue was not somebody else's life but her own; she could see her life disintegrating, crumbling away before her eyes. How had it started? How had this situation come about? How did all such situations come about but by little things piling on little things. One stick, one straw, one piece of wood, all entwined; another stick, another straw, another piece of wood, and soon you had a little dam; and a little dam grew with every layer until it stretched across the river of your life and you were cut off, cut off from the other part of you, that part of you that held your heart, and, in her case, cut off from her own flesh and blood, from her son. But the son, in this moment, was a secondary loss; it was the father she was thinking about; Corny was going to sell up. He had stood fast from the beginning; he had bought the garage in the face of opposition. Everybody had said he had been done. Four thousand for a place like that! He must have been bonkers, was the general opinion. Oh yes, it would be a good thing if the road went through, but would it go through? Corny had held on, held on to the threadbare hope of the road going through. And the road hadn't gone through, yet still he had held on. Something would turn up, something; he knew it would. She could feel him stroking her hair in the darkness of the night, talking faith into himself, recharging himself for another day. "You'll see, Mary Ann, you'll see. Something'll turn up, and then I'll make it all up to you. I'll buy you the biggest car you ever saw. I'll have the house rebuilt; you'll have so many new clothes that Lettice will think she's a rag-woman." Corny, in the dark of the night, talking faith into himself and her. And now he was going to sell up. He couldn't, he couldn't.

"What's come over you?"

Mary Ann turned and looked up the path to where Michael was standing in the doorway, so like his father that he could be his young brother. She did not answer him but walked towards him, her face grim with the defiance his tone had evoked in her.

"How in the name of God have you got yourself mixed up with that lot?"

"I'm not mixed up with that lot; I've never seen them in my life before, except Jimmy."

She glared at him as she passed him, and she was going across the hall when his voice came to her, softly now, saying, "You take my advice and get yourself off home this very minute. Don't be such a blasted little fool."

"You mind your own business, our Michael. You're so blooming smug you make me sick."

"And you're so blooming pig-headed you're messing up your life. Corny is right in the stand he's taking. Everybody is with him."

She was at the foot of the stairs now, and she turned to face him, crying, "I don't care if the whole world is with him. I don't need your sympathy or anybody else's. I can stand on my own feet. And you mind your own business and gather all your own forces to run your own life. You're not dead yet; you may have a long way to go, so don't crow."

She was at the top of the stairs when Michael's voice came from the foot, crying at her, "Who's crowing? Be your age, and stop acting like little Mary Ann Shaughnessy."

As Mary Ann burst into her room she heard her mother's voice crying, "Michael!" and his voice trailing away, saying, "Aw well, somebody's got to. . . ."

And then she was brought to a stop by the sight of Rose Mary standing near the window. She was looking straight at her, her face tear-stained and her lips trembling. "I saw Jimmy, Mam," she said.

"Get into bed. I told you to get into bed."

"I want to go back home, Mam."

"Get into bed, Rose Mary."

"I want our David, Mam, and me dad. I miss them. I miss our David, Mam."

"Rose Mary, what did I say?"

"Could I just go over the morrow and——"

Mary Ann's hand came none too gently across Rose Mary's buttocks, and Rose Mary let out a loud cry, and when the hand came again she let out another. A minute later the door burst open and there stood Lizzie.

"You've got no need to take it out of the child. Michael was right; you've got to come to your senses. And don't you smack her again; she's done nothing. The only thing she wants is to go home to her father and her brother."

"She happens to be my child, Mother." Mary Ann always addressed Lizzie as mother in times of stress. "And I'll do what I like with her, as you did with me."

"Well, you smack her again if you dare!" Lizzie's face was dark with temper, and Mary Ann's equally so as she snapped back, "I'll smack her when I like. She happens to be mine, and I'll thank you not to interfere. And I'd better inform you now that this is the last night you'll have to give me shelter; I'm going to find a place for us both to-morrow."

"You're mad, girl, that's what you are, mad. It's a pity Corny didn't use his hands on you and beat some sense into you. He's slipped up somewhere."

The door banged and Mary Ann turned slowly round to see her daughter sitting up in bed, her face puckered, her arms held out towards her, and, rushing to her, she hugged her to her breast. Then throwing herself on the bed, she cradled the child in her arms and they both cried together.

13

The following morning Mary Ann went to Newcastle, and she took Rose Mary with her. Lizzie had shed tears in front of her before she left the house, saying, "Don't be silly, lass, don't be silly. We've all said things we're sorry for, but it's just because we're all concerned for you."

She had replied to her mother, "It's all right, it's all right, I know." She had sounded very subdued, and she was very subdued. Inside, she felt lifeless, half dead. She left Lizzie with the impression that she was going after a job, and she was, but it wasn't the real reason for her visit to Newcastle.

First, she must go and see Mr. Quinton. It was many years since she had seen Bob Quinton. At different periods in her life he had loomed large, and when he appeared on her horizon it had always spelt trouble, mostly for her da, because her da had thought Mr. Quinton wanted her ma, and he had at one time. But all that was in the past. She was going to Mr. Quinton now to ask him how she could get in touch with Mr. Blenkinsop.

Mary Ann was not shown into Mr. Quinton's presence immediately. The girl in the enquiries office wanted to know her business, and when she said it was private, the girl stared at her, then she took her time before she lifted the receiver and began to speak.

Mary Ann's spirits were so low at this moment that she couldn't take offence.

When the girl stopped speaking she looked up at Mary Ann and said, "Miss Taylor will see if he's in; you had better take a seat."

Mary Ann had hardly sat herself down and pulled Rose Mary's coat straight when the phone rang again, and the girl, looking up, said, "He'll see you."

It was almost at the same moment that Mary Ann heard a remembered voice coming from the adjoining room. The intersecting door was opened by a woman, and, behind her, appeared Mr. Quinton. "Well, hello, Mary Ann." He held out his hand as he crossed towards her.

"Hello, Mr. Quinton."

"Oh, it is good to see you. It's years since I clapped eyes on you." He held on to her hand. "And this, I bet, is Rose Mary. When was it I last saw her?" He bent down to Rose Mary. "When was it when I last saw you?" He chucked her under the chin. "At your christening, I think."

"That's right," said Mary Ann.

"Come on, come in." He pushed them both before him, past the staring young lady at the desk, and the smiling elderly secretary, through the secretary's office and into a third room.

"Sit yourself down." He stood back from her and looked at her. "You haven't altered a scrap. You know, you never age, Mary Ann."

"Aw, I wish you were speaking the truth." She moved her head sadly. "I feel an old woman at this moment."

"Old woman? Nonsense." He waved his hand at her and pulled his chair from behind the desk to the side of it, so that he was near to her, and he sat looking at her hard before he asked quietly, "How's Lizzie?"

"Oh, she's fine."

"And Mike?"

"He's fine, too."

"And how's that big fellow of yours?"

Mary Ann's face became stiff for a moment, and then she said, "Oh, he's quite well."

Bob Quinton stared at her; then he looked at the child and smiled widely, and put out his hand once again and chucked her chin. And Rose Mary giggled just a little bit.

"Mr. Quinton, I've come to ask you if you could give me Mr. Blenkinsop's address. I . . . I understand you're going to build his factory for him?"

"Yes, I am, I'm very pleased to say." He bent his body in a deep bow towards her. "It's a very big contract."

"Yes." Mary Ann nodded.

"And you want his address?"

"Yes, please. If you would."

Bob Quinton narrowed his eyes at Mary Ann. There was something here that wasn't quite right. He had heard from Blenkinsop that he was putting the petrol side of the business in young Boyle's hands. He had intended to pay him a visit this very morning and congratulate him, yet here was his wife looking for Mr. Blenkinsop on the side. Why hadn't she asked Corny for the address? Mary Ann was a fixer; she had fixed so many people's lives that at one time he had attributed to her special powers. But the powers she had possessed were of innocence, the power attached to love, the great love that she bore her father. Yet the Mary Ann sitting before him now looked deflated, sort of lost. She didn't look possessed of any special power. He glanced at the child again; then, getting to his feet, he said, "What about a cup of coffee, eh? You'd like one?"

"I would, thank you." Mary Ann nodded at him.

"And milk for this lady?" He tugged gently at Rose Mary's hair.

"If you please," said Mary Ann.

"Come along. No, I don't mean you." He flapped his hand at Mary Ann. "I mean this young lady. She'll have to go and help Mrs. Morton fetch it."

He pulled open the office door and said, "Mrs. Morton, do you think you could take this young lady over to Simpson's and bring a tray of coffee?" Then leaning over towards his secretary, he said softly, "I would ask Miss Jennings to do it but I don't think I can trust her to bring the coffee and the child both back safely. What do you say?"

Mrs. Morton gave him a tight smile. Then, holding her hand out to Rose Mary, she said,

"Come along, my dear."

Rose Mary hesitated and looked through the door towards her mother. And when she saw Mary Ann nod her head she gave her hand to the secretary.

Back in the room, Bob Quinton resumed his seat, and, bending towards Mary Ann, one elbow on his knee, he held out his hand, palm upwards, saying, "Come on, spit it out. What's the trouble?"

"Oh." Mary Ann looked away from him. "Corny. Corny and I have had a bit of a disagreement."

"Corny?" Although he had wondered why she hadn't asked Corny for Mr. Blenkinsop's address he hadn't, for a moment, thought the trouble was with him. Her da again, yes, because Mike, being Mike, was unpredictable. There had been some talk years ago about him carrying on with a young girl. But Mary Ann having trouble with Corny. Why? He understood they were crazy about each other. He remembered Corny from far back when, as a boy, Mary Ann had championed him. Surely nothing could go wrong between those two. But things did go wrong between people who loved each other. He had only to look at his own life. He said gently, "You and Corny . . . I can't take that in, Mary Ann."

"Nor can I." There were tears in her eyes.

"A woman?"

"Oh, no, no!" She sounded for a moment like the old spirited Mary Ann, and he smiled at her, then said, "What then?"

"Oh, it started with the children."

"The children?"

She nodded. Then, haltingly, she gave him a brief outline of what had happened, and finished with, "I heard yesterday he's going to sell out to Mr. Blenkinsop, and he mustn't do it, Mr. Quinton, he mustn't. He's worked and slaved, he's lived just to make the place pay, and now it's in his hands and it's going to be a big thing he's going to sell up."

"Well, you know, Mary Ann, I think the cure lies with you. You could stop all this by going back."

Mary Ann straightened her shoulders and leant her back against the chair, and then she said sadly, "He doesn't want me any more. If he had wanted me badly he would have come and fetched me."

"Aw! Aw! Mary Ann." Bob Quinton rose to his feet and flapped his hands in the air as if wafting flies away. "A woman's point of view again. Aw! Aw! Mary Ann. The medieval approach . . . is that what you want?"

"No. No, you misunderstand me."

"No, I don't. I don't. But you, above all people, I would have thought would have tackled this situation with reason. You, who have patched up so many lives, are now quite willing to sit back and watch your own be smashed up on an issue of chivalry, because that's what it amounts to."

"Oh no, it doesn't, Mr. Quinton." Mary Ann shook her head widely. "You're misconstruing everything; in fact, you're just like all the others."

"What, has your da said something similar, and your mother?"

"Everybody has."

"Well, I think they're right. But look; the time's going on and the child will be back in a moment. What do you want to see Mr. Blenkinsop for? To ask him not to buy Corny out?"

"Yes, that's it."

"Well, have you thought of the possibility that if he doesn't sell to him he'll sell to someone else?"

"Yes, I have. But . . . but if Mr. Blenkinsop makes it clear that he doesn't want to buy and that he won't give the business to anyone else if Corny goes then there'll be no point, will there, because he won't get very much for it as it stands, just what we paid. And we've hardly paid anything off the mortgage—you don't in the first few years, do you?"

A slow smile spread across Bob Quinton's face, and he moved his head from side to side as he said, "I'm glad to see that little scheming brain of yours can still work. And now it's my turn to act fairy godmother in a small way, because I'm meeting Mr. Blenkinsop in exactly"—he looked down at his watch—"twenty-five minutes from now. He's picking me up and we're going round the site. You know, I intended to look in on you to-day. . . . Ah, here they come with the coffee." He went swiftly towards the door and took the tray from his secretary. "And cakes! Who likes cakes with cream on?"

"I do."

Bob Quinton looked down towards Rose Mary as his secretary said, "She picked them."

"Well, she'll have to eat them," said Bob, laughing.

"I can't eat all the six. Anyway, Mam only lets me have one." Rose Mary smiled towards her mother. Then, still looking at her, she added, "But I could take one in a bag for David, couldn't I, Mam?"

"Rose Mary! said Mary Ann chidingly, and Rose Mary bowed her head.

It was half an hour later, and Mary Ann was sitting in the same chair, looking at Mr. Blenkinsop, and Mr. Blenkinsop was looking at her, and a heavy silence had fallen on them. They had the office to themselves, for Bob Quinton had thoughtfully conducted Rose Mary to the next room.

Mr. Blenkinsop now blinked rapidly, placed his hands together as if in prayer, then rubbed the palms one against the other before he said, "How did you come to know that I was going to buy your husband out?"

"Jimmy . . . our boy, he came round last night to the farm and told me. He . . . he thought I should know."

"Jimmy." Mr. Blenkinsop's lips were pursed, then again he said, "Jimmy." And now his eyes rolled back and he inspected a corner of the ceiling for a moment before saying, "Well, well!" Then, rising from his chair, he walked about the room. When he came to a standstill, he said, "And you don't want your husband to sell?"

"No." She screwed her head round. "He's worked so hard, and he's doing it because . . . well, of what I told you . . . the trouble between us."

"He's a fool."

"What!"

Mr. Blenkinsop walked round to face Mary Ann. "I said he's a fool. He shouldn't put up with this situation; he should have gone to the farm and picked you up and taken you home and spanked you."

"You think he should?" Mary Ann smiled a weak smile.

"I do."

"You don't think I should have gone crawling back?"

"He shouldn't have given you time to do anything; he should have followed you straightaway, got you by the scruff of the neck and yanked you home." He was smiling as he spoke, and Mary Ann, swallowing deeply, said, "You know, Mr. Blenkinsop, you're the only one who has said that, except . . . except his grannie. Everybody else seems to think that I should have gone back on my own."

"We . . . ell." He drew out the word. "Perhaps I'm used to dealing with American women, but under the same circumstances if their man hadn't come haring after them and grabbed them up and yanked them home. . . . We . . . ell."

"That's what a man would do if he cared for a woman, wouldn't he, Mr. Blenkinsop?"

"Yes. Yes." Mr. Blenkinsop suddenly stopped in his walking again. Then, thrusting his neck out and bringing his head down, he said, "Ah, no. Hold it a minute. Don't let's jump to conclusions. I'm saying that's what men should do, but we're talking about your man, and if he didn't do that then there's a very good reason for it. I've a very high opinion of your husband, Mrs. Boyle. I haven't known him very long but I take him to be a man of his word, a man of strong character, an honest man. Now a man with these characteristics doesn't stay put for nothing. Is there something more in it than what you've told me, eh?"

Mary Ann lowered her head. "Perhaps. It's a long story. It's got to do with the children. You see, he's always maintained that David would talk if they were separated, I think I told you. He's been on like this for a couple of years now. And Rose Mary getting lost proved him right, and we quarrelled, and I said something to him I shouldn't have done. It's that I think that has prevented him from coming to me."

"Ah, well now, if you know that you've put a stumbling block in the way of him coming for you, it's up to you to remove it, isn't it? Fair's fair."

Mary Ann rose to her feet and, going to the desk and picking up her bag and gloves, said, "About the business of buying him out, is there anything signed yet?"

There was a long pause before Mr. Blenkinsop said, "No, no, not yet."

"Could . . . could you be persuaded to change your mind and say you don't want it, I mean say that you are not going to buy the place after all?"

"Well, seeing that he wants to sell, if I don't buy somebody else will, and that wouldn't suit my plans."

Mary Ann turned towards him but didn't look at him as she said, "You . . . you could say that if he sold out to anyone else you would stick to your original plan and put the buildings on the west side, Riley's side."

Mr. Blenkinsop's head went back and he laughed a loud laugh. Then, mopping his eyes, he said, "You should have been in business, Mrs. Boyle, but . . . leave it to me. . . . Mind, I'm not promising anything." He wagged his finger at her.

"Thank you."

"Well now, come along, I can drop you off at the end of the farm lane. How's that?"

Mary Ann should have said, "No thank you, I've got other business to do in Newcastle," there was a job to be found, but she was tired and weary and so utterly, utterly miserable that she said, "I'd be glad of a lift."

It was about twenty minutes later that Mr. Blenkinsop halted the car at the end of the farm lane and watched Bob Quinton assist Mary and Rose Mary to alight, and after the goodbyes were said and Bob Quinton was once more seated beside him he drove off.

Mr. Blenkinsop drove in silence for some minutes before saying, "Well!"

"Yes, well," replied Bob Quinton.

"What's all this about, do you know?"

"About you buying Corny out?"

"Yes."

"I only know what she told me, that you're going to buy the garage and run it in your own company."

"Well! Well! Well!" The car took an S-bend, and when they were on the straight again Mr. Blenkinsop said, "When I go back to the States I'm going to tell this story like that play that is running, you know, 'A funny thing happened to me on the way to . . .' I'd better say on the way to a little garage tucked up a side-lane. Because, you know, I don't know a blasted thing about me going to buy him out."

"You don't?" Bob Quinton turned fully round in his seat.

"No, not a thing; it's all new to me. I did say to him jokingly, when I first told him of my plans, 'You wouldn't like to sell out?' and he said flatly and firmly no."

"Well, I'll be jiggered. But she said the boy, Jimmy, or some such name, the boy who works there, he came and told her last night."

"Yes, that's what she told me too. Well! It would appear that Jimmy knows more about my business than I do myself. Perhaps he's thought-reading, perhaps I do want to buy the garage. I don't know. But we'll find out when we meet Mr. Boyle, eh?" Mr. Blenkinsop glanced with a merry twinkle in his eye at Bob Quinton, and, together, they laughed.

A few minutes later they drew up outside the garage and Corny came to meet them.

During the last few days Corny had averaged a loss of a pound a day weight, this was due more to worry than to the scrappy meals he had prepared for himself. And only an hour ago he had decided he couldn't go through another day, more important still, another night of this. Whether she came back or not he would have to see her, talk to her before this thing got absolutely out of hand. There was a fear in him that it was already out of hand, the situation had galloped ahead, dragging them both with it. He had been saying to himself during the last two days what Mike had been saying to him from the beginning: why hadn't he stopped her, grabbed her up, brought her back and shaken some sense into her? But he had let her go; he had played the big fellow, the master of his house, the master of his fate who couldn't be . . . the master of his wife, the big fellow who couldn't keep his family together. He had reached the stage where he was telling himself that he had been to blame from the beginning, that he should never have suggested the twins being separated. Yet the truth in him refuted this, and he knew that he had done right, and the proof of this was now dashing round the place chattering twenty-to-the-dozen. Further proof was, his son had seemed to come alive before his eyes; he was no longer the shadow of his sister, he was an individual; the buried assertiveness that had at times erupted in temper was now verbal. There was no longer any fear of the boy being submerged by Rose Mary. . . . She could come back at any minute . . . any minute.

Last night he had sat in the screaming loneliness of the kitchen and wondered what Mary Ann was doing, but whatever she was doing, he imagined she would be doing it in more comfort than if she were here. She had never really considered this her home. That fact had slipped out time and time again. In her mind, home was still the farm, with its big kitchen, and roaring fire, and well-laden table, and its sitting-room, comfortable, yet elegant in the way her mother had arranged things. It seemed ironic to him that it had to be at the moment when he had prospects of giving her a replica of her childhood home that she should walk out on him.

He hadn't fallen asleep until after three o'clock, and he had been awakened at six by a hammering on the door. It was a motorist requiring petrol. That was another funny thing; he'd never had so much work in for months as he had in the last few days. Nor had so many cars passed up and down the road; it was as if the word had gone round. He had been thankful in a way that he had been kept busy during the day, yet all the while under his ribs was this great tearing ache.

A car coming on to the drive brought him out of the garage, and he now walked towards where Mr. Blenkinsop was getting out of it on one side, and Mr. Quinton the other. He nodded to each but did not smile.

"Hello, Corny."

"Hello, Mr. Quinton."

"It's a long time since we met."

"Yes, it is that." Corny jerked his head, whilst wiping his hands on a piece of clean rag. He brought his gaze from Bob Quinton and looked at Mr. Blenkinsop. The American had him fixed with a hard stare. He returned the stare for a moment; then said, "Anything wrong, sir?"

"Well, that's according to how you look at it. Can I have a chat with you?"

Corny's eyes narrowed just the slightest. "Yes, certainly." He turned and went towards the office, the two men following. When they were inside there wasn't much room. Corny indicated that Mr. Blenkinsop should take the one seat, but Mr. Blenkinsop waved it aside, and, coming to the point straight away, said, "What's this about you wanting to sell out?"

"Sell out? Me wanting to sell out?" The whole of Corny's face was puckered. "I don't know what you're getting at, sir."

Mr. Blenkinsop flashed a glance towards Bob Quinton, and the two men smiled, and Bob said, "Curiouser and curiouser."

"You've said it," said Mr. Blenkinsop. "Curiouser and curiouser."

"Who said I was going to sell out? And who am I going to sell to?"

"I was informed this morning that you were selling out to me."

"You! . . . I don't get it."

"Well, to be quite frank, Mr. Boyle, neither do I, so I'd better put you in the picture as much as I can see of it. . . . I had a visit from your wife this morning."

Corny's mouth opened the slightest, then closed again. He made no comment and waited for Mr. Blenkinsop to continue.

"She came to ask me not to buy you out."

Corny's head moved from side to side, and then he said, "I don't understand. There's been no talk of you buying me out, has there?"

"No, not to my knowledge, but she had been told that you were going to sell out to me, and apparently this upset her. She knows how much stock you lay on the place and how hard you've worked and she didn't want me to reap the benefit." Mr. Blenkinsop laughed.

"But I don't see how. I've never said any such thing to her." His head dropped. "I suppose it's no news to you that there's a bit of trouble between us?"

"No, it's no news," said Mr. Blenkinsop flatly.

"Well, how did she get this idea?" Corny looked from Mr. Blenkinsop to Bob Quinton.

"Well, as far as I can gather," said Mr. Blenkinsop, "it came from you. You told your assistant, Jimmy, that you were going to sell out, and he goes and tells your wife."

"Jimmy!"

"Yes, Jimmy."

"He went and told her that?"

Almost before he was finished speaking Corny was out of the office door, and the two men looked at each other as they heard him bellowing, "Jimmy! Jimmy! Here a minute . . . in the office."

As Corny re-entered the office Jimmy came on his heels. He stood in the doorway, covered with oil and grease. You could say he was covered in it from his head to his feet. He, too, had a piece of rag in his hands, which he kept twisting round and round. He looked at the American and his grin widened; he looked at the strange man; then he looked at Corny, and from his boss's expression he knew that there was . . . summat up.

"You've been to the farm to . . . to see Mrs. Boyle," said Corny now.

"Aw, that." The grin spread over Jimmy's face and he said, "Well, I took the lads. You see, one of the fellows had set the piece she did, I mean Mrs. Boyle, to a tune."

"What are you talking about now?" said Corny roughly.

Jimmy again glanced from one to the other, then went on. "Just what I said. I went to the farm with the lads because of the piece Mrs. Boyle had written, the pop piece." He stopped, and again his glance flicked over the three men. And then he gabbled on, "She had the idea that if she wrote a pop piece it could bring in some money, and it could you know. It still could, it's good. Duke, our Group leader, he says it's good; he says she's got the idea. We're going to play it on Saturday night at 'The Well'. She got the idea because of what you said . . . sir." He nodded at the American. "You said she acts like a woman, you remember? An' I said to the boss here it was a good line, and so she worked on it and she said not to tell you." He was nodding at Corny now, and Corny said quickly, "Stop jabbering, Jimmy; that's not what I want to know. What else did you tell Mrs. Boyle when you saw her?"

The silly expression slid from Jimmy's face, and it was with a straight countenance that he said, "Nowt."

"Did you tell her that I was going to sell out, that Mr. Blenkinsop was wanting to buy me out?"

Jimmy now looked down at his feet. Then he looked at his hands and began to pull the rag apart. Next he looked at the men, one after the other; but not at their faces, his glance was directed somewhere at waist level. At last, after a gulp in his throat, he said, "Well, I . . . I did say that."

"But what for?"

Jimmy's head now came up quickly and, staring with a straight face at Corny, he said, "I thought it would bring her back, that's what. She knows what stock you put on the place. I thought she'd come haring back straight away. She's miserable, an' you're as miserable as sin, it's awful workin' here like this, so, well I got wonderin' what I could do, an' I just thought up that. But it didn't work. But . . . but how did you know about it?" His glance swept the other men again, and he chewed on his lip as the explanation came to him, even before Corny said, "She went to Mr. Blenkinsop here and asked him not to go through with it."

"Cor! I never thought she'd do that; I just thought she'd pack up an' grab Rose Mary and come haring back. I expected her to be here when I got in this mornin' . . . I'm sorry, boss." He was looking with a sideward glance at Corny, and Corny's voice was low as he said, "All right, Jimmy, you tried. I won't forget it. Go on."

The three now looked at each other for a moment; then Corny turned away and stood gazing out of the window while Mr. Blenkinsop said, "I wouldn't mind a factory full of that type."

"Nor me," said Bob Quinton. "It rather gives the lie to the thoughtless modern youth; at least, that they are all tarred with the same brush."

There followed another silence. Then Mr. Blenkinsop said, "You know, I feel very guilty about the situation; I feel I'm the cause of it."

"No, sir, don't think that." Corny turned towards him. "This started long before you came on the scene, and now it's up to me to put an end to it."

"You're going to fetch her?" asked Bob quietly.

"Yes, I would have done it before if I hadn't been so pig-headed. You climb up so far in your own estimation and it's a devil of a job to get down again." He looked from one to the other. "If you'll excuse me I want to get the boy ready; I'll take him with me."

"You go ahead." Mr. Blenkinsop nodded at him and patted his shoulder as he went out of the office, and then he looked at Bob Quinton and they raised their eyebrows at each other, and Bob said under his breath, "It's a pity he's been driven to do this."

"What? Go for her?"

"Yes; it won't do her any good in the future making him climb down."

"I know what you mean." Mr. Blenkinsop nodded. "Pity she couldn't have met him halfway."

Bob Quinton jerked his chin upwards and, nodding at Mr. Blenkinsop, he said, "That's an idea. That-is-an-idea."

"What do you mean?"

"Just a minute, I'll tell you." He put his head out of the door in time to see Corny taking David into the house and he called to him, "Do you mind if I use your phone?"

"Go ahead," Corny shouted back.

The next minute Bob was dialling the farm number. The phone had been switched to Mike's office in the yard and it was Michael who answered.

"Hello, Michael," said Bob. "This is Quinton here. Remember me?"

"Of course, of course."

"Look, I'm in a bit of a hurry. Is Mary Ann anywhere about?"

"She's over in the house."

"Could you get her for me? Or switch over to the house? You are on the phone in the house, aren't you?"

"Yes, yes, I'll do that. Hold on a minute."

It was some seconds later when Mary Ann said, "Hello, Mr. Quinton."

"Listen, Mary Ann. There's no time for polite cross-talk. I'm at the garage and as usual you're getting your way, Corny is coming over for you. . . . Are you there?"

"Yes." Mary Ann's voice was scarcely audible.

"As I said, you've got your way. I only hope you don't live to regret it; no man likes to come crawling on his knees." Bob Quinton jerked his head towards Mr. Blenkinsop as he spoke, and Mr. Blenkinsop jerked his head back at him.

"Oh. Oh, I don't want him to come crawling on his knees, I don't. Believe me, I don't."

"Well, you can't do much to stop him now; he's practically on his way; he's gone upstairs to have a wash and get the boy ready, and that shouldn't take him more than fifteen minutes."

"I . . . I could . . ."

"What?"

"I . . . I don't know. Oh, I want to come home, Mr. Quinton, I want to come home."

"Well then, what about doing it now?"

"But we'd likely miss each other. Anyway it wouldn't make much difference now because he'd think I'd only done it because you'd told me to. But . . . but I was going to come, I really was, I was going to come back after dinner."

"Look, listen to me. It's twenty-past twelve. There's the Gateshead bus if I'm not mistaken, passes along the main road around half-past. You and Rose Mary could sprint up that road in five minutes. It's only a fifteen-minute run in the bus to the bottom of the road here. It would be extraordinary if just as you were getting off the bus you should see the car coming down the lane. What about it?"

"Yes, yes." She was gasping as if she was already running. "Yes, I'll do that and . . . and even if I miss him I'll be there when he gets back. Thanks, thanks, Mr. Quinton."

"You did the same for me once. I always like to pay my debts. Get going, Mary Ann. Presto!" He put down the receiver, then passed his hand over the top of his head, and, looking at Mr. Blenkinsop, he said, "And she did, you know. She fixed my life for me years ago, and I have never forgotten it. . . . Well now, what we've got to do is to try to delay the laddie a little if he comes down within the next fifteen minutes. Have you time on your hands?"

"I've time for this," said Mr. Blenkinsop, "all the time that's needed. . . ."

Upstairs, Corny was saying, "Wash your ears. Wash them well now; get all the dirt out."

"Washed 'em, Da-ad, clean."

"Run and get your pants, then, the grey ones. And your blue shirt."

"Clean sand-ams, Da-ad?"

"Yes, and your clean sandals."

Corny scrubbed at the grease on his arms. The sink was in a mess; there was no hot water; he had let the back-boiler go out last night. He thickened his hands with scouring powder. It was like the thing. No hot water when he wanted to get the grease off, and she would go mad when she saw the state of the sink, of the bathroom, of the whole house. He stopped the rubbing of his hands for a second. What had he been thinking of? Why had he been so damned stubborn? He knew her; he knew she hadn't meant what she had said; he knew quite well that she'd had no real intention of walking out on him, that she had expected him to prevent her. Why hadn't he? Just why hadn't he? Looking back now over the interminable space of time since he stood on the road calling after her, he saw himself on that day as a stubborn, pig-headed, high and mighty individual. He saw himself on that day as a man still young, but he felt young no longer; the last few days had laid the years on him.

"Da-ad." David stood in the doorway, dressed in his clean clothes, and he looked from Corny down to his feet, and Corny said, "That's fine . . . fine."

"Goin' ride, Da-ad?"

"Yes," said Corny. "We're going to see your mam and Rose Mary." Corny did not look at his son when he gave him this news, but after a moment, during which David made no sound, he turned his head sharply. There stood the boy, his face awash with tears. The silent crying tore at Corny as no loud bellowing could have, and when, within the next moment, David had rushed to him and buried his face in his thigh he wiped a hand quickly, then placed it gently on the boy's head. This was only the second time he had seen David cry since that first wild outburst of grief when Rose Mary was lost, and it had been a similar crying, a silent, compressed crying, an adult sort of crying. There came to his mind the look he used to see in the boy's eyes when he was defiant, the look that had made him say, "That fellow knows what he's up to; he's having me on." He realized, as he stroked his son's hair, that there was a depth in this child, an understanding that was beyond his years. Perhaps it had matured because it had not been diluted by speech.

He bent to him now and said, "Come on. Come on. You don't want your mam to see you with your face all red, do you?"

David shook his head, then gave a little smile.

It was a full fifteen minutes later when they came down the stairs together, and Corny was not a little suprised to see that Mr. Blenkinsop and Bob Quinton were still about the place. But Mr. Blenkinsop gave an explanation for this immediately.

"You don't mind?" he said, "We've been looking at the spare piece of land, getting ideas . . . you don't mind?"

"Mind!" Corny shook his head.

"We would like to tell you what we think could be done, subject to your approval, of course. But that'll come later, eh?"

"Yes, if you don't mind."

Mr. Blenkinsop now stood directly in front of Corny and said, "How about to-morrow morning? . . . Is that all right with you, Mr. Quinton?" He looked at Bob Quinton; and Bob nodded, then said, "Hold on a minute. I'd better look and see." And then he proceeded to take a book from his pocket and study it.

Corny's eyes flicked from one to the other. They were blocking his path into the garage and the car. He didn't want to be brusque, or off-hand, but they knew where he was going, so why must they fiddle on.

"Yes, that'll do me fine," said Bob Quinton, glancing at Mr. Blenkinsop, and Mr. Blenkinsop, turning his attention again to Corny, said, "All right, will eleven suit you?"

"Any time, any time," said Corny. "I'll be here."

"Well now, that's settled. And now you're wanting to be off."

"If you don't mind."

"And we'd better be making a move, too. What about lunch? Have you any arrangements?" Mr. Blenkinsop moved slowly from Corny's path, and as Corny hurried into the garage he heard Bob Quinton say, "Nothing in particular, but you come and lunch with me. I have a favourite place and. . . ."

Their voices trailed away and Corny pulled open the car door and lifted David up on to the seat. A minute later he was behind the wheel and had driven the car to the garage opening. But there he stopped. You just wouldn't believe it, he said to himself; you'd just think they were doing it on purpose, for there was Mr. Blenkinsop's car right across his path and his engine had stalled. He put his head out of the window and called, "Anything wrong?"

"No, no," Mr. Blenkinsop shouted back to him. "She"ll get going in a minute; she has these spasms."

Corny sat gripping the wheel. If he had to get out and see to that car he would go bonkers.

For three long, long minutes he sat waiting. Then with an exclamation he thrust open the door and went towards the big low car, and just as he reached it and bent his head down to Mr. Blenkinsop's the engine started with a roar.

Mr. Blenkinsop was very apologetic. "It's a long time since she's done it; I'll have to get you to have a look at the plugs."

"They were all right last week."

"Oh yes, I forgot you did her over. Well, it's something; she's as temperamental as a thoroughbred foal. I've always said cars have personalities. I believe it, I do."

Mr. Blenkinsop had turned his head towards Bob Quinton, and it seemed to Corny that Bob Quinton was enjoying Mr. Blenkinsop's predicament, for he was trying not to laugh.

"Ah, well, I'd better get out of your road before she has another tantrum. Sorry about all this." Mr. Blenkinsop again smiled at Corny, and Corny straightening himself, managed to say evenly, "That's all right."

He got into the Rover again and the next minute he was driving on to the road. The American's car, he noticed through his driving mirror, was again stationary. Well, it could remain stationary until he came back. But whatever was wrong with it, it didn't seem to be upsetting Mr. Blenkinsop very much for he was laughing his head off. Americans were odd—he had thought that when he was over there years ago—nice but odd, unpredictable like.

He turned his eyes now down to David, and the boy looked up at him, and they smiled.

When he rounded the bend he saw in the distance the bus pulling to a stop at the bottom of the road. He saw two people alight, a mother and child; he saw the conductor bend down and speak to the child; and it didn't dawn on him who the woman and child were until the car had almost reached them.

Mary Ann! Mary Ann had come back on her own. . . . Aw, Mary Ann.

He stopped the car and stared at her through the windscreen. She was some yards away and she, too, had stopped and was staring towards him. Then the next minute, as if activated by the same spring, they moved. Corny out of the car, and she towards him. They were conscious of the children's high-pitched, delighted screams, but at this moment they were something apart, something separate from themselves. Eye holding eye they stared at each other as they moved closer, and when his arms came out she flung herself into them, pressing herself against his hard, bony body, crying, "Oh, Corny! Oh, Corny!"

"Mary Ann. Mary Ann." His voice was as broken as hers. He put his face down and buried it in her hair.

"I'm sorry. I'm sorry. Oh, Corny, I'm sorry."

"So am I. So am I."

"I shouldn't have done it. I shouldn't. I never meant it. I never meant to leave you; I must have been barmy. . . . I had to come; I couldn't stand it any longer." She lifted her streaming face upwards and simulated surprise as he said, softly, "I was coming for you."

"You were?"

He nodded at her, then said under his breath, "I've nearly been round the bend."

"So have I. . . .Oh, I've missed you. Oh Corny! Corny. . . . And home . . . and everything. Oh, I wanted to be home, Corny. I . . . I never want to see the farm again. . . . Well, not for weeks."

With a sudden movement he pressed her to him again; then said, "Let's get back."

They came out of their world to see Rose Mary and David standing, hand in hand, looking at them.

Both of the children now recognized that the gate into their parents' world was open again and, with a bound, they dashed to them, Rose Mary towards Corny, who hoisted her up into the air, and David towards his mother. Mary Ann lifted the boy into her arms, and he hugged her neck, and when Mary Ann heard him say, "Oh, Mam . . . Mam," the words as distinct as Rose Mary would have said them, she experienced a feeling of deep remorse and guilt.

Corny had been right. Her son was talking, and it was she herself who had prevented him from talking. She herself, who prayed each night that God would give him speech, had kept the seal pressed tightly on his lips; and the seal had been Rose Mary. And she had done it, as she knew now, not so much because she couldn't bear the thought of the twins being separated, but because she couldn't bear the thought of herself being separated from either of them. It was funny, the things that had to happen to you before you could be made to see your real motives.

"Oh, Dad. Dad." Rose Mary was moving her hands over Corny's face. "Oh, I've missed you, Dad. And our David. Oh, I have."

As the child's voice broke, Corny said briskly, "Come on, let's get back home." He put her down on the ground and put his arm out and drew Mary Ann to him; and she put David down, and together they went to the car, the children following.

A few minutes later they were back on the drive, and as they piled out, Jimmy came running down the length of the garage. The grin was splitting his face as he stopped in front of Mary Ann, and with his head on one side he said, "Ee! But I'm glad to see you back, Mrs. Boyle."

"I'm glad to be back, Jimmy."

Mary Ann's voice was very subdued and slightly dignified. He jerked his head at her twice. Then looking towards Rose Mary, he said, "Hello there, young 'un."

"Hello, Jimmy." Rose Mary ran to him and clasped his greasy sleeve, and he cried to her, "Look, you'll get all muck and oil and then your ma'll skelp me."

"She wouldn't. . . . Oh, lovely! We're home." Rose Mary gave a leap in the air, then swung round and grabbed David with such force that he almost fell over backwards; then she herself almost fell over backwards, metaphorically speaking, when her brother said to her, "Give over." Rose Mary stood still looking at him; then, glancing towards her mother and father, she cried, "He said give over. Did you hear him, Mam? A big word, give over, he said. David can talk proper, Mam."

"Yes," said Mary Ann, avoiding looking at Corny. Then she turned away and walked towards the house, and Corny followed her. And when Rose Mary, pulling David by the hand, came scrambling behind her father he turned, and, bending to them, said under his breath, "Stay out to play for a while."

"But, Dad, we've got our good things on."

"It's all right. Just for a little bit. Don't get mucked up. I'll give you a shout in a minute."

David pulled his hand from Rose Mary's and, turning about, ran back to where Jimmy stood. But Rose Mary continued to look at her dad. She wanted to go upstairs and get out of her good things; she had been in them far too long. Anyway, her dad should know that she couldn't play in her good things.

"But, Dad, it won't take a minute."

"Rose Mary! Stay out until I call, you understand?"

"Yes, Dad." Rose Mary remained still as Corny walked away from her and into the house; and as she stood, it came to her that their David had gone off on his own. She turned quickly about and watched David following Jimmy into the garage. He hadn't shouted to her to come on, or anything.

A funny little feeling came over Rose Mary. She couldn't understand it. All she could do was associate it with the feeling she got when Miss Plum, after being nice to her, turned nasty. The feeling spurted her now towards the garage. She was back home with her mam and dad and their David, and their David couldn't get along without her. . . .

Upstairs, in the kitchen, Corny sat in the big chair with Mary Ann curled up in his arms, very like a child herself. There was a tenderness between them, a new tentative tenderness, a tenderness that made them humble and honest. Mary Ann moved her finger slowly round the shirt button on his chest and looked at it as she said, "It's taught me a lesson. I don't think I'll ever need another."

"You're not the only one."

"Talk about purgatory. If purgatory is anything like this last few days I'm going to make sure that I'm not going to be a candidate for it. And you know," she glanced up at him, "they were awful. Everyone of them, they were all against me."

"Don't be silly."

"I'm not, Corny. It's true; even me da."

"Your da against you!" Corny jerked his head up and laughed.

"I'm telling you. As for my mother, I wouldn't have believed it. Even after she came to see you she made you out to be the golden boy."

Again Corny laughed. "Well, that's a change," he said.

"You should have seen the send-off she gave me when I came away. She was crying all over me. They all were, or nearly so. They were glad to see the back of me."

"Now, don't you be silly." He took her chin in his hands and moved her head slowly back and forward. "They took the attitude they did because they knew I'm no use without you."

She lowered her lids, then muttered, "You mean, they knew I was no use without you."

"Well, let's say forty-nine, fifty-one. But I know this much; they were all upset and they did their best to put things right. But it took Jimmy to do the thinking."

"Jimmy?" She screwed up her eyes at him.

"Yes. That tale about me selling out seemed to do the trick, didn't it?"

Mary Ann pulled herself upwards from him with a jerk and, with her two hands flat on his chest, she stared at him as she said, "You mean to say that was all a put-up job, you sent Jimmy?"

"Oh, no, no, no! Don't let's start. Now, let's get this right . . . right from the beginning, from the word go. I knew nothing about it until an hour ago."

Mary Ann was making small movements with her head. Then she asked softly, "You weren't going to sell out to Mr. Blenkinsop?"

"No, I never dreamt of it. Now ask yourself, as if I would, getting this far, after all this struggle. No, it was his idea. He thought . . . well. . . ." Corny lowered his head and shook it. "He thought it might bring you back and try to prevent me doing anything silly."

Mary Ann brought one hand from Corny's chest and put it across her mouth. "And I went to Mr. Blenkinsop and . . . and asked him not to buy you out, and. . . . Oh! Oh! I didn't only see him, I . . . I first went to Bob Quinton. Oh, what will they think? They'll think I'm batty."

"They'll think nothing of the kind; they've been here."

"No!"

"Yes. Now don't get het up. They wanted to know what it was all about. And that's how I found out that Jimmy had been to you with this tale."

"Oh, wait till I see him."

"Now, now." He took hold of her by the shoulders and shook her gently. "Think, just think, if he hadn't given you that yarn we might have gone on and on. There's no telling. Anything could have happened . . . Mary Ann." He bent his head towards her. "I just don't want to think about it; it frightens me; it frightens me still. I'm just going to be thankful that you're back." He smiled softly at her; then added slowly, "And take mighty good care in the future—you don't leave this house without me unless I have a chain attached to you."

He held her tightly; and as he stroked her hair he said, "And you won't go for Jimmy?"

She moved her face against him, and after a moment she said, "Fancy him thinking all that up."

"I've always told you that that lad has a head on his shoulders. There's a lot goes on behind that silly-looking face of his. And he's loyal, and that means a great deal these days. When things get going I'll see he's all right. . . . You know, I could have kissed him this morning when he owned up to telling you that tale, and to know you still cared enough to stop me doing something silly."

Mary Ann gazed into his face, her own face serious now, as she said, "I've never stopped caring. . . . Corny, promise me, promise me that if I ever forget about this time and what's happened and I try to do anything stupid again, you'll shake the life out of me, or box my ears."

"Box your ears?" He pulled his chin in. "You try anything on, me lady, and I won't stop at boxing your ears; I'll take me grannie's advice and I'll black your eyes. 'You should have blacked her eyes,' she said."

"What! your grannie . . . she said that?"

"She did. And much more."

"But, Corny, she . . . she was the only one who was on my side; she called you worse than dirt; she . . . Oh . . . Oh!" Mary Ann bit on her lip to try and prevent herself from laughing. "The crafty old fox!"

"Ee! me grannie." There was a look of wonderment on Corny's face. "She's wise, you know."

They began to laugh, their bodies pressed tight again, rocking backwards and forwards. They laughed, but their laughter was not merry; it was the kind of laughter one laughs after getting a fright, the laughter that gushes forth when the danger is passed.

14

They'd had a meal; Mary Ann had cleaned up the house; she was now going to bake something nice for tea; but before she started she felt she must have a word with Jimmy. she had just put the bread-board and cooking utensils on the table near the window when she saw him crossing the yard with some pieces of wood in his arms. Quickly she tapped on the window and motioned to him that she wanted to see him. In a minute she was down the back stairs and in the yard, and there he was, waiting for her at the gate. She walked up to him slowly and looked at him for a second or so before saying, "You should take up writing short stories, Jimmy."

"Me! Short stories, Mrs. Boyle? I couldn't write, me spellin's terrible."

"That doesn't stop you telling the tale, does it?" She looked up at him under her eyelids.

"Aw, that. Eeh! Well, I thought you would never come back. You see." He stooped and placed the wood against the railings; then, straightening up but still keeping his head bent, he gazed at his feet as he said, "You see, me mam always said it started over nothin', and neither of them would give in. Both of them were at work, you see, and me dad was on the night shift and we hardly ever saw him. Ships that passed in the night, he said they were. And they had a row, and she walked out. There was only me at home, 'cos me only sister, she's married. It was awful being in the house and nobody there, I mean no woman. I never forget that year, and so I felt a bit worried like about . . . about the boss and you."

"Aw, Jimmy, I'm sorry. I didn't know. But I'm glad you got worried about us. Thanks . . . thanks a lot." She put out her hands and clasped his arms, bringing the colour flooding over his long face, and for a moment he was definitely embarrassed. Then, his natural humour coming to his aid, he slanted his gaze at her as he asked, "It'll be all right for me to play me trombone then, Mrs. Boyle?"

She gave him a sharp push as she laughed. "You! That's blackmail. Go on with you."

He was chuckling as he stooped to pick up the wood, and she looked down on him and said, "I might stand for your trombone wailing, but I'll never stand for you having long hair like that crowd of yours."

"Aw." He straightened and jerked his head back. "Funny thing about that. Your dad got under Duke's skin a bit. My! I thought for a minute there was goin' to be bust-up, but after we got back Duke began to talk about breakin' the barrier with a new gimmick, and he came up with the idea of shavin' their heads."

"No!" Mary Ann was covering her face with her hands.

"Aye, it's a fact. He's thinking of shaving up the sides and just leavin' a rim over the top here"—he demonstrated to her—"like a comb, you know, and callin' us 'The Cocks'."

"The Cocks!" squeaked Mary Ann, still laughing.

"Aye, that's what he says."

"Why not shave the lot off and call yourselves 'The Men'? That would break the sound barrier, at least among all the long-haired loonies. . . . THE MEN!" She wagged her finger up and down. "And underneath you could have 'Versus the rest'."

"Ee! you can think quick, can't you, Mrs. Boyle? That isn't half bad. 'The Men . . . versus the rest'. I'll tell him, I'll tell him what you said."

"You do, Jimmy. Tell him I'll put words to all his tunes if they all get their hair cut."

"Aye, I will."

"Jim-my!"

"Ee! There's the boss bellowin'. I'll get it in the neck." He turned from her and ran with the wood towards the back door of the garage, and, as he neared it, Rose Mary emerged and, seeing Mary Ann, came swiftly towards her, crying, "Mam! Mam! Wait a minute."

"Yes, dear?" Mary Ann held out her arm and put it round Rose Mary and hugged her to her side as she looked down and listened to her saying, "Mam, it's our David. He won't do anythin'."

"Do anything? What do you mean?"

"Well, he won't play with me."

"Nonsense." Mary Ann pressed Rose Mary from her. "David won't play with you? Of course he will. Where is he?"

"He's with me dad, under the car."

"Under the car?"

"He wanted me to get under but I wouldn't, and me dad said I hadn't to anyway. Me dad told David to go and play on the old car with me, but he wouldn't. He waited till me dad got under the car and he crawled under with him. And they were laughin' . . . an' Jimmy an' all."

Taking Rose Mary's hand, Mary Ann said, "Come on," and with something of her old sprightliness, she marched towards the garage. David under a car! Thick with oil and grease! She had enough of that when she had Corny's things to see to.

Half-way up the garage, she saw Corny's legs sticking out from beneath a car, and next to the legs were those of David. His buttocks, too, were also in sight as he was lying on his stomach.

When she stood over the two pairs of legs she said, softly, "David, aren't you going to play with Rose Mary?"

She waited for a moment, and when no reply came she said sharply, "David!"

There was a wriggle of the buttocks and David emerged, rolled on to his back, stared up at her and said, by way of enquiry, "Mam?"

Mary Ann looked down at her grease- and oil-smeared son. She wanted to grab him by the shoulders, yank him upstairs, take his clothes off, and put him in the bath. She kept her voice calm as she said, "Aren't you going to play with Rose Mary on the old car?"

"No, Mam. Helpin' Da-ad." He held up one hand to her, and in it was a spanner.

Corny's voice now came from under the car, saying, "Give it me here, the big one, the one with the wide handle. Then go and play with Rose Mary."

"No, Da-ad." David was again lying on his stomach, only his heels visible now, and his muffled voice came to Mary Ann and Rose Mary, saying, "No, Da-ad, don't want to. This spinner?"

Mary Ann waited for Corny to say something. He had stopped tapping with the hammer. She could imagine him lying on his back, his eyes tightly closed, biting on his lip as he realized a new situation had arisen, a new situation that she would have to face. And not only herself but Rose Mary also. Her little daughter would need to be helped to face it, helped to watch calmly this severed part of her making his own decisions, choosing his own pleasures, living his own life. She gripped Rose Mary's hand tightly as she called in a light voice, her words addressed to her son but their meaning meant for her husband, "It's all right. Rose Mary's coming upstairs to help me bake something nice for tea . . . aren't you, Rose Mary?" She looked down into her daughter's straight face. Then, bending swiftly down, she called under the car in a jocular fashion, "But don't either of you dare to come up those stairs in that condition; I'll bring a bucket of hot water down for you to get the thick of it off."

"We hear." Following on Corny's laughing answer, David now piped in, "We hear. We hear, Mam."

Mary Ann moved away and drew Rose Mary with her, but all the way down the garage Rose Mary walked with her head turned over her shoulder, looking back at the car and David's feet, and she didn't speak until they reached the kitchen, not until Mary Ann said, "Go and get your cooking apron, and your board and rolling pin, and you can make some tea-cakes, eh?" And then, her lip quivering, she looked at her mother and said, "But, Mam, David doesn't want to play with me any more. Now he can talk he doesn't want to play with me any more."

"Of course, he does, dear. He's just new-fangled with the idea of helping your dad. That'll wear off. We'll go to the sands to-morrow if it's fine and, you'll see, he'll be like he was before. Go on now and get your things out and help me, because, you know, you're a big girl; you're six, and you should help me."

"Yes, Mam."

Mary Ann went to the table and made great play of setting about her cooking. New-fangled because he was helping his dad. Things would be like they were before. No. She was confronted with the stark truth that things would never be like they were before, for David had become Corny's; of his own choice, the boy had taken his father. As, years ago, she had taken her father and left her mother to their Michael, now David had taken Corny and left her to Rose Mary. Oh, she knew there would be times when he needed her, like there had been times when she had needed her mother, but it would never really be the same again. They might always be a close-knit unit, but within the unit one of her angels would fight his twin, and herself, for his independence. It was only in this moment that she realized that David was like neither Corny nor her; he was like her da, like Mike. He had been slow to talk, but now he had started he would have his say and fight for the right to have it.

"Mam, will I put some lemon peel in me tea-cakes?"

Mary Ann turned smilingly towards Rose Mary, saying, "Yes, yes, that's an idea; David likes lemon peel, doesn't he?"

"Yes, Mam. Mam, will I make my tea-cakes just for David and me?"

"Yes, you do that, I'll make some for your dad and you make some for David. That's a good idea."

Rose Mary smiled, then said, "Don't say I've made them until he's eaten one, then he'll get a gliff, eh?"

"All right. And make them so nice he won't believe you've made them."

"Yes, and he'll want me to make them every day. He'll keep me at it, and I won't be able to have any play or anything."

"Well, if he does," said Mary Ann, measuring the flour into a bowl, "you'll just have to say, 'Now look, I'll make them for you twice a week, but that's all, because I want to play sometime'. You'll have to be firm."

"Yes, I will." Rose Mary clattered her dishes on to the board, and after a pause she said, "But I wouldn't mind baking tea-cakes for David every day. I wouldn't mind, Mam."

"It wouldn't be good for him," said Mary Ann. "You won't have to give him all his own way."

"No, I won't."

Mary Ann turned to glance at her daughter. She was busily arranging her little rolling-pin and cutter, her knife and her basin, and as she did so she said, as if to herself, "But I wouldn't mind. I wouldn't mind, not really."

Mary Ann turned her head slowly round and looked out of the window. David, almost with one blow, had cut the cord that had held them together. He had flung it aside and darted away, as it were, leaving Rose Mary holding one end in her hand, reluctant to let go, bewildered at being severed from her root.

The plait of joy and sorrow that went to make up life was so closely entwined that you could hardly disentangle the strands. She wanted to gather her daughter into her arms and try to explain things to her, but she knew it did not lie in her power to do this; only unfolding years and life itself could explain, within a little, the independence of a spirit.

15

It was Sunday again and, outwardly, life had returned to normal; not that Corny's frequent diving upstairs was his normal procedure. Sometimes Mary Ann had never seen him from breakfast until lunch time, except when she took his coffee down, but now it seemed he didn't want to let her out of his sight. He came upstairs on any little pretext just to look at her, to make sure she was really there. It was a similar pattern to the first month after they were married.

But it was almost two o'clock now and Corny hadn't got back for his dinner. There had been a breakdown along the road and he had been called to see to it. She went into the front room and looked out of the window. She couldn't keep the children waiting much longer; yet Corny liked them all to sit down together, especially for a Sunday dinner. And she had made a lovely dinner . . . roast pork, and all the trimmings, and a lemon meringue pie for after. Rose Mary came into the room now, accompanied by David, and asked, "Is me dad comin', Mam?"

"I can't see him yet."

"Oh, I'm hungry."

"Me an' all," said David.

They were standing one on each side of her, and she put her arms around them and pressed them tightly to her. And they both gripped her round the waist, joining her in the circle of their arms.

She smiled softly as she looked down on them. Oh, she was lucky . . . lucky. She must never forget that. No, she never would she assured herself. She thanked God for her angels and that everything in her life was all right again. . . . But not quite.

It being Sunday, and Jimmy content to stay on duty, they should have all being going to the farm, but there had been no mention of the farm to-day. Corny had remembered what she had said: "I never want to see the farm again. Well, not for weeks and weeks." And so he had not brought up the subject. Yet here she was, and had been all day, wishing she was going to see her ma and da and their Michael and Sarah, and sit round the big table and have a marvellous tea—that she hadn't had to get ready—and laugh . . . above all, laugh.

What was the matter with her that she could change her mind so quickly? A couple of days ago she had been glad to see the last of them. Did that include her da?

She bowed her head and released her hold on the children, and turning away, went into the kitchen.

She had just looked into the oven to see that everything hadn't been kizzened up, when Jimmy's voice came from the bottom of the stairs, calling, "Mrs. Boyle!"

She hurried to the landing and looked down on him. "Yes, Jimmy."

"The boss has just phoned from the crossroads to tell you he'll be back in ten minutes."

"Thanks, Jimmy."

"That's givin' you time to dish up; he wants it on the table." Jimmy laughed, and she laughed back. Funny, how she had come to like Jimmy. Before, he had simply been a daft youngster, but now she saw him in a different light altogether. She asked him now, "Will you have room for a bite when I put it out?"

"Corners everywhere, Mrs. Boyle."

She flapped her hand at him and said, "All right, I'll give you a knock when it's ready."

"Ta, ta, Mrs. Boyle. . . ."

Twenty minutes later Corny was washed and sitting at the table and doing justice to Mary Ann's cooking, and every now and again he would look at her and smile with some part of his face. Then he would look at the children. He caused Rose Mary to laugh and almost choke when he winked at her.

After Mary Ann had thumped her on the back and made her drink some water, Rose Mary, her face streaming, said, "It was a piece of scrancham, my best bit, it was nice and crackly. . . . Can I have another piece, Mam?"

"Yes, but mind how you eat it. Don't go and choke yourself this time."

After Mary Ann had helped Rose Mary to the pork rind she said to David, "You want some too, David?"

"No, Mam." David looked up at her; then immediately followed this by asking, "Goin' farm, 'safter-noon?"

Mary Ann resumed her seat, and David looked from her to his father, and Corny, after glancing at Mary Ann's downcast eyes looked towards his plate, and said, "No, not this afternoon. But we might take a dander down to your Great-gran McBride's."

"Oh, yes, Dad," put in Rose Mary, and both she and David made excited noises, interspersed with cries of, "Oh! Great-gran McBride."

Corny now said softly to Mary Ann, "All right?"

"Yes," she replied, but there was little enthusiasm in her voice. Not that she didn't like going to Fanny's, but free Sundays had always been reserved for the farm. She told herself that if she was strong enough she would say to Corny now, "We'll go to the farm." But it was early yet to face her family and the hostility they might still be feeling towards her; and this included Mr. Lord. She felt as if she had been thrust out by them all. The feeling touched on the primitive. As, in the dark past, some erring member of a tribe was cast aside, so had her family treated her . . . or so she felt; and the feeling wasn't lessened by the knowledge that it was all her own fault. . . .

Dinner over, the dishes washed, the kitchen tidy, Mary Ann set about getting the children ready before she saw to herself.

In the bedroom Corny was changing his shirt. He was in the act of pulling it over his head when he heard a car come on to the drive. His ear was like a thermometer where cars were concerned. He looked at himself in the mirror. When the cars began coming on to the garage drive thick and fast he felt his temperature would go up so high he'd blow his top. He was grinning at himself in pleasurable anticipation of this happening when he swung round on the sound of a well-known voice coming from the stairs, crying, "Anybody in?"

It was Mike. He was through the door and on to the landing in a second, but not before Mary Ann, half dressed, with the children coming behind her.

They all stood on the landing looking down the stairs. Corny was exclaiming loudly, as were both the children, but Mary Ann remained quiet. She watched her father coming towards her, followed by her mother, and behind her mother slowly came Sarah, and behind Sarah, as always, Michael.

The hard knot came struggling up from her chest and lodged itself in her throat, and when her da put his arms around her shoulders she felt it would choke her. But when her mother, smiling gently at her, bent and kissed her, it bolted out from her mouth in the form of an agonised sob.

"Oh, there, there, child." Lizzie enfolded her as if indeed she was still a child, and she sounded very much like it at this moment, so much so that the twins stopped their gabbling and gazed at their mother. Then Rose Mary, tears suddenly spouting from her eyes, darted towards her, crying, "Oh, Mam! Mam!" And David stood stiffly by, his lips quivering.

"Aw, Mary Ann," Sarah lumbered towards her. "Don't . . . don't cry like that. We just had to come. I'm sorry if it's upset you."

Mary Ann, gasping and sniffing now, put her hand out to Sarah and shook her head wildly as she spluttered, "It hasn't. It hasn't; it's just . . . Oh!" Her glance flashed from one to the other of this, her family, and she spread her arms wide as if to enfold them all. "It's just that I'm so glad to see you."

Corny was standing by her side now, holding her, and he looked at her family, endorsing her sentiments, saying briefly, "Me an' all."

"Well," said Michael, who always had a levelling influence on any disturbance, "I don't like buses with standing room only. We're almost crushed to death in here, so if I'm not going to be offered a seat I'm going down into the garage to find an empty car. . . . And it's about time we were offered a cup of tea, if you ask me, we must have been here three minutes flat."

"Go on with you." Corny pushed Michael in the back and into the kitchen, and Lizzie, following Sarah into the bedroom to take off their outdoor things, shouted, "I'll see to it, Mary Ann, although it isn't fifteen minutes since they all had tea."

The children, returning to normal, followed their father and uncle. This left Mary Ann on the landing with Mike. Again he put his arm around her shoulders and, pressing her tightly to him, asked under his breath, "How's things?"

Shyly she glanced up at him. "Fine, Da."

"Sure?"

"Yes. Better than before, I think. I've learned a lesson."

"Don't we all?" He moved his head slowly above hers. "I've been sick over the last couple of days wondering, and your mother has an' all, and the others." He was referring to Michael and Sarah. "The house hasn't been the same; it was like something hanging over us."

Mary Ann moved slowly from the protection of his arm and went into the front room, and he followed her, and when they were quite alone he said, "You won't hold it against us for the way we went on? We only acted for your own good; we knew that you would never be happy away from him."

"I know, Dad, I know." Her head was drooping. "It seemed hard to bear at the time because nobody seemed to see my side of it, but now, looking back, I realize I hadn't much on my side, except temper."

"Oh, you weren't all to blame. Oh no." Mike jerked his head. "The big fellow's as stubborn as a mule. But, as I said, we knew that, separated, you would both wither. . . . You know, lass." He took her chin in his one hand. "In a way, it's the pattern of Lizzie's and my life all over again; except"—he wrinkled his nose and added quizzically—"except for my weakness, for I can't ever see you havin' to cart Corny home mortal drunk."

"Ah, Da, don't, don't." She turned her eyes away from him, and he said, "Aw, I can face the truth now, but as I was saying, the pattern of your life is much the same as ours. I knew I was no good without Liz, and he knows he wouldn't be any good without you; we're two of a kind, Corny and me. There's only one woman for us. There might be little side slips, occasioned by glandular disturbances in the difficult years." He pushed her gently and laughed, and caused her to laugh, too, and say, "Oh, Da . . . Da, you're awful. Anyway"—her smile broadened—"when Corny reaches his glandular disturbance I'll be ready and——"

Mary Ann's voice was suddenly cut off by the sound of a band playing; at least it sounded like a band, and it wasn't coming from the wireless in the next room; it was coming from outside, from down below on the drive. She almost jumped towards the window, Mike with her, and together they stood staring down at the four instrumentalists.

"In the name of God!" said Mike, then continued to gaze downwards with his mouth open. Now glancing at Mary Ann, he added, "Did you ever see anything like them in all your born days?"

Mary Ann put her fingers across her mouth. "They've shaved off their hair, nearly all of it."

"Shaved off their . . . !" Mike narrowed his eyes as he peered downwards. "You mean to say that's the blasted lot that came to our place the other night?"

Mary Ann nodded. "He said they might; Jimmy said they might . . . Corny! Corny!" she called now over her shoulder, and almost before she had finished calling his name Corny was in the room, accompanied by Lizzie and Michael.

"What's all the racket?"

"Look at this."

"Aw," Corny leaned over her and looked down on to the drive. "This is going a bit too far. I'll tear Jimmy apart; you see if I don't."

"Corny!" Mary Ann gripped his arm as he turned to go. "Don't . . . don't say anything to him, because . . . well, he only tried to help me. You see," she spread a quick glance round the rest of them now and said, "I . . . I wrote some words and one of them set them to music; that's what they came to let me hear the other night."

"Well I never! Hitting the pops!" Mike was grinning now, his attitude entirely different from what it had been a moment ago. "And you wrote the words?" There was pride in his voice.

"Yes, Da."

"What are they?" asked Michael.

"Oh, I've forgotten; I've got them written down in the other room."

"Well, go and get them," said Mike now, "and we'll all join in. Listen to it! It's as good as you hear on 'Juke Box Jury'. I'm telling you that. Anyway, it's got a tune. What you call it?"

Mary Ann turned as she reached the door. "She Acts Like Woman."

"She acts like a woman?" Lizzie was looking quizzically at Mary Ann, who, her face very red now, said, "It . . . it was something Mr. Blenkinsop said about me; well . . . about me going for Jimmy practising his trombone." She looked down and tried to stop herself laughing. "He said I acted like a woman."

"Well, I never!" said Lizzie. "And you turned it into a song?"

"Sort of."

"Well, go on; go on and get the words," said Mike, pushing Mary Ann out of the door.

It was plain that Mike was tickled and amused at the situation. But Corny wasn't amused; he didn't mind Jimmy practising now and again, but that was different from having that queer-looking squad doing a rehearsal on his drive, and a car might draw up at any minute. He turned from the others, who were now crowded round the window, and, running swiftly downstairs, he went past the instrumentalists and made straight for Jimmy, who was standing well away from the group and inside the garage.

Jimmy seemed to be expecting him, and he didn't give him time to start before getting in, "Now look, boss, it isn't my fault; I didn't ask them here. I told them not to start, but you might as well talk to the wall."

"SHE ACTS LIKE A WOMAN."

The group had become vocal; the voices soared now, and Corny, without speaking, turned and looked towards the performers. They had looked funny enough with their hair on, but now they looked ridiculous; their scalps bare except for a fringe of hair running from the top of the brow to the nape of the neck, they appeared to him like relics of a prehistoric tribe.

"SHE ACTS LIKE A WOMAN."

"Look!" shouted Corny above the falsetto pitch. "Drop it a minute."

Duke, his fringe of red hair making him look more odd than the rest, glanced towards Corny and said, "Why?"

"Because I say so," shouted Corny.

"You don't like it?"

"Look," Corny said, "we won't talk about liking or disliking anything at the moment. What I want to point out is that this isn't the place for practising."

Duke stared at Corny, and his eyes narrowed as he said, "I thought you were all right; Jimmy said you didn't mind."

"I don't mind Jimmy practisin' when he's got nothing else to do, but he'll certainly not do it on the main drive."

"Aw." Duke's head nodded backwards. "See what you mean. But do you like it? It's the thing your missus wrote. I had to alter bits here and there you know. . . ."

Corny rubbed his hand hard across his face, then said patiently, "It was very good of you to take it up, but look, go to the back." He pointed to the garage. "Go and play it there; you won't be in anybody's way there; then perhaps I'll tell you what I think of it."

"It's very kind of you, I'm sure." This cocky comment came from Poodle and brought Corny flashing round to say, "Now look, me young cock-a-doodle or whatever you're supposed to be; mind what you say and how you say it. Now"—he spread his hands out indicating the lot of them—"get yourself through there before I change me mind."

The four boys went past him and into the garage; their steps were slow, and the glances they bestowed on him told him they were quite indifferent to anything his mind might do.

"For two pins!"

"Corny!" Mary Ann touched his sleeve, and he turned quickly to her. "I'm sorry."

Now he gave a forced laugh. "What's there to be sorry about? But you see"—his voice dropped—"I couldn't have them on the drive, could I?"

"No, no, of course not." She agreed wholly with him. "But I'm sorry that I ever thought about writing that bloomin' stuff."

"Don't you be sorry." He grinned widely at her. "They've made something out of it; they're going to play out at the back. Come on upstairs and let's have a look at the words and see how it goes."

"You're sure you don't mind?" Her voice was very small, and he became quite still as he looked at her, and after a moment he said, "I mind nothing, nothing at all as long as you're with me."

"Oh, Corny." Their hands held and gripped painfully for a moment; then they were out on the drive, their hands still joined, running towards the front door. But when about three steps from it, Mary Ann pulled them to a stop and on a groan, she said, "Oh no! Oh, no!"

"What is it?"

"Look down there. Am I seeing things or is that me grannie?"

"Good God! It's her all right."

"Oh, Corny. To-day of all days. And remember what happened when she was here last. Oh, Corny!"

"Look. Go upstairs and warn the others. I'll hold her off for a minute; I'll go and meet her."

Mary Ann seemed glued to the ground, until he pushed her, saying, "Go on, go on. You're not the only who's going to welcome this visit . . . think of Mike."

The next minute Mary Ann was racing up the stairs.

"Ma! Da!" She burst into the kitchen where they were all gathered now, and, after swallowing deeply, she brought out, "Me grannie! She's coming up the road."

"What?" Lizzie, the teapot in her hand, swung round, "No!"

"It is. It is. Corny's gone to meet her."

Mike turned slowly from the window and looked at Lizzie, and Lizzie, looking straight back at him, said, "She must have gone to the house and found nobody there."

Mike moved further from the window. He didn't speak, only lowered his lids and rubbed his teeth across each other, making a sound that wasn't quite a grind.

"How she can come back here after things I said to her the other day I don't know." Mary Ann was shaking her head when Mike said, "The one that can snub that woman won't be from this earth, lass; he'll have to be from another planet, with powers greater than any we can dream of; that woman's got a hide like a herd of rhinoceroses pressed together."

"Laugh at her."

They all turned their eyes towards Sarah, and she smiled her beautiful smile, saying, "It's about the only thing, failing a man from another planet, that will make a dent in the rhinoceros's hide." She was looking at Mike as she spoke.

"You're right. You're right." Mike nodded his head at her. "As always, Sarah, you're right. And that's what we'll do, eh?" He looked from one to the other now with the eagerness of a boy, finally letting his eyes come to rest on Mary Ann, and he added, "What do you say?"

"You know me." Mary Ann gave a quizzical smile. "I'll promise God's honour, and then she's only to open her mouth and say something nasty about Corny, the bairns, or . . . well, any one of you." She spread her arms wide. "You know me."

They all looked at her; there was a chuckle here and there, then they were all laughing, and at the height of it the group outside suddenly blared forth "She acts like a Woman". But even this combination couldn't drown Mrs. McMullen's voice as she came up the stairs.

No one went towards the door, and when Corny thrust it open and ushered the old woman in he did so with a flourish. "Look!" he cried. "It's Gran. I saw her coming up the road. . . ."

"All right. All right," Mrs. McMullen interrupted him sharply. "Don't go on. I don't need any introduction; they know me now. No need to act like a circus master." She moved forward, her glance sweeping over the crowded room. "Looks like a cattle market," she said. "Still, it doesn't take many to fill this place. Let's sit down."

It was Michael who brought a chair towards her; and when she was seated she looked directly at Lizzie, saying, "You could have told me, couldn't you, you were all going out jaunting? It would have saved me legs. But I'm of no importance; I'm young enough to trek the God-forsaken road."

"I didn't see any need to tell you we were going out, Mother; I didn't know you were coming."

"You know if I'm coming any day I come on a Sunday."

"It must be five weeks since you came; do you expect me to wait in for you?"

"No, I don't; I don't expect any consideration from anybody, so I'm not disappointed when I don't get it. . . . What's that racket out there?" She turned her head sharply towards the window. "What is it?"

"It's a group." Corny now walked past her and looked down into the yard before turning to her and saying, "They're playing a thing of Mary Ann's; she wrote the words. It'll likely get into the Top Twenty." He winked at Mike, who was standing to the side of him.

"Am I going to get a drink of tea?" Mrs. McMullen was again looking at her daughter—she was adept at turning conversations into side channels when the subject wasn't pleasing to her, and any achievement of her grand-daughter's was certainly not pleasing her.

"Well, give yourself a chance to get your hat and coat off; the tea's all ready, just waiting for you."

Lizzie accompanied this with small shakes of her head that spoke plainly of her irritation, and Mrs. McMullen, after raising her eyebrows, folded her hands on her lap and bowed her head, and her whole attitude said, There now. Would you believe it? Would you believe that anybody could speak to me in such a fashion after asking them a civil question?

Then her head was brought up quickly by a concerted drawn-out wail and she cried, "Stop that lot! Who are they, anyway? And why do you let them carry on here?" she pulled herself to her feet and moved a few steps to the window and glared down on to the group, and its open-mouthed audience of Rose Mary and David.

All those standing behind her mingled their glances knowingly. Mrs. McMullen remained silent for a moment; then, turning her head over her shoulder, she looked at Corny and asked, "What are they?"

"What do you mean, Gran, what are they?"

"Just what I said: what are they? They're not human beings; don't tell me that; they look like something Doctor Who left lying around."

There was a splutter of laughter from Michael and Sarah, and Mary Ann, too, had her work cut out not to bellow, but on principle she wouldn't laugh at anything her grannie said.

"What are they singing? She . . . what?"

"'She acts like a woman'," said Corny, his grin wide now. "It's the title of the song Mary Ann wrote. Look, the words are here." He looked about him, and Mike, picking up the sheet of paper from the table, handed it to him with an exchange of glances.

"Look." Corny thrust the paper in front of Mrs. McMullen. "Read them; then you'll be able to sing with the group."

Mrs. McMullen's look should have withered Corny. She grabbed the paper from his hand and, holding it well from her as if it smelt, she read aloud, "She acts like a Woman. Man, I'm telling you she acts like a woman." Then only her muttering was heard until she came to the end. And now, handing the sheet back to Corny, she stared at him a moment blankly before emitting one word, "Edifying!" She turned about and resumed her seat; then repeated, "Edifying. Very edifying, I must say. But I'm not surprised; nothing could surprise me."

Mary Ann's face looked tight now, and Corny was signalling to her above her head of her grannie when that old lady explained the reason for her visit. She did it in clipped, precise tones, talking rapidly.

"Well, I didn't come here to read trash, or to look at four imbeciles; nor yet to listen to that awful wailing. I came to tell you me news."

Her statement, and the way she issued it, had the power to catch and hold all their attention.

"I've won a car," said Mrs. McMullen flatly.

There was a long pause before anybody spoke; then Lizzie said, "A car, Mother?"

"Yes; you're not deaf, are you? I said a car. An' don't look so surprised. Why shouldn't I win a car? There's no law against an elderly person winning a car, is there?"

"No, no, of course not." Lizzie's voice was sharp. "I was only surprised that you had won a car. But I'm glad, I'm glad."

"You won a car, Gran?" Corny was standing in front of the old lady. "What make is it?"

"They call it a Wolseley."

"A Wolseley!" The expanse of Corny's face widened.

"Do I have to repeat everything? A Wolseley."

Corny now looked towards Mary Ann; then to Lizzie; then his glance flashed to Mike, Michael and Sarah, before coming to rest on Mrs. McMullen's unblinking eyes again. Now he asked, "How did you win it, Gran? Bingo?"

"I don't go to bingo, I'll have you understand. No, I won it with a couplet for Pieman's Pies. A good couplet that had a real rhyme in it, and sense: 'Don't buy a pig-in-a-poke, buy a pig in a pie, Pieman's pie'."

Now the old lady's eyes flicked for a moment in Mary Ann's direction, and Mary Ann caught their malevolent gleam. Oh, she was an old bitch. yes, that's what she was, an old bitch. A couplet that rhymed, with sense in it. 'Don't buy a pig-in-a-poke, buy a pig in a pie'. But fancy her of all women writing a couplet of any kind! She herself had sent in slogans for years; slogans for corn flakes, sauce, soap, boot polish, the lot, and what had she got? Nothing; not even a consolation prize. Yet here, this old tyke could win a car. There was no justice. It wouldn't have mattered if anyone else in the world had won a car with a couplet except her grannie, because her grannie was the least deserving of luck.

"And that's not all." Mrs. McMullen's head was now swaying like a golliwog's.

"Don't tell me you've won the chauffeur and all." This was from Michael, and his grandmother turned her head swiftly in his direction and said, "No. No, I didn't win a chauffeur, but I won a fortnight's holiday in Spain."

Nobody spoke; nobody moved. It would have to be her, thought Sarah. Why couldn't it have been my mam and dad? What use will she make of a car, or a fortnight in Spain?

Mike thought that the truest saying in the world was that the devil looked after his own. Lizzie thought, "What is this going to mean?"

And Mary Ann thought, "I just can't believe it. It isn't fair." And some small section of her mind took up her childhood attitude and asked what God was about anyway, for in dealing out prizes to this old witch he had certainly slipped up.

Corny, still standing in front of the old lady, said, "A fortnight in Spain? That's hard lines all round."

"Hard lines all round? What do you mean?" Mrs. McMullen picked him up even before he fell.

"Well, I mean you not being able to go to Spain, or use the car."

"What makes you think that I'm not going to use the car or go to Spain?"

Corny opened his mouth, straightened his shoulders, blinked his eyes, then closed his mouth as he continued to look at this amazing old woman. And she, staring back at him with her round dark eyes, said, "I'm going to use me car all right."

"But you'll have to get somebody to drive it," Michael put in.

"There'll be plenty to drive it, falling over themselves to drive it. Oh, I'm not worried about that. They'll break their necks for free jaunts."

"But where are you going to keep it?" asked Michael.

Mrs. McMullen now looked back at Corny, and for a moment he thought she was going to say, "In your garage," but she didn't.

"Outside the front door," she said. "Like everybody else in the street."

"A Wolseley outside the front door!" There was a shocked note in Corny's voice at the thought of a Wolseley being left out in all weathers.

"Why not? There's not a garage within half-a-mile of my street, and there's cars dotted all over the place. I've had an old wreck near my window for two years. And the Baileys across the road have just got a cover for theirs. Well, I can get a cover for mine."

A silence fell on the room again. Corny turned away. He didn't look at anyone, not even at Mary Ann, for the thought in his mind was: a Wolseley, a new Wolseley, standing outside a front door, subject to hail, rain and shine. It was too much for him.

"Did you win them both together, I mean the car, and the trip abroad?" asked Michael now.

"Yes, I did. It depended on how many points the judges gave you for the correct answers to the puzzle and the couplet, an' I got the highest."

"What are you going to do about Spain?" Michael had more sense than to say, "You can't go to Spain, Gran."

"I'm going."

"Don't be silly." Lizzie seemed to come alive at last. She swung round, grabbed up the teapot, went to the little tea table, and began pouring out the tea.

"That's a nice attitude to take, isn't it? I'm not in me grave yet."

Again Lizzie swung round, the teapot still in her hand. "I didn't suggest you were in your grave; but I do maintain that you're too old to go off to Spain on your own."

"Who said I was goin' on me own?"

Lizzie stood still now; they all stood still and waited.

"It's for two people."

Lizzie took in a deep breath, but didn't say anything.

"I suppose you think I can't get anybody to go with me."

"Well, I wouldn't bank on it," said Lizzie now. "Who's going to go traipsing off to Spain with . . . ?" She just stopped herself from saying "with an old woman". But Mrs. McMullen supplied the missing words. "Go on," she said. "Who's going to go traipsing off to Spain with an old woman like me? . . . And who should I ask but you, me own daughter?"

"Me!" Lizzie gaped at her mother. Then thrusting her arm backwards, she put the teapot on the edge of the table. It was only Mike's hand, moving swiftly towards it, that stopped it from toppling off.

"Now look here, Mother. Now get this into your head right away——"

"All right, all right, don't start. But I'm just putting it to you. Who's got more right to have a share of me success than me daughter? And on the other hand, who's duty is it to see to me but me daughter's? And there's a third thing. I remember years ago, years and years ago when you were young and bonny you saying how you'd like to go to Spain. You wanted to meet a Spaniard in those days. You thought the contrast with your fairness and his darkness would look well. Aye, and it would have. An, it's not too late; your life's not over yet. And if anyone deserves a holiday, it's you. A real holiday . . . a real one."

There was a movement behind the old woman as Mike went quietly out of the room, and now Lizzie, bending down to her mother, hissed at her, "Look. Now look, Mother. Don't you start on any of your underground tactics, because they won't work. I'm not going to Spain with you, now let that sink right in, and say no more about it, not another word."

With this, Lizzie straightened herself up, glared at her mother for a moment; then she too went out of the room.

It was at this moment that the group down below, after having stopped, struck up again, and Mrs. McMullen, turning towards Michael with ill-concealed fury, cried, "Shut that blasted window or I'll throw something out on that lot!"

"The window's closed, Gran," said Michael quietly.

"Well, it doesn't seem like it." She looked round from one to the other. Then, turning her gimlet eyes towards the window again, she said, "You can't expect noise or anything else to be kept out of this little mousehole; it's a tunnel for wind and weather."

Corny planted himself deliberately in front of Mary Ann and swung her round and pushed her out of the door; and when she was on the landing she stood with her face cupped in her hands. She would hit her, she would. The wicked old . . . ! She wasn't really stumped for words—they were all there in her mind—but she wasn't in the habit of voicing swear words.

She walked slowly across the little landing towards the bedroom door; then came to an abrupt halt. The door was open and in the reflection of the wardrobe mirror she saw her ma and da. Mike had his arms around Lizzie and she had her arms around him. Mary Ann didn't turn away. Years ago she had joyed in watching such reunions between her parents—it meant that everything was all right—and as she looked at them the anger died in her. Mike's voice came to her softly now, saying, "I wouldn't mind, Liz, You can; it's up to you."

"Don't be silly, man. When I travel I'll travel with you or not at all. As for the Spaniard . . . I got him years ago."

Mary Ann turned away, and as she did so the kitchen door opened and Corny came on to the landing. "All right?" he whispered down to her.

She nodded and pointed towards the bedroom, and after catching a glimpse of Mike with Lizzie in his arms, Corny turned quickly away.

Taking Mary Ann into the sitting room, he said quietly, "Your world all right now?"

She nodded and dropped her head slowly on to his breast. Then she muttered, "Why couldn't I have won that car and the trip abroad instead of that old devil? I would have loved you to have had a Wolseley."

"Look." He took her by the shoulders and brought his face down to hers. "I don't want a Wolseley; I've got everything. I'll be so busy in a little while that I won't know where to put meself. As for money . . . well"—he moved his head slowly—"there won't be any more worries about that. Yet all that is on the side; the main thing is I've got you. You've always been all I wanted; you'll go on being all I want. I want you to get that in your head. Make it stick. You understand?"

Mary Ann's eyes were moist as she gazed up into his face. He hadn't mentioned the children, just her. She buried her head again, and he held her tightly. Then after a moment he said, "Do you know what? I know a way we could get her car."

She screwed up her face and he bent his head and touched her nose lightly with his lips as he said, "You could bring her to live here and I could garage——"

"Oh, you!" She punched at him with her two fists.

"Well, it's a way. I mean we'd be sure of the car. And just think . . . a Wolseley!"

"Corny Boyle." Again she was punching at him as he laughed. "Do you want me stark staring mad?"

His arms enfolding her once more, he rocked her backwards and forwards. "I want you any way . . . any way, Mary Ann Boyle. As long as you . . ." He released one arm and, throwing it dramatically upwards, thrust back his head and bellowed, "ACT LIKE A WOMAN."

"Oh, Corny! Corny! Oh, you're daft." She was shaking with her laughter.

"Come on," he said, hugging her to his side. "We'd better get next door and see the end of Dame McMullen's pantomime."

When they reached the landing, there was Mike and Lizzie coming towards the kitchen door, and Corny, taking up another dramatic pose, cried in an undertone, "United we stand, divided we fall. Forward, the Shaughnessy McBoyles!" And on this he thrust open the door and, with an exaggerated bow, he ushered each of them into the room. Mike followed Lizzie. Both were laughing. Mary Ann, following Mike, caught at his hand, and her other hand she placed in Corny's. She was happy . . . happy.

"Mam! Mam!"

"Ma-am!"

But when she heard her children call she released her hold on her father and husband, and, running back to the top of the stairs, she spread her arms wide to her angels. And as she held them she thought that it was odd but during the last few telling days, although she had not forgotten about her angels, they had been thrust into the background, and she had thought only of their father.

And that's how it should be at times; and that's how it must be . . . in the future.

Mary Ann and Bill

To Foster and Rose Mary.
A generation does not divide us.

1

WORDS

Mary Ann sat in the living-room above the garage and looked at her children, and she wondered, and not for the first time, why it was possible that you could be driven almost demented by those you loved most; if it wasn't Corny, it was one of the twins driving her to the point where she wanted to break things.

When the great stroke of luck had befallen them a few months earlier she had thought that all was set fair now for peace, plenty, and pleasure. She couldn't have been more mistaken.

Peace, with that noise going on across the road! What had once been fields overlaid by a wide canopy of sky that she could look into from the bedroom window, was now a contorted mass of scaffolding and buildings in the process of erection. Even to the side of the house, on the spare bit of land, there was hammering and battering and clanking going on all hours of the day; and whereas, at one time, they were lucky to get half-a-dozen customers for petrol during the day, now the custom was so thick they never seemed to close.

This white elephant of a garage, off the beaten track from the main road, which they had supported for seven years in the hope that the road would be extended to take them in had never materialised. Instead, Mr. Blenkinsop, the American, had. And Mr. Blenkinsop had transformed Green Lane and Boyle's garage into a place where the last thing one expected now was peace.

As for plenty, Corny had always said that when his ship came in he'd build her a fine house on this very spot, or anywhere else she liked; they'd get a spanking new car; they'd take a holiday, not a fortnight, but a month, and abroad, and it would be first-class for them from beginning to end; no mediocre boarding-houses for Mrs. Mary Ann Boyle. These were the things he had promised her just before he went to sleep at nights, and she forgot about them the next day, knowing they were but dreams. Yet when the miracle happened and he could have built them a house, bought a smashing car, especially as he was in the business, and taken them for a holiday, what had happened? He couldn't leave the garage; he had to be here at Mr. Blenkinsop's beck and call. As for the house, that would have to wait; let Mr. Blenkinsop get the factory up first and let him get the garage premises extended on the spare land, and then he would think about the house. As for the holiday, well, she could take a week off if she liked, but he couldn't come along. . . . So much for plenty.

And pleasure? Oh! pleasure. She had never had less pleasure in her life than during these last few months. Corny was so tired when he came upstairs that he couldn't even look at the television. As for going out, say to Newcastle, to the pictures, even that was a thing of the past since the miracle had happened.

All she seemed to do now was to cook because there was always somebody popping in for lunch. Mr. Blenkinsop and his cousin Dan from Doncaster, who was now in charge of the works, and other big pots who were interested in the new factory. She had liked doing it at first because she liked being told she was a smashing cook, but she found you could weary of praise when a mountain of dishes kept you going well into the afternoon; and a box of chocolates and a bunch of flowers failed to soothe you since they couldn't wipe up.

And besides the peace, plenty and pleasure, there were the twins. She had always considered she could manage the twins. Even during all those long years when David hadn't been able to speak and his dumbness made him obstinate she had been able to cope with him, but since he had begun to talk six months ago she had found him almost unmanageable. He would lapse into long aggravating silences, during which no one could get a word out of him; but when he did talk the substance of his conversation was such as to make you wonder how on earth he had come by his knowledge, and sometimes create in you a desire to brain him for his precociousness, and at other times to laugh until you cried at his patter.

But this evening she felt no way inclined to laugh at her small son. Anyway, he was in one of his obstinate moods and she could also say that so was she herself. She was fed up to the teeth with this day and all its happenings; from early morning she had been on the go. She had made arrangements to go and get her hair done when Corny had phoned up to say that Mr. Dan Blenkinsop had just come in from Doncaster; how about a cuppa? And she had made a cuppa, and over it Mr. Blenkinsop had been so talkative and charming that the time had gone by and now it was too late for her to keep her appointment in Felling, and her hair looked like nothing on earth, and Corny had accepted the invitation of Mr. Blenkinsop for them all to go to Doncaster tomorrow. . . . Well, she wasn't going. She would just tell Corny and he could phone and call it off; she wasn't going looking a mess like this. In any case it was he who accepted the invitation and not her. He had jumped at it like a schoolboy, saying, "Oh, that'll be grand, a day out. And the twins will be over the moon to see the boys."

She had memories of the last time the twins and Mr. Daniel Blenkinsop's four sons had met. Neither the house nor the garage had returned to order for a week afterwards.

But in the meantime she would use the promised trip—about which their father had already informed them—as a means of making the children come clean regarding why David had been kept in at school.

"You tell me what he's been up to, Rose Mary, or there'll be no trip to Doncaster tomorrow for anybody."

Rose Mary lowered her eyes from her mother's face and slid them towards her brother, but David had his gaze fixed intently on the mantelpiece and, because it meant he had to look over the top of his mother's head, his chin was up and out, and Rose Mary knew from experience it was a bad sign. Their David never talked when he pushed his chin out, no matter what he was looking at. There was a vague yearning in the back of her mind for the time past when their David couldn't talk at all. Everything had been lovely then. She had looked after him and talked for him, and he yelled if he couldn't be with her, but now the tables were turned so completely that he yelled if she insisted on being with him. The only thing their David wanted to do now was to muck about with cars, and get all greased up. He didn't play any more. She didn't see why she kept sticking up for him, she didn't. But when she saw her mother's hand jerk forward suddenly and grip David by the shoulders and heard her voice angry sounding as she cried, "Don't put on that defiant air with me! I warn you; you'll go straight to bed. That's after you get a jolly good smacked backside," she shouted as loudly, "Aw, Mam, don't. Don't bray him. He'll tell you."

Rose Mary was hanging on to her mother's arm now, and, her lips trembling and her voice full of tears, she looked at her brother and cried, "Well, tell her you! If you don't I will, 'cos I'm not goin' to not go to Doncaster the morrow through you. See! 'Cos you won't play with me if we don't go, so tell her."

Both Mary Ann and Rose Mary now concentrated their gaze on David; and David stared back into his mother's eyes and remained mute, and Mary Ann had her work cut out not to box his ears instantly.

Aiming to keep in command of the situation, Mary Ann turned her eyes slowly away from her son's penetrating stare and, looking at her daughter, said, "Well, it's up to you."

Rose Mary swallowed; then, her head drooping on to her chest, she whispered, "He swore."

"SWORE!" Mary Ann again looked at her son. "You swore? Who did you swear at?"

Rose Mary once more supplied the information. "At Miss Plum."

"You didn't, David; you didn't swear at Miss Plum!" Mary Ann was really shocked.

David's round face stretched slightly as he pulled his lower lip downwards and pushed his arched eyebrows towards the rim of his ginger hair.

"What did you say?" Mary Ann's voice was tight, and when the only response she got was the further pulling down of his lip and the further pushing up of his eyebrows she put the question to Rose Mary, "What did he say?"

Rose Mary blinked, then bit on the nail of her middle finger before she said, "Lots."

"Lots! You mean he swore more than once?"

"Ah-ha."

Mary Ann closed her eyes for a moment. She knew this would happen some time or another. The boy spent too much time down in that garage and with the workmen on the site, and knowing some of the adjectives used by the workmen, she trembled to think which one of them he had levelled at his teacher.

"Go on, tell me," she said. She addressed her daughter.

Rose Mary nipped at her lower lip; then, wagging her head from side to side, she cast a glance at her brother, who was now staring straight at her, and said, "Fumblegillgoozle."

"Fumble-gill . . . ? But that's not a word. I mean, that's not swearing."

The twins now exchanged a deep look which Mary Ann could not interpret, and she said, "Well, it isn't. It's a made-up word, isn't it?"

"Yes. Yes, Mam; but Miss Plum said that he said it like swearin'."

Mary Ann hadn't a doubt but that her son could put the inflection on fumble-gill-goozle to make it sound like swearing. He was learning words, he was fascinated by words, and he had a way with his inflection. "Is that all he said?"

"No, Mam." Again the brother and sister exchanged a deep glance before Rose Mary, continuing with the betrayal, whispered, "Antimacassar."

Again Mary Ann closed her eyes, this time to prevent herself from laughing outright. When she opened them she looked directly at her son and said, "Antimacassar and fumblegillgoozle aren't swear words. But it all depends how you use them, and you know that, don't you, dear?"

"Yes, Mam." It was the first time he had spoken since he had come into the house, and the sound of his own voice was like an ice breaker cleaving a way through his imposed silence, for now he added rapidly, "I don't like Miss Plum, Mam. She's big. And I don't like her hands. And when she bends over you you can see right down her throat, and she'd had onions. And she marked me sums wrong and they weren't wrong; and she gave Tony Gibbs ten, and he's a fool. Tony Gibbs is a fool. An I told her I'm not sittin' next to her at mass on Sunday any more. I told her I'm goin' to sit with Rose Mary. . . ."

"Yes, yes, he did, Mam. He told Miss Plum that."

Rose Mary's face was alight with her pleasure. For many months now she had been deprived of her twin's company in so many ways, and to be separated from him in church was to her the last straw. It had been Miss Plum's idea to keep them apart, hoping that the separation might go some way towards enabling David to break the dominance of his sister. Undoubtedly this strategy had helped towards David's independence, but now there was nobody more aware than David that he did not need Miss Plum's help, or that of anyone else for that matter, to make him talk.

"You cheeked Miss Plum, David?"

"No, no, I just told her."

"You must have cheeked her." Mary Ann was bending towards him. "What else did you say?"

David looked up into his mother's face. His eyes were twinkling now, and the corner of his mouth was moving up into a quirk, when Rose Mary spluttered, he spluttered too, until Mary Ann said sharply, "Stop it! Stop it, the both of you. Now I want to know what else you said."

They stopped their giggling and David lapsed into his silence again and Rose Mary said, ". . . Gordon Bennett, Mam, and Blimey Riley."

Mary Ann swallowed deeply. Gordon Bennett was a saying that Jimmy down below in the garage often resorted to. He didn't swear much in front of the children but his intonation when he said "Gordon Bennett!" spoke volumes. And Blimey Riley. Well, that was one Corny often came out with when he was exasperated. He would exclaim between gritted teeth "Bl-i-mey, Riley!" and it certainly sounded more like swearing than swearing. So, in a way, David had sworn.

Poor Miss Plum; she had her sympathy. She had thirty-eight in her class and she needed only two or three Davids to drive her round the bend. She said now sternly, "Miss Plum had every right to keep you in, and if I had been her I would have given you the ruler across your knuckles." She looked from one straight face to the other. "And don't think you're out of the wood yet. Wait till I tell your father about this. Now go and get yourselves washed and then come back and have your tea. And there's no play for you until I say so, understand?"

They stared at her for a moment longer, then as if governed by the same impulse they turned together and went out of the room, and as they passed through the door she cried after them, "What is that you said, David?"

She was on the landing now looking down at her son. She took him by the shoulders again and shook him. "Tell me what you said."

When she paused for a moment and his head stopped bobbing, he spluttered, "Rub-rubber guts."

Mary Ann drew in a deep breath that seemed to swell her small body to twice its size, and she twisted him round and grabbed him by the collar and thrust him into the bedroom to the accompanying pleas of Rose Mary, crying, "Oh, no, Mam! Oh, no! Don't, don't Mam. Don't bray him."

With one hand she thrust Rose Mary back on to the landing, then, standing with her back to the bedroom door, she swiftly stripped down David's short pants and laid the imprint of her hand four times across his buttocks. And then she released him and, panting, stood looking down at him.

She was looking now not at a cheeky little devil, but at a little boy with the tears squeezing from under his tightly closed lids, and she had the desire to grab him up into her arms and soothe him and pet him and say, "There, there! I'm sorry, darling, I'm sorry." But no; Master David had to be taught a lesson. Rubber guts, indeed!

When she turned and hurried from the room she almost fell over Rose Mary, and she yelled at her, "Get into that bathroom and get yourself washed! You're as bad as he is. Wait till your father comes in. There's going to be a change in this house; you see if there isn't."

"Oh, Mam, Mam, you shouldn't; you shouldn't have hit our David. I'll tell me da of you. I will. I will."

Now Rose Mary found herself lifted by the collar and thrust into the bathroom and her dress whipped up and her knickers whipped down, and she screamed open murder as Mary Ann's hand contacted her rounded buttocks. And when it was over she sat on the floor and looked up at Mary Ann and cried between her gasping, "I don't love you. I don't love you. I'm going away. I'm going away to Gran's. And I'll take our David with me. I will, I will. I don't love you."

Mary Ann went out, banging the bathroom door after her; and on the landing once more she put her hand up and cupped her face. "I don't love you. I don't love you." The words were like a knife going into her. Although she knew it was a momentary spasm, and one she had indulged in many a time herself, it had the power to send her spirits into the depths.

She was just going into the kitchen when Corny came bounding up the stairs. "What's the matter? I could hear her screaming downstairs. What's up?"

Mary Ann sat down on a chair and looked up at her tall, homely-looking red-haired husband, and what she said was, "Oh, Corny!"

Dropping on to his hunkers, Corny gathered her hands into his and gazed into her twisted face as he asked softly, "What is it, love? What's the matter? What's happened?"

"I . . . I don't know whether to laugh or cry. I . . . I think I'll cry. . . . I've had to skelp both their behinds."

"Well, it won't be the first time. But what's it about, anyway?"

"He's . . . he's had one of his defiant moods on. They were kept in at school. He's been swearing at Miss Plum."

"No!" He sat back on his hunkers; then grinned, "Swearing? What did he say?"

"Antimacassar." She watched him droop his head on to his chest, and when his eyes, wide and merry, came up to meet hers, she said, "And fumblegillgoozle."

". . . Fumble-what?"

"That's what I said, fumble-what. It's one he's made up. Fumble-gill-goozle. Have you ever heard anything like it?"

He shook his head.

"But that isn't the worst. . . . Gordon Bennett."

"Oh, no!"

"Yes, Gordon Bennett. And you can imagine the emphasis he would put on it. And wait for it, Mr. Boyle." She inclined her head towards him. "Blimey, Riley!"

He took one of his hands from hers and covered his mouth to smother his laughter; then his shoulders began to shake.

"And he called me rubber guts."

The next minute his arms were around her and their heads were together.

After a moment she pressed herself away from him and, looking into his face, she said, "We can laugh, but, you know, it's serious. He's got this thing about words; you never know what he's coming out with next. And I've told you he spends far too much time down in the garage, and on the site, and you can't put a gag in men's mouths."

"Well, he doesn't hear anything really bad down in the garage. There's only Jimmy there; he might come out with a damn and an occasional bloody."

"It's plenty."

"Aw." He rose to his feet. "If he hears nothing worse than that he won't come to much harm."

"He does hear worse than that on the site."

"Well, I can't tie him up, and I can't keep my eye on him all the time, we've just got to let things take their course. He's a lad, Mary Ann. You see—" he turned to her again—"all his life, not being able to talk, he was cut off. To him it must feel as if he'd been born just six months ago, and from the minute he found his voice, he's been experimenting. Let him be and don't worry. Come on, up you get." He pulled her to her feet, then ended, "It's a break you need. Tomorrow's a day out; it'll do you good."

She looked up at him, saying coolly, "A day out you said? Who for? The Blenkinsop boys?"

"Oh, it won't be a repeat of the time they were here. There's plenty of room up at their place. That big field beyond. And then there's the ponies and what not. Once you get there you won't see them or ours until we're coming back. I've got a feeling it's going to be a good day. . . . Come on, let me inject you with that feeling, Mrs. Boyle." Swiftly he picked her up in his arms and kissed her hard, and when he put her down again he said, "There, how's that? Feel the difference?" And when she replied, "Not that you'd notice," he said, "You know, the trouble with you, Mrs. Boyle, is you're growing old."

She didn't laugh with him or retaliate in any way but, going into the scullery to start the tea, she thought, "Yes, I am growing old. I'm twenty-seven." And the train of thought caught a grievance that was in her mind a lot of late, that asked her what had she done with her life? What was she doing with her life? The answer came as before, nothing, except cooking and cleaning, and washing and shopping, and worrying, and waiting for Corny to come up from the garage so she would have company; then watching him going to sleep watching the telly. Then awakening to it all over again the following morning.

Yes; she was twenty-seven, and she was getting old.

2

THE DAY OUT

Rose Mary looked up unsmiling into her mother's face. Although she loved her mother again this morning she wasn't really kind with her, because she hadn't said she was sorry about braying them last night.

They had an arrangement regarding clearing the air after incidents like last night. Whoever was at fault was to be the one to say sorry, and then everybody was kind again. There was no doubt in Rose Mary's mind that her mam was at fault for braying them, because, she reasoned, Miss Plum had punished David for swearing, or for sounding like swearing, and it was awful of her mam to lather into him again.

When Mary Ann said, "Now, let either of you get a mark on your clothes and you're for it. Do you hear me?" she said stiffly, "Yes, Mam."

"Do you hear me, David?"

". . . Yes, Mam."

"Well, remember it. Now go downstairs, but don't you move away from the garage drive. And don't go into the garage. Understand?"

They both looked at her silently, then turned and walked slowly away.

The scene outside was most unusually quiet today. There were no cranes and grabs clanking across the road; no sound of men's voices shouting; no lorries churning up the mud in the lane; and for once no car standing at the petrol tanks opposite the wide space that led into the hangar-like shed that constituted the workshop and garage.

Bringing her eyes to David, who was standing with his hands thrust deep into his pockets, Rose Mary now said, "She never said she was sorry."

He returned her glance and wagged his head twice before saying, "I don't care."

"Neither do I."

"I know some more words." He slanted his eyes at her.

"Eeh! our David. You'd better not. Mam'll give it to you. . . . What are they?" She leant her head towards him, and he grinned at her, then whispered "Skinnymalink."

"Oh, that's not a word; I know that one."

He jerked his head; then said, "Well, you don't know skilligalee."

"Eeh! skilligalee." She whispered the word back at him. "Where did you get it?"

"One of the men." His chin was jerking again.

"Is it a bad swear?"

"Ah-ha."

"Eeh! our David. Mam'll tan you purple if she hears it."

He grinned at her again, then walked jauntingly towards the opening of the garage, and Rose Mary followed him. And there they both stopped and looked into the dim interior where Jimmy was standing talking to a shock-haired, tight-trousered young man, whom they recognized as Poodle-Patter, the nickname given to one of the group with which Jimmy played.

As David went to move forward Rose Mary pulled him back, saying, "Don't go in; Mam'll be down in a minute, and you know what she said."

"I'm not going in; I'm just going to the office door."

"Eeh! our David." Rose Mary remained where she was, but David moved forward, and at the office door he stopped and cocked his ear to hear Jimmy say, "Yes, I know I could get more money at Baxter's but I don't want to go, man."

"You must be barmy." Poodle-Patter dug Jimmy in the chest with his fist. "Five quid a week more and you're turning your nose up at it."

"I'm not turning me nose up at it, man. It's just that I'm well set here. I'm all right."

"How long is it since you had a rise?"

"Couple of months since."

"How much?"

"Ten bob."

"Ten bob!" Poodle-Patter's nose crinkled in scorn. Then leaning towards Jimmy, he said, "You want to come in with us in the car, don't you?"

"You know I do."

"Well then you'll have to do something about it. Duke's got his eye on this mini-bus. He can get it for two hundred if we put the money down flat, I told you, but if it's spread over it'll mean another thirty quid on it, and as Duke says somebody's got to take the responsibility of the never-never and he's not going to. He's been done afore, you remember? It's cash and equal shares: forty quid each, then we'll all have a say in it."

"Forty quid!" Jimmy's voice was scornful. I couldn't raise forty shillings at the minute, and you know it. Look here, Poodle." He now dug his finger into Poodle's chest. "You an' Duke an' the rest talkin' about responsibilities, well, I've got responsibilities; and to me mam. There's only one wage comin' into our house, and that's mine; and there's three of us to keep on it, with Theresa still at school. You can tell Duke from me he can buy his blasted car and count me out."

"Ah, don't get ratty, man; you know we wouldn't do anything without you. Anyway, you're necessary to our lot and we know it; there's not one of us knows owt about a car, we'd have to pay God knows what for repairs. You've kept The Duchess going over the last year when she should have been on the scrap heap. I don't know how you've done it. I said so to Dave and Barny. 'I don't know how Jimmy does it,' I said. Look." Poodle-Patter moved nearer to Jimmy, his voice wheedling now, "I'm not asking you to do anything out of line, I'm only saying make a move. Everybody should make a move, and you've been in this dump long enough. And it isn't as if you're not sure of a job. I tell you, Baxter's are wantin' somebody like you, a bloke with experience. And that's the basic they're paying, fifteen quid a week. Will you think on it?"

"Look!" Jimmy bowed his head while thrusting his fist out towards Poodle, and Poodle, playfully gripping it between his hands, wagged it, saying, "That's a boy! That's a boy! Sleep on it. There's no real hurry, not really; The Duchess has carried us a good many trips, she'll carry us a few more. I'll tell Duke you're considering it. Look, I must be off. See you, fellow."

Poodle now punched Jimmy once more in the chest, then turned swiftly towards the garage opening, and when he passed Rose Mary he put his hand out and chucked her chin, saying, "O-o-oh! hello there, gorgeous."

Rose Mary blinked her eyes and tossed her head. She wasn't displeased with the title of gorgeous. All Jimmy's band called her gorgeous, but Jimmy didn't because he knew her dad wouldn't have let him.

As she saw David move further into the garage she whispered hoarsely, "No, our David! Mam'll be down in a second; you'll only get wrong."

David didn't appear to hear her, for he walked towards Jimmy, who was now standing with his two hands on the bonnet of a car, his head bent forward as if he was thinking deeply, and he looked up at him for some seconds before he said, "Jimmy."

"Oh; hello there." Jimmy straightened himself up, then grinned down at the small boy. "By, you look smashin'. I never knew you looked like that; it must be 'cos you've been washed."

David did not grin back at his friend but considered him seriously for a moment before saying, "You wouldn't leave here, would you, Jimmy?"

"Leave here? . . . Aw." Jimmy jerked his chin to the side. Then looking down slantwise at David, he said, "Trust you to hear things you shouldn't. You've got lugs on you like a cuddy."

"But you wouldn't, would you, Jimmy?"

"No."

"But you'd get five pounds more at Baxter's."

"Aye, I'd get five pounds more at Baxter's, so what?"

"Why . . . why don't you ask Dad for more money?"

"Look." Jimmy dropped on his hunkers and, his face level with David's, he was about to put his hands on his shoulders when he stopped himself and exclaimed, "Eeh! I just need to do that and I'll have your man knock the daylights out of me." He rubbed the palms of his oily hands together and said, slowly now, "Your dad gave me a rise just a while ago. That's the second one in six months, and who knows, maybe I'll get another one shortly. I'm satisfied, so what is there to worry about?"

David stared unblinkingly into the long, kindly face. Although Jimmy neither came upstairs for meals nor slept in their house he considered him part of his family; he liked him next to his mam and dad. He didn't place Rose Mary in his list of affections; because Rose Mary was already inside of him, part of himself. He might fight with her, tease her and torment her, but he also listened to her and considered her views and demands as if they were issuing from his own brain. He asked now quietly, "Will they put you out of the band if you don't help to buy the car?"

Jimmy put his head on one side and began to chuckle; then he shook it slowly before he said, "You know, you're a rum customer. You know what I think? I think you've been here afore. Me mother always says that some folks have been here afore. She says that they couldn't know what to do at an early age unless they had learned it in another life." He drooped his head to the other side, adding, "You don't know what I'm on about do you? But to answer your question. Aye, very likely if I don't fork out they might. . . ."

At this moment there came the toot-toot of a motor-horn and Jimmy, stretching his long length upwards, exclaimed, as he smiled at David, "Ah, here we go again," then went out towards the petrol pumps and the customer.

David was once more standing beside Rose Mary when Mary Ann and Corny appeared on the drive. He watched his father walk slowly towards Jimmy, then stand waiting while Jimmy took the money from the driver, saying, "A pound and sixpence."

The man in the car handing Jimmy two pound notes, said, "I'm sorry I haven't any less," and Jimmy replied, "That's all right, sir, I'll get you the change."

Within seconds he came back from the office and, looking at Corny, said, "I haven't got it in the till; can you change it, boss?"

"No, not a pound note," said Corny, then bending towards the man in the car, he said, "We'll call it straight." He nodded towards Jimmy, and Jimmy handed the man the pound note back again.

"That's very kind of you." The driver smiled up at Corny, saying, "I'll have to remember to call this way when I'm coming back and do the same again."

They all laughed now.

As the car drove away Mary Ann said to no one in particular, "That's the third time to my knowledge you've run out of change in a fortnight. Oh! Oh!" She raised her hand, "It's only sixpence I know. It was only threepence before, and a shilling before that. But what's a shilling? And what's sixpence? And what's threepence in a fortnight? Only one and nine. But there's fifty-two weeks in a year. Cut those by half, and you have twenty-six one and ninepences. At least." She turned round now and confronted both Corny and Jimmy.

There was a grin on Jimmy's face but he remained silent. There was a grin on Corny's face too, and he said airily, "Yes, twenty-six one and ninepences up the flue. . . . But, Mrs. Boyle." He walked towards her, then took her arm and led her into the garage towards their car. "Did you hear what that gentleman said? I'll call this way when I'm coming back. Now. He's no fool, and he knows I'm no fool; I'm not going to do that every time he calls in. But the impression is made, the good impression. He'll tell his friends. He won't say they'll get cheaper petrol here, or that this garage bloke doesn't care about money; he'll say, 'Go to Boyle's, you'll get the service. It's a good garage.' Aw, to heck!" He pulled open the car door. "What does it matter? We needn't worry about the coppers any longer. Get yourself in, woman." He slapped at her bottom. "Aren't I always telling you them days are gone? Come on you two." He yanked the children into the back of the car, and as he started her up he said in grave, dignified tones, "Remember, Mrs. Boyle, you're married to a man with a bank balance that is getting blacker and blacker every week. Twenty-six one and ninepences. . . . Rabbit feed!"

When she dug him in the ribs he laughed; then pushing his head out of the window, he called to Jimmy, saying, "Now, you'll lock up at six and see everything's O.K. before you leave . . . right?"

"Don't you worry, boss. Have a nice time."

And Mary Ann called, "And don't forget to turn the gas off. I've left it in the oven for you, a pie; it just needs warming. Half-an-hour."

"Right-o, Mrs. Boyle. Thanks. Thanks. . . . Bye-bye, nippers." He waved to the children, and they waved to him.

As the car swung into the road Mary Ann sat back and sighed. It was nice after all to get away for a day, away from the honk-honks, the smell of petrol and the irritations, which were still present even when the banging and noise had ceased. She sighed again. She would enjoy today. Yes, she would enjoy today. And it went without saying that the twins would; they loved the Blenkinsop horde. She was about to turn to them when the unusual quiet that prevailed in the back of the car was forced on her notice and she nipped at her lip to suppress her smile. The events of last night were evidently still with them and they were expecting her to say she was sorry. Well, they could expect. Rubber guts, indeed!

Corny, too, noticing the absence of chatter remarked under his breath, "No talkie-talkie from backie-backie" and she replied softly and in the same idiom, "Coventry. Waiting for sorry-sorry, but no feely like it."

When Rose Mary saw her mam and dad laughing quietly together she felt slightly peeved; she hadn't been able to make out what they were talking about. She wanted to lean over and say, "What you laughing at, Mam?" She always liked to be in on a joke. But she wasn't kind with her mam. Yet she was still kind with her dad, so she could talk to him.

She leaned towards Corny now and said, "Do you know Annabel Morton, Dad?"

"Annabel Morton? No." His head went up as if he was thinking. "Never heard of her in me life."

"Oh, Dad!" Rose Mary pushed him in the back. "You do know Annabel Morton. I'm always talking about Annabel Morton. She's a beast, and she's Miss Plum's favourite. You do know Annabel Morton."

"Oh . . . h! that Annabel Morton. Oh yes, I know that stinker. She's dreadful; she's terrible; she's horrible; she's. . . ."

"Dad! you're takin' the micky."

"Oh, no, I'm not; I'm just agreeing with all you've said about Annabel Morton. What's she done now . . . that Annabel Morton?"

"Well, yesterday dinner-time, after we came out of the hall, Patricia Gibbs was telling me about the girl who lives next door to her and who's going to be married in a long white dress with a train, and a wreath and veil and everything, and she's going to marry a priest."

Mary Ann's head, on the point of jerking round, stopped abruptly and she continued to gaze ahead while she waited and left the sorting of this one to Corny.

"Oh, she's going to marry a priest, is she? Is she a Catholic?"

"No; she said she wasn't, but she's going to marry a priest."

"It'll be a minister she's going to marry."

"No, no, I said that, 'cos I know they're called ministers, and misters, but she said no, he was a priest and she was going to marry him."

"Oh, I think she made a mistake," said Corny. "It wouldn't be—"

"It wasn't a mistake, Dad. And as we were talkin' about it Annabel Morton had her lugs cocked and she said Patricia Gibbs was barmy and she'd picked a barmy one to tell it to, and she meant me, and I slapped her face for her."

After a short pause Corny said, "In a way, I think Annabel Morton was right this time. I think Patricia Gibbs is a bit barmy if she says that the girl is going to marry a priest."

There was another short silence before Rose Mary said, "Well, why can't priests marry, Dad?"

Corny was saved from trying to explain a situation that was beyond his understanding by his son saying, "'Cos they can't marry people, women, you nit, they can only marry nuns."

The car seemed to do a side-step. In the middle of a splutter Mary Ann cried, "Careful!'n' Then with her head down she said, "Look where you're going."

"They don't marry nuns. Eeh! our David. Nuns can't marry; they're angels."

There was a short silence now as David tried to digest this. Then he put the question to his father's back. "They're not, Dad, are they? Nuns aren't angels. They've got legs, haven't they?"

The car took another erratic course before Corny replied thickly, "Well, angels could have legs. . . . Speaking of legs—" Corny now aimed to direct the conversation into safer channels. "Did you bring your football boots?"

"No, Dad."

"Well, you won't have any toes left in your shoes when Brian and Rex get that ball going."

"Do you think we'll see Susan and Diana?" asked Rose Mary now.

"Perhaps," said Corny. "We'll see Susan, anyway."

"Well, we didn't last time; she was away on the complement."

"Continent."

"Yes, Dad; that's what I said, complement."

Another short pause before Rose Mary stated, "I like Susan; she's nice. She said I'm going to be tall like you, Dad. I want to be tall, I don't want to be little."

"Stabbed in the back." Mary Ann muttered the words below her breath, and Corny muttered back, "Better give in and get it over."

"Susan says when you're tall you can. . . ."

Mary Ann turned around and surveyed her offspring, looking first at Rose Mary, then at David, then back to Rose Mary again. She said quietly, "I'm sorry."

Rose Mary wriggled her bottom on the seat, drew her lower lip right into her mouth, drooped her head, then wagged it from side to side before raising it sideways and glancing at David.

David's reactions had not been so obvious. All he did was to sit on his hands and lower his lids.

Then, again as if released by one spring, they were standing up and their arms were about Mary Ann's neck and they were laughing as they cried, "Oh, Mam! Mam!"

"There now. There now. You'll choke me. Sit down. Sit down."

David sat back on the seat, but Rose Mary lingered. Her mouth rubbing against Mary Ann's ear, she whispered, "I was only having you on, Mam. I don't care how big I am."

Mary Ann kissed the face so like her own; and when she was settled in her seat again she looked at Corny, whose amused glance flashed to hers, and she thought, as she had done so often as a child, It's going to be a lovely day, beautiful.

*   *   *

The Dan Blenkinsops lived in an old house on the outskirts of Doncaster. It had the added attraction of a tennis court, a paddock, and a strip of woodland.

Dan and Ida Blenkinsop had six children, four boys and two girls. Tommy, the youngest, was eight; Rex was ten; Brian, eleven; and Roland, thirteen; then there was Susan, fifteen, and Diana, nineteen.

Mary Ann had met all the family with the exception of Diana, and she was looking forward to meeting Mr. Blenkinsop's eldest daughter, for she would likely see a great deal of her in the future as she was going to act as secretary to her father who was now in the position of managing director of the English side of Blenkinsop's Packing Company.

Mary Ann was now sitting in the corner of a luxurious couch which was upholstered in pale blue satin and bore the imprint of grubby hands and, even worse, dirty feet. She looked about her at the lovely pieces of furniture, all, to her mind, ill-treated; cups and glasses standing on the grand piano; a conglomeration of boys' implements, all of a destructive nature ranging from catapults to guns, and including a bow and arrow, lay piled on what was evidently an antique desk. The Chinese carpet showed the tread of dirty shoes all over it, and from where she sat she could see into the hall and to the bottom of the stairs where a long coloured scarf hung like a limp flag from the banisters. She could see shoes lying jumbled on the parquet floor, and coats and sweaters heaped on a chair.

Mary Ann smiled to herself. It took all sorts to make a world. And in this world of the Blenkinsops there was evidently no discipline but a lot of fun. Also, she sensed there was a lot of money squandered needlessly. Yet, she had to admit, the children didn't act spoilt. They were very good-mannered and charming—that's when they were forced to stand, or to sit still for a moment, but most of the time they seemed to be bounding, jumping or rushing somewhere, yelling, shouting and calling as they went. And their mother wasn't in the least affected by it.

Mary Ann now watched Mrs. Blenkinsop come into the room. She never seemed to hurry. She was tall and rather graceful, with black hair and black eyes, in sharp contrast to her husband who was very fair, and, incidentally, much shorter than his wife.

Mrs. Blenkinsop came straight towards Mary Ann, saying, "Diana's coming; you've got to pin her down when you can." She sank on to the couch, adding, "She's making the best of the time left to her. She loves riding; she's never stopped all the holidays. Ah." She turned her face towards Mary Ann, "But they're only young once, aren't they?"

She was speaking as if to an equal, and quite suddenly Mary Ann again felt old, like she had done last night. Mrs. Blenkinsop must be forty if she was a day, but her words seemed to imply that they were both of a similar age and frivolity was past them.

Mr. Blenkinsop now came across the room, walking with Corny. He was saying, "Well, the main office is ready and that's all that matters at present. Get the brain working and the body will take care of itself." He laughed his hearty laugh, adding, "Anyway, from Monday next that'll be my headquarters and. . . ." He paused and looked towards the door and, his voice rising, he added, "And that of my able secretary, Miss Diana Blenkinsop."

From the very first sight of the tall, leggy, blonde-headed, extremely modern-looking Diana, Mary Ann experienced a feeling of apprehension, even danger, for there arose in her immediately the fighting protective feeling that she had lived with, and acted on, during the years of her childhood . . . and after. The feeling had centred then around her father, but now it wasn't her father who was bringing it to the fore, but her husband.

She looked at Corny standing in front of the girl who was almost his height, and his ordinary looking face, which at times appeared handsome to her, was, she imagined, looking its most attractive at this moment. The girl, she noted, had almond-shaped, wide-spaced blue eyes and she was using them unblinkingly on Corny. It wasn't until her father drew her attention away by saying, "And this is Mrs. Boyle," that she turned from him.

Mary Ann didn't stand up. She was at a disadvantage sitting down, but she knew she would be dwarfed still further if she got to her feet.

"This is Diana. Now you two will be bumping into each other pretty often, I'm sure, so the sooner you get acquainted the better."

Diana lowered herself down on to the arm of the couch, and Mary Ann was forced to put her head well back to look up at her, and she made herself speak pleasantly to the disdainful-looking madam, as she had already dubbed her.

"Will this be your first post as secretary?"

"No." The voice was cool, matching the whole appearance. "I've been with Kent, the solicitor, for three months. . . ."

"Oh, and then she was with Broadbent's." It was her mother speaking now. "She was there for nearly six months, weren't you, dear?" It was as if Mrs. Blenkinsop was emphasising that her daughter wasn't without experience.

"You're going to find it a change from a solicitor's." They all looked at Corny. He was seated opposite the couch and he was looking directly at Diana Blenkinsop, and she looked back at him as she asked politely, "What way, different?"

"Oh." He jerked his head. "Well, a bit rougher, I should say. There are nearly two hundred chaps knocking around there and you'll be the only female. Oh, of course, except Mary Ann." He now looked towards Mary Ann, and she looked back at him. Oh of course, except Mary Ann, he had said. She wasn't a female; she was just some gender that passed unnoticed among two hundred men.

"Oh, we're not worried about Diana." Mrs. Blenkinsop was walking towards the french windows. "She can take care of herself." She cast a smiling glance back to her daughter before going on to the terrace and calling, "Roland. Brian. Lunch. Bring them in . . . lunch."

Mr. Blenkinsop now seated himself beside Mary Ann and began to talk to her. She had a feeling that he was trying to be kind, going out of his way to be kind. When she looked at him she thought he was in much the same position as herself, being small. Perhaps he was being kind because he knew what it felt like to be confronted by the big types, either male or female.

His effort was checked by the avalanche of his four boys and their sister, Susan, together with her own two. They all came into the room yelling at the top of their voices; even Rose Mary and David. She wanted to check them but resisted. And then Rose Mary had hold of her hands, gabbling, "Oh, Mam! Mam, you just come and see them. They're beautiful, lovely, aren't they, David?"

"Oh yes. Come and see them, Mam, will you, 'cos they're super."

She smiled her bewilderment not only from one to the other, but also to the group of Blenkinsops, who were all around the couch now, and they explained in a chorus, "The puppies. . . . The Grip's had puppies."

Fancy calling a dog, a female dog, The Grip; yet she remembered her one and only encounter with the family's bull terrier, and the name, she imagined, wasn't entirely inappropriate, although they had assured her The Grip was as gentle as a kitten . . . with people. With other dogs it was a different matter, they explained. Apparently, she had earned her title from her power to hang on to any four-footed creature which earned her dislike. But now The Grip had had puppies. It was odd that anything so fierce was capable of motherhood. Mary Ann widened her eyes and showed pleased surprise and assured them that she would love to see The Grip's puppies.

"But not before lunch," said Mrs. Blenkinsop emphatically, as she shooed the children into the hall, with orders to wash.

A few minutes later they were all in the dining-room, and Mary Ann was both impressed and saddened by the quality of the silver and china used, and the chips and cracks in the latter. And she was almost horrified at the toe and heel indentations on the legs of the period table and chairs. It was all right being free and easy, she thought, but the condition of this beautiful furniture almost amounted to vandalism. But, as her dad was always saying, it took all kinds.

The lunch, she considered, was very ordinary, and the food would have been completely dull if it hadn't been enlivened with wine. She took note that Corny allowed his glass to be filled up three times, and also that the two Blenkinsop girls and Roland were allowed wine, and the boy was only thirteen. By the end of the lunch she told herself this was an entirely different way of living from her own; nevertheless, she preferred her own every time.

The children's demands that they should go to see the puppies cut short any lingering over coffee, and Mary Ann wasn't displeased that they should get outside, because she was finding herself irritated by Diana Blenkinsop's supercilious attitude, and more so because it seemed lost on Corny, for he was talking to her as if he had known her all his life; and she had even condescended to laugh at something he said.

But one thing Mary Ann told herself as she walked down the garden by Mr. Blenkinsop's side, nodding politely as he talked without really paying much attention to what he was saying, was that when they left here she must say nothing detrimental about Diana Blenkinsop. She must keep her spleen to herself; all the books told you that you got off on the wrong foot when you showed your jealousy. Not that she was jealous. Oh no; it was only that Corny had seemingly found Diana Blenkinsop attractive, and if she should voice the opposite view about her it would only show her less attractive by comparison. . . . That's what all the books said.

They came to the paddock and the stables, and here, in a wire-netting enclosure, were The Grip and her six offspring.

The barking and yapping of the young puppies was overlaid by the exclamations of admiration from the children.

Mr. Blenkinsop stooped down and picked up one of the puppies and, putting it into Rose Mary's arms, said, "There. What does it feel like?"

"Oh, Mam! Mam!" Rose Mary was laughing hysterically as she strained her face away from the puppy's tongue and endeavoured to hang on to his wriggling body.

"She may drop it," said Mary Ann anxiously, and Mr. Blenkinsop said, "It's all right,

I've got him. But she mustn't drop this one because he's the prize pup. Thirty-five guineas' worth there. He goes tomorrow."

"Thirty-five guineas!" Corny was making appreciative movements with his head.

"Yes. It seems a lot," said Mr. Blenkinsop, "but she's a thoroughbred. And what's more, I'm going to be out of pocket by the time they all go. You have no idea . . . I'm telling you you've no idea what it takes to feed these youngsters. But, thank goodness, they'll all be gone by the end of the month, with the exception of Bill there." He pointed to where David was scratching the tummy of one of the pups who was lying on its back. "He's the runt."

"What's the matter with him?" Mary Ann asked politely.

"Oh, nothing really, except that his chest is too broad. It's supposed to be broad—these brindles are noted for their chests, but they've got to have legs to support them, like this one here." He took the puppy from Rose Mary's arms and held it up. "You see, his front legs are as straight as broom shanks, but when Bill there grows, his weight will make him bandy. But he's full of life. He's a lad, is Bill."

"Dad!" Amid the hubbub David's voice went unheard. "Dad! Dad!" He tugged at his father's sleeve.

"Yes, what is it?" Corny bent over David, and David looked up into his father's eyes, then down at the puppy lying on its back. "Aw-w! I don't know about that." Corny straightened up; then looked at Mary Ann and said under his breath, "He's after a pup."

Mary Ann gave him one telling look. A pup indeed! she had enough to put up with without a dog going mad around the house. Oh, no! She was about to turn away in the hope of drawing her offspring with her when David's voice hit her, crying loudly, "Mam! Mam!" And she looked down at him and said under her breath, "No, David."

But Rose Mary had picked up the scent now. Standing close to Mary Ann she caressed her hand and looked up at her pleadingly, saying, "Couldn't we, Mam? Couldn't we?"

"No! And that's final. And stop it." Mary Ann was hissing now.

It would seem that Mr. Blenkinsop had not heard any of the exchanges, at least he gave a good imitation of being unaware of what was going on, for, stooping down, he picked up the now bounding puppy and, bringing it over the wire, held it in front of Mary Ann and said, engagingly, "Can I make you a present of him?"

"WH . . . !" Mary Ann swallowed, blinked her eyes, glanced wildly around her, then was forced to take the puppy into her arms, and her acceptance or refusal was drowned by the shrieks of delight from both Rose Mary and David, and these were echoed by the entire male side of the Blenkinsop family.

"Oh good. I'm glad you're going to have Bill," cried Roland; and Brian, endorsing his brother's words, said, "We wondered what would happen to him. We wouldn't be able to keep him, you see, not with The Grip. Sort of mother and son, you know."

And so Mary Ann, who didn't want a dog, who had never really been fond of dogs, well, not since she was a child, who felt herself cramped and restricted in the confines of her four small rooms, and whose life at the moment seemed full of drudgery and empty of anything creative, was now to be saddled with a dog, and, of all breeds, a bull terrier, which type was known for its ferocity. She'd go mad. And this, without taking into account the future, in which Diana Blenkinsop portended to move large. But with eleven people all milling around, all expounding in different ways on Bill's virtues, what could you do but just smile. She was still smiling when Diana, staring her straight in the face, said, "Runts are always unpredictable, but the best of luck." Whereupon, Mary Ann had an almost uncontrollable desire to reach up and slap her face. Eeh! she'd be glad when she was home.

It was a quarter to one when Corny was roused from a deep sleep by a small hand on his face and a voice whispering, "Dad! Dad!"

"Yes . . . yes. What is it?"

"It's Bill, Dad. He's howling. He's crying."

"Look, Rose Mary!" Corny too was whispering hoarsely now. "Go on back to bed."

"But he misses his mam, Dad. And it's the first night. Could we not bring him up . . . ?"

"No! Definitely no. Get back to bed."

"But, Dad."

"Look. Do you want your backside skelped? Go on; you'll wake your mam, and David."

"David's awake, Dad; he's on the landing, top of the stairs."

"Oh my God! The words were muttered thickly as Corny dragged himself out of bed, and, pushing Rose Mary before him, he groped his way out of the dark room and on to the darker landing.

"David!"

"Yes, Dad."

"Get yourself back into bed this instant."

There was no movement from the head of the stairs.

"Do you hear me?" Corny felt his son groping his way across the landing; then he followed him into the small room and switched on the light, and, looking from one to the other, he said, "Bill's not coming upstairs. That was agreed last night. Now, wasn't it? He's got to sleep downstairs. You know what your mother said; you were lucky that she brought him. Now don't press your luck, and get back into bed, both of you!"

The last three words were like the crack of a whip. With a lift of his hand he hoisted David into the upper bunk, and without another word he switched off the light and groped his way back into his own room again.

Corny hadn't slept side by side with Mary Ann for eight years not to know when she was asleep or awake, even if she was silent. As he wriggled himself down under the clothes he said, "Don't say it," and for answer she replied very quietly, "I'm going to say it. You evaded the issue when we came to bed by very conveniently going straight to sleep, but I saw you giving Mr. Blenkinsop the wink to pass the puppy on to me. You wanted that dog as much as they did, and you saw the only way to get it was to put me on the spot. Well now, you got your way and what are you going to do about it? Just listen to him."

For a moment they lay and listened to the heart-rending howls that came up through the floor boards from the garage where Bill was ensconced in a blanket-lined wash-basket. Corny, making no reference to the duplicity of which he was accused, grunted, "He'll get used to it."

"But what are we going to do until he does? He's been like that for the last two hours."

"You've been awake all that time?" He turned quickly and drew her into his arms, where she lay unyielding against him.

"I'm sorry, love; I'm sorry. But . . . but they wanted him. Yes, yes, I know I did an' all. I've always wanted a dog about the place, and he's cute. You'll get to like him. He's cute." He squeezed her.

"O-o-o-o! Ow'll! Wow! Wow! WO-OW-OOO!"

"Oh my God!" Corny pulled the clothes over their heads, and as Mary Ann pushed them back again she remarked coolly, "You'll get used to it."

"Now, look; don't take that attitude. Very likely I will get used to it. I'll have to, won't I? But don't be snooty and so damn self-righteous."

Corny turned round on to his other side again and again put his head under the bedclothes. . . .

At half-past-two, dragging on his trousers with such ferocity that he pulled off the brace belt, he went from the room and down the stairs and, unlocking the garage, grabbed up the yapping pup and marched upstairs with it to the kitchen where, dragging a cushion from a chair, he put it inside the fender, near the oven, and plonked the now quiet animal into the middle of it. Bending down close to it, he growled, "Now, another word out of you, just one more peep, and out of the window you go."

Bill stared up at Corny with his small round eyes, then he opened his mouth and yawned widely. He understood. The first round had been won.

Mary Ann arose at half past six. She didn't always get up so early, and after the night she'd had she needed extra rest, but something told her that she should rise. Perhaps it was the small scufflings from behind the wall to the right of her.

When she entered the kitchen she stopped dead, absolutely dead, and so did Bill.

Bill was in the middle of disembowelling the armchair; he was covered all over with kapok, and he gave two delicate sneezes to rid his nose of the fluff adhering to it; then he jumped down from the chair and bounded towards her. Mary Ann let him jump around her feet as she leant against the door, with one hand on the knob and the other across her mouth. Inside the fender was the remains of a cushion; on the hearth rug was what had once been a tea towel; the woollen hand-knitted tea-cosy that she had bought from the bazaar just a few weeks ago had almost returned to its original state of unknitted wool. Great lengths of it stretched from one corner of the room to the other, and the legs of a chair had taken on the appearance of a loom. All that was left of the tea cosy was the pink woollen rose that had adorned the top. And pervading this chaos was a peculiar smell. It was what her da had been wont to call a widdle scent. He had said that animals didn't smell, they just gave off a widdle scent.

Widdle scent! Three puddles and two mounds of dark matter, the result, no doubt, of the extra mince with which the children had fed him.

"Get away!" Her voice was almost a thin scream. She slapped her hand so hard on his rump that he was bowled over sideways. But Bill was a friendly, forgiving chap, and he showed it by again jumping up at her. For this show of affection he found himself being lifted by the scruff of the neck and thrown into the scullery and the door banged on him. Well, well; that's what a fellow got for simply passing the time until people turned up.

Mary Ann now stalked into the bedroom, and when she ripped the bedclothes from her husband he sat bolt upright, spluttering, "W . . . what . . . What is it? what's the matter?"

"Would you mind coming into the kitchen."

"Aw, Lord!" Corny flopped back on to the bed again. "He's wet. All right, he's wet. I'll wipe it up."

"Corny!"

He opened his eyes, there was a danger signal in that note. He got out of the bed and followed Mary Ann out of the room and into the kitchen. There he took one look then closed his eyes tightly and muttered deeply and thickly, "Oh, Christopher Colombus!"

When he opened his eyes again she was standing a yard from him, the tears glazing her cheeks, and he went to her and said softly, "I'm sorry, love, I'm sorry. I'll keep him downstairs. I promise."

"Have . . . have you seen the chair?"

He looked towards the disembowelled chair. Then drooping his head, he said, "I'll get you another. This very day, I'll get you another, a better one."

"It's . . . it's one of a pair. It's spoilt the pair." Her whole face was trembling.

"I'll get you a pair. It doesn't matter about that, but . . . but I'll kill him for this, see if I don't. Where is he?"

Corny would have had to be deaf not to know where Bill was, and he made for the scullery door, only to stop before opening it and say, "I'd better get my things on first."

A few minutes later, carrying Bill by the scruff of the neck, he took him downstairs and thrust him into the basket in the garage, and, holding him there, he addressed him. "Look here. The quicker you learn to put up with this the better for all concerned. This is your home. Now understand that, this basket, this place." He beat the side of the basket with his hand and rolled his head to indicate the garage.

Bill, sitting on his hindquarters, now thrust out the tip of a very pink tongue, and, lifting his right front paw, he wagged it at Corny, and Corny rubbing his hand across his brow, said, "Aw, man, it's no use; you won't last a week at this rate, she won't put up with it. And I don't blame her. Look, if I'd had any idea of what you were going to do upstairs you could have yelled your lungs out; and you will the night."

The paw was still flapping at him, and after raising his eyes heavenwards and shaking his head he took it and said, "All right, all right. But I'm warning you. You've got to stay mum if you want to last out here."

3

LIKE MOTHER LIKE DAUGHTER

This was the third time Rose Mary had been to confession. She had been frightened the first time, but she wasn't any more. Father Carey was nice, but she wouldn't like to go to Father Doughty. Eeh! no. They said he gave you awful penances like standing on your head and walking on glass on your bare feet, but Father Carey just said, "Say one Our Father and three Hail Marys." She liked Father Carey. She was trying to explain to him now a particular kind of sin; the sin of telling her mother she didn't love her while all the time she loved her a lot, heaps and heaps.

"Why do you keep telling your mother you don't love her?" The priest's voice was very soothing.

"'Cos of Bill."

"Bill?"

"Our dog."

"OO-h!"

"Mam says we've got to get rid of him."

"She doesn't like Bill?"

"No; 'cos he tore up the chair and the tea-towels, and he howls all night, and he makes widdles and dollops all over the place if he's let upstairs."

The priest cleared his throat and it was some seconds before he was able to say, "Well, you must train your dog."

"He doesn't want to be trained, Father; he jumps all over you and licks you. He's nice, Father."

There was another silence before the priest said, "What kind of a dog is he?"

"He's a bull terrier, Father." Rose Mary thought the priest groaned. "Father." She craned her face up to the dark mesh that separated her from the faint outline of the hand that was cupping the youthful cheek of Father Carey. "Will you pray that she'll like him, Father, make something happen sort of that she'll like him?"

The hand moved on the face and she could see the mouth now, the lips moving one over the other; then the priest said, "You want a miracle."

Rose Mary's eyebrows, stretching upwards, seemed to make her grow taller because she was now seeing Father Carey's whole head as she exclaimed on a high note, "Oh yes, please,

Father. Oh yes! that would do it, a miracle."

The priest's voice was hurried now and slightly stern and very dampening as he said, "You've got to pray awfully hard for miracles, awfully hard; they're not easily come by; you've got to work at them. What you'll have to do is to be very good and please your mother and keep the dog out of her way for a time while you train it."

"Yes, Father." Her voice was meek but some part of her mind was answering him in a different tone altogether, saying, "Ah, man, we've done all that."

"Now, for you penance say one 'Our Father' and three 'Hail Marys', and be a good girl."

It was dismissal, but she knelt on; and then she said, "But I haven't said me act of contrition, Father."

Her eyebrows again moved upwards because she thought she heard the priest saying, "Oh, lord!" Like that, like their David said sometimes, not holy-like at all.

"Make a good act of contrition."

"Oh, my God, I am very sorry that I have sinned against Thee because Thou are so good and by the help of Thy Holy Grace I'll never sin again. In the name of the Father, SonHolyGhostAmen. Ta-rah, Father."

"Good night, my child." The priest was coughing badly now.

She left the confessional with her head bowed, her hands joined, and she acted holy all the way to the rail of Our Lady's altar. And there she said her penance; and there, very much as her mother had done not so many years ago, she laid her problems before the Holy Family, and not only the problem of the dog, but the problem that was really, in a way, more important.

She would like to have told Father Carey about this other problem but it was a jumbled confused mass of impressions in her mind; there was nothing clear cut about it as there was about Bill. Bill either went or he stayed; yet this other problem, in a way, was also about going and staying, and it concerned her mam and dad and . . . her. She always thought of Diana Blenkinsop as her. She didn't like Diana Blenkinsop, and this troubled her too because she liked all the other Blenkinsops, all the boys and Susan, and Mr. Blenkinsop and Mrs. . . . Well, she liked Mrs. Blenkinsop a little bit, not a lot, but she hated Diana, 'cos Diana made her da laugh, and that made her mam angry, proper angry.

Diana Blenkinsop was always coming to the garage for this and that. She hadn't seen her herself because she was at school, but she had heard her mam asking her dad at night why she had to leave her office so often. She had asked did Diana want her dad to sharpen her pencils for her. That could have been funny but it wasn't; it was sort of frightening. And now, even when she tried to explain this problem to Our Lady, who was holding Jesus and looking down on her, she found she couldn't formulate her fears into words; all she could say was, "Please, Holy Mary, will you make me mam happy again and laughin' like, like she was a while back."

David was waiting for her outside of the church. He was kicking his toecaps alternately against the kerb. She said to him immediately, "Did you ask him to do something about Bill?"

He looked sideways at her before drooping his head; then he replied briefly, "No."

"Oh, our David . . . you!" She walked away, and he followed her, just a step behind, and she said over her shoulder, "You're no help, are you? Yet what will you do if she won't let us keep him?" She slowed her step and they walked together now, glancing at each other.

"Father Carey says we want a miracle. He's going to try."

"Don't be daft."

"I'm not daft, our David. That's what he said. But he said we'll have to work at it."

"How?"

She shrugged her shoulders. "Train Bill."

"Train Bill!" he repeated scornfully; then added, "You know what Dad said."

Yes, she knew what her dad had said: anybody who could train Bill would qualify for a lion tamer. Not that Bill was like a lion, he was just playful, slap-happy like. She said now, "I hope he hasn't yapped all day."

"Some hope."

"You're some help, our David." Her voice was high. "You do nothing about anything, never."

"I do so."

They were standing confronting each other in the middle of the street now. "I do something about lots of things you don't know about."

"Like what?"

"Never you mind."

"Tuppence you don't fight." They turned their heads quickly and looked at the man who was passing them with a broad grin on his face, and they both walked away, Rose Mary remarking, "Cheeky thing."

They were unusually quiet on the bus journey home, but it wasn't their nice conductor so there were no remarks made, and once they got off at the end of the road they ran all the way up the lane.

This time last year the lane had been bordered by hedges; now there was no hedge on the left side and the area appeared to be a moving mass of men and machinery. Just before they reached the white stones that edged the garage drive the buzzer went and all around them became black with men hurrying towards cars and motor-bikes.

They both ran into the garage, as they always did, to say "Hello!" to Corny and to see how Bill was faring, but tonight their steps were checked at the entrance, for there stood their dad leaning nonchalantly against the side of a car talking to Diana Blenkinsop. They were looking at each other and smiling, and Rose Mary turned away as Corny put his head back and laughed; then she turned quickly back again as she realized there was no excited yapping or bounding body tripping them up. David must have sensed this at the same time because he called loudly to Corny, saying, "Dad! Dad! where's Bill?"

"Oh." Corny straightened his back; then pointing, he said, "He's out the back in the woodshed; he's been under my feet and nearly driven me mad." He jerked his head in the direction of the far end of the garage.

The children stared at him for a moment, then transferred their gaze to Diana Blenkinsop, and she, looking down at them, said, "Hello there. Had a nice day?"

When neither of them answered, Corny said, "You're being spoken to. Miss Blenkinsop was asking you a question." His voice and face were stiff.

"Yes," said Rose Mary.

"Yes," said David. Then together they walked away down the garage.

"Hello there, nippers." They both turned their heads in the direction of a car that was standing over the repair well, and they called back to the figure squatting underneath, "Hello, Jimmy, we're going to see Bill."

"Oh, Bill. Coo! he's been a devil the day."

They said nothing to this but went through the small door that led on to open ground and across it to the shed.

Bill's whining faded away as they unlatched the door, and then they were almost smothered with shavings.

"Oh, Bill! Bill!" Rose Mary turned her face away from the licking tongue and David, falling back on to his heels, cried, "Hold it! Hold it!" Then, oblivious of the dirt, they were both kneeling on the floor, holding the dog between them, and Bill quivered his pleasure from his nose to the extreme tip of his tail.

When eventually they got to their feet and ran back to the garage Bill was bounding between them, barking joyously now. As they neared the small door David stopped, and, grabbing at Bill's collar, said, "You go and ask Mam for a piece for me and I'll take him down into the field."

Rose Mary's face puckered. This wasn't fair; yet it would be more unfair to take Bill back into the garage and have him getting wrong, so she cried, "Well, don't go far away mind, 'cos if you do I won't bring you any. Just the first field."

He was running from her now, with Bill at his heels, and Rose Mary, too, ran into the garage. But once through the door she stopped, for her mother was in the garage. She was standing some yards away from her father and Diana Blenkinsop, but Diana was talking to her. She was smiling as she said, "It's patience that's needed. You've got to have a way with animals, they need handling. With some you've got to take a firm hand. I think Bill's one of the latter."

There was a slight pause before Mary Ann said, in a voice that sounded cool and thin to Rose Mary, "And he's not the only one."

There was a funny silence in the garage now and all of a sudden her mother turned towards her, as if she had known all the time she was there, and grabbing her hand, took her through the small door again, across the open ground and through the gate into their back yard, and she never let loose of her hand until they reached the landing. Then quite suddenly she stopped and leant against the wall and put her two hands over her face.

"Oh, Mam. Mam." Rose Mary had her arms around her waist now. "Don't cry. Oh, don't cry. Please, please, Mam."

Mary Ann stumbled blindly into the kitchen and, sitting down in the armchair, turned her face into the corner of it.

"Oh, Mam." Rose Mary was stroking her hair. "I hate Diana Blenkinsop, I do, I do. I hope she dies. I'll scratch her face for her so I will."

Mary Ann raised her head, her eyes still closed, and she gulped in her throat a number of times before she said, "Be quiet. Be quiet." She did not say, "How do you know I'm crying because of Diana Blenkinsop?" This was her child, flesh of her flesh, brain of her brain. She herself hadn't to be told when, as a child, she had watched her mother suffer.

She was about to get to her feet when the sound of Corny's quick heavy tread came to them, and she muttered under her breath, "Go on out to play; don't hang around. Do you hear? Go out to play."

Rose Mary was going out of the kitchen as her father burst in. He banged the door behind him and stood against it and he looked to where Mary Ann was taking the tea-cloth from the sideboard drawer. It was some seconds before he spoke, and this alone was evidence of his anger.

"Now look, we've got to have this out."

Mary Ann spread the cloth over the table, stroking down the edges, then turned to the sideboard again to get the cutlery. And now he was standing behind her. "Listen to me." When his hand came on her shoulder and he swung her round she sprang from him, her face dark with anger as she cried, "Yes, I'll listen to you. But what are you going to tell me; that I've got a vivid imagination? That it's all in my mind?"

"You insulted her."

"WHAT! I INSULTED HER! . . . All right then, I insulted her. Now perhaps it'll get through that thick skin of hers that it isn't a done thing to throw herself at a married man."

"Aw, don't be so ridiculous, woman."

"Ridiculous am I? She's been down below—" she thumbed the floor—"She's been down below three times today to my knowledge."

"Her father sent her. He wanted some papers, consumption of petrol. . . ."

"Consumption, me grannie's aunt! Every day last week she was in the garage. Every time I went down I saw her there. Consumption of petrol! Papers! Huh! They've got a phone attached from the main office to yours, haven't they? Look, Corny." Her voice suddenly dropped. "You're no fool, and you know I'm no fool. If this had been happening to somebody else you'd say that girl wants a kick in the backside, that's what you'd say. You would say she's taking advantage of her father's position; you'd say she's a supercilious big-headed madam. And there's something else you would say. You would say she's sex mad."

Corny's face was a dull red—it seemed to have caught alight from his hair—and his voice had a blustering note as he answered, "All right, all right. Say she's all that, say you've hit the nail on the head, now what about me? It takes two to make a deal. What kind of a fool do you take me for?"

"A big one." Her voice was quiet and bitter. "Somebody's going to get hurt before this play is over and it won't be Miss Diana Blenkinsop. You'll be just one of the male heads she's cracked in passing. She's out for scalps. She's the same type as her mother; I can imagine the same thing happening years ago. . . ."

"Aw, for God's sake!" He put his hand up to his brow. "Mrs. Blenkinsop now."

"No, it isn't Mrs. Blenkinsop now. We'll stick to her daughter; that's quite enough to be going on with."

They were staring at each other in bitter, painful silence. Then Corny, his head moving in small jerks and his body seeming to slump, said quietly, "Ah, Mary Ann, what's happened? Look." He moved a step nearer to her. "You know how I feel. God in Heaven, woman, there's never been anybody in my life but you. You know in your heart all this is bunkum; there's only you for me, ever . . . ever."

She gulped in her throat but her eyes held his steadily as she said, "Yes, I know there's only me for you; and you know I'm safely tucked away in these four small rooms, cooking, cleaning, washing, looking after the children. I'm for you up here, but downstairs you're having your fun. All right, all right." She lifted her hand. "It could be innocent on your side, but I know girls, and I'm telling you, that girl is in deadly earnest. And in your heart of hearts you know it too."

She drew in a deep breath now before adding, "We've talked about this in the past, haven't we, about men going off on the side and coming back and being forgiven? And women doing the same thing. And we've agreed that neither of us could tolerate that; neither of us could take back the soiled article, because that's what it is. The old-fashioned term of the woman being soiled still held good for us." She moved away from him back to the sideboard, and from there she said, "It's up to you."

His body seemed on the point of exploding with the rising tide of anger as he stalked to the door, and from there he turned and bawled at her, "Aye, it's up to me! And I'm not going to jeopardise all I've worked for to pander to your jealous whims. If you had any blooming sense, woman, you would realize that although Mr. Rodney Blenkinsop put me on my feet I've still got to depend on Dan Blenkinsop. He could just as easily contract with Riley's on the other side of the field for his petrol, or Baxter's. They're breaking their necks to get in, Baxter's are. There's nothing signed or sealed and you know that. Rodney Blenkinsop said he'd do this and he'd do that for me, but there's no contract. Dan Blenkinsop could back out the morrow; he could make some excuse to Mr. Rodney about it. He's in America, and it's a long way off, and I could be flat on my face before he comes back, and it would all be because my wife wouldn't allow me to speak to an attractive young lass. That's the trouble, isn't it? Because she's tall and elegant and attractive you can't bear it. Well, you might have something more to bear than that afore you've finished. You say it's up to me, and it is, and I'm telling you straight, I'm not jeopardising my future, all our futures, because you're bitchy. If she comes into the place I'm speaking to her; I say, if she comes in; it's ten-to-one she's along in the office now telling her father about the reception she got from you. And this could be the beginning of the end, Mrs. Boyle, 'cos families are funny things, especially fathers and daughters, and he thinks the sun shines out of her. Now you really have something to worry about."

The kitchen door banged; the bottom door banged; and Mary Ann hadn't moved. For years she had prayed that some day Corny would have a break. She had seen the break as the road going through. They had bought the place eight years ago on the supposition that the by-road was going to connect the two main roads, one in and one out of the town, and thereby making the garage a thriving one. But the council had put paid to that scheme and they had merely existed for years, until the American, Mr. Blenkinsop, had come on the scene and had seen the waste land across the road as a site for his factory. After testing Corny as to his honesty, with regard to a repair bill, he had decided to build the main gates facing the garage, and to make use of his petrol station and the spare land for garaging and lorry repairs. They had looked upon it as a sort of miracle. Now she was learning that miracles have their drawbacks, for she knew that she would give ten years of her life if the clock could be turned back for six months and Mr. Blenkinsop had decided to build his gates facing on to Riley's garage on the further road. . . .

Downstairs in the office Corny sat on the high stool, his elbows on the desk, his hand cupping his forehead. What had happened to her? This was crazy, crazy. They should be on top of the world. Instead. . . .

"Good night, boss; I'm away."

"Oh, good night, Jimmy. Is it that time?"

"Not me usual, but I asked you, you know. We're going to Blyth to play for a dance. I told you, you know."

"Oh aye." Corny nodded.

"I'll make up for it." Jimmy hesitated in the doorway.

"Oh, that's all right, Jimmy. Go on, go on, enjoy yourself."

"Thank you, boss. . . . Boss." Jimmy's long body was bent forward a little.

"Yes, Jimmy?"

Jimmy lowered his head, then he rubbed his none too clean hands over his hair and said, 'Aw, it doesn't matter. Good night, boss."

"Good night, Jimmy."

Corny got to his feet and went into the garage, and as he did so a car came on to the drive. The driver wanted five gallons of petrol. When he went back into the office for change he pulled open the till, took out the silver and his hand moved to the side where a short while ago he had seen a ten shilling note. Now there were only pound notes. He picked up four half-crowns from the silver till and went out on to the drive.

Once more in the office he pulled the till open and looked at it. There had been a ten shilling note there just before he went upstairs. He had been checking the takings when he saw Diana crossing the drive. He had purposely gone out of the office and into the garage because he didn't want her coming in here. He didn't admit to himself the place was too small to hold both of them without coming into contact, and he feared contact with her. No petrol had been sold while he was talking to her, nor when Mary Ann came on the scene. How long had he been upstairs? Five minutes, ten minutes, not more. But Jimmy could have filled a tank during that time. Well, he could soon check on that.

He went out and looked at the registers on the tanks and when he returned the number corresponded with the amounts he had put in the book earlier.

Here was another problem.

Again he dropped his elbows on the desk and supported his head. There were only two people who had access to this till, Jimmy and himself.

Jimmy had been with him since he was a nipper and he had never done this before. But there was always a first time, there was always a circumstance that pressed you just a little bit too much, and the group's car was the circumstance in Jimmy's case. But pinching from him! He had only noticed the deficiencies during the past three weeks, but it could have been going on for months, even years; not notes, but a bit of silver here and there. But now apparently he was getting reckless. Or, on the other hand—Corny's jaw tightened—he might be thinking that his boss's mind was preoccupied with other things and would be above noticing the cash desk. Aye, that was likely it. What had he wanted to say to him before he left? He'd a guilty look on his face; perhaps he had wanted to own up.

Well, there were two courses he could take. He could tackle him with it and perhaps give him the sack, or take temptation out of his way by getting a cash register in. But if he did the latter he still wouldn't be able to trust him.

Aw, God above, what with one thing and another life wasn't worth living. Why was it things had turned out like this? He had thought that when his break came he would be on top of the world; and he wasn't on top of the world, the world was on top of him.

4

SUNDAY AFTERNOON

Sunday's pattern ran along set lines. Corny went to first Mass; the children went to ten o'clock, often accompanied by Mary Ann, after she had prepared a cold lunch to come back to.

The afternoon pattern varied slightly. Either they went to the farm or the children's grandparents visited them, or they they all went to Michael's and Sarah's. Sometimes if the day was very fine the combined family would take a run out to the coast, but once a week they all met, and today Mike and Lizzie Shaughnessy were coming. Michael and Sarah would have accompanied them but they were on holiday.

At lunch Rose Mary tried to break the unhappy silence, but only succeeded in creating more tension when she remarked, "Me granda loves Bill 'cos he's like me granda, somehow, is Bill."

This remark had brought her mother's wrath on her and Mary Ann had exclaimed on a high note, "Don't be ridiculous, Rose Mary. And don't dare say any such thing when your granda arrives."

Yet when the silence fell on them again and there was only the sound of their eating and the scraping of cutlery on the plates she thought that, in a strange way, Rose Mary was right; that dog was like her father, not in looks, because it was an ugly beast, and her father, although nearing fifty, was still a handsome-looking man, but the animal had traits very like those in her da. Once he had set his mind on a thing nothing or no one would turn him away from it.

In the dog's case it was bent on making this room its headquarters. Three times this morning she had pushed him downstairs; the last time she had amost thrown him down.

At two o'clock they stood before her, all scrubbed and clean, wearing their Sunday best, and she looked from one to the other as she said, "Now, you get messed up before your granda and grandma comes and see what I'll do." She wagged her finger, first at Rose Mary, and then at David. "Let him out of that shed if you dare. Mind I'm warning you."

As they stared back at her she read their minds. "She's cruel. Mam's cruel."

The phone ringing broke their concentration; the phone was connected with the office downstairs and Corny was downstairs. Mary Ann hesitated a moment before picking it up, and then his voice came to her.

"Your mother's just phoned. She says Gran's arrived; she'll have to bring her along."

Mary Ann closed her eyes.

"Are you there?"

She forced herself to say "Yes." Where did he think she was?

"Look, honey." His voice was low. "This has got to stop."

She glanced round at the children. They were both still looking at her, and she motioned them away with her hand, and as they went out of the door she said stiffly into the phone, "I didn't start it."

"Well, neither did I. Look, love, I tell you there's not a thing in it. Believe me. . . . Look, your mam and dad's coming; they'll smell a rat if we go on like this."

"Is that all you're afraid of?"

The shout he gave into the phone made her pull her head sharply back.

"I'm afraid of nothing. I've told you I've done nothing to be afraid of. You'd drive a man mad. I'm tellin' you mind, if you go on like this you'll get what you're askin' for."

When she heard the phone being banged down she put the receiver back and put her hand up to her lips to stop their trembling. She had her head bowed as she went on to the landing but she brought it up with a jerk when she saw the two of them standing looking at her. The next minute they were on her. Their arms about her, their heads buried in her waist, they enfolded her in silent sympathy, and she had to bite tight on her lips to stop herself from breaking down.

"Come on. Come on." She ruffled their heads; then exclaimed, "Aw, now look what I've gone and done, and me going for you to keep tidy." She looked down into their faces, and they stared back at her. Then she said brokenly, "Come on, I'll tidy you up," and, still clinging to her, they went into the bedroom. And as she combed their hair she thought, they're so big a part of me, there's nothing I think that they don't sense and she pulled them towards her again and kissed them one after the other. And then she was crying softly, and Rose Mary was crying softly, and David was blinking hard and sucking his bottom lip right into his mouth.

"If you wanted a dog, why didn't you get a dog, not an ugly beast like that?" Gran was addressing Mary Ann pointedly, and Mary Ann, as always, was praying that she be given the power to answer her grandmother civilly. This woman who had been the torment of her da's life, the thorn in the side of her mother, and the constant pinprick—and that was putting it mildly—in her own.

Grandma McMullen never seemed to get any older. Her well-preserved body, her jet black hair piled high on her head, her thick-skinned face and round black eyes looked ageless. Mary Ann could never imagine her dying, although she wished it every time they met; but this, she knew was the vainest of all her wishes.

She replied to her now, "I didn't want the dog; I didn't bring it here."

"Oh! Oh!" Mrs. McMullen swung her head widely, taking in her daughter, Lizzie and her son-in-law Mike, and Corny, and then she appealed to an invisible figure standing somewhere near the window. "Did you hear that? The world is coming to an end; somebody's got one over on her at last. . . ."

As Mary Ann went into the scullery, Lizzie rose to her feet, saying, "You're in one of your good moods today, aren't you, Mother?" Then she went hastily towards the door between the kitchen and scullery and closed it and, coming towards her mother again, ended, "Now I warned you before we came away, no one's got to put up with your tongue."

Mrs. McMullen slowly bowed her head, then brought it up sideways and again she appealed to the imaginary figure near the window, "Well! Do you hear that?" she said. "Do you hear that? It's come to something when you can't open your mouth. Look." She now confronted her daughter with a hard black stare. "I was meaning to be funny. Hasn't anybody got a sense of humour around here?"

"You could have fooled me."

"What!" The old lady turned and glared at her son-in-law's back as it moved towards the door leading out on to the landing, and as Mike went through it she said in no small voice, "Yes, I could have fooled you; it wouldn't take much to do that."

Lizzie almost sprang towards the other door now and, banging it closed, she cried under her breath, "Now that's finished it. Now I warn you; this is the last time you come out with us."

Mrs. McMullen stared at her daughter again. Then, her head wagging and her mouth working as if she was chewing on gum, she said, "You were glad enough to come in me car."

"Oh, my goodness!" Lizzie put her hand to her head and was about to turn from her mother but confronted her again, crying, "Your reasoning has always been a mystery to me, Mother. It still is. We've got a car of our own; we didn't need yours to come in. You got Fred Tyler to bring you to the farm today so that Corny could look it over."

"No such thing. Who told you that?"

"Fred Tyler told me that, if you want to know. You told him it would be a free ride as he wanted to visit his folks in Felling."

"He's a liar."

"Oh well, that's all right then, he's a liar and you don't want Corny to look her over." She glanced swiftly at Corny, and Corny who had remained silent all this while looked at Gran, and Gran looked at him, and after a moment she said, "I'll pay you; I don't want you to do it for nothing. But those other beggars in Shields, they sting me to death. They sent me in a bill for seven pounds. Where am I going to find seven pounds?"

Before Corny could answer, Lizzie said, "You shouldn't be keeping the car, you can't afford to run it. You know you can't. You should have sold it the minute you won it. Now it's going to rack and ruin standing outside your front door. What do you want with a car, anyway, at your age?"

"It's my car and I'll keep it as long as I like, and I'll thank you to mind your own business. As for age; if you had half as much life in you as I have you'd be more spry than you are now."

As Lizzie looked down on her mother she wondered how, during all these long years of torment, she had prevented herself from striking her; for most of her life she'd had this kind of thing to deal with. Age had not softened her mother or changed her, except for the worst.

"What's wrong with her?" asked Corny flatly now.

"I don't know. That's what you'll have to find out. She goes pink-pink-pink-pink, like that. Fred Tyler says he thinks it's just due to verberration."

"Verberration? You mean vibration?"

"I mean verberration. That's what he said. I'm not daft."

No, she wasn't daft, not her. Corny, looking down on Mrs. McMullen, hardened his heart enough to say, "If it's anything big I won't be able to tackle her; I've got too much in."

"How can it be anything big, it was new only a few months ago."

"Lots of things go wrong with new cars."

"Not with this one. You said it was one of the best."

"So it is. But still things can go wrong. And I'm telling you, if it's anything that's going to take time you'll have to get it fixed elsewhere."

He felt mean acting like this, but once he started doing her repairs she'd never be off the door. When she had won the car he had offered to buy it from her, but no; and now it was being ruined standing out in all weathers and had depreciated by hundreds already. He turned abruptly and went out.

On the drive he found Mike. He was standing quietly smoking and looking towards the chaotic jumble of machinery on the other side of the road; he grinned at him and said, "I suppose you know by now why she came. She's after you for free repairs. If you once start she'll have you at it."

"She'll not. I told her, if it's anything big she can take it elsewhere."

"Aw, she's a crafty old bitch if ever there was one." Mike squared his teeth on the stem of his pipe, then turned and walked with Corny towards the Wolseley. But before Corny lifted the bonnet he said, "I'd better put on a set of overalls else I'll get me head in me hands."

When he returned and began to tap various parts of the car engine, Mike stood watching him in silence for a few minutes, then he asked casually, "What's up, Corny?"

Corny's eyes flicked towards Mike; then he turned his attention again to the car. You couldn't keep much from Mike; in any case, the feeling between himself and Mary Ann was sticking out like a sore thumb.

"Serious?" asked Mike quietly.

"Could be." There was a pause before Corny straightened himself and, looking at Mike said, "She's mad."

Mike was smiling tolerantly. "Haven't noticed it up to now. Quick-tempered like. Takes after her male parent—" his smile widened—"but mad? Well—" he shook his head—"what's made her mad, Corny?"

"Come in here a minute." Corny led the way into his office, where, having closed the door, he confronted Mike and said plainly. "She thinks I'm gone on somebody else."

They stared at each other. They were both about the same height, touching six foot two, and they could have been father and son in that their hair was almost the same hue of red. But whereas Corny's body was thin and sinewy, Mike's was heavily built.

Mike took the pipe from his mouth and tapped it against the palm of his hand, but still kept his eyes on Corny as he asked quietly, "Well, are you?"

Corny tossed his head. It was an impatient gesture, and it was some seconds before he said "Look; it's like this, Mike." He now went on to explain how Diana Blenkinsop came into the picture, and when he had finished there was a long pause before Mike said, "Well, as I see it, she's got a point, Corny. Oh! Oh!" he held up his hand. "Hold your horses; don't go down me throat. I've been through this meself, you remember?" His mouth moved up at one corner. "It nearly spoilt your wedding. I don't need to go through all that again, do I? But I'm just telling you I know how you feel. . . ."

"But Mike, man, I don't really feel anything for her, not really. She's nice to natter to, she gives you a sort of kick. . . . Well. . . ." Again he tossed his head. "When anybody seeks you out it gives you a kick whether it's man, woman or child. You know that yourself."

"Aye, as you say, I know that meself; but I'm going to say this to you, Corny. It's a dangerous game to play. But for Mary Ann confronting me with the truth about that little bitch who had almost hypnotised me, well I don't know where I'd be the day. It was a sort of madness. At least it was in my case; I was clawing my way back to youth, willing my dreams to take shape in the daylight. Aw, lad, I know all about it. But in your case you haven't reached that stage yet; you're young. But young or not, this could be serious. You know, Mary Ann's nature is like a fiddle string, the slightest touch and it vibrates. God forgive me, but I made it vibrate more than enough when she was young. I was a heart scald to her, and she doesn't want to go through that again, Corny, not in any way."

Corny sat slowly down on the high stool and he bowed his head as he said, "You know how I feel about her. I don't need to put it into words; you know the whole story. Ever since I was an ignorant nipper, a loud-mouth lout, she has stood by me, defended me, and I could have loved her for that alone, but I loved her for herself. I still do. God, she knows it. But Mike, that doesn't mean to say I daren't look at another lass."

"No, no, it doesn't; of course it doesn't. ·. . . What does she look like, this Diana

Blenkinsop?"

Corny raised his eyebrows and smiled wryly. "The lot. Straight off the front of a magazine. Long legs, no bust, flaxen hair down her back, blue eyes, red lips, and five foot ten."

Mike took the flat of his hand and flapped it against his brow as he said, "And you wonder why she's up in the air. Why man, you know she hates being small, and for you to look at anybody an inch taller would be enough, but five foot ten, and all that thrown in, aw, Corny, that isn't playing the game."

"Well," Corny got up from the seat and his voice was serious, "game or no game, Mike, I've got to be civil to her; she's Dan Blenkinsop's daughter and he's in charge here while Mr. Rodney's in America. Even when he's back Dan'll still be in charge. As I tried to explain to Mary Ann, at this stage he could make or break me."

"And so you've got to suck up to his daughter."

"NO!" The word was a bark. "And don't use that expression to me, Mike. I suck up to nobody; never have. If I'd been that way inclined I'd be further on the day, I suppose."

"I'm sorry, Corny." Mike put his hand on Corny's shoulder. "I shouldn't have put it like that, it was too raw. But you feel you've got to be nice to her?"

Corny's face was sullen and his lips were tight as he said, "I feel I haven't got to do as me wife says and tell her to stay to hell out of the garage, and when she brings a message from her father I haven't got to say to her, 'Look I don't want anything by hand, use the phone'."

"Aye. Aye, I know it's awkward, but remember, Corny, Mary Ann's got her side to it. Anyway, we all run into patches like this, and they pass."

"Patches! They're more than patches that hit me. My life is either as dull as ditch water with nothing happening, or everything's coming at me from all sides at once. I've got another thing on my mind and all . . . Jimmy."

"Jimmy?"

"Aye, he's helping himself to bits of cash." He nodded towards the till.

"Jimmy! I can't believe that; he's a good lad, I would have said he's as straight at a die."

"So would I, staked me life on it; but he's after a car. That gang of his want a new van to hold them and their instruments, and naturally he's expected to pig in. If he was on his own he likely could, but with his mother to see to money's tight. I've given him two ten bob rises this year, I can't give him any more at the present. I've promised him I'll put him on a better basis at the end of the year. I'll know where I stand then. The factory should be up and if I get my way I'll be under contract to Mr. Blenkinsop, Mr. Rodney, not Dan, and then to hell with them all. But in the meantime I'm not putting Jimmy's money up and then not being able to pull it down again if things don't go the way they should."

"Aye, I see your point, but I wouldn't have believed it about Jimmy if you hadn't told me yourself. You've got proof?"

"Well, there's ten shilling notes been slipping away once or twice a week. I haven't kept a tag on the silver, the Lord knows how much of that's gone. . . . Aw come on." He moved towards the door. "I'd better see to the old faggot's machine."

As they went on the the drive again the children came tearing round the end of the garage, with Bill on their heels, and Rose Mary cried, "Granda! Granda! Look at him jumping. Up Bill! Up Bill!" She held her hand brow high and Bill leapt at it, but when he dropped to the ground again he fell on his side and rolled on to his back, and Mike laughed and Corny was forced to smile. "It's his legs," he said . . . "they just won't hold that chest of his. That's why we got him. He was the runt. But runt or not, he's a thoroughbred, he's a good dog, Mike."

Mike, looking at Bill, nodded, saying, "Yes, he looks a fine fellow. I wouldn't like him to get a hold of my leg when he's a few months older. Just look at those jaws."

As the children dashed away again with Bill tearing after them, Corny said, "She hates the sight of him."

"Well, you can't say he's a pretty dog; women like something nice to look at."

"Nice to look at!" Corny jerked his chin. "That dog's got character." He now turned and grinned widely at Mike and there was a chuckle in his voice as he said, "I'll say he has. Oh lad, if you could have seen the kitchen on that first night you would have thought a ship load of rats had been at it." He gave a deep gurgle. "She nearly went daft. Mind, I could have killed him meself, but after, when I thought about it, I had to laugh. He reminded me of Joe. Do you remember the dog I had as a lad? I used to bring him to me grannie's."

"Oh, Joe, Oh yes, I remember you and Joe. Didn't you nearly break Fanny's neck with him once?"

"Yes, I had him on a piece of rope and there was a kid from upstairs came in. She had a cat in her arms and Joe dived and hurled me across the room, and he took me grannie's legs from under her, and she grabbed at the tablecloth as she went down. She had just put out four plates of stew. Oh, I never forget that night." He was laughing loudly. "I can see her, to this day, sitting on the floor covered in it, and Joe, flat out under the table, looking at her. Eeh! my, we had to run. And I daren't show me face in the door for days after. . . . But it might have killed her, the fall she took."

They were both laughing now.

"It would take more than that to kill Fanny," said Mike. "By the way, how is she?"

"Oh, grand. I saw her last week. She's got a new lease of life. Going to bingo now."

"No!"

"Aye; she had won thirty-six bob and she was standing treats as if it was thirty-six thousand. You know her."

"Oh aye, I know Fanny. I wish there were more like her. . . ."

It was about half-an-hour later when Lizzie put her head out of the window and called, "Tea's ready!" and Mike called back, "Coming!" Then looking at Corny, who was still tinkering with the engine, he said, "I would leave that and let her get on with it, we'd better not keep them waiting, we don't want any more black looks." Then turning round, he called, "Rose Mary! David! Come on; tea up."

"Granda! Dad!" Rose Mary came running up to the car. "Have you seen Bill?"

Corny brought his head up so quickly from the engine that it bumped the top of the bonnet, and, rubbing it, he screwed up his face as he said. "Have we seen Bill? You're asking me when you've had him all afternoon?"

"Well, he was with us a minute ago and now he's gone." She looked over the road and called, "Is he there, David?" and David came running and shouting, "No, I can't see him."

"Where had you him last?" asked Mike, and Rose Mary answered, "Down in the field, Granda. We came round the back way and on to the drive, and we thought he'd be here."

"Oh Lord!" Corny covered his face with one hand, then, oblivious of the grease on it, he pushed it upwards through his hair and said, "Ten to one he's upstairs."

"No." Mike moved quickly now towards the door of the house, saying, "I'm going to enjoy this."

"You'll be the only one, then," said Corny, pulling off his overalls and throwing them into the front of the garage.

When he reached the stairs he expected to find Mary Ann at the top with the dog by the scruff of the neck, but there was no one to be seen, not even Mike or the children.

On entering the kitchen he stood within the door taking in the scene. Bill was seated inside the fender, his rump to the stove that housed a back boiler and was comfortably warm. His mouth was wide open, his tongue lolling out of one side, and with his small round black eyes he was appraising the company, one after the other.

Lizzie stood staring down at him. Mary Ann, too, stood staring at him, but from the distance of the scullery doorway, her mouth grim, one hand on her hip, her pose alone spelling battle. The children stood close to Mike by the side of the table, their attention riveted on Bill.

And Mrs. McMullen. Well, Mrs. McMullen sat in the big chair to the side of the fireplace and she glared at Bill, and her look seemed to bring his eyes to focus finally on her, and as they stared at each other she passed sentence. "Dogs like him want puttin' down when they're young," she said: "they're a dangerous breed, they can't be trusted with children. Once they get their teeth in they hang on. Killed a bairn they did. It was in the papers not so long ago. Just give him another couple of months, and you won't be able to do anything with him, you'll find yourself in Court with a summons and a hospital bill to pay for somebody's leg, that is if he hasn't finished them off."

"He could be trained," said Lizzie.

"What, to finish them off?" laughed Mike.

Lizzie ignored this and, looking abruptly at her mother, said, "Give him a chance, he's only a puppy."

"Puppy! He's as big as a house end now, what'll he be like when he's fully grown? This poky room won't hold him. It doesn't hold much now, but wait till he's reached his size. . . ."

"Then we'll move into a bigger house to accommodate him."

They now all looked at Corny as he moved past Mary Ann and went into the scullery to wash his hands.

"Oh, you're going to break eggs with a big stick. You're a long time moving into your bigger houses."

As the kettle boiled Mary Ann went to the gas stove and from there she heard Corny mutter over the sink, "Break eggs with a big stick, the old buzzard."

If only everything had been all right, Mary Ann knew that at this minute she would have been standing close to his side and he would have made her giggle. She also knew that she would even have taken Bill's part, simply because her grannie didn't like him.

As she made the tea Corny stood drying his hands watching her, and when she went to pass him to get the tea stand from the cupboard he suddenly caught her by the arm, and they stared at each other for a moment; then quickly his mouth dropped on hers, hard, possessively. When he looked at her again her eyes were gushing tears and he put his arms about her, whispering. "Don't. Don't. Don't let her see you crying, for God's sake; that'll give her too much satisfaction. Go on. Go on." He pushed her towards the sink. "See to your face, I'll take the tea in."

As he passed her with the tray he put out his free hand and touched her hair, and this did not help to ease her crying.

"You didn't tell me what was wrong with her, the car?" Gran greeted him as he entered the room again, and he said, "It was a hole in the exhaust; I've done what I can."

"How much will it be?"

"I'll send me bill in," he said.

"Well, don't forget," she answered.

It would just serve her damn well right if he did send a bill in. And wouldn't she get a shock? He could imagine her coming storming up here, raising the roof on him.

The talk was falsely animated during the meal. It was Corny who kept the conversation going, and in this he was aided by Mike.

Mary Ann, from her place at the bottom of the table, poured out the tea, and from her seat, if she cast her eyes to the right, she could see Bill. He had settled down by the stove with his head lying on his front paws. He looked utterly relaxed. She found herself wishing she could like him; she wished she could put up with him for everybody's sake, especially now that her grannie couldn't stand him. There must be something good about the beast if her grannie didn't like him.

There was always a climax when Mrs. McMullen visited her relations. It came earlier than usual during this visit, just as tea was finished.

It should happen that Bill had found the stove slightly too warm for his thin coat and had moved from the inside of the fender to the outside, and this brought him to the foot of "Gran's chair". When she left the table and went to sit down there was Bill. He was not impeding her; she could have sat down and not even touched him, but that wasn't Gran's way. Taking her foot, she gave him a sharp dig in the ribs. The result was surprising but, as she herself had stated earlier, predictable.

Bill had been happy today, as he had never been since he had left his mother. He was in a warm place which was permeated with nice smells. He had discovered he was very fond of biscuits, not the broken biscuits that you got with your dinner, but biscuits with chocolate on them. He knew he was going to develop a real taste for biscuits with chocolate on them. Chocolate had a particular smell and there was a strong smell of chocolate in this room. He knew that if he waited long enough and quietly enough he would be rewarded. That was, until the thing hit him in the ribs. His reaction to the pain was for his jaws to spring open, then snap closed, and to give vent to a cry that was part yelp, part yap, and part growl, and all the time he felt the pain he jumped madly around the room dodging under one object after another.

"There! There! What did I tell you? He's dangerous. He went for me."

"He did no such thing!" Lizzie was yelling at her mother. "You asked for it."

"I asked for what?"

"You should have left him alone."

"Don't chase him, let up," cried Corny.

"Look, stop it!" Mary Ann was shouting at the twins now. "You'll have the things off the table."

"Here he is! Here he is!" Mike reached down behind the couch and grabbed at Bill's collar, and, pulling him up, he thrust him wriggling and squirming into David's arms and David, now looking fearfully up at his mother, said, "He didn't do it. He didn't start it, Mam, it was Gran. She kicked him. I saw her; she kicked him."

"I did nothing of the sort, boy. Well! would you believe it?"

"Yes, you did, Gran, I saw you." Rose Mary was now standing by David's side confronting the old woman, and Mrs. McMullen, looking from one to the other of her great-grandchildren, didn't know which she disliked most, or whether her dislike for them was greater than that for their mother. But that couldn't possibly be. Nevertheless, she knew that there was a time when it was advisable to retreat, and so with great dignity she sat down in her chair again and, her chin moving upwards, she made a statement, which was sinisterly prophetic in this case.

"Every dog has his day," she said.

David stared at her; then grinning he said flippantly, "Aye, and a bitch has two afternoons."

Such a reply coming from her great-grandson not only brought Mrs. McMullen's eyebrows almost up to her hairline but also created an amazed silence in the room, and an assortment of astounded expressions.

Still holding on to the wriggling dog, David now looked apprehensively from one face to the other. He'd get wrong, he knew he would. He felt a little afraid, until all of a sudden there came a sound like an explosion. It was his granda and his dad bursting out laughing together. His granda had his hand on his dad's shoulder and he was roaring. And his grandma too, she was laughing with her head down and her face covered. But his mam wasn't laughing. The next minute she had hold of his collar and was pushing him and Bill outside while Rose Mary came after them shouting, "No Mam. No Mam."

On the landing, Mary Ann looked down at her son and hissed under her breath, "David!

where on earth did you hear that?"

"It . . . it wasn't swearin', Mam."

Mary Ann swallowed deeply. "It was a kind of swearing."

At this David shook his head and glanced at Rose Mary, and Rose Mary said, "Not really, Mam, not proper swearin'."

"Who told you it?"

David blinked and hitched Bill further up into his arms and had to avoid his licking tongue before he said, "Nobody, Mam; I just heard it."

"Where?"

David glanced at Rose Mary again, then looked down but didn't answer, and Mary Ann wanted to take him by the shoulders and shake him. But that meant shaking that animal too and then anything might happen. "Where?" she repeated.

It was Rose Mary who answered for him. "Jimmy. Jimmy says that, Mam."

Mary Ann straightened herself up. Jimmy? Well, wait until she saw him tomorrow. "Take that animal downstairs and lock him up," she said.

Neither of them moved. They were looking up at her, blinking all the while.

"You heard what I said."

"She kicked him, Mam. He wouldn't have done anything if she hadn't have kicked him." As David spoke the door opened and Corny and Mike came on to the landing. They were still laughing. Mary Ann did not look at them but at the children and repeated, "Take him downstairs."

They both glanced at their father and grandfather, then went slowly down the stairs, and Mary Ann turned and looked at these two whom she loved so deeply that the feeling often brought nothing but pain, and she saw them now as a couple of boys. They were leaning against each other and she hissed at them under her breath, "Stop it! D'you hear? Stop it!"

Mike now put his hand out towards her, spluttering, "And a bitch has two afternoons."

As she saw their laughter mounting she pushed them towards the bedroom, and once inside she cried, "If you must act like bairns do it in here."

"Sh . . . she wants her hat and coat," Mike gasped; "She's going . . . we're going. We're going out on a wave. We always go out on a wave when she's about."

She picked up her grannie's coat and went out and into the kitchen, there to be met by the standing figure of Mrs. McMullen.

Mary Ann didn't hand her grannie her hat and coat; instead, she handed them to her mother, and it was Lizzie who went to help the old lady into her things, only to be repulsed with the words, "Thank you! I can see to meself."

And that was all Mrs. McMullen said until they reached the bottom of the stairs, and there, turning and looking straight into Mary Ann's face, she remarked, "They're a credit to you. They're a pair you could take anywhere. You must be proud of them."

The pressure of her mother's fingers on her arm stilled her retort, and Lizzie, bending down, kissed her and whispered, "I'll ring you later."

When her da kissed her his eyes were still wet and gleaming, but he said nothing more, he just patted her cheek and went towards the car.

She did not wait to see them off but returned upstairs, and a few minutes later Corny entered the room. He came straight towards her, the twinkle deep in his eye, but he did not repeat the joke; instead, he picked her up in his arms as he had been wont to do and sat down with her in the big chair, and when he pressed her face into his neck her body began to shake, but not with laughter; she was picking up where she had left off in the scullery earlier on.

5

GETTING ACQUAINTED

"Now Rose Mary, if I've told you once I've told you a hundred times, he can't come upstairs; he's all right where he is."

"But listen to him, Mam, he's yelling the place down. He's lonely. He likes people, he does; he only cries when he's by hisself. . . ."

Mary Ann had turned her head away, but now she brought her gaze down to her daughter again as she said patiently, "He's a puppy, Rose Mary, he's got to learn. He won't learn if you give in to him."

Rose Mary's lips trembled as she muttered, "I worry all day 'bout him, shut up in there in the dark. I'm frightened of the dark, you know I am, Mam, and he—"

"Rose Mary!" It came on a high note, but when she saw her daughter's face crumpling into tears she knew that this would continue all the way to school, and all during Miss Plum's questioning, and she was forced to compromise. "Look," she said; "you can go and let him out. He can run round behind the garage, but see that the lane gate is closed, for mind—" she bent down towards her daughter—"if he gets out on the road among all those lorries he could be killed."

"Yes, I know, Mam. All right, Mam, I'll fasten the gate tight." Swiftly now Rose Mary's arms came up and hugged her mother around the neck. "Thanks, Mam. . . . Ta. I'll tell our David."

David was standing in grim silence at the bottom of the stairs waiting for her, and she dashed at him, whispering hoarsely, "Mam says we can let him out and he can run in the back."

"She did?"

"Yes. Come on, hurry, 'cos we'll miss the bus else."

They raced round the side of the building, through the wooden gate that was laced with wire netting, and to the wood-shed, and when they released Bill he showed his thanks by bounding around them until David grabbed his collar and, pressing on his hindquarters to keep him still, said, "Now look; you behave yourself and we'll take you out the night, eh?" He wanted to rub his face against the dog but refrained. But Rose Mary, dropping on to her hunkers, cupped the long snout in her hands, and as she bent to kiss it the slobbering tongue covered her face in one stroke from chin to brow, and she almost fell over laughing.

When they ran to the gate Bill galloped with them, but when he realized he wasn't going to be allowed through he stood up on his hind legs against the wire netting and howled. He howled and he howled until gradually he tired and then he reduced his howling to a whimper before turning forlornly away to investigate the open area.

He found it a place of little interest, except for the wooden wall of the garage out of which a number of quaint smells oozed, none of them very alluring. The investigation over, he returned to the gate and discovered that if he kept to one side of it he could see occasional activity on a small patch of road fronting the garage. It was as he lay gazing in this direction, and bored to extinction, that he saw coming towards him an apparition which brought his body springing upwards. When the apparition reached the other side of the gate and pressed its nose against the wire netting and so touched his, the effect was like an electric shock. It shot up his bony muzzle, along his spine and right to the end of his tail, where it recharged itself and retraced its path.

Bill hadn't seen one of his own kind since he had left his family, and now he was being confronted by a female. That she wasn't of his own breed, nor yet could lay claim to being a thoroughbred didn't trouble him. He couldn't have cared less that she wasn't a simple cross between a poodle and a terrier, and that obvious other breeds could be detected in her ancestry; to him she was the most fascinating creature he had encountered so far in his young life, and urges, entirely new to him, were acting like crossed wires under his coat, for ripples of delight were darting off at tangents through every part of his body.

He said a breathless, "Hello," and she answered with a cool, "Hello." And then she indicated by turning her back on him and taking a few steps from the gate that she wouldn't mind if he accompanied her.

There was nothing Bill wanted more at this moment than to accompany this witch, and when she returned to the gate, squatted, and gave him absolute proof of her feeling for him, there arose in him a blind fury against the barrier between them, and nothing or no one was going to prevent him from breaking it down. To this end he got his teeth into the bottom strand of the wire netting and he pulled, and he tugged, and he bit while the temptress walked up and down on the other side of the gate giving him encouragement in the way she knew best.

When Bill had made a hole big enough to get his head through the lady walked away again, and when she realized he wasn't following she stood looking at him in some disappointment; then, like many another lady before her, she suddenly got fed up with the whole business and trotted off.

Bill, now working with intensified fury, enlarged the hole, and with a wriggle he was through. Like lightning he was on the garage drive, then on the road, and across it. He pulled up once to sniff at what was left of a thorn bush, which confirmed that she had passed this way, and then he was running amidst the tangle of building material, cranes, grabs and lorries. . . .

Mary Ann was feeling somewhat better this morning, though not exactly light in heart; she would never feel like that again until Miss Blenkinsop decided to take a position elsewhere, and as things stood she couldn't see her doing that. But last night Corny had been his old self and he had assured her that in the whole wide world she was the only one that mattered to him, and she believed him. But that was last night, in the darkness, with her head buried on his chest; this morning, in the stark light of day, and the time approaching ten minutes to nine when Miss Blenkinsop would be arriving, bringing her car on the drive with a flourish and pulling up, with a screech of brakes, at the garage door, she wasn't so sure. Anyway madam would be disappointed this morning, for it would be Jimmy who would take her car and park it in the garage, because Corny had gone into Shields on business.

Even knowing that she wouldn't witness Corny greeting Diana Blenkinsop as he did most mornings, Mary Ann found herself standing to the side of the front room window which overlooked the drive. She wondered what madam would be wearing this morning; perhaps a mini skirt. No, she wouldn't dare wear a mini skirt, not with her height.

The drive was empty of cars and people, and after a moment Mary Ann's gaze was drawn across the road and to a section practically opposite the window, where last week they had started to excavate the land prior to building an underground car park beneath one of the factory shops. The excavations had reached the point where the hole was about twenty feet deep. On the edge of it a grab was working. At present it was stationary. Her eyes were passing over it when they were brought leaping back to take in a black and white figure standing on top of the grab itself.

Bill! No, it couldn't be, he was in the yard. But . . . but there was only one Bill, there could only be one Bill hereabouts and that was him. He had got out. Then something happened that caused her to push up the window and yell at the top of her voice, "Stop it! Stop it!"

As she ran down the stairs she could still see the wide grin on the grab operator's face as he leant from the cab pointing out the dog to his mates, and even before he pulled the lever gently to set the grab in motion Mary Ann had known what he was about to do.

When she reached the driveway she saw the grab swinging into mid-air, with the petrified dog clinging with its two front paws to one of the supporting chains, while its hind legs slithered here and there on the muddy surface of the lid. The operator was doing it for a laugh. If he opened the grab the dog would fall between the lips, but he was just having a laugh and the men on the rim were guffawing loudly.

"Stop it! Stop it this minute!" She was below the cab now yelling up at the man. "You cruel, sadistic devil, you! Stop it, I tell you."

"What do you say, missus?"

The grin was wider now.

"You heard what I said. You'll hear of this. That's my dog."

"He's all right; he's just havin' an obstacle put in his way, he's after a bitch. He's all right." The man flapped his hand at her.

"You'll be far from all right when my husband finishes with you."

"Oh aye? Just make the appointment then, missus, just make the appointment. Tell him any time."

"Stop that thing."

"I'd better not, missus. Better get it to the bottom, break his neck else. Would you like his neck broke?"

When the grab hit the bottom of the hole she watched Bill fall off into the mud, then make an attempt to crawl out of it. But the harder he paddled the more he stuck.

"Oh, you're a horrible swine. That's what you are, a horrible swine." There were tears in her voice as she yelled, not only at the crane man now but at the men standing further along the rim. Then before anyone knew what she was up to she was slipping and sliding down the wet clay face of the hole.

Mary Ann wasn't aware of the scene behind her now, but a man in a trilby hat and leather jacket had come up to the crane demanding, "What's this? What's up?"

"Aw, it was just a joke."

"A joke?" The man bawled. "What's that woman doing down there? What's this anyway?"

"The dog was on the grab," one of the men put in sheepishly, "and Sam let him down."

"You did what!" The man looked up at the operator.

"He's not hurt. He was just sitting there and I set it moving."

The two men stared at one another for a moment; then the man in the trilby hat said, "I'll bloody well set you moving after this." Then going over the rim himself, he reached Mary Ann just as she fell flat on her face in the quagmire with Bill in her arms.

When he pulled her to her feet he said, "Give him here." But Bill refused to be parted from Mary Ann. His whole body quivering, he clung on to the shoulder of her dress and as the man's hand came on to him he made a pitiful sound and Mary Ann gasped, "It's all right, I can manage him."

"Look; you'll have to let me help you; you can't walk in this." Without further words he put his arm around her waist and lifted her sucking feet from out of the mud, and like a mother carrying a child on her hip he bore her to the far side of the hole where the ground was comparatively dry, then mounted a ladder that had been laid against the sloping ground.

When he reached the rim he put her on her feet and steadied her, saying, "There, there;

you're all right."

"Th-thank you."

"'Struth! we're in a mess." He knocked lumps of mud from his jacket, then added, "Somebody'll pay for this. Come on."

As they walked back around the perimeter of the hole he said, "You're Mrs. Boyle, aren't you? Used to be Shaughnessy?"

"Yes. Yes, that's right."

"You don't remember me? Aw well, it's not the time to press an introduction. You'd better get yourself into the house and get that stuff off you, and him." He nodded towards Bill who was still clinging tenaciously to Mary Ann's shoulder.

Mary Ann looked at her rescuer. She didn't remember ever having seen him before; but then his face was all bespattered and his clothes were in a similar plight to her own, which made her say, "I think you need cleaning up an' all. Would you like to come inside? You're about the same build as . . . as my husband, you could have a change of clothes if you like."

"Well, that's very nice of you. I wouldn't mind getting out of this clobber at the moment."

When they came to the grab the operator was busily at work, as were his mates, and the man muttered, "I'll see to them later."

There were two other people who had witnessed the incident, Jimmy and Diana Blenkinsop. Jimmy, his long face stretched even to a greater length, said, "Eeh! Mrs. Boyle, you shouldn't have gone down there."

Diana Blenkinsop gave a little laugh, and she said, "You have got yourself into a mess, haven't you? He would have got out on his own you know; he comes from a very tenacious breed."

"AND SO DO I!" said Mary Ann, pausing slightly before marching across the road, followed by the man.

When they reached the drive he said under his breath, "Friend of yours?"

"What do you think?" She glanced sideways at him, and he grinned back at her, and the grin stirred a faint memory in her mind. She had seen him before but she couldn't place him.

After scraping their feet on the scraper let into the wall, she led the way upstairs, and on the landing she pointed to a door, saying, "That's the bathroom. There's plenty of hot water. I'll bring you some clean clothes as soon as I get the thick off."

"Don't hurry." He was grinning again. "And I think you'd better start on the bold boy first; if you let him down he'll leave you some trade marks."

"Yes, you're right." She laughed at the man. She liked his voice, his easy manner. He was nice.

In the scullery, when she attempted to put Bill into the sink he dug his claws into her shoulder again and hung on to her, and she stroked his muddy head with her equally muddy hand and said, "It's all right. It's all right, I won't hurt you."

When finally she had him standing in the sink he sat down quite suddenly as if his legs would no longer support him, and when he looked up at her and made a little whining sound she laughed again and said, "It's all right, I'm not going to drown you."

When he was clean she put him inside the fender and, pressing him firmly downwards, commanded sternly, "Now stay. Stay. I'll be back." Then she scrambled into the bedroom, whipped some clean things for herself out of the wardrobe, together with a shirt and old trousers and a coat of Corny's, and going to the bathroom door called, "I'm leaving the things outside."

The voice came to her cheerily, "Right-o. Thanks. Thanks a lot. I could stay in here all day."

As she heard the swish of water she smiled and hurried into the scullery again, and there she stripped her clothes off, washed her face, legs and arms in the sink, and got into her clean clothes; and she was in the kitchen again before a tap came on the door.

When he entered the room she looked at him and laughed with him as he said, "All made to measure. Would you believe it? Except that your man's a bit longer in the leg than me, we must be of a size."

"You are." She nodded at him. "Would you like a drink of something, I've got the kettle on?"

"Now that's very nice of you, but I should be getting back, that lot will be having a holiday knowing I'm out of the way for five minutes. . . . On the other hand, they'll be expecting me to blow me top and are likely playing wary, so yes, thanks, I'll take that drink."

He sat down by the side of the table and as she went into the scullery he called to her, "His nibs has settled down all right, not a peep out of him."

"I think he's still suffering from shock," she called back.

"Well, aye, it would be a shock to the poor little beggar to find himself whisked into mid-air like that. That Fred Tyler's an empty-headed nowt, if ever there was one. If it had been his mother on top of the grab he would have done the same. By the way, don't you remember me?"

She came to the scullery door and stared at him. Yes, yes, she had seen him somewhere before. He was a very attractive looking fellow; black hair, deep brown eyes, squarish face, well built.

"Fillimore Street. you know, behind Burton Street and Mulhattan's Hall. We used to live next to the Scallans, the daughter who married Jack McBride. They were Salvationists, and old Fanny nearly went barmy."

"Murgatroyd!" Mary Ann was pointing at him, her finger wagging. "Yes, yes, of course, Murgatroyd. Johnny Murgatroyd, of course."

"I used to chase you round the back lanes and try to scare the wits out of you."

She laughed widely as she recalled the big lanky fellow swooping down on her from the street corner when she was returning from school; especially would he swoop on St. Patrick's Day, because she was green and he was blue.

She brought the cups of coffee to the table, and as she sat down she said, "Well, well, after all these years, and you've got to rescue me as an introduction."

"Aye," he said; "funny that. Pity the TV cameras hadn't been there, it would have caused a laugh him going down on the grab," he nodded towards Bill, "and the three of us then slithering on our bellies." He jerked his head at her and paused before saying, "You should make up a song about that an' all."

Her eyes widened, but before she could say anything he said, "Oh, I know quite a lot about you; I thought that song you made up for Duke and them was really fine."

"You know Duke?"

"We live next door to him in Jarrow."

"It's a small world." She shook her head.

"You've said it. By!" he said, "they're a lot, that group. I don't know why Jimmy strings along with them. Me mother's threatened to get the polis time and time again. They come back from a do on a Saturday night—or a Sunday morning—and start raising the place. Drums, guitars, mouth organs, the lot."

"You live with you mother?" Her head was bowed enquiringly towrds him. "You're not married?"

For reply he jerked his chin upwards; then running his hand through his hair he said, "Nearly came off two years ago, but she changed her mind."

"I'm sorry."

"Oh, don't be." He was grinning again. "She's got a bairn now and she goes about like something the cat dragged in. Talk about counting your blessings; it nearly made me go to church the last time I saw her. . . ."

They were laughing uproariously when the door opened and they both turned and looked at Corny.

Mary Ann got to her feet, saying, "You've missed it all. This is Johnny Murgatroyd. He. . . ."

Corny came forward, saying, "Jimmy's told me something of it. It was very good of you." His voice had a slightly stiff note to it.

Johnny Murgatroyd was on his feet now, his hand extended. "Oh, that's all right. It was a sort of re-introduction. We know each other; brought up back to back so to speak. I used to chase her when she was a nipper."

"Oh, yes." Corny gave a weak smile; then looked from the fellow's coat to his trousers; and Mary Ann said, "We were covered from head to foot in slime. I've lent him your things. That's all right, isn't it?"

"Oh aye. Yes, yes." He nodded his head airily; then looking towards the fireplace, he asked, "How did he get out?"

"Don't ask me; I haven't had time to investigate that yet. But there's one thing certain, it's frightened the life out of him."

Corny was on his hunkers by the fender and he stroked Bill's back, saying, "All right old chap?" but Bill made no move towards him.

"He's shivering." He looked up at Mary Ann.

"I had to wash him and, as I said, he got an awful shock and I think he's still frightened."

"Well, I'd better be on me way."

They both turned towards Johnny Murgatroyd. "If you could give me a sheet of paper to put round my old duds I'd be grateful." He smiled at Mary Ann and added, "Then I'll see to somebody taking over from me and dash home and make a change and let you have your things back." He nodded at Corny now, and Corny said, "Oh, there's no hurry."

"Good job we're much of a build." Johnny's engaging grin widened, and Corny said, "Aye, it is." He stared at the man, he was about an inch shorter than himself but of a thicker build and good looking in a sort of way. He was the kind of fellow that women would fall over their feet for.

"Many thanks. I'm grateful."

"You're welcome," said Corny.

"I'll pop in again and have a word with you, if that's all right." He looked at Mary Ann, and Mary Ann resisted looking towards Corny before saying, "Yes, yes, of course, Johnny."

Five minutes later, after seeing their visitor away, they returned upstairs, and Mary Ann said, "You didn't mind me lending him your things?"

"No, no, of course not."

She stared at him. "But I couldn't do anything else, he was in such a mess, and I would never have got out of there but for him."

"Oh, I suppose somebody would have dragged you out. They would have sent down the grab again."

As he turned away she looked at his back, and then she nipped on her lip to stop herself from smiling and forced herself to say casually, "Yes, I suppose so, but he seemed the only one who wanted to. It was nice meeting him again after all this time."

"Yes, yes, very nice I should say." He was talking from the scullery now. "And he's going to drop in again. Never waited to be asked. Bit fresh, if you ask me. Going to make you pay for the rescue."

"Well, that's an attitude to take." She was looking at him from the doorway as he poured himself out some coffee, and her control went by the board. "You've got room to talk, haven't you? You can laugh and joke with whom you choose, but because you came in and found me laughing with a man that's all wrong. And after he had done me a great service. I don't think your lady friend has ever done you a service, but then," she closed her eyes and bobbed her head, "I may be mistaken."

She had turned into the kitchen again and like a flash he was after her.

Pulling her round to him, he ground out under his breath, "Now look you here. We straightened me out last night, now I'm going to straighten you out . . . before it goes any further. Johnny Murgatroyd is a womaniser. That is the first time I've met him to speak to, but I've heard quite a lot about him. He was going to be married a while ago but the lass found out he was keeping a woman in Wallsend, and apparently she wasn't the first, and she won't be the last; so Mrs. Boyle, take heed to what I'm saying. No more tête-à-têtes with Mr. Johnny Murgatroyd."

"You're hurting my shoulders."

"I'll hurt more than your shoulders if I've got to tell you about this again, I'll skelp your lug for you."

"Just you try it on."

"Don't tempt me."

She watched him stalk from the room; then she sat down on the chair near the fireplace, and again she was biting on her lip. But now she let the smile spread over her face. It filled her eyes and sank into her being, filling her with a warmth.

A movement to the side of her brought her eyes to Bill. He was on his feet, and slowly stepping over the fender he put his two front paws on her knees and leapt up on to her lap, and there, laying his muzzle between her breasts, he gazed up at her. And she looked back at him. Then after a moment she said to herself, "Well, well, who would have thought it?" and her arms went round him and she hugged him to her.

6

WHAT'S GOOD FOR THE GOOSE

"It is, our David. It is because of the miracle Father Carey made."

"Don't be daft."

"I'm not, our David, I'm not daft. I told you I told Father Carey in confession and he said it wanted a miracle, and he made it. Mam was going to throw Bill out. You know she was. She wasn't going to let us keep him, and now she has him all the time and he won't leave her, and she's trainin' him herself. It couldn't have happened if Father Carey hadn't. . . ."

They had just got off the bus in Felling and were walking up Stuart Crescent making for Carlisle Street where the school was, and David, jumping into the gutter and kicking at a pebble, said, "It's 'cos Mam got him out of the hole and he was frightened and she was nice to him, that's why."

"'Tisn't. He was frightened of the dark and being tied up and being by hisself. But that didn't make him keep with Mam all the time, like now. You don't believe anything, our David, like you used to. It is a miracle, so!"

David glanced at her and grinned, but she didn't grin back at him. Since he had begun to talk he had moved further and further away from her. At first he had been all for their dad. He was still for their dad; but now he was for other people too, like Jimmy. He was always trailing round after Jimmy. Yet there were odd times when he wanted to be near her, and he would look at her and grin, like he was doing now, and she would feel happy. Only she couldn't feel happy this morning; she had too much on her mind. She said suddenly, "Do you like Diana Blenkinsop?"

When his reply came with startling suddenness she was in the gutter beside him. "You don't? Why?"

David kicked another pebble, then started to dribble it along the roadway. Why didn't he like Diana Blenkinsop? When the answer came to him he turned his head and gave it to Rose Mary: "'Cos me mam doesn't like her."

"Oh, David." She was running by his side now. She didn't like Diana Blenkinsop because her dad liked Diana Blenkinsop. And David didn't like Diana Blenkinsop because her mam didn't like Diana Blenkinsop. You see, it was all the same. She said now, "They were talking about her again last night."

"I know." He kept his gaze concentrated on his dribbling feet; the stone veered off into the middle of the road and as he went to follow it Rose Mary grabbed him, crying, "Eeh no! The cars." And they returned to the pavement and for a while walked in sedate silence.

When they came in sight of the school gate Rose Mary's step slowed and she said, "There's that Annabel Morton talkin' to Patricia Gibbs. Patricia promised to bring me a book full of pictures, but she only promised so's she could get you to carry it back."

David's glance was slanted at her again, his eyebrows showing a surprised lift in their middle, and she nodded at him and said, "She's gone on you."

"Polony!"

"It isn't polony, she's sucking up. She wants to be asked to tea, but she's not me best friend and I'm not goin' to."

Annabel Morton was nearly eight and a big girl for her age, and, as Sarah Flannagan had hated Mary Ann as a child, so Annabel Morton hated Mary Ann's daughter, and the feeling was reciprocated in full. When Annabel's voice, addressing no one in particular, said, "Somebody stinks," Rose Mary turned on her like a flash of lightning, crying, "You! You don't know what you're talking about. Scent doesn't stink, it smells. It's scent, me mam's."

"It's scent, me mam's," mimicked Annabel to her solitary listener. "But it still stinks, doesn't it?"

"You're a pig!" Rose Mary did not yell this statement, she hissed it under her breath and she embroidered it by adding, "If you lift a pig up by its tail its eyes'll drop out. Mind somebody doesn't do that to you."

This would take some beating, and at the moment Annabel could find nothing with which to match it, and so Rose Mary, having won the first round of the day, put on her swanky walk, which wobbled her buttocks, which in turn swung her short skirt from side to side. The result was entertaining, or annoying; it all depended on the frame of mind of the onlooker. . . .

It was in the middle of the morning, after they had had their milk, that they started to paint. Rose Mary liked the painting lesson, she was good at it. The whole class were doing a mural on history. It was depicting Bonnie Prince Charlie and Flora Macdonald. Each table was doing a section, and then they would put it altogether and it would fill one wall of the classroom. Rose Mary and Patricia Gibbs and her brother, Tony, were doing the water section with the boat on it. Rose Mary had just mixed up a beautiful deep blue for the water under the boat when Patricia dug her in the ribs with her elbow, at the same time withdrawing from under her painting board a big flat book.

They both looked about the room to ascertain the whereabouts of Miss Plum and saw that they were safe, for she was at the far end showing Cissie Trent what to do. Cissie Trent was dim and took a lot of showing. Patricia quickly flicked over the pages and pointed to a coloured plate and looked at Rose Mary, and Rose Mary looked at the picture. For a moment she couldn't make out what it was. And then she saw it was all about a man and a woman; the woman had hardly anything on the top of her, and the man had long hair right past his shoulders. He was lying on a kind of bed thing and the woman was bending over him with a knife in her hand. Eeh! it looked awful. She looked at Patricia and Patricia looked at her and, her eyes round and bright, she whispered, "She's going to cut his hair off. It's called Samson and De-lie-la-la."

". . . Sam . . . son and De-lie-la-la?" Rose Mary's lips moved widely over the name. "What's she doing?"

"I told you: she's going to cut his hair off."

"Eeh! what for?"

"So's he won't be able to do anything."

"What is he going to do?"

"Things."

"What things? . . . Like what things? Playing a group?"

That explanation was as good as any for Patricia, and she nodded as she smiled, "Yes. Ah-ha."

Rose Mary considered a moment before saying, "But that's daft. How can cutting his hair off stop him playing in a . . . ?"

They both felt the hot breath on their necks and turned startled eyes towards the face of Annabel Morton. But Annabel was looking at the picture. Then she looked from one to the other, and she said, "Mushrooms."

The word was like a sentence of death to both of them. Mushrooms was the word in current use in the classroom to express deep astonishment, amazement, or horror. The book was whipped from sight and pushed under Rose Mary's drawing board, and they both attacked their painting with such energy that they were panting when Miss Plum loomed up before them.

"Which of you is hiding a book?"

Patricia looked at Rose Mary, but Rose Mary was staring at Miss Plum.

"Come on. Come on, hand it over."

Still Rose Mary didn't move.

"Rose Mary! Have you got that book?"

Rose Mary's fingers groped under the pad and she pulled out the book and handed it up to Miss Plum. She had done this without taking her startled gaze from the teacher.

Miss Plum now flicked over the pages of the book, her eyes jerking from one art plate to another, and when her eyes came to rest on Bacchus in his gross nudity sporting with equally bare frolicking females she swallowed deeply; then looking at the children again she said, "Who owns this book?"

"I do, Miss," said Patricia.

"Where did you get it?"

"From home, Miss. It's . . . it's me brother's. I took a loan of it."

Again Miss Plum swallowed, twice this time, before saying, "When you go home tonight tell your mother, not your brother, that I have this book, Patricia; and tell her I would like to see her. . . . But anyway I will give you a note."

"Yes, Miss."

"Now get on with your work, both of you, and I'll deal with you later."

They both resumed their painting, but with less energy now; and after a while Rose Mary, in a tear-filled voice, whispered, "You've got me wrong, Patricia Gibbs."

"Well, you wanted to see it."

"No I didn't; I didn't ask to see your nasty book."

"'Tisn't nasty."

"Yes, it is. She had no clothes on her. . . ." She dare not pronounce the word breast.

"'Tisn't nasty," repeated Patricia. "Our John says it's art. He goes to the art classes at night, he should know." Her voice sank lower. "Miss Plum's a nit. . . ."

The result of this little episode was that Rose Mary was met at the gate by Annabel; tactics vary very little with the years. Annabel did what Sarah Flannagan used to do to Mary Ann. She allowed Rose Mary to pass, then fired her dart. "Dirty pictures," she said. And when Rose Mary flung round to confront her she repeated loudly and with a defiant thrusting out of her chin, "DIRTY PICTURES!"

What could one say to this? You couldn't give the answer "I'm not," nor could you give the answer "They weren't," because in the back of her mind she felt they were.

David was waiting for her at the corner of the railings. He knew all about it, all the class knew about it. Rose Mary thought the whole school knew about it, and soon everybody who went to church would know about it.

She was crying when they got on the bus and their special conductor said, "Aye, aye! What's this? Got the cane?"

Rose Mary shook her head, then lowered it.

"Well, this is a change; I've never seen you blubbing afore. Something serious happened the day? You set the school on fire?"

Setting the school on fire would have been nothing to the heinous crime for which she was being blamed.

"What's she done?" The conductor was now addressing David pointedly, and David, after glancing at Rose Mary, craned his neck up, indicating that what he had to say must be whispered, and when the conductor put his ear down to him he said, in a voice that was threaded with what might be termed glee, "She was looking at mucky pictures."

The conductor's head jerked up. "Good God! You don't say?"

"I wasn't." Rose Mary hadn't heard what David had said, but the conductor's reactions told her as plainly as if he had shouted it. She now dug David in the arm with her fist, crying, "I wasn't, our David!" Then looking up at the conductor, she said, "I didn't. They were in a book, in Patricia Gibbs's book. She was just showing me."

"Oh!" The conductor was trying hard to keep his face straight. He pushed his cap on to the back of his head and said, "And the teacher caught you at it?"

Rose Mary nodded.

"Too bad! Too bad!" With his knee he gently nudged David's hip, and this caused David to bow his head and put his hand tightly across his mouth.

Rose Mary was still protesting her innocence not only to the conductor and their David now and the man and woman who were sitting behind them and who were very interested in the tragedy, but also to the two men who were sitting on the other side of the bus.

When she alighted from the bus she imagined that everybody in it suddenly burst out laughing. But then it might only be the funny noise the wheels were making; anyway, she continued to cry and protest at intervals until she reached the house, the kitchen, and Mary Ann. . . .

"It's all right. It's all right," said Mary Ann. " Now let's get this straight. . . . And you David," she reached out and pushed David to one side, "take that grin off your face and stop sniggering, it's nothing to laugh at. Now tell me all about it." She sat down on the chair and drew Rose Mary on to her knee, and Rose Mary told her and finished, "I only saw that one, Mam, honest, the one with the man and the woman called Sam-son and De-lie-la-la. She hadn't much clothes on and he had long hair, and that was all."

Mary Ann took a firm hold on her face muscles and forbade herself to smile. "Well, now, Samson and De-lie-la- I mean Delilah. She's called Delilah. Say Delilah."

"De-lie-la-ha."

". . . It's all right. Don't worry, you'll get it. Well, that isn't a dirty picture."

"It isn't, Mam?"

"No, no; it's a great picture, it's very famous. There's a story about Samson and Delilah."

So Mary Ann told Rose Mary, and David, the story of Samson and Delilah, and she ended with, "All his strength was in his hair, you see. Once he was without his hair, Delilah knew that he wouldn't be able to do anything, win battles and things like that, all his strength would go, all his power, and so she cut off his hair."

"And did it, Mam? I mean, didn't he fight any more battles after, and things?"

"No, no, he didn't." She didn't go on to explain the gory details of what happened to Samson after this, she left it at that. Instead, she said, "There, you weren't looking at a mucky picture, you were looking at a great picture. And when you go back to school tomorrow you can tell Annabel Morton that. And if Miss Plum says anything more to you about it you tell her what I've said, that Samson and Delilah is a great picture and there's nothing to be ashamed of in looking at it."

"Yes, Mam." Rose Mary's voice was small. She couldn't see herself telling Miss Plum that, but she was comforted nevertheless. And wait until she saw that Annabel Morton, just wait.

"Go on now and get washed and then have your tea. Afterwards you can take Bill out and have a scamper."

"Has he been out today, Mam?" asked David now, as he rolled Bill on his back on the mat.

"I took him down the road at dinner-time and left him in the yard a while after, but that's all. He could do with a run. Go on now and get washed, tea's ready."

They both now ran out of the room, leaving the door open and calling to Bill; and Mary Ann went into the scullery while Bill stood on the mat looking first one way, and then the other, finally he walked towards the scullery.

7

MATERIAL AND IMAGINATION

The idea come to Mary Ann a fortnight after the incident of the grab. She sat down, as she usually did after she had finished washing the dinner dishes, with a cup of tea and a book. Sometimes she gave herself fifteen minutes, sometimes half-an-hour, it all depended on her interest in what she was reading. There was no chance to read once the children were home, and this was the only time of the day when there seemed to be an interval between the chores. But the pattern over the last two weeks had changed, for as soon as she sat down Bill moved from the fireplace and took up his position on her lap. She was amused at the dog's sudden devotion to her, and not at all displeased, although she still protested to Corny, "I don't want the thing up here, but he's quiet and behaving himself—at least at present, but should he start again . . . well." And to the children, when they grumbled, "He doesn't want to stay out, Mam; he'll come if you'll come," she would say, "Don't be so silly. Put his lead on and take him over the fields. He's got to have a run, and I can't take him out all the time. And don't tug him. And tell him to heel, and sit, and when he does it pat his head."

When she talked to them like this they would stare at her in a disconcerting way and she always had to busy herself in order not to laugh in front of them, because the transference of

Bill's affection from them to herself was really funny when she came to think of it. And now here he was on her lap again, and every time she lifted the book up he would push his muzzle in front of it and open his mouth and laugh at her.

Mary Ann was convinced that he was laughing; his lolling tongue, the light in his eyes, the way his dewlaps quivered, he couldn't be doing anything else but laughing.

She had got into the habit over the last few afternoons of talking to him. "I'd like to read if you don't mind," she said to him. "Oh, you do? Well, do you know this is the only time of the day I have to myself? . . . What do I want time to myself for? . . . Don't ask such a silly question. Oh, you know it's a silly question, do you, and you're sorry." She put her head on one side and surveyed him; then touching his muzzle with her finger she said, "You know you are the ugliest thing I've ever seen in my life, at least the ugliest dog, but you've got something. . . . What? I don't know, you tell me. We've all got something, you say? Oh yes, very likely. . . . How do you see us, Bill, eh? What do you call us in your mind? Big he, and little she? Angel one, and angel two?"

She laughed at the description of her family and Bill wriggled on her knee, then let his front paws go slack around her hips and placed his muzzle in his favourite position, the hollow of her breasts, and she stroked his head and stared at him, and he stared back at her.

How long they remained like this she wasn't sure but when she next spoke aloud she said, "It's an idea. Why not? It's worth trying; dafter things than that have been known to succeed. I've seen nothing like it in any of the papers. There's Dorfy of course. She writes dialect pieces in the Shields Gazette, but this would be from a dog's point of view, how he sees us. I could make it funny. Yes, if I tried I could make it funny. . . . Ooh, I'm sorry." She had jumped up so quickly that Bill found himself sprawling on the floor and she stooped down and soothed his rumpled feelings. Then looking into his eyes again she said, "It would be funny, wouldn't it, if it came off." And now there came into her mind the picture of Diana Blenkinsop.

Diana Blenkinsop, and life from the viewpoint of a dog would appear to have no connection whatever, but in Mary Ann's mind they were closely linked.

During the next three weeks the house was like a simmering kettle, on the point of boiling but never reaching it.

Mary Ann was in a state of suppressed excitement. She was hugging a secret to herself, and if things worked out, as she prayed they would, that would show them. When her thoughts took this line she saw the picture of Corny and Diana Blenkinsop standing together. Twice in the last week she had seen Diana come out of Corny's office; once she had seen their heads together under the bonnet of her car. She was the type, Mary Ann decided, that would go to any lengths to get what she wanted, even to messing up the engine of her car.

She had written, and written, and re-written three five hundred word snippets about Bill, supposedly his outlook on life, and last Monday she had sent them to the editor of the *Newcastle Courier*. Now the sight of the postman coming along the road would drive her down the stairs to meet him at the door, but here it was Friday and she had received no reply, not even an acknowledgement. But then, she hadn't received the stuff back either, so perhaps no news was good news. . . .

Corny's life over the last three weeks had been one of irritation. First in his mind was the fact that Mary Ann was playing up. She was up to something, he could tell. He only hoped to God it wasn't anything against Diana Blenkinsop, but knowing to what limits she had gone to put things right for her father, one such effort incidentally, resulting in him losing one hand, he was more than a little worried as to what lengths she would go with regard to himself. And then there was Jimmy. For two pins he would give him the sack, but where would he get another like him. Jimmy could turn a car inside out. He was a good worker;

give him a job and he stuck at it until it was finished, but the quality didn't make up for being light fingered. Two ten shilling notes had gone from the till this week. The second one he had marked, but when later he had asked Jimmy if he had change for a pound note on him, and Jimmy had given him a ten shilling note and ten shillings worth of silver, it hadn't been the marked note. He was cute was Jimmy; and that was the worst type of thief, a cute one.

And then there was Mr. Blenkinsop. He had come into the garage yesterday and looked around for quite a while before he said, "You all right, Corny?" and he'd replied, "Yes, I'm all right. What makes you think I'm not?"

"The little lady all right, Mary Ann?"

"Yes, yes, she's all right."

Then Mr. Blenkinsop had jerked his head and said "Oh, I was just wondering."

He didn't ask him what was making him wonder, he daren't. Had he noticed that his daughter was never away from the garage? Even lunch times now she would come in. She said it was the quickest way to the hill beyond; she sunbathed there when it was fine. She'd even brought her lunch twice or thrice and had it out there. He wished to God she hadn't come to work here. Nothing had been the same since. He was all mixed up inside. He kept telling himself that the next time she put her nose in the door he would ignore her, but when he heard her say "Cor-ny!" in that particular way she had, he found himself looking at her and smiling at her, and saying, "Yes. Yes. Yes." He agreed with every damn thing she said.

But yesterday she had said, "I wonder what you would be like in a fight, Corny?" and he had said, "Fight? Who should I fight?"

She had shrugged her shoulders. "I was just wondering."

"You don't wonder things like that without a reason." He had stopped smiling at her, but she had continued to smile at him; then walking away she said, "Do you know that our handsome ganger is upstairs?"

He made himself utter a small "Huh!" when she turned and confronted him, then shook his head and said, "Well, what would you like to make of that? She's known Johnny Murgatroyd since they were bairns." He had then nodded his head in a cautionary fashion towards her as he said, "You're a starter, Diana, aren't you?"

"What do you mean, a starter?"

"You know what I mean all right. They could say the same about you. You're in here with me, but you're not going to lose your good name because of that, are you?"

"I might." She walked a step towards him. "Perhaps I have already."

He gulped in his throat, rubbed his hands with an imaginary piece of rag, then said, "You want your backside smacked, that's what you want. Go on outside and do your sunbathing."

"You're trying to make me out a child, Cor-ny, aren't you?" she said. "But you know I'm not. We both know I'm not, so. . . ." She tossed her blonde head backwards and her hair jumped from her shoulders as if it were alive. "We've got to face up to these things. But there's plenty of time, it'll grow on you. I'm in no hurry."

She went out through the small door in the back wall of the garage, and Corny went to a car, lifted the bonnet and bent over the engine with his hands gripping the framework. My God! what was he to do? She was a little bitch. No, she was a big bitch; a long-legged, beautiful, attractive big bitch. He hated her. No. No, he didn't, he. . . . His head went further down over the engine. He wouldn't even allow himself to think the word. . . .

And the children? Rose Mary was unhappy for a number of reasons. Their David didn't want to play with her at all. Even when they came home from school he didn't want to play with her like he used to. He would yell at her and say, "I'm going with the cars." She didn't want to go into the garage with the cars but she wanted to be near David. And she wanted to be near Bill, but Bill, after ten or fifteen minutes' romping, would make straight for the house and upstairs and their mam. She was glad that Bill liked her mam because now they could keep him. But he just liked her mam and he didn't like her. Well, if he liked her he didn't want to stay with her, he just wanted to stay with her mam. She couldn't understand it.

And then there was her dad. He used to come and play with them when they were in bed. If he was late coming upstairs he would always come into the room and have a game with them. That was, up till lately. Now, even if she kept awake until he came in, he would just kiss her and say good night and God bless, and that was all.

And her mam. Her mam was worried and she knew what her mam was worried about 'cos she had seen her standing to the side of the curtains looking down on to the drive, watching her dad and Diana Blenkinsop. Yet her mam hadn't cried these last few weeks. Of the two, it was her dad she was more worried about. Her dad . . . and Diana Blenkinsop. . . .

And David. David, too, had his worries. David's worries were deep; they were things not to be talked about. You didn't think too much about them but you did something to try to get them to go away. His worries were concerned, first with Jimmy, secondly with his dad. About Jimmy he was doing something definite; with regard to the problem of his dad he was working something out.

In a way it was David who had inherited his mother's ingenuity.

8

BEN

The phone rang about quarter-to-seven. It was Lizzie. "Is that you, Mary Ann?" she said.

"Yes, Mam."

"I've got some rather sad news for you. Ben is going fast. Tony's just been down, and he says that Ben asked for you, just as if you were in the house. 'Where's Mary Ann?' he said. He's rambling a little, but I wondered whether you'd like to come and see him."

"Oh, yes, Mam, yes. I didn't know he was ill."

"He's only been bad since Tuesday. But he's a good age, you know."

"What's Mr. Lord going to do without him?"

"That's what we're all asking, lass. But he's got Tony and Lettice."

"I know, I know, but they're not Ben; Ben's been with him nearly all his life."

"Can you come?"

"Yes, Mam, yes, of course. I was just going to get them ready for bed but Corny will see them, he's just downstairs."

"All right, dear. We'll expect you in an hour or so."

"Bye-bye Mam."

"Bye-bye, dear."

She had put the phone down before she realized that Corny wouldn't be able to run her over, somebody must be here with the children. She could have asked her da to pick her up; but it didn't matter, she'd get the bus.

She ran downstairs and into the office where Corny was sitting at the desk. She forgot for the moment that there was any coldness between them and she said, "Ben . . . Ben's dying. Mam's just phoned, he'd like to see me. Will you put the children to bed?"

He was on his feet looking down at her and he shook his head, saying, "Aw, poor old Ben. But still he's getting on, it's to be expected. . . . He asked for you?"

"Mam said so."

"Well, get yourself away. But look—" He put out his hand towards her and she turned as she was going through the door. "I won't be able to run you over. Are they coming for you?"

"I forgot to ask Dad."

"I'll get on to them."

"No, no, it doesn't matter. He could be busy or anything; I'll get the bus at the corner. If I hurry I'll get the ten past seven." She was running up the stairs again.

Five minutes later, when she came down, Corny was waiting for her on the drive. "Get your Dad to bring you back mind."

"Oh, he'll do that." She looked up at him. "Don't let them stay up late, will you?"

"Leave that to me." He nodded at her.

"And . . . and Bill; don't leave him on his own upstairs, will you not? He might start tearing the place up again."

He smiled wryly at her, then said, "We couldn't risk that could we?" They stared at each other for a moment; then as she turned away he said to her quietly, "Forgotten something?" She paused, then looked down at her handbag before saying, "No I don't think so."

"Well, if that's how you want it, it's up to you."

She walked away from him with a quick light step, the only thing about her that was light at the moment.

Whenever they left each other for any length of time she always kissed him, and he her; it might only be a peck on the cheek but it was a symbol that they were close—kind, as Rose Mary would have said.

The sketches she had been writing around Bill during the last three weeks had provided tangents for her thoughts along which to escape from the thing that was filling her mind; the thing that was making her sad deep inside, and not a little fearful. Her impetuous battling character was not coming to her aid over the business of Corny's attraction for Diana Blenkinsop, and no matter what excuse he gave about having to be civil to the girl because of her father she knew it was just an excuse, and she knew that he knew it too. He was attracted to Diana Blenkinsop.

She had always felt she knew more about the workings of a man's mind than she did a woman's. This was likely, because since she was a small child she had dissected her father's character, sorting out his good points from his bad ones, but loving him all the while. But in her husband's case her reaction to the dissection was different. She had worked and schemed to turn her father's eye and thoughts away from another woman and back to her mother, but she couldn't do that with regard to her husband. She knew that she would never work or scheme to keep Corny, not when there was another woman involved. He would have to stay with her because he loved her, because he found her more attractive than any other woman. He would have to stay with her because her love for him alone would satisfy him. This was one time she could not fight.

She was lost in her thinking and did not notice the car, which had just flashed by, come to a stop until it backed towards her.

"Hello there. Waiting for the bus?"

"Oh, hello, Johnny. Yes, yes, I'm going home; I mean to my mother's." She still couldn't get out of the habit of thinking of the farm as her home, although Corny had impressed upon her that she had one home now and it was where he lived.

"Get in then; I'll run you along."

"Oh, no, no, Johnny; the bus will be here in a minute, it's due. I won't take you out of your way."

"You won't take me out of my way. I'm at a loose end, you'll be doing me a kindness. Come on, get in."

She stood looking down at him. Corny didn't like this man, he liked him as little as she did Diana Blenkinsop. He'd be wild if he knew she had taken a lift from him, but it seemed silly not to, and he'd get her there in a quarter of the time.

When he leant forward and pushed open the door she could do nothing but slide into the seat beside him. He looked different tonight, very smart, handsome in fact. He was wearing a shirt and tie that the adverts would have described as impeccable, and his light grey suit looked expensive. He had told her that he sometimes picked up fifty pounds a week when bonuses were good. He had been foreman at Quinton's for five years and Bob Quinton thought very highly of him. Johnny wasn't bashful about himself. His car too, was a good one, and she knew it would take something to run. The way he looked now he had no connection with the ganger on the site.

"Why didn't your hubby run you along?"

When she explained he said, "Oh, oh, I see." Then added "You know, I'll like meeting your mam and dad again. I wonder whether they'll remember me?" He grinned at her.

She had been going to say to him, "Will you drop me at the end of the road," but when, in his mind's eye, he was already seeing himself talking to her parents she couldn't do anything else but allow him to drive her up to the farm.

Lizzie was waiting on the lawn for her. She had been expecting to see her hurrying along the road; remembering that the children couldn't be left alone she had phoned the house to say that Mike would come and pick Mary Ann up, but Corny had said she had been gone some time and would already be on the bus. But here she was getting out of a car with a man.

Mary Ann kissed Lizzie, then said, "Do you know who this is, Mam?"

Lizzie looked at the man before her. Her face was straight. She shook her head and said, "Yes, and no. I feel I should know you."

"Johnny Murgatroyd."

"Murgatroyd. Oh yes." Lizzie smiled now. "Of course, of course. But you've changed somewhat since those days."

"I . . . I told you about him getting me and Bill out of the mud, you remember?"

"Yes, you did. Come in." Lizzie led the way into the house and Mike got up from his seat and put down his pipe and took Mary Ann in his arms and kissed her; then looking across the big farm kitchen to where the man was standing just inside the door, he said, "Hello."

"You don't remember me either?" Johnny came forward.

"Yes, yes, I do, Johnny Murgatroyd."

Johnny turned round and looked from one to the other. "Recognised at last. No more an orphan. Daddy! Daddy! I've come home."

They all laughed. "Oh, you'd take some forgetting." Mike jerked his head. "You were a bit of a devil if I remember. How have you come here?" He looked at Mary Ann and Mary Ann said, "I was waiting for the bus, Da, and . . . and Johnny was passing and he gave me a lift."

"Oh, I see. Sit down, sit down."

Johnny Murgatroyd sat down, and he looked at Mike. Mike had said, You'll take some forgetting; well, and so would he. He had a vivid memory of battling, boozing Mike Shaughnessy. Who would have imagined that he would have settled down and had all this? A farm, and a grand house. It's funny how some people fell on their feet. Well, he'd have a grand house one day, just wait and see. Great oaks from little acorns grow.

"Will you have a cup of tea before you go up?" Lizzie was looking at Mary Ann.

"No, Mam; it's no time since I had a meal, I'll go now. But perhaps Johnny here would like one?"

"I never say no to a cuppa." He was laughing up at Lizzie.

"Thanks for the lift, Johnny, I'll be seeing you."

"You will. Oh, you will." He nodded at her, and she went out and through the familiar farmyard and up the hill to the house where lived Mr. Lord, the man who had shaped all their destinies . . . with her help.

She went in the back way as she always did, and it was strange not to see Ben, either in the kitchen or coming from the hall.

Tony met her and kissed her on the cheek. Whenever he did this she was made to wonder how different her life would have been if she had married him as Mr. Lord had schemed she should. But it had been Corny who had filled her horizon since the day she had championed the raggy, tousled-haired individual against Mr. Lord himself. And Tony had married Lettice, a divorcee, and they were both happy, ideally happy. It shone out of their faces whenever she saw them together. And now, as Lettice came towards her, the look was still there, which made her feel a little sad, even a little jealous.

"Hello, my dear," Lettice kissed her warmly, then asked, "Are you going into the drawing-room first?"

"Is there time? I mean, how is Ben now?"

"Oh, he's dozing, he keeps waking up at intervals. Just go and say hello first."

Mr. Lord was sitting, as usual, in his winged chair; during the day he would face the window and look on to the garden, but in the evening he would set himself to the side of the big open fire.

He did not turn his head when she entered the room. His hands, in characteristic pose, were resting on the arms of the chair, but tonight his chin wasn't up and out, it was bent deep into his chest. She reached him before she said, "Hello." She had always greeted him with "Hello." He brought his head round to her and a faint light of pleasure came into his pale, watery, blue eyes.

"Hello, my dear," he said; then he shook his head slowly and said, "Sad night, sad night."

"Yes."

"Sit close to me, here." He pointed to his knee, and she brought a stool from one side of the fireplace and sat where he had bidden her.

"Part of me will go with him."

She made no answer to this. She knew it was so.

"A great part." He stared at her for a moment before he said, "I have bullied him all his life, shouted, ranted and bullied him, and if we lived for another fifty years together I would continue to do so; it was my way with him. He understood it and never murmured."

There was a great lump in her throat as she said, "You were his life, you were all he had and ever wanted; he was never hurt by anything you said or did."

He moved his head slowly, then said, "He wasn't a poor man, I'm generous in my way; he could have left me years ago. . . . I wish I had gone before him. But it won't be long anyway before we're together again."

"Oh." Her voice broke as she whispered, "Oh, don't say that. And . . . and it's better this way. If he had been left alone he would have had no one, not really, because there was only you in his life, whereas you've got"—she paused—"all of us."

He raised his head and looked at her, then put out his long, thin, blue-veined hand and cupped her chin, "Yes, I've got all of you. But the only one I really ever wanted was you. You know that, child, don't you?"

She was crying openly now and she took his hand and pressed it to her cheek, and he said, "There, there. Go on, go on up. Twice today he has spoken your name. I know he would like to see you."

She rose to her feet without further words and went out into the hall. The drawing-room door was open and through it she saw Lettice and Tony standing together. When they turned and saw her they came swiftly to her and Lettice put her arm around her shoulders and said, "Don't cry, don't upset yourself. Would you like a drink, a sherry, before you go up?"

"No; no, thanks." Mary Ann wiped her face with her handkerchief, then said, "I'd better go now."

"Yes, do," said Lettice, "and get it over with, and I'll make some coffee." She nodded to Tony and he walked up the stairs by Mary Ann's side, and when they entered Ben's room a nurse rose from the side of the bed and, coming towards them, said, "He's awake."

Mary Ann went forward and stood gazing down on Ben. He looked a very, very old man, much older than his eighty years. She bent over him and said softly, "Hello, Ben."

His thin wrinkled lips moved in a semblance of a smile. Ben had rarely smiled. He had in a way grumbled at others, herself included, as much as his master had grumbled at him. He had never shown any affection towards her. At first he had shown open hostility and jealousy, because from a child she had inveigled herself into his master's good books by being what he considered perky and cheeky, whereas his life-long service elicited nothing but the whiplash of a tongue that was for ever expressing the bitterness of life.

"Mary . . . Mary Ann."

"Yes, Ben."

His lips mouthed words that were soundless; then again they moved and he said, "See to him, he needs you, master needs you."

"Yes, Ben. Don't worry, I'll see to him." She did not say that his master had his grandson and his grandson's wife to see to him, for she knew that she, and she alone, could fill the void that Ben would leave in Mr. Lord's life. Even when he had been given a great grandson the boy had not taken her place; and that was very strange when you came to think about it.

"Good girl."

The tears were flowing down her face again. When she felt the rustle of the nurse's skirt at her side she bent down and kissed the hollow cheek, and Ben closed his eyes.

Tony led her from the room and down the stairs, and in the drawing-room Lettice was waiting, and she said, "There, sit down and have your coffee."

"It's awful . . . it's awful. Death is awful."

"It's got to come to us all," said Tony solemnly. "But poor old Ben's done nothing but work all his days, yet we couldn't stop him."

"He wouldn't have lived to this age if we'd been able to," said Lettice. "Work was his life, working for grandad."

"There aren't many left like him," said Tony. "They don't make them any more."

No, thought Mary Ann, they didn't make Bens any more, not men who were willing to give their lives to others; it was every man for himself these days. The world of Ben and Mr. Lord was passing; it had almost gone. It would vanish entirely, at least from their sphere, when Mr. Lord died, but she prayed that that wouldn't be for a long time yet.

After a while she asked, "How's Peter?"

"Oh, fine. We had a letter from him this morning," said Lettice. "I say fine, but he has his troubles." She smiled. "He informs us that he doesn't like the new sports master. His name is Mr. Tollett, and they have nicknamed him Tightrope Tollett. I can't see the connection but likely they can. How are the twins?"

"Oh, they're grand."

"I hear you've got a dog," said Tony now, grinning slyly.

"Yes," said Mary Ann; "a bull terrier."

"So I heard. You pick the breeds."

"I didn't pick him."

"I understand he created a little disorder in the kitchen."

"A little disorder is right," said Mary Ann. "If I'd had a gun I would have shot him on the spot. Well," she rose to her feet, "I'd better be going; I've left Corny to see to them and they play him up."

"Are you going to look in on grandad again?" asked Lettice.

"Yes, just to say good night. . . ."

Ten minutes later Mary Ann entered the farm kitchen again and stopped just within the door and looked to where Johnny Murgatroyd was still sitting at the table. He called across the room to her, "You haven't been long."

As she walked towards her mother she said to him, "You needn't have waited."

"Oh, I had nothing better to do."

"How did you find him?" said Lizzie.

"Very low; they don't think he'll last the night."

"Poor old Ben," said Mike. "He was a good man . . . a good man." He knocked out the doddle from his pipe on the hob of the fire. "The old fellow's going to be lost. Things won't be the same."

Lizzie said now, "You'll have to pop over and see Mr. Lord more often. In spite of Tony and Lettice he'll miss Ben greatly."

"Yes," said Mary Ann, "I mean to. And now," she fastened the top button of her coat, "I'd better get back."

"Aren't you going to have something to drink?" said Lizzie.

"No; no thanks, Mam, I've just had a cup of coffee with Lettice and Tony."

As they all went through the hall to the front door Mary Ann said, "You'll phone me when it happens?"

"Yes, of course, dear," said Lizzie.

On the drive Johnny held out his hand to Mike, saying, "Well, it's been nice meeting up with you again, and you, Mrs. S."

"It's been nice seeing you, Johnny, and talking about old times," said Lizzie. "Any time you're passing you must look in."

"Yes, yes I will. I won't need another invitation, and don't forget you asked me."

She laughed at him; then looked at Mary Ann whose face was straight and she said, "Don't worry, dear."

As they drove along the lane, Johnny aiming to be sympathetic, said, "It's a pity about the old fellow but we've all got to go some time. Your dad tells me he's eighty. Well, he's had a good run for his money."

Mary Ann made no answer to this. Good run for his money. We've all to go some time. All trite expressions meaning nothing. Death was a frightful thing; it was the final of all final things. She knew she shouldn't think like this. Her religion should help her, for wasn't there a life after death, but she couldn't see it. She often thought about death and the fact that it was so final worried her, but it was a thing you couldn't talk about. People didn't want to talk about death. If you talked about death you were classed as morbid. And if you told the priest of your thoughts in confession all you got was you must pray for faith. Lord I believe, help thou my unbelief. At times she got all churned up inside with one thing and another. She thought too much . . . "What did you say, Johnny?"

"You were miles away. I was saying that I bet you a quid you don't know who I'm taking out the morrow?"

"Now why should I?" she smiled slightly at him. "I don't know anybody you know."

"But you do. You know this one all right."

Her thoughts took her back to Burton Street and the surrounding district. Who did she knew there that he knew? The only person who was in her life from that district was Sarah, who was now her sister-in-law. "You've got me puzzled," she said; "I still don't know anyone that you know."

"Think hard."

She thought hard, then said, "I give up."

"What about Miss Blenkinsop?"

Her surprise lifted her around on the seat and she exclaimed loudly, "What! You and Diana Blenkinsop? You're joking."

"No, no, I'm not joking." His tone was slightly huffed. "Why should I be joking?" He gave a swift glance at her. "Because she's the boss's daughter and I'm a ganger? Do I look like a ganger?" He took one hand from the wheel and draped it down the front of himself.

"No, no, I didn't mean that." But she had meant that.

"I'm going places, Mary Ann."

"I've no doubt of that, Johnny." Her smile had widened.

"Do you know something?"

"What?"

"You should be thanking me for telling you, it'll get her out of your hair."

"What do you mean?" Her body had jerked round again.

"Oh, oh, you know what I mean."

"I don't."

"Now, now, Mary Ann, don't let us hide our heads in the sand; you know for a fact that she's got her sights set on your man. Everybody on the job knows it."

She felt she wanted to be sick, literally sick. She swallowed deeply and took in a great intake of breath before she forced herself to say on an airy note, "Well, I don't care what they know on the job, it's of no importance. She can have her sights set at any angle, she'll only be wasting her time."

"Oh, I'm glad you're not worried."

"I'm not worried." She sounded cool, confident, and he glanced quickly at her, the corner of his mouth turned upwards. "Still, I think, me taking her over should help you to be less worried than not being worried, if you get what I mean."

She remained quiet, thinking. Yes, indeed, this would make her less worried, this would show Corny what kind of a girl he was almost going overboard for. The only snag was it couldn't last because when Mr. and Mrs. Blenkinsop got wind of it there'd be an explosion, because beneath all their camaraderie they were snobbish, especially Mrs. Blenkinsop; she kept open house but she vetted the entrants. Mary Ann felt there had been more than a touch of condescension about the invitation that was extended to themselves; it was a sort of boss's wife being nice to an employee's family, attitude. But Corny was no employee of Mr. Blenkinsop.

When they reached the road opposite the garage Corny was serving petrol and he jerked his head up and became quite still as he looked at Mary Ann getting out of the car and the face that was grinning at her from the window. When Johnny Murgatroyd waved to him he made no response but turned and attended to the customer.

A few minutes later he mounted the stairs, telling himself to go carefully.

Mary Ann was in the bedroom with the children and he had to wait a full ten minutes before she came into the kitchen. Her face was not showing sorrow for Ben, nor yet mischievous elation at being driven up to the door by Johnny Murgatroyd; it had a sort of neutral look that took some of the wind out of his sails. He watched her pat Bill and say, "Down! Down!" before he forced himself to say calmly, "How did you find him?"

"He won't last the night."

In an ordinary way he would have said, "I'm sorry about that," but instead he said, "Where did you pick that one up?"

She turned and looked at him over her shoulder. "You mean Johnny?"

"Well, he didn't look like Cliff Michelmore, or Danny Blanchflower, or the Shah of

Persia."

She had a desire to burst out laughing, and she turned her head away and replied coolly, "I didn't pick him up, he picked me up while I was waiting for the bus."

He screwed his face up and peered at her back. "You mean when you were going?"

She turned to him and inclined her head slowly downwards, giving emphasis to his words as she repeated them, "Yes, when I was going."

"Then he must have waited for you?"

"Yes, he waited for me, and dad saw nothing immoral in it; neither did Mam."

"You mean he took you right to the farm?"

"He took me right to the farm. Isn't it awful, scandalous?" She shook her head in mock horror at herself, and he said quickly, "Now, you can drop that. And if you've got any sense you'll drop him. And the next time he offers to give you a lift you'll tell him what to do."

"But perhaps I haven't got any sense, Corny, perhaps I'm like you."

"Oh, my God!" He put his hand to his brow and turned from her and leaned his shoulder against the mantelpiece. Then pulling himself upwards again he shouted at her, "Look! I don't let myself be seen around the town in a car with someone that's notorious, and he is notorious. No decent girl would be seen within a mile of him."

"Really! You surprise me."

"I'm warning you." He took a step forward, his teeth grinding against each other. "You'd better not go too far."

Quite suddenly the jocularity was ripped from her tone and she cried back at him, "You telling me not to go too far! You telling me you wouldn't be seen in the town with anyone like him! No. No, you wouldn't be seen round the town with Miss Blenkinsop because there's no need, you have the privacy of the garage, and the office, haven't you?"

There was silence that only waited to be shattered, then he cried, "You're mad, that's what you are, mad. And you'll get what you're asking for." He marched towards the door, pulled it open, then turned and shouted, "There'll be nobody but yourself to blame when I walk out. Now remember that. It won't be Diana who has caused it, but you, you and your rotten, jealous mind."

When the lower door banged the house shook.

In the bedroom the children lay in their bunks perfectly still. Rose Mary was in the bottom bunk and she stared upwards, waiting for David to make a move, and when he didn't she got out of the bunk and, standing on tiptoes, touched his shoulder. But he gave no sign. His face was almost covered by the blanket, and when she pulled it down his eyes were wide open, and they stared at each other.

9

ROSE MARY'S SICKNESS

The following morning the postman brought Mary Ann a letter and she wanted to cry, "Look! look! would you believe it." It was from the editor of the *Newcastle Courier* and it said simply, "Dear Mrs. Boyle, I am very interested in your doggy sketches and if you would care to call on me at three o'clock on Monday afternoon we could discuss their publication, subject to alteration and cutting. Yours sincerely, Albert Newman."

At eleven o'clock her mother phoned to say Ben had died a half-an-hour earlier. She didn't know when the funeral would be, likely about Wednesday, and, of course, she would be going? Yes, said Mary Ann, she'd be there.

"Are you coming over tomorrow?" Lizzie had asked, and Mary Ann answered, "I think we'll leave it this week, Mam." There was a long pause before Lizzie had replied, "All right, just as you say."

Sunday was a long nightmare with Corny working frantically down below in the garage; the children haunting her, not wanting to leave her for a minute, even David; and Bill having another spasm of tearing up everything in sight, until she cried, "Take him out and keep him out. And keep yourselves out too."

And they had dragged Bill out and gone into the field behind the house and sat in the derelict car, but they hadn't played.

And so came Monday.

Rose Mary said she felt sick and didn't think she could go to school. "You're going," said Mary Ann. She remembered back to the days when she had been so concerned about her father that she had made herself sick and used it as pretence to be off school.

"If she says she's sick, she's sick." Corny was standing on the landing and he looked through the open door into the bedroom, and Mary Ann looked back at him and said nothing.

"You can't send her to school if she's sick."

"Very well; she's sick and she needn't go to school."

Her attitude was infuriating to him, he wanted to break things.

So Rose Mary didn't go to school, but Mary Ann saw that she stayed in bed all morning. She also saw that the enforced inactivity was almost driving her daughter wild, so she allowed her to get up for lunch, and after it, when she asked if she could take Bill for a walk, Mary Ann said, "Yes, and tell your father I'm going into town to do some shopping."

Rose Mary stared at her, her eyes wide.

"Do as I tell you. Take Bill. Put his lead on."

Bill showed great reluctance, as always, to being moved out of the kitchen, and Mary Ann had to carry him downstairs. Then hurrying back and into the bedroom she made her face up, put on her best suit and hat, looked at herself critically in the mirror, then went out with only a handbag.

Corny noticed this as she crossed the drive; she was carrying no shopping bag and she had on her best clothes. He wanted to dash after her and demand where she was going. He almost called to her, but Jimmy checked him.

"Boss!"

"What is it now?"

Jimmy looked down towards his feet, rubbing his hands together. "There's something I want to say."

"Oh, aye." Corny narrowed his eyes at the young fellow.

"I'm sorry, but . . . but . . . but I've just got to."

"Well, whatever it is, you needn't take a week about it. Come into the office; it's about time you had it off your chest."

Jimmy's head came up and he stared at his boss striding towards the office, then he followed him. There was nothing much escaped the boss.

"Well, say your piece." Corny sat himself down on the high stool and looked at the figures in the open book before him, and Jimmy stood just within the door and again he looked down, and now he said, "I want to give me notice in."

"What!"

"I'm sorry, boss, but I think it's best."

"Oh you do, do you? And why do you want to give your notice in?"

"Well, we all need a change now and again," Jimmy grinned sheepishly.

"More money, I suppose?"

"Aye, more money, boss."

"You're not getting enough here and not making enough on the side?"

Jimmy stared at him, then said, "Well the tips are few and far between."

Corny was on the point of saying, "Well, I'm not referring to your tips, I'm referring to your light fingers," but perhaps it was better to let things be this way. He'd never get another like Jimmy for work, but then he'd never get another who would help himself to the takings; he'd see to that before anyone else started. But he couldn't resist one thrust. "I suppose you've got nearly enough to stand your share in the car by now?"

"Well, not quite, boss, not quite."

"Oh well, you've still got time, haven't you?" Corny got up from the seat and walked past Jimmy, keeping his eyes on him all the time, and Jimmy returned his stare unblinking. So that was it, he knew. He had known all along.

When Corny reached the drive again his thoughts reverted to Mary Ann. Where was she off to, dressed up like that? Where? WHERE? It couldn't be Murgatroyd. The funeral? No, no, it would be too soon for that. She didn't know yet anyway; and she wouldn't go in that cocky red hat. But perhaps she was going home for something. He would get on to the farm and have a word with Mike, not Lizzie. No; Mike understood things.

Mike answered from the milking parlour. No, Mary Ann wasn't coming there, not to his knowledge.

"What do you think about Johnny Murgatroyd?" Corny asked, and Mike replied "Johnny? Oh, Johnny's all right. A bit of a lad I understand, but there's no harm in him. Why do you ask? . . . Oh, because he brought her home? Oh, don't worry about that, lad. Anyway, as far as I've been able to gather there's only one fellow in her life, and also, I was given to understand, there was only one lass in yours. Does that still hold, Corny?"

"Of course, it does, Mike. I've told you."

"Is that dame still paying her daily visits?"

There was a pause before Corny said, "I can't tell her to clear out."

"You could, you know. And it would clear matters up quicker than a dose of salts."

"It's easier said than done, Mike."

"Aye, everything's easier said than done."

"You have no idea at all where she might be going?"

"Not in the wide world. I'll tap Lizzie, and if I hear anything I'll give you a ring."

"Don't let on I've phoned you, Mike."

"No, no; I can keep me big mouth shut when it's necessary. Good-bye, lad, and don't worry."

"Good-bye, Mike."

And then he found out where she was, who she was all dolled up for, at least he imagined he had. He was directing the backing of a lorry out of the drive when he heard one of the men on the site shout, "Where's the boss?" And another, on a laugh, saying, "Which one?"

"Murgatroyd."

"Oh, he's gone into Newcastle. A bit of special business I understand." There was another laugh. "Swinburne's taken over. He's at yon side of number three shed; they're digging out there."

This news had an opposite effect on Corny to what might have been expected. His rage seeped away and of a sudden he felt tired and very much alone. He went upstairs and into the kitchen and sat down at the table and, putting his elbows on it, he rested his head in his hands. Well, he had asked for it, and he was getting it. Being Mary Ann she would take nothing lying down. He had threatened to walk out on her but it looked like she wasn't going to give him a chance. How had all this come about? . . .

Rose Mary, in her childish way, was wondering the same thing. Why weren't they all happy like they used to be? Why wasn't everything nice and lovely? The answer was Diana Blenkinsop. She threw the ball for Bill and he fetched it. She threw it again and he fetched it; but the third time she threw it he turned and walked in the direction of the house and she had to run after him and put his lead on.

He was always wanting to be in the house and near her mam. When she had asked for an explanation from her father concerning Bill's change of face he had said that Bill likely felt safer in the house since he had got the fright on the grab, and as it was their mam who had got him out of the hole, he had become attached to her.

She wished she had been the one who had got him out of the hole, and then he wouldn't have wanted to leave her. Everybody was leaving her, their David, and Bill, and now. . . . She wouldn't let her thoughts travel any further along this frightening road. She walked the length of the field, then looked to the top of it where it adjoined the garage, where the men were building the big workshop. As she started up the field someone waved to her from the foot of the scaffolding and after a moment she waved back.

Then she was away, dashing up the field, dragging Bill with her.

"Hello, Rose Mary." Mr. Blenkinsop looked down on her as she stood panting. "Why aren't you at school?"

"I was sick and couldn't go."

"Oh, I'm sorry to hear that. Are you better now?"

"Yes, thank you."

"Eating too many sweets I suppose?" He bent down to her, smiling into her face, but she didn't smile back as she said, "No, I didn't have any sweets, I didn't want any."

He straightened up and surveyed her for a moment. This wasn't the Rose Mary Boyle that he had come to know. He was well schooled in childish ailments, and the look on her face wasn't derived from a tummy upset, if he was any judge. Tummy upsets were soon forgotten when children got out into the open air, especially with a dog. He'd had a feeling recently that things weren't as harmonious as they might be in the little house above the garage. He began to walk away from the building and down the field, and Rose Mary walked with him. Mr. Blenkinsop knew it wasn't good tactics to quiz children, but very often it was the only way anyone could get any information. He said, "I haven't seen your mother for days, how is she?"

There was a pause before Rose Mary answered, "Not very well. She's gone into Newcastle; she's got her best things on."

She looked up at him and he looked down at her again, and she answered the question in his eyes by saying, "She doesn't put her best things on except for something special."

He nodded his head slowly at her. "And what's this special thing your mother's gone into Newcastle for . . . with her best things on?" He nodded his head slowly at her.

"I don't know."

"You don't know?"

"No, and me dad doesn't know. She just said for me to tell him that she was going shopping and she didn't take a basket, and she never goes shopping in her best things."

They stopped and were holding each other's gaze. "You have no idea why she went into Newcastle?" He bent his head slightly downwards now and she answered, "I think I have."

"Can you tell me?" His voice was very low.

"It's . . . it's because me dad's going to leave us."

He straightened up, his shoulders back, his chin tucked into his neck, and it was a full minute before he said, "Your dad . . . your father's going to leave you?"

"He said he was on Friday night."

He gave a little laugh now, then drew in a long breath before exclaiming, "O . . . h!

mothers and fathers always argue and have little fights and say they're going to leave each other, but they never do. I shouldn't worry."

"Mr. Blenkinsop."

"Yes, what is it?" He was bending over her again, his face full of sympathy, and he watched her lips moving around the words "Would you" like a deaf-mute straining to talk. It wasn't until he said, "Tell me. Come along, you can tell me what's troubling you. I won't tell anyone, I promise," that she startled him by saying, "Would . . . would you send your Diana away, please?"

He was standing straight again, his eyes screwed up. His mind was working furiously; a voice inside him was bawling "No, no, this can't be." Yet in an odd way he knew, he had known it all along. But he said to her quietly, "Why do you want me to send Diana away, Rose Mary?"

"Because . . ." She closed her eyes now and bent her head.

"Come on, tell me." He put his finger under her chin and raised her head, and she said, "Because she's going to take me dad away."

"God Almighty!" It was a deep oath. If she'd broken up this happy family, he'd break her neck; as much as he loved her he'd break her neck. She was like her mother. How could women be such devils. And how could men love them for being devils.

He knew that all good looking men were a challenge to his wife and must be brought to her feet, but once there she let them go. Some of them, he remembered with shame for her, had crawled away broken. Time had taught him to understand his wife; for her to be entirely happy she must have these little diversions, these diversions that kept her ego balanced. She had said to him, "At heart I'm a one man woman, and men are fools if they can't see that. It's up to them."

Diana had had boys fluttering round her since she was ten. She had already been engaged and broken it off, but she had never tried, as far as she knew anyway, to capture a married man. Boyle was a big, attractive-looking fellow in his way, an honest fellow too. It was his honesty that had decided his cousin, Rodney, to build the plant on this side of the spare land. He was no empty-headed fool was young Boyle, but on the other hand he was the type that if he reached Diana's feet and she kicked him, he'd break. Self-esteem would see to that.

Well, whatever he had to do, he must do it warily, for his daughter, he knew, was as headstrong as an unbroken colt, and a jerk on the reins at this stage might send her off, dragging Boyle with her.

He put his hand on Rose Mary's head and, bringing his face close to hers, said, "Now you're not to worry any more. Do you hear me? Everything's going to be all right."

"You'll send her away?"

"I don't know what I'm going to do yet. This is just between you and me. You won't tell anyone will you what you've told me?"

"Oh, no. But our David knows."

"He does?"

"Yes."

"But he doesn't know that you were going to tell me?"

"Oh, no."

"Well then, you go on home, and remember not a word to anybody. Not even to David. Promise?"

"Promise." She made a cross on the yoke of her dress somewhere in the region of her heart and he patted her head again and said, "Go on now." And she turned from him, Bill pulling her into a run as she went towards home. And Mr. Blenkinsop walked slowly up the field towards the building, and again he said deep, in his throat, "God Almighty!"

10

FAME AND FORTUNE

Meanwhile Mary Ann was in Newcastle sitting in an office opposite a small bald-headed man. Mr. Newman was smiling broadly at Mary Ann as he said, "I have found them very refreshing, very amusing, something different."

"Thank you."

"Have you done much of this kind of thing?"

"I've been scribbling all my life but I've never had anything published."

"Well, it's about time you did, isn't it?"

She smiled back at him and said, "You're very kind."

"Oh, we can't afford to be kind in this business, Mrs. Boyle. If work hasn't merit it doesn't get published on sympathy, or because," he poked his head forward, "you happen to know the editor."

They were laughing.

"Have you any more of these ready?"

"I've got another three." She opened her bag and handed him an envelope, and he said, "Good. Good," and as he pulled the scripts out he added, "The main thing is will you be able to keep up this kind of humour; you know humorous stuff is the most difficult to write."

"It's always come easy to me. Well, what I mean is, I can write something funny where I could never write an essay or descriptive stuff."

"You never know what you can do until you try. By the way, I was thinking that it would be a good idea just to sign these articles 'Bill', no name or anything. You see they're supposed to be written by him. Well, what do you think about that?"

What did she think about it? Not much. It was half the pleasure, all the pleasure in fact to see one's name in print, and, let's face it, for other people to see your name in print.

He said on a thin laugh, "I know how you feel about this, but take my advice and let them be written by Bill, the bull terrier, and they'll likely catch on, much more so than if they were written by Mrs. Mary Boyle."

"Mary Ann Boyle."

He inclined his head towards her, "Mrs. Mary Ann Boyle. Well, you see?"

Yes, she saw, and she smiled back at him.

"I like the way you started the first one. It got me reading straight away." He picked up one of the scripts from the table and read:

'There is a tide in the affairs of men which, taken at the flood, leads on to fortune. So said some fellow. And there is a day in the span of a dog which decides what kind of dog's life he's going to have.

'Most kids know to some extent where they'll be for the first few years, but a dog knows, as soon as he stops sucking out he goes, so naturally he goes on sucking as long as the skin of his belly will stand it. I did, I was the biggest sucker in the business.'

He looked across at Mary Ann and said, "It's fresh. I mean fresh, you know which kind?"

"Yes, yes, I know which kind." She was laughing again.

He turned over a couple of pages and pointed, saying, "This bit where you bring him home and he names you all: Big he, Little she, Angel one and Angel two. Where did you get the idea from?"

"Oh, it was the day he got hung up on the grab and the craneman dropped him into the hole. You know, it's in the third one."

"Oh yes, I had a good laugh over that one. I passed it on to my assistant and he said you had a wonderful imagination."

She shook her head slowly. "It actually happened, just as I put it down."

"You're joking?"

"No, no, I'm not."

"And from hating his guts you took to him as it says here?"

"Yes, that's how it happened."

"And you mean to say the one about him getting you up in the middle of the night and then finding the place in shreds in the morning is true?"

"Yes, honest, everything."

"Well, well, but nobody will believe it. This Bill must be a lad."

"He is, but since the business of the grab he won't leave me. And the second one, that one you've got in you hand," she pointed, "that's about him getting into our bed in the middle of the night, and Corny, my husband, waking up and finding a black wet muzzle an inch from his face; if it had been a hand grenade he couldn't have moved faster. Poor Bill didn't know what had hit him."

Mr. Newman was laughing again, then he said, "I may have to tighten things up here and there, do you mind?"

"No, not at all. I'm only too pleased that you like them."

"Oh, I like them all right. I only hope that they catch on. You never can tell. I aim to print one each Saturday for a few weeks. It would be very nice if the younger generation scrambled for the paper to find out what Bill had been up to during the week, wouldn't it?"

She shook her head slowly. "It would be marvellous."

"Well, now, down to basic facts. How about ten guineas."

"Ten guineas?" Her brows puckered slightly, and at this he said, "For each publication," and as her face cleared he laughed and added, "Oh, we're not as bad as that."

"I'd be very grateful for ten guineas."

He rose to his feet and, holding out his hand, said, "Let's hope this is the beginning of a long and successful series concerning one Bill, a bull terrier."

"I hope so, too," . . .

When she was outside she walked in a daze until she reached the bottom of Northumberland Street, and there she thought, I'll phone him and tell him. She knew it would be better this way, because under the circumstances she couldn't go back and look at him and say, "I'm going to do a series for *The Courier*," not with this other thing between them. And also, on the phone she wouldn't see his face, or witness his reactions, and so there was a chance she would remain calm.

When she heard his voice she said, "It's me, Corny."

"Oh!"

"I'm . . . I'm in Newcastle."

"So you're in Newcastle!"

She closed her eyes. "I . . . I thought I would phone you, I've something to tell you."

There was a short silence, and then his voice came rasping at her, "Oh, you have, have you? And you haven't the courage to face me. Whose idea was it that you should phone it?

Is he holding your hand . . . breathing down your neck?" The last was almost a yell and she took the earphone away from her face and stared at it in utter perplexity for a moment, until his voice came at her again, louder now, "If you're there, Mr. Murgatroyd, let me tell you this. . . ."

She didn't hear his next words for his voice was so loud it blurred the line and she mouthed to herself, "Murgatroyd! Murgatroyd! He must be barmy."

When the line became silent again she said, "Are you finished?" and the answer she got was, "Go to hell!"

When she heard the receiver being banged down she leant against the wall of the kiosk. Well, if she wanted her own back she was certainly getting it. But she didn't want her own back, not in this way.

It was as she was passing the station on the way to the bus terminus that a lorry drew up alongside the kerb and a voice hailed her, "Hi, there!"

When she turned round and saw Johnny's grinning face looking down at her she said aloud, "Oh, no! No!"

"You going back home?"

She ran across the pavement and to the door of the cab and, looking up at him, she said, "Yes I'm going back but not with you."

"What's up?" His face was straight.

"Nothing. Nothing."

"There must be something for you to jump the gun like that. I haven't asked you to go back with me, but I was going to." The grin almost re-appeared and then, getting down from the cab, he said, "What is it?"

"Look, Johnny, just leave me and get back."

"No, no, I'm not going back." He thrust his hands into his pockets. "I want to know what's up. It concerns me doesn't it?"

"Look, Johnny, it's like this," she said breathlessly. "I came in this afternoon to meet the editor of the *Newcastle Courier* and I didn't tell Corny because, well, well we had a bit of a row. But just a minute ago I phoned him and," she put her hand up to her brow, "he nearly bawled my head off; he . . . he thinks I'm here with you."

"Huh! you're kiddin'. What gave him that idea?"

"You know as much as I do about that."

"He must be do-lally."

"I think we're all going do-lally."

He laughed at her now. "All right," he said. "I wouldn't embarrass you for the world . . . Mrs. Boyle. I'll tell you what I'll do. I'll go straight to the garage when I get back and. . . ."

"Oh, no! No!"

"Now look." He lifted his hand and patted her shoulder gently. "Leave this to me. I'm the soul of tact. I am. I am. I'll do it innocently; I'll tell him exactly what I came into Newcastle for, it's in the back there." He pointed to an odd-shaped piece of machinery in the lorry. "I'll do it when he's filling me up. I'll ask after you and the children and when you get home he'll be eating out of your hand. Now go and have a cup of tea. Don't get the next bus, give me time."

"Oh, Johnny." Her shoulders drooped. "What a mess!"

"We all find ourselves in it some time or other. The only consolation I can offer you is you're not alone. Go on now, have a cuppa. Be seeing you." He pulled himself up into the cab and she walked away and did as he advised and went into a café and had a cup of tea.

Corny didn't exactly eat out of her hand when she arrived home. He looked at her as she crossed the drive going towards the front door, then turned away, and it was a full fifteen minutes before he came upstairs and stood inside the kitchen with his back to the door and watched her as she stood cutting bread at the side table. After gulping deep in his throat he muttered, "I'm sorry about this afternoon."

She didn't move, nor speak, but when she felt him standing behind her she began to tremble.

"I'm sorry I went on like that."

Still she didn't answer. She piled the bread on the plate now and when she went to move away he touched her lightly on the arm, saying quietly, "What was it you wanted to tell me?"

"Nothing."

"Come on now." He pulled her round to him, but she held the plate in both hands, and it kept them apart.

"You didn't get dressed up and go into Newcastle and then go into a phone box and call me for nothing. I said I'm sorry. In a way . . . well, you should be glad I'm jealous of him."

She didn't speak or look at him as he took the plate from her hands and put it on the table, but when he went to put his arms around her she drew back from him, and his brows gathered and his teeth met tightly for a moment. But he forced himself to repeat quietly, "Come on, tell me what it is."

She looked at him now and, her voice cool, she said, "I've had some articles accepted by *The Courier*. The editor asked to see them this afternoon."

"You have?" His expression was one of surprise and pleasure and he repeated, "You have. And by *The Courier*. Lord, that's a good start. Well, well." He nodded his head at her. "I've told you all along you'd do it. And to get into *The Courier* is something. By, I'd say it is. What are they about?"

"Bill."

"What!" His cheeks were pushing his eyes into deep hollows; his whole face was screwed up with astonishment. "Bill? You've written articles on Bill?"

"Yes, on Bill."

"What about?"

"Oh!" She turned to the table. "Just things he does."

"Well I never!" His voice sounded a little flat now. "Are they funny like?"

"You'll have to judge for yourself when you read them."

"I will. Yes," he nodded at her again, "I'll read them after tea. By the way, what are they giving you?"

"Ten guineas."

"Each?" His voice was high.

"Yes," she paused, then added, "He's got six. If they take on I'll be doing them every week."

Into the silence that now fell on them Jimmy's voice came from the bottom of the stairs, calling, "Are you there, boss?" and when Corny went on to the landing Jimmy looked up at him and said, "Bloke's asking for you."

"All right, I'll be down." Corny looked back towards the kitchen but he didn't return to it; he went slowly down the stairs, and at the bottom he paused for a moment. Ten guineas a time. It would make her feel independent of him. He didn't like it, he didn't like it at all. It was a thing he had about money. He never wanted her to have anything in that line but what he provided.

11

THE WILL

Ben was buried on Wednesday. It was the first time Mary Ann had been to a cremation, and although the disposal seemed more final than burying, there was a greater sense of peace about the whole thing than if they had stood round an open grave. She'd always had a horror of graves and coffins, but this way of going was clean somehow.

As the curtains glided on silent rails and covered up the last move Ben's earthly body was to experience she fancied she saw him young again. Yet she had never even seen a picture of Ben when he was young. His back had been bent the first time she had clapped eyes on him when he had opened the door to her that morning in the far, far past, the morning she had gone in search of . . . 'the Lord' to beg him to give her da a job. It was Ben who had tried to throw her out of the house; it was Ben who had been jealous of her; but it was Ben who had, in his own strange way, come to depend on her because he realized that through her, and only her, would his master know life again.

She walked with Corny out of the little chapel. They followed behind Tony and Lettice. Then came her mother and father, and Michael and Sarah. Sarah always came last so that her shambling walk would not impede others. Mr. Lord was not at the funeral, it would have been too much for him.

Tony, looking at Mary Ann, now said, "Will you come back to the house?"

"If you don't mind, Tony, I'd rather go home. I'll—"

"He asked for you. There's a will to be read and he asked us all to be there."

She glanced at Corny but his look was non-committal. It said, "It's up to you."

"It won't take long." It was Mike speaking to her now. "And you could do with a cup of tea. There's nothing to rush for anyway. The children will be all right with Jimmy when they get back from school."

When they reached the house they took their coats off in the hall, then filed into the drawing-room. The day was very warm, almost like a June day, not one in early September, but Mr. Lord was sitting close to the fire.

Mary Ann went straight to him. She did not, as usual, say, "Hello," nor did he speak to her, but when she put her hand on his he took it and held it gently, and she sat down by his side.

When they were all seated Lettice served the tea that the daily woman had brought in; then she tried, with the help of Tony, to make conversation, but found it rather difficult with Mr. Lord sitting silent, and Mary Ann having little to say either.

It was almost twenty minutes later when, the trolley removed, Mr. Lord looked at Tony and said, "Will you bring me that letter from the desk?" And when the letter was in his hand he looked at it, then at the assembled company and said. "This is Ben's will. I don't know what it holds, only that it wasn't drawn up by a solicitor. He wrote it out himself about five or six years ago and had it witnessed by my gardener and his wife, then he put it into my keeping, and he didn't mention it from that day." He paused and swallowed and his Adam's apple sent ripples down the loose skin of his neck. "I will get my grandson to read it to you. Whatever it holds, his wishes will be carried out to the letter."

Tony split the long envelope open with a paper knife, then drew out a single foolscap sheet, and after unfolding it he scanned the heading, then looked from one to the other before he began to read. "This is my last will and testament and I make it on the first day of December, nineteen hundred and sixty-two. My estate is invested in three building societies and up to date the total is nine thousand three hundred and twenty-five pounds, and God willing it may grow. I'm in my right mind and I wish to dispose of it as follows: I wish to leave one thousand pounds to Peter Brown, my master's great-grandson. This to be kept in trust for him until the age of sixteen, because at sixteen I think a boy needs a lot of things, which are mostly not good for him, at least so he is told, but by the age of twenty-one when it appears right and proper he should have these things very often the taste for them has gone.

"When I say I leave nothing to my young master, Mr. Tony Brown, I am sure he will understand, because he has all he needs and more. To his wife, Madam Lettice, I leave my grateful thanks for the kindness and consideration she has shewn me since she has become mistress of this house. Never did I think I could tolerate a woman running my master's house but I found that my young master's wife was an exception.

"To my master, I leave the memory of my utter devotion. There has been no one in my life for fifty-two years other than himself; he knows this.

"To Michael Shaughnessy, farmer on my master's estate, I leave the sum of three hundred pounds because here was a man big enough and bold enough to overcome the dirty deals life has a habit of dealing out."

At this point Tony raised his eyes and smiled towards Mike, and Mike, his eyes wide, his lips apart, his head moving slightly, looked back at him in amazement. Then Tony resumed his reading.

"Now I come to the main recipient of my estate, namely Mary Ann Shaughnessy. Although she is now Mrs. Mary Ann Boyle I still think of her as Mary Ann Shaughnessy. After the above commitments have been met I wish her to have whatever is left. I do this because, when, as a loving, cheeky, fearless child, she came into my master's life, he became alive again. She turned him from an embittered man, upon whom I, with all my devotion, was unable to make any impression, into a human being once more. You will forgive me, Master, for stating this so plainly, but you and I know it to be true. It was this child, this Mary Ann Shaughnessy, who melted the ice around your heart.

"There is another reason, Mary Ann, why I want you to have and enjoy the money I have worked for, but which brought me no comfort, no pleasure. It is because right from the first you were kind to me, and concerned for me, even when you feared me, so I. . . ."

Tony's words were cut off by the sound of choked, painful sobbing. Mary Ann was bent forward, her face buried in her hands.

"There now, there now." Lizzie was at one side of her and Lettice at the other. The men were on their feet, with the exception of Mr. Lord. Mr. Lord's face was turned towards the fire and his jaw bones showed white under his blue-veined skin.

Lettice now led Mary Ann into her room and there Mary Ann dropped on to the couch, her face still covered with her hands, and her sobbing increased until it racked her whole body.

When Corny came to her side he put his hands on her shoulders and, shaking her gently, said, "Come on now, give over, stop it." But his attention only seemed to make her worse.

Now Tony came on the scene. He had a glass in his hand and, bending over the back of the couch, he coaxed her: "Come on. Come on, dear, drink this."

But Mary Ann continued to sob and he handed the glass to Lizzie, saying, "Make her drink it; I must get back to grandfather, he's upset."

"Mary Ann, stop it! Do you hear?" Corny had pushed Lizzie aside almost roughly and was once more gripping Mary Ann's shoulders, and Lizzie, her voice steely now, said,

"Don't Corny, don't. Let her cry it out. She needs to cry." She looked at him full in the face, then more gently she said, "Leave her for a while, she'll be all right."

He straightened up and stared at her, at this woman who had never wanted him for her daughter. They had always been good friends, but he often wondered what went on under Lizzie's poised and tactful exterior.

He walked slowly out of the room and closed the door behind him, and when he looked across the wide hall there was Mike standing at the bottom of the stairs, his elbow resting on the balustrade. Corny went up to him and Mike said, "It was the shock; it was a shock to me an' all. Three hundred pounds!" He shook his head slowly. "Fancy old Ben thinking of me." Then taking a deep breath he added, "This is going to make a difference, isn't it? It's a small fortune she's got. Nearly eight thousand pounds I should imagine by the time it's all worked out. Of course, there'll be death duties to pay." He stared at Corny now. "You don't look very happy about it, lad."

Corny stared back at Mike. He could speak the truth to his father-in-law; they were brothers under the skin. He said bluntly, "No, I'm not happy about it. What do you think it'll do to her?"

"Do to her? Well, knowing Mary Ann, not much."

"Huh!" Corny tossed his head. "You think so? Well I see it differently."

"What do you mean?"

"Oh, nothing." He brought his shoulders hunching up cupping his head. The action looked as if he was retreating from something, and Mike said, "Don't be daft, man; money will make no difference to Mary Ann. You should know that."

Corny turned slowly towards him and quietly he asked him, "How would you have felt if it had been left to Lizzie?"

Mike opened his mouth to speak, then closed it again. Aye, how would he have felt if it had been left to Lizzie? It would have made her independent of him. It didn't do for a woman to have money, at least not more than the man she was married to. He stared back into Corny's eyes and said, "Aye, I see what you mean."

12

SAMSON AGAIN

On the Thursday night, David leant over his bunk and, looking down on to Rose Mary, whispered "We could cut it off."

"What?" she whispered back at him.

"Her hair."

"Whose?"

"Don't be goofy, you know whose, Diana Blenkinsop's."

Rose Mary was sitting bolt upright now, her face only inches from her brother's hanging upside down in mid air, and she said, "Eeh! our David, that's wicked. Whatever gave you that idea?"

"Mam."

"Mam?"

"Yes, 'bout Samson."

"Samson?"

"Don't be so mutton-nappered. You remember, she told us the story about Samson. When he had his hair cut off he couldn't do nothin'."

"But Samson was a man."

"It's all the same. And she would look different with her hair off, all like that." He took one hand from the edge of the bunk and traced his finger in a jagged line around his neck, and Rose Mary exclaimed on a horrified note, "Eeh! you dursen't."

"I dare."

And as she stared at him she knew he dared.

"They're still not kind," he said.

"I asked Mr. Blenkinsop to send her away."

David swung himself down from the bunk and, crouching on the floor at her side, exclaimed incredulously, "When?"

"Last Monday, when I pretended I was sick." She crimped her face at him. "I only wanted to stay off so I could see Mr. Blenkinsop."

"And what did he say?"

"He said I hadn't to worry; he would see to it."

"Well, he hasn't, has he?"

She shook her head slowly, and he stared back at her through the dim light, looking deep into her eyes and appealing to her to solve this problem, as he had been wont to do, but inarticulately, before he could speak; and she answered the look in his eyes by whispering very low, "I'll die if she takes me dad away."

As he continued to stare at her, his mind registered the death-like process they would go through if Diana Blenkinsop did take their dad away. At the end of his thinking he added to himself, And Jimmy and all. But he comforted himself on this point. Jimmy wouldn't go; he could stop that, he would see to that the morrow.

Rose Mary broke into his thoughts now, saying, "But you couldn't reach."

"If the sun's shining and it's hot like it was the day, she'll go down and lie on the bank sun bathing. She lies with her hair all out at the back. The men on the scaffolding were watchin' her the day, and laughin'."

"But you've got to go to school."

"I could have a headache."

Again they were staring at each other. Then Rose Mary whispered, "But me mam won't stand for me being off again, I can't say I'm sick again."

"I'll do it on me own."

"Eeh! no, our David, I should be with you."

"I'll be all right." He nodded at her. "If it's sunny in the mornin' I'll say me head's bad."

The door opening suddenly brought both their heads towards the light and their mother.

"What are you doing out of bed?"

"I've . . . I've got a bad head."

"You didn't say anything about a bad head when you came to bed. Go on, get up." She hoisted him up into the bunk, then tucked the clothes around him and said, "Go to sleep and your headache will be gone when you wake up." Then she tucked Rose Mary in again and, going towards the door, said, "Now no more talking. Get yourselves to sleep."

Back in the living-room she sat down near the fire. Bill was lying on the mat, and when he rose and went to climb on to her knee she said, "No, no!" But he stood with his front paws on her lap looking at her and again she said, "No!" and on this he dropped his heavy body down and lay by the side of her chair.

There was a magazine lying on the little table to the side of her. She picked it up, then put it down again. She couldn't read, she couldn't settle to anything. She felt that she was moving into a world of delirium. She still wanted to cry when she thought of Ben and what he had done for her, but she mustn't start that again.

Last night she had cried until she fell asleep, and this morning she had felt terrible; and the feeling wasn't caused by her crying alone but by Corny's attitude to this great slice of luck that had befallen her. He wasn't pleased that Ben had left her the money, in fact he was angry. She had wanted to say to him, "But we'll share it, we've shared everything"; yet she didn't because they weren't sharing everything as of old. She couldn't share even the surface of his affection with Diana Blenkinsop.

The odd thing about the money was that she hadn't brought up the subject to him, or he to her. She had hardly seen him since this morning. He had come up to dinner and eaten it in silence and then had gone straight down again. The same had happened at teatime. And now it was almost nine o'clock and he was still downstairs. He would have to come up some time and he'd have to talk about it some time.

It was half-an-hour later when he entered the room. She had his supper ready on the table and she said to him, "Tea or coffee?"

"Tea," he answered.

That was all, just "Tea." When she had made the tea and they were seated at the table she said quietly, "Tony phoned. He . . . he wants me to go to Newcastle on Monday to see the bank manager and Mr. Lord's solicitor."

He had a piece of cold ham poised before his mouth when, turning his head slightly towards her, he said flatly, "Well, what about it?"

"O . . . oh!" She was on her feet, her hands gripping the edge of the table. "You're wild, aren't you? You're wild because Ben left me that money."

He put the ham in his mouth and chewed on it before he replied grimly, "The word isn't wild, I just think it's a mistake you being left it. It was hard enough living with you before, but God knows what it'll be like now with fame and fortune hitting you at one go."

Her face slowly stretched in amazement as she looked at him and she repeated, "What did you say?"

"You heard me."

"Yes, I heard you. It was hard enough living with me before. Well! well! Now I'm learning something. Hard enough living with me. . . ." Her voice rose almost to a squeak.

"Yes, yes, it was if you want to know, because for years I've had to contend with your home. This was never your home, as I've told you before. This was just a little shack that I provided for you, it wasn't home, you never referred to it as home. But the farm was home, wasn't it? Then your mother never wanting me to have you, because I was just a mechanic, and she's never let me forget it."

"Oh! Corny Boyle. How can you sit there and spit out such lies. Mam's been wonderful to you; she's been. . . ."

"Oh yes, she's been wonderful to me, like Tony has, the great Mr. Lord's grandson, the man you should have married, the man your mother wanted you to marry, the man Mr. Lord created for you. Aye, created." He raised his hand high in the air. "And did he not prepare you for such an elevated station by sending you to a convent and giving you big ideas. . . . Oh aye, they're all wonderful."

Mary Ann stepped back from the table still keeping her eyes on him. She had never imagined for a moment he thought like this, but all these things must have been fermenting in his mind for years.

He had stopped his eating and was staring down at his plate, and she had the urge to run to him and put her arms about him and say, "Oh, you silly billy! You're jealous, and you haven't got one real reason in the world to be jealous of me. As for money, take the lot, put it in the business, do what you like with it, it doesn't matter. What matters is that everything should be all right between us, that we should be . . . kind." But she smothered the urge;

nothing had changed, there was still Diana Blenkinsop.

She turned away and went into the kitchen and stood looking out of the small window and watched the lights of the cars flashing by on the main road half a mile away.

After a while she heard him pushing his chair back, and then his voice came from the scullery door, saying, "I'm sorry. You enjoy you money. Take the holiday you've always been on about. I'm off to bed, I'm tired."

She made no response by word or movement. He had said he was sorry in a voice that was still full of bitterness. "Take a holiday," he had said. Well, perhaps she would do that. She would take the children and go away some place. It would give him time to think and sort himself out. On the other hand it might give him time to throw himself into the waiting arms of Diana Blenkinsop. Well, if that's what he wanted then he must have it. She could see not greater purgatory in life than living with someone who didn't really want you.

13

MR. BLENKINSOP'S STRATEGY

On Friday morning Mr. Blenkinsop arrived at the office not at nine o'clock, but nearer ten, because he hadn't come from Newcastle, where he stayed during the week, but from his home in Doncaster.

Last night, unknown to his daughter, he had returned home because he wanted to talk to his wife privately, and urgently.

During the journey he had rehearsed what he was going to say to her. He would begin with: "Now look here, Ida, you've been against her going to America." And doubtless she would come back at him immediately and he would let her have her say because he, too, hadn't taken to the idea when his cousin, Rodney, first suggested that Diana should go out to Detroit. The idea was that mixing business with pleasure she would take up a post in the factory out there with a view to coming back and acting as manageress over the women's department. Recently, however, he had changed his views about this matter and had put it to his wife that it might be a good thing for their daughter to have this experience. But Ida wouldn't hear of it. The family would be broken up soon enough, she had protested; she wasn't going to force any member to leave it.

Yet how would she react when she learnt that the member in question could be preparing to fly from the nest at any moment. He wasn't considering Corny's power of resistance, because few men, he imagined, could resist anyone as luscious as his daughter, especially a man who had been married for seven or eight years. It was a crucial time in marriage; there was a great deal of truth in the seven year itch. Moreover, he knew that when Diana set her mind on anything she would have it, even if when she got it she smashed it into smithereens, as she had done with many a toy she had craved for as a child. Now her toys were men.

But when Mr. Blenkinsop reached home he found his wife knew all about the business. At least that was the impression he got as soon as he entered the house. She was entertaining three friends to tea. From the drawing-room window she had seen him getting out of his car on the drive and had met him in the hall, saying rapidly under her breath, "I expected you.

Say nothing about it though when you come in; Florence and Kate are here. Jessie Reeves popped in unexpectedly. I'm wondering if she knows anything; Kate gave me a funny look when she came in. The Reeveses were out Chalford way on Sunday too. They might have seen them, but say nothing." She turned from him and led the way back into the drawing-room and, a little mystified, he followed her.

Chalford! it wasn't likely Boyle took her to Chalford on Sunday.

He greeted the three ladies, talked with them, joked with them and half-an-hour later saw them to their cars. Yet again he was obstructed from having any private conversation with his wife by his family descending on him and demanding to know what had brought him back on a Thursday night.

"It's my house. I can come back any time I like." He pushed at the boys' heads, hugged Susan to him, then demanded to know what was happening to their homework; and eventually he returned to the drawing-room and closed the door. Looking at his wife he let out a long slow breath and said, "Well!"

"Yes, indeed." Ida Blenkinsop draped one arm over the head of the couch and lifted her slim legs up on to it before adding, "You can exclaim, well! Of all the people she could take up with! When I think of her turning her nose up at Reg Foster, and Brian, and Charles. And look what Charles will be one of these days, he's nearly reached three thousand now. The trouble with this one is, he looks all right, too all right I understand, but what he'll sound like is another thing, and how he'll act is yet another."

Dan Blenkinsop stood with his back to the fire, his hands in his pockets, looking at his wife. He was puzzled and becoming more puzzled every moment. He said now, "How did you get to know?"

"Well, Kate ran into them on Sunday. She thought nothing of it; they were on the bridge looking at the water near Chalford. She saw them getting into this big car and thought, Oh! But then on Wednesday she was with John in Newcastle and there they met them again, and John recognized the fellow. He says he is well over thirty and a womaniser. He worked on a building in Newcastle that John designed. . . ."

"What! Look, Ida." Dan screwed up his eyes and flapped his hand in front of his face in an effort to check her flow. "Look, stop a minute and tell me who you're talking about."

"Who I'm talking about?" She swung her legs off the couch. "Diana, of course, and your ganger."

"My ganger?" He stepped off the Chinese hearthrug and moved towards her, his chin thrust out enquiringly, and he repeated, "My ganger?"

"Yes, a man called Murgatroyd. John Murgatroyd."

There was a chair near the head of the couch and Dan lowered himself on to it; then bending towards his wife he said, "You mean that Diana's going out with Murgatroyd, the ganger?"

"What do you think I've been talking about. And"—she spread out her hands widely—"what's brought you back tonight? I thought that's what you'd come about."

Dan took his handkerchief from his pocket and wiped his brow.

"It wasn't that?"

He now looked up under his lids at his wife and said slowly, "It was about Diana, but not with Murgatroyd. You mean to say she's been going out with Johnny Murgatroyd?"

"You know him?" She shook her head. "Of course you know him; what am I talking about? But what is he like? He's just an ordinary workman isn't he? And why have you come if not about that? Is anything else wrong?"

Again he mopped his brow as he said patiently, "Not wrong; I would say a little complicated. I came out tonight, dear, to suggest that it would be as well if you changed your mind about her going to America. You know she wanted to go, but you were so dead against it she allowed herself to be persuaded."

"Now don't rub it in, Dan." Ida Blenkinsop turned her face away, and her husband said quickly, "I'm not rubbing it in, but I think it would be the best thing under the circumstances, because I've got something else to tell you."

Her face was towards him again, her eyes wide with enquiry.

"She's causing havoc in the Boyle family."

"You mean with him . . . Corny?"

"Yes, with him, Corny."

"You're joking. That's as bad as the ganger."

"It might appear so on the surface. To my mind it's much worse. The ganger happens to be single; Corny's got a wife and two children, and even the children are aware of the situation."

"Oh Dan!" She had risen to her feet. "You're exaggerating." Her tone was airy.

Dan now got to his feet and, his voice patient no longer, he snapped, "I'm not exaggerating, Ida, and I'm really concerned, not for our daughter but for the Boyle family. I tell you the children know. That little girl came to me, and you know what she said? She asked me if I would send Diana away because she didn't want to lose her daddy."

"Good gracious! I've never heard of such a thing. That's precociousness. She's like her mother that child. . . ."

"Ida! you've got to face up to this. If Diana doesn't go hay-wire with Boyle she'll go it with Murgatroyd. But I want to see that she doesn't go it with young Boyle. That's a nice family and I would never forgive myself if she broke it up. But I know what you're thinking. Oh, yes I do. You would rather she amused herself in that direction than go for Murgatroyd, because you think she's safe with Boyle, him being married, whereas she could get tied up with . . . the ganger, and then you'd have to bury you head in the sand. Now from tomorrow night I'm going to tell her she's finished down there at the factory. I'm going to tell her I've heard from Rodney and he's renewed his invitation for her to go out to him. I'm going to get through to Rodney tonight and explain things, and there'll be a letter for her from him early next week endorsing all I've said."

Ida Blenkinsop put her hand up to her cheek and walked across the room to the window, where she stood for a few minutes before coming back. Then looking at her husband she said, "What if she meets a Boyle or a Murgatroyd out there?"

"We'll have to take our chance on that. But there's one thing I'm determined on, she's not going to break up the Boyle family to afford herself a little amusement, and as long as she's within walking distance of him, or driving distance for that matter, she'll see him as a challenge."

"It's the wife's fault." Ida Blenkinsop jerked her chin to the side. "She should look after her man and see that he doesn't stray. Little women are all alike; they're all tongue and no talent. I could never stand little women, not really."

As he took her arm and smiled at her and said, "Come on, let's have something to eat, I'm hungry," he was thinking: And neither can your daughter, for he now sensed that Diana's hunting of Corny was as much to vex his wife as to satisfy her craving for male adulation.

It was about twenty past ten on the Friday morning when Mr. Blenkinsop came into the garage. Corny was at the far door and when he saw him he felt the muscles of his stomach tense. Diana had left the garage only a few minutes earlier. He had been in the pit under the car and he had caught sight of her legs first, long, slim, brown . . . and bare. She was wearing a mini skirt but he couldn't see the bottom of it, only the length of her legs.

When she bent down and her face came on a level with his he couldn't look at it for a moment, yet when he looked away his eyes were drawn to her thighs, which were partly exposed and within inches of his hands.

"Good morning." That was all she had said but she could make it sound like the opening bars of an overture. She was wearing a scent that wiped out the smell of the petrol and oil. She looked fresh, young, and beautiful, so beautiful that he ached as he looked at her. He wetted his lips and said, "Hello, there."

"Busy?"

"No, this is a new form of exercise; they say it prevents you from getting old."

She laughed softly. "You're the type that'll never grow old, Corny."

"Nice of you to say so, but you see before you a man literally prone with age.."

She laughed softly. "When you feel like that it's a sure sign you need a change."

"I'm inclined to agree with you."

"It's a beautiful day."

"I hadn't really noticed, not until a minute ago." He wasn't used to paying compliments and the thought that he had done so brought the blood rushing to his face, but when she laughed out loud he knew a moment's fear in case the sound carried upwards and into the house.

"Do you know something?"

"What?"

"You're very, very nice, Mr. Cornelius Boyle."

He lowered his eyes from hers for a moment, looked at the spanner in his right hand, moved his lips outwards, then drew them in tight between his teeth before he replied, "And you know something?"

"What?"

"You are more than nice, Miss Diana Blenkinsop, much, much more than nice." He dare not allow himself to look into her eyes; his gaze was fixed on her hair where it fell over her shoulders and rested on the points of her small breasts.

"Dad! Dad! where's Jimmy?"

He blinked quickly, his body jerked as if he had been dreaming and, turning his head, he looked at the face of his son peering at him from yon side of the car, and he said, "He . . . he's about somewhere. In . . . in the yard, I think."

David did not say, "All right, Dad," and run off; he still knelt on the edge of the well, his head inclined to one shoulder, and he gazed at his dad then at the other face beyond his dad.

"Well, I must be off. I'm looking for Father. He hasn't turned up yet; I thought he might be wandering around the works."

"I haven't seen him."

Her face became still; her eyes looked into his. "We'll meet again." Her smile showed all her teeth, like a telly advert. When her face lifted from his he watched her body unfold, he watched her legs as they walked away, then he turned again slowly on to his back and lay gasping for a moment.

What was going to be the outcome of it? They were nearing some point of revelation. He knew it and she knew it. Dear God, what was he going to do? Mary Ann. Oh, Mary Ann. He wanted help. He thought of Mike, but Mike could do nothing more. There was no alternative only his own reserves, and God knew they were pretty weak at the moment.

"Dad!"

He had forgotten about David and he turned his head towards him, saying, "You still there, what do you want?"

"Can I help you?"

"No, no. I thought you had a bad head?"

"I have."

"Well, go out in the fresh air."

"Yes, Dad."

After David moved away he lay until he felt his stomach heaving as if he were going to be sick, and he crawled from under the car and went to the back gate and took in great draughts of fresh air. As she said, it was a beautiful morning, like a summer's day; the world was bright, she was bright and beautiful and young, so young. . . . Mary Ann was young, yet Mary Ann was like a child compared with her, because Diana had knowledge that Mary Ann had no notion of. Diana had a knowledge of men, what they wanted, what they needed. She was like a woman made out of history, all the Salomes, all the Cleopatras, all the essence of all the women who had made love their business.

It was as he turned into the garage again that he saw Mr. Blenkinsop at the far door. "Hello, there. Can I have a word with you, Corny?"

Mr. Blenkinsop was looking at him in an odd way and the sweat began to run down from his oxters and soak his shirt.

"Yes, yes," he nodded his head quickly. "Would you like to come into the office?" He led the way into his office and there he said, "Take a seat."

Mr. Blenkinsop sat down on the only chair, and Corny did not perch himself on the high stool but stood with his back to his desk and pressed his hips against it as if for support, and as he looked at Mr. Blenkinsop's bent head his sweating increased, and he ran a finger round the neck of his overalls. Then Mr. Blenkinsop raised his head and said, "I don't like to probe into a man's private life but this is one time when I'm forced to. I want to ask you what you know about Johnny Murgatroyd?"

The question came as such a surprise that Corny gaped for a moment, then said, "Johnny? Johnny Murgatroyd?"

"Yes."

"Well, as you say, a man's private life is his own, but one hears things. What has he been up to?"

"It's not what he's been up to but what he might be up to." The words were slow and meaningful, yet Corny didn't get the gist of them until a thought struck him. Was he trying to tell him something about Mary Ann and Murgatroyd? The thought brought him from the desk and he stretched himself upwards before he said, "What do you want to say, Mr. Blenkinsop?"

"Well, it's rather a delicate matter, Corny. I. . . ."

Corny felt himself bridling. He'd say it was a delicate matter; and what damn business was it of his anyway. He said stiffly, "My wife's known Johnny Murgatroyd since they were children together. They lived next door to each other so to speak."

"Oh, I didn't know that, but one hears things you know. Do you think there's any truth in the rumour that he's had a number of women, not girls, women, if you follow me?"

"Yes, I follow you." Corny nodded at him slowly. "But as I said, and as you said, the man's life's his own, it's nobody's business except his and those concerned."

"Quite right, quite right." Mr. Blenkinsop made a movement that expressed his understanding, and then he said, "I agree with you, a man's life is his own and he can do what he likes with it, until it impinges on your daughter's life and then one sees it differently."

Corny had been standing straight, almost rigid, and now he brought his head down. It moved lower and lower and his eyes held Mr. Blenkinsop's for a full minute before he said, "Murgatroyd and Diana?"

"Yes, Murgatroyd and Diana."

Now his shoulders were moving upwards again, taking his head with them, and he made a sound like a laugh as he said, "No, no, you've been listening to rumours, Mr. Blenkinsop. Diana going with Murgatroyd? Never!"

The laughing sound he made increased. There was an assurance about it until Mr. Blenkinsop, getting to his feet, said, "I haven't been listening to rumours, Corny; I only wish I had. She's going around with him. She was at a dance last Saturday night with him. I went to the house where she is staying. They're very nice people, he calls for her there. She was out with him all day on Sunday and she didn't get back until turned one o'clock on Monday morning. She's seen him every night this week and has never been in before twelve. Mrs. Foster, the woman she's staying with, was glad I called. She's been a little worried, not because she knows anything against Murgatroyd but because she thinks he's too old for her and," he pursed his lips, "not quite her class."

Corny was leaning against the edge of the desk again. He was staring down at his feet. Again he was feeling sick but it was a different kind of sickness now. It was a sickness bred of shame, self-recrimination, and the feeling that only a man gets when he knows he's been made a fool of, when he's been taken for a ride, a long, long ride; when he's been used, laughed at.

Johnny Murgatroyd, the scum of the earth. And where sex was concerned he was the scum of the earth. Her father had said that she was out with him until one o'clock in the morning. Well, no one could be out with a man like Johnny Murgatroyd and not know what it was all about. Oh, God! He was so sick, sick to the core of him. And not ten minutes ago she had looked into his eyes and promised him anything he had in mind to ask. Or had she? Had it just been his imagination? NO. NO. It had not been his imagination. He had been neither drunk nor daft these past weeks, but one thing he had been, and that was besotted by a cheap sexy slut.

Mr. Blenkinsop had been talking for some minutes and he hadn't heard him and he brought his attention back to him again to hear him say, "Rodney wanted her to go to America and I think the only way to nip this in the bud is to send her packing, so to speak. Of course, her mother and I will miss her terribly but we can't stand by and let her ruin her life. And you know young girls are very headstrong; when they get it into their head they're in love they imagine they'll die if they don't get their way. Yet with a girl like Diana she'll be in and out of love, if I know anything, for a good many years to come. . . . I hope you don't mind me asking about Murgatroyd, but if there's nothing you really know against him, well, that's that."

Corny found his voice to say, "I only know he's unmarried and women seem to like him."

"Oh yes, yes." Mr. Blenkinsop was walking out of the office now and he smiled over his shoulder at Corny and said, "There's no doubt about that. He's a very, very presentable man, but I don't want him," his voice dropped and he repeated, "I don't want him for a son-in-law, you understand?"

Corny understood. He also hoped in this moment that Mr. Blenkinsop would get him for a son-in-law. He hoped that Murgatroyd would in some way manage to marry Diana Blenkinsop, and by God it would serve her right.

"Well, I must get off now, but thanks, Corny. You really don't mind me having asked you about him?"

"Oh no, not at all."

"Thanks. Good-bye."

"Good-bye, Mr. Blenkinsop."

He returned to the office, and now he did sit on his stool and he supported his slumped shoulders by crossing his arms on the desk. And in this moment he felt so low, so belittled there was no hole so small that he couldn't have crawled into.

Mary Ann opened the sideboard drawer and took out a pair of binoculars. They had originally been used by some naval man but now looked very much the worse for wear. She had picked them up in a second-hand shop about two years ago, around the time that Corny was taking an interest in bird life to while away the time between passing motorists. He had said to her one day, "You wouldn't believe it but I've seen ten different kinds of birds on the spare land this morning. I couldn't make out half of them, only to see that they were different. You can't get near enough to them. What you want are field glasses when looking at birds."

She had said, "I'll get you a book on the different types of birds; you can get them in that small series." She hadn't thought about the glasses until she had seen them lying among some junk in a dirty-looking shop in a back street in Newcastle. She had been amazed that she had been asked three pounds for them, but she had paid it, and Corny had had a lot of fun out of the glasses. That was until the stroke of luck came, and he had never touched the glasses since. But she had. She had used these glasses day after day over the past weeks, round about dinner time, because it was at dinner time that Diana Blenkinsop sauntered over the spare land. When it was fine she had her lunch out there on the knoll; even when it was raining she would saunter down the field, past the derelict old car that the children played with, down to where the land rose to form the knoll, and where, Mary Ann knew, the men, as they sat munching their bait, would be able to see her plainly standing silhouetted against the sky.

As time went on it was a compelling urge that made her take up the field glasses. She always seemed to know the time when the figure would appear from the side of the half-erected car park. This sprang from the same instinct that told her when Diana Blenkinsop was down in the garage. She seemed to be able to smell her there. The feeling would bring her to a stop in the middle of some job and carry her to the front room, to the side of the window, and as sure as life a few minutes later she would see the tall, lithe figure sauntering across the drive.

She stood now to the side of the scullery window and lifted the glasses to her eyes. Yes, there she was already ensconced, and she must have had her lunch because she was sunbathing. She was lying spreadeagled like a body being sacrificed to the sun.

She was brazen, utterly brazen. Mary Ann's lips tightened. She looked all legs, bare legs. Oh, men! Couldn't Corny see what she was?

Her attention was now brought from the knoll to the derelict car and the figure that had just emerged from the shelter of it. It was David. When she realized that her son was going towards Diana Blenkinsop there entered into her a deeper note of bitterness. Even children were attracted to her. Not Rose Mary. No. No female would be. When she saw David drop on to the ground she screwed up her eyes and re-focused the glasses. What on earth was he doing? He was crawling, up the side of the knoll, right behind the prone figure.

What . . . on . . . earth . . . was he up to? Perhaps he was playing a game? He was going to give her a fright.

When he was within less than an arm's length of Diana Blenkinsop she saw him stop, and then her heart almost ceased to beat when his hand, holding something in it from which the sun glinted as if from steel, moved towards the head lying on the grass.

She gripped the glasses tightly to her face as she cried, "David! David! Don't! Don't!" The next minute she saw Diana Blenkinsop spring to her feet and hold her head. Then David turned and ran down the hill, and Diana after him.

Now she herself was flying down the back stairs, through the yard and on to the open space behind the garage, there to see Diana Blenkinsop belabouring David about the head and shoulders.

No tigress could have covered the distance quicker and, tearing her son from the enraged girl, she cried, "You! You great big useless hussy, take that!"

She'd had to reach up some distance to deliver the blow, but such was its force that it made Diana Blenkinsop reel backwards and she stood for a moment cupping her face before she cried, "How dare you! HOW DARE YOU!"

"You say how dare I? You have the nerve to say how dare I? And you beating my son?"

"Beating your son?" Diana Blenkinsop was spitting the words at Mary Ann now. "Yes, and I'll beat him again. Just look. See what he's done?" She lifted the front of her hair to show a jagged line about six inches from the bottom and two inches in width. "He was cutting my hair off, the horrible little tyke." She was glaring down at David, and David, from the shelter of his mother's waist, slanted his eyes up to her and clung tighter to Mary Ann.

"Whatever he did, you've got no right to lay hands on him; you should have come to me."

"Come to you!" The words held deep scorn. "And what would you have done? You can't control any member of your family from your dog upwards. Your children take no more notice of you than your husband does."

Mary Ann found difficulty in breathing, and her words came as a hissed whisper through her trembling lips. "You cheap, loose individual, you!"

There was a slight pause before Diana said, "You had better be careful, but whatever I am, I can lay no claim to commonness." Her lip curled on the word. "There's a difference, Mrs. Boyle."

At this point she raised her eyes from Mary Ann's face to the small garage door and her head wagged slightly as she watched Corny come and stand beside his wife. He was looking at her as he had never looked at her before and he said quietly, "Yes, as you say, Diana, there is a difference between cheap and common, yet some folks can be both."

As Diana stared into the face that was almost on a level with her own, she knew that her power over this man was gone. He had likely heard about Johnny. Oh well, what did it matter. The sea was teeming with such fish. She said to him, "Your son tried to cut my hair off."

Corny cast a swift glance down at David; then looking back at her, he said, "Did he now!"

"Yes, he did now." She mimicked his inflexion, then added, "And your wife struck me."

"Oh, she did, did she?" Now he looked down at Mary Ann. But Mary Ann did not return his glance; she was staring at the girl, sensing something had happened, even before this incident, between her and Corny.

"Yes, she did. She's keeping true to type, the back street type."

Corny took a step from Mary Ann's side as he said grimly, "I'll have you remember it's my wife you're talking about."

"Oh, la-la! Aren't we becoming loyal all of a sudden! You must have lost your amnesia. How does it feel to remember you've got a wife?"

Corny's arms were stiff by his sides, his muscles tense, his finger nails digging into his palms. He was getting all he had asked for, and more. God, how could he have been so blind! Could it be that just over half an hour ago there was some part of him that had loved this hussy. Aye, he'd have to admit it, some part of him had loved her; not in the way he loved Mary Ann but in a way that was like a craving for drugs, or drink. And now there was nobody in the wide world he hated as he did her.

He watched her coming nearer to him, her eyes fixed scornfully on his. She passed him without a word, but when she came to Mary Ann she paused slightly, and looking down at her, said, "I should give him back his trousers, it might help him to find out whether he's a man or not."

Mary Ann was in front of him, hanging on to his upraised arm. The trembling of his body went through hers. She did not look up at his face but kept her eyes fixed on the arm she was holding, yet she knew that he was watching the figure moving towards the small door in the garage. When she felt he could see her no longer she released her hold, but still not looking at him she said under her breath, "You'd better come upstairs . . . and you an' all." She put out her hand and pulled David towards her, and with him by her side she walked slowly forward. But she had covered more than half of the open space before she heard the crunch of Corny's steps behind her.

In the kitchen she was glad to sit down; every bone in her body was shaking. She did not know whether it was with anger or relief; anger at the things that girl had said, or relief at the knowledge that whatever had been between her and Corny was finished, dead.

When she saw Corny enter the room, she bowed her head against the look on his face. The thing might be dead but she felt he was suffering the loss as if of a beloved one. . . . It wasn't over yet then.

She had to do something to ease the embarrassment between them so she pulled David towards her, and, her voice trembling, she asked him, "Tell me, what made you do it?"

David stood before her with his head bent. When he raised his eyes he didn't look at her, but at his father who was standing with his elbows resting on the mantelpiece, his back towards them, and he said, "Because of Samson."

"Samson!" Mary Ann gazed at her son in perplexity. Then she asked, "Which Samson?"

"The Samson you told me and Rose Mary about with the long hair."

Mary Ann shook her head slightly and waited.

"Well, you said that when his hair was cut he couldn't do anything, he was no use. You said everything was in his hair, an' I thought"—he glanced quickly at his father's back again, then ended on a high cracked note, "I thought she couldn't do anything if her hair. . . ."

When his voice broke he screwed up his eyes tightly and the tears welled from between his lashes, and Mary Ann drew him into her arms and held him for a moment. Then rising from her chair, she took him by the hand and into the bathroom, and before she washed his face she held him again, and kissed him and murmured over him, "Oh David. David." And he cried now with his eyes open and whispered, "He won't go, will he, Mam? Dad won't go?" And she whispered back, "No, no. Don't worry; you've made it all right."

Whether he had or not, at least he had been the means of proving to her that Diana Blenkinsop was gone. But the question now was, had her effect on Corny been such that their life, as it had once been, was a thing so dead that it could never be revived?

14

THE ETHICS OF STEALING

It was just after three o'clock when David approached Jimmy for the second time that day. "Are you still busy?" he said to him.

"Aye," said Jimmy, without looking at him.

"I told you I've got somethin' to show you."

"And I told you I don't want to see it."

David stood looking at Jimmy's bent body; he was cleaning an engine that was jacked upon a low platform.

"It won't take five minutes, Jimmy."

"I told you I haven't got five minutes. And what if your dad comes and finds me away from my job?" He straightened up and looked down on the small boy, and David looked back at him and said, "But you're goin' the night."

"Aye, I'm goin' the night, and a bloomin' good job an' all."

David now turned from him and went to the door of the shed and looked into the yard, then coming back he whispered, "Will you not go away until I come back, I mean into the garage, I've got something for you?"

"I'll be here for the next half hour or so," said Jimmy flatly.

Jimmy watched the boy run out of the shed and across the yard, and he shook his head and muttered to himself, "Who would believe it, eh, who would believe it?"

In less than five minutes David was back in the shed, and when he closed the door Jimmy shouted at him, "Leave that open, I want to see."

"Just for a minute, Jimmy. I'll switch the light on."

He now came and stood in front of Jimmy. He was holding in his hands a cocoa tin with a lid on it and he held it out, saying, "It's for you, for the car, so you won't have to go."

Jimmy bent his thin bony body over David and he said one word, "Eh?"

"You wanted money for the car, for your share. I haven't got it all but there's a lot, and me pocket money an' all. I only kept sixpence back of me pocket money and put the other one and six in."

"Chree-ist!" exclaimed Jimmy. "Don't tell me you've been taking it for me?" He was showing not only his teeth but his gums, and his face looked comical, but he didn't feel comical. He knew the kid had been pinching for weeks now and he knew that when the boss twigged the money was missing he would get the blame of it. He had wanted to tip the boss the wink, but he found he couldn't. How could you tell him his own bairn was a thief? He couldn't do it, he liked the boss. The only thing he could do was to leave and let him find out for himself. The boss was always easy with money, and he had been very easy these past few months when it had been flooding in, and he himself could have made quite a bit on the side but he wasn't given that way. But he would never have guessed in a month of Sundays that the young 'un was taking it for him, for the car. He remembered the day Poodle Patter had come into the garage and tried to persuade him to go to Baxter's. The kid had been listening then. Crikey! what was he to do now? He dropped on to an upturned wooden box and, looking at David, said, "Aw man, you're daft, barmy, clean barmy."

With the change in Jimmy's attitude David's face brightened and he pulled the lid off the tin and emptied the contents on to the bench. There were ten shilling notes, pound notes, and one five-pound note.

Jimmy closed his eyes, then put his hand over them, and when he heard David say excitedly, "There's nearly ten pounds. You won't have to go now, will you?" he looked at the boy and said slowly, "David man, don't you know you've been stealin'? Don't you know you'll get something for your corner for this?"

"It isn't lock-up stealing, Jimmy, not real stealing, it's just from Dad, and he's got lots of money, and he doesn't bother about change, you know he doesn't. He said, 'What's sixpence?'"

"Aye, he might have said what's sixpence, man, but look, these are not just sixpences, there's a fiver. When, in the name of God, did you take that?"

"Just a while back."

"Oh crikey!"

"You won't go now, Jimmy, will you?"

Jimmy looked down into the round face that was wearing an almost angelic expression and he was lost for words. This here kid was a corker. You never knew what he was going to get up to next; but to pinch for him! It put a different complexion on the whole thing. He'd have to do something about it.

He gathered up the money and put it back into the tin and, gazing down at David, he said, "Now look; I've got a little job I want you to do for me. Now will you stay here and do it until I come back?"

"Aye, Jimmy, I'll do it for you, but," he paused, "you won't leave, will you?"

Jimmy looked back into the now solemn countenance, and he jerked his head and rubbed his lips with his tongue before saying, "We'll see. We'll see. Only you stick at this job. Now take that bit of glass paper and get a polish on this rod. I want to see me face in it. Right?"

"Right, Jimmy."

Corny was in the office. The till was open and he was looking at the contents. He slanted his eyes towards Jimmy as he stood at the door but he didn't speak, and Jimmy said, "Could I have a word with you, boss?"

Still Corny didn't answer. There was a five-pound note missing from the till. He wanted to turn on this lad and say, "Hand it over before I knock it out of you!" but in another hour or so he would be gone and that would be that. And, by damn, he'd see that the new one who was starting on Monday didn't grease his finger at his expense.

Jimmy didn't know how to begin, and the boss wasn't being very helpful. He looked in a bit of a stew. Well that to-do at dinner-time with that piece and the missus was enough to put anybody in a stew, but he didn't think the missus would be troubled any more by Miss Blenkinsop, and that was a good thing. He had been sorry for the missus lately, and he couldn't for the life of him understand the boss. He said now, "There was a reason, boss, why I wanted to leave."

"I've no doubt about that." Corny's voice was cold.

Coo! he was in a stew. And now having to tell him what his lad had been up to was a bit thick, but there was no other way out of it. "You . . . I don't know whether you've noticed anything about the takings, boss, but . . . but there's been money going."

Corny slid from the stool and stared at Jimmy and he said, "Aye, aye, Jimmy, there's been money going. But it's rather late in the day isn't it to give me an explanation?"

As Jimmy stared back into Corny's eyes, he realized the thing he had feared, the thing he was leaving for had already happened; the boss had known about it all along and thought it was him. Aw, crikey! He wagged his head from side to side, then thrusting the tin towards Corny, he said, "It's all in there. But . . . but it wasn't me that took it."

Corny looked at the cocoa tin, then lifted the lid. Following this he turned out the contents on to the desk and picked up the five-pound note. Slowly now he turned round and looked at Jimmy, then he said, "Well, if you didn't take it, who did? The fairies? There's only you and me dealing with money here."

Jimmy bowed his head. "You remember Poodle Patter coming and tryin' to get me to go a share in the car for the band, boss?"

Corny made no response and Jimmy went on, "He was at me to go to Baxter's for more money, and to get rid of him I said I would think about it. Well, there was somebody listening and they thought up a way to get the money for me." He lifted his head and looked at Corny and said simply, "Young David."

Corny stared at him. He stared and he continued to stare until Jimmy said, "I'm sorry, boss."

"Our David!" It was a mere whisper, and Jimmy nodded his head once. "You mean he's been stealing from the—" he thumbed the till, "all this time, under my nose?"

Jimmy said nothing until Corny asked, "How long have you known about this?"

"Oh," Jimmy wagged his head in characteristic fashion, "it was the week you got Bill I think. Aye, about that time, because he remembered you telling me to tell the man to keep the change. You said, 'What's sixpence.' I saw him at it through the window the first time, but I thought I was mistaken until the next time he came in an' I watched him."

"But why didn't you tell me, Jimmy?" Corny's voice had risen now.

"Aw, boss, ask yourself. Anyway, I tried twice but both times you were in a bit of a stew about something and I thought I'd better not make matters worse."

"You know what you are, Jimmy, you're a fool, that's what you are, you're a long, lanky fool!" Corny was shouting now. "I've known this money's been going all the time, but I thought it was you."

"Aye." Jimmy jerked his head. "I know that."

"Well, you didn't think I was so green as not to miss pound notes and ten shilling notes going out of the till, did you?"

"Well, you didn't say nowt, boss. Anyway," he now hunched his shoulders up, "I couldn't give him away; he sort of, well likes me and trails after me. Aw, I just couldn't, so I thought it was better to clear out an' you find out for yourself. But then, well he brings me the tin and tells me he's done it for me so's I won't go."

"Oh, my God!" Corny sat down heavily on the stool and, leaning his elbow on the desk, he supported his head. He'd go barmy. After a moment he looked at Jimmy and said, "You know I don't want you to go, don't you?"

"I don't want to go either boss."

"You've got fixed up at Baxter's."

"Aye, I start on Monday."

"Could you back out?"

Jimmy looked down towards his boots, then said, "Aye, I could, but then you've got the other fellow startin' Monday."

"Oh, that can be fixed," said Corny. "We've said for some time we could do with another hand. And he's young and I won't have time to see to him myself and train him. How about it?"

"Suits me, boss." Jimmy was grinning slightly, and Corny got off the stool and went towards him and again he said, "You're a fool, Jimmy. No matter who it is—now you listen to me, man, woman or child—don't you take the rap for anybody, not for a thing like that, for stealing." He drew in a long breath, then putting his hand out and gripping Jimmy's shoulder he said, "Nevertheless, thanks. And I won't forget you for this. Now where is he?"

"I set him cleaning a rod in the shed. You won't come down too hard on him, will you?"

"You leave it to me. This is one lesson he's got to learn and the hard way."

As Jimmy walked quickly by Corny's side he asked, under his breath, "Where's Mrs. Boyle?"

For answer Corny said, "It'll be all over by the time she gets downstairs."

David stopped rubbing the rod as soon as he caught sight of his father. Jimmy wasn't there, there was just his dad, and when he saw the look on his face he began to tremble.

"So you've been stealing from me?" Corny was towering over him.

"N . . . not pro . . . proper stealing, Dad." It was as if he had gone back six months and was learning to pronounce his words again.

"There's only one form of stealing. If you take something that doesn't belong to you that's stealing, proper stealing."

"I . . . I d-didn't want J-J-Jimmy to go, D-Dad."

"Jimmy could have asked me for the money. If Jimmy had wanted a share in that car he could have got the money. He didn't want you to steal for him."

"You said it di-didn't matter, Dad."

"What didn't matter?"

"Mo-money."

Corny remembered faintly saying, "What's money for but to go round."

"You knew it mattered, didn't you? If it didn't matter why did you do it on the sly? Why did you go to the office when I wasn't there and take money out of the till if it didn't matter? You knew it was stealing. You wouldn't go upstairs and open your mother's purse and take money out, would you?"

David was past answering. He was staring at Corny, his eyes stretched to their limit.

"Take your pants down."

"N-n-no, Dad. P-please, Dad."

"You'll take your pants down, or I will."

"M-Mam!"

"Your mother isn't here and if she was that wouldn't stop me from braying you. Come on." He made a grab at him and in a second he had pulled the short trousers down over David's hips, but even before he had swung him round and over his knee David had started to holla, and when Corny's hand descended on his buttocks for the first time he let out a high piercing scream.

Ten times Corny's hand contacted his son's buttocks and it must have been around the sixth ear-splitting scream that Rose Mary entered the drive.

She knew that noise, she knew who cried like that. She ran to the garage and was borne in the direction of the hullabaloo, and she was just rushing through the small door when she saw her mother coming from the yard. She was running like mad towards the repair shed.

"Corny! what are you doing? Leave him go!"

When Mary Ann went to grab her son from her husband's hands he thrust her aside, and as he stood David on his feet he cried at her, "Now don't start until you know what it's all about."

"I don't care what it's all about; there's no need to murder him."

"I wasn't murdering him, I was twanking his backside. And he's lucky to get off with just that. Do you know what he's been doing?"

Mary Ann said nothing, she just stared at her son. His face was scarlet and awash with tears, and from his face she looked to his thin bare legs and the side of his buttocks that outdid his face in colour.

"He's been stealing. This is the one that's been taking the money from the till, and all the while I thought it was Jimmy."

Mary Ann couldn't speak for a moment, then she whispered, "Oh, no! Oh, no!"

"Oh, yes."

"David! you couldn't."

Now David did a very strange thing. He did not run to his mother where he knew he would find comfort, but he turned to the man who had been thrashing him, and laying his head against his waist he put his arms around his hips and choked as he spluttered, "Oh! Oh! Oh! Dad."

Corny swallowed deeply, wet his lips, then bending down he pulled up the trousers and fastened them round his son's waist.

Rose Mary had been standing at her mother's side, absolutely too shocked to utter a word. Their mam smacked their bottoms sometimes, but . . . but she had never seen anybody get smacked like her dad had smacked David. He said David had stolen money. Eeh! it was a lie because David never did anything without telling her. He would not even steal without telling her. But then David wouldn't steal; he knew it was a sin, and he'd have to go to confession and tell Father Carey. Their dad was awful. She didn't love their dad. Poor, poor David. Her feelings now lifted her in a jump to her brother's side, and David did another surprising thing. With the flat of one hand he pushed her away, and whether it was with surprise or whether she tripped over one of the jutting pieces of wood that supported the engine on the bench, she fell backwards. And now she let out a howl.

She howled until she reached the kitchen and Mary Ann, taking her by the shoulders, shook her gently, saying, "Now stop it. You weren't hurt; stop it, I tell you."

"He . . . he pushed me, our David pushed me."

"He didn't mean to, he was upset."

"Dad said he stole. He's tellin' lies, isn't he?"

"If your dad said he stole, then he stole. And that's what he's been thrashed for. Now go to the bathroom and don't pester him or question him because he's upset. Run the bath for me."

"Have . . . have we to go to bed, Mam?"

"No, I'm just going to give David a bath, then he'll feel better." She did not add, "It might ease the pain of his bottom."

As Rose Mary went slowly out of the kitchen Corny came in and stood near the table, but he didn't look at Mary Ann as he gave her the explanation for David stealing the money. When he had finished there was a pause, and then she said, "You'll have to make it up to Jimmy somehow."

"Yes, yes, I intend to."

He now said, "I can't understand how he could do it under my nose."

Mary Ann went into the scullery and put the kettle on the gas and she stood near the stove for a moment and turned her face towards the kitchen door. She wanted to shout out, "It shouldn't surprise you; anybody could have walked off with the garage these past few weeks and I doubt if you would have noticed." But of course she didn't. That was over, over and done with; except that the corpse was still lying between them and nothing would be the same again until it was removed. And the only way to remove such a corpse was to talk about it, and that was going to be very difficult for them both.

15

PATTERNS OF LIFE

"It's a wonder you're not struck down dead, Rose Mary Boyle. Eeh! I just don't know how you can. Like me mam says, if you got paid for being a liar you'd own the world."

"I'm not a liar, Annabel Morton, and I'm not like you, thank goodness; I'm not a common, ignorant, big-mouthed pig!"

"No, of course, you're not, you're a common, ignorant, big-mouthed idiot, that's what you are."

"What is this?" The cool voice of Miss Plum brought Annabel Morton round to face their teacher, and Miss Plum raised her hand and said, "School hasn't begun yet and you've started."

Rose Mary warmed suddenly to her teacher. "She's always on, Miss Plum, she never lets up. She's always at me and our David, isn't she, David?"

David made no response. He was still in a way suffering from the effect of Friday, having his ears boxed by Diana Blenkinsop, then being thrashed almost within an inch of his life, at least that's what Rose Mary had told him had happened. But in any case the effects of the thrashing had caused him to be sick on Saturday, really sick; nervous tummy, his mam had called it. Then on Sunday his Grannie McMullen had come. She had heard about him trying to cut somebody's hair off. His grannie heard everything; she was the devil's mam, their Rose Mary said, and he could believe it. She hadn't heard about the money he had taken, and for that at least he was thankful. But she had heard about all the money his mam was getting because Ben had died. She had wanted to know what his mam was going to do with it and his mam had said they were going to have a bungalow built at the bottom of the field.

If he had known his mother was going to get all that money he would never have taken any from the till because yesterday she had given Jimmy the money he wanted for his share in the car.

The money was making things exciting and he felt he was missing a lot having to come to school; and here was Miss Plum at them already. Well, if she wasn't at them she soon would be; he could tell by the look on her face and the way she had shut up their Rose Mary.

And Miss Plum had shut up Rose Mary, she shut her up with one word, "ENOUGH!" Then after a pause she turned to Annabel Morton and said, "You are not to call people liars, Annabel."

"Yes, Miss Plum," said Annabel meekly, before adding, "But she is, Miss Plum. Do you know what she said? She said her mam's been left a fortune an' she's going to build a bungalow and going to give their house to Jimmy, who works in the garage. And she said her mother's a writer and she gets lots of money from the *Newcastle Courier*. . . ."

"Well, she does, you! She does." Rose Mary was poking her chin out at the unbelieving individual.

"That's enough." Miss Plum's voice was stern now, "And Annabel is quite right this time, you are lying, and you've got to. . . ."

Miss Plum was utterly amazed as Rose Mary slapped at her skirt and dared to say, "You! you're as bad as she is. It's true . . . tis!"

"Don't do that!" Miss Plum had caught the hand and slapped it twice. "You're a naughty girl, Rose Mary; I'll take you to the. . . . Oooh!"

Miss Plum couldn't believe it was happening. Only the pain in her shin where David's hard toecap had kicked her proved to her that it had happened. Rose Mary Boyle had slapped at her and David Boyle had kicked her. "Well!" She seemed to swell to twice her height and twice her breadth. As her hands went out to descend on them they turned and fled.

David was now racing across the school yard in and out of the children with Rose Mary hanging on to his hand, but just as they reached the gate he pulled her to a skidding stop. And there he turned and looked at the sea of faces mostly on his eye level, except the enraged countenance of Miss Plum. And it was to her he shouted one word, "HELL!"

Then running again, almost flying, they scampered up the road and they didn't seem to draw breath until they reached the bus stop, and there Rose Mary, gasping, stared at her brother, at their David, who had sworn a terrible word at Miss Plum. She, herself, had slapped at Miss Plum's dress but their David had kicked Miss Plum, he had kicked her on the shin and made her yell; and then he had said that word.

Quite suddenly the enormity of this crime and its penalty, of which she would be called upon to share, was too much for her and she burst out crying.

David stood looking at her helplessly. He didn't feel at all repentant, at least not yet. After a moment he said, "Here's the bus."

She was still crying as they boarded the bus. It was their nice conductor and he said, "Hello. What's up with you two? It isn't ten minutes ago I dropped you. This day's flashed by."

They didn't answer, and when they were seated he came up to them and, bending down, said, "What's happened this time?" And Rose Mary, sniffing and gulping, said, "She called me a liar, Annabel Morton, and the teacher came and she took her part and . . . and I said I wasn't a liar and I put my hand out, like that." She tapped the conductor's coat. "And she slapped my hand." She paused and cast a glance at David, but David was looking down at his finger nail as it intently cleaned its opposite number, and raising her face further to the conductor she whispered, "He kicked her."

"He did!" The conductor's voice was laden with awe. "Go on."

Rose Mary closed her eyes and nodded her head and went to impart something even worse. Placing her mouth near his ear, she whispered, "He swore."

He brought his face fully round to hers, trying to shut the laughter out of it by stretching his eyes and keeping his lips firm; then he said, "He swore, did he?" Now his mouth was near her ear. "What did he say?"

". . . Hell."

"HELL!" The conductor straightened up and cast a glance at the interested passengers around them, and his look warned them not to titter.

"By! He's done it now, hasn't he?" The conductor looked at David's bowed head. "Once upon a time he never opened his mouth, did he? And now, by, he's not only opened it, he's using it, isn't he?" He was talking as if David wasn't there, and Rose Mary nodded at him, then said, "We'll get wrong."

"Oh, I wouldn't worry." The conductor jerked his head now.

"But we will; we'll be taken to the priest." She turned her head swiftly to look at the man behind her who had made a funny noise, but the man's face was straight.

"What do you think he'll give you?"

"Who?"

"The priest, when you're taken to him?"

"Likely a whole decade of the Rosary, I usually only get one Our Father and three Hail Marys."

Now the conductor turned abruptly away, saying, "Fares, please. Fares, please," as he went down the bus.

He was a long time down the bus because everybody was talking to him, and some people were laughing. Rose Mary thought she would never laugh again.

When they stood on the platform waiting for the bus to stop the conductor put his hand on David's head and said, "You'll do, young 'un, you'll do," and David grinned weakly at him. He felt he stood well in the conductor's estimation. For a moment he wished the bus conductor was his dad, at least for the next hour or so.

When they entered the lane Rose Mary started crying again, and once more he took hold of her hand, a thing he hadn't done, except when he pulled her out of the school yard, for a long, long time.

When they came in sight of the garage he drew her to a stop and they stared at each other. Rose Mary was frightened. He was frightened, but he wasn't crying. When she said to him, "We'll get wrong," he made no reply, and they walked on again.

It had never entered their heads to run anywhere else but home.

When Mary Ann, having made the bed and tidied the room, went to adjust the curtains she imagined she was seeing things when she saw them hand in hand walking slowly across the drive towards the front door. She pressed her face near the window for a moment; then she turned and flew down the stairs, and as she opened the door Corny was approaching them from the garage, and they both asked the same thing in different ways: "What's the matter? Why have you come home?"

"Mi . . . Miss Plum, Mam."

"Miss Plum! What's she done?"

"She wouldn't believe us."

Mary Ann bent down towards Rose Mary. "She wouldn't believe you? What did you tell her?"

"About everything in the school yard. Annabel Morton called me a liar, and a pig, and then she told Miss Plum what I'd said and Miss Plum said I was lying an' all. And I didn't mean to slap her, Mam, I didn't; I just touched her skirt like that." She flicked at her mother's hand now. "And she slapped me, she slapped me twice. And then David. . . ." She turned and looked at her brother, but David was looking up at Corny, staring up at him, fear in his eyes again, and Corny said, "Yes, well? What did David do?"

Rose Mary waited for David to go on with the tale, but David remained mute and she said, "He only did it because she slapped me, Mam, that's why."

"All right, all right," said Mary Ann patiently, "but tell me what he did."

"He . . . he kicked her, and he said. . . ."

"You kicked Miss Plum?" Mary Ann was confronting her son, and David looked at her unblinking but said nothing.

"How could you, David?"

"He only did it because she was hitting me, Mam."

Mary Ann took in a deep breath and Corny let out a slow one, and then Mary Ann asked of her daughter, "What else did he do?"

Rose Mary's head drooped slightly to the side, her eyes filled with tears again, she blinked and gulped but couldn't bring herself to repeat the terrible thing their David had said to Miss Plum, and so Corny, looking at his son, asked him quietly, "What else did you do, David?" And David looked back at his father and said briefly, "Swore."

Corny moved his tongue round his mouth as if he were trying to erase a substance that was sticking to his teeth, and then he asked, "What did you say?"

There was quite a pause before David said, "Hell!"

". . . Hell?"

"Uh-huh!"

"Why?" Corny felt he had to pursue this, and seriously, but David went mute again, and Rose Mary, now that the worst was over, quickly took up the story. "He grabbed me by the hand and pulled me away from Miss Plum and it was as we were going through the gate he turned back and he shouted it at her."

Both Corny and Mary Ann saw the scene vividly in their minds, and simultaneously they turned away and Mary Ann said, "Come along, come upstairs."

They had hardly entered the room when the phone rang and, Corny picking it up, said, "Yes?" and Jimmy answered. "It's the schoolmistress. She wants to know are the bairns back."

"Put her on." Corny now looked at Mary Ann and she reached out and took the phone from him; then with her other hand she waved the children out of the room, whispering, "Go into the sitting-room, I'll be there in a minute."

"Mrs. Boyle?"

"Yes, this is Mrs. Boyle."

"Have the children returned home?"

"Yes, they've just got in, Miss Swatland." Mary Ann's voice was stiff.

"I suppose they've given you their version of the incident?"

"Yes, Miss Swatland."

"They were very naughty you know, Mrs. Boyle. Of course, being twins it's understandable that they'll defend each other, but in this case they were very, very naughty. Do you know that David kicked Miss Plum?"

"I understand that he did."

"And that Rose Mary slapped her?"

"I don't think Rose Mary slapped her. She made a movement with her hand at her skirt; there's quite a difference."

There was a short silence on the line now, then Miss Swatland said, "Rose Mary has a vivid imagination, Mrs. Boyle. This isn't a bad thing unless it gets out of hand and then there's a very thin line between imagination and lies."

"Rose Mary wasn't telling lies, Miss Swatland."

There was a gentle laugh on the other end of the line. "Oh, Mrs. Boyle you don't know what Rose Mary says at school, what she said today. I understand she said you had come into a fortune, and you were giving your garage boy your house and building a bungalow, besides which you were writing for *The Courier,* and on and on."

"Which are all true, Miss Swatland."

There was a longer pause now, and the sound of whispering came to Mary Ann and she glanced at Corny and inclined her head towards him.

Miss Swatland was speaking again. "Well, you must admit, Mrs. Boyle, such things don't happen in the usual course of events, and when a child relates them one is apt to think they are exaggerating, to say the least. Miss Plum wasn't to know of your good fortune."

"Miss Plum could have thought there may have been some truth in the child's prattle. It isn't unheard of for people to win the pools, is it, although I haven't won the pools. And I think when a child is using her imagination, even when there isn't any truth as a basis, it doesn't help her to be told she is a liar."

"Miss Plum has a lot of small children to cope with, Mrs. Boyle. . . ."

"I'm quite well aware of that. Well, she'll have two less in the future, Miss Swatland, because I'm going to take the children away."

"Oh, that is up to you, Mrs. Boyle."

"Yes, it's up to me, Miss Swatland. Good day."

"Good day, Mrs. Boyle."

Mary Ann put the phone down and looked up at Corny, and Corny said, "Take them away? But where will you send them?"

"Her to the Convent, and him to St. Joseph's Preparatory."

As he turned away from her and walked towards the window she said quietly, "We can do it between us." Then going swiftly to the sideboard drawer, she took from her bag an envelope and went to his side and handed it to him, saying, "That's for you. You won't be able to actually get the money until it goes through probate, but it's just to let you know that it's yours."

"What is it?"

"Open it and see."

He looked at her a full minute before he did as she bade him, then when he saw the solicitor's letter he bit on his lip and handed it back to her, saying, "I can't take it."

"Corny! Look at me."

He looked at her.

"We . . . we've always shared everything and I won't spend another penny of the money unless you take half. I mean it. That's to go straight into your personal account when it comes through. It's not going into the business, it's for you to do as you like with. I don't want you to put any of it towards the bungalow, and I won't, that's to come out of the business. You always intended to build a house, didn't you?"

He had his head bowed deep on his chest and he said, "Mary Ann."

She didn't answer him, she waited, but he seemed incapable of going on. When she saw his jaw bones working and the knuckles shining white through his clenched fists she turned away and said, "What about us going down to Fanny's this afternoon. We've never been for ages."

It was still a while before he answered, and then he said briefly, "Aye."

"The . . . the children would love it, and there's something I want to give her."

Again she went to her bag and took out another envelope, and as she looked at it she said, "It's wonderful to be able to do things you've dreamed about."

He half turned his head towards her, his eyes still cast down, and she looked towards him and said, "It's fifty pounds. They gave me an advance. Oh, I'm dying to see her face when she. . . ."

"Oh, God!"

She watched him swing himself round from the window and go to the chair by the fireside and, dropping into it, bury his face in his hands, and when he muttered thickly, "Coals of fire," she could say nothing, only stand by the table and press her hands flat on it and look down on them and wait.

Corny squeezed his face between his hard palms. She was going to give his grannie fifty pounds. Nobody, not one of her ten sons and daughters she had alive, or any of her offspring, had ever given her fifty shillings, except perhaps himself—he had always seen to his grannie—but Mary Ann was going to give her fifty pounds; only she would have thought about giving her fifty pounds; only she would have thought about saying I'll not spend a penny of my money unless you take half. And he had been such a blind and bloody fool that he had let his thoughts and feelings slide from her. For weeks now there had been superimposed on her a pair of long, brown legs and a face that he had thought beautiful. In this moment he couldn't imagine what had possessed him not to see through the slut the moment he clapped eyes on her, but the point was he hadn't. Instead some part of him had gone down before her like dry grass before a fire.

For days now he had been consumed with shame, yet he kept telling himself that nothing had happened, not really. He hadn't been with her, he hadn't kissed her, he hadn't even touched her. That was funny. He had never once touched her hand, yet he was feeling as guilty as if he had gone the whole hog, and he knew why, oh aye, he knew why, because deep in his heart he had wanted to. Mary Ann had sensed this and nothing would be right between them until he could tell her, until he could own up.

"Mary . . . Mary Ann."

"Yes."

"I'm . . . Oh, God, Mary Ann, I'm sorry." He gazed up at her, his voice low and thick. "Oh, God, Mary Ann, I am, I am. To the very heart of me I'm sorry. As long as I live I'll never hurt you again." His eyes were tightly closed now, screwed deep into their sockets, and when her arms went round him and he pulled her on to his knee, she held his head tightly against her and for a moment she couldn't believe that the shaking of his body was caused by his crying. Corny crying. She had first met him when she was seven and he had been in her life since and she had never known him to cry.

The tears were raining from her own eyes now, dropping down her cheeks and on to his hair, and she moved her face in it and tried to stop him talking. Some of his words she couldn't catch, they were so thick and broken and mumbled, but others she picked out and hugged to her heart, such as "Nothing happened, nothing, ever. Believe me, believe me—never touched her—not her hand. Like madness—As long as I live I swear to you I'll never hurt you again . . . never in that way. Oh, Mary Ann. Why? Why?"

"It's all right, it's all right." She held his head more tightly and rocked him as she repeated. "It's all right. It's all over now, it's all right," and while she rocked him she thought of the time just before she got married when her da had become fascinated by that young girl, and after she herself had exposed the girl for what she was her da had struck her, and then he had gone out into the night and the storm, and her mother had thought he had gone for good, but in the early dawn Michael had found him in the barn, exhausted and her mother had taken the lantern and gone to him. It was odd, she thought, how patterns of life were repeated.

16

FANNY

The children bounced on the back seat of the car chanting, "Great . . . gran . . . Mac . . . Bride's!" and each time they bounced Bill fell against one or the other, until he felt forced to protest.

Mary Ann, screwing up her face against his howling, turned round and, dragging him up, hoisted him over the seat on to her knee.

"Ah, Mam, he was all right."

Mary Ann looked over her shoulder at Rose Mary and said, "He sounded all right, didn't he? A little more of that and he would have been sick."

Bill settled down quietly on her knee, and the children took up their chants again, and Corny drove in silence. He felt washed out, drained, but quiet inside. The turmoil had gone.

Mary Ann, too, felt quiet inside, spent. She had to talk to the children but all the while her mind was on other things. She thought in a way it was a good thing they were going to Fanny's. Life became normal when in Fanny's company.

Most of the Jarrow that they passed through wasn't familiar any longer. New blocks of flats, new squares, new roads; soon even Burton Street and Mulhattan's Hall would be gone. As a child she had longed to get away from the poverty of this district, from the meanness of Burton Street and the cramping quarters of Mulhattan's Hall where there were five two-roomed flats and privacy was a thing you could only dream of. Yet now, as the car drew towards the house, she thought, Once they pull it down that'll be the end of Jarrow—at least for me. And, what was more serious, once they pulled it down it certainly would be the end of Jarrow for the Hall's oldest occupant.

Fanny spied them from the window and she was at the door to greet them in her characteristic fashion.

"In the name of God, has your place been burned down! It's no use coming here for lodgings, I can't put you up . . . Hello, me bairns. Good God Almighty! what's this you've brought?" She pointed to the dog and Rose Mary shouted, "Can't you see, Great-gran, it's a dog."

"It's Bill. I told you about him, Great-gran," said David. "You know."

Fanny bent towards David and, digging him in the chest with her finger, said, "Aye, you told me about a dog, but you wouldn't call him a dog, would you? Snakes alive! I've never seen anything so ugly in me life. Get your things off, get your things off all of you, the kettle's on. How are you lass?" She bent and kissed Mary Ann. Then looking at her grandson, she said, "It's no use askin' you how you are, you're never anythin' but all right." She paused now and added, "There's always a first time. What's the matter with you? Have you got a cold?"

Corny stretched his face and rubbed at his eyes, saying, "Yes, I've got a bit of a snifter."

"It looks like it an' all. Well, you keep it to yourself, I don't want any of it. Well, sit yourselves down, can't you. Go on."

When they were all seated she looked from one to the other and said, "You might have given me a bit of warnin', to descend on me like this. You're not exactly manna from heaven, an' I haven't a thing in for the tea."

"Well, if you don't want us we can go."

She took her hand and pushed at Corny's head. "You'll go soon enough if I have any of your old buck."

"How you keeping, Fanny?" Mary Ann now asked, and Fanny, lowering her flabby body down on to a straight-backed chair, said, "Aw, well, lass, you know by rights I should be dead. Sometimes I think I am and they've forgotten to screw me down. Look, what's he up to, sniffing over there?" She pointed to Bill who was investigating beneath the bed in the far corner of the room.

"It's likely the last two months' washing attracting his attention," said Corny.

"Mind it, you. I don't put me dirty washing under the bed." She nodded straight-faced at him. "All my dirty washing goes on the line, outside."

They were all laughing together now and Mary Ann thought, Oh, it's good to be with Fanny.

"And what have me bonnie bairns been doin'?" Fanny embraced the two standing before her, and Rose Mary, laughing up at her, said, "Oh, lots and lots, Great-gran."

"Such as what?"

Oh. Rose Mary looked at David, then glanced back at her mother, and when she finally looked at Fanny again she was nipping her lower lip, and Fanny said, "Oh, it's like that, is it?"

"It's like that," said Mary Ann. "We won't go into it now, it's too painful."

"Aw." Fanny nodded her head while she cast a glance down on the averted eyes of her great-grandson, and, bending down to him, she whispered, "What you been up to this time, young fellow me lad? You murdered somebody?"

When David's head began to swing and his lips to work one against the other, Mary Ann put in, "I might as well tell you. They both ran away from school this morning."

"You're jokin'!"

"I'm not joking, Fanny; they're both very wicked. You won't believe what I'm going to tell you, but Rose Mary there slapped her teacher, and David, well he not only kicked her in the shins but swore at her. Now I bet you won't believe that of your great-grandchildren."

Fanny, dropping her gaze to the two lowered heads, said, "Never in this wide world, I wouldn't believe it if the Lord himself came down and said, 'Fanny McBride, if you don't take my word for it you'll go to hell'."

Rose Mary's head came up with a jerk. "That's what he said, Great-gran. It's true, it is, it's true. He did, he said that word to Miss Plum."

"Hell? Never!"

"He did, didn't you, David?"

There was pride in Rose Mary's tone now, and Fanny, pulling herself to her feet and pressing her forearm over her great sagging breasts, turned away, saying, "This is too much. It's the biggest surprise of me life. I'm away to get the cups, I must have a sup tea to get over that shock . . . Mary Ann, can you help me a minute?"

Mary Ann reached the scullery just seconds after Fanny and found her standing near the shallow stone sink over which there was no tap. Fanny motioned her to close the door. Then her body, shaking all over, she gave way to her laughter, and Mary Ann, standing close to her, laughed with her.

"He told her to go to hell?"

"As far as I can gather."

"And he kicked her shins?"

"Yes, oh yes. The headmistress was on the phone a minute or so after they got in."

"He's a lad; he's going to be a handful."

"You're telling me, Fanny."

Fanny dried her eyes; then patting Mary Ann on the cheek she said, "Aw, it's good to see you, lass. I had the blues this mornin'. You know, I get them every now and again, but they were of a very dark hue the day, and I lay thinkin', Tuesday, what'm I gona do with meself all day. But I said a little prayer and left it to Him, and here you are, lass. But tell me," she bent her face close to Mary Ann, "is everything all right?"

There was a pause before Mary Ann said, "Yes, Fanny."

"There's been somethin' up, hasn't there?"

Mary Ann now lowered her head and said in a whisper, "Yes, Fanny."

"I knew it. When he popped in last week-end there was somethin' about him. It's gone now. I looked at his face when he came in at the door and I knew it was gone. But he's been in trouble, hasn't he?"

Mary Ann turned her face away as she said, "You could call it that, Fanny."

"Money?"

"Oh, no, Fanny."

"Not the business then?" Fanny's eyebrows moved upwards.

"No."

There was a longer pause before Fanny whispered, "You're not tellin' me that my Corny would ever look at. . . ."

"Fanny." Mary Ann gripped the old woman's hands. "I'll pop in some time towards the week-end, when I'm down for my shopping, and tell you about it, eh?"

Fanny's head moved stiffly and she said, "Aye, lass, do that, do that." Then, turning to the rack where the cups hung, she asked in a louder tone, "What brought you down the day anyway?"

Now her tone was lighter and louder, Mary Ann answered, "Well, we wanted to see you."

"I'm flattered I'm sure, but is that all? I've never seen the gang of you on a Tuesday afore in me life."

"I had a present for you and I wanted to give it to you myself."

Fanny turned round with four cups in her hand and she said, "A present for me? Well now; why do you have to bring me a present on a Tuesday afternoon, it isn't me birthday? And it's neither a feast, fast, or day of obligation as far as I can gather, and it's weeks off Christmas. Why a present?"

"Must there be a reason why I want to give a present?" Mary Ann poked her face at Fanny across the table. "I just want to give you a present, that's all. Here, give me those." She took the cups from Fanny's hands and placed them on the saucers on the tray, and as she did so she said, "You could do with some new ones."

"Aye, I could that. Those that aren't cracked or chipped haven't a handle to support them. Aw, but what does it matter? Go on, I want to see this present you've brought me."

She stopped just within the kitchen and, nodding towards Bill where he lay on the floor by the side of the bed, she said, "I'm glad of one thing, it's not him."

As she went to the hob to lift up the teapot that was for ever stewing there she said, "Well, come on, where's that present." And when she turned round, the teapot in her hand, Mary Ann handed her the envelope.

Fanny put the teapot on the table, then with her two hands she felt all round the envelope, and the thickness of it, and she looked at Mary Ann, then at Corny, and from him to the children, and they looked at her, waiting for her reactions.

"Well, go on, open it." Mary Ann could have been back twelve years in the past, bringing her friend a present on her birthday, or at Christmas, and saying to her, "Well go on, open it!"

Fanny put her finger under the flap but had some difficulty in splitting open the long brown envelope, and when at last the jagged edges sprang apart she stared at the money.

Slowly she withdrew the notes. They were five pounds notes and were held together by an elastic band, and her mouth dropped into a huge gape as she flicked the edge of them one after the other. They appeared to her as a never-ending stream. She lifted her eyes and looked at Mary Ann. Her expression didn't show pleasure, and you couldn't say she looked surprised, not just surprised; amazed, yes. She now looked at Corny and said, "What is this?" Then, her eyes blinking a little and the suspicion of a smile reaching her lips, she said, "You won the pools?"

"No." Corny shook his head. "Mary Ann's come into some money."

Fanny now looked at Mary Ann again and she said, "You've come into money, lass? From where?"

"You remember Ben, Fanny, you know who used to look after Mr. Lord."

"Aye."

"Well, he died, and . . . and he left me nearly all his money, over eight thousand pounds."

"Eight thousand pounds!" It was only a whisper from Fanny now, and Corny, sensing the flood of emotion that was rising in his grannie, hoped to check it by saying, "Aye, and she's throwing it about right, left and centre; she's thrown half of it my way."

"Half of it?" Fanny turned her attention to Corny now, but her eyes seemed glazed and out of focus. "Well, aye, that's understandable. But me. All this?"

"It isn't that much, Fanny, it's only fifty pounds." Mary Ann's voice was soft, and Fanny now looked at her and her lips trembled before she brought out, "Fifty you say? Only fifty pounds. Lass, do you realize that I've never had fifty pounds in me hand in me life afore. I've . . . I've never seen fifty pounds all at once in me life afore. And . . . and what am I going to do with it?"

"Light the fire with it if you like, Fanny," Mary Ann was smiling gently.

Fanny put the envelope down on the table and, turning from them, her shoulders hunched, she went towards the scullery again, only to be stopped by Corny saying, "Come on now, none of that."

A moment ago Fanny's body had been shaking with laughter, now it was shaking with her sobbing.

When Corny sat her down in her chair, Mary Ann put her arms around her shoulders and, her own voice near tears too, she said, "Oh, Fanny, look, I wanted to make you happy, not to see you bubble. Come on now, come on."

But the more Mary Ann persuaded, the more Fanny cried, difficult, hard crying, crying that was wrenched up from far below her brusque, jocular, life hardened exterior.

Now the children were standing at her knees, Rose Mary with the tears running down her face and David with his tongue probing one cheek after the other in an effort not to join her.

While this was all going on Bill had been lying quietly enough on the old clippie mat by the side of Fanny's bed. He liked this room. There were smells here quite different from those at home; there was a spice about the smells here that reminded him of the morning he had met that girl, the one who had led him to the grab, and of the one solitary lamp-post he had yet encountered.

From under the bed there was wafted to him at the present moment the musty, stingy, yet bracing aroma that had attracted him as soon as he entered the room. They had said he hadn't to go near it, but it was drawing him, inching him towards it. He turned one fishy eye in the direction of his people. They were all gathered round a chair, nobody was looking at him. The smell said, "Come on; it's now or never." And so, without rising, he wriggled forward and there it was, the source of this delight. It was soft and deep and warm. He pushed his nose into it. It gave him a tickly feeling that urged him to play, so he took a mouthful of it and shook it. But when it fell over his head he didn't care much for that, so he wriggled to get from under it, but the more he wriggled the more it enfolded him. This was too much of a good thing. If he didn't do something about it he'd be smothered, so, biting and scrambling, he fought until he was free.

He had reached the other side of the bed and brought the thing with him. He was in the open now, and knew how to deal with it. The smell was more exciting in the open, it was sending shivers all over him. When he saw all the feathers floating about him he growled his delight, and dashing round the bed he dragged the old eiderdown with him.

"Look. Look what he's got, Dad. Bill!"

"Oh, godfathers! Here, you rattlesnake you, give that to me."

"Don't pull it, Corny, don't pull it, it'll only make him worse."

"In the name of God! how did he get hold of that."

"You shouldn't leave such things under the bed." Corny was yelling at Fanny now, and she, getting to her feet, flapped her hands here and there to ward off the rain of feathers.

"Corny! Corny, I'm telling you, don't pull it. I'll get him. Leave it, just leave it; you're making him worse. And you let go, David."

Bill had never had such a game in his life. He growled his delight; he knew the more he pulled the more feathers he could raise; and his people were enjoying it too. Like all his breed he loved to give pleasure to humans, if not to his own species, so he pulled and he pulled.

"Let me get behind him." Mary Ann was yelling at the top of her voice. "Leave go, Rose Mary. Are you all mad? Do you hear me, the lot of you! Don't pull it!"

When at last it got through to the children and Corny that they were only adding havoc to chaos, Bill had sole possession of the tattered eiderdown again and they could hardly see each other through the cloud of feathers.

They drew the down up their nostrils then sneezed it out. When they opened their mouths to speak they swallowed feathers. They were all spluttering and coughing and flapping their hands as if they were warding off a swarm of bees.

After sneezing violently, Mary Ann cried, "Leave . . . leave him to me. Now, now just keep quiet and leave him to me." Then she moved slowly towards Bill who was at the far side of the table, quiet now, stretched out to his full length with his front paws lying on the edge of the eiderdown and his blunt snout resting between them.

"Bill. Bill darling. Go . . . od boy. Give it to mother. That's a go-od boy. Bestest boy in the worldie world." She was almost crooning as she approached him, and Bill looked at her lovingly. Here was his best pal, here was the one he liked best of the lot. Here was someone who understood him, who talked with him and played with him when the others weren't around. Well now he would give her a game like she had never had before.

When he up and dashed from her, dragging the eiderdown with him, she threw herself full length on it, and the result was disastrous. Pulled to an abrupt stop his never very steady legs gave way and he overbalanced and landed against Fanny's feet, and in the process of scrambling up again he dashed between them, and over she went.

Corny was standing within a yard of her, and springing forward he grabbed at her as she fell, hoping to break her fall; and luckily he did. It was also lucky for him that the old chair was behind him and he found himself almost pushed through the sagging bottom of it with Fanny's weight on top of him.

There was a moment of utter silence in the room; then it was broken by a rumble of laughter, a rumble that could only erupt from a chest as deep as Fanny's.

Corny, from his cramped, contorted position, had the wind knocked out of him, but the shaking body of his grannie raised in him a chuckle, then a laugh, then a roar. And now Rose Mary and David, each tugging at Fanny's hands, joined in with a high squealing glee.

And Mary Ann?

Mary Ann was lying on the eiderdown, her face buried in the crook of her elbow. When she raised her head it was to look into the eyes of Bill, who was prone once more, his muzzle flat out, staring at her. She now looked about her, at the shambles the room represented, then ceilingwards, at the feathers floating and settling everywhere, then she looked at the huddle of her family in and around the battered armchair, and she joined her voice to theirs. She laughed and laughed until she felt that if she didn't stop she'd be ill. But it was cathartic laughter; it was what they needed to dispel the last of the nightmare. And it could never have come about except at Fanny's. Oh, thank God for Fanny. . . . And Bill. Oh, yes. She put out her hand towards Bill and he wriggled his body forward. Oh yes, and Bill.